5—

E. Nesbit – 7 books in 1

The Railway Children,
Five Children and It,
The Phoenix and the Carpet,
The Story of the Amulet,
The Story of the Treasure-Seekers,
The Would-Be-Goods,
and
The Enchanted Castle

Shoes and Ships and Sealing Wax

Visit our website, ShoesAndShipsAndSealingWax.com, for more great books!

The Railway Children

To my dear son Paul Bland, behind whose knowledge of railways my ignorance confidently shelters.

Chapter 1. The Beginning of Things.

They were not railway children to begin with. I don't suppose they had ever thought about railways except as a means of getting to Maskelyne and Cook's, the Pantomime, Zoological Gardens, and Madame Tussaud's. They were just ordinary suburban children, and they lived with their Father and Mother in an ordinary red-brick-fronted villa, with coloured glass in the front door, a tiled passage that was called a hall, a bath-room with hot and cold water, electric bells, French windows, and a good deal of white paint, and 'every modern convenience', as the house-agents say.

There were three of them. Roberta was the eldest. Of course, Mothers never have favourites, but if their Mother HAD had a favourite, it might have been Roberta. Next came Peter, who wished to be an Engineer when he grew up; and the youngest was Phyllis, who meant extremely well.

Mother did not spend all her time in paying dull calls to dull ladies, and sitting dully at home waiting for dull ladies to pay calls to her. She was almost always there, ready to play with the children, and read to them, and help them to do their home-lessons. Besides this she used to write stories for them while they were at school, and read them aloud after tea, and she always made up funny pieces of poetry for their birthdays and for other great occasions, such as the christening of the new kittens, or the refurnishing of the doll's house, or the time when they were getting over the mumps.

These three lucky children always had everything they needed: pretty clothes, good fires, a lovely nursery with heaps of toys, and a Mother Goose wall-paper. They had a kind and merry nursemaid, and a dog who was called James, and who was their very own. They also had a Father who was just perfect—never cross, never unjust, and always ready for a game—at least, if at any time he was NOT ready, he always had an excellent reason for it, and explained the reason to the children so interestingly and funnily that they felt sure he couldn't help himself.

You will think that they ought to have been very happy. And so they were, but they did not know HOW happy till the pretty life in the Red Villa was over and done with, and they had to live a very different life indeed.

The dreadful change came quite suddenly.

Peter had a birthday—his tenth. Among his other presents was a model engine more perfect than you could ever have dreamed of. The other presents were full of charm, but the Engine was fuller of charm than any of the others were.

Its charm lasted in its full perfection for exactly three days. Then, owing either to Peter's inexperience or Phyllis's good intentions, which had been rather pressing, or to some other cause, the Engine suddenly went off with a bang. James was so frightened that he went out and did not come back all day. All the Noah's Ark people who were in the tender were broken to bits, but nothing else was hurt except the poor little engine and the feelings of Peter. The others said he cried over it—but of course boys of ten do not cry, however terrible the tragedies may be which darken their lot. He said that his eyes were red because he had a cold. This turned out to be true, though Peter did not know it was when he said it, the next day he had to go to bed and stay there. Mother began to be afraid that he might be sickening for measles, when suddenly he sat up in bed and said:

"I hate gruel—I hate barley water—I hate bread and milk. I want to get up and have something REAL to eat."

"What would you like?" Mother asked.

"A pigeon-pie," said Peter, eagerly, "a large pigeon-pie. A very large one."

So Mother asked the Cook to make a large pigeon-pie. The pie was made. And when the pie was made, it was cooked. And when it was cooked, Peter ate some of it. After that his cold was better. Mother made a piece of poetry to amuse him while the pie was being made. It began by saying what an unfortunate but worthy boy Peter was, then it went on:

He had an engine that he loved
With all his heart and soul,
And if he had a wish on earth
It was to keep it whole.

One day—my friends, prepare your minds;
I'm coming to the worst—
Quite suddenly a screw went mad,
And then the boiler burst!

With gloomy face he picked it up
And took it to his Mother,
Though even he could not suppose
That she could make another;

For those who perished on the line
He did not seem to care,
His engine being more to him
Than all the people there.

And now you see the reason why
Our Peter has been ill:
He soothes his soul with pigeon-pie
His gnawing grief to kill.

He wraps himself in blankets warm
And sleeps in bed till late,
Determined thus to overcome
His miserable fate.

And if his eyes are rather red,
His cold must just excuse it:
Offer him pie; you may be sure
He never will refuse it.

Father had been away in the country for three or four days. All Peter's hopes for the curing of his afflicted Engine were now fixed on his Father, for Father was most wonderfully clever with his fingers. He could mend all sorts of things. He had often acted as veterinary surgeon to the wooden rocking-horse; once he had saved its life when all human aid was despaired of, and the poor creature was given up for lost, and even the carpenter said he didn't see his way to do anything. And it was

Father who mended the doll's cradle when no one else could; and with a little glue and some bits of wood and a pen-knife made all the Noah's Ark beasts as strong on their pins as ever they were, if not stronger.

Peter, with heroic unselfishness, did not say anything about his Engine till after Father had had his dinner and his after-dinner cigar. The unselfishness was Mother's idea—but it was Peter who carried it out. And needed a good deal of patience, too.

At last Mother said to Father, "Now, dear, if you're quite rested, and quite comfy, we want to tell you about the great railway accident, and ask your advice."

"All right," said Father, "fire away!"

So then Peter told the sad tale, and fetched what was left of the Engine.

"Hum," said Father, when he had looked the Engine over very carefully.

The children held their breaths.

"Is there NO hope?" said Peter, in a low, unsteady voice.

"Hope? Rather! Tons of it," said Father, cheerfully; "but it'll want something besides hope—a bit of brazing say, or some solder, and a new valve. I think we'd better keep it for a rainy day. In other words, I'll give up Saturday afternoon to it, and you shall all help me."

"CAN girls help to mend engines?" Peter asked doubtfully.

"Of course they can. Girls are just as clever as boys, and don't you forget it! How would you like to be an engine-driver, Phil?"

"My face would be always dirty, wouldn't it?" said Phyllis, in unenthusiastic tones, "and I expect I should break something."

"I should just love it," said Roberta—"do you think I could when I'm grown up, Daddy? Or even a stoker?"

"You mean a fireman," said Daddy, pulling and twisting at the engine. "Well, if you still wish it, when you're grown up, we'll see about making you a fire-woman. I remember when I was a boy—"

Just then there was a knock at the front door.

"Who on earth!" said Father. "An Englishman's house is his castle, of course, but I do wish they built semi-detached villas with moats and drawbridges."

Ruth—she was the parlour-maid and had red hair—came in and said that two gentlemen wanted to see the master.

"I've shown them into the Library, Sir," said she.

"I expect it's the subscription to the Vicar's testimonial," said Mother, "or else it's the choir holiday fund. Get rid of them quickly, dear. It does break up an evening so, and it's nearly the children's bedtime."

But Father did not seem to be able to get rid of the gentlemen at all quickly.

"I wish we HAD got a moat and drawbridge," said Roberta; "then, when we didn't want people, we could just pull up the drawbridge and no one else could get in. I expect Father will have forgotten about when he was a boy if they stay much longer."

Mother tried to make the time pass by telling them a new fairy story about a Princess with green eyes, but it was difficult because they could hear the voices of Father and the gentlemen in the Library, and Father's voice sounded louder and different to the voice he generally used to people who came about testimonials and holiday funds.

Then the Library bell rang, and everyone heaved a breath of relief.

"They're going now," said Phyllis; "he's rung to have them shown out."

But instead of showing anybody out, Ruth showed herself in, and she looked queer, the children thought.

"Please'm," she said, "the Master wants you to just step into the study. He looks like the dead, mum; I think he's had bad news. You'd best prepare yourself for the worst, 'm—p'raps it's a death in the family or a bank busted or—"

"That'll do, Ruth," said Mother gently; "you can go."

Then Mother went into the Library. There was more talking. Then the bell rang again, and Ruth fetched a cab. The children heard boots go out and down the steps. The cab drove away, and the front door shut. Then Mother came in. Her dear face was as white as her lace collar, and her eyes looked very big and shining. Her mouth looked like just a line of pale red—her lips were thin and not their proper shape at all.

"It's bedtime," she said. "Ruth will put you to bed."

"But you promised we should sit up late tonight because Father's come home," said Phyllis.

"Father's been called away—on business," said Mother. "Come, darlings, go at once."

They kissed her and went. Roberta lingered to give Mother an extra hug and to whisper:

"It wasn't bad news, Mammy, was it? Is anyone dead—or—"

"Nobody's dead—no," said Mother, and she almost seemed to push Roberta away. "I can't tell you anything tonight, my pet. Go, dear, go NOW."

So Roberta went.

Ruth brushed the girls' hair and helped them to undress. (Mother almost always did this herself.) When she had turned down the gas and left them she found Peter, still dressed, waiting on the stairs.

"I say, Ruth, what's up?" he asked.

"Don't ask me no questions and I won't tell you no lies," the red- headed Ruth replied. "You'll know soon enough."

Late that night Mother came up and kissed all three children as they lay asleep. But Roberta was the only one whom the kiss woke, and she lay mousey-still, and said nothing.

"If Mother doesn't want us to know she's been crying," she said to herself as she heard through the dark the catching of her Mother's breath, "we WON'T know it. That's all."

When they came down to breakfast the next morning, Mother had already gone out.

"To London," Ruth said, and left them to their breakfast.

"There's something awful the matter," said Peter, breaking his egg. "Ruth told me last night we should know soon enough."

"Did you ASK her?" said Roberta, with scorn.

"Yes, I did!" said Peter, angrily. "If you could go to bed without caring whether Mother was worried or not, I couldn't. So there."

"I don't think we ought to ask the servants things Mother doesn't tell us," said Roberta.

"That's right, Miss Goody-goody," said Peter, "preach away."

"I'm not goody," said Phyllis, "but I think Bobbie's right this time."

"Of course. She always is. In her own opinion," said Peter.

"Oh, DON'T!" cried Roberta, putting down her egg-spoon; "don't let's be horrid to each other. I'm sure some dire calamity is happening. Don't let's make it worse!"

"Who began, I should like to know?" said Peter.

Roberta made an effort, and answered:—

"I did, I suppose, but—"

"Well, then," said Peter, triumphantly. But before he went to school he thumped his sister between the shoulders and told her to cheer up.

The children came home to one o'clock dinner, but Mother was not there. And she was not there at tea-time.

It was nearly seven before she came in, looking so ill and tired that the children felt they could not ask her any questions. She sank into an arm-chair. Phyllis took the long pins out of her hat, while Roberta took off her gloves, and Peter unfastened her walking-shoes and fetched her soft velvety slippers for her.

When she had had a cup of tea, and Roberta had put eau-de-Cologne on her poor head that ached, Mother said:—

"Now, my darlings, I want to tell you something. Those men last night did bring very bad news, and Father will be away for some time. I am very worried about it, and I want you all to help me, and not to make things harder for me."

"As if we would!" said Roberta, holding Mother's hand against her face.

"You can help me very much," said Mother, "by being good and happy and not quarrelling when I'm away"—Roberta and Peter exchanged guilty glances—"for I shall have to be away a good deal."

"We won't quarrel. Indeed we won't," said everybody. And meant it, too.

"Then," Mother went on, "I want you not to ask me any questions about this trouble; and not to ask anybody else any questions."

Peter cringed and shuffled his boots on the carpet.

"You'll promise this, too, won't you?" said Mother.

"I did ask Ruth," said Peter, suddenly. "I'm very sorry, but I did."

"And what did she say?"

"She said I should know soon enough."

"It isn't necessary for you to know anything about it," said Mother; "it's about business, and you never do understand business, do you?"

"No," said Roberta; "is it something to do with Government?" For Father was in a Government Office.

"Yes," said Mother. "Now it's bed-time, my darlings. And don't YOU worry. It'll all come right in the end."

"Then don't YOU worry either, Mother," said Phyllis, "and we'll all be as good as gold."

Mother sighed and kissed them.

"We'll begin being good the first thing tomorrow morning," said Peter, as they went upstairs.

"Why not NOW?" said Roberta.

"There's nothing to be good ABOUT now, silly," said Peter.

"We might begin to try to FEEL good," said Phyllis, "and not call names."

"Who's calling names?" said Peter. "Bobbie knows right enough that when I say 'silly', it's just the same as if I said Bobbie."

"WELL," said Roberta.

"No, I don't mean what you mean. I mean it's just a—what is it Father calls it?—a germ of endearment! Good night."

The girls folded up their clothes with more than usual neatness— which was the only way of being good that they could think of.

"I say," said Phyllis, smoothing out her pinafore, "you used to say it was so dull—nothing happening, like in books. Now something HAS happened."

"I never wanted things to happen to make Mother unhappy," said Roberta. "Everything's perfectly horrid."

Everything continued to be perfectly horrid for some weeks.

Mother was nearly always out. Meals were dull and dirty. The between-maid was sent away, and Aunt Emma came on a visit. Aunt Emma was much older than Mother. She was going abroad to be a governess. She was very busy getting her clothes ready, and they were very ugly, dingy clothes, and she had them always littering about, and the sewing-machine seemed to whir—on and on all day and most of the night. Aunt Emma believed in keeping children in their proper places. And they more than returned the compliment. Their idea of Aunt Emma's proper place was anywhere where they were not. So they saw very little of her. They preferred the company of the servants, who were more amusing. Cook, if in a good temper, could sing comic songs, and the housemaid, if she happened not to be offended with you, could imitate a hen that has laid an egg, a bottle of champagne being opened, and could mew like two cats fighting. The servants never told the children what the bad news was that the gentlemen had brought to Father. But they kept hinting that they could tell a great deal if they chose—and this was not comfortable.

One day when Peter had made a booby trap over the bath-room door, and it had acted beautifully as Ruth passed through, that red-haired parlour-maid caught him and boxed his ears.

"You'll come to a bad end," she said furiously, "you nasty little limb, you! If you don't mend your ways, you'll go where your precious Father's gone, so I tell you straight!"

Roberta repeated this to her Mother, and next day Ruth was sent away.

Then came the time when Mother came home and went to bed and stayed there two days and the Doctor came, and the children crept wretchedly about the house and wondered if the world was coming to an end.

Mother came down one morning to breakfast, very pale and with lines on her face that used not to be there. And she smiled, as well as she could, and said:—

"Now, my pets, everything is settled. We're going to leave this house, and go and live in the country. Such a ducky dear little white house. I know you'll love it."

A whirling week of packing followed—not just packing clothes, like when you go to the seaside, but packing chairs and tables, covering their tops with sacking and their legs with straw.

All sorts of things were packed that you don't pack when you go to the seaside. Crockery, blankets, candlesticks, carpets, bedsteads, saucepans, and even fenders and fire-irons.

The house was like a furniture warehouse. I think the children enjoyed it very much. Mother was very busy, but not too busy now to talk to them, and read to them, and even to make a bit of poetry for Phyllis to cheer her up when she fell down with a screwdriver and ran it into her hand.

"Aren't you going to pack this, Mother?" Roberta asked, pointing to the beautiful cabinet inlaid with red turtleshell and brass.

"We can't take everything," said Mother.

"But we seem to be taking all the ugly things," said Roberta.

"We're taking the useful ones," said Mother; "we've got to play at being Poor for a bit, my chickabiddy."

When all the ugly useful things had been packed up and taken away in a van by men in green-baize aprons, the two girls and Mother and Aunt Emma slept in the two spare rooms where the furniture was all pretty. All their beds had gone. A bed was made up for Peter on the drawing-room sofa.

"I say, this is larks," he said, wriggling joyously, as Mother tucked him up. "I do like moving! I wish we moved once a month."

Mother laughed.

"I don't!" she said. "Good night, Peterkin."

As she turned away Roberta saw her face. She never forgot it.

"Oh, Mother," she whispered all to herself as she got into bed, "how brave you are! How I love you! Fancy being brave enough to laugh when you're feeling like THAT!"

Next day boxes were filled, and boxes and more boxes; and then late in the afternoon a cab came to take them to the station.

Aunt Emma saw them off. They felt that THEY were seeing HER off, and they were glad of it.

"But, oh, those poor little foreign children that she's going to governess!" whispered Phyllis. "I wouldn't be them for anything!"

At first they enjoyed looking out of the window, but when it grew dusk they grew sleepier and sleepier, and no one knew how long they had been in the train when they were roused by Mother's shaking them gently and saying:—

"Wake up, dears. We're there."

They woke up, cold and melancholy, and stood shivering on the draughty platform while the baggage was taken out of the train. Then the engine, puffing and blowing, set to work again, and dragged the train away. The children watched the tail-lights of the guard's van disappear into the darkness.

This was the first train the children saw on that railway which was in time to become so very dear to them. They did not guess then how they would grow to love the railway, and how soon it would become the centre of their new life, nor what wonders and changes it would bring to them. They only shivered and sneezed and hoped the walk to the new house would not be long. Peter's nose was colder than he ever remembered it to have been before. Roberta's hat was crooked, and the elastic seemed tighter than usual. Phyllis's shoe-laces had come undone.

"Come," said Mother, "we've got to walk. There aren't any cabs here."

The walk was dark and muddy. The children stumbled a little on the rough road, and once Phyllis absently fell into a puddle, and was picked up damp and unhappy. There were no gas-lamps on the road, and the road was uphill. The cart went at a foot's pace, and they followed the gritty crunch of its wheels. As their eyes got used to the darkness, they could see the mound of boxes swaying dimly in front of them.

A long gate had to be opened for the cart to pass through, and after that the road seemed to go across fields—and now it went down hill. Presently a great dark lumpish thing showed over to the right.

"There's the house," said Mother. "I wonder why she's shut the shutters."

"Who's SHE?" asked Roberta.

"The woman I engaged to clean the place, and put the furniture straight and get supper."

There was a low wall, and trees inside.

"That's the garden," said Mother.

"It looks more like a dripping-pan full of black cabbages," said Peter.

The cart went on along by the garden wall, and round to the back of the house, and here it clattered into a cobble-stoned yard and stopped at the back door.

There was no light in any of the windows.

Everyone hammered at the door, but no one came.

The man who drove the cart said he expected Mrs. Viney had gone home.

"You see your train was that late," said he.

"But she's got the key," said Mother. "What are we to do?"

"Oh, she'll have left that under the doorstep," said the cart man; "folks do hereabouts." He took the lantern off his cart and stooped.

"Ay, here it is, right enough," he said.

He unlocked the door and went in and set his lantern on the table.

"Got e'er a candle?" said he.

"I don't know where anything is." Mother spoke rather less cheerfully than usual.

He struck a match. There was a candle on the table, and he lighted it. By its thin little glimmer the children saw a large bare kitchen with a stone floor. There were no curtains, no hearth-rug. The kitchen table from home stood in the middle of the room. The chairs were in one corner, and the pots, pans, brooms, and crockery in another. There was no fire, and the black grate showed cold, dead ashes.

As the cart man turned to go out after he had brought in the boxes, there was a rustling, scampering sound that seemed to come from inside the walls of the house.

"Oh, what's that?" cried the girls.

"It's only the rats," said the cart man. And he went away and shut the door, and the sudden draught of it blew out the candle.

"Oh, dear," said Phyllis, "I wish we hadn't come!" and she knocked a chair over.

"ONLY the rats!" said Peter, in the dark.

Chapter 2. Peter's Coal-Mine.

"What fun!" said Mother, in the dark, feeling for the matches on the table. "How frightened the poor mice were—I don't believe they were rats at all."

She struck a match and relighted the candle and everyone looked at each other by its winky, blinky light.

"Well," she said, "you've often wanted something to happen and now it has. This is quite an adventure, isn't it? I told Mrs. Viney to get us some bread and butter, and meat and things, and to have supper ready. I suppose she's laid it in the dining-room. So let's go and see."

The dining-room opened out of the kitchen. It looked much darker than the kitchen when they went in with the one candle. Because the kitchen was whitewashed, but the dining-room was dark wood from floor to ceiling, and across the ceiling there were heavy black beams. There was a muddled maze of dusty furniture—the breakfast- room furniture from the old home where they had lived all their lives. It seemed a very long time ago, and a very long way off.

There was the table certainly, and there were chairs, but there was no supper.

"Let's look in the other rooms," said Mother; and they looked. And in each room was the same kind of blundering half-arrangement of furniture, and fire-irons and crockery, and all sorts of odd things on the floor, but there was nothing to eat; even in the pantry there were only a rusty cake-tin and a broken plate with whitening mixed in it.

"What a horrid old woman!" said Mother; "she's just walked off with the money and not got us anything to eat at all."

"Then shan't we have any supper at all?" asked Phyllis, dismayed, stepping back on to a soap-dish that cracked responsively.

"Oh, yes," said Mother, "only it'll mean unpacking one of those big cases that we put in the cellar. Phil, do mind where you're walking to, there's a dear. Peter, hold the light."

The cellar door opened out of the kitchen. There were five wooden steps leading down. It wasn't a proper cellar at all, the children thought, because its ceiling went up as high as the kitchen's. A bacon-rack hung under its ceiling. There was wood in it, and coal. Also the big cases.

Peter held the candle, all on one side, while Mother tried to open the great packing-case. It was very securely nailed down.

"Where's the hammer?" asked Peter.

"That's just it," said Mother. "I'm afraid it's inside the box. But there's a coal-shovel—and there's the kitchen poker."

And with these she tried to get the case open.

"Let me do it," said Peter, thinking he could do it better himself. Everyone thinks this when he sees another person stirring a fire, or opening a box, or untying a knot in a bit of string.

"You'll hurt your hands, Mammy," said Roberta; "let me."

"I wish Father was here," said Phyllis; "he'd get it open in two shakes. What are you kicking me for, Bobbie?"

"I wasn't," said Roberta.

Just then the first of the long nails in the packing-case began to come out with a scrunch. Then a lath was raised and then another, till all four stood up with the long nails in them shining fiercely like iron teeth in the candle-light.

"Hooray!" said Mother; "here are some candles—the very first thing! You girls go and light them. You'll find some saucers and things. Just drop a little candle-grease in the saucer and stick the candle upright in it."

"How many shall we light?"

"As many as ever you like," said Mother, gaily. "The great thing is to be cheerful. Nobody can be cheerful in the dark except owls and dormice."

So the girls lighted candles. The head of the first match flew off and stuck to Phyllis's finger; but, as Roberta said, it was only a little burn, and she might have had to be a Roman martyr and be burned whole if she had happened to live in the days when those things were fashionable.

Then, when the dining-room was lighted by fourteen candles, Roberta fetched coal and wood and lighted a fire.

"It's very cold for May," she said, feeling what a grown-up thing it was to say.

The fire-light and the candle-light made the dining-room look very different, for now you could see that the dark walls were of wood, carved here and there into little wreaths and loops.

The girls hastily 'tidied' the room, which meant putting the chairs against the wall, and piling all the odds and ends into a corner and partly hiding them with the big leather arm-chair that Father used to sit in after dinner.

"Bravo!" cried Mother, coming in with a tray full of things. "This is something like! I'll just get a tablecloth and then—"

The tablecloth was in a box with a proper lock that was opened with a key and not with a shovel, and when the cloth was spread on the table, a real feast was laid out on it.

Everyone was very, very tired, but everyone cheered up at the sight of the funny and delightful supper. There were biscuits, the Marie and the plain kind, sardines, preserved ginger, cooking raisins, and candied peel and marmalade.

"What a good thing Aunt Emma packed up all the odds and ends out of the Store cupboard," said Mother. "Now, Phil, DON'T put the marmalade spoon in among the sardines."

"No, I won't, Mother," said Phyllis, and put it down among the Marie biscuits.

"Let's drink Aunt Emma's health," said Roberta, suddenly; "what should we have done if she hadn't packed up these things? Here's to Aunt Emma!"

And the toast was drunk in ginger wine and water, out of willow- patterned tea-cups, because the glasses couldn't be found.

They all felt that they had been a little hard on Aunt Emma. She wasn't a nice cuddly person like Mother, but after all it was she who had thought of packing up the odds and ends of things to eat.

It was Aunt Emma, too, who had aired all the sheets ready; and the men who had moved the furniture had put the bedsteads together, so the beds were soon made.

"Good night, chickies," said Mother. "I'm sure there aren't any rats. But I'll leave my door open, and then if a mouse comes, you need only scream, and I'll come and tell it exactly what I think of it."

Then she went to her own room. Roberta woke to hear the little travelling clock chime two. It sounded like a church clock ever so far away, she always thought. And she heard, too, Mother still moving about in her room.

Next morning Roberta woke Phyllis by pulling her hair gently, but quite enough for her purpose.

"Wassermarrer?" asked Phyllis, still almost wholly asleep.

"Wake up! wake up!" said Roberta. "We're in the new house—don't you remember? No servants or anything. Let's get up and begin to be useful. We'll just creep down mouse-quietly, and have everything beautiful before Mother gets up. I've woke Peter. He'll be dressed as soon as we are."

So they dressed quietly and quickly. Of course, there was no water in their room, so when they got down they washed as much as they thought was necessary under the spout of the pump in the yard. One pumped and the other washed. It was splashy but interesting.

"It's much more fun than basin washing," said Roberta. "How sparkly the weeds are between the stones, and the moss on the roof—oh, and the flowers!"

The roof of the back kitchen sloped down quite low. It was made of thatch and it had moss on it, and house-leeks and stonecrop and wallflowers, and even a clump of purple flag-flowers, at the far corner.

"This is far, far, far and away prettier than Edgecombe Villa," said Phyllis. "I wonder what the garden's like."

"We mustn't think of the garden yet," said Roberta, with earnest energy. "Let's go in and begin to work."

They lighted the fire and put the kettle on, and they arranged the crockery for breakfast; they could not find all the right things, but a glass ash-tray made an excellent salt-cellar, and a newish baking-tin seemed as if it would do to put bread on, if they had any.

When there seemed to be nothing more that they could do, they went out again into the fresh bright morning.

"We'll go into the garden now," said Peter. But somehow they couldn't find the garden. They went round the house and round the house. The yard occupied the back, and across it were stables and outbuildings. On the other three sides the house stood simply in a field, without a yard of garden to divide it from the short smooth turf. And yet they had certainly seen the garden wall the night before.

It was a hilly country. Down below they could see the line of the railway, and the black yawning mouth of a tunnel. The station was out of sight. There was a great bridge with tall arches running across one end of the valley.

"Never mind the garden," said Peter; "let's go down and look at the railway. There might be trains passing."

"We can see them from here," said Roberta, slowly; "let's sit down a bit."

So they all sat down on a great flat grey stone that had pushed itself up out of the grass; it was one of many that lay about on the hillside, and when Mother came out to look for them at eight o'clock, she found them deeply asleep in a contented, sun-warmed bunch.

They had made an excellent fire, and had set the kettle on it at about half-past five. So that by eight the fire had been out for some time, the water had all boiled away, and the bottom was burned out of the kettle. Also they had not thought of washing the crockery before they set the table.

"But it doesn't matter—the cups and saucers, I mean," said Mother. "Because I've found another room—I'd quite forgotten there was one. And it's magic! And I've boiled the water for tea in a saucepan."

The forgotten room opened out of the kitchen. In the agitation and half darkness the night before its door had been mistaken for a cupboard's. It was a little square room, and on its table, all nicely set out, was a joint of cold roast beef, with bread, butter, cheese, and a pie.

"Pie for breakfast!" cried Peter; "how perfectly ripping!"

"It isn't pigeon-pie," said Mother; "it's only apple. Well, this is the supper we ought to have had last night. And there was a note from Mrs. Viney. Her son-in-law has broken his arm, and she had to get home early. She's coming this morning at ten."

That was a wonderful breakfast. It is unusual to begin the day with cold apple pie, but the children all said they would rather have it than meat.

"You see it's more like dinner than breakfast to us," said Peter, passing his plate for more, "because we were up so early."

The day passed in helping Mother to unpack and arrange things. Six small legs quite ached with running about while their owners carried clothes and crockery and all sorts of things to their proper places. It was not till quite late in the afternoon that Mother said:—

"There! That'll do for to-day. I'll lie down for an hour, so as to be as fresh as a lark by supper-time."

Then they all looked at each other. Each of the three expressive countenances expressed the same thought. That thought was double, and consisted, like the bits of information in the Child's Guide to Knowledge, of a question and an answer.

Q. Where shall we go?

A. To the railway.

So to the railway they went, and as soon as they started for the railway they saw where the garden had hidden itself. It was right behind the stables, and it had a high wall all round.

"Oh, never mind about the garden now!" cried Peter. "Mother told me this morning where it was. It'll keep till to-morrow. Let's get to the railway."

The way to the railway was all down hill over smooth, short turf with here and there furze bushes and grey and yellow rocks sticking out like candied peel from the top of a cake.

The way ended in a steep run and a wooden fence—and there was the railway with the shining metals and the telegraph wires and posts and signals.

They all climbed on to the top of the fence, and then suddenly there was a rumbling sound that made them look along the line to the right, where the dark mouth of a tunnel opened itself in the face of a rocky cliff; next moment a train had rushed out of the tunnel with a shriek and a snort, and had slid noisily past them. They felt the rush of its passing, and the pebbles on the line jumped and rattled under it as it went by.

"Oh!" said Roberta, drawing a long breath; "it was like a great dragon tearing by. Did you feel it fan us with its hot wings?"

"I suppose a dragon's lair might look very like that tunnel from the outside," said Phyllis.

But Peter said:—

"I never thought we should ever get as near to a train as this. It's the most ripping sport!"

"Better than toy-engines, isn't it?" said Roberta.

(I am tired of calling Roberta by her name. I don't see why I should. No one else did. Everyone else called her Bobbie, and I don't see why I shouldn't.)

"I don't know; it's different," said Peter. "It seems so odd to see ALL of a train. It's awfully tall, isn't it?"

"We've always seen them cut in half by platforms," said Phyllis.

"I wonder if that train was going to London," Bobbie said. "London's where Father is."

"Let's go down to the station and find out," said Peter.

So they went.

They walked along the edge of the line, and heard the telegraph wires humming over their heads. When you are in the train, it seems such a little way between post and post, and one after another the posts seem to catch up the wires almost more quickly than you can count them. But when you have to walk, the posts seem few and far between.

But the children got to the station at last.

Never before had any of them been at a station, except for the purpose of catching trains—or perhaps waiting for them—and always with grown-ups in attendance, grown-ups who were not themselves interested in stations, except as places from which they wished to get away.

Never before had they passed close enough to a signal-box to be able to notice the wires, and to hear the mysterious 'ping, ping,' followed by the strong, firm clicking of machinery.

The very sleepers on which the rails lay were a delightful path to travel by—just far enough apart to serve as the stepping-stones in a game of foaming torrents hastily organised by Bobbie.

Then to arrive at the station, not through the booking office, but in a freebooting sort of way by the sloping end of the platform. This in itself was joy.

Joy, too, it was to peep into the porters' room, where the lamps are, and the Railway almanac on the wall, and one porter half asleep behind a paper.

There were a great many crossing lines at the station; some of them just ran into a yard and stopped short, as though they were tired of business and meant to retire for good. Trucks stood on the rails here, and on one side was a great heap of coal—not a loose heap, such as you see in your coal cellar, but a sort of solid building of coals with large square blocks of coal outside used just as though they were bricks, and built up till the heap looked like the picture of the Cities of the Plain in 'Bible Stories for Infants.' There was a line of whitewash near the top of the coaly wall.

When presently the Porter lounged out of his room at the twice-repeated tingling thrill of a gong over the station door, Peter said, "How do you do?" in his best manner, and hastened to ask what the white mark was on the coal for.

"To mark how much coal there be," said the Porter, "so as we'll know if anyone nicks it. So don't you go off with none in your pockets, young gentleman!"

This seemed, at the time but a merry jest, and Peter felt at once that the Porter was a friendly sort with no nonsense about him. But later the words came back to Peter with a new meaning.

Have you ever gone into a farmhouse kitchen on a baking day, and seen the great crock of dough set by the fire to rise? If you have, and if you were at that time still young enough to be interested in everything you saw, you will remember that you found yourself quite unable to resist the temptation to poke your finger into the soft round of dough that curved inside the pan like a giant mushroom. And you will remember that your finger made a dent in the dough, and that slowly, but quite surely, the dent disappeared, and the dough looked quite the same as it did before you touched it. Unless, of course, your hand was extra dirty, in which case, naturally, there would be a little black mark.

Well, it was just like that with the sorrow the children had felt at Father's going away, and at Mother's being so unhappy. It made a deep impression, but the impression did not last long.

They soon got used to being without Father, though they did not forget him; and they got used to not going to school, and to seeing very little of Mother, who was now almost all day shut up in her upstairs room writing, writing, writing. She used to come down at tea-time and read aloud the stories she had written. They were lovely stories.

The rocks and hills and valleys and trees, the canal, and above all, the railway, were so new and so perfectly pleasing that the remembrance of the old life in the villa grew to seem almost like a dream.

Mother had told them more than once that they were 'quite poor now,' but this did not seem to be anything but a way of speaking. Grown- up people, even Mothers, often make remarks that don't seem to mean anything in particular, just for the sake of saying something, seemingly. There was always enough to eat, and they wore the same kind of nice clothes they had always worn.

But in June came three wet days; the rain came down, straight as lances, and it was very, very cold. Nobody could go out, and everybody shivered. They all went up to the door of Mother's room and knocked.

"Well, what is it?" asked Mother from inside.

"Mother," said Bobbie, "mayn't I light a fire? I do know how."

And Mother said: "No, my ducky-love. We mustn't have fires in June—coal is so dear. If you're cold, go and have a good romp in the attic. That'll warm you."

"But, Mother, it only takes such a very little coal to make a fire."

"It's more than we can afford, chickeny-love," said Mother, cheerfully. "Now run away, there's darlings—I'm madly busy!"

"Mother's always busy now," said Phyllis, in a whisper to Peter. Peter did not answer. He shrugged his shoulders. He was thinking.

Thought, however, could not long keep itself from the suitable furnishing of a bandit's lair in the attic. Peter was the bandit, of course. Bobbie was his lieutenant, his band of trusty robbers, and, in due course, the parent of Phyllis, who was the captured maiden for whom a magnificent ransom—in horse-beans—was unhesitatingly paid.

They all went down to tea flushed and joyous as any mountain brigands.

But when Phyllis was going to add jam to her bread and butter, Mother said:—

"Jam OR butter, dear—not jam AND butter. We can't afford that sort of reckless luxury nowadays."

Phyllis finished the slice of bread and butter in silence, and followed it up by bread and jam. Peter mingled thought and weak tea.

After tea they went back to the attic and he said to his sisters:—

"I have an idea."

"What's that?" they asked politely.

"I shan't tell you," was Peter's unexpected rejoinder.

"Oh, very well," said Bobbie; and Phil said, "Don't, then."

"Girls," said Peter, "are always so hasty tempered."

"I should like to know what boys are?" said Bobbie, with fine disdain. "I don't want to know about your silly ideas."

"You'll know some day," said Peter, keeping his own temper by what looked exactly like a miracle; "if you hadn't been so keen on a row, I might have told you about it being only noble-heartedness that made me not tell you my idea. But now I shan't tell you anything at all about it—so there!"

And it was, indeed, some time before he could be induced to say anything, and when he did it wasn't much. He said:—

"The only reason why I won't tell you my idea that I'm going to do is because it MAY be wrong, and I don't want to drag you into it."

"Don't you do it if it's wrong, Peter," said Bobbie; "let me do it." But Phyllis said:—

"*I* should like to do wrong if YOU'RE going to!"

"No," said Peter, rather touched by this devotion; "it's a forlorn hope, and I'm going to lead it. All I ask is that if Mother asks where I am, you won't blab."

"We haven't got anything TO blab," said Bobbie, indignantly.

"Oh, yes, you have!" said Peter, dropping horse-beans through his fingers. "I've trusted you to the death. You know I'm going to do a lone adventure—and some people might think it wrong—I don't. And if Mother asks where I am, say I'm playing at mines."

"What sort of mines?"

"You just say mines."

"You might tell US, Pete."

"Well, then, COAL-mines. But don't you let the word pass your lips on pain of torture."

"You needn't threaten," said Bobbie, "and I do think you might let us help."

"If I find a coal-mine, you shall help cart the coal," Peter condescended to promise.

"Keep your secret if you like," said Phyllis.

"Keep it if you CAN," said Bobbie.

"I'll keep it, right enough," said Peter.

Between tea and supper there is an interval even in the most greedily regulated families. At this time Mother was usually writing, and Mrs. Viney had gone home.

Two nights after the dawning of Peter's idea he beckoned the girls mysteriously at the twilight hour.

"Come hither with me," he said, "and bring the Roman Chariot."

The Roman Chariot was a very old perambulator that had spent years of retirement in the loft over the coach-house. The children had oiled its works till it glided noiseless as a pneumatic bicycle, and answered to the helm as it had probably done in its best days.

"Follow your dauntless leader," said Peter, and led the way down the hill towards the station.

Just above the station many rocks have pushed their heads out through the turf as though they, like the children, were interested in the railway.

In a little hollow between three rocks lay a heap of dried brambles and heather.

Peter halted, turned over the brushwood with a well-scarred boot, and said:—

"Here's the first coal from the St. Peter's Mine. We'll take it home in the chariot. Punctuality and despatch. All orders carefully attended to. Any shaped lump cut to suit regular customers."

The chariot was packed full of coal. And when it was packed it had to be unpacked again because it was so heavy that it couldn't be got up the hill by the three children, not even when Peter harnessed himself to the handle with his braces, and firmly grasping his waistband in one hand pulled while the girls pushed behind.

Three journeys had to be made before the coal from Peter's mine was added to the heap of Mother's coal in the cellar.

Afterwards Peter went out alone, and came back very black and mysterious.

"I've been to my coal-mine," he said; "to-morrow evening we'll bring home the black diamonds in the chariot."

It was a week later that Mrs. Viney remarked to Mother how well this last lot of coal was holding out.

The children hugged themselves and each other in complicated wriggles of silent laughter as they listened on the stairs. They had all forgotten by now that there had ever been any doubt in Peter's mind as to whether coal-mining was wrong.

But there came a dreadful night when the Station Master put on a pair of old sand shoes that he had worn at the seaside in his summer holiday, and crept out very quietly to the yard where the Sodom and Gomorrah heap of coal was, with the whitewashed line round it. He crept out there, and he waited like a cat by a mousehole. On the top of the heap something small and dark was scrabbling and rattling furtively among the coal.

The Station Master concealed himself in the shadow of a brake-van that had a little tin chimney and was labelled:—

G. N. and S. R. 34576 Return at once to White Heather Sidings

and in this concealment he lurked till the small thing on the top of the heap ceased to scrabble and rattle, came to the edge of the heap, cautiously let itself down, and lifted something after it. Then the arm of the Station Master was raised, the hand of the Station Master fell on a collar, and there was Peter firmly held by the jacket, with an old carpenter's bag full of coal in his trembling clutch.

"So I've caught you at last, have I, you young thief?" said the Station Master.

"I'm not a thief," said Peter, as firmly as he could. "I'm a coal-miner."

"Tell that to the Marines," said the Station Master.

"It would be just as true whoever I told it to," said Peter.

"You're right there," said the man, who held him. "Stow your jaw, you young rip, and come along to the station."

"Oh, no," cried in the darkness an agonised voice that was not Peter's.

"Not the POLICE station!" said another voice from the darkness.

"Not yet," said the Station Master. "The Railway Station first. Why, it's a regular gang. Any more of you?"

"Only us," said Bobbie and Phyllis, coming out of the shadow of another truck labelled Staveley Colliery, and bearing on it the legend in white chalk: 'Wanted in No. 1 Road.'

"What do you mean by spying on a fellow like this?" said Peter, angrily.

"Time someone did spy on you, *I* think," said the Station Master. "Come along to the station."

"Oh, DON'T!" said Bobbie. "Can't you decide NOW what you'll do to us? It's our fault just as much as Peter's. We helped to carry the coal away—and we knew where he got it."

"No, you didn't," said Peter.

"Yes, we did," said Bobbie. "We knew all the time. We only pretended we didn't just to humour you."

Peter's cup was full. He had mined for coal, he had struck coal, he had been caught, and now he learned that his sisters had 'humoured' him.

"Don't hold me!" he said. "I won't run away."

The Station Master loosed Peter's collar, struck a match and looked at them by its flickering light.

"Why," said he, "you're the children from the Three Chimneys up yonder. So nicely dressed, too. Tell me now, what made you do such a thing? Haven't you ever been to church or learned your catechism or anything, not to know it's wicked to steal?" He spoke much more gently now, and Peter said:—

"I didn't think it was stealing. I was almost sure it wasn't. I thought if I took it from the outside part of the heap, perhaps it would be. But in the middle I thought I could fairly count it only mining. It'll take thousands of years for you to burn up all that coal and get to the middle parts."

"Not quite. But did you do it for a lark or what?"

"Not much lark carting that beastly heavy stuff up the hill," said Peter, indignantly.

"Then why did you?" The Station Master's voice was so much kinder now that Peter replied:—

"You know that wet day? Well, Mother said we were too poor to have a fire. We always had fires when it was cold at our other house, and—"

"DON'T!" interrupted Bobbie, in a whisper.

"Well," said the Station Master, rubbing his chin thoughtfully, "I'll tell you what I'll do. I'll look over it this once. But you remember, young gentleman, stealing is stealing, and what's mine isn't yours, whether you call it mining or whether you don't. Run along home."

"Do you mean you aren't going to do anything to us? Well, you are a brick," said Peter, with enthusiasm.

"You're a dear," said Bobbie.

"You're a darling," said Phyllis.

"That's all right," said the Station Master.

And on this they parted.

"Don't speak to me," said Peter, as the three went up the hill. "You're spies and traitors—that's what you are."

But the girls were too glad to have Peter between them, safe and free, and on the way to Three Chimneys and not to the Police Station, to mind much what he said.

"We DID say it was us as much as you," said Bobbie, gently.

"Well—and it wasn't."

"It would have come to the same thing in Courts with judges," said Phyllis. "Don't be snarky, Peter. It isn't our fault your secrets are so jolly easy to find out." She took his arm, and he let her.

"There's an awful lot of coal in the cellar, anyhow," he went on.

"Oh, don't!" said Bobbie. "I don't think we ought to be glad about THAT."

"I don't know," said Peter, plucking up a spirit. "I'm not at all sure, even now, that mining is a crime."

But the girls were quite sure. And they were also quite sure that he was quite sure, however little he cared to own it.

Chapter 3. The Old Gentleman.

After the adventure of Peter's Coal-mine, it seemed well to the children to keep away from the station—but they did not, they could not, keep away from the railway. They had lived all their lives in a street where cabs and omnibuses rumbled by at all hours, and the carts of butchers and bakers and candlestick makers (I never saw a candlestick-maker's cart; did you?) might occur at any moment. Here in the deep silence of the sleeping country the only things that went by were the trains. They seemed to be all that was left to link the children to the old life that had once been theirs. Straight down the hill in front of Three Chimneys the daily passage of their six feet began to mark a path across the crisp, short turf. They began to know the hours when certain trains passed, and they gave names to them. The 9.15 up was called the Green Dragon. The 10.7 down was the Worm of Wantley. The midnight town express, whose shrieking rush they sometimes woke from their dreams to hear, was the Fearsome Fly-by-night. Peter got up once, in chill starshine, and, peeping at it through his curtains, named it on the spot.

It was by the Green Dragon that the old gentleman travelled. He was a very nice-looking old gentleman, and he looked as if he were nice, too, which is not at all the same thing. He had a fresh-coloured, clean-shaven face and white hair, and he wore rather odd-shaped collars and a top-hat that wasn't exactly the same kind as other people's. Of course the children didn't see all this at first. In fact the first thing they noticed about the old gentleman was his hand.

It was one morning as they sat on the fence waiting for the Green Dragon, which was three and a quarter minutes late by Peter's Waterbury watch that he had had given him on his last birthday.

"The Green Dragon's going where Father is," said Phyllis; "if it were a really real dragon, we could stop it and ask it to take our love to Father."

"Dragons don't carry people's love," said Peter; "they'd be above it."

"Yes, they do, if you tame them thoroughly first. They fetch and carry like pet spaniels," said Phyllis, "and feed out of your hand. I wonder why Father never writes to us."

"Mother says he's been too busy," said Bobbie; "but he'll write soon, she says."

"I say," Phyllis suggested, "let's all wave to the Green Dragon as it goes by. If it's a magic dragon, it'll understand and take our loves to Father. And if it isn't, three waves aren't much. We shall never miss them."

So when the Green Dragon tore shrieking out of the mouth of its dark lair, which was the tunnel, all three children stood on the railing and waved their pocket-handkerchiefs without stopping to think whether they were clean handkerchiefs or the reverse. They were, as a matter of fact, very much the reverse.

And out of a first-class carriage a hand waved back. A quite clean hand. It held a newspaper. It was the old gentleman's hand.

After this it became the custom for waves to be exchanged between the children and the 9.15.

And the children, especially the girls, liked to think that perhaps the old gentleman knew Father, and would meet him 'in business,' wherever that shady retreat might be, and tell him how his three children stood on a rail far away in the green country and waved their love to him every morning, wet or fine.

For they were now able to go out in all sorts of weather such as they would never have been allowed to go out in when they lived in their villa house. This was Aunt Emma's doing, and the children felt more and more that they had not been quite fair to this unattractive aunt, when they found how useful were the long gaiters and waterproof coats that they had laughed at her for buying for them.

Mother, all this time, was very busy with her writing. She used to send off a good many long blue envelopes with stories in them—and large envelopes of different sizes and colours used to come to her. Sometimes she would sigh when she opened them and say:—

"Another story come home to roost. Oh, dear, Oh, dear!" and then the children would be very sorry.

But sometimes she would wave the envelope in the air and say:— "Hooray, hooray. Here's a sensible Editor. He's taken my story and this is the proof of it."

At first the children thought 'the Proof' meant the letter the sensible Editor had written, but they presently got to know that the proof was long slips of paper with the story printed on them.

Whenever an Editor was sensible there were buns for tea.

One day Peter was going down to the village to get buns to celebrate the sensibleness of the Editor of the Children's Globe, when he met the Station Master.

Peter felt very uncomfortable, for he had now had time to think over the affair of the coal-mine. He did not like to say "Good morning" to the Station Master, as you usually do to anyone you meet on a lonely road, because he had a hot feeling, which spread even to his ears, that the Station Master might not care to speak to a person who had stolen coals. 'Stolen' is a nasty word, but Peter felt it was the right one. So he looked down, and said Nothing.

It was the Station Master who said "Good morning" as he passed by. And Peter answered, "Good morning." Then he thought:—

"Perhaps he doesn't know who I am by daylight, or he wouldn't be so polite."

And he did not like the feeling which thinking this gave him. And then before he knew what he was going to do he ran after the Station Master, who stopped when he heard Peter's hasty boots crunching the road, and coming up with him very breathless and with his ears now quite magenta-coloured, he said:—

"I don't want you to be polite to me if you don't know me when you see me."

"Eh?" said the Station Master.

"I thought perhaps you didn't know it was me that took the coals," Peter went on, "when you said 'Good morning.' But it was, and I'm sorry. There."

"Why," said the Station Master, "I wasn't thinking anything at all about the precious coals. Let bygones be bygones. And where were you off to in such a hurry?"

"I'm going to buy buns for tea," said Peter.

"I thought you were all so poor," said the Station Master.

"So we are," said Peter, confidentially, "but we always have three pennyworth of halfpennies for tea whenever Mother sells a story or a poem or anything."

"Oh," said the Station Master, "so your Mother writes stories, does she?"

"The beautifulest you ever read," said Peter.

"You ought to be very proud to have such a clever Mother."

"Yes," said Peter, "but she used to play with us more before she had to be so clever."

"Well," said the Station Master, "I must be getting along. You give us a look in at the Station whenever you feel so inclined. And as to coals, it's a word that—well—oh, no, we never mention it, eh?"

"Thank you," said Peter. "I'm very glad it's all straightened out between us." And he went on across the canal bridge to the village to get the buns, feeling more comfortable in his mind than he had felt since the hand of the Station Master had fastened on his collar that night among the coals.

Next day when they had sent the threefold wave of greeting to Father by the Green Dragon, and the old gentleman had waved back as usual, Peter proudly led the way to the station.

"But ought we?" said Bobbie.

"After the coals, she means," Phyllis explained.

"I met the Station Master yesterday," said Peter, in an offhand way, and he pretended not to hear what Phyllis had said; "he expresspecially invited us to go down any time we liked."

"After the coals?" repeated Phyllis. "Stop a minute—my bootlace is undone again."

"It always IS undone again," said Peter, "and the Station Master was more of a gentleman than you'll ever be, Phil—throwing coal at a chap's head like that."

Phyllis did up her bootlace and went on in silence, but her shoulders shook, and presently a fat tear fell off her nose and splashed on the metal of the railway line. Bobbie saw it.

"Why, what's the matter, darling?" she said, stopping short and putting her arm round the heaving shoulders.

"He called me un-un-ungentlemanly," sobbed Phyllis. "I didn't never call him unladylike, not even when he tied my Clorinda to the firewood bundle and burned her at the stake for a martyr."

Peter had indeed perpetrated this outrage a year or two before.

"Well, you began, you know," said Bobbie, honestly, "about coals and all that. Don't you think you'd better both unsay everything since the wave, and let honour be satisfied?"

"I will if Peter will," said Phyllis, sniffling.

"All right," said Peter; "honour is satisfied. Here, use my hankie, Phil, for goodness' sake, if you've lost yours as usual. I wonder what you do with them."

"You had my last one," said Phyllis, indignantly, "to tie up the rabbit-hutch door with. But you're very ungrateful. It's quite right what it says in the poetry book about sharper than a serpent it is to have a toothless child—but it means ungrateful when it says toothless. Miss Lowe told me so."

"All right," said Peter, impatiently, "I'm sorry. THERE! Now will you come on?"

They reached the station and spent a joyous two hours with the Porter. He was a worthy man and seemed never tired of answering the questions that begin with "Why—" which many people in higher ranks of life often seem weary of.

He told them many things that they had not known before—as, for instance, that the things that hook carriages together are called couplings, and that the pipes like great serpents that hang over the couplings are meant to stop the train with.

"If you could get a holt of one o' them when the train is going and pull 'em apart," said he, "she'd stop dead off with a jerk."

"Who's she?" said Phyllis.

"The train, of course," said the Porter. After that the train was never again 'It' to the children.

"And you know the thing in the carriages where it says on it, 'Five pounds' fine for improper use.' If you was to improperly use that, the train 'ud stop."

"And if you used it properly?" said Roberta.

"It 'ud stop just the same, I suppose," said he, "but it isn't proper use unless you're being murdered. There was an old lady once—someone kidded her on it was a refreshment-room bell, and she used it improper, not being in danger of her life, though hungry, and when the train stopped and the guard came along expecting to find someone weltering in their last moments, she says, "Oh, please, Mister, I'll take a glass of stout and a bath bun," she says. And the train was seven minutes behind her time as it was."

"What did the guard say to the old lady?"

"*I* dunno," replied the Porter, "but I lay she didn't forget it in a hurry, whatever it was."

In such delightful conversation the time went by all too quickly.

The Station Master came out once or twice from that sacred inner temple behind the place where the hole is that they sell you tickets through, and was most jolly with them all.

"Just as if coal had never been discovered," Phyllis whispered to her sister.

He gave them each an orange, and promised to take them up into the signal-box one of these days, when he wasn't so busy.

Several trains went through the station, and Peter noticed for the first time that engines have numbers on them, like cabs.

"Yes," said the Porter, "I knowed a young gent as used to take down the numbers of every single one he seed; in a green note-book with silver corners it was, owing to his father being very well-to-do in the wholesale stationery."

Peter felt that he could take down numbers, too, even if he was not the son of a wholesale stationer. As he did not happen to have a green leather note-book with silver corners, the Porter gave him a yellow envelope and on it he noted:—

379 663

and felt that this was the beginning of what would be a most interesting collection.

That night at tea he asked Mother if she had a green leather note- book with silver corners. She had not; but when she heard what he wanted it for she gave him a little black one.

"It has a few pages torn out," said she; "but it will hold quite a lot of numbers, and when it's full I'll give you another. I'm so glad you like the railway. Only, please, you mustn't walk on the line."

"Not if we face the way the train's coming?" asked Peter, after a gloomy pause, in which glances of despair were exchanged.

"No—really not," said Mother.

Then Phyllis said, "Mother, didn't YOU ever walk on the railway lines when you were little?"

Mother was an honest and honourable Mother, so she had to say, "Yes."

"Well, then," said Phyllis.

"But, darlings, you don't know how fond I am of you. What should I do if you got hurt?"

"Are you fonder of us than Granny was of you when you were little?" Phyllis asked. Bobbie made signs to her to stop, but Phyllis never did see signs, no matter how plain they might be.

Mother did not answer for a minute. She got up to put more water in the teapot.

"No one," she said at last, "ever loved anyone more than my mother loved me."

Then she was quiet again, and Bobbie kicked Phyllis hard under the table, because Bobbie understood a little bit the thoughts that were making Mother so quiet—the thoughts of the time when Mother was a little girl and was all the world to HER mother. It seems so easy and natural to run to Mother when one is in trouble. Bobbie understood a little how people do not leave off running to their mothers when they are in trouble even when they are grown up, and she thought she knew a little what it must be to be sad, and have no mother to run to any more.

So she kicked Phyllis, who said:—

"What are you kicking me like that for, Bob?"

And then Mother laughed a little and sighed and said:—

"Very well, then. Only let me be sure you do know which way the trains come—and don't walk on the line near the tunnel or near corners."

"Trains keep to the left like carriages," said Peter, "so if we keep to the right, we're bound to see them coming."

"Very well," said Mother, and I dare say you think that she ought not to have said it. But she remembered about when she was a little girl herself, and she did say it—and neither her own children nor you nor any other children in the world could ever understand exactly what it cost her to do it. Only some few of you, like Bobbie, may understand a very little bit.

It was the very next day that Mother had to stay in bed because her head ached so. Her hands were burning hot, and she would not eat anything, and her throat was very sore.

"If I was you, Mum," said Mrs. Viney, "I should take and send for the doctor. There's a lot of catchy complaints a-going about just now. My sister's eldest—she took a chill and it went to her inside, two years ago come Christmas, and she's never been the same gell since."

Mother wouldn't at first, but in the evening she felt so much worse that Peter was sent to the house in the village that had three laburnum trees by the gate, and on the gate a brass plate with W. W. Forrest, M.D., on it.

W. W. Forrest, M.D., came at once. He talked to Peter on the way back. He seemed a most charming and sensible man, interested in railways, and rabbits, and really important things.

When he had seen Mother, he said it was influenza.

"Now, Lady Grave-airs," he said in the hall to Bobbie, "I suppose you'll want to be head-nurse."

"Of course," said she.

"Well, then, I'll send down some medicine. Keep up a good fire. Have some strong beef tea made ready to give her as soon as the fever goes down. She can have grapes now, and beef essence—and soda-water and milk, and you'd better get in a bottle of brandy. The best brandy. Cheap brandy is worse than poison."

She asked him to write it all down, and he did.

When Bobbie showed Mother the list he had written, Mother laughed. It WAS a laugh, Bobbie decided, though it was rather odd and feeble.

"Nonsense," said Mother, laying in bed with eyes as bright as beads. "I can't afford all that rubbish. Tell Mrs. Viney to boil two pounds of scrag-end of the neck for your dinners to-morrow, and I can have some of the broth. Yes, I should like some more water now, love. And will you get a basin and sponge my hands?"

Roberta obeyed. When she had done everything she could to make Mother less uncomfortable, she went down to the others. Her cheeks were very red, her lips set tight, and her eyes almost as bright as Mother's.

She told them what the Doctor had said, and what Mother had said.

"And now," said she, when she had told all, "there's no one but us to do anything, and we've got to do it. I've got the shilling for the mutton."

"We can do without the beastly mutton," said Peter; "bread and butter will support life. People have lived on less on desert islands many a time."

"Of course," said his sister. And Mrs. Viney was sent to the village to get as much brandy and soda-water and beef tea as she could buy for a shilling.

"But even if we never have anything to eat at all," said Phyllis, "you can't get all those other things with our dinner money."

"No," said Bobbie, frowning, "we must find out some other way. Now THINK, everybody, just as hard as ever you can."

They did think. And presently they talked. And later, when Bobbie had gone up to sit with Mother in case she wanted anything, the other two were very busy with scissors and a white sheet, and a paint brush, and the pot of Brunswick black that Mrs. Viney used for grates and fenders. They did not manage to do what they wished, exactly, with the first sheet, so they took another out of the linen cupboard. It did not occur to them that they were spoiling good sheets which cost good money. They only knew that they were making a good—but what they were making comes later.

Bobbie's bed had been moved into Mother's room, and several times in the night she got up to mend the fire, and to give her mother milk and soda-water. Mother talked to herself a good deal, but it did not seem to mean anything. And once she woke up suddenly and called out: "Mamma, mamma!" and Bobbie knew she was calling for Granny, and that she had forgotten that it was no use calling, because Granny was dead.

In the early morning Bobbie heard her name and jumped out of bed and ran to Mother's bedside.

"Oh—ah, yes—I think I was asleep," said Mother. "My poor little duck, how tired you'll be—I do hate to give you all this trouble."

"Trouble!" said Bobbie.

"Ah, don't cry, sweet," Mother said; "I shall be all right in a day or two."

And Bobbie said, "Yes," and tried to smile.

When you are used to ten hours of solid sleep, to get up three or four times in your sleep-time makes you feel as though you had been up all night. Bobbie felt quite stupid and her eyes were sore and stiff, but she tidied the room, and arranged everything neatly before the Doctor came.

This was at half-past eight.

"Everything going on all right, little Nurse?" he said at the front door. "Did you get the brandy?"

"I've got the brandy," said Bobbie, "in a little flat bottle."

"I didn't see the grapes or the beef tea, though," said he.

"No," said Bobbie, firmly, "but you will to-morrow. And there's some beef stewing in the oven for beef tea."

"Who told you to do that?" he asked.

"I noticed what Mother did when Phil had mumps."

"Right," said the Doctor. "Now you get your old woman to sit with your mother, and then you eat a good breakfast, and go straight to bed and sleep till dinner-time. We can't afford to have the head- nurse ill."

He was really quite a nice doctor.

When the 9.15 came out of the tunnel that morning the old gentleman in the first-class carriage put down his newspaper, and got ready to wave his hand to the three children on the fence. But this morning there were not three. There was only one. And that was Peter.

Peter was not on the railings either, as usual. He was standing in front of them in an attitude like that of a show-man showing off the animals in a menagerie, or of the kind clergyman when he points with a wand at the 'Scenes from Palestine,' when there is a magic-lantern and he is explaining it.

Peter was pointing, too. And what he was pointing at was a large white sheet nailed against the fence. On the sheet there were thick black letters more than a foot long.

Some of them had run a little, because of Phyllis having put the Brunswick black on too eagerly, but the words were quite easy to read.

And this what the old gentleman and several other people in the train read in the large black letters on the white sheet:—

LOOK OUT AT THE STATION.

A good many people did look out at the station and were disappointed, for they saw nothing unusual. The old gentleman looked out, too, and at first he too saw nothing more unusual than the gravelled platform and the sunshine and the wallflowers and forget-me-nots in the station borders. It was only just as the train was beginning to puff and pull itself together to start again that he saw Phyllis. She was quite out of breath with running.

"Oh," she said, "I thought I'd missed you. My bootlaces would keep coming down and I fell over them twice. Here, take it."

She thrust a warm, dampish letter into his hand as the train moved.

He leaned back in his corner and opened the letter. This is what he read:—

> "Dear Mr. We do not know your name.
>
> Mother is ill and the doctor says to give her the things at the end of the letter, but she says she can't aford it, and to get mutton for us and she will have the broth. We do not know anybody here but you, because Father is away and we do not know the address. Father will pay you, or if he has lost all his money, or anything, Peter will pay you when he is a man. We promise it on our honer. I.O.U. for all the things Mother wants.
>
> "sined Peter.

"Will you give the parsel to the Station Master, because of us not knowing what train you come down by? Say it is for Peter that was sorry about the coals and he will know all right.

"Roberta. "Phyllis. "Peter."

Then came the list of things the Doctor had ordered.

The old gentleman read it through once, and his eyebrows went up. He read it twice and smiled a little. When he had read it thrice, he put it in his pocket and went on reading The Times.

At about six that evening there was a knock at the back door. The three children rushed to open it, and there stood the friendly Porter, who had told them so many interesting things about railways. He dumped down a big hamper on the kitchen flags.

"Old gent," he said; "he asked me to fetch it up straight away."

"Thank you very much," said Peter, and then, as the Porter lingered, he added:—

"I'm most awfully sorry I haven't got twopence to give you like Father does, but—"

"You drop it if you please," said the Porter, indignantly. "I wasn't thinking about no tuppences. I only wanted to say I was sorry your Mamma wasn't so well, and to ask how she finds herself this evening—and I've fetched her along a bit of sweetbrier, very sweet to smell it is. Twopence indeed," said he, and produced a bunch of sweetbrier from his hat, "just like a conjurer," as Phyllis remarked afterwards.

"Thank you very much," said Peter, "and I beg your pardon about the twopence."

"No offence," said the Porter, untruly but politely, and went.

Then the children undid the hamper. First there was straw, and then there were fine shavings, and then came all the things they had asked for, and plenty of them, and then a good many things they had not asked for; among others peaches and port wine and two chickens, a cardboard box of big red roses with long stalks, and a tall thin green bottle of lavender water, and three smaller fatter bottles of eau-de-Cologne. There was a letter, too.

"Dear Roberta and Phyllis and Peter," it said; "here are the things you want. Your mother will want to know where they came from. Tell her they were sent by a friend who heard she was ill. When she is well again you must tell her all about it, of course. And if she says you ought not to have asked for the things, tell her that I say you were quite right, and that I hope she will forgive me for taking the liberty of allowing myself a very great pleasure."

The letter was signed G. P. something that the children couldn't read.

"I think we WERE right," said Phyllis.

"Right? Of course we were right," said Bobbie.

"All the same," said Peter, with his hands in his pockets, "I don't exactly look forward to telling Mother the whole truth about it."

"We're not to do it till she's well," said Bobbie, "and when she's well we shall be so happy we shan't mind a little fuss like that. Oh, just look at the roses! I must take them up to her."

"And the sweetbrier," said Phyllis, sniffing it loudly; "don't forget the sweetbrier."

"As if I should!" said Roberta. "Mother told me the other day there was a thick hedge of it at her mother's house when she was a little girl."

Chapter 4. The Engine-Burglar.

What was left of the second sheet and the Brunswick black came in very nicely to make a banner bearing the legend

SHE IS NEARLY WELL THANK YOU

and this was displayed to the Green Dragon about a fortnight after the arrival of the wonderful hamper. The old gentleman saw it, and waved a cheerful response from the train. And when this had been done the children saw that now was the time when they must tell Mother what they had done when she was ill. And it did not seem nearly so easy as they had thought it would be. But it had to be done. And it was done. Mother was extremely angry. She was seldom angry, and now she was angrier than they had ever known her. This was horrible. But it was much worse when she suddenly began to cry. Crying is catching, I believe, like measles and whooping-cough. At any rate, everyone at once found itself taking part in a crying- party.

Mother stopped first. She dried her eyes and then she said:—

"I'm sorry I was so angry, darlings, because I know you didn't understand."

"We didn't mean to be naughty, Mammy," sobbed Bobbie, and Peter and Phyllis sniffed.

"Now, listen," said Mother; "it's quite true that we're poor, but we have enough to live on. You mustn't go telling everyone about our affairs—it's not right. And you must never, never, never ask strangers to give you things. Now always remember that—won't you?"

They all hugged her and rubbed their damp cheeks against hers and promised that they would.

"And I'll write a letter to your old gentleman, and I shall tell him that I didn't approve—oh, of course I shall thank him, too, for his kindness. It's YOU I don't approve of, my darlings, not the old gentleman. He was as kind as ever he could be. And you can give the letter to the Station Master to give him—and we won't say any more about it."

Afterwards, when the children were alone, Bobbie said:—

"Isn't Mother splendid? You catch any other grown-up saying they were sorry they had been angry."

"Yes," said Peter, "she IS splendid; but it's rather awful when she's angry."

"She's like Avenging and Bright in the song," said Phyllis. "I should like to look at her if it wasn't so awful. She looks so beautiful when she's really downright furious."

They took the letter down to the Station Master.

"I thought you said you hadn't got any friends except in London," said he.

"We've made him since," said Peter.

"But he doesn't live hereabouts?"

"No—we just know him on the railway."

Then the Station Master retired to that sacred inner temple behind the little window where the tickets are sold, and the children went down to the Porters' room and talked to the Porter. They learned several interesting things from him—among others that his name was Perks, that he was married and had three children, that the lamps in front of engines are called head-lights and the ones at the back tail-lights.

"And that just shows," whispered Phyllis, "that trains really ARE dragons in disguise, with proper heads and tails."

It was on this day that the children first noticed that all engines are not alike.

"Alike?" said the Porter, whose name was Perks, "lor, love you, no, Miss. No more alike nor what you an' me are. That little 'un without a tender as went by just now all on her own, that was a tank, that was—she's off to do some shunting t'other side o' Maidbridge. That's as it might be you, Miss. Then there's goods engines, great, strong things with three wheels each side—joined with rods to strengthen 'em—as it might be me. Then there's main- line engines as it might be this 'ere young gentleman when he grows up and wins all the races at 'is school—so he will. The main-line engine she's built for speed as well as power. That's one to the 9.15 up."

"The Green Dragon," said Phyllis.

"We calls her the Snail, Miss, among ourselves," said the Porter. "She's oftener be'ind'and nor any train on the line."

"But the engine's green," said Phyllis.

"Yes, Miss," said Perks, "so's a snail some seasons o' the year."

The children agreed as they went home to dinner that the Porter was most delightful company.

Next day was Roberta's birthday. In the afternoon she was politely but firmly requested to get out of the way and keep there till tea- time.

"You aren't to see what we're going to do till it's done; it's a glorious surprise," said Phyllis.

And Roberta went out into the garden all alone. She tried to be grateful, but she felt she would much rather have helped in whatever it was than have to spend her birthday afternoon by herself, no matter how glorious the surprise might be.

Now that she was alone, she had time to think, and one of the things she thought of most was what mother had said in one of those feverish nights when her hands were so hot and her eyes so bright.

The words were: "Oh, what a doctor's bill there'll be for this!"

She walked round and round the garden among the rose-bushes that hadn't any roses yet, only buds, and the lilac bushes and syringas and American currants, and the more she thought of the doctor's bill, the less she liked the thought of it.

And presently she made up her mind. She went out through the side door of the garden and climbed up the steep field to where the road runs along by the canal. She walked along until she came to the bridge that crosses the canal and leads to the village, and here she waited. It was very pleasant in the sunshine to lean one's elbows on the warm stone of the bridge and look down at the blue water of the canal. Bobbie had never seen any other canal, except the Regent's Canal, and the water of that is not at all a pretty colour. And she had never seen any river at all except the Thames, which also would be all the better if its face was washed.

Perhaps the children would have loved the canal as much as the railway, but for two things. One was that they had found the railway FIRST—on that first, wonderful morning when the house and the country and the moors and rocks and great hills were all new to them. They had not found the canal till some days later. The other reason was that everyone on the railway had been kind to them—the Station Master, the Porter, and the old gentleman who waved. And the people on the canal were anything but kind.

The people on the canal were, of course, the bargees, who steered the slow barges up and down, or walked beside the old horses that trampled up the mud of the towing-path, and strained at the long tow-ropes.

Peter had once asked one of the bargees the time, and had been told to "get out of that," in a tone so fierce that he did not stop to say anything about his having just as much right on the towing-path as the man himself. Indeed, he did not even think of saying it till some time later.

Then another day when the children thought they would like to fish in the canal, a boy in a barge threw lumps of coal at them, and one of these hit Phyllis on the back of the neck. She was just stooping down to tie up her bootlace—and though the coal hardly hurt at all it made her not care very much about going on fishing.

On the bridge, however, Roberta felt quite safe, because she could look down on the canal, and if any boy showed signs of meaning to throw coal, she could duck behind the parapet.

Presently there was a sound of wheels, which was just what she expected.

The wheels were the wheels of the Doctor's dogcart, and in the cart, of course, was the Doctor.

He pulled up, and called out:—

"Hullo, head nurse! Want a lift?"

"I wanted to see you," said Bobbie.

"Your mother's not worse, I hope?" said the Doctor.

"No—but—"

"Well, skip in, then, and we'll go for a drive."

Roberta climbed in and the brown horse was made to turn round—which it did not like at all, for it was looking forward to its tea—I mean its oats.

"This IS jolly," said Bobbie, as the dogcart flew along the road by the canal.

"We could throw a stone down any one of your three chimneys," said the Doctor, as they passed the house.

"Yes," said Bobbie, "but you'd have to be a jolly good shot."

"How do you know I'm not?" said the Doctor. "Now, then, what's the trouble?"

Bobbie fidgeted with the hook of the driving apron.

"Come, out with it," said the Doctor.

"It's rather hard, you see," said Bobbie, "to out with it; because of what Mother said."

"What DID Mother say?"

"She said I wasn't to go telling everyone that we're poor. But you aren't everyone, are you?"

"Not at all," said the Doctor, cheerfully. "Well?"

"Well, I know doctors are very extravagant—I mean expensive, and Mrs. Viney told me that her doctoring only cost her twopence a week because she belonged to a Club."

"Yes?"

"You see she told me what a good doctor you were, and I asked her how she could afford you, because she's much poorer than we are. I've been in her house and I know. And then she told me about the Club, and I thought I'd ask you—and—oh, I don't want Mother to be worried! Can't we be in the Club, too, the same as Mrs. Viney?"

The Doctor was silent. He was rather poor himself, and he had been pleased at getting a new family to attend. So I think his feelings at that minute were rather mixed.

"You aren't cross with me, are you?" said Bobbie, in a very small voice.

The Doctor roused himself.

"Cross? How could I be? You're a very sensible little woman. Now look here, don't you worry. I'll make it all right with your Mother, even if I have to make a special brand-new Club all for her. Look here, this is where the Aqueduct begins."

"What's an Aque—what's its name?" asked Bobbie.

"A water bridge," said the Doctor. "Look."

The road rose to a bridge over the canal. To the left was a steep rocky cliff with trees and shrubs growing in the cracks of the rock. And the canal here left off running along the top of the hill and started to run on a bridge of its own—a great bridge with tall arches that went right across the valley.

Bobbie drew a long breath.

"It IS grand, isn't it?" she said. "It's like pictures in the History of Rome."

"Right!" said the Doctor, "that's just exactly what it IS like. The Romans were dead nuts on aqueducts. It's a splendid piece of engineering."

"I thought engineering was making engines."

"Ah, there are different sorts of engineering—making road and bridges and tunnels is one kind. And making fortifications is another. Well, we must be turning back. And, remember, you aren't to worry about doctor's bills or you'll be ill yourself, and then I'll send you in a bill as long as the aqueduct."

When Bobbie had parted from the Doctor at the top of the field that ran down from the road to Three Chimneys, she could not feel that she had done wrong. She knew that Mother would perhaps think differently. But Bobbie felt that for once she was the one who was right, and she scrambled down the rocky slope with a really happy feeling.

Phyllis and Peter met her at the back door. They were unnaturally clean and neat, and Phyllis had a red bow in her hair. There was only just time for Bobbie to make herself tidy and tie up her hair with a blue bow before a little bell rang.

"There!" said Phyllis, "that's to show the surprise is ready. Now you wait till the bell rings again and then you may come into the dining-room."

So Bobbie waited.

"Tinkle, tinkle," said the little bell, and Bobbie went into the dining-room, feeling rather shy. Directly she opened the door she found herself, as it seemed, in a new world of light and flowers and singing. Mother and Peter and Phyllis were standing in a row at the end of the table. The shutters were shut and there were twelve candles on the table, one for each of Roberta's years. The table was covered with a sort of pattern of flowers, and at Roberta's place was a thick wreath of forget-me-nots and several most interesting little packages. And Mother and Phyllis and Peter were singing—to the first part of the tune of St. Patrick's Day. Roberta knew that Mother had written the words on purpose for her birthday. It was a little way of Mother's on birthdays. It had begun on Bobbie's fourth birthday when Phyllis was a baby. Bobbie remembered learning the verses to say to Father 'for a surprise.' She wondered if Mother had remembered, too. The four-year-old verse had been:—

> Daddy dear, I'm only four
> And I'd rather not be more.
>
> Four's the nicest age to be,
> Two and two and one and three.
>
> What I love is two and two,
> Mother, Peter, Phil, and you.
>
> What you love is one and three,
> Mother, Peter, Phil, and me.
>
> Give your little girl a kiss
> Because she learned and told you this.

The song the others were singing now went like this:—

> Our darling Roberta,
> No sorrow shall hurt her
> If we can prevent it
> Her whole life long.
>
> Her birthday's our fete day,
> We'll make it our great day,
> And give her our presents
> And sing her our song.
>
> May pleasures attend her
> And may the Fates send her
> The happiest journey
> Along her life's way.
>
> With skies bright above her
> And dear ones to love her!
> Dear Bob! Many happy
> Returns of the day!

When they had finished singing they cried, "Three cheers for our Bobbie!" and gave them very loudly. Bobbie felt exactly as though she were going to cry—you know that odd feeling in the bridge of your nose and the pricking in your eyelids? But before she had time to begin they were all kissing and hugging her.

"Now," said Mother, "look at your presents."

They were very nice presents. There was a green and red needle-book that Phyllis had made herself in secret moments. There was a darling little silver brooch of Mother's shaped like a buttercup, which Bobbie had known and loved for years, but which she had never, never thought would come to be her very own. There was also a pair of blue glass vases from Mrs. Viney. Roberta had seen and admired them in the village shop. And there were three birthday cards with pretty pictures and wishes.

Mother fitted the forget-me-not crown on Bobbie's brown head.

"And now look at the table," she said.

There was a cake on the table covered with white sugar, with 'Dear Bobbie' on it in pink sweets, and there were buns and jam; but the nicest thing was that the big table was almost covered with flowers- -wallflowers were laid all round the tea-tray—there was a ring of forget-me-nots round each plate. The cake had a wreath of white lilac round it, and in the middle was something that looked like a pattern all done with single blooms of lilac or wallflower or laburnum.

"It's a map—a map of the railway!" cried Peter. "Look—those lilac lines are the metals—and there's the station done in brown wallflowers. The laburnum is the train, and there are the signal- boxes, and the road up to here—and those fat red daisies are us three waving to the old gentleman—that's him, the pansy in the laburnum train."

"And there's 'Three Chimneys' done in the purple primroses," said Phyllis. "And that little tiny rose-bud is Mother looking out for us when we're late for tea. Peter invented it all, and we got all the flowers from the station. We thought you'd like it better."

"That's my present," said Peter, suddenly dumping down his adored steam-engine on the table in front of her. Its tender had been lined with fresh white paper, and was full of sweets.

"Oh, Peter!" cried Bobbie, quite overcome by this munificence, "not your own dear little engine that you're so fond of?"

"Oh, no," said Peter, very promptly, "not the engine. Only the sweets."

Bobbie couldn't help her face changing a little—not so much because she was disappointed at not getting the engine, as because she had thought it so very noble of Peter, and now she felt she had been silly to think it. Also she felt she must have seemed greedy to expect the engine as well as the sweets. So her face changed. Peter saw it. He hesitated a minute; then his face changed, too, and he said: "I mean not ALL the engine. I'll let you go halves if you like."

"You're a brick," cried Bobbie; "it's a splendid present." She said no more aloud, but to herself she said:—

"That was awfully jolly decent of Peter because I know he didn't mean to. Well, the broken half shall be my half of the engine, and I'll get it mended and give it back to Peter for his birthday."— "Yes, Mother dear, I should like to cut the cake," she added, and tea began.

It was a delightful birthday. After tea Mother played games with them—any game they liked—and of course their first choice was blindman's-buff, in the course of which Bobbie's forget-me-not wreath twisted itself crookedly over one of her ears and stayed there. Then, when it was near bed-time and time to calm down, Mother had a lovely new story to read to them.

"You won't sit up late working, will you, Mother?" Bobbie asked as they said good night.

And Mother said no, she wouldn't—she would only just write to Father and then go to bed.

But when Bobbie crept down later to bring up her presents—for she felt she really could not be separated from them all night—Mother was not writing, but leaning her head on her arms and her arms on the table. I think it was rather good of Bobbie to slip quietly away, saying over and over, "She doesn't want me to know she's unhappy, and I won't know; I won't know." But it made a sad end to the birthday.

* * * * * *

The very next morning Bobbie began to watch her opportunity to get Peter's engine mended secretly. And the opportunity came the very next afternoon.

Mother went by train to the nearest town to do shopping. When she went there, she always went to the Post-office. Perhaps to post her letters to Father, for she never gave them to the children or Mrs. Viney to post, and she never went to the village herself. Peter and Phyllis went with her. Bobbie wanted an excuse not to go, but try as she would she couldn't think of a good one. And just when she felt that all was lost, her frock caught on a big nail by the kitchen door and there was a great criss-cross tear all along the front of the skirt. I assure you this was really an accident. So the others pitied her and went without her, for there was no time for her to change, because they were rather late already and had to hurry to the station to catch the train.

When they had gone, Bobbie put on her everyday frock, and went down to the railway. She did not go into the station, but she went along the line to the end of the platform where the engine is when the down train is alongside the platform—the place where there are a water tank and a long, limp, leather hose, like an elephant's trunk. She hid behind a bush on the other side of the railway. She had the toy engine done up in brown paper, and she waited patiently with it under her arm.

Then when the next train came in and stopped, Bobbie went across the metals of the up-line and stood beside the engine. She had never been so close to an engine before. It looked much larger and harder than she had expected, and it made her feel very small indeed, and, somehow, very soft—as if she could very, very easily be hurt rather badly.

"I know what silk-worms feel like now," said Bobbie to herself.

The engine-driver and fireman did not see her. They were leaning out on the other side, telling the Porter a tale about a dog and a leg of mutton.

"If you please," said Roberta—but the engine was blowing off steam and no one heard her.

"If you please, Mr. Engineer," she spoke a little louder, but the Engine happened to speak at the same moment, and of course Roberta's soft little voice hadn't a chance.

It seemed to her that the only way would be to climb on to the engine and pull at their coats. The step was high, but she got her knee on it, and clambered into the cab; she stumbled and fell on hands and knees on the base of the great heap of coals that led up to the square opening in the tender. The engine was not above the weaknesses of its fellows; it was making a great deal more noise than there was the slightest need for. And just as Roberta fell on the coals, the engine-driver, who had turned without seeing her, started the engine, and when Bobbie had picked herself up, the train was moving—not fast, but much too fast for her to get off.

All sorts of dreadful thoughts came to her all together in one horrible flash. There were such things as express trains that went on, she supposed, for hundreds of miles without stopping. Suppose this should be one of them? How would she get home again? She had no money to pay for the return journey.

"And I've no business here. I'm an engine-burglar—that's what I am," she thought. "I shouldn't wonder if they could lock me up for this." And the train was going faster and faster.

There was something in her throat that made it impossible for her to speak. She tried twice. The men had their backs to her. They were doing something to things that looked like taps.

Suddenly she put out her hand and caught hold of the nearest sleeve. The man turned with a start, and he and Roberta stood for a minute looking at each other in silence. Then the silence was broken by them both.

The man said, "Here's a bloomin' go!" and Roberta burst into tears.

The other man said he was blooming well blest—or something like it- -but though naturally surprised they were not exactly unkind.

"You're a naughty little gell, that's what you are," said the fireman, and the engine-driver said:—

"Daring little piece, I call her," but they made her sit down on an iron seat in the cab and told her to stop crying and tell them what she meant by it.

She did stop, as soon as she could. One thing that helped her was the thought that Peter would give almost his ears to be in her place—on a real engine—really going. The children had often wondered whether any engine-driver could be found noble enough to take them for a ride on an engine—and now there she was. She dried her eyes and sniffed earnestly.

"Now, then," said the fireman, "out with it. What do you mean by it, eh?"

"Oh, please," sniffed Bobbie.

"Try again," said the engine-driver, encouragingly.

Bobbie tried again.

"Please, Mr. Engineer," she said, "I did call out to you from the line, but you didn't hear me—and I just climbed up to touch you on the arm—quite gently I meant to do it—and then I fell into the coals—and I am so sorry if I frightened you. Oh, don't be cross— oh, please don't!" She sniffed again.

"We ain't so much CROSS," said the fireman, "as interested like. It ain't every day a little gell tumbles into our coal bunker outer the sky, is it, Bill? What did you DO it for—eh?"

"That's the point," agreed the engine-driver; "what did you do it FOR?"

Bobbie found that she had not quite stopped crying. The engine- driver patted her on the back and said: "Here, cheer up, Mate. It ain't so bad as all that 'ere, I'll be bound."

"I wanted," said Bobbie, much cheered to find herself addressed as 'Mate'—"I only wanted to ask you if you'd be so kind as to mend this." She picked up the brown-paper parcel from among the coals and undid the string with hot, red fingers that trembled.

Her feet and legs felt the scorch of the engine fire, but her shoulders felt the wild chill rush of the air. The engine lurched and shook and rattled, and as they shot under a bridge the engine seemed to shout in her ears.

The fireman shovelled on coals.

Bobbie unrolled the brown paper and disclosed the toy engine.

"I thought," she said wistfully, "that perhaps you'd mend this for me—because you're an engineer, you know."

The engine-driver said he was blowed if he wasn't blest.

"I'm blest if I ain't blowed," remarked the fireman.

But the engine-driver took the little engine and looked at it—and the fireman ceased for an instant to shovel coal, and looked, too.

"It's like your precious cheek," said the engine-driver—"whatever made you think we'd be bothered tinkering penny toys?"

"I didn't mean it for precious cheek," said Bobbie; "only everybody that has anything to do with railways is so kind and good, I didn't think you'd mind. You don't really—do you?" she added, for she had seen a not unkindly wink pass between the two.

"My trade's driving of an engine, not mending her, especially such a hout-size in engines as this 'ere," said Bill. "An' 'ow are we a- goin' to get you back to your sorrowing friends and relations, and all be forgiven and forgotten?"

"If you'll put me down next time you stop," said Bobbie, firmly, though her heart beat fiercely against her arm as she clasped her hands, "and lend me the money for a third-class ticket, I'll pay you back—honour bright. I'm not a confidence trick like in the newspapers—really, I'm not."

"You're a little lady, every inch," said Bill, relenting suddenly and completely. "We'll see you gets home safe. An' about this engine—Jim—ain't you got ne'er a pal as can use a soldering iron? Seems to me that's about all the little bounder wants doing to it."

"That's what Father said," Bobbie explained eagerly. "What's that for?"

She pointed to a little brass wheel that he had turned as he spoke.

"That's the injector."

"In—what?"

"Injector to fill up the boiler."

"Oh," said Bobbie, mentally registering the fact to tell the others; "that IS interesting."

"This 'ere's the automatic brake," Bill went on, flattered by her enthusiasm. "You just move this 'ere little handle—do it with one finger, you can—and the train jolly soon stops. That's what they call the Power of Science in the newspapers."

He showed her two little dials, like clock faces, and told her how one showed how much steam was going, and the other showed if the brake was working properly.

By the time she had seen him shut off steam with a big shining steel handle, Bobbie knew more about the inside working of an engine than she had ever thought there was to know, and Jim had promised that his second cousin's wife's brother should solder the toy engine, or Jim would know the reason why. Besides all the knowledge she had gained Bobbie felt that she and Bill and Jim were now friends for life, and that they had wholly and forever forgiven her for stumbling uninvited among the sacred coals of their tender.

At Stacklepoole Junction she parted from them with warm expressions of mutual regard. They handed her over to the guard of a returning train—a friend of theirs—and she had the joy of knowing what guards do in their secret fastnesses, and understood how, when you pull the communication cord in railway carriages, a wheel goes round under the guard's nose and a loud bell rings in his ears. She asked the guard why his van smelt so fishy, and learned that he had to carry a lot of fish every day, and that the wetness in the hollows of the corrugated floor had all drained out of boxes full of plaice and cod and mackerel and soles and smelts.

Bobbie got home in time for tea, and she felt as though her mind would burst with all that had been put into it since she parted from the others. How she blessed the nail that had torn her frock!

"Where have you been?" asked the others.

"To the station, of course," said Roberta. But she would not tell a word of her adventures till the day appointed, when she mysteriously led them to the station at the hour of the 3.19's transit, and proudly introduced them to her friends, Bill and Jim. Jim's second cousin's wife's brother had not been unworthy of the sacred trust reposed in him. The toy engine was, literally, as good as new.

"Good-bye—oh, good-bye," said Bobbie, just before the engine screamed ITS good-bye. "I shall always, always love you—and Jim's second cousin's wife's brother as well!"

And as the three children went home up the hill, Peter hugging the engine, now quite its own self again, Bobbie told, with joyous leaps of the heart, the story of how she had been an Engine-burglar.

Chapter 5. Prisoners and Captives.

It was one day when Mother had gone to Maidbridge. She had gone alone, but the children were to go to the station to meet her. And, loving the station as they did, it was only natural that they should be there a good hour before there was any chance of Mother's train arriving, even if the train were punctual, which was most unlikely. No doubt they would have been just as early, even if it had been a fine day, and all the delights of woods and fields and rocks and rivers had been open to them. But it happened to be a very wet day and, for July, very cold. There was a wild wind that drove flocks of dark purple clouds across the sky "like herds of dream- elephants," as Phyllis said. And the rain stung sharply, so that the way to the station was finished at a run. Then the rain fell faster and harder, and beat slantwise against the windows of the booking office and of the chill place that had General Waiting Room on its door.

"It's like being in a besieged castle," Phyllis said; "look at the arrows of the foe striking against the battlements!"

"It's much more like a great garden-squirt," said Peter.

They decided to wait on the up side, for the down platform looked very wet indeed, and the rain was driving right into the little bleak shelter where down-passengers have to wait for their trains.

The hour would be full of incident and of interest, for there would be two up trains and one down to look at before the one that should bring Mother back.

"Perhaps it'll have stopped raining by then," said Bobbie; "anyhow, I'm glad I brought Mother's waterproof and umbrella."

They went into the desert spot labelled General Waiting Room, and the time passed pleasantly enough in a game of advertisements. You know the game, of course? It is something like dumb Crambo. The players take it in turns to go out, and then come back and look as like some advertisement as they can, and the others have to guess what advertisement it is meant to be. Bobbie came in and sat down under Mother's umbrella and made a sharp face, and everyone knew she was the fox who sits under the umbrella in the advertisement. Phyllis tried to make a Magic Carpet of Mother's waterproof, but it would not stand out stiff and raft-like as a Magic Carpet should, and nobody could guess it. Everyone thought Peter was carrying things a little too far when he blacked his face all over with coal- dust and struck a spidery attitude and said he was the blot that advertises somebody's Blue Black Writing Fluid.

It was Phyllis's turn again, and she was trying to look like the Sphinx that advertises What's-his-name's Personally Conducted Tours up the Nile when the sharp ting of the signal announced the up train. The children rushed out to see it pass. On its engine were the particular driver and fireman who were now numbered among the children's dearest friends. Courtesies passed between them. Jim asked after the toy engine, and Bobbie pressed on his acceptance a moist, greasy package of toffee that she had made herself.

Charmed by this attention, the engine-driver consented to consider her request that some day he would take Peter for a ride on the engine.

"Stand back, Mates," cried the engine-driver, suddenly, "and horf she goes."

And sure enough, off the train went. The children watched the tail- lights of the train till it disappeared round the curve of the line, and then turned to go back to the dusty freedom of the General Waiting Room and the joys of the advertisement game.

They expected to see just one or two people, the end of the procession of passengers who had given up their tickets and gone away. Instead, the platform round the door of the station had a dark blot round it, and the dark blot was a crowd of people.

"Oh!" cried Peter, with a thrill of joyous excitement, "something's happened! Come on!"

They ran down the platform. When they got to the crowd, they could, of course, see nothing but the damp backs and elbows of the people on the crowd's outside. Everybody was talking at once. It was evident that something had happened.

"It's my belief he's nothing worse than a natural," said a farmerish-looking person. Peter saw his red, clean-shaven face as he spoke.

"If you ask me, I should say it was a Police Court case," said a young man with a black bag.

"Not it; the Infirmary more like—"

Then the voice of the Station Master was heard, firm and official:—

"Now, then—move along there. I'll attend to this, if YOU please."

But the crowd did not move. And then came a voice that thrilled the children through and through. For it spoke in a foreign language. And, what is more, it was a language that they had never heard. They had heard French spoken and German. Aunt Emma knew German, and used to sing a song about bedeuten and zeiten and bin and sin. Nor was it Latin. Peter had been in Latin for four terms.

It was some comfort, anyhow, to find that none of the crowd understood the foreign language any better than the children did.

"What's that he's saying?" asked the farmer, heavily.

"Sounds like French to me," said the Station Master, who had once been to Boulogne for the day.

"It isn't French!" cried Peter.

"What is it, then?" asked more than one voice. The crowd fell back a little to see who had spoken, and Peter pressed forward, so that when the crowd closed up again he was in the front rank.

"I don't know what it is," said Peter, "but it isn't French. I know that." Then he saw what it was that the crowd had for its centre. It was a man—the man, Peter did not doubt, who had spoken in that strange tongue. A man with long hair and wild eyes, with shabby clothes of a cut Peter had not seen before—a man whose hands and lips trembled, and who spoke again as his eyes fell on Peter.

"No, it's not French," said Peter.

"Try him with French if you know so much about it," said the farmer- man.

"Parlay voo Frongsay?" began Peter, boldly, and the next moment the crowd recoiled again, for the man with the wild eyes had left leaning against the wall, and had sprung forward and caught Peter's hands, and begun to pour forth a flood of words which, though he could not understand a word of them, Peter knew the sound of.

"There!" said he, and turned, his hands still clasped in the hands of the strange shabby figure, to throw a glance of triumph at the crowd; "there; THAT'S French."

"What does he say?"

"I don't know." Peter was obliged to own it.

"Here," said the Station Master again; "you move on if you please. I'LL deal with this case."

A few of the more timid or less inquisitive travellers moved slowly and reluctantly away. And Phyllis and Bobbie got near to Peter. All three had been TAUGHT French at school. How deeply they now wished that they had LEARNED it! Peter shook his head at the stranger, but he also shook his hands as warmly and looked at him as kindly as he could. A person in the crowd, after some hesitation, said suddenly, "No comprenny!" and then, blushing deeply, backed out of the press and went away.

"Take him into your room," whispered Bobbie to the Station Master. "Mother can talk French. She'll be here by the next train from Maidbridge."

The Station Master took the arm of the stranger, suddenly but not unkindly. But the man wrenched his arm away, and cowered back coughing and trembling and trying to push the Station Master away.

"Oh, don't!" said Bobbie; "don't you see how frightened he is? He thinks you're going to shut him up. I know he does—look at his eyes!"

"They're like a fox's eyes when the beast's in a trap," said the farmer.

"Oh, let me try!" Bobbie went on; "I do really know one or two French words if I could only think of them."

Sometimes, in moments of great need, we can do wonderful things— things that in ordinary life we could hardly even dream of doing. Bobbie had never been anywhere near the top of her French class, but she must have learned something without knowing it, for now, looking at those wild, hunted eyes, she actually remembered and, what is more, spoke, some French words. She said:—

"Vous attendre. Ma mere parlez Francais. Nous—what's the French for 'being kind'?"

Nobody knew.

"Bong is 'good,'" said Phyllis.

"Nous etre bong pour vous."

I do not know whether the man understood her words, but he understood the touch of the hand she thrust into his, and the kindness of the other hand that stroked his shabby sleeve.

She pulled him gently towards the inmost sanctuary of the Station Master. The other children followed, and the Station Master shut the door in the face of the crowd, which stood a little while in the booking office talking and looking at the fast closed yellow door, and then by ones and twos went its way, grumbling.

Inside the Station Master's room Bobbie still held the stranger's hand and stroked his sleeve.

"Here's a go," said the Station Master; "no ticket—doesn't even know where he wants to go. I'm not sure now but what I ought to send for the police."

"Oh, DON'T!" all the children pleaded at once. And suddenly Bobbie got between the others and the stranger, for she had seen that he was crying.

By a most unusual piece of good fortune she had a handkerchief in her pocket. By a still more uncommon accident the handkerchief was moderately clean. Standing in front of the stranger, she got out the handkerchief and passed it to him so that the others did not see.

"Wait till Mother comes," Phyllis was saying; "she does speak French beautifully. You'd just love to hear her."

"I'm sure he hasn't done anything like you're sent to prison for," said Peter.

"Looks like without visible means to me," said the Station Master. "Well, I don't mind giving him the benefit of the doubt till your Mamma comes. I SHOULD like to know what nation's got the credit of HIM, that I should."

Then Peter had an idea. He pulled an envelope out of his pocket, and showed that it was half full of foreign stamps.

"Look here," he said, "let's show him these—"

Bobbie looked and saw that the stranger had dried his eyes with her handkerchief. So she said: "All right."

They showed him an Italian stamp, and pointed from him to it and back again, and made signs of question with their eyebrows. He shook his head. Then they showed him a Norwegian stamp—the common blue kind it was—and again he signed No. Then they showed him a Spanish one, and at that he took the envelope from Peter's hand and searched among the stamps with a hand that trembled. The hand that he reached out at last, with a gesture as of one answering a question, contained a RUSSIAN stamp.

"He's Russian," cried Peter, "or else he's like 'the man who was'— in Kipling, you know."

The train from Maidbridge was signalled.

"I'll stay with him till you bring Mother in," said Bobbie.

"You're not afraid, Missie?"

"Oh, no," said Bobbie, looking at the stranger, as she might have looked at a strange dog of doubtful temper. "You wouldn't hurt me, would you?"

She smiled at him, and he smiled back, a queer crooked smile. And then he coughed again. And the heavy rattling swish of the incoming train swept past, and the Station Master and Peter and Phyllis went out to meet it. Bobbie was still holding the stranger's hand when they came back with Mother.

The Russian rose and bowed very ceremoniously.

Then Mother spoke in French, and he replied, haltingly at first, but presently in longer and longer sentences.

The children, watching his face and Mother's, knew that he was telling her things that made her angry and pitying, and sorry and indignant all at once.

"Well, Mum, what's it all about?" The Station Master could not restrain his curiosity any longer.

"Oh," said Mother, "it's all right. He's a Russian, and he's lost his ticket. And I'm afraid he's very ill. If you don't mind, I'll take him home with me now. He's really quite worn out. I'll run down and tell you all about him to-morrow."

"I hope you won't find you're taking home a frozen viper," said the Station Master, doubtfully.

"Oh, no," Mother said brightly, and she smiled; "I'm quite sure I'm not. Why, he's a great man in his own country, writes books— beautiful books—I've read some of them; but I'll tell you all about it to-morrow."

She spoke again in French to the Russian, and everyone could see the surprise and pleasure and gratitude in his eyes. He got up and politely bowed to the Station Master, and offered his arm most ceremoniously to Mother. She took it, but anybody could have seen that she was helping him along, and not he her.

"You girls run home and light a fire in the sitting-room," Mother said, "and Peter had better go for the Doctor."

But it was Bobbie who went for the Doctor.

"I hate to tell you," she said breathlessly when she came upon him in his shirt sleeves, weeding his pansy-bed, "but Mother's got a very shabby Russian, and I'm sure he'll have to belong to your Club. I'm certain he hasn't got any money. We found him at the station."

"Found him! Was he lost, then?" asked the Doctor, reaching for his coat.

"Yes," said Bobbie, unexpectedly, "that's just what he was. He's been telling Mother the sad, sweet story of his life in French; and she said would you be kind enough to come directly if you were at home. He has a dreadful cough, and he's been crying."

The Doctor smiled.

"Oh, don't," said Bobbie; "please don't. You wouldn't if you'd seen him. I never saw a man cry before. You don't know what it's like."

Dr. Forrest wished then that he hadn't smiled.

When Bobbie and the Doctor got to Three Chimneys, the Russian was sitting in the arm-chair that had been Father's, stretching his feet to the blaze of a bright wood fire, and sipping the tea Mother had made him.

"The man seems worn out, mind and body," was what the Doctor said; "the cough's bad, but there's nothing that can't be cured. He ought to go straight to bed, though—and let him have a fire at night."

"I'll make one in my room; it's the only one with a fireplace," said Mother. She did, and presently the Doctor helped the stranger to bed.

There was a big black trunk in Mother's room that none of the children had ever seen unlocked. Now, when she had lighted the fire, she unlocked it and took some clothes out—men's clothes—and set them to air by the newly lighted fire. Bobbie, coming in with more wood for the fire, saw the mark on the night-shirt, and looked over to the open trunk. All the things she could see were men's clothes. And the name marked on the shirt was Father's name. Then Father hadn't taken his clothes with him. And that night-shirt was one of Father's new ones. Bobbie remembered its being made, just before Peter's birthday. Why hadn't Father taken his clothes? Bobbie slipped from the room. As she went she heard the key turned in the lock of the trunk. Her heart was beating horribly. WHY hadn't Father taken his clothes? When Mother came out of the room, Bobbie flung tightly clasping arms round her waist, and whispered:—

"Mother—Daddy isn't—isn't DEAD, is he?"

"My darling, no! What made you think of anything so horrible?"

"I—I don't know," said Bobbie, angry with herself, but still clinging to that resolution of hers, not to see anything that Mother didn't mean her to see.

Mother gave her a hurried hug. "Daddy was quite, QUITE well when I heard from him last," she said, "and he'll come back to us some day. Don't fancy such horrible things, darling!"

Later on, when the Russian stranger had been made comfortable for the night, Mother came into the girls' room. She was to sleep there in Phyllis's bed, and Phyllis was to have a mattress on the floor, a most amusing adventure for Phyllis. Directly Mother came in, two white figures started up, and two eager voices called:—

"Now, Mother, tell us all about the Russian gentleman."

A white shape hopped into the room. It was Peter, dragging his quilt behind him like the tail of a white peacock.

"We have been patient," he said, "and I had to bite my tongue not to go to sleep, and I just nearly went to sleep and I bit too hard, and it hurts ever so. DO tell us. Make a nice long story of it."

"I can't make a long story of it to-night," said Mother; "I'm very tired."

Bobbie knew by her voice that Mother had been crying, but the others didn't know.

"Well, make it as long as you can," said Phil, and Bobbie got her arms round Mother's waist and snuggled close to her.

"Well, it's a story long enough to make a whole book of. He's a writer; he's written beautiful books. In Russia at the time of the Czar one dared not say anything about the rich people doing wrong, or about the things that ought to be done to make poor people better and happier. If one did one was sent to prison."

"But they CAN'T," said Peter; "people only go to prison when they've done wrong."

"Or when the Judges THINK they've done wrong," said Mother. "Yes, that's so in England. But in Russia it was different. And he wrote a beautiful book about poor people and how to help them. I've read it. There's nothing in it but goodness and kindness. And they sent him to prison for it. He was three years in a horrible dungeon, with hardly any light, and all damp and dreadful. In prison all alone for three years."

Mother's voice trembled a little and stopped suddenly.

"But, Mother," said Peter, "that can't be true NOW. It sounds like something out of a history book—the Inquisition, or something."

"It WAS true," said Mother; "it's all horribly true. Well, then they took him out and sent him to Siberia, a convict chained to other convicts—wicked men who'd done all sorts of crimes—a long chain of them, and they walked, and walked, and walked, for days and weeks, till he thought they'd never stop walking. And overseers went behind them with whips—yes, whips—to beat them if they got tired. And some of them went lame, and some fell down, and when they couldn't get up and go on, they beat them, and then left them to die. Oh, it's all too terrible! And at last he got to the mines, and he was condemned to stay there for life—for life, just for writing a good, noble, splendid book."

"How did he get away?"

"When the war came, some of the Russian prisoners were allowed to volunteer as soldiers. And he volunteered. But he deserted at the first chance he got and—"

"But that's very cowardly, isn't it"—said Peter—"to desert? Especially when it's war."

"Do you think he owed anything to a country that had done THAT to him? If he did, he owed more to his wife and children. He didn't know what had become of them."

"Oh," cried Bobbie, "he had THEM to think about and be miserable about TOO, then, all the time he was in prison?"

"Yes, he had them to think about and be miserable about all the time he was in prison. For anything he knew they might have been sent to prison, too. They did those things in Russia. But while he was in the mines some friends managed to get a message to him that his wife and children had escaped and come to England. So when he deserted he came here to look for them."

"Had he got their address?" said practical Peter.

"No; just England. He was going to London, and he thought he had to change at our station, and then he found he'd lost his ticket and his purse."

"Oh, DO you think he'll find them?—I mean his wife and children, not the ticket and things."

"I hope so. Oh, I hope and pray that he'll find his wife and children again."

Even Phyllis now perceived that mother's voice was very unsteady.

"Why, Mother," she said, "how very sorry you seem to be for him!"

Mother didn't answer for a minute. Then she just said, "Yes," and then she seemed to be thinking. The children were quiet.

Presently she said, "Dears, when you say your prayers, I think you might ask God to show His pity upon all prisoners and captives."

"To show His pity," Bobbie repeated slowly, "upon all prisoners and captives. Is that right, Mother?"

"Yes," said Mother, "upon all prisoners and captives. All prisoners and captives."

Chapter 6. Saviours of the Train.

The Russian gentleman was better the next day, and the day after that better still, and on the third day he was well enough to come into the garden. A basket chair was put for him and he sat there, dressed in clothes of Father's which were too big for him. But when Mother had hemmed up the ends of the sleeves and the trousers, the clothes did well enough. His was a kind face now that it was no longer tired and frightened, and he smiled at the children whenever he saw them. They wished very much that he could speak English. Mother wrote several letters to people she thought might know whereabouts in England a Russian gentleman's wife and family might possibly be; not to the people she used to know before she came to live at Three Chimneys—she never wrote to any of them—but strange people—Members of Parliament and Editors of papers, and Secretaries of Societies.

And she did not do much of her story-writing, only corrected proofs as she sat in the sun near the Russian, and talked to him every now and then.

The children wanted very much to show how kindly they felt to this man who had been sent to prison and to Siberia just for writing a beautiful book about poor people. They could smile at him, of course; they could and they did. But if you smile too constantly, the smile is apt to get fixed like the smile of the hyaena. And then it no longer looks friendly, but simply silly. So they tried other ways, and brought him flowers till the place where he sat was surrounded by little fading bunches of clover and roses and Canterbury bells.

And then Phyllis had an idea. She beckoned mysteriously to the others and drew them into the back yard, and there, in a concealed spot, between the pump and the water-butt, she said:—

"You remember Perks promising me the very first strawberries out of his own garden?" Perks, you will recollect, was the Porter. "Well, I should think they're ripe now. Let's go down and see."

Mother had been down as she had promised to tell the Station Master the story of the Russian Prisoner. But even the charms of the railway had been unable to tear the children away from the neighbourhood of the interesting stranger. So they had not been to the station for three days.

They went now.

And, to their surprise and distress, were very coldly received by Perks.

"'Ighly honoured, I'm sure," he said when they peeped in at the door of the Porters' room. And he went on reading his newspaper.

There was an uncomfortable silence.

"Oh, dear," said Bobbie, with a sigh, "I do believe you're CROSS."

"What, me? Not me!" said Perks loftily; "it ain't nothing to me."

"What AIN'T nothing to you?" said Peter, too anxious and alarmed to change the form of words.

"Nothing ain't nothing. What 'appens either 'ere or elsewhere," said Perks; "if you likes to 'ave your secrets, 'ave 'em and welcome. That's what I say."

The secret-chamber of each heart was rapidly examined during the pause that followed. Three heads were shaken.

"We haven't got any secrets from YOU," said Bobbie at last.

"Maybe you 'ave, and maybe you 'aven't," said Perks; "it ain't nothing to me. And I wish you all a very good afternoon." He held up the paper between him and them and went on reading.

"Oh, DON'T!" said Phyllis, in despair; "this is truly dreadful! Whatever it is, do tell us."

"We didn't mean to do it whatever it was."

No answer. The paper was refolded and Perks began on another column.

"Look here," said Peter, suddenly, "it's not fair. Even people who do crimes aren't punished without being told what it's for—as once they were in Russia."

"I don't know nothing about Russia."

"Oh, yes, you do, when Mother came down on purpose to tell you and Mr. Gills all about OUR Russian."

"Can't you fancy it?" said Perks, indignantly; "don't you see 'im a- asking of me to step into 'is room and take a chair and listen to what 'er Ladyship 'as to say?"

"Do you mean to say you've not heard?"

"Not so much as a breath. I did go so far as to put a question. And he shuts me up like a rat-trap. 'Affairs of State, Perks,' says he. But I did think one o' you would 'a' nipped down to tell me— you're here sharp enough when you want to get anything out of old Perks"—Phyllis flushed purple as she thought of the strawberries— "information about locomotives or signals or the likes," said Perks.

"We didn't know you didn't know."

"We thought Mother had told you."

"Wewantedtotellyouonlywethoughtitwouldbestalenews."

The three spoke all at once.

Perks said it was all very well, and still held up the paper. Then Phyllis suddenly snatched it away, and threw her arms round his neck.

"Oh, let's kiss and be friends," she said; "we'll say we're sorry first, if you like, but we didn't really know that you didn't know."

"We are so sorry," said the others.

And Perks at last consented to accept their apologies.

Then they got him to come out and sit in the sun on the green Railway Bank, where the grass was quite hot to touch, and there, sometimes speaking one at a time, and sometimes all together, they told the Porter the story of the Russian Prisoner.

"Well, I must say," said Perks; but he did not say it—whatever it was.

"Yes, it is pretty awful, isn't it?" said Peter, "and I don't wonder you were curious about who the Russian was."

"I wasn't curious, not so much as interested," said the Porter.

"Well, I do think Mr. Gills might have told you about it. It was horrid of him."

"I don't keep no down on 'im for that, Missie," said the Porter; "cos why? I see 'is reasons. 'E wouldn't want to give away 'is own side with a tale like that 'ere. It ain't human nature. A man's got to stand up for his own side whatever they does. That's what it means by Party Politics. I should 'a' done the same myself if that long-'aired chap 'ad 'a' been a Jap."

"But the Japs didn't do cruel, wicked things like that," said Bobbie.

"P'r'aps not," said Perks, cautiously; "still you can't be sure with foreigners. My own belief is they're all tarred with the same brush."

"Then why were you on the side of the Japs?" Peter asked.

"Well, you see, you must take one side or the other. Same as with Liberals and Conservatives. The great thing is to take your side and then stick to it, whatever happens."

A signal sounded.

"There's the 3.14 up," said Perks. "You lie low till she's through, and then we'll go up along to my place, and see if there's any of them strawberries ripe what I told you about."

"If there are any ripe, and you DO give them to me," said Phyllis, "you won't mind if I give them to the poor Russian, will you?"

Perks narrowed his eyes and then raised his eyebrows.

"So it was them strawberries you come down for this afternoon, eh?" said he.

This was an awkward moment for Phyllis. To say "yes" would seem rude and greedy, and unkind to Perks. But she knew if she said "no," she would not be pleased with herself afterwards. So—

"Yes," she said, "it was."

"Well done!" said the Porter; "speak the truth and shame the—"

"But we'd have come down the very next day if we'd known you hadn't heard the story," Phyllis added hastily.

"I believe you, Missie," said Perks, and sprang across the line six feet in front of the advancing train.

The girls hated to see him do this, but Peter liked it. It was so exciting.

The Russian gentleman was so delighted with the strawberries that the three racked their brains to find some other surprise for him. But all the racking did not bring out any idea more novel than wild cherries. And this idea occurred to them next morning. They had seen the blossom on the trees in the spring, and they knew where to look for wild cherries now that cherry time was here. The trees grew all up and along the rocky face of the cliff out of which the mouth of the tunnel opened. There were all sorts of trees there, birches and beeches and baby oaks and hazels, and among them the cherry blossom had shone like snow and silver.

The mouth of the tunnel was some way from Three Chimneys, so Mother let them take their lunch with them in a basket. And the basket would do to bring the cherries back in if they found any. She also lent them her silver watch so that they should not be late for tea. Peter's Waterbury had taken it into its head not to go since the day when Peter dropped it into the water-butt. And they started. When they got to the top of the cutting, they leaned over the fence and looked down to where the railway lines lay at the bottom of what, as Phyllis said, was exactly like a mountain gorge.

"If it wasn't for the railway at the bottom, it would be as though the foot of man had never been there, wouldn't it?"

The sides of the cutting were of grey stone, very roughly hewn. Indeed, the top part of the cutting had been a little natural glen that had been cut deeper to bring it down to the level of the tunnel's mouth. Among the rocks, grass and flowers grew, and seeds dropped by birds in the crannies of the stone had taken root and grown into bushes and trees that overhung the cutting. Near the tunnel was a flight of steps leading down to the line—just wooden bars roughly fixed into the earth—a very steep and narrow way, more like a ladder than a stair.

"We'd better get down," said Peter; "I'm sure the cherries would be quite easy to get at from the side of the steps. You remember it was there we picked the cherry blossoms that we put on the rabbit's grave."

So they went along the fence towards the little swing gate that is at the top of these steps. And they were almost at the gate when Bobbie said:—

"Hush. Stop! What's that?"

"That" was a very odd noise indeed—a soft noise, but quite plainly to be heard through the sound of the wind in tree branches, and the hum and whir of the telegraph wires. It was a sort of rustling, whispering sound. As they listened it stopped, and then it began again.

And this time it did not stop, but it grew louder and more rustling and rumbling.

"Look"—cried Peter, suddenly—"the tree over there!"

The tree he pointed at was one of those that have rough grey leaves and white flowers. The berries, when they come, are bright scarlet, but if you pick them, they disappoint you by turning black before you get them home. And, as Peter pointed, the tree was moving—not just the way trees ought to move when the wind blows through them, but all in one piece, as though it were a live creature and were walking down the side of the cutting.

"It's moving!" cried Bobbie. "Oh, look! and so are the others. It's like the woods in Macbeth."

"It's magic," said Phyllis, breathlessly. "I always knew this railway was enchanted."

It really did seem a little like magic. For all the trees for about twenty yards of the opposite bank seemed to be slowly walking down towards the railway line, the tree with the grey leaves bringing up the rear like some old shepherd driving a flock of green sheep.

"What is it? Oh, what is it?" said Phyllis; "it's much too magic for me. I don't like it. Let's go home."

But Bobbie and Peter clung fast to the rail and watched breathlessly. And Phyllis made no movement towards going home by herself.

The trees moved on and on. Some stones and loose earth fell down and rattled on the railway metals far below.

"It's ALL coming down," Peter tried to say, but he found there was hardly any voice to say it with. And, indeed, just as he spoke, the great rock, on the top of which the walking trees were, leaned slowly forward. The trees, ceasing to walk, stood still and shivered. Leaning with the rock, they seemed to hesitate a moment, and then rock and trees and grass and bushes, with a rushing sound, slipped right away from the face of the cutting and fell on the line with a blundering crash that could have been heard half a mile off. A cloud of dust rose up.

"Oh," said Peter, in awestruck tones, "isn't it exactly like when coals come in?—if there wasn't any roof to the cellar and you could see down."

"Look what a great mound it's made!" said Bobbie.

"Yes," said Peter, slowly. He was still leaning on the fence. "Yes," he said again, still more slowly.

Then he stood upright.

"The 11.29 down hasn't gone by yet. We must let them know at the station, or there'll be a most frightful accident."

"Let's run," said Bobbie, and began.

But Peter cried, "Come back!" and looked at Mother's watch. He was very prompt and businesslike, and his face looked whiter than they had ever seen it.

"No time," he said; "it's two miles away, and it's past eleven."

"Couldn't we," suggested Phyllis, breathlessly, "couldn't we climb up a telegraph post and do something to the wires?"

"We don't know how," said Peter.

"They do it in war," said Phyllis; "I know I've heard of it."

"They only CUT them, silly," said Peter, "and that doesn't do any good. And we couldn't cut them even if we got up, and we couldn't get up. If we had anything red, we could get down on the line and wave it."

"But the train wouldn't see us till it got round the corner, and then it could see the mound just as well as us," said Phyllis; "better, because it's much bigger than us."

"If we only had something red," Peter repeated, "we could go round the corner and wave to the train."

"We might wave, anyway."

"They'd only think it was just US, as usual. We've waved so often before. Anyway, let's get down."

They got down the steep stairs. Bobbie was pale and shivering. Peter's face looked thinner than usual. Phyllis was red-faced and damp with anxiety.

"Oh, how hot I am!" she said; "and I thought it was going to be cold; I wish we hadn't put on our—" she stopped short, and then ended in quite a different tone—"our flannel petticoats."

Bobbie turned at the bottom of the stairs.

"Oh, yes," she cried; "THEY'RE red! Let's take them off."

They did, and with the petticoats rolled up under their arms, ran along the railway, skirting the newly fallen mound of stones and rock and earth, and bent, crushed, twisted trees. They ran at their best pace. Peter led, but the girls were not far behind. They reached the corner that hid the mound from the straight line of railway that ran half a mile without curve or corner.

"Now," said Peter, taking hold of the largest flannel petticoat.

"You're not"—Phyllis faltered—"you're not going to TEAR them?"

"Shut up," said Peter, with brief sternness.

"Oh, yes," said Bobbie, "tear them into little bits if you like. Don't you see, Phil, if we can't stop the train, there'll be a real live accident, with people KILLED. Oh, horrible! Here, Peter, you'll never tear it through the band!"

She took the red flannel petticoat from him and tore it off an inch from the band. Then she tore the other in the same way.

"There!" said Peter, tearing in his turn. He divided each petticoat into three pieces. "Now, we've got six flags." He looked at the watch again. "And we've got seven minutes. We must have flagstaffs."

The knives given to boys are, for some odd reason, seldom of the kind of steel that keeps sharp. The young saplings had to be broken off. Two came up by the roots. The leaves were stripped from them.

"We must cut holes in the flags, and run the sticks through the holes," said Peter. And the holes were cut. The knife was sharp enough to cut flannel with. Two of the flags were set up in heaps of loose stones between the sleepers of the down line. Then Phyllis and Roberta took each a flag, and stood ready to wave it as soon as the train came in sight.

"I shall have the other two myself," said Peter, "because it was my idea to wave something red."

"They're our petticoats, though," Phyllis was beginning, but Bobbie interrupted—

"Oh, what does it matter who waves what, if we can only save the train?"

Perhaps Peter had not rightly calculated the number of minutes it would take the 11.29 to get from the station to the place where they were, or perhaps the train was late. Anyway, it seemed a very long time that they waited.

Phyllis grew impatient. "I expect the watch is wrong, and the train's gone by," said she.

Peter relaxed the heroic attitude he had chosen to show off his two flags. And Bobbie began to feel sick with suspense.

It seemed to her that they had been standing there for hours and hours, holding those silly little red flannel flags that no one would ever notice. The train wouldn't care. It would go rushing by them and tear round the corner and go crashing into that awful mound. And everyone would be killed. Her hands grew very cold and trembled so that she could hardly hold the flag. And then came the distant rumble and hum of the metals, and a puff of white steam showed far away along the stretch of line.

"Stand firm," said Peter, "and wave like mad! When it gets to that big furze bush step back, but go on waving! Don't stand ON the line, Bobbie!"

The train came rattling along very, very fast.

"They don't see us! They won't see us! It's all no good!" cried Bobbie.

The two little flags on the line swayed as the nearing train shook and loosened the heaps of loose stones that held them up. One of them slowly leaned over and fell on the line. Bobbie jumped forward and caught it up, and waved it; her hands did not tremble now.

It seemed that the train came on as fast as ever. It was very near now.

"Keep off the line, you silly cuckoo!" said Peter, fiercely.

"It's no good," Bobbie said again.

"Stand back!" cried Peter, suddenly, and he dragged Phyllis back by the arm.

But Bobbie cried, "Not yet, not yet!" and waved her two flags right over the line. The front of the engine looked black and enormous. It's voice was loud and harsh.

"Oh, stop, stop, stop!" cried Bobbie. No one heard her. At least Peter and Phyllis didn't, for the oncoming rush of the train covered the sound of her voice with a mountain of sound. But afterwards she used to wonder whether the engine itself had not heard her. It seemed almost as though it had—for it slackened swiftly, slackened and stopped, not twenty yards from the place where Bobbie's two flags waved over the line. She saw the great black engine stop dead, but somehow she could not stop waving the flags. And when the driver and the fireman had got off the engine and Peter and Phyllis had gone to meet them and pour out their excited tale of the awful mound just round the corner, Bobbie still waved the flags but more and more feebly and jerkily.

When the others turned towards her she was lying across the line with her hands flung forward and still gripping the sticks of the little red flannel flags.

The engine-driver picked her up, carried her to the train, and laid her on the cushions of a first-class carriage.

"Gone right off in a faint," he said, "poor little woman. And no wonder. I'll just 'ave a look at this 'ere mound of yours, and then we'll run you back to the station and get her seen to."

It was horrible to see Bobbie lying so white and quiet, with her lips blue, and parted.

"I believe that's what people look like when they're dead," whispered Phyllis.

"DON'T!" said Peter, sharply.

They sat by Bobbie on the blue cushions, and the train ran back. Before it reached their station Bobbie had sighed and opened her eyes, and rolled herself over and begun to cry. This cheered the others wonderfully. They had seen her cry before, but they had never seen her faint, nor anyone else, for the matter of that. They had not known what to do when she was fainting, but now she was only crying they could thump her on the back and tell her not to, just as they always did. And presently, when she stopped crying, they were able to laugh at her for being such a coward as to faint.

When the station was reached, the three were the heroes of an agitated meeting on the platform.

The praises they got for their "prompt action," their "common sense," their "ingenuity," were enough to have turned anybody's head. Phyllis enjoyed herself thoroughly. She had never been a real heroine before, and the feeling was delicious. Peter's ears got very red. Yet he, too, enjoyed himself. Only Bobbie wished they all wouldn't. She wanted to get away.

"You'll hear from the Company about this, I expect," said the Station Master.

Bobbie wished she might never hear of it again. She pulled at Peter's jacket.

"Oh, come away, come away! I want to go home," she said.

So they went. And as they went Station Master and Porter and guards and driver and fireman and passengers sent up a cheer.

"Oh, listen," cried Phyllis; "that's for US!"

"Yes," said Peter. "I say, I am glad I thought about something red, and waving it."

"How lucky we DID put on our red flannel petticoats!" said Phyllis.

Bobbie said nothing. She was thinking of the horrible mound, and the trustful train rushing towards it.

"And it was US that saved them," said Peter.

"How dreadful if they had all been killed!" said Phyllis; "wouldn't it, Bobbie?"

"We never got any cherries, after all," said Bobbie.

The others thought her rather heartless.

Chapter 7. For Valour.

I hope you don't mind my telling you a good deal about Roberta. The fact is I am growing very fond of her. The more I observe her the more I love her. And I notice all sorts of things about her that I like.

For instance, she was quite oddly anxious to make other people happy. And she could keep a secret, a tolerably rare accomplishment. Also she had the power of silent sympathy. That sounds rather dull, I know, but it's not so dull as it sounds. It just means that a person is able to know that you are unhappy, and to love you extra on that account, without bothering you by telling you all the time how sorry she is for you. That was what Bobbie was like. She knew that Mother was unhappy—and that Mother had not told her the reason. So she just loved Mother more and never said a single word that could let Mother know how earnestly her little girl wondered what Mother was unhappy about. This needs practice. It is not so easy as you might think.

Whatever happened—and all sorts of nice, pleasant ordinary things happened—such as picnics, games, and buns for tea, Bobbie always had these thoughts at the back of her mind. "Mother's unhappy. Why? I don't know. She doesn't want me to know. I won't try to find out. But she IS unhappy. Why? I don't know. She doesn't—" and so on, repeating and repeating like a tune that you don't know the stopping part of.

The Russian gentleman still took up a good deal of everybody's thoughts. All the editors and secretaries of Societies and Members of Parliament had answered Mother's letters as politely as they knew how; but none of them could tell where the wife and children of Mr. Szezcpansky would be likely to be. (Did I tell you that the Russian's very Russian name was that?)

Bobbie had another quality which you will hear differently described by different people. Some of them call it interfering in other people's business—and some call it "helping lame dogs over stiles," and some call it "loving-kindness." It just means trying to help people.

She racked her brains to think of some way of helping the Russian gentleman to find his wife and children. He had learned a few words of English now. He could say "Good morning," and "Good night," and "Please," and "Thank you," and "Pretty," when the children brought him flowers, and "Ver' good," when they asked him how he had slept.

The way he smiled when he "said his English," was, Bobbie felt, "just too sweet for anything." She used to think of his face because she fancied it would help her to some way of helping him. But it did not. Yet his being there cheered her because she saw that it made Mother happier.

"She likes to have someone to be good to, even beside us," said Bobbie. "And I know she hated to let him have Father's clothes. But I suppose it 'hurt nice,' or she wouldn't have."

For many and many a night after the day when she and Peter and Phyllis had saved the train from wreck by waving their little red flannel flags, Bobbie used to wake screaming and shivering, seeing again that horrible mound, and the poor, dear trustful engine rushing on towards it—just thinking that it was doing its swift duty, and that everything was clear and safe. And then a warm thrill of pleasure used to run through her at the remembrance of how she and Peter and Phyllis and the red flannel petticoats had really saved everybody.

One morning a letter came. It was addressed to Peter and Bobbie and Phyllis. They opened it with enthusiastic curiosity, for they did not often get letters.

The letter said:—

> "Dear Sir, and Ladies,
>
> —It is proposed to make a small presentation to you, in commemoration of your prompt and courageous action in warning the train on the --- inst., and thus averting what must, humanly speaking, have been a terrible accident.
>
> The presentation will take place at the --- Station at three o'clock on the 30th inst., if this time and place will be convenient to you.
>
> "Yours faithfully,
>
> "Jabez Inglewood.
> "Secretary, Great Northern and Southern Railway Co."

There never had been a prouder moment in the lives of the three children. They rushed to Mother with the letter, and she also felt proud and said so, and this made the children happier than ever.

"But if the presentation is money, you must say, 'Thank you, but we'd rather not take it,'" said Mother. "I'll wash your Indian muslins at once," she added. "You must look tidy on an occasion like this."

"Phil and I can wash them," said Bobbie, "if you'll iron them, Mother."

Washing is rather fun. I wonder whether you've ever done it? This particular washing took place in the back kitchen, which had a stone floor and a very big stone sink under its window.

"Let's put the bath on the sink," said Phyllis; "then we can pretend we're out-of-doors washerwomen like Mother saw in France."

"But they were washing in the cold river," said Peter, his hands in his pockets, "not in hot water."

"This is a HOT river, then," said Phyllis; "lend a hand with the bath, there's a dear."

"I should like to see a deer lending a hand," said Peter, but he lent his.

"Now to rub and scrub and scrub and rub," said Phyllis, hopping joyously about as Bobbie carefully carried the heavy kettle from the kitchen fire.

"Oh, no!" said Bobbie, greatly shocked; "you don't rub muslin. You put the boiled soap in the hot water and make it all frothy-lathery- -and then you shake the muslin and squeeze it, ever so gently, and all the dirt comes out. It's only clumsy things like tablecloths and sheets that have to be rubbed."

The lilac and the Gloire de Dijon roses outside the window swayed in the soft breeze.

"It's a nice drying day—that's one thing," said Bobbie, feeling very grown up. "Oh, I do wonder what wonderful feelings we shall have when we WEAR the Indian muslin dresses!"

"Yes, so do I," said Phyllis, shaking and squeezing the muslin in quite a professional manner.

"NOW we squeeze out the soapy water. NO—we mustn't twist them—and then rinse them. I'll hold them while you and Peter empty the bath and get clean water."

"A presentation! That means presents," said Peter, as his sisters, having duly washed the pegs and wiped the line, hung up the dresses to dry. "Whatever will it be?"

"It might be anything," said Phyllis; "what I've always wanted is a baby elephant—but I suppose they wouldn't know that."

"Suppose it was gold models of steam-engines?" said Bobbie.

"Or a big model of the scene of the prevented accident," suggested Peter, "with a little model train, and dolls dressed like us and the engine-driver and fireman and passengers."

"Do you LIKE," said Bobbie, doubtfully, drying her hands on the rough towel that hung on a roller at the back of the scullery door, "do you LIKE us being rewarded for saving a train?"

"Yes, I do," said Peter, downrightly; "and don't you try to come it over us that you don't like it, too. Because I know you do."

"Yes," said Bobbie, doubtfully, "I know I do. But oughtn't we to be satisfied with just having done it, and not ask for anything more?"

"Who did ask for anything more, silly?" said her brother; "Victoria Cross soldiers don't ASK for it; but they're glad enough to get it all the same. Perhaps it'll be medals. Then, when I'm very old indeed, I shall show them to my grandchildren and say, 'We only did our duty,' and they'll be awfully proud of me."

"You have to be married," warned Phyllis, "or you don't have any grandchildren."

"I suppose I shall HAVE to be married some day," said Peter, "but it will be an awful bother having her round all the time. I'd like to marry a lady who had trances, and only woke up once or twice a year."

"Just to say you were the light of her life and then go to sleep again. Yes. That wouldn't be bad," said Bobbie.

"When *I* get married," said Phyllis, "I shall want him to want me to be awake all the time, so that I can hear him say how nice I am."

"I think it would be nice," said Bobbie, "to marry someone very poor, and then you'd do all the work and he'd love you most frightfully, and see the blue wood smoke curling up among the trees from the domestic hearth as he came home from work every night. I say—we've got to answer that letter and say that the time and place WILL be convenient to us. There's the soap, Peter. WE'RE both as clean as clean. That pink box of writing paper you had on your birthday, Phil."

It took some time to arrange what should be said. Mother had gone back to her writing, and several sheets of pink paper with scalloped gilt edges and green four-leaved shamrocks in the corner were spoiled before the three had decided what to say. Then each made a copy and signed it with its own name.

The threefold letter ran:—

> "Dear Mr. Jabez Inglewood,
>
> —Thank you very much. We did not want to be rewarded but only to save the train, but we are glad you think so and thank you very much. The time and place you say will be quite convenient to us. Thank you very much.
>
> "Your affecate little friend,"

Then came the name, and after it:—

> "P.S. Thank you very much."

"Washing is much easier than ironing," said Bobbie, taking the clean dry dresses off the line. "I do love to see things come clean. Oh- -I don't know how we shall wait till it's time to know what presentation they're going to present!"

When at last—it seemed a very long time after—it was THE day, the three children went down to the station at the proper time. And everything that happened was so odd that it seemed like a dream. The Station Master came out to meet them—in his best clothes, as Peter noticed at once—and led them into the waiting room where once they had played the advertisement game. It looked quite different now. A carpet had been put down—and there were pots of roses on the mantelpiece and on the window ledges—green branches stuck up, like holly and laurel are at Christmas, over the framed advertisement of Cook's Tours and the Beauties of Devon and the Paris Lyons Railway. There were quite a number of people there besides the Porter—two or three ladies in smart dresses, and quite a crowd of gentlemen in high hats and frock coats—besides everybody who belonged to the station. They recognized several people who had been in the train on the red-flannel-petticoat day. Best of all their own old gentleman was there, and his coat and hat and collar seemed more than ever different from anyone else's. He shook hands with them and then everybody sat down on chairs, and a gentleman in spectacles—they found out afterwards that he was the District Superintendent—began quite a long speech—very clever indeed. I am not going to write the speech down. First, because you would think it dull; and secondly, because it made all the children blush so, and get so hot about the ears that I am quite anxious to get away from this part of the subject; and thirdly, because the gentleman took so many words to say what he had to say that I really haven't time to write them down. He said all sorts of nice things about the children's bravery and presence of mind, and when he had done he sat down, and everyone who was there clapped and said, "Hear, hear."

And then the old gentleman got up and said things, too. It was very like a prize-giving. And then he called the children one by one, by their names, and gave each of them a beautiful gold watch and chain. And inside the watches were engraved after the name of the watch's new owner:—

"From the Directors of the Northern and Southern Railway in grateful recognition of the courageous and prompt action which averted an accident on --- 1905."

The watches were the most beautiful you can possibly imagine, and each one had a blue leather case to live in when it was at home.

"You must make a speech now and thank everyone for their kindness," whispered the Station Master in Peter's ear and pushed him forward. "Begin 'Ladies and Gentlemen,'" he added.

Each of the children had already said "Thank you," quite properly.

"Oh, dear," said Peter, but he did not resist the push.

"Ladies and Gentlemen," he said in a rather husky voice. Then there was a pause, and he heard his heart beating in his throat. "Ladies and Gentlemen," he went on with a rush, "it's most awfully good of you, and we shall treasure the watches all our lives—but really we don't deserve it because what we did wasn't anything, really. At least, I mean it was awfully exciting, and what I mean to say—thank you all very, very much."

The people clapped Peter more than they had done the District Superintendent, and then everybody shook hands with them, and as soon as politeness would let them, they got away, and tore up the hill to Three Chimneys with their watches in their hands.

It was a wonderful day—the kind of day that very seldom happens to anybody and to most of us not at all.

"I did want to talk to the old gentleman about something else," said Bobbie, "but it was so public—like being in church."

"What did you want to say?" asked Phyllis.

"I'll tell you when I've thought about it more," said Bobbie.

So when she had thought a little more she wrote a letter.

> "My dearest old gentleman," it said; "I want most awfully to ask you something. If you could get out of the train and go by the next, it would do. I do not want you to give me anything. Mother says we ought not to. And besides, we do not want any THINGS. Only to talk to you about a Prisoner and Captive.
>
> Your loving little friend,
>
> "Bobbie."

She got the Station Master to give the letter to the old gentleman, and next day she asked Peter and Phyllis to come down to the station with her at the time when the train that brought the old gentleman from town would be passing through.

She explained her idea to them—and they approved thoroughly.

They had all washed their hands and faces, and brushed their hair, and were looking as tidy as they knew how. But Phyllis, always unlucky, had upset a jug of lemonade down the front of her dress. There was no time to change—and the wind happening to blow from the coal yard, her frock was soon powdered with grey, which stuck to the sticky lemonade stains and made her look, as Peter said, "like any little gutter child."

It was decided that she should keep behind the others as much as possible.

"Perhaps the old gentleman won't notice," said Bobbie. "The aged are often weak in the eyes."

There was no sign of weakness, however, in the eyes, or in any other part of the old gentleman, as he stepped from the train and looked up and down the platform.

The three children, now that it came to the point, suddenly felt that rush of deep shyness which makes your ears red and hot, your hands warm and wet, and the tip of your nose pink and shiny.

"Oh," said Phyllis, "my heart's thumping like a steam-engine—right under my sash, too."

"Nonsense," said Peter, "people's hearts aren't under their sashes."

"I don't care—mine is," said Phyllis.

"If you're going to talk like a poetry-book," said Peter, "my heart's in my mouth."

"My heart's in my boots—if you come to that," said Roberta; "but do come on—he'll think we're idiots."

"He won't be far wrong," said Peter, gloomily. And they went forward to meet the old gentleman.

"Hullo," he said, shaking hands with them all in turn. "This is a very great pleasure."

"It WAS good of you to get out," Bobbie said, perspiring and polite.

He took her arm and drew her into the waiting room where she and the others had played the advertisement game the day they found the Russian. Phyllis and Peter followed. "Well?" said the old gentleman, giving Bobbie's arm a kind little shake before he let it go. "Well? What is it?"

"Oh, please!" said Bobbie.

"Yes?" said the old gentleman.

"What I mean to say—" said Bobbie.

"Well?" said the old gentleman.

"It's all very nice and kind," said she.

"But?" he said.

"I wish I might say something," she said.

"Say it," said he.

"Well, then," said Bobbie—and out came the story of the Russian who had written the beautiful book about poor people, and had been sent to prison and to Siberia for just that.

"And what we want more than anything in the world is to find his wife and children for him," said Bobbie, "but we don't know how. But you must be most horribly clever, or you wouldn't be a Direction of the Railway. And if YOU knew how—and would? We'd rather have that than anything else in the world. We'd go without the watches, even, if you could sell them and find his wife with the money."

And the others said so, too, though not with so much enthusiasm.

"Hum," said the old gentleman, pulling down the white waistcoat that had the big gilt buttons on it, "what did you say the name was— Fryingpansky?"

"No, no," said Bobbie earnestly. "I'll write it down for you. It doesn't really look at all like that except when you say it. Have you a bit of pencil and the back of an envelope?" she asked.

The old gentleman got out a gold pencil-case and a beautiful, sweet- smelling, green Russian leather note-book and opened it at a new page.

"Here," he said, "write here."

She wrote down "Szezcpansky," and said:—

"That's how you write it. You CALL it Shepansky."

The old gentleman took out a pair of gold-rimmed spectacles and fitted them on his nose. When he had read the name, he looked quite different.

"THAT man? Bless my soul!" he said. "Why, I've read his book! It's translated into every European language. A fine book—a noble book. And so your mother took him in—like the good Samaritan. Well, well. I'll tell you what, youngsters—your mother must be a very good woman."

"Of course she is," said Phyllis, in astonishment.

"And you're a very good man," said Bobbie, very shy, but firmly resolved to be polite.

"You flatter me," said the old gentleman, taking off his hat with a flourish. "And now am I to tell you what I think of you?"

"Oh, please don't," said Bobbie, hastily.

"Why?" asked the old gentleman.

"I don't exactly know," said Bobbie. "Only—if it's horrid, I don't want you to; and if it's nice, I'd rather you didn't."

The old gentleman laughed.

"Well, then," he said, "I'll only just say that I'm very glad you came to me about this—very glad, indeed. And I shouldn't be surprised if I found out something very soon. I know a great many Russians in London, and every Russian knows HIS name. Now tell me all about yourselves."

He turned to the others, but there was only one other, and that was Peter. Phyllis had disappeared.

"Tell me all about yourself," said the old gentleman again. And, quite naturally, Peter was stricken dumb.

"All right, we'll have an examination," said the old gentleman; "you two sit on the table, and I'll sit on the bench and ask questions."

He did, and out came their names and ages—their Father's name and business—how long they had lived at Three Chimneys and a great deal more.

The questions were beginning to turn on a herring and a half for three halfpence, and a pound of lead and a pound of feathers, when the door of the waiting room was kicked open by a boot; as the boot entered everyone could see that its lace was coming undone—and in came Phyllis, very slowly and carefully.

In one hand she carried a large tin can, and in the other a thick slice of bread and butter.

"Afternoon tea," she announced proudly, and held the can and the bread and butter out to the old gentleman, who took them and said:—

"Bless my soul!"

"Yes," said Phyllis.

"It's very thoughtful of you," said the old gentleman, "very."

"But you might have got a cup," said Bobbie, "and a plate."

"Perks always drinks out of the can," said Phyllis, flushing red. "I think it was very nice of him to give it me at all—let alone cups and plates," she added.

"So do I," said the old gentleman, and he drank some of the tea and tasted the bread and butter.

And then it was time for the next train, and he got into it with many good-byes and kind last words.

"Well," said Peter, when they were left on the platform, and the tail-lights of the train disappeared round the corner, "it's my belief that we've lighted a candle to-day—like Latimer, you know, when he was being burned—and there'll be fireworks for our Russian before long."

And so there were.

It wasn't ten days after the interview in the waiting room that the three children were sitting on the top of the biggest rock in the field below their house watching the 5.15 steam away from the station along the bottom of the valley. They saw, too, the few people who had got out at the station straggling up the road towards the village—and they saw one person leave the road and open the gate that led across the fields to Three Chimneys and to nowhere else.

"Who on earth!" said Peter, scrambling down.

"Let's go and see," said Phyllis.

So they did. And when they got near enough to see who the person was, they saw it was their old gentleman himself, his brass buttons winking in the afternoon sunshine, and his white waistcoat looking whiter than ever against the green of the field.

"Hullo!" shouted the children, waving their hands.

"Hullo!" shouted the old gentleman, waving his hat.

Then the three started to run—and when they got to him they hardly had breath left to say:—

"How do you do?"

"Good news," said he. "I've found your Russian friend's wife and child—and I couldn't resist the temptation of giving myself the pleasure of telling him."

But as he looked at Bobbie's face he felt that he COULD resist that temptation.

"Here," he said to her, "you run on and tell him. The other two will show me the way."

Bobbie ran. But when she had breathlessly panted out the news to the Russian and Mother sitting in the quiet garden—when Mother's face had lighted up so beautifully, and she had said half a dozen quick French words to the Exile—Bobbie wished that she had NOT carried the news. For the Russian sprang up with a cry that made Bobbie's heart leap and then tremble—a cry of love and longing such as she had never heard. Then he took Mother's hand and kissed it gently and reverently—and then he sank down in his chair and covered his face with his hands and sobbed. Bobbie crept away. She did not want to see the others just then.

But she was as gay as anybody when the endless French talking was over, when Peter had torn down to the village for buns and cakes, and the girls had got tea ready and taken it out into the garden.

The old gentleman was most merry and delightful. He seemed to be able to talk in French and English almost at the same moment, and Mother did nearly as well. It was a delightful time. Mother seemed as if she could not make enough fuss about the old gentleman, and she said yes at once when he asked if he might present some "goodies" to his little friends.

The word was new to the children—but they guessed that it meant sweets, for the three large pink and green boxes, tied with green ribbon, which he took out of his bag, held unheard-of layers of beautiful chocolates.

The Russian's few belongings were packed, and they all saw him off at the station.

Then Mother turned to the old gentleman and said:—

"I don't know how to thank you for EVERYTHING. It has been a real pleasure to me to see you. But we live very quietly. I am so sorry that I can't ask you to come and see us again."

The children thought this very hard. When they HAD made a friend— and such a friend—they would dearly have liked him to come and see them again.

What the old gentleman thought they couldn't tell. He only said:—

"I consider myself very fortunate, Madam, to have been received once at your house."

"Ah," said Mother, "I know I must seem surly and ungrateful—but—"

"You could never seem anything but a most charming and gracious lady," said the old gentleman, with another of his bows.

And as they turned to go up the hill, Bobbie saw her Mother's face.

"How tired you look, Mammy," she said; "lean on me."

"It's my place to give Mother my arm," said Peter. "I'm the head man of the family when Father's away."

Mother took an arm of each.

"How awfully nice," said Phyllis, skipping joyfully, "to think of the dear Russian embracing his long-lost wife. The baby must have grown a lot since he saw it."

"Yes," said Mother.

"I wonder whether Father will think I'VE grown," Phyllis went on, skipping still more gaily. "I have grown already, haven't I, Mother?"

"Yes," said Mother, "oh, yes," and Bobbie and Peter felt her hands tighten on their arms.

"Poor old Mammy, you ARE tired," said Peter.

Bobbie said, "Come on, Phil; I'll race you to the gate."

And she started the race, though she hated doing it. YOU know why Bobbie did that. Mother only thought that Bobbie was tired of walking slowly. Even Mothers, who love you better than anyone else ever will, don't always understand.

Chapter 8. The Amateur Firemen.

"That's a likely little brooch you've got on, Miss," said Perks the Porter; "I don't know as ever I see a thing more like a buttercup without it WAS a buttercup."

"Yes," said Bobbie, glad and flushed by this approval. "I always thought it was more like a buttercup almost than even a real one— and I NEVER thought it would come to be mine, my very own—and then Mother gave it to me for my birthday."

"Oh, have you had a birthday?" said Perks; and he seemed quite surprised, as though a birthday were a thing only granted to a favoured few.

"Yes," said Bobbie; "when's your birthday, Mr. Perks?" The children were taking tea with Mr. Perks in the Porters' room among the lamps and the railway almanacs. They had brought their own cups and some jam turnovers. Mr. Perks made tea in a beer can, as usual, and everyone felt very happy and confidential.

"My birthday?" said Perks, tipping some more dark brown tea out of the can into Peter's cup. "I give up keeping of my birthday afore you was born."

"But you must have been born SOMETIME, you know," said Phyllis, thoughtfully, "even if it was twenty years ago—or thirty or sixty or seventy."

"Not so long as that, Missie," Perks grinned as he answered. "If you really want to know, it was thirty-two years ago, come the fifteenth of this month."

"Then why don't you keep it?" asked Phyllis.

"I've got something else to keep besides birthdays," said Perks, briefly.

"Oh! What?" asked Phyllis, eagerly. "Not secrets?"

"No," said Perks, "the kids and the Missus."

It was this talk that set the children thinking, and, presently, talking. Perks was, on the whole, the dearest friend they had made. Not so grand as the Station Master, but more approachable—less powerful than the old gentleman, but more confidential.

"It seems horrid that nobody keeps his birthday," said Bobbie. "Couldn't WE do something?"

"Let's go up to the Canal bridge and talk it over," said Peter. "I got a new gut line from the postman this morning. He gave it me for a bunch of roses that I gave him for his sweetheart. She's ill."

"Then I do think you might have given her the roses for nothing," said Bobbie, indignantly.

"Nyang, nyang!" said Peter, disagreeably, and put his hands in his pockets.

"He did, of course," said Phyllis, in haste; "directly we heard she was ill we got the roses ready and waited by the gate. It was when you were making the brekker-toast. And when he'd said 'Thank you' for the roses so many times—much more than he need have—he pulled out the line and gave it to Peter. It wasn't exchange. It was the grateful heart."

"Oh, I BEG your pardon, Peter," said Bobbie, "I AM so sorry."

"Don't mention it," said Peter, grandly, "I knew you would be."

So then they all went up to the Canal bridge. The idea was to fish from the bridge, but the line was not quite long enough.

"Never mind," said Bobbie. "Let's just stay here and look at things. Everything's so beautiful."

It was. The sun was setting in red splendour over the grey and purple hills, and the canal lay smooth and shiny in the shadow—no ripple broke its surface. It was like a grey satin ribbon between the dusky green silk of the meadows that were on each side of its banks.

"It's all right," said Peter, "but somehow I can always see how pretty things are much better when I've something to do. Let's get down on to the towpath and fish from there."

Phyllis and Bobbie remembered how the boys on the canal-boats had thrown coal at them, and they said so.

"Oh, nonsense," said Peter. "There aren't any boys here now. If there were, I'd fight them."

Peter's sisters were kind enough not to remind him how he had NOT fought the boys when coal had last been thrown. Instead they said, "All right, then," and cautiously climbed down the steep bank to the towing-path. The line was carefully baited, and for half an hour they fished patiently and in vain. Not a single nibble came to nourish hope in their hearts.

All eyes were intent on the sluggish waters that earnestly pretended they had never harboured a single minnow when a loud rough shout made them start.

"Hi!" said the shout, in most disagreeable tones, "get out of that, can't you?"

An old white horse coming along the towing-path was within half a dozen yards of them. They sprang to their feet and hastily climbed up the bank.

"We'll slip down again when they've gone by," said Bobbie.

But, alas, the barge, after the manner of barges, stopped under the bridge.

"She's going to anchor," said Peter; "just our luck!"

The barge did not anchor, because an anchor is not part of a canal- boat's furniture, but she was moored with ropes fore and aft—and the ropes were made fast to the palings and to crowbars driven into the ground.

"What you staring at?" growled the Bargee, crossly.

"We weren't staring," said Bobbie; "we wouldn't be so rude."

"Rude be blessed," said the man; "get along with you!"

"Get along yourself," said Peter. He remembered what he had said about fighting boys, and, besides, he felt safe halfway up the bank. "We've as much right here as anyone else."

"Oh, 'AVE you, indeed!" said the man. "We'll soon see about that." And he came across his deck and began to climb down the side of his barge.

"Oh, come away, Peter, come away!" said Bobbie and Phyllis, in agonised unison.

"Not me," said Peter, "but YOU'D better."

The girls climbed to the top of the bank and stood ready to bolt for home as soon as they saw their brother out of danger. The way home lay all down hill. They knew that they all ran well. The Bargee did not look as if HE did. He was red-faced, heavy, and beefy.

But as soon as his foot was on the towing-path the children saw that they had misjudged him.

He made one spring up the bank and caught Peter by the leg, dragged him down—set him on his feet with a shake—took him by the ear—and said sternly:—

"Now, then, what do you mean by it? Don't you know these 'ere waters is preserved? You ain't no right catching fish 'ere—not to say nothing of your precious cheek."

Peter was always proud afterwards when he remembered that, with the Bargee's furious fingers tightening on his ear, the Bargee's crimson countenance close to his own, the Bargee's hot breath on his neck, he had the courage to speak the truth.

"I WASN'T catching fish," said Peter.

"That's not YOUR fault, I'll be bound," said the man, giving Peter's ear a twist—not a hard one—but still a twist.

Peter could not say that it was. Bobbie and Phyllis had been holding on to the railings above and skipping with anxiety. Now suddenly Bobbie slipped through the railings and rushed down the bank towards Peter, so impetuously that Phyllis, following more temperately, felt certain that her sister's descent would end in the waters of the canal. And so it would have done if the Bargee hadn't let go of Peter's ear—and caught her in his jerseyed arm.

"Who are you a-shoving of?" he said, setting her on her feet.

"Oh," said Bobbie, breathless, "I'm not shoving anybody. At least, not on purpose. Please don't be cross with Peter. Of course, if it's your canal, we're sorry and we won't any more. But we didn't know it was yours."

"Go along with you," said the Bargee.

"Yes, we will; indeed we will," said Bobbie, earnestly; "but we do beg your pardon—and really we haven't caught a single fish. I'd tell you directly if we had, honour bright I would."

She held out her hands and Phyllis turned out her little empty pocket to show that really they hadn't any fish concealed about them.

"Well," said the Bargee, more gently, "cut along, then, and don't you do it again, that's all."

The children hurried up the bank.

"Chuck us a coat, M'ria," shouted the man. And a red-haired woman in a green plaid shawl came out from the cabin door with a baby in her arms and threw a coat to him. He put it on, climbed the bank, and slouched along across the bridge towards the village.

"You'll find me up at the 'Rose and Crown' when you've got the kid to sleep," he called to her from the bridge.

When he was out of sight the children slowly returned. Peter insisted on this.

"The canal may belong to him," he said, "though I don't believe it does. But the bridge is everybody's. Doctor Forrest told me it's public property. I'm not going to be bounced off the bridge by him or anyone else, so I tell you."

Peter's ear was still sore and so were his feelings.

The girls followed him as gallant soldiers might follow the leader of a forlorn hope.

"I do wish you wouldn't," was all they said.

"Go home if you're afraid," said Peter; "leave me alone. I'M not afraid."

The sound of the man's footsteps died away along the quiet road. The peace of the evening was not broken by the notes of the sedge- warblers or by the voice of the woman in the barge, singing her baby to sleep. It was a sad song she sang. Something about Bill Bailey and how she wanted him to come home.

The children stood leaning their arms on the parapet of the bridge; they were glad to be quiet for a few minutes because all three hearts were beating much more quickly.

"I'm not going to be driven away by any old bargeman, I'm not," said Peter, thickly.

"Of course not," Phyllis said soothingly; "you didn't give in to him! So now we might go home, don't you think?"

"NO," said Peter.

Nothing more was said till the woman got off the barge, climbed the bank, and came across the bridge.

She hesitated, looking at the three backs of the children, then she said, "Ahem."

Peter stayed as he was, but the girls looked round.

"You mustn't take no notice of my Bill," said the woman; "'is bark's worse'n 'is bite. Some of the kids down Farley way is fair terrors. It was them put 'is back up calling out about who ate the puppy-pie under Marlow bridge."

"Who DID?" asked Phyllis.

"*I* dunno," said the woman. "Nobody don't know! But somehow, and I don't know the why nor the wherefore of it, them words is p'ison to a barge-master. Don't you take no notice. 'E won't be back for two hours good. You might catch a power o' fish afore that. The light's good an' all," she added.

"Thank you," said Bobbie. "You're very kind. Where's your baby?"

"Asleep in the cabin," said the woman. "'E's all right. Never wakes afore twelve. Reg'lar as a church clock, 'e is."

"I'm sorry," said Bobbie; "I would have liked to see him, close to."

"And a finer you never did see, Miss, though I says it." The woman's face brightened as she spoke.

"Aren't you afraid to leave it?" said Peter.

"Lor' love you, no," said the woman; "who'd hurt a little thing like 'im? Besides, Spot's there. So long!"

The woman went away.

"Shall we go home?" said Phyllis.

"You can. I'm going to fish," said Peter briefly.

"I thought we came up here to talk about Perks's birthday," said Phyllis.

"Perks's birthday'll keep."

So they got down on the towing-path again and Peter fished. He did not catch anything.

It was almost quite dark, the girls were getting tired, and as Bobbie said, it was past bedtime, when suddenly Phyllis cried, "What's that?"

And she pointed to the canal boat. Smoke was coming from the chimney of the cabin, had indeed been curling softly into the soft evening air all the time—but now other wreaths of smoke were rising, and these were from the cabin door.

"It's on fire—that's all," said Peter, calmly. "Serve him right."

"Oh—how CAN you?" cried Phyllis. "Think of the poor dear dog."

"The BABY!" screamed Bobbie.

In an instant all three made for the barge.

Her mooring ropes were slack, and the little breeze, hardly strong enough to be felt, had yet been strong enough to drift her stern against the bank. Bobbie was first—then came Peter, and it was Peter who slipped and fell. He went into the canal up to his neck, and his feet could not feel the bottom, but his arm was on the edge of the barge. Phyllis caught at his hair. It hurt, but it helped him to get out. Next minute he had leaped on to the barge, Phyllis following.

"Not you!" he shouted to Bobbie; "ME, because I'm wet."

He caught up with Bobbie at the cabin door, and flung her aside very roughly indeed; if they had been playing, such roughness would have made Bobbie weep with tears of rage and pain. Now, though he flung her on to the edge of the hold, so that her knee and her elbow were grazed and bruised, she only cried:—

"No—not you—ME," and struggled up again. But not quickly enough.

Peter had already gone down two of the cabin steps into the cloud of thick smoke. He stopped, remembered all he had ever heard of fires, pulled his soaked handkerchief out of his breast pocket and tied it over his mouth. As he pulled it out he said:—

"It's all right, hardly any fire at all."

And this, though he thought it was a lie, was rather good of Peter. It was meant to keep Bobbie from rushing after him into danger. Of course it didn't.

The cabin glowed red. A paraffin lamp was burning calmly in an orange mist.

"Hi," said Peter, lifting the handkerchief from his mouth for a moment. "Hi, Baby—where are you?" He choked.

"Oh, let ME go," cried Bobbie, close behind him. Peter pushed her back more roughly than before, and went on.

Now what would have happened if the baby hadn't cried I don't know— but just at that moment it DID cry. Peter felt his way through the dark smoke, found something small and soft and warm and alive, picked it up and backed out, nearly tumbling over Bobbie who was close behind. A dog snapped at his leg—tried to bark, choked.

"I've got the kid," said Peter, tearing off the handkerchief and staggering on to the deck.

Bobbie caught at the place where the bark came from, and her hands met on the fat back of a smooth-haired dog. It turned and fastened its teeth on her hand, but very gently, as much as to say:—

"I'm bound to bark and bite if strangers come into my master's cabin, but I know you mean well, so I won't REALLY bite."

Bobbie dropped the dog.

"All right, old man. Good dog," said she. "Here—give me the baby, Peter; you're so wet you'll give it cold."

Peter was only too glad to hand over the strange little bundle that squirmed and whimpered in his arms.

"Now," said Bobbie, quickly, "you run straight to the 'Rose and Crown' and tell them. Phil and I will stay here with the precious. Hush, then, a dear, a duck, a darling! Go NOW, Peter! Run!"

"I can't run in these things," said Peter, firmly; "they're as heavy as lead. I'll walk."

"Then I'LL run," said Bobbie. "Get on the bank, Phil, and I'll hand you the dear."

The baby was carefully handed. Phyllis sat down on the bank and tried to hush the baby. Peter wrung the water from his sleeves and knickerbocker legs as well as he could, and it was Bobbie who ran like the wind across the bridge and up the long white quiet twilight road towards the 'Rose and Crown.'

There is a nice old-fashioned room at the 'Rose and Crown; where Bargees and their wives sit of an evening drinking their supper beer, and toasting their supper cheese at a glowing basketful of coals that sticks out into the room under a great hooded chimney and is warmer and prettier and more comforting than any other fireplace *I* ever saw.

There was a pleasant party of barge people round the fire. You might not have thought it pleasant, but they did; for they were all friends or acquaintances, and they liked the same sort of things, and talked the same sort of talk. This is the real secret of pleasant society. The Bargee Bill, whom the children had found so disagreeable, was considered excellent company by his mates. He was telling a tale of his own wrongs—always a thrilling subject. It was his barge he was speaking about.

"And 'e sent down word 'paint her inside hout,' not namin' no colour, d'ye see? So I gets a lotter green paint and I paints her stem to stern, and I tell yer she looked A1. Then 'E comes along and 'e says, 'Wot yer paint 'er all one colour for?' 'e says. And I says, says I, 'Cause I thought she'd look fust-rate,' says I, 'and I think so still.' An' he says, 'DEW yer? Then ye can just pay for the bloomin' paint yerself,' says he. An' I 'ad to, too." A murmur of sympathy ran round the room. Breaking noisily in on it came Bobbie. She burst open the swing door—crying breathlessly:—

"Bill! I want Bill the Bargeman."

There was a stupefied silence. Pots of beer were held in mid-air, paralysed on their way to thirsty mouths.

"Oh," said Bobbie, seeing the bargewoman and making for her. "Your barge cabin's on fire. Go quickly."

The woman started to her feet, and put a big red hand to her waist, on the left side, where your heart seems to be when you are frightened or miserable.

"Reginald Horace!" she cried in a terrible voice; "my Reginald Horace!"

"All right," said Bobbie, "if you mean the baby; got him out safe. Dog, too." She had no breath for more, except, "Go on—it's all alight."

Then she sank on the ale-house bench and tried to get that breath of relief after running which people call the 'second wind.' But she felt as though she would never breathe again.

Bill the Bargee rose slowly and heavily. But his wife was a hundred yards up the road before he had quite understood what was the matter.

Phyllis, shivering by the canal side, had hardly heard the quick approaching feet before the woman had flung herself on the railing, rolled down the bank, and snatched the baby from her.

"Don't," said Phyllis, reproachfully; "I'd just got him to sleep."

* * * * * *

Bill came up later talking in a language with which the children were wholly unfamiliar. He leaped on to the barge and dipped up pails of water. Peter helped him and they put out the fire. Phyllis, the bargewoman, and the baby—and presently Bobbie, too— cuddled together in a heap on the bank.

"Lord help me, if it was me left anything as could catch alight," said the woman again and again.

But it wasn't she. It was Bill the Bargeman, who had knocked his pipe out and the red ash had fallen on the hearth-rug and smouldered there and at last broken into flame. Though a stern man he was just. He did not blame his wife for what was his own fault, as many bargemen, and other men, too, would have done.

* * * * * *

Mother was half wild with anxiety when at last the three children turned up at Three Chimneys, all very wet by now, for Peter seemed to have come off on the others. But when she had disentangled the truth of what had happened from their mixed and incoherent narrative, she owned that they had done quite right, and could not possibly have done otherwise. Nor did she put any obstacles in the way of their accepting the cordial invitation with which the bargeman had parted from them.

"Ye be here at seven to-morrow," he had said, "and I'll take you the entire trip to Farley and back, so I will, and not a penny to pay. Nineteen locks!"

They did not know what locks were; but they were at the bridge at seven, with bread and cheese and half a soda cake, and quite a quarter of a leg of mutton in a basket.

It was a glorious day. The old white horse strained at the ropes, the barge glided smoothly and steadily through the still water. The sky was blue overhead. Mr. Bill was as nice as anyone could possibly be. No one would have thought that he could be the same man who had held Peter by the ear. As for Mrs. Bill, she had always been nice, as Bobbie said, and so had the baby, and even Spot, who might have bitten them quite badly if he had liked.

"It was simply ripping, Mother," said Peter, when they reached home very happy, very tired, and very dirty, "right over that glorious aqueduct. And locks—you don't know what they're like. You sink into the ground and then, when you feel you're never going to stop going down, two great black gates open slowly, slowly—you go out, and there you are on the canal just like you were before."

"I know," said Mother, "there are locks on the Thames. Father and I used to go on the river at Marlow before we were married."

"And the dear, darling, ducky baby," said Bobbie; "it let me nurse it for ages and ages—and it WAS so good. Mother, I wish we had a baby to play with."

"And everybody was so nice to us," said Phyllis, "everybody we met. And they say we may fish whenever we like. And Bill is going to show us the way next time he's in these parts. He says we don't know really."

"He said YOU didn't know," said Peter; "but, Mother, he said he'd tell all the bargees up and down the canal that we were the real, right sort, and they were to treat us like good pals, as we were."

"So then I said," Phyllis interrupted, "we'd always each wear a red ribbon when we went fishing by the canal, so they'd know it was US, and we were the real, right sort, and be nice to us!"

"So you've made another lot of friends," said Mother; "first the railway and then the canal!"

"Oh, yes," said Bobbie; "I think everyone in the world is friends if you can only get them to see you don't want to be UN-friends."

"Perhaps you're right," said Mother; and she sighed. "Come, Chicks. It's bedtime."

"Yes," said Phyllis. "Oh dear—and we went up there to talk about what we'd do for Perks's birthday. And we haven't talked a single thing about it!"

"No more we have," said Bobbie; "but Peter's saved Reginald Horace's life. I think that's about good enough for one evening."

"Bobbie would have saved him if I hadn't knocked her down; twice I did," said Peter, loyally.

"So would I," said Phyllis, "if I'd known what to do."

"Yes," said Mother, "you've saved a little child's life. I do think that's enough for one evening. Oh, my darlings, thank God YOU'RE all safe!"

Chapter 9. The Pride of Perks.

It was breakfast-time. Mother's face was very bright as she poured the milk and ladled out the porridge.

"I've sold another story, Chickies," she said; "the one about the King of the Mussels, so there'll be buns for tea. You can go and get them as soon as they're baked. About eleven, isn't it?"

Peter, Phyllis, and Bobbie exchanged glances with each other, six glances in all. Then Bobbie said:—

"Mother, would you mind if we didn't have the buns for tea to-night, but on the fifteenth? That's next Thursday."

"*I* don't mind when you have them, dear," said Mother, "but why?"

"Because it's Perks's birthday," said Bobbie; "he's thirty-two, and he says he doesn't keep his birthday any more, because he's got other things to keep—not rabbits or secrets—but the kids and the missus."

"You mean his wife and children," said Mother.

"Yes," said Phyllis; "it's the same thing, isn't it?"

"And we thought we'd make a nice birthday for him. He's been so awfully jolly decent to us, you know, Mother," said Peter, "and we agreed that next bun-day we'd ask you if we could."

"But suppose there hadn't been a bun-day before the fifteenth?" said Mother.

"Oh, then, we meant to ask you to let us anti—antipate it, and go without when the bun-day came."

"Anticipate," said Mother. "I see. Certainly. It would be nice to put his name on the buns with pink sugar, wouldn't it?"

"Perks," said Peter, "it's not a pretty name."

"His other name's Albert," said Phyllis; "I asked him once."

"We might put A. P.," said Mother; "I'll show you how when the day comes."

This was all very well as far as it went. But even fourteen halfpenny buns with A. P. on them in pink sugar do not of themselves make a very grand celebration.

"There are always flowers, of course," said Bobbie, later, when a really earnest council was being held on the subject in the hay-loft where the broken chaff-cutting machine was, and the row of holes to drop hay through into the hay-racks over the mangers of the stables below.

"He's got lots of flowers of his own," said Peter.

"But it's always nice to have them given you," said Bobbie, "however many you've got of your own. We can use flowers for trimmings to the birthday. But there must be something to trim besides buns."

"Let's all be quiet and think," said Phyllis; "no one's to speak until it's thought of something."

So they were all quiet and so very still that a brown rat thought that there was no one in the loft and came out very boldly. When Bobbie sneezed, the rat was quite shocked and hurried away, for he saw that a hay-loft where such things could happen was no place for a respectable middle-aged rat that liked a quiet life.

"Hooray!" cried Peter, suddenly, "I've got it." He jumped up and kicked at the loose hay.

"What?" said the others, eagerly.

"Why, Perks is so nice to everybody. There must be lots of people in the village who'd like to help to make him a birthday. Let's go round and ask everybody."

"Mother said we weren't to ask people for things," said Bobbie, doubtfully.

"For ourselves, she meant, silly, not for other people. I'll ask the old gentleman too. You see if I don't," said Peter.

"Let's ask Mother first," said Bobbie.

"Oh, what's the use of bothering Mother about every little thing?" said Peter, "especially when she's busy. Come on. Let's go down to the village now and begin."

So they went. The old lady at the Post-office said she didn't see why Perks should have a birthday any more than anyone else.

"No," said Bobbie, "I should like everyone to have one. Only we know when his is."

"Mine's to-morrow," said the old lady, "and much notice anyone will take of it. Go along with you."

So they went.

And some people were kind, and some were crusty. And some would give and some would not. It is rather difficult work asking for things, even for other people, as you have no doubt found if you have ever tried it.

When the children got home and counted up what had been given and what had been promised, they felt that for the first day it was not so bad. Peter wrote down the lists of the things in the little pocket-book where he kept the numbers of his engines. These were the lists:—

GIVEN. A tobacco pipe from the sweet shop. Half a pound of tea from the grocer's. A woollen scarf slightly faded from the draper's, which was the other side of the grocer's. A stuffed squirrel from the Doctor.

PROMISED. A piece of meat from the butcher. Six fresh eggs from the woman who lived in the old turnpike cottage. A piece of honeycomb and six bootlaces from the cobbler, and an iron shovel from the blacksmith's.

Very early next morning Bobbie got up and woke Phyllis. This had been agreed on between them. They had not told Peter because they thought he would think it silly. But they told him afterwards, when it had turned out all right.

They cut a big bunch of roses, and put it in a basket with the needle-book that Phyllis had made for Bobbie on her birthday, and a very pretty blue necktie of Phyllis's. Then they wrote on a paper: 'For Mrs. Ransome, with our best love, because it is her birthday,' and they put the paper in the basket, and they took it to the Post- office, and went in and put it on the counter and ran away before the old woman at the Post-office had time to get into her shop.

When they got home Peter had grown confidential over helping Mother to get the breakfast and had told her their plans.

"There's no harm in it," said Mother, "but it depends HOW you do it. I only hope he won't be offended and think it's CHARITY. Poor people are very proud, you know."

"It isn't because he's poor," said Phyllis; "it's because we're fond of him."

"I'll find some things that Phyllis has outgrown," said Mother, "if you're quite sure you can give them to him without his being offended. I should like to do some little thing for him because he's been so kind to you. I can't do much because we're poor ourselves. What are you writing, Bobbie?"

"Nothing particular," said Bobbie, who had suddenly begun to scribble. "I'm sure he'd like the things, Mother."

The morning of the fifteenth was spent very happily in getting the buns and watching Mother make A. P. on them with pink sugar. You know how it's done, of course? You beat up whites of eggs and mix powdered sugar with them, and put in a few drops of cochineal. And then you make a cone of clean, white paper with a little hole at the pointed end, and put the pink egg-sugar in at the big end. It runs slowly out at the pointed end, and you write the letters with it just as though it were a great fat pen full of pink sugar-ink.

The buns looked beautiful with A. P. on every one, and, when they were put in a cool oven to set the sugar, the children went up to the village to collect the honey and the shovel and the other promised things.

The old lady at the Post-office was standing on her doorstep. The children said "Good morning," politely, as they passed.

"Here, stop a bit," she said.

So they stopped.

"Those roses," said she.

"Did you like them?" said Phyllis; "they were as fresh as fresh. *I* made the needle-book, but it was Bobbie's present." She skipped joyously as she spoke.

"Here's your basket," said the Post-office woman. She went in and brought out the basket. It was full of fat, red gooseberries.

"I dare say Perks's children would like them," said she.

"You ARE an old dear," said Phyllis, throwing her arms around the old lady's fat waist. "Perks WILL be pleased."

"He won't be half so pleased as I was with your needle-book and the tie and the pretty flowers and all," said the old lady, patting Phyllis's shoulder. "You're good little souls, that you are. Look here. I've got a pram round the back in the wood-lodge. It was got for my Emmie's first, that didn't live but six months, and she never had but that one. I'd like Mrs. Perks to have it. It 'ud be a help to her with that great boy of hers. Will you take it along?"

"OH!" said all the children together.

When Mrs. Ransome had got out the perambulator and taken off the careful papers that covered it, and dusted it all over, she said:—

"Well, there it is. I don't know but what I'd have given it to her before if I'd thought of it. Only I didn't quite know if she'd accept of it from me. You tell her it was my Emmie's little one's pram—"

"Oh, ISN'T it nice to think there is going to be a real live baby in it again!"

"Yes," said Mrs. Ransome, sighing, and then laughing; "here, I'll give you some peppermint cushions for the little ones, and then you run along before I give you the roof off my head and the clothes off my back."

All the things that had been collected for Perks were packed into the perambulator, and at half-past three Peter and Bobbie and Phyllis wheeled it down to the little yellow house where Perks lived.

The house was very tidy. On the window ledge was a jug of wild- flowers, big daisies, and red sorrel, and feathery, flowery grasses.

There was a sound of splashing from the wash-house, and a partly washed boy put his head round the door.

"Mother's a-changing of herself," he said.

"Down in a minute," a voice sounded down the narrow, freshly scrubbed stairs.

The children waited. Next moment the stairs creaked and Mrs. Perks came down, buttoning her bodice. Her hair was brushed very smooth and tight, and her face shone with soap and water.

"I'm a bit late changing, Miss," she said to Bobbie, "owing to me having had a extry clean-up to-day, along o' Perks happening to name its being his birthday. I don't know what put it into his head to think of such a thing. We keeps the children's birthdays, of course; but him and me—we're too old for such like, as a general rule."

"We knew it was his birthday," said Peter, "and we've got some presents for him outside in the perambulator.

As the presents were being unpacked, Mrs. Perks gasped. When they were all unpacked, she surprised and horrified the children by sitting suddenly down on a wooden chair and bursting into tears.

"Oh, don't!" said everybody; "oh, please don't!" And Peter added, perhaps a little impatiently: "What on earth is the matter? You don't mean to say you don't like it?"

Mrs. Perks only sobbed. The Perks children, now as shiny-faced as anyone could wish, stood at the wash-house door, and scowled at the intruders. There was a silence, an awkward silence.

"DON'T you like it?" said Peter, again, while his sisters patted Mrs. Perks on the back.

She stopped crying as suddenly as she had begun.

"There, there, don't you mind me. I'M all right!" she said. "Like it? Why, it's a birthday such as Perks never 'ad, not even when 'e was a boy and stayed with his uncle, who was a corn chandler in his own account. He failed afterwards. Like it? Oh—" and then she went on and said all sorts of things that I won't write down, because I am sure that Peter and Bobbie and Phyllis would not like me to. Their ears got hotter and hotter, and their faces redder and redder, at the kind things Mrs. Perks said. They felt they had done nothing to deserve all this praise.

At last Peter said: "Look here, we're glad you're pleased. But if you go on saying things like that, we must go home. And we did want to stay and see if Mr. Perks is pleased, too. But we can't stand this."

"I won't say another single word," said Mrs. Perks, with a beaming face, "but that needn't stop me thinking, need it? For if ever—"

"Can we have a plate for the buns?" Bobbie asked abruptly. And then Mrs. Perks hastily laid the table for tea, and the buns and the honey and the gooseberries were displayed on plates, and the roses were put in two glass jam jars, and the tea-table looked, as Mrs. Perks said, "fit for a Prince."

"To think!" she said, "me getting the place tidy early, and the little 'uns getting the wild-flowers and all—when never did I think there'd be anything more for him except the ounce of his pet particular that I got o' Saturday and been saving up for 'im ever since. Bless us! 'e IS early!"

Perks had indeed unlatched the latch of the little front gate.

"Oh," whispered Bobbie, "let's hide in the back kitchen, and YOU tell him about it. But give him the tobacco first, because you got it for him. And when you've told him, we'll all come in and shout, 'Many happy returns!'"

It was a very nice plan, but it did not quite come off. To begin with, there was only just time for Peter and Bobbie and Phyllis to rush into the wash-house, pushing the young and open-mouthed Perks children in front of them. There was not time to shut the door, so that, without at all meaning it, they had to listen to what went on in the kitchen. The wash-house was a tight fit for the Perks children and the Three Chimneys children, as well as all the wash- house's proper furniture, including the mangle and the copper.

"Hullo, old woman!" they heard Mr. Perks's voice say; "here's a pretty set-out!"

"It's your birthday tea, Bert," said Mrs. Perks, "and here's a ounce of your extry particular. I got it o' Saturday along o' your happening to remember it was your birthday to-day."

"Good old girl!" said Mr. Perks, and there was a sound of a kiss.

"But what's that pram doing here? And what's all these bundles? And where did you get the sweetstuff, and—"

The children did not hear what Mrs. Perks replied, because just then Bobbie gave a start, put her hand in her pocket, and all her body grew stiff with horror.

"Oh!" she whispered to the others, "whatever shall we do? I forgot to put the labels on any of the things! He won't know what's from who. He'll think it's all US, and that we're trying to be grand or charitable or something horrid."

"Hush!" said Peter.

And then they heard the voice of Mr. Perks, loud and rather angry.

"I don't care," he said; "I won't stand it, and so I tell you straight."

"But," said Mrs. Perks, "it's them children you make such a fuss about—the children from the Three Chimneys."

"I don't care," said Perks, firmly, "not if it was a angel from Heaven. We've got on all right all these years and no favours asked. I'm not going to begin these sort of charity goings-on at my time of life, so don't you think it, Nell."

"Oh, hush!" said poor Mrs Perks; "Bert, shut your silly tongue, for goodness' sake. The all three of 'ems in the wash-house a-listening to every word you speaks."

"Then I'll give them something to listen to," said the angry Perks; "I've spoke my mind to them afore now, and I'll do it again," he added, and he took two strides to the wash-house door, and flung it wide open—as wide, that is, as it would go, with the tightly packed children behind it.

"Come out," said Perks, "come out and tell me what you mean by it. 'Ave I ever complained to you of being short, as you comes this charity lay over me?"

"OH!" said Phyllis, "I thought you'd be so pleased; I'll never try to be kind to anyone else as long as I live. No, I won't, not never."

She burst into tears.

"We didn't mean any harm," said Peter.

"It ain't what you means so much as what you does," said Perks.

"Oh, DON'T!" cried Bobbie, trying hard to be braver than Phyllis, and to find more words than Peter had done for explaining in. "We thought you'd love it. We always have things on our birthdays."

"Oh, yes," said Perks, "your own relations; that's different."

"Oh, no," Bobbie answered. "NOT our own relations. All the servants always gave us things at home, and us to them when it was their birthdays. And when it was mine, and Mother gave me the brooch like a buttercup, Mrs. Viney gave me two lovely glass pots, and nobody thought she was coming the charity lay over us."

"If it had been glass pots here," said Perks, "I wouldn't ha' said so much. It's there being all this heaps and heaps of things I can't stand. No—nor won't, neither."

"But they're not all from us—" said Peter, "only we forgot to put the labels on. They're from all sorts of people in the village."

"Who put 'em up to it, I'd like to know?" asked Perks.

"Why, we did," sniffed Phyllis.

Perks sat down heavily in the elbow-chair and looked at them with what Bobbie afterwards described as withering glances of gloomy despair.

"So you've been round telling the neighbours we can't make both ends meet? Well, now you've disgraced us as deep as you can in the neighbourhood, you can just take the whole bag of tricks back w'ere it come from. Very much obliged, I'm sure. I don't doubt but what you meant it kind, but I'd rather not be acquainted with you any longer if it's all the same to you." He deliberately turned the chair round so that his back was turned to the children. The legs of the chair grated on the brick floor, and that was the only sound that broke the silence.

Then suddenly Bobbie spoke.

"Look here," she said, "this is most awful."

"That's what I says," said Perks, not turning round.

"Look here," said Bobbie, desperately, "we'll go if you like—and you needn't be friends with us any more if you don't want, but—"

"WE shall always be friends with YOU, however nasty you are to us," sniffed Phyllis, wildly.

"Be quiet," said Peter, in a fierce aside.

"But before we go," Bobbie went on desperately, "do let us show you the labels we wrote to put on the things."

"I don't want to see no labels," said Perks, "except proper luggage ones in my own walk of life. Do you think I've kept respectable and outer debt on what I gets, and her having to take in washing, to be give away for a laughing-stock to all the neighbours?"

"Laughing?" said Peter; "you don't know."

"You're a very hasty gentleman," whined Phyllis; "you know you were wrong once before, about us not telling you the secret about the Russian. Do let Bobbie tell you about the labels!"

"Well. Go ahead!" said Perks, grudgingly.

"Well, then," said Bobbie, fumbling miserably, yet not without hope, in her tightly stuffed pocket, "we wrote down all the things everybody said when they gave us the things, with the people's names, because Mother said we ought to be careful—because—but I wrote down what she said—and you'll see."

But Bobbie could not read the labels just at once. She had to swallow once or twice before she could begin.

Mrs. Perks had been crying steadily ever since her husband had opened the wash-house door. Now she caught her breath, choked, and said:—

"Don't you upset yourself, Missy. *I* know you meant it kind if he doesn't."

"May I read the labels?" said Bobbie, crying on to the slips as she tried to sort them. "Mother's first. It says:—

"'Little Clothes for Mrs. Perks's children.' Mother said, 'I'll find some of Phyllis's things that she's grown out of if you're quite sure Mr. Perks wouldn't be offended and think it's meant for charity. I'd like to do some little thing for him, because he's so kind to you. I can't do much because we're poor ourselves.'"

Bobbie paused.

"That's all right," said Perks, "your Ma's a born lady. We'll keep the little frocks, and what not, Nell."

"Then there's the perambulator and the gooseberries, and the sweets," said Bobbie, "they're from Mrs. Ransome. She said: 'I dare say Mr. Perks's children would like the sweets. And the perambulator was got for my Emmie's first—it didn't live but six months, and she's never had but that one. I'd like Mrs. Perks to have it. It would be a help with her fine boy. I'd have given it before if I'd been sure she'd accept of it from me.' She told me to tell you," Bobbie added, "that it was her Emmie's little one's pram."

"I can't send that pram back, Bert," said Mrs Perks, firmly, "and I won't. So don't you ask me—"

"I'm not a-asking anything," said Perks, gruffly.

"Then the shovel," said Bobbie. "Mr. James made it for you himself. And he said—where is it? Oh, yes, here! He said, 'You tell Mr. Perks it's a pleasure to make a little trifle for a man as is so much respected,' and then he said he wished he could shoe your children and his own children, like they do the horses, because, well, he knew what shoe leather was."

"James is a good enough chap," said Perks.

"Then the honey," said Bobbie, in haste, "and the boot-laces. HE said he respected a man that paid his way—and the butcher said the same. And the old turnpike woman said many was the time you'd lent her a hand with her garden when you were a lad—and things like that came home to roost—I don't know what she meant. And everybody who gave anything said they liked you, and it was a very good idea of ours; and nobody said anything about charity or anything horrid like that. And the old gentleman gave Peter a gold pound for you, and said you were a man who knew your work. And I thought you'd LOVE to know how fond people are of you, and I never was so unhappy in my life. Good-bye. I hope you'll forgive us some day—"

She could say no more, and she turned to go.

"Stop," said Perks, still with his back to them; "I take back every word I've said contrary to what you'd wish. Nell, set on the kettle."

"We'll take the things away if you're unhappy about them," said Peter; "but I think everybody'll be most awfully disappointed, as well as us."

"I'm not unhappy about them," said Perks; "I don't know," he added, suddenly wheeling the chair round and showing a very odd-looking screwed-up face, "I don't know as ever I was better pleased. Not so much with the presents—though they're an A1 collection—but the kind respect of our neighbours. That's worth having, eh, Nell?"

"I think it's all worth having," said Mrs. Perks, "and you've made a most ridiculous fuss about nothing, Bert, if you ask me."

"No, I ain't," said Perks, firmly; "if a man didn't respect hisself, no one wouldn't do it for him."

"But everyone respects you," said Bobbie; "they all said so."

"I knew you'd like it when you really understood," said Phyllis, brightly.

"Humph! You'll stay to tea?" said Mr. Perks.

Later on Peter proposed Mr. Perks's health. And Mr. Perks proposed a toast, also honoured in tea, and the toast was, "May the garland of friendship be ever green," which was much more poetical than anyone had expected from him.

* * * * * *

"Jolly good little kids, those," said Mr. Perks to his wife as they went to bed.

"Oh, they're all right, bless their hearts," said his wife; "it's you that's the aggravatingest old thing that ever was. I was ashamed of you—I tell you"

"You didn't need to be, old gal. I climbed down handsome soon as I understood it wasn't charity. But charity's what I never did abide, and won't neither."

* * * * * *

All sorts of people were made happy by that birthday party. Mr. Perks and Mrs. Perks and the little Perkses by all the nice things and by the kind thoughts of their neighbours; the Three Chimneys children by the success, undoubted though unexpectedly delayed, of their plan; and Mrs. Ransome every time she saw the fat Perks baby in the perambulator. Mrs. Perks made quite a round of visits to thank people for their kind birthday presents, and after each visit felt that she had a better friend than she had thought.

"Yes," said Perks, reflectively, "it's not so much what you does as what you means; that's what I say. Now if it had been charity—"

"Oh, drat charity," said Mrs. Perks; "nobody won't offer you charity, Bert, however much you was to want it, I lay. That was just friendliness, that was."

When the clergyman called on Mrs. Perks, she told him all about it. "It WAS friendliness, wasn't it, Sir?" said she.

"I think," said the clergyman, "it was what is sometimes called loving-kindness."

So you see it was all right in the end. But if one does that sort of thing, one has to be careful to do it in the right way. For, as Mr. Perks said, when he had time to think it over, it's not so much what you do, as what you mean.

Chapter 10. The Terrible Secret.

When they first went to live at Three Chimneys, the children had talked a great deal about their Father, and had asked a great many questions about him, and what he was doing and where he was and when he would come home. Mother always answered their questions as well as she could. But as the time went on they grew to speak less of him. Bobbie had felt almost from the first that for some strange miserable reason these questions hurt Mother and made her sad. And little by little the others came to have this feeling, too, though they could not have put it into words.

One day, when Mother was working so hard that she could not leave off even for ten minutes, Bobbie carried up her tea to the big bare room that they called Mother's workshop. It had hardly any furniture. Just a table and a chair and a rug. But always big pots of flowers on the window-sills and on the mantelpiece. The children saw to that. And from the three long uncurtained windows the beautiful stretch of meadow and moorland, the far violet of the hills, and the unchanging changefulness of cloud and sky.

"Here's your tea, Mother-love," said Bobbie; "do drink it while it's hot."

Mother laid down her pen among the pages that were scattered all over the table, pages covered with her writing, which was almost as plain as print, and much prettier. She ran her hands into her hair, as if she were going to pull it out by handfuls.

"Poor dear head," said Bobbie, "does it ache?"

"No—yes—not much," said Mother. "Bobbie, do you think Peter and Phil are FORGETTING Father?"

"NO," said Bobbie, indignantly. "Why?"

"You none of you ever speak of him now."

Bobbie stood first on one leg and then on the other.

"We often talk about him when we're by ourselves," she said.

"But not to me," said Mother. "Why?"

Bobbie did not find it easy to say why.

"I—you—" she said and stopped. She went over to the window and looked out.

"Bobbie, come here," said her Mother, and Bobbie came.

"Now," said Mother, putting her arm round Bobbie and laying her ruffled head against Bobbie's shoulder, "try to tell me, dear."

Bobbie fidgeted.

"Tell Mother."

"Well, then," said Bobbie, "I thought you were so unhappy about Daddy not being here, it made you worse when I talked about him. So I stopped doing it."

"And the others?"

"I don't know about the others," said Bobbie. "I never said anything about THAT to them. But I expect they felt the same about it as me."

"Bobbie dear," said Mother, still leaning her head against her, "I'll tell you. Besides parting from Father, he and I have had a great sorrow—oh, terrible—worse than anything you can think of, and at first it did hurt to hear you all talking of him as if everything were just the same. But it would be much more terrible if you were to forget him. That would be worse than anything."

"The trouble," said Bobbie, in a very little voice—"I promised I would never ask you any questions, and I never have, have I? But— the trouble—it won't last always?"

"No," said Mother, "the worst will be over when Father comes home to us."

"I wish I could comfort you," said Bobbie.

"Oh, my dear, do you suppose you don't? Do you think I haven't noticed how good you've all been, not quarrelling nearly as much as you used to—and all the little kind things you do for me—the flowers, and cleaning my shoes, and tearing up to make my bed before I get time to do it myself?"

Bobbie HAD sometimes wondered whether Mother noticed these things.

"That's nothing," she said, "to what—"

"I MUST get on with my work," said Mother, giving Bobbie one last squeeze. "Don't say anything to the others."

That evening in the hour before bed-time instead of reading to the children Mother told them stories of the games she and Father used to have when they were children and lived near each other in the country—tales of the adventures of Father with Mother's brothers when they were all boys together. Very funny stories they were, and the children laughed as they listened.

"Uncle Edward died before he was grown up, didn't he?" said Phyllis, as Mother lighted the bedroom candles.

"Yes, dear," said Mother, "you would have loved him. He was such a brave boy, and so adventurous. Always in mischief, and yet friends with everybody in spite of it. And your Uncle Reggie's in Ceylon— yes, and Father's away, too. But I think they'd all like to think we'd enjoyed talking about the things they used to do. Don't you think so?"

"Not Uncle Edward," said Phyllis, in a shocked tone; "he's in Heaven."

"You don't suppose he's forgotten us and all the old times, because God has taken him, any more than I forget him. Oh, no, he remembers. He's only away for a little time. We shall see him some day."

"And Uncle Reggie—and Father, too?" said Peter.

"Yes," said Mother. "Uncle Reggie and Father, too. Good night, my darlings."

"Good night," said everyone. Bobbie hugged her mother more closely even than usual, and whispered in her ear, "Oh, I do love you so, Mummy—I do—I do—"

When Bobbie came to think it all over, she tried not to wonder what the great trouble was. But she could not always help it. Father was not dead—like poor Uncle Edward—Mother had said so. And he was not ill, or Mother would have been with him. Being poor wasn't the trouble. Bobbie knew it was something nearer the heart than money could be.

"I mustn't try to think what it is," she told herself; "no, I mustn't. I AM glad Mother noticed about us not quarrelling so much. We'll keep that up."

And alas, that very afternoon she and Peter had what Peter called a first-class shindy.

They had not been a week at Three Chimneys before they had asked Mother to let them have a piece of garden each for their very own, and she had agreed, and the south border under the peach trees had been divided into three pieces and they were allowed to plant whatever they liked there.

Phyllis had planted mignonette and nasturtium and Virginia Stock in hers. The seeds came up, and though they looked just like weeds, Phyllis believed that they would bear flowers some day. The Virginia Stock justified her faith quite soon, and her garden was gay with a band of bright little flowers, pink and white and red and mauve.

"I can't weed for fear I pull up the wrong things," she used to say comfortably; "it saves such a lot of work."

Peter sowed vegetable seeds in his—carrots and onions and turnips. The seed was given to him by the farmer who lived in the nice black- and-white, wood-and-plaster house just beyond the bridge. He kept turkeys and guinea fowls, and was a most amiable man. But Peter's vegetables never had much of a chance, because he liked to use the earth of his garden for digging canals, and making forts and earthworks for his toy soldiers. And the seeds of vegetables rarely come to much in a soil that is constantly disturbed for the purposes of war and irrigation.

Bobbie planted rose-bushes in her garden, but all the little new leaves of the rose-bushes shrivelled and withered, perhaps because she moved them from the other part of the garden in May, which is not at all the right time of year for moving roses. But she would not own that they were dead, and hoped on against hope, until the day when Perks came up to see the garden, and told her quite plainly that all her roses were as dead as doornails.

"Only good for bonfires, Miss," he said. "You just dig 'em up and burn 'em, and I'll give you some nice fresh roots outer my garden; pansies, and stocks, and sweet willies, and forget-me-nots. I'll bring 'em along to-morrow if you get the ground ready."

So next day she set to work, and that happened to be the day when Mother had praised her and the others about not quarrelling. She moved the rose-bushes and carried them to the other end of the garden, where the rubbish heap was that they meant to make a bonfire of when Guy Fawkes' Day came.

Meanwhile Peter had decided to flatten out all his forts and earthworks, with a view to making a model of the railway-tunnel, cutting, embankment, canal, aqueduct, bridges, and all.

So when Bobbie came back from her last thorny journey with the dead rose-bushes, he had got the rake and was using it busily.

"*I* was using the rake," said Bobbie.

"Well, I'm using it now," said Peter.

"But I had it first," said Bobbie.

"Then it's my turn now," said Peter. And that was how the quarrel began.

"You're always being disagreeable about nothing," said Peter, after some heated argument.

"I had the rake first," said Bobbie, flushed and defiant, holding on to its handle.

"Don't—I tell you I said this morning I meant to have it. Didn't I, Phil?"

Phyllis said she didn't want to be mixed up in their rows. And instantly, of course, she was.

"If you remember, you ought to say."

"Of course she doesn't remember—but she might say so."

"I wish I'd had a brother instead of two whiny little kiddy sisters," said Peter. This was always recognised as indicating the high-water mark of Peter's rage.

Bobbie made the reply she always made to it.

"I can't think why little boys were ever invented," and just as she said it she looked up, and saw the three long windows of Mother's workshop flashing in the red rays of the sun. The sight brought back those words of praise:—

"You don't quarrel like you used to do."

"OH!" cried Bobbie, just as if she had been hit, or had caught her finger in a door, or had felt the hideous sharp beginnings of toothache.

"What's the matter?" said Phyllis.

Bobbie wanted to say: "Don't let's quarrel. Mother hates it so," but though she tried hard, she couldn't. Peter was looking too disagreeable and insulting.

"Take the horrid rake, then," was the best she could manage. And she suddenly let go her hold on the handle. Peter had been holding on to it too firmly and pullingly, and now that the pull the other way was suddenly stopped, he staggered and fell over backward, the teeth of the rake between his feet.

"Serve you right," said Bobbie, before she could stop herself.

Peter lay still for half a moment—long enough to frighten Bobbie a little. Then he frightened her a little more, for he sat up— screamed once—turned rather pale, and then lay back and began to shriek, faintly but steadily. It sounded exactly like a pig being killed a quarter of a mile off.

Mother put her head out of the window, and it wasn't half a minute after that she was in the garden kneeling by the side of Peter, who never for an instant ceased to squeal.

"What happened, Bobbie?" Mother asked.

"It was the rake," said Phyllis. "Peter was pulling at it, so was Bobbie, and she let go and he went over."

"Stop that noise, Peter," said Mother. "Come. Stop at once."

Peter used up what breath he had left in a last squeal and stopped.

"Now," said Mother, "are you hurt?"

"If he was really hurt, he wouldn't make such a fuss," said Bobbie, still trembling with fury; "he's not a coward!"

"I think my foot's broken off, that's all," said Peter, huffily, and sat up. Then he turned quite white. Mother put her arm round him.

"He IS hurt," she said; "he's fainted. Here, Bobbie, sit down and take his head on your lap."

Then Mother undid Peter's boots. As she took the right one off, something dripped from his foot on to the ground. It was red blood. And when the stocking came off there were three red wounds in Peter's foot and ankle, where the teeth of the rake had bitten him, and his foot was covered with red smears.

"Run for water—a basinful," said Mother, and Phyllis ran. She upset most of the water out of the basin in her haste, and had to fetch more in a jug.

Peter did not open his eyes again till Mother had tied her handkerchief round his foot, and she and Bobbie had carried him in and laid him on the brown wooden settle in the dining-room. By this time Phyllis was halfway to the Doctor's.

Mother sat by Peter and bathed his foot and talked to him, and Bobbie went out and got tea ready, and put on the kettle.

"It's all I can do," she told herself. "Oh, suppose Peter should die, or be a helpless cripple for life, or have to walk with crutches, or wear a boot with a sole like a log of wood!"

She stood by the back door reflecting on these gloomy possibilities, her eyes fixed on the water-butt.

"I wish I'd never been born," she said, and she said it out loud.

"Why, lawk a mercy, what's that for?" asked a voice, and Perks stood before her with a wooden trug basket full of green-leaved things and soft, loose earth.

"Oh, it's you," she said. "Peter's hurt his foot with a rake—three great gaping wounds, like soldiers get. And it was partly my fault."

"That it wasn't, I'll go bail," said Perks. "Doctor seen him?"

"Phyllis has gone for the Doctor."

"He'll be all right; you see if he isn't," said Perks. "Why, my father's second cousin had a hay-fork run into him, right into his inside, and he was right as ever in a few weeks, all except his being a bit weak in the head afterwards, and they did say that it was along of his getting a touch of the sun in the hay-field, and not the fork at all. I remember him well. A kind-'earted chap, but soft, as you might say."

Bobbie tried to let herself be cheered by this heartening reminiscence.

"Well," said Perks, "you won't want to be bothered with gardening just this minute, I dare say. You show me where your garden is, and I'll pop the bits of stuff in for you. And I'll hang about, if I may make so free, to see the Doctor as he comes out and hear what he says. You cheer up, Missie. I lay a pound he ain't hurt, not to speak of."

But he was. The Doctor came and looked at the foot and bandaged it beautifully, and said that Peter must not put it to the ground for at least a week.

"He won't be lame, or have to wear crutches or a lump on his foot, will he?" whispered Bobbie, breathlessly, at the door.

"My aunt! No!" said Dr. Forrest; "he'll be as nimble as ever on his pins in a fortnight. Don't you worry, little Mother Goose."

It was when Mother had gone to the gate with the Doctor to take his last instructions and Phyllis was filling the kettle for tea, that Peter and Bobbie found themselves alone.

"He says you won't be lame or anything," said Bobbie.

"Oh, course I shan't, silly," said Peter, very much relieved all the same.

"Oh, Peter, I AM so sorry," said Bobbie, after a pause.

"That's all right," said Peter, gruffly.

"It was ALL my fault," said Bobbie.

"Rot," said Peter.

"If we hadn't quarrelled, it wouldn't have happened. I knew it was wrong to quarrel. I wanted to say so, but somehow I couldn't."

"Don't drivel," said Peter. "I shouldn't have stopped if you HAD said it. Not likely. And besides, us rowing hadn't anything to do with it. I might have caught my foot in the hoe, or taken off my fingers in the chaff-cutting machine or blown my nose off with fireworks. It would have been hurt just the same whether we'd been rowing or not."

"But I knew it was wrong to quarrel," said Bobbie, in tears, "and now you're hurt and—"

"Now look here," said Peter, firmly, "you just dry up. If you're not careful, you'll turn into a beastly little Sunday-school prig, so I tell you."

"I don't mean to be a prig. But it's so hard not to be when you're really trying to be good."

(The Gentle Reader may perhaps have suffered from this difficulty.)

"Not it," said Peter; "it's a jolly good thing it wasn't you was hurt. I'm glad it was ME. There! If it had been you, you'd have been lying on the sofa looking like a suffering angel and being the light of the anxious household and all that. And I couldn't have stood it."

"No, I shouldn't," said Bobbie.

"Yes, you would," said Peter.

"I tell you I shouldn't."

"I tell you you would."

"Oh, children," said Mother's voice at the door. "Quarrelling again? Already?"

"We aren't quarrelling—not really," said Peter. "I wish you wouldn't think it's rows every time we don't agree!" When Mother had gone out again, Bobbie broke out:—

"Peter, I AM sorry you're hurt. But you ARE a beast to say I'm a prig."

"Well," said Peter unexpectedly, "perhaps I am. You did say I wasn't a coward, even when you were in such a wax. The only thing is—don't you be a prig, that's all. You keep your eyes open and if you feel priggishness coming on just stop in time. See?"

"Yes," said Bobbie, "I see."

"Then let's call it Pax," said Peter, magnanimously: "bury the hatchet in the fathoms of the past. Shake hands on it. I say, Bobbie, old chap, I am tired."

He was tired for many days after that, and the settle seemed hard and uncomfortable in spite of all the pillows and bolsters and soft folded rugs. It was terrible not to be able to go out. They moved the settle to the window, and from there Peter could see the smoke of the trains winding along the valley. But he could not see the trains.

At first Bobbie found it quite hard to be as nice to him as she wanted to be, for fear he should think her priggish. But that soon wore off, and both she and Phyllis were, as he observed, jolly good sorts. Mother sat with him when his sisters were out. And the words, "he's not a coward," made Peter determined not to make any fuss about the pain in his foot, though it was rather bad, especially at night.

Praise helps people very much, sometimes.

There were visitors, too. Mrs. Perks came up to ask how he was, and so did the Station Master, and several of the village people. But the time went slowly, slowly.

"I do wish there was something to read," said Peter. "I've read all our books fifty times over."

"I'll go to the Doctor's," said Phyllis; "he's sure to have some."

"Only about how to be ill, and about people's nasty insides, I expect," said Peter.

"Perks has a whole heap of Magazines that came out of trains when people are tired of them," said Bobbie. "I'll run down and ask him."

So the girls went their two ways.

Bobbie found Perks busy cleaning lamps.

"And how's the young gent?" said he.

"Better, thanks," said Bobbie, "but he's most frightfully bored. I came to ask if you'd got any Magazines you could lend him."

"There, now," said Perks, regretfully, rubbing his ear with a black and oily lump of cotton waste, "why didn't I think of that, now? I was trying to think of something as 'ud amuse him only this morning, and I couldn't think of anything better than a guinea-pig. And a young chap I know's going to fetch that over for him this tea-time."

"How lovely! A real live guinea! He will be pleased. But he'd like the Magazines as well."

"That's just it," said Perks. "I've just sent the pick of 'em to Snigson's boy—him what's just getting over the pewmonia. But I've lots of illustrated papers left."

He turned to the pile of papers in the corner and took up a heap six inches thick.

"There!" he said. "I'll just slip a bit of string and a bit of paper round 'em."

He pulled an old newspaper from the pile and spread it on the table, and made a neat parcel of it.

"There," said he, "there's lots of pictures, and if he likes to mess 'em about with his paint-box, or coloured chalks or what not, why, let him. *I* don't want 'em."

"You're a dear," said Bobbie, took the parcel, and started. The papers were heavy, and when she had to wait at the level-crossing while a train went by, she rested the parcel on the top of the gate. And idly she looked at the printing on the paper that the parcel was wrapped in.

Suddenly she clutched the parcel tighter and bent her head over it. It seemed like some horrible dream. She read on—the bottom of the column was torn off—she could read no farther.

She never remembered how she got home. But she went on tiptoe to her room and locked the door. Then she undid the parcel and read that printed column again, sitting on the edge of her bed, her hands and feet icy cold and her face burning. When she had read all there was, she drew a long, uneven breath.

"So now I know," she said.

What she had read was headed, 'End of the Trial. Verdict. Sentence.'

The name of the man who had been tried was the name of her Father. The verdict was 'Guilty.' And the sentence was 'Five years' Penal Servitude.'

"Oh, Daddy," she whispered, crushing the paper hard, "it's not true- -I don't believe it. You never did it! Never, never, never!"

There was a hammering on the door.

"What is it?" said Bobbie.

"It's me," said the voice of Phyllis; "tea's ready, and a boy's brought Peter a guinea-pig. Come along down."

And Bobbie had to.

Chapter 11. The Hound in the Red Jersey.

Bobbie knew the secret now. A sheet of old newspaper wrapped round a parcel—just a little chance like that—had given the secret to her. And she had to go down to tea and pretend that there was nothing the matter. The pretence was bravely made, but it wasn't very successful.

For when she came in, everyone looked up from tea and saw her pink- lidded eyes and her pale face with red tear-blotches on it.

"My darling," cried Mother, jumping up from the tea-tray, "whatever IS the matter?"

"My head aches, rather," said Bobbie. And indeed it did.

"Has anything gone wrong?" Mother asked.

"I'm all right, really," said Bobbie, and she telegraphed to her Mother from her swollen eyes this brief, imploring message—"NOT before the others!"

Tea was not a cheerful meal. Peter was so distressed by the obvious fact that something horrid had happened to Bobbie that he limited his speech to repeating, "More bread and butter, please," at startlingly short intervals. Phyllis stroked her sister's hand under the table to express sympathy, and knocked her cup over as she did it. Fetching a cloth and wiping up the spilt milk helped Bobbie a little. But she thought that tea would never end. Yet at last it did end, as all things do at last, and when Mother took out the tray, Bobbie followed her.

"She's gone to own up," said Phyllis to Peter; "I wonder what she's done."

"Broken something, I suppose," said Peter, "but she needn't be so silly over it. Mother never rows for accidents. Listen! Yes, they're going upstairs. She's taking Mother up to show her—the water-jug with storks on it, I expect it is."

Bobbie, in the kitchen, had caught hold of Mother's hand as she set down the tea-things.

"What is it?" Mother asked.

But Bobbie only said, "Come upstairs, come up where nobody can hear us."

When she had got Mother alone in her room she locked the door and then stood quite still, and quite without words.

All through tea she had been thinking of what to say; she had decided that "I know all," or "All is known to me," or "The terrible secret is a secret no longer," would be the proper thing. But now that she and her Mother and that awful sheet of newspaper were alone in the room together, she found that she could say nothing.

Suddenly she went to Mother and put her arms round her and began to cry again. And still she could find no words, only, "Oh, Mammy, oh, Mammy, oh, Mammy," over and over again.

Mother held her very close and waited.

Suddenly Bobbie broke away from her and went to her bed. From under her mattress she pulled out the paper she had hidden there, and held it out, pointing to her Father's name with a finger that shook.

"Oh, Bobbie," Mother cried, when one little quick look had shown her what it was, "you don't BELIEVE it? You don't believe Daddy did it?"

"NO," Bobbie almost shouted. She had stopped crying.

"That's all right," said Mother. "It's not true. And they've shut him up in prison, but he's done nothing wrong. He's good and noble and honourable, and he belongs to us. We have to think of that, and be proud of him, and wait."

Again Bobbie clung to her Mother, and again only one word came to her, but now that word was "Daddy," and "Oh, Daddy, oh, Daddy, oh, Daddy!" again and again.

"Why didn't you tell me, Mammy?" she asked presently.

"Are you going to tell the others?" Mother asked.

"No."

"Why?"

"Because—"

"Exactly," said Mother; "so you understand why I didn't tell you. We two must help each other to be brave."

"Yes," said Bobbie; "Mother, will it make you more unhappy if you tell me all about it? I want to understand."

So then, sitting cuddled up close to her Mother, Bobbie heard "all about it." She heard how those men, who had asked to see Father on that remembered last night when the Engine was being mended, had come to arrest him, charging him with selling State secrets to the Russians—with being, in fact, a spy and a traitor. She heard about the trial, and about the evidence—letters, found in Father's desk at the office, letters that convinced the jury that Father was guilty.

"Oh, how could they look at him and believe it!" cried Bobbie; "and how could ANY one do such a thing!"

"SOMEONE did it," said Mother, "and all the evidence was against Father. Those letters—"

"Yes. How did the letters get into his desk?"

"Someone put them there. And the person who put them there was the person who was really guilty."

"HE must be feeling pretty awful all this time," said Bobbie, thoughtfully.

"I don't believe he had any feelings," Mother said hotly; "he couldn't have done a thing like that if he had."

"Perhaps he just shoved the letters into the desk to hide them when he thought he was going to be found out. Why don't you tell the lawyers, or someone, that it must have been that person? There wasn't anyone that would have hurt Father on purpose, was there?"

"I don't know—I don't know. The man under him who got Daddy's place when he—when the awful thing happened—he was always jealous of your Father because Daddy was so clever and everyone thought such a lot of him. And Daddy never quite trusted that man."

"Couldn't we explain all that to someone?"

"Nobody will listen," said Mother, very bitterly, "nobody at all. Do you suppose I've not tried everything? No, my dearest, there's nothing to be done. All we can do, you and I and Daddy, is to be brave, and patient, and—" she spoke very softly—"to pray, Bobbie, dear."

"Mother, you've got very thin," said Bobbie, abruptly.

"A little, perhaps."

"And oh," said Bobbie, "I do think you're the bravest person in the world as well as the nicest!"

"We won't talk of all this any more, will we, dear?" said Mother; "we must bear it and be brave. And, darling, try not to think of it. Try to be cheerful, and to amuse yourself and the others. It's much easier for me if you can be a little bit happy and enjoy things. Wash your poor little round face, and let's go out into the garden for a bit."

The other two were very gentle and kind to Bobbie. And they did not ask her what was the matter. This was Peter's idea, and he had drilled Phyllis, who would have asked a hundred questions if she had been left to herself.

A week later Bobbie managed to get away alone. And once more she wrote a letter. And once more it was to the old gentleman.

> "My dear Friend," she said, "you see what is in this paper. It is not true. Father never did it. Mother says someone put the papers in Father's desk, and she says the man under him that got Father's place afterwards was jealous of Father, and Father suspected him a long time. But nobody listens to a word she says, but you are so good and clever, and you found out about the Russian gentleman's wife directly. Can't you find out who did the treason because he wasn't Father upon my honour; he is an Englishman and uncapable to do such things, and then they would let Father out of prison. It is dreadful, and Mother is getting so thin. She told us once to pray for all prisoners and captives. I see now. Oh, do help me—there is only just Mother and me know, and we can't do anything. Peter and Phil don't know. I'll pray for you twice every day as long as I live if you'll only try—just try to find out. Think if it was YOUR Daddy, what you would feel. Oh, do, do, DO help me. With love
>
> "I remain Your affectionately little friend
> "Roberta.
>
> P.S. Mother would send her kind regards if she knew I am writing— but it is no use telling her I am, in case you can't do anything. But I know you will. Bobbie with best love."

She cut the account of her Father's trial out of the newspaper with Mother's big cutting-out scissors, and put it in the envelope with her letter.

Then she took it down to the station, going out the back way and round by the road, so that the others should not see her and offer to come with her, and she gave the letter to the Station Master to give to the old gentleman next morning.

"Where HAVE you been?" shouted Peter, from the top of the yard wall where he and Phyllis were.

"To the station, of course," said Bobbie; "give us a hand, Pete."

She set her foot on the lock of the yard door. Peter reached down a hand.

"What on earth?" she asked as she reached the wall-top—for Phyllis and Peter were very muddy. A lump of wet clay lay between them on the wall, they had each a slip of slate in a very dirty hand, and behind Peter, out of the reach of accidents, were several strange rounded objects rather like very fat sausages, hollow, but closed up at one end.

"It's nests," said Peter, "swallows' nests. We're going to dry them in the oven and hang them up with string under the eaves of the coach-house."

"Yes," said Phyllis; "and then we're going to save up all the wool and hair we can get, and in the spring we'll line them, and then how pleased the swallows will be!"

"I've often thought people don't do nearly enough for dumb animals," said Peter with an air of virtue. "I do think people might have thought of making nests for poor little swallows before this."

"Oh," said Bobbie, vaguely, "if everybody thought of everything, there'd be nothing left for anybody else to think about."

"Look at the nests—aren't they pretty?" said Phyllis, reaching across Peter to grasp a nest.

"Look out, Phil, you goat," said her brother. But it was too late; her strong little fingers had crushed the nest.

"There now," said Peter.

"Never mind," said Bobbie.

"It IS one of my own," said Phyllis, "so you needn't jaw, Peter. Yes, we've put our initial names on the ones we've done, so that the swallows will know who they've got to be so grateful to and fond of."

"Swallows can't read, silly," said Peter.

"Silly yourself," retorted Phyllis; "how do you know?"

"Who thought of making the nests, anyhow?" shouted Peter.

"I did," screamed Phyllis.

"Nya," rejoined Peter, "you only thought of making hay ones and sticking them in the ivy for the sparrows, and they'd have been sopping LONG before egg-laying time. It was me said clay and swallows."

"I don't care what you said."

"Look," said Bobbie, "I've made the nest all right again. Give me the bit of stick to mark your initial name on it. But how can you? Your letter and Peter's are the same. P. for Peter, P. for Phyllis."

"I put F. for Phyllis," said the child of that name. "That's how it sounds. The swallows wouldn't spell Phyllis with a P., I'm certain- sure."

"They can't spell at all," Peter was still insisting.

"Then why do you see them always on Christmas cards and valentines with letters round their necks? How would they know where to go if they couldn't read?"

"That's only in pictures. You never saw one really with letters round its neck."

"Well, I have a pigeon, then; at least Daddy told me they did. Only it was under their wings and not round their necks, but it comes to the same thing, and—"

"I say," interrupted Bobbie, "there's to be a paperchase to-morrow."

"Who?" Peter asked.

"Grammar School. Perks thinks the hare will go along by the line at first. We might go along the cutting. You can see a long way from there."

The paperchase was found to be a more amusing subject of conversation than the reading powers of swallows. Bobbie had hoped it might be. And next morning Mother let them take their lunch and go out for the day to see the paperchase.

"If we go to the cutting," said Peter, "we shall see the workmen, even if we miss the paperchase."

Of course it had taken some time to get the line clear from the rocks and earth and trees that had fallen on it when the great landslip happened. That was the occasion, you will remember, when the three children saved the train from being wrecked by waving six little red-flannel-petticoat flags. It is always interesting to watch people working, especially when they work with such interesting things as spades and picks and shovels and planks and barrows, when they have cindery red fires in iron pots with round holes in them, and red lamps hanging near the works at night. Of course the children were never out at night; but once, at dusk, when Peter had got out of his bedroom skylight on to the roof, he had seen the red lamp shining far away at the edge of the cutting. The children had often been down to watch the work, and this day the interest of picks and spades, and barrows being wheeled along planks, completely put the paperchase out of their heads, so that they quite jumped when a voice just behind them panted, "Let me pass, please." It was the hare—a big-boned, loose-limbed boy, with dark hair lying flat on a very damp forehead. The bag of torn paper under his arm was fastened across one shoulder by a strap. The children stood back. The hare ran along the line, and the workmen leaned on their picks to watch him. He ran on steadily and disappeared into the mouth of the tunnel.

"That's against the by-laws," said the foreman.

"Why worry?" said the oldest workman; "live and let live's what I always say. Ain't you never been young yourself, Mr. Bates?"

"I ought to report him," said the foreman.

"Why spoil sport's what I always say."

"Passengers are forbidden to cross the line on any pretence," murmured the foreman, doubtfully.

"He ain't no passenger," said one of the workmen.

"Nor 'e ain't crossed the line, not where we could see 'im do it," said another.

"Nor yet 'e ain't made no pretences," said a third.

"And," said the oldest workman, "'e's outer sight now. What the eye don't see the 'art needn't take no notice of's what I always say."

And now, following the track of the hare by the little white blots of scattered paper, came the hounds. There were thirty of them, and they all came down the steep, ladder-like steps by ones and twos and threes and sixes and sevens. Bobbie and Phyllis and Peter counted them as they passed. The foremost ones hesitated a moment at the foot of the ladder, then their eyes caught the gleam of scattered whiteness along the line and they turned towards the tunnel, and, by ones and twos and threes and sixes and sevens, disappeared in the dark mouth of it. The last one, in a red jersey, seemed to be extinguished by the darkness like a candle that is blown out.

"They don't know what they're in for," said the foreman; "it isn't so easy running in the dark. The tunnel takes two or three turns."

"They'll take a long time to get through, you think?" Peter asked.

"An hour or more, I shouldn't wonder."

"Then let's cut across the top and see them come out at the other end," said Peter; "we shall get there long before they do."

The counsel seemed good, and they went.

They climbed the steep steps from which they had picked the wild cherry blossom for the grave of the little wild rabbit, and reaching the top of the cutting, set their faces towards the hill through which the tunnel was cut. It was stiff work.

"It's like Alps," said Bobbie, breathlessly.

"Or Andes," said Peter.

"It's like Himmy what's its names?" gasped Phyllis. "Mount Everlasting. Do let's stop."

"Stick to it," panted Peter; "you'll get your second wind in a minute."

Phyllis consented to stick to it—and on they went, running when the turf was smooth and the slope easy, climbing over stones, helping themselves up rocks by the branches of trees, creeping through narrow openings between tree trunks and rocks, and so on and on, up and up, till at last they stood on the very top of the hill where they had so often wished to be.

"Halt!" cried Peter, and threw himself flat on the grass. For the very top of the hill was a smooth, turfed table-land, dotted with mossy rocks and little mountain-ash trees.

The girls also threw themselves down flat.

"Plenty of time," Peter panted; "the rest's all down hill."

When they were rested enough to sit up and look round them, Bobbie cried:—

"Oh, look!"

"What at?" said Phyllis.

"The view," said Bobbie.

"I hate views," said Phyllis, "don't you, Peter?"

"Let's get on," said Peter.

"But this isn't like a view they take you to in carriages when you're at the seaside, all sea and sand and bare hills. It's like the 'coloured counties' in one of Mother's poetry books."

"It's not so dusty," said Peter; "look at the Aqueduct straddling slap across the valley like a giant centipede, and then the towns sticking their church spires up out of the trees like pens out of an inkstand. *I* think it's more like

> "There could he see the banners
> Of twelve fair cities shine."

"I love it," said Bobbie; "it's worth the climb."

"The paperchase is worth the climb," said Phyllis, "if we don't lose it. Let's get on. It's all down hill now."

"*I* said that ten minutes ago," said Peter.

"Well, I'VE said it now," said Phyllis; "come on."

"Loads of time," said Peter. And there was. For when they had got down to a level with the top of the tunnel's mouth—they were a couple of hundred yards out of their reckoning and had to creep along the face of the hill—there was no sign of the hare or the hounds.

"They've gone long ago, of course," said Phyllis, as they leaned on the brick parapet above the tunnel.

"I don't think so," said Bobbie, "but even if they had, it's ripping here, and we shall see the trains come out of the tunnel like dragons out of lairs. We've never seen that from the top side before."

"No more we have," said Phyllis, partially appeased.

It was really a most exciting place to be in. The top of the tunnel seemed ever so much farther from the line than they had expected, and it was like being on a bridge, but a bridge overgrown with bushes and creepers and grass and wild-flowers.

"I KNOW the paperchase has gone long ago," said Phyllis every two minutes, and she hardly knew whether she was pleased or disappointed when Peter, leaning over the parapet, suddenly cried:—

"Look out. Here he comes!"

They all leaned over the sun-warmed brick wall in time to see the hare, going very slowly, come out from the shadow of the tunnel.

"There, now," said Peter, "what did I tell you? Now for the hounds!"

Very soon came the hounds—by ones and twos and threes and sixes and sevens—and they also were going slowly and seemed very tired. Two or three who lagged far behind came out long after the others.

"There," said Bobbie, "that's all—now what shall we do?"

"Go along into the tulgy wood over there and have lunch," said Phyllis; "we can see them for miles from up here."

"Not yet," said Peter. "That's not the last. There's the one in the red jersey to come yet. Let's see the last of them come out."

But though they waited and waited and waited, the boy in the red jersey did not appear.

"Oh, let's have lunch," said Phyllis; "I've got a pain in my front with being so hungry. You must have missed seeing the red-jerseyed one when he came out with the others—"

But Bobbie and Peter agreed that he had not come out with the others.

"Let's get down to the tunnel mouth," said Peter; "then perhaps we shall see him coming along from the inside. I expect he felt spun- chuck, and rested in one of the manholes. You stay up here and watch, Bob, and when I signal from below, you come down. We might miss seeing him on the way down, with all these trees."

So the others climbed down and Bobbie waited till they signalled to her from the line below. And then she, too, scrambled down the roundabout slippery path among roots and moss till she stepped out between two dogwood trees and joined the others on the line. And still there was no sign of the hound with the red jersey.

"Oh, do, DO let's have something to eat," wailed Phyllis. "I shall die if you don't, and then you'll be sorry."

"Give her the sandwiches, for goodness' sake, and stop her silly mouth," said Peter, not quite unkindly. "Look here," he added, turning to Bobbie, "perhaps we'd better have one each, too. We may need all our strength. Not more than one, though. There's no time."

"What?" asked Bobbie, her mouth already full, for she was just as hungry as Phyllis.

"Don't you see," replied Peter, impressively, "that red-jerseyed hound has had an accident—that's what it is. Perhaps even as we speak he's lying with his head on the metals, an unresisting prey to any passing express—"

"Oh, don't try to talk like a book," cried Bobbie, bolting what was left of her sandwich; "come on. Phil, keep close behind me, and if a train comes, stand flat against the tunnel wall and hold your petticoats close to you."

"Give me one more sandwich," pleaded Phyllis, "and I will."

"I'm going first," said Peter; "it was my idea," and he went.

Of course you know what going into a tunnel is like? The engine gives a scream and then suddenly the noise of the running, rattling train changes and grows different and much louder. Grown-up people pull up the windows and hold them by the strap. The railway carriage suddenly grows like night—with lamps, of course, unless you are in a slow local train, in which case lamps are not always provided. Then by and by the darkness outside the carriage window is touched by puffs of cloudy whiteness, then you see a blue light on the walls of the tunnel, then the sound of the moving train changes once more, and you are out in the good open air again, and grown-ups let the straps go. The windows, all dim with the yellow breath of the tunnel, rattle down into their places, and you see once more the dip and catch of the telegraph wires beside the line, and the straight-cut hawthorn hedges with the tiny baby trees growing up out of them every thirty yards.

All this, of course, is what a tunnel means when you are in a train. But everything is quite different when you walk into a tunnel on your own feet, and tread on shifting, sliding stones and gravel on a path that curves downwards from the shining metals to the wall. Then you see slimy, oozy trickles of water running down the inside of the tunnel, and you notice that the bricks are not red or brown, as they are at the tunnel's mouth, but dull, sticky, sickly green. Your voice, when you speak, is quite changed from what it was out in the sunshine, and it is a long time before the tunnel is quite dark.

It was not yet quite dark in the tunnel when Phyllis caught at Bobbie's skirt, ripping out half a yard of gathers, but no one noticed this at the time.

"I want to go back," she said, "I don't like it. It'll be pitch dark in a minute. I WON'T go on in the dark. I don't care what you say, I WON'T."

"Don't be a silly cuckoo," said Peter; "I've got a candle end and matches, and—what's that?"

"That" was a low, humming sound on the railway line, a trembling of the wires beside it, a buzzing, humming sound that grew louder and louder as they listened.

"It's a train," said Bobbie.

"Which line?"

"Let me go back," cried Phyllis, struggling to get away from the hand by which Bobbie held her.

"Don't be a coward," said Bobbie; "it's quite safe. Stand back."

"Come on," shouted Peter, who was a few yards ahead. "Quick! Manhole!"

The roar of the advancing train was now louder than the noise you hear when your head is under water in the bath and both taps are running, and you are kicking with your heels against the bath's tin sides. But Peter had shouted for all he was worth, and Bobbie heard him. She dragged Phyllis along to the manhole. Phyllis, of course, stumbled over the wires and grazed both her legs. But they dragged her in, and all three stood in the dark, damp, arched recess while the train roared louder and louder. It seemed as if it would deafen them. And, in the distance, they could see its eyes of fire growing bigger and brighter every instant.

"It IS a dragon—I always knew it was—it takes its own shape in here, in the dark," shouted Phyllis. But nobody heard her. You see the train was shouting, too, and its voice was bigger than hers.

And now, with a rush and a roar and a rattle and a long dazzling flash of lighted carriage windows, a smell of smoke, and blast of hot air, the train hurtled by, clanging and jangling and echoing in the vaulted roof of the tunnel. Phyllis and Bobbie clung to each other. Even Peter caught hold of Bobbie's arm, "in case she should be frightened," as he explained afterwards.

And now, slowly and gradually, the tail-lights grew smaller and smaller, and so did the noise, till with one last WHIZ the train got itself out of the tunnel, and silence settled again on its damp walls and dripping roof.

"OH!" said the children, all together in a whisper.

Peter was lighting the candle end with a hand that trembled.

"Come on," he said; but he had to clear his throat before he could speak in his natural voice.

"Oh," said Phyllis, "if the red-jerseyed one was in the way of the train!"

"We've got to go and see," said Peter.

"Couldn't we go and send someone from the station?" said Phyllis.

"Would you rather wait here for us?" asked Bobbie, severely, and of course that settled the question.

So the three went on into the deeper darkness of the tunnel. Peter led, holding his candle end high to light the way. The grease ran down his fingers, and some of it right up his sleeve. He found a long streak from wrist to elbow when he went to bed that night.

It was not more than a hundred and fifty yards from the spot where they had stood while the train went by that Peter stood still, shouted "Hullo," and then went on much quicker than before. When the others caught him up, he stopped. And he stopped within a yard of what they had come into the tunnel to look for. Phyllis saw a gleam of red, and shut her eyes tight. There, by the curved, pebbly down line, was the red-jerseyed hound. His back was against the wall, his arms hung limply by his sides, and his eyes were shut.

"Was the red, blood? Is he all killed?" asked Phyllis, screwing her eyelids more tightly together.

"Killed? Nonsense!" said Peter. "There's nothing red about him except his jersey. He's only fainted. What on earth are we to do?"

"Can we move him?" asked Bobbie.

"I don't know; he's a big chap."

"Suppose we bathe his forehead with water. No, I know we haven't any, but milk's just as wet. There's a whole bottle."

"Yes," said Peter, "and they rub people's hands, I believe."

"They burn feathers, I know," said Phyllis.

"What's the good of saying that when we haven't any feathers?"

"As it happens," said Phyllis, in a tone of exasperated triumph, "I've got a shuttlecock in my pocket. So there!"

And now Peter rubbed the hands of the red-jerseyed one. Bobbie burned the feathers of the shuttlecock one by one under his nose, Phyllis splashed warmish milk on his forehead, and all three kept on saying as fast and as earnestly as they could:—

"Oh, look up, speak to me! For my sake, speak!"

Chapter 12. What Bobbie Brought Home.

"Oh, look up! Speak to me! For MY sake, speak!" The children said the words over and over again to the unconscious hound in a red jersey, who sat with closed eyes and pale face against the side of the tunnel.

"Wet his ears with milk," said Bobbie. "I know they do it to people that faint—with eau-de-Cologne. But I expect milk's just as good."

So they wetted his ears, and some of the milk ran down his neck under the red jersey. It was very dark in the tunnel. The candle end Peter had carried, and which now burned on a flat stone, gave hardly any light at all.

"Oh, DO look up," said Phyllis. "For MY sake! I believe he's dead."

"For MY sake," repeated Bobbie. "No, he isn't."

"For ANY sake," said Peter; "come out of it." And he shook the sufferer by the arm.

And then the boy in the red jersey sighed, and opened his eyes, and shut them again and said in a very small voice, "Chuck it."

"Oh, he's NOT dead," said Phyllis. "I KNEW he wasn't," and she began to cry.

"What's up? I'm all right," said the boy.

"Drink this," said Peter, firmly, thrusting the nose of the milk bottle into the boy's mouth. The boy struggled, and some of the milk was upset before he could get his mouth free to say:—

"What is it?"

"It's milk," said Peter. "Fear not, you are in the hands of friends. Phil, you stop bleating this minute."

"Do drink it," said Bobbie, gently; "it'll do you good."

So he drank. And the three stood by without speaking to him.

"Let him be a minute," Peter whispered; "he'll be all right as soon as the milk begins to run like fire through his veins."

He was.

"I'm better now," he announced. "I remember all about it." He tried to move, but the movement ended in a groan. "Bother! I believe I've broken my leg," he said.

"Did you tumble down?" asked Phyllis, sniffing.

"Of course not—I'm not a kiddie," said the boy, indignantly; "it was one of those beastly wires tripped me up, and when I tried to get up again I couldn't stand, so I sat down. Gee whillikins! it does hurt, though. How did YOU get here?"

"We saw you all go into the tunnel and then we went across the hill to see you all come out. And the others did—all but you, and you didn't. So we are a rescue party," said Peter, with pride.

"You've got some pluck, I will say," remarked the boy.

"Oh, that's nothing," said Peter, with modesty. "Do you think you could walk if we helped you?"

"I could try," said the boy.

He did try. But he could only stand on one foot; the other dragged in a very nasty way.

"Here, let me sit down. I feel like dying," said the boy. "Let go of me—let go, quick—" He lay down and closed his eyes. The others looked at each other by the dim light of the little candle.

"What on earth!" said Peter.

"Look here," said Bobbie, quickly, "you must go and get help. Go to the nearest house."

"Yes, that's the only thing," said Peter. "Come on."

"If you take his feet and Phil and I take his head, we could carry him to the manhole."

They did it. It was perhaps as well for the sufferer that he had fainted again.

"Now," said Bobbie, "I'll stay with him. You take the longest bit of candle, and, oh—be quick, for this bit won't burn long."

"I don't think Mother would like me leaving you," said Peter, doubtfully. "Let me stay, and you and Phil go."

"No, no," said Bobbie, "you and Phil go—and lend me your knife. I'll try to get his boot off before he wakes up again."

"I hope it's all right what we're doing," said Peter.

"Of course it's right," said Bobbie, impatiently. "What else WOULD you do? Leave him here all alone because it's dark? Nonsense. Hurry up, that's all."

So they hurried up.

Bobbie watched their dark figures and the little light of the little candle with an odd feeling of having come to the end of everything. She knew now, she thought, what nuns who were bricked up alive in convent walls felt like. Suddenly she gave herself a little shake.

"Don't be a silly little girl," she said. She was always very angry when anyone else called her a little girl, even if the adjective that went first was not "silly" but "nice" or "good" or "clever." And it was only when she was very angry with herself that she allowed Roberta to use that expression to Bobbie.

She fixed the little candle end on a broken brick near the red-jerseyed boy's feet. Then she opened Peter's knife. It was always hard to manage—a halfpenny was generally needed to get it open at all. This time Bobbie somehow got it open with her thumbnail. She broke the nail, and it hurt horribly. Then she cut the boy's bootlace, and got the boot off. She tried to pull off his stocking, but his leg was dreadfully swollen, and it did not seem to be the proper shape. So she cut the stocking down, very slowly and carefully. It was a brown, knitted stocking, and she wondered who had knitted it, and whether it was the boy's mother, and whether she was feeling anxious about him, and how she would feel when he was brought home with his leg broken. When Bobbie had got the stocking off and saw the poor leg, she felt as though the tunnel was growing darker, and the ground felt unsteady, and nothing seemed quite real.

"SILLY little girl!" said Roberta to Bobbie, and felt better.

"The poor leg," she told herself; "it ought to have a cushion—ah!"

She remembered the day when she and Phyllis had torn up their red flannel petticoats to make danger signals to stop the train and prevent an accident. Her flannel petticoat to-day was white, but it would be quite as soft as a red one. She took it off.

"Oh, what useful things flannel petticoats are!" she said; "the man who invented them ought to have a statue directed to him." And she said it aloud, because it seemed that any voice, even her own, would be a comfort in that darkness.

"WHAT ought to be directed? Who to?" asked the boy, suddenly and very feebly.

"Oh," said Bobbie, "now you're better! Hold your teeth and don't let it hurt too much. Now!"

She had folded the petticoat, and lifting his leg laid it on the cushion of folded flannel.

"Don't faint again, PLEASE don't," said Bobbie, as he groaned. She hastily wetted her handkerchief with milk and spread it over the poor leg.

"Oh, that hurts," cried the boy, shrinking. "Oh—no, it doesn't—it's nice, really."

"What's your name?" said Bobbie.

"Jim."

"Mine's Bobbie."

"But you're a girl, aren't you?"

"Yes, my long name's Roberta."

"I say—Bobbie."

"Yes?"

"Wasn't there some more of you just now?"

"Yes, Peter and Phil—that's my brother and sister. They've gone to get someone to carry you out."

"What rum names. All boys'."

"Yes—I wish I was a boy, don't you?"

"I think you're all right as you are."

"I didn't mean that—I meant don't you wish YOU were a boy, but of course you are without wishing."

"You're just as brave as a boy. Why didn't you go with the others?"

"Somebody had to stay with you," said Bobbie.

"Tell you what, Bobbie," said Jim, "you're a brick. Shake." He reached out a red-jerseyed arm and Bobbie squeezed his hand.

"I won't shake it," she explained, "because it would shake YOU, and that would shake your poor leg, and that would hurt. Have you got a hanky?"

"I don't expect I have." He felt in his pocket. "Yes, I have. What for?"

She took it and wetted it with milk and put it on his forehead.

"That's jolly," he said; "what is it?"

"Milk," said Bobbie. "We haven't any water—"

"You're a jolly good little nurse," said Jim.

"I do it for Mother sometimes," said Bobbie—"not milk, of course, but scent, or vinegar and water. I say, I must put the candle out now, because there mayn't be enough of the other one to get you out by."

"By George," said he, "you think of everything."

Bobbie blew. Out went the candle. You have no idea how black- velvety the darkness was.

"I say, Bobbie," said a voice through the blackness, "aren't you afraid of the dark?"

"Not—not very, that is—"

"Let's hold hands," said the boy, and it was really rather good of him, because he was like most boys of his age and hated all material tokens of affection, such as kissing and holding of hands. He called all such things "pawings," and detested them.

The darkness was more bearable to Bobbie now that her hand was held in the large rough hand of the red-jerseyed sufferer; and he, holding her little smooth hot paw, was surprised to find that he did not mind it so much as he expected. She tried to talk, to amuse him, and "take his mind off" his sufferings, but it is very difficult to go on talking in the dark, and presently they found themselves in a silence, only broken now and then by a—

"You all right, Bobbie?"

or an—

"I'm afraid it's hurting you most awfully, Jim. I AM so sorry."

And it was very cold.

* * * * * *

Peter and Phyllis tramped down the long way of the tunnel towards daylight, the candle-grease dripping over Peter's fingers. There were no accidents unless you count Phyllis's catching her frock on a wire, and tearing a long, jagged slit in it, and tripping over her bootlace when it came undone, or going down on her hands and knees, all four of which were grazed.

"There's no end to this tunnel," said Phyllis—and indeed it did seem very very long.

"Stick to it," said Peter; "everything has an end, and you get to it if you only keep all on."

Which is quite true, if you come to think of it, and a useful thing to remember in seasons of trouble—such as measles, arithmetic, impositions, and those times when you are in disgrace, and feel as though no one would ever love you again, and you could never—never again—love anybody.

"Hurray," said Peter, suddenly, "there's the end of the tunnel—looks just like a pin-hole in a bit of black paper, doesn't it?"

The pin-hole got larger—blue lights lay along the sides of the tunnel. The children could see the gravel way that lay in front of them; the air grew warmer and sweeter. Another twenty steps and they were out in the good glad sunshine with the green trees on both sides.

Phyllis drew a long breath.

"I'll never go into a tunnel again as long as ever I live," said she, "not if there are twenty hundred thousand millions hounds inside with red jerseys and their legs broken."

"Don't be a silly cuckoo," said Peter, as usual. "You'd HAVE to."

"I think it was very brave and good of me," said Phyllis.

"Not it," said Peter; "you didn't go because you were brave, but because Bobbie and I aren't skunks. Now where's the nearest house, I wonder? You can't see anything here for the trees."

"There's a roof over there," said Phyllis, pointing down the line.

"That's the signal-box," said Peter, "and you know you're not allowed to speak to signalmen on duty. It's wrong."

"I'm not near so afraid of doing wrong as I was of going into that tunnel," said Phyllis. "Come on," and she started to run along the line. So Peter ran, too.

It was very hot in the sunshine, and both children were hot and breathless by the time they stopped, and bending their heads back to look up at the open windows of the signal-box, shouted "Hi!" as loud as their breathless state allowed. But no one answered. The signal-box stood quiet as an empty nursery, and the handrail of its steps was hot to the hands of the children as they climbed softly up. They peeped in at the open door. The signalman was sitting on a chair tilted back against the wall. His head leaned sideways, and his mouth was open. He was fast asleep.

"My hat!" cried Peter; "wake up!" And he cried it in a terrible voice, for he knew that if a signalman sleeps on duty, he risks losing his situation, let alone all the other dreadful risks to trains which expect him to tell them when it is safe for them to go their ways.

The signalman never moved. Then Peter sprang to him and shook him. And slowly, yawning and stretching, the man awoke. But the moment he WAS awake he leapt to his feet, put his hands to his head "like a mad maniac," as Phyllis said afterwards, and shouted:—

"Oh, my heavens—what's o'clock?"

"Twelve thirteen," said Peter, and indeed it was by the white-faced, round-faced clock on the wall of the signal-box.

The man looked at the clock, sprang to the levers, and wrenched them this way and that. An electric bell tingled—the wires and cranks creaked, and the man threw himself into a chair. He was very pale, and the sweat stood on his forehead "like large dewdrops on a white cabbage," as Phyllis remarked later. He was trembling, too; the children could see his big hairy hands shake from side to side, "with quite extra-sized trembles," to use the subsequent words of Peter. He drew long breaths. Then suddenly he cried, "Thank God, thank God you come in when you did—oh, thank God!" and his shoulders began to heave and his face grew red again, and he hid it in those large hairy hands of his.

"Oh, don't cry—don't," said Phyllis, "it's all right now," and she patted him on one big, broad shoulder, while Peter conscientiously thumped the other.

But the signalman seemed quite broken down, and the children had to pat him and thump him for quite a long time before he found his handkerchief—a red one with mauve and white horseshoes on it—and mopped his face and spoke. During this patting and thumping interval a train thundered by.

"I'm downright shamed, that I am," were the words of the big signalman when he had stopped crying; "snivelling like a kid." Then suddenly he seemed to get cross. "And what was you doing up here, anyway?" he said; "you know it ain't allowed."

"Yes," said Phyllis, "we knew it was wrong—but I wasn't afraid of doing wrong, and so it turned out right. You aren't sorry we came."

"Lor' love you—if you hadn't 'a' come—" he stopped and then went on. "It's a disgrace, so it is, sleeping on duty. If it was to come to be known—even as it is, when no harm's come of it."

"It won't come to be known," said Peter; "we aren't sneaks. All the same, you oughtn't to sleep on duty—it's dangerous."

"Tell me something I don't know," said the man, "but I can't help it. I know'd well enough just how it 'ud be. But I couldn't get off. They couldn't get no one to take on my duty. I tell you I ain't had ten minutes' sleep this last five days. My little chap's ill—pewmonia, the Doctor says—and there's no one but me and 'is little sister to do for him. That's where it is. The gell must 'ave her sleep. Dangerous? Yes, I believe you. Now go and split on me if you like."

"Of course we won't," said Peter, indignantly, but Phyllis ignored the whole of the signalman's speech, except the first six words.

"You asked us," she said, "to tell you something you don't know. Well, I will. There's a boy in the tunnel over there with a red jersey and his leg broken."

"What did he want to go into the blooming tunnel for, then?" said the man.

"Don't you be so cross," said Phyllis, kindly. "WE haven't done anything wrong except coming and waking you up, and that was right, as it happens."

Then Peter told how the boy came to be in the tunnel.

"Well," said the man, "I don't see as I can do anything. I can't leave the box."

"You might tell us where to go after someone who isn't in a box, though," said Phyllis.

"There's Brigden's farm over yonder—where you see the smoke a- coming up through the trees," said the man, more and more grumpy, as Phyllis noticed.

"Well, good-bye, then," said Peter.

But the man said, "Wait a minute." He put his hand in his pocket and brought out some money—a lot of pennies and one or two shillings and sixpences and half-a-crown. He picked out two shillings and held them out.

"Here," he said. "I'll give you this to hold your tongues about what's taken place to-day."

There was a short, unpleasant pause. Then:—

"You ARE a nasty man, though, aren't you?" said Phyllis.

Peter took a step forward and knocked the man's hand up, so that the shillings leapt out of it and rolled on the floor.

"If anything COULD make me sneak, THAT would!" he said. "Come, Phil," and marched out of the signal-box with flaming cheeks.

Phyllis hesitated. Then she took the hand, still held out stupidly, that the shillings had been in.

"I forgive you," she said, "even if Peter doesn't. You're not in your proper senses, or you'd never have done that. I know want of sleep sends people mad. Mother told me. I hope your little boy will soon be better, and—"

"Come on, Phil," cried Peter, eagerly.

"I give you my sacred honour-word we'll never tell anyone. Kiss and be friends," said Phyllis, feeling how noble it was of her to try to make up a quarrel in which she was not to blame.

The signalman stooped and kissed her.

"I do believe I'm a bit off my head, Sissy," he said. "Now run along home to Mother. I didn't mean to put you about—there."

So Phil left the hot signal-box and followed Peter across the fields to the farm.

When the farm men, led by Peter and Phyllis and carrying a hurdle covered with horse-cloths, reached the manhole in the tunnel, Bobbie was fast asleep and so was Jim. Worn out with the pain, the Doctor said afterwards.

"Where does he live?" the bailiff from the farm asked, when Jim had been lifted on to the hurdle.

"In Northumberland," answered Bobbie.

"I'm at school at Maidbridge," said Jim. "I suppose I've got to get back there, somehow."

"Seems to me the Doctor ought to have a look in first," said the bailiff.

"Oh, bring him up to our house," said Bobbie. "It's only a little way by the road. I'm sure Mother would say we ought to."

"Will your Ma like you bringing home strangers with broken legs?"

"She took the poor Russian home herself," said Bobbie. "I know she'd say we ought."

"All right," said the bailiff, "you ought to know what your Ma 'ud like. I wouldn't take it upon me to fetch him up to our place without I asked the Missus first, and they call me the Master, too."

"Are you sure your Mother won't mind?" whispered Jim.

"Certain," said Bobbie.

"Then we're to take him up to Three Chimneys?" said the bailiff.

"Of course," said Peter.

"Then my lad shall nip up to Doctor's on his bike, and tell him to come down there. Now, lads, lift him quiet and steady. One, two, three!"

* * * * * *

Thus it happened that Mother, writing away for dear life at a story about a Duchess, a designing villain, a secret passage, and a missing will, dropped her pen as her work-room door burst open, and turned to see Bobbie hatless and red with running.

"Oh, Mother," she cried, "do come down. We found a hound in a red jersey in the tunnel, and he's broken his leg and they're bringing him home."

"They ought to take him to the vet," said Mother, with a worried frown; "I really CAN'T have a lame dog here."

"He's not a dog, really—he's a boy," said Bobbie, between laughing and choking.

"Then he ought to be taken home to his mother."

"His mother's dead," said Bobbie, "and his father's in Northumberland. Oh, Mother, you will be nice to him? I told him I was sure you'd want us to bring him home. You always want to help everybody."

Mother smiled, but she sighed, too. It is nice that your children should believe you willing to open house and heart to any and every one who needs help. But it is rather embarrassing sometimes, too, when they act on their belief.

"Oh, well," said Mother, "we must make the best of it."

When Jim was carried in, dreadfully white and with set lips whose red had faded to a horrid bluey violet colour, Mother said:—

"I am glad you brought him here. Now, Jim, let's get you comfortable in bed before the Doctor comes!"

And Jim, looking at her kind eyes, felt a little, warm, comforting flush of new courage.

"It'll hurt rather, won't it?" he said. "I don't mean to be a coward. You won't think I'm a coward if I faint again, will you? I really and truly don't do it on purpose. And I do hate to give you all this trouble."

"Don't you worry," said Mother; "it's you that have the trouble, you poor dear—not us."

And she kissed him just as if he had been Peter. "We love to have you here—don't we, Bobbie?"

"Yes," said Bobbie—and she saw by her Mother's face how right she had been to bring home the wounded hound in the red jersey.

Chapter 13. The Hound's Grandfather.

Mother did not get back to her writing all that day, for the red-jerseyed hound whom the children had brought to Three Chimneys had to be put to bed. And then the Doctor came, and hurt him most horribly. Mother was with him all through it, and that made it a little better than it would have been, but "bad was the best," as Mrs. Viney said.

The children sat in the parlour downstairs and heard the sound of the Doctor's boots going backwards and forwards over the bedroom floor. And once or twice there was a groan.

"It's horrible," said Bobbie. "Oh, I wish Dr. Forrest would make haste. Oh, poor Jim!"

"It IS horrible," said Peter, "but it's very exciting. I wish Doctors weren't so stuck-up about who they'll have in the room when they're doing things. I should most awfully like to see a leg set. I believe the bones crunch like anything."

"Don't!" said the two girls at once.

"Rubbish!" said Peter. "How are you going to be Red Cross Nurses, like you were talking of coming home, if you can't even stand hearing me say about bones crunching? You'd have to HEAR them crunch on the field of battle—and be steeped in gore up to the elbows as likely as not, and—"

"Stop it!" cried Bobbie, with a white face; "you don't know how funny you're making me feel."

"Me, too," said Phyllis, whose face was pink.

"Cowards!" said Peter.

"I'm not," said Bobbie. "I helped Mother with your rake-wounded foot, and so did Phil—you know we did."

"Well, then!" said Peter. "Now look here. It would be a jolly good thing for you if I were to talk to you every day for half an hour about broken bones and people's insides, so as to get you used to it."

A chair was moved above.

"Listen," said Peter, "that's the bone crunching."

"I do wish you wouldn't," said Phyllis. "Bobbie doesn't like it."

"I'll tell you what they do," said Peter. I can't think what made him so horrid. Perhaps it was because he had been so very nice and kind all the earlier part of the day, and now he had to have a change. This is called reaction. One notices it now and then in oneself. Sometimes when one has been extra good for a longer time than usual, one is suddenly attacked by a violent fit of not being good at all. "I'll tell you what they do," said Peter; "they strap the broken man down so that he can't resist or interfere with their doctorish designs, and then someone holds his head, and someone holds his leg—the broken one, and pulls it till the bones fit in— with a crunch, mind you! Then they strap it up and—let's play at bone-setting!"

"Oh, no!" said Phyllis.

But Bobbie said suddenly: "All right—LET'S! I'll be the doctor, and Phil can be the nurse. You can be the broken boner; we can get at your legs more easily, because you don't wear petticoats."

"I'll get the splints and bandages," said Peter; "you get the couch of suffering ready."

The ropes that had tied up the boxes that had come from home were all in a wooden packing-case in the cellar. When Peter brought in a trailing tangle of them, and two boards for splints, Phyllis was excitedly giggling.

"Now, then," he said, and lay down on the settle, groaning most grievously.

"Not so loud!" said Bobbie, beginning to wind the rope round him and the settle. "You pull, Phil."

"Not so tight," moaned Peter. "You'll break my other leg."

Bobbie worked on in silence, winding more and more rope round him.

"That's enough," said Peter. "I can't move at all. Oh, my poor leg!" He groaned again.

"SURE you can't move?" asked Bobbie, in a rather strange tone.

"Quite sure," replied Peter. "Shall we play it's bleeding freely or not?" he asked cheerfully.

"YOU can play what you like," said Bobbie, sternly, folding her arms and looking down at him where he lay all wound round and round with cord. "Phil and I are going away. And we shan't untie you till you promise never, never to talk to us about blood and wounds unless we say you may. Come, Phil!"

"You beast!" said Peter, writhing. "I'll never promise, never. I'll yell, and Mother will come."

"Do," said Bobbie, "and tell her why we tied you up! Come on, Phil. No, I'm not a beast, Peter. But you wouldn't stop when we asked you and—"

"Yah," said Peter, "it wasn't even your own idea. You got it out of Stalky!"

Bobbie and Phil, retiring in silent dignity, were met at the door by the Doctor. He came in rubbing his hands and looking pleased with himself.

"Well," he said, "THAT job's done. It's a nice clean fracture, and it'll go on all right, I've no doubt. Plucky young chap, too—hullo! what's all this?"

His eye had fallen on Peter who lay mousy-still in his bonds on the settle.

"Playing at prisoners, eh?" he said; but his eyebrows had gone up a little. Somehow he had not thought that Bobbie would be playing while in the room above someone was having a broken bone set.

"Oh, no!" said Bobbie, "not at PRISONERS. We were playing at setting bones. Peter's the broken boner, and I was the doctor."

The Doctor frowned.

"Then I must say," he said, and he said it rather sternly, "that's it's a very heartless game. Haven't you enough imagination even to faintly picture what's been going on upstairs? That poor chap, with the drops of sweat on his forehead, and biting his lips so as not to cry out, and every touch on his leg agony and—"

"YOU ought to be tied up," said Phyllis; "you're as bad as—"

"Hush," said Bobbie; "I'm sorry, but we weren't heartless, really."

"I was, I suppose," said Peter, crossly. "All right, Bobbie, don't you go on being noble and screening me, because I jolly well won't have it. It was only that I kept on talking about blood and wounds. I wanted to train them for Red Cross Nurses. And I wouldn't stop when they asked me."

"Well?" said Dr. Forrest, sitting down.

"Well—then I said, 'Let's play at setting bones.' It was all rot. I knew Bobbie wouldn't. I only said it to tease her. And then when she said 'yes,' of course I had to go through with it. And they tied me up. They got it out of Stalky. And I think it's a beastly shame."

He managed to writhe over and hide his face against the wooden back of the settle.

"I didn't think that anyone would know but us," said Bobbie, indignantly answering Peter's unspoken reproach. "I never thought of your coming in. And hearing about blood and wounds does really make me feel most awfully funny. It was only a joke our tying him up. Let me untie you, Pete."

"I don't care if you never untie me," said Peter; "and if that's your idea of a joke—"

"If I were you," said the Doctor, though really he did not quite know what to say, "I should be untied before your Mother comes down. You don't want to worry her just now, do you?"

"I don't promise anything about not saying about wounds, mind," said Peter, in very surly tones, as Bobbie and Phyllis began to untie the knots.

"I'm very sorry, Pete," Bobbie whispered, leaning close to him as she fumbled with the big knot under the settle; "but if you only knew how sick you made me feel."

"You've made ME feel pretty sick, I can tell you," Peter rejoined. Then he shook off the loose cords, and stood up.

"I looked in," said Dr. Forrest, "to see if one of you would come along to the surgery. There are some things that your Mother will want at once, and I've given my man a day off to go and see the circus; will you come, Peter?"

Peter went without a word or a look to his sisters.

The two walked in silence up to the gate that led from the Three Chimneys field to the road. Then Peter said:—

"Let me carry your bag. I say, it is heavy—what's in it?"

"Oh, knives and lancets and different instruments for hurting people. And the ether bottle. I had to give him ether, you know— the agony was so intense."

Peter was silent.

"Tell me all about how you found that chap," said Dr. Forrest.

Peter told. And then Dr. Forrest told him stories of brave rescues; he was a most interesting man to talk to, as Peter had often remarked.

Then in the surgery Peter had a better chance than he had ever had of examining the Doctor's balance, and his microscope, and his scales and measuring glasses. When all the things were ready that Peter was to take back, the Doctor said suddenly:—

"You'll excuse my shoving my oar in, won't you? But I should like to say something to you."

"Now for a rowing," thought Peter, who had been wondering how it was that he had escaped one.

"Something scientific," added the Doctor.

"Yes," said Peter, fiddling with the fossil ammonite that the Doctor used for a paper-weight.

"Well then, you see. Boys and girls are only little men and women. And WE are much harder and hardier than they are—" (Peter liked the "we." Perhaps the Doctor had known he would.) — "and much stronger, and things that hurt THEM don't hurt US. You know you mustn't hit a girl—"

"I should think not, indeed," muttered Peter, indignantly.

"Not even if she's your own sister. That's because girls are so much softer and weaker than we are; they have to be, you know," he added, "because if they weren't, it wouldn't be nice for the babies. And that's why all the animals are so good to the mother animals. They never fight them, you know."

"I know," said Peter, interested; "two buck rabbits will fight all day if you let them, but they won't hurt a doe."

"No; and quite wild beasts—lions and elephants—they're immensely gentle with the female beasts. And we've got to be, too."

"I see," said Peter.

"And their hearts are soft, too," the Doctor went on, "and things that we shouldn't think anything of hurt them dreadfully. So that a man has to be very careful, not only of his fists, but of his words. They're awfully brave, you know," he went on. "Think of Bobbie waiting alone in the tunnel with that poor chap. It's an odd thing — the softer and more easily hurt a woman is the better she can screw herself up to do what HAS to be done. I've seen some brave women— your Mother's one," he ended abruptly.

"Yes," said Peter.

"Well, that's all. Excuse my mentioning it. But nobody knows everything without being told. And you see what I mean, don't you?"

"Yes," said Peter. "I'm sorry. There!"

"Of course you are! People always are—directly they understand. Everyone ought to be taught these scientific facts. So long!"

They shook hands heartily. When Peter came home, his sisters looked at him doubtfully.

"It's Pax," said Peter, dumping down the basket on the table. "Dr. Forrest has been talking scientific to me. No, it's no use my telling you what he said; you wouldn't understand. But it all comes to you girls being poor, soft, weak, frightened things like rabbits, so us men have just got to put up with them. He said you were female beasts. Shall I take this up to Mother, or will you?"

"I know what BOYS are," said Phyllis, with flaming cheeks; "they're just the nastiest, rudest—"

"They're very brave," said Bobbie, "sometimes."

"Ah, you mean the chap upstairs? I see. Go ahead, Phil—I shall put up with you whatever you say because you're a poor, weak, frightened, soft—"

"Not if I pull your hair you won't," said Phyllis, springing at him.

"He said 'Pax,'" said Bobbie, pulling her away. "Don't you see," she whispered as Peter picked up the basket and stalked out with it, "he's sorry, really, only he won't say so? Let's say we're sorry."

"It's so goody goody," said Phyllis, doubtfully; "he said we were female beasts, and soft and frightened—"

"Then let's show him we're not frightened of him thinking us goody goody," said Bobbie; "and we're not any more beasts than he is."

And when Peter came back, still with his chin in the air, Bobbie said:—

"We're sorry we tied you up, Pete."

"I thought you would be," said Peter, very stiff and superior.

This was hard to bear. But—

"Well, so we are," said Bobbie. "Now let honour be satisfied on both sides."

"I did call it Pax," said Peter, in an injured tone.

"Then let it BE Pax," said Bobbie. "Come on, Phil, let's get the tea. Pete, you might lay the cloth."

"I say," said Phyllis, when peace was really restored, which was not till they were washing up the cups after tea, "Dr. Forrest didn't REALLY say we were female beasts, did he?"

"Yes," said Peter, firmly, "but I think he meant we men were wild beasts, too."

"How funny of him!" said Phyllis, breaking a cup.

* * * * * *

"May I come in, Mother?" Peter was at the door of Mother's writing room, where Mother sat at her table with two candles in front of her. Their flames looked orange and violet against the clear grey blue of the sky where already a few stars were twinkling.

"Yes, dear," said Mother, absently, "anything wrong?" She wrote a few more words and then laid down her pen and began to fold up what she had written. "I was just writing to Jim's grandfather. He lives near here, you know."

"Yes, you said so at tea. That's what I want to say. Must you write to him, Mother? Couldn't we keep Jim, and not say anything to his people till he's well? It would be such a surprise for them."

"Well, yes," said Mother, laughing, "I think it would."

"You see," Peter went on, "of course the girls are all right and all that—I'm not saying anything against THEM. But I should like it if I had another chap to talk to sometimes."

"Yes," said Mother, "I know it's dull for you, dear. But I can't help it. Next year perhaps I can send you to school—you'd like that, wouldn't you?"

"I do miss the other chaps, rather," Peter confessed; "but if Jim could stay after his leg was well, we could have awful larks."

"I've no doubt of it," said Mother. "Well—perhaps he could, but you know, dear, we're not rich. I can't afford to get him everything he'll want. And he must have a nurse."

"Can't you nurse him, Mother? You do nurse people so beautifully."

"That's a pretty compliment, Pete—but I can't do nursing and my writing as well. That's the worst of it."

"Then you MUST send the letter to his grandfather?"

"Of course—and to his schoolmaster, too. We telegraphed to them both, but I must write as well. They'll be most dreadfully anxious."

"I say, Mother, why can't his grandfather pay for a nurse?" Peter suggested. "That would be ripping. I expect the old boy's rolling in money. Grandfathers in books always are."

"Well, this one isn't in a book," said Mother, "so we mustn't expect him to roll much."

"I say," said Peter, musingly, "wouldn't it be jolly if we all WERE in a book, and you were writing it? Then you could make all sorts of jolly things happen, and make Jim's legs get well at once and be all right to-morrow, and Father come home soon and—"

"Do you miss your Father very much?" Mother asked, rather coldly, Peter thought.

"Awfully," said Peter, briefly.

Mother was enveloping and addressing the second letter.

"You see," Peter went on slowly, "you see, it's not only him BEING Father, but now he's away there's no other man in the house but me— that's why I want Jim to stay so frightfully much. Wouldn't you like to be writing that book with us all in it, Mother, and make Daddy come home soon?"

Peter's Mother put her arm round him suddenly, and hugged him in silence for a minute. Then she said:—

"Don't you think it's rather nice to think that we're in a book that God's writing? If I were writing the book, I might make mistakes. But God knows how to make the story end just right—in the way that's best for us."

"Do you really believe that, Mother?" Peter asked quietly.

"Yes," she said, "I do believe it—almost always—except when I'm so sad that I can't believe anything. But even when I can't believe it, I know it's true—and I try to believe. You don't know how I try, Peter. Now take the letters to the post, and don't let's be sad any more. Courage, courage! That's the finest of all the virtues! I dare say Jim will be here for two or three weeks yet."

For what was left of the evening Peter was so angelic that Bobbie feared he was going to be ill. She was quite relieved in the morning to find him plaiting Phyllis's hair on to the back of her chair in quite his old manner.

It was soon after breakfast that a knock came at the door. The children were hard at work cleaning the brass candlesticks in honour of Jim's visit.

"That'll be the Doctor," said Mother; "I'll go. Shut the kitchen door—you're not fit to be seen."

But it wasn't the Doctor. They knew that by the voice and by the sound of the boots that went upstairs. They did not recognise the sound of the boots, but everyone was certain that they had heard the voice before.

There was a longish interval. The boots and the voice did not come down again.

"Who can it possibly be?" they kept on asking themselves and each other.

"Perhaps," said Peter at last, "Dr. Forrest has been attacked by highwaymen and left for dead, and this is the man he's telegraphed for to take his place. Mrs. Viney said he had a local tenant to do his work when he went for a holiday, didn't you, Mrs. Viney?"

"I did so, my dear," said Mrs. Viney from the back kitchen.

"He's fallen down in a fit, more likely, said Phyllis, "all human aid despaired of. And this is his man come to break the news to Mother."

"Nonsense!" said Peter, briskly; "Mother wouldn't have taken the man up into Jim's bedroom. Why should she? Listen—the door's opening. Now they'll come down. I'll open the door a crack."

He did.

"It's not listening," he replied indignantly to Bobbie's scandalised remarks; "nobody in their senses would talk secrets on the stairs. And Mother can't have secrets to talk with Dr. Forrest's stable-man- -and you said it was him."

"Bobbie," called Mother's voice.

They opened the kitchen door, and Mother leaned over the stair railing.

"Jim's grandfather has come," she said; "wash your hands and faces and then you can see him. He wants to see you!" The bedroom door shut again.

"There now!" said Peter; "fancy us not even thinking of that! Let's have some hot water, Mrs. Viney. I'm as black as your hat."

The three were indeed dirty, for the stuff you clean brass candlesticks with is very far from cleaning to the cleaner.

They were still busy with soap and flannel when they heard the boots and the voice come down the stairs and go into the dining-room. And when they were clean, though still damp—because it takes such a long time to dry your hands properly, and they were very impatient to see the grandfather—they filed into the dining-room.

Mother was sitting in the window-seat, and in the leather-covered armchair that Father always used to sit in at the other house sat—

THEIR OWN OLD GENTLEMAN!

"Well, I never did," said Peter, even before he said, "How do you do?" He was, as he explained afterwards, too surprised even to remember that there was such a thing as politeness—much less to practise it.

"It's our own old gentleman!" said Phyllis.

"Oh, it's you!" said Bobbie. And then they remembered themselves and their manners and said, "How do you do?" very nicely.

"This is Jim's grandfather, Mr. —" said Mother, naming the old gentleman's name.

"How splendid!" said Peter; "that's just exactly like a book, isn't it, Mother?"

"It is, rather," said Mother, smiling; "things do happen in real life that are rather like books, sometimes."

"I am so awfully glad it IS you," said Phyllis; "when you think of the tons of old gentlemen there are in the world—it might have been almost anyone."

"I say, though," said Peter, "you're not going to take Jim away, though, are you?"

"Not at present," said the old gentleman. "Your Mother has most kindly consented to let him stay here. I thought of sending a nurse, but your Mother is good enough to say that she will nurse him herself."

"But what about her writing?" said Peter, before anyone could stop him. "There won't be anything for him to eat if Mother doesn't write."

"That's all right," said Mother, hastily.

The old gentleman looked very kindly at Mother.

"I see," he said, "you trust your children, and confide in them."

"Of course," said Mother.

"Then I may tell them of our little arrangement," he said. "Your Mother, my dears, has consented to give up writing for a little while and to become a Matron of my Hospital."

"Oh!" said Phyllis, blankly; "and shall we have to go away from Three Chimneys and the Railway and everything?"

"No, no, darling," said Mother, hurriedly.

"The Hospital is called Three Chimneys Hospital," said the old gentleman, "and my unlucky Jim's the only patient, and I hope he'll continue to be so. Your Mother will be Matron, and there'll be a hospital staff of a housemaid and a cook—till Jim's well."

"And then will Mother go on writing again?" asked Peter.

"We shall see," said the old gentleman, with a slight, swift glance at Bobbie; "perhaps something nice may happen and she won't have to."

"I love my writing," said Mother, very quickly.

"I know," said the old gentleman; "don't be afraid that I'm going to try to interfere. But one never knows. Very wonderful and beautiful things do happen, don't they? And we live most of our lives in the hope of them. I may come again to see the boy?"

"Surely," said Mother, "and I don't know how to thank you for making it possible for me to nurse him. Dear boy!"

"He kept calling Mother, Mother, in the night," said Phyllis. "I woke up twice and heard him."

"He didn't mean me," said Mother, in a low voice to the old gentleman; "that's why I wanted so much to keep him."

The old gentleman rose.

"I'm so glad," said Peter, "that you're going to keep him, Mother."

"Take care of your Mother, my dears," said the old gentleman. "She's a woman in a million."

"Yes, isn't she?" whispered Bobbie.

"God bless her," said the old gentleman, taking both Mother's hands, "God bless her! Ay, and she shall be blessed. Dear me, where's my hat? Will Bobbie come with me to the gate?"

At the gate he stopped and said:—

"You're a good child, my dear—I got your letter. But it wasn't needed. When I read about your Father's case in the papers at the time, I had my doubts. And ever since I've known who you were, I've been trying to find out things. I haven't done very much yet. But I have hopes, my dear—I have hopes."

"Oh!" said Bobbie, choking a little.

"Yes—I may say great hopes. But keep your secret a little longer. Wouldn't do to upset your Mother with a false hope, would it?"

"Oh, but it isn't false!" said Bobbie; "I KNOW you can do it. I knew you could when I wrote. It isn't a false hope, is it?"

"No," he said, "I don't think it's a false hope, or I wouldn't have told you. And I think you deserve to be told that there IS a hope."

"And you don't think Father did it, do you? Oh, say you don't think he did."

"My dear," he said, "I'm perfectly CERTAIN he didn't."

If it was a false hope, it was none the less a very radiant one that lay warm at Bobbie's heart, and through the days that followed lighted her little face as a Japanese lantern is lighted by the candle within.

Chapter 14. The End.

Life at the Three Chimneys was never quite the same again after the old gentleman came to see his grandson. Although they now knew his name, the children never spoke of him by it—at any rate, when they were by themselves. To them he was always the old gentleman, and I think he had better be the old gentleman to us, too. It wouldn't make him seem any more real to you, would it, if I were to tell you that his name was Snooks or Jenkins (which it wasn't)?—and, after all, I must be allowed to keep one secret. It's the only one; I have told you everything else, except what I am going to tell you in this chapter, which is the last. At least, of course, I haven't told you EVERYTHING. If I were to do that, the book would never come to an end, and that would be a pity, wouldn't it?

Well, as I was saying, life at Three Chimneys was never quite the same again. The cook and the housemaid were very nice (I don't mind telling you their names—they were Clara and Ethelwyn), but they told Mother they did not seem to want Mrs. Viney, and that she was an old muddler. So Mrs. Viney came only two days a week to do washing and ironing. Then Clara and Ethelwyn said they could do the work all right if they weren't interfered with, and that meant that the children no longer got the tea and cleared it away and washed up the tea-things and dusted the rooms.

This would have left quite a blank in their lives, although they had often pretended to themselves and to each other that they hated housework. But now that Mother had no writing and no housework to do, she had time for lessons. And lessons the children had to do. However nice the person who is teaching you may be, lessons are lessons all the world over, and at their best are worse fun than peeling potatoes or lighting a fire.

On the other hand, if Mother now had time for lessons, she also had time for play, and to make up little rhymes for the children as she used to do. She had not had much time for rhymes since she came to Three Chimneys.

There was one very odd thing about these lessons. Whatever the children were doing, they always wanted to be doing something else. When Peter was doing his Latin, he thought it would be nice to be learning History like Bobbie. Bobbie would have preferred Arithmetic, which was what Phyllis happened to be doing, and Phyllis of course thought Latin much the most interesting kind of lesson. And so on.

So, one day, when they sat down to lessons, each of them found a little rhyme at its place. I put the rhymes in to show you that their Mother really did understand a little how children feel about things, and also the kind of words they use, which is the case with very few grown-up people. I suppose most grown-ups have very bad memories, and have forgotten how they felt when they were little. Of course, the verses are supposed to be spoken by the children.

PETER

I once thought Caesar easy pap—
How very soft I must have been!
When they start Caesar with a chap
He little know what that will mean.
Oh, verbs are silly stupid things.
I'd rather learn the dates of kings!

BOBBIE

The worst of all my lesson things
Is learning who succeeded who
In all the rows of queens and kings,
With dates to everything they do:
With dates enough to make you sick;—
I wish it was Arithmetic!

PHYLLIS

Such pounds and pounds of apples fill
My slate—what is the price you'd spend?
You scratch the figures out until
You cry upon the dividend.
I'd break the slate and scream for joy
If I did Latin like a boy!

This kind of thing, of course, made lessons much jollier. It is something to know that the person who is teaching you sees that it is not all plain sailing for you, and does not think that it is just your stupidness that makes you not know your lessons till you've learned them!

Then as Jim's leg got better it was very pleasant to go up and sit with him and hear tales about his school life and the other boys. There was one boy, named Parr, of whom Jim seemed to have formed the lowest possible opinion, and another boy named Wigsby Minor, for whose views Jim had a great respect. Also there were three brothers named Paley, and the youngest was called Paley Terts, and was much given to fighting.

Peter drank in all this with deep joy, and Mother seemed to have listened with some interest, for one day she gave Jim a sheet of paper on which she had written a rhyme about Parr, bringing in Paley and Wigsby by name in a most wonderful way, as well as all the reasons Jim had for not liking Parr, and Wigsby's wise opinion on the matter. Jim was immensely pleased. He had never had a rhyme written expressly for him before. He read it till he knew it by heart and then he sent it to Wigsby, who liked it almost as much as Jim did. Perhaps you may like it, too.

THE NEW BOY

His name is Parr: he says that he
Is given bread and milk for tea.
He says his father killed a bear.
He says his mother cuts his hair.

He wears goloshes when it's wet.
I've heard his people call him "Pet"!
He has no proper sense of shame;
He told the chaps his Christian name.

He cannot wicket-keep at all,
He's frightened of a cricket ball.
He reads indoors for hours and hours.
He knows the names of beastly flowers.

He says his French just like Mossoo—
A beastly stuck-up thing to do—
He won't keep *cave*, shirks his turn
And says he came to school to learn!

He won't play football, says it hurts;

He wouldn't fight with Paley Terts;
He couldn't whistle if he tried,
And when we laughed at him he cried!

Now Wigsby Minor says that Parr
Is only like all new boys are.
I know when *I* first came to school
I wasn't such a jolly fool!

Jim could never understand how Mother could have been clever enough to do it. To the others it seemed nice, but natural. You see they had always been used to having a mother who could write verses just like the way people talk, even to the shocking expression at the end of the rhyme, which was Jim's very own.

Jim taught Peter to play chess and draughts and dominoes, and altogether it was a nice quiet time.

Only Jim's leg got better and better, and a general feeling began to spring up among Bobbie, Peter, and Phyllis that something ought to be done to amuse him; not just games, but something really handsome. But it was extraordinarily difficult to think of anything.

"It's no good," said Peter, when all of them had thought and thought till their heads felt quite heavy and swollen; "if we can't think of anything to amuse him, we just can't, and there's an end of it. Perhaps something will just happen of its own accord that he'll like."

"Things DO happen by themselves sometimes, without your making them," said Phyllis, rather as though, usually, everything that happened in the world was her doing.

"I wish something would happen," said Bobbie, dreamily, "something wonderful."

And something wonderful did happen exactly four days after she had said this. I wish I could say it was three days after, because in fairy tales it is always three days after that things happen. But this is not a fairy story, and besides, it really was four and not three, and I am nothing if not strictly truthful.

They seemed to be hardly Railway children at all in those days, and as the days went on each had an uneasy feeling about this which Phyllis expressed one day.

"I wonder if the Railway misses us," she said, plaintively. "We never go to see it now."

"It seems ungrateful," said Bobbie; "we loved it so when we hadn't anyone else to play with."

"Perks is always coming up to ask after Jim," said Peter, "and the signalman's little boy is better. He told me so."

"I didn't mean the people," explained Phyllis; "I meant the dear Railway itself."

"The thing I don't like," said Bobbie, on this fourth day, which was a Tuesday, "is our having stopped waving to the 9.15 and sending our love to Father by it."

"Let's begin again," said Phyllis. And they did.

Somehow the change of everything that was made by having servants in the house and Mother not doing any writing, made the time seem extremely long since that strange morning at the beginning of things, when they had got up so early and burnt the bottom out of the kettle and had apple pie for breakfast and first seen the Railway.

It was September now, and the turf on the slope to the Railway was dry and crisp. Little long grass spikes stood up like bits of gold wire, frail blue harebells trembled on their tough, slender stalks, Gipsy roses opened wide and flat their lilac-coloured discs, and the golden stars of St. John's Wort shone at the edges of the pool that lay halfway to the Railway. Bobbie gathered a generous handful of the flowers and thought how pretty they would look lying on the green-and-pink blanket of silk-waste that now covered Jim's poor broken leg.

"Hurry up," said Peter, "or we shall miss the 9.15!"

"I can't hurry more than I am doing," said Phyllis. "Oh, bother it! My bootlace has come undone AGAIN!"

"When you're married," said Peter, "your bootlace will come undone going up the church aisle, and your man that you're going to get married to will tumble over it and smash his nose in on the ornamented pavement; and then you'll say you won't marry him, and you'll have to be an old maid."

"I shan't," said Phyllis. "I'd much rather marry a man with his nose smashed in than not marry anybody."

"It would be horrid to marry a man with a smashed nose, all the same," went on Bobbie. "He wouldn't be able to smell the flowers at the wedding. Wouldn't that be awful!"

"Bother the flowers at the wedding!" cried Peter. "Look! the signal's down. We must run!"

They ran. And once more they waved their handkerchiefs, without at all minding whether the handkerchiefs were clean or not, to the 9.15.

"Take our love to Father!" cried Bobbie. And the others, too, shouted:—

"Take our love to Father!"

The old gentleman waved from his first-class carriage window. Quite violently he waved. And there was nothing odd in that, for he always had waved. But what was really remarkable was that from every window handkerchiefs fluttered, newspapers signalled, hands waved wildly. The train swept by with a rustle and roar, the little pebbles jumped and danced under it as it passed, and the children were left looking at each other.

"Well!" said Peter.

"WELL!" said Bobbie.

"*WELL!*" said Phyllis.

"Whatever on earth does that mean?" asked Peter, but he did not expect any answer.

"*I* don't know," said Bobbie. "Perhaps the old gentleman told the people at his station to look out for us and wave. He knew we should like it!"

Now, curiously enough, this was just what had happened. The old gentleman, who was very well known and respected at his particular station, had got there early that morning, and he had waited at the door where the young man stands holding the interesting machine that clips the tickets, and he had said something to every single passenger who passed through that door. And after nodding to what the old gentleman had said—and the nods expressed every shade of surprise, interest, doubt, cheerful pleasure, and grumpy agreement— each passenger had gone on to the platform and read one certain part of his newspaper. And when the passengers got into the train, they had told the other passengers who were already there what the old gentleman had said, and then the other passengers had also looked at their newspapers and seemed very astonished and, mostly, pleased. Then, when the train passed the fence where the three children were, newspapers and hands and handkerchiefs were waved madly, till all that side of the train was fluttery with white like the pictures of the King's Coronation in the biograph at Maskelyne and Cook's. To the children it almost seemed as though the train itself was alive, and was at last responding to the love that they had given it so freely and so long.

"It is most extraordinarily rum!" said Peter.

"Most stronery!" echoed Phyllis.

But Bobbie said, "Don't you think the old gentleman's waves seemed more significating than usual?"

"No," said the others.

"I do," said Bobbie. "I thought he was trying to explain something to us with his newspaper."

"Explain what?" asked Peter, not unnaturally.

"*I* don't know," Bobbie answered, "but I do feel most awfully funny. I feel just exactly as if something was going to happen."

"What is going to happen," said Peter, "is that Phyllis's stocking is going to come down."

This was but too true. The suspender had given way in the agitation of the waves to the 9.15. Bobbie's handkerchief served as first aid to the injured, and they all went home.

Lessons were more than usually difficult to Bobbie that day. Indeed, she disgraced herself so deeply over a quite simple sum about the division of 48 pounds of meat and 36 pounds of bread among 144 hungry children that Mother looked at her anxiously.

"Don't you feel quite well, dear?" she asked.

"I don't know," was Bobbie's unexpected answer. "I don't know how I feel. It isn't that I'm lazy. Mother, will you let me off lessons to-day? I feel as if I wanted to be quite alone by myself."

"Yes, of course I'll let you off," said Mother; "but—"

Bobbie dropped her slate. It cracked just across the little green mark that is so useful for drawing patterns round, and it was never the same slate again. Without waiting to pick it up she bolted. Mother caught her in the hall feeling blindly among the waterproofs and umbrellas for her garden hat.

"What is it, my sweetheart?" said Mother. "You don't feel ill, do you?"

"I DON'T know," Bobbie answered, a little breathlessly, "but I want to be by myself and see if my head really IS all silly and my inside all squirmy-twisty."

"Hadn't you better lie down?" Mother said, stroking her hair back from her forehead.

"I'd be more alive in the garden, I think," said Bobbie.

But she could not stay in the garden. The hollyhocks and the asters and the late roses all seemed to be waiting for something to happen. It was one of those still, shiny autumn days, when everything does seem to be waiting.

Bobbie could not wait.

"I'll go down to the station," she said, "and talk to Perks and ask about the signalman's little boy."

So she went down. On the way she passed the old lady from the Post- office, who gave her a kiss and a hug, but, rather to Bobbie's surprise, no words except:—

"God bless you, love—" and, after a pause, "run along—do."

The draper's boy, who had sometimes been a little less than civil and a little more than contemptuous, now touched his cap, and uttered the remarkable words:—

"'Morning, Miss, I'm sure—"

The blacksmith, coming along with an open newspaper in his hand, was even more strange in his manner. He grinned broadly, though, as a rule, he was a man not given to smiles, and waved the newspaper long before he came up to her. And as he passed her, he said, in answer to her "Good morning":—

"Good morning to you, Missie, and many of them! I wish you joy, that I do!"

"Oh!" said Bobbie to herself, and her heart quickened its beats, "something IS going to happen! I know it is—everyone is so odd, like people are in dreams."

The Station Master wrung her hand warmly. In fact he worked it up and down like a pump-handle. But he gave her no reason for this unusually enthusiastic greeting. He only said:—

"The 11.54's a bit late, Miss—the extra luggage this holiday time," and went away very quickly into that inner Temple of his into which even Bobbie dared not follow him.

Perks was not to be seen, and Bobbie shared the solitude of the platform with the Station Cat. This tortoiseshell lady, usually of a retiring disposition, came to-day to rub herself against the brown stockings of Bobbie with arched back, waving tail, and reverberating purrs.

"Dear me!" said Bobbie, stooping to stroke her, "how very kind everybody is to-day—even you, Pussy!"

Perks did not appear until the 11.54 was signalled, and then he, like everybody else that morning, had a newspaper in his hand.

"Hullo!" he said, "'ere you are. Well, if THIS is the train, it'll be smart work! Well, God bless you, my dear! I see it in the paper, and I don't think I was ever so glad of anything in all my born days!" He looked at Bobbie a moment, then said, "One I must have, Miss, and no offence, I know, on a day like this 'ere!" and with that he kissed her, first on one cheek and then on the other.

"You ain't offended, are you?" he asked anxiously. "I ain't took too great a liberty? On a day like this, you know—"

"No, no," said Bobbie, "of course it's not a liberty, dear Mr. Perks; we love you quite as much as if you were an uncle of ours— but—on a day like WHAT?"

"Like this 'ere!" said Perks. "Don't I tell you I see it in the paper?"

"Saw WHAT in the paper?" asked Bobbie, but already the 11.54 was steaming into the station and the Station Master was looking at all the places where Perks was not and ought to have been.

Bobbie was left standing alone, the Station Cat watching her from under the bench with friendly golden eyes.

Of course you know already exactly what was going to happen. Bobbie was not so clever. She had the vague, confused, expectant feeling that comes to one's heart in dreams. What her heart expected I can't tell—perhaps the very thing that you and I know was going to happen—but her mind expected nothing; it was almost blank, and felt nothing but tiredness and stupidness and an empty feeling, like your body has when you have been a long walk and it is very far indeed past your proper dinner-time.

Only three people got out of the 11.54. The first was a countryman with two baskety boxes full of live chickens who stuck their russet heads out anxiously through the wicker bars; the second was Miss Peckitt, the grocer's wife's cousin, with a tin box and three brown- paper parcels; and the third—

"Oh! my Daddy, my Daddy!" That scream went like a knife into the heart of everyone in the train, and people put their heads out of the windows to see a tall pale man with lips set in a thin close line, and a little girl clinging to him with arms and legs, while his arms went tightly round her.

* * * * * *

"I knew something wonderful was going to happen," said Bobbie, as they went up the road, "but I didn't think it was going to be this. Oh, my Daddy, my Daddy!"

"Then didn't Mother get my letter?" Father asked.

"There weren't any letters this morning. Oh! Daddy! it IS really you, isn't it?"

The clasp of a hand she had not forgotten assured her that it was. "You must go in by yourself, Bobbie, and tell Mother quite quietly that it's all right. They've caught the man who did it. Everyone knows now that it wasn't your Daddy."

"*I* always knew it wasn't," said Bobbie. "Me and Mother and our old gentleman."

"Yes," he said, "it's all his doing. Mother wrote and told me you had found out. And she told me what you'd been to her. My own little girl!" They stopped a minute then.

And now I see them crossing the field. Bobbie goes into the house, trying to keep her eyes from speaking before her lips have found the right words to "tell Mother quite quietly" that the sorrow and the struggle and the parting are over and done, and that Father has come home.

I see Father walking in the garden, waiting—waiting. He is looking at the flowers, and each flower is a miracle to eyes that all these months of Spring and Summer have seen only flagstones and gravel and a little grudging grass. But his eyes keep turning towards the house. And presently he leaves the garden and goes to stand outside the nearest door. It is the back door, and across the yard the swallows are circling. They are getting ready to fly away from cold winds and keen frost to the land where it is always summer. They are the same swallows that the children built the little clay nests for.

Now the house door opens. Bobbie's voice calls:—

"Come in, Daddy; come in!"

He goes in and the door is shut. I think we will not open the door or follow him. I think that just now we are not wanted there. I think it will be best for us to go quickly and quietly away. At the end of the field, among the thin gold spikes of grass and the harebells and Gipsy roses and St. John's Wort, we may just take one last look, over our shoulders, at the white house where neither we nor anyone else is wanted now.

Five Children and It

To John Bland

My Lamb, you are so very small,
You have not learned to read at all.
Yet never a printed book withstands
The urgence of your dimpled hands.
So, though this book is for yourself,
Let mother keep it on the shelf
Till you can read. O days that Pass,
That day will come too soon, alas!

Chapter 1. Beautiful as the Day

The house was three miles from the station, but before the dusty hired fly had rattled along for five minutes the children began to put their heads out of the carriage window and to say, 'Aren't we nearly there?' And every time they passed a house, which was not very often, they all said, 'Oh, is THIS it?' But it never was, till they reached the very top of the hill, just past the chalk-quarry and before you come to the gravel-pit. And then there was a white house with a green garden and an orchard beyond, and mother said, 'Here we are!'

'How white the house is,' said Robert.

'And look at the roses,' said Anthea.

'And the plums,' said Jane.

'It is rather decent,' Cyril admitted.

The Baby said, 'Wanty go walky'; and the fly stopped with a last rattle and jolt.

Everyone got its legs kicked or its feet trodden on in the scramble to get out of the carriage that very minute, but no one seemed to mind. Mother, curiously enough, was in no hurry to get out; and even when she had come down slowly and by the step, and with no jump at all, she seemed to wish to see the boxes carried in, and even to pay the driver, instead of joining in that first glorious rush round the garden and the orchard and the thorny, thistly, briery, brambly wilderness beyond the broken gate and the dry fountain at the side of the house. But the children were wiser, for once. It was not really a pretty house at all; it was quite ordinary, and mother thought it was rather inconvenient, and was quite annoyed at there being no shelves, to speak of, and hardly a cupboard in the place. Father used to say that the ironwork on the roof and coping was like an architect's nightmare. But the house was deep in the country, with no other house in sight, and the children had been in London for two years, without so much as once going to the seaside even for a day by an excursion train, and so the White House seemed to them a sort of Fairy Palace set down in an Earthly Paradise. For London is like prison for children, especially if their relations are not rich.

Of course there are the shops and the theatres, and Maskelyne and Cook's, and things, but if your people are rather poor you don't get taken to the theatres, and you can't buy things out of the shops; and London has none of those nice things that children may play with without hurting the things or themselves - such as trees and sand and woods and waters. And nearly everything in London is the wrong sort of shape - all straight lines and flat streets, instead of being all sorts of odd shapes, like things are in the country. Trees are all different, as you know, and I am sure some tiresome person must have told you that there are no two blades of grass exactly alike. But in streets, where the blades of grass don't grow, everything is like everything else. This is why so many children who live in towns are so extremely naughty. They do not know what is the matter with them, and no more do their fathers and mothers, aunts, uncles, cousins, tutors, governesses, and nurses; but I know. And so do you now. Children in the country are naughty sometimes, too, but that is for quite different reasons.

The children had explored the gardens and the outhouses thoroughly before they were caught and cleaned for tea, and they saw quite well that they were certain to be happy at the White House. They thought so from the first moment, but when they found the back of the house covered with jasmine, an in white flower, and smelling like a bottle of the most expensive scent that is ever given for a birthday present; and when they had seen the lawn, all green and smooth, and quite different from the brown grass in the gardens at Camden Town; and when they had found the stable with a loft over it and some old hay still left, they were almost certain; and when Robert had found the broken swing and tumbled out of it and got a lump on his head the size of an egg, and Cyril had nipped his finger in the door of a hutch that seemed made to keep rabbits in, if you ever had any, they had no longer any doubts whatever.

The best part of it all was that there were no rules about not going to places and not doing things. In London almost everything is labelled 'You mustn't touch,' and though the label is invisible, it's just as bad, because you know it's there, or if you don't you jolly soon get told.

The White House was on the edge of a hill, with a wood behind it - and the chalk-quarry on one side and the gravel-pit on the other. Down at the bottom of the hill was a level plain, with queer-shaped white buildings where people burnt lime, and a big red brewery and other houses; and when the big chimneys were smoking and the sun was setting, the valley looked as if it was filled with golden mist, and the limekilns and oast-houses glimmered and glittered till they were like an enchanted city out of the Arabian Nights.

Now that I have begun to tell you about the place, I feel that I could go on and make this into a most interesting story about all the ordinary things that the children did - just the kind of things you do yourself, you know - and you would believe every word of it; and when I told about the children's being tiresome, as you are sometimes, your aunts would perhaps write in the margin of the story with a pencil, 'How true!' or 'How like life!'and you would see it and very likely be annoyed. So I will only tell you the really astonishing things that happened, and you may leave the book about quite safely, for no aunts and uncles either are likely to write 'How true!' on the edge of the story. Grown-up people find it very difficult to believe really wonderful things, unless they have what they call proof. But children will believe almost anything, and grown-ups know this. That is why they tell you that the earth is round like an orange, when you can see perfectly well that it is flat and lumpy; and why they say that the earth goes round the sun, when you can see for yourself any day that the sun gets up in the morning and goes to bed at night like a good sun as it is, and the earth knows its place, and lies as still as a mouse. Yet I daresay you believe all that about the earth and the sun, and if so you will find it quite easy to believe that before Anthea and Cyril and the others had been a week in the country they had found a fairy. At least they called it that, because that was what it called itself; and of course it knew best, but it was not at all like any fairy you ever saw or heard of or read about.

It was at the gravel-pits. Father had to go away suddenly on business, and mother had gone away to stay with Granny, who was not very well. They both went in a great hurry, and when they were gone the house seemed dreadfully quiet and empty, and the children wandered from one room to another and looked at the bits of paper and string on the floors left over from the packing, and not yet cleared up, and wished they had something to do. It was Cyril who said:

'I say, let's take our Margate spades and go and dig in the gravel-pits. We can pretend it's seaside.'

'Father said it was once,' Anthea said; 'he says there are shells there thousands of years old.'

So they went. Of course they had been to the edge of the gravel-pit and looked over, but they had not gone down into it for fear father should say they mustn't play there, and the same with the chalk-quarry. The gravel-pit is not really dangerous if you don't try to climb down the edges, but go the slow safe way round by the road, as if you were a cart.

Each of the children carried its own spade, and took it in turns to carry the Lamb. He was the baby, and they called him that because 'Baa' was the first thing he ever said. They called Anthea 'Panther', which seems silly when you read it, but when you say it it sounds a little like her name.

The gravel-pit is very large and wide, with grass growing round the edges at the top, and dry stringy wildflowers, purple and yellow. It is like a giant's wash-hand basin. And there are mounds of gravel, and holes in the sides of the basin where gravel has been taken out, and high up in the steep sides there are the little holes that are the little front doors of the little sand-martins' little houses.

The children built a castle, of course, but castle-building is rather poor fun when you have no hope of the swishing tide ever coming in to fill up the moat and wash away the drawbridge, and, at the happy last, to wet everybody up to the waist at least.

Cyril wanted to dig out a cave to play smugglers in, but the others thought it might bury them alive, so it ended in all spades going to work to dig a hole through the castle to Australia. These children, you see, believed that the world was round, and that on the other side the little Australian boys and girls were really walking wrong way up, like flies on the ceiling, with their heads hanging down into the air.

The children dug and they dug and they dug, and their hands got sandy and hot and red, and their faces got damp and shiny. The Lamb had tried to eat the sand, and had cried so hard when he found that it was not, as he had supposed, brown sugar, that he was now tired out, and was lying asleep in a warm fat bunch in the middle of the half-finished castle. This left his brothers and sisters free to work really hard, and the hole that was to come out in Australia soon grew so deep that Jane, who was called Pussy for short, begged the others to Stop.

'Suppose the bottom of the hole gave way suddenly,' she said, 'and you tumbled out among the little Australians, all the sand would get in their eyes.'

'Yes,' said Robert; 'and they would hate us, and throw stones at us, and not let us see the kangaroos, or opossums, or blue-gums, or Emu Brand birds, or anything.'

Cyril and Anthea knew that Australia was not quite so near as all that, but they agreed to stop using the spades and go on with their hands. This was quite easy, because the sand at the bottom of the hole was very soft and fine and dry, like sea-sand. And there were little shells in it.

'Fancy it having been wet sea here once, all sloppy and shiny,' said Jane, 'with fishes and conger-eels and coral and mermaids.'

'And masts of ships and wrecked Spanish treasure. I wish we could find a gold doubloon, or something,' Cyril said.

'How did the sea get carried away?' Robert asked.

'Not in a pail, silly,' said his brother. 'Father says the earth got too hot underneath, like you do in bed sometimes, so it just hunched up its shoulders, and the sea had to slip off, like the blankets do off us, and the shoulder was left sticking out, and turned into dry land. Let's go and look for shells; I think that little cave looks likely, and I see something sticking out there like a bit of wrecked ship's anchor, and it's beastly hot in the Australian hole.'

The others agreed, but Anthea went on digging. She always liked to finish a thing when she had once begun it. She felt it would be a disgrace to leave that hole without getting through to Australia.

The cave was disappointing, because there were no shells, and the wrecked ship's anchor turned out to be only the broken end of a pickaxe handle, and the cave party were just making up their minds that the sand makes you thirstier when it is not by the seaside, and someone had suggested going home for lemonade, when Anthea suddenly screamed:

'Cyril! Come here! Oh, come quick! It's alive! It'll get away! Quick!'

They all hurried back.

'It's a rat, I shouldn't wonder,' said Robert. 'Father says they infest old places - and this must be pretty old if the sea was here thousands of years ago.'

'Perhaps it is a snake,' said Jane, shuddering.

'Let's look,' said Cyril, jumping into the hole. 'I'm not afraid of snakes. I like them. If it is a snake I'll tame it, and it will follow me everywhere, and I'll let it sleep round my neck at night.'

'No, you won't,' said Robert firmly. He shared Cyril's bedroom. 'But you may if it's a rat.'

'Oh, don't be silly!' said Anthea; 'it's not a rat, it's MUCH bigger. And it's not a snake. It's got feet; I saw them; and fur! No - not the spade. You'll hurt it! Dig with your hands.'

'And let IT hurt ME instead! That's so likely, isn't it?' said Cyril, seizing a spade.

'Oh, don't!' said Anthea. 'Squirrel, DON'T. I - it sounds silly, but it said something. It really and truly did.'

'What?'

'It said, "You let me alone".'

But Cyril merely observed that his sister must have gone off her nut, and he and Robert dug with spades while Anthea sat on the edge of the hole, jumping up and down with hotness and anxiety. They dug carefully, and presently everyone could see that there really was something moving in the bottom of the Australian hole.

Then Anthea cried out, 'I'M not afraid. Let me dig,' and fell on her knees and began to scratch like a dog does when he has suddenly remembered where it was that he buried his bone.

'Oh, I felt fur,' she cried, half laughing and half crying. 'I did indeed! I did!' when suddenly a dry husky voice in the sand made them all jump back, and their hearts jumped nearly as fast as they did.

'Let me alone,' it said. And now everyone heard the voice and looked at the others to see if they had too.

'But we want to see you,' said Robert bravely.

'I wish you'd come out,' said Anthea, also taking courage.

'Oh, well - if that's your wish,' the voice said, and the sand stirred and spun and scattered, and something brown and furry and fat came rolling out into the hole and the sand fell off it, and it sat there yawning and rubbing the ends of its eyes with its hands.

'I believe I must have dropped asleep,' it said, stretching itself.

The children stood round the hole in a ring, looking at the creature they had found. It was worth looking at. Its eyes were on long horns like a snail's eyes, and it could move them in and out like telescopes; it had ears like a bat's ears, and its tubby body was shaped like a spider's and covered with thick soft fur; its legs and arms were furry too, and it had hands and feet like a monkey's.

'What on earth is it?' Jane said. 'Shall we take it home?'

The thing turned its long eyes to look at her, and said: 'Does she always talk nonsense, or is it only the rubbish on her head that makes her silly?'

It looked scornfully at Jane's hat as it spoke.

'She doesn't mean to be silly,' Anthea said gently; we none of us do, whatever you may think! Don't be frightened; we don't want to hurt you, you know.'

'Hurt ME!' it said. 'ME frightened? Upon my word! Why, you talk as if I were nobody in particular.' All its fur stood out like a cat's when it is going to fight.

'Well,' said Anthea, still kindly, 'perhaps if we knew who you are in particular we could think of something to say that wouldn't make you cross. Everything we've said so far seems to have. Who are you? And don't get angry! Because really we don't know.'

'You don't know?' it said. 'Well, I knew the world had changed - but - well, really - do you mean to tell me seriously you don't know a Psammead when you see one?'

'A Sammyadd? That's Greek to me.'

'So it is to everyone,' said the creature sharply. 'Well, in plain English, then, a SAND-FAIRY. Don't you know a Sand-fairy when you see one?'

It looked so grieved and hurt that Jane hastened to say, 'Of course I see you are, now. It's quite plain now one comes to look at you.'

'You came to look at me, several sentences ago,' it said crossly, beginning to curl up again in the sand.

'Oh - don't go away again! Do talk some more,' Robert cried. 'I didn't know you were a Sand-fairy, but I knew directly I saw you that you were much the wonderfullest thing I'd ever seen.'

The Sand-fairy seemed a shade less disagreeable after this.

'It isn't talking I mind,' it said, 'as long as you're reasonably civil. But I'm not going to make polite conversation for you. If you talk nicely to me, perhaps I'll answer you, and perhaps I won't. Now say something.'

Of course no one could think of anything to say, but at last Robert thought of 'How long have you lived here?' and he said it at once.

'Oh, ages - several thousand years,' replied the Psammead.

'Tell us all about it. Do.'

'It's all in books.'

'You aren't!' Jane said. 'Oh, tell us everything you can about yourself! We don't know anything about you, and you are so nice.'

The Sand-fairy smoothed his long rat-like whiskers and smiled between them.

'Do please tell!' said the children all together.

It is wonderful how quickly you get used to things, even the most astonishing. Five minutes before, the children had had no more idea than you that there was such a thing as a sand-fairy in the world, and now they were talking to it as though they had known it all their lives. It drew its eyes in and said:

'How very sunny it is - quite like old times. Where do you get your Megatheriums from now?'

'What?' said the children all at once. It is very difficult always to remember that 'what' is not polite, especially in moments of surprise or agitation.

'Are Pterodactyls plentiful now?' the Sand-fairy went on.

The children were unable to reply.

'What do you have for breakfast?' the Fairy said impatiently, 'and who gives it you?'

'Eggs and bacon, and bread-and-milk, and porridge and things. Mother gives it us. What are Mega-what's-its-names and Ptero-what-do-you-call-thems? And does anyone have them for breakfast?'

'Why, almost everyone had Pterodactyl for breakfast in my time! Pterodactyls were something like crocodiles and something like birds - I believe they were very good grilled. You see it was like this: of course there were heaps of sand-fairies then, and in the morning early you went out and hunted for them, and when you'd found one it gave you your wish. People used to send their little boys down to the seashore early in the morning before breakfast to get the day's wishes, and very often the eldest boy in the family would be told to wish for a Megatherium, ready jointed for cooking. It was as big as an elephant, you see, so there was a good deal of meat on it. And if they wanted fish, the Ichthyosaurus was asked for - he was twenty to forty feet long, so there was plenty of him. And for poultry there was the Plesiosaurus; there were nice pickings on that too. Then the other children could wish for other things. But when people had dinner-parties it was nearly always Megatheriums; and Ichthyosaurus, because his fins were a great delicacy and his tail made soup.'

'There must have been heaps and heaps of cold meat left over,' said Anthea, who meant to be a good housekeeper some day.

'Oh no,' said the Psammead, 'that would never have done. Why, of course at sunset what was left over turned into stone. You find the stone bones of the Megatherium and things all over the place even now, they tell me.'

'Who tell you?' asked Cyril; but the Sand-fairy frowned and began to dig very fast with its furry hands.

'Oh, don't go!' they all cried; 'tell us more about it when it was Megatheriums for breakfast! Was the world like this then?'

It stopped digging.

'Not a bit,' it said; 'it was nearly all sand where I lived, and coal grew on trees, and the periwinkles were as big as tea-trays - you find them now; they're turned into stone. We sand-fairies used to live on the seashore, and the children used to come with their little flint-spades and flint-pails and make castles for us to live in. That's thousands of years ago, but I hear that children still build castles on the sand. It's difficult to break yourself of a habit.'

'But why did you stop living in the castles?' asked Robert.

'It's a sad story,' said the Psammead gloomily. 'It was because they WOULD build moats to the castles, and the nasty wet bubbling sea used to come in, and of course as soon as a sand-fairy got wet it caught cold, and generally died. And so there got to be fewer and fewer, and, whenever you found a fairy and had a wish, you used to wish for a Megatherium, and eat twice as much as you wanted, because it might be weeks before you got another wish.'

'And did YOU get wet?' Robert inquired.

The Sand-fairy shuddered. 'Only once,' it said; 'the end of the twelfth hair of my top left whisker - I feel the place still in damp weather. It was only once, but it was quite enough for me. I went away as soon as the sun had dried my poor dear whisker. I scurried away to the back of the beach, and dug myself a house deep in warm dry sand, and there I've been ever since. And the sea changed its lodgings afterwards. And now I'm not going to tell you another thing.'

'Just one more, please,' said the children. 'Can you give wishes now?'

'Of course,' said it; 'didn't I give you yours a few minutes ago? You said, "I wish you'd come out," and I did.'

'Oh, please, mayn't we have another?'

'Yes, but be quick about it. I'm tired of you.'

I daresay you have often thought what you would do if you had three wishes given you, and have despised the old man and his wife in the black-pudding story, and felt certain that if you had the chance you could think of three really useful wishes without a moment's hesitation. These children had often talked this matter over, but, now the chance had suddenly come to them, they could not make up their minds.

'Quick,' said the Sand-fairy crossly. No one could think of anything, only Anthea did manage to remember a private wish of her own and jane's which they had never told the boys. She knew the boys would not care about it - but still it was better than nothing.

'I wish we were all as beautiful as the day,' she said in a great hurry.

The children looked at each other, but each could see that the others were not any better-looking than usual. The Psammead pushed out its long eyes, and seemed to be holding its breath and swelling itself out till it was twice as fat and furry as before. Suddenly it let its breath go in a long sigh.

'I'm really afraid I can't manage it,' it said apologetically; 'I must be out of practice.'

The children were horribly disappointed.

'Oh, DO try again!' they said.

'Well,' said the Sand-fairy, 'the fact is, I was keeping back a little strength to give the rest of you your wishes with. If you'll be contented with one wish a day amongst the lot of you I daresay I can screw myself up to it. Do you agree to that?'

'Yes, oh yes!' said Jane and Anthea. The boys nodded. They did not believe the Sand-fairy could do it. You can always make girls believe things much easier than you can boys.

It stretched out its eyes farther than ever, and swelled and swelled and swelled.

'I do hope it won't hurt itself,' said Anthea.

'Or crack its skin,' Robert said anxiously.

Everyone was very much relieved when the Sand-fairy, after getting so big that it almost filled up the hole in the sand, suddenly let out its breath and went back to its proper size.

'That's all right,' it said, panting heavily. 'It'll come easier to-morrow.'

'Did it hurt much?' asked Anthea.

'Only my poor whisker, thank you,' said he, 'but you're a kind and thoughtful child. Good day.'

It scratched suddenly and fiercely with its hands and feet, and disappeared in the sand. Then the children looked at each other, and each child suddenly found itself alone with three perfect strangers, all radiantly beautiful.

They stood for some moments in perfect silence. Each thought that its brothers and sisters had wandered off, and that these strange children had stolen up unnoticed while it was watching the swelling form of the Sand-fairy. Anthea spoke first -

'Excuse me,' she said very politely to Jane, who now had enormous blue eyes and a cloud of russet hair, 'but have you seen two little boys and a little girl anywhere about?'

'I was just going to ask you that,' said Jane. And then Cyril cried:

'Why, it's YOU! I know the hole in your pinafore! You ARE Jane, aren't you? And you're the Panther; I can see your dirty handkerchief that you forgot to change after you'd cut your thumb! Crikey! The wish has come off, after all. I say, am I as handsome as you are?'

'If you're Cyril, I liked you much better as you were before,' said Anthea decidedly. 'You look like the picture of the young chorister, with your golden hair; you'll die young, I shouldn't wonder. And if that's Robert, he's like an Italian organ-grinder. His hair's all black.'

'You two girls are like Christmas cards, then - that's all - silly Christmas cards,' said Robert angrily. 'And jane's hair is simply carrots.'

It was indeed of that Venetian tint so much admired by artists.

'Well, it's no use finding fault with each other,' said Anthea; 'let's get the Lamb and lug it home to dinner. The servants will admire us most awfully, you'll see.'

Baby was just waking when they got to him, and not one of the children but was relieved to find that he at least was not as beautiful as the day, but just the same as usual.

'I suppose he's too young to have wishes naturally,' said Jane. 'We shall have to mention him specially next time.'

Anthea ran forward and held out her arms.

'Come to own Panther, ducky,' she said.

The Baby looked at her disapprovingly, and put a sandy pink thumb in his mouth, Anthea was his favourite sister.

'Come then,' she said.

'G'way long!' said the Baby.

'Come to own Pussy,' said Jane.

'Wants my Panty,' said the Lamb dismally, and his lip trembled.

'Here, come on, Veteran,' said Robert, 'come and have a yidey on Yobby's back.'

'Yah, narky narky boy,' howled the Baby, giving way altogether. Then the children knew the worst. THE BABY DID NOT KNOW THEM!

They looked at each other in despair, and it was terrible to each, in this dire emergency, to meet only the beautiful eyes of perfect strangers, instead of the merry, friendly, commonplace, twinkling, jolly little eyes of its own brothers and sisters.

'This is most truly awful,' said Cyril when he had tried to lift up the Lamb, and the Lamb had scratched like a cat and bellowed like a bull. 'We've got to MAKE FRIENDS with him! I can't carry him home screaming like that. Fancy having to make friends with our own baby! - it's too silly.'

That, however, was exactly what they had to do. It took over an hour, and the task was not rendered any easier by the fact that the Lamb was by this time as hungry as a lion and as thirsty as a desert.

At last he consented to allow these strangers to carry him home by turns, but as he refused to hold on to such new acquaintances he was a dead weight and most exhausting.

'Thank goodness, we're home!' said Jane, staggering through the iron gate to where Martha, the nursemaid, stood at the front door shading her eyes with her hand and looking out anxiously. 'Here! Do take Baby!'

Martha snatched the Baby from her arms.

'Thanks be, HE'S safe back,' she said. 'Where are the others, and whoever to goodness gracious are all of you?'

'We're US, of course,' said Robert.

'And who's US, when you're at home?' asked Martha scornfully.

'I tell you it's US, only we're beautiful as the day,' said Cyril. 'I'm Cyril, and these are the others, and we're jolly hungry. Let us in, and don't be a silly idiot.'

Martha merely dratted Cyril's impudence and tried to shut the door in his face.

'I know we LOOK different, but I'm Anthea, and we're so tired, and it's long past dinner-time.'

'Then go home to your dinners, whoever you are; and if our children put you up to this playacting you can tell them from me they'll catch it, so they know what to expect!' With that she did bang the door. Cyril rang the bell violently. No answer. Presently cook put her head out of a bedroom window and said:

'If you don't take yourselves off, and that precious sharp, I'll go and fetch the police.' And she slammed down the window.

'It's no good,' said Anthea. 'Oh, do, do come away before we get sent to prison!'

The boys said it was nonsense, and the law of England couldn't put you in prison for just being as beautiful as the day, but all the same they followed the others out into the lane.

'We shall be our proper selves after sunset, I suppose,' said Jane.

'I don't know,' Cyril said sadly; 'it mayn't be like that now - things have changed a good deal since Megatherium times.'

'Oh,' cried Anthea suddenly, 'perhaps we shall turn into stone at sunset, like the Megatheriums did, so that there mayn't be any of us left over for the next day.'

She began to cry, so did Jane. Even the boys turned pale. No one had the heart to say anything.

It was a horrible afternoon. There was no house near where the children could beg a crust of bread or even a glass of water. They were afraid to go to the village, because they had seen Martha go down there with a basket, and there was a local constable. True, they were all as beautiful as the day, but that is a poor comfort when you are as hungry as a hunter and as thirsty as a sponge.

Three times they tried in vain to get the servants in the White House to let them in and listen to their tale. And then Robert went alone, hoping to be able to climb in at one of the back windows and so open the door to the others. But all the windows were out of reach, and Martha emptied a toilet-jug of cold water over him from a top window, and said:

'Go along with you, you nasty little Eyetalian monkey."

It came at last to their sitting down in a row under the hedge, with their feet in a dry ditch, waiting for sunset, and wondering whether, when the sun did set, they would turn into stone, or only into their own old natural selves; and each of them still felt lonely and among strangers, and tried not to look at the others, for, though their voices were their own, their faces were so radiantly beautiful as to be quite irritating to look at.

'I don't believe we SHALL turn to stone,' said Robert, breaking a long miserable silence, 'because the Sand-fairy said he'd give us another wish to-morrow, and he couldn't if we were stone, could he?'

The others said 'No,' but they weren't at all comforted.

Another silence, longer and more miserable, was broken by Cyril's suddenly saying, 'I don't want to frighten you girls, but I believe it's beginning with me already. My foot's quite dead. I'm turning to stone, I know I am, and so will you in a minute.'

'Never mind,' said Robert kindly, 'perhaps you'll be the only stone one, and the rest of us will be all right, and we'll cherish your statue and hang garlands on it.'

But when it turned out that Cyril's foot had only gone to sleep through his sitting too long with it under him, and when it came to life in an agony of pins and needles, the others were quite cross.

'Giving us such a fright for nothing!' said Anthea.

The third and miserablest silence of all was broken by Jane. She said: 'If we DO come out of this all right, we'll ask the Sammyadd to make it so that the servants don't notice anything different, no matter what wishes we have.'

The others only grunted. They were too wretched even to make good resolutions.

At last hunger and fright and crossness and tiredness - four very nasty things - all joined together to bring one nice thing, and that was sleep. The children lay asleep in a row, with their beautiful eyes shut and their beautiful mouths open. Anthea woke first. The sun had set, and the twilight was coming on.

Anthea pinched herself very hard, to make sure, and when she found she could still feel pinching she decided that she was not stone, and then she pinched the others. They, also, were soft.

'Wake up,' she said, almost in tears of joy; 'it's all right, we're not stone. And oh, Cyril, how nice and ugly you do look, with your old freckles and your brown hair and your little eyes. And so do you all!' she added, so that they might not feel jealous.

When they got home they were very much scolded by Martha, who told them about the strange children.

'A good-looking lot, I must say, but that impudent.'

'I know,' said Robert, who knew by experience how hopeless it would be to try to explain things to Martha.

'And where on earth have you been all this time, you naughty little things, you?'

'In the lane.'

'Why didn't you come home hours ago?'

'We couldn't because of THEM,' said Anthea.

'Who?'

'The children who were as beautiful as the day. They kept us there till after sunset. We couldn't come back till they'd gone. You don't know how we hated them! Oh, do, do give us some supper - we are so hungry.'

'Hungry! I should think so,' said Martha angrily; 'out all day like this. Well, I hope it'll be a lesson to you not to go picking up with strange children - down here after measles, as likely as not! Now mind, if you see them again, don't you speak to them - not one word nor so much as a look - but come straight away and tell me. I'll spoil their beauty for them!'

'If ever we DO see them again we'll tell you,' Anthea said; and Robert, fixing his eyes fondly on the cold beef that was being brought in on a tray by cook, added in heartfelt undertones -

'And we'll take jolly good care we never DO see them again.'

And they never have.

Chapter 2. Golden Guineas

Anthea woke in the morning from a very real sort of dream, in which she was walking in the Zoological Gardens on a pouring wet day without any umbrella. The animals seemed desperately unhappy because of the rain, and were all growling gloomily. When she awoke, both the growling and the rain went on just the same. The growling was the heavy regular breathing of her sister Jane, who had a slight cold and was still asleep. The rain fell in slow drops on to Anthea's face from the wet corner of a bath-towel which her brother Robert was gently squeezing the water out of, to wake her up, as he now explained.

'Oh, drop it!' she said rather crossly; so he did, for he was not a brutal brother, though very ingenious in apple-pie beds, booby-traps, original methods of awakening sleeping relatives, and the other little accomplishments which make home happy.

'I had such a funny dream,' Anthea began.

'So did I,' said Jane, wakening suddenly and without warning. 'I dreamed we found a Sand-fairy in the gravel-pits, and it said it was a Sammyadd, and we might have a new wish every day, and -'

'But that's what I dreamed,' said Robert. 'I was just going to tell you - and we had the first wish directly it said so. And I dreamed you girls were donkeys enough to ask for us all to be beautiful as the day, and we jolly well were, and it was perfectly beastly.'

'But CAN different people all dream the same thing?' said Anthea, sitting up in bed, 'because I dreamed all that as well as about the Zoo and the rain; and Baby didn't know us in my dream, and the servants shut us out of the house because the radiantness of our beauty was such a complete disguise, and -'

The voice of the eldest brother sounded from across the landing.

'Come on, Robert,' it said, 'you'll be late for breakfast again - unless you mean to shirk your bath like you did on Tuesday.'

'I say, come here a sec,' Robert replied. 'I didn't shirk it; I had it after brekker in father's dressing-room, because ours was emptied away.'

Cyril appeared in the doorway, partially clothed.

'Look here,' said Anthea, 'we've all had such an odd dream. We've all dreamed we found a Sand-fairy.'

Her voice died away before Cyril's contemptuous glance. 'Dream?' he said, 'you little sillies, it's TRUE. I tell you it all happened. That's why I'm so keen on being down early. We'll go up there directly after brekker, and have another wish. Only we'll make up our minds, solid, before we go, what it is we do want, and no one must ask for anything unless the others agree first. No more peerless beauties for this child, thank you. Not if I know it!'

The other three dressed, with their mouths open. If all that dream about the Sand-fairy was real, this real dressing seemed very like a dream, the girls thought. Jane felt that Cyril was right, but Anthea was not sure, till after they had seen Martha and heard her full and plain reminders about their naughty conduct the day before. Then Anthea was sure. 'Because,' said she, 'servants never dream anything but the things in the Dream-book, like snakes and oysters and going to a wedding - that means a funeral, and snakes are a false female friend, and oysters are babies.'

'Talking of babies,' said Cyril, 'where's the Lamb?' 'Martha's going to take him to Rochester to see her cousins. Mother said she might. She's dressing him now,' said Jane, 'in his very best coat and hat. Bread-and-butter, please.'

'She seems to like taking him too,' said Robert in a tone of wonder.

'Servants do like taking babies to see their relations,' Cyril said. 'I've noticed it before - especially in their best things.'

'I expect they pretend they're their own babies, and that they're not servants at all, but married to noble dukes of high degree, and they say the babies are the little dukes and duchesses,' Jane suggested dreamily, taking more marmalade. 'I expect that's what Martha'll say to her cousin. She'll enjoy herself most frightfully-'

'She won't enjoy herself most frightfully carrying our infant duke to Rochester,' said Robert, 'not if she's anything like me - she won't.'

'Fancy walking to Rochester with the Lamb on your back! Oh, crikey!' said Cyril in full agreement.

'She's going by carrier,' said Jane. 'Let's see them off, then we shall have done a polite and kindly act, and we shall be quite sure we've got rid of them for the day.'

So they did.

Martha wore her Sunday dress of two shades of purple, so tight in the chest that it made her stoop, and her blue hat with the pink cornflowers and white ribbon. She had a yellow-lace collar with a green bow. And the Lamb had indeed his very best cream-coloured silk coat and hat. It was a smart party that the carrier's cart picked up at the Cross Roads. When its white tilt and red wheels had slowly vanished in a swirl of chalk-dust -

'And now for the Sammyadd!' said Cyril, and off they went.

As they went they decided on the wish they would ask for. Although they were all in a great hurry they did not try to climb down the sides of the gravel-pit, but went round by the safe lower road, as if they had been carts. They had made a ring of stones round the place where the Sand-fairy had disappeared, so they easily found the spot. The sun was burning and bright, and the sky was deep blue - without a cloud. The sand was very hot to touch.

'Oh - suppose it was only a dream, after all,' Robert said as the boys uncovered their spades from the sand-heap where they had buried them and began to dig.

'Suppose you were a sensible chap,' said Cyril; 'one's quite as likely as the other!' 'Suppose you kept a civil tongue in your head,' Robert snapped.

'Suppose we girls take a turn,' said Jane, laughing. 'You boys seem to be getting very warm.'

'Suppose you don't come shoving your silly oar in,' said Robert, who was now warm indeed.

'We won't,' said Anthea quickly. 'Robert dear, don't be so grumpy - we won't say a word, you shall be the one to speak to the Fairy and tell him what we've decided to wish for. You'll say it much better than we shall.'

'Suppose you drop being a little humbug,' said Robert, but not crossly. 'Look out - dig with your hands, now!'

So they did, and presently uncovered the spider-shaped brown hairy body, long arms and legs, bat's ears and snail's eyes of the Sand-fairy himself. Everyone drew a deep breath of satisfaction, for now of course it couldn't have been a dream.

The Psammead sat up and shook the sand out of its fur.

'How's your left whisker this morning?' said Anthea politely.

'Nothing to boast of,' said it, 'it had rather a restless night. But thank you for asking.'

'I say,' said Robert, 'do you feel up to giving wishes to-day, because we very much want an extra besides the regular one? The extra's a very little one,' he added reassuringly.

'Humph!' said the Sand-fairy. (If you read this story aloud, please pronounce 'humph' exactly as it is spelt, for that is how he said it.) 'Humph! Do you know, until I heard you being disagreeable to each other just over my head, and so loud too, I really quite thought I had dreamed you all. I do have very odd dreams sometimes.'

'Do you?'Jane hurried to say, so as to get away from the subject of disagreeableness. 'I wish,' she added politely, 'you'd tell us about your dreams - they must be awfully interesting.'

'Is that the day's wish?' said the Sand-fairy, yawning.

Cyril muttered something about 'just like a girl,' and the rest stood silent. If they said 'Yes,' then good-bye to the other wishes they had decided to ask for. If they said 'No,' it would be very rude, and they had all been taught manners, and had learned a little too, which is not at all the same thing. A sigh of relief broke from all lips when the Sand-fairy said:

'If I do I shan't have strength to give you a second wish; not even good tempers, or common sense, or manners, or little things like that.'

'We don't want you to put yourself out at all about these things, we can manage them quite well ourselves,' said Cyril eagerly; while the others looked guiltily at each other, and wished the Fairy would not keep all on about good tempers, but give them one good rowing if it wanted to, and then have done with it.

'Well,' said the Psammead, putting out his long snail's eyes so suddenly that one of them nearly went into the round boy's eyes of Robert, 'let's have the little wish first.'

'We don't want the servants to notice the gifts you give us.'

'Are kind enough to give us,' said Anthea in a whisper.

'Are kind enough to give us, I mean,' said Robert.

The Fairy swelled himself out a bit, let his breath go, and said -

'I've done THAT for you - it was quite easy. People don't notice things much, anyway. What's the next wish?'

'We want,' said Robert slowly, 'to be rich beyond the dreams of something or other.'

'Avarice,' said Jane.

'So it is,' said the Fairy unexpectedly. 'But it won't do you much good, that's one comfort,' it muttered to itself. 'Come - I can't go beyond dreams, you know! How much do you want, and will you have it in gold or notes?'

'Gold, please - and millions of it.'

'This gravel-pit full be enough?' said the Fairy in an off-hand manner.

'Oh YES!'

'Then get out before I begin, or you'll be buried alive in it.'

It made its skinny arms so long, and waved them so frighteningly, that the children ran as hard as they could towards the road by which carts used to come to the gravel-pits. Only Anthea had presence of mind enough to shout a timid 'Good-morning, I hope your whisker will be better to-morrow,' as she ran.

On the road they turned and looked back, and they had to shut their eyes, and open them very slowly, a little bit at a time, because the sight was too dazzling for their eyes to be able to bear it. It was something like trying to look at the sun at high noon on Midsummer Day. For the whole of the sand-pit was full, right up to the very top, with new shining gold pieces, and all the little sand-martins' little front doors were covered out of sight. Where the road for the carts wound into the gravel-pit the gold lay in heaps like stones lie by the roadside, and a great bank of shining gold shelved down from where it lay flat and smooth between the tall sides of the gravel-pit. And all the gleaming heap was minted gold. And on the sides and edges of these countless coins the midday sun shone and sparkled, and glowed and gleamed till the quarry looked like the mouth of a smelting furnace, or one of the fairy halls that you see sometimes in the sky at sunset.

The children stood with their mouths open, and no one said a word.

At last Robert stopped and picked up one of the loose coins from the edge of the heap by the cart-road, and looked at it. He looked on both sides. Then he said in a low voice, quite different to his own, 'It's not sovereigns.'

'It's gold, anyway,' said Cyril. And now they all began to talk at once. They all picked up the golden treasure by handfuls, and let it run through their fingers like water, and the chink it made as it fell was wonderful music. At first they quite forgot to think of spending the money, it was so nice to play with. Jane sat down between two heaps of gold and Robert began to bury her, as you bury your father in sand when you are at the seaside and he has gone to sleep on the beach with his newspaper over his face. But Jane was not half buried before she cried out, 'Oh, stop, it's too heavy! It hurts!

Robert said 'Bosh!' and went on.

'Let me out, I tell you,' cried Jane, and was taken out, very white, and trembling a little.

'You've no idea what it's like,' said she; 'it's like stones on you - or like chains.'

'Look here,' Cyril said, 'if this is to do us any good, it's no good our staying gasping at it like this. Let's fill our pockets and go and buy things. Don't you forget, it won't last after sunset. I wish we'd asked the Sammyadd why things don't turn to stone. Perhaps this will. I'll tell you what, there's a pony and cart in the village.'

'Do you want to buy that?' asked Jane.

'No, silly - we'll HIRE it. And then we'll go to Rochester and buy heaps and heaps of things. Look here, let's each take as much as we can carry. But it's not sovereigns. They've got a man's head on one side and a thing like the ace of spades on the other. Fill your pockets with it, I tell you, and come along. You can jaw as we go - if you must jaw.'

Cyril sat down and began to fill his pockets. 'You made fun of me for getting father to have nine pockets in my Norfolks,' said he, 'but now you see!'

They did. For when Cyril had filled his nine pockets and his handkerchief and the space between himself and his shirt front with the gold coins, he had to stand up. But he staggered, and had to sit down again in a hurry-

'Throw out some of the cargo,' said Robert. 'You'll sink the ship, old chap. That comes of nine pockets.'

And Cyril had to.

Then they set off to walk to the village. It was more than a mile, and the road was very dusty indeed, and the sun seemed to get hotter and hotter, and the gold in their pockets got heavier and heavier.

It was Jane who said, 'I don't see how we're to spend it all. There must be thousands of pounds among the lot of us. I'm going to leave some of mine behind this stump in the hedge. And directly we get to the village we'll buy some biscuits; I know it's long past dinner-time.' She took out a handful or two of gold and hid it in the hollows of an old hornbeam. 'How round and yellow they are,' she said. 'Don't you wish they were gingerbread nuts and we were going to eat them?'

'Well, they're not, and we're not,' said Cyril. 'Come on!'

But they came on heavily and wearily. Before they reached the village, more than one stump in the hedge concealed its little hoard of hidden treasure. Yet they reached the village with about twelve hundred guineas in their pockets. But in spite of this inside wealth they looked quite ordinary outside, and no one would have thought they could have more than a half-crown each at the outside. The haze of heat, the blue of the wood smoke, made a sort of dim misty cloud over the red roofs of the village. The four sat down heavily on the first bench they came to- It happened to be outside the Blue Boar Inn.

It was decided that Cyril should go into the Blue Boar and ask for ginger-beer, because, as Anthea said, 'It is not wrong for men to go into public houses, only for children. And Cyril is nearer to being a man than us, because he is the eldest.' So he went. The others sat in the sun and waited.

'Oh, hats, how hot it is!' said Robert. 'Dogs put their tongues out when they're hot; I wonder if it would cool us at all to put out ours?'

'We might try,'Jane said; and they all put their tongues out as far as ever they could go, so that it quite stretched their throats, but it only seemed to make them thirstier than ever, besides annoying everyone who went by. So they took their tongues in again, just as Cyril came back with the ginger-beer.

'I had to pay for it out of my own two-and-sevenpence, though, that I was going to buy rabbits with,' he said. 'They wouldn't change the gold. And when I pulled out a handful the man just laughed and said it was card-counters. And I got some sponge-cakes too, out of a glass jar on the bar-counter. And some biscuits with caraways in.'

The sponge-cakes were both soft and dry and the biscuits were dry too, and yet soft, which biscuits ought not to be. But the ginger-beer made up for everything.

'It's my turn now to try to buy something with the money,' Anthea said, 'I'm next eldest. Where is the pony-cart kept?'

It was at The Chequers, and Anthea went in the back way to the yard, because they all knew that little girls ought not to go into the bars of public-houses. She came out, as she herself said, 'pleased but not proud'.

'He'll be ready in a brace of shakes, he says,' she remarked, 'and he's to have one sovereign - or whatever it is - to drive us in to Rochester and back, besides waiting there till we've got everything we want. I think I managed very well.'

'You think yourself jolly clever, I daresay,' said Cyril moodily. 'How did you do it?'

'I wasn't jolly clever enough to go taking handfuls of money out of my pocket, to make it seem cheap, anyway,' she retorted. 'I just found a young man doing something to a horse's leg with a sponge and a pail. And I held out one sovereign, and I said, "Do you know what this is?" He said, "No," and he'd call his father. And the old man came, and he said it was a spade guinea; and he said was it my own to do as I liked with, and I said "Yes"; and I asked about the pony-cart, and I said he could have the guinea if he'd drive us in to Rochester. And his name is S. Crispin. And he said, "Right oh".'

It was a new sensation to be driven in a smart pony-trap along pretty country roads, it was very pleasant too (which is not always the case with new sensations), quite apart from the beautiful plans of spending the money which each child made as they went along, silently of course and quite to itself, for they felt it would never have done to let the old innkeeper hear them talk in the affluent sort of way they were thinking. The old man put them down by the bridge at their request.

'If you were going to buy a carriage and horses, where would you go?' asked Cyril, as if he were only asking for the sake of something to say.

'Billy Peasemarsh, at the Saracen's Head,' said the old man promptly. 'Though all forbid I should recommend any man where it's a question of horses, no more than I'd take anybody else's recommending if I was a-buying one. But if your pa's thinking of a turnout of any sort, there ain't a straighter man in Rochester, nor a civiller spoken, than Billy, though I says it.'

'Thank you,' said Cyril. 'The Saracen's Head.'

And now the children began to see one of the laws of nature turn upside down and stand on its head like an acrobat. Any grown-up persons would tell you that money is hard to get and easy to spend. But the fairy money had been easy to get, and spending it was not only hard, it was almost impossible. The tradespeople of Rochester seemed to shrink, to a trades-person, from the glittering fairy gold ('furrin money' they called it, for the most part). To begin with, Anthea, who had had the misfortune to sit on her hat earlier in the day, wished to buy another. She chose a very beautiful one, trimmed with pink roses and the blue breasts of peacocks. It was marked in the window, 'Paris Model, three guineas'.

'I'm glad,' she said, 'because, if it says guineas, it means guineas, and not sovereigns, which we haven't got.'

But when she took three of the spade guineas in her hand, which was by this time rather dirty owing to her not having put on gloves before going to the gravel-pit, the black-silk young lady in the shop looked very hard at her, and went and whispered something to an older and uglier lady, also in black silk, and then they gave her back the money and said it was not current coin.

'It's good money,' said Anthea, 'and it's my own.'

'I daresay,' said the lady, 'but it's not the kind of money that's fashionable now, and we don't care about taking it.'

'I believe they think we've stolen it,' said Anthea, rejoining the others in the street; 'if we had gloves they wouldn't think we were so dishonest. It's my hands being so dirty fills their minds with doubts.'

So they chose a humble shop, and the girls bought cotton gloves, the kind at sixpence three-farthings, but when they offered a guinea the woman looked at it through her spectacles and said she had no change; so the gloves had to be paid for out of Cyril's two-and-sevenpence that he meant to buy rabbits with, and so had the green imitation crocodile-skin purse at ninepence-halfpenny which had been bought at the same time. They tried several more shops, the kinds where you buy toys and scent, and silk handkerchiefs and books, and fancy boxes of stationery, and photographs of objects of interest in the vicinity. But nobody cared to change a guinea that day in Rochester, and as they went from shop to shop they got dirtier and dirtier, and their hair got more and more untidy, and Jane slipped and fell down on a part of the road where a water-cart had just gone by. Also they got very hungry, but they found no one would give them anything to eat for their guineas. After trying two pastrycooks in vain, they became so hungry, perhaps from the smell of the cake in the shops, as Cyril suggested, that they formed a plan of campaign in whispers and carried it out in desperation. They marched into a third pastrycook's - Beale his name was - and before the people behind the counter could interfere each child had seized three new penny buns, clapped the three together between its dirty hands, and taken a big bite out of the triple sandwich. Then they stood at bay, with the twelve buns in their hands and their mouths very full indeed. The shocked pastrycook bounded round the corner.

'Here,' said Cyril, speaking as distinctly as he could, and holding out the guinea he got ready before entering the shop, 'pay yourself out of that.'

Mr Beale snatched the coin, bit it, and put it in his pocket.

'Off you go,' he said, brief and stern like the man in the song.

'But the change?' said Anthea, who had a saving mind.

'Change!' said the man. 'I'll change you! Hout you goes; and you may think yourselves lucky I don't send for the police to find out where you got it!'

In the Castle Gardens the millionaires finished the buns, and though the curranty softness of these were delicious, and acted like a charm in raising the spirits of the party, yet even the stoutest heart quailed at the thought of venturing to sound Mr Billy Peasemarsh at the Saracen's Head on the subject of a horse and carriage. The boys would have given up the idea, but Jane was always a hopeful child, and Anthea generally an obstinate one, and their earnestness prevailed.

The whole party, by this time indescribably dirty, therefore betook itself to the Saracen's Head. The yard-method of attack having been successful at The Chequers was tried again here. Mr Peasemarsh was in the yard, and Robert opened the business in these terms -

'They tell me you have a lot of horses and carriages to sell.' It had been agreed that Robert should be spokesman, because in books it is always the gentlemen who buy horses, and not ladies, and Cyril had had his go at the Blue Boar.

'They tell you true, young man,' said Mr Peasemarsh. He was a long lean man, with very blue eyes and a tight mouth and narrow lips.

'We should like to buy some, please,' said Robert politely.

'I daresay you would.'

'Will you show us a few, please? To choose from.' 'Who are you a-kiddin of?' inquired Mr Billy Peasemarsh. 'Was you sent here of a message?'

'I tell you,' said Robert, 'we want to buy some horses and carriages, and a man told us you were straight and civil spoken, but I shouldn't wonder if he was mistaken.'

'Upon my sacred!' said Mr Peasemarsh. 'Shall I trot the whole stable out for your Honour's worship to see? Or shall I send round to the Bishop's to see if he's a nag or two to dispose of?'

'Please do,' said Robert, 'if it's not too much trouble. It would be very kind of you.'

Mr Peasemarsh put his hands in his pockets and laughed, and they did not like the way he did it. Then he shouted 'Willum!'

A stooping ostler appeared in a stable door.

'Here, Willum, come and look at this 'ere young dook! Wants to buy the whole stud, lock, stock, and bar'l. And ain't got tuppence in his pocket to bless hisself with, I'll go bail!'

Willum's eyes followed his master's pointing thumb with contemptuous interest.

'Do 'e, for sure?' he said.

But Robert spoke, though both the girls were now pulling at his jacket and begging him to 'come along'. He spoke, and he was very angry; he said:

'I'm not a young duke, and I never pretended to be. And as for tuppence - what do you call this?' And before the others could stop him he had pulled out two fat handfuls of shining guineas, and held them out for Mr Peasemarsh to look at. He did look. He snatched one up in his finger and thumb. He bit it, and Jane expected him to say, 'The best horse in my stables is at your service.' But the others knew better. Still it was a blow, even to the most desponding, when he said shortly:

'Willum, shut the yard doors,' and Willum grinned and went to shut them.

'Good-afternoon,' said Robert hastily; 'we shan't buy any of your horses now, whatever you say, and I hope it'll be a lesson to you.' He had seen a little side gate open, and was moving towards it as he spoke. But Billy Peasemarsh put himself in the way.

'Not so fast, you young off-scouring!' he said. 'Willum, fetch the pleece.'

Willum went. The children stood huddled together like frightened sheep, and Mr Peasemarsh spoke to them till the pleece arrived. He said many things. Among other things he said:

'Nice lot you are, aren't you, coming tempting honest men with your guineas!'

'They ARE our guineas,' said Cyril boldly.

'Oh, of course we don't know all about that, no more we don't - oh no - course not! And dragging little gells into it, too. 'Ere - I'll let the gells go if you'll come along to the pleece quiet.'

'We won't be let go,' said Jane heroically; 'not without the boys. It's our money just as much as theirs, you wicked old man.'

'Where'd you get it, then?' said the man, softening slightly, which was not at all what the boys expected when Jane began to call names.

Jane cast a silent glance of agony at the others.

'Lost your tongue, eh? Got it fast enough when it's for calling names with. Come, speak up! Where'd you get it?'

'Out of the gravel-pit,' said truthful Jane.

'Next article,' said the man.

'I tell you we did,' Jane said. 'There's a fairy there - all over brown fur - with ears like a bat's and eyes like a snail's, and he gives you a wish a day, and they all come true.'

'Touched in the head, eh?' said the man in a low voice, 'all the more shame to you boys dragging the poor afflicted child into your sinful burglaries.'

'She's not mad; it's true,' said Anthea; 'there is a fairy. If I ever see him again I'll wish for something for you; at least I would if vengeance wasn't wicked - so there!'

'Lor' lumme,' said Billy Peasemarsh, 'if there ain't another on 'em!'

And now Willum came -back with a spiteful grin on his face, and at his back a policeman, with whom Mr Peasemarsh spoke long in a hoarse earnest whisper.

'I daresay you're right,' said the policeman at last. 'Anyway, I'll take 'em up on a charge of unlawful possession, pending inquiries. And the magistrate will deal with the case. Send the afflicted ones to a home, as likely as not, and the boys to a reformatory. Now then, come along, youngsters! No use making a fuss. You bring the gells along, Mr Peasemarsh, sir, and I'll shepherd the boys.'

Speechless with rage and horror, the four children were driven along the streets of Rochester. Tears of anger and shame blinded them, so that when Robert ran right into a passer-by he did not recognize her till a well—known voice said, 'Well, if ever I did! Oh, Master Robert, whatever have you been a doing of now?' And another voice, quite as well known, said, 'Panty; want go own Panty!'

They had run into Martha and the baby!

Martha behaved admirably. She refused to believe a word of the policeman's story, or of Mr Peasemarsh's either, even when they made Robert turn out his pockets in an archway and show the guineas.

'I don't see nothing,' she said. 'You've gone out of your senses, you two! There ain't any gold there - only the poor child's hands, all over crock and dirt, and like the very chimbley. Oh, that I should ever see the day!'

And the children thought this very noble of Martha, even if rather wicked, till they remembered how the Fairy had promised that the servants should never notice any of the fairy gifts. So of course Martha couldn't see the gold, and so was only speaking the truth, and that was quite right, of course, but not extra noble.

It was getting dusk when they reached the police-station. The policeman told his tale to an inspector, who sat in a large bare room with a thing like a clumsy nursery-fender at one end to put prisoners in. Robert wondered whether it was a cell or a dock.

'Produce the coins, officer,' said the inspector.

'Turn out your pockets,' said the constable.

Cyril desperately plunged his hands in his pockets, stood still a moment, and then began to laugh - an odd sort of laugh that hurt, and that felt much more like crying. His pockets were empty. So were the pockets of the others. For of course at sunset all the fairy gold had vanished away.

'Turn out your pockets, and stop that noise,' said the inspector.

Cyril turned out his pockets, every one of the nine which enriched his Norfolk suit. And every pocket was empty.

'Well!' said the inspector.

'I don't know how they done it - artful little beggars! They walked in front of me the 'ole way, so as for me to keep my eye on them and not to attract a crowd and obstruct the traffic.'

'It's very remarkable,' said the inspector, frowning.

'If you've quite done a-browbeating of the innocent children,' said Martha, 'I'll hire a private carriage and we'll drive home to their papa's mansion. You'll hear about this again, young man! - I told you they hadn't got any gold, when you were pretending to see it in their poor helpless hands. It's early in the day for a constable on duty not to be able to trust his own eyes. As to the other one, the less said the better; he keeps the Saracen's Head, and he knows best what his liquor's like.'

'Take them away, for goodness' sake,' said the inspector crossly. But as they left the police-station he said, 'Now then!' to the policeman and Mr Pease- marsh, and he said it twenty times as crossly as he had spoken to Martha.

Martha was as good as her word. She took them home in a very grand carriage, because the carrier's cart was gone, and, though she had stood by them so nobly with the police, she was so angry with them as soon as they were alone for 'trapseing into Rochester by themselves', that none of them dared to mention the old man with the pony-cart from the village who was waiting for them in Rochester. And so, after one day of boundless wealth, the children found themselves sent to bed in deep disgrace, and only enriched by two pairs of cotton gloves, dirty inside because of the state of the hands they had been put on to cover, an imitation crocodile-skin purse, and twelve penny buns long since digested.

The thing that troubled them most was the fear that the old gentleman's guinea might have disappeared at sunset with all the rest, so they went down to the village next day to apologize for not meeting him in Rochester, and to see. They found him very friendly. The guinea had NOT disappeared, and he had bored a hole in it and hung it on his watch-chain. As for the guinea the baker took, the children felt they could not care whether it had vanished or not, which was not perhaps very honest, but on the other hand was not wholly unnatural. But afterwards this preyed on Anthea's mind, and at last she secretly sent twelve stamps by post to 'Mr Beale, Baker, Rochester'. Inside she wrote, 'To pay for the buns.' I hope the guinea did disappear, for that pastrycook was really not at all a nice man, and, besides, penny buns are seven for sixpence in all really respectable shops.

Chapter 3. Being Wanted

The morning after the children had been the possessors of boundless wealth, and had been unable to buy anything really useful or enjoyable with it, except two pairs of cotton gloves, twelve penny buns, an imitation crocodile-skin purse, and a ride in a pony-cart, they awoke without any of the enthusiastic happiness which they had felt on the previous day when they remembered how they had had the luck to find a Psammead, or Sand-fairy; and to receive its promise to grant them a new wish every day. For now they had had two wishes, Beauty and Wealth, and neither had exactly made them happy. But the happening of strange things, even if they are not completely pleasant things, is more amusing than those times when nothing happens but meals, and they are not always completely pleasant, especially on the days when it is cold mutton or hash.

There was no chance of talking things over before breakfast, because everyone overslept itself, as it happened, and it needed a vigorous and determined struggle to get dressed so as to be only ten minutes late for breakfast. During this meal some efforts were made to deal with the question of the Psammead in an impartial spirit, but it is very difficult to discuss anything thoroughly and at the same time to attend faithfully to your baby brother's breakfast needs. The Baby was particularly lively that morning. He not only wriggled his body through the bar of his high chair, and hung by his head, choking and purple, but he collared a tablespoon with desperate suddenness, hit Cyril heavily on the head with it, and then cried because it was taken away from him. He put his fat fist in his bread-and-milk, and demanded 'nam', which was only allowed for tea. He sang, he put his feet on the table - he clamoured to 'go walky'. The conversation was something like this:

'Look here - about that Sand-fairy - Look out! - he'll have the milk over.'

Milk removed to a safe distance.

'Yes - about that Fairy - No, Lamb dear, give Panther the narky poon.'

Then Cyril tried. 'Nothing we've had yet has turned out - He nearly had the mustard that time!'

'I wonder whether we'd better wish - Hullo! you've done it now, my boy!' And, in a flash of glass and pink baby-paws, the bowl of golden carp in the middle of the table rolled on its side, and poured a flood of mixed water and goldfish into the Baby's lap and into the laps of the others.

Everyone was almost as much upset as the goldfish: the Lamb only remaining calm. When the pool on the floor had been mopped up, and the leaping, gasping goldfish had been collected and put back in the water, the Baby was taken away to be entirely redressed by Martha, and most of the others had to change completely. The pinafores and jackets that had been bathed in goldfish-and-water were hung out to dry, and then it turned out that Jane must either mend the dress she had torn the day before or appear all day in her best petticoat. It was white and soft and frilly, and trimmed with lace, and very, very pretty, quite as pretty as a frock, if not more so. Only it was NOT a frock, and Martha's word was law. She wouldn't let Jane wear her best frock, and she refused to listen for a moment to Robert's suggestion that Jane should wear her best petticoat and call it a dress.

'It's not respectable,' she said. And when people say that, it's no use anyone's saying anything. You will find this out for yourselves some day.

So there was nothing for it but for Jane to mend her frock. The hole had been torn the day before when she happened to tumble down in the High Street of Rochester, just where a water-cart had passed on its silvery way. She had grazed her knee, and her stocking was much more than grazed, and her dress was cut by the same stone which had attended to the knee and the stocking. Of course the others were not such sneaks as to abandon a comrade in misfortune, so they all sat on the grass-plot round the sundial, and Jane darned away for dear life. The Lamb was still in the hands of Martha having its clothes changed, so conversation was possible.

Anthea and Robert timidly tried to conceal their inmost thought, which was that the Psammead was not to be trusted; but Cyril said:

'Speak out - say what you've got to say - I hate hinting, and "don't know", and sneakish ways like that.'

So then Robert said, as in honour bound: 'Sneak yourself - Anthea and me weren't so goldfishy as you two were, so we got changed quicker, and we've had time to think it over, and if you ask me -'

'I didn't ask you,' said Jane, biting off a needleful of thread as she had always been strictly forbidden to do.

'I don't care who asks or who doesn't,' said Robert, but Anthea and I think the Sammyadd is a spiteful brute. If it can give us our wishes I suppose it can give itself its own, and I feel almost sure it wishes every time that our wishes shan't do us any good. Let's let the tiresome beast alone, and just go and have a jolly good game of forts, on our own, in the chalk-pit.'

(You will remember that the happily situated house where these children were spending their holidays lay between a chalk-quarry and a gravel-pit.)

Cyril and Jane were more hopeful - they generally were.

'I don't think the Sammyadd does it on purpose,' Cyril said; 'and, after all, it WAS silly to wish for boundless wealth. Fifty pounds in two-shilling pieces would have been much more sensible. And wishing to be beautiful as the day was simply donkeyish. I don't want to be disagreeable, but it was. We must try to find a really useful wish, and wish it.'

Jane dropped her work and said:

'I think so too, it's too silly to have a chance like this and not use it. I never heard of anyone else outside a book who had such a chance; there must be simply heaps of things we could wish for that wouldn't turn out Dead Sea fish, like these two things have. Do let's think hard, and wish something nice, so that we can have a real jolly day - what there is left of it.'

Jane darned away again like mad, for time was indeed getting on, and everyone began to talk at once. If you had been there you could not possibly have made head or tail of the talk, but these children were used to talking 'by fours', as soldiers march, and each of them could say what it had to say quite comfortably, and listen to the agreeable sound of its own voice, and at the same time have three-quarters of two sharp ears to spare for listening to what the others said. That is an easy example in multiplication of vulgar fractions, but, as I daresay you can't do even that, I won't ask you to tell me whether $3/4 \times 2 = 1\ 1/2$, but I will ask you to believe me that this was the amount of ear each child was able to lend to the others. Lending ears was common in Roman times, as we learn from Shakespeare; but I fear I am getting too instructive.

When the frock was darned, the start for the gravel-pit was delayed by Martha's insisting on everybody's washing its hands - which was nonsense, because nobody had been doing anything at all, except Jane, and how can you get dirty doing nothing? That is a difficult question, and I cannot answer it on paper. In real life I could very soon show you - or you me, which is much more likely.

During the conversation in which the six ears were lent (there were four children, so THAT sum comes right), it had been decided that fifty pounds in two-shilling pieces was the right wish to have. And the lucky children, who could have anything in the wide world by just wishing for it, hurriedly started for the gravel-pit to express their wishes to the Psammead. Martha caught them at the gate, and insisted on their taking the Baby with them.

'Not want him indeed! Why, everybody 'ud want him, a duck! with all their hearts they would; and you know you promised your ma to take him out every blessed day,' said Martha.

'I know we did,' said Robert in gloom, 'but I wish the Lamb wasn't quite so young and small. It would be much better fun taking him out.'

'He'll mend of his youngness with time,' said Martha; 'and as for his smallness, I don't think you'd fancy carrying of him any more, however big he was. Besides he can walk a bit, bless his precious fat legs, a ducky! He feels the benefit of the new-laid air, so he does, a pet!' With this and a kiss, she plumped the Lamb into Anthea's arms, and went back to make new pinafores on the sewing-machine. She was a rapid performer on this instrument.

The Lamb laughed with pleasure, and said, 'Walky wif Panty,' and rode on Robert's back with yells of joy, and tried to feed Jane with stones, and altogether made himself so agreeable that nobody could long be sorry that he was of the party.

The enthusiastic Jane even suggested that they should devote a week's wishes to assuring the Baby's future, by asking such gifts for him as the good fairies give to Infant Princes in proper fairy-tales, but Anthea soberly reminded her that as the Sand-fairy's wishes only lasted till sunset they could not ensure any benefit to the Baby's later years; and Jane owned that it would be better to wish for fifty pounds in two-shilling pieces, and buy the Lamb a three-pound-fifteen rocking-horse, like those in the Army and Navy Stores list, with part of the money.

It was settled that, as soon as they had wished for the money and got it, they would get Mr Crispin to drive them into Rochester again, taking Martha with them, if they could not get out of taking her. And they would make a list of the things they really wanted before they started. Full of high hopes and excellent resolutions, they went round the safe slow cart-road to the gravel-pits, and as they went in between the mounds of gravel a sudden thought came to them, and would have turned their ruddy cheeks pale if they had been children in a book. Being real live children, it only made them stop and look at each other with rather blank and silly expressions. For now they remembered that yesterday, when they had asked the Psammead for boundless wealth, and it was getting ready to fill the quarry with the minted gold of bright guineas - millions of them - it had told the children to run along outside the quarry for fear they should be buried alive in the heavy splendid treasure. And they had run. And so it happened that they had not had time to mark the spot where the Psammead was, with a ring of stones, as before. And it was this thought that put such silly expressions on their faces.

'Never mind,' said the hopeful Jane, 'we'll soon find him.'

But this, though easily said, was hard in the doing. They looked and they looked, and though they found their seaside spades, nowhere could they find the Sand-fairy.

At last they had to sit down and rest - not at all because they were weary or disheartened, of course, but because the Lamb insisted on being put down, and you cannot look very carefully after anything you may have happened to lose in the sand if you have an active baby to look after at the same time. Get someone to drop your best knife in the sand next time you go to the seaside, and then take your baby brother with you when you go to look for it, and you will see that I am right.

The Lamb, as Martha had said, was feeling the benefit of the country air, and he was as frisky as a sandhopper. The elder ones longed to go on talking about the new wishes they would have when (or if) they found the Psammead again. But the Lamb wished to enjoy himself.

He watched his opportunity and threw a handful of sand into Anthea's face, and then suddenly burrowed his own head in the sand and waved his fat legs in the air. Then of course the sand got into his eyes, as it had into Anthea's, and he howled.

The thoughtful Robert had brought one solid brown bottle of ginger-beer with him, relying on a thirst that had never yet failed him. This had to be uncorked hurriedly - it was the only wet thing within reach, and it was necessary to wash the sand out of the Lamb's eyes somehow. Of course the ginger hurt horribly, and he howled more than ever. And, amid his anguish of kicking, the bottle was upset and the beautiful ginger-beer frothed out into the sand and was lost for ever.

It was then that Robert, usually a very patient brother, so far forgot himself as to say:

'Anybody would want him, indeed! Only they don't; Martha doesn't, not really, or she'd jolly well keep him with her. He's a little nuisance, that's what he is. It's too bad. I only wish everybody DID want him with all their hearts; we might get some peace in our lives.'

The Lamb stopped howling now, because Jane had suddenly remembered that there is only one safe way of taking things out of little children's eyes, and that is with your own soft wet tongue. It is quite easy if you love the Baby as much as you ought to.

Then there was a little silence. Robert was not proud of himself for having been so cross, and the others were not proud of him either. You often notice that sort of silence when someone has said something it ought not to - and everyone else holds its tongue and waits for the one who oughtn't to have said it is sorry.

The silence was broken by a sigh - a breath suddenly let out. The children's heads turned as if there had been a string tied to each nose, and someone had pulled all the strings at once.

And everyone saw the Sand-fairy sitting quite close to them, with the expression which it used as a smile on its hairy face.

'Good-morning,' it said; 'I did that quite easily! Everyone wants him now.'

'It doesn't matter,' said Robert sulkily, because he knew he had been behaving rather like a pig. 'No matter who wants him - there's no one here to - anyhow.'

'Ingratitude,' said the Psammead, 'is a dreadful vice.'

'We're not ungrateful,'Jane made haste to say, 'but we didn't REALLY want that wish. Robert only just said it. Can't you take it back and give us a new one?'

'No - I can't,' the Sand-fairy said shortly; 'chopping and changing - it's not business. You ought to be careful what you do wish. There was a little boy once, he'd wished for a Plesiosaurus instead of an Ichthyosaurus, because he was too lazy to remember the easy names of everyday things, and his father had been very vexed with him, and had made him go to bed before tea-time, and wouldn't let him go out in the nice flint boat along with the other children - it was the annual school-treat next day - and he came and flung himself down near me on the morning of the treat, and he kicked his little prehistoric legs about and said he wished he was dead. And of course then he was.'

'How awful!' said the children all together.

'Only till sunset, of course,' the Psammead said; 'still it was quite enough for his father and mother. And he caught it when he woke up - I can tell you. He didn't turn to stone - I forget why - but there must have been some reason. They didn't know being dead is only being asleep, and you're bound to wake up somewhere or other, either where you go to sleep or in some better place. You may be sure he caught it, giving them such a turn. Why, he wasn't allowed to taste Megatherium for a month after that. Nothing but oysters and periwinkles, and common things like that.'

All the children were quite crushed by this terrible tale. They looked at the Psammead in horror. Suddenly the Lamb perceived that something brown and furry was near him.

'Poof, poof, poofy,' he said, and made a grab.

'It's not a pussy,' Anthea was beginning, when the Sand-fairy leaped back.

'Oh, my left whisker!' it said; 'don't let him touch me. He's wet.'

Its fur stood on end with horror - and indeed a good deal of the ginger-beer had been spilt on the blue smock of the Lamb.

The Psammead dug with its hands and feet, and vanished in an instant and a whirl of sand.

The children marked the spot with a ring of stones.

'We may as well get along home,' said Robert. 'I'll say I'm sorry; but anyway if it's no good it's no harm, and we know where the sandy thing is for to-morrow.'

The others were noble. No one reproached Robert at all. Cyril picked up the Lamb, who was now quite himself again, and off they went by the safe cart-road.

The cart-road from the gravel-pits joins the road almost directly.

At the gate into the road the party stopped to shift the Lamb from Cyril's back to Robert's. And as they paused a very smart open carriage came in sight, with a coachman and a groom on the box, and inside the carriage a lady - very grand indeed, with a dress all white lace and red ribbons and a parasol all red and white - and a white fluffy dog on her lap with a red ribbon round its neck. She looked at the children, and particularly at the Baby, and she smiled at him. The children were used to this, for the Lamb was, as all the servants said, a 'very taking child'. So they waved their hands politely to the lady and expected her to drive on. But she did not. Instead she made the coachman stop. And she beckoned to Cyril, and when he went up to the carriage she said:

'What a dear darling duck of a baby! Oh, I SHOULD so like to adopt it! Do you think its mother would mind?'

'She'd mind very much indeed,' said Anthea shortly.

'Oh, but I should bring it up in luxury, you know. I am Lady Chittenden. You must have seen my photograph in the illustrated papers. They call me a beauty, you know, but of course that's all nonsense. Anyway -'

She opened the carriage door and jumped out. She had the wonderfullest red high-heeled shoes with silver buckles. 'Let me hold him a minute,' she said. And she took the Lamb and held him very awkwardly, as if she was not used to babies.

Then suddenly she jumped into the carriage with the Lamb in her arms and slammed the door and said, 'Drive on!'

The Lamb roared, the little white dog barked, and the coachman hesitated.

'Drive on, I tell you!' cried the lady; and the coachman did, for, as he said afterwards, it was as much as his place was worth not to.

The four children looked at each other, and then with one accord they rushed after the carriage and held on behind. Down the dusty road went the smart carriage, and after it, at double-quick time, ran the twinkling legs of the Lamb's brothers and sisters.

The Lamb howled louder and louder, but presently his howls changed by slow degree to hiccupy gurgles, and then all was still and they knew he had gone to sleep.

The carriage went on, and the eight feet that twinkled through the dust were growing quite stiff and tired before the carriage stopped at the lodge of a grand park. The children crouched down behind the carriage, and the lady got out. She looked at the Baby as it lay on the carriage seat, and hesitated.

'The darling - I won't disturb it,' she said, and went into the lodge to talk to the woman there about a setting of Buff Orpington eggs that had not turned out well.

The coachman and footman sprang from the box and bent over the sleeping Lamb.

'Fine boy - wish he was mine,' said the coachman.

'He wouldn't favour YOU much,' said the groom sourly; 'too 'andsome.'

The coachman pretended not to hear. He said:

'Wonder at her now - I do really! Hates kids. Got none of her own, and can't abide other folkses'.'

The children, crouching in the white dust under the carriage, exchanged uncomfortable glances.

'Tell you what,' the coachman went on firmly, 'blowed if I don't hide the little nipper in the hedge and tell her his brothers took 'im! Then I'll come back for him afterwards.'

'No, you don't,' said the footman. 'I've took to that kid so as never was. If anyone's to have him, it's me - so there!'

'Stow your gab!' the coachman rejoined. 'You don't want no kids, and, if you did, one kid's the same as another to you. But I'm a married man and a judge of breed. I knows a first-rate yearling when I sees him. I'm a-goin' to 'ave him, an' least said soonest mended.'

'I should 'a' thought,' said the footman sneeringly, you'd a'most enough. What with Alfred, an' Albert, an' Louise, an' Victor Stanley, and Helena Beatrice, and another -'

The coachman hit the footman in the chin - the foot- man hit the coachman in the waistcoat - the next minute the two were fighting here and there, in and out, up and down, and all over everywhere, and the little dog jumped on the box of the carriage and began barking like mad.

Cyril, still crouching in the dust, waddled on bent legs to the side of the carriage farthest from the battlefield. He unfastened the door of the carriage - the two men were far too much occupied with their quarrel to notice anything - took the Lamb in his arms, and, still stooping, carried the sleeping baby a dozen yards along the road to where a stile led into a wood. The others followed, and there among the hazels and young oaks and sweet chestnuts, covered by high strong-scented bracken, they all lay hidden till the angry voices of the men were hushed at the angry voice of the red-and-white lady, and, after a long and anxious search, the carriage at last drove away.

'My only hat!' said Cyril, drawing a deep breath as the sound of wheels at last died away. 'Everyone DOES want him now - and no mistake! That Sammyadd has done us again! Tricky brute! For any sake, let's get the kid safe home.'

So they peeped out, and finding on the right hand only lonely white road, and nothing but lonely white road on the left, they took courage, and the road, Anthea carrying the sleeping Lamb.

Adventures dogged their footsteps. A boy with a bundle of faggots on his back dropped his bundle by the roadside and asked to look at the Baby, and then offered to carry him; but Anthea was not to be caught that way twice. They all walked on, but the boy followed, and Cyril and Robert couldn't make him go away till they had more than once invited him to smell their fists. Afterwards a little girl in a blue-and-white checked pinafore actually followed them for a quarter of a mile crying for 'the precious Baby', and then she was only got rid of by threats of tying her to a tree in the wood with all their pocket-handkerchiefs. 'So that the bears can come and eat you as soon as it gets dark,' said Cyril severely. Then she went off crying. It presently seemed wise, to the brothers and sisters of the Baby, who was wanted by everyone, to hide in the hedge whenever they saw anyone coming, and thus they managed to prevent the Lamb from arousing the inconvenient affection of a milkman, a stone-breaker, and a man who drove a cart with a paraffin barrel at the back of it. They were nearly home when the worst thing of all happened. Turning a corner suddenly they came upon two vans, a tent, and a company of gipsies encamped by the side of the road. The vans were hung all round with wicker chairs and cradles, and flower-stands and feather brushes. A lot of ragged children were industriously making dust-pies in the road, two men lay on the grass smoking, and three women were doing the family washing in an old red watering-can with the top broken off.

In a moment all the gipsies, men, women, and children, surrounded Anthea and the Baby.

'Let me hold him, little lady,' said one of the gipsy women, who had a mahogany-coloured face and dust-coloured hair; 'I won't hurt a hair of his head, the little picture!'

'I'd rather not,' said Anthea.

'Let me have him,' said the other woman, whose face was also of the hue of mahogany, and her hair jet-black, in greasy curls. 'I've nineteen of my own, so I have.'

'No,' said Anthea bravely, but her heart beat so that it nearly choked her.

Then one of the men pushed forward.

'Swelp me if it ain't!' he cried, 'my own long-lost cheild! Have he a strawberry mark on his left ear? No? Then he's my own babby, stolen from me in hinnocent hinfancy. 'And 'im over - and we'll not 'ave the law on yer this time.'

He snatched the Baby from Anthea, who turned scarlet and burst into tears of pure rage.

The others were standing quite still; this was much the most terrible thing that had ever happened to them. Even being taken up by the police in Rochester was nothing to this. Cyril was quite white, and his hands trembled a little, but he made a sign to the others to shut up. He was silent a minute, thinking hard. Then he said:

'We don't want to keep him if he's yours. But you see he's used to us. You shall have him if you want him.'

'No, no!' cried Anthea - and Cyril glared at her.

'Of course we want him,' said the women, trying to get the Baby out of the man's arms. The Lamb howled loudly.

'Oh, he's hurt!' shrieked Anthea; and Cyril, in a savage undertone, bade her 'Stow it!'

'You trust to me,' he whispered. 'Look here,' he went on, 'he's awfully tiresome with people he doesn't know very well. Suppose we stay here a bit till he gets used to you, and then when it's bedtime I give you my word of honour we'll go away and let you keep him if you want to. And then when we're gone you can decide which of you is to have him, as you all want him so much.'

'That's fair enough,' said the man who was holding the Baby, trying to loosen the red neckerchief which the Lamb had caught hold of and drawn round his mahogany throat so tight that he could hardly breathe. The gipsies whispered together, and Cyril took the chance to whisper too. He said, 'Sunset! we'll get away then.'

And then his brothers and sisters were filled with wonder and admiration at his having been so clever as to remember this.

'Oh, do let him come to us!' said Jane. 'See we'll sit down here and take care of him for you till he gets used to you.'

'What about dinner?' said Robert suddenly. The others looked at him with scorn. 'Fancy bothering about your beastly dinner when your br - I mean when the Baby' - Jane whispered hotly. Robert carefully winked at her and went on:

'You won't mind my just running home to get our dinner?' he said to the gipsy; 'I can bring it out here in a basket.'

His brother and sisters felt themselves very noble, and despised him. They did not know his thoughtful secret intention. But the gipsies did in a minute. 'Oh yes!' they said; 'and then fetch the police with a pack of lies about it being your baby instead of ours! D'jever catch a weasel asleep?' they asked.

'If you're hungry you can pick a bit along of us,' said the light-haired gipsy woman, not unkindly. 'Here, Levi, that blessed kid'll howl all his buttons off. Give him to the little lady, and let's see if they can't get him used to us a bit.'

So the Lamb was handed back; but the gipsies crowded so closely that he could not possibly stop howling. Then the man with the red handkerchief said:

'Here, Pharaoh, make up the fire; and you girls see to the pot. Give the kid a chanst.' So the gipsies, very much against their will, went off to their work, and the children and the Lamb were left sitting on the grass.

'He'll be all right at sunset,'Jane whispered. 'But, oh, it is awful! Suppose they are frightfully angry when they come to their senses! They might beat us, or leave us tied to trees, or something.'

'No, they won't,' Anthea said. ('Oh, my Lamb, don't cry any more, it's all right, Panty's got oo, duckie!) They aren't unkind people, or they wouldn't be going to give us any dinner.'

'Dinner?' said Robert. 'I won't touch their nasty dinner. It would choke me!'

The others thought so too then. But when the dinner was ready - it turned out to be supper, and happened between four and five - they were all glad enough to take what they could get. It was boiled rabbit, with onions, and some bird rather like a chicken, but stringier about its legs and with a stronger taste. The Lamb had bread soaked in hot water and brown sugar sprinkled on the top. He liked this very much, and consented to let the two gipsy women feed him with it, as he sat on Anthea's lap. All that long hot afternoon Robert and Cyril and Anthea and Jane had to keep the Lamb amused and happy, while the gipsies looked eagerly on. By the time the shadows grew long and black across the meadows he had really 'taken to' the woman with the light hair, and even consented to kiss his hand to the children, and to stand up and bow, with his hand on his chest - 'like a gentleman' - to the two men. The whole gipsy camp was in raptures with him, and his brothers and sisters could not help taking some pleasure in showing off his accomplishments to an audience so interested and enthusiastic. But they longed for sunset.

'We're getting into the habit of longing for sunset,' Cyril whispered. 'How I do wish we could wish something really sensible, that would be of some use, so that we should be quite sorry when sunset came.'

The shadows got longer and longer, and at last there were no separate shadows any more, but one soft glowing shadow over everything; for the sun was out of sight - behind the hill - but he had not really set yet. The people who make the laws about lighting bicycle lamps are the people who decide when the sun sets; he has to do it, too, to the minute, or they would know the reason why!

But the gipsies were getting impatient.

'Now, young uns,' the red-handkerchief man said,'it's time you were laying of your heads on your pillowses - so it is! The kid's all right and friendly with us now - so you just hand him over and sling that hook o' yours like you said.'

The women and children came crowding round the Lamb, arms were held out, fingers snapped invitingly, friendly faces beaming with admiring smiles; but all failed to tempt the loyal Lamb. He clung with arms and legs to Jane, who happened to be holding him, and uttered the gloomiest roar of the whole day.

'It's no good,' the woman said, 'hand the little poppet over, miss. We'll soon quiet him.'

And still the sun would not set.

'Tell her about how to put him to bed,' whispered Cyril; 'anything to gain time - and be ready to bolt when the sun really does make up its silly old mind to set.'

'Yes, I'll hand him over in just one minute,' Anthea began, talking very fast - 'but do let me just tell you he has a warm bath every night and cold in the morning, and he has a crockery rabbit to go into the warm bath with him, and little Samuel saying his prayers in white china on a red cushion for the cold bath; and if you let the soap get into his eyes, the Lamb -'

'Lamb kyes,' said he - he had stopped roaring to listen.

The woman laughed. 'As if I hadn't never bath'd a babby!' she said. 'Come - give us a hold of him. Come to 'Melia, my precious.'

'G'way, ugsie!' replied the Lamb at once.

'Yes, but,' Anthea went on, 'about his meals; you really MUST let me tell you he has an apple or a banana every morning, and bread-and-milk for breakfast, and an egg for his tea sometimes, and -'

'I've brought up ten,' said the black-ringleted woman, 'besides the others. Come, miss, 'and 'im over - I can't bear it no longer. I just must give him a hug.'

'We ain't settled yet whose he's to be, Esther,' said one of the men.

'It won't be you, Esther, with seven of 'em at your tail a'ready.'

'I ain't so sure of that,' said Esther's husband.

'And ain't I nobody, to have a say neither?' said the husband of 'Melia.

Zillah, the girl, said, 'An' me? I'm a single girl - and no one but 'im to look after - I ought to have him.'

'Hold yer tongue!'

'Shut your mouth!'

'Don't you show me no more of your imperence!'

Everyone was getting very angry. The dark gipsy faces were frowning and anxious-looking. Suddenly a change swept over them, as if some invisible sponge had wiped away these cross and anxious expressions, and left only a blank.

The children saw that the sun really HAD set. But they were afraid to move. And the gipsies were feeling so muddled, because of the invisible sponge that had washed all the feelings of the last few hours out of their hearts, that they could not say a word.

The children hardly dared to breathe. Suppose the gipsies, when they recovered speech, should be furious to think how silly they had been all day.

It was an awkward moment. Suddenly Anthea, greatly daring, held out the Lamb to the red-handkerchief man.

'Here he is!' she said.

The man drew back. 'I shouldn't like to deprive you, miss,' he said hoarsely.

'Anyone who likes can have my share of him,' said the other man.

'After all, I've got enough of my own,' said Esther.

'He's a nice little chap, though,' said Amelia. She was the only one who now looked affectionately at the whimpering Lamb.

Zillah said, 'If I don't think I must have had a touch of the sun. I don't want him.'

'Then shall we take him away?' said Anthea.

'Well, suppose you do,' said Pharaoh heartily, 'and we'll say no more about it!'

And with great haste all the gipsies began to be busy about their tents for the night. All but Amelia. She went with the children as far as the bend in the road - and there she said:

'Let me give him a kiss, miss - I don't know what made us go for to behave so silly. Us gipsies don't steal babies, whatever they may tell you when you're naughty. We've enough of our own, mostly. But I've lost all mine.'

She leaned towards the Lamb; and he, looking in her eyes, unexpectedly put up a grubby soft paw and stroked her face.

'Poor, poor!' said the Lamb. And he let the gipsy woman kiss him, and, what is more, he kissed her brown cheek in return - a very nice kiss, as all his kisses are, and not a wet one like some babies give. The gipsy woman moved her finger about on his forehead, as if she had been writing something there, and the same with his chest and his hands and his feet; then she said:

'May he be brave, and have the strong head to think with, and the strong heart to love with, and the strong hands to work with, and the strong feet to travel with, and always come safe home to his own.' Then she said something in a strange language no one could understand, and suddenly added:

'Well, I must be saying "so long" - and glad to have made your acquaintance.' And she turned and went back to her home - the tent by the grassy roadside.

The children looked after her till she was out of sight. Then Robert said, 'How silly of her! Even sunset didn't put her right. What rot she talked!'

'Well,' said Cyril, 'if you ask me, I think it was rather decent of her -'

'Decent?' said Anthea; 'it was very nice indeed of her. I think she's a dear.'

'She's just too frightfully nice for anything,' said Jane.

And they went home - very late for tea and unspeakably late for dinner. Martha scolded, of course. But the Lamb was safe.

'I say - it turned out we wanted the Lamb as much as anyone,' said Robert, later.

'Of course.'

'But do you feel different about it now the sun's set?'

'No,' said all the others together. 'Then it's lasted over sunset with us.'

'No, it hasn't,' Cyril explained. 'The wish didn't do anything to US. We always wanted him with all our hearts when we were our proper selves, only we were all pigs this morning; especially you, Robert.' Robert bore this much with a strange calm.

'I certainly THOUGHT I didn't want him this morning,' said he. 'Perhaps I was a pig. But everything looked so different when we thought we were going to lose him.'

Chapter 4. Wings

The next day was very wet - too wet to go out, and far too wet to think of disturbing a Sand-fairy so sensitive to water that he still, after thousands of years, felt the pain of once having had his left whisker wetted. It was a long day, and it was not till the afternoon that all the children suddenly decided to write letters to their mother. It was Robert who had the misfortune to upset the ink-pot - an unusually deep and full one - straight into that part of Anthea's desk where she had long pretended that an arrangement of gum and cardboard painted with Indian ink was a secret drawer. It was not exactly Robert's fault; it was only his misfortune that he chanced to be lifting the ink across the desk just at the moment when Anthea had got it open, and that that same moment should have been the one chosen by the Lamb to get under the table and break his squeaking bird. There was a sharp convenient wire inside the bird, and of course the Lamb ran the wire into Robert's leg at once; and so, without anyone's meaning to, the secret drawer was flooded with ink. At the same time a stream was poured over Anthea's half-finished letter. So that her letter was something like this:

> DARLING MOTHER, I hope you are quite well, and I hope Granny is better. The other day we ...

Then came a flood of ink, and at the bottom these words in pencil -

> It was not me upset the ink, but it took such a time clearing up, so no more as it is post-time.
>
> - From your loving daughter,
> ANTHEA.

Robert's letter had not even been begun. He had been drawing a ship on the blotting-paper while he was trying to think of what to say. And of course after the ink was upset he had to help Anthea to clean out her desk, and he promised to make her another secret drawer, better than the other. And she said, 'Well, make it now.' So it was post-time and his letter wasn't done. And the secret drawer wasn't done either.

Cyril wrote a long letter, very fast, and then went to set a trap for slugs that he had read about in the Home-made Gardener, and when it was post-time the letter could not be found, and it never was found. Perhaps the slugs ate it.

jane's letter was the only one that went. She meant to tell her mother all about the Psammead - in fact -they had all meant to do this - but she spent so long thinking how to spell the word that there was no time to tell the story properly, and it is useless to tell a story unless you do tell it properly, so she had to be contented with this -

> MY DEAR MOTHER DEAR,
>
> We are all as as good as we can, like you told us to, and the Lamb has a little cold, but Martha says it is nothing, only he upset the goldfish into himself yesterday morning. When we were up at the sand-pit the other day we went round by the safe way where carts go, and we found a —

Half an hour went by before Jane felt quite sure that they could none of them spell Psammead. And they could not find it in the dictionary either, though they looked. Then Jane hastily finished her letter.

> We found a strange thing, but it is nearly post-time, so no more at present from your little girl,
> JANE.
>
> Ps. - If you could have a wish come true, what would you have?

Then the postman was heard blowing his horn, and Robert rushed out in the rain to stop his cart and give him the letter. And that was how it happened that, though all the children meant to tell their mother about the Sand-fairy, somehow or other she never got to know. There were other reasons why she never got to know, but these come later.

The next day Uncle Richard came and took them all to Maidstone in a wagonette - all except the Lamb. Uncle Richard was the very best kind of uncle. He bought them toys at Maidstone. He took them into a shop and let them choose exactly what they wanted, without any restrictions about price, and no nonsense about things being instructive. It is very wise to let children choose exactly what they like, because they are very foolish and inexperienced, and sometimes they will choose a really instructive thing without meaning to. This happened to Robert, who chose, at the last moment, and in a great hurry, a box with pictures on it of winged bulls with men's heads and winged men with eagles' heads. He thought there would be animals inside, the same as on the box. When he got it home it was a Sunday puzzle about ancient Nineveh! The others chose in haste, and were happy at leisure. Cyril had a model engine, and the girls had two dolls, as well as a china tea-set with forget-me-nots on it, to be 'between them'. The boys' 'between them' was bow and arrows.

Then Uncle Richard took them on the beautiful Medway in a boat, and then they all had tea at a beautiful pastrycook's, and when they reached home it was far too late to have any wishes that day.

They did not tell Uncle Richard anything about the Psammead. I do not know why. And they do not know why. But I daresay you can guess.

The day after Uncle Richard had behaved so handsomely was a very hot day indeed. The people who decide what the weather is to be, and put its orders down for it in the newspapers every morning, said afterwards that it was the hottest day there had been for years. They had ordered it to be 'warmer - some showers', and warmer it certainly was. In fact it was so busy being warmer that it had no time to attend to the order about showers, so there weren't any.

Have you ever been up at five o'clock on a fine summer morning? It is very beautiful. The sunlight is pinky and yellowy, and all the grass and trees are covered with dew-diamonds. And all the shadows go the opposite way to the way they do in the evening, which is very interesting and makes you feel as though you were in a new other world.

Anthea awoke at five. She had made herself wake, and I must tell you how it is done, even if it keeps you waiting for the story to go on.

You get into bed at night, and lie down quite flat on your little back with your hands straight down by your sides. Then you say 'I must wake up at five' (or six, or seven, or eight, or nine, or whatever the time is that you want), and as you say it you push your chin down on to your chest and then bang your head back on the pillow. And you do this as many times as there are ones in the time you want to wake up at. (It is quite an easy sum.) Of course everything depends on your really wanting to get up at five (or six, or seven, or eight, or nine); if you don't really want to, it's all of no use. But if you do - well, try it and see. Of course in this, as in doing Latin proses or getting into mischief, practice makes perfect. Anthea was quite perfect.

At the very moment when she opened her eyes she heard the black-and-gold clock down in the dining-room strike eleven. So she knew it was three minutes to five. The black-and-gold clock always struck wrong, but it was all right when you knew what it meant. It was like a person talking a foreign language. If you know the language it is just as easy to understand as English. And Anthea knew the clock language. She was very sleepy, but she jumped out of bed and put her face and hands into a basin of cold water. This is a fairy charm that prevents your wanting to get back into bed again. Then she dressed, and folded up her nightgown. She did not tumble it together by the sleeves, but folded it by the seams from the hem, and that will show you the kind of well-brought-up little girl she was.

Then she took her shoes in her hand and crept softly down the stairs. She opened the dining-room window and climbed out. It would have been just as easy to go out by the door, but the window was more romantic, and less likely to be noticed by Martha.

'I will always get up at five,' she said to herself. 'It was quite too awfully pretty for anything.'

Her heart was beating very fast, for she was carrying out a plan quite her own. She could not be sure that it was a good plan, but she was quite sure that it would not be any better if she were to tell the others about it. And she had a feeling that, right or wrong, she would rather go through with it alone. She put on her shoes under the iron veranda, on the red-and-yellow shining tiles, and then she ran straight to the sand-pit, and found the Psammead's place, and dug it out; it was very cross indeed.

'It's too bad,' it said, fluffing up its fur like pigeons do their feathers at Christmas time. 'The weather's arctic, and it's the middle of the night.'

'I'm so sorry,' said Anthea gently, and she took off her white pinafore and covered the Sand-fairy up with it, all but its head, its bat's ears, and its eyes that were like a snail's eyes.

'Thank you,' it said, 'that's better. What's the wish this morning?'

'I don't know,' said she; 'that's just it. You see we've been very unlucky, so far. I wanted to talk to you about it. But - would you mind not giving me any wishes till after breakfast? It's so hard to talk to anyone if they jump out at you with wishes you don't really want!'

'You shouldn't say you wish for things if you don't wish for them. In the old days people almost always knew whether it was Megatherium or Ichthyosaurus they really wanted for dinner.'

'I'll try not,' said Anthea, 'but I do wish -'

'Look out!' said the Psammead in a warning voice, and it began to blow itself out.

'Oh, this isn't a magic wish - it's just - I should be so glad if you'd not swell yourself out and nearly burst to give me anything just now. Wait till the others are here.'

'Well, well,' it said indulgently, but it shivered.

'Would you,' asked Anthea kindly - 'would you like to come and sit on my lap? You'd be warmer, and I could turn the skirt of my frock up round you. I'd be very careful.'

Anthea had never expected that it would, but it did.

'Thank you,' it said; 'you really are rather thoughtful.' It crept on to her lap and snuggled down, and she put her arms round it with a rather frightened gentleness. 'Now then!' it said.

'Well then,' said Anthea, 'everything we have wished has turned out rather horrid. I wish you would advise us. You are so old, you must be very wise.'

'I was always generous from a child,' said the Sand-fairy. 'I've spent the whole of my waking hours in giving. But one thing I won't give - that's advice.'

'You see,' Anthea went on, it's such a wonderful thing - such a splendid, glorious chance. It's so good and kind and dear of you to give us our wishes, and it seems such a pity it should all be wasted just because we are too silly to know what to wish for.'

Anthea had meant to say that - and she had not wanted to say it before the others. It's one thing to say you're silly, and quite another to say that other people are.

'Child,' said the Sand-fairy sleepily, 'I can only advise you to think before you speak -'

'But I thought you never gave advice.'

'That piece doesn't count,' it said. 'You'll never take it! Besides, it's not original. It's in all the copy-books.'

'But won't you just say if you think wings would be a silly wish?'

'Wings?' it said. 'I should think you might do worse. Only, take care you aren't flying high at sunset. There was a little Ninevite boy I heard of once. He was one of King Sennacherib's sons, and a traveller brought him a Psammead. He used to keep it in a box of sand on the palace terrace. It was a dreadful degradation for one of us, of course; still the boy was the Assyrian King's son. And one day he wished for wings and got them. But he forgot that they would turn into stone at sunset, and when they did he fell slap on to one of the winged lions at the top of his father's great staircase; and what with HIS stone wings and the lions' stone wings - well, it's not a pretty story! But I believe the boy enjoyed himself very much till then.'

'Tell me,' said Anthea, 'why don't our wishes turn into stone now? Why do they just vanish?'

'Autres temps, autres moeurs,' said the creature.

'Is that the Ninevite language?' asked Anthea, who had learned no foreign language at school except French.

'What I mean is,' the Psammead went on, 'that in the old days people wished for good solid everyday gifts - Mammoths and Pterodactyls and things - and those could be turned into stone as easy as not. But people wish such high-flying fanciful things nowadays. How are you going to turn being beautiful as the day, or being wanted by everybody, into stone? You see it can't be done. And it would never do to have two rules, so they simply vanish. If being beautiful as the day COULD be turned into stone it would last an awfully long time, you know - much longer than you would. Just look at the Greek statues. It's just as well as it is. Good-bye. I AM so sleepy.'

It jumped off her lap - dug frantically, and vanished.

Anthea was late for breakfast. It was Robert who quietly poured a spoonful of treacle down the Lamb's frock, so that he had to be taken away and washed thoroughly directly after breakfast. And it was of course a very naughty thing to do; yet it served two purposes - it delighted the Lamb, who loved above all things to be completely sticky, and it engaged Martha's attention so that the others could slip away to the sand-pit without the Lamb.

They did it, and in the lane Anthea, breathless from the scurry of that slipping, panted out -

'I want to propose we take turns to wish. Only, nobody's to have a wish if the others don't think it's a nice wish. Do you agree?'

'Who's to have first wish?' asked Robert cautiously.

'Me, if you don't mind,' said Anthea apologetically. 'And I've thought about it - and it's wings.'

There was a silence. The others rather wanted to find fault, but it was hard, because the word 'wings' raised a flutter of joyous excitement in every breast.

'Not so dusty,' said Cyril generously; and Robert added, 'Really, Panther, you're not quite such a fool as you look.'

Jane said, 'I think it would be perfectly lovely. It's like a bright dream of delirium.' They found the Sand-fairy easily. Anthea said:

'I wish we all had beautiful wings to fly with.'

The Sand-fairy blew himself out, and next moment each child felt a funny feeling, half heaviness and half lightness, on its shoulders. The Psammead put its head on one side and turned its snail's eyes from one to the other.

'Not so dusty,' it said dreamily. 'But really, Robert, you're not quite such an angel as you look.' Robert almost blushed.

The wings were very big, and more beautiful than you can possibly imagine - for they were soft and smooth, and every feather lay neatly in its place. And the feathers were of the most lovely mixed changing colours, like the rainbow, or iridescent glass, or the beautiful scum that sometimes floats on water that is not at all nice to drink.

'Oh - but can we fly?'Jane said, standing anxiously first on one foot and then on the other.

'Look out!' said Cyril; 'you're treading on my wing.'

'Does it hurt?' asked Anthea with interest; but no one answered, for Robert had spread his wings and jumped up, and now he was slowly rising in the air. He looked very awkward in his knickerbocker suit - his boots in particular hung helplessly, and seemed much larger than when he was standing in them. But the others cared but little how he looked - or how they looked, for that matter. For now they all spread out their wings and rose in the air. Of course you all know what flying feels like, because everyone has dreamed about flying, and it seems so beautifully easy - only, you can never remember how you did it; and as a rule you have to do it without wings, in your dreams, which is more clever and uncommon, but not so easy to remember the rule for. Now the four children rose flapping from the ground, and you can't think how good the air felt running against their faces. Their wings were tremendously wide when they were spread out, and they had to fly quite a long way apart so as not to get in each other's way. But little things like this are easily learned.

All the words in the English Dictionary, and in the Greek Lexicon as well, are, I find, of no use at all to tell you exactly what it feels like to be flying, so I will not try. But I will say that to look DOWN on the fields and woods, instead of along at them, is something like looking at a beautiful live map, where, instead of silly colours on paper, you have real moving sunny woods and green fields laid out one after the other. As Cyril said, and I can't think where he got hold of such a strange expression, 'It does you a fair treat!'. It was most wonderful and more like real magic than any wish the children had had yet. They flapped and flew and sailed on their great rainbow wings, between green earth and blue sky; and they flew right over Rochester and then swerved round towards Maidstone, and presently they all began to feel extremely hungry. Curiously enough, this happened when they were flying rather low, and just as they were crossing an orchard where some early plums shone red and ripe.

They paused on their wings. I cannot explain to you how this is done, but it is something like treading water when you are swimming, and hawks do it extremely well.

'Yes, I daresay,' said Cyril, though no one had spoken. 'But stealing is stealing even if you've got wings.'

'Do you really think so?' said Jane briskly. 'If you've got wings you're a bird, and no one minds birds breaking the commandments. At least, they MAY mind, but the birds always do it, and no one scolds them or sends them to prison.'

It was not so easy to perch on a plum-tree as you might think, because the rainbow wings were so very large; but somehow they all managed to do it, and the plums were certainly very sweet and juicy.

Fortunately, it was not till they had all had quite as many plums as were good for them that they saw a stout man, who looked exactly as though he owned the plum-trees, come hurrying through the orchard gate with a thick stick, and with one accord they disentangled their wings from the plum-laden branches and began to fly.

The man stopped short, with his mouth open. For he had seen the boughs of his trees moving and twitching, and he had said to himself, 'The young varmints - at it again!' And he had come out at once, for the lads of the village had taught him in past seasons that plums want looking after. But when he saw the rainbow wings flutter up out of the plum-tree he felt that he must have gone quite mad, and he did not like the feeling at all. And when Anthea looked down and saw his mouth go slowly open, and stay so, and his face become green and mauve in patches, she called out:

'Don't be frightened,' and felt hastily in her pocket for a threepenny-bit with a hole in it, which she had meant to hang on a ribbon round her neck, for luck. She hovered round the unfortunate plum-owner, and said, 'We have had some of your plums; we thought it wasn't stealing, but now I am not so sure. So here's some money to pay for them.'

She swooped down towards the terror-stricken grower of plums, and slipped the coin into the pocket of his jacket, and in a few flaps she had rejoined the others.

The farmer sat down on the grass, suddenly and heavily.

'Well - I'm blessed!' he said. 'This here is what they call delusions, I suppose. But this here threepenny' - he had pulled it out and bitten it - 'THAT'S real enough. Well, from this day forth I'll be a better man. It's the kind of thing to sober a chap for life, this is. I'm glad it was only wings, though. I'd rather see birds as aren't there, and couldn't be, even if they pretend to talk, than some things as I could name.'

He got up slowly and heavily, and went indoors, and he was so nice to his wife that day that she felt quite happy, and said to herself, 'Law, whatever have a-come to the man!' and smartened herself up and put a blue ribbon bow at the place where her collar fastened on, and looked so pretty that he was kinder than ever. So perhaps the winged children really did do one good thing that day. If so, it was the only one; for really there is nothing like wings for getting you into trouble. But, on the other hand, if you are in trouble, there is nothing like wings for getting you out of it.

This was the case in the matter of the fierce dog who sprang out at them when they had folded up their wings as small as possible and were going up to a farm door to ask for a crust of bread and cheese, for in spite of the plums they were soon just as hungry as ever again.

Now there is no doubt whatever that, if the four had been ordinary wingless children, that black and fierce dog would have had a good bite out of the brown-stockinged leg of Robert, who was the nearest. But at first growl there was a flutter of wings, and the dog was left to strain at his chain and stand on his hind-legs as if he were trying to fly too.

They tried several other farms, but at those where there were no dogs the people were far too frightened to do anything but scream; and at last when it was nearly four o'clock, and their wings were getting miserably stiff and tired, they alighted on a church-tower and held a council of war.

'We can't possibly fly all the way home without dinner or tea,' said Robert with desperate decision.

'And nobody will give us any dinner, or even lunch, let alone tea,' said Cyril.

'Perhaps the clergyman here might,' suggested Anthea. 'He must know all about angels -'

'Anybody could see we're not that,' said Jane. 'Look at Robert's boots and Squirrel's plaid necktie.'

'Well,' said Cyril firmly, 'if the country you're in won't SELL provisions, you TAKE them. In wars I mean. I'm quite certain you do. And even in other stories no good brother would allow his little sisters to starve in the midst of plenty.'

'Plenty?' repeated Robert hungrily; and the others looked vaguely round the bare leads of the church- tower, and murmured, 'In the midst of?'

'Yes,' said Cyril impressively. 'There is a larder window at the side of the clergyman's house, and I saw things to eat inside - custard pudding and cold chicken and tongue - and pies - and jam. It's rather a high window - but with wings -'

'How clever of you!' said Jane.

'Not at all,' said Cyril modestly; 'any born general - Napoleon or the Duke of Marlborough - would have seen it just the same as I did.'

'It seems very wrong,' said Anthea.

'Nonsense,' said Cyril. 'What was it Sir Philip Sidney said when the soldier wouldn't stand him a drink? - "My necessity is greater than his".'

'We'll club our money, though, and leave it to pay for the things, won't we?' Anthea was persuasive, and very nearly in tears, because it is most trying to feel enormously hungry and unspeakably sinful at one and the same time.

'Some of it,' was the cautious reply.

Everyone now turned out its pockets on the lead roof of the tower, where visitors for the last hundred and fifty years had cut their own and their sweethearts' initials with penknives in the soft lead. There was five-and-sevenpence-halfpenny altogether, and even the upright Anthea admitted that that was too much to pay for four peoples dinners. Robert said he thought eighteen pence.

And half-a-crown was finally agreed to be 'handsome'.

So Anthea wrote on the back of her last term's report, which happened to be in her pocket, and from which she first tore her own name and that of the school, the following letter:

> DEAR REVEREND CLERGYMAN,
>
> We are very hungry indeed because of having to fly all day, and we think it is not stealing when you are starving to death. We are afraid to ask you for fear you should say 'No', because of course you know

> about angels, but you would not think we were angels. We will only take the nessessities of life, and no pudding or pie, to show you it is not grediness but true starvation that makes us make your larder stand and deliver. But we are not highwaymen by trade.

'Cut it short,' said the others with one accord. And Anthea hastily added:

> Our intentions are quite honourable if you only knew. And here is half-a-crown to show we are sinseer and grateful. Thank you for your kind hospitality.
>
> FROM Us FOUR.

The half-crown was wrapped in this letter, and all the children felt that when the clergyman had read it he would understand everything, as well as anyone could who had not seen the wings.

'Now,' said Cyril, "of course there's some risk; we'd better fly straight down the other side of the tower and then flutter low across the churchyard and in through the shrubbery. There doesn't seem to be anyone about. But you never know. The window looks out into the shrubbery. It is embowered in foliage, like a window in a story. I'll go in and get the things. Robert and Anthea can take them as I hand them out through the window; and Jane can keep watch - her eyes are sharp - and whistle if she sees anyone about. Shut up, Robert! She can whistle quite well enough for that, anyway. It ought not to be a very good whistle - it'll sound more natural and birdlike. Now then - off we go!'

I cannot pretend that stealing is right. I can only say that on this occasion it did not look like stealing to the hungry four, but appeared in the light of a fair and reasonable business transaction. They had never happened to learn that a tongue - hardly cut into - a chicken and a half, a loaf of bread, and a syphon of soda-water cannot be bought in shops for half-a-crown. These were the necessaries of life, which Cyril handed out of the larder window when, quite unobserved and without hindrance or adventure, he had led the others to that happy spot. He felt that to refrain from jam, apple turnovers, cake, and mixed candied peel was a really heroic act - and I agree with him. He was also proud of not taking the custard pudding - and there I think he was wrong - because if he had taken it there would have been a difficulty about returning the dish; no one, however starving, has a right to steal china pie-dishes with little pink flowers on them. The soda-water syphon was different. They could not do without something to drink, and as the maker's name was on it they felt sure it would be returned to him wherever they might leave it. If they had time they would take it back themselves. The man appeared to live in Rochester, which would not be much out of their way home.

Everything was carried up to the top of the tower, and laid down on a sheet of kitchen paper which Cyril had found on the top shelf of the larder. As he unfolded it, Anthea said, 'I don't think THAT'S a necessity of life.'

'Yes, it is,' said he. 'We must put the things down somewhere to cut them up; and I heard father say the other day people got diseases from germans in rain-water. Now there must be lots of rain-water here - and when it dries up the germans are left, and they'd get into the things, and we should all die of scarlet fever.'

'What are germans?'

'Little waggly things you see with microscopes,' said Cyril, with a scientific air. 'They give you every illness you can think of! I'm sure the paper was a necessary, just as much as the bread and meat and water. Now then! Oh, my eyes, I am hungry!'

I do not wish to describe the picnic party on the top of the tower. You can imagine well enough what it is like to carve a chicken and a tongue with a knife that has only one blade - and that snapped off short about half-way down. But it was done. Eating with your fingers is greasy and difficult - and paper dishes soon get to look very spotty and horrid. But one thing you CAN'T imagine, and that is how soda-water behaves when you try to drink it straight out of a syphon - especially a quite full one. But if imagination will not help you, experience will, and you can easily try it for yourself if you can get a grown-up to give you the syphon. If you want to have a really thorough experience, put the tube in your mouth and press the handle very suddenly and very hard. You had better do it when you are alone - and out of doors is best for this experiment.

However you eat them, tongue and chicken and new bread are very good things, and no one minds being sprinkled a little with soda-water on a really fine hot day. So that everyone enjoyed the dinner very much indeed, and everyone ate as much as it possibly could: first, because it was extremely hungry; and secondly, because, as I said, tongue and chicken and new bread are very nice.

Now, I daresay you will have noticed that if you have to wait for your dinner till long after the proper time, and then eat a great deal more dinner than usual, and sit in the hot sun on the top of a church-tower - or even anywhere else - you become soon and strangely sleepy. Now Anthea and Jane and Cyril and Robert were very like you in many ways, and when they had eaten all they could, and drunk all there was, they became sleepy, strangely and soon - especially Anthea, because she had got up so early.

One by one they left off talking and leaned back, and before it was a quarter of an hour after dinner they had all curled round and tucked themselves up under their large soft warm wings and were fast asleep. And the sun was sinking slowly in the west. (I must say it was in the west, because it is usual in books to say so, for fear careless people should think it was setting in the east. In point of fact, it was not exactly in the west either - but that's near enough.) The sun, I repeat, was sinking slowly in the west, and the children slept warmly and happily on - for wings are cosier than eiderdown quilts to sleep under. The shadow of the church-tower fell across the churchyard, and across the Vicarage, and across the field beyond; and presently there were no more shadows, and the sun had set, and the wings were gone. And still the children slept. But not for long. Twilight is very beautiful, but it is chilly; and you know, however sleepy you are, you wake up soon enough if your brother or sister happens to be up first and pulls your blankets off you. The four wingless children shivered and woke. And there they were - on the top of a church-tower in the dusky twilight, with blue stars coming out by ones and twos and tens and twenties over their heads - miles away from home, with three-and-three-halfpence in their pockets, and a doubtful act about the necessities of life to be accounted for if anyone found them with the soda-water syphon.

They looked at each other. Cyril spoke first, picking up the syphon:

'We'd better get along down and get rid of this beastly thing. It's dark enough to leave it on the clergyman's doorstep, I should think. Come on.'

There was a little turret at the corner of the tower, and the little turret had a door in it. They had noticed this when they were eating, but had not explored it, as you would have done in their place. Because, of course, when you have wings, and can explore the whole sky, doors seem hardly worth exploring.

Now they turned towards it.

'Of course,' said Cyril, 'this is the way down.'

It was. But the door was locked on the inside!

And the world was growing darker and darker. And they were miles from home. And there was the soda-water syphon.

I shall not tell you whether anyone cried, nor if so, how many cried, nor who cried. You will be better employed in making up your minds what you would have done if you had been in their place.

Whether anyone cried or not, there was certainly an interval during which none of the party was quite itself. When they grew calmer, Anthea put her handkerchief in her pocket and her arm round Jane, and said:

'It can't be for more than one night. We can signal with our handkerchiefs in the morning. They'll be dry then. And someone will come up and let us out -'

'And find the syphon,' said Cyril gloomily; 'and we shall be sent to prison for stealing -'

'You said it wasn't stealing. You said you were sure it wasn't.'

'I'm not sure NOW,' said Cyril shortly.

'Let's throw the beastly thing slap away among the trees,' said Robert, 'then no one can do anything to us.'

'Oh yes' - Cyril's laugh was not a lighthearted one - 'and hit some chap on the head, and be murderers as well as - as the other thing.'

'But we can't stay up here all night,' said Jane; 'and I want my tea.'

'You CAN'T want your tea,' said Robert; 'you've only just had your dinner.'

'But I do want it,' she said; 'especially when you begin talking about stopping up here all night. Oh, Panther - I want to go home! I want to go home!'

'Hush, hush,' Anthea said. 'Don't, dear. It'll be all right, somehow. Don't, don't -'

'Let her cry,' said Robert desperately; 'if she howls loud enough, someone may hear and come and let us out.'

'And see the soda-water thing,' said Anthea swiftly. 'Robert, don't be a brute. Oh, Jane, do try to be a man! It's just the same for all of us.'

Jane did try to 'be a man' - and reduced her howls to sniffs.

There was a pause. Then Cyril said slowly, 'Look here. We must risk that syphon. I'll button it up inside my jacket - perhaps no one will notice it. You others keep well in front of me. There are lights in the clergyman's house. They've not gone to bed yet. We must just yell as loud as ever we can. Now all scream when I say three. Robert, you do the yell like the railway engine, and I'll do the coo-ee like father's. The girls can do as they please. One, two, three!'

A fourfold yell rent the silent peace of the evening, and a maid at one of the Vicarage windows paused with her hand on the blind-cord.

'One, two, three!' Another yell, piercing and complex, startled the owls and starlings to a flutter of feathers in the belfry below. The maid fled from the Vicarage window and ran down the Vicarage stairs and into the Vicarage kitchen, and fainted as soon as she had explained to the man-servant and the cook and the cook's cousin that she had seen a ghost. It was quite untrue, of course, but I suppose the girl's nerves were a little upset by the yelling.

'One, two, three!' The Vicar was on his doorstep by this time, and there was no mistaking the yell that greeted him.

'Goodness me,' he said to his wife, 'my dear, someone's being murdered in the church! Give me my hat and a thick stick, and tell Andrew to come after me. I expect it's the lunatic who stole the tongue.'

The children had seen the flash of light when the Vicar opened his front door. They had seen his dark form on the doorstep, and they had paused for breath, and also to see what he would do.

When he turned back for his hat, Cyril said hastily:

'He thinks he only fancied he heard something. You don't half yell! Now! One, two, three!'

It was certainly a whole yell this time, and the Vicar's wife flung her arms round her husband and screamed a feeble echo of it.

'You shan't go!' she said, 'not alone. Jessie!' - the maid unfainted and came out of the kitchen - 'send Andrew at once. There's a dangerous lunatic in the church, and he must go immediately and catch it.'

'I expect he WILL catch it too,' said Jessie to herself as she went through the kitchen door. 'Here, Andrew,' she said, there's someone screaming like mad in the church, and the missus says you're to go along and catch it.'

'Not alone, I don't,' said Andrew in low firm tones. To his master he merely said, 'Yes, sir.'

'You heard those screams?'

'I did think I noticed a sort of something,' said Andrew.

'Well, come on, then,' said the Vicar. 'My dear, I MUST go!' He pushed her gently into the sitting-room, banged the door, and rushed out, dragging Andrew by the arm.

A volley of yells greeted them. As it died into silence Andrew shouted, 'Hullo, you there! Did you call?'

'Yes,' shouted four far-away voices.

'They seem to be in the air,' said the Vicar. 'Very remarkable.'

'Where are you?' shouted Andrew: and Cyril replied in his deepest voice, very slow and loud:

'CHURCH! TOWER! TOP!'

'Come down, then!' said Andrew; and the same voice replied:

'CAN'T! DOOR LOCKED!'

'My goodness!' said the Vicar. 'Andrew, fetch the stable lantern. Perhaps it would be as well to fetch another man from the village.'

'With the rest of the gang about, very likely. No, sir; if this 'ere ain't a trap - well, may I never! There's cook's cousin at the back door now. He's a keeper, sir, and used to dealing with vicious characters. And he's got his gun, sir.'

'Hullo there!' shouted Cyril from the church-tower; 'come up and let us out.'

'We're a-coming,' said Andrew. 'I'm a-going to get a policeman and a gun.'

'Andrew, Andrew,' said the Vicar, 'that's not the truth.'

'It's near enough, sir, for the likes of them.'

So Andrew fetched the lantern and the cook's cousin; and the Vicar's wife begged them all to be very careful.

They went across the churchyard - it was quite dark now - and as they went they talked. The Vicar was certain a lunatic was on the church-tower - the one who had written the mad letter, and taken the cold tongue and things. Andrew thought it was a 'trap'; the cook's cousin alone was calm. 'Great cry, little wool,' said he; 'dangerous chaps is quieter.' He was not at all afraid. But then he had a gun. That was why he was asked to lead the way up the worn steep dark steps of the church-tower. He did lead the way, with the lantern in one hand and the gun in the other. Andrew went next. He pretended afterwards that this was because he was braver than his master, but really it was because he thought of traps, and he did not like the idea of being behind the others for fear someone should come softly up behind him and catch hold of his legs in the dark. They went on and on, and round and round the little corkscrew staircase - then through the bell-ringers' loft, where the bell-ropes hung with soft furry ends like giant caterpillars - then up another stair into the belfry, where the big quiet bells are - and then on, up a ladder with broad steps - and then up a little stone stair. And at the top of that there was a little door. And the door was bolted on the stair side.

The cook's cousin, who was a gamekeeper, kicked at the door, and said:

'Hullo, you there!'

The children were holding on to each other on the other side of the door, and trembling with anxiousness - and very hoarse with their howls. They could hardly speak, but Cyril managed to reply huskily:

'Hullo, you there!'

'How did you get up there?'

It was no use saying 'We flew up', so Cyril said:

'We got up - and then we found the door was locked and we couldn't get down. Let us out - do.'

'How many of you are there?' asked the keeper.

'Only four,' said Cyril.

'Are you armed?'

'Are we what?'

'I've got my gun handy - so you'd best not try any tricks,' said the keeper. 'If we open the door, will you promise to come quietly down, and no nonsense?'

'Yes - oh YES!' said all the children together.

'Bless me,' said the Vicar, 'surely that was a female voice?'

'Shall I open the door, Sir?' said the keeper. Andrew went down a few steps, 'to leave room for the others' he said afterwards.

'Yes,' said the Vicar, 'open the door. Remember,' he said through the keyhole, 'we have come to release you. You will keep your promise to refrain from violence?'

'How this bolt do stick,' said the keeper; 'anyone 'ud think it hadn't been drawed for half a year.' As a matter of fact it hadn't.

When all the bolts were drawn, the keeper spoke deep-chested words through the keyhole.

'I don't open,' said he, 'till you've gone over to the other side of the tower. And if one of you comes at me I fire. Now!'

'We're all over on the other side,' said the voices.

The keeper felt pleased with himself, and owned himself a bold man when he threw open that door, and, stepping out into the leads, flashed the full light of the stable lantern on to the group of desperadoes standing against the parapet on the other side of the tower.

He lowered his gun, and he nearly dropped the lantern.

'So help me,' he cried, 'if they ain't a pack of kiddies!'

The Vicar now advanced.

'How did you come here?' he asked severely. 'Tell me at once. '

'Oh, take us down,' said Jane, catching at his coat, 'and we'll tell you anything you like. You won't believe us, but it doesn't matter. Oh, take us down!'

The others crowded round him, with the same entreaty. All but Cyril. He had enough to do with the soda-water syphon, which would keep slipping down under his jacket. It needed both hands to keep it steady in its place.

But he said, standing as far out of the lantern light as possible:

'Please do take us down.'

So they were taken down. It is no joke to go down a strange church-tower in the dark, but the keeper helped them - only, Cyril had to be independent because of the soda-water syphon. It would keep trying to get away. Half-way down the ladder it all but escaped. Cyril just caught it by its spout, and as nearly as possible lost his footing. He was trembling and pale when at last they reached the bottom of the winding stair and stepped out on to the flags of the church-porch.

Then suddenly the keeper caught Cyril and Robert each by an arm.

'You bring along the gells, sir,' said he; 'you and Andrew can manage them.'

'Let go!' said Cyril; 'we aren't running away. We haven't hurt your old church. Leave go!'

'You just come along,' said the keeper; and Cyril dared not oppose him with violence, because just then the syphon began to slip again.

So they were all marched into the Vicarage study, and the Vicar's wife came rushing in.

'Oh, William, are you safe?' she cried.

Robert hastened to allay her anxiety.

'Yes,' he said, 'he's quite safe. We haven't hurt him at all. And please, we're very late, and they'll be anxious at home. Could you send us home in your carriage?'

'Or perhaps there's a hotel near where we could get a carriage from,' said Anthea. 'Martha will be very anxious as it is.'

The Vicar had sunk into a chair, overcome by emotion and amazement.

Cyril had also sat down, and was leaning forward with his elbows on his knees because of that soda-water syphon.

'But how did you come to be locked up in the church-tower?' asked the Vicar.

'We went up,' said Robert slowly, 'and we were tired, and we all went to sleep, and when we woke up we found the door was locked, so we yelled.'

'I should think you did!' said the Vicar's wife. 'Frightening everybody out of their wits like this! You ought to be ashamed of yourselves.'

'We are,' said Jane gently.

'But who locked the door?' asked the Vicar.

'I don't know at all,' said Robert, with perfect truth. 'Do please send us home.'

'Well, really,' said the Vicar, 'I suppose we'd better. Andrew, put the horse to, and you can take them home.'

'Not alone, I don't,' said Andrew to himself.

'And,' the Vicar went on, 'let this be a lesson to you ...' He went on talking, and the children listened miserably. But the keeper was not listening. He was looking at the unfortunate Cyril. He knew all about poachers of course, so he knew how people look when they're hiding something. The Vicar had just got to the part about trying to grow up to be a blessing to your parents, and not a trouble and a disgrace, when the keeper suddenly said:

'Arst him what he's got there under his jacket'; and Cyril knew that concealment was at an end. So he stood up, and squared his shoulders and tried to look noble, like the boys in books that no one can look in the face of and doubt that they come of brave and noble families and will be faithful to the death, and he pulled out the soda-water syphon and said:

'Well, there you are, then.'

There was a silence. Cyril went on - there was nothing else for it:

'Yes, we took this out of your larder, and some chicken and tongue and bread. We were very hungry, and we didn't take the custard or jam. We only took bread and meat and water - and we couldn't help its being the soda kind -just the necessaries of life; and we left half-a-crown to pay for it, and we left a letter. And we're very sorry. And my father will pay a fine or anything you like, but don't send us to prison. Mother would be so vexed. You know what you said about not being a disgrace. Well, don't you go and do it to us - that's all! We're as sorry as we can be. There!'

'However did you get up to the larder window?' said Mrs Vicar.

'I can't tell you that,' said Cyril firmly.

'Is this the whole truth you've been telling me?' asked the clergyman.

'No,' answered Jane suddenly; 'it's all true, but it's not the whole truth. We can't tell you that. It's no good asking. Oh, do forgive us and take us home!' She ran to the Vicar's wife and threw her arms round her. The Vicar's wife put her arms round Jane, and the keeper whispered behind his hand to the Vicar:

'They're all right, sir - I expect it's a pal they're standing by. Someone put 'em up to it, and they won't peach. Game little kids.'

'Tell me,' said the Vicar kindly, 'are you screening someone else? Had anyone else anything to do with this?'

'Yes,' said Anthea, thinking of the Psammead; 'but it wasn't their fault.'

'Very well, my dears,' said the Vicar, 'then let's say no more about it. Only just tell us why you wrote such an odd letter.'

'I don't know,' said Cyril. 'You see, Anthea wrote it in such a hurry, and it really didn't seem like stealing then. But afterwards, when we found we couldn't get down off the church-tower, it seemed just exactly like it. We are all very sorry -'

'Say no more about it,' said the Vicar's wife; 'but another time just think before you take other people's tongues. Now - some cake and milk before you go home?'

When Andrew came to say that the horse was put to, and was he expected to be led alone into the trap that he had plainly seen from the first, he found the children eating cake and drinking milk and laughing at the Vicar's jokes. Jane was sitting on the Vicar's wife's lap.

So you see they got off better than they deserved.

The gamekeeper, who was the cook's cousin, asked leave to drive home with them, and Andrew was only too glad to have someone to protect him from the trap he was so certain of.

When the wagonette reached their own house, between the chalk-quarry and the gravel-pit, the children were very sleepy, but they felt that they and the keeper were friends for life.

Andrew dumped the children down at the iron gate without a word. 'You get along home,' said the Vicarage cook's cousin, who was a gamekeeper. 'I'll get me home on Shanks' mare.'

So Andrew had to drive off alone, which he did not like at all, and it was the keeper that was cousin to the Vicarage cook who went with the children to the door, and, when they had been swept to bed in a whirlwind of reproaches, remained to explain to Martha and the cook and the housemaid exactly what had happened. He explained so well that Martha was quite amiable the next morning.

After that he often used to come over and see Martha; and in the end - but that is another story, as dear Mr Kipling says.

Martha was obliged to stick to what she had said the night before about keeping the children indoors the next day for a punishment. But she wasn't at all snarky about it, and agreed to let Robert go out for half an hour to get something he particularly wanted. This, of course, was the day's wish.

Robert rushed to the gravel-pit, found the Psammead, and presently wished for - But that, too, is another story.

Chapter 6. A Castle and No Dinner

The others were to be kept in as a punishment for the misfortunes of the day before. Of course Martha thought it was naughtiness, and not misfortune - so you must not blame her. She only thought she was doing her duty. You know grown-up people often say they do not like to punish you, and that they only do it for your own good, and that it hurts them as much as it hurts you - and this is really very often the truth.

Martha certainly hated having to punish the children quite as much as they hated to be punished. For one thing, she knew what a noise there would be in the house all day. And she had other reasons.

'I declare,' she said to the cook, 'it seems almost a shame keeping of them indoors this lovely day; but they are that audacious, they'll be walking in with their heads knocked off some of these days, if I don't put my foot down. You make them a cake for tea to-morrow, dear. And we'll have Baby along of us soon as we've got a bit forrard with our work. Then they can have a good romp with him out of the way. Now, Eliza, come, get on with them beds. Here's ten o'clock nearly, and no rabbits caught!'

People say that in Kent when they mean 'and no work done'.

So all the others were kept in, but Robert, as I have said, was allowed to go out for half an hour to get something they all wanted. And that, of course, was the day's wish. He had no difficulty in finding the Sand-fairy, for the day was already so hot that it had actually, for the first time, come out of its own accord, and it was sitting in a sort of pool of soft sand, stretching itself, and trimming its whiskers, and turning its snail's eyes round and round.

'Ha!' it said when its left eye saw Robert; 'I've been looking out for you. Where are the rest of you? Not smashed themselves up with those wings, I hope?'

'No,' said Robert; 'but the wings got us into a row, just like all the wishes always do. So the others are kept indoors, and I was only let out for half-an-hour - to get the wish. So please let me wish as quickly as I can.'

'Wish away,' said the Psammead, twisting itself round in the sand. But Robert couldn't wish away. He forgot all the things he had been thinking about, and nothing would come into his head but little things for himself, like toffee, a foreign stamp album, or a clasp- knife with three blades and a corkscrew. He sat down to think better, but it was no use. He could only think of things the others would not have cared for - such as a football, or a pair of leg-guards, or to be able to lick Simpkins minor thoroughly when he went back to school.

'Well,' said the Psammead at last, 'you'd better hurry up with that wish of yours. Time flies.'

'I know it does,' said Robert. 'I can't think what to wish for. I wish you could give one of the others their wish without their having to come here to ask for it. Oh, DON'T!'

But it was too late. The Psammead had blown itself out to about three times its proper size, and now it collapsed like a pricked bubble, and with a deep sigh leaned back against the edge of its sand-pool, quite faint with the effort.

'There!' it said in a weak voice; 'it was tremendously hard - but I did it. Run along home, or they're sure to wish for something silly before you get there.'

They were - quite sure; Robert felt this, and as he ran home his mind was deeply occupied with the sort of wishes he might find they had wished in his absence. They might wish for rabbits, or white mice, or chocolate, or a fine day to-morrow, or even - and that was most likely - someone might have said, 'I do wish to goodness Robert would hurry up.' Well, he WAS hurrying up, and so they would have their wish, and the day would be wasted. Then he tried to think what they could wish for - something that would be amusing indoors. That had been his own difficulty from the beginning. So few things are amusing indoors when the sun is shining outside and you mayn't go out, however much you want to. Robert was running as fast as he could, but when he turned the corner that ought to have brought him within sight of the architect's nightmare - the ornamental iron-work on the top of the house - he opened his eyes so wide that he had to drop into a walk; for you cannot run with your eyes wide open. Then suddenly he stopped short, for there was no house to be seen. The front-garden railings were gone too, and where the house had stood - Robert rubbed his eyes and looked again. Yes, the others HAD wished - there was no doubt about that - and they must have wished that they lived in a castle; for there the castle stood black and stately, and very tall and broad, with battlements and lancet windows, and eight great towers; and, where the garden and the orchard had been, there were white things dotted like mushrooms. Robert walked slowly on, and as he got nearer he saw that these were tents) and men in armour were walking about among the tents - crowds and crowds of them.

'Oh, crikey!' said Robert fervently. 'They HAVE! They've wished for a castle, and it's being besieged! It's just like that Sand-fairy! I wish we'd never seen the beastly thing!'

At the little window above the great gateway, across the moat that now lay where the garden had been but half an hour ago, someone was waving something pale dust-coloured. Robert thought it was one of Cyril's handkerchiefs. They had never been white since the day when he had upset the bottle of 'Combined Toning and Fixing Solution' into the drawer where they were. Robert waved back, and immediately felt that he had been unwise. For his signal had been seen by the besieging force, and two men in steel-caps were coming towards him. They had high brown boots on their long legs, and they came towards him with such great strides that Robert remembered the shortness of his own legs and did not run away. He knew it would be useless to himself, and he feared it might be irritating to the foe. So he stood still, and the two men seemed quite pleased with him.

'By my halidom,' said one, 'a brave varlet this!'

Robert felt pleased at being CALLED brave, and somehow it made him FEEL brave. He passed over the 'varlet'. It was the way people talked in historical romances for the young, he knew, and it was evidently not meant for rudeness. He only hoped he would be able to understand what they said to him. He had not always been able quite to follow the conversations in the historical romances for the young.

'His garb is strange,' said the other. 'Some outlandish treachery, belike.'

'Say, lad, what brings thee hither?'

Robert knew this meant, 'Now then, youngster, what are you up to here, eh?' - so he said:

'If you please, I want to go home.'

'Go, then!' said the man in the longest boots; 'none hindereth, and nought lets us to follow. Zooks!' he added in a cautious undertone, 'I misdoubt me but he beareth tidings to the besieged.'

'Where dwellest thou, young knave?' inquired the man with the largest steel-cap.

'Over there,' said Robert; and directly he had said it he knew he ought to have said 'Yonder!'

'Ha - sayest so?' rejoined the longest boots. 'Come hither, boy. This is a matter for our leader.'

And to the leader Robert was dragged forthwith - by the reluctant ear.

The leader was the most glorious creature Robert had ever seen. He was exactly like the pictures Robert had so often admired in the historical romances. He had armour, and a helmet, and a horse, and a crest, and feathers, and a shield, and a lance, and a sword. His armour and his weapons were all, I am almost sure, of quite different periods. The shield was thirteenth-century, while the sword was of the pattern used in the Peninsular War. The cuirass was of the time of Charles I, and the helmet dated from the Second Crusade. The arms on the shield were very grand - three red running lions on a blue ground. The tents were of the latest brand and the whole appearance of camp, army, and leader might have been a shock to some. But Robert was dumb with admiration, and it all seemed to him perfectly correct, because he knew no more of heraldry or archaeology than the gifted artists who usually drew the pictures for the historical romances. The scene was indeed 'exactly like a picture'. He admired it all so much that he felt braver than ever.

'Come hither, lad,' said the glorious leader, when the men in Cromwellian steel-caps had said a few low eager words. And he took off his helmet, because he could not see properly with it on. He had a kind face, and long fair hair. 'Have no fear; thou shalt take no scathe,' he said.

Robert was glad of that. He wondered what 'scathe' was, and if it was nastier than the senna tea which he had to take sometimes.

'Unfold thy tale without alarm,' said the leader kindly. 'Whence comest thou, and what is thine intent?'

'My what?' said Robert.

'What seekest thou to accomplish? What is thine errand, that thou wanderest here alone among these rough men-at-arms? Poor child, thy mother's heart aches for thee e'en now, I'll warrant me.'

'I don't think so,' said Robert; 'you see, she doesn't know I'm out.'

The leader wiped away a manly tear, exactly as a leader in a historical romance would have done, and said:

'Fear not to speak the truth, my child; thou hast nought to fear from Wulfric de Talbot.'

Robert had a wild feeling that this glorious leader of the besieging party - being himself part of a wish - would be able to understand better than Martha, or the gipsies, or the policeman in Rochester, or the clergyman of yesterday, the true tale of the wishes and the Psammead. The only difficulty was that he knew he could never remember enough 'quothas' and 'beshrew me's', and things like that, to make his talk sound like the talk of a boy in a historical romance. However, he began boldly enough, with a sentence straight out of Ralph de Courcy; or, The Boy Crusader. He said:

'Grammercy for thy courtesy, fair sir knight. The fact is, it's like this - and I hope you're not in a hurry, because the story's rather a breather. Father and mother are away, and when we were down playing in the sand-pits we found a Psammead.'

'I cry thee mercy! A Sammyadd?' said the knight.

'Yes, a sort of - of fairy, or enchanter - yes, that's it, an enchanter; and he said we could have a wish every day, and we wished first to be beautiful.'

'Thy wish was scarce granted,' muttered one of the men-at-arms, looking at Robert, who went on as if he had not heard, though he thought the remark very rude indeed.

'And then we wished for money - treasure, you know; but we couldn't spend it. And yesterday we wished for wings, and we got them, and we had a ripping time to begin with -'

'Thy speech is strange and uncouth,' said Sir Wulfric de Talbot. 'Repeat thy words - what hadst thou?'

'A ripping - I mean a jolly - no - we were contented with our lot - that's what I mean; only, after that we got into an awful fix.'

'What is a fix? A fray, mayhap?'

'No - not a fray. A - a - a tight place.'

'A dungeon? Alas for thy youthful fettered limbs!' said the knight, with polite sympathy.

'It wasn't a dungeon. We just - just encountered undeserved misfortunes,' Robert explained, 'and to-day we are punished by not being allowed to go out. That's where I live,' - he pointed to the castle. 'The others are in there, and they're not allowed to go out. It's all the Psammead's - I mean the enchanter's fault. I wish we'd never seen him.'

'He is an enchanter of might?'

'Oh yes - of might and main. Rather!'

'And thou deemest that it is the spells of the enchanter whom thou hast angered that have lent strength to the besieging party,' said the gallant leader; 'but know thou that Wulfric de Talbot needs no enchanter's aid to lead his followers to victory.'

'No, I'm sure you don't,' said Robert, with hasty courtesy; 'of course not - you wouldn't, you know. But, all the same, it's partly his fault, but we're most to blame. You couldn't have done anything if it hadn't been for us.'

'How now, bold boy?' asked Sir Wulfric haughtily. 'Thy speech is dark, and eke scarce courteous. Unravel me this riddle!'

'Oh,' said Robert desperately, 'of course you don't know it, but you're not REAL at all. You're only here because the others must have been idiots enough to wish for a castle - and when the sun sets you'll just vanish away, and it'll be all right.'

The captain and the men-at-arms exchanged glances, at first pitying, and then sterner, as the longest-booted man said, 'Beware, noble my lord; the urchin doth but feign madness to escape from our clutches. Shall we not bind him?'

'I'm no more mad than you are,' said Robert angrily, 'perhaps not so much - only, I was an idiot to think you'd understand anything. Let me go - I haven't done anything to you.'

'Whither?' asked the knight, who seemed to have believed all the enchanter story till it came to his own share in it. 'Whither wouldst thou wend?'

'Home, of course.' Robert pointed to the castle.

'To carry news of succour? Nay!'

'All right then,' said Robert, struck by a sudden idea; 'then let me go somewhere else.' His mind sought eagerly among his memories of the historical romance.

'Sir Wulfric de Talbot,' he said slowly, 'should think foul scorn to - to keep a chap - I mean one who has done him no hurt - when he wants to cut off quietly - I mean to depart without violence.'

'This to my face! Beshrew thee for a knave!' replied Sir Wulfric. But the appeal seemed to have gone home. 'Yet thou sayest sooth,' he added thoughtfully. 'Go where thou wilt,' he added nobly, 'thou art free. Wulfric de Talbot warreth not with babes, and Jakin here shall bear thee company.' 'All right,' said Robert wildly. 'Jakin will enjoy himself, I think. Come on, Jakin. Sir Wulfric, I salute thee.'

He saluted after the modern military manner, and set off running to the sand-pit, Jakin's long boots keeping up easily.

He found the Fairy. He dug it up, he woke it up, he implored it to give him one more wish.

'I've done two to-day already,' it grumbled, 'and one was as stiff a bit of work as ever I did.'

'Oh, do, do, do, do, DO!' said Robert, while Jakin looked on with an expression of open-mouthed horror at the strange beast that talked, and gazed with its snail's eyes at him.

'Well, what is it?' snapped the Psammead, with cross sleepiness.

'I wish I was with the others,' said Robert. And the Psammead began to swell. Robert never thought of wishing the castle and the siege away. Of course he knew they had all come out of a wish, but swords and daggers and pikes and lances seemed much too real to be wished away. Robert lost consciousness for an instant. When he opened his eyes the others were crowding round him.

'We never heard you come in,' they said. 'How awfully jolly of you to wish it to give us our wish!'

'Of course we understood that was what you'd done.'

'But you ought to have told us. Suppose we'd wished something silly.'

'Silly?' said Robert, very crossly indeed. 'How much sillier could you have been, I'd like to know? You nearly settled ME - I can tell you.'

Then he told his story, and the others admitted that it certainly had been rough on him. But they praised his courage and cleverness so much that he presently got back his lost temper, and felt braver than ever, and consented to be captain of the besieged force.

'We haven't done anything yet,' said Anthea comfortably; 'we waited for you. We're going to shoot at them through these little loopholes with the bow and arrows uncle gave you, and you shall have first shot.'

'I don't think I would,' said Robert cautiously; 'you don't know what they're like near to. They've got REAL bows and arrows - an awful length - and swords and pikes and daggers, and all sorts of sharp things. They're all quite, quite real. It's not just a - a picture, or a vision, or anything; they can hurt us - or kill us even, I shouldn't wonder. I can feel my ear all sore still. Look here - have you explored the castle? Because I think we'd better let them alone as long as they let us alone. I heard that Jakin man say they weren't going to attack till just before sundown. We can be getting ready for the attack. Are there any soldiers in the castle to defend it?'

'We don't know,' said Cyril. 'You see, directly I'd wished we were in a besieged castle, everything seemed to go upside down, and,when it came straight we looked out of the window, and saw the camp and things and you - and of course we kept on looking at everything. Isn't this room jolly? It's as real as real!'

It was. It was square, with stone walls four feet thick, and great beams for ceiling. A low door at the corner led to a flight of steps, up and down. The children went down; they found themselves in a great arched gatehouse - the enormous doors were shut and barred. There was a window in a little room at the bottom of the round turret up which the stair wound, rather larger than the other windows, and looking through it they saw that the drawbridge was up and the portcullis down; the moat looked very wide and deep. Opposite the great door that led to the moat was another great door, with a little door in it. The children went through this, and found themselves in a big paved courtyard, with the great grey walls of the castle rising dark and heavy on all four sides.

Near the middle of the courtyard stood Martha, moving her right hand backwards and forwards in the air. The cook was stooping down and moving her hands, also in a very curious way. But. the oddest and at the same time most terrible thing was the Lamb, who was sitting on nothing, about three feet from the ground, laughing happily.

The children ran towards him. Just as Anthea was reaching out her arms to take him, Martha said crossly, 'Let him alone - do, miss, when he is good.'

'But what's he DOING?' said Anthea.

'Doing? Why, a-setting in his high chair as good as gold, a precious, watching me doing of the ironing. Get along with you, do - my iron's cold again.'

She went towards the cook, and seemed to poke an invisible fire with an unseen poker - the cook seemed to be putting an unseen dish into an invisible oven.

'Run along with you, do,' she said; 'I'm behindhand as it is. You won't get no dinner if you come a-hindering of me like this. Come, off you goes, or I'll pin a dishcloth to some of your tails.'

'You're sure the Lamb's all right?' asked Jane anxiously.

'Right as ninepence, if you don't come unsettling of him. I thought you'd like to be rid of him for to-day; but take him, if you want him, for gracious' sake.'

'No, no,' they said, and hastened away. They would have to defend the castle presently, and the Lamb was safer even suspended in mid-air in an invisible kitchen than in the guardroom of a besieged castle. They went through the first doorway they came to, and sat down helplessly on a wooden bench that ran along the room inside.

'How awful!' said Anthea and Jane together; and Jane added, 'I feel as if I was in a mad asylum.'

'What does it mean?' Anthea said. 'It's creepy; I don't like it. I wish we'd wished for something plain - a rocking-horse, or a donkey, or something.'

'It's no use wishing NOW,' said Robert bitterly; and Cyril said:

'Do dry up a sec; I want to think.'

He buried his face in his hands, and the others looked about them. They were in a long room with an arched roof. There were wooden tables along it, and one across at the end of the room, on a sort of raised platform. The room was very dim and dark. The floor was strewn with dry things like sticks, and they did not smell nice.

Cyril sat up suddenly and said:

'Look here - it's all right. I think it's like this. You know, we wished that the servants shouldn't notice any difference when we got wishes. And nothing happens to the Lamb unless we specially wish it to. So of course they don't notice the castle or anything. But then the castle is on the same place where our house was - is, I mean - and the servants have to go on being in the house, or else they would notice. But you can't have a castle mixed up with our house - and so we can't see the house, because we see the castle; and they can't see the castle, because they go on seeing the house; and so -'

'Oh, DON'T!' said Jane; 'you make my head go all swimmy, like being on a roundabout. It doesn't matter! Only, I hope we shall be able to see our dinner, that's all - because if it's invisible it'll be unfeelable as well, and then we can't eat it! I KNOW it will, because I tried to feel if I could feel the Lamb's chair, and there was nothing under him at all but air. And we can't eat air, and I feel just as if I hadn't had any breakfast for years and years.'

'It's no use thinking about it,' said Anthea. 'Let's go on exploring. Perhaps we might find something to eat.'

This lighted hope in every breast, and they went on exploring the castle. But though it was the most perfect and delightful castle you can possibly imagine, and furnished in the most complete and beautiful manner, neither food nor men-at-arms were to be found in it. 'If only you'd thought of wishing to be besieged in a castle thoroughly garrisoned and provisioned!' said Jane reproachfully.

'You can't think of everything, you know,' said Anthea. 'I should think it must be nearly dinner-time by now.'

It wasn't; but they hung about watching the strange movements of the servants in the middle of the courtyard, because, of course, they couldn't be sure where the dining-room of the invisible house was. Presently they saw Martha carrying an invisible tray across the courtyard, for it seemed that, by the most fortunate accident, the dining-room of the house and the banqueting-hall of the castle were in the same place. But oh, how their hearts sank when they perceived that the tray was invisible!

They waited in wretched silence while Martha went through the form of carving an unseen leg of mutton and serving invisible greens and potatoes with a spoon that no one could see. When she had left the room, the children looked at the empty table, and then at each other.

'This is worse than anything,' said Robert, who had not till now been particularly keen on his dinner.

'I'm not so very hungry,' said Anthea, trying to make the best of things, as usual.

Cyril tightened his belt ostentatiously. Jane burst into tears.

Chapter 7. A Siege and Bed

The children were sitting in the gloomy banqueting-hall, at the end of one of the long bare wooden tables. There was now no hope. Martha had brought in the dinner, and the dinner was invisible, and unfeelable too; for, when they rubbed their hands along the table, they knew but too well that for them there was nothing there BUT table.

Suddenly Cyril felt in his pocket.

'Right, oh!' he cried. 'Look here! Biscuits.'

Rather broken and crumbled, certainly, but still biscuits. Three whole ones, and a generous handful of crumbs and fragments.

'I got them this morning - cook - and I'd quite forgotten,' he explained as he divided them with scrupulous fairness into four heaps.

They were eaten in a happy silence, though they tasted a little oddly, because they had been in Cyril's pocket all the morning with a hank of tarred twine, some green fir-cones, and a ball of cobbler's wax.

'Yes, but look here, Squirrel,' said Robert; 'you're so clever at explaining about invisibleness and all that. How is it the biscuits are here, and all the bread and meat and things have disappeared?'

'I don't know,' said Cyril after a pause, 'unless it's because WE had them. Nothing about us has changed. Everything's in my pocket all right.'

'Then if we HAD the mutton it would be real,' said Robert. 'Oh, don't I wish we could find it!'

'But we can't find it. I suppose it isn't ours till we've got it in our mouths.'

'Or in our pockets,' said Jane, thinking of the biscuits.

'Who puts mutton in their pockets, goose-girl?' said Cyril. 'But I know - at any rate, I'll try it!'

He leaned over the table with his face about an inch from it, and kept opening and shutting his mouth as if he were taking bites out of air.

'It's no good,' said Robert in deep dejection. 'You'll only - Hullo!'

Cyril stood up with a grin of triumph, holding a square piece of bread in his mouth. It was quite real. Everyone saw it. It is true that, directly he bit a piece off, the rest vanished; but it was all right, because he knew he had it in his hand though he could neither see nor feel it. He took another bite from the air between his fingers, and it turned into bread as he bit. The next moment all the others were following his example, and opening and shutting their mouths an inch or so from the bare-looking table. Robert captured a slice of mutton, and - but I think I will draw a veil over the rest of this painful scene. It is enough to say that they all had enough mutton, and that when Martha came to change the plates she said she had never seen such a mess in all her born days.

The pudding was, fortunately, a plain suet roly-poly, and in answer to Martha's questions the children all with one accord said that they would NOT have treacle on it - nor jam, nor sugar - 'Just plain, please,' they said. Martha said, 'Well, I never - what next, I wonder!' and went away.

Then ensued another scene on which I will not dwell, for nobody looks nice picking up slices of suet pudding from the table in its mouth, like a dog. The great thing, after all, was that they had had dinner; and now everyone felt more courage to prepare for the attack that was to be delivered before sunset. Robert, as captain, insisted on climbing to the top of one of the towers to reconnoitre, so up they all went. And now they could see all round the castle, and could see, too, that beyond the moat, on every side, the tents of the besieging party were pitched. Rather uncomfortable shivers ran down the children's backs as they saw that all the men were very busy cleaning or sharpening their arms, re-stringing their bows, and polishing their shields. A large party came along the road, with horses dragging along the great trunk of a tree; and Cyril felt quite pale, because he knew this was for a battering-ram.

'What a good thing we've got a moat,' he said; 'and what a good thing the drawbridge is up - I should never have known how to work it.'

'Of course it would be up in a besieged castle.'

'You'd think there ought to have been soldiers in it, wouldn't you?' said Robert.

'You see you don't know how long it's been besieged,' said Cyril darkly; 'perhaps most of the brave defenders were killed quite early in the siege and all the provisions eaten, and now there are only a few intrepid survivors - that's us, and we are going to defend it to the death.'

'How do you begin - defending to the death, I mean?' asked Anthea.

'We ought to be heavily armed - and then shoot at them when they advance to the attack.'

'They used to pour boiling lead down on besiegers when they got too close,' said Anthea. 'Father showed me the holes on purpose for pouring it down through at Bodiam Castle. And there are holes like it in the gate-tower here.'

'I think I'm glad it's only a game; it IS only a game, isn't it?' said Jane.

But no one answered.

The children found plenty of strange weapons in the castle, and if they were armed at all it was soon plain that they would be, as Cyril said, 'armed heavily' - for these swords and lances and crossbows were far too weighty even for Cyril's manly strength; and as for the longbows, none of the children could even begin to bend them. The daggers were better; but Jane hoped that the besiegers would not come close enough for daggers to be of any use.

'Never mind, we can hurl them like javelins,' said Cyril, 'or drop them on people's heads. I say - there are lots of stones on the other side of the courtyard. If we took some of those up, just to drop on their heads if they were to try swimming the moat.'

So a heap of stones grew apace, up in the room above the gate; and another heap, a shiny spiky dangerous-looking heap, of daggers and knives.

As Anthea was crossing the courtyard for more stones, a sudden and valuable idea came to her. She went to Martha and said, 'May we have just biscuits for tea? We're going to play at besieged castles, and we'd like the biscuits to provision the garrison. Put mine in my pocket, please, my hands are so dirty. And I'll tell the others to fetch theirs.'

This was indeed a happy thought, for now with four generous handfuls of air, which turned to biscuit as Martha crammed it into their pockets, the garrison was well provisioned till sundown.

They brought up some iron pots of cold water to pour on the besiegers instead of hot lead, with which the castle did not seem to be provided.

The afternoon passed with wonderful quickness. It was very exciting; but none of them, except Robert, could feel all the time that this was real deadly dangerous work. To the others, who had only seen the camp and the besiegers from a distance, the whole thing seemed half a game of make-believe, and half a splendidly distinct and perfectly safe dream. But it was only now and then that Robert could feel this.

When it seemed to be tea-time the biscuits were eaten with water from the deep well in the courtyard, drunk out of horns. Cyril insisted on putting by eight of the biscuits, in case anyone should feel faint in stress of battle.

just as he was putting away the reserve biscuits in a sort of little stone cupboard without a door, a sudden sound made him drop three. It was the loud fierce cry of a trumpet.

'You see it IS real,' said Robert, 'and they are going to attack.'

All rushed to the narrow windows.

'Yes,' said Robert, 'they're all coming out of their tents and moving about like ants. There's that Jakin dancing about where the bridge joins on. I wish he could see me put my tongue out at him! Yah!'

The others were far too pale to wish to put their tongues out at anybody. They looked at Robert with surprised respect. Anthea said:

'You really ARE brave, Robert.'

'Rot!' Cyril's pallor turned to redness now, all in a minute. 'He's been getting ready to be brave all the afternoon. And I wasn't ready, that's all. I shall be braver than he is in half a jiffy.'

'Oh dear!' said Jane, 'what does it matter which of you is the bravest? I think Cyril was a perfect silly to wish for a castle, and I don't want to play.'

'It ISN'T' - Robert was beginning sternly, but Anthea interrupted -

'Oh yes, you do,' she said coaxingly; 'it's a very nice game, really, because they can't possibly get in, and if they do the women and children are always spared by civilized armies.'

'But are you quite, quite sure they ARE civilized?' asked Jane, panting. 'They seem to be such a long time ago.'

'Of course they are.' Anthea pointed cheerfully through the narrow window. 'Why, look at the little flags on their lances, how bright they are - and how fine the leader is! Look, that's him - isn't it, Robert? - on the grey horse.'

Jane consented to look, and the scene was almost too pretty to be alarming. The green turf, the white tents, the flash of pennoned lances, the gleam of armour, and the bright colours of scarf and tunic - it was just like a splendid coloured picture. The trumpets were sounding, and when the trumpets stopped for breath the children could hear the cling-clang of armour and the murmur of voices.

A trumpeter came forward to the edge of the moat, which now seemed very much narrower than at first, and blew the longest and loudest blast they had yet heard. When the blaring noise had died away, a man who was with the trumpeter shouted:

'What ho, within there!' and his voice came plainly to the garrison in the gate-house.

'Hullo there!' Robert bellowed back at once.

'In the name of our Lord the King, and of our good lord and trusty leader Sir Wulfric de Talbot, we summon this castle to surrender - on pain of fire and sword and no quarter. Do ye surrender?'

'No,' bawled Robert, 'of course we don't! Never,

Never, NEVER!'

The man answered back:

'Then your fate be on your own heads.'

'Cheer,' said Robert in a fierce whisper. 'Cheer to show them we aren't afraid, and rattle the daggers to make more noise. One, two, three! Hip, hip, hooray! Again - Hip, hip, hooray! One more - Hip, hip, hooray!' The cheers were rather high and weak, but the rattle of the daggers lent them strength and depth.

There was another shout from the camp across the moat - and then the beleaguered fortress felt that the attack had indeed begun.

It was getting rather dark in the room above the great gate, and Jane took a very little courage as she remembered that sunset couldn't be far off now.

'The moat is dreadfully thin,' said Anthea.

'But they can't get into the castle even if they do swim over,' said Robert. And as he spoke he heard feet on the stair outside - heavy feet and the clank of steel. No one breathed for a moment. The steel and the feet went on up the turret stairs. Then Robert sprang softly to the door. He pulled off his shoes.

'Wait here,' he whispered, and stole quickly and softly after the boots and the spur-clank. He peeped into the upper room. The man was there - and it was Jakin, all dripping with moat-water, and he was fiddling about with the machinery which Robert felt sure worked the drawbridge. Robert banged the door suddenly, and turned the great key in the lock, just as Jakin sprang to the inside of the door. Then he tore downstairs and into the little turret at the foot of the tower where the biggest window was.

'We ought to have defended THIS!' he cried to the others as they followed him. He was just in time. Another man had swum over, and his fingers were on the window-ledge. Robert never knew how the man had managed to climb up out of the water. But he saw the clinging fingers, and hit them as hard as he could with an iron bar that he caught up from the floor. The man fell with a plop-plash into the moat-water. In another moment Robert was outside the little room, had banged its door and was shooting home the enormous bolts, and calling to Cyril to lend a hand.

Then they stood in the arched gate-house, breathing hard and looking at each other. Jane's mouth was open.

'Cheer up, Janey,' said Robert - 'it won't last much longer.'

There was a creaking above, and something rattled and shook. The pavement they stood on seemed to tremble. Then a crash told them that the drawbridge had been lowered to its place.

'That's that beast Jakin,' said Robert. 'There's still the portcullis; I'm almost certain that's worked from lower down.'

And now the drawbridge rang and echoed hollowly to the hoofs of horses and the tramp of armed men. 'Up - quick!' cried Robert. 'Let's drop things on them.'

Even the girls were feeling almost brave now. They followed Robert quickly, and under his directions began to drop stones out through the long narrow windows. There was a confused noise below, and some groans.

'Oh dear!' said Anthea, putting down the stone she was just going to drop out. 'I'm afraid we've hurt somebody!'

Robert caught up the stone in a fury.

'I should just hope we HAD!' he said; 'I'd give something for a jolly good boiling kettle of lead. Surrender, indeed!'

And now came more tramping, and a pause, and then the thundering thump of the battering-ram. And the little room was almost quite dark.

'We've held it,' cried Robert, 'we won't surrender! The sun MUST set in a minute. Here - they're all jawing underneath again. Pity there's no time to get more stones! Here, pour that water down on them. It's no good, of course, but they'll hate it.'

'Oh dear!' said Jane; 'don't you think we'd better surrender?'

'Never!' said Robert; 'we'll have a parley if you like, but we'll never surrender. Oh, I'll be a soldier when I grow up - you just see if I don't. I won't go into the Civil Service, whatever anyone says.'

'Let's wave a handkerchief and ask for a parley,' Jane pleaded. 'I don't believe the sun's going to set to-night at all.'

'Give them the water first - the brutes!' said the bloodthirsty Robert. So Anthea tilted the pot over the nearest lead-hole, and poured. They heard a splash below, but no one below seemed to have felt it. And again the ram battered the great door. Anthea paused.

'How idiotic,' said Robert, lying flat on the floor and putting one eye to the lead hole. 'Of course the holes go straight down into the gate-house - that's for when the enemy has got past the door and the portcullis, and almost all is lost. Here, hand me the pot.' He crawled on to the three-cornered window-ledge in the middle of the wall, and, taking the pot from Anthea, poured the water out through the arrow-slit.

And as he began to pour, the noise of the battering-ram and the trampling of the foe and the shouts of 'Surrender!' and 'De Talbot for ever!' all suddenly stopped and went out like the snuff of a candle; the little dark room seemed to whirl round and turn topsy-turvy, and when the children came to themselves there they were safe and sound, in the big front bedroom of their own house - the house with the ornamental nightmare iron-top to the roof.

They all crowded to the window and looked out. The moat and the tents and the besieging force were all gone - and there was the garden with its tangle of dahlias and marigolds and asters and late roses, and the spiky iron railings and the quiet white road.

Everyone drew a deep breath.

'And that's all right!' said Robert. 'I told you so! And, I say, we didn't surrender, did we?'

'Aren't you glad now I wished for a castle?' asked Cyril.

'I think I am NOW,' said Anthea slowly. 'But I wouldn't wish for it again, I think, Squirrel dear!'

'Oh, it was simply splendid!' said Jane unexpectedly. 'I wasn't frightened a bit.'

'Oh, I say!' Cyril was beginning, but Anthea stopped him.

'Look here,' she said, 'it's just come into my head. This is the very first thing we've wished for that hasn't got us into a row. And there hasn't been the least little scrap of a row about this. Nobody's raging downstairs, we're safe and sound, we've had an awfully jolly day - at least, not jolly exactly, but you know what I mean. And we know now how brave Robert is - and Cyril too, of course,' she added hastily, 'and Jane as well. And we haven't got into a row with a single grown-up.'

The door was opened suddenly and fiercely.

'You ought to be ashamed of yourselves,' said the voice of Martha, and they could tell by her voice that she was very angry indeed. 'I thought you couldn't last through the day without getting up to some doggery! A person can't take a breath of air on the front doorstep but you must be emptying the wash-hand jug on to their heads! Off you go to bed, the lot of you, and try to get up better children in the morning. Now then - don't let me have to tell you twice. If I find any of you not in bed in ten minutes I'll let you know it, that's all! A new cap, and everything!'

She flounced out amid a disregarded chorus of regrets and apologies. The children were very sorry, but really it was not their faults. You can't help it if you are pouring water on a besieging foe, and your castle suddenly changes into your house - and everything changes with it except the water, and that happens to fall on somebody else's clean cap.

'I don't know why the water didn't change into nothing, though,' said Cyril.

'Why should it?' asked Robert. 'Water's water all the world over.' 'I expect the castle well was the same as ours in the stable-yard,' said Jane. And that was really the case.

'I thought we couldn't get through a wish-day without a row,' said Cyril; 'it was much too good to be true. Come on, Bobs, my military hero. If we lick into bed sharp she won't be so frumious, and perhaps she'll bong us up some supper. I'm jolly hungry! Good-night, kids.'

'Good-night. I hope the castle won't come creeping back in the night,' said Jane.

'Of course it won't,' said Anthea briskly, 'but Martha will - not in the night, but in a minute. Here, turn round, I'll get that knot out of your pinafore strings.'

'Wouldn't it have been degrading for Sir Wulfric de Talbot,' said Jane dreamily, 'if he could have known that half the besieged garrison wore pinafores?'

'And the other half knickerbockers. Yes - frightfully. Do stand still - you're only tightening the knot,' said Anthea.

Chapter 8. Bigger Than the Baker's Boy

'Look here,' said Cyril. 'I've got an idea.'

'Does it hurt much?' said Robert sympathetically.

'Don't be a jackape! I'm not humbugging.'

'Shut up, Bobs!' said Anthea.

'Silence for the Squirrel's oration,' said Robert.

Cyril balanced himself on the edge of the water-butt in the backyard, where they all happened to be, and spoke.

'Friends, Romans, countrymen - and women - we found a Sammyadd. We have had wishes. We've had wings, and being beautiful as the day - ugh! - that was pretty jolly beastly if you like - and wealth and castles, and that rotten gipsy business with the Lamb. But we're no forrader. We haven't really got anything worth having for our wishes.'

'We've had things happening,' said Robert; 'that's always something.'

'It's not enough, unless they're the right things,' said Cyril firmly. 'Now I've been thinking -' 'Not really?' whispered Robert.

'In the silent what's-its-names of the night. It's like suddenly being asked something out of history - the date of the Conquest or something; you know it all right all the time, but when you're asked it all goes out of your head. Ladies and gentlemen, you know jolly well that when we're all rotting about in the usual way heaps of things keep cropping up, and then real earnest wishes come into the heads of the beholder -'

'Hear, hear!' said Robert.

'- of the beholder, however stupid he is,' Cyril went on. 'Why, even Robert might happen to think of a really useful wish if he didn't injure his poor little brains trying so hard to think. - Shut up, Bobs, I tell you! - You'll have the whole show over.'

A struggle on the edge of a water-butt is exciting, but damp. When it was over, and the boys were partially dried, Anthea said:

'It really was you began it, Bobs. Now honour is satisfied, do let Squirrel go on. We're wasting the whole morning.'

'Well then,' said Cyril, still wringing the water out of the tails of his jacket, 'I'll call it pax if Bobs will.'

'Pax then,' said Robert sulkily. 'But I've got a lump as big as a cricket ball over my eye.'

Anthea patiently offered a dust-coloured handkerchief, and Robert bathed his wounds in silence. 'Now, Squirrel,' she said.

'Well then - let's just play bandits, or forts, or soldiers, or any of the old games. We're dead sure to think of something if we try not to. You always do.'

The others consented. Bandits was hastily chosen for the game. 'It's as good as anything else,' said Jane gloomily. It must be owned that Robert was at first but a half-hearted bandit, but when Anthea had borrowed from Martha the red-spotted handkerchief in which the keeper had brought her mushrooms that morning, and had tied up Robert's head with it so that he could be the wounded hero who had saved the bandit captain's life the day before, he cheered up wonderfully. All were soon armed. Bows and arrows slung on the back look well; and umbrellas and cricket stumps stuck through the belt give a fine impression of the wearer's being armed to the teeth. The white cotton hats that men wear in the country nowadays have a very brigandish effect when a few turkey's feathers are stuck in them. The Lamb's mail-cart was covered with a red-and-blue checked tablecloth, and made an admirable baggage-wagon. The Lamb asleep inside it was not at all in the way. So the banditti set out along the road that led to the sand-pit.

'We ought to be near the Sammyadd,' said Cyril, 'in case we think of anything suddenly.'

It is all very well to make up your minds to play bandits - or chess, or ping-pong, or any other agreeable game - but it is not easy to do it with spirit when all the wonderful wishes you can think of, or can't think of, are waiting for you round the corner. The game was dragging a little, and some of the bandits were beginning to feel that the others were disagreeable things, and were saying so candidly, when the baker's boy came along the road with loaves in a basket. The opportunity was not one to be lost.

'Stand and deliver!' cried Cyril.

'Your money or your life!' said Robert.

And they stood on each side of the baker's boy. Unfortunately, he did not seem to enter into the spirit of the thing at all. He was a baker's boy of an unusually large size. He merely said:

'Chuck it now, d'ye hear!' and pushed the bandits aside most disrespectfully.

Then Robert lassoed him with jane's skipping-rope, and instead of going round his shoulders, as Robert intended, it went round his feet and tripped him up. The basket was upset, the beautiful new loaves went bumping and bouncing all over the dusty chalky road. The girls ran to pick them up, and all in a moment Robert and the baker's boy were fighting it out, man to man, with Cyril to see fair play, and the skipping-rope twisting round their legs like an interested snake that wished to be a peacemaker. It did not succeed; indeed the way the boxwood handles sprang up and hit the fighters on the shins and ankles was not at all peace-making. I know this is the second fight - or contest - in this chapter, but I can't help it. It was that sort of day. You know yourself there are days when rows seem to keep on happening, quite without your meaning them to. If I were a writer of tales of adventure such as those which used to appear in The Boys of England when I was young, of course I should be able to describe the fight, but I cannot do it. I never can see what happens during a fight, even when it is only dogs. Also, if I had been one of these Boys of England writers, Robert would have got the best of it. But I am like George Washington - I cannot tell a lie, even about a cherry-tree, much less about a fight, and I cannot conceal from you that Robert was badly beaten, for the second time that day. The baker's boy blacked his other eye, and, being ignorant of the first rules of fair play and gentlemanly behaviour, he also pulled Robert's hair, and kicked him on the knee. Robert always used to say he could have licked the butcher if it hadn't been for the girls. But I am not sure. Anyway, what happened was this, and very painful it was to self-respecting boys.

Cyril was just tearing off his coat so as to help his brother in proper style, when Jane threw her arms round his legs and began to cry and ask him not to go and be beaten too. That 'too' was very nice for Robert, as you can imagine - but it was nothing to what he felt when Anthea rushed in between him and the baker's boy, and caught that unfair and degraded fighter round the waist, imploring him not to fight any more.

'Oh, don't hurt my brother any more!' she said in floods of tears. 'He didn't mean it - it's only play. And I'm sure he's very sorry.'

You see how unfair this was to Robert. Because, if the baker's boy had had any right and chivalrous instincts, and had yielded to Anthea's pleading and accepted her despicable apology, Robert could not, in honour, have done anything to him at a future time. But Robert's fears, if he had any, were soon dispelled. Chivalry was a stranger to the breast of the baker's boy. He pushed Anthea away very roughly, and he chased Robert with kicks and unpleasant conversation right down the road to the sand-pit, and there, with one last kick, he landed him in a heap of sand.

'I'll larn you, you young varmint!' he said, and went off to pick up his loaves and go about his business. Cyril, impeded by Jane, could do nothing without hurting her, for she clung round his legs with the strength of despair. The baker's boy went off red and damp about the face; abusive to the last, he called them a pack of silly idiots, and disappeared round the corner. Then Jane's grasp loosened. Cyril turned away in silent dignity to follow Robert, and the girls followed him, weeping without restraint.

It was not a happy party that flung itself down in the sand beside the sobbing Robert. For Robert was sobbing - mostly with rage. Though of course I know that a really heroic boy is always dry-eyed after a fight. But then he always wins, which had not been the case with Robert.

Cyril was angry with Jane; Robert was furious with Anthea; the girls were miserable; and not one of the four was pleased with the baker's boy. There was, as French writers say, 'a silence full of emotion'.

Then Robert dug his toes and his hands into the sand and wriggled in his rage. 'He'd better wait till I'm grown up - the cowardly brute! Beast! - I hate him! But I'll pay him out. Just because he's bigger than me.'

'You began,' said Jane incautiously.

'I know I did, silly - but I was only rotting - and he kicked me - look here —'

Robert tore down a stocking and showed a purple bruise touched up with red. 'I only wish I was bigger than him, that's all.'

He dug his fingers in the sand, and sprang up, for his hand had touched something furry. It was the Psammead, of course - 'On the look-out to make sillies of them as usual,' as Cyril remarked later. And of course the next moment Robert's wish was granted, and he was bigger than the baker's boy. Oh, but much, much bigger. He was bigger than the big policeman who used to be at the crossing at the Mansion House years ago - the one who was so kind in helping old ladies over the crossing - and he was the biggest man I have ever seen, as well as the kindest. No one had a foot-rule in its pocket, so Robert could not be measured - but he was taller than your father would be if he stood on your mother's head, which I am sure he would never be unkind enough to do. He must have been ten or eleven feet high, and as broad as a boy of that height ought to be. his Norfolk suit had fortunately grown too, and now he stood up in it - with one of his enormous stockings turned down to show the gigantic bruise on his vast leg. Immense tears of fury still stood on his flushed giant face. He looked so surprised, and he was so large to be wearing an Eton collar, that the others could not help laughing.

'The Sammyadd's done us again,' said Cyril.

'Not us - ME,' said Robert. 'If you'd got any decent feeling you'd try to make it make you the same size. You've no idea how silly it feels,' he added thoughtlessly.

'And I don't want to; I can jolly well see how silly it looks,' Cyril was beginning; but Anthea said:

'Oh, DON'T! I don't know what's the matter with you boys to-day. Look here, Squirrel, let's play fair. It is hateful for poor old Bobs, all alone up there. Let's ask the Sammyadd for another wish, and, if it will, I do really think we ought to be made the same size.'

The others agreed, but not gaily; but when they found the Psammead, it wouldn't.

'Not I,' it said crossly, rubbing its face with its feet. He's a rude violent boy, and it'll do him good to be the wrong size for a bit. What did he want to come digging me out with his nasty wet hands for? He nearly touched me! He's a perfect savage. A boy of the Stone Age would have had more sense.'

Robert's hands had indeed been wet - with tears.

'Go away and leave me in peace, do,' the Psammead went on. 'I can't think why you don't wish for something sensible - something to eat or drink, or good manners, or good tempers. Go along with you, do!'

It almost snarled as it shook its whiskers, and turned a sulky brown back on them. The most hopeful felt that further parley was vain. They turned again to the colossal Robert.

'Whatever shall we do?' they said; and they all said it.

'First,' said Robert grimly, 'I'm going to reason with that baker's boy. I shall catch him at the end of the road.'

'Don't hit a chap littler than yourself, old man,' said Cyril.

'Do I look like hitting him?' said Robert scornfully. 'Why, I should KILL him. But I'll give him something to remember. Wait till I pull up my stocking.' He pulled up his stocking, which was as large as a small bolster-case, and strode off. His strides were six or seven feet long, so that it was quite easy for him to be at the bottom of the hill, ready to meet the baker's boy when he came down swinging the empty basket to meet his master's cart, which had been leaving bread at the cottages along the road.

Robert crouched behind a haystack in the farmyard, that is at the corner, and when he heard the boy come whistling along, he jumped out at him and caught him by the collar.

'Now,' he said, and his voice was about four times its usual size, just as his body was four times its, 'I'm going to teach you to kick boys smaller than you.'

He lifted up the baker's boy and set him on the top of the haystack, which was about sixteen feet from the ground, and then he sat down on the roof of the cowshed and told the baker's boy exactly what he thought of him. I don't think the boy heard it all - he was in a sort of trance of terror. When Robert had said everything he could think of, and some things twice over, he shook the boy and said:

'And now get down the best way you can,' and left him.

I don't know how the baker's boy got down, but I do know that he missed the cart, and got into the very hottest of hot water when he turned up at last at the bakehouse. I am sorry for him, but, after all, it was quite right that he should be taught that English boys mustn't use their feet when they fight, but their fists. Of course the water he got into only became hotter when he tried to tell his master about the boy he had licked and the giant as high as a church, because no one could possibly believe such a tale as that. Next day the tale was believed - but that was too late to be of any use to the baker's boy.

When Robert rejoined the others he found them in the garden. Anthea had thoughtfully asked Martha to let them have dinner out there - because the dining-room was rather small, and it would have been so awkward to have a brother the size of Robert in there. The Lamb, who had slept peacefully during the whole stormy morning, was now found to be sneezing, and Martha said he had a cold and would be better indoors.

'And really it's just as well,' said Cyril, 'for I don't believe he'd ever have stopped screaming if he'd once seen you the awful size you are!'

Robert was indeed what a draper would call an 'out-size' in boys. He found himself able to step right over the iron gate in the front garden.

Martha brought out the dinner - it was cold veal and baked potatoes, with sago pudding and stewed plums to follow.

She of course did not notice that Robert was anything but the usual size, and she gave him as much meat and potatoes as usual and no more. You have no idea how small your usual helping of dinner looks when you are many times your proper size. Robert groaned, and asked for more bread. But Martha would not go on giving more bread for ever. She was in a hurry, because the keeper intended to call on his way to Benenhurst Fair, and she wished to be dressed smartly before he came.

'I wish WE were going to the Fair,' said Robert.

'You can't go anywhere that size,' said Cyril.

'Why not?' said Robert. 'They have giants at fairs, much bigger ones than me.'

'Not much, they don't,' Cyril was beginning, when Jane screamed 'Oh!' with such loud suddenness that they all thumped her on the back and asked whether she had swallowed a plum-stone.

'No,' she said, breathless from being thumped, 'it's - it's not a plum-stone. it's an idea. Let's take Robert to the Fair, and get them to give us money for showing him! Then we really shall get something out of the old Sammyadd at last!'

'Take me, indeed!' said Robert indignantly. 'Much more likely me take you!'

And so it turned out. The idea appealed irresistibly to everyone but Robert, and even he was brought round by Anthea's suggestion that he should have a double share of any money they might make. There was a little old pony-trap in the coach-house - the kind that is called a governess-cart. It seemed desirable to get to the Fair as quickly as possible, so Robert - who could now take enormous steps and so go very fast indeed - consented to wheel the others in this. It was as easy to him now as wheeling the Lamb in the mail-cart had been in the morning. The Lamb's cold prevented his being of the party.

It was a strange sensation being wheeled in a pony-carriage by a giant. Everyone enjoyed the journey except Robert and the few people they passed on the way. These mostly went into what looked like some kind of standing-up fits by the roadside, as Anthea said. Just outside Benenhurst, Robert hid in a barn, and the others went on to the Fair.

There were some swings, and a hooting tooting blaring merry-go-round, and a shooting-gallery and coconut shies. Resisting an impulse to win a coconut - or at least to attempt the enterprise - Cyril went up to the woman who was loading little guns before the array of glass bottles on strings against a sheet of canvas.

'Here you are, little gentleman!' she said. 'Penny a shot!'

'No, thank you,' said Cyril, 'we are here on business, not on pleasure. Who's the master?'

'The what?'

'The master - the head - the boss of the show.'

'Over there,' she said, pointing to a stout man in a dirty linen jacket who was sleeping in the sun; 'but I don't advise you to wake him sudden. His temper's contrary, especially these hot days. Better have a shot while you're waiting.'

'It's rather important,' said Cyril. 'It'll be very profitable to him. I think he'll be sorry if we take it away.'

'Oh, if it's money in his pocket,' said the woman. 'No kid now? What is it?'

'It's a GIANT.'

'You ARE kidding?'

'Come along and see,' said Anthea.

The woman looked doubtfully at them, then she called to a ragged little girl in striped stockings and a dingy white petticoat that came below her brown frock, and leaving her in charge of the 'shooting-gallery' she turned to Anthea and said, 'Well, hurry up! But if you ARE kidding, you'd best say so. I'm as mild as milk myself, but my Bill he's a fair terror and -'

Anthea led the way to the barn. 'It really IS a giant,' she said. 'He's a giant little boy - in Norfolks like my brother's there. And we didn't bring him up to the Fair because people do stare so, and they seem to go into kind of standing-up fits when they see him. And we thought perhaps you'd like to show him and get pennies; and if you like to pay us something, you can - only, it'll have to be rather a lot, because we promised him he should have a double share of whatever we made.'

The woman murmured something indistinct, of which the children could only hear the words, 'Swelp me!' 'balmy,' and 'crumpet,' which conveyed no definite idea to their minds. She had taken Anthea's hand, and was holding it very firmly; and Anthea could not help wondering what would happen if Robert should have wandered off or turned his proper size during the interval. But she knew that the Psammead's gifts really did last till sunset, however inconvenient their lasting might be; and she did not think, somehow, that Robert would care to go out alone while he was that size.

When they reached the barn and Cyril called 'Robert!' there was a stir among the loose hay, and Robert began to come out. His hand and arm came first - then a foot and leg. When the woman saw the hand she said 'My!' but when she saw the foot she said 'Upon my civvy!' and when, by slow and heavy degrees, the whole of Robert's enormous bulk was at last completely disclosed, she drew a long breath and began to say many things, compared with which 'balmy' and 'crumpet' seemed quite ordinary. She dropped into understandable English at last.

'What'll you take for him?' she said excitedly. 'Anything in reason. We'd have a special van built - leastways, I know where there's a second-hand one would do up handsome - what a baby elephant had, as died. What'll you take? He's soft, ain't he? Them giants mostly is - but I never see - no, never! What'll you take? Down on the nail. We'll treat him like a king, and give him first-rate grub and a doss fit for a bloomin' dook. He must be dotty or he wouldn't need you kids to cart him about. What'll you take for him?'

'They won't take anything,' said Robert sternly. 'I'm no more soft than you are - not so much, I shouldn't wonder. I'll come and be a show for to-day if you'll give me' - he hesitated at the enormous price he was about to ask - 'if you'll give me fifteen shillings.'

'Done,' said the woman, so quickly that Robert felt he had been unfair to himself, and wished he had asked thirty. 'Come on now - and see my Bill - and we'll fix a price for the season. I dessay you might get as much as two quid a week reg'lar. Come on - and make yourself as small as you can, for gracious' sake!'

This was not very small, and a crowd gathered quickly, so that it was at the head of an enthusiastic procession that Robert entered the trampled meadow where the Fair was held, and passed over the stubbly yellow dusty grass to the door of the biggest tent. He crept in, and the woman went to call her Bill.

He was the big sleeping man, and he did not seem at all pleased at being awakened. Cyril, watching through a slit in the tent, saw him scowl and shake a heavy fist and a sleepy head. Then the woman went on speaking very fast. Cyril heard 'Strewth,' and 'biggest draw you ever, so help me!' and he began to share Robert's feeling that fifteen shillings was indeed far too little. Bill slouched up to the tent and entered. When he beheld the magnificent proportions of Robert he said but little - 'Strike me pink!' were the only words the children could afterwards remember - but he produced fifteen shillings, mainly in sixpences and coppers, and handed it to Robert.

'We'll fix up about what you're to draw when the show's over to-night,' he said with hoarse heartiness. 'Lor' love a duck! you'll be that happy with us you'll never want to leave us. Can you do a song now - or a bit of a breakdown?'

'Not to-day,' said Robert, rejecting the idea of trying to sing 'As once in May', a favourite of his mother's, and the only song he could think of at the moment.

'Get Levi and clear them bloomin' photos out. Clear the tent. Stick up a curtain or suthink,' the man went on. 'Lor', what a pity we ain't got no tights his size! But we'll have 'em before the week's out. Young man, your fortune's made. It's a good thing you came to me, and not to some chaps as I could tell you on. I've known blokes as beat their giants, and starved 'em too; so I'll tell you straight, you're in luck this day if you never was afore. 'Cos I'm a lamb, I am - and I don't deceive you.'

'I'm not afraid of anyone's beating ME,' said Robert, looking down on the 'lamb'. Robert was crouched on his knees, because the tent was not big enough for him to stand upright in, but even in that position he could still look down on most people. 'But I'm awfully hungry. I wish you'd get me something to eat.'

'Here, 'Becca,' said the hoarse Bill. 'Get him some grub - the best you've got, mind!' Another whisper followed, of which the children only heard, 'Down in black and white - first thing to-morrow.'

Then the woman went to get the food - it was only bread and cheese when it came, but it was delightful to the large and empty Robert; and the man went to post sentinels round the tent, to give the alarm if Robert should attempt to escape with his fifteen shillings.

'As if we weren't honest,' said Anthea indignantly when the meaning of the sentinels dawned on her.

Then began a very strange and wonderful afternoon.

Bill was a man who knew his business. In a very little while, the photographic views, the spyglasses you look at them through, so that they really seem rather real, and the lights you see them by, were all packed away. A curtain - it was an old red-and-black carpet really - was run across the tent. Robert was concealed behind, and Bill was standing on a trestle-table outside the tent making a speech. It was rather a good speech. It began by saying that the giant it was his privilege to introduce to the public that day was the eldest son of the Emperor of San Francisco, compelled through an unfortunate love affair with the Duchess of the Fiji Islands to leave his own country and take refuge in England - the land of liberty - where freedom was the right of every man, no matter how big he was. It ended by the announcement that the first twenty who came to the tent door should see the giant for threepence apiece. 'After that,' said Bill, 'the price is riz, and I don't undertake to say what it won't be riz to. So now's yer time.'

A young man squiring his sweetheart on her afternoon out was the first to come forward. For that occasion his was the princely attitude - no expense spared - money no object. His girl wished to see the giant? Well, she should see the giant, even though seeing the giant cost threepence each and the other entertainments were all penny ones.

The flap of the tent was raised - the couple entered. Next moment a wild shriek from the girl thrilled through all present. Bill slapped his leg. 'That's done the trick!' he whispered to 'Becca. It was indeed a splendid advertisement of the charms of Robert. When the girl came out she was pale and trembling, and a crowd was round the tent.

'What was it like?' asked a bailiff.

'Oh! - horrid! - you wouldn't believe,' she said. 'It's as big as a barn, and that fierce. It froze the blood in my bones. I wouldn't ha' missed seeing it for anything.'

The fierceness was only caused by Robert's trying not to laugh. But the desire to do that soon left him, and before sunset he was more inclined to cry than to laugh, and more inclined to sleep than either. For, by ones and twos and threes, people kept coming in all the afternoon, and Robert had to shake hands with those who wished it, and allow himself to be punched and pulled and patted and thumped, so that people might make sure he was really real.

The other children sat on a bench and watched and waited, and were very bored indeed. It seemed to them that this was the hardest way of earning money that could have been invented. And only fifteen shillings! Bill had taken four times that already, for the news of the giant had spread, and tradespeople in carts, and gentlepeople in carriages, came from far and near. One gentleman with an eyeglass, and a very large yellow rose in his buttonhole, offered Robert, in an obliging whisper, ten pounds a week to appear at the Crystal Palace. Robert had to say 'No'.

'I can't,' he said regretfully. 'It's no use promising what you can't do.'

'Ah, poor fellow, bound for a term of years, I suppose! Well, here's my card; when your time's up come to me.'

'I will - if I'm the same size then,' said Robert truthfully.

'If you grow a bit, so much the better,' said the gentleman. When he had gone, Robert beckoned Cyril and said:

'Tell them I must and will have an easy. And I want my tea.'

Tea was provided, and a paper hastily pinned on the tent. It said:

CLOSED FOR HALF AN HOUR
WHILE THE GIANT GETS HIS TEA

Then there was a hurried council.

'How am I to get away?' said Robert. 'I've been thinking about it all the afternoon.'

'Why, walk out when the sun sets and you're your right size. They can't do anything to us.'

Robert opened his eyes. 'Why, they'd nearly kill us,' he said, 'when they saw me get my right size. No, we must think of some other way. We MUST be alone when the sun sets.'

'I know,' said Cyril briskly, and he went to the door, outside which Bill was smoking a clay pipe and talking in a low voice to 'Becca. Cyril heard him say - 'Good as havin' a fortune left you.'

'Look here,' said Cyril, 'you can let people come in again in a minute. He's nearly finished his tea. But he must be left alone when the sun sets. He's very queer at that time of day, and if he's worried I won't answer for the consequences.'

'Why - what comes over him?' asked Bill.

'I don't know; it's - it's a sort of a change,' said Cyril candidly. 'He isn't at all like himself - you'd hardly know him. He's very queer indeed. Someone'll get hurt if he's not alone about sunset.' This was true.

'He'll pull round for the evening, I s'pose?'

'Oh yes - half an hour after sunset he'll be quite himself again.'

'Best humour him,' said the woman.

And so, at what Cyril judged was about half an hour before sunset, the tent was again closed 'whilst the giant gets his supper'.

The crowd was very merry about the giant's meals and their coming so close together.

'Well, he can pick a bit,' Bill owned. 'You see he has to eat hearty, being the size he is.'

Inside the tent the four children breathlessly arranged a plan of retreat. 'You go NOW,' said Cyril to the girls, 'and get along home as fast as you can. Oh, never mind the beastly pony-cart; we'll get that to-morrow. Robert and I are dressed the same. We'll manage somehow, like Sydney Carton did. Only, you girls MUST get out, or it's all no go. We can run, but you can't - whatever you may think. No, Jane, it's no good Robert going out and knocking people down. The police would follow him till he turned his proper size, and then arrest him like a shot. Go you must! If you don't, I'll never speak to you again. It was you got us into this mess really, hanging round people's legs the way you did this morning. Go, I tell you!'

And Jane and Anthea went.

'We're going home,' they said to Bill. 'We're leaving the giant with you. Be kind to him.' And that, as Anthea said afterwards, was very deceitful, but what were they to do?

When they had gone, Cyril went to Bill.

'Look here,' he said, 'he wants some ears of corn - there's some in the next field but one. I'll just run and get it. Oh, and he says can't you loop up the tent at the back a bit? He says he's stifling for a breath of air. I'll see no one peeps in at him. I'll cover him up, and he can take a nap while I go for the corn. He WILL have it - there's no holding him when he gets like this.'

The giant was made comfortable with a heap of sacks and an old tarpaulin. The curtain was looped up, and the brothers were left alone. They matured their plan in whispers. Outside, the merry-go-round blared out its comic tunes, screaming now and then to attract public notice.

Half a minute after the sun had set, a boy in a Norfolk suit came out past Bill.

'I'm off for the corn,' he said, and mingled quickly with the crowd.

At the same instant a boy came out of the back of the tent past 'Becca, posted there as sentinel.

'I'm off after the corn,' said this boy also. And he, too, moved away quietly and was lost in the crowd. The front-door boy was Cyril; the back-door was Robert - now, since sunset, once more his proper size. They walked quickly through the field, and along the road, where Robert caught Cyril up. Then they ran. They were home as soon as the girls were, for it was a long way, and they ran most of it. It was indeed a very long way, as they found when they had to go and drag the pony-trap home next morning, with no enormous Robert to wheel them in it as if it were a mail-cart, and they were babies and he was their gigantic nursemaid.

I cannot possibly tell you what Bill and 'Becca said when they found that the giant had gone. For one thing, I do not know.

Chapter 9. Grown Up

Cyril had once pointed out that ordinary life is full of occasions on which a wish would be most useful. And this thought filled his mind when he happened to wake early on the morning after the morning after Robert had wished to be bigger than the baker's boy, and had been it. The day that lay between these two days had been occupied entirely by getting the governess-cart home from Benenhurst.

Cyril dressed hastily; he did not take a bath, because tin baths are so noisy, and he had no wish to rouse Robert, and he slipped off alone, as Anthea had once done, and ran through the dewy morning to the sand-pit. He dug up the Psammead very carefully and kindly, and began the conversation by asking it whether it still felt any ill effects from the contact with the tears of Robert the day before yesterday. The Psammead was in a good temper. It replied politely.

'And now, what can I do for you?' it said. 'I suppose you've come here so early to ask for something for yourself, something your brothers and sisters aren't to know about eh? Now, do be persuaded for your own good! Ask for a good fat Megatherium and have done with it.'

'Thank you - not to-day, I think,' said Cyril cautiously. 'What I really wanted to say was - you know how you're always wishing for things when you're playing at anything?'

'I seldom play,' said the Psammead coldly.

'Well, you know what I mean,' Cyril went on impatiently. 'What I want to say is: won't you let us have our wish just when we think of it, and just where we happen to be? So that we don't have to come and disturb you again,' added the crafty Cyril.

'It'll only end in your wishing for something you don't really want, like you did about the castle,' said the Psammead, stretching its brown arms and yawning. 'It's always the same since people left off eating really wholesome things. However, have it your own way. Good-bye.'

'Good-bye,' said Cyril politely.

'I'll tell you what,' said the Psammead suddenly, shooting out its long snail's eyes - 'I'm getting tired of you - all of you. You have no more sense than so many oysters. Go along with you!' And Cyril went.

'What an awful long time babies STAY babies,' said Cyril after the Lamb had taken his watch out of his pocket while he wasn't noticing, and with coos and clucks of naughty rapture had opened the case and used the whole thing as a garden spade, and when even immersion in a wash-hand basin had failed to wash the mould from the works and make the watch go again. Cyril had said several things in the heat of the moment; but now he was calmer, and had even consented to carry the Lamb part of the way to the woods. Cyril had persuaded the others to agree to his plan, and not to wish for anything more till they really did wish it. Meantime it seemed good to go to the woods for nuts, and on the mossy grass under a sweet chestnut-tree the five were sitting. The Lamb was pulling up the moss by fat handfuls, and Cyril was gloomily contemplating the ruins of his watch.

'He does grow,' said Anthea. 'Doesn't oo, precious?'

'Me grow,' said the Lamb cheerfully - 'me grow big boy, have guns an' mouses - an' - an' ...' Imagination or vocabulary gave out here. But anyway it was the longest speech the Lamb had ever made, and it charmed everyone, even Cyril, who tumbled the Lamb over and rolled him in the moss to the music of delighted squeals.

'I suppose he'll be grown up some day,' Anthea was saying, dreamily looking up at the blue of the sky that showed between the long straight chestnut-leaves. But at that moment the Lamb, struggling gaily with Cyril, thrust a stoutly-shod little foot against his brother's chest; there was a crack! - the innocent Lamb had broken the glass of father's second-best Waterbury watch, which Cyril had borrowed without leave.

'Grow up some day!' said Cyril bitterly, plumping the Lamb down on the grass. 'I daresay he will when nobody wants him to. I wish to goodness he would -'

'OH, take care!' cried Anthea in an agony of apprehension. But it was too late - like music to a song her words and Cyril's came out together - Anthea - 'Oh, take care!' Cyril - 'Grow up now!'

The faithful Psammead was true to its promise, and there, before the horrified eyes of its brothers and sisters, the Lamb suddenly and violently grew up. It was the most terrible moment. The change was not so sudden as the wish-changes usually were. The Baby's face changed first. It grew thinner and larger, lines came in the forehead, the eyes grew more deep-set and darker in colour, the mouth grew longer and thinner; most terrible of all, a little dark moustache appeared on the lip of one who was still - except as to the face - a two-year-old baby in a linen smock and white open-work socks.

'Oh, I wish it wouldn't! Oh, I wish it wouldn't! You boys might wish as well!' They all wished hard, for the sight was enough to dismay the most heartless. They all wished so hard, indeed, that they felt quite giddy and almost lost consciousness; but the wishing was quite vain, for, when the wood ceased to whirl round, their dazzled eyes were riveted at once by the spectacle of a very proper-looking young man in flannels and a straw hat - a young man who wore the same little black moustache which just before they had actually seen growing upon the Baby's lip. This, then, was the Lamb - grown up! Their own Lamb! It was a terrible moment. The grown-up Lamb moved gracefully across the moss and settled himself against the trunk of the sweet chestnut. He tilted the straw hat over his eyes. He was evidently weary. He was going to sleep. The Lamb - the original little tiresome beloved Lamb often went to sleep at odd times and in unexpected places. Was this new Lamb in the grey flannel suit and the pale green necktie like the other Lamb? or had his mind grown up together with his body?

That was the question which the others, in a hurried council held among the yellowing bracken a few yards from the sleeper, debated eagerly.

'Whichever it is, it'll be just as awful,' said Anthea. 'If his inside senses are grown up too, he won't stand our looking after him; and if he's still a baby inside of him how on earth are we to get him to do anything? And it'll be getting on for dinner-time in a minute 'And we haven't got any nuts,' said Jane.

'Oh, bother nuts!' said Robert; 'but dinner's different - I didn't have half enough dinner yesterday. Couldn't we tie him to the tree and go home to our dinners and come back afterwards?'

'A fat lot of dinner we should get if we went back without the Lamb!' said Cyril in scornful misery. 'And it'll be just the same if we go back with him in the state he is now. Yes, I know it's my doing; don't rub it in! I know I'm a beast, and not fit to live; you can take that for settled, and say no more about it. The question is, what are we going to do?'

'Let's wake him up, and take him into Rochester or Maidstone and get some grub at a pastrycook's,' said Robert hopefully.

'Take him?' repeated Cyril. 'Yes - do! It's all MY fault - I don't deny that - but you'll find you've got your work cut out for you if you try to take that young man anywhere. The Lamb always was spoilt, but now he's grown up he's a demon - simply. I can see it. Look at his mouth.'

'Well then,' said Robert, 'let's wake him up and see what HE'LL do. Perhaps HE'LL take us to Maidstone and stand Sam. He ought to have a lot of money in the pockets of those extra-special bags. We MUST have dinner, anyway.'

They drew lots with little bits of bracken. It fell to Jane's lot to waken the grown-up Lamb.

She did it gently by tickling his nose with a twig of wild honeysuckle. He said 'Bother the flies!' twice, and then opened his eyes.

'Hullo, kiddies!' he said in a languid tone, 'still here? What's the giddy hour? You'll be late for your grub!'

'I know we shall,' said Robert bitterly.

'Then cut along home,' said the grown-up Lamb.

'What about your grub, though?' asked Jane.

'Oh, how far is it to the station, do you think? I've a sort of notion that I'll run up to town and have some lunch at the club.'

Blank misery fell like a pall on the four others. The Lamb - alone - unattended - would go to town and have lunch at a club! Perhaps he would also have tea there. Perhaps sunset would come upon him amid the dazzling luxury of club-land, and a helpless cross sleepy baby would find itself alone amid unsympathetic waiters, and would wail miserably for 'Panty' from the depths of a club arm-chair! The picture moved Anthea almost to tears.

'Oh no, Lamb ducky, you mustn't do that!' she cried incautiously.

The grown-up Lamb frowned. 'My dear Anthea,' he said, 'how often am I to tell you that my name is Hilary or St Maur or Devereux? - any of my baptismal names are free to my little brothers and sisters, but NOT "Lamb" - a relic of foolish and far-off childhood.'

This was awful. He was their elder brother now, was he? Well, of course he was, if he was grown up - since they weren't. Thus, in whispers, Anthea and Robert.

But the almost daily adventures resulting from the Psammead wishes were making the children wise beyond their years.

'Dear Hilary,' said Anthea, and the others choked at the name, 'you know father didn't wish you to go to London. He wouldn't like us to be left alone without you to take care of us. Oh, deceitful beast that I am!' she added to herself.

'Look here,' said Cyril, 'if you're our elder brother, why not behave as such and take us over to Maidstone and give us a jolly good blow-out, and we'll go on the river afterwards?'

'I'm infinitely obliged to you,' said the Lamb courteously, 'but I should prefer solitude. Go home to your lunch - I mean your dinner. Perhaps I may look in about tea-time - or I may not be home till after you are in your beds.'

Their beds! Speaking glances flashed between the wretched four. Much bed there would be for them if they went home without the Lamb.

'We promised mother not to lose sight of you if we took you out,' Jane said before the others could stop her.

'Look here, Jane,' said the grown-up Lamb, putting his hands in his pockets and looking down at her, 'little girls should be seen and not heard. You kids must learn not to make yourselves a nuisance. Run along home now - and perhaps, if you're good, I'll give you each a penny to-morrow.'

'Look here,' said Cyril, in the best 'man to man' tone at his command, 'where are you going, old man? You might let Bobs and me come with you - even if you don't want the girls.'

This was really rather noble of Cyril, for he never did care much about being seen in public with the Lamb, who of course after sunset would be a baby again.

The 'man to man' tone succeeded.

'I shall just run over to Maidstone on my bike,' said the new Lamb airily, fingering the little black moustache. 'I can lunch at The Crown - and perhaps I'll have a pull on the river; but I can't take you all on the machine - now, can I? Run along home, like good children.'

The position was desperate. Robert exchanged a despairing look with Cyril. Anthea detached a pin from her waistband, a pin whose withdrawal left a gaping chasm between skirt and bodice, and handed it furtively to Robert - with a grimace of the darkest and deepest meaning. Robert slipped away to the road. There, sure enough, stood a bicycle - a beautiful new free-wheel. Of course Robert understood at once that if the Lamb was grown up he MUST have a bicycle. This had always been one of Robert's own reasons for wishing to be grown up. He hastily began to use the pin - eleven punctures in the back tyre, seven in the front. He would have made the total twenty-two but for the rustling of the yellow hazel-leaves, which warned him of the approach of the others. He hastily leaned a hand on each wheel, and was rewarded by the 'whish' of what was left of the air escaping from eighteen neat pin-holes.

'Your bike's run down,' said Robert, wondering how he could so soon have learned to deceive.

'So it is,' said Cyril.

'It's a puncture,' said Anthea, stooping down, and standing up again with a thorn which she had got ready for the purpose. 'Look here.'

The grown-up Lamb (or Hilary, as I suppose one must now call him) fixed his pump and blew up the tyre. The punctured state of it was soon evident.

'I suppose there's a cottage somewhere near - where one could get a pail of water?' said the Lamb.

There was; and when the number of punctures had been made manifest, it was felt to be a special blessing that the cottage provided 'teas for cyclists'. It provided an odd sort of tea-and-hammy meal for the Lamb and his brothers. This was paid for out of the fifteen shillings which had been earned by Robert when he was a giant - for the Lamb, it appeared, had unfortunately no money about him. This was a great disappointment for the others; but it is a thing that will happen, even to the most grown-up of us. However, Robert had enough to eat, and that was something. Quietly but persistently the miserable four took it in turns to try to persuade the Lamb (or St Maur) to spend the rest of the day in the woods. There was not very much of the day left by the time he had mended the eighteenth puncture. He looked up from the completed work with a sigh of relief, and suddenly put his tie straight.

'There's a lady coming,' he said briskly - 'for goodness' sake, get out of the way. Go home - hide - vanish somehow! I can't be seen with a pack of dirty kids.' His brothers and sisters were indeed rather dirty, because, earlier in the day, the Lamb, in his infant state, had sprinkled a good deal of garden soil over them. The grown-up Lamb's voice was so tyrant-like, as Jane said afterwards, that they actually retreated to the back garden, and left him with his little moustache and his flannel suit to meet alone the young lady, who now came up the front garden wheeling a bicycle.

The woman of the house came out, and the young lady spoke to her - the Lamb raised his hat as she passed him - and the children could not hear what she said, though they were craning round the corner by the pig-pail and listening with all their ears. They felt it to be 'perfectly fair,' as Robert said, 'with that wretched Lamb in that condition.'

When the Lamb spoke in a languid voice heavy with politeness, they heard well enough.

'A puncture?' he was saying. 'Can I not be of any assistance? If you could allow me -?'

There was a stifled explosion of laughter behind the pig-pail - the grown-up Lamb (otherwise Devereux) turned the tail of an angry eye in its direction.

'You're very kind,' said the lady, looking at the Lamb. She looked rather shy, but, as the boys put it, there didn't seem to be any nonsense about her.

'But oh,' whispered Cyril behind the pig-pail, 'I should have thought he'd had enough bicycle-mending for one day - and if she only knew that really and truly he's only a whiny-piny, silly little baby!'

'He's not,' Anthea murmured angrily. 'He's a dear - if people only let him alone. It's our own precious Lamb still, whatever silly idiots may turn him into - isn't he, Pussy?'

Jane doubtfully supposed so.

Now, the Lamb - whom I must try to remember to call St Maur - was examining the lady's bicycle and talking to her with a very grown-up manner indeed. No one could possibly have supposed, to see and hear him, that only that very morning he had been a chubby child of two years breaking other people's Waterbury watches. Devereux (as he ought to be called for the future) took out a gold watch when he had mended the lady's bicycle, and all the onlookers behind the pig-pail said 'Oh!' - because it seemed so unfair that the Baby, who had only that morning destroyed two cheap but honest watches, should now, in the grown-upness Cyril's folly had raised him to, have a real gold watch - with a chain and seals!

Hilary (as I will now term him) withered his brothers and sisters with a glance, and then said to the lady - with whom he seemed to be quite friendly:

'If you will allow me, I will ride with you as far as the Cross Roads; it is getting late, and there are tramps about.'

No one will ever know what answer the young lady intended to give to this gallant offer, for, directly Anthea heard it made, she rushed out, knocking against the pig-pail, which overflowed in a turbid stream, and caught the Lamb (I suppose I ought to say Hilary) by the arm. The others followed, and in an instant the four dirty children were visible, beyond disguise.

'Don't let him,' said Anthea to the lady, and she spoke with intense earnestness; 'he's not fit to go with anyone!'

'Go away, little girl!' said St Maur (as we will now call him) in a terrible voice. 'Go home at once!'

'You'd much better not have anything to do with him,' the now reckless Anthea went on. 'He doesn't know who he is. He's something very different from what you think he is.'

'What do you mean?' asked the lady not unnaturally, while Devereux (as I must term the grown-up Lamb) tried vainly to push Anthea away. The others backed her up, and she stood solid as a rock.

'You just let him go with you,' said Anthea, 'you'll soon see what I mean! How would you like to suddenly see a poor little helpless baby spinning along downhill beside you with its feet up on a bicycle it had lost control of?'

The lady had turned rather pale.

'Who are these very dirty children?' she asked the grown-up Lamb (sometimes called St Maur in these pages).

'I don't know,' he lied miserably.

'Oh, Lamb! how can you?' cried Jane - 'when you know perfectly well you're our own little baby brother that we're so fond of. We're his big brothers and sisters,' she explained, turning to the lady, who with trembling hands was now turning her bicycle towards the gate, 'and we've got to take care of him. And we must get him home before sunset, or I don't know whatever will become of us. You see, he's sort of under a spell - enchanted - you know what I mean!'

Again and again the Lamb (Devereux, I mean) had tried to stop Jane's eloquence, but Robert and Cyril held him, one by each leg, and no proper explanation was possible. The lady rode hastily away, and electrified her relatives at dinner by telling them of her escape from a family of dangerous lunatics. 'The little girl's eyes were simply those of a maniac. I can't think how she came to be at large,' she said.

When her bicycle had whizzed away down the road, Cyril spoke gravely.

'Hilary, old chap,' he said, 'you must have had a sunstroke or something. And the things you've been saying to that lady! Why, if we were to tell you the things you've said when you are yourself again, say tomorrow morning, you wouldn't even understand them - let alone believe them! You trust to me, old chap, and come home now, and if you're not yourself in the morning we'll ask the milkman to ask the doctor to come.'

The poor grown-up Lamb (St Maur was really one of his Christian names) seemed now too bewildered to resist.

'Since you seem all to be as mad as the whole worshipful company of hatters,' he said bitterly, 'I suppose I HAD better take you home. But you're not to suppose I shall pass this over. I shall have something to say to you all to-morrow morning.'

'Yes, you will, my Lamb,' said Anthea under her breath, 'but it won't be at all the sort of thing you think it's going to be.'

In her heart she could hear the pretty, soft little loving voice of the baby Lamb - so different from the affected tones of the dreadful grown-up Lamb (one of whose names was Devereux) - saying, 'Me love Panty - wants to come to own Panty.'

'Oh, let's get home, for goodness' sake,' she said. 'You shall say whatever you like in the morning - if you can,' she added in a whisper. It was a gloomy party that went home through the soft evening. During Anthea's remarks Robert had again made play with the pin and the bicycle tyre and the Lamb (whom they had to call St Maur or Devereux or Hilary) seemed really at last to have had his fill of bicycle-mending. So the machine was wheeled.

The sun was just on the point of setting when they arrived at the White House. The four elder children would have liked to linger in the lane till the complete sunsetting turned the grown-up Lamb (whose Christian names I will not further weary you by repeating) into their own dear tiresome baby brother. But he, in his grown-upness, insisted on going on, and thus he was met in the front garden by Martha.

Now you remember that, as a special favour, the Psammead had arranged that the servants in the house should never notice any change brought about by the wishes of the children. Therefore Martha merely saw the usual party, with the baby Lamb, about whom she had been desperately anxious all the afternoon, trotting beside Anthea on fat baby legs, while the children, of course, still saw the grown-up Lamb (never mind what names he was christened by), and Martha rushed at him and caught him in her arms, exclaiming:

'Come to his own Martha, then - a precious poppet!'

The grown-up Lamb (whose names shall now be buried in oblivion) struggled furiously. An expression of intense horror and annoyance was seen on his face. But Martha was stronger than he. She lifted him up and carried him into the house. None of the children will ever forget that picture. The neat grey-flannel-suited grown-up young man with the green tie and the little black moustache - fortunately, he was slightly built, and not tall - struggling in the sturdy arms of Martha, who bore him away helpless, imploring him, as she went, to be a good boy now, and come and have his nice bremmilk! Fortunately, the sun set as they reached the doorstep, the bicycle disappeared, and Martha was seen to carry into the house the real live darling sleepy two-year-old Lamb. The grown-up Lamb (nameless henceforth) was gone for ever.

'For ever,' said Cyril, 'because, as soon as ever the Lamb's old enough to be bullied, we must jolly well begin to bully him, for his own sake - so that he mayn't grow up like that.'

'You shan't bully him,' said Anthea stoutly; 'not if I can stop it.'

'We must tame him by kindness,' said Jane.

'You see,' said Robert, 'if he grows up in the usual way, there'll be plenty of time to correct him as he goes along. The awful thing to-day was his growing up so suddenly. There was no time to improve him at all.'

'He doesn't want any improving,' said Anthea as the voice of the Lamb came cooing through the open door, just as she had heard it in her heart that afternoon:

'Me loves Panty - wants to come to own Panty!'

Chapter 10. Scalps

Probably the day would have been a greater success if Cyril had not been reading The Last of the Mohicans. The story was running in his head at breakfast, and as he took his third cup of tea he said dreamily, 'I wish there were Red Indians in England - not big ones, you know, but little ones, just about the right size for us to fight.'

Everyone disagreed with him at the time, and no one attached any importance to the incident. But when they went down to the sand-pit to ask for a hundred pounds in two-shilling pieces with Queen Victoria's head on, to prevent mistakes - which they had always felt to be a really reasonable wish that must turn out well - they found out that they had done it again! For the Psammead, which was very cross and sleepy, said:

'Oh, don't bother me. You've had your wish.'

'I didn't know it,' said Cyril.

'Don't you remember yesterday?' said the Sand-fairy, still more disagreeably. 'You asked me to let you have your wishes wherever you happened to be, and you wished this morning, and you've got it.'

'Oh, have we?' said Robert. 'What is it?'

'So you've forgotten?' said the Psammead, beginning to burrow. 'Never mind; you'll know soon enough. And I wish you joy of it! A nice thing you've let yourselves in for!'

'We always do, somehow,' said Jane sadly.

And now the odd thing was that no one could remember anyone's having wished for anything that morning. The wish about the Red Indians had not stuck in anyone's head. It was a most anxious morning. Everyone was trying to remember what had been wished for, and no one could, and everyone kept expecting something awful to happen every minute. It was most agitating; they knew, from what the Psammead had said, that they must have wished for something more than usually undesirable, and they spent several hours in most agonizing uncertainty. It was not till nearly dinner-time that Jane tumbled over The Last of the Mohicans - which had, of course, been left face downwards on the floor - and when Anthea had picked her and the book up she suddenly said, 'I know!' and sat down flat on the carpet.

'Oh, Pussy, how awful! It was Indians he wished for - Cyril - at breakfast, don't you remember? He said, "I wish there were Red Indians in England," - and now there are, and they're going about scalping people all over the country, like as not.'

'Perhaps they're only in Northumberland and Durham,' said Jane soothingly. It was almost impossible to believe that it could really hurt people much to be scalped so far away as that.

'Don't you believe it!' said Anthea. 'The Sammyadd said we'd let ourselves in for a nice thing. That means they'll come HERE. And suppose they scalped the Lamb!'

'Perhaps the scalping would come right again at sunset,' said Jane; but she did not speak so hopefully as usual.

'Not it!' said Anthea. 'The things that grow out of the wishes don't go. Look at the fifteen shillings! Pussy, I'm going to break something, and you must let me have every penny of money you've got. The Indians will come HERE, don't you see? That spiteful Psammead as good as said so. You see what my plan is? Come on!'

Jane did not see at all. But she followed her sister meekly into their mother's bedroom.

Anthea lifted down the heavy water-jug - it had a pattern of storks and long grasses on it, which Anthea never forgot. She carried it into the dressing-room, and carefully emptied the water out of it into the bath. Then she took the jug back into the bedroom and dropped it on the floor. You know how a jug always breaks if you happen to drop it by accident. If you happen to drop it on purpose, it is quite different. Anthea dropped that jug three times, and it was as unbroken as ever. So at last she had to take her father's boot-tree and break the jug with that in cold blood. It was heartless work.

Next she broke open the missionary-box with the poker. Jane told her that it was wrong, of course, but Anthea shut her lips very tight and then said:

'Don't be silly - it's a matter of life and death.'

There was not very much in the missionary-box - only seven-and-fourpence - but the girls between them had nearly four shillings. This made over eleven shillings, as you will easily see.

Anthea tied up the money in a corner of her pocket-handkerchief. 'Come on, Jane!' she said, and ran down to the farm. She knew that the farmer was going into Rochester that afternoon. In fact it had been arranged that he was to take the four children with him. They had planned this in the happy hour when they believed that they were going to get that hundred pounds, in two-shilling pieces, out of the Psammead. They had arranged to pay the farmer two shillings each for the ride. Now Anthea hastily explained to him that they could not go, but would he take Martha and the Baby instead? He agreed, but he was not pleased to get only half-a-crown instead of eight shillings.

Then the girls ran home again. Anthea was agitated, but not flurried. When she came to think it over afterwards, she could not help seeing that she had acted with the most far-seeing promptitude, just like a born general. She fetched a little box from her corner drawer, and went to find Martha, who was laying the cloth and not in the best of tempers.

'Look here,' said Anthea. 'I've broken the toilet-jug in mother's room.'

'Just like you - always up to some mischief,' said Martha, dumping down a salt-cellar with a bang.

'Don't be cross, Martha dear,' said Anthea. 'I've got enough money to pay for a new one - if only you'll be a dear and go and buy it for us. Your cousins keep a china-shop, don't they? And I would like you to get it to-day, in case mother comes home to-morrow. You know she said she might, perhaps.'

'But you're all going into town yourselves,' said Martha.

'We can't afford to, if we get the new jug,' said Anthea; 'but we'll pay for you to go, if you'll take the Lamb. And I say, Martha, look here - I'll give you my Liberty box, if you'll go. Look, it's most awfully pretty - all inlaid with real silver and ivory and ebony like King Solomon's temple.'

'I see,' said Martha; 'no, I don't want your box, miss. What you want is to get the precious Lamb off your hands for the afternoon. Don't you go for to think I don't see through you!'

This was so true that Anthea longed to deny it at once - Martha had no business to know so much. But she held her tongue.

Martha set down the bread with a bang that made it jump off its trencher.

'I DO want the jug got,' said Anthea softly. 'You WILL go, won't you?'

'Well, just for this once, I don't mind; but mind you don't get into none of your outrageous mischief while I'm gone - that's all!'

'He's going earlier than he thought,' said Anthea eagerly. 'You'd better hurry and get dressed. Do put on that lovely purple frock, Martha, and the hat with the pink cornflowers, and the yellow-lace collar. Jane'll finish laying the cloth, and I'll wash the Lamb and get him ready.'

As she washed the unwilling Lamb, and hurried him into his best clothes, Anthea peeped out of the window from time to time; so far all was well - she could see no Red Indians. When with a rush and a scurry and some deepening of the damask of Martha's complexion she and the Lamb had been got off, Anthea drew a deep breath.

'HE'S safe!' she said, and, to Jane's horror, flung herself down on the floor and burst into floods of tears. Jane did not understand at all how a person could be so brave and like a general, and then suddenly give way and go flat like an air-balloon when you prick it. It is better not to go flat, of course, but you will observe that Anthea did not give way till her aim was accomplished. She had got the dear Lamb out of danger - she felt certain the Red Indians would be round the White House or nowhere - the farmer's cart would not come back till after sunset, so she could afford to cry a little. It was partly with joy that she cried, because she had done what she meant to do. She cried for about three minutes, while Jane hugged her miserably and said at five-second intervals, 'Don't cry, Panther dear!'

Then she jumped up, rubbed her eyes hard with the corner of her pinafore, so that they kept red for the rest of the day, and started to tell the boys. But just at that moment cook rang the dinner-bell, and nothing could be said till they had all been helped to minced beef. Then cook left the room, and Anthea told her tale. But it is a mistake to tell a thrilling tale when people are eating minced beef and boiled potatoes. There seemed somehow to be something about the food that made the idea of Red Indians seem flat and unbelievable. The boys actually laughed, and called Anthea a little silly.

'Why,' said Cyril, 'I'm almost sure it was before I said that, that Jane said she wished it would be a fine day.'

'It wasn't,' said Jane briefly.

'Why, if it was Indians,' Cyril went on - 'salt, please, and mustard - I must have something to make this mush go down - if it was Indians, they'd have been infesting the place long before this - you know they would. I believe it's the fine day.'

'Then why did the Sammyadd say we'd let ourselves in for a nice thing?' asked Anthea. She was feeling very cross. She knew she had acted with nobility and discretion, and after that it was very hard to be called a little silly, especially when she had the weight of a burglared missionary-box and about seven-and-fourpence, mostly in coppers, lying like lead upon her conscience.

There was a silence, during which cook took away the mincy plates and brought in the treacle-pudding. As soon as she had retired, Cyril began again.

'Of course I don't mean to say,' he admitted, 'that it wasn't a good thing to get Martha and the Lamb out of the light for the afternoon; but as for Red Indians - why, you know jolly well the wishes always come that very minute. If there was going to be Red Indians, they'd be here now.'

'I expect they are,' said Anthea; 'they're lurking amid the undergrowth, for anything you know. I do think you're most beastly unkind.'

'Indians almost always DO lurk, really, though, don't they?' put in Jane, anxious for peace.

No, they don't,' said Cyril tartly. 'And I'm not unkind, I'm only truthful. And I say it was utter rot breaking the water-jug; and as for the missionary-box, I believe it's a treason-crime, and I shouldn't wonder if you could be hanged for it, if any of us was to split -'

'Shut up, can't you?' said Robert; but Cyril couldn't. You see, he felt in his heart that if there SHOULD be Indians they would be entirely his own fault, so he did not wish to believe in them. And trying not to believe things when in your heart you are almost sure they are true, is as bad for the temper as anything I know.

'It's simply idiotic,' he said, 'talking about Indians, when you can see for yourselves that it's Jane who's got her wish. Look what a fine day it is - OH - '

He had turned towards the window to point out the fineness of the day - the others turned too - and a frozen silence caught at Cyril, and none of the others felt at all like breaking it. For there, peering round the corner of the window, among the red leaves of the Virginia creeper, was a face - a brown face, with a long nose and a tight mouth and very bright eyes. And the face was painted in coloured patches. It had long black hair, and in the hair were feathers!

Every child's mouth in the room opened, and stayed open. The treacle-pudding was growing white and cold on their plates. No one could move.

Suddenly the feathered head was cautiously withdrawn, and the spell was broken. I am sorry to say that Anthea's first words were very like a girl.

'There, now!' she said. 'I told you so!'

Treacle-pudding had now definitely ceased to charm. Hastily wrapping their portions in a Spectator of the week before the week before last, they hid them behind the crinkled-paper stove-ornament, and fled upstairs to reconnoitre and to hold a hurried council.

'Pax,' said Cyril handsomely when they reached their mother's bedroom. 'Panther, I'm sorry if I was a brute.'

'All right,' said Anthea, 'but you see now!'

No further trace of Indians, however, could be discerned from the windows.

'Well,' said Robert, 'what are we to do?'

'The only thing I can think of,' said Anthea, who was now generally admitted to be the heroine of the day, 'is - if we dressed up as like Indians as we can, and looked out of the windows, or even went out. They might think we were the powerful leaders of a large neighbouring tribe, and - and not do anything to us, you know, for fear of awful vengeance.'

'But Eliza, and the cook?' said Jane.

'You forget - they can't notice anything,' said Robert. 'They wouldn't notice anything out of the way, even if they were scalped or roasted at a slow fire.'

'But would they come right at sunset?'

'Of course. You can't be really scalped or burned to death without noticing it, and you'd be sure to notice it next day, even if it escaped your attention at the time,' said Cyril. 'I think Anthea's right, but we shall want a most awful lot of feathers.'

'I'll go down to the hen-house,' said Robert. 'There's one of the turkeys in there - it's not very well. I could cut its feathers without it minding much. It's very bad - doesn't seem to care what happens to it. Get me the cutting-out scissors.'

Earnest reconnoitring convinced them all that no Indians were in the poultry-yard. Robert went. In five minutes he came back - pale, but with many feathers.

'Look here,' he said, 'this is jolly serious. I cut off the feathers, and when I turned to come out there was an Indian squinting at me from under the old hen-coop. I just brandished the feathers and yelled, and got away before he could get the coop off the top of himself. Panther, get the coloured blankets off our beds, and look slippy, can't you?'

It is wonderful how like an Indian you can make yourselves with blankets and feathers and coloured scarves. Of course none of the children happened to have long black hair, but there was a lot of black calico that had been got to cover school-books with. They cut strips of this into a sort of fine fringe, and fastened it round their heads with the amber-coloured ribbons off the girls' Sunday dresses. Then they stuck turkeys' feathers in the ribbons. The calico looked very like long black hair, especially when the strips began to curl up a bit.

'But our faces,' said Anthea, 'they're not at all the right colour. We're all rather pale, and I'm sure I don't know why, but Cyril is the colour of putty.'

'I'm not,' said Cyril.

'The real Indians outside seem to be brownish,' said Robert hastily. 'I think we ought to be really RED - it's sort of superior to have a red skin, if you are one.'

The red ochre cook used for the kitchen bricks seemed to be about the reddest thing in the house. The children mixed some in a saucer with milk, as they had seen cook do for the kitchen floor. Then they carefully painted each other's faces and hands with it, till they were quite as red as any Red Indian need be - if not redder.

They knew at once that they must look very terrible when they met Eliza in the passage, and she screamed aloud. This unsolicited testimonial pleased them very much. Hastily telling her not to be a goose, and that it was only a game, the four blanketed, feathered, really and truly Redskins went boldly out to meet the foe. I say boldly. That is because I wish to be polite. At any rate, they went.

Along the hedge dividing the wilderness from the garden was a row of dark heads, all highly feathered.

'It's our only chance,' whispered Anthea. 'Much better than to wait for their blood-freezing attack. We must pretend like mad. Like that game of cards where you pretend you've got aces when you haven't. Fluffing they call it, I think. Now then. Whoop!'

With four wild war-whoops - or as near them as English children could be expected to go without any previous practice - they rushed through the gate and struck four warlike attitudes in face of the line of Red Indians. These were all about the same height, and that height was Cyril's.

'I hope to goodness they can talk English,' said Cyril through his attitude.

Anthea knew they could, though she never knew how she came to know it. She had a white towel tied to a walking-stick. This was a flag of truce, and she waved it, in the hope that the Indians would know what it was. Apparently they did - for one who was browner than the others stepped forward.

'Ye seek a pow-wow?' he said in excellent English. 'I am Golden Eagle, of the mighty tribe of Rock-dwellers.' 'And I,' said Anthea, with a sudden inspiration, 'am the Black Panther - chief of the - the - the - Mazawattee tribe. My brothers - I don't mean - yes, I do - the tribe - I mean the Mazawattees - are in ambush below the brow of yonder hill.'

'And what mighty warriors be these?' asked Golden Eagle, turning to the others.

Cyril said he was the great chief Squirrel, of the Moning Congo tribe, and, seeing that Jane was sucking her thumb and could evidently think of no name for herself, he added, 'This great warrior is Wild Cat - Pussy Ferox we call it in this land - leader of the vast Phiteezi tribe.'

'And thou, valorous Redskin?' Golden Eagle inquired suddenly of Robert, who, taken unawares, could only reply that he was Bobs, leader of the Cape Mounted Police.

'And now,' said Black Panther, 'our tribes, if we just whistle them up, will far outnumber your puny forces; so resistance is useless. Return, therefore, to your own land, O brother, and smoke pipes of peace in your wampums with your squaws and your medicine-men, and dress yourselves in the gayest wigwams, and eat happily of the juicy fresh-caught moccasins.'

'You've got it all wrong,' murmured Cyril angrily. But Golden Eagle only looked inquiringly at her.

'Thy customs are other than ours, O Black Panther,' he said. 'Bring up thy tribe, that we may hold pow-wow in state before them, as becomes great chiefs.'

'We'll bring them up right enough,' said Anthea, 'with their bows and arrows, and tomahawks, and scalping-knives, and everything you can think of, if you don't look sharp and go.'

She spoke bravely enough, but the hearts of all the children were beating furiously, and their breath came in shorter and shorter gasps. For the little real Red Indians were closing up round them - coming nearer and nearer with angry murmurs - so that they were the centre of a crowd of dark, cruel faces.

'It's no go,' whispered Robert. 'I knew it wouldn't be. We must make a bolt for the Psammead. It might help us. If it doesn't - well, I suppose we shall come alive again at sunset. I wonder if scalping hurts as much as they say.'

'I'll wave the flag again,' said Anthea. 'If they stand back, we'll run for it.'

She waved the towel, and the chief commanded his followers to stand back. Then, charging wildly at the place where the line of Indians was thinnest, the four children started to run. Their first rush knocked down some half-dozen Indians, over whose blanketed bodies the children leaped, and made straight for the sand-Pit. This was no time for the safe easy way by which carts go down - right over the edge of the sand-pit they went, among the yellow and pale purple flowers and dried grasses, past the little sand-martins' little front doors, skipping, clinging, bounding, stumbling, sprawling, and finally rolling.

Yellow Eagle and his followers came up with them just at the very spot where they had seen the Psammead that morning.

Breathless and beaten, the wretched children now awaited their fate. Sharp knives and axes gleamed round them, but worse than these was the cruel light in the eyes of Golden Eagle and his followers.

'Ye have lied to us, O Black Panther of the Mazawattees - and thou, too, Squirrel of the Moning Congos. These also, Pussy Ferox of the Phiteezi, and Bobs of the Cape Mounted Police - these also have lied to us, if not with their tongue, yet by their silence. Ye have lied under the cover of the Truce-flag of the Pale-face. Ye have no followers. Your tribes are far away - following the hunting trail. What shall be their doom?' he concluded, turning with a bitter smile to the other Red Indians.

'Build we the fire!' shouted his followers; and at once a dozen ready volunteers started to look for fuel. The four children, each held between two strong little Indians, cast despairing glances round them. Oh, if they could only see the Psammead!

'Do you mean to scalp us first and then roast us?' asked Anthea desperately.

'Of course!' Redskin opened his eyes at her. 'It's always done.'

The Indians had formed a ring round the children, and now sat on the ground gazing at their captives. There was a threatening silence.

Then slowly, by twos and threes, the Indians who had gone to look for firewood came back, and they came back empty-handed. They had not been able to find a single stick of wood, for a fire! No one ever can, as a matter of fact, in that part of Kent.

The children drew a deep breath of relief, but it ended in a moan of terror. For bright knives were being brandished all about them. Next moment each child was seized by an Indian; each closed its eyes and tried not to scream. They waited for the sharp agony of the knife. It did not come. Next moment they were released, and fell in a trembling heap. Their heads did not hurt at all. They only felt strangely cool! Wild war-whoops rang in their ears. When they ventured to open their eyes they saw four of their foes dancing round them with wild leaps and screams, and each of the four brandished in his hand a scalp of long flowing black hair. They put their hands to their heads - their own scalps were safe! The poor untutored savages had indeed scalped the children. But they had only, so to speak, scalped them of the black calico ringlets!

The children fell into each other's arms, sobbing and laughing.

'Their scalps are ours,' chanted the chief; 'ill-rooted were their ill-fated hairs! They came off in the hands of the victors - without struggle, without resistance, they yielded their scalps to the conquering Rock-dwellers! Oh, how little a thing is a scalp so lightly won!'

'They'll take our real ones in a minute; you see if they don't,' said Robert, trying to rub some of the red ochre off his face and hands on to his hair.

'Cheated of our just and fiery revenge are we,' the chant went on - 'but there are other torments than the scalping-knife and the flames. Yet is the slow fire the correct thing. O strange unnatural country, wherein a man may find no wood to burn his enemy! - Ah, for the boundless forests of my native land, where the great trees for thousands of miles grow but to furnish firewood wherewithal to burn our foes. Ah, would we were but in our native forest once more!'

Suddenly, like a flash of lightning, the golden gravel shone all round the four children instead of the dusky figures. For every single Indian had vanished on the instant at their leader's word. The Psammead must have been there all the time. And it had given the Indian chief his wish.

Martha brought home a jug with a pattern of storks and long grasses on it. Also she brought back all Anthea's money.

'My cousin, she give me the jug for luck; she said it was an odd one what the basin of had got smashed.'

'Oh, Martha, you arc a dear!' sighed Anthea, throwing her arms round her.

'Yes,' giggled Martha, 'you'd better make the most of me while you've got me. I shall give your ma notice directly minute she comes back.'

'Oh, Martha, we haven't been so very horrid to you, have we?' asked Anthea, aghast.

'Oh, it ain't that, miss.' Martha giggled more than ever. 'I'm a-goin' to be married. It's Beale the gamekeeper. He's been a-proposin' to me off and on ever since you come home from the clergyman's where you got locked up on the church-tower. And to-day I said the word an' made him a happy man.'

Anthea put the seven-and-fourpence back in the missionary-box, and pasted paper over the place where the poker had broken it. She was very glad to be able to do this, and she does not know to this day whether breaking open a missionary-box is or is not a hanging matter.

Chapter 11. The Last Wish

Of course you, who see above that this is the eleventh (and last) chapter, know very well that the day of which this chapter tells must be the last on which Cyril, Anthea, Robert, and Jane will have a chance of getting anything out of the Psammead, or Sand-fairy.

But the children themselves did not know this. They were full of rosy visions, and, whereas on other days they had often found it extremely difficult to think of anything really nice to wish for, their brains were now full of the most beautiful and sensible ideas. 'This,' as Jane remarked afterwards, 'is always the way.' Everyone was up extra early that morning, and these plans were hopefully discussed in the garden before breakfast. The old idea of one hundred pounds in modern florins was still first favourite, but there were others that ran it close - the chief of these being the 'pony each' idea. This had a great advantage. You could wish for a pony each during the morning, ride it all day, have it vanish at sunset, and wish it back again next day. Which would be an economy of litter and stabling. But at breakfast two things happened. First, there was a letter from mother. Granny was better, and mother and father hoped to be home that very afternoon. A cheer arose. And of course this news at once scattered all the before-breakfast wish-ideas. For everyone saw quite plainly that the wish for the day must be something to please mother and not to please themselves.

'I wonder what she WOULD like,' pondered Cyril.

'She'd like us all to be good,' said Jane primly.

'Yes - but that's so dull for us,' Cyril rejoined; 'and, besides, I should hope we could be that without sand-fairies to help us. No; it must be something splendid, that we couldn't possibly get without wishing for.'

'Look out,' said Anthea in a warning voice; 'don't forget yesterday. Remember, we get our wishes now just wherever we happen to be when we say "I wish". Don't let's let ourselves in for anything silly - to-day of all days.'

'All right,' said Cyril. 'You needn't jaw.'

Just then Martha came in with a jug full of hot water for the teapot - and a face full of importance for the children.

'A blessing we're all alive to eat our breakfasses!' she said darkly.

'Why, whatever's happened?' everybody asked.

'Oh, nothing,' said Martha, 'only it seems nobody's safe from being murdered in their beds nowadays.'

'Why,' said Jane as an agreeable thrill of horror ran down her back and legs and out at her toes, 'has anyone been murdered in their beds?'

'Well - not exactly,' said Martha; 'but they might just as well. There's been burglars over at Peasmarsh Place - Beale's just told me - and they've took every single one of Lady Chittenden's diamonds and jewels and things, and she's a-goin' out of one fainting fit into another, with hardly time to say "Oh, my diamonds!" in between. And Lord Chittenden's away in London.'

'Lady Chittenden,' said Anthea; 'we've seen her. She wears a red-and-white dress, and she has no children of her own and can't abide other folkses'.'

'That's her,' said Martha. 'Well, she's put all her trust in riches, and you see how she's served. They say the diamonds and things was worth thousands of thousands of pounds. There was a necklace and a river - whatever that is - and no end of bracelets; and a tarrer and ever so many rings. But there, I mustn't stand talking and all the place to clean down afore your ma comes home.'

'I don't see why she should ever have had such lots of diamonds,' said Anthea when Martha had flounced off. 'She was rather a nasty lady, I thought. And mother hasn't any diamonds, and hardly any jewels - the topaz necklace, and the sapphire ring daddy gave her when they were engaged, and the garnet star, and the little pearl brooch with great-grandpapa's hair in it - that's about all.'

'When I'm grown up I'll buy mother no end of diamonds,' said Robert, 'if she wants them. I shall make so much money exploring in Africa I shan't know what to do with it.'

'Wouldn't it be jolly,' said Jane dreamily, 'if mother could find all those lovely things, necklaces and rivers of diamonds and tarrers?'

'TI—ARAS,' said Cyril.

'Ti—aras, then - and rings and everything in her room when she came home? I wish she would.' The others gazed at her in horror.

'Well, she WILL,' said Robert; 'you've wished, my good Jane - and our only chance now is to find the Psammead, and if it's in a good temper it MAY take back the wish and give us another. If not - well - goodness knows what we're in for! - the police, of course, and - don't cry, silly! We'll stand by you. Father says we need never be afraid if we don't do anything wrong and always speak the truth.'

But Cyril and Anthea exchanged gloomy glances. They remembered how convincing the truth about the Psammead had been once before when told to the police.

It was a day of misfortunes. Of course the Psammead could not be found. Nor the jewels, though every one Of the children searched their mother's room again and again.

'Of course,' Robert said, 'WE couldn't find them. It'll be mother who'll do that. Perhaps she'll think they've been in the house for years and years, and never know they are the stolen ones at all.'

'Oh yes!' Cyril was very scornful; 'then mother will be a receiver of stolen goods, and you know jolly well what THAT'S worse than.'

Another and exhaustive search of the sand-pit failed to reveal the Psammead, so the children went back to the house slowly and sadly.

'I don't care,' said Anthea stoutly, 'we'll tell mother the truth, and she'll give back the jewels - and make everything all right.'

'Do you think so?' said Cyril slowly. 'Do you think she'll believe us? Could anyone believe about a Sammyadd unless they'd seen it? She'll think we're pretending. Or else she'll think we're raving mad, and then we shall be sent to Bedlam. How would you like it?' - he turned suddenly on the miserable Jane - 'how would you like it, to be shut up in an iron cage with bars and padded walls, and nothing to do but stick straws in your hair all day, and listen to the howlings and ravings of the other maniacs? Make up your minds to it, all of you. It's no use telling mother.'

'But it's true,' said Jane.

'Of course it is, but it's not true enough for grown-up people to believe it,' said Anthea. 'Cyril's right. Let's put flowers in all the vases, and try not to think about diamonds. After all, everything has come right in the end all the other times.'

So they filled all the pots they could find with flowers - asters and zinnias, and loose-leaved late red roses from the wall of the stable-yard, till the house was a perfect bower.

And almost as soon as dinner was cleared away mother arrived, and was clasped in eight loving arms. It was very difficult indeed not to tell her all about the Psammead at once, because they had got into the habit of telling her everything. But they did succeed in not telling her. Mother, on her side, had plenty to tell them - about Granny, and Granny's pigeons, and Auntie Emma's lame tame donkey. She was very delighted with the flowery-boweryness of the house; and everything seemed so natural and pleasant, now that she was home again, that the children almost thought they must have dreamed the Psammead.

But, when mother moved towards the stairs to go UP to her bedroom and take off her bonnet, the eight arms clung round her just as if she only had two children, one the Lamb and the other an octopus.

'Don't go up, mummy darling,' said Anthea; 'let me take your things up for you.'

'Or I will,' said Cyril.

'We want you to come and look at the rose-tree,' said Robert.

'Oh, don't go up!' said Jane helplessly.

'Nonsense, dears,' said mother briskly, 'I'm not such an old woman yet that I can't take my bonnet off in the proper place. Besides, I must wash these black hands of mine.'

So up she went, and the children, following her, exchanged glances of gloomy foreboding.

Mother took off her bonnet - it was a very pretty hat, really, with white roses on it - and when she had taken it off she went to the dressing-table to do her pretty hair.

On the table between the ring-stand and the pincushion lay a green leather case. Mother opened it.

'Oh, how lovely!' she cried. It was a ring, a large pearl with shining many-lighted diamonds set round it. 'Wherever did this come from?' mother asked, trying it on her wedding finger, which it fitted beautifully. 'However did it come here?'

'I don't know,' said each of the children truthfully.

'Father must have told Martha to put it here,' mother said. 'I'll run down and ask her.'

'Let me look at it,' said Anthea, who knew Martha would not be able to see the ring. But when Martha was asked, of course she denied putting the ring there, and so did Eliza and cook.

Mother came back to her bedroom, very much interested and pleased about the ring. But, when she opened the dressing-table drawer and found a long case containing an almost priceless diamond necklace, she was more interested still, though not so pleased. In the wardrobe, when she went to put away her 'bonnet', she found a tiara and several brooches, and the rest of the jewellery turned up in various parts of the room during the next half-hour. The children looked more and more uncomfortable, and now Jane began to sniff.

Mother looked at her gravely.

'Jane,' she said, 'I am sure you know something about this. Now think before you speak, and tell me the truth.'

'We found a Fairy,' said Jane obediently.

'No nonsense, please,' said her mother sharply.

'Don't be silly, Jane,' Cyril interrupted. Then he went on desperately. 'Look here, mother, we've never seen the things before, but Lady Chittenden at Peasmarsh Place lost all her jewellery by wicked burglars last night. Could this possibly be it?'

All drew a deep breath. They were saved.

'But how could they have put it here? And why should they?' asked mother, not unreasonably. 'Surely it would have been easier and safer to make off with it?'

'Suppose,' said Cyril, 'they thought it better to wait for - for sunset - nightfall, I mean, before they went off with it. No one but us knew that you were coming back to-day.'

'I must send for the police at once,' said mother distractedly. 'Oh, how I wish daddy were here!'

'Wouldn't it be better to wait till he DOES come?' asked Robert, knowing that his father would not be home before sunset.

'No, no; I can't wait a minute with all this on my mind,' cried mother. 'All this' was the heap of jewel-cases on the bed. They put them all in the wardrobe, and mother locked it. Then mother called Martha.

'Martha,' she said, 'has any stranger been into MY room since I've been away? Now, answer me truthfully.'

'No, mum,' answered Martha; 'leastways, what I mean to say -'

She stopped.

'Come,' said her mistress kindly; 'I see someone has. You must tell me at once. Don't be frightened. I'm sure you haven't done anything wrong.'

Martha burst into heavy sobs.

'I was a-goin' to give you warning this very day, mum, to leave at the end of my month, so I was - on account of me being going to make a respectable young man happy. A gamekeeper he is by trade, mum - and I wouldn't deceive you - of the name of Beale. And it's as true as I stand here, it was your coming home in such a hurry, and no warning given, out of the kindness of his heart it was, as he says, "Martha, my beauty," he says - which I ain't and never was, but you know how them men will go on - "I can't see you a-toiling and a-moiling and not lend a 'elping 'and; which mine is a strong arm and it's yours, Martha, my dear," says he. And so he helped me a-cleanin' of the windows, but outside, mum, the whole time, and me in; if I never say another breathing word it's the gospel truth.'

'Were you with him the whole time?' asked her mistress.

'Him outside and me in, I was,' said Martha; 'except for fetching up a fresh pail and the leather that that slut of a Eliza'd hidden away behind the mangle.'

'That will do,' said the children's mother. 'I am not pleased with you, Martha, but you have spoken the truth, and that counts for something.'

When Martha had gone, the children clung round their mother.

'Oh, mummy darling,' cried Anthea, 'it isn't Beale's fault, it isn't really! He's a great dear; he is, truly and honourably, and as honest as the day. Don't let the police take him, mummy! Oh, don't, don't, don't!'

It was truly awful. Here was an innocent man accused of robbery through that silly wish of Jane's, and it was absolutely useless to tell the truth. All longed to, but they thought of the straws in the hair and the shrieks of the other frantic maniacs, and they could not do it.

'Is there a cart hereabouts?' asked mother feverishly. 'A trap of any sort? I must drive in to Rochester and tell the police at once.'

All the children sobbed, 'There's a cart at the farm, but, oh, don't go! - don't go! - oh, don't go! - wait till daddy comes home!'

Mother took not the faintest notice. When she had set her mind on a thing she always went straight through with it; she was rather like Anthea in this respect.

'Look here, Cyril,' she said, sticking on her hat with long sharp violet-headed pins, 'I leave you in charge. Stay in the dressing-room. You can pretend to be swimming boats in the bath, or something. Say I gave you leave. But stay there, with the landing door open; I've locked the other. And don't let anyone go into my room. Remember, no one knows the jewels are there except me, and all of you, and the wicked thieves who put them there. Robert, you stay in the garden and watch the windows. If anyone tries to get in you must run and tell the two farm men that I'll send up to wait in the kitchen. I'll tell them there are dangerous characters about - that's true enough.

Now, remember, I trust you both. But I don't think they'll try it till after dark, so you're quite safe. Good-bye, darlings.'

And she locked her bedroom door and went off with the key in her pocket.

The children could not help admiring the dashing and decided way in which she had acted. They thought how useful she would have been in organizing escape from some of the tight places in which they had found themselves of late in consequence of their ill-timed wishes.

'She's a born general,' said Cyril - 'but I don't know what's going to happen to us. Even if the girls were to hunt for that beastly Sammyadd and find it, and get it to take the jewels away again, mother would only think we hadn't looked out properly and let the burglars sneak in and nick them - or else the police will think WE'VE got them - or else that she's been fooling them. Oh, it's a pretty decent average ghastly mess this time, and no mistake!'

He savagely made a paper boat and began to float it in the bath, as he had been told to do.

Robert went into the garden and sat down on the worn yellow grass, with his miserable head between his helpless hands.

Anthea and Jane whispered together in the passage downstairs, where the coconut matting was - with the hole in it that you always caught your foot in if you were not careful. Martha's voice could be heard in the kitchen - grumbling loud and long.

'It's simply quite too dreadfully awful,' said Anthea. 'How do you know all the diamonds are there, too? If they aren't, the police will think mother and father have got them, and that they've only given up some of them for a kind of desperate blind. And they'll be put in prison, and we shall be branded outcasts, the children of felons. And it won't be at all nice for father and mother either,' she added, by a candid afterthought.

'But what can WE do?' asked Jane.

'Nothing - at least we might look for the Psammead again. It's a very, very hot day. He may have come out to warm that whisker of his.'

'He won't give us any more beastly wishes to-day,' said Jane flatly. 'He gets crosser and crosser every time we see him. I believe he hates having to give wishes.'

Anthea had been shaking her head gloomily - now she stopped shaking it so suddenly that it really looked as though she were pricking up her ears.

'What is it?' asked Jane. 'Oh, have you thought of something?'

'Our one chance,' cried Anthea dramatically; 'the last lone-lorn forlorn hope. Come on.'

At a brisk trot she led the way to the sand-pit. Oh, joy! - there was the Psammead, basking in a golden sandy hollow and preening its whiskers happily in the glowing afternoon sun. The moment it saw them it whisked round and began to burrow - it evidently preferred its own company to theirs. But Anthea was too quick for it. She caught it by its furry shoulders gently but firmly, and held it.

'Here - none of that!' said the Psammead. 'Leave go of me, will you?'

But Anthea held him fast.

'Dear kind darling Sammyadd,' she said breathlessly.

'Oh yes - it's all very well,' it said; 'you want another wish, I expect. But I can't keep on slaving from morning till night giving people their wishes. I must have SOME time to myself.'

'Do you hate giving wishes?' asked Anthea gently, and her voice trembled with excitement.

'Of course I do,' it said. 'Leave go of me or I'll bite! - I really will - I mean it. Oh, well, if you choose to risk it.'

Anthea risked it and held on.

'Look here,' she said, 'don't bite me - listen to reason. If you'll only do what we want to-day, we'll never ask you for another wish as long as we live.'

The Psammead was much moved.

'I'd do anything,' it said in a tearful voice. 'I'd almost burst myself to give you one wish after another, as long as I held out, if you'd only never, never ask me to do it after to-day. If you knew how I hate to blow myself out with other people's wishes, and how frightened I am always that I shall strain a muscle or something. And then to wake up every morning and know you've GOT to do it. You don't know what it is - you don't know what it is, you don't!' Its voice cracked with emotion, and the last 'don't' was a squeak.

Anthea set it down gently on the sand.

'It's all over now,' she said soothingly. 'We promise faithfully never to ask for another wish after to-day.' 'Well, go ahead,' said the Psammead; 'let's get it over.'

'How many can you do?'

'I don't know - as long as I can hold out.'

'Well, first, I wish Lady Chittenden may find she's never lost her jewels.'

The Psammead blew itself out, collapsed, and said, 'Done.'

'I wish, said Anthea more slowly, 'mother mayn't get to the police.'

'Done,' said the creature after the proper interval.

'I wish,' said Jane suddenly, 'mother could forget all about the diamonds.'

'Done,' said the Psammead; but its voice was weaker.

'Wouldn't you like to rest a little?' asked Anthea considerately.

'Yes, please,' said the Psammead; 'and, before we go further, will you wish something for me?'

'Can't you do wishes for yourself?'

'Of course not,' it said; 'we were always expected to give each other our wishes - not that we had any to speak of in the good old Megatherium days. Just wish, will you, that you may never be able, any of you, to tell anyone a word about ME.'

'Why?' asked Jane.

'Why, don't you see, if you told grown-ups I should have no peace of my life. They'd get hold of me, and they wouldn't wish silly things like you do, but real earnest things; and the scientific people would hit on some way of making things last after sunset, as likely as not; and they'd ask for a graduated income-tax, and old-age pensions and manhood suffrage, and free secondary education, and dull things like that; and get them, and keep them, and the whole world would be turned topsy-turvy. Do wish it! Quick!'

Anthea repeated the Psammead's wish, and it blew itself out to a larger size than they had yet seen it attain.

'And now,' it said as it collapsed, 'can I do anything more for you?'

'Just one thing; and I think that clears everything up, doesn't it, Jane? I wish Martha to forget about the diamond ring, and mother to forget about the keeper cleaning the windows.' 'It's like the "Brass Bottle",' said Jane.

'Yes, I'm glad we read that or I should never have thought of it.'

'Now,' said the Psammead faintly, 'I'm almost worn out. Is there anything else?'

'No; only thank you kindly for all you've done for us, and I hope you'll have a good long sleep, and I hope we shall see you again some day.'

'Is that a wish?' it said in a weak voice.

'Yes, please,' said the two girls together.

Then for the last time in this story they saw the Psammead blow itself out and collapse suddenly. It nodded to them, blinked its long snail's eyes, burrowed, and disappeared, scratching fiercely to the last, and the sand closed over it.

'I hope we've done right?' said Jane.

'I'm sure we have,' said Anthea. 'Come on home and tell the boys.'

Anthea found Cyril glooming over his paper boats, and told him. Jane told Robert. The two tales were only just ended when mother walked in, hot and dusty. She explained that as she was being driven into Rochester to buy the girls' autumn school-dresses the axle had broken, and but for the narrowness of the lane and the high soft hedges she would have been thrown out. As it was, she was not hurt, but she had had to walk home. 'And oh, my dearest dear chicks,' she said, 'I am simply dying for a cup of tea! Do run and see if the kettle boils!'

'So you see it's all right,' Jane whispered. 'She doesn't remember.'

'No more does Martha,' said Anthea, who had been to ask after the state of the kettle.

As the servants sat at their tea, Beale the gamekeeper dropped in. He brought the welcome news that Lady Chittenden's diamonds had not been lost at all. Lord Chittenden had taken them to be re-set and cleaned, and the maid who knew about it had gone for a holiday. So that was all right.

'I wonder if we ever shall see the Psammead again,' said Jane wistfully as they walked in the garden, while mother was putting the Lamb to bed.

'I'm sure we shall,' said Cyril, 'if you really wished it.'

'We've promised never to ask it for another wish,' said Anthea.

'I never want to,' said Robert earnestly.

They did see it again, of course, but not in this story. And it was not in a sand-pit either, but in a very, very, very different place. It was in a — But I must say no more.

The Phoenix and the Carpet

To My Dear Godson HUBERT GRIFFITH
and his sister MARGARET

To Hubert

Dear Hubert, if I ever found
A wishing-carpet lying round,
I'd stand upon it, and I'd say:
'Take me to Hubert, right away!'
And then we'd travel very far
To where the magic countries are
That you and I will never see,
And choose the loveliest gifts for you, from me.

But oh! alack! and well-a-day!
No wishing-carpets come my way.
I never found a Phoenix yet,
And Psammeads are so hard to get!
So I give you nothing fine—
Only this book your book and mine,
And hers, whose name by yours is set;
Your book, my book, the book of Margaret!

E. Nesbit, Dymchurch, September 1904

Chapter 1. The Egg

It began with the day when it was almost the Fifth of November, and a doubt arose in some breast—Robert's, I fancy—as to the quality of the fireworks laid in for the Guy Fawkes celebration.

'They were jolly cheap,' said whoever it was, and I think it was Robert, 'and suppose they didn't go off on the night? Those Prosser kids would have something to snigger about then.'

'The ones *I* got are all right,' Jane said; 'I know they are, because the man at the shop said they were worth thribble the money—'

'I'm sure thribble isn't grammar,' Anthea said.

'Of course it isn't,' said Cyril; 'one word can't be grammar all by itself, so you needn't be so jolly clever.'

Anthea was rummaging in the corner-drawers of her mind for a very disagreeable answer, when she remembered what a wet day it was, and how the boys had been disappointed of that ride to London and back on the top of the tram, which their mother had promised them as a reward for not having once forgotten, for six whole days, to wipe their boots on the mat when they came home from school.

So Anthea only said, 'Don't be so jolly clever yourself, Squirrel. And the fireworks look all right, and you'll have the eightpence that your tram fares didn't cost to-day, to buy something more with. You ought to get a perfectly lovely Catharine wheel for eightpence.'

'I daresay,' said Cyril, coldly; 'but it's not YOUR eightpence anyhow—'

'But look here,' said Robert, 'really now, about the fireworks. We don't want to be disgraced before those kids next door. They think because they wear red plush on Sundays no one else is any good.'

'I wouldn't wear plush if it was ever so—unless it was black to be beheaded in, if I was Mary Queen of Scots,' said Anthea, with scorn.

Robert stuck steadily to his point. One great point about Robert is the steadiness with which he can stick.

'I think we ought to test them,' he said.

'You young duffer,' said Cyril, 'fireworks are like postage-stamps. You can only use them once.'

'What do you suppose it means by "Carter's tested seeds" in the advertisement?'

There was a blank silence. Then Cyril touched his forehead with his finger and shook his head.

'A little wrong here,' he said. 'I was always afraid of that with poor Robert. All that cleverness, you know, and being top in algebra so often—it's bound to tell—'

'Dry up,' said Robert, fiercely. 'Don't you see? You can't TEST seeds if you do them ALL. You just take a few here and there, and if those grow you can feel pretty sure the others will be—what do you call it?—Father told me—"up to sample". Don't you think we ought to sample the fire-works? Just shut our eyes and each draw one out, and then try them.'

'But it's raining cats and dogs,' said Jane.

'And Queen Anne is dead,' rejoined Robert. No one was in a very good temper. 'We needn't go out to do them; we can just move back the table, and let them off on the old tea-tray we play toboggans with. I don't know what YOU think, but *I* think it's time we did something, and that would be really useful; because then we shouldn't just HOPE the fireworks would make those Prossers sit up—we should KNOW.'

'It WOULD be something to do,' Cyril owned with languid approval.

So the table was moved back. And then the hole in the carpet, that had been near the window till the carpet was turned round, showed most awfully. But Anthea stole out on tip-toe, and got the tray when cook wasn't looking, and brought it in and put it over the hole.

Then all the fireworks were put on the table, and each of the four children shut its eyes very tight and put out its hand and grasped something. Robert took a cracker, Cyril and Anthea had Roman candles; but Jane's fat paw closed on the gem of the whole collection, the Jack-in-the-box that had cost two shillings, and one at least of the party—I will not say which, because it was sorry afterwards—declared that Jane had done it on purpose. Nobody was pleased. For the worst of it was that these four children, with a very proper dislike of anything even faintly bordering on the sneakish, had a law, unalterable as those of the Medes and Persians, that one had to stand by the results of a toss-up, or a drawing of lots, or any other appeal to chance, however much one might happen to dislike the way things were turning out.

'I didn't mean to,' said Jane, near tears. 'I don't care, I'll draw another—'

'You know jolly well you can't,' said Cyril, bitterly. 'It's settled. It's Medium and Persian. You've done it, and you'll have to stand by it—and us too, worse luck. Never mind. YOU'LL have your pocket-money before the Fifth. Anyway, we'll have the Jack-in-the-box LAST, and get the most out of it we can.'

So the cracker and the Roman candles were lighted, and they were all that could be expected for the money; but when it came to the Jack-in-the-box it simply sat in the tray and laughed at them, as Cyril said. They tried to light it with paper and they tried to light it with matches; they tried to light it with Vesuvian fusees from the pocket of father's second-best overcoat that was hanging in the hall. And then Anthea slipped away to the cupboard under the stairs where the brooms and dustpans were kept, and the rosiny fire-lighters that smell so nice and like the woods where pine-trees grow, and the old newspapers and the bees-wax and turpentine, and the horrid and stiff dark rags that are used for cleaning brass and furniture, and the paraffin for the lamps. She came back with a little pot that had once cost sevenpence-halfpenny when it was full of red-currant jelly; but the jelly had been all eaten long ago, and now Anthea had filled the jar with paraffin. She came in, and she threw the paraffin over the tray just at the moment when Cyril was trying with the twenty-third match to light the Jack-in-the-box. The Jack-in-the-box did not catch fire any more than usual, but the paraffin acted quite differently, and in an instant a hot flash of flame leapt up and burnt off Cyril's eyelashes, and scorched the faces of all four before they could spring back. They backed, in four instantaneous bounds, as far as they could, which was to the wall, and the pillar of fire reached from floor to ceiling.

'My hat,' said Cyril, with emotion, 'You've done it this time, Anthea.'

The flame was spreading out under the ceiling like the rose of fire in Mr Rider Haggard's exciting story about Allan Quatermain. Robert and Cyril saw that no time was to be lost. They turned up the edges of the carpet, and kicked them over the tray. This cut off the column of fire, and it disappeared and there was nothing left but smoke and a dreadful smell of lamps that have been turned too low.

All hands now rushed to the rescue, and the paraffin fire was only a bundle of trampled carpet, when suddenly a sharp crack beneath their feet made the amateur firemen start back. Another crack—the carpet moved as if it had had a cat wrapped in it; the Jack-in-the-box had at last allowed itself to be lighted, and it was going off with desperate violence inside the carpet.

Robert, with the air of one doing the only possible thing, rushed to the window and opened it. Anthea screamed, Jane burst into tears, and Cyril turned the table wrong way up on top of the carpet heap. But the firework went on, banging and bursting and spluttering even underneath the table.

Next moment mother rushed in, attracted by the howls of Anthea, and in a few moments the firework desisted and there was a dead silence, and the children stood looking at each other's black faces, and, out of the corners of their eyes, at mother's white one.

The fact that the nursery carpet was ruined occasioned but little surprise, nor was any one really astonished that bed should prove the immediate end of the adventure. It has been said that all roads lead to Rome; this may be true, but at any rate, in early youth I am quite sure that many roads lead to BED, and stop there—or YOU do.

The rest of the fireworks were confiscated, and mother was not pleased when father let them off himself in the back garden, though he said, 'Well, how else can you get rid of them, my dear?'

You see, father had forgotten that the children were in disgrace, and that their bedroom windows looked out on to the back garden. So that they all saw the fireworks most beautifully, and admired the skill with which father handled them.

Next day all was forgotten and forgiven; only the nursery had to be deeply cleaned (like spring-cleaning), and the ceiling had to be whitewashed.

And mother went out; and just at tea-time next day a man came with a rolled-up carpet, and father paid him, and mother said—

'If the carpet isn't in good condition, you know, I shall expect you to change it.' And the man replied—

'There ain't a thread gone in it nowhere, mum. It's a bargain, if ever there was one, and I'm more'n 'arf sorry I let it go at the price; but we can't resist the lydies, can we, sir?' and he winked at father and went away.

Then the carpet was put down in the nursery, and sure enough there wasn't a hole in it anywhere.

As the last fold was unrolled something hard and loud-sounding bumped out of it and trundled along the nursery floor. All the children scrambled for it, and Cyril got it. He took it to the gas. It was shaped like an egg, very yellow and shiny, half-transparent, and it had an odd sort of light in it that changed as you held it in different ways. It was as though it was an egg with a yolk of pale fire that just showed through the stone.

'I MAY keep it, mayn't I, mother?' Cyril asked.

And of course mother said no; they must take it back to the man who had brought the carpet, because she had only paid for a carpet, and not for a stone egg with a fiery yolk to it.

So she told them where the shop was, and it was in the Kentish Town Road, not far from the hotel that is called the Bull and Gate. It was a poky little shop, and the man was arranging furniture outside on the pavement very cunningly, so that the more broken parts should show as little as possible. And directly he saw the children he knew them again, and he began at once, without giving them a chance to speak.

'No you don't' he cried loudly; 'I ain't a-goin' to take back no carpets, so don't you make no bloomin' errer. A bargain's a bargain, and the carpet's puffik throughout.'

'We don't want you to take it back,' said Cyril; 'but we found something in it.'

'It must have got into it up at your place, then,' said the man, with indignant promptness, 'for there ain't nothing in nothing as I sell. It's all as clean as a whistle.'

'I never said it wasn't CLEAN,' said Cyril, 'but—'

'Oh, if it's MOTHS,' said the man, 'that's easy cured with borax. But I expect it was only an odd one. I tell you the carpet's good through and through. It hadn't got no moths when it left my 'ands—not so much as an hegg.'

'But that's just it,' interrupted Jane; 'there WAS so much as an egg.'

The man made a sort of rush at the children and stamped his foot.

'Clear out, I say!' he shouted, 'or I'll call for the police. A nice thing for customers to 'ear you a-coming 'ere a-charging me with finding things in goods what I sells. 'Ere, be off, afore I sends you off with a flea in your ears. Hi! constable—'

The children fled, and they think, and their father thinks, that they couldn't have done anything else. Mother has her own opinion.

But father said they might keep the egg.

'The man certainly didn't know the egg was there when he brought the carpet,' said he, 'any more than your mother did, and we've as much right to it as he had.'

So the egg was put on the mantelpiece, where it quite brightened up the dingy nursery. The nursery was dingy, because it was a basement room, and its windows looked out on a stone area with a rockery made of clinkers facing the windows. Nothing grew in the rockery except London pride and snails.

The room had been described in the house agent's list as a 'convenient breakfast-room in basement,' and in the daytime it was rather dark. This did not matter so much in the evenings when the gas was alight, but then it was in the evening that the blackbeetles got so sociable, and used to come out of the low cupboards on each side of the fireplace where their homes were, and try to make friends with the children. At least, I suppose that was what they wanted, but the children never would.

On the Fifth of November father and mother went to the theatre, and the children were not happy, because the Prossers next door had lots of fireworks and they had none.

They were not even allowed to have a bonfire in the garden.

'No more playing with fire, thank you,' was father's answer, when they asked him.

When the baby had been put to bed the children sat sadly round the fire in the nursery.

'I'm beastly bored,' said Robert.

'Let's talk about the Psammead,' said Anthea, who generally tried to give the conversation a cheerful turn.

'What's the good of TALKING?' said Cyril. 'What I want is for something to happen. It's awfully stuffy for a chap not to be allowed out in the evenings. There's simply nothing to do when you've got through your homers.'

Jane finished the last of her home-lessons and shut the book with a bang.

'We've got the pleasure of memory,' said she. 'Just think of last holidays.'

Last holidays, indeed, offered something to think of—for they had been spent in the country at a white house between a sand-pit and a gravel-pit, and things had happened. The children had found a Psammead, or sand-fairy, and it had let them have anything they wished for—just exactly anything, with no bother about its not being really for their good, or anything like that. And if you want to know what kind of things they wished for, and how their wishes turned out you can read it all in a book called Five Children and It (It was the Psammead). If you've not read it, perhaps I ought to tell you that the fifth child was the baby brother, who was called the Lamb, because the first thing he ever said was 'Baa!' and that the other children were not particularly handsome, nor were they extra clever, nor extraordinarily good. But they were not bad sorts on the whole; in fact, they were rather like you.

'I don't want to think about the pleasures of memory,' said Cyril; 'I want some more things to happen.'

'We're very much luckier than any one else, as it is,' said Jane. 'Why, no one else ever found a Psammead. We ought to be grateful.'

'Why shouldn't we GO ON being, though?' Cyril asked—'lucky, I mean, not grateful. Why's it all got to stop?'

'Perhaps something will happen,' said Anthea, comfortably. 'Do you know, sometimes I think we are the sort of people that things DO happen to.'

'It's like that in history,' said Jane: 'some kings are full of interesting things, and others—nothing ever happens to them, except their being born and crowned and buried, and sometimes not that.'

'I think Panther's right,' said Cyril: 'I think we are the sort of people things do happen to. I have a sort of feeling things would happen right enough if we could only give them a shove. It just wants something to start it. That's all.'

'I wish they taught magic at school,' Jane sighed. 'I believe if we could do a little magic it might make something happen.'

'I wonder how you begin?' Robert looked round the room, but he got no ideas from the faded green curtains, or the drab Venetian blinds, or the worn brown oil-cloth on the floor. Even the new carpet suggested nothing, though its pattern was a very wonderful one, and always seemed as though it were just going to make you think of something.

'I could begin right enough,' said Anthea; 'I've read lots about it. But I believe it's wrong in the Bible.'

'It's only wrong in the Bible because people wanted to hurt other people. I don't see how things can be wrong unless they hurt somebody, and we don't want to hurt anybody; and what's more, we jolly well couldn't if we tried. Let's get the Ingoldsby Legends. There's a thing about Abra-cadabra there,' said Cyril, yawning. 'We may as well play at magic. Let's be Knights Templars. They were awfully gone on magic. They used to work spells or something with a goat and a goose. Father says so.'

'Well, that's all right,' said Robert, unkindly; 'you can play the goat right enough, and Jane knows how to be a goose.'

'I'll get Ingoldsby,' said Anthea, hastily. 'You turn up the hearthrug.'

So they traced strange figures on the linoleum, where the hearthrug had kept it clean. They traced them with chalk that Robert had nicked from the top of the mathematical master's desk at school. You know, of course, that it is stealing to take a new stick of chalk, but it is not wrong to take a broken piece, so long as you only take one. (I do not know the reason of this rule, nor who made it.) And they chanted all the gloomiest songs they could think of. And, of course, nothing happened. So then Anthea said, 'I'm sure a magic fire ought to be made of sweet-smelling wood, and have magic gums and essences and things in it.'

'I don't know any sweet-smelling wood, except cedar,' said Robert; 'but I've got some ends of cedar-wood lead pencil.'

So they burned the ends of lead pencil. And still nothing happened.

'Let's burn some of the eucalyptus oil we have for our colds,' said Anthea.

And they did. It certainly smelt very strong. And they burned lumps of camphor out of the big chest. It was very bright, and made a horrid black smoke, which looked very magical. But still nothing happened. Then they got some clean tea-cloths from the dresser drawer in the kitchen, and waved them over the magic chalk-tracings, and sang 'The Hymn of the Moravian Nuns at Bethlehem', which is very impressive. And still nothing happened. So they waved more and more wildly, and Robert's tea-cloth caught the golden egg and whisked it off the mantelpiece, and it fell into the fender and rolled under the grate.

'Oh, crikey!' said more than one voice.

And every one instantly fell down flat on its front to look under the grate, and there lay the egg, glowing in a nest of hot ashes.

'It's not smashed, anyhow,' said Robert, and he put his hand under the grate and picked up the egg. But the egg was much hotter than any one would have believed it could possibly get in such a short time, and Robert had to drop it with a cry of 'Bother!' It fell on the top bar of the grate, and bounced right into the glowing red-hot heart of the fire.

'The tongs!' cried Anthea. But, alas, no one could remember where they were. Every one had forgotten that the tongs had last been used to fish up the doll's teapot from the bottom of the water- butt, where the Lamb had dropped it. So the nursery tongs were resting between the water-butt and the dustbin, and cook refused to lend the kitchen ones.

'Never mind,' said Robert, 'we'll get it out with the poker and the shovel.'

'Oh, stop,' cried Anthea. 'Look at it! Look! look! look! I do believe something IS going to happen!'

For the egg was now red-hot, and inside it something was moving. Next moment there was a soft cracking sound; the egg burst in two, and out of it came a flame-coloured bird. It rested a moment among the flames, and as it rested there the four children could see it growing bigger and bigger under their eyes.

Every mouth was a-gape, every eye a-goggle.

The bird rose in its nest of fire, stretched its wings, and flew out into the room. It flew round and round, and round again, and where it passed the air was warm. Then it perched on the fender. The children looked at each other. Then Cyril put out a hand towards the bird. It put its head on one side and looked up at him, as you may have seen a parrot do when it is just going to speak, so that the children were hardly astonished at all when it said, 'Be careful; I am not nearly cool yet.'

They were not astonished, but they were very, very much interested.

They looked at the bird, and it was certainly worth looking at. Its feathers were like gold. It was about as large as a bantam, only its beak was not at all bantam-shaped. 'I believe I know what it is,' said Robert. 'I've seen a picture.'

He hurried away. A hasty dash and scramble among the papers on father's study table yielded, as the sum-books say, 'the desired result'. But when he came back into the room holding out a paper, and crying, 'I say, look here,' the others all said 'Hush!' and he hushed obediently and instantly, for the bird was speaking.

'Which of you,' it was saying, 'put the egg into the fire?'

'He did,' said three voices, and three fingers pointed at Robert.

The bird bowed; at least it was more like that than anything else.

'I am your grateful debtor,' it said with a high-bred air.

The children were all choking with wonder and curiosity—all except Robert. He held the paper in his hand, and he KNEW. He said so. He said—

'*I* know who you are.'

And he opened and displayed a printed paper, at the head of which was a little picture of a bird sitting in a nest of flames.

'You are the Phoenix,' said Robert; and the bird was quite pleased.

'My fame has lived then for two thousand years,' it said. 'Allow me to look at my portrait.' It looked at the page which Robert, kneeling down, spread out in the fender, and said—

'It's not a flattering likeness ... And what are these characters?' it asked, pointing to the printed part.

'Oh, that's all dullish; it's not much about YOU, you know,' said Cyril, with unconscious politeness; 'but you're in lots of books.'

'With portraits?' asked the Phoenix.

'Well, no,' said Cyril; 'in fact, I don't think I ever saw any portrait of you but that one, but I can read you something about yourself, if you like.'

The Phoenix nodded, and Cyril went off and fetched Volume X of the old Encyclopedia, and on page 246 he found the following:—

'Phoenix - in ornithology, a fabulous bird of antiquity.'

'Antiquity is quite correct,' said the Phoenix, 'but fabulous—well, do I look it?'

Every one shook its head. Cyril went on—

'The ancients speak of this bird as single, or the only one of its kind.'

'That's right enough,' said the Phoenix.

'They describe it as about the size of an eagle.'

'Eagles are of different sizes,' said the Phoenix; 'it's not at all a good description.'

All the children were kneeling on the hearthrug, to be as near the Phoenix as possible.

'You'll boil your brains,' it said. 'Look out, I'm nearly cool now;' and with a whirr of golden wings it fluttered from the fender to the table. It was so nearly cool that there was only a very faint smell of burning when it had settled itself on the table-cloth.

'It's only a very little scorched,' said the Phoenix, apologetically; 'it will come out in the wash. Please go on reading.'

The children gathered round the table.

'The size of an eagle,' Cyril went on, 'its head finely crested with a beautiful plumage, its neck covered with feathers of a gold colour, and the rest of its body purple; only the tail white, and the eyes sparkling like stars. They say that it lives about five hundred years in the wilderness, and when advanced in age it builds itself a pile of sweet wood and aromatic gums, fires it with the wafting of its wings, and thus burns itself; and that from its ashes arises a worm, which in time grows up to be a Phoenix. Hence the Phoenicians gave—'

'Never mind what they gave,' said the Phoenix, ruffling its golden feathers. 'They never gave much, anyway; they always were people who gave nothing for nothing. That book ought to be destroyed. It's most inaccurate. The rest of my body was never purple, and as for my—tail—well, I simply ask you, IS it white?'

It turned round and gravely presented its golden tail to the children.

'No. it's not,' said everybody.

'No, and it never was,' said the Phoenix. 'And that about the worm is just a vulgar insult. The Phoenix has an egg, like all respectable birds. It makes a pile—that part's all right—and it lays its egg, and it burns itself; and it goes to sleep and wakes up in its egg, and comes out and goes on living again, and so on for ever and ever. I can't tell you how weary I got of it—such a restless existence; no repose.'

'But how did your egg get HERE?' asked Anthea.

'Ah, that's my life-secret,' said the Phoenix. 'I couldn't tell it to any one who wasn't really sympathetic. I've always been a misunderstood bird. You can tell that by what they say about the worm. I might tell YOU,' it went on, looking at Robert with eyes that were indeed starry. 'You put me on the fire—' Robert looked uncomfortable.

'The rest of us made the fire of sweet-scented woods and gums, though,' said Cyril.

'And—and it was an accident my putting you on the fire,' said Robert, telling the truth with some difficulty, for he did not know how the Phoenix might take it. It took it in the most unexpected manner.

'Your candid avowal,' it said, 'removes my last scruple. I will tell you my story.'

'And you won't vanish, or anything sudden will you?, asked Anthea, anxiously.

'Why?' it asked, puffing out the golden feathers, 'do you wish me to stay here?'

'Oh YES,' said every one, with unmistakable sincerity.

'Why?' asked the Phoenix again, looking modestly at the table-cloth.

'Because,' said every one at once, and then stopped short; only Jane added after a pause, 'you are the most beautiful person we've ever seen.' 'You are a sensible child,' said the Phoenix, 'and I will NOT vanish or anything sudden. And I will tell you my tale. I had resided, as your book says, for many thousand years in the wilderness, which is a large, quiet place with very little really good society, and I was becoming weary of the monotony of my existence. But I acquired the habit of laying my egg and burning myself every five hundred years—and you know how difficult it is to break yourself of a habit.'

'Yes,' said Cyril; 'Jane used to bite her nails.'

'But I broke myself of it,' urged Jane, rather hurt, 'You know I did.'

'Not till they put bitter aloes on them,' said Cyril.

'I doubt,' said the bird, gravely, 'whether even bitter aloes (the aloe, by the way, has a bad habit of its own, which it might well cure before seeking to cure others; I allude to its indolent practice of flowering but once a century), I doubt whether even bitter aloes could have cured ME. But I WAS cured. I awoke one morning from a feverish dream—it was getting near the time for me to lay that tiresome fire and lay that tedious egg upon it—and I saw two people, a man and a woman. They were sitting on a carpet—and when I accosted them civilly they narrated to me their life-story, which, as you have not yet heard it, I will now proceed to relate. They were a prince and princess, and the story of their parents was one which I am sure you will like to hear. In early youth the mother of the princess happened to hear the story of a certain enchanter, and in that story I am sure you will be interested. The enchanter—'

'Oh, please don't,' said Anthea. 'I can't understand all these beginnings of stories, and you seem to be getting deeper and deeper in them every minute. Do tell us your OWN story. That's what we really want to hear.'

'Well,' said the Phoenix, seeming on the whole rather flattered, 'to cut about seventy long stories short (though *I* had to listen to them all—but to be sure in the wilderness there is plenty of time), this prince and princess were so fond of each other that they did not want any one else, and the enchanter—don't be alarmed, I won't go into his history—had given them a magic carpet (you've heard of a magic carpet?), and they had just sat on it and told it to take them right away from every one—and it had brought them to the wilderness. And as they meant to stay there they had no further use for the carpet, so they gave it to me. That was indeed the chance of a lifetime!'

'I don't see what you wanted with a carpet,' said Jane, 'when you've got those lovely wings.'

'They ARE nice wings, aren't they?' said the Phoenix, simpering and spreading them out. 'Well, I got the prince to lay out the carpet, and I laid my egg on it; then I said to the carpet, "Now, my excellent carpet, prove your worth. Take that egg somewhere where it can't be hatched for two thousand years, and where, when that time's up, some one will light a fire of sweet wood and aromatic gums, and put the egg in to hatch;" and you see it's all come out exactly as I said. The words were no sooner out of my beak than egg and carpet disappeared. The royal lovers assisted to arrange my pile, and soothed my last moments. I burnt myself up and knew no more till I awoke on yonder altar.'

It pointed its claw at the grate.

'But the carpet,' said Robert, 'the magic carpet that takes you anywhere you wish. What became of that?'

'Oh, THAT?' said the Phoenix, carelessly—'I should say that that is the carpet. I remember the pattern perfectly.'

It pointed as it spoke to the floor, where lay the carpet which mother had bought in the Kentish Town Road for twenty-two shillings and ninepence.

At that instant father's latch-key was heard in the door.

'OH,' whispered Cyril, 'now we shall catch it for not being in bed!'

'Wish yourself there,' said the Phoenix, in a hurried whisper, 'and then wish the carpet back in its place.'

No sooner said than done. It made one a little giddy, certainly, and a little breathless; but when things seemed right way up again, there the children were, in bed, and the lights were out.

They heard the soft voice of the Phoenix through the darkness.

'I shall sleep on the cornice above your curtains,' it said. 'Please don't mention me to your kinsfolk.'

'Not much good,' said Robert, 'they'd never believe us. I say,' he called through the half-open door to the girls; 'talk about adventures and things happening. We ought to be able to get some fun out of a magic carpet AND a Phoenix.'

'Rather,' said the girls, in bed.

'Children,' said father, on the stairs, 'go to sleep at once. What do you mean by talking at this time of night?'

No answer was expected to this question, but under the bedclothes Cyril murmured one.

'Mean?' he said. 'Don't know what we mean. I don't know what anything means.'

'But we've got a magic carpet AND a Phoenix,' said Robert.

'You'll get something else if father comes in and catches you,' said Cyril. 'Shut up, I tell you.'

Robert shut up. But he knew as well as you do that the adventures of that carpet and that Phoenix were only just beginning.

Father and mother had not the least idea of what had happened in their absence. This is often the case, even when there are no magic carpets or Phoenixes in the house.

The next morning—but I am sure you would rather wait till the next chapter before you hear about THAT.

Chapter 2. The Topless Tower

The children had seen the Phoenix-egg hatched in the flames in their own nursery grate, and had heard from it how the carpet on their own nursery floor was really the wishing carpet, which would take them anywhere they chose. The carpet had transported them to bed just at the right moment, and the Phoenix had gone to roost on the cornice supporting the window-curtains of the boys' room.

'Excuse me,' said a gentle voice, and a courteous beak opened, very kindly and delicately, the right eye of Cyril. 'I hear the slaves below preparing food. Awaken! A word of explanation and arrangement ... I do wish you wouldn't—'

The Phoenix stopped speaking and fluttered away crossly to the cornice-pole; for Cyril had hit out, as boys do when they are awakened suddenly, and the Phoenix was not used to boys, and his feelings, if not his wings, were hurt.

'Sorry,' said Cyril, coming awake all in a minute. 'Do come back! What was it you were saying? Something about bacon and rations?'

The Phoenix fluttered back to the brass rail at the foot of the bed.

'I say—you ARE real,' said Cyril. 'How ripping! And the carpet?'

'The carpet is as real as it ever was,' said the Phoenix, rather contemptuously; 'but, of course, a carpet's only a carpet, whereas a Phoenix is superlatively a Phoenix.'

'Yes, indeed,' said Cyril, 'I see it is. Oh, what luck! Wake up, Bobs! There's jolly well something to wake up for today. And it's Saturday, too.'

'I've been reflecting,' said the Phoenix, 'during the silent watches of the night, and I could not avoid the conclusion that you were quite insufficiently astonished at my appearance yesterday. The ancients were always VERY surprised. Did you, by chance, EXPECT my egg to hatch?'

'Not us,' Cyril said.

'And if we had,' said Anthea, who had come in in her nightie when she heard the silvery voice of the Phoenix, 'we could never, never have expected it to hatch anything so splendid as you.'

The bird smiled. Perhaps you've never seen a bird smile?

'You see,' said Anthea, wrapping herself in the boys' counterpane, for the morning was chill, 'we've had things happen to us before;' and she told the story of the Psammead, or sand-fairy.

'Ah yes,' said the Phoenix; 'Psammeads were rare, even in my time. I remember I used to be called the Psammead of the Desert. I was always having compliments paid me; I can't think why.'

'Can YOU give wishes, then?' asked Jane, who had now come in too.

'Oh, dear me, no,' said the Phoenix, contemptuously, 'at least— but I hear footsteps approaching. I hasten to conceal myself.' And it did.

I think I said that this day was Saturday. It was also cook's birthday, and mother had allowed her and Eliza to go to the Crystal Palace with a party of friends, so Jane and Anthea of course had to help to make beds and to wash up the breakfast cups, and little things like that. Robert and Cyril intended to spend the morning in conversation with the Phoenix, but the bird had its own ideas about this.

'I must have an hour or two's quiet,' it said, 'I really must. My nerves will give way unless I can get a little rest. You must remember it's two thousand years since I had any conversation—I'm out of practice, and I must take care of myself. I've often been told that mine is a valuable life.' So it nestled down inside an old hatbox of father's, which had been brought down from the box-room some days before, when a helmet was suddenly needed for a game of tournaments, with its golden head under its golden wing, and went to sleep. So then Robert and Cyril moved the table back and were going to sit on the carpet and wish themselves somewhere else. But before they could decide on the place, Cyril said—

'I don't know. Perhaps it's rather sneakish to begin without the girls.'

'They'll be all the morning,' said Robert, impatiently. And then a thing inside him, which tiresome books sometimes call the 'inward monitor', said, 'Why don't you help them, then?'

Cyril's 'inward monitor' happened to say the same thing at the same moment, so the boys went and helped to wash up the tea-cups, and to dust the drawing-room. Robert was so interested that he proposed to clean the front doorsteps—a thing he had never been allowed to do. Nor was he allowed to do it on this occasion. One reason was that it had already been done by cook.

When all the housework was finished, the girls dressed the happy, wriggling baby in his blue highwayman coat and three-cornered hat, and kept him amused while mother changed her dress and got ready to take him over to granny's. Mother always went to granny's every Saturday, and generally some of the children went with her; but today they were to keep house. And their hearts were full of joyous and delightful feelings every time they remembered that the house they would have to keep had a Phoenix in it, AND a wishing carpet.

You can always keep the Lamb good and happy for quite a long time if you play the Noah's Ark game with him. It is quite simple. He just sits on your lap and tells you what animal he is, and then you say the little poetry piece about whatever animal he chooses to be.

Of course, some of the animals, like the zebra and the tiger, haven't got any poetry, because they are so difficult to rhyme to. The Lamb knows quite well which are the poetry animals.

'I'm a baby bear!' said the Lamb, snugging down; and Anthea began:

'I love my little baby bear,
I love his nose and toes and hair;
I like to hold him in my arm,
And keep him VERY safe and warm.'

And when she said 'very', of course there was a real bear's hug.

Then came the eel, and the Lamb was tickled till he wriggled exactly like a real one:

'I love my little baby eel,
He is so squidglety to feel;
He'll be an eel when he is big—
But now he's just—a—tiny SNIG!'

Perhaps you didn't know that a snig was a baby eel? It is, though, and the Lamb knew it.

'Hedgehog now-!' he said; and Anthea went on:

'My baby hedgehog, how I like ye,
Though your back's so prickly-spiky;
Your front is very soft, I've found,
So I must love you front ways round!'

And then she loved him front ways round, while he squealed with pleasure.

It is a very baby game, and, of course, the rhymes are only meant for very, very small people—not for people who are old enough to read books, so I won't tell you any more of them.

By the time the Lamb had been a baby lion and a baby weazel, and a baby rabbit and a baby rat, mother was ready; and she and the Lamb, having been kissed by everybody and hugged as thoroughly as it is possible to be when you're dressed for out-of-doors, were seen to the tram by the boys. When the boys came back, every one looked at every one else and said—

'Now!'

They locked the front door and they locked the back door, and they fastened all the windows. They moved the table and chairs off the carpet, and Anthea swept it.

'We must show it a LITTLE attention,' she said kindly. 'We'll give it tea-leaves next time. Carpets like tea-leaves.'

Then every one put on its out-door things, because as Cyril said, they didn't know where they might be going, and it makes people stare if you go out of doors in November in pinafores and without hats.

Then Robert gently awoke the Phoenix, who yawned and stretched itself, and allowed Robert to lift it on to the middle of the carpet, where it instantly went to sleep again with its crested head tucked under its golden wing as before. Then every one sat down on the carpet.

'Where shall we go?' was of course the question, and it was warmly discussed. Anthea wanted to go to Japan. Robert and Cyril voted for America, and Jane wished to go to the seaside.

'Because there are donkeys there,' said she.

'Not in November, silly,' said Cyril; and the discussion got warmer and warmer, and still nothing was settled.

'I vote we let the Phoenix decide,' said Robert, at last. So they stroked it till it woke. 'We want to go somewhere abroad,' they said, 'and we can't make up our minds where.'

'Let the carpet make up ITS mind, if it has one,' said the Phoenix. 'Just say you wish to go abroad.'

So they did; and the next moment the world seemed to spin upside down, and when it was right way up again and they were ungiddy enough to look about them, they were out of doors.

Out of doors—this is a feeble way to express where they were. They were out of—out of the earth, or off it. In fact, they were floating steadily, safely, splendidly, in the crisp clear air, with the pale bright blue of the sky above them, and far down below the pale bright sun-diamonded waves of the sea. The carpet had stiffened itself somehow, so that it was square and firm like a raft, and it steered itself so beautifully and kept on its way so flat and fearless that no one was at all afraid of tumbling off. In front of them lay land.

'The coast of France,' said the Phoenix, waking up and pointing with its wing. 'Where do you wish to go? I should always keep one wish, of course—for emergencies—otherwise you may get into an emergency from which you can't emerge at all.'

But the children were far too deeply interested to listen.

'I tell you what,' said Cyril: 'let's let the thing go on and on, and when we see a place we really want to stop at—why, we'll just stop. Isn't this ripping?'

'It's like trains,' said Anthea, as they swept over the low-lying coast-line and held a steady course above orderly fields and straight roads bordered with poplar trees—'like express trains, only in trains you never can see anything because of grown-ups wanting the windows shut; and then they breathe on them, and it's like ground glass, and nobody can see anything, and then they go to sleep.'

'It's like tobogganing,' said Robert, 'so fast and smooth, only there's no door-mat to stop short on—it goes on and on.'

'You darling Phoenix,' said Jane, 'it's all your doing. Oh, look at that ducky little church and the women with flappy cappy things on their heads.'

'Don't mention it,' said the Phoenix, with sleepy politeness.

'OH!' said Cyril, summing up all the rapture that was in every heart. 'Look at it all—look at it—and think of the Kentish Town Road!'

Every one looked and every one thought. And the glorious, gliding, smooth, steady rush went on, and they looked down on strange and beautiful things, and held their breath and let it go in deep sighs, and said 'Oh!' and 'Ah!' till it was long past dinner-time.

It was Jane who suddenly said, 'I wish we'd brought that jam tart and cold mutton with us. It would have been jolly to have a picnic in the air.'

The jam tart and cold mutton were, however, far away, sitting quietly in the larder of the house in Camden Town which the children were supposed to be keeping. A mouse was at that moment tasting the outside of the raspberry jam part of the tart (she had nibbled a sort of gulf, or bay, through the pastry edge) to see whether it was the sort of dinner she could ask her little mouse-husband to sit down to. She had had a very good dinner herself. It is an ill wind that blows nobody any good.

'We'll stop as soon as we see a nice place,' said Anthea. 'I've got threepence, and you boys have the fourpence each that your trams didn't cost the other day, so we can buy things to eat. I expect the Phoenix can speak French.'

The carpet was sailing along over rocks and rivers and trees and towns and farms and fields. It reminded everybody of a certain time when all of them had had wings, and had flown up to the top of a church tower, and had had a feast there of chicken and tongue and new bread and soda-water. And this again reminded them how hungry they were. And just as they were all being reminded of this very strongly indeed, they saw ahead of them some ruined walls on a hill, and strong and upright, and really, to look at, as good as new—a great square tower.

'The top of that's just the exactly same size as the carpet,' said Jane. '*I* think it would be good to go to the top of that, because then none of the Abby-what's-its-names—I mean natives—would be able to take the carpet away even if they wanted to. And some of us could go out and get things to eat—buy them honestly, I mean, not take them out of larder windows.'

'I think it would be better if we went—' Anthea was beginning; but Jane suddenly clenched her hands.

'I don't see why I should never do anything I want, just because I'm the youngest. I wish the carpet would fit itself in at the top of that tower—so there!'

The carpet made a disconcerting bound, and next moment it was hovering above the square top of the tower. Then slowly and carefully it began to sink under them. It was like a lift going down with you at the Army and Navy Stores.

'I don't think we ought to wish things without all agreeing to them first,' said Robert, huffishly. 'Hullo! What on earth?'

For unexpectedly and greyly something was coming up all round the four sides of the carpet. It was as if a wall were being built by magic quickness. It was a foot high—it was two feet high—three, four, five. It was shutting out the light—more and more.

Anthea looked up at the sky and the walls that now rose six feet above them.

'We're dropping into the tower,' she screamed. 'THERE WASN'T ANY TOP TO IT. So the carpet's going to fit itself in at the bottom.'

Robert sprang to his feet.

'We ought to have—Hullo! an owl's nest.' He put his knee on a jutting smooth piece of grey stone, and reached his hand into a deep window slit—broad to the inside of the tower, and narrowing like a funnel to the outside.

'Look sharp!' cried every one, but Robert did not look sharp enough. By the time he had drawn his hand out of the owl's nest—there were no eggs there—the carpet had sunk eight feet below him.

'Jump, you silly cuckoo!' cried Cyril, with brotherly anxiety.

But Robert couldn't turn round all in a minute into a jumping position. He wriggled and twisted and got on to the broad ledge, and by the time he was ready to jump the walls of the tower had risen up thirty feet above the others, who were still sinking with the carpet, and Robert found himself in the embrasure of a window; alone, for even the owls were not at home that day. The wall was smoothish; there was no climbing up, and as for climbing down—Robert hid his face in his hands, and squirmed back and back from the giddy verge, until the back part of him was wedged quite tight in the narrowest part of the window slit.

He was safe now, of course, but the outside part of his window was like a frame to a picture of part of the other side of the tower. It was very pretty, with moss growing between the stones and little shiny gems; but between him and it there was the width of the tower, and nothing in it but empty air. The situation was terrible. Robert saw in a flash that the carpet was likely to bring them into just the same sort of tight places that they used to get into with the wishes the Psammead granted them.

And the others—imagine their feelings as the carpet sank slowly and steadily to the very bottom of the tower, leaving Robert clinging to the wall. Robert did not even try to imagine their feelings—he had quite enough to do with his own; but you can.

As soon as the carpet came to a stop on the ground at the bottom of the inside of the tower it suddenly lost that raft-like stiffness which had been such a comfort during the journey from Camden Town to the topless tower, and spread itself limply over the loose stones and little earthy mounds at the bottom of the tower, just exactly like any ordinary carpet. Also it shrank suddenly, so that it seemed to draw away from under their feet, and they stepped quickly off the edges and stood on the firm ground, while the carpet drew itself in till it was its proper size, and no longer fitted exactly into the inside of the tower, but left quite a big space all round it.

Then across the carpet they looked at each other, and then every chin was tilted up and every eye sought vainly to see where poor Robert had got to. Of course, they couldn't see him.

'I wish we hadn't come,' said Jane.

'You always do,' said Cyril, briefly. 'Look here, we can't leave Robert up there. I wish the carpet would fetch him down.'

The carpet seemed to awake from a dream and pull itself together. It stiffened itself briskly and floated up between the four walls of the tower. The children below craned their heads back, and nearly broke their necks in doing it. The carpet rose and rose. It hung poised darkly above them for an anxious moment or two; then it dropped down again, threw itself on the uneven floor of the tower, and as it did so it tumbled Robert out on the uneven floor of the tower.

'Oh, glory!' said Robert, 'that was a squeak. You don't know how I felt. I say, I've had about enough for a bit. Let's wish ourselves at home again and have a go at that jam tart and mutton. We can go out again afterwards.'

'Righto!' said every one, for the adventure had shaken the nerves of all. So they all got on to the carpet again, and said—

'I wish we were at home.'

And lo and behold, they were no more at home than before. The carpet never moved. The Phoenix had taken the opportunity to go to sleep. Anthea woke it up gently.

'Look here,' she said.

'I'm looking,' said the Phoenix.

'We WISHED to be at home, and we're still here,' complained Jane.

'No,' said the Phoenix, looking about it at the high dark walls of the tower. 'No; I quite see that.'

'But we wished to be at home,' said Cyril.

'No doubt,' said the bird, politely.

'And the carpet hasn't moved an inch,' said Robert.

'No,' said the Phoenix, 'I see it hasn't.'

'But I thought it was a wishing carpet?'

'So it is,' said the Phoenix.

'Then why—?' asked the children, altogether.

'I did tell you, you know,' said the Phoenix, 'only you are so fond of listening to the music of your own voices. It is, indeed, the most lovely music to each of us, and therefore—'

'You did tell us WHAT?' interrupted an Exasperated.

'Why, that the carpet only gives you three wishes a day and YOU'VE HAD THEM.'

There was a heartfelt silence.

'Then how are we going to get home?' said Cyril, at last.

'I haven't any idea,' replied the Phoenix, kindly. 'Can I fly out and get you any little thing?'

'How could you carry the money to pay for it?'

'It isn't necessary. Birds always take what they want. It is not regarded as stealing, except in the case of magpies.'

The children were glad to find they had been right in supposing this to be the case, on the day when they had wings, and had enjoyed somebody else's ripe plums.

'Yes; let the Phoenix get us something to eat, anyway,' Robert urged—' ('If it will be so kind you mean,' corrected Anthea, in a whisper); 'if it will be so kind, and we can be thinking while it's gone.'

So the Phoenix fluttered up through the grey space of the tower and vanished at the top, and it was not till it had quite gone that Jane said—

'Suppose it never comes back.'

It was not a pleasant thought, and though Anthea at once said, 'Of course it will come back; I'm certain it's a bird of its word,' a further gloom was cast by the idea. For, curiously enough, there was no door to the tower, and all the windows were far, far too high to be reached by the most adventurous climber. It was cold, too, and Anthea shivered.

'Yes,' said Cyril, 'it's like being at the bottom of a well.'

The children waited in a sad and hungry silence, and got little stiff necks with holding their little heads back to look up the inside of the tall grey tower, to see if the Phoenix were coming.

At last it came. It looked very big as it fluttered down between the walls, and as it neared them the children saw that its bigness was caused by a basket of boiled chestnuts which it carried in one claw. In the other it held a piece of bread. And in its beak was a very large pear. The pear was juicy, and as good as a very small drink. When the meal was over every one felt better, and the question of how to get home was discussed without any disagreeableness. But no one could think of any way out of the difficulty, or even out of the tower; for the Phoenix, though its beak and claws had fortunately been strong enough to carry food for them, was plainly not equal to flying through the air with four well-nourished children.

'We must stay here, I suppose,' said Robert at last, 'and shout out every now and then, and some one will hear us and bring ropes and ladders, and rescue us like out of mines; and they'll get up a subscription to send us home, like castaways.'

'Yes; but we shan't be home before mother is, and then father'll take away the carpet and say it's dangerous or something,' said Cyril.

'I DO wish we hadn't come,' said Jane.

And every one else said 'Shut up,' except Anthea, who suddenly awoke the Phoenix and said—

'Look here, I believe YOU can help us. Oh, I do wish you would!'

'I will help you as far as lies in my power,' said the Phoenix, at once. 'What is it you want now?'

'Why, we want to get home,' said every one.

'Oh,' said the Phoenix. 'Ah, hum! Yes. Home, you said? Meaning?'

'Where we live—where we slept last night—where the altar is that your egg was hatched on.'

'Oh, there!' said the Phoenix. 'Well, I'll do my best.' It fluttered on to the carpet and walked up and down for a few minutes in deep thought. Then it drew itself up proudly.

'I CAN help you,' it said. 'I am almost sure I can help you. Unless I am grossly deceived I can help you. You won't mind my leaving you for an hour or two?' and without waiting for a reply it soared up through the dimness of the tower into the brightness above.

'Now,' said Cyril, firmly, 'it said an hour or two. But I've read about captives and people shut up in dungeons and catacombs and things awaiting release, and I know each moment is an eternity. Those people always do something to pass the desperate moments. It's no use our trying to tame spiders, because we shan't have time.'

'I HOPE not,' said Jane, doubtfully.

'But we ought to scratch our names on the stones or something.'

'I say, talking of stones,' said Robert, 'you see that heap of stones against the wall over in that corner. Well, I'm certain there's a hole in the wall there—and I believe it's a door. Yes, look here—the stones are round like an arch in the wall; and here's the hole—it's all black inside.'

He had walked over to the heap as he spoke and climbed up to it—dislodged the top stone of the heap and uncovered a little dark space.

Next moment every one was helping to pull down the heap of stones, and very soon every one threw off its jacket, for it was warm work.

'It IS a door,' said Cyril, wiping his face, 'and not a bad thing either, if—'

He was going to add 'if anything happens to the Phoenix,' but he didn't for fear of frightening Jane. He was not an unkind boy when he had leisure to think of such things.

The arched hole in the wall grew larger and larger. It was very, very black, even compared with the sort of twilight at the bottom of the tower; it grew larger because the children kept pulling off the stones and throwing them down into another heap. The stones must have been there a very long time, for they were covered with moss, and some of them were stuck together by it. So it was fairly hard work, as Robert pointed out.

When the hole reached to about halfway between the top of the arch and the tower, Robert and Cyril let themselves down cautiously on the inside, and lit matches. How thankful they felt then that they had a sensible father, who did not forbid them to carry matches, as some boys' fathers do. The father of Robert and Cyril only insisted on the matches being of the kind that strike only on the box.

'It's not a door, it's a sort of tunnel,' Robert cried to the girls, after the first match had flared up, flickered, and gone out. 'Stand off—we'll push some more stones down!'

They did, amid deep excitement. And now the stone heap was almost gone—and before them the girls saw the dark archway leading to unknown things. All doubts and fears as to getting home were forgotten in this thrilling moment. It was like Monte Cristo—it was like—

'I say,' cried Anthea, suddenly, 'come out! There's always bad air in places that have been shut up. It makes your torches go out, and then you die. It's called fire-damp, I believe. Come out, I tell you.'

The urgency of her tone actually brought the boys out—and then every one took up its jacket and fanned the dark arch with it, so as to make the air fresh inside. When Anthea thought the air inside 'must be freshened by now,' Cyril led the way into the arch.

The girls followed, and Robert came last, because Jane refused to tail the procession lest 'something' should come in after her, and catch at her from behind. Cyril advanced cautiously, lighting match after match, and peerIng before him.

'It's a vaulting roof,' he said, 'and it's all stone—all right, Panther, don't keep pulling at my jacket! The air must be all right because of the matches, silly, and there are—look out—there are steps down.'

'Oh, don't let's go any farther,' said Jane, in an agony of reluctance (a very painful thing, by the way, to be in). 'I'm sure there are snakes, or dens of lions, or something. Do let's go back, and come some other time, with candles, and bellows for the fire-damp.'

'Let me get in front of you, then,' said the stern voice of Robert, from behind. 'This is exactly the place for buried treasure, and I'm going on, anyway; you can stay behind if you like.'

And then, of course, Jane consented to go on.

So, very slowly and carefully, the children went down the steps—there were seventeen of them—and at the bottom of the steps were more passages branching four ways, and a sort of low arch on the right-hand side made Cyril wonder what it could be, for it was too low to be the beginning of another passage.

So he knelt down and lit a match, and stooping very low he peeped in.

'There's SOMETHING,' he said, and reached out his hand. It touched something that felt more like a damp bag of marbles than anything else that Cyril had ever touched.

'I believe it IS a buried treasure,' he cried.

And it was; for even as Anthea cried, 'Oh, hurry up, Squirrel—fetch it out!' Cyril pulled out a rotting canvas bag—about as big as the paper ones the greengrocer gives you with Barcelona nuts in for sixpence.

'There's more of it, a lot more,' he said.

As he pulled the rotten bag gave way, and the gold coins ran and span and jumped and bumped and chinked and clinked on the floor of the dark passage.

I wonder what you would say if you suddenly came upon a buried treasure? What Cyril said was, 'Oh, bother—I've burnt my fingers!' and as he spoke he dropped the match. 'AND IT WAS THE LAST!' he added.

There was a moment of desperate silence. Then Jane began to cry.

'Don't,' said Anthea, 'don't, Pussy—you'll exhaust the air if you cry. We can get out all right.'

'Yes,' said Jane, through her sobs, 'and find the Phoenix has come back and gone away again—because it thought we'd gone home some other way, and—Oh, I WISH we hadn't come.'

Every one stood quite still—only Anthea cuddled Jane up to her and tried to wipe her eyes in the dark.

'D-DON'T,' said Jane; 'that's my EAR—I'm not crying with my ears.'

'Come, let's get on out,' said Robert; but that was not so easy, for no one could remember exactly which way they had come. It is very difficult to remember things in the dark, unless you have matches with you, and then of course it is quite different, even if you don't strike one.

Every one had come to agree with Jane's constant wish—and despair was making the darkness blacker than ever, when quite suddenly the floor seemed to tip up—and a strong sensation of being in a whirling lift came upon every one. All eyes were closed—one's eyes always are in the dark, don't you think? When the whirling feeling stopped, Cyril said 'Earthquakes!' and they all opened their eyes.

They were in their own dingy breakfast-room at home, and oh, how light and bright and safe and pleasant and altogether delightful it seemed after that dark underground tunnel! The carpet lay on the floor, looking as calm as though it had never been for an excursion in its life. On the mantelpiece stood the Phoenix, waiting with an air of modest yet sterling worth for the thanks of the children.

'But how DID you do it?' they asked, when every one had thanked the Phoenix again and again.

'Oh, I just went and got a wish from your friend the Psammead.'

'But how DID you know where to find it?'

'I found that out from the carpet; these wishing creatures always know all about each other—they're so clannish; like the Scots, you know—all related.'

'But, the carpet can't talk, can it?'

'No.'

'Then how—'

'How did I get the Psammead's address? I tell you I got it from the carpet.'

'DID it speak then?'

'No,' said the Phoenix, thoughtfully, 'it didn't speak, but I gathered my information from something in its manner. I was always a singularly observant bird.'

it was not till after the cold mutton and the jam tart, as well as the tea and bread-and-butter, that any one found time to regret the golden treasure which had been left scattered on the floor of the underground passage, and which, indeed, no one had thought of till now, since the moment when Cyril burnt his fingers at the flame of the last match.

'What owls and goats we were!' said Robert. 'Look how we've always wanted treasure—and now—'

'Never mind,' said Anthea, trying as usual to make the best of it. 'We'll go back again and get it all, and then we'll give everybody presents.'

More than a quarter of an hour passed most agreeably in arranging what presents should be given to whom, and, when the claims of generosity had been satisfied, the talk ran for fifty minutes on what they would buy for themselves.

It was Cyril who broke in on Robert's almost too technical account of the motor-car on which he meant to go to and from school—

'There!' he said. 'Dry up. It's no good. We can't ever go back. We don't know where it is.'

'Don't YOU know?' Jane asked the Phoenix, wistfully.

'Not in the least,' the Phoenix replied, in a tone of amiable regret.

'Then we've lost the treasure,' said Cyril. And they had.

'But we've got the carpet and the Phoenix,' said Anthea.

'Excuse me,' said the bird, with an air of wounded dignity, 'I do SO HATE to seem to interfere, but surely you MUST mean the Phoenix and the carpet?'

Chapter 3. The Queen Cook

It was on a Saturday that the children made their first glorious journey on the wishing carpet. Unless you are too young to read at all, you will know that the next day must have been Sunday.

Sunday at 18, Camden Terrace, Camden Town, was always a very pretty day. Father always brought home flowers on Saturday, so that the breakfast-table was extra beautiful. In November, of course, the flowers were chrysanthemums, yellow and coppery coloured. Then there were always sausages on toast for breakfast, and these are rapture, after six days of Kentish Town Road eggs at fourteen a shilling.

On this particular Sunday there were fowls for dinner, a kind of food that is generally kept for birthdays and grand occasions, and there was an angel pudding, when rice and milk and oranges and white icing do their best to make you happy.

After dinner father was very sleepy indeed, because he had been working hard all the week; but he did not yield to the voice that said, 'Go and have an hour's rest.' He nursed the Lamb, who had a horrid cough that cook said was whooping-cough as sure as eggs, and he said—

'Come along, kiddies; I've got a ripping book from the library, called The Golden Age, and I'll read it to you.'

Mother settled herself on the drawing-room sofa, and said she could listen quite nicely with her eyes shut. The Lamb snugged into the 'armchair corner' of daddy's arm, and the others got into a happy heap on the hearth-rug. At first, of course, there were too many feet and knees and shoulders and elbows, but real comfort was actually settling down on them, and the Phoenix and the carpet were put away on the back top shelf of their minds (beautiful things that could be taken out and played with later), when a surly solid knock came at the drawing-room door. It opened an angry inch, and the cook's voice said, 'Please, m', may I speak to you a moment?'

Mother looked at father with a desperate expression. Then she put her pretty sparkly Sunday shoes down from the sofa, and stood up in them and sighed.

'As good fish in the sea,' said father, cheerfully, and it was not till much later that the children understood what he meant.

Mother went out into the passage, which is called 'the hall', where the umbrella-stand is, and the picture of the 'Monarch of the Glen' in a yellow shining frame, with brown spots on the Monarch from the damp in the house before last, and there was cook, very red and damp in the face, and with a clean apron tied on all crooked over the dirty one that she had dished up those dear delightful chickens in. She stood there and she seemed to get redder and damper, and she twisted the corner of her apron round her fingers, and she said very shortly and fiercely—

'If you please ma'am, I should wish to leave at my day month.' Mother leaned against the hatstand. The children could see her looking pale through the crack of the door, because she had been very kind to the cook, and had given her a holiday only the day before, and it seemed so very unkind of the cook to want to go like this, and on a Sunday too.

'Why, what's the matter?' mother said.

'It's them children,' the cook replied, and somehow the children all felt that they had known it from the first. They did not remember having done anything extra wrong, but it is so frightfully easy to displease a cook. 'It's them children: there's that there new carpet in their room, covered thick with mud, both sides, beastly yellow mud, and sakes alive knows where they got it. And all that muck to clean up on a Sunday! It's not my place, and it's not my intentions, so I don't deceive you, ma'am, and but for them limbs, which they is if ever there was, it's not a bad place, though I says it, and I wouldn't wish to leave, but—'

'I'm very sorry,' said mother, gently. 'I will speak to the children. And you had better think it over, and if you REALLY wish to go, tell me to-morrow.'

Next day mother had a quiet talk with cook, and cook said she didn't mind if she stayed on a bit, just to see.

But meantime the question of the muddy carpet had been gone into thoroughly by father and mother. Jane's candid explanation that the mud had come from the bottom of a foreign tower where there was buried treasure was received with such chilling disbelief that the others limited their defence to an expression of sorrow, and of a determination 'not to do it again'. But father said (and mother agreed with him, because mothers have to agree with fathers, and not because it was her own idea) that children who coated a carpet on both sides with thick mud, and when they were asked for an explanation could only talk silly nonsense—that meant Jane's truthful statement—were not fit to have a carpet at all, and, indeed, SHOULDN'T have one for a week!

So the carpet was brushed (with tea-leaves, too) which was the only comfort Anthea could think of) and folded up and put away in the cupboard at the top of the stairs, and daddy put the key in his trousers pocket. 'Till Saturday,' said he.

'Never mind,' said Anthea, 'we've got the Phoenix.'

But, as it happened, they hadn't. The Phoenix was nowhere to be found, and everything had suddenly settled down from the rosy wild beauty of magic happenings to the common damp brownness of ordinary November life in Camden Town—and there was the nursery floor all bare boards in the middle and brown oilcloth round the outside, and the bareness and yellowness of the middle floor showed up the blackbeetles with terrible distinctness, when the poor things came out in the evening, as usual, to try to make friends with the children. But the children never would.

The Sunday ended in gloom, which even junket for supper in the blue Dresden bowl could hardly lighten at all. Next day the Lamb's cough was worse. It certainly seemed very whoopy, and the doctor came in his brougham carriage.

Every one tried to bear up under the weight of the sorrow which it was to know that the wishing carpet was locked up and the Phoenix mislaid. A good deal of time was spent in looking for the Phoenix.

'It's a bird of its word,' said Anthea. 'I'm sure it's not deserted us. But you know it had a most awfully long fly from wherever it was to near Rochester and back, and I expect the poor thing's feeling tired out and wants rest. I am sure we may trust it.'

The others tried to feel sure of this, too, but it was hard.

No one could be expected to feel very kindly towards the cook, since it was entirely through her making such a fuss about a little foreign mud that the carpet had been taken away.

'She might have told us,' said Jane, 'and Panther and I would have cleaned it with tea-leaves.'

'She's a cantankerous cat,' said Robert.

'I shan't say what I think about her,' said Anthea, primly, 'because it would be evil speaking, lying, and slandering.'

'It's not lying to say she's a disagreeable pig, and a beastly blue-nosed Bozwoz,' said Cyril, who had read The Eyes of Light, and intended to talk like Tony as soon as he could teach Robert to talk like Paul.

And all the children, even Anthea, agreed that even if she wasn't a blue-nosed Bozwoz, they wished cook had never been born.

But I ask you to believe that they didn't do all the things on purpose which so annoyed the cook during the following week, though I daresay the things would not have happened if the cook had been a favourite. This is a mystery. Explain it if you can. The things that had happened were as follows:

Sunday.—Discovery of foreign mud on both sides of the carpet.

Monday.—Liquorice put on to boil with aniseed balls in a saucepan. Anthea did this, because she thought it would be good for the Lamb's cough. The whole thing forgotten, and bottom of saucepan burned out. It was the little saucepan lined with white that was kept for the baby's milk.

Tuesday.—A dead mouse found in pantry. Fish-slice taken to dig grave with. By regrettable accident fish-slice broken. Defence: 'The cook oughtn't to keep dead mice in pantries.'

Wednesday.—Chopped suet left on kitchen table. Robert added chopped soap, but he says he thought the suet was soap too.

Thursday.—Broke the kitchen window by falling against it during a perfectly fair game of bandits in the area.

Friday.—Stopped up grating of kitchen sink with putty and filled sink with water to make a lake to sail paper boats in. Went away and left the tap running. Kitchen hearthrug and cook's shoes ruined.

On Saturday the carpet was restored. There had been plenty of time during the week to decide where it should be asked to go when they did get it back.

Mother had gone over to granny's, and had not taken the Lamb because he had a bad cough, which, cook repeatedly said, was whooping-cough as sure as eggs is eggs.

'But we'll take him out, a ducky darling,' said Anthea. 'We'll take him somewhere where you can't have whooping-cough.

Don't be so silly, Robert. If he DOES talk about it no one'll take any notice. He's always talking about things he's never seen.'

So they dressed the Lamb and themselves in out-of-doors clothes, and the Lamb chuckled and coughed, and laughed and coughed again, poor dear, and all the chairs and tables were moved off the carpet by the boys, while Jane nursed the Lamb, and Anthea rushed through the house in one last wild hunt for the missing Phoenix.

'It's no use waiting for it,' she said, reappearing breathless in the breakfast-room. 'But I know it hasn't deserted us. It's a bird of its word.'

'Quite so,' said the gentle voice of the Phoenix from beneath the table.

Every one fell on its knees and looked up, and there was the Phoenix perched on a crossbar of wood that ran across under the table, and had once supported a drawer, in the happy days before the drawer had been used as a boat, and its bottom unfortunately trodden out by Raggett's Really Reliable School Boots on the feet of Robert.

'I've been here all the time,' said the Phoenix, yawning politely behind its claw. 'If you wanted me you should have recited the ode of invocation; it's seven thousand lines long, and written in very pure and beautiful Greek.'

'Couldn't you tell it us in English?' asked Anthea.

'It's rather long, isn't it?' said Jane, jumping the Lamb on her knee.

'Couldn't you make a short English version, like Tate and Brady?'

'Oh, come along, do,' said Robert, holding out his hand. 'Come along, good old Phoenix.'

'Good old BEAUTIFUL Phoenix,' it corrected shyly.

'Good old BEAUTIFUL Phoenix, then. Come along, come along,' said Robert, impatiently, with his hand still held out.

The Phoenix fluttered at once on to his wrist.

'This amiable youth,' it said to the others, 'has miraculously been able to put the whole meaning of the seven thousand lines of Greek invocation into one English hexameter—a little misplaced some of the words—but

'Oh, come along, come along, good old beautiful Phoenix!'

'Not perfect, I admit—but not bad for a boy of his age.'

'Well, now then,' said Robert, stepping back on to the carpet with the golden Phoenix on his wrist.

'You look like the king's falconer,' said Jane, sitting down on the carpet with the baby on her lap.

Robert tried to go on looking like it. Cyril and Anthea stood on the carpet.

'We shall have to get back before dinner,' said Cyril, 'or cook will blow the gaff.'

'She hasn't sneaked since Sunday,' said Anthea.

'She—' Robert was beginning, when the door burst open and the cook, fierce and furious, came in like a whirlwind and stood on the corner of the carpet, with a broken basin in one hand and a threat in the other, which was clenched.

'Look 'ere!' she cried, 'my only basin; and what the powers am I to make the beefsteak and kidney pudding in that your ma ordered for your dinners? You don't deserve no dinners, so yer don't.'

'I'm awfully sorry, cook,' said Anthea gently; 'it was my fault, and I forgot to tell you about it. It got broken when we were telling our fortunes with melted lead, you know, and I meant to tell you.'

'Meant to tell me,' replied the cook; she was red with anger, and really I don't wonder—'meant to tell! Well, *I* mean to tell, too. I've held my tongue this week through, because the missus she said to me quiet like, "We mustn't expect old heads on young shoulders," but now I shan't hold it no longer. There was the soap you put in our pudding, and me and Eliza never so much as breathed it to your ma—though well we might—and the saucepan, and the fish-slice, and—My gracious cats alive! what 'ave you got that blessed child dressed up in his outdoors for?'

'We aren't going to take him out,' said Anthea; 'at least—' She stopped short, for though they weren't going to take him out in the Kentish Town Road, they certainly intended to take him elsewhere. But not at all where cook meant when she said 'out'. This confused the truthful Anthea.

'Out!' said the cook, 'that I'll take care you don't;' and she snatched the Lamb from the lap of Jane, while Anthea and Robert caught her by the skirts and apron. 'Look here,' said Cyril, in stern desperation, 'will you go away, and make your pudding in a pie-dish, or a flower-pot, or a hot-water can, or something?'

'Not me,' said the cook, briefly; 'and leave this precious poppet for you to give his deathercold to.'

'I warn you,' said Cyril, solemnly. 'Beware, ere yet it be too late.'

'Late yourself the little popsey-wopsey,' said the cook, with angry tenderness. 'They shan't take it out, no more they shan't. And—Where did you get that there yellow fowl?' She pointed to the Phoenix.

Even Anthea saw that unless the cook lost her situation the loss would be theirs.

'I wish,' she said suddenly, 'we were on a sunny southern shore, where there can't be any whooping-cough.'

She said it through the frightened howls of the Lamb, and the sturdy scoldings of the cook, and instantly the giddy-go-round-and-falling-lift feeling swept over the whole party, and the cook sat down flat on the carpet, holding the screaming Lamb tight to her stout print-covered self, and calling on St Bridget to help her. She was an Irishwoman.

The moment the tipsy-topsy-turvy feeling stopped, the cook opened her eyes, gave one sounding screech and shut them again, and Anthea took the opportunity to get the desperately howling Lamb into her own arms.

'It's all right,' she said; 'own Panther's got you. Look at the trees, and the sand, and the shells, and the great big tortoises. Oh DEAR, how hot it is!'

It certainly was; for the trusty carpet had laid itself out on a southern shore that was sunny and no mistake, as Robert remarked. The greenest of green slopes led up to glorious groves where palm-trees and all the tropical flowers and fruits that you read of in Westward Ho! and Fair Play were growing in rich profusion. Between the green, green slope and the blue, blue sea lay a stretch of sand that looked like a carpet of jewelled cloth of gold, for it was not greyish as our northern sand is, but yellow and changing—opal-coloured like sunshine and rainbows. And at the very moment when the wild, whirling, blinding, deafening, tumbling upside-downness of the carpet-moving stopped, the children had the happiness of seeing three large live turtles waddle down to the edge of the sea and disappear in the water. And it was hotter than you can possibly imagine, unless you think of ovens on a baking-day.

Every one without an instant's hesitation tore off its London-in-November outdoor clothes, and Anthea took off the Lamb's highwayman blue coat and his three-cornered hat, and then his jersey, and then the Lamb himself suddenly slipped out of his little blue tight breeches and stood up happy and hot in his little white shirt.

'I'm sure it's much warmer than the seaside in the summer,' said Anthea. 'Mother always lets us go barefoot then.'

So the Lamb's shoes and socks and gaiters came off, and he stood digging his happy naked pink toes into the golden smooth sand.

'I'm a little white duck-dickie,' said he—'a little white duck-dickie what swims,' and splashed quacking into a sandy pool.

'Let him,' said Anthea; 'it can't hurt him. Oh, how hot it is!'

The cook suddenly opened her eyes and screamed, shut them, screamed again, opened her eyes once more and said—

'Why, drat my cats alive, what's all this? It's a dream, I expect. Well, it's the best I ever dreamed. I'll look it up in the dream-book to-morrow. Seaside and trees and a carpet to sit on. I never did!'

'Look here,' said Cyril, 'it isn't a dream; it's real.'

'Ho yes!' said the cook; 'they always says that in dreams.'

'It's REAL, I tell you,' Robert said, stamping his foot. 'I'm not going to tell you how it's done, because that's our secret.' He winked heavily at each of the others in turn. 'But you wouldn't go away and make that pudding, so we HAD to bring you, and I hope you like it.'

'I do that, and no mistake,' said the cook unexpectedly; 'and it being a dream it don't matter what I say; and I WILL say, if it's my last word, that of all the aggravating little varmints—'

'Calm yourself, my good woman,' said the Phoenix.

'Good woman, indeed,' said the cook; 'good woman yourself.' Then she saw who it was that had spoken. 'Well, if I ever,' said she; 'this is something like a dream! Yellow fowls a-talking and all! I've heard of such, but never did I think to see the day.'

'Well, then,' said Cyril, impatiently, 'sit here and see the day now. It's a jolly fine day. Here, you others—a council!' They walked along the shore till they were out of earshot of the cook, who still sat gazing about her with a happy, dreamy, vacant smile.

'Look here,' said Cyril, 'we must roll the carpet up and hide it, so that we can get at it at any moment. The Lamb can be getting rid of his whooping-cough all the morning, and we can look about; and if the savages on this island are cannibals, we'll hook it, and take her back. And if not, we'll LEAVE HER HERE.'

'Is that being kind to servants and animals, like the clergyman said?' asked Jane.

'Nor she isn't kind,' retorted Cyril.

'Well—anyway,' said Anthea, 'the safest thing is to leave the carpet there with her sitting on it. Perhaps it'll be a lesson to her, and anyway, if she thinks it's a dream it won't matter what she says when she gets home.'

So the extra coats and hats and mufflers were piled on the carpet. Cyril shouldered the well and happy Lamb, the Phoenix perched on Robert's wrist, and 'the party of explorers prepared to enter the interior'.

The grassy slope was smooth, but under the trees there were tangled creepers with bright, strange-shaped flowers, and it was not easy to walk.

'We ought to have an explorer's axe,' said Robert. 'I shall ask father to give me one for Christmas.'

There were curtains of creepers with scented blossoms hanging from the trees, and brilliant birds darted about quite close to their faces.

'Now, tell me honestly,' said the Phoenix, 'are there any birds here handsomer than I am? Don't be afraid of hurting my feelings—I'm a modest bird, I hope.'

'Not one of them,' said Robert, with conviction, 'is a patch upon you!'

'I was never a vain bird,' said the Phoenix, 'but I own that you confirm my own impression. I will take a flight.' It circled in the air for a moment, and, returning to Robert's wrist, went on, 'There is a path to the left.'

And there was. So now the children went on through the wood more quickly and comfortably, the girls picking flowers and the Lamb inviting the 'pretty dickies' to observe that he himself was a 'little white real-water-wet duck!'

And all this time he hadn't whooping-coughed once.

The path turned and twisted, and, always threading their way amid a tangle of flowers, the children suddenly passed a corner and found themselves in a forest clearing, where there were a lot of pointed huts—the huts, as they knew at once, of SAVAGES.

The boldest heart beat more quickly. Suppose they WERE cannibals. It was a long way back to the carpet.

'Hadn't we better go back?' said Jane. 'Go NOW,' she said, and her voice trembled a little. 'Suppose they eat us.'

'Nonsense, Pussy,' said Cyril, firmly. 'Look, there's a goat tied up. That shows they don't eat PEOPLE.'

'Let's go on and say we're missionaries,' Robert suggested.

'I shouldn't advise THAT,' said the Phoenix, very earnestly.

'Why not?'

'Well, for one thing, it isn't true,' replied the golden bird.

It was while they stood hesitating on the edge of the clearing that a tall man suddenly came out of one of the huts. He had hardly any clothes, and his body all over was a dark and beautiful coppery colour—just like the chrysanthemums father had brought home on Saturday. In his hand he held a spear. The whites of his eyes and the white of his teeth were the only light things about him, except that where the sun shone on his shiny brown body it looked white, too. If you will look carefully at the next shiny savage you meet with next to nothing on, you will see at once—if the sun happens to be shining at the time—that I am right about this.

The savage looked at the children. Concealment was impossible. He uttered a shout that was more like 'Oo goggery bag-wag' than anything else the children had ever heard, and at once brown coppery people leapt out of every hut, and swarmed like ants about the clearing. There was no time for discussion, and no one wanted to discuss anything, anyhow. Whether these coppery people were cannibals or not now seemed to matter very little.

Without an instant's hesitation the four children turned and ran back along the forest path; the only pause was Anthea's. She stood back to let Cyril pass, because he was carrying the Lamb, who screamed with delight. (He had not whooping-coughed a single once since the carpet landed him on the island.)

'Gee-up, Squirrel; gee-gee,' he shouted, and Cyril did gee-up. The path was a shorter cut to the beach than the creeper-covered way by which they had come, and almost directly they saw through the trees the shining blue-and-gold-and-opal of sand and sea.

'Stick to it,' cried Cyril, breathlessly.

They did stick to it; they tore down the sands—they could hear behind them as they ran the patter of feet which they knew, too well, were copper-coloured.

The sands were golden and opal-coloured—and BARE. There were wreaths of tropic seaweed, there were rich tropic shells of the kind you would not buy in the Kentish Town Road under at least fifteen pence a pair. There were turtles basking lumpily on the water's edge—but no cook, no clothes, and no carpet.

'On, on! Into the sea!' gasped Cyril. 'They MUST hate water. I've—heard—savages always—dirty.'

Their feet were splashing in the warm shallows before his breathless words were ended. The calm baby-waves were easy to go through. It is warm work running for your life in the tropics, and the coolness of the water was delicious. They were up to their arm-pits now, and Jane was up to her chin.

'Look!' said the Phoenix. 'What are they pointing at?'

The children turned; and there, a little to the west was a head—a head they knew, with a crooked cap upon it. It was the head of the cook.

For some reason or other the savages had stopped at the water's edge and were all talking at the top of their voices, and all were pointing copper-coloured fingers, stiff with interest and excitement, at the head of the cook.

The children hurried towards her as quickly as the water would let them.

'What on earth did you come out here for?' Robert shouted; 'and where on earth's the carpet?'

'It's not on earth, bless you,' replied the cook, happily; 'it's UNDER ME—in the water. I got a bit warm setting there in the sun, and I just says, "I wish I was in a cold bath"—just like that—and next minute here I was! It's all part of the dream.'

Every one at once saw how extremely fortunate it was that the carpet had had the sense to take the cook to the nearest and largest bath—the sea, and how terrible it would have been if the carpet had taken itself and her to the stuffy little bath-room of the house in Camden Town!

'Excuse me,' said the Phoenix's soft voice, breaking in on the general sigh of relief, 'but I think these brown people want your cook.'

'To—to eat?' whispered Jane, as well as she could through the water which the plunging Lamb was dashing in her face with happy fat hands and feet.

'Hardly,' rejoined the bird. 'Who wants cooks to EAT? Cooks are ENGAGED, not eaten. They wish to engage her.'

'How can you understand what they say?' asked Cyril, doubtfully.

'It's as easy as kissing your claw,' replied the bird. 'I speak and understand ALL languages, even that of your cook, which is difficult and unpleasing. It's quite easy, when you know how it's done. It just comes to you. I should advise you to beach the carpet and land the cargo—the cook, I mean. You can take my word for it, the copper-coloured ones will not harm you now.'

It is impossible not to take the word of a Phoenix when it tells you to. So the children at once got hold of the corners of the carpet, and, pulling it from under the cook, towed it slowly in through the shallowing water, and at last spread it on the sand. The cook, who had followed, instantly sat down on it, and at once the copper-coloured natives, now strangely humble, formed a ring round the carpet, and fell on their faces on the rainbow-and-gold sand. The tallest savage spoke in this position, which must have been very awkward for him; and Jane noticed that it took him quite a long time to get the sand out of his mouth afterwards.

'He says,' the Phoenix remarked after some time, 'that they wish to engage your cook permanently.'

'Without a character?' asked Anthea, who had heard her mother speak of such things.

'They do not wish to engage her as cook, but as queen; and queens need not have characters.'

There was a breathless pause.

'WELL,' said Cyril, 'of all the choices! But there's no accounting for tastes.'

Every one laughed at the idea of the cook's being engaged as queen; they could not help it.

'I do not advise laughter,' warned the Phoenix, ruffling out his golden feathers, which were extremely wet. 'And it's not their own choice. It seems that there is an ancient prophecy of this copper-coloured tribe that a great queen should some day arise out of the sea with a white crown on her head, and—and—well, you see! There's the crown!'

It pointed its claw at cook's cap; and a very dirty cap it was, because it was the end of the week.

'That's the white crown,' it said; 'at least, it's nearly white—very white indeed compared to the colour THEY are—and anyway, it's quite white enough.'

Cyril addressed the cook. 'Look here!' said he, 'these brown people want you to be their queen. They're only savages, and they don't know any better. Now would you really like to stay? or, if you'll promise not to be so jolly aggravating at home, and not to tell any one a word about to-day, we'll take you back to Camden Town.'

'No, you don't,' said the cook, in firm, undoubting tones. 'I've always wanted to be the Queen, God bless her! and I always thought what a good one I should make; and now I'm going to. IF it's only in a dream, it's well worth while. And I don't go back to that nasty underground kitchen, and me blamed for everything; that I don't, not till the dream's finished and I wake up with that nasty bell a rang-tanging in my ears—so I tell you.'

'Are you SURE,' Anthea anxiously asked the Phoenix, 'that she will be quite safe here?'

'She will find the nest of a queen a very precious and soft thing,' said the bird, solemnly.

'There—you hear,' said Cyril. 'You're in for a precious soft thing, so mind you're a good queen, cook. It's more than you'd any right to expect, but long may you reign.'

Some of the cook's copper-coloured subjects now advanced from the forest with long garlands of beautiful flowers, white and sweet-scented, and hung them respectfully round the neck of their new sovereign.

'What! all them lovely bokays for me!' exclaimed the enraptured cook. 'Well, this here is something LIKE a dream, I must say.'

She sat up very straight on the carpet, and the copper-coloured ones, themselves wreathed in garlands of the gayest flowers, madly stuck parrot feathers in their hair and began to dance. It was a dance such as you have never seen; it made the children feel almost sure that the cook was right, and that they were all in a dream. Small, strange-shaped drums were beaten, odd-sounding songs were sung, and the dance got faster and faster and odder and odder, till at last all the dancers fell on the sand tired out.

The new queen, with her white crown-cap all on one side, clapped wildly.

'Brayvo!' she cried, 'brayvo! It's better than the Albert Edward Music-hall in the Kentish Town Road. Go it again!'

But the Phoenix would not translate this request into the copper-coloured language; and when the savages had recovered their breath, they implored their queen to leave her white escort and come with them to their huts.

'The finest shall be yours, O queen,' said they.

'Well—so long!' said the cook, getting heavily on to her feet, when the Phoenix had translated this request. 'No more kitchens and attics for me, thank you. I'm off to my royal palace, I am; and I only wish this here dream would keep on for ever and ever.'

She picked up the ends of the garlands that trailed round her feet, and the children had one last glimpse of her striped stockings and worn elastic-side boots before she disappeared into the shadow of the forest, surrounded by her dusky retainers, singing songs of rejoicing as they went.

'WELL!' said Cyril, 'I suppose she's all right, but they don't seem to count us for much, one way or the other.'

'Oh,' said the Phoenix, 'they think you're merely dreams. The prophecy said that the queen would arise from the waves with a white crown and surrounded by white dream-children. That's about what they think YOU are!'

'And what about dinner?' said Robert, abruptly.

'There won't be any dinner, with no cook and no pudding-basin,' Anthea reminded him; 'but there's always bread-and-butter.'

'Let's get home,' said Cyril.

The Lamb was furiously unwishful to be dressed in his warm clothes again, but Anthea and Jane managed it, by force disguised as coaxing, and he never once whooping-coughed.

Then every one put on its own warm things and took its place on the carpet.

A sound of uncouth singing still came from beyond the trees where the copper-coloured natives were crooning songs of admiration and respect to their white-crowned queen. Then Anthea said 'Home,' just as duchesses and other people do to their coachmen, and the intelligent carpet in one whirling moment laid itself down in its proper place on the nursery floor. And at that very moment Eliza opened the door and said—

'Cook's gone! I can't find her anywhere, and there's no dinner ready. She hasn't taken her box nor yet her outdoor things. She just ran out to see the time, I shouldn't wonder—the kitchen clock never did give her satisfaction—and she's got run over or fell down in a fit as likely as not. You'll have to put up with the cold bacon for your dinners; and what on earth you've got your outdoor things on for I don't know. And then I'll slip out and see if they know anything about her at the police-station.'

But nobody ever knew anything about the cook any more, except the children, and, later, one other person.

Mother was so upset at losing the cook, and so anxious about her, that Anthea felt most miserable, as though she had done something very wrong indeed. She woke several times in the night, and at last decided that she would ask the Phoenix to let her tell her mother all about it. But there was no opportunity to do this next day, because the Phoenix, as usual, had gone to sleep in some out-of-the-way spot, after asking, as a special favour, not to be disturbed for twenty-four hours.

The Lamb never whooping-coughed once all that Sunday, and mother and father said what good medicine it was that the doctor had given him. But the children knew that it was the southern shore where you can't have whooping-cough that had cured him. The Lamb babbled of coloured sand and water, but no one took any notice of that. He often talked of things that hadn't happened.

It was on Monday morning, very early indeed, that Anthea woke and suddenly made up her mind. She crept downstairs in her night-gown (it was very chilly), sat down on the carpet, and with a beating heart wished herself on the sunny shore where you can't have whooping-cough, and next moment there she was.

The sand was splendidly warm. She could feel it at once, even through the carpet. She folded the carpet, and put it over her shoulders like a shawl, for she was determined not to be parted from it for a single instant, no matter how hot it might be to wear.

Then trembling a little, and trying to keep up her courage by saying over and over, 'It is my DUTY, it IS my duty,' she went up the forest path.

'Well, here you are again,' said the cook, directly she saw Anthea. 'This dream does keep on!'

The cook was dressed in a white robe; she had no shoes and stockings and no cap and she was sitting under a screen of palm-leaves, for it was afternoon in the island, and blazing hot. She wore a flower wreath on her hair, and copper-coloured boys were fanning her with peacock's feathers.

'They've got the cap put away,' she said. 'They seem to think a lot of it. Never saw one before, I expect.'

'Are you happy?' asked Anthea, panting; the sight of the cook as queen quite took her breath away.

'I believe you, my dear,' said the cook, heartily. 'Nothing to do unless you want to. But I'm getting rested now. Tomorrow I'm going to start cleaning out my hut, if the dream keeps on, and I shall teach them cooking; they burns everything to a cinder now unless they eats it raw.'

'But can you talk to them?'

'Lor' love a duck, yes!' the happy cook-queen replied; 'it's quite easy to pick up. I always thought I should be quick at foreign languages. I've taught them to understand "dinner," and "I want a drink," and "You leave me be," already.'

'Then you don't want anything?' Anthea asked earnestly and anxiously.

'Not me, miss; except if you'd only go away. I'm afraid of me waking up with that bell a-going if you keep on stopping here a-talking to me. Long as this here dream keeps up I'm as happy as a queen.'

'Goodbye, then,' said Anthea, gaily, for her conscience was clear now.

She hurried into the wood, threw herself on the ground, and said 'Home'—and there she was, rolled in the carpet on the nursery floor.

'SHE'S all right, anyhow,' said Anthea, and went back to bed. 'I'm glad somebody's pleased. But mother will never believe me when I tell her.'

The story is indeed a little difficult to believe. Still, you might try.

Chapter 4. Two Bazaars

Mother was really a great dear. She was pretty and she was loving, and most frightfully good when you were ill, and always kind, and almost always just. That is, she was just when she understood things. But of course she did not always understand things. No one understands everything, and mothers are not angels, though a good many of them come pretty near it. The children knew that mother always WANTED to do what was best for them, even if she was not clever enough to know exactly what was the best. That was why all of them, but much more particularly Anthea, felt rather uncomfortable at keeping the great secret from her of the wishing carpet and the Phoenix. And Anthea, whose inside mind was made so that she was able to be much more uncomfortable than the others, had decided that she MUST tell her mother the truth, however little likely it was that her mother would believe it.

'Then I shall have done what's right,' said she to the Phoenix; 'and if she doesn't believe me it won't be my fault—will it?'

'Not in the least,' said the golden bird. 'And she won't, so you're quite safe.'

Anthea chose a time when she was doing her home-lessons—they were Algebra and Latin, German, English, and Euclid—and she asked her mother whether she might come and do them in the drawing-room—'so as to be quiet,' she said to her mother; and to herself she said, 'And that's not the real reason. I hope I shan't grow up a LIAR.'

Mother said, 'Of course, dearie,' and Anthea started swimming through a sea of x's and y's and z's. Mother was sitting at the mahogany bureau writing letters.

'Mother dear,' said Anthea.

'Yes, love-a-duck,' said mother.

'About cook,' said Anthea. '*I* know where she is.'

'Do you, dear?' said mother. 'Well, I wouldn't take her back after the way she has behaved.'

'It's not her fault,' said Anthea. 'May I tell you about it from the beginning?'

Mother laid down her pen, and her nice face had a resigned expression. As you know, a resigned expression always makes you want not to tell anybody anything.

'It's like this,' said Anthea, in a hurry: 'that egg, you know, that came in the carpet; we put it in the fire and it hatched into the Phoenix, and the carpet was a wishing carpet—and—'

'A very nice game, darling,' said mother, taking up her pen. 'Now do be quiet. I've got a lot of letters to write. I'm going to Bournemouth to-morrow with the Lamb—and there's that bazaar.'

Anthea went back to x y z, and mother's pen scratched busily.

'But, mother,' said Anthea, when mother put down the pen to lick an envelope, 'the carpet takes us wherever we like—and—'

'I wish it would take you where you could get a few nice Eastern things for my bazaar,' said mother. 'I promised them, and I've no time to go to Liberty's now.'

'It shall,' said Anthea, 'but, mother—'

'Well, dear,' said mother, a little impatiently, for she had taken up her pen again.

'The carpet took us to a place where you couldn't have whooping-cough, and the Lamb hasn't whooped since, and we took cook because she was so tiresome, and then she would stay and be queen of the savages. They thought her cap was a crown, and—'

'Darling one,' said mother, 'you know I love to hear the things you make up—but I am most awfully busy.'

'But it's true,' said Anthea, desperately.

'You shouldn't say that, my sweet,' said mother, gently. And then Anthea knew it was hopeless.

'Are you going away for long?' asked Anthea.

'I've got a cold,' said mother, 'and daddy's anxious about it, and the Lamb's cough.'

'He hasn't coughed since Saturday,' the Lamb's eldest sister interrupted.

'I wish I could think so,' mother replied. 'And daddy's got to go to Scotland. I do hope you'll be good children.'

'We will, we will,' said Anthea, fervently. 'When's the bazaar?'

'On Saturday,' said mother, 'at the schools. Oh, don't talk any more, there's a treasure! My head's going round, and I've forgotten how to spell whooping-cough.'

Mother and the Lamb went away, and father went away, and there was a new cook who looked so like a frightened rabbit that no one had the heart to do anything to frighten her any more than seemed natural to her.

The Phoenix begged to be excused. It said it wanted a week's rest, and asked that it might not be disturbed. And it hid its golden gleaming self, and nobody could find it.

So that when Wednesday afternoon brought an unexpected holiday, and every one decided to go somewhere on the carpet, the journey had to be undertaken without the Phoenix. They were debarred from any carpet excursions in the evening by a sudden promise to mother, exacted in the agitation of parting, that they would not be out after six at night, except on Saturday, when they were to go to the bazaar, and were pledged to put on their best clothes, to wash themselves to the uttermost, and to clean their nails—not with scissors, which are scratchy and bad, but with flat-sharpened ends of wooden matches, which do no harm to any one's nails.

'Let's go and see the Lamb,' said Jane.

But every one was agreed that if they appeared suddenly in Bournemouth it would frighten mother out of her wits, if not into a fit. So they sat on the carpet, and thought and thought and thought till they almost began to squint.

'Look here,' said Cyril, 'I know. Please carpet, take us somewhere where we can see the Lamb and mother and no one can see us.'

'Except the Lamb,' said Jane, quickly.

And the next moment they found themselves recovering from the upside-down movement—and there they were sitting on the carpet, and the carpet was laid out over another thick soft carpet of brown pine-needles. There were green pine-trees overhead, and a swift clear little stream was running as fast as ever it could between steep banks—and there, sitting on the pine-needle carpet, was mother, without her hat; and the sun was shining brightly, although it was November—and there was the Lamb, as jolly as jolly and not whooping at all.

'The carpet's deceived us,' said Robert, gloomily; 'mother will see us directly she turns her head.'

But the faithful carpet had not deceived them.

Mother turned her dear head and looked straight at them, and DID NOT SEE THEM!

'We're invisible,' Cyril whispered: 'what awful larks!'

But to the girls it was not larks at all. It was horrible to have mother looking straight at them, and her face keeping the same, just as though they weren't there.

'I don't like it,' said Jane. 'Mother never looked at us like that before. Just as if she didn't love us—as if we were somebody else's children, and not very nice ones either—as if she didn't care whether she saw us or not.'

'It is horrid,' said Anthea, almost in tears.

But at this moment the Lamb saw them, and plunged towards the carpet, shrieking, 'Panty, own Panty—an' Pussy, an' Squiggle—an' Bobs, oh, oh!'

Anthea caught him and kissed him, so did Jane; they could not help it—he looked such a darling, with his blue three-cornered hat all on one side, and his precious face all dirty—quite in the old familiar way.

'I love you, Panty; I love you—and you, and you, and you,' cried the Lamb.

It was a delicious moment. Even the boys thumped their baby brother joyously on the back.

Then Anthea glanced at mother—and mother's face was a pale sea-green colour, and she was staring at the Lamb as if she thought he had gone mad. And, indeed, that was exactly what she did think.

'My Lamb, my precious! Come to mother,' she cried, and jumped up and ran to the baby.

She was so quick that the invisible children had to leap back, or she would have felt them; and to feel what you can't see is the worst sort of ghost-feeling. Mother picked up the Lamb and hurried away from the pinewood.

'Let's go home,' said Jane, after a miserable silence. 'It feels just exactly as if mother didn't love us.'

But they couldn't bear to go home till they had seen mother meet another lady, and knew that she was safe. You cannot leave your mother to go green in the face in a distant pinewood, far from all human aid, and then go home on your wishing carpet as though nothing had happened.

When mother seemed safe the children returned to the carpet, and said 'Home'—and home they went.

'I don't care about being invisible myself,' said Cyril, 'at least, not with my own family. It would be different if you were a prince, or a bandit, or a burglar.'

And now the thoughts of all four dwelt fondly on the dear greenish face of mother.

'I wish she hadn't gone away,' said Jane; 'the house is simply beastly without her.'

'I think we ought to do what she said,' Anthea put in. 'I saw something in a book the other day about the wishes of the departed being sacred.'

'That means when they've departed farther off,' said Cyril. 'India's coral or Greenland's icy, don't you know; not Bournemouth. Besides, we don't know what her wishes are.'

'She SAID'—Anthea was very much inclined to cry—'she said, "Get Indian things for my bazaar;" but I know she thought we couldn't, and it was only play.'

'Let's get them all the same,' said Robert. 'We'll go the first thing on Saturday morning.'

And on Saturday morning, the first thing, they went.

There was no finding the Phoenix, so they sat on the beautiful wishing carpet, and said—

'We want Indian things for mother's bazaar. Will you please take us where people will give us heaps of Indian things?'

The docile carpet swirled their senses away, and restored them on the outskirts of a gleaming white Indian town. They knew it was Indian at once, by the shape of the domes and roofs; and besides, a man went by on an elephant, and two English soldiers went along the road, talking like in Mr Kipling's books—so after that no one could have any doubt as to where they were. They rolled up the carpet and Robert carried it, and they walked bodily into the town.

It was very warm, and once more they had to take off their London-in-November coats, and carry them on their arms.

The streets were narrow and strange, and the clothes of the people in the streets were stranger and the talk of the people was strangest of all.

'I can't understand a word,' said Cyril. 'How on earth are we to ask for things for our bazaar?'

'And they're poor people, too,' said Jane; 'I'm sure they are. What we want is a rajah or something.'

Robert was beginning to unroll the carpet, but the others stopped him, imploring him not to waste a wish.

'We asked the carpet to take us where we could get Indian things for bazaars,' said Anthea, 'and it will.'

Her faith was justified.

Just as she finished speaking a very brown gentleman in a turban came up to them and bowed deeply. He spoke, and they thrilled to the sound of English words.

'My ranee, she think you very nice childs. She asks do you lose yourselves, and do you desire to sell carpet? She see you from her palkee. You come see her—yes?'

They followed the stranger, who seemed to have a great many more teeth in his smile than are usual, and he led them through crooked streets to the ranee's palace. I am not going to describe the ranee's palace, because I really have never seen the palace of a ranee, and Mr Kipling has. So you can read about it in his books. But I know exactly what happened there.

The old ranee sat on a low-cushioned seat, and there were a lot of other ladies with her—all in trousers and veils, and sparkling with tinsel and gold and jewels. And the brown, turbaned gentleman stood behind a sort of carved screen, and interpreted what the children said and what the queen said. And when the queen asked to buy the carpet, the children said 'No.'

'Why?' asked the ranee.

And Jane briefly said why, and the interpreter interpreted. The queen spoke, and then the interpreter said—

'My mistress says it is a good story, and you tell it all through without thought of time.'

And they had to. It made a long story, especially as it had all to be told twice—once by Cyril and once by the interpreter. Cyril rather enjoyed himself. He warmed to his work, and told the tale of the Phoenix and the Carpet, and the Lone Tower, and the Queen-Cook, in language that grew insensibly more and more Arabian Nightsy, and the ranee and her ladies listened to the interpreter, and rolled about on their fat cushions with laughter.

When the story was ended she spoke, and the interpreter explained that she had said, 'Little one, thou art a heaven-born teller of tales,' and she threw him a string of turquoises from round her neck.

'OH, how lovely!' cried Jane and Anthea.

Cyril bowed several times, and then cleared his throat and said—

'Thank her very, very much; but I would much rather she gave me some of the cheap things in the bazaar. Tell her I want them to sell again, and give the money to buy clothes for poor people who haven't any.'

'Tell him he has my leave to sell my gift and clothe the naked with its price,' said the queen, when this was translated.

But Cyril said very firmly, 'No, thank you. The things have got to be sold to-day at our bazaar, and no one would buy a turquoise necklace at an English bazaar. They'd think it was sham, or else they'd want to know where we got it.'

So then the queen sent out for little pretty things, and her servants piled the carpet with them.

'I must needs lend you an elephant to carry them away,' she said, laughing.

But Anthea said, 'If the queen will lend us a comb and let us wash our hands and faces, she shall see a magic thing. We and the carpet and all these brass trays and pots and carved things and stuffs and things will just vanish away like smoke.'

The queen clapped her hands at this idea, and lent the children a sandal-wood comb inlaid with ivory lotus-flowers. And they washed their faces and hands in silver basins. Then Cyril made a very polite farewell speech, and quite suddenly he ended with the words—

'And I wish we were at the bazaar at our schools.'

And of course they were. And the queen and her ladies were left with their mouths open, gazing at the bare space on the inlaid marble floor where the carpet and the children had been.

'That is magic, if ever magic was!' said the queen, delighted with the incident; which, indeed, has given the ladies of that court something to talk about on wet days ever since.

Cyril's stories had taken some time, so had the meal of strange sweet foods that they had had while the little pretty things were being bought, and the gas in the schoolroom was already lighted. Outside, the winter dusk was stealing down among the Camden Town houses.

'I'm glad we got washed in India,' said Cyril. 'We should have been awfully late if we'd had to go home and scrub.'

'Besides,' Robert said, 'it's much warmer washing in India. I shouldn't mind it so much if we lived there.'

The thoughtful carpet had dumped the children down in a dusky space behind the point where the corners of two stalls met. The floor was littered with string and brown paper, and baskets and boxes were heaped along the wall.

The children crept out under a stall covered with all sorts of table-covers and mats and things, embroidered beautifully by idle ladies with no real work to do. They got out at the end, displacing a sideboard-cloth adorned with a tasteful pattern of blue geraniums. The girls got out unobserved, so did Cyril; but Robert, as he cautiously emerged, was actually walked on by Mrs Biddle, who kept the stall. Her large, solid foot stood firmly on the small, solid hand of Robert and who can blame Robert if he DID yell a little?

A crowd instantly collected. Yells are very unusual at bazaars, and every one was intensely interested. It was several seconds before the three free children could make Mrs Biddle understand that what she was walking on was not a schoolroom floor, or even, as she presently supposed, a dropped pin-cushion, but the living hand of a suffering child. When she became aware that she really had hurt him, she grew very angry indeed. When people have hurt other people by accident, the one who does the hurting is always much the angriest. I wonder why.

'I'm very sorry, I'm sure,' said Mrs Biddle; but she spoke more in anger than in sorrow. 'Come out! whatever do you mean by creeping about under the stalls, like earwigs?'

'We were looking at the things in the corner.'

'Such nasty, prying ways,' said Mrs Biddle, 'will never make you successful in life. There's nothing there but packing and dust.'

'Oh, isn't there!' said Jane. 'That's all you know.'

'Little girl, don't be rude,' said Mrs Biddle, flushing violet.

'She doesn't mean to be; but there ARE some nice things there, all the same,' said Cyril; who suddenly felt how impossible it was to inform the listening crowd that all the treasures piled on the carpet were mother's contributions to the bazaar. No one would believe it; and if they did, and wrote to thank mother, she would think—well, goodness only knew what she would think. The other three children felt the same.

'I should like to see them,' said a very nice lady, whose friends had disappointed her, and who hoped that these might be belated contributions to her poorly furnished stall.

She looked inquiringly at Robert, who said, 'With pleasure, don't mention it,' and dived back under Mrs Biddle's stall.

'I wonder you encourage such behaviour,' said Mrs Biddle. 'I always speak my mind, as you know, Miss Peasmarsh; and, I must say, I am surprised.' She turned to the crowd. 'There is no entertainment here,' she said sternly. 'A very naughty little boy has accidentally hurt himself, but only slightly. Will you please disperse? It will only encourage him in naughtiness if he finds himself the centre of attraction.'

The crowd slowly dispersed. Anthea, speechless with fury, heard a nice curate say, 'Poor little beggar!' and loved the curate at once and for ever.

Then Robert wriggled out from under the stall with some Benares brass and some inlaid sandalwood boxes.

'Liberty!' cried Miss Peasmarsh. 'Then Charles has not forgotten, after all.'

'Excuse me,' said Mrs Biddle, with fierce politeness, 'these objects are deposited behind MY stall. Some unknown donor who does good by stealth, and would blush if he could hear you claim the things. Of course they are for me.'

'My stall touches yours at the corner,' said poor Miss Peasmarsh, timidly, 'and my cousin did promise—'

The children sidled away from the unequal contest and mingled with the crowd. Their feelings were too deep for words—till at last Robert said—

'That stiff-starched PIG!'

'And after all our trouble! I'm hoarse with gassing to that trousered lady in India.'

'The pig-lady's very, very nasty,' said Jane.

It was Anthea who said, in a hurried undertone, 'She isn't very nice, and Miss Peasmarsh is pretty and nice too. Who's got a pencil?'

it was a long crawl, under three stalls, but Anthea did it. A large piece of pale blue paper lay among the rubbish in the corner.

She folded it to a square and wrote upon it, licking the pencil at every word to make it mark quite blackly: 'All these Indian things are for pretty, nice Miss Peasmarsh's stall.' She thought of adding, 'There is nothing for Mrs Biddle;' but she saw that this might lead to suspicion, so she wrote hastily: 'From an unknown donna,' and crept back among the boards and trestles to join the others.

So that when Mrs Biddle appealed to the bazaar committee, and the corner of the stall was lifted and shifted, so that stout clergymen and heavy ladies could get to the corner without creeping under stalls, the blue paper was discovered, and all the splendid, shining Indian things were given over to Miss Peasmarsh, and she sold them all, and got thirty-five pounds for them.

'I don't understand about that blue paper,' said Mrs Biddle. 'It looks to me like the work of a lunatic. And saying you were nice and pretty! It's not the work of a sane person.'

Anthea and Jane begged Miss Peasmarsh to let them help her to sell the things, because it was their brother who had announced the good news that the things had come. Miss Peasmarsh was very willing, for now her stall, that had been SO neglected, was surrounded by people who wanted to buy, and she was glad to be helped. The children noted that Mrs Biddle had not more to do in the way of selling than she could manage quite well. I hope they were not glad—for you should forgive your enemies, even if they walk on your hands and then say it is all your naughty fault. But I am afraid they were not so sorry as they ought to have been.

It took some time to arrange the things on the stall. The carpet was spread over it, and the dark colours showed up the brass and silver and ivory things. It was a happy and busy afternoon, and when Miss Peasmarsh and the girls had sold every single one of the little pretty things from the Indian bazaar, far, far away, Anthea and Jane went off with the boys to fish in the fishpond, and dive into the bran-pie, and hear the cardboard band, and the phonograph, and the chorus of singing birds that was done behind a screen with glass tubes and glasses of water.

They had a beautiful tea, suddenly presented to them by the nice curate, and Miss Peasmarsh joined them before they had had more than three cakes each. It was a merry party, and the curate was extremely pleasant to every one, 'even to Miss Peasmarsh,' as Jane said afterwards.

'We ought to get back to the stall,' said Anthea, when no one could possibly eat any more, and the curate was talking in a low voice to Miss Peas marsh about 'after Easter'.

'There's nothing to go back for,' said Miss Peasmarsh gaily; 'thanks to you dear children we've sold everything.'

'There—there's the carpet,' said Cyril.

'Oh,' said Miss Peasmarsh, radiantly, 'don't bother about the carpet. I've sold even that. Mrs Biddle gave me ten shillings for it. She said it would do for her servant's bedroom.'

'Why,' said Jane, 'her servants don't HAVE carpets. We had cook from her, and she told us so.'

'No scandal about Queen Elizabeth, if YOU please,' said the curate, cheerfully; and Miss Peasmarsh laughed, and looked at him as though she had never dreamed that any one COULD be so amusing. But the others were struck dumb. How could they say, 'The carpet is ours!' For who brings carpets to bazaars?

The children were now thoroughly wretched. But I am glad to say that their wretchedness did not make them forget their manners, as it does sometimes, even with grown-up people, who ought to know ever so much better.

They said, 'Thank you very much for the jolly tea,' and 'Thanks for being so jolly,' and 'Thanks awfully for giving us such a jolly time;' for the curate had stood fish-ponds, and bran-pies, and phonographs, and the chorus of singing birds, and had stood them like a man. The girls hugged Miss Peasmarsh, and as they went away they heard the curate say—

'Jolly little kids, yes, but what about—you will let it be directly after Easter. Ah, do say you will—'

And Jane ran back and said, before Anthea could drag her away, 'What are you going to do after Easter?'

Miss Peasmarsh smiled and looked very pretty indeed. And the curate said—

'I hope I am going to take a trip to the Fortunate Islands.'

'I wish we could take you on the wishing carpet,' said Jane.

'Thank you,' said the curate, 'but I'm afraid I can't wait for that. I must go to the Fortunate Islands before they make me a bishop. I should have no time afterwards.'

'I've always thought I should marry a bishop,' said Jane: 'his aprons would come in so useful. Wouldn't YOU like to marry a bishop, Miss Peasmarsh?'

It was then that they dragged her away.

As it was Robert's hand that Mrs Biddle had walked on, it was decided that he had better not recall the incident to her mind, and so make her angry again. Anthea and Jane had helped to sell things at the rival stall, so they were not likely to be popular.

A hasty council of four decided that Mrs Biddle would hate Cyril less than she would hate the others, so the others mingled with the crowd, and it was he who said to her—

'Mrs Biddle, WE meant to have that carpet. Would you sell it to us? We would give you—'

'Certainly not,' said Mrs Biddle. 'Go away, little boy.'

There was that in her tone which showed Cyril, all too plainly, the hopelessness of persuasion. He found the others and said—

'It's no use; she's like a lioness robbed of its puppies. We must watch where it goes—and— Anthea, I don't care what you say. It's our own carpet. It wouldn't be burglary. It would be a sort of forlorn hope rescue party—heroic and daring and dashing, and not wrong at all.'

The children still wandered among the gay crowd—but there was no pleasure there for them any more. The chorus of singing birds sounded just like glass tubes being blown through water, and the phonograph simply made a horrid noise, so that you could hardly hear yourself speak. And the people were buying things they couldn't possibly want, and it all seemed very stupid. And Mrs Biddle had bought the wishing carpet for ten shillings. And the whole of life was sad and grey and dusty, and smelt of slight gas escapes, and hot people, and cake and crumbs, and all the children were very tired indeed.

They found a corner within sight of the carpet, and there they waited miserably, till it was far beyond their proper bedtime. And when it was ten the people who had bought things went away, but the people who had been selling stayed to count up their money.

'And to jaw about it,' said Robert. 'I'll never go to another bazaar as long as ever I live. My hand is swollen as big as a pudding. I expect the nails in her horrible boots were poisoned.'

Just then some one who seemed to have a right to interfere said—

'Everything is over now; you had better go home.'

So they went. And then they waited on the pavement under the gas lamp, where ragged children had been standing all the evening to listen to the band, and their feet slipped about in the greasy mud till Mrs Biddle came out and was driven away in a cab with the many things she hadn't sold, and the few things she had bought—among others the carpet. The other stall-holders left their things at the school till Monday morning, but Mrs Biddle was afraid some one would steal some of them, so she took them in a cab.

The children, now too desperate to care for mud or appearances, hung on behind the cab till it reached Mrs Biddle's house. When she and the carpet had gone in and the door was shut Anthea said—

'Don't let's burgle—I mean do daring and dashing rescue acts—till we've given her a chance. Let's ring and ask to see her.'

The others hated to do this, but at last they agreed, on condition that Anthea would not make any silly fuss about the burglary afterwards, if it really had to come to that.

So they knocked and rang, and a scared-looking parlourmaid opened the front door. While they were asking for Mrs Biddle they saw her. She was in the dining-room, and she had already pushed back the table and spread out the carpet to see how it looked on the floor.

'I knew she didn't want it for her servants' bedroom,' Jane muttered.

Anthea walked straight past the uncomfortable parlourmaid, and the others followed her. Mrs Biddle had her back to them, and was smoothing down the carpet with the same boot that had trampled on the hand of Robert. So that they were all in the room, and Cyril, with great presence of mind, had shut the room door before she saw them.

'Who is it, Jane?' she asked in a sour voice; and then turning suddenly, she saw who it was. Once more her face grew violet—a deep, dark violet. 'You wicked daring little things!' she cried, 'how dare you come here? At this time of night, too. Be off, or I'll send for the police.'

'Don't be angry,' said Anthea, soothingly, 'we only wanted to ask you to let us have the carpet. We have quite twelve shillings between us, and—'

'How DARE you?' cried Mrs Biddle, and her voice shook with angriness.

'You do look horrid,' said Jane suddenly.

Mrs Biddle actually stamped that booted foot of hers. 'You rude, barefaced child!' she said.

Anthea almost shook Jane; but Jane pushed forward in spite of her.

'It really IS our nursery carpet,' she said, 'you ask ANY ONE if it isn't.'

'Let's wish ourselves home,' said Cyril in a whisper.

'No go,' Robert whispered back, 'she'd be there too, and raving mad as likely as not. Horrid thing, I hate her!'

'I wish Mrs Biddle was in an angelic good temper,' cried Anthea, suddenly. 'It's worth trying,' she said to herself.

Mrs Biddle's face grew from purple to violet, and from violet to mauve, and from mauve to pink. Then she smiled quite a jolly smile.

'Why, so I am!' she said, 'what a funny idea! Why shouldn't I be in a good temper, my dears.'

Once more the carpet had done its work, and not on Mrs Biddle alone. The children felt suddenly good and happy.

'You're a jolly good sort,' said Cyril. 'I see that now. I'm sorry we vexed you at the bazaar to-day.'

'Not another word,' said the changed Mrs Biddle. 'Of course you shall have the carpet, my dears, if you've taken such a fancy to it. No, no; I won't have more than the ten shillings I paid.'

'It does seem hard to ask you for it after you bought it at the bazaar,' said Anthea; 'but it really IS our nursery carpet. It got to the bazaar by mistake, with some other things.'

'Did it really, now? How vexing!' said Mrs Biddle, kindly. 'Well, my dears, I can very well give the extra ten shillings; so you take your carpet and we'll say no more about it. Have a piece of cake before you go! I'm so sorry I stepped on your hand, my boy. Is it all right now?'

'Yes, thank you,' said Robert. 'I say, you ARE good.'

'Not at all,' said Mrs Biddle, heartily. 'I'm delighted to be able to give any little pleasure to you dear children.'

And she helped them to roll up the carpet, and the boys carried it away between them.

'You ARE a dear,' said Anthea, and she and Mrs Biddle kissed each other heartily.

'WELL!' said Cyril as they went along the street.

'Yes,' said Robert, 'and the odd part is that you feel just as if it was REAL—her being so jolly, I mean—and not only the carpet making her nice.'

'Perhaps it IS real,' said Anthea, 'only it was covered up with crossness and tiredness and things, and the carpet took them away.'

'I hope it'll keep them away,' said Jane; 'she isn't ugly at all when she laughs.'

The carpet has done many wonders in its day; but the case of Mrs Biddle is, I think, the most wonderful. For from that day she was never anything like so disagreeable as she was before, and she sent a lovely silver tea-pot and a kind letter to Miss Peasmarsh when the pretty lady married the nice curate; just after Easter it was, and they went to Italy for their honeymoon.

Chapter 5. The Temple

'I wish we could find the Phoenix,' said Jane. 'It's much better company than the carpet.'

'Beastly ungrateful, little kids are,' said Cyril.

'No, I'm not; only the carpet never says anything, and it's so helpless. It doesn't seem able to take care of itself. It gets sold, and taken into the sea, and things like that. You wouldn't catch the Phoenix getting sold.'

It was two days after the bazaar. Every one was a little cross—some days are like that, usually Mondays, by the way. And this was a Monday.

'I shouldn't wonder if your precious Phoenix had gone off for good,' said Cyril; 'and I don't know that I blame it. Look at the weather!'

'It's not worth looking at,' said Robert. And indeed it wasn't.

'The Phoenix hasn't gone—I'm sure it hasn't,' said Anthea. 'I'll have another look for it.'

Anthea looked under tables and chairs, and in boxes and baskets, in mother's work-bag and father's portmanteau, but still the Phoenix showed not so much as the tip of one shining feather.

Then suddenly Robert remembered how the whole of the Greek invocation song of seven thousand lines had been condensed by him into one English hexameter, so he stood on the carpet and chanted—

'Oh, come along, come along, you good old beautiful Phoenix,'

and almost at once there was a rustle of wings down the kitchen stairs, and the Phoenix sailed in on wide gold wings.

'Where on earth HAVE you been?' asked Anthea. 'I've looked everywhere for you.'

'Not EVERYWHERE,' replied the bird, 'because you did not look in the place where I was. Confess that that hallowed spot was overlooked by you.'

'WHAT hallowed spot?' asked Cyril, a little impatiently, for time was hastening on, and the wishing carpet still idle.

'The spot,' said the Phoenix, 'which I hallowed by my golden presence was the Lutron.'

'The WHAT?'

'The bath—the place of washing.'

'I'm sure you weren't,' said Jane. 'I looked there three times and moved all the towels.'

'I was concealed,' said the Phoenix, 'on the summit of a metal column—enchanted, I should judge, for it felt warm to my golden toes, as though the glorious sun of the desert shone ever upon it.'

'Oh, you mean the cylinder,' said Cyril: 'it HAS rather a comforting feel, this weather. And now where shall we go?'

And then, of course, the usual discussion broke out as to where they should go and what they should do. And naturally, every one wanted to do something that the others did not care about.

'I am the eldest,' Cyril remarked, 'let's go to the North Pole.'

'This weather! Likely!' Robert rejoined. 'Let's go to the Equator.'

'I think the diamond mines of Golconda would be nice,' said Anthea; 'don't you agree, Jane?'

'No, I don't,' retorted Jane, 'I don't agree with you. I don't agree with anybody.'

The Phoenix raised a warning claw.

'If you cannot agree among yourselves, I fear I shall have to leave you,' it said.

'Well, where shall we go? You decide!' said all.

'If I were you,' said the bird, thoughtfully, 'I should give the carpet a rest. Besides, you'll lose the use of your legs if you go everywhere by carpet. Can't you take me out and explain your ugly city to me?'

'We will if it clears up,' said Robert, without enthusiasm. 'Just look at the rain. And why should we give the carpet a rest?'

'Are you greedy and grasping, and heartless and selfish?' asked the bird, sharply.

'NO!' said Robert, with indignation.

'Well then!' said the Phoenix. 'And as to the rain—well, I am not fond of rain myself. If the sun knew *I* was here—he's very fond of shining on me because I look so bright and golden. He always says I repay a little attention. Haven't you some form of words suitable for use in wet weather?'

'There's "Rain, rain, go away,"' said Anthea; 'but it never DOES go.'

'Perhaps you don't say the invocation properly,' said the bird.

'Rain, rain, go away,
Come again another day,
Little baby wants to play,'

said Anthea.

'That's quite wrong; and if you say it in that sort of dull way, I can quite understand the rain not taking any notice. You should open the window and shout as loud as you can—

'Rain, rain, go away,
Come again another day;
Now we want the sun, and so,
Pretty rain, be kind and go!

'You should always speak politely to people when you want them to do things, and especially when it's going away that you want them to do. And to-day you might add—

'Shine, great sun, the lovely Phoe-
Nix is here, and wants to be
Shone on, splendid sun, by thee!'

'That's poetry!' said Cyril, decidedly.

'It's like it,' said the more cautious Robert.

'I was obliged to put in "lovely",' said the Phoenix, modestly, 'to make the line long enough.'

'There are plenty of nasty words just that length,' said Jane; but every one else said 'Hush!' And then they opened the window and shouted the seven lines as loud as they could, and the Phoenix said all the words with them, except 'lovely', and when they came to that it looked down and coughed bashfully.

The rain hesitated a moment and then went away.

'There's true politeness,' said the Phoenix, and the next moment it was perched on the window-ledge, opening and shutting its radiant wings and flapping out its golden feathers in such a flood of glorious sunshine as you sometimes have at sunset in autumn time. People said afterwards that there had not been such sunshine in December for years and years and years.

'And now,' said the bird, 'we will go out into the city, and you shall take me to see one of my temples.'

'Your temples?'

'I gather from the carpet that I have many temples in this land.'

'I don't see how you CAN find anything out from it,' said Jane: 'it never speaks.'

'All the same, you can pick up things from a carpet,' said the bird; 'I've seen YOU do it. And I have picked up several pieces of information in this way. That papyrus on which you showed me my picture—I understand that it bears on it the name of the street of your city in which my finest temple stands, with my image graved in stone and in metal over against its portal.'

'You mean the fire insurance office,' said Robert. 'It's not really a temple, and they don't—'

'Excuse me,' said the Phoenix, coldly, 'you are wholly misinformed. It IS a temple, and they do.'

'Don't let's waste the sunshine,' said Anthea; 'we might argue as we go along, to save time.'

So the Phoenix consented to make itself a nest in the breast of Robert's Norfolk jacket, and they all went out into the splendid sunshine. The best way to the temple of the Phoenix seemed to be to take the tram, and on the top of it the children talked, while the Phoenix now and then put out a wary beak, cocked a cautious eye, and contradicted what the children were saying.

It was a delicious ride, and the children felt how lucky they were to have had the money to pay for it. They went with the tram as far as it went, and when it did not go any farther they stopped too, and got off. The tram stops at the end of the Gray's Inn Road, and it was Cyril who thought that one might well find a short cut to the Phoenix Office through the little streets and courts that lie tightly packed between Fetter Lane and Ludgate Circus. Of course, he was quite mistaken, as Robert told him at the time, and afterwards Robert did not forbear to remind his brother how he had said so. The streets there were small and stuffy and ugly, and crowded with printers' boys and binders' girls coming out from work; and these stared so hard at the pretty red coats and caps of the sisters that they wished they had gone some other way. And the printers and binders made very personal remarks, advising Jane to get her hair cut, and inquiring where Anthea had bought that hat. Jane and Anthea scorned to reply, and Cyril and Robert found that they were hardly a match for the rough crowd. They could think of nothing nasty enough to say. They turned a corner sharply, and then Anthea pulled Jane into an archway, and then inside a door; Cyril and Robert quickly followed, and the jeering crowd passed by without seein them.

Anthea drew a long breath.

'How awful!' she said. 'I didn't know there were such people, except in books.'

'It was a bit thick; but it's partly you girls' fault, coming out in those flashy coats.'

'We thought we ought to, when we were going out with the Phoenix,' said Jane; and the bird said, 'Quite right, too'—and incautiously put out his head to give her a wink of encouragement.

And at the same instant a dirty hand reached through the grim balustrade of the staircase beside them and clutched the Phoenix, and a hoarse voice said—

'I say, Urb, blowed if this ain't our Poll parrot what we lost. Thank you very much, lidy, for bringin' 'im home to roost.'

The four turned swiftly. Two large and ragged boys were crouched amid the dark shadows of the stairs. They were much larger than Robert and Cyril, and one of them had snatched the Phoenix away and was holding it high above their heads.

'Give me that bird,' said Cyril, sternly: 'it's ours.'

'Good arternoon, and thankin' you,' the boy went on, with maddening mockery. 'Sorry I can't give yer tuppence for yer trouble—but I've 'ad to spend my fortune advertising for my vallyable bird in all the newspapers. You can call for the reward next year.'

'Look out, Ike,' said his friend, a little anxiously; 'it 'ave a beak on it.'

'It's other parties as'll have the Beak on to 'em presently,' said Ike, darkly, 'if they come a-trying to lay claims on my Poll parrot. You just shut up, Urb. Now then, you four little gells, get out er this.'

'Little girls!' cried Robert. 'I'll little girl you!'

He sprang up three stairs and hit out.

There was a squawk—the most bird-like noise any one had ever heard from the Phoenix—and a fluttering, and a laugh in the darkness, and Ike said—

'There now, you've been and gone and strook my Poll parrot right in the fevvers—strook 'im something crool, you 'ave.'

Robert stamped with fury. Cyril felt himself growing pale with rage, and with the effort of screwing up his brain to make it clever enough to think of some way of being even with those boys. Anthea and Jane were as angry as the boys, but it made them want to cry. Yet it was Anthea who said—

'Do, PLEASE, let us have the bird.'

'Dew, PLEASE, get along and leave us an' our bird alone.'

'If you don't,' said Anthea, 'I shall fetch the police.'

'You better!' said he who was named Urb. 'Say, Ike, you twist the bloomin' pigeon's neck; he ain't worth tuppence.'

'Oh, no,' cried Jane, 'don't hurt it. Oh, don't; it is such a pet.'

'I won't hurt it,' said Ike; 'I'm 'shamed of you, Urb, for to think of such a thing. Arf a shiner, miss, and the bird is yours for life.'

'Half a WHAT?' asked Anthea.

'Arf a shiner, quid, thick 'un—half a sov, then.'

'I haven't got it—and, besides, it's OUR bird,' said Anthea.

'Oh, don't talk to him,' said Cyril and then Jane said suddenly—

'Phoenix—dear Phoenix, we can't do anything. YOU must manage it.'

'With pleasure,' said the Phoenix—and Ike nearly dropped it in his amazement.

'I say, it do talk, suthin' like,' said he.

'Youths,' said the Phoenix, 'sons of misfortune, hear my words.'

'My eyes!' said Ike.

'Look out, Ike,' said Urb, 'you'll throttle the joker—and I see at wunst 'e was wuth 'is weight in flimsies.'oo

'Hearken, O Eikonoclastes, despiser of sacred images—and thou, Urbanus, dweller in the sordid city. Forbear this adventure lest a worse thing befall.'

'Luv' us!' said Ike, 'ain't it been taught its schoolin' just!'

'Restore me to my young acolytes and escape unscathed. Retain me—and—'

'They must ha' got all this up, case the Polly got pinched,' said Ike. 'Lor' lumme, the artfulness of them young uns!'

'I say, slosh 'em in the geseech and get clear off with the swag's wot I say,' urged Herbert.

'Right O,' said Isaac.

'Forbear,' repeated the Phoenix, sternly. 'Who pinched the click off of the old bloke in Aldermanbury?' it added, in a changed tone.

'Who sneaked the nose-rag out of the young gell's 'and in Bell Court? Who—'

'Stow it,' said Ike. 'You! ugh! yah!—leave go of me. Bash him off, Urb; 'e'll have my bloomin' eyes outer my ed.'

There were howls, a scuffle, a flutter; Ike and Urb fled up the stairs, and the Phoenix swept out through the doorway. The children followed and the Phoenix settled on Robert, 'like a butterfly on a rose,' as Anthea said afterwards, and wriggled into the breast of his Norfolk jacket, 'like an eel into mud,' as Cyril later said.

'Why ever didn't you burn him? You could have, couldn't you?' asked Robert, when the hurried flight through the narrow courts had ended in the safe wideness of Farringdon Street.

'I could have, of course,' said the bird, 'but I didn't think it would be dignified to allow myself to get warm about a little thing like that. The Fates, after all, have not been illiberal to me. I have a good many friends among the London sparrows, and I have a beak and claws.'

These happenings had somewhat shaken the adventurous temper of the children, and the Phoenix had to exert its golden self to hearten them up.

Presently the children came to a great house in Lombard Street, and there, on each side of the door, was the image of the Phoenix carved in stone, and set forth on shining brass were the words—

PHOENIX FIRE OFFICE

'One moment,' said the bird. 'Fire? For altars, I suppose?'

'*I* don't know,' said Robert; he was beginning to feel shy, and that always made him rather cross.

'Oh, yes, you do,' Cyril contradicted. 'When people's houses are burnt down the Phoenix gives them new houses. Father told me; I asked him.'

'The house, then, like the Phoenix, rises from its ashes? Well have my priests dealt with the sons of men!'

'The sons of men pay, you know,' said Anthea; 'but it's only a little every year.'

'That is to maintain my priests,' said the bird, 'who, in the hour of affliction, heal sorrows and rebuild houses. Lead on; inquire for the High Priest. I will not break upon them too suddenly in all my glory. Noble and honour-deserving are they who make as nought the evil deeds of the lame-footed and unpleasing Hephaestus.'

'I don't know what you're talking about, and I wish you wouldn't muddle us with new names. Fire just happens. Nobody does it—not as a deed, you know,' Cyril explained. 'If they did the Phoenix wouldn't help them, because its a crime to set fire to things. Arsenic, or something they call it, because it's as bad as poisoning people. The Phoenix wouldn't help THEM—father told me it wouldn't.'

'My priests do well,' said the Phoenix. 'Lead on.'

'I don't know what to say,' said Cyril; and the Others said the same.

'Ask for the High Priest,' said the Phoenix. 'Say that you have a secret to unfold that concerns my worship, and he will lead you to the innermost sanctuary.'

So the children went in, all four of them, though they didn't like it, and stood in a large and beautiful hall adorned with Doulton tiles, like a large and beautiful bath with no water in it, and stately pillars supporting the roof. An unpleasing representation of the Phoenix in brown pottery disfigured one wall. There were counters and desks of mahogany and brass, and clerks bent over the desks and walked behind the counters. There was a great clock over an inner doorway.

'Inquire for the High Priest,' whispered the Phoenix.

An attentive clerk in decent black, who controlled his mouth but not his eyebrows, now came towards them. He leaned forward on the counter, and the children thought he was going to say, 'What can I have the pleasure of showing you?' like in a draper's; instead of which the young man said—

'And what do YOU want?'

'We want to see the High Priest.'

'Get along with you,' said the young man.

An elder man, also decent in black coat, advanced.

'Perhaps it's Mr Blank' (not for worlds would I give the name). 'He's a Masonic High Priest, you know.'

A porter was sent away to look for Mr Asterisk (I cannot give his name), and the children were left there to look on and be looked on by all the gentlemen at the mahogany desks. Anthea and Jane thought that they looked kind. The boys thought they stared, and that it was like their cheek.

The porter returned with the news that Mr Dot Dash Dot (I dare not reveal his name) was out, but that Mr—

Here a really delightful gentleman appeared. He had a beard and a kind and merry eye, and each one of the four knew at once that this was a man who had kiddies of his own and could understand what you were talking about. Yet it was a difficult thing to explain.

'What is it?' he asked. 'Mr'—he named the name which I will never reveal—'is out. Can I do anything?'

'Inner sanctuary,' murmured the Phoenix.

'I beg your pardon,' said the nice gentleman, who thought it was Robert who had spoken.

'We have something to tell you,' said Cyril, 'but'—he glanced at the porter, who was lingering much nearer than he need have done—'this is a very public place.'

The nice gentleman laughed.

'Come upstairs then,' he said, and led the way up a wide and beautiful staircase. Anthea says the stairs were of white marble, but I am not sure. On the corner-post of the stairs, at the top, was a beautiful image of the Phoenix in dark metal, and on the wall at each side was a flat sort of image of it.

The nice gentleman led them into a room where the chairs, and even the tables, were covered with reddish leather. He looked at the children inquiringly.

'Don't be frightened,' he said; 'tell me exactly what you want.'

'May I shut the door?' asked Cyril.

The gentleman looked surprised, but he shut the door.

'Now,' said Cyril, firmly, 'I know you'll be awfully surprised, and you'll think it's not true and we are lunatics; but we aren't, and it is. Robert's got something inside his Norfolk—that's Robert, he's my young brother. Now don't be upset and have a fit or anything sir. Of course, I know when you called your shop the "Phoenix" you never thought there was one; but there is—and Robert's got it buttoned up against his chest!'

'If it's an old curio in the form of a Phoenix, I dare say the Board—' said the nice gentleman, as Robert began to fumble with his buttons.

'It's old enough,' said Anthea, 'going by what it says, but—'

'My goodness gracious!' said the gentleman, as the Phoenix, with one last wriggle that melted into a flutter, got out of its nest in the breast of Robert and stood up on the leather-covered table.

'What an extraordinarily fine bird!' he went on. 'I don't think I ever saw one just like it.'

'I should think not,' said the Phoenix, with pardonable pride. And the gentleman jumped.

'Oh, it's been taught to speak! Some sort of parrot, perhaps?'

'I am,' said the bird, simply, 'the Head of your House, and I have come to my temple to receive your homage. I am no parrot'—its beak curved scornfully—'I am the one and only Phoenix, and I demand the homage of my High Priest.'

'In the absence of our manager,' the gentleman began, exactly as though he were addressing a valued customer—'in the absence of our manager, I might perhaps be able—What am I saying?' He turned pale, and passed his hand across his brow. 'My dears,' he said, 'the weather is unusually warm for the time of year, and I don't feel quite myself. Do you know, for a moment I really thought that that remarkable bird of yours had spoken and said it was the Phoenix, and, what's more, that I'd believed it.'

'So it did, sir,' said Cyril, 'and so did you.'

'It really—Allow me.'

A bell was rung. The porter appeared.

'Mackenzie,' said the gentleman, 'you see that golden bird?'

'Yes, sir.'

The other breathed a sigh of relief.

'It IS real, then?'

'Yes, sir, of course, sir. You take it in your hand, sir,' said the porter, sympathetically, and reached out his hand to the Phoenix, who shrank back on toes curved with agitated indignation.

'Forbear!' it cried; 'how dare you seek to lay hands on me?'

The porter saluted.

'Beg pardon, sir,' he said, 'I thought you was a bird.'

'I AM a bird—THE bird—the Phoenix.'

'Of course you are, sir,' said the porter. 'I see that the first minute, directly I got my breath, sir.'

'That will do,' said the gentleman. 'Ask Mr Wilson and Mr Sterry to step up here for a moment, please.'

Mr Sterry and Mr Wilson were in their turn overcome by amazement—quickly followed by conviction. To the surprise of the children every one in the office took the Phoenix at its word, and after the first shock of surprise it seemed to be perfectly natural to every one that the Phoenix should be alive, and that, passing through London, it should call at its temple.

'We ought to have some sort of ceremony,' said the nicest gentleman, anxiously. 'There isn't time to summon the directors and shareholders—we might do that tomorrow, perhaps. Yes, the board-room would be best. I shouldn't like it to feel we hadn't done everything in our power to show our appreciation of its condescension in looking in on us in this friendly way.'

The children could hardly believe their ears, for they had never thought that any one but themselves would believe in the Phoenix. And yet every one did; all the men in the office were brought in by twos and threes, and the moment the Phoenix opened its beak it convinced the cleverest of them, as well as those who were not so clever. Cyril wondered how the story would look in the papers next day. He seemed to see the posters in the streets:

PHOENIX FIRE OFFICE
THE PHOENIX AT ITS TEMPLE
MEETING TO WELCOME IT
DELIGHT OF THE MANAGER AND EVERYBODY.

'Excuse our leaving you a moment,' said the nice gentleman, and he went away with the others; and through the half-closed door the children could hear the sound of many boots on stairs, the hum of excited voices explaining, suggesting, arguing, the thumpy drag of heavy furniture being moved about.

The Phoenix strutted up and down the leather-covered table, looking over its shoulder at its pretty back.

'You see what a convincing manner I have,' it said proudly.

And now a new gentleman came in and said, bowing low—

'Everything is prepared—we have done our best at so short a notice; the meeting—the ceremony—will be in the board-room. Will the Honourable Phoenix walk—it is only a few steps—or would it like to be—would it like some sort of conveyance?'

'My Robert will bear me to the board-room, if that be the unlovely name of my temple's inmost court,' replied the bird.

So they all followed the gentleman. There was a big table in the board-room, but it had been pushed right up under the long windows at one side, and chairs were arranged in rows across the room—like those you have at schools when there is a magic lantern on 'Our Eastern Empire', or on 'The Way We Do in the Navy'. The doors were of carved wood, very beautiful, with a carved Phoenix above. Anthea noticed that the chairs in the front rows were of the kind that her mother so loved to ask the price of in old furniture shops, and never could buy, because the price was always nearly twenty pounds each. On the mantelpiece were some heavy bronze candlesticks and a clock, and on the top of the clock was another image of the Phoenix.

'Remove that effigy,' said the Phoenix to the gentlemen who were there, and it was hastily taken down. Then the Phoenix fluttered to the middle of the mantelpiece and stood there, looking more golden than ever. Then every one in the house and the office came in—from the cashier to the women who cooked the clerks' dinners in the beautiful kitchen at the top of the house. And every one bowed to the Phoenix and then sat down in a chair.

'Gentlemen,' said the nicest gentleman, 'we have met here today—'

The Phoenix was turning its golden beak from side to side.

'I don't notice any incense,' it said, with an injured sniff. A hurried consultation ended in plates being fetched from the kitchen. Brown sugar, sealing-wax, and tobacco were placed on these, and something from a square bottle was poured over it all. Then a match was applied. It was the only incense that was handy in the Phoenix office, and it certainly burned very briskly and smoked a great deal.

'We have met here today,' said the gentleman again, 'on an occasion unparalleled in the annals of this office. Our respected Phoenix—'

'Head of the House,' said the Phoenix, in a hollow voice.

'I was coming to that. Our respected Phoenix, the Head of this ancient House, has at length done us the honour to come among us. I think I may say, gentlemen, that we are not insensible to this honour, and that we welcome with no uncertain voice one whom we have so long desired to see in our midst.'

Several of the younger clerks thought of saying 'Hear, hear,' but they feared it might seem disrespectful to the bird.

'I will not take up your time,' the speaker went on, 'by recapitulating the advantages to be derived from a proper use of our system of fire insurance. I know, and you know, gentlemen, that our aim has ever been to be worthy of that eminent bird whose name we bear, and who now adorns our mantelpiece with his presence. Three cheers, gentlemen, for the winged Head of the House!'

The cheers rose, deafening. When they had died away the Phoenix was asked to say a few words.

It expressed in graceful phrases the pleasure it felt in finding itself at last in its own temple.

'And,' it went on, 'You must not think me wanting in appreciation of your very hearty and cordial reception when I ask that an ode may be recited or a choric song sung. It is what I have always been accustomed to.'

The four children, dumb witnesses of this wonderful scene, glanced a little nervously across the foam of white faces above the sea of black coats. It seemed to them that the Phoenix was really asking a little too much.

'Time presses,' said the Phoenix, 'and the original ode of invocation is long, as well as being Greek; and, besides, it's no use invoking me when here I am; but is there not a song in your own tongue for a great day such as this?'

Absently the manager began to sing, and one by one the rest joined—

> 'Absolute security!
> No liability!
> All kinds of property insured against fire.
> Terms most favourable,
> Expenses reasonable,
> Moderate rates for annual Insurance.'

'That one is NOT my favourite,' interrupted the Phoenix, 'and I think you've forgotten part of it.'

The manager hastily began another—

> 'O Golden Phoenix, fairest bird,
> The whole great world has often heard
> Of all the splendid things we do,
> Great Phoenix, just to honour you.'

'That's better,' said the bird. And every one sang—

> 'Class one, for private dwelling-house,
> For household goods and shops allows;
> Provided these are built of brick
> Or stone, and tiled and slated thick.'

'Try another verse,' said the Phoenix, 'further on.'

And again arose the voices of all the clerks and employees and managers and secretaries and cooks—

> 'In Scotland our insurance yields
> The price of burnt-up stacks in fields.'

'Skip that verse,' said the Phoenix.

> 'Thatched dwellings and their whole contents
> We deal with—also with their rents;
> Oh, glorious Phoenix, look and see
> That these are dealt with in class three.
>
> 'The glories of your temple throng
> Too thick to go in any song;
> And we attend, O good and wise,
> To "days of grace" and merchandise.
>
> 'When people's homes are burned away
> They never have a cent to pay
> If they have done as all should do,
> O Phoenix, and have honoured you.
>
> 'So let us raise our voice and sing
> The praises of the Phoenix King.
> In classes one and two and three,
> Oh, trust to him, for kind is he!'

'I'm sure YOU'RE very kind,' said the Phoenix; 'and now we must be going. And thank you very much for a very pleasant time. May you all prosper as you deserve to do, for I am sure a nicer, pleasanter-spoken lot of temple attendants I have never met, and never wish to meet. I wish you all good-day!'

It fluttered to the wrist of Robert and drew the four children from the room. The whole of the office staff followed down the wide stairs and filed into their accustomed places, and the two most important officials stood on the steps bowing till Robert had buttoned the golden bird in his Norfolk bosom, and it and he and the three other children were lost in the crowd.

The two most important gentlemen looked at each other earnestly and strangely for a moment, and then retreated to those sacred inner rooms, where they toil without ceasing for the good of the House.

And the moment they were all in their places—managers, secretaries, clerks, and porters—they all started, and each looked cautiously round to see if any one was looking at him. For each thought that he had fallen asleep for a few minutes, and had dreamed a very odd dream about the Phoenix and the board-room. And, of course, no one mentioned it to any one else, because going to sleep at your office is a thing you simply MUST NOT do.

The extraordinary confusion of the board-room, with the remains of the incense in the plates, would have shown them at once that the visit of the Phoenix had been no dream, but a radiant reality, but no one went into the board-room again that day; and next day, before the office was opened, it was all cleaned and put nice and tidy by a lady whose business asking questions was not part of. That is why Cyril read the papers in vain on the next day and the day after that; because no sensible person thinks his dreams worth putting in the paper, and no one will ever own that he has been asleep in the daytime.

The Phoenix was very pleased, but it decided to write an ode for itself. It thought the ones it had heard at its temple had been too hastily composed. Its own ode began—

> 'For beauty and for modest worth
> The Phoenix has not its equal on earth.'

And when the children went to bed that night it was still trying to cut down the last line to the proper length without taking out any of what it wanted to say.

That is what makes poetry so difficult.

Chapter 6. Doing Good

'We shan't be able to go anywhere on the carpet for a whole week, though,' said Robert.

'And I'm glad of it,' said Jane, unexpectedly.

'Glad?' said Cyril; 'GLAD?'

It was breakfast-time, and mother's letter, telling them how they were all going for Christmas to their aunt's at Lyndhurst, and how father and mother would meet them there, having been read by every one, lay on the table, drinking hot bacon-fat with one corner and eating marmalade with the other.

'Yes, glad,' said Jane. 'I don't want any more things to happen just now. I feel like you do when you've been to three parties in a week—like we did at granny's once—and extras in between, toys and chocs and things like that. I want everything to be just real, and no fancy things happening at all.' 'I don't like being obliged to keep things from mother,' said Anthea. 'I don't know why, but it makes me feel selfish and mean.'

'If we could only get the mater to believe it, we might take her to the jolliest places,' said Cyril, thoughtfully. 'As it is, we've just got to be selfish and mean—if it is that—but I don't feel it is.'

'I KNOW it isn't, but I FEEL it is,' said Anthea, 'and that's just as bad.'

'It's worse,' said Robert; 'if you knew it and didn't feel it, it wouldn't matter so much.'

'That's being a hardened criminal, father says,' put in Cyril, and he picked up mother's letter and wiped its corners with his handkerchief, to whose colour a trifle of bacon-fat and marmalade made but little difference.

'We're going to-morrow, anyhow,' said Robert. 'Don't,' he added, with a good-boy expression on his face—'don't let's be ungrateful for our blessings; don't let's waste the day in saying how horrid it is to keep secrets from mother, when we all know Anthea tried all she knew to give her the secret, and she wouldn't take it. Let's get on the carpet and have a jolly good wish. You'll have time enough to repent of things all next week.'

'Yes,' said Cyril, 'let's. It's not really wrong.'

'Well, look here,' said Anthea. 'You know there's something about Christmas that makes you want to be good—however little you wish it at other times. Couldn't we wish the carpet to take us somewhere where we should have the chance to do some good and kind action? It would be an adventure just the same,' she pleaded.

'I don't mind,' said Cyril. 'We shan't know where we're going, and that'll be exciting. No one knows what'll happen. We'd best put on our outers in case—'

'We might rescue a traveller buried in the snow, like St Bernard dogs, with barrels round our necks,' said Jane, beginning to be interested.

'Or we might arrive just in time to witness a will being signed—more tea, please,' said Robert, 'and we should see the old man hide it away in the secret cupboard; and then, after long years, when the rightful heir was in despair, we should lead him to the hidden panel and—'

'Yes,' interrupted Anthea; 'or we might be taken to some freezing garret in a German town, where a poor little pale, sick child—'

'We haven't any German money,' interrupted Cyril, 'so THAT'S no go. What I should like would be getting into the middle of a war and getting hold of secret intelligence and taking it to the general, and he would make me a lieutenant or a scout, or a hussar.'

When breakfast was cleared away, Anthea swept the carpet, and the children sat down on it, together with the Phoenix, who had been especially invited, as a Christmas treat, to come with them and witness the good and kind action they were about to do.

Four children and one bird were ready, and the wish was wished.

Every one closed its eyes, so as to feel the topsy-turvy swirl of the carpet's movement as little as possible.

When the eyes were opened again the children found themselves on the carpet, and the carpet was in its proper place on the floor of their own nursery at Camden Town.

'I say,' said Cyril, 'here's a go!'

'Do you think it's worn out? The wishing part of it, I mean?' Robert anxiously asked the Phoenix.

'It's not that,' said the Phoenix; 'but—well—what did you wish—?'

'Oh! I see what it means,' said Robert, with deep disgust; 'it's like the end of a fairy story in a Sunday magazine. How perfectly beastly!'

'You mean it means we can do kind and good actions where we are? I see. I suppose it wants us to carry coals for the cook or make clothes for the bare heathens. Well, I simply won't. And the last day and everything. Look here!' Cyril spoke loudly and firmly. 'We want to go somewhere really interesting, where we have a chance of doing something good and kind; we don't want to do it here, but somewhere else. See? Now, then.'

The obedient carpet started instantly, and the four children and one bird fell in a heap together, and as they fell were plunged in perfect darkness.

'Are you all there?' said Anthea, breathlessly, through the black dark. Every one owned that it was there.

'Where are we? Oh! how shivery and wet it is! Ugh!—oh!—I've put my hand in a puddle!'

'Has any one got any matches?' said Anthea, hopelessly. She felt sure that no one would have any.

It was then that Robert, with a radiant smile of triumph that was quite wasted in the darkness, where, of course, no one could see anything, drew out of his pocket a box of matches, struck a match and lighted a candle—two candles. And every one, with its mouth open, blinked at the sudden light.

'Well done Bobs,' said his sisters, and even Cyril's natural brotherly feelings could not check his admiration of Robert's foresight.

'I've always carried them about ever since the lone tower day,' said Robert, with modest pride. 'I knew we should want them some day. I kept the secret well, didn't I?'

'Oh, yes,' said Cyril, with fine scorn. 'I found them the Sunday after, when I was feeling in your Norfolks for the knife you borrowed off me. But I thought you'd only sneaked them for Chinese lanterns, or reading in bed by.'

'Bobs,' said Anthea, suddenly, 'do you know where we are? This is the underground passage, and look there—there's the money and the money-bags, and everything.'

By this time the ten eyes had got used to the light of the candles, and no one could help seeing that Anthea spoke the truth.

'It seems an odd place to do good and kind acts in, though,' said Jane. 'There's no one to do them to.'

'Don't you be too sure,' said Cyril; 'just round the next turning we might find a prisoner who has languished here for years and years, and we could take him out on our carpet and restore him to his sorrowing friends.'

'Of course we could,' said Robert, standing up and holding the candle above his head to see further off; 'or we might find the bones of a poor prisoner and take them to his friends to be buried properly—that's always a kind action in books, though I never could see what bones matter.'

'I wish you wouldn't,' said Jane.

'I know exactly where we shall find the bones, too,' Robert went on. 'You see that dark arch just along the passage? Well, just inside there—'

'If you don't stop going on like that,' said Jane, firmly, 'I shall scream, and then I'll faint—so now then!'

'And *I* will, too,' said Anthea.

Robert was not pleased at being checked in his flight of fancy.

'You girls will never be great writers,' he said bitterly. 'They just love to think of things in dungeons, and chains, and knobbly bare human bones, and—'

Jane had opened her mouth to scream, but before she could decide how you began when you wanted to faint, the golden voice of the Phoenix spoke through the gloom.

'Peace!' it said; 'there are no bones here except the small but useful sets that you have inside you. And you did not invite me to come out with you to hear you talk about bones, but to see you do some good and kind action.'

'We can't do it here,' said Robert, sulkily.

'No,' rejoined the bird. 'The only thing we can do here, it seems, is to try to frighten our little sisters.'

'He didn't, really, and I'm not so VERY little,' said Jane, rather ungratefully.

Robert was silent. It was Cyril who suggested that perhaps they had better take the money and go.

'That wouldn't be a kind act, except to ourselves; and it wouldn't be good, whatever way you look at it,' said Anthea, 'to take money that's not ours.'

'We might take it and spend it all on benefits to the poor and aged,' said Cyril.

'That wouldn't make it right to steal,' said Anthea, stoutly.

'I don't know,' said Cyril. They were all standing up now. 'Stealing is taking things that belong to some one else, and there's no one else.'

'It can't be stealing if—'

'That's right,' said Robert, with ironical approval; 'stand here all day arguing while the candles burn out. You'll like it awfully when it's all dark again—and bony.'

'Let's get out, then,' said Anthea. 'We can argue as we go.' So they rolled up the carpet and went. But when they had crept along to the place where the passage led into the topless tower they found the way blocked by a great stone, which they could not move.

'There!' said Robert. 'I hope you're satisfied!'

'Everything has two ends,' said the Phoenix, softly; 'even a quarrel or a secret passage.'

So they turned round and went back, and Robert was made to go first with one of the candles, because he was the one who had begun to talk about bones. And Cyril carried the carpet.

'I wish you hadn't put bones into our heads,' said Jane, as they went along.

'I didn't; you always had them. More bones than brains,' said Robert.

The passage was long, and there were arches and steps and turnings and dark alcoves that the girls did not much like passing. The passage ended in a flight of steps. Robert went up them.

Suddenly he staggered heavily back on to the following feet of Jane, and everybody screamed, 'Oh! what is it?'

'I've only bashed my head in,' said Robert, when he had groaned for some time; 'that's all. Don't mention it; I like it. The stairs just go right slap into the ceiling, and it's a stone ceiling. You can't do good and kind actions underneath a paving-stone.'

'Stairs aren't made to lead just to paving-stones as a general rule,' said the Phoenix. 'Put your shoulder to the wheel.'

'There isn't any wheel,' said the injured Robert, still rubbing his head.

But Cyril had pushed past him to the top stair, and was already shoving his hardest against the stone above. Of course, it did not give in the least.

'If it's a trap-door—' said Cyril. And he stopped shoving and began to feel about with his hands.

'Yes, there is a bolt. I can't move it.'

By a happy chance Cyril had in his pocket the oil-can of his father's bicycle; he put the carpet down at the foot of the stairs, and he lay on his back, with his head on the top step and his feet straggling down among his young relations, and he oiled the bolt till the drops of rust and oil fell down on his face. One even went into his mouth—open, as he panted with the exertion of keeping up this unnatural position. Then he tried again, but still the bolt would not move. So now he tied his handkerchief—the one with the bacon-fat and marmalade on it—to the bolt, and Robert's handkerchief to that, in a reef knot, which cannot come undone however much you pull, and, indeed, gets tighter and tighter the more you pull it. This must not be confused with a granny knot, which comes undone if you look at it. And then he and Robert pulled, and the girls put their arms round their brothers and pulled too, and suddenly the bolt gave way with a rusty scrunch, and they all rolled together to the bottom of the stairs—all but the Phoenix, which had taken to its wings when the pulling began.

Nobody was hurt much, because the rolled-up carpet broke their fall; and now, indeed, the shoulders of the boys were used to some purpose, for the stone allowed them to heave it up. They felt it give; dust fell freely on them.

'Now, then,' cried Robert, forgetting his head and his temper, 'push all together. One, two, three!'

The stone was heaved up. It swung up on a creaking, unwilling hinge, and showed a growing oblong of dazzling daylight; and it fell back with a bang against something that kept it upright. Every one climbed out, but there was not room for every one to stand comfortably in the little paved house where they found themselves, so when the Phoenix had fluttered up from the darkness they let the stone down, and it closed like a trap-door, as indeed it was.

You can have no idea how dusty and dirty the children were. Fortunately there was no one to see them but each other. The place they were in was a little shrine, built on the side of a road that went winding up through yellow-green fields to the topless tower. Below them were fields and orchards, all bare boughs and brown furrows, and little houses and gardens. The shrine was a kind of tiny chapel with no front wall—just a place for people to stop and rest in and wish to be good. So the Phoenix told them. There was an image that had once been brightly coloured, but the rain and snow had beaten in through the open front of the shrine, and the poor image was dull and weather-stained. Under it was written: 'St Jean de Luz. Priez pour nous.' It was a sad little place, very neglected and lonely, and yet it was nice, Anthea thought, that poor travellers should come to this little rest-house in the hurry and worry of their journeyings and be quiet for a few minutes, and think about being good. The thought of St Jean de Luz—who had, no doubt, in his time, been very good and kind—made Anthea want more than ever to do something kind and good.

'Tell us,' she said to the Phoenix, 'what is the good and kind action the carpet brought us here to do?'

'I think it would be kind to find the owners of the treasure and tell them about it,' said Cyril.

'And give it them ALL?' said Jane.

'Yes. But whose is it?'

'I should go to the first house and ask the name of the owner of the castle,' said the golden bird, and really the idea seemed a good one.

They dusted each other as well as they could and went down the road. A little way on they found a tiny spring, bubbling out of the hillside and falling into a rough stone basin surrounded by draggled hart's-tongue ferns, now hardly green at all. Here the children washed their hands and faces and dried them on their pocket-handkerchiefs, which always, on these occasions, seem unnaturally small. Cyril's and Robert's handkerchiefs, indeed, rather undid the effects of the wash. But in spite of this the party certainly looked cleaner than before.

The first house they came to was a little white house with green shutters and a slate roof. It stood in a prim little garden, and down each side of the neat path were large stone vases for flowers to grow in; but all the flowers were dead now.

Along one side of the house was a sort of wide veranda, built of poles and trellis-work, and a vine crawled all over it. It was wider than our English verandas, and Anthea thought it must look lovely when the green leaves and the grapes were there; but now there were only dry, reddish-brown stalks and stems, with a few withered leaves caught in them.

The children walked up to the front door. It was green and narrow. A chain with a handle hung beside it, and joined itself quite openly to a rusty bell that hung under the porch. Cyril had pulled the bell and its noisy clang was dying away before the terrible thought came to all. Cyril spoke it.

'My hat!' he breathed. 'We don't know any French!'

At this moment the door opened. A very tall, lean lady, with pale ringlets like whitey-brown paper or oak shavings, stood before them. She had an ugly grey dress and a black silk apron. Her eyes were small and grey and not pretty, and the rims were red, as though she had been crying.

She addressed the party in something that sounded like a foreign language, and ended with something which they were sure was a question. Of course, no one could answer it.

'What does she say?' Robert asked, looking down into the hollow of his jacket, where the Phoenix was nestling. But before the Phoenix could answer, the whitey-brown lady's face was lighted up by a most charming smile.

'You—you ar-r-re fr-r-rom the England!' she cried. 'I love so much the England. Mais entrez—entrez donc tous! Enter, then—enter all. One essuyes his feet on the carpet.' She pointed to the mat.

'We only wanted to ask—'

'I shall say you all that what you wish,' said the lady. 'Enter only!'

So they all went in, wiping their feet on a very clean mat, and putting the carpet in a safe corner of the veranda.

'The most beautiful days of my life,' said the lady, as she shut the door, 'did pass themselves in England. And since long time I have not heard an English voice to repeal me the past.'

This warm welcome embarrassed every one, but most the boys, for the floor of the hall was of such very clean red and white tiles, and the floor of the sitting-room so very shiny—like a black looking-glass—that each felt as though he had on far more boots than usual, and far noisier.

There was a wood fire, very small and very bright, on the hearth—neat little logs laid on brass fire-dogs. Some portraits of powdered ladies and gentlemen hung in oval frames on the pale walls. There were silver candlesticks on the mantelpiece, and there were chairs and a table, very slim and polite, with slender legs. The room was extremely bare, but with a bright foreign bareness that was very cheerful, in an odd way of its own. At the end of the polished table a very un-English little boy sat on a footstool in a high-backed, uncomfortable-looking chair. He wore black velvet, and the kind of collar—all frills and lacey— that Robert would rather have died than wear; but then the little French boy was much younger than Robert.

'Oh, how pretty!' said every one. But no one meant the little French boy, with the velvety short knickerbockers and the velvety short hair.

What every one admired was a little, little Christmas-tree, very green, and standing in a very red little flower-pot, and hung round with very bright little things made of tinsel and coloured paper. There were tiny candles on the tree, but they were not lighted yet.

'But yes—is it not that it is genteel?' said the lady. 'Sit down you then, and let us see.'

The children sat down in a row on the stiff chairs against the wall, and the lady lighted a long, slim red taper at the wood flame, and then she drew the curtains and lit the little candles, and when they were all lighted the little French boy suddenly shouted, 'Bravo, ma tante! Oh, que c'est gentil,' and the English children shouted 'Hooray!'

Then there was a struggle in the breast of Robert, and out fluttered the Phoenix—spread his gold wings, flew to the top of the Christmas-tree, and perched there.

'Ah! catch it, then,' cried the lady; 'it will itself burn—your genteel parrakeet!'

'It won't,' said Robert, 'thank you.'

And the little French boy clapped his clean and tidy hands; but the lady was so anxious that the Phoenix fluttered down and walked up and down on the shiny walnut-wood table.

'Is it that it talks?' asked the lady.

And the Phoenix replied in excellent French. It said, 'Parfaitement, madame!'

'Oh, the pretty parrakeet,' said the lady. 'Can it say still of other things?'

And the Phoenix replied, this time in English, 'Why are you sad so near Christmas-time?'

The children looked at it with one gasp of horror and surprise, for the youngest of them knew that it is far from manners to notice that strangers have been crying, and much worse to ask them the reason of their tears. And, of course, the lady began to cry again, very much indeed, after calling the Phoenix a bird without a heart; and she could not find her handkerchief, so Anthea offered hers, which was still very damp and no use at all. She also hugged the lady, and this seemed to be of more use than the handkerchief, so that presently the lady stopped crying, and found her own handkerchief and dried her eyes, and called Anthea a cherished angel.

'I am sorry we came just when you were so sad,' said Anthea, 'but we really only wanted to ask you whose that castle is on the hill.'

'Oh, my little angel,' said the poor lady, sniffing, 'to-day and for hundreds of years the castle is to us, to our family. To-morrow it must that I sell it to some strangers—and my little Henri, who ignores all, he will not have never the lands paternal. But what will you? His father, my brother—Mr the Marquis—has spent much of money, and it the must, despite the sentiments of familial respect, that I admit that my sainted father he also—'

'How would you feel if you found a lot of money—hundreds and thousands of gold pieces?' asked Cyril.

The lady smiled sadly.

'Ah! one has already recounted to you the legend?' she said. 'It is true that one says that it is long time; oh! but long time, one of our ancestors has hid a treasure—of gold, and of gold, and of gold—enough to enrich my little Henri for the life. But all that, my children, it is but the accounts of fays—'

'She means fairy stories,' whispered the Phoenix to Robert. 'Tell her what you have found.'

So Robert told, while Anthea and Jane hugged the lady for fear she should faint for joy, like people in books, and they hugged her with the earnest, joyous hugs of unselfish delight.

'It's no use explaining how we got in,' said Robert, when he had told of the finding of the treasure, 'because you would find it a little difficult to understand, and much more difficult to believe. But we can show you where the gold is and help you to fetch it away.'

The lady looked doubtfully at Robert as she absently returned the hugs of the girls.

'No, he's not making it up,' said Anthea; 'it's true, TRUE, TRUE!—and we are so glad.'

'You would not be capable to torment an old woman?' she said; 'and it is not possible that it be a dream.'

'It really IS true,' said Cyril; 'and I congratulate you very much.'

His tone of studied politeness seemed to convince more than the raptures of the others.

'If I do not dream,' she said, 'Henri come to Manon—and you—you shall come all with me to Mr the Curate. Is it not?'

Manon was a wrinkled old woman with a red and yellow handkerchief twisted round her head. She took Henri, who was already sleepy with the excitement of his Christmas-tree and his visitors, and when the lady had put on a stiff black cape and a wonderful black silk bonnet and a pair of black wooden clogs over her black cashmere house-boots, the whole party went down the road to a little white house—very like the one they had left—where an old priest, with a good face, welcomed them with a politeness so great that it hid his astonishment.

The lady, with her French waving hands and her shrugging French shoulders and her trembling French speech, told the story. And now the priest, who knew no English, shrugged HIS shoulders and waved HIS hands and spoke also in French.

'He thinks,' whispered the Phoenix, 'that her troubles have turned her brain. What a pity you know no French!'

'I do know a lot of French,' whispered Robert, indignantly; 'but it's all about the pencil of the gardener's son and the penknife of the baker's niece—nothing that anyone ever wants to say.'

'If *I* speak,' the bird whispered, 'he'll think HE'S mad, too.'

'Tell me what to say.'

'Say "C'est vrai, monsieur. Venez donc voir,"' said the Phoenix; and then Robert earned the undying respect of everybody by suddenly saying, very loudly and distinctly—

'Say vray, mossoo; venny dong vwaw.'

The priest was disappointed when he found that Robert's French began and ended with these useful words; but, at any rate, he saw that if the lady was mad she was not the only one, and he put on a big beavery hat, and got a candle and matches and a spade, and they all went up the hill to the wayside shrine of St John of Luz.

'Now,' said Robert, 'I will go first and show you where it is.'

So they prised the stone up with a corner of the spade, and Robert did go first, and they all followed and found the golden treasure exactly as they had left it. And every one was flushed with the joy of performing such a wonderfully kind action.

Then the lady and the priest clasped hands and wept for joy, as French people do, and knelt down and touched the money, and talked very fast and both together, and the lady embraced all the children three times each, and called them 'little garden angels,' and then she and the priest shook each other by both hands again, and talked, and talked, and talked, faster and more Frenchy than you would have believed possible. And the children were struck dumb with joy and pleasure.

'Get away NOW,' said the Phoenix softly, breaking in on the radiant dream.

So the children crept away, and out through the little shrine, and the lady and the priest were so tearfully, talkatively happy that they never noticed that the guardian angels had gone.

The 'garden angels' ran down the hill to the lady's little house, where they had left the carpet on the veranda, and they spread it out and said 'Home,' and no one saw them disappear, except little Henri, who had flattened his nose into a white button against the window-glass, and when he tried to tell his aunt she thought he had been dreaming. So that was all right.

'It is much the best thing we've done,' said Anthea, when they talked it over at tea-time. 'In the future we'll only do kind actions with the carpet.'

'Ahem!' said the Phoenix.

'I beg your pardon?' said Anthea.

'Oh, nothing,' said the bird. 'I was only thinking!'

Chapter 7. Mews From Persia

When you hear that the four children found themselves at Waterloo Station quite un-taken-care-of, and with no one to meet them, it may make you think that their parents were neither kind nor careful. But if you think this you will be wrong. The fact is, mother arranged with Aunt Emma that she was to meet the children at Waterloo, when they went back from their Christmas holiday at Lyndhurst. The train was fixed, but not the day. Then mother wrote to Aunt Emma, giving her careful instructions about the day and the hour, and about luggage and cabs and things, and gave the letter to Robert to post. But the hounds happened to meet near Rufus Stone that morning, and what is more, on the way to the meet they met Robert, and Robert met them, and instantly forgot all about posting Aunt Emma's letter, and never thought of it again until he and the others had wandered three times up and down the platform at Waterloo—which makes six in all—and had bumped against old gentlemen, and stared in the faces of ladies, and been shoved by people in a hurry, and 'by-your-leaved' by porters with trucks, and were quite, quite sure that Aunt Emma was not there. Then suddenly the true truth of what he had forgotten to do came home to Robert, and he said, 'Oh, crikey!' and stood still with his mouth open, and let a porter with a Gladstone bag in each hand and a bundle of umbrellas under one arm blunder heavily into him, and never so much as said, 'Where are you shoving to now?' or, 'Look out where you're going, can't you?' The heavier bag smote him at the knee, and he staggered, but he said nothing.

When the others understood what was the matter I think they told Robert what they thought of him.

'We must take the train to Croydon,' said Anthea, 'and find Aunt Emma.'

'Yes,' said Cyril, 'and precious pleased those Jevonses would be to see us and our traps.'

Aunt Emma, indeed, was staying with some Jevonses—very prim people. They were middle-aged and wore very smart blouses, and they were fond of matinees and shopping, and they did not care about children.

'I know MOTHER would be pleased to see us if we went back,' said Jane.

'Yes, she would, but she'd think it was not right to show she was pleased, because it's Bob's fault we're not met. Don't I know the sort of thing?' said Cyril. 'Besides, we've no tin. No; we've got enough for a growler among us, but not enough for tickets to the New Forest. We must just go home. They won't be so savage when they find we've really got home all right. You know auntie was only going to take us home in a cab.'

'I believe we ought to go to Croydon,' Anthea insisted.

'Aunt Emma would be out to a dead cert,' said Robert. 'Those Jevonses go to the theatre every afternoon, I believe. Besides, there's the Phoenix at home, AND the carpet. I vote we call a four-wheeled cabman.'

A four-wheeled cabman was called—his cab was one of the old-fashioned kind with straw in the bottom—and he was asked by Anthea to drive them very carefully to their address. This he did, and the price he asked for doing so was exactly the value of the gold coin grandpapa had given Cyril for Christmas. This cast a gloom; but Cyril would never have stooped to argue about a cab-fare, for fear the cabman should think he was not accustomed to take cabs whenever he wanted them. For a reason that was something like this he told the cabman to put the luggage on the steps, and waited till the wheels of the growler had grittily retired before he rang the bell.

'You see,' he said, with his hand on the handle, 'we don't want cook and Eliza asking us before HIM how it is we've come home alone, as if we were babies.'

Here he rang the bell; and the moment its answering clang was heard, every one felt that it would be some time before that bell was answered. The sound of a bell is quite different, somehow, when there is anyone inside the house who hears it. I can't tell you why that is—but so it is.

'I expect they're changing their dresses,' said Jane.

'Too late,' said Anthea, 'it must be past five. I expect Eliza's gone to post a letter, and cook's gone to see the time.'

Cyril rang again. And the bell did its best to inform the listening children that there was really no one human in the house. They rang again and listened intently. The hearts of all sank low. It is a terrible thing to be locked out of your own house, on a dark, muggy January evening.

'There is no gas on anywhere,' said Jane, in a broken voice.

'I expect they've left the gas on once too often, and the draught blew it out, and they're suffocated in their beds. Father always said they would some day,' said Robert cheerfully.

'Let's go and fetch a policeman,' said Anthea, trembling.

'And be taken up for trying to be burglars—no, thank you,' said Cyril. 'I heard father read out of the paper about a young man who got into his own mother's house, and they got him made a burglar only the other day.'

'I only hope the gas hasn't hurt the Phoenix,' said Anthea. 'It said it wanted to stay in the bathroom cupboard, and I thought it would be all right, because the servants never clean that out. But if it's gone and got out and been choked by gas—And besides, directly we open the door we shall be choked, too. I KNEW we ought to have gone to Aunt Emma, at Croydon. Oh, Squirrel, I wish we had. Let's go NOW.'

'Shut up,' said her brother, briefly. 'There's some one rattling the latch inside.' Every one listened with all its ears, and every one stood back as far from the door as the steps would allow.

The latch rattled, and clicked. Then the flap of the letter-box lifted itself—every one saw it by the flickering light of the gas-lamp that shone through the leafless lime-tree by the gate—a golden eye seemed to wink at them through the letter-slit, and a cautious beak whispered—

'Are you alone?'

'It's the Phoenix,' said every one, in a voice so joyous, and so full of relief, as to be a sort of whispered shout.

'Hush!' said the voice from the letter-box slit. 'Your slaves have gone a-merry-making. The latch of this portal is too stiff for my beak. But at the side—the little window above the shelf whereon your bread lies—it is not fastened.'

'Righto!' said Cyril.

And Anthea added, 'I wish you'd meet us there, dear Phoenix.'

The children crept round to the pantry window. It is at the side of the house, and there is a green gate labelled 'Tradesmen's Entrance', which is always kept bolted. But if you get one foot on the fence between you and next door, and one on the handle of the gate, you are over before you know where you are. This, at least, was the experience of Cyril and Robert, and even, if the truth must be told, of Anthea and Jane. So in almost no time all four were in the narrow gravelled passage that runs between that house and the next.

Then Robert made a back, and Cyril hoisted himself up and got his knicker-bockered knee on the concrete window-sill. He dived into the pantry head first, as one dives into water, and his legs waved in the air as he went, just as your legs do when you are first beginning to learn to dive. The soles of his boots—squarish muddy patches—disappeared.

'Give me a leg up,' said Robert to his sisters.

'No, you don't,' said Jane firmly. 'I'm not going to be left outside here with just Anthea, and have something creep up behind us out of the dark. Squirrel can go and open the back door.'

A light had sprung awake in the pantry. Cyril always said the Phoenix turned the gas on with its beak, and lighted it with a waft of its wing; but he was excited at the time, and perhaps he really did it himself with matches, and then forgot all about it. He let the others in by the back door. And when it had been bolted again the children went all over the house and lighted every single gas-jet they could find. For they couldn't help feeling that this was just the dark dreary winter's evening when an armed burglar might easily be expected to appear at any moment. There is nothing like light when you are afraid of burglars—or of anything else, for that matter.

And when all the gas-jets were lighted it was quite clear that the Phoenix had made no mistake, and that Eliza and cook were really out, and that there was no one in the house except the four children, and the Phoenix, and the carpet, and the blackbeetles who lived in the cupboards on each side of the nursery fire-place. These last were very pleased that the children had come home again, especially when Anthea had lighted the nursery fire. But, as usual, the children treated the loving little blackbeetles with coldness and disdain.

I wonder whether you know how to light a fire? I don't mean how to strike a match and set fire to the corners of the paper in a fire someone has laid ready, but how to lay and light a fire all by yourself. I will tell you how Anthea did it, and if ever you have to light one yourself you may remember how it is done. First, she raked out the ashes of the fire that had burned there a week ago—for Eliza had actually never done this, though she had had plenty of time. In doing this Anthea knocked her knuckle and made it bleed. Then she laid the largest and handsomest cinders in the bottom of the grate. Then she took a sheet of old newspaper (you ought never to light a fire with to-day's newspaper—it will not burn well, and there are other reasons against it), and tore it into four quarters, and screwed each of these into a loose ball, and put them on the cinders; then she got a bundle of wood and broke the string, and stuck the sticks in so that their front ends rested on the bars, and the back ends on the back of the paper balls. In doing this she cut her finger slightly with the string, and when she broke it, two of the sticks jumped up and hit her on the cheek. Then she put more cinders and some bits of coal—no dust. She put most of that on her hands, but there seemed to be enough left for her face. Then she lighted the edges of the paper balls, and waited till she heard the fizz-crack-crack-fizz of the wood as it began to burn. Then she went and washed her hands and face under the tap in the back kitchen.

Of course, you need not bark your knuckles, or cut your finger, or bruise your cheek with wood, or black yourself all over; but otherwise, this is a very good way to light a fire in London. In the real country fires are lighted in a different and prettier way.

But it is always good to wash your hands and face afterwards, wherever you are.

While Anthea was delighting the poor little blackbeetles with the cheerful blaze, Jane had set the table for—I was going to say tea, but the meal of which I am speaking was not exactly tea. Let us call it a tea-ish meal. There was tea, certainly, for Anthea's fire blazed and crackled so kindly that it really seemed to be affectionately inviting the kettle to come and sit upon its lap. So the kettle was brought and tea made. But no milk could be found—so every one had six lumps of sugar to each cup instead. The things to eat, on the other hand, were nicer than usual. The boys looked about very carefully, and found in the pantry some cold tongue, bread, butter, cheese, and part of a cold pudding—very much nicer than cook ever made when they were at home. And in the kitchen cupboard was half a Christmassy cake, a pot of strawberry jam, and about a pound of mixed candied fruit, with soft crumbly slabs of delicious sugar in each cup of lemon, orange, or citron.

It was indeed, as Jane said, 'a banquet fit for an Arabian Knight.'

The Phoenix perched on Robert's chair, and listened kindly and politely to all they had to tell it about their visit to Lyndhurst, and underneath the table, by just stretching a toe down rather far, the faithful carpet could be felt by all—even by Jane, whose legs were very short.

'Your slaves will not return to-night,' said the Phoenix. 'They sleep under the roof of the cook's stepmother's aunt, who is, I gather, hostess to a large party to-night in honour of her husband's cousin's sister-in-law's mother's ninetieth birthday.'

'I don't think they ought to have gone without leave,' said Anthea, 'however many relations they have, or however old they are; but I suppose we ought to wash up.'

'It's not our business about the leave,' said Cyril, firmly, 'but I simply won't wash up for them. We got it, and we'll clear it away; and then we'll go somewhere on the carpet. It's not often we get a chance of being out all night. We can go right away to the other side of the equator, to the tropical climes, and see the sun rise over the great Pacific Ocean.'

'Right you are,' said Robert. 'I always did want to see the Southern Cross and the stars as big as gas-lamps.'

'DON'T go,' said Anthea, very earnestly, 'because I COULDN'T. I'm SURE mother wouldn't like us to leave the house and I should hate to be left here alone.'

'I'd stay with you,' said Jane loyally.

'I know you would,' said Anthea gratefully, 'but even with you I'd much rather not.'

'Well,' said Cyril, trying to be kind and amiable, 'I don't want you to do anything you think's wrong, BUT—'

He was silent; this silence said many things.

'I don't see,' Robert was beginning, when Anthea interrupted—

'I'm quite sure. Sometimes you just think a thing's wrong, and sometimes you KNOW. And this is a KNOW time.'

The Phoenix turned kind golden eyes on her and opened a friendly beak to say—

'When it is, as you say, a "know time", there is no more to be said. And your noble brothers would never leave you.'

'Of course not,' said Cyril rather quickly. And Robert said so too.

'I myself,' the Phoenix went on, 'am willing to help in any way possible. I will go personally—either by carpet or on the wing—and fetch you anything you can think of to amuse you during the evening. In order to waste no time I could go while you wash up.—Why,' it went on in a musing voice, 'does one wash up teacups and wash down the stairs?'

'You couldn't wash stairs up, you know,' said Anthea, 'unless you began at the bottom and went up feet first as you washed. I wish cook would try that way for a change.'

'I don't,' said Cyril, briefly. 'I should hate the look of her elastic-side boots sticking up.'

'This is mere trifling,' said the Phoenix. 'Come, decide what I shall fetch for you. I can get you anything you like.'

But of course they couldn't decide. Many things were suggested—a rocking-horse, jewelled chessmen, an elephant, a bicycle, a motor-car, books with pictures, musical instruments, and many other things. But a musical instrument is agreeable only to the player, unless he has learned to play it really well; books are not sociable, bicycles cannot be ridden without going out of doors, and the same is true of motor-cars and elephants. Only two people can play chess at once with one set of chessmen (and anyway it's very much too much like lessons for a game), and only one can ride on a rocking-horse. Suddenly, in the midst of the discussion, the Phoenix spread its wings and fluttered to the floor, and from there it spoke.

'I gather,' it said, 'from the carpet, that it wants you to let it go to its old home, where it was born and brought up, and it will return within the hour laden with a number of the most beautiful and delightful products of its native land.'

'What IS its native land?'

'I didn't gather. But since you can't agree, and time is passing, and the tea-things are not washed down—I mean washed up—'

'I votes we do,' said Robert. 'It'll stop all this jaw, anyway. And it's not bad to have surprises. Perhaps it's a Turkey carpet, and it might bring us Turkish delight.'

'Or a Turkish patrol,' said Robert.

'Or a Turkish bath,' said Anthea.

'Or a Turkish towel,' said Jane.

'Nonsense,' Robert urged, 'it said beautiful and delightful, and towels and baths aren't THAT, however good they may be for you. Let it go. I suppose it won't give us the slip,' he added, pushing back his chair and standing up.

'Hush!' said the Phoenix; 'how can you? Don't trample on its feelings just because it's only a carpet.'

'But how can it do it—unless one of us is on it to do the wishing?' asked Robert. He spoke with a rising hope that it MIGHT be necessary for one to go and why not Robert? But the Phoenix quickly threw cold water on his new-born dream.

'Why, you just write your wish on a paper, and pin it on the carpet.'

So a leaf was torn from Anthea's arithmetic book, and on it Cyril wrote in large round-hand the following:

> We wish you to go to your dear native home, and bring back the most beautiful and delightful productions of it you can—and not to be gone long, please.
>
> (Signed) CYRIL.
> ROBERT.
> ANTHEA.
> JANE.

Then the paper was laid on the carpet.

'Writing down, please,' said the Phoenix; 'the carpet can't read a paper whose back is turned to it, any more than you can.'

It was pinned fast, and the table and chairs having been moved, the carpet simply and suddenly vanished, rather like a patch of water on a hearth under a fierce fire. The edges got smaller and smaller, and then it disappeared from sight.

'It may take it some time to collect the beautiful and delightful things,' said the Phoenix. 'I should wash up—I mean wash down.'

So they did. There was plenty of hot water left in the kettle, and every one helped—even the Phoenix, who took up cups by their handles with its clever claws and dipped them in the hot water, and then stood them on the table ready for Anthea to dry them. But the bird was rather slow, because, as it said, though it was not above any sort of honest work, messing about with dish-water was not exactly what it had been brought up to. Everything was nicely washed up, and dried, and put in its proper place, and the dish-cloth washed and hung on the edge of the copper to dry, and the tea-cloth was hung on the line that goes across the scullery. (If you are a duchess's child, or a king's, or a person of high social position's child, you will perhaps not know the difference between a dish-cloth and a tea-cloth; but in that case your nurse has been better instructed than you, and she will tell you all about it.) And just as eight hands and one pair of claws were being dried on the roller-towel behind the scullery door there came a strange sound from the other side of the kitchen wall—the side where the nursery was. It was a very strange sound, indeed—most odd, and unlike any other sounds the children had ever heard. At least, they had heard sounds as much like it as a toy engine's whistle is like a steam siren's.

'The carpet's come back,' said Robert; and the others felt that he was right.

'But what has it brought with it?' asked Jane. 'It sounds like Leviathan, that great beast.'

'It couldn't have been made in India, and have brought elephants? Even baby ones would be rather awful in that room,' said Cyril. 'I vote we take it in turns to squint through the keyhole.'

They did—in the order of their ages. The Phoenix, being the eldest by some thousands of years, was entitled to the first peep. But—

'Excuse me,' it said, ruffling its golden feathers and sneezing softly; 'looking through keyholes always gives me a cold in my golden eyes.'

So Cyril looked.

'I see something grey moving,' said he.

'It's a zoological garden of some sort, I bet,' said Robert, when he had taken his turn. And the soft rustling, bustling, ruffling, scuffling, shuffling, fluffling noise went on inside.

'*I* can't see anything,' said Anthea, 'my eye tickles so.'

Then Jane's turn came, and she put her eye to the keyhole.

'It's a giant kitty-cat,' she said; 'and it's asleep all over the floor.'

'Giant cats are tigers—father said so.'

'No, he didn't. He said tigers were giant cats. It's not at all the same thing.'

'It's no use sending the carpet to fetch precious things for you if you're afraid to look at them when they come,' said the Phoenix, sensibly. And Cyril, being the eldest, said—

'Come on,' and turned the handle.

The gas had been left full on after tea, and everything in the room could be plainly seen by the ten eyes at the door. At least, not everything, for though the carpet was there it was invisible, because it was completely covered by the hundred and ninety-nine beautiful objects which it had brought from its birthplace.

'My hat!' Cyril remarked. 'I never thought about its being a PERSIAN carpet.'

Yet it was now plain that it was so, for the beautiful objects which it had brought back were cats—Persian cats, grey Persian cats, and there were, as I have said, 199 of them, and they were sitting on the carpet as close as they could get to each other. But the moment the children entered the room the cats rose and stretched, and spread and overflowed from the carpet to the floor, and in an instant the floor was a sea of moving, mewing pussishness, and the children with one accord climbed to the table, and gathered up their legs, and the people next door knocked on the wall—and, indeed, no wonder, for the mews were Persian and piercing.

'This is pretty poor sport,' said Cyril. 'What's the matter with the bounders?'

'I imagine that they are hungry,' said the Phoenix. 'If you were to feed them—'

'We haven't anything to feed them with,' said Anthea in despair, and she stroked the nearest Persian back. 'Oh, pussies, do be quiet—we can't hear ourselves think.'

She had to shout this entreaty, for the mews were growing deafening, 'and it would take pounds' and pounds' worth of cat's-meat.'

'Let's ask the carpet to take them away,' said Robert. But the girls said 'No.'

'They are so soft and pussy,' said Jane.

'And valuable,' said Anthea, hastily. 'We can sell them for lots and lots of money.'

'Why not send the carpet to get food for them?' suggested the Phoenix, and its golden voice came harsh and cracked with the effort it had to be make to be heard above the increasing fierceness of the Persian mews.

So it was written that the carpet should bring food for 199 Persian cats, and the paper was pinned to the carpet as before.

The carpet seemed to gather itself together, and the cats dropped off it, as raindrops do from your mackintosh when you shake it. And the carpet disappeared.

Unless you have had one-hundred and ninety-nine well-grown Persian cats in one small room, all hungry, and all saying so in unmistakable mews, you can form but a poor idea of the noise that now deafened the children and the Phoenix. The cats did not seem to have been at all properly brought up. They seemed to have no idea of its being a mistake in manners to ask for meals in a strange house—let alone to howl for them—and they mewed, and they mewed, and they mewed, and they mewed, till the children poked their fingers into their ears and waited in silent agony, wondering why the whole of Camden Town did not come knocking at the door to ask what was the matter, and only hoping that the food for the cats would come before the neighbours did—and before all the secret of the carpet and the Phoenix had to be given away beyond recall to an indignant neighbourhood.

The cats mewed and mewed and twisted their Persian forms in and out and unfolded their Persian tails, and the children and the Phoenix huddled together on the table.

The Phoenix, Robert noticed suddenly, was trembling.

'So many cats,' it said, 'and they might not know I was the Phoenix. These accidents happen so quickly. It quite un-mans me.'

This was a danger of which the children had not thought.

'Creep in,' cried Robert, opening his jacket.

And the Phoenix crept in—only just in time, for green eyes had glared, pink noses had sniffed, white whiskers had twitched, and as Robert buttoned his coat he disappeared to the waist in a wave of eager grey Persian fur. And on the instant the good carpet slapped itself down on the floor. And it was covered with rats—three hundred and ninety-eight of them, I believe, two for each cat.

'How horrible!' cried Anthea. 'Oh, take them away!'

'Take yourself away,' said the Phoenix, 'and me.'

'I wish we'd never had a carpet,' said Anthea, in tears.

They hustled and crowded out of the door, and shut it, and locked it. Cyril, with great presence of mind, lit a candle and turned off the gas at the main.

'The rats'll have a better chance in the dark,' he said.

The mewing had ceased. Every one listened in breathless silence. We all know that cats eat rats—it is one of the first things we read in our little brown reading books; but all those cats eating all those rats—it wouldn't bear thinking of.

Suddenly Robert sniffed, in the silence of the dark kitchen, where the only candle was burning all on one side, because of the draught.

'What a funny scent!' he said.

And as he spoke, a lantern flashed its light through the window of the kitchen, a face peered in, and a voice said—

'What's all this row about? You let me in.'

It was the voice of the police!

Robert tip-toed to the window, and spoke through the pane that had been a little cracked since Cyril accidentally knocked it with a walking-stick when he was playing at balancing it on his nose. (It was after they had been to a circus.)

'What do you mean?' he said. 'There's no row. You listen; everything's as quiet as quiet.' And indeed it was.

The strange sweet scent grew stronger, and the Phoenix put out its beak.

The policeman hesitated.

'They're MUSK-rats,' said the Phoenix. 'I suppose some cats eat them—but never Persian ones. What a mistake for a well-informed carpet to make! Oh, what a night we're having!'

'Do go away,' said Robert, nervously. 'We're just going to bed—that's our bedroom candle; there isn't any row. Everything's as quiet as a mouse.'

A wild chorus of mews drowned his words, and with the mews were mingled the shrieks of the musk-rats. What had happened? Had the cats tasted them before deciding that they disliked the flavour?

'I'm a-coming in,' said the policeman. 'You've got a cat shut up there.'

'A cat,' said Cyril. 'Oh, my only aunt! A cat!'

'Come in, then,' said Robert. 'It's your own look out. I advise you not. Wait a shake, and I'll undo the side gate.'

He undid the side gate, and the policeman, very cautiously, came in. And there in the kitchen, by the light of one candle, with the mewing and the screaming going like a dozen steam sirens, twenty waiting on motor-cars, and half a hundred squeaking pumps, four agitated voices shouted to the policeman four mixed and wholly different explanations of the very mixed events of the evening.

Did you ever try to explain the simplest thing to a policeman?

Chapter 8. The Cats, The Cow, and The Burglar

The nursery was full of Persian cats and musk-rats that had been brought there by the wishing carpet. The cats were mewing and the musk-rats were squeaking so that you could hardly hear yourself speak. In the kitchen were the four children, one candle, a concealed Phoenix, and a very visible policeman.

'Now then, look here,' said the Policeman, very loudly, and he pointed his lantern at each child in turn, 'what's the meaning of this here yelling and caterwauling. I tell you you've got a cat here, and some one's a ill-treating of it. What do you mean by it, eh?'

It was five to one, counting the Phoenix; but the policeman, who was one, was of unusually fine size, and the five, including the Phoenix, were small. The mews and the squeaks grew softer, and in the comparative silence, Cyril said—

'It's true. There are a few cats here. But we've not hurt them. It's quite the opposite. We've just fed them.'

'It don't sound like it,' said the policeman grimly.

'I daresay they're not REAL cats,' said Jane madly, perhaps they're only dream-cats.'

'I'll dream-cat you, my lady,' was the brief response of the force.

'If you understood anything except people who do murders and stealings and naughty things like that, I'd tell you all about it,' said Robert; 'but I'm certain you don't. You're not meant to shove your oar into people's private cat-keepings. You're only supposed to interfere when people shout "murder" and "stop thief" in the street. So there!'

The policeman assured them that he should see about that; and at this point the Phoenix, who had been making itself small on the pot-shelf under the dresser, among the saucepan lids and the fish- kettle, walked on tip-toed claws in a noiseless and modest manner, and left the room unnoticed by any one.

'Oh, don't be so horrid,' Anthea was saying, gently and earnestly. 'We LOVE cats—dear pussy-soft things. We wouldn't hurt them for worlds. Would we, Pussy?'

And Jane answered that of course they wouldn't. And still the policeman seemed unmoved by their eloquence.

'Now, look here,' he said, 'I'm a-going to see what's in that room beyond there, and—'

His voice was drowned in a wild burst of mewing and squeaking. And as soon as it died down all four children began to explain at once; and though the squeaking and mewing were not at their very loudest, yet there was quite enough of both to make it very hard for the policeman to understand a single word of any of the four wholly different explanations now poured out to him.

'Stow it,' he said at last. 'I'm a-goin' into the next room in the execution of my duty. I'm a-goin' to use my eyes—my ears have gone off their chumps, what with you and them cats.'

And he pushed Robert aside, and strode through the door.

'Don't say I didn't warn you,' said Robert.

'It's tigers REALLY,' said Jane. 'Father said so. I wouldn't go in, if I were you.'

But the policeman was quite stony; nothing any one said seemed to make any difference to him. Some policemen are like this, I believe. He strode down the passage, and in another moment he would have been in the room with all the cats and all the rats (musk), but at that very instant a thin, sharp voice screamed from the street outside—

'Murder—murder! Stop thief!'

The policeman stopped, with one regulation boot heavily poised in the air.

'Eh?' he said.

And again the shrieks sounded shrilly and piercingly from the dark street outside.

'Come on,' said Robert. 'Come and look after cats while somebody's being killed outside.' For Robert had an inside feeling that told him quite plainly WHO it was that was screaming.

'You young rip,' said the policeman, 'I'll settle up with you bimeby.'

And he rushed out, and the children heard his boots going weightily along the pavement, and the screams also going along, rather ahead of the policeman; and both the murder-screams and the policeman's boots faded away in the remote distance.

Then Robert smacked his knickerbocker loudly with his palm, and said—

'Good old Phoenix! I should know its golden voice anywhere.'

And then every one understood how cleverly the Phoenix had caught at what Robert had said about the real work of a policeman being to look after murderers and thieves, and not after cats, and all hearts were filled with admiring affection.

'But he'll come back,' said Anthea, mournfully, 'as soon as it finds the murderer is only a bright vision of a dream, and there isn't one at all really.'

'No he won't,' said the soft voice of the clever Phoenix, as it flew in. 'HE DOES NOT KNOW WHERE YOUR HOUSE IS. I heard him own as much to a fellow mercenary. Oh! what a night we are having! Lock the door, and let us rid ourselves of this intolerable smell of the perfume peculiar to the musk-rat and to the house of the trimmers of beards. If you'll excuse me, I will go to bed. I am worn out.'

It was Cyril who wrote the paper that told the carpet to take away the rats and bring milk, because there seemed to be no doubt in any breast that, however Persian cats may be, they must like milk.

'Let's hope it won't be musk-milk,' said Anthea, in gloom, as she pinned the paper face-downwards on the carpet. 'Is there such a thing as a musk-cow?' she added anxiously, as the carpet shrivelled and vanished. 'I do hope not. Perhaps really it WOULD have been wiser to let the carpet take the cats away. It's getting quite late, and we can't keep them all night.'

'Oh, can't we?' was the bitter rejoinder of Robert, who had been fastening the side door. 'You might have consulted me,' he went on. 'I'm not such an idiot as some people.'

'Why, whatever—'

'Don't you see? We've jolly well GOT to keep the cats all night—oh, get down, you furry beasts!—because we've had three wishes out of the old carpet now, and we can't get any more till to-morrow.'

The liveliness of Persian mews alone prevented the occurrence of a dismal silence.

Anthea spoke first.

'Never mind,' she said. 'Do you know, I really do think they're quieting down a bit. Perhaps they heard us say milk.'

'They can't understand English,' said Jane. 'You forget they're Persian cats, Panther.'

'Well,' said Anthea, rather sharply, for she was tired and anxious, 'who told you "milk" wasn't Persian for milk. Lots of English words are just the same in French—at least I know "miaw" is, and "croquet", and "fiance". Oh, pussies, do be quiet! Let's stroke them as hard as we can with both hands, and perhaps they'll stop.'

So every one stroked grey fur till their hands were tired, and as soon as a cat had been stroked enough to make it stop mewing it was pushed gently away, and another mewing mouser was approached by the hands of the strokers. And the noise was really more than half purr when the carpet suddenly appeared in its proper place, and on it, instead of rows of milk-cans, or even of milk-jugs, there was a COW. Not a Persian cow, either, nor, most fortunately, a musk-cow, if there is such a thing, but a smooth, sleek, dun-coloured Jersey cow, who blinked large soft eyes at the gas-light and mooed in an amiable if rather inquiring manner.

Anthea had always been afraid of cows; but now she tried to be brave.

'Anyway, it can't run after me,' she said to herself 'There isn't room for it even to begin to run.'

The cow was perfectly placid. She behaved like a strayed duchess till some one brought a saucer for the milk, and some one else tried to milk the cow into it. Milking is very difficult. You may think it is easy, but it is not. All the children were by this time strung up to a pitch of heroism that would have been impossible to them in their ordinary condition. Robert and Cyril held the cow by the horns; and Jane, when she was quite sure that their end of the cow was quite secure, consented to stand by, ready to hold the cow by the tail should occasion arise. Anthea, holding the saucer, now advanced towards the cow. She remembered to have heard that cows, when milked by strangers, are susceptible to the soothing influence of the human voice. So, clutching her saucer very tight, she sought for words to whose soothing influence the cow might be susceptible. And her memory, troubled by the events of the night, which seemed to go on and on for ever and ever, refused to help her with any form of words suitable to address a Jersey cow in.

'Poor pussy, then. Lie down, then, good dog, lie down!' was all that she could think of to say, and she said it.

And nobody laughed. The situation, full of grey mewing cats, was too serious for that. Then Anthea, with a beating heart, tried to milk the cow. Next moment the cow had knocked the saucer out of her hand and trampled on it with one foot, while with the other three she had walked on a foot each of Robert, Cyril, and Jane.

Jane burst into tears. 'Oh, how much too horrid everything is!' she cried. 'Come away. Let's go to bed and leave the horrid cats with the hateful cow. Perhaps somebody will eat somebody else. And serve them right.'

They did not go to bed, but they had a shivering council in the drawing-room, which smelt of soot—and, indeed, a heap of this lay in the fender. There had been no fire in the room since mother went away, and all the chairs and tables were in the wrong places, and the chrysanthemums were dead, and the water in the pot nearly dried up. Anthea wrapped the embroidered woolly sofa blanket round Jane and herself, while Robert and Cyril had a struggle, silent and brief, but fierce, for the larger share of the fur hearthrug.

'It is most truly awful,' said Anthea, 'and I am so tired. Let's let the cats loose.'

'And the cow, perhaps?' said Cyril. 'The police would find us at once. That cow would stand at the gate and mew—I mean moo—to come in. And so would the cats. No; I see quite well what we've got to do. We must put them in baskets and leave them on people's doorsteps, like orphan foundlings.'

'We've got three baskets, counting mother's work one,' said Jane brightening.

'And there are nearly two hundred cats,' said Anthea, 'besides the cow—and it would have to be a different-sized basket for her; and then I don't know how you'd carry it, and you'd never find a doorstep big enough to put it on. Except the church one—and—'

'Oh, well,' said Cyril, 'if you simply MAKE difficulties—'

'I'm with you,' said Robert. 'Don't fuss about the cow, Panther. It's simply GOT to stay the night, and I'm sure I've read that the cow is a remunerating creature, and that means it will sit still and think for hours. The carpet can take it away in the morning. And as for the baskets, we'll do them up in dusters, or pillow-cases, or bath-towels. Come on, Squirrel. You girls can be out of it if you like.'

His tone was full of contempt, but Jane and Anthea were too tired and desperate to care; even being 'out of it', which at other times they could not have borne, now seemed quite a comfort. They snuggled down in the sofa blanket, and Cyril threw the fur hearthrug over them.

'Ah, he said, 'that's all women are fit for—to keep safe and warm, while the men do the work and run dangers and risks and things.'

'I'm not,' said Anthea, 'you know I'm not.' But Cyril was gone.

It was warm under the blanket and the hearthrug, and Jane snuggled up close to her sister; and Anthea cuddled Jane closely and kindly, and in a sort of dream they heard the rise of a wave of mewing as Robert opened the door of the nursery. They heard the booted search for baskets in the back kitchen. They heard the side door open and close, and they knew that each brother had gone out with at least one cat. Anthea's last thought was that it would take at least all night to get rid of one hundred and ninety-nine cats by twos. There would be ninety-nine journeys of two cats each, and one cat over.

'I almost think we might keep the one cat over,' said Anthea. 'I don't seem to care for cats just now, but I daresay I shall again some day.' And she fell asleep. Jane also was sleeping.

It was Jane who awoke with a start, to find Anthea still asleep. As, in the act of awakening, she kicked her sister, she wondered idly why they should have gone to bed in their boots; but the next moment she remembered where they were.

There was a sound of muffled, shuffled feet on the stairs. Like the heroine of the classic poem, Jane 'thought it was the boys', and as she felt quite wide awake, and not nearly so tired as before, she crept gently from Anthea's side and followed the footsteps. They went down into the basement; the cats, who seemed to have fallen into the sleep of exhaustion, awoke at the sound of the approaching footsteps and mewed piteously. Jane was at the foot of the stairs before she saw it was not her brothers whose coming had roused her and the cats, but a burglar. She knew he was a burglar at once, because he wore a fur cap and a red and black charity-check comforter, and he had no business where he was.

If you had been stood in Jane's shoes you would no doubt have run away in them, appealing to the police and neighbours with horrid screams. But Jane knew better. She had read a great many nice stories about burglars, as well as some affecting pieces of poetry, and she knew that no burglar will ever hurt a little girl if he meets her when burgling. Indeed, in all the cases Jane had read of, his burglarishness was almost at once forgotten in the interest he felt in the little girl's artless prattle. So if Jane hesitated for a moment before addressing the burglar, it was only because she could not at once think of any remark sufficiently prattling and artless to make a beginning with. In the stories and the affecting poetry the child could never speak plainly, though it always looked old enough to in the pictures. And Jane could not make up her mind to lisp and 'talk baby', even to a burglar. And while she hesitated he softly opened the nursery door and went in.

Jane followed—just in time to see him sit down flat on the floor, scattering cats as a stone thrown into a pool splashes water.

She closed the door softly and stood there, still wondering whether she COULD bring herself to say, 'What's 'oo doing here, Mithter Wobber?' and whether any other kind of talk would do.

Then she heard the burglar draw a long breath, and he spoke.

'It's a judgement,' he said, 'so help me bob if it ain't. Oh, 'ere's a thing to 'appen to a chap! Makes it come 'ome to you, don't it neither? Cats an' cats an' cats. There couldn't be all them cats. Let alone the cow. If she ain't the moral of the old man's Daisy. She's a dream out of when I was a lad—I don't mind 'er so much. 'Ere, Daisy, Daisy?'

The cow turned and looked at him.

'SHE'S all right,' he went on. 'Sort of company, too. Though them above knows how she got into this downstairs parlour. But them cats—oh, take 'em away, take 'em away! I'll chuck the 'ole show—Oh, take 'em away.'

'Burglar,' said Jane, close behind him, and he started convulsively, and turned on her a blank face, whose pale lips trembled. 'I can't take those cats away.'

'Lor' lumme!' exclaimed the man; 'if 'ere ain't another on 'em. Are you real, miss, or something I'll wake up from presently?'

'I am quite real,' said Jane, relieved to find that a lisp was not needed to make the burglar understand her. 'And so,' she added, 'are the cats.'

'Then send for the police, send for the police, and I'll go quiet. If you ain't no realler than them cats, I'm done, spunchuck—out of time. Send for the police. I'll go quiet. One thing, there'd not be room for 'arf them cats in no cell as ever *I* see.'

He ran his fingers through his hair, which was short, and his eyes wandered wildly round the roomful of cats.

'Burglar,' said Jane, kindly and softly, 'if you didn't like cats, what did you come here for?'

'Send for the police,' was the unfortunate criminal's only reply. 'I'd rather you would—honest, I'd rather.'

'I daren't,' said Jane, 'and besides, I've no one to send. I hate the police. I wish he'd never been born.'

'You've a feeling 'art, miss,' said the burglar; 'but them cats is really a little bit too thick.'

'Look here,' said Jane, 'I won't call the police. And I am quite a real little girl, though I talk older than the kind you've met before when you've been doing your burglings. And they are real cats—and they want real milk—and—Didn't you say the cow was like somebody's Daisy that you used to know?'

'Wish I may die if she ain't the very spit of her,' replied the man.

'Well, then,' said Jane—and a thrill of joyful pride ran through her—'perhaps you know how to milk cows?'

'Perhaps I does,' was the burglar's cautious rejoinder.

'Then,' said Jane, 'if you will ONLY milk ours—you don't know how we shall always love you.'

The burglar replied that loving was all very well.

'If those cats only had a good long, wet, thirsty drink of milk,' Jane went on with eager persuasion, 'they'd lie down and go to sleep as likely as not, and then the police won't come back. But if they go on mewing like this he will, and then I don't know what'll become of us, or you either.'

This argument seemed to decide the criminal. Jane fetched the wash-bowl from the sink, and he spat on his hands and prepared to milk the cow. At this instant boots were heard on the stairs.

'It's all up,' said the man, desperately, 'this 'ere's a plant. 'ERE'S the police.' He made as if to open the window and leap from it.

'It's all right, I tell you,' whispered Jane, in anguish. 'I'll say you're a friend of mine, or the good clergyman called in, or my uncle, or ANYTHIING—only do, do, do milk the cow. Oh, DON'T go—oh—oh, thank goodness it's only the boys!'

It was; and their entrance had awakened Anthea, who, with her brothers, now crowded through the doorway. The man looked about him like a rat looks round a trap.

'This is a friend of mine,' said Jane; 'he's just called in, and he's going to milk the cow for us. ISN'T it good and kind of him?'

She winked at the others, and though they did not understand they played up loyally.

'How do?' said Cyril, 'Very glad to meet you. Don't let us interrupt the milking.'

'I shall 'ave a 'ead and a 'arf in the morning, and no bloomin' error,' remarked the burglar; but he began to milk the cow.

Robert was winked at to stay and see that he did not leave off milking or try to escape, and the others went to get things to put the milk in; for it was now spurting and foaming in the wash-bowl, and the cats had ceased from mewing and were crowding round the cow, with expressions of hope and anticipation on their whiskered faces.

'We can't get rid of any more cats,' said Cyril, as he and his sisters piled a tray high with saucers and soup-plates and platters and pie-dishes, 'the police nearly got us as it was. Not the same one—a much stronger sort. He thought it really was a foundling orphan we'd got. If it hadn't been for me throwing the two bags of cat slap in his eye and hauling Robert over a railing, and lying like mice under a laurel-bush—Well, it's jolly lucky I'm a good shot, that's all. He pranced off when he'd got the cat-bags off his face—thought we'd bolted. And here we are.'

The gentle samishness of the milk swishing into the hand-bowl seemed to have soothed the burglar very much. He went on milking in a sort of happy dream, while the children got a cup and ladled the warm milk out into the pie-dishes and plates, and platters and saucers, and set them down to the music of Persian purrs and lappings.

'It makes me think of old times,' said the burglar, smearing his ragged coat-cuff across his eyes—'about the apples in the orchard at home, and the rats at threshing time, and the rabbits and the ferrets, and how pretty it was seeing the pigs killed.'

Finding him in this softened mood, Jane said—

'I wish you'd tell us how you came to choose our house for your burglaring to-night. I am awfully glad you did. You have been so kind. I don't know what we should have done without you,' she added hastily. 'We all love you ever so. Do tell us.'

The others added their affectionate entreaties, and at last the burglar said—

'Well, it's my first job, and I didn't expect to be made so welcome, and that's the truth, young gents and ladies. And I don't know but what it won't be my last. For this 'ere cow, she reminds me of my father, and I know 'ow 'e'd 'ave 'ided me if I'd laid 'ands on a 'a'penny as wasn't my own.'

'I'm sure he would,' Jane agreed kindly; 'but what made you come here?'

'Well, miss,' said the burglar, 'you know best 'ow you come by them cats, and why you don't like the police, so I'll give myself away free, and trust to your noble 'earts. (You'd best bale out a bit, the pan's getting fullish.) I was a-selling oranges off of my barrow—for I ain't a burglar by trade, though you 'ave used the name so free—an' there was a lady bought three 'a'porth off me. An' while she was a-pickin' of them out—very careful indeed, and I'm always glad when them sort gets a few over-ripe ones—there was two other ladies talkin' over the fence. An' one on 'em said to the other on 'em just like this—

"'I've told both gells to come, and they can doss in with M'ria and Jane, 'cause their boss and his missis is miles away and the kids too. So they can just lock up the 'ouse and leave the gas a-burning, so's no one won't know, and get back bright an' early by 'leven o'clock. And we'll make a night of it, Mrs Prosser, so we will. I'm just a-going to run out to pop the letter in the post." And then the lady what had chosen the three ha'porth so careful, she said: "Lor, Mrs Wigson, I wonder at you, and your hands all over suds. This good gentleman'll slip it into the post for yer, I'll be bound, seeing I'm a customer of his." So they give me the letter, and of course I read the direction what was written on it afore I shoved it into the post. And then when I'd sold my barrowful, I was a-goin' 'ome with the chink in my pocket, and I'm blowed if some bloomin' thievin' beggar didn't nick the lot whilst I was just a-wettin' of my whistle, for callin' of oranges is dry work. Nicked the bloomin' lot 'e did—and me with not a farden to take 'ome to my brother and his missus.'

'How awful!' said Anthea, with much sympathy.

'Horful indeed, miss, I believe yer,' the burglar rejoined, with deep feeling. 'You don't know her temper when she's roused. An' I'm sure I 'ope you never may, neither. And I'd 'ad all my oranges off of 'em. So it came back to me what was wrote on the ongverlope, and I says to myself, "Why not, seein' as I've been done myself, and if they keeps two slaveys there must be some pickings?" An' so 'ere I am. But them cats, they've brought me back to the ways of honestness. Never no more.'

'Look here,' said Cyril, 'these cats are very valuable—very indeed. And we will give them all to you, if only you will take them away.'

'I see they're a breedy lot,' replied the burglar. 'But I don't want no bother with the coppers. Did you come by them honest now? Straight?'

'They are all our very own,' said Anthea, 'we wanted them, but the confidement—'

'Consignment,' whispered Cyril.

'was larger than we wanted, and they're an awful bother. If you got your barrow, and some sacks or baskets, your brother's missus would be awfully pleased. My father says Persian cats are worth pounds and pounds each.'

'Well,' said the burglar—and he was certainly moved by her remarks—'I see you're in a hole—and I don't mind lending a helping 'and. I don't ask 'ow you come by them. But I've got a pal—'e's a mark on cats. I'll fetch him along, and if he thinks they'd fetch anything above their skins I don't mind doin' you a kindness.'

'You won't go away and never come back,' said Jane, 'because I don't think I COULD bear that.'

The burglar, quite touched by her emotion, swore sentimentally that, alive or dead, he would come back.

Then he went, and Cyril and Robert sent the girls to bed and sat up to wait for his return. It soon seemed absurd to await him in a state of wakefulness, but his stealthy tap on the window awoke them readily enough. For he did return, with the pal and the barrow and the sacks. The pal approved of the cats, now dormant in Persian repletion, and they were bundled into the sacks, and taken away on the barrow—mewing, indeed, but with mews too sleepy to attract public attention.

'I'm a fence—that's what I am,' said the burglar gloomily. 'I never thought I'd come down to this, and all acause er my kind 'eart.'

Cyril knew that a fence is a receiver of stolen goods, and he replied briskly—

'I give you my sacred the cats aren't stolen. What do you make the time?'

'I ain't got the time on me,' said the pal—'but it was just about chucking-out time as I come by the "Bull and Gate". I shouldn't wonder if it was nigh upon one now.'

When the cats had been removed, and the boys and the burglar had parted with warm expressions of friendship, there remained only the cow.

'She must stay all night,' said Robert. 'Cook'll have a fit when she sees her.'

'All night?' said Cyril. 'Why—it's tomorrow morning if it's one. We can have another wish!'

So the carpet was urged, in a hastily written note, to remove the cow to wherever she belonged, and to return to its proper place on the nursery floor. But the cow could not be got to move on to the carpet. So Robert got the clothes line out of the back kitchen, and tied one end very firmly to the cow's horns, and the other end to a bunched-up corner of the carpet, and said 'Fire away.'

And the carpet and cow vanished together, and the boys went to bed, tired out and only too thankful that the evening at last was over.

Next morning the carpet lay calmly in its place, but one corner was very badly torn. It was the corner that the cow had been tied on to.

Chapter 9. The Burglar's Bride

The morning after the adventure of the Persian cats, the musk-rats, the common cow, and the uncommon burglar, all the children slept till it was ten o'clock; and then it was only Cyril who woke; but he attended to the others, so that by half past ten every one was ready to help to get breakfast. It was shivery cold, and there was but little in the house that was really worth eating.

Robert had arranged a thoughtful little surprise for the absent servants. He had made a neat and delightful booby trap over the kitchen door, and as soon as they heard the front door click open and knew the servants had come back, all four children hid in the cupboard under the stairs and listened with delight to the entrance—the tumble, the splash, the scuffle, and the remarks of the servants. They heard the cook say it was a judgement on them for leaving the place to itself; she seemed to think that a booby trap was a kind of plant that was quite likely to grow, all by itself, in a dwelling that was left shut up. But the housemaid, more acute, judged that someone must have been in the house—a view confirmed by the sight of the breakfast things on the nursery table.

The cupboard under the stairs was very tight and paraffiny, however, and a silent struggle for a place on top ended in the door bursting open and discharging Jane, who rolled like a football to the feet of the servants.

'Now,' said Cyril, firmly, when the cook's hysterics had become quieter, and the housemaid had time to say what she thought of them, 'don't you begin jawing us. We aren't going to stand it. We know too much. You'll please make an extra special treacle roley for dinner, and we'll have a tinned tongue.'

'I daresay,' said the housemaid, indignant, still in her outdoor things and with her hat very much on one side. 'Don't you come a-threatening me, Master Cyril, because I won't stand it, so I tell you. You tell your ma about us being out? Much I care! She'll be sorry for me when she hears about my dear great-aunt by marriage as brought me up from a child and was a mother to me. She sent for me, she did, she wasn't expected to last the night, from the spasms going to her legs—and cook was that kind and careful she couldn't let me go alone, so—'

'Don't,' said Anthea, in real distress. 'You know where liars go to, Eliza—at least if you don't—'

'Liars indeed!' said Eliza, 'I won't demean myself talking to you.'

'How's Mrs Wigson?' said Robert, 'and DID you keep it up last night?'

The mouth of the housemaid fell open.

'Did you doss with Maria or Emily?' asked Cyril.

'How did Mrs Prosser enjoy herself?' asked Jane.

'Forbear,' said Cyril, 'they've had enough. Whether we tell or not depends on your later life,' he went on, addressing the servants. 'If you are decent to us we'll be decent to you. You'd better make that treacle roley—and if I were you, Eliza, I'd do a little housework and cleaning, just for a change.'

The servants gave in once and for all.

'There's nothing like firmness,' Cyril went on, when the breakfast things were cleared away and the children were alone in the nursery. 'People are always talking of difficulties with servants. It's quite simple, when you know the way. We can do what we like now and they won't peach. I think we've broken THEIR proud spirit. Let's go somewhere by carpet.'

'I wouldn't if I were you,' said the Phoenix, yawning, as it swooped down from its roost on the curtain pole. 'I've given you one or two hints, but now concealment is at an end, and I see I must speak out.'

It perched on the back of a chair and swayed to and fro, like a parrot on a swing.

'What's the matter now?' said Anthea. She was not quite so gentle as usual, because she was still weary from the excitement of last night's cats. 'I'm tired of things happening. I shan't go anywhere on the carpet. I'm going to darn my stockings.'

'Darn!' said the Phoenix, 'darn! From those young lips these strange expressions—'

'Mend, then,' said Anthea, 'with a needle and wool.'

The Phoenix opened and shut its wings thoughtfully.

'Your stockings,' it said, 'are much less important than they now appear to you. But the carpet—look at the bare worn patches, look at the great rent at yonder corner. The carpet has been your faithful friend—your willing servant. How have you requited its devoted service?'

'Dear Phoenix,' Anthea urged, 'don't talk in that horrid lecturing tone. You make me feel as if I'd done something wrong. And really it is a wishing carpet, and we haven't done anything else to it—only wishes.'

'Only wishes,' repeated the Phoenix, ruffling its neck feathers angrily, 'and what sort of wishes? Wishing people to be in a good temper, for instance. What carpet did you ever hear of that had such a wish asked of it? But this noble fabric, on which you trample so recklessly' (every one removed its boots from the carpet and stood on the linoleum), 'this carpet never flinched. It did what you asked, but the wear and tear must have been awful. And then last night—I don't blame you about the cats and the rats, for those were its own choice; but what carpet could stand a heavy cow hanging on to it at one corner?'

'I should think the cats and rats were worse,' said Robert, 'look at all their claws.'

'Yes,' said the bird, 'eleven thousand nine hundred and forty of them—I daresay you noticed? I should be surprised if these had not left their mark.'

'Good gracious,' said Jane, sitting down suddenly on the floor, and patting the edge of the carpet softly; 'do you mean it's WEARING OUT?'

'Its life with you has not been a luxurious one,' said the Phoenix.

'French mud twice. Sand of sunny shores twice. Soaking in southern seas once. India once. Goodness knows where in Persia once. musk-rat-land once. And once, wherever the cow came from. Hold your carpet up to the light, and with cautious tenderness, if YOU please.'

With cautious tenderness the boys held the carpet up to the light; the girls looked, and a shiver of regret ran through them as they saw how those eleven thoousand nine hundred and forty claws had run through the carpet. It was full of little holes: there were some large ones, and more than one thin place. At one corner a strip of it was torn, and hung forlornly.

'We must mend it,' said Anthea; 'never mind about my stockings. I can sew them up in lumps with sewing cotton if there's no time to do them properly. I know it's awful and no girl would who respected herself, and all that; but the poor dear carpet's more important than my silly stockings. Let's go out now this very minute.'

So out they all went, and bought wool to mend the carpet; but there is no shop in Camden Town where you can buy wishing-wool, no, nor in Kentish Town either. However, ordinary Scotch heather-mixture fingering seemed good enough, and this they bought, and all that -day Jane and Anthea darned and darned and darned. The boys went out for a walk in the afternoon, and the gentle Phoenix paced up and down the table—for exercise, as it said—and talked to the industrious girls about their carpet.

'It is not an ordinary, ignorant, innocent carpet from Kidderminster,' it said, 'it is a carpet with a past—a Persian past. Do you know that in happier years, when that carpet was the property of caliphs, viziers, kings, and sultans, it never lay on a floor?'

'I thought the floor was the proper home of a carpet,' Jane interrupted.

'Not of a MAGIC carpet,' said the Phoenix; 'why, if it had been allowed to lie about on floors there wouldn't be much of it left now. No, indeed! It has lived in chests of cedarwood, inlaid with pearl and ivory, wrapped in priceless tissues of cloth of gold, embroidered with gems of fabulous value. It has reposed in the sandal-wood caskets of princesses, and in the rose-attar-scented treasure-houses of kings. Never, never, had any one degraded it by walking on it—except in the way of business, when wishes were required, and then they always took their shoes off. And YOU—'

'Oh, DON'T!' said Jane, very near tears. 'You know you'd never have been hatched at all if it hadn't been for mother wanting a carpet for us to walk on.'

'You needn't have walked so much or so hard!' said the bird, 'but come, dry that crystal tear, and I will relate to you the story of the Princess Zulieka, the Prince of Asia, and the magic carpet.'

'Relate away,' said Anthea—'I mean, please do.'

'The Princess Zulieka, fairest of royal ladies,' began the bird, 'had in her cradle been the subject of several enchantments. Her grandmother had been in her day—'

But what in her day Zulieka's grandmother had been was destined never to be revealed, for Cyril and Robert suddenly burst into the room, and on each brow were the traces of deep emotion. On Cyril's pale brow stood beads of agitation and perspiration, and on the scarlet brow of Robert was a large black smear.

'What ails ye both?' asked the Phoenix, and it added tartly that story-telling was quite impossible if people would come interrupting like that.

'Oh, do shut up, for any sake!' said Cyril, sinking into a chair.

Robert smoothed the ruffled golden feathers, adding kindly—

'Squirrel doesn't mean to be a beast. It's only that the MOST AWFUL thing has happened, and stories don't seem to matter so much. Don't be cross. You won't be when you've heard what's happened.'

'Well, what HAS happened?' said the bird, still rather crossly; and Anthea and Jane paused with long needles poised in air, and long needlefuls of Scotch heather-mixture fingering wool drooping from them.

'The most awful thing you can possibly think of,' said Cyril. 'That nice chap—our own burglar—the police have got him, on suspicion of stolen cats. That's what his brother's missis told me.'

'Oh, begin at the beginning!' cried Anthea impatiently.

'Well, then, we went out, and down by where the undertaker's is, with the china flowers in the window—you know. There was a crowd, and of course we went to have a squint. And it was two bobbies and our burglar between them, and he was being dragged along; and he said, "I tell you them cats was GIVE me. I got 'em in exchange for me milking a cow in a basement parlour up Camden Town way."

'And the people laughed. Beasts! And then one of the policemen said perhaps he could give the name and address of the cow, and he said, no, he couldn't; but he could take them there if they'd only leave go of his coat collar, and give him a chance to get his breath. And the policeman said he could tell all that to the magistrate in the morning. He didn't see us, and so we came away.'

'Oh, Cyril, how COULD you?' said Anthea.

'Don't be a pudding-head,' Cyril advised. 'A fat lot of good it would have done if we'd let him see us. No one would have believed a word we said. They'd have thought we were kidding. We did better than let him see us. We asked a boy where he lived and he told us, and we went there, and it's a little greengrocer's shop, and we bought some Brazil nuts. Here they are.' The girls waved away the Brazil nuts with loathing and contempt.

'Well, we had to buy SOMETHING, and while we were making up our minds what to buy we heard his brother's missis talking. She said when he came home with all them miaoulers she thought there was more in it than met the eye. But he WOULD go out this morning with the two likeliest of them, one under each arm. She said he sent her out to buy blue ribbon to put round their beastly necks, and she said if he got three months' hard it was her dying word that he'd got the blue ribbon to thank for it; that, and his own silly thieving ways, taking cats that anybody would know he couldn't have come by in the way of business, instead of things that wouldn't have been missed, which Lord knows there are plenty such, and—'

'Oh, STOP!' cried Jane. And indeed it was time, for Cyril seemed like a clock that had been wound up, and could not help going on. 'Where is he now?'

'At the police-station,' said Robert, for Cyril was out of breath. 'The boy told us they'd put him in the cells, and would bring him up before the Beak in the morning. I thought it was a jolly lark last night—getting him to take the cats—but now—'

'The end of a lark,' said the Phoenix, 'is the Beak.'

'Let's go to him,' cried both the girls jumping up. 'Let's go and tell the truth. They MUST believe us.'

'They CAN'T,' said Cyril. 'Just think! If any one came to you with such a tale, you couldn't believe it, however much you tried. We should only mix things up worse for him.'

'There must be something we could do,' said Jane, sniffing very much—'my own dear pet burglar! I can't bear it. And he was so nice, the way he talked about his father, and how he was going to be so extra honest. Dear Phoenix, you MUST be able to help us. You're so good and kind and pretty and clever. Do, do tell us what to do.'

The Phoenix rubbed its beak thoughtfully with its claw.

'You might rescue him,' it said, 'and conceal him here, till the law-supporters had forgotten about him.'

'That would be ages and ages,' said Cyril, 'and we couldn't conceal him here. Father might come home at any moment, and if he found the burglar here HE wouldn't believe the true truth any more than the police would. That's the worst of the truth. Nobody ever believes it. Couldn't we take him somewhere else?'

Jane clapped her hands.

'The sunny southern shore!' she cried, 'where the cook is being queen. He and she would be company for each other!'

And really the idea did not seem bad, if only he would consent to go.

So, all talking at once, the children arranged to wait till evening, and then to seek the dear burglar in his lonely cell.

Meantime Jane and Anthea darned away as hard as they could, to make the carpet as strong as possible. For all felt how terrible it would be if the precious burglar, while being carried to the sunny southern shore, were to tumble through a hole in the carpet, and be lost for ever in the sunny southern sea.

The servants were tired after Mrs Wigson's party, so every one went to bed early, and when the Phoenix reported that both servants were snoring in a heartfelt and candid manner, the children got up—they had never undressed; just putting their nightgowns on over their things had been enough to deceive

Eliza when she came to turn out the gas. So they were ready for anything, and they stood on the carpet and said—

'I wish we were in our burglar's lonely cell.' and instantly they were.

I think every one had expected the cell to be the 'deepest dungeon below the castle moat'. I am sure no one had doubted that the burglar, chained by heavy fetters to a ring in the damp stone wall, would be tossing uneasily on a bed of straw, with a pitcher of water and a mouldering crust, untasted, beside him. Robert, remembering the underground passage and the treasure, had brought a candle and matches, but these were not needed.

The cell was a little white-washed room about twelve feet long and six feet wide. On one side of it was a sort of shelf sloping a little towards the wall. On this were two rugs, striped blue and yellow, and a water-proof pillow. Rolled in the rugs, and with his head on the pillow, lay the burglar, fast asleep. (He had had his tea, though this the children did not know—it had come from the coffee-shop round the corner, in very thick crockery.) The scene was plainly revealed by the light of a gas-lamp in the passage outside, which shone into the cell through a pane of thick glass over the door.

'I shall gag him,' said Cyril, 'and Robert will hold him down. Anthea and Jane and the Phoenix can whisper soft nothings to him while he gradually awakes.'

This plan did not have the success it deserved, because the burglar, curiously enough, was much stronger, even in his sleep, than Robert and Cyril, and at the first touch of their hands he leapt up and shouted out something very loud indeed.

Instantly steps were heard outside. Anthea threw her arms round the burglar and whispered—

'It's us—the ones that gave you the cats. We've come to save you, only don't let on we're here. Can't we hide somewhere?'

Heavy boots sounded on the flagged passage outside, and a firm voice shouted—

'Here—you—stop that row, will you?'

'All right, governor,' replied the burglar, still with Anthea's arms round him; 'I was only a-talking in my sleep. No offence.'

It was an awful moment. Would the boots and the voice come in. Yes! No! The voice said—

'Well, stow it, will you?'

And the boots went heavily away, along the passage and up some sounding stone stairs.

'Now then,' whispered Anthea.

'How the blue Moses did you get in?' asked the burglar, in a hoarse whisper of amazement.

'On the carpet,' said Jane, truly.

'Stow that,' said the burglar. 'One on you I could 'a' swallowed, but four—AND a yellow fowl.'

'Look here,' said Cyril, sternly, 'you wouldn't have believed any one if they'd told you beforehand about your finding a cow and all those cats in our nursery.'

'That I wouldn't,' said the burglar, with whispered fervour, 'so help me Bob, I wouldn't.'

'Well, then,' Cyril went on, ignoring this appeal to his brother, 'just try to believe what we tell you and act accordingly. It can't do you any HARM, you know,' he went on in hoarse whispered earnestness. 'You can't be very much worse off than you are now, you know. But if you'll just trust to us we'll get you out of this right enough. No one saw us come in. The question is, where would you like to go?'

'I'd like to go to Boolong,' was the instant reply of the burglar. 'I've always wanted to go on that there trip, but I've never 'ad the ready at the right time of the year.'

'Boolong is a town like London,' said Cyril, well meaning, but inaccurate, 'how could you get a living there?'

The burglar scratched his head in deep doubt.

'It's 'ard to get a 'onest living anywheres nowadays,' he said, and his voice was sad.

'Yes, isn't it?' said Jane, sympathetically; 'but how about a sunny southern shore, where there's nothing to do at all unless you want to.'

'That's my billet, miss,' replied the burglar. 'I never did care about work—not like some people, always fussing about.'

'Did you never like any sort of work?' asked Anthea, severely.

'Lor', lumme, yes,' he answered, 'gardening was my 'obby, so it was. But father died afore 'e could bind me to a nurseryman, an'- -'

'We'll take you to the sunny southern shore,' said Jane; 'you've no idea what the flowers are like.'

'Our old cook's there,' said Anthea. 'She's queen—'

'Oh, chuck it,' the burglar whispered, clutching at his head with both hands. 'I knowed the first minute I see them cats and that cow as it was a judgement on me. I don't know now whether I'm a-standing on my hat or my boots, so help me I don't. If you CAN get me out, get me, and if you can't, get along with you for goodness' sake, and give me a chanst to think about what'll be most likely to go down with the Beak in the morning.'

'Come on to the carpet, then,' said Anthea, gently shoving. The others quietly pulled, and the moment the feet of the burglar were planted on the carpet Anthea wished:

'I wish we were all on the sunny southern shore where cook is.'

And instantly they were. There were the rainbow sands, the tropic glories of leaf and flower, and there, of course, was the cook, crowned with white flowers, and with all the wrinkles of crossness and tiredness and hard work wiped out of her face.

'Why, cook, you're quite pretty!' Anthea said, as soon as she had got her breath after the tumble-rush-whirl of the carpet. The burglar stood rubbing his eyes in the brilliant tropic sunlight, and gazing wildly round him on the vivid hues of the tropic land.

'Penny plain and tuppence coloured!' he exclaimed pensively, 'and well worth any tuppence, however hard-earned.'

The cook was seated on a grassy mound with her court of copper-coloured savages around her. The burglar pointed a grimy finger at these.

'Are they tame?' he asked anxiously. 'Do they bite or scratch, or do anything to yer with poisoned arrows or oyster shells or that?'

'Don't you be so timid,' said the cook. 'Look'e 'ere, this 'ere's only a dream what you've come into, an' as it's only a dream there's no nonsense about what a young lady like me ought to say or not, so I'll say you're the best-looking fellow I've seen this many a day. And the dream goes on and on, seemingly, as long as you behaves. The things what you has to eat and drink tastes just as good as real ones, and—'

'Look 'ere,' said the burglar, 'I've come 'ere straight outer the pleece station. These 'ere kids'll tell you it ain't no blame er mine.'

'Well, you WERE a burglar, you know,' said the truthful Anthea gently.

'Only because I was druv to it by dishonest blokes, as well you knows, miss,' rejoined the criminal. 'Blowed if this ain't the 'ottest January as I've known for years.'

'Wouldn't you like a bath?' asked the queen, 'and some white clothes like me?'

'I should only look a juggins in 'em, miss, thanking you all the same,' was the reply; 'but a bath I wouldn't resist, and my shirt was only clean on week before last.'

Cyril and Robert led him to a rocky pool, where he bathed luxuriously. Then, in shirt and trousers he sat on the sand and spoke.

'That cook, or queen, or whatever you call her—her with the white bokay on her 'ed—she's my sort. Wonder if she'd keep company!'

'I should ask her.'

'I was always a quick hitter,' the man went on; 'it's a word and a blow with me. I will.'

In shirt and trousers, and crowned with a scented flowery wreath which Cyril hastily wove as they returned to the court of the queen, the burglar stood before the cook and spoke.

'Look 'ere, miss,' he said. 'You an' me being' all forlorn-like, both on us, in this 'ere dream, or whatever you calls it, I'd like to tell you straight as I likes yer looks.'

The cook smiled and looked down bashfully.

'I'm a single man—what you might call a batcheldore. I'm mild in my 'abits, which these kids'll tell you the same, and I'd like to 'ave the pleasure of walkin' out with you next Sunday.'

'Lor!' said the queen cook, "ow sudden you are, mister.'

'Walking out means you're going to be married,' said Anthea. 'Why not get married and have done with it? *I* would.'

'I don't mind if I do,' said the burglar. But the cook said—

'No, miss. Not me, not even in a dream. I don't say anythink ag'in the young chap's looks, but I always swore I'd be married in church, if at all—and, anyway, I don't believe these here savages would know how to keep a registering office, even if I was to show them. No, mister, thanking you kindly, if you can't bring a clergyman into the dream I'll live and die like what I am.'

'Will you marry her if we get a clergyman?' asked the match-making Anthea.

'I'm agreeable, miss, I m sure,' said he, pulling his wreath straight. "Ow this 'ere bokay do tiddle a chap's ears to be sure!'

So, very hurriedly, the carpet was spread out, and instructed to fetch a clergyman. The instructions were written on the inside of Cyril's cap with a piece of billiard chalk Robert had got from the marker at the hotel at Lyndhurst. The carpet disappeared, and more quickly than you would have thought possible it came back, bearing on its bosom the Reverend Septimus Blenkinsop.

The Reverend Septimus was rather a nice young man, but very much mazed and muddled, because when he saw a strange carpet laid out at his feet, in his own study, he naturally walked on it to examine it more closely. And he happened to stand on one of the thin places that Jane and Anthea had darned, so that he was half on wishing carpet and half on plain Scotch heather-mixture fingering, which has no magic properties at all.

The effect of this was that he was only half there—so that the children could just see through him, as though he had been a ghost. And as for him, he saw the sunny southern shore, the cook and the burglar and the children quite plainly; but through them all he saw, quite plainly also, his study at home, with the books and the pictures and the marble clock that had been presented to him when he left his last situation.

He seemed to himself to be in a sort of insane fit, so that it did not matter what he did—and he married the burglar to the cook. The cook said that she would rather have had a solider kind of a clergyman, one that you couldn't see through so plain, but perhaps this was real enough for a dream.

And of course the clergyman, though misty, was really real, and able to marry people, and he did. When the ceremony was over the clergyman wandered about the island collecting botanical specimens, for he was a great botanist, and the ruling passion was strong even in an insane fit.

There was a splendid wedding feast. Can you fancy Jane and Anthea, and Robert and Cyril, dancing merrily in a ring, hand-in-hand with copper-coloured savages, round the happy couple, the queen cook and the burglar consort? There were more flowers gathered and thrown than you have ever even dreamed of, and before the children took carpet for home the now married-and-settled burglar made a speech.

'Ladies and gentlemen,' he said, 'and savages of both kinds, only I know you can't understand what I'm a saying of, but we'll let that pass. If this is a dream, I'm on. If it ain't, I'm onner than ever. If it's betwixt and between—well, I'm honest, and I can't say more. I don't want no more 'igh London society—I've got some one to put my arm around of; and I've got the whole lot of this 'ere island for my allotment, and if I don't grow some broccoli as'll open the judge's eye at the cottage flower shows, well, strike me pink! All I ask is, as these young gents and ladies'll bring some parsley seed into the dream, and a penn'orth of radish seed, and threepenn'orth of onion, and I wouldn't mind goin' to fourpence or fippence for mixed kale, only I ain't got a brown, so I don't deceive you. And there's one thing more, you might take away the parson. I don't like things what I can see 'alf through, so here's how!' He drained a coconut-shell of palm wine.

It was now past midnight—though it was tea-time on the island.

With all good wishes the children took their leave. They also collected the clergyman and took him back to his study and his presentation clock.

The Phoenix kindly carried the seeds next day to the burglar and his bride, and returned with the most satisfactory news of the happy pair.

'He's made a wooden spade and started on his allotment,' it said, 'and she is weaving him a shirt and trousers of the most radiant whiteness.'

The police never knew how the burglar got away. In Kentish Town Police Station his escape is still spoken of with bated breath as the Persian mystery.

As for the Reverend Septimus Blenkinsop, he felt that he had had a very insane fit indeed, and he was sure it was due to over-study. So he planned a little dissipation, and took his two maiden aunts to Paris, where they enjoyed a dazzling round of museums and picture galleries, and came back feeling that they had indeed seen life. He never told his aunts or any one else about the marriage on the island—because no one likes it to be generally known if he has had insane fits, however interesting and unusual.

Chapter 10. The Hole in the Carpet

Hooray! hooray! hooray!
Mother comes home to-day;
Mother comes home to-day,
Hooray! hooray! hooray!'

Jane sang this simple song directly after breakfast, and the Phoenix shed crystal tears of affectionate sympathy.

'How beautiful,' it said, 'is filial devotion!'

'She won't be home till past bedtime, though,' said Robert. 'We might have one more carpet-day.'

He was glad that mother was coming home—quite glad, very glad; but at the same time that gladness was rudely contradicted by a quite strong feeling of sorrow, because now they could not go out all day on the carpet.

'I do wish we could go and get something nice for mother, only she'd want to know where we got it,' said Anthea. 'And she'd never, never believe it, the truth. People never do, somehow, if it's at all interesting.'

'I'll tell you what,' said Robert. 'Suppose we wished the carpet to take us somewhere where we could find a purse with money in it—then we could buy her something.'

'Suppose it took us somewhere foreign, and the purse was covered with strange Eastern devices, embroidered in rich silks, and full of money that wasn't money at all here, only foreign curiosities, then we couldn't spend it, and people would bother about where we got it, and we shouldn't know how on earth to get out of it at all.'

Cyril moved the table off the carpet as he spoke, and its leg caught in one of Anthea's darns and ripped away most of it, as well as a large slit in the carpet.

'Well, now you HAVE done it,' said Robert.

But Anthea was a really first-class sister. She did not say a word till she had got out the Scotch heather-mixture fingering wool and the darning-needle and the thimble and the scissors, and by that time she had been able to get the better of her natural wish to be thoroughly disagreeable, and was able to say quite kindly—

'Never mind, Squirrel, I'll soon mend it.'

Cyril thumped her on the back. He understood exactly how she had felt, and he was not an ungrateful brother.

'Respecting the purse containing coins,' the Phoenix said, scratching its invisible ear thoughtfully with its shining claw, 'it might be as well, perhaps, to state clearly the amount which you wish to find, as well as the country where you wish to find it, and the nature of the coins which you prefer. It would be indeed a cold moment when you should find a purse containing but three oboloi.'

'How much is an oboloi?'

'An obol is about twopence halfpenny,' the Phoenix replied.

'Yes,' said Jane, 'and if you find a purse I suppose it is only because some one has lost it, and you ought to take it to the policeman.'

'The situation,' remarked the Phoenix, 'does indeed bristle with difficulties.'

'What about a buried treasure,' said Cyril, 'and every one was dead that it belonged to?'

'Mother wouldn't believe THAT,' said more than one voice.

'Suppose,' said Robert—'suppose we asked to be taken where we could find a purse and give it back to the person it belonged to, and they would give us something for finding it?'

'We aren't allowed to take money from strangers. You know we aren't, Bobs,' said Anthea, making a knot at the end of a needleful of Scotch heather-mixture fingering wool (which is very wrong, and you must never do it when you are darning).

'No, THAT wouldn't do,' said Cyril. 'Let's chuck it and go to the North Pole, or somewhere really interesting.'

'No,' said the girls together, 'there must be SOME way.'

'Wait a sec,' Anthea added. 'I've got an idea coming. Don't speak.'

There was a silence as she paused with the darning-needle in the air! Suddenly she spoke:

'I see. Let's tell the carpet to take us somewhere where we can get the money for mother's present, and—and—and get it some way that she'll believe in and not think wrong.'

'Well, I must say you are learning the way to get the most out of the carpet,' said Cyril. He spoke more heartily and kindly than usual, because he remembered how Anthea had refrained from snarking him about tearing the carpet.

'Yes,' said the Phoenix, 'you certainly are. And you have to remember that if you take a thing out it doesn't stay in.'

No one paid any attention to this remark at the time, but afterwards every one thought of it.

'Do hurry up, Panther,' said Robert; and that was why Anthea did hurry up, and why the big darn in the middle of the carpet was all open and webby like a fishing net, not tight and close like woven cloth, which is what a good, well-behaved darn should be.

Then every one put on its outdoor things, the Phoenix fluttered on to the mantelpiece and arranged its golden feathers in the glass, and all was ready. Every one got on to the carpet.

'Please go slowly, dear carpet,' Anthea began; we like to see where we're going.' And then she added the difficult wish that had been decided on.

Next moment the carpet, stiff and raftlike, was sailing over the roofs of Kentish Town.

'I wish—No, I don't mean that. I mean it's a PITY we aren't higher up,' said Anthea, as the edge of the carpet grazed a chimney-pot.

'That's right. Be careful,' said the Phoenix, in warning tones. 'If you wish when you're on a wishing carpet, you DO wish, and there's an end of it.'

So for a short time no one spoke, and the carpet sailed on in calm magnificence over St Pancras and King's Cross stations and over the crowded streets of Clerkenwell.

'We're going out Greenwich way,' said Cyril, as they crossed the streak of rough, tumbled water that was the Thames. 'We might go and have a look at the Palace.'

On and on the carpet swept, still keeping much nearer to the chimney-pots than the children found at all comfortable. And then, just over New Cross, a terrible thing happened.

Jane and Robert were in the middle of the carpet. Part of them was on the carpet, and part of them—the heaviest part—was on the great central darn.

'It's all very misty,' said Jane; 'it looks partly like out of doors and partly like in the nursery at home. I feel as if I was going to have measles; everything looked awfully rum then, remember.'

'I feel just exactly the same,' Robert said.

'It's the hole,' said the Phoenix; 'it's not measles whatever that possession may be.'

And at that both Robert and Jane suddenly, and at once, made a bound to try and get on to the safer part of the carpet, and the darn gave way and their boots went up, and the heavy heads and bodies of them went down through the hole, and they landed in a position something between sitting and sprawling on the flat leads on the top of a high, grey, gloomy, respectable house whose address was 705, Amersham Road, New Cross.

The carpet seemed to awaken to new energy as soon as it had got rid of their weight, and it rose high in the air. The others lay down flat and peeped over the edge of the rising carpet.

'Are you hurt?' cried Cyril, and Robert shouted 'No,' and next moment the carpet had sped away, and Jane and Robert were hidden from the sight of the others by a stack of smoky chimneys.

'Oh, how awful!' said Anthea.

'It might have been worse,' said the Phoenix. 'What would have been the sentiments of the survivors if that darn had given way when we were crossing the river?'

'Yes, there's that,' said Cyril, recovering himself. 'They'll be all right. They'll howl till some one gets them down, or drop tiles into the front garden to attract attention of passersby. Bobs has got my one-and-fivepence—lucky you forgot to mend that hole in my pocket, Panther, or he wouldn't have had it. They can tram it home.'

But Anthea would not be comforted.

'It's all my fault,' she said. 'I KNEW the proper way to darn, and I didn't do it. It's all my fault. Let's go home and patch the carpet with your Etons—something really strong—and send it to fetch them.'

'All right,' said Cyril; 'but your Sunday jacket is stronger than my Etons. We must just chuck mother's present, that's all. I wish—'

'Stop!' cried the Phoenix; 'the carpet is dropping to earth.'

And indeed it was.

It sank swiftly, yet steadily, and landed on the pavement of the Deptford Road. It tipped a little as it landed, so that Cyril and Anthea naturally walked off it, and in an instant it had rolled itself up and hidden behind a gate-post. It did this so quickly that not a single person in the Deptford Road noticed it. The Phoenix rustled its way into the breast of Cyril's coat, and almost at the same moment a well-known voice remarked—

'Well, I never! What on earth are you doing here?'

They were face to face with their pet uncle—their Uncle Reginald.

'We DID think of going to Greenwich Palace and talking about Nelson,' said Cyril, telling as much of the truth as he thought his uncle could believe.

'And where are the others?' asked Uncle Reginald.

'I don't exactly know,' Cyril replied, this time quite truthfully.

'Well,' said Uncle Reginald, 'I must fly. I've a case in the County Court. That's the worst of being a beastly solicitor. One can't take the chances of life when one gets them. If only I could come with you to the Painted Hall and give you lunch at the "Ship" afterwards! But, alas! it may not be.'

The uncle felt in his pocket.

'*I* mustn't enjoy myself,' he said, 'but that's no reason why you shouldn't. Here, divide this by four, and the product ought to give you some desired result. Take care of yourselves. Adieu.'

And waving a cheery farewell with his neat umbrella, the good and high-hatted uncle passed away, leaving Cyril and Anthea to exchange eloquent glances over the shining golden sovereign that lay in Cyril's hand.

'Well!' said Anthea.

'Well!' said Cyril.

'Well!' said the Phoenix.

'Good old carpet!' said Cyril, joyously.

'It WAS clever of it—so adequate and yet so simple,' said the Phoenix, with calm approval.

'Oh, come on home and let's mend the carpet. I am a beast. I'd forgotten the others just for a minute,' said the conscience-stricken Anthea.

They unrolled the carpet quickly and slyly—they did not want to attract public attention—and the moment their feet were on the carpet Anthea wished to be at home, and instantly they were.

The kindness of their excellent uncle had made it unnecessary for them to go to such extremes as Cyril's Etons or Anthea's Sunday jacket for the patching of the carpet.

Anthea set to work at once to draw the edges of the broken darn together, and Cyril hastily went out and bought a large piece of the marble-patterned American oil-cloth which careful housewives use to cover dressers and kitchen tables. It was the strongest thing he could think of.

Then they set to work to line the carpet throughout with the oil-cloth. The nursery felt very odd and empty without the others, and Cyril did not feel so sure as he had done about their being able to 'tram it' home. So he tried to help Anthea, which was very good of him, but not much use to her.

The Phoenix watched them for a time, but it was plainly growing more and more restless. It fluffed up its splendid feathers, and stood first on one gilded claw and then on the other, and at last it said—

'I can bear it no longer. This suspense! My Robert—who set my egg to hatch—in the bosom of whose Norfolk raiment I have nestled so often and so pleasantly! I think, if you'll excuse me—'

'Yes—DO,' cried Anthea, 'I wish we'd thought of asking you before.'

Cyril opened the window. The Phoenix flapped its sunbright wings and vanished.

'So THAT'S all right,' said Cyril, taking up his needle and instantly pricking his hand in a new place.

Of course I know that what you have really wanted to know about all this time is not what Anthea and Cyril did, but what happened to Jane and Robert after they fell through the carpet on to the leads of the house which was called number 705, Amersham Road.

But I had to tell you the other first. That is one of the most annoying things about stories, you cannot tell all the different parts of them at the same time.

Robert's first remark when he found himself seated on the damp, cold, sooty leads was—

'Here's a go!'

Jane's first act was tears.

'Dry up, Pussy; don't be a little duffer,' said her brother, kindly, 'it'll be all right.'

And then he looked about, just as Cyril had known he would, for something to throw down, so as to attract the attention of the wayfarers far below in the street. He could not find anything. Curiously enough, there were no stones on the leads, not even a loose tile. The roof was of slate, and every single slate knew its place and kept it. But, as so often happens, in looking for one thing he found another. There was a trap-door leading down into the house.

And that trap-door was not fastened.

'Stop snivelling and come here, Jane,' he cried, encouragingly. 'Lend a hand to heave this up. If we can get into the house, we might sneak down without meeting any one, with luck. Come on.'

They heaved up the door till it stood straight up, and, as they bent to look into the hole below, the door fell back with a hollow clang on the leads behind, and with its noise was mingled a blood-curdling scream from underneath.

'Discovered!' hissed Robert. 'Oh, my cats alive!'

They were indeed discovered.

They found themselves looking down into an attic, which was also a lumber-room. It had boxes and broken chairs, old fenders and picture-frames, and rag-bags hanging from nails.

In the middle of the floor was a box, open, half full of clothes. Other clothes lay on the floor in neat piles. In the middle of the piles of clothes sat a lady, very fat indeed, with her feet sticking out straight in front of her. And it was she who had screamed, and who, in fact, was still screaming.

'Don't!' cried Jane, 'please don't! We won't hurt you.'

'Where are the rest of your gang?' asked the lady, stopping short in the middle of a scream.

'The others have gone on, on the wishing carpet,' said Jane truthfully.

'The wishing carpet?' said the lady.

'Yes,' said Jane, before Robert could say 'You shut up!' 'You must have read about it. The Phoenix is with them.'

Then the lady got up, and picking her way carefully between the piles of clothes she got to the door and through it. She shut it behind her, and the two children could hear her calling 'Septimus! Septimus!' in a loud yet frightened way.

'Now,' said Robert quickly; 'I'll drop first.'

He hung by his hands and dropped through the trap-door.

'Now you. Hang by your hands. I'll catch you. Oh, there's no time for jaw. Drop, I say.'

Jane dropped.

Robert tried to catch her, and even before they had finished the breathless roll among the piles of clothes, which was what his catching ended in, he whispered—

'We'll hide—behind those fenders and things; they'll think we've gone along the roofs. Then, when all is calm, we'll creep down the stairs and take our chance.'

They hastily hid. A corner of an iron bedstead stuck into Robert's side, and Jane had only standing room for one foot—but they bore it—and when the lady came back, not with Septimus, but with another lady, they held their breath and their hearts beat thickly.

'Gone!' said the first lady; 'poor little things—quite mad, my dear—and at large! We must lock this room and send for the police.'

'Let me look out,' said the second lady, who was, if possible, older and thinner and primmer than the first. So the two ladies dragged a box under the trap-door and put another box on the top of it, and then they both climbed up very carefully and put their two trim, tidy heads out of the trap-door to look for the 'mad children'.

'Now,' whispered Robert, getting the bedstead leg out of his side.

They managed to creep out from their hiding-place and out through the door before the two ladies had done looking out of the trap-door on to the empty leads.

Robert and Jane tiptoed down the stairs—one flight, two flights. Then they looked over the banisters. Horror! a servant was coming up with a loaded scuttle.

The children with one consent crept swiftly through the first open door.

The room was a study, calm and gentlemanly, with rows of books, a writing table, and a pair of embroidered slippers warming themselves in the fender. The children hid behind the window-curtains. As they passed the table they saw on it a missionary-box with its bottom label torn off, open and empty.

'Oh, how awful!' whispered Jane. 'We shall never get away alive.'

'Hush!' said Robert, not a moment too soon, for there were steps on the stairs, and next instant the two ladies came into the room. They did not see the children, but they saw the empty missionary box.

'I knew it,' said one. 'Selina, it WAS a gang. I was certain of it from the first. The children were not mad. They were sent to distract our attention while their confederates robbed the house.'

'I am afraid you are right,' said Selina; 'and WHERE ARE THEY NOW?'

'Downstairs, no doubt, collecting the silver milk-jug and sugar-basin and the punch-ladle that was Uncle Joe's, and Aunt Jerusha's teaspoons. I shall go down.'

'Oh, don't be so rash and heroic,' said Selina. 'Amelia, we must call the police from the window. Lock the door. I WILL—I will—'

The words ended in a yell as Selina, rushing to the window, came face to face with the hidden children.

'Oh, don't!' said Jane; 'how can you be so unkind? We AREN'T burglars, and we haven't any gang, and we didn't open your missionary-box. We opened our own once, but we didn't have to use the money, so our consciences made us put it back and—DON'T! Oh, I wish you wouldn't—'

Miss Selina had seized Jane and Miss Amelia captured Robert. The children found themselves held fast by strong, slim hands, pink at the wrists and white at the knuckles.

'We've got YOU, at any rate,' said Miss Amelia. 'Selina, your captive is smaller than mine. You open the window at once and call "Murder!" as loud as you can.

Selina obeyed; but when she had opened the window, instead of calling 'Murder!' she called 'Septimus!' because at that very moment she saw her nephew coming in at the gate.

In another minute he had let himself in with his latch-key and had mounted the stairs. As he came into the room Jane and Robert each uttered a shriek of joy so loud and so sudden that the ladies leaped with surprise, and nearly let them go.

'It's our own clergyman,' cried Jane.

'Don't you remember us?' asked Robert. 'You married our burglar for us—don't you remember?'

'I KNEW it was a gang,' said Amelia. 'Septimus, these abandoned children are members of a desperate burgling gang who are robbing the house. They have already forced the missionary-box and purloined its contents.'

The Reverend Septimus passed his hand wearily over his brow.

'I feel a little faint,' he said, 'running upstairs so quickly.'

'We never touched the beastly box,' said Robert.

'Then your confederates did,' said Miss Selina.

'No, no,' said the curate, hastily. '*I* opened the box myself. This morning I found I had not enough small change for the Mothers' Independent Unity Measles and Croup Insurance payments. I suppose this is NOT a dream, is it?'

'Dream? No, indeed. Search the house. I insist upon it.'

The curate, still pale and trembling, searched the house, which, of course, was blamelessly free of burglars.

When he came back he sank wearily into his chair.

'Aren't you going to let us go?' asked Robert, with furious indignation, for there is something in being held by a strong lady that sets the blood of a boy boiling in his veins with anger and despair. 'We've never done anything to you. It's all the carpet. It dropped us on the leads. WE couldn't help it. You know how it carried you over to the island, and you had to marry the burglar to the cook.'

'Oh, my head!' said the curate.

'Never mind your head just now,' said Robert; 'try to be honest and honourable, and do your duty in that state of life!'

'This is a judgement on me for something, I suppose,' said the Reverend Septimus, wearily, 'but I really cannot at the moment remember what.'

'Send for the police,' said Miss Selina.

'Send for a doctor,' said the curate.

'Do you think they ARE mad, then,' said Miss Amelia.

'I think I am,' said the curate.

Jane had been crying ever since her capture. Now she said—'You aren't now, but perhaps you will be, if—And it would serve you jolly well right, too.'

'Aunt Selina,' said the curate, 'and Aunt Amelia, believe me, this is only an insane dream. You will realize it soon. It has happened to me before. But do not let us be unjust, even in a dream. Do not hold the children; they have done no harm. As I said before, it was I who opened the box.'

The strong, bony hands unwillingly loosened their grasp. Robert shook himself and stood in sulky resentment. But Jane ran to the curate and embraced him so suddenly that he had not time to defend himself.

'You're a dear,' she said. 'It IS like a dream just at first, but you get used to it. Now DO let us go. There's a good, kind, honourable clergyman.'

'I don't know,' said the Reverend Septimus; 'it's a difficult problem. It is such a very unusual dream. Perhaps it's only a sort of other life—quite real enough for you to be mad in. And if you're mad, there might be a dream-asylum where you'd be kindly treated, and in time restored, cured, to your sorrowing relatives. It is very hard to see your duty plainly, even in ordinary life, and these dream-circumstances are so complicated—'

'If it's a dream,' said Robert, 'you will wake up directly, and then you'd be sorry if you'd sent us into a dream-asylum, because you might never get into the same dream again and let us out, and so we might stay there for ever, and then what about our sorrowing relatives who aren't in the dreams at all?'

But all the curate could now say was, 'Oh, my head!'

And Jane and Robert felt quite ill with helplessness and hopelessness. A really conscientious curate is a very difficult thing to manage.

And then, just as the hopelessness and the helplessness were getting to be almost more than they could bear, the two children suddenly felt that extraordinary shrinking feeling that you always have when you are just going to vanish. And the next moment they had vanished, and the Reverend Septimus was left alone with his aunts.

'I knew it was a dream,' he cried, wildly. 'I've had something like it before. Did you dream it too, Aunt Selina, and you, Aunt Amelia? I dreamed that you did, you know.'

Aunt Selina looked at him and then at Aunt Amelia. Then she said boldly—

'What do you mean? WE haven't been dreaming anything. You must have dropped off in your chair.'

The curate heaved a sigh of relief.

'Oh, if it's only *I*,' he said; 'if we'd all dreamed it I could never have believed it, never!'

Afterwards Aunt Selina said to the other aunt—

'Yes, I know it was an untruth, and I shall doubtless be punished for it in due course. But I could see the poor dear fellow's brain giving way before my very eyes. He couldn't have stood the strain of three dreams. It WAS odd, wasn't it? All three of us dreaming the same thing at the same moment. We must never tell dear Seppy. But I shall send an account of it to the Psychical Society, with stars instead of names, you know.'

And she did. And you can read all about it in one of the society's fat Blue-books.

Of course, you understand what had happened? The intelligent Phoenix had simply gone straight off to the Psammead, and had wished Robert and Jane at home. And, of course, they were at home at once. Cyril and Anthea had not half finished mending the carpet.

When the joyful emotions of reunion had calmed down a little, they all went out and spent what was left of Uncle Reginald's sovereign in presents for mother. They bought her a pink silk handkerchief, a pair of blue and white vases, a bottle of scent, a packet of Christmas candles, and a cake of soap shaped and coloured like a tomato, and one that was so like an orange that almost any one you had given it to would have tried to peel it—if they liked oranges, of course. Also they bought a cake with icing on, and the rest of the money they spent on flowers to put in the vases.

When they had arranged all the things on a table, with the candles stuck up on a plate ready to light the moment mother's cab was heard, they washed themselves thoroughly and put on tidier clothes.

Then Robert said, 'Good old Psammead,' and the others said so too.

'But, really, it's just as much good old Phoenix,' said Robert. 'Suppose it hadn't thought of getting the wish!'

'Ah!' said the Phoenix, 'it is perhaps fortunate for you that I am such a competent bird.'

'There's mother's cab,' cried Anthea, and the Phoenix hid and they lighted the candles, and next moment mother was home again.

She liked her presents very much, and found their story of Uncle Reginald and the sovereign easy and even pleasant to believe.

'Good old carpet,' were Cyril's last sleepy words.

'What there is of it,' said the Phoenix, from the cornice-pole.

Chapter 11. The Beginning of the End

'Well, I MUST say,' mother said, looking at the wishing carpet as it lay, all darned and mended and backed with shiny American cloth, on the floor of the nursery—'I MUST say I've never in my life bought such a bad bargain as that carpet.'

A soft 'Oh!' of contradiction sprang to the lips of Cyril, Robert, Jane, and Anthea. Mother looked at them quickly, and said—

'Well, of course, I see you've mended it very nicely, and that was sweet of you, dears.'

'The boys helped too,' said the dears, honourably.

'But, still—twenty-two and ninepence! It ought to have lasted for years. It's simply dreadful now. Well, never mind, darlings, you've done your best. I think we'll have coconut matting next time. A carpet doesn't have an easy life of it in this room, does it?'

'It's not our fault, mother, is it, that our boots are the really reliable kind?' Robert asked the question more in sorrow than in anger.

'No, dear, we can't help our boots,' said mother, cheerfully, 'but we might change them when we come in, perhaps. It's just an idea of mine. I wouldn't dream of scolding on the very first morning after I've come home. Oh, my Lamb, how could you?'

This conversation was at breakfast, and the Lamb had been beautifully good until every one was looking at the carpet, and then it was for him but the work of a moment to turn a glass dish of syrupy blackberry jam upside down on his young head. It was the work of a good many minutes and several persons to get the jam off him again, and this interesting work took people's minds off the carpet, and nothing more was said just then about its badness as a bargain and about what mother hoped for from coconut matting.

When the Lamb was clean again he had to be taken care of while mother rumpled her hair and inked her fingers and made her head ache over the difficult and twisted house-keeping accounts which cook gave her on dirty bits of paper, and which were supposed to explain how it was that cook had only fivepence-half-penny and a lot of unpaid bills left out of all the money mother had sent her for house-keeping. Mother was very clever, but even she could not quite understand the cook's accounts.

The Lamb was very glad to have his brothers and sisters to play with him. He had not forgotten them a bit, and he made them play all the old exhausting games: 'Whirling Worlds', where you swing the baby round and round by his hands; and 'Leg and Wing', where you swing him from side to side by one ankle and one wrist. There was also climbing Vesuvius. In this game the baby walks up you, and when he is standing on your shoulders, you shout as loud as you can, which is the rumbling of the burning mountain, and then tumble him gently on to the floor, and roll him there, which is the destruction of Pompeii.

'All the same, I wish we could decide what we'd better say next time mother says anything about the carpet,' said Cyril, breathlessly ceasing to be a burning mountain.

'Well, you talk and decide,' said Anthea; 'here, you lovely ducky Lamb. Come to Panther and play Noah's Ark.'

The Lamb came with his pretty hair all tumbled and his face all dusty from the destruction of Pompeii, and instantly became a baby snake, hissing and wriggling and creeping in Anthea's arms, as she said—

'I love my little baby snake,
He hisses when he is awake,
He creeps with such a wriggly creep,
He wriggles even in his sleep.'

'Crocky,' said the Lamb, and showed all his little teeth. So Anthea went on—

'I love my little crocodile,
I love his truthful toothful smile;
It is so wonderful and wide,
I like to see it—FROM OUTSIDE.'

'Well, you see,' Cyril was saying; 'it's just the old bother. Mother can't believe the real true truth about the carpet, and—'

'You speak sooth, O Cyril,' remarked the Phoenix, coming out from the cupboard where the blackbeetles lived, and the torn books, and the broken slates, and odd pieces of toys that had lost the rest of themselves. 'Now hear the wisdom of Phoenix, the son of the Phoenix—'

'There is a society called that,' said Cyril.

'Where is it? And what is a society?' asked the bird.

'It's a sort of joined-together lot of people—a sort of brotherhood—a kind of—well, something very like your temple, you know, only quite different.'

'I take your meaning,' said the Phoenix. 'I would fain see these calling themselves Sons of the Phoenix'

'But what about your words of wisdom?'

'Wisdom is always welcome,' said the Phoenix.

'Pretty Polly!' remarked the Lamb, reaching his hands towards the golden speaker.

The Phoenix modestly retreated behind Robert, and Anthea hastened to distract the attention of the Lamb by murmuring—

"I love my little baby rabbit;
But oh! he has a dreadful habit
Of paddling out among the rocks
And soaking both his bunny socks.'

'I don't think you'd care about the sons of the Phoenix, really,' said Robert. 'I have heard that they don't do anything fiery. They only drink a great deal. Much more than other people, because they drink lemonade and fizzy things, and the more you drink of those the more good you get.'

'In your mind, perhaps,' said Jane; 'but it wouldn't be good in your body. You'd get too balloony.'

The Phoenix yawned.

'Look here,' said Anthea; 'I really have an idea. This isn't like a common carpet. It's very magic indeed. Don't you think, if we put Tatcho on it, and then gave it a rest, the magic part of it might grow, like hair is supposed to do?'

'It might,' said Robert; 'but I should think paraffin would do as well—at any rate as far as the smell goes, and that seems to be the great thing about Tatcho.'

But with all its faults Anthea's idea was something to do, and they did it.

It was Cyril who fetched the Tatcho bottle from father's washhand-stand. But the bottle had not much in it.

'We mustn't take it all,' Jane said, 'in case father's hair began to come off suddenly. If he hadn't anything to put on it, it might all drop off before Eliza had time to get round to the chemist's for another bottle. It would be dreadful to have a bald father, and it would all be our fault.'

'And wigs are very expensive, I believe,' said Anthea. 'Look here, leave enough in the bottle to wet father's head all over with in case any emergency emerges—and let's make up with paraffin. I expect it's the smell that does the good really—and the smell's exactly the same.'

So a small teaspoonful of the Tatcho was put on the edges of the worst darn in the carpet and rubbed carefully into the roots of the hairs of it, and all the parts that there was not enough Tatcho for had paraffin rubbed into them with a piece of flannel. Then the flannel was burned. It made a gay flame, which delighted the Phoenix and the Lamb.

'How often,' said mother, opening the door—'how often am I to tell you that you are NOT to play with paraffin? What have you been doing?'

'We have burnt a paraffiny rag,' Anthea answered.

It was no use telling mother what they had done to the carpet. She did not know it was a magic carpet, and no one wants to be laughed at for trying to mend an ordinary carpet with lamp-oil.

'Well, don't do it again,' said mother. 'And now, away with melancholy! Father has sent a telegram. Look!' She held it out, and the children, holding it by its yielding corners, read—

'Box for kiddies at Garrick.
Stalls for us, Haymarket.
Meet Charing Cross, 6.30.'

'That means,' said mother, 'that you're going to see "The Water Babies" all by your happy selves, and father and I will take you and fetch you. Give me the Lamb, dear, and you and Jane put clean lace in your red evening frocks, and I shouldn't wonder if you found they wanted ironing. This paraffin smell is ghastly. Run and get out your frocks.'

The frocks did want ironing—wanted it rather badly, as it happened; for, being of tomato-Coloured Liberty silk, they had been found very useful for tableaux vivants when a red dress was required for Cardinal Richelieu. They were very nice tableaux, these, and I wish I could tell you about them; but one cannot tell everything in a story. You would have been specially interested in hearing about the tableau of the Princes in the Tower, when one of the pillows burst, and the youthful Princes were so covered with feathers that the picture might very well have been called 'Michaelmas Eve; or, Plucking the Geese'.

Ironing the dresses and sewing the lace in occupied some time, and no one was dull, because there was the theatre to look forward to, and also the possible growth of hairs on the carpet, for which every one kept looking anxiously. By four o'clock Jane was almost sure that several hairs were beginning to grow.

The Phoenix perched on the fender, and its conversation, as usual, was entertaining and instructive—like school prizes are said to be. But it seemed a little absent-minded, and even a little sad.

'Don't you feel well, Phoenix, dear?' asked Anthea, stooping to take an iron off the fire.

'I am not sick,' replied the golden bird, with a gloomy shake of the head; 'but I am getting old.'

'Why, you've hardly been hatched any time at all.'

'Time,' remarked the Phoenix, 'is measured by heartbeats. I'm sure the palpitations I've had since I've known you are enough to blanch the feathers of any bird.'

'But I thought you lived 500 years,' said Robert, and you've hardly begun this set of years. Think of all the time that's before you.'

'Time,' said the Phoenix, 'is, as you are probably aware, merely a convenient fiction. There is no such thing as time. I have lived in these two months at a pace which generously counterbalances 500 years of life in the desert. I am old, I am weary. I feel as if I ought to lay my egg, and lay me down to my fiery sleep. But unless I'm careful I shall be hatched again instantly, and that is a misfortune which I really do not think I COULD endure. But do not let me intrude these desperate personal reflections on your youthful happiness. What is the show at the theatre to-night? Wrestlers? Gladiators? A combat of cameleopards and unicorns?'

'I don't think so,' said Cyril; 'it's called "The Water Babies", and if it's like the book there isn't any gladiating in it. There are chimney-sweeps and professors, and a lobster and an otter and a salmon, and children living in the water.'

'It sounds chilly.' The Phoenix shivered, and went to sit on the tongs.

'I don't suppose there will be REAL water,' said Jane. 'And theatres are very warm and pretty, with a lot of gold and lamps. Wouldn't you like to come with us?'

'*I* was just going to say that,' said Robert, in injured tones, 'only I know how rude it is to interrupt. Do come, Phoenix, old chap; it will cheer you up. It'll make you laugh like any thing. Mr Bourchier always makes ripping plays. You ought to have seen "Shock-headed Peter" last year.'

'Your words are strange,' said the Phoenix, 'but I will come with you. The revels of this Bourchier, of whom you speak, may help me to forget the weight of my years.' So that evening the Phoenix snugged inside the waistcoat of Robert's Etons—a very tight fit it seemed both to Robert and to the Phoenix—and was taken to the play.

Robert had to pretend to be cold at the glittering, many-mirrored restaurant where they ate dinner, with father in evening dress, with a very shiny white shirt-front, and mother looking lovely in her grey evening dress, that changes into pink and green when she moves. Robert pretended that he was too cold to take off his great-coat, and so sat sweltering through what would otherwise have been a most thrilling meal. He felt that he was a blot on the smart beauty of the family, and he hoped the Phoenix knew what he was suffering for its sake. Of course, we are all pleased to suffer for the sake of others, but we like them to know it unless we are the very best and noblest kind of people, and Robert was just ordinary.

Father was full of jokes and fun, and every one laughed all the time, even with their mouths full, which is not manners. Robert thought father would not have been quite so funny about his keeping his over-coat on if father had known all the truth. And there Robert was probably right.

When dinner was finished to the last grape and the last paddle in the finger glasses—for it was a really truly grown-up dinner—the children were taken to the theatre, guided to a box close to the stage, and left.

Father's parting words were: 'Now, don't you stir out of this box, whatever you do. I shall be back before the end of the play. Be good and you will be happy. Is this zone torrid enough for the abandonment of great-coats, Bobs? No? Well, then, I should say you were sickening for something—mumps or measles or thrush or teething. Goodbye.'

He went, and Robert was at last able to remove his coat, mop his perspiring brow, and release the crushed and dishevelled Phoenix. Robert had to arrange his damp hair at the looking-glass at the back of the box, and the Phoenix had to preen its disordered feathers for some time before either of them was fit to be seen.

They were very, very early. When the lights went up fully, the Phoenix, balancing itself on the gilded back of a chair, swayed in ecstasy.

'How fair a scene is this!' it murmured; 'how far fairer than my temple! Or have I guessed aright? Have you brought me hither to lift up my heart with emotions of joyous surprise? Tell me, my Robert, is it not that this, THIS is my true temple, and the other was but a humble shrine frequented by outcasts?'

'I don't know about outcasts,' said Robert, 'but you can call this your temple if you like. Hush! the music is beginning.'

I am not going to tell you about the play. As I said before, one can't tell everything, and no doubt you saw 'The Water Babies' yourselves. If you did not it was a shame, or, rather, a pity.

What I must tell you is that, though Cyril and Jane and Robert and Anthea enjoyed it as much as any children possibly could, the pleasure of the Phoenix was far, far greater than theirs.

'This is indeed my temple,' it said again and again. 'What radiant rites! And all to do honour to me!'

The songs in the play it took to be hymns in its honour. The choruses were choric songs in its praise. The electric lights, it said, were magic torches lighted for its sake, and it was so charmed with the footlights that the children could hardly persuade it to sit still. But when the limelight was shown it could contain its approval no longer. It flapped its golden wings, and cried in a voice that could be heard all over the theatre:

'Well done, my servants! Ye have my favour and my countenance!'

Little Tom on the stage stopped short in what he was saying. A deep breath was drawn by hundreds of lungs, every eye in the house turned to the box where the luckless children cringed, and most people hissed, or said 'Shish!' or 'Turn them out!'

Then the play went on, and an attendant presently came to the box and spoke wrathfully.

'It wasn't us, indeed it wasn't,' said Anthea, earnestly; 'it was the bird.'

The man said well, then, they must keep their bird very quiet. 'Disturbing every one like this,' he said.

'It won't do it again,' said Robert, glancing imploringly at the golden bird; 'I'm sure it won't.'

'You have my leave to depart,' said the Phoenix gently.

'Well, he is a beauty, and no mistake,' said the attendant, 'only I'd cover him up during the acts. It upsets the performance.'

And he went.

'Don't speak again, there's a dear,' said Anthea; 'you wouldn't like to interfere with your own temple, would you?'

So now the Phoenix was quiet, but it kept whispering to the children. It wanted to know why there was no altar, no fire, no incense, and became so excited and fretful and tiresome that four at least of the party of five wished deeply that it had been left at home.

What happened next was entirely the fault of the Phoenix. It was not in the least the fault of the theatre people, and no one could ever understand afterwards how it did happen. No one, that is, except the guilty bird itself and the four children. The Phoenix was balancing itself on the gilt back of the chair, swaying backwards and forwards and up and down, as you may see your own domestic parrot do. I mean the grey one with the red tail. All eyes were on the stage, where the lobster was delighting the audience with that gem of a song, 'If you can't walk straight, walk sideways!' when the Phoenix murmured warmly—

'No altar, no fire, no incense!' and then, before any of the children could even begin to think of stopping it, it spread its bright wings and swept round the theatre, brushing its gleaming feathers against delicate hangings and gilded woodwork.

It seemed to have made but one circular wing-sweep, such as you may see a gull make over grey water on a stormy day. Next moment it was perched again on the chair-back—and all round the theatre, where it had passed, little sparks shone like tinsel seeds, then little smoke wreaths curled up like growing plants—little flames opened like flower-buds. People whispered—then people shrieked.

'Fire! Fire!' The curtain went down—the lights went up.

'Fire!' cried every one, and made for the doors.

'A magnificent idea!' said the Phoenix, complacently. 'An enormous altar—fire supplied free of charge. Doesn't the incense smell delicious?'

The only smell was the stifling smell of smoke, of burning silk, or scorching varnish.

The little flames had opened now into great flame-flowers. The people in the theatre were shouting and pressing towards the doors.

'Oh, how COULD you!' cried Jane. 'Let's get out.'

'Father said stay here,' said Anthea, very pale, and trying to speak in her ordinary voice.

'He didn't mean stay and be roasted,' said Robert. 'No boys on burning decks for me, thank you.'

'Not much,' said Cyril, and he opened the door of the box.

But a fierce waft of smoke and hot air made him shut it again. It was not possible to get out that way.

They looked over the front of the box. Could they climb down?

It would be possible, certainly; but would they be much better off?

'Look at the people,' moaned Anthea; 'we couldn't get through.'

And, indeed, the crowd round the doors looked as thick as flies in the jam-making season.

'I wish we'd never seen the Phoenix,' cried Jane.

Even at that awful moment Robert looked round to see if the bird had overheard a speech which, however natural, was hardly polite or grateful.

The Phoenix was gone.

'Look here,' said Cyril, 'I've read about fires in papers; I'm sure it's all right. Let's wait here, as father said.'

'We can't do anything else,' said Anthea bitterly.

'Look here,' said Robert, 'I'm NOT frightened—no, I'm not. The Phoenix has never been a skunk yet, and I'm certain it'll see us through somehow. I believe in the Phoenix!'

'The Phoenix thanks you, O Robert,' said a golden voice at his feet, and there was the Phoenix itself, on the Wishing Carpet.

'Quick!' it said. 'Stand on those portions of the carpet which are truly antique and authentic—and—'

A sudden jet of flame stopped its words. Alas! the Phoenix had unconsciously warmed to its subject, and in the unintentional heat of the moment had set fire to the paraffin with which that morning the children had anointed the carpet. It burned merrily. The children tried in vain to stamp it out. They had to stand back and let it burn itself out. When the paraffin had burned away it was found that it had taken with it all the darns of Scotch heather-mixture fingering. Only the fabric of the old carpet was left—and that was full of holes.

'Come,' said the Phoenix, 'I'm cool now.'

The four children got on to what was left of the carpet. Very careful they were not to leave a leg or a hand hanging over one of the holes. It was very hot—the theatre was a pit of fire. Every one else had got out.

Jane had to sit on Anthea's lap.

'Home!' said Cyril, and instantly the cool draught from under the nursery door played upon their legs as they sat. They were all on the carpet still, and the carpet was lying in its proper place on the nursery floor, as calm and unmoved as though it had never been to the theatre or taken part in a fire in its life.

Four long breaths of deep relief were instantly breathed. The draught which they had never liked before was for the moment quite pleasant. And they were safe. And every one else was safe. The theatre had been quite empty when they left. Every one was sure of that.

They presently found themselves all talking at once. Somehow none of their adventures had given them so much to talk about. None other had seemed so real.

'Did you notice—?' they said, and 'Do you remember—?'

When suddenly Anthea's face turned pale under the dirt which it had collected on it during the fire.

'Oh,' she cried, 'mother and father! Oh, how awful! They'll think we're burned to cinders. Oh, let's go this minute and tell them we aren't.'

'We should only miss them,' said the sensible Cyril.

'Well—YOU go then,' said Anthea, 'or I will. Only do wash your face first. Mother will be sure to think you are burnt to a cinder if she sees you as black as that, and she'll faint or be ill or something. Oh, I wish we'd never got to know that Phoenix.'

'Hush!' said Robert; 'it's no use being rude to the bird. I suppose it can't help its nature. Perhaps we'd better wash too. Now I come to think of it my hands are rather—'

No one had noticed the Phoenix since it had bidden them to step on the carpet. And no one noticed that no one had noticed.

All were partially clean, and Cyril was just plunging into his great-coat to go and look for his parents—he, and not unjustly, called it looking for a needle in a bundle of hay—when the sound of father's latchkey in the front door sent every one bounding up the stairs.

'Are you all safe?' cried mother's voice; 'are you all safe?' and the next moment she was kneeling on the linoleum of the hall, trying to kiss four damp children at once, and laughing and crying by turns, while father stood looking on and saying he was blessed or something.

'But how did you guess we'd come home,' said Cyril, later, when every one was calm enough for talking.

'Well, it was rather a rum thing. We heard the Garrick was on fire, and of course we went straight there,' said father, briskly. 'We couldn't find you, of course—and we couldn't get in—but the firemen told us every one was safely out. And then I heard a voice at my ear say, "Cyril, Anthea, Robert, and Jane"—and something touched me on the shoulder. It was a great yellow pigeon, and it got in the way of my seeing who'd spoken. It fluttered off, and then some one said in the other ear, "They're safe at home"; and when I turned again, to see who it was speaking, hanged if there wasn't that confounded pigeon on my other shoulder. Dazed by the fire, I suppose. Your mother said it was the voice of—'

'I said it was the bird that spoke,' said mother, 'and so it was. Or at least I thought so then. It wasn't a pigeon. It was an orange-coloured cockatoo. I don't care who it was that spoke. It was true and you're safe.'

Mother began to cry again, and father said bed was a good place after the pleasures of the stage.

So every one went there.

Robert had a talk to the Phoenix that night.

'Oh, very well,' said the bird, when Robert had said what he felt, 'didn't you know that I had power over fire? Do not distress yourself. I, like my high priests in Lombard Street, can undo the work of flames. Kindly open the casement.'

It flew out.

That was why the papers said next day that the fire at the theatre had done less damage than had been anticipated. As a matter of fact it had done none, for the Phoenix spent the night in putting things straight. How the management accounted for this, and how many of the theatre officials still believe that they were mad on that night will never be known.

Next day mother saw the burnt holes in the carpet.

'It caught where it was paraffiny,' said Anthea.

'I must get rid of that carpet at once,' said mother.

But what the children said in sad whispers to each other, as they pondered over last night's events, was—

'We must get rid of that Phoenix.'

Chapter 12. The End of the End

'Egg, toast, tea, milk, tea-cup and saucer, egg-spoon, knife, butter—that's all, I think,' remarked Anthea, as she put the last touches to mother's breakfast-tray, and went, very carefully up the stairs, feeling for every step with her toes, and holding on to the tray with all her fingers. She crept into mother's room and set the tray on a chair. Then she pulled one of the blinds up very softly.

'Is your head better, mammy dear?' she asked, in the soft little voice that she kept expressly for mother's headaches. 'I've brought your brekkie, and I've put the little cloth with clover-leaves on it, the one I made you.'

'That's very nice,' said mother sleepily.

Anthea knew exactly what to do for mothers with headaches who had breakfast in bed. She fetched warm water and put just enough eau de Cologne in it, and bathed mother's face and hands with the sweet-scented water. Then mother was able to think about breakfast.

'But what's the matter with my girl?' she asked, when her eyes got used to the light.

'Oh, I'm so sorry you're ill,' Anthea said. 'It's that horrible fire and you being so frightened. Father said so. And we all feel as if it was our faults. I can't explain, but—'

'It wasn't your fault a bit, you darling goosie,' mother said. 'How could it be?'

'That's just what I can't tell you,' said Anthea. 'I haven't got a futile brain like you and father, to think of ways of explaining everything.'

Mother laughed.

'My futile brain—or did you mean fertile?—anyway, it feels very stiff and sore this morning—but I shall be quite all right by and by. And don't be a silly little pet girl. The fire wasn't your faults. No; I don't want the egg, dear. I'll go to sleep again, I think. Don't you worry. And tell cook not to bother me about meals. You can order what you like for lunch.'

Anthea closed the door very mousily, and instantly went downstairs and ordered what she liked for lunch. She ordered a pair of turkeys, a large plum-pudding, cheese-cakes, and almonds and raisins.

Cook told her to go along, do. And she might as well not have ordered anything, for when lunch came it was just hashed mutton and semolina pudding, and cook had forgotten the sippets for the mutton hash and the semolina pudding was burnt.

When Anthea rejoined the others she found them all plunged in the gloom where she was herself. For every one knew that the days of the carpet were now numbered. Indeed, so worn was it that you could almost have numbered its threads.

So that now, after nearly a month of magic happenings, the time was at hand when life would have to go on in the dull, ordinary way and Jane, Robert, Anthea, and Cyril would be just in the same position as the other children who live in Camden Town, the children whom these four had so often pitied, and perhaps a little despised.

'We shall be just like them,' Cyril said.

'Except,' said Robert, 'that we shall have more things to remember and be sorry we haven't got.'

'Mother's going to send away the carpet as soon as she's well enough to see about that coconut matting. Fancy us with coconut-matting—us! And we've walked under live coconut-trees on the island where you can't have whooping-cough.'

'Pretty island,' said the Lamb; 'paint-box sands and sea all shiny sparkly.'

His brothers and sisters had often wondered whether he remembered that island. Now they knew that he did.

'Yes,' said Cyril; 'no more cheap return trips by carpet for us—that's a dead cert.'

They were all talking about the carpet, but what they were all thinking about was the Phoenix.

The golden bird had been so kind, so friendly, so polite, so instructive—and now it had set fire to a theatre and made mother ill.

Nobody blamed the bird. It had acted in a perfectly natural manner. But every one saw that it must not be asked to prolong its visit. Indeed, in plain English it must be asked to go!

The four children felt like base spies and treacherous friends; and each in its mind was saying who ought not to be the one to tell the Phoenix that there could no longer be a place for it in that happy home in Camden Town. Each child was quite sure that one of them ought to speak out in a fair and manly way, but nobody wanted to be the one.

They could not talk the whole thing over as they would have liked to do, because the Phoenix itself was in the cupboard, among the blackbeetles and the odd shoes and the broken chessmen.

But Anthea tried.

'It's very horrid. I do hate thinking things about people, and not being able to say the things you're thinking because of the way they would feel when they thought what things you were thinking, and wondered what they'd done to make you think things like that, and why you were thinking them.'

Anthea was so anxious that the Phoenix should not understand what she said that she made a speech completely baffling to all. It was not till she pointed to the cupboard in which all believed the Phoenix to be that Cyril understood.

'Yes,' he said, while Jane and Robert were trying to tell each other how deeply they didn't understand what Anthea were saying; 'but after recent eventfulnesses a new leaf has to be turned over, and, after all, mother is more important than the feelings of any of the lower forms of creation, however unnatural.'

'How beautifully you do do it,' said Anthea, absently beginning to build a card-house for the Lamb—'mixing up what you're saying, I mean. We ought to practise doing it so as to be ready for mysterious occasions. We're talking about THAT,' she said to Jane and Robert, frowning, and nodding towards the cupboard where the Phoenix was. Then Robert and Jane understood, and each opened its mouth to speak.

'Wait a minute,' said Anthea quickly; 'the game is to twist up what you want to say so that no one can understand what you're saying except the people you want to understand it, and sometimes not them.'

'The ancient philosophers,' said a golden voice, 'Well understood the art of which you speak.'

Of course it was the Phoenix, who had not been in the cupboard at all, but had been cocking a golden eye at them from the cornice during the whole conversation.

'Pretty dickie!' remarked the Lamb. 'CANARY dickie!'

'Poor misguided infant,' said the Phoenix.

There was a painful pause; the four could not but think it likely that the Phoenix had understood their very veiled allusions, accompanied as they had been by gestures indicating the cupboard. For the Phoenix was not wanting in intelligence.

'We were just saying—' Cyril began, and I hope he was not going to say anything but the truth. Whatever it was he did not say it, for the Phoenix interrupted him, and all breathed more freely as it spoke.

'I gather,' it said, 'that you have some tidings of a fatal nature to communicate to our degraded black brothers who run to and fro for ever yonder.' It pointed a claw at the cupboard, where the blackbeetles lived.

'Canary TALK,' said the Lamb joyously; 'go and show mammy.'

He wriggled off Anthea's lap.

'Mammy's asleep,' said Jane, hastily. 'Come and be wild beasts in a cage under the table.'

But the Lamb caught his feet and hands, and even his head, so often and so deeply in the holes of the carpet that the cage, or table, had to be moved on to the linoleum, and the carpet lay bare to sight with all its horrid holes.

'Ah,' said the bird, 'it isn't long for this world.'

'No,' said Robert; 'everything comes to an end. It's awful.'

'Sometimes the end is peace,' remarked the Phoenix. 'I imagine that unless it comes soon the end of your carpet will be pieces.'

'Yes,' said Cyril, respectfully kicking what was left of the carpet. The movement of its bright colours caught the eye of the Lamb, who went down on all fours instantly and began to pull at the red and blue threads.

'Aggedydaggedygaggedy,' murmured the Lamb; 'daggedy ag ag ag!'

And before any one could have winked (even if they had wanted to, and it would not have been of the slightest use) the middle of the floor showed bare, an island of boards surrounded by a sea of linoleum. The magic carpet was gone, AND SO WAS THE LAMB!

There was a horrible silence. The Lamb—the baby, all alone—had been wafted away on that untrustworthy carpet, so full of holes and magic. And no one could know where he was. And no one could follow him because there was now no carpet to follow on.

Jane burst into tears, but Anthea, though pale and frantic, was dry-eyed.

'It MUST be a dream,' she said.

'That's what the clergyman said,' remarked Robert forlornly; 'but it wasn't, and it isn't.'

'But the Lamb never wished,' said Cyril; 'he was only talking Bosh.'

'The carpet understands all speech,' said the Phoenix, 'even Bosh. I know not this Boshland, but be assured that its tongue is not unknown to the carpet.'

'Do you mean, then,' said Anthea, in white terror, 'that when he was saying "Agglety dag," or whatever it was, that he meant something by it?'

'All speech has meaning,' said the Phoenix.

'There I think you're wrong,' said Cyril; 'even people who talk English sometimes say things that don't mean anything in particular.'

'Oh, never mind that now,' moaned Anthea; 'you think "Aggety dag" meant something to him and the carpet?'

'Beyond doubt it held the same meaning to the carpet as to the luckless infant,' the Phoenix said calmly.

'And WHAT did it mean? Oh WHAT?'

'Unfortunately,' the bird rejoined, 'I never studied Bosh.'

Jane sobbed noisily, but the others were calm with what is sometimes called the calmness of despair. The Lamb was gone—the Lamb, their own precious baby brother—who had never in his happy little life been for a moment out of the sight of eyes that loved him—he was gone. He had gone alone into the great world with no other companion and protector than a carpet with holes in it. The children had never really understood before what an enormously big place the world is. And the Lamb might be anywhere in it!

'And it's no use going to look for him.' Cyril, in flat and wretched tones, only said what the others were thinking.

'Do you wish him to return?' the Phoenix asked; it seemed to speak with some surprise.

'Of course we do!' cried everybody.

'Isn't he more trouble than he's worth?' asked the bird doubtfully.

'No, no. Oh, we do want him back! We do!'

'Then,' said the wearer of gold plumage, 'if you'll excuse me, I'll just pop out and see what I can do.'

Cyril flung open the window, and the Phoenix popped out.

'Oh, if only mother goes on sleeping! Oh, suppose she wakes up and wants the Lamb! Oh, suppose the servants come! Stop crying, Jane. It's no earthly good. No, I'm not crying myself—at least I wasn't till you said so, and I shouldn't anyway if—if there was any mortal thing we could do. Oh, oh, oh!'

Cyril and Robert were boys, and boys never cry, of course. Still, the position was a terrible one, and I do not wonder that they made faces in their efforts to behave in a really manly way.

And at this awful moment mother's bell rang.

A breathless stillness held the children. Then Anthea dried her eyes. She looked round her and caught up the poker. She held it out to Cyril.

'Hit my hand hard,' she said; 'I must show mother some reason for my eyes being like they are. Harder,' she cried as Cyril gently tapped her with the iron handle. And Cyril, agitated and trembling, nerved himself to hit harder, and hit very much harder than he intended.

Anthea screamed.

'Oh, Panther, I didn't mean to hurt, really,' cried Cyril, clattering the poker back into the fender.

'It's—all—right,' said Anthea breathlessly, clasping the hurt hand with the one that wasn't hurt; 'it's—getting—red.'

It was—a round red and blue bump was rising on the back of it. 'Now, Robert,' she said, trying to breathe more evenly, 'you go out—oh, I don't know where—on to the dustbin—anywhere—and I shall tell mother you and the Lamb are out.'

Anthea was now ready to deceive her mother for as long as ever she could. Deceit is very wrong, we know, but it seemed to Anthea that it was her plain duty to keep her mother from being frightened about the Lamb as long as possible. And the Phoenix might help.

'It always has helped,' Robert said; 'it got us out of the tower, and even when it made the fire in the theatre it got us out all right. I'm certain it will manage somehow.'

Mother's bell rang again.

'Oh, Eliza's never answered it,' cried Anthea; 'she never does. Oh, I must go.'

And she went.

Her heart beat bumpingly as she climbed the stairs. Mother would be certain to notice her eyes—well, her hand would account for that. But the Lamb—

'No, I must NOT think of the Lamb, she said to herself, and bit her tongue till her eyes watered again, so as to give herself something else to think of. Her arms and legs and back, and even her tear-reddened face, felt stiff with her resolution not to let mother be worried if she could help it.

She opened the door softly.

'Yes, mother?' she said.

'Dearest,' said mother, 'the Lamb—'

Anthea tried to be brave. She tried to say that the Lamb and Robert were out. Perhaps she tried too hard. Anyway, when she opened her mouth no words came. So she stood with it open. It seemed easier to keep from crying with one's mouth in that unusual position.

'The Lamb,' mother went on; 'he was very good at first, but he's pulled the toilet-cover off the dressing-table with all the brushes and pots and things, and now he's so quiet I'm sure he's in some dreadful mischief. And I can't see him from here, and if I'd got out of bed to see I'm sure I should have fainted.'

'Do you mean he's HERE?' said Anthea.

'Of course he's here,' said mother, a little impatiently. 'Where did you think he was?'

Anthea went round the foot of the big mahogany bed. There was a pause.

'He's not here NOW,' she said.

That he had been there was plain, from the toilet-cover on the floor, the scattered pots and bottles, the wandering brushes and combs, all involved in the tangle of ribbons and laces which an open drawer had yielded to the baby's inquisitive fingers.

'He must have crept out, then,' said mother; 'do keep him with you, there's a darling. If I don't get some sleep I shall be a wreck when father comes home.'

Anthea closed the door softly. Then she tore downstairs and burst into the nursery, crying—

'He must have wished he was with mother. He's been there all the time. "Aggety dag—"'

The unusual word was frozen on her lip, as people say in books.

For there, on the floor, lay the carpet, and on the carpet, surrounded by his brothers and by Jane, sat the Lamb. He had covered his face and clothes with vaseline and violet powder, but he was easily recognizable in spite of this disguise.

'You are right,' said the Phoenix, who was also present; 'it is evident that, as you say, "Aggety dag" is Bosh for "I want to be where my mother is," and so the faithful carpet understood it.'

'But how,' said Anthea, catching up the Lamb and hugging him—'how did he get back here?'

'Oh,' said the Phoenix, 'I flew to the Psammead and wished that your infant brother were restored to your midst, and immediately it was so.'

'Oh, I am glad, I am glad!' cried Anthea, still hugging the baby. 'Oh, you darling! Shut up, Jane! I don't care HOW much he comes off on me! Cyril! You and Robert roll that carpet up and put it in the beetle-cupboard. He might say "Aggety dag" again, and it might mean something quite different next time. Now, my Lamb, Panther'll clean you a little. Come on.'

'I hope the beetles won't go wishing,' said Cyril, as they rolled up the carpet.

Two days later mother was well enough to go out, and that evening the coconut matting came home. The children had talked and talked, and thought and thought, but they had not found any polite way of telling the Phoenix that they did not want it to stay any longer.

The days had been days spent by the children in embarrassment, and by the Phoenix in sleep.

And, now the matting was laid down, the Phoenix awoke and fluttered down on to it.

It shook its crested head.

'I like not this carpet,' it said; 'it is harsh and unyielding, and it hurts my golden feet.'

'We've jolly well got to get used to its hurting OUR golden feet,' said Cyril.

'This, then,' said the bird, 'supersedes the Wishing Carpet.'

'Yes,' said Robert, 'if you mean that it's instead of it.'

'And the magic web?' inquired the Phoenix, with sudden eagerness.

'It's the rag-and-bottle man's day to-morrow,' said Anthea, in a low voice; 'he will take it away.'

The Phoenix fluttered up to its favourite perch on the chair-back.

'Hear me!' it cried, 'oh youthful children of men, and restrain your tears of misery and despair, for what must be must be, and I would not remember you, thousands of years hence, as base ingrates and crawling worms compact of low selfishness.'

'I should hope not, indeed,' said Cyril.

'Weep not,' the bird went on; 'I really do beg that you won't weep.

I will not seek to break the news to you gently. Let the blow fall at once. The time has come when I must leave you.'

All four children breathed forth a long sigh of relief.

'We needn't have bothered so about how to break the news to it,' whispered Cyril.

'Ah, sigh not so,' said the bird, gently. 'All meetings end in partings. I must leave you. I have sought to prepare you for this. Ah, do not give way!'

'Must you really go—so soon?' murmured Anthea. It was what she had often heard her mother say to calling ladies in the afternoon.

'I must, really; thank you so much, dear,' replied the bird, just as though it had been one of the ladies.

'I am weary,' it went on. 'I desire to rest—after all the happenings of this last moon I do desire really to rest, and I ask of you one last boon.'

'Any little thing we can do,' said Robert.

Now that it had really come to parting with the Phoenix, whose favourite he had always been, Robert did feel almost as miserable as the Phoenix thought they all did.

'I ask but the relic designed for the rag-and-bottle man. Give me what is left of the carpet and let me go.'

'Dare we?' said Anthea. 'Would mother mind?'

'I have dared greatly for your sakes,' remarked the bird.

'Well, then, we will,' said Robert.

The Phoenix fluffed out its feathers joyously.

'Nor shall you regret it, children of golden hearts,' it said. 'Quick—spread the carpet and leave me alone; but first pile high the fire. Then, while I am immersed in the sacred preliminary rites, do ye prepare sweet-smelling woods and spices for the last act of parting.'

The children spread out what was left of the carpet. And, after all, though this was just what they would have wished to have happened, all hearts were sad. Then they put half a scuttle of coal on the fire and went out, closing the door on the Phoenix—left, at last, alone with the carpet.

'One of us must keep watch,' said Robert, excitedly, as soon as they were all out of the room, 'and the others can go and buy sweet woods and spices. Get the very best that money can buy, and plenty of them. Don't let's stand to a threepence or so. I want it to have a jolly good send-off. It's the only thing that'll make us feel less horrid inside.'

It was felt that Robert, as the pet of the Phoenix, ought to have the last melancholy pleasure of choosing the materials for its funeral pyre.

'I'll keep watch if you like,' said Cyril. 'I don't mind. And, besides, it's raining hard, and my boots let in the wet. You might call and see if my other ones are "really reliable" again yet.'

So they left Cyril, standing like a Roman sentinel outside the door inside which the Phoenix was getting ready for the great change, and they all went out to buy the precious things for the last sad rites.

'Robert is right,' Anthea said; 'this is no time for being careful about our money. Let's go to the stationer's first, and buy a whole packet of lead-pencils. They're cheaper if you buy them by the packet.'

This was a thing that they had always wanted to do, but it needed the great excitement of a funeral pyre and a parting from a beloved Phoenix to screw them up to the extravagance.

The people at the stationer's said that the pencils were real cedar-wood, so I hope they were, for stationers should always speak the truth. At any rate they cost one-and-fourpence. Also they spent sevenpence three-farthings on a little sandal-wood box inlaid with ivory.

'Because,' said Anthea, 'I know sandalwood smells sweet, and when it's burned it smells very sweet indeed.'

'Ivory doesn't smell at all,' said Robert, 'but I expect when you burn it it smells most awful vile, like bones.'

At the grocer's they bought all the spices they could remember the names of—shell-like mace, cloves like blunt nails, peppercorns, the long and the round kind; ginger, the dry sort, of course; and the beautiful bloom-covered shells of fragrant cinnamon. Allspice too, and caraway seeds (caraway seeds that smelt most deadly when the time came for burning them).

Camphor and oil of lavender were bought at the chemist's, and also a little scent sachet labelled 'Violettes de Parme'.

They took the things home and found Cyril still on guard. When they had knocked and the golden voice of the Phoenix had said 'Come in,' they went in.

There lay the carpet—or what was left of it—and on it lay an egg, exactly like the one out of which the Phoenix had been hatched.

The Phoenix was walking round and round the egg, clucking with joy and pride.

'I've laid it, you see,' it said, 'and as fine an egg as ever I laid in all my born days.'

Every one said yes, it was indeed a beauty.

The things which the children had bought were now taken out of their papers and arranged on the table, and when the Phoenix had been persuaded to leave its egg for a moment and look at the materials for its last fire it was quite overcome.

'Never, never have I had a finer pyre than this will be. You shall not regret it,' it said, wiping away a golden tear. 'Write quickly: "Go and tell the Psammead to fulfil the last wish of the Phoenix, and return instantly".'

But Robert wished to be polite and he wrote—

'Please go and ask the Psammead to be so kind as to fulfil the Phoenix's last wish, and come straight back, if you please.' The paper was pinned to the carpet, which vanished and returned in the flash of an eye.

Then another paper was written ordering the carpet to take the egg somewhere where it wouldn't be hatched for another two thousand years. The Phoenix tore itself away from its cherished egg, which it watched with yearning tenderness till, the paper being pinned on, the carpet hastily rolled itself up round the egg, and both vanished for ever from the nursery of the house in Camden Town.

'Oh, dear! oh, dear! oh, dear!' said everybody.

'Bear up,' said the bird; 'do you think *I* don't suffer, being parted from my precious new-laid egg like this? Come, conquer your emotions and build my fire.'

'OH!' cried Robert, suddenly, and wholly breaking down, 'I can't BEAR you to go!'

The Phoenix perched on his shoulder and rubbed its beak softly against his ear.

'The sorrows of youth soon appear but as dreams,' it said. 'Farewell, Robert of my heart. I have loved you well.'

The fire had burnt to a red glow. One by one the spices and sweet woods were laid on it. Some smelt nice and some—the caraway seeds and the Violettes de Parme sachet among them—smelt worse than you would think possible.

'Farewell, farewell, farewell, farewell!' said the Phoenix, in a far-away voice.

'Oh, GOOD-BYE,' said every one, and now all were in tears.

The bright bird fluttered seven times round the room and settled in the hot heart of the fire. The sweet gums and spices and woods flared and flickered around it, but its golden feathers did not burn. It seemed to grow red-hot to the very inside heart of it—and then before the eight eyes of its friends it fell together, a heap of white ashes, and the flames of the cedar pencils and the sandal-wood box met and joined above it.

'Whatever have you done with the carpet?' asked mother next day.

'We gave it to some one who wanted it very much. The name began with a P,' said Jane.

The others instantly hushed her.

'Oh, well, it wasn't worth twopence,' said mother.

'The person who began with P said we shouldn't lose by it,' Jane went on before she could be stopped.

'I daresay!' said mother, laughing.

But that very night a great box came, addressed to the children by all their names. Eliza never could remember the name of the carrier who brought it. It wasn't Carter Paterson or the Parcels Delivery.

It was instantly opened. It was a big wooden box, and it had to be opened with a hammer and the kitchen poker; the long nails came squeaking out, and boards scrunched as they were wrenched off. Inside the box was soft paper, with beautiful Chinese patterns on it—blue and green and red and violet. And under the paper—well, almost everything lovely that you can think of. Everything of reasonable size, I mean; for, of course, there were no motors or flying machines or thoroughbred chargers. But there really was almost everything else. Everything that the children had always wanted—toys and games and books, and chocolate and candied cherries and paint-boxes and photographic cameras, and all the presents they had always wanted to give to father and mother and the Lamb, only they had never had the money for them. At the very bottom of the box was a tiny golden feather. No one saw it but Robert, and he picked it up and hid it in the breast of his jacket, which had been so often the nesting-place of the golden bird. When he went to bed the feather was gone. It was the last he ever saw of the Phoenix.

Pinned to the lovely fur cloak that mother had always wanted was a paper, and it said—

'In return for the carpet. With gratitude.—P.'

You may guess how father and mother talked it over. They decided at last the person who had had the carpet, and whom, curiously enough, the children were quite unable to describe, must be an insane millionaire who amused himself by playing at being a rag-and-bone man. But the children knew better.

They knew that this was the fulfilment, by the powerful Psammead, of the last wish of the Phoenix, and that this glorious and delightful boxful of treasures was really the very, very, very end of the Phoenix and the Carpet.

The Story of the Amulet

To Dr Wallis Budge of the British Museum as a small token of gratitude for his unfailing kindness and help in the making of it

Chapter 1. The Psammead

There were once four children who spent their summer holidays in a white house, happily situated between a sandpit and a chalkpit. One day they had the good fortune to find in the sandpit a strange creature. Its eyes were on long horns like snail's eyes, and it could move them in and out like telescopes. It had ears like a bat's ears, and its tubby body was shaped like a spider's and covered with thick soft fur—and it had hands and feet like a monkey's. It told the children—whose names were Cyril, Robert, Anthea, and Jane—that it was a Psammead or sand-fairy. (Psammead is pronounced Sammy-ad.) It was old, old, old, and its birthday was almost at the very beginning of everything. And it had been buried in the sand for thousands of years. But it still kept its fairylikeness, and part of this fairylikeness was its power to give people whatever they wished for. You know fairies have always been able to do this. Cyril, Robert, Anthea, and Jane now found their wishes come true; but, somehow, they never could think of just the right things to wish for, and their wishes sometimes turned out very oddly indeed. In the end their unwise wishings landed them in what Robert called 'a very tight place indeed', and the Psammead consented to help them out of it in return for their promise never never to ask it to grant them any more wishes, and never to tell anyone about it, because it did not want to be bothered to give wishes to anyone ever any more. At the moment of parting Jane said politely—

'I wish we were going to see you again some day.'

And the Psammead, touched by this friendly thought, granted the wish. The book about all this is called Five Children and It, and it ends up in a most tiresome way by saying—

'The children DID see the Psammead again, but it was not in the sandpit; it was—but I must say no more—'

The reason that nothing more could be said was that I had not then been able to find out exactly when and where the children met the Psammead again. Of course I knew they would meet it, because it was a beast of its word, and when it said a thing would happen, that thing happened without fail. How different from the people who tell us about what weather it is going to be on Thursday next, in London, the South Coast, and Channel!

The summer holidays during which the Psammead had been found and the wishes given had been wonderful holidays in the country, and the children had the highest hopes of just such another holiday for the next summer. The winter holidays were beguiled by the wonderful happenings of The Phoenix and the Carpet, and the loss of these two treasures would have left the children in despair, but for the splendid hope of their next holiday in the country. The world, they felt, and indeed had some reason to feel, was full of wonderful things—and they were really the sort of people that wonderful things happen to. So they looked forward to the summer holiday; but when it came everything was different, and very, very horrid. Father had to go out to Manchuria to telegraph news about the war to the tiresome paper he wrote for—the Daily Bellower, or something like that, was its name. And Mother, poor dear Mother, was away in Madeira, because she had been very ill. And The Lamb—I mean the baby—was with her. And Aunt Emma, who was Mother's sister, had suddenly married Uncle Reginald, who was Father's brother, and they had gone to China, which is much too far off for you to expect to be asked to spend the holidays in, however fond your aunt and uncle may be of you. So the children were left in the care of old Nurse, who lived in Fitzroy Street, near the British Museum, and though she was always very kind to them, and indeed spoiled them far more than would be good for the most grown-up of us, the four children felt perfectly wretched, and when the cab had driven off with Father and all his boxes and guns and the sheepskin, with blankets and the aluminium mess-kit inside it, the stoutest heart quailed, and the girls broke down altogether, and sobbed in each other's arms, while the boys each looked out of one of the long gloomy windows of the parlour, and tried to pretend that no boy would be such a muff as to cry.

I hope you notice that they were not cowardly enough to cry till their Father had gone; they knew he had quite enough to upset him without that. But when he was gone everyone felt as if it had been trying not to cry all its life, and that it must cry now, if it died for it. So they cried.

Tea—with shrimps and watercress—cheered them a little. The watercress was arranged in a hedge round a fat glass salt-cellar, a tasteful device they had never seen before. But it was not a cheerful meal.

After tea Anthea went up to the room that had been Father's, and when she saw how dreadfully he wasn't there, and remembered how every minute was taking him further and further from her, and nearer and nearer to the guns of the Russians, she cried a little more. Then she thought of Mother, ill and alone, and perhaps at that very moment wanting a little girl to put eau-de-cologne on her head, and make her sudden cups of tea, and she cried more than ever. And then she remembered what Mother had said, the night before she went away, about Anthea being the eldest girl, and about trying to make the others happy, and things like that. So she stopped crying, and thought instead. And when she had thought as long as she could bear she washed her face and combed her hair, and went down to the others, trying her best to look as though crying were an exercise she had never even heard of.

She found the parlour in deepest gloom, hardly relieved at all by the efforts of Robert, who, to make the time pass, was pulling Jane's hair—not hard, but just enough to tease.

'Look here,' said Anthea. 'Let's have a palaver.' This word dated from the awful day when Cyril had carelessly wished that there were Red Indians in England—and there had been. The word brought back memories of last summer holidays and everyone groaned; they thought of the white house with the beautiful tangled garden—late roses, asters, marigold, sweet mignonette, and feathery asparagus—of the wilderness which someone had once meant to make into an orchard, but which was now, as Father said, 'five acres of thistles haunted by the ghosts of baby cherry-trees'. They thought of the view across the valley, where the lime-kilns looked like Aladdin's palaces in the sunshine, and they thought of their own sandpit, with its fringe of yellowy grasses and pale-stringy-stalked wild flowers, and the little holes in the cliff that were the little sand-martins' little front doors. And they thought of the free fresh air smelling of thyme and sweetbriar, and the scent of the wood-smoke from the cottages in the lane—and they looked round old Nurse's stuffy parlour, and Jane said—

'Oh, how different it all is!'

It was. Old Nurse had been in the habit of letting lodgings, till Father gave her the children to take care of. And her rooms were furnished 'for letting'. Now it is a very odd thing that no one ever seems to furnish a room 'for letting' in a bit the same way as one would furnish it for living in. This room had heavy dark red stuff curtains—the colour that blood would not make a stain on—with coarse lace curtains inside. The carpet was yellow, and violet, with bits of grey and brown oilcloth in odd places. The fireplace had shavings and tinsel in it. There was a very varnished mahogany chiffonier, or sideboard, with a lock that wouldn't act. There were hard chairs—far too many of them—with crochet antimacassars slipping off their seats, all of which sloped the wrong way. The table wore a cloth of a cruel green colour with a yellow chain-stitch pattern round it. Over the fireplace was a looking-glass that made you look much uglier than you really were, however plain you might be to begin with. Then there was a mantelboard with maroon plush and wool fringe that did not match the plush; a dreary clock like a black marble tomb—it was silent as the grave too, for it had long since forgotten how to tick. And there were painted glass vases that never had any flowers in, and a painted tambourine that no one ever played, and painted brackets with nothing on them.

'And maple-framed engravings of the Queen, the Houses of Parliament, the Plains of Heaven, and of a blunt-nosed woodman's flat return.'

There were two books—last December's Bradshaw, and an odd volume of Plumridge's Commentary on Thessalonians. There were—but I cannot dwell longer on this painful picture. It was indeed, as Jane said, very different.

'Let's have a palaver,' said Anthea again.

'What about?' said Cyril, yawning.

'There's nothing to have ANYTHING about,' said Robert kicking the leg of the table miserably.

'I don't want to play,' said Jane, and her tone was grumpy.

Anthea tried very hard not to be cross. She succeeded.

'Look here,' she said, 'don't think I want to be preachy or a beast in any way, but I want to what Father calls define the situation. Do you agree?'

'Fire ahead,' said Cyril without enthusiasm.

'Well then. We all know the reason we're staying here is because Nurse couldn't leave her house on account of the poor learned gentleman on the top-floor. And there was no one else Father could entrust to take care of us—and you know it's taken a lot of money, Mother's going to Madeira to be made well.'

Jane sniffed miserably.

'Yes, I know,' said Anthea in a hurry, 'but don't let's think about how horrid it all is. I mean we can't go to things that cost a lot, but we must do SOMETHING. And I know there are heaps of things you can see in London without paying for them, and I thought we'd go and see them. We are all quite old now, and we haven't got The Lamb—'

Jane sniffed harder than before.

'I mean no one can say "No" because of him, dear pet. And I thought we MUST get Nurse to see how quite old we are, and let us go out by ourselves, or else we shall never have any sort of a time at all. And I vote we see everything there is, and let's begin by asking Nurse to give us some bits of bread and we'll go to St James's Park. There are ducks there, I know, we can feed them. Only we must make Nurse let us go by ourselves.'

'Hurrah for liberty!' said Robert, 'but she won't.'

'Yes she will,' said Jane unexpectedly. '*I* thought about that this morning, and I asked Father, and he said yes; and what's more he told old Nurse we might, only he said we must always say where we wanted to go, and if it was right she would let us.'

'Three cheers for thoughtful Jane,' cried Cyril, now roused at last from his yawning despair. 'I say, let's go now.'

So they went, old Nurse only begging them to be careful of crossings, and to ask a policeman to assist in the more difficult cases. But they were used to crossings, for they had lived in Camden Town and knew the Kentish Town Road where the trams rush up and down like mad at all hours of the day and night, and seem as though, if anything, they would rather run over you than not.

They had promised to be home by dark, but it was July, so dark would be very late indeed, and long past bedtime.

They started to walk to St James's Park, and all their pockets were stuffed with bits of bread and the crusts of toast, to feed the ducks with. They started, I repeat, but they never got there.

Between Fitzroy Street and St James's Park there are a great many streets, and, if you go the right way you will pass a great many shops that you cannot possibly help stopping to look at. The children stopped to look at several with gold-lace and beads and pictures and jewellery and dresses, and hats, and oysters and lobsters in their windows, and their sorrow did not seem nearly so impossible to bear as it had done in the best parlour at No. 300, Fitzroy Street.

Presently, by some wonderful chance turn of Robert's (who had been voted Captain because the girls thought it would be good for him— and indeed he thought so himself—and of course Cyril couldn't vote against him because it would have looked like a mean jealousy), they came into the little interesting criss-crossy streets that held the most interesting shops of all—the shops where live things were sold. There was one shop window entirely filled with cages, and all sorts of beautiful birds in them. The children were delighted till they remembered how they had once wished for wings themselves, and had had them—and then they felt how desperately unhappy anything with wings must be if it is shut up in a cage and not allowed to fly.

'It must be fairly beastly to be a bird in a cage,' said Cyril. 'Come on!'

They went on, and Cyril tried to think out a scheme for making his fortune as a gold-digger at Klondyke, and then buying all the caged birds in the world and setting them free. Then they came to a shop that sold cats, but the cats were in cages, and the children could not help wishing someone would buy all the cats and put them on hearthrugs, which are the proper places for cats. And there was the dog-shop, and that was not a happy thing to look at either, because all the dogs were chained or caged, and all the dogs, big and little, looked at the four children with sad wistful eyes and wagged beseeching tails as if they were trying to say, 'Buy me! buy me! buy me! and let me go for a walk with you; oh, do buy me, and buy my poor brothers too! Do! do! do!' They almost said, 'Do! do! do!' plain to the ear, as they whined; all but one big Irish terrier, and he growled when Jane patted him.

'Grrrrr,' he seemed to say, as he looked at them from the back corner of his eye—'YOU won't buy me. Nobody will—ever—I shall die chained up—and I don't know that I care how soon it is, either!'

I don't know that the children would have understood all this, only once they had been in a besieged castle, so they knew how hateful it is to be kept in when you want to get out.

Of course they could not buy any of the dogs. They did, indeed, ask the price of the very, very smallest, and it was sixty-five pounds—but that was because it was a Japanese toy spaniel like the Queen once had her portrait painted with, when she was only Princess of Wales. But the children thought, if the smallest was all that money, the biggest would run into thousands—so they went on.

And they did not stop at any more cat or dog or bird shops, but passed them by, and at last they came to a shop that seemed as though it only sold creatures that did not much mind where they were—such as goldfish and white mice, and sea-anemones and other aquarium beasts, and lizards and toads, and hedgehogs and tortoises, and tame rabbits and guinea-pigs. And there they stopped for a long time, and fed the guinea-pigs with bits of bread through the cage-bars, and wondered whether it would be possible to keep a sandy-coloured double-lop in the basement of the house in Fitzroy Street.

'I don't suppose old Nurse would mind VERY much,' said Jane. 'Rabbits are most awfully tame sometimes. I expect it would know her voice and follow her all about.'

'She'd tumble over it twenty times a day,' said Cyril; 'now a snake—'

'There aren't any snakes, said Robert hastily, 'and besides, I never could cotton to snakes somehow—I wonder why.'

'Worms are as bad,' said Anthea, 'and eels and slugs—I think it's because we don't like things that haven't got legs.'

'Father says snakes have got legs hidden away inside of them,' said Robert.

'Yes—and he says WE'VE got tails hidden away inside us—but it doesn't either of it come to anything REALLY,' said Anthea. 'I hate things that haven't any legs.'

'It's worse when they have too many,' said Jane with a shudder, 'think of centipedes!'

They stood there on the pavement, a cause of some inconvenience to the passersby, and thus beguiled the time with conversation. Cyril was leaning his elbow on the top of a hutch that had seemed empty when they had inspected the whole edifice of hutches one by one, and he was trying to reawaken the interest of a hedgehog that had curled itself into a ball earlier in the interview, when a small, soft voice just below his elbow said, quietly, plainly and quite unmistakably—not in any squeak or whine that had to be translated—but in downright common English—

'Buy me—do—please buy me!'

Cyril started as though he had been pinched, and jumped a yard away from the hutch.

'Come back—oh, come back!' said the voice, rather louder but still softly; 'stoop down and pretend to be tying up your bootlace—I see it's undone, as usual.'

Cyril mechanically obeyed. He knelt on one knee on the dry, hot dusty pavement, peered into the darkness of the hutch and found himself face to face with—the Psammead!

It seemed much thinner than when he had last seen it. It was dusty and dirty, and its fur was untidy and ragged. It had hunched itself up into a miserable lump, and its long snail's eyes were drawn in quite tight so that they hardly showed at all.

'Listen,' said the Psammead, in a voice that sounded as though it would begin to cry in a minute, 'I don't think the creature who keeps this shop will ask a very high price for me. I've bitten him more than once, and I've made myself look as common as I can. He's never had a glance from my beautiful, beautiful eyes. Tell the others I'm here—but tell them to look at some of those low, common beasts while I'm talking to you. The creature inside mustn't think you care much about me, or he'll put a price upon me far, far beyond your means. I remember in the dear old days last summer you never had much money. Oh—I never thought I should be so glad to see you—I never did.' It sniffed, and shot out its long snail's eyes expressly to drop a tear well away from its fur. 'Tell the others I'm here, and then I'll tell you exactly what to do about buying me.' Cyril tied his bootlace into a hard knot, stood up and addressed the others in firm tones—

'Look here,' he said, 'I'm not kidding—and I appeal to your honour,' an appeal which in this family was never made in vain. 'Don't look at that hutch—look at the white rat. Now you are not to look at that hutch whatever I say.'

He stood in front of it to prevent mistakes.

'Now get yourselves ready for a great surprise. In that hutch there's an old friend of ours—DON'T look!—Yes; it's the Psammead, the good old Psammead! it wants us to buy it. It says you're not to look at it. Look at the white rat and count your money! On your honour don't look!'

The others responded nobly. They looked at the white rat till they quite stared him out of countenance, so that he went and sat up on his hind legs in a far corner and hid his eyes with his front paws, and pretended he was washing his face.

Cyril stooped again, busying himself with the other bootlace and listened for the Psammead's further instructions.

'Go in,' said the Psammead, 'and ask the price of lots of other things. Then say, "What do you want for that monkey that's lost its tail—the mangy old thing in the third hutch from the end." Oh—don't mind MY feelings—call me a mangy monkey—I've tried hard enough to look like one! I don't think he'll put a high price on me—I've bitten him eleven times since I came here the day before yesterday. If he names a bigger price than you can afford, say you wish you had the money.'

'But you can't give us wishes. I've promised never to have another wish from you,' said the bewildered Cyril.

'Don't be a silly little idiot,' said the Sand-fairy in trembling but affectionate tones, 'but find out how much money you've got between you, and do exactly what I tell you.'

Cyril, pointing a stiff and unmeaning finger at the white rat, so as to pretend that its charms alone employed his tongue, explained matters to the others, while the Psammead hunched itself, and bunched itself, and did its very best to make itself look uninteresting. Then the four children filed into the shop.

'How much do you want for that white rat?' asked Cyril.

'Eightpence,' was the answer.

'And the guinea-pigs?'

'Eighteenpence to five bob, according to the breed.'

'And the lizards?'

'Ninepence each.'

'And toads?'

'Fourpence. Now look here,' said the greasy owner of all this caged life with a sudden ferocity which made the whole party back hurriedly on to the wainscoting of hutches with which the shop was lined. 'Lookee here. I ain't agoin' to have you a comin' in here a turnin' the whole place outer winder, an' prizing every animile in the stock just for your larks, so don't think it! If you're a buyer, BE a buyer—but I never had a customer yet as wanted to buy mice, and lizards, and toads, and guineas all at once. So hout you goes.'

'Oh! wait a minute,' said the wretched Cyril, feeling how foolishly yet well-meaningly he had carried out the Psammead's instructions. 'Just tell me one thing. What do you want for the mangy old monkey in the third hutch from the end?'

The shopman only saw in this a new insult.

'Mangy young monkey yourself,' said he; 'get along with your blooming cheek. Hout you goes!'

'Oh! don't be so cross,' said Jane, losing her head altogether, 'don't you see he really DOES want to know THAT!'

'Ho! does 'e indeed,' sneered the merchant. Then he scratched his ear suspiciously, for he was a sharp business man, and he knew the ring of truth when he heard it. His hand was bandaged, and three minutes before he would have been glad to sell the 'mangy old monkey' for ten shillings. Now— 'Ho! 'e does, does 'e,' he said, 'then two pun ten's my price. He's not got his fellow that monkey ain't, nor yet his match, not this side of the equator, which he comes from. And the only one ever seen in London. Ought to be in the Zoo. Two pun ten, down on the nail, or hout you goes!'

The children looked at each other—twenty-three shillings and fivepence was all they had in the world, and it would have been merely three and fivepence, but for the sovereign which Father had given to them 'between them' at parting. 'We've only twenty-three shillings and fivepence,' said Cyril, rattling the money in his pocket.

'Twenty-three farthings and somebody's own cheek,' said the dealer, for he did not believe that Cyril had so much money.

There was a miserable pause. Then Anthea remembered, and said—

'Oh! I WISH I had two pounds ten.'

'So do I, Miss, I'm sure,' said the man with bitter politeness; 'I wish you 'ad, I'm sure!'

Anthea's hand was on the counter, something seemed to slide under it. She lifted it. There lay five bright half sovereigns.

'Why, I HAVE got it after all,' she said; 'here's the money, now let's have the Sammy,... the monkey I mean.'

The dealer looked hard at the money, but he made haste to put it in his pocket.

'I only hope you come by it honest,' he said, shrugging his shoulders. He scratched his ear again.

'Well!' he said, 'I suppose I must let you have it, but it's worth thribble the money, so it is—'

He slowly led the way out to the hutch—opened the door gingerly, and made a sudden fierce grab at the Psammead, which the Psammead acknowledged in one last long lingering bite.

'Here, take the brute,' said the shopman, squeezing the Psammead so tight that he nearly choked it. 'It's bit me to the marrow, it have.'

The man's eyes opened as Anthea held out her arms.

'Don't blame me if it tears your face off its bones,' he said, and the Psammead made a leap from his dirty horny hands, and Anthea caught it in hers, which were not very clean, certainly, but at any rate were soft and pink, and held it kindly and closely.

'But you can't take it home like that,' Cyril said, 'we shall have a crowd after us,' and indeed two errand boys and a policeman had already collected.

'I can't give you nothink only a paper-bag, like what we put the tortoises in,' said the man grudgingly.

So the whole party went into the shop, and the shopman's eyes nearly came out of his head when, having given Anthea the largest paper-bag he could find, he saw her hold it open, and the Psammead carefully creep into it. 'Well!' he said, 'if that there don't beat cockfighting! But p'raps you've met the brute afore.'

'Yes,' said Cyril affably, 'he's an old friend of ours.'

'If I'd a known that,' the man rejoined, 'you shouldn't a had him under twice the money. 'Owever,' he added, as the children disappeared, 'I ain't done so bad, seeing as I only give five bob for the beast. But then there's the bites to take into account!'

The children trembling in agitation and excitement, carried home the Psammead, trembling in its paper-bag.

When they got it home, Anthea nursed it, and stroked it, and would have cried over it, if she hadn't remembered how it hated to be wet.

When it recovered enough to speak, it said—

'Get me sand; silver sand from the oil and colour shop. And get me plenty.'

They got the sand, and they put it and the Psammead in the round bath together, and it rubbed itself, and rolled itself, and shook itself and scraped itself, and scratched itself, and preened itself, till it felt clean and comfy, and then it scrabbled a hasty hole in the sand, and went to sleep in it.

The children hid the bath under the girls' bed, and had supper. Old Nurse had got them a lovely supper of bread and butter and fried onions. She was full of kind and delicate thoughts.

When Anthea woke the next morning, the Psammead was snuggling down between her shoulder and Jane's.

'You have saved my life,' it said. 'I know that man would have thrown cold water on me sooner or later, and then I should have died. I saw him wash out a guinea-pig's hutch yesterday morning. I'm still frightfully sleepy, I think I'll go back to sand for another nap. Wake the boys and this dormouse of a Jane, and when you've had your breakfasts we'll have a talk.'

'Don't YOU want any breakfast?' asked Anthea.

'I daresay I shall pick a bit presently,' it said; 'but sand is all I care about—it's meat and drink to me, and coals and fire and wife and children.' With these words it clambered down by the bedclothes and scrambled back into the bath, where they heard it scratching itself out of sight.

'Well!' said Anthea, 'anyhow our holidays won't be dull NOW. We've found the Psammead again.'

'No,' said Jane, beginning to put on her stockings. 'We shan't be dull—but it'll be only like having a pet dog now it can't give us wishes.'

'Oh, don't be so discontented,' said Anthea. 'If it can't do anything else it can tell us about Megatheriums and things.'

Chapter 2. The Half Amulet

Long ago—that is to say last summer—the children, finding themselves embarrassed by some wish which the Psammead had granted them, and which the servants had not received in a proper spirit, had wished that the servants might not notice the gifts which the Psammead gave. And when they parted from the Psammead their last wish had been that they should meet it again. Therefore they HAD met it (and it was jolly lucky for the Psammead, as Robert pointed out). Now, of course, you see that the Psammead's being where it was, was the consequence of one of their wishes, and therefore was a Psammead-wish, and as such could not be noticed by the servants. And it was soon plain that in the Psammead's opinion old Nurse was still a servant, although she had now a house of her own, for she never noticed the Psammead at all. And that was as well, for she would never have consented to allow the girls to keep an animal and a bath of sand under their bed.

When breakfast had been cleared away—it was a very nice breakfast with hot rolls to it, a luxury quite out of the common way—Anthea went and dragged out the bath, and woke the Psammead.

It stretched and shook itself.

'You must have bolted your breakfast most unwholesomely,' it said, 'you can't have been five minutes over it.'

'We've been nearly an hour,' said Anthea. 'Come—you know you promised.'

'Now look here,' said the Psammead, sitting back on the sand and shooting out its long eyes suddenly, 'we'd better begin as we mean to go on. It won't do to have any misunderstanding, so I tell you plainly that—'

'Oh, PLEASE,' Anthea pleaded, 'do wait till we get to the others. They'll think it most awfully sneakish of me to talk to you without them; do come down, there's a dear.'

She knelt before the sand-bath and held out her arms. The Psammead must have remembered how glad it had been to jump into those same little arms only the day before, for it gave a little grudging grunt, and jumped once more.

Anthea wrapped it in her pinafore and carried it downstairs. It was welcomed in a thrilling silence. At last Anthea said, 'Now then!'

'What place is this?' asked the Psammead, shooting its eyes out and turning them slowly round.

'It's a sitting-room, of course,' said Robert.

'Then I don't like it,' said the Psammead.

'Never mind,' said Anthea kindly; 'we'll take you anywhere you like if you want us to. What was it you were going to say upstairs when I said the others wouldn't like it if I stayed talking to you without them?'

It looked keenly at her, and she blushed.

'Don't be silly,' it said sharply. 'Of course, it's quite natural that you should like your brothers and sisters to know exactly how good and unselfish you were.'

'I wish you wouldn't,' said Jane. 'Anthea was quite right. What was it you were going to say when she stopped you?'

'I'll tell you,' said the Psammead, 'since you're so anxious to know. I was going to say this. You've saved my life—and I'm not ungrateful—but it doesn't change your nature or mine. You're still very ignorant, and rather silly, and I am worth a thousand of you any day of the week.'

'Of course you are!' Anthea was beginning but it interrupted her.

'It's very rude to interrupt,' it said; 'what I mean is that I'm not going to stand any nonsense, and if you think what you've done is to give you the right to pet me or make me demean myself by playing with you, you'll find out that what you think doesn't matter a single penny. See? It's what *I* think that matters.'

'I know,' said Cyril, 'it always was, if you remember.'

'Well,' said the Psammead, 'then that's settled. We're to be treated as we deserve. I with respect, and all of you with—but I don't wish to be offensive. Do you want me to tell you how I got into that horrible den you bought me out of? Oh, I'm not ungrateful! I haven't forgotten it and I shan't forget it.'

'Do tell us,' said Anthea. 'I know you're awfully clever, but even with all your cleverness, I don't believe you can possibly know how—how respectfully we do respect you. Don't we?'

The others all said yes—and fidgeted in their chairs. Robert spoke the wishes of all when he said—

'I do wish you'd go on.' So it sat up on the green-covered table and went on.

'When you'd gone away,' it said, 'I went to sand for a bit, and slept. I was tired out with all your silly wishes, and I felt as though I hadn't really been to sand for a year.'

'To sand?' Jane repeated.

'Where I sleep. You go to bed. I go to sand.'

Jane yawned; the mention of bed made her feel sleepy.

'All right,' said the Psammead, in offended tones. 'I'm sure *I* don't want to tell you a long tale. A man caught me, and I bit him. And he put me in a bag with a dead hare and a dead rabbit. And he took me to his house and put me out of the bag into a basket with holes that I could see through. And I bit him again. And then he brought me to this city, which I am told is called the Modern Babylon—though it's not a bit like the old Babylon—and he sold me to the man you bought me from, and then I bit them both. Now, what's your news?'

'There's not quite so much biting in our story,' said Cyril regretfully; 'in fact, there isn't any. Father's gone to Manchuria, and Mother and The Lamb have gone to Madeira because Mother was ill, and don't I just wish that they were both safe home again.'

Merely from habit, the Sand-fairy began to blow itself out, but it stopped short suddenly.

'I forgot,' it said; 'I can't give you any more wishes.'

'No—but look here,' said Cyril, 'couldn't we call in old Nurse and get her to say SHE wishes they were safe home. I'm sure she does.'

'No go,' said the Psammead. 'It's just the same as your wishing yourself if you get some one else to wish for you. It won't act.'

'But it did yesterday—with the man in the shop,' said Robert.

'Ah yes,' said the creature, 'but you didn't ASK him to wish, and you didn't know what would happen if he did. That can't be done again. It's played out.'

'Then you can't help us at all,' said Jane; 'oh—I did think you could do something; I've been thinking about it ever since we saved your life yesterday. I thought you'd be certain to be able to fetch back Father, even if you couldn't manage Mother.'

And Jane began to cry.

'Now DON'T,' said the Psammead hastily; 'you know how it always upsets me if you cry. I can't feel safe a moment. Look here; you must have some new kind of charm.'

'That's easier said than done.'

'Not a bit of it,' said the creature; 'there's one of the strongest charms in the world not a stone's throw from where you bought me yesterday. The man that I bit so—the first one, I mean—went into a shop to ask how much something cost—I think he said it was a concertina—and while he was telling the man in the shop how much too much he wanted for it, I saw the charm in a sort of tray, with a lot of other things. If you can only buy THAT, you will be able to have your heart's desire.'

The children looked at each other and then at the Psammead. Then Cyril coughed awkwardly and took sudden courage to say what everyone was thinking.

'I do hope you won't be waxy,' he said; 'but it's like this: when you used to give us our wishes they almost always got us into some row or other, and we used to think you wouldn't have been pleased if they hadn't. Now, about this charm—we haven't got over and above too much tin, and if we blue it all on this charm and it turns out to be not up to much—well—you see what I'm driving at, don't you?'

'I see that YOU don't see more than the length of your nose, and THAT'S not far,' said the Psammead crossly. 'Look here, I HAD to give you the wishes, and of course they turned out badly, in a sort of way, because you hadn't the sense to wish for what was good for you. But this charm's quite different. I haven't GOT to do this for you, it's just my own generous kindness that makes me tell you about it. So it's bound to be all right. See?'

'Don't be cross,' said Anthea, 'Please, PLEASE don't. You see, it's all we've got; we shan't have any more pocket-money till Daddy comes home—unless he sends us some in a letter. But we DO trust you. And I say all of you,' she went on, 'don't you think it's worth spending ALL the money, if there's even the chanciest chance of getting Father and Mother back safe NOW? Just think of it! Oh, do let's!'

'*I* don't care what you do,' said the Psammead; 'I'll go back to sand again till you've made up your minds.'

'No, don't!' said everybody; and Jane added, 'We are quite mind made-up—don't you see we are? Let's get our hats. Will you come with us?'

'Of course,' said the Psammead; 'how else would you find the shop?'

So everybody got its hat. The Psammead was put into a flat bass-bag that had come from Farringdon Market with two pounds of filleted plaice in it. Now it contained about three pounds and a quarter of solid Psammead, and the children took it in turns to carry it.

'It's not half the weight of The Lamb,' Robert said, and the girls sighed.

The Psammead poked a wary eye out of the top of the basket every now and then, and told the children which turnings to take.

'How on earth do you know?' asked Robert. 'I can't think how you do it.'

And the Psammead said sharply, 'No—I don't suppose you can.'

At last they came to THE shop. It had all sorts and kinds of things in the window—concertinas, and silk handkerchiefs, china vases and tea-cups, blue Japanese jars, pipes, swords, pistols, lace collars, silver spoons tied up in half-dozens, and wedding-rings in a red lacquered basin. There were officers' epaulets and doctors' lancets. There were tea-caddies inlaid with red turtle-shell and brass curly-wurlies, plates of different kinds of money, and stacks of different kinds of plates. There was a beautiful picture of a little girl washing a dog, which Jane liked very much. And in the middle of the window there was a dirty silver tray full of mother-of-pearl card counters, old seals, paste buckles, snuff-boxes, and all sorts of little dingy odds and ends.

The Psammead put its head quite out of the fish-basket to look in the window, when Cyril said—

'There's a tray there with rubbish in it.'

And then its long snail's eyes saw something that made them stretch out so much that they were as long and thin as new slate-pencils. Its fur bristled thickly, and its voice was quite hoarse with excitement as it whispered—

'That's it! That's it! There, under that blue and yellow buckle, you can see a bit sticking out. It's red. Do you see?'

'Is it that thing something like a horse-shoe?' asked Cyril. 'And red, like the common sealing-wax you do up parcels with?' 'Yes, that's it,' said the Psammead. 'Now, you do just as you did before. Ask the price of other things. That blue buckle would do. Then the man will get the tray out of the window. I think you'd better be the one,' it said to Anthea. 'We'll wait out here.'

So the others flattened their noses against the shop window, and presently a large, dirty, short-fingered hand with a very big diamond ring came stretching through the green half-curtains at the back of the shop window and took away the tray.

They could not see what was happening in the interview between Anthea and the Diamond Ring, and it seemed to them that she had had time—if she had had money—to buy everything in the shop before the moment came when she stood before them, her face wreathed in grins, as Cyril said later, and in her hand the charm.

It was made of a red, smooth, softly shiny stone.

'I've got it,' Anthea whispered, just opening her hand to give the others a glimpse of it. 'Do let's get home. We can't stand here like stuck-pigs looking at it in the street.'

So home they went. The parlour in Fitzroy Street was a very flat background to magic happenings. Down in the country among the flowers and green fields anything had seemed—and indeed had been—possible. But it was hard to believe that anything really wonderful could happen so near the Tottenham Court Road. But the Psammead was there—and it in itself was wonderful. And it could talk—and it had shown them where a charm could be bought that would make the owner of it perfectly happy. So the four children hurried home, taking very long steps, with their chins stuck out, and their mouths shut very tight indeed. They went so fast that the Psammead was quite shaken about in its fish-bag, but it did not say anything—perhaps for fear of attracting public notice.

They got home at last, very hot indeed, and set the Psammead on the green tablecloth.

'Now then!' said Cyril.

But the Psammead had to have a plate of sand fetched for it, for it was quite faint. When it had refreshed itself a little it said—

'Now then! Let me see the charm,' and Anthea laid it on the green table-cover. The Psammead shot out his long eyes to look at it, then it turned them reproachfully on Anthea and said—

'But there's only half of it here!'

This was indeed a blow.

'It was all there was,' said Anthea, with timid firmness. She knew it was not her fault. 'There should be another piece,' said the Psammead, 'and a sort of pin to fasten the two together.'

'Isn't half any good?'—'Won't it work without the other bit?'—'It cost seven-and-six.'—'Oh, bother, bother, bother!'—'Don't be silly little idiots!' said everyone and the Psammead altogether.

Then there was a wretched silence. Cyril broke it—

'What shall we do?'

'Go back to the shop and see if they haven't got the other half,' said the Psammead. 'I'll go to sand till you come back. Cheer up! Even the bit you've got is SOME good, but it'll be no end of a bother if you can't find the other.'

So Cyril went to the shop. And the Psammead to sand. And the other three went to dinner, which was now ready. And old Nurse was very cross that Cyril was not ready too.

The three were watching at the windows when Cyril returned, and even before he was near enough for them to see his face there was something about the slouch of his shoulders and set of his knickerbockers and the way he dragged his boots along that showed but too plainly that his errand had been in vain.

'Well?' they all said, hoping against hope on the front-door step.

'No go,' Cyril answered; 'the man said the thing was perfect. He said it was a Roman lady's locket, and people shouldn't buy curios if they didn't know anything about arky—something or other, and that he never went back on a bargain, because it wasn't business, and he expected his customers to act the same. He was simply nasty—that's what he was, and I want my dinner.'

It was plain that Cyril was not pleased.

The unlikeliness of anything really interesting happening in that parlour lay like a weight of lead on everyone's spirits. Cyril had his dinner, and just as he was swallowing the last mouthful of apple-pudding there was a scratch at the door. Anthea opened it and in walked the Psammead.

'Well,' it said, when it had heard the news, 'things might be worse. Only you won't be surprised if you have a few adventures before you get the other half. You want to get it, of course.'

'Rather,' was the general reply. 'And we don't mind adventures.'

'No,' said the Psammead, 'I seem to remember that about you. Well, sit down and listen with all your ears. Eight, are there? Right—I am glad you know arithmetic. Now pay attention, because I don't intend to tell you everything twice over.'

As the children settled themselves on the floor—it was far more comfortable than the chairs, as well as more polite to the Psammead, who was stroking its whiskers on the hearth-rug—a sudden cold pain caught at Anthea's heart. Father—Mother—the darling Lamb—all far away. Then a warm, comfortable feeling flowed through her. The Psammead was here, and at least half a charm, and there were to be adventures. (If you don't know what a cold pain is, I am glad for your sakes, and I hope you never may.)

'Now,' said the Psammead cheerily, 'you are not particularly nice, nor particularly clever, and you're not at all good-looking. Still, you've saved my life—oh, when I think of that man and his pail of water!—so I'll tell you all I know. At least, of course I can't do that, because I know far too much. But I'll tell you all I know about this red thing.'

'Do! Do! Do! Do!' said everyone.

'Well, then,' said the Psammead. 'This thing is half of an Amulet that can do all sorts of things; it can make the corn grow, and the waters flow, and the trees bear fruit, and the little new beautiful babies come. (Not that babies ARE beautiful, of course,' it broke off to say, 'but their mothers think they are—and as long as you think a thing's true it IS true as far as you're concerned.)'

Robert yawned.

The Psammead went on.

'The complete Amulet can keep off all the things that make people unhappy—jealousy, bad temper, pride, disagreeableness, greediness, selfishness, laziness. Evil spirits, people called them when the Amulet was made. Don't you think it would be nice to have it?'

'Very,' said the children, quite without enthusiasm.

'And it can give you strength and courage.'

'That's better,' said Cyril.

'And virtue.'

'I suppose it's nice to have that,' said Jane, but not with much interest.

'And it can give you your heart's desire.'

'Now you're talking,' said Robert.

'Of course I am,' retorted the Psammead tartly, 'so there's no need for you to.'

'Heart's desire is good enough for me,' said Cyril.

'Yes, but,' Anthea ventured, 'all that's what the WHOLE charm can do. There's something that the half we've got can win off its own bat—isn't there?' She appealed to the Psammead. It nodded.

'Yes,' it said; 'the half has the power to take you anywhere you like to look for the other half.'

This seemed a brilliant prospect till Robert asked—

'Does it know where to look?'

The Psammead shook its head and answered, 'I don't think it's likely.'

'Do you?'

'No.'

'Then,' said Robert, 'we might as well look for a needle in a bottle of hay. Yes—it IS bottle, and not bundle, Father said so.'

'Not at all,' said the Psammead briskly-, 'you think you know everything, but you are quite mistaken. The first thing is to get the thing to talk.'

'Can it?' Jane questioned. Jane's question did not mean that she thought it couldn't, for in spite of the parlour furniture the feeling of magic was growing deeper and thicker, and seemed to fill the room like a dream of a scented fog.

'Of course it can. I suppose you can read.'

'Oh yes!' Everyone was rather hurt at the question.

'Well, then—all you've got to do is to read the name that's written on the part of the charm that you've got. And as soon as you say the name out loud the thing will have power to do—well, several things.'

There was a silence. The red charm was passed from hand to hand.

'There's no name on it,' said Cyril at last.

'Nonsense,' said the Psammead; 'what's that?'

'Oh, THAT!' said Cyril, 'it's not reading. It looks like pictures of chickens and snakes and things.'

'I've no patience with you,' said the Psammead; 'if you can't read you must find some one who can. A priest now?'

'We don't know any priests,' said Anthea; 'we know a clergyman—he's called a priest in the prayer-book, you know—but he only knows Greek and Latin and Hebrew, and this isn't any of those—I know.'

The Psammead stamped a furry foot angrily.

'I wish I'd never seen you,' it said; 'you aren't any more good than so many stone images. Not so much, if I'm to tell the truth. Is there no wise man in your Babylon who can pronounce the names of the Great Ones?'

'There's a poor learned gentleman upstairs,' said Anthea, 'we might try him. He has a lot of stone images in his room, and iron-looking ones too—we peeped in once when he was out. Old Nurse says he doesn't eat enough to keep a canary alive. He spends it all on stones and things.'

'Try him,' said the Psammead, 'only be careful. If he knows a greater name than this and uses it against you, your charm will be of no use. Bind him first with the chains of honour and upright dealing. And then ask his aid—oh, yes, you'd better all go; you can put me to sand as you go upstairs. I must have a few minutes' peace and quietness.'

So the four children hastily washed their hands and brushed their hair—this was Anthea's idea—and went up to knock at the door of the 'poor learned gentleman', and to 'bind him with the chains of honour and upright dealing'.

The learned gentleman had let his dinner get quite cold. It was mutton chop, and as it lay on the plate it looked like a brown island in the middle of a frozen pond, because the grease of the gravy had become cold, and consequently white. It looked very nasty, and it was the first thing the children saw when, after knocking three times and receiving no reply, one of them ventured to turn the handle and softly to open the door. The chop was on the end of a long table that ran down one side of the room. The table had images on it and queer-shaped stones, and books. And there were glass cases fixed against the wall behind, with little strange things in them. The cases were rather like the ones you see in jewellers' shops.

The 'poor learned gentleman' was sitting at a table in the window, looking at something very small which he held in a pair of fine pincers. He had a round spy-glass sort of thing in one eye—which reminded the children of watchmakers, and also of the long snail's eyes of the Psammead. The gentleman was very long and thin, and his long, thin boots stuck out under the other side of his table. He did not hear the door open, and the children stood hesitating. At last Robert gave the door a push, and they all started back, for in the middle of the wall that the door had hidden was a mummy-case—very, very, very big—painted in red and yellow and green and black, and the face of it seemed to look at them quite angrily.

You know what a mummy-case is like, of course? If you don't you had better go to the British Museum at once and find out. Anyway, it is not at all the sort of thing that you expect to meet in a top-floor front in Bloomsbury, looking as though it would like to know what business YOU had there.

So everyone said, 'Oh!' rather loud, and their boots clattered as they stumbled back.

The learned gentleman took the glass out of his eye and said—'I beg your pardon,' in a very soft, quiet pleasant voice—the voice of a gentleman who has been to Oxford.

'It's us that beg yours,' said Cyril politely. 'We are sorry to disturb you.'

'Come in,' said the gentleman, rising—with the most distinguished courtesy, Anthea told herself. 'I am delighted to see you. Won't you sit down? No, not there; allow me to move that papyrus.'

He cleared a chair, and stood smiling and looking kindly through his large, round spectacles.

'He treats us like grown-ups,' whispered Robert, 'and he doesn't seem to know how many of us there are.'

'Hush,' said Anthea, 'it isn't manners to whisper. You say, Cyril—go ahead.'

'We're very sorry to disturb you,' said Cyril politely, 'but we did knock three times, and you didn't say "Come in", or "Run away now", or that you couldn't be bothered just now, or to come when you weren't so busy, or any of the things people do say when you knock at doors, so we opened it. We knew you were in because we heard you sneeze while we were waiting.'

'Not at all,' said the gentleman; 'do sit down.'

'He has found out there are four of us,' said Robert, as the gentleman cleared three more chairs. He put the things off them carefully on the floor. The first chair had things like bricks that tiny, tiny birds' feet have walked over when the bricks were soft, only the marks were in regular lines. The second chair had round things on it like very large, fat, long, pale beads. And the last chair had a pile of dusty papers on it. The children sat down.

'We know you are very, very learned,' said Cyril, 'and we have got a charm, and we want you to read the name on it, because it isn't in Latin or Greek, or Hebrew, or any of the languages WE know—'

'A thorough knowledge of even those languages is a very fair foundation on which to build an education,' said the gentleman politely.

'Oh!' said Cyril blushing, 'but we only know them to look at, except Latin—and I'm only in Caesar with that.' The gentleman took off his spectacles and laughed. His laugh sounded rusty, Cyril thought, as though it wasn't often used.

'Of course!' he said. 'I'm sure I beg your pardon. I think I must have been in a dream. You are the children who live downstairs, are you not? Yes. I have seen you as I have passed in and out. And you have found something that you think to be an antiquity, and you've brought it to show me? That was very kind. I should like to inspect it."

'I'm afraid we didn't think about your liking to inspect it,' said the truthful Anthea. 'It was just for US because we wanted to know the name on it—'

'Oh, yes—and, I say,' Robert interjected, 'you won't think it rude of us if we ask you first, before we show it, to be bound in the what-do-you-call-it of—'

'In the bonds of honour and upright dealing,' said Anthea.

'I'm afraid I don't quite follow you,' said the gentleman, with gentle nervousness.

'Well, it's this way,' said Cyril. 'We've got part of a charm. And the Sammy—I mean, something told us it would work, though it's only half a one; but it won't work unless we can say the name that's on it. But, of course, if you've got another name that can lick ours, our charm will be no go; so we want you to give us your word of honour as a gentleman—though I'm sure, now I've seen you, that it's not necessary; but still I've promised to ask you, so we must. Will you please give us your honourable word not to say any name stronger than the name on our charm?'

The gentleman had put on his spectacles again and was looking at Cyril through them. He now said: 'Bless me!' more than once, adding, 'Who told you all this?'

'I can't tell you,' said Cyril. 'I'm very sorry, but I can't.'

Some faint memory of a far-off childhood must have come to the learned gentleman just then, for he smiled. 'I see,' he said. 'It is some sort of game that you are engaged in? Of course! Yes! Well, I will certainly promise. Yet I wonder how you heard of the names of power?'

'We can't tell you that either,' said Cyril; and Anthea said, 'Here is our charm,' and held it out.

With politeness, but without interest, the gentleman took it. But after the first glance all his body suddenly stiffened, as a pointer's does when he sees a partridge.

'Excuse me,' he said in quite a changed voice, and carried the charm to the window. He looked at it; he turned it over. He fixed his spy-glass in his eye and looked again. No one said anything. Only Robert made a shuffling noise with his feet till Anthea nudged him to shut up. At last the learned gentleman drew a long breath.

'Where did you find this?' he asked.

'We didn't find it. We bought it at a shop. Jacob Absalom the name is—not far from Charing Cross,' said Cyril.

'We gave seven-and-sixpence for it,' added Jane.

'It is not for sale, I suppose? You do not wish to part with it? I ought to tell you that it is extremely valuable — extraordinarily valuable, I may say.'

'Yes,' said Cyril, 'we know that, so of course we want to keep it.'

'Keep it carefully, then,' said the gentleman impressively; 'and if ever you should wish to part with it, may I ask you to give me the refusal of it?'

'The refusal?'

'I mean, do not sell it to anyone else until you have given me the opportunity of buying it.'

'All right,' said Cyril, 'we won't. But we don't want to sell it. We want to make it do things.'

'I suppose you can play at that as well as at anything else,' said the gentleman; 'but I'm afraid the days of magic are over.'

'They aren't REALLY,' said Anthea earnestly. 'You'd see they aren't if I could tell you about our last summer holidays. Only I mustn't. Thank you very much. And can you read the name?'

'Yes, I can read it.'

'Will you tell it us?'

'The name,' said the gentleman, 'is Ur Hekau Setcheh.'

'Ur Hekau Setcheh,' repeated Cyril. 'Thanks awfully. I do hope we haven't taken up too much of your time.'

'Not at all,' said the gentleman. 'And do let me entreat you to be very, very careful of that most valuable specimen.'

They said 'Thank you' in all the different polite ways they could think of, and filed out of the door and down the stairs. Anthea was last. Half-way down to the first landing she turned and ran up again.

The door was still open, and the learned gentleman and the mummy-case were standing opposite to each other, and both looked as though they had stood like that for years.

The gentleman started when Anthea put her hand on his arm.

'I hope you won't be cross and say it's not my business,' she said, 'but do look at your chop! Don't you think you ought to eat it? Father forgets his dinner sometimes when he's writing, and Mother always says I ought to remind him if she's not at home to do it herself, because it's so bad to miss your regular meals. So I thought perhaps you wouldn't mind my reminding you, because you don't seem to have anyone else to do it.'

She glanced at the mummy-case; IT certainly did not look as though it would ever think of reminding people of their meals.

The learned gentleman looked at her for a moment before he said—

'Thank you, my dear. It was a kindly thought. No, I haven't anyone to remind me about things like that.'

He sighed, and looked at the chop.

'It looks very nasty,' said Anthea.

'Yes,' he said, 'it does. I'll eat it immediately, before I forget.'

As he ate it he sighed more than once. Perhaps because the chop was nasty, perhaps because he longed for the charm which the children did not want to sell, perhaps because it was so long since anyone cared whether he ate his chops or forgot them.

Anthea caught the others at the stair-foot. They woke the Psammead, and it taught them exactly how to use the word of power, and to make the charm speak. I am not going to tell you how this is done, because you might try to do it. And for you any such trying would be almost sure to end in disappointment. Because in the first place it is a thousand million to one against your ever getting hold of the right sort of charm, and if you did, there would be hardly any chance at all of your finding a learned gentleman clever enough and kind enough to read the word for you.

The children and the Psammead crouched in a circle on the floor—in the girls' bedroom, because in the parlour they might have been interrupted by old Nurse's coming in to lay the cloth for tea—and the charm was put in the middle of the circle.

The sun shone splendidly outside, and the room was very light. Through the open window came the hum and rattle of London, and in the street below they could hear the voice of the milkman.

When all was ready, the Psammead signed to Anthea to say the word. And she said it. Instantly the whole light of all the world seemed to go out. The room was dark. The world outside was dark—darker than the darkest night that ever was. And all the sounds went out too, so that there was a silence deeper than any silence you have ever even dreamed of imagining. It was like being suddenly deaf and blind, only darker and quieter even than that.

But before the children had got over the sudden shock of it enough to be frightened, a faint, beautiful light began to show in the middle of the circle, and at the same moment a faint, beautiful voice began to speak. The light was too small for one to see anything by, and the voice was too small for you to hear what it said. You could just see the light and just hear the voice.

But the light grew stronger. It was greeny, like glow-worms' lamps, and it grew and grew till it was as though thousands and thousands of glow-worms were signalling to their winged sweethearts from the middle of the circle. And the voice grew, not so much in loudness as in sweetness (though it grew louder, too), till it was so sweet that you wanted to cry with pleasure just at the sound of it. It was like nightingales, and the sea, and the fiddle, and the voice of your mother when you have been a long time away, and she meets you at the door when you get home.

And the voice said—

'Speak. What is it that you would hear?'

I cannot tell you what language the voice used. I only know that everyone present understood it perfectly. If you come to think of it, there must be some language that everyone could understand, if we only knew what it was. Nor can I tell you how the charm spoke, nor whether it was the charm that spoke, or some presence in the charm. The children could not have told you either. Indeed, they could not look at the charm while it was speaking, because the light was too bright. They looked instead at the green radiance on the faded Kidderminster carpet at the edge of the circle. They all felt very quiet, and not inclined to ask questions or fidget with their feet. For this was not like the things that had happened in the country when the Psammead had given them their wishes. That had been funny somehow, and this was not. It was something like Arabian Nights magic, and something like being in church. No one cared to speak.

It was Cyril who said at last—

'Please we want to know where the other half of the charm is.'

'The part of the Amulet which is lost,' said the beautiful voice, 'was broken and ground into the dust of the shrine that held it. It and the pin that joined the two halves are themselves dust, and the dust is scattered over many lands and sunk in many seas.'

'Oh, I say!' murmured Robert, and a blank silence fell.

'Then it's all up?' said Cyril at last; 'it's no use our looking for a thing that's smashed into dust, and the dust scattered all over the place.'

'If you would find it,' said the voice, 'You must seek it where it still is, perfect as ever.'

'I don't understand,' said Cyril.

'In the Past you may find it,' said the voice.

'I wish we MAY find it,' said Cyril.

The Psammead whispered crossly, 'Don't you understand? The thing existed in the Past. If you were in the Past, too, you could find it. It's very difficult to make you understand things. Time and space are only forms of thought.'

'I see,' said Cyril.

'No, you don't,' said the Psammead, 'and it doesn't matter if you don't, either. What I mean is that if you were only made the right way, you could see everything happening in the same place at the same time. Now do you see?'

'I'm afraid *I* don't,' said Anthea; 'I'm sorry I'm so stupid.'

'Well, at any rate, you see this. That lost half of the Amulet is in the Past. Therefore it's in the Past we must look for it. I mustn't speak to the charm myself. Ask it things! Find out!'

'Where can we find the other part of you?' asked Cyril obediently.

'In the Past,' said the voice.

'What part of the Past?'

'I may not tell you. If you will choose a time, I will take you to the place that then held it. You yourselves must find it.'

'When did you see it last?' asked Anthea—'I mean, when was it taken away from you?'

The beautiful voice answered—

'That was thousands of years ago. The Amulet was perfect then, and lay in a shrine, the last of many shrines, and I worked wonders. Then came strange men with strange weapons and destroyed my shrine, and the Amulet they bore away with many captives. But of these, one, my priest, knew the word of power, and spoke it for me, so that the Amulet became invisible, and thus returned to my shrine, but the shrine was broken down, and ere any magic could rebuild it one spoke a word before which my power bowed down and was still. And the Amulet lay there, still perfect, but enslaved. Then one coming with stones to rebuild the shrine, dropped a hewn stone on the Amulet as it lay, and one half was sundered from the other. I had no power to seek for that which was lost. And there being none to speak the word of power, I could not rejoin it. So the Amulet lay in the dust of the desert many thousand years, and at last came a small man, a conqueror with an army, and after him a crowd of men who sought to seem wise, and one of these found half the Amulet and brought it to this land. But none could read the name. So I lay still. And this man dying and his son after him, the Amulet was sold by those who came after to a merchant, and from him you bought it, and it is here, and now, the name of power having been spoken, I also am here.'

This is what the voice said. I think it must have meant Napoleon by the small man, the conqueror. Because I know I have been told that he took an army to Egypt, and that afterwards a lot of wise people went grubbing in the sand, and fished up all sorts of wonderful things, older than you would think possible. And of these I believe this charm to have been one, and the most wonderful one of all.

Everyone listened: and everyone tried to think. It is not easy to do this clearly when you have been listening to the kind of talk I have told you about.

At last Robert said—

'Can you take us into the Past—to the shrine where you and the other thing were together. If you could take us there, we might find the other part still there after all these thousands of years.'

'Still there? silly!' said Cyril. 'Don't you see, if we go back into the Past it won't be thousands of years ago. It will be NOW for us—won't it?' He appealed to the Psammead, who said—

'You're not so far off the idea as you usually are!'

'Well,' said Anthea, 'will you take us back to when there was a shrine and you were safe in it—all of you?'

'Yes,' said the voice. 'You must hold me up, and speak the word of power, and one by one, beginning with the first-born, you shall pass through me into the Past. But let the last that passes be the one that holds me, and let him not lose his hold, lest you lose me, and so remain in the Past for ever.'

'That's a nasty idea,' said Robert.

'When you desire to return,' the beautiful voice went on, 'hold me up towards the East, and speak the word. Then, passing through me, you shall return to this time and it shall be the present to you.'

'But how—' A bell rang loudly.

'Oh crikey!' exclaimed Robert, 'that's tea! Will you please make it proper daylight again so that we can go down. And thank you so much for all your kindness.'

'We've enjoyed ourselves very much indeed, thank you!' added Anthea politely.

The beautiful light faded slowly. The great darkness and silence came and these suddenly changed to the dazzlement of day and the great soft, rustling sound of London, that is like some vast beast turning over in its sleep.

The children rubbed their eyes, the Psammead ran quickly to its sandy bath, and the others went down to tea. And until the cups were actually filled tea seemed less real than the beautiful voice and the greeny light.

After tea Anthea persuaded the others to allow her to hang the charm round her neck with a piece of string.

'It would be so awful if it got lost,' she said: 'it might get lost anywhere, you know, and it would be rather beastly for us to have to stay in the Past for ever and ever, wouldn't it?'

Chapter 4. Eight Thousand Years Ago

Next morning Anthea got old Nurse to allow her to take up the 'poor learned gentleman's' breakfast. He did not recognize her at first, but when he did he was vaguely pleased to see her.

'You see I'm wearing the charm round my neck,' she said; 'I'm taking care of it—like you told us to.'

'That's right,' said he; 'did you have a good game last night?'

'You will eat your breakfast before it's cold, won't you?' said Anthea. 'Yes, we had a splendid time. The charm made it all dark, and then greeny light, and then it spoke. Oh! I wish you could have heard it—it was such a darling voice—and it told us the other half of it was lost in the Past, so of course we shall have to look for it there!'

The learned gentleman rubbed his hair with both hands and looked anxiously at Anthea.

'I suppose it's natural—youthful imagination and so forth,' he said. 'Yet someone must have ... Who told you that some part of the charm was missing?'

'I can't tell you,' she said. 'I know it seems most awfully rude, especially after being so kind about telling us the name of power, and all that, but really, I'm not allowed to tell anybody anything about the—the—the person who told me. You won't forget your breakfast, will you?'

The learned gentleman smiled feebly and then frowned—not a cross-frown, but a puzzle-frown.

'Thank you,' he said, 'I shall always be pleased if you'll look in—any time you're passing you know—at least ...'

'I will,' she said; 'goodbye. I'll always tell you anything I MAY tell.'

He had not had many adventures with children in them, and he wondered whether all children were like these. He spent quite five minutes in wondering before he settled down to the fifty-second chapter of his great book on 'The Secret Rites of the Priests of Amen Ra'.

It is no use to pretend that the children did not feel a good deal of agitation at the thought of going through the charm into the Past. That idea, that perhaps they might stay in the Past and never get back again, was anything but pleasing. Yet no one would have dared to suggest that the charm should not be used; and though each was in its heart very frightened indeed, they would all have joined in jeering at the cowardice of any one of them who should have uttered the timid but natural suggestion, 'Don't let's!'

It seemed necessary to make arrangements for being out all day, for there was no reason to suppose that the sound of the dinner-bell would be able to reach back into the Past, and it seemed unwise to excite old Nurse's curiosity when nothing they could say—not even the truth—could in any way satisfy it. They were all very proud to think how well they had understood what the charm and the Psammead had said about Time and Space and things like that, and they were perfectly certain that it would be quite impossible to make old Nurse understand a single word of it. So they merely asked her to let them take their dinner out into Regent's Park—and this, with the implied cold mutton and tomatoes, was readily granted.

'You can get yourselves some buns or sponge-cakes, or whatever you fancy-like,' said old Nurse, giving Cyril a shilling. 'Don't go getting jam-tarts, now—so messy at the best of times, and without forks and plates ruination to your clothes, besides your not being able to wash your hands and faces afterwards.'

So Cyril took the shilling, and they all started off. They went round by the Tottenham Court Road to buy a piece of waterproof sheeting to put over the Psammead in case it should be raining in the Past when they got there. For it is almost certain death to a Psammead to get wet.

The sun was shining very brightly, and even London looked pretty. Women were selling roses from big baskets-full, and Anthea bought four roses, one each, for herself and the others. They were red roses and smelt of summer—the kind of roses you always want so desperately at about Christmas-time when you can only get mistletoe, which is pale right through to its very scent, and holly which pricks your nose if you try to smell it. So now everyone had a rose in its buttonhole, and soon everyone was sitting on the grass in Regent's Park under trees whose leaves would have been clean, clear green in the country, but here were dusty and yellowish, and brown at the edges.

'We've got to go on with it,' said Anthea, 'and as the eldest has to go first, you'll have to be last, Jane. You quite understand about holding on to the charm as you go through, don't you, Pussy?'

'I wish I hadn't got to be last,' said Jane.

'You shall carry the Psammead if you like,' said Anthea. 'That is,' she added, remembering the beast's queer temper, 'if it'll let you.'

The Psammead, however, was unexpectedly amiable.

'*I* don't mind,' it said, 'who carries me, so long as it doesn't drop me. I can't bear being dropped.'

Jane with trembling hands took the Psammead and its fish-basket under one arm. The charm's long string was hung round her neck. Then they all stood up. Jane held out the charm at arm's length, and Cyril solemnly pronounced the word of power.

As he spoke it the charm grew tall and broad, and he saw that Jane was just holding on to the edge of a great red arch of very curious shape. The opening of the arch was small, but Cyril saw that he could go through it. All round and beyond the arch were the faded trees and trampled grass of Regent's Park, where the little ragged children were playing Ring-o'-Roses. But through the opening of it shone a blaze of blue and yellow and red. Cyril drew a long breath and stiffened his legs so that the others should not see that his knees were trembling and almost knocking together. 'Here goes!' he said, and, stepping up through the arch, disappeared. Then followed Anthea. Robert, coming next, held fast, at Anthea's suggestion, to the sleeve of Jane, who was thus dragged safely through the arch. And as soon as they were on the other side of the arch there was no more arch at all and no more Regent's Park either, only the charm in Jane's hand, and it was its proper size again. They were now in a light so bright that they winked and blinked and rubbed their eyes. During this dazzling interval Anthea felt for the charm and pushed it inside Jane's frock, so that it might be quite safe. When their eyes got used to the new wonderful light the children looked around them. The sky was very, very blue, and it sparkled and glittered and dazzled like the sea at home when the sun shines on it.

They were standing on a little clearing in a thick, low forest; there were trees and shrubs and a close, thorny, tangly undergrowth. In front of them stretched a bank of strange black mud, then came the browny-yellowy shining ribbon of a river. Then more dry, caked mud and more greeny-browny jungle. The only things that told that human people had been there were the clearing, a path that led to it, and an odd arrangement of cut reeds in the river.

They looked at each other.

'Well!' said Robert, 'this IS a change of air!'

It was. The air was hotter than they could have imagined, even in London in August.

'I wish I knew where we were,' said Cyril.

'Here's a river, now—I wonder whether it's the Amazon or the Tiber, or what.'

'It's the Nile,' said the Psammead, looking out of the fish-bag.

'Then this is Egypt,' said Robert, who had once taken a geography prize.

'I don't see any crocodiles,' Cyril objected. His prize had been for natural history.

The Psammead reached out a hairy arm from its basket and pointed to a heap of mud at the edge of the water.

'What do you call that?' it said; and as it spoke the heap of mud slid into the river just as a slab of damp mixed mortar will slip from a bricklayer's trowel.

'Oh!' said everybody.

There was a crashing among the reeds on the other side of the water.

'And there's a river-horse!' said the Psammead, as a great beast like an enormous slaty-blue slug showed itself against the black bank on the far side of the stream.

'It's a hippopotamus,' said Cyril; 'it seems much more real somehow than the one at the Zoo, doesn't it?'

'I'm glad it's being real on the other side of the river,' said Jane. And now there was a crackling of reeds and twigs behind them. This was horrible. Of course it might be another hippopotamus, or a crocodile, or a lion—or, in fact, almost anything.

'Keep your hand on the charm, Jane,' said Robert hastily. 'We ought to have a means of escape handy. I'm dead certain this is the sort of place where simply anything might happen to us.'

'I believe a hippopotamus is going to happen to us,' said Jane—'a very, very big one.'

They had all turned to face the danger.

'Don't be silly little duffers,' said the Psammead in its friendly, informal way; 'it's not a river-horse. It's a human.'

It was. It was a girl—of about Anthea's age. Her hair was short and fair, and though her skin was tanned by the sun, you could see that it would have been fair too if it had had a chance. She had every chance of being tanned, for she had no clothes to speak of, and the four English children, carefully dressed in frocks, hats, shoes, stockings, coats, collars, and all the rest of it, envied her more than any words of theirs or of mine could possibly say. There was no doubt that here was the right costume for that climate.

She carried a pot on her head, of red and black earthenware. She did not see the children, who shrank back against the edge of the jungle, and she went forward to the brink of the river to fill her pitcher. As she went she made a strange sort of droning, humming, melancholy noise all on two notes. Anthea could not help thinking that perhaps the girl thought this noise was singing.

The girl filled the pitcher and set it down by the river bank. Then she waded into the water and stooped over the circle of cut reeds. She pulled half a dozen fine fish out of the water within the reeds, killing each as she took it out, and threading it on a long osier that she carried. Then she knotted the osier, hung it on her arm, picked up the pitcher, and turned to come back. And as she turned she saw the four children. The white dresses of Jane and Anthea stood out like snow against the dark forest background. She screamed and the pitcher fell, and the water was spilled out over the hard mud surface and over the fish, which had fallen too. Then the water slowly trickled away into the deep cracks.

'Don't be frightened,' Anthea cried, 'we won't hurt you.'

'Who are you?' said the girl.

Now, once for all, I am not going to be bothered to tell you how it was that the girl could understand Anthea and Anthea could understand the girl. YOU, at any rate, would not understand ME, if I tried to explain it, any more than you can understand about time and space being only forms of thought. You may think what you like. Perhaps the children had found out the universal language which everyone can understand, and which wise men so far have not found. You will have noticed long ago that they were singularly lucky children, and they may have had this piece of luck as well as others. Or it may have been that ... but why pursue the question further? The fact remains that in all their adventures the muddle-headed inventions which we call foreign languages never bothered them in the least. They could always understand and be understood. If you can explain this, please do. I daresay I could understand your explanation, though you could never understand mine.

So when the girl said, 'Who are you?' everyone understood at once, and Anthea replied—

'We are children—just like you. Don't be frightened. Won't you show us where you live?'

Jane put her face right into the Psammead's basket, and burrowed her mouth into its fur to whisper—

'Is it safe? Won't they eat us? Are they cannibals?'

The Psammead shrugged its fur.

'Don't make your voice buzz like that, it tickles my ears,' it said rather crossly. 'You can always get back to Regent's Park in time if you keep fast hold of the charm,' it said.

The strange girl was trembling with fright.

Anthea had a bangle on her arm. It was a sevenpenny-halfpenny trumpery thing that pretended to be silver; it had a glass heart of turquoise blue hanging from it, and it was the gift of the maid-of-all-work at the Fitzroy Street house. 'Here,' said Anthea, 'this is for you. That is to show we will not hurt you. And if you take it I shall know that you won't hurt us.'

The girl held out her hand. Anthea slid the bangle over it, and the girl's face lighted up with the joy of possession.

'Come,' she said, looking lovingly at the bangle; 'it is peace between your house and mine.'

She picked up her fish and pitcher and led the way up the narrow path by which she had come and the others followed.

'This is something like!' said Cyril, trying to be brave.

'Yes!' said Robert, also assuming a boldness he was far from feeling, 'this really and truly IS an adventure! Its being in the Past makes it quite different from the Phoenix and Carpet happenings.'

The belt of thick-growing acacia trees and shrubs—mostly prickly and unpleasant-looking—seemed about half a mile across. The path was narrow and the wood dark. At last, ahead, daylight shone through the boughs and leaves.

The whole party suddenly came out of the wood's shadow into the glare of the sunlight that shone on a great stretch of yellow sand, dotted with heaps of grey rocks where spiky cactus plants showed gaudy crimson and pink flowers among their shabby, sand-peppered leaves. Away to the right was something that looked like a grey-brown hedge, and from beyond it blue smoke went up to the bluer sky. And over all the sun shone till you could hardly bear your clothes.

'That is where I live,' said the girl pointing.

'I won't go,' whispered Jane into the basket, 'unless you say it's all right.'

The Psammead ought to have been touched by this proof of confidence. Perhaps, however, it looked upon it as a proof of doubt, for it merely snarled—

'If you don't go now I'll never help you again.'

'OH,' whispered Anthea, 'dear Jane, don't! Think of Father and Mother and all of us getting our heart's desire. And we can go back any minute. Come on!'

'Besides,' said Cyril, in a low voice, 'the Psammead must know there's no danger or it wouldn't go. It's not so over and above brave itself. Come on!'

This Jane at last consented to do.

As they got nearer to the browny fence they saw that it was a great hedge about eight feet high, made of piled-up thorn bushes.

'What's that for?' asked Cyril.

'To keep out foes and wild beasts,' said the girl.

'I should think it ought to, too,' said he. 'Why, some of the thorns are as long as my foot.'

There was an opening in the hedge, and they followed the girl through it. A little way further on was another hedge, not so high, also of dry thorn bushes, very prickly and spiteful-looking, and within this was a sort of village of huts.

There were no gardens and no roads. Just huts built of wood and twigs and clay, and roofed with great palm-leaves, dumped down anywhere. The doors of these houses were very low, like the doors of dog-kennels. The ground between them was not paths or streets, but just yellow sand trampled very hard and smooth.

In the middle of the village there was a hedge that enclosed what seemed to be a piece of ground about as big as their own garden in Camden Town.

No sooner were the children well within the inner thorn hedge than dozens of men and women and children came crowding round from behind and inside the huts.

The girl stood protectingly in front of the four children, and said—

'They are wonder-children from beyond the desert. They bring marvellous gifts, and I have said that it is peace between us and them.'

She held out her arm with the Lowther Arcade bangle on it.

The children from London, where nothing now surprises anyone, had never before seen so many people look so astonished.

They crowded round the children, touching their clothes, their shoes, the buttons on the boys' jackets, and the coral of the girls' necklaces.

'Do say something,' whispered Anthea.

'We come,' said Cyril, with some dim remembrance of a dreadful day when he had had to wait in an outer office while his father interviewed a solicitor, and there had been nothing to read but the Daily Telegraph—'we come from the world where the sun never sets. And peace with honour is what we want. We are the great Anglo-Saxon or conquering race. Not that we want to conquer YOU,' he added hastily. 'We only want to look at your houses and your—well, at all you've got here, and then we shall return to our own place, and tell of all that we have seen so that your name may be famed.'

Cyril's speech didn't keep the crowd from pressing round and looking as eagerly as ever at the clothing of the children. Anthea had an idea that these people had never seen woven stuff before, and she saw how wonderful and strange it must seem to people who had never had any clothes but the skins of beasts. The sewing, too, of modern clothes seemed to astonish them very much. They must have been able to sew themselves, by the way, for men who seemed to be the chiefs wore knickerbockers of goat-skin or deer-skin, fastened round the waist with twisted strips of hide. And the women wore long skimpy skirts of animals' skins. The people were not very tall, their hair was fair, and men and women both had it short. Their eyes were blue, and that seemed odd in Egypt. Most of them were tattooed like sailors, only more roughly.

'What is this? What is this?' they kept asking touching the children's clothes curiously.

Anthea hastily took off Jane's frilly lace collar and handed it to the woman who seemed most friendly.

'Take this,' she said, 'and look at it. And leave us alone. We want to talk among ourselves.'

She spoke in the tone of authority which she had always found successful when she had not time to coax her baby brother to do as he was told. The tone was just as successful now. The children were left together and the crowd retreated. It paused a dozen yards away to look at the lace collar and to go on talking as hard as it could.

The children will never know what those people said, though they knew well enough that they, the four strangers, were the subject of the talk. They tried to comfort themselves by remembering the girl's promise of friendliness, but of course the thought of the charm was more comfortable than anything else. They sat down on the sand in the shadow of the hedged-round place in the middle of the village, and now for the first time they were able to look about them and to see something more than a crowd of eager, curious faces.

They here noticed that the women wore necklaces made of beads of different coloured stone, and from these hung pendants of odd, strange shapes, and some of them had bracelets of ivory and flint.

'I say,' said Robert, 'what a lot we could teach them if we stayed here!'

'I expect they could teach us something too,' said Cyril. 'Did you notice that flint bracelet the woman had that Anthea gave the collar to? That must have taken some making. Look here, they'll get suspicious if we talk among ourselves, and I do want to know about how they do things. Let's get the girl to show us round, and we can be thinking about how to get the Amulet at the same time. Only mind, we must keep together.'

Anthea beckoned to the girl, who was standing a little way off looking wistfully at them, and she came gladly.

'Tell us how you make the bracelets, the stone ones,' said Cyril.

'With other stones,' said the girl; 'the men make them; we have men of special skill in such work.'

'Haven't you any iron tools?'

'Iron,' said the girl, 'I don't know what you mean.' It was the first word she had not understood.

'Are all your tools of flint?' asked Cyril. 'Of course,' said the girl, opening her eyes wide.

I wish I had time to tell you of that talk. The English children wanted to hear all about this new place, but they also wanted to tell of their own country. It was like when you come back from your holidays and you want to hear and to tell everything at the same time. As the talk went on there were more and more words that the girl could not understand, and the children soon gave up the attempt to explain to her what their own country was like, when they began to see how very few of the things they had always thought they could not do without were really not at all necessary to life.

The girl showed them how the huts were made—indeed, as one was being made that very day she took them to look at it. The way of building was very different from ours. The men stuck long pieces of wood into a piece of ground the size of the hut they wanted to make. These were about eight inches apart; then they put in another row about eight inches away from the first, and then a third row still further out. Then all the space between was filled up with small branches and twigs, and then daubed over with black mud worked with the feet till it was soft and sticky like putty.

The girl told them how the men went hunting with flint spears and arrows, and how they made boats with reeds and clay. Then she explained the reed thing in the river that she had taken the fish out of. It was a fish-trap—just a ring of reeds set up in the water with only one little opening in it, and in this opening, just below the water, were stuck reeds slanting the way of the river's flow, so that the fish, when they had swum sillily in, sillily couldn't get out again. She showed them the clay pots and jars and platters, some of them ornamented with black and red patterns, and the most wonderful things made of flint and different sorts of stone, beads, and ornaments, and tools and weapons of all sorts and kinds.

'It is really wonderful,' said Cyril patronizingly, 'when you consider that it's all eight thousand years ago—'

'I don't understand you,' said the girl.

'It ISN'T eight thousand years ago,' whispered Jane. 'It's NOW—and that's just what I don't like about it. I say, DO let's get home again before anything more happens. You can see for yourselves the charm isn't here.'

'What's in that place in the middle?' asked Anthea, struck by a sudden thought, and pointing to the fence.

'That's the secret sacred place,' said the girl in a whisper. 'No one knows what is there. There are many walls, and inside the insidest one IT is, but no one knows what IT is except the headsmen.'

'I believe YOU know,' said Cyril, looking at her very hard.

'I'll give you this if you'll tell me,' said Anthea taking off a bead-ring which had already been much admired.

'Yes,' said the girl, catching eagerly at the ring. 'My father is one of the heads, and I know a water charm to make him talk in his sleep. And he has spoken. I will tell you. But if they know I have told you they will kill me. In the insidest inside there is a stone box, and in it there is the Amulet. None knows whence it came. It came from very far away.'

'Have you seen it?' asked Anthea.

The girl nodded.

'Is it anything like this?' asked Jane, rashly producing the charm.

The girl's face turned a sickly greenish-white.

'Hide it, hide it,' she whispered. 'You must put it back. If they see it they will kill us all. You for taking it, and me for knowing that there was such a thing. Oh, woe—woe! why did you ever come here?'

'Don't be frightened,' said Cyril. 'They shan't know. Jane, don't you be such a little jack-ape again—that's all. You see what will happen if you do. Now, tell me—' He turned to the girl, but before he had time to speak the question there was a loud shout, and a man bounded in through the opening in the thorn-hedge.

'Many foes are upon us!' he cried. 'Make ready the defences!'

His breath only served for that, and he lay panting on the ground. 'Oh, DO let's go home!' said Jane. 'Look here—I don't care—I WILL!'

She held up the charm. Fortunately all the strange, fair people were too busy to notice HER. She held up the charm. And nothing happened.

'You haven't said the word of power,' said Anthea.

Jane hastily said it—and still nothing happened.

'Hold it up towards the East, you silly!' said Robert.

'Which IS the East?' said Jane, dancing about in her agony of terror.

Nobody knew. So they opened the fish-bag to ask the Psammead.

And the bag had only a waterproof sheet in it.

The Psammead was gone.

'Hide the sacred thing! Hide it! Hide it!' whispered the girl.

Cyril shrugged his shoulders, and tried to look as brave as he knew he ought to feel.

'Hide it up, Pussy,' he said. 'We are in for it now. We've just got to stay and see it out.'

Chapter 5. The Fight in The Village

Here was a horrible position! Four English children, whose proper date was A.D. 1905, and whose proper address was London, set down in Egypt in the year 6000 B.C. with no means whatever of getting back into their own time and place. They could not find the East, and the sun was of no use at the moment, because some officious person had once explained to Cyril that the sun did not really set in the West at all—nor rise in the East either, for the matter of that.

The Psammead had crept out of the bass-bag when they were not looking and had basely deserted them.

An enemy was approaching. There would be a fight. People get killed in fights, and the idea of taking part in a fight was one that did not appeal to the children.

The man who had brought the news of the enemy still lay panting on the sand. His tongue was hanging out, long and red, like a dog's. The people of the village were hurriedly filling the gaps in the fence with thorn-bushes from the heap that seemed to have been piled there ready for just such a need. They lifted the cluster-thorns with long poles—much as men at home, nowadays, lift hay with a fork.

Jane bit her lip and tried to decide not to cry.

Robert felt in his pocket for a toy pistol and loaded it with a pink paper cap. It was his only weapon.

Cyril tightened his belt two holes.

And Anthea absently took the drooping red roses from the buttonholes of the others, bit the ends of the stalks, and set them in a pot of water that stood in the shadow by a hut door. She was always rather silly about flowers.

'Look here!' she said. 'I think perhaps the Psammead is really arranging something for us. I don't believe it would go away and leave us all alone in the Past. I'm certain it wouldn't.'

Jane succeeded in deciding not to cry—at any rate yet.

'But what can we do?' Robert asked.

'Nothing,' Cyril answered promptly, 'except keep our eyes and ears open. Look! That runner chap's getting his wind. Let's go and hear what he's got to say.'

The runner had risen to his knees and was sitting back on his heels. Now he stood up and spoke. He began by some respectful remarks addressed to the heads of the village. His speech got more interesting when he said—

'I went out in my raft to snare ibises, and I had gone up the stream an hour's journey. Then I set my snares and waited. And I heard the sound of many wings, and looking up, saw many herons circling in the air. And I saw that they were afraid; so I took thought. A beast may scare one heron, coming upon it suddenly, but no beast will scare a whole flock of herons. And still they flew and circled, and would not light. So then I knew that what scared the herons must be men, and men who knew not our ways of going softly so as to take the birds and beasts unawares. By this I knew they were not of our race or of our place. So, leaving my raft, I crept along the river bank, and at last came upon the strangers. They are many as the sands of the desert, and their spear-heads shine red like the sun. They are a terrible people, and their march is towards US. Having seen this, I ran, and did not stay till I was before you.'

'These are YOUR folk,' said the headman, turning suddenly and angrily on Cyril, 'you came as spies for them.'

'We did NOT,' said Cyril indignantly. 'We wouldn't be spies for anything. I'm certain these people aren't a bit like us. Are they now?' he asked the runner.

'No,' was the answer. 'These men's faces were darkened, and their hair black as night. Yet these strange children, maybe, are their gods, who have come before to make ready the way for them.'

A murmur ran through the crowd.

'No, NO,' said Cyril again. 'We are on your side. We will help you to guard your sacred things.'

The headman seemed impressed by the fact that Cyril knew that there WERE sacred things to be guarded. He stood a moment gazing at the children. Then he said—

'It is well. And now let all make offering, that we may be strong in battle.'

The crowd dispersed, and nine men, wearing antelope-skins, grouped themselves in front of the opening in the hedge in the middle of the village. And presently, one by one, the men brought all sorts of things—hippopotamus flesh, ostrich-feathers, the fruit of the date palms, red chalk, green chalk, fish from the river, and ibex from the mountains; and the headman received these gifts. There was another hedge inside the first, about a yard from it, so that there was a lane inside between the hedges. And every now and then one of the headmen would disappear along this lane with full hands and come back with hands empty.

'They're making offerings to their Amulet,' said Anthea. 'We'd better give something too.'

The pockets of the party, hastily explored, yielded a piece of pink tape, a bit of sealing-wax, and part of the Waterbury watch that Robert had not been able to help taking to pieces at Christmas and had never had time to rearrange. Most boys have a watch in this condition. They presented their offerings, and Anthea added the red roses.

The headman who took the things looked at them with awe, especially at the red roses and the Waterbury-watch fragment.

'This is a day of very wondrous happenings,' he said. 'I have no more room in me to be astonished. Our maiden said there was peace between you and us. But for this coming of a foe we should have made sure.'

The children shuddered.

'Now speak. Are you upon our side?'

'YES. Don't I keep telling you we are?' Robert said. 'Look here. I will give you a sign. You see this.' He held out the toy pistol. 'I shall speak to it, and if it answers me you will know that I and the others are come to guard your sacred thing—that we've just made the offerings to.'

'Will that god whose image you hold in your hand speak to you alone, or shall I also hear it?' asked the man cautiously.

'You'll be surprised when you DO hear it,' said Robert. 'Now, then.' He looked at the pistol and said—

'If we are to guard the sacred treasure within'—he pointed to the hedged-in space—'speak with thy loud voice, and we shall obey.'

He pulled the trigger, and the cap went off. The noise was loud, for it was a two-shilling pistol, and the caps were excellent.

Every man, woman, and child in the village fell on its face on the sand. The headman who had accepted the test rose first.

'The voice has spoken,' he said. 'Lead them into the ante-room of the sacred thing.'

So now the four children were led in through the opening of the hedge and round the lane till they came to an opening in the inner hedge, and they went through an opening in that, and so passed into another lane.

All the hedges were of brushwood and thorns.

'It's like the maze at Hampton Court,' whispered Anthea.

The lanes were all open to the sky, but the little hut in the middle of the maze was round-roofed, and a curtain of skins hung over the doorway.

'Here you may wait,' said their guide, 'but do not dare to pass the curtain.' He himself passed it and disappeared.

'But look here,' whispered Cyril, 'some of us ought to be outside in case the Psammead turns up.'

'Don't let's get separated from each other, whatever we do,' said Anthea. 'It's quite bad enough to be separated from the Psammead. We can't do anything while that man is in there. Let's all go out into the village again. We can come back later now we know the way in. That man'll have to fight like the rest, most likely, if it comes to fighting. If we find the Psammead we'll go straight home. It must be getting late, and I don't much like this mazy place.'

They went out and told the headman that they would protect the treasure when the fighting began. And now they looked about them and were able to see exactly how a first-class worker in flint flakes and notches an arrow-head or the edge of an axe—an advantage which no other person now alive has ever enjoyed. The boys found the weapons most interesting. The arrow-heads were not on arrows such as you shoot from a bow, but on javelins, for throwing from the hand. The chief weapon was a stone fastened to a rather short stick something like the things gentlemen used to carry about and call life-preservers in the days of the garrotters.

Then there were long things like spears or lances, with flint knives—horribly sharp—and flint battle-axes.

Everyone in the village was so busy that the place was like an ant-heap when you have walked into it by accident. The women were busy and even the children.

Quite suddenly all the air seemed to glow and grow red—it was like the sudden opening of a furnace door, such as you may see at Woolwich Arsenal if you ever have the luck to be taken there—and then almost as suddenly it was as though the furnace doors had been shut. For the sun had set, and it was night.

The sun had that abrupt way of setting in Egypt eight thousand years ago, and I believe it has never been able to break itself of the habit, and sets in exactly the same manner to the present day. The girl brought the skins of wild deer and led the children to a heap of dry sedge.

'My father says they will not attack yet. Sleep!' she said, and it really seemed a good idea. You may think that in the midst of all these dangers the children would not have been able to sleep—but somehow, though they were rather frightened now and then, the feeling was growing in them—deep down and almost hidden away, but still growing—that the Psammead was to be trusted, and that they were really and truly safe. This did not prevent their being quite as much frightened as they could bear to be without being perfectly miserable.

'I suppose we'd better go to sleep,' said Robert. 'I don't know what on earth poor old Nurse will do with us out all night; set the police on our tracks, I expect. I only wish they could find us! A dozen policemen would be rather welcome just now. But it's no use getting into a stew over it,' he added soothingly. 'Good night.'

And they all fell asleep.

They were awakened by long, loud, terrible sounds that seemed to come from everywhere at once—horrible threatening shouts and shrieks and howls that sounded, as Cyril said later, like the voices of men thirsting for their enemies' blood.

'It is the voice of the strange men,' said the girl, coming to them trembling through the dark. 'They have attacked the walls, and the thorns have driven them back. My father says they will not try again till daylight. But they are shouting to frighten us. As though we were savages! Dwellers in the swamps!' she cried indignantly.

All night the terrible noise went on, but when the sun rose, as abruptly as he had set, the sound suddenly ceased.

The children had hardly time to be glad of this before a shower of javelins came hurtling over the great thorn-hedge, and everyone sheltered behind the huts. But next moment another shower of weapons came from the opposite side, and the crowd rushed to other shelter. Cyril pulled out a javelin that had stuck in the roof of the hut beside him. Its head was of brightly burnished copper.

Then the sound of shouting arose again and the crackle of dried thorns. The enemy was breaking down the hedge. All the villagers swarmed to the point whence the crackling and the shouting came; they hurled stones over the hedges, and short arrows with flint heads. The children had never before seen men with the fighting light in their eyes. It was very strange and terrible, and gave you a queer thick feeling in your throat; it was quite different from the pictures of fights in the illustrated papers at home.

It seemed that the shower of stones had driven back the besiegers. The besieged drew breath, but at that moment the shouting and the crackling arose on the opposite side of the village and the crowd hastened to defend that point, and so the fight swayed to and fro across the village, for the besieged had not the sense to divide their forces as their enemies had done.

Cyril noticed that every now and then certain of the fighting-men would enter the maze, and come out with brighter faces, a braver aspect, and a more upright carriage.

'I believe they go and touch the Amulet,' he said. 'You know the Psammead said it could make people brave.'

They crept through the maze, and watching they saw that Cyril was right. A headman was standing in front of the skin curtain, and as the warriors came before him he murmured a word they could not hear, and touched their foreheads with something that they could not see. And this something he held in his hands. And through his fingers they saw the gleam of a red stone that they knew.

The fight raged across the thorn-hedge outside. Suddenly there was a loud and bitter cry.

'They're in! They're in! The hedge is down!'

The headman disappeared behind the deer-skin curtain.

'He's gone to hide it,' said Anthea. 'Oh, Psammead dear, how could you leave us!'

Suddenly there was a shriek from inside the hut, and the headman staggered out white with fear and fled out through the maze. The children were as white as he.

'Oh! What is it? What is it?' moaned Anthea. 'Oh, Psammead, how could you! How could you!'

And the sound of the fight sank breathlessly, and swelled fiercely all around. It was like the rising and falling of the waves of the sea.

Anthea shuddered and said again, 'Oh, Psammead, Psammead!'

'Well?' said a brisk voice, and the curtain of skins was lifted at one corner by a furry hand, and out peeped the bat's ears and snail's eyes of the Psammead.

Anthea caught it in her arms and a sigh of desperate relief was breathed by each of the four.

'Oh! which IS the East!' Anthea said, and she spoke hurriedly, for the noise of wild fighting drew nearer and nearer.

'Don't choke me,' said the Psammead, 'come inside.'

The inside of the hut was pitch dark.

'I've got a match,' said Cyril, and struck it. The floor of the hut was of soft, loose sand.

'I've been asleep here,' said the Psammead; 'most comfortable it's been, the best sand I've had for a month. It's all right. Everything's all right. I knew your only chance would be while the fight was going on. That man won't come back. I bit him, and he thinks I'm an Evil Spirit. Now you've only got to take the thing and go.'

The hut was hung with skins. Heaped in the middle were the offerings that had been given the night before, Anthea's roses fading on the top of the heap. At one side of the hut stood a large square stone block, and on it an oblong box of earthenware with strange figures of men and beasts on it.

'Is the thing in there?' asked Cyril, as the Psammead pointed a skinny finger at it.

'You must judge of that,' said the Psammead. 'The man was just going to bury the box in the sand when I jumped out at him and bit him.'

'Light another match, Robert,' said Anthea. 'Now, then quick! which is the East?'

'Why, where the sun rises, of course!'

'But someone told us—'

'Oh! they'll tell you anything!' said the Psammead impatiently, getting into its bass-bag and wrapping itself in its waterproof sheet.

'But we can't see the sun in here, and it isn't rising anyhow,' said Jane.

'How you do waste time!' the Psammead said. 'Why, the East's where the shrine is, of course. THERE!'

It pointed to the great stone.

And still the shouting and the clash of stone on metal sounded nearer and nearer. The children could hear that the headmen had surrounded the hut to protect their treasure as long as might be from the enemy. But none dare to come in after the Psammead's sudden fierce biting of the headman.

'Now, Jane,' said Cyril, very quickly. 'I'll take the Amulet, you stand ready to hold up the charm, and be sure you don't let it go as you come through.'

He made a step forward, but at that instant a great crackling overhead ended in a blaze of sunlight. The roof had been broken in at one side, and great slabs of it were being lifted off by two spears. As the children trembled and winked in the new light, large dark hands tore down the wall, and a dark face, with a blobby fat nose, looked over the gap. Even at that awful moment Anthea had time to think that it was very like the face of Mr Jacob Absalom, who had sold them the charm in the shop near Charing Cross.

'Here is their Amulet,' cried a harsh, strange voice; 'it is this that makes them strong to fight and brave to die. And what else have we here—gods or demons?'

He glared fiercely at the children, and the whites of his eyes were very white indeed. He had a wet, red copper knife in his teeth. There was not a moment to lose.

'Jane, JANE, QUICK!' cried everyone passionately.

Jane with trembling hands held up the charm towards the East, and Cyril spoke the word of power. The Amulet grew to a great arch. Out beyond it was the glaring Egyptian sky, the broken wall, the cruel, dark, big-nosed face with the red, wet knife in its gleaming teeth. Within the arch was the dull, faint, greeny-brown of London grass and trees.

'Hold tight, Jane!' Cyril cried, and he dashed through the arch, dragging Anthea and the Psammead after him. Robert followed, clutching Jane. And in the ears of each, as they passed through the arch of the charm, the sound and fury of battle died out suddenly and utterly, and they heard only the low, dull, discontented hum of vast London, and the peeking and patting of the sparrows on the gravel and the voices of the ragged baby children playing Ring-o'-Roses on the yellow trampled grass. And the charm was a little charm again in Jane's hand, and there was the basket with their dinner and the bathbuns lying just where they had left it.

'My hat!' said Cyril, drawing a long breath; 'that was something like an adventure.'

'It was rather like one, certainly,' said the Psammead.

They all lay still, breathing in the safe, quiet air of Regent's Park.

'We'd better go home at once,' said Anthea presently. 'Old Nurse will be most frightfully anxious. The sun looks about the same as it did when we started yesterday. We've been away twenty-four hours.' 'The buns are quite soft still,' said Cyril, feeling one; 'I suppose the dew kept them fresh.'

They were not hungry, curiously enough.

They picked up the dinner-basket and the Psammead-basket, and went straight home.

Old Nurse met them with amazement.

'Well, if ever I did!' she said. 'What's gone wrong? You've soon tired of your picnic.'

The children took this to be bitter irony, which means saying the exact opposite of what you mean in order to make yourself disagreeable; as when you happen to have a dirty face, and someone says, 'How nice and clean you look!'

'We're very sorry,' began Anthea, but old Nurse said—

'Oh, bless me, child, I don't care! Please yourselves and you'll please me. Come in and get your dinners comf'table. I've got a potato on a-boiling.'

When she had gone to attend to the potatoes the children looked at each other. Could it be that old Nurse had so changed that she no longer cared that they should have been away from home for twenty-four hours—all night in fact—without any explanation whatever?

But the Psammead put its head out of its basket and said—

'What's the matter? Don't you understand? You come back through the charm-arch at the same time as you go through it. This isn't tomorrow!' 'Is it still yesterday?' asked Jane.

'No, it's today. The same as it's always been. It wouldn't do to go mixing up the present and the Past, and cutting bits out of one to fit into the other.'

'Then all that adventure took no time at all?'

'You can call it that if you like,' said the Psammead. 'It took none of the modern time, anyhow.'

That evening Anthea carried up a steak for the learned gentleman's dinner. She persuaded Beatrice, the maid-of-all-work, who had given her the bangle with the blue stone, to let her do it. And she stayed and talked to him, by special invitation, while he ate the dinner.

She told him the whole adventure, beginning with—

'This afternoon we found ourselves on the bank of the River Nile,' and ending up with, 'And then we remembered how to get back, and there we were in Regent's Park, and it hadn't taken any time at all.'

She did not tell anything about the charm or the Psammead, because that was forbidden, but the story was quite wonderful enough even as it was to entrance the learned gentleman.

'You are a most unusual little girl,' he said. 'Who tells you all these things?'

'No one,' said Anthea, 'they just happen.'

'Make-believe,' he said slowly, as one who recalls and pronounces a long-forgotten word.

He sat long after she had left him. At last he roused himself with a start.

'I really must take a holiday,' he said; 'my nerves must be all out of order. I actually have a perfectly distinct impression that the little girl from the rooms below came in and gave me a coherent and graphic picture of life as I conceive it to have been in pre-dynastic Egypt. Strange what tricks the mind will play! I shall have to be more careful.'

He finished his bread conscientiously, and actually went for a mile walk before he went back to his work.

Chapter 6. The Way to Babylon

'How many miles to Babylon?
Three score and ten!
Can I get there by candle light?
Yes, and back again!'

Jane was singing to her doll, rocking it to and fro in the house which she had made for herself and it. The roof of the house was the dining-table, and the walls were tablecloths and antimacassars hanging all round, and kept in their places by books laid on their top ends at the table edge.

The others were tasting the fearful joys of domestic tobogganing. You know how it is done—with the largest and best tea-tray and the surface of the stair carpet. It is best to do it on the days when the stair rods are being cleaned, and the carpet is only held by the nails at the top. Of course, it is one of the five or six thoroughly tip-top games that grown-up people are so unjust to—and old Nurse, though a brick in many respects, was quite enough of a standard grown-up to put her foot down on the tobogganing long before any of the performers had had half enough of it. The tea-tray was taken away, and the baffled party entered the sitting-room, in exactly the mood not to be pleased if they could help it.

So Cyril said, 'What a beastly mess!'

And Robert added, 'Do shut up, Jane!'

Even Anthea, who was almost always kind, advised Jane to try another song. 'I'm sick to death of that,' said she.

It was a wet day, so none of the plans for seeing all the sights of London that can be seen for nothing could be carried out. Everyone had been thinking all the morning about the wonderful adventures of the day before, when Jane had held up the charm and it had turned into an arch, through which they had walked straight out of the present time and the Regent's Park into the land of Egypt eight thousand years ago. The memory of yesterday's happenings was still extremely fresh and frightening, so that everyone hoped that no one would suggest another excursion into the past, for it seemed to all that yesterday's adventures were quite enough to last for at least a week. Yet each felt a little anxious that the others should not think it was afraid, and presently Cyril, who really was not a coward, began to see that it would not be at all nice if he should have to think himself one. So he said—

'I say—about that charm—Jane—come out. We ought to talk about it, anyhow.'

'Oh, if that's all,' said Robert.

Jane obediently wriggled to the front of her house and sat there.

She felt for the charm, to make sure that it was still round her neck.

'It ISN'T all,' said Cyril, saying much more than he meant because he thought Robert's tone had been rude—as indeed it had.

'We ought to go and look for that Amulet. What's the good of having a first-class charm and keeping it idle, just eating its head off in the stable.'

'I'M game for anything, of course,' said Robert; but he added, with a fine air of chivalry, 'only I don't think the girls are keen today somehow.'

'Oh, yes; I am,' said Anthea hurriedly. 'If you think I'm afraid, I'm not.'

'I am though,' said Jane heavily; 'I didn't like it, and I won't go there again—not for anything I won't.'

'We shouldn't go THERE again, silly,' said Cyril; 'it would be some other place.'

'I daresay; a place with lions and tigers in it as likely as not.'

Seeing Jane so frightened, made the others feel quite brave. They said they were certain they ought to go.

'It's so ungrateful to the Psammead not to,' Anthea added, a little primly.

Jane stood up. She was desperate.

'I won't!' she cried; 'I won't, I won't, I won't! If you make me I'll scream and I'll scream, and I'll tell old Nurse, and I'll get her to burn the charm in the kitchen fire. So now, then!'

You can imagine how furious everyone was with Jane for feeling what each of them had felt all the morning. In each breast the same thought arose, 'No one can say it's OUR fault.' And they at once began to show Jane how angry they all felt that all the fault was hers. This made them feel quite brave.

> 'Tell-tale tit, its tongue shall be split,
> And all the dogs in our town shall have a little bit,'

sang Robert.

'It's always the way if you have girls in anything.' Cyril spoke in a cold displeasure that was worse than Robert's cruel quotation, and even Anthea said, 'Well, I'M not afraid if I AM a girl,' which of course, was the most cutting thing of all.

Jane picked up her doll and faced the others with what is sometimes called the courage of despair.

'I don't care,' she said; 'I won't, so there! It's just silly going to places when you don't want to, and when you don't know what they're going to be like! You can laugh at me as much as you like. You're beasts—and I hate you all!'

With these awful words she went out and banged the door.

Then the others would not look at each other, and they did not feel so brave as they had done.

Cyril took up a book, but it was not interesting to read. Robert kicked a chair-leg absently. His feet were always eloquent in moments of emotion. Anthea stood pleating the end of the tablecloth into folds—she seemed earnestly anxious to get all the pleats the same size. The sound of Jane's sobs had died away.

Suddenly Anthea said, 'Oh! let it be "pax"—poor little Pussy—you know she's the youngest.'

'She called us beasts,' said Robert, kicking the chair suddenly.

'Well, said Cyril, who was subject to passing fits of justice, 'we began, you know. At least you did.' Cyril's justice was always uncompromising.

'I'm not going to say I'm sorry if you mean that,' said Robert, and the chair-leg cracked to the kick he gave as he said it.

'Oh, do let's,' said Anthea, 'we're three to one, and Mother does so hate it if we row. Come on. I'll say I'm sorry first, though I didn't say anything, hardly.'

'All right, let's get it over,' said Cyril, opening the door.'Hi—you—Pussy!'

Far away up the stairs a voice could be heard singing brokenly, but still defiantly—

> 'How many miles (sniff) to Babylon?
> Three score and ten! (sniff)
> Can I get there by candle light?
> Yes (sniff), and back again!'

It was trying, for this was plainly meant to annoy. But Anthea would not give herself time to think this. She led the way up the stairs, taking three at a time, and bounded to the level of Jane, who sat on the top step of all, thumping her doll to the tune of the song she was trying to sing.

'I say, Pussy, let it be pax! We're sorry if you are—'

It was enough. The kiss of peace was given by all. Jane being the youngest was entitled to this ceremonial. Anthea added a special apology of her own.

'I'm sorry if I was a pig, Pussy dear,' she said—'especially because in my really and truly inside mind I've been feeling a little as if I'd rather not go into the Past again either. But then, do think. If we don't go we shan't get the Amulet, and oh, Pussy, think if we could only get Father and Mother and The Lamb safe back! We MUST go, but we'll wait a day or two if you like and then perhaps you'll feel braver.'

'Raw meat makes you brave, however cowardly you are,' said Robert, to show that there was now no ill-feeling, 'and cranberries—that's what Tartars eat, and they're so brave it's simply awful. I suppose cranberries are only for Christmas time, but I'll ask old Nurse to let you have your chop very raw if you like.'

'I think I could be brave without that,' said Jane hastily; she hated underdone meat. 'I'll try.'

At this moment the door of the learned gentleman's room opened, and he looked out.

'Excuse me,' he said, in that gentle, polite weary voice of his, 'but was I mistaken in thinking that I caught a familiar word just now? Were you not singing some old ballad of Babylon?'

'No,' said Robert, 'at least Jane was singing "How many miles," but I shouldn't have thought you could have heard the words for—'

He would have said, 'for the sniffing,' but Anthea pinched him just in time.

'I did not hear ALL the words,' said the learned gentleman. 'I wonder would you recite them to me?'

So they all said together—

'How many miles to Babylon?
Three score and ten!
Can I get there by candle light?
Yes, and back again!'

'I wish one could,' the learned gentleman said with a sigh.

'Can't you?' asked Jane.

'Babylon has fallen,' he answered with a sigh. 'You know it was once a great and beautiful city, and the centre of learning and Art, and now it is only ruins, and so covered up with earth that people are not even agreed as to where it once stood.'

He was leaning on the banisters, and his eyes had a far-away look in them, as though he could see through the staircase window the splendour and glory of ancient Babylon.

'I say,' Cyril remarked abruptly. 'You know that charm we showed you, and you told us how to say the name that's on it?'

'Yes!'

'Well, do you think that charm was ever in Babylon?'

'It's quite possible,' the learned gentleman replied. 'Such charms have been found in very early Egyptian tombs, yet their origin has not been accurately determined as Egyptian. They may have been brought from Asia. Or, supposing the charm to have been fashioned in Egypt, it might very well have been carried to Babylon by some friendly embassy, or brought back by the Babylonish army from some Egyptian campaign as part of the spoils of war. The inscription may be much later than the charm. Oh yes! it is a pleasant fancy, that that splendid specimen of yours was once used amid Babylonish surroundings.' The others looked at each other, but it was Jane who spoke.

'Were the Babylon people savages, were they always fighting and throwing things about?' For she had read the thoughts of the others by the unerring light of her own fears.

'The Babylonians were certainly more gentle than the Assyrians,' said the learned gentleman. 'And they were not savages by any means. A very high level of culture,' he looked doubtfully at his audience and went on, 'I mean that they made beautiful statues and jewellery, and built splendid palaces. And they were very learned — they had glorious libraries and high towers for the purpose of astrological and astronomical observation.'

'Er?' said Robert.

'I mean for — star-gazing and fortune-telling,' said the learned gentleman, 'and there were temples and beautiful hanging gardens—'

'I'll go to Babylon if you like,' said Jane abruptly, and the others hastened to say 'Done!' before she should have time to change her mind.

'Ah,' said the learned gentleman, smiling rather sadly, 'one can go so far in dreams, when one is young.' He sighed again, and then adding with a laboured briskness, 'I hope you'll have a — a — jolly game,' he went into his room and shut the door.

'He said "jolly" as if it was a foreign language,' said Cyril. 'Come on, let's get the Psammead and go now. I think Babylon seems a most frightfully jolly place to go to.'

So they woke the Psammead and put it in its bass-bag with the waterproof sheet, in case of inclement weather in Babylon. It was very cross, but it said it would as soon go to Babylon as anywhere else. 'The sand is good thereabouts,' it added.

Then Jane held up the charm, and Cyril said—

'We want to go to Babylon to look for the part of you that was lost. Will you please let us go there through you?'

'Please put us down just outside,' said Jane hastily; 'and then if we don't like it we needn't go inside.'

'Don't be all day,' said the Psammead.

So Anthea hastily uttered the word of power, without which the charm could do nothing.

'Ur—Hekau—Setcheh!' she said softly, and as she spoke the charm grew into an arch so tall that the top of it was close against the bedroom ceiling. Outside the arch was the bedroom painted chest-of-drawers and the Kidderminster carpet, and the washhand-stand with the riveted willow-pattern jug, and the faded curtains, and the dull light of indoors on a wet day. Through the arch showed the gleam of soft green leaves and white blossoms. They stepped forward quite happily. Even Jane felt that this did not look like lions, and her hand hardly trembled at all as she held the charm for the others to go through, and last, slipped through herself, and hung the charm, now grown small again, round her neck.

The children found themselves under a white-blossomed, green-leafed fruit-tree, in what seemed to be an orchard of such trees, all white-flowered and green-foliaged. Among the long green grass under their feet grew crocuses and lilies, and strange blue flowers. In the branches overhead thrushes and blackbirds were singing, and the coo of a pigeon came softly to them in the green quietness of the orchard.

'Oh, how perfectly lovely!' cried Anthea.

'Why, it's like home exactly—I mean England—only everything's bluer, and whiter, and greener, and the flowers are bigger.'

The boys owned that it certainly was fairly decent, and even Jane admitted that it was all very pretty.

'I'm certain there's nothing to be frightened of here,' said Anthea.

'I don't know,' said Jane. 'I suppose the fruit-trees go on just the same even when people are killing each other. I didn't half like what the learned gentleman said about the hanging gardens. I suppose they have gardens on purpose to hang people in. I do hope this isn't one.'

'Of course it isn't,' said Cyril. 'The hanging gardens are just gardens hung up—*I* think on chains between houses, don't you know, like trays. Come on; let's get somewhere.'

They began to walk through the cool grass. As far as they could see was nothing but trees, and trees and more trees. At the end of their orchard was another one, only separated from theirs by a little stream of clear water. They jumped this, and went on. Cyril, who was fond of gardening—which meant that he liked to watch the gardener at work—was able to command the respect of the others by telling them the names of a good many trees. There were nut-trees and almond-trees, and apricots, and fig-trees with their big five-fingered leaves. And every now and then the children had to cross another brook.

'It's like between the squares in Through the Looking-glass,' said Anthea.

At last they came to an orchard which was quite different from the other orchards. It had a low building in one corner.

'These are vines,' said Cyril superiorly, 'and I know this is a vineyard. I shouldn't wonder if there was a wine-press inside that place over there.'

At last they got out of the orchards and on to a sort of road, very rough, and not at all like the roads you are used to. It had cypress trees and acacia trees along it, and a sort of hedge of tamarisks, like those you see on the road between Nice and Cannes, or near Littlehampton, if you've only been as far as that.

And now in front of them they could see a great mass of buildings. There were scattered houses of wood and stone here and there among green orchards, and beyond these a great wall that shone red in the early morning sun. The wall was enormously high—more than half the height of St Paul's—and in the wall were set enormous gates that shone like gold as the rising sun beat on them. Each gate had a solid square tower on each side of it that stood out from the wall and rose above it. Beyond the wall were more towers and houses, gleaming with gold and bright colours. Away to the left ran the steel-blue swirl of a great river. And the children could see, through a gap in the trees, that the river flowed out from the town under a great arch in the wall.

'Those feathery things along by the water are palms,' said Cyril instructively.

'Oh, yes; you know everything,' Robert replied. 'What's all that grey-green stuff you see away over there, where it's all flat and sandy?'

'All right,' said Cyril loftily, '*I* don't want to tell you anything. I only thought you'd like to know a palm-tree when you saw it again.'

'Look!' cried Anthea; 'they're opening the gates.'

And indeed the great gates swung back with a brazen clang, and instantly a little crowd of a dozen or more people came out and along the road towards them.

The children, with one accord, crouched behind the tamarisk hedge.

'I don't like the sound of those gates,' said Jane. 'Fancy being inside when they shut. You'd never get out.'

'You've got an arch of your own to go out by,' the Psammead put its head out of the basket to remind her. 'Don't behave so like a girl. If I were you I should just march right into the town and ask to see the king.'

There was something at once simple and grand about this idea, and it pleased everyone.

So when the work-people had passed (they WERE work-people, the children felt sure, because they were dressed so plainly—just one long blue shirt thing—of blue or yellow) the four children marched boldly up to the brazen gate between the towers. The arch above the gate was quite a tunnel, the walls were so thick.

'Courage,' said Cyril. 'Step out. It's no use trying to sneak past. Be bold!'

Robert answered this appeal by unexpectedly bursting into 'The British Grenadiers', and to its quick-step they approached the gates of Babylon.

'Some talk of Alexander,
And some of Hercules,
Of Hector and Lysander,
And such great names as these.
But of all the gallant heroes ...'

This brought them to the threshold of the gate, and two men in bright armour suddenly barred their way with crossed spears.

'Who goes there?' they said.

(I think I must have explained to you before how it was that the children were always able to understand the language of any place they might happen to be in, and to be themselves understood. If not, I have no time to explain it now.)

'We come from very far,' said Cyril mechanically. 'From the Empire where the sun never sets, and we want to see your King.'

'If it's quite convenient,' amended Anthea. 'The King (may he live for ever!),' said the gatekeeper, 'is gone to fetch home his fourteenth wife. Where on earth have you come from not to know that?'

'The Queen then,' said Anthea hurriedly, and not taking any notice of the question as to where they had come from.

'The Queen,' said the gatekeeper, '(may she live for ever!) gives audience today three hours after sunrising.'

'But what are we to do till the end of the three hours?' asked Cyril.

The gatekeeper seemed neither to know nor to care. He appeared less interested in them than they could have thought possible. But the man who had crossed spears with him to bar the children's way was more human.

'Let them go in and look about them,' he said. 'I'll wager my best sword they've never seen anything to come near our little—village.' He said it in the tone people use for when they call the Atlantic Ocean the 'herring pond'.

The gatekeeper hesitated.

'They're only children, after all,' said the other, who had children of his own. 'Let me off for a few minutes, Captain, and I'll take them to my place and see if my good woman can't fit them up in something a little less outlandish than their present rig. Then they can have a look round without being mobbed. May I go?'

'Oh yes, if you like,' said the Captain, 'but don't be all day.'

The man led them through the dark arch into the town. And it was very different from London. For one thing, everything in London seems to be patched up out of odds and ends, but these houses seemed to have been built by people who liked the same sort of things. Not that they were all alike, for though all were squarish, they were of different sizes, and decorated in all sorts of different ways, some with paintings in bright colours, some with black and silver designs. There were terraces, and gardens, and balconies, and open spaces with trees. Their guide took them to a little house in a back street, where a kind-faced woman sat spinning at the door of a very dark room.

'Here,' he said, 'just lend these children a mantle each, so that they can go about and see the place till the Queen's audience begins. You leave that wool for a bit, and show them round if you like. I must be off now.'

The woman did as she was told, and the four children, wrapped in fringed mantles, went with her all about the town, and oh! how I wish I had time to tell you all that they saw. It was all so wonderfully different from anything you have ever seen. For one thing, all the houses were dazzlingly bright, and many of them covered with pictures. Some had great creatures carved in stone at each side of the door. Then the people—there were no black frock-coats and tall hats; no dingy coats and skirts of good, useful, ugly stuffs warranted to wear. Everyone's clothes were bright and beautiful with blue and scarlet and green and gold.

The market was brighter than you would think anything could be. There were stalls for everything you could possibly want—and for a great many things that if you wanted here and now, want would be your master. There were pineapples and peaches in heaps—and stalls of crockery and glass things, beautiful shapes and glorious colours, there were stalls for necklaces, and clasps, and bracelets, and brooches, for woven stuffs, and furs, and embroidered linen. The children had never seen half so many beautiful things together, even at Liberty's. It seemed no time at all before the woman said—

'It's nearly time now. We ought to be getting on towards the palace. It's as well to be early.' So they went to the palace, and when they got there it was more splendid than anything they had seen yet.

For it was glowing with colours, and with gold and silver and black and white—like some magnificent embroidery. Flight after flight of broad marble steps led up to it, and at the edges of the stairs stood great images, twenty times as big as a man—images of men with wings like chain armour, and hawks' heads, and winged men with the heads of dogs. And there were the statues of great kings.

Between the flights of steps were terraces where fountains played, and the Queen's Guard in white and scarlet, and armour that shone like gold, stood by twos lining the way up the stairs; and a great body of them was massed by the vast door of the palace itself, where it stood glittering like an impossibly radiant peacock in the noon-day sun.

All sorts of people were passing up the steps to seek audience of the Queen. Ladies in richly-embroidered dresses with fringy flounces, poor folks in plain and simple clothes, dandies with beards oiled and curled.

And Cyril, Robert, Anthea and Jane, went with the crowd.

At the gate of the palace the Psammead put one eye cautiously out of the basket and whispered—

'I can't be bothered with queens. I'll go home with this lady. I'm sure she'll get me some sand if you ask her to.'

'Oh! don't leave us,' said Jane. The woman was giving some last instructions in Court etiquette to Anthea, and did not hear Jane.

'Don't be a little muff,' said the Psammead quite fiercely. 'It's not a bit of good your having a charm. You never use it. If you want me you've only got to say the name of power and ask the charm to bring me to you.'

'I'd rather go with you,' said Jane. And it was the most surprising thing she had ever said in her life.

Everyone opened its mouth without thinking of manners, and Anthea, who was peeping into the Psammead's basket, saw that its mouth opened wider than anybody's.

'You needn't gawp like that,' Jane went on. 'I'm not going to be bothered with queens any more than IT is. And I know, wherever it is, it'll take jolly good care that it's safe.'

'She's right there,' said everyone, for they had observed that the Psammead had a way of knowing which side its bread was buttered.

She turned to the woman and said, 'You'll take me home with you, won't you? And let me play with your little girls till the others have done with the Queen.'

'Surely I will, little heart!' said the woman.

And then Anthea hurriedly stroked the Psammead and embraced Jane, who took the woman's hand, and trotted contentedly away with the Psammead's bag under the other arm.

The others stood looking after her till she, the woman, and the basket were lost in the many-coloured crowd. Then Anthea turned once more to the palace's magnificent doorway and said—

'Let's ask the porter to take care of our Babylonian overcoats.'

So they took off the garments that the woman had lent them and stood amid the jostling petitioners of the Queen in their own English frocks and coats and hats and boots.

'We want to see the Queen,' said Cyril; 'we come from the far Empire where the sun never sets!'

A murmur of surprise and a thrill of excitement ran through the crowd. The door-porter spoke to a black man, he spoke to someone else. There was a whispering, waiting pause. Then a big man, with a cleanly-shaven face, beckoned them from the top of a flight of red marble steps.

They went up; the boots of Robert clattering more than usual because he was so nervous. A door swung open, a curtain was drawn back. A double line of bowing forms in gorgeous raiment formed a lane that led to the steps of the throne, and as the children advanced hurriedly there came from the throne a voice very sweet and kind.

'Three children from the land where the sun never sets! Let them draw hither without fear.'

In another minute they were kneeling at the throne's foot, saying, 'O Queen, live for ever!' exactly as the woman had taught them. And a splendid dream-lady, all gold and silver and jewels and snowy drift of veils, was raising Anthea, and saying—

'Don't be frightened, I really am SO glad you came! The land where the sun never sets! I am delighted to see you! I was getting quite too dreadfully bored for anything!'

And behind Anthea the kneeling Cyril whispered in the ears of the respectful Robert—

'Bobs, don't say anything to Panther. It's no use upsetting her, but we didn't ask for Jane's address, and the Psammead's with her.'

'Well,' whispered Robert, 'the charm can bring them to us at any moment. IT said so.'

'Oh, yes,' whispered Cyril, in miserable derision, 'WE'RE all right, of course. So we are! Oh, yes! If we'd only GOT the charm.'

Then Robert saw, and he murmured, 'Crikey!' at the foot of the throne of Babylon; while Cyril hoarsely whispered the plain English fact—

'Jane's got the charm round her neck, you silly cuckoo.'

'Crikey!' Robert repeated in heart-broken undertones.

Chapter 7. 'The Deepest Dungeon Below The Castle Moat'

The Queen threw three of the red and gold embroidered cushions off the throne on to the marble steps that led up to it.

'Just make yourselves comfortable there,' she said. 'I'm simply dying to talk to you, and to hear all about your wonderful country and how you got here, and everything, but I have to do justice every morning. Such a bore, isn't it? Do you do justice in your own country?'

'No, said Cyril; 'at least of course we try to, but not in this public sort of way, only in private.' 'Ah, yes,' said the Queen, 'I should much prefer a private audience myself—much easier to manage. But public opinion has to be considered. Doing justice is very hard work, even when you're brought up to it.'

'We don't do justice, but we have to do scales, Jane and me,' said Anthea, 'twenty minutes a day. It's simply horrid.'

'What are scales?' asked the Queen, 'and what is Jane?'

'Jane is my little sister. One of the guards-at-the-gate's wife is taking care of her. And scales are music.'

'I never heard of the instrument,' said the Queen. 'Do you sing?'

'Oh, yes. We can sing in parts,' said Anthea.

'That IS magic,' said the Queen. 'How many parts are you each cut into before you do it?'

'We aren't cut at all,' said Robert hastily. 'We couldn't sing if we were. We'll show you afterwards.'

'So you shall, and now sit quiet like dear children and hear me do justice. The way I do it has always been admired. I oughtn't to say that ought I? Sounds so conceited. But I don't mind with you, dears. Somehow I feel as though I'd known you quite a long time already.'

The Queen settled herself on her throne and made a signal to her attendants. The children, whispering together among the cushions on the steps of the throne, decided that she was very beautiful and very kind, but perhaps just the least bit flighty.

The first person who came to ask for justice was a woman whose brother had taken the money the father had left for her. The brother said it was the uncle who had the money. There was a good deal of talk and the children were growing rather bored, when the Queen suddenly clapped her hands, and said—

'Put both the men in prison till one of them owns up that the other is innocent.'

'But suppose they both did it?' Cyril could not help interrupting.

'Then prison's the best place for them,' said the Queen.

'But suppose neither did it.'

'That's impossible,' said the Queen; 'a thing's not done unless someone does it. And you mustn't interrupt.'

Then came a woman, in tears, with a torn veil and real ashes on her head—at least Anthea thought so, but it may have been only road-dust. She complained that her husband was in prison.

'What for?' said the Queen.

'They SAID it was for speaking evil of your Majesty,' said the woman, 'but it wasn't. Someone had a spite against him. That was what it was.'

'How do you know he hadn't spoken evil of me?' said the Queen.

'No one could,' said the woman simply, 'when they'd once seen your beautiful face.'

'Let the man out,' said the Queen, smiling. 'Next case.'

The next case was that of a boy who had stolen a fox. 'Like the Spartan boy,' whispered Robert. But the Queen ruled that nobody could have any possible reason for owning a fox, and still less for stealing one. And she did not believe that there were any foxes in Babylon; she, at any rate, had never seen one. So the boy was released.

The people came to the Queen about all sorts of family quarrels and neighbourly misunderstandings—from a fight between brothers over the division of an inheritance, to the dishonest and unfriendly conduct of a woman who had borrowed a cooking-pot at the last New Year's festival, and not returned it yet.

And the Queen decided everything, very, very decidedly indeed. At last she clapped her hands quite suddenly and with extreme loudness, and said—

'The audience is over for today.'

Everyone said, 'May the Queen live for ever!' and went out.

And the children were left alone in the justice-hall with the Queen of Babylon and her ladies.

'There!' said the Queen, with a long sigh of relief. 'THAT'S over! I couldn't have done another stitch of justice if you'd offered me the crown of Egypt! Now come into the garden, and we'll have a nice, long, cosy talk.'

She led them through long, narrow corridors whose walls they somehow felt, were very, very thick, into a sort of garden courtyard. There were thick shrubs closely planted, and roses were trained over trellises, and made a pleasant shade—needed, indeed, for already the sun was as hot as it is in England in August at the seaside.

Slaves spread cushions on a low, marble terrace, and a big man with a smooth face served cool drink in cups of gold studded with beryls. He drank a little from the Queen's cup before handing it to her.

'That's rather a nasty trick,' whispered Robert, who had been carefully taught never to drink out of one of the nice, shiny, metal cups that are chained to the London drinking fountains without first rinsing it out thoroughly.

The Queen overheard him.

'Not at all,' said she. 'Ritti-Marduk is a very clean man. And one has to have SOME ONE as taster, you know, because of poison.'

The word made the children feel rather creepy; but Ritti-Marduk had tasted all the cups, so they felt pretty safe. The drink was delicious—very cold, and tasting like lemonade and partly like penny ices.

'Leave us,' said the Queen. And all the Court ladies, in their beautiful, many-folded, many-coloured, fringed dresses, filed out slowly, and the children were left alone with the Queen.

'Now,' she said, 'tell me all about yourselves.'

They looked at each other.

'You, Bobs,' said Cyril.

'No—Anthea,' said Robert.

'No—you—Cyril,' said Anthea. 'Don't you remember how pleased the Queen of India was when you told her all about us?'

Cyril muttered that it was all very well, and so it was. For when he had told the tale of the Phoenix and the Carpet to the Ranee, it had been only the truth—and all the truth that he had to tell. But now it was not easy to tell a convincing story without mentioning the Amulet—which, of course, it wouldn't have done to mention—and without owning that they were really living in London, about 2,500 years later than the time they were talking in.

Cyril took refuge in the tale of the Psammead and its wonderful power of making wishes come true. The children had never been able to tell anyone before, and Cyril was surprised to find that the spell which kept them silent in London did not work here. 'Something to do with our being in the Past, I suppose,' he said to himself.

'This is MOST interesting,' said the Queen. 'We must have this Psammead for the banquet tonight. Its performance will be one of the most popular turns in the whole programme. Where is it?'

Anthea explained that they did not know; also why it was that they did not know.

'Oh, THAT'S quite simple,' said the Queen, and everyone breathed a deep sigh of relief as she said it.

'Ritti-Marduk shall run down to the gates and find out which guard your sister went home with.'

'Might he'—Anthea's voice was tremulous—'might he—would it interfere with his meal-times, or anything like that, if he went NOW?'

'Of course he shall go now. He may think himself lucky if he gets his meals at any time,' said the Queen heartily, and clapped her hands.

'May I send a letter?' asked Cyril, pulling out a red-backed penny account-book, and feeling in his pockets for a stump of pencil that he knew was in one of them.

'By all means. I'll call my scribe.'

'Oh, I can scribe right enough, thanks,' said Cyril, finding the pencil and licking its point. He even had to bite the wood a little, for it was very blunt.

'Oh, you clever, clever boy!' said the Queen. 'DO let me watch you do it!'

Cyril wrote on a leaf of the book—it was of rough, woolly paper, with hairs that stuck out and would have got in his pen if he had been using one, and ruled for accounts.

'Hide IT most carefully before you come here,' he wrote, 'and don't mention it—and destroy this letter. Everything is going A1. The Queen is a fair treat. There's nothing to be afraid of.'

'What curious characters, and what a strange flat surface!' said the Queen. 'What have you inscribed?'

'I've 'scribed,' replied Cyril cautiously, 'that you are fair, and a—and like a—like a festival; and that she need not be afraid, and that she is to come at once.'

Ritti-Marduk, who had come in and had stood waiting while Cyril wrote, his Babylonish eyes nearly starting out of his Babylonish head, now took the letter, with some reluctance.

'O Queen, live for ever! Is it a charm?' he timidly asked. 'A strong charm, most great lady?'

'YES,' said Robert, unexpectedly, 'it IS a charm, but it won't hurt anyone until you've given it to Jane. And then she'll destroy it, so that it CAN'T hurt anyone. It's most awful strong!—as strong as—Peppermint!' he ended abruptly.

'I know not the god,' said Ritti-Marduk, bending timorously.

'She'll tear it up directly she gets it,' said Robert, 'That'll end the charm. You needn't be afraid if you go now.'

Ritti-Marduk went, seeming only partly satisfied; and then the Queen began to admire the penny account-book and the bit of pencil in so marked and significant a way that Cyril felt he could not do less than press them upon her as a gift. She ruffled the leaves delightedly.

'What a wonderful substance!' she said. 'And with this style you make charms? Make a charm for me! Do you know,' her voice sank to a whisper, 'the names of the great ones of your own far country?'

'Rather!' said Cyril, and hastily wrote the names of Alfred the Great, Shakespeare, Nelson, Gordon, Lord Beaconsfield, Mr Rudyard Kipling, and Mr Sherlock Holmes, while the Queen watched him with 'unbaited breath', as Anthea said afterwards.

She took the book and hid it reverently among the bright folds of her gown.

'You shall teach me later to say the great names,' she said. 'And the names of their Ministers—perhaps the great Nisroch is one of them?'

'I don't think so,' said Cyril. 'Mr Campbell Bannerman's Prime Minister and Mr Burns a Minister, and so is the Archbishop of Canterbury, I think, but I'm not sure—and Dr Parker was one, I know, and—'

'No more,' said the Queen, putting her hands to her ears. 'My head's going round with all those great names. You shall teach them to me later—because of course you'll make us a nice long visit now you have come, won't you? Now tell me—but no, I am quite tired out with your being so clever. Besides, I'm sure you'd like ME to tell YOU something, wouldn't you?'

'Yes,' said Anthea. 'I want to know how it is that the King has gone—'

'Excuse me, but you should say "the King may-he-live-for-ever",' said the Queen gently.

'I beg your pardon,' Anthea hastened to say—'the King may-he-live-for-ever has gone to fetch home his fourteenth wife? I don't think even Bluebeard had as many as that. And, besides, he hasn't killed YOU at any rate.'

The Queen looked bewildered.

'She means,' explained Robert, 'that English kings only have one wife—at least, Henry the Eighth had seven or eight, but not all at once.'

'In our country,' said the Queen scornfully, 'a king would not reign a day who had only one wife. No one would respect him, and quite right too.'

'Then are all the other thirteen alive?' asked Anthea.

'Of course they are—poor mean-spirited things! I don't associate with them, of course, I am the Queen: they're only the wives.'

'I see,' said Anthea, gasping.

'But oh, my dears,' the Queen went on, 'such a to-do as there's been about this last wife! You never did! It really was TOO funny. We wanted an Egyptian princess. The King may-he-live-for-ever has got a wife from most of the important nations, and he had set his heart on an Egyptian one to complete his collection. Well, of course, to begin with, we sent a handsome present of gold. The Egyptian king sent back some horses—quite a few; he's fearfully stingy!—and he said he liked the gold very much, but what they were really short of was lapis lazuli, so of course we sent him some. But by that time he'd begun to use the gold to cover the beams of the roof of the Temple of the Sun-God, and he hadn't nearly enough to finish the job, so we sent some more. And so it went on, oh, for years. You see each journey takes at least six months. And at last we asked the hand of his daughter in marriage.'

'Yes, and then?' said Anthea, who wanted to get to the princess part of the story.

'Well, then,' said the Queen, 'when he'd got everything out of us that he could, and only given the meanest presents in return, he sent to say he would esteem the honour of an alliance very highly, only unfortunately he hadn't any daughter, but he hoped one would be born soon, and if so, she should certainly be reserved for the King of Babylon!'

'What a trick!' said Cyril.

'Yes, wasn't it? So then we said his sister would do, and then there were more gifts and more journeys; and now at last the tiresome, black-haired thing is coming, and the King may-he-live-for-ever has gone seven days' journey to meet her at Carchemish. And he's gone in his best chariot, the one inlaid with lapis lazuli and gold, with the gold-plated wheels and onyx-studded hubs—much too great an honour in my opinion. She'll be here tonight; there'll be a grand banquet to celebrate her arrival. SHE won't be present, of course. She'll be having her baths and her anointings, and all that sort of thing. We always clean our foreign brides very carefully. It takes two or three weeks. Now it's dinnertime, and you shall eat with me, for I can see that you are of high rank.' She led them into a dark, cool hall, with many cushions on the floor. On these they sat and low tables were brought—beautiful tables of smooth, blue stone mounted in gold. On these, golden trays were placed; but there were no knives, or forks, or spoons. The children expected the Queen to call for them; but no. She just ate with her fingers, and as the first dish was a great tray of boiled corn, and meat and raisins all mixed up together, and melted fat poured all over the tray, it was found difficult to follow her example with anything like what we are used to think of as good table manners. There were stewed quinces afterwards, and dates in syrup, and thick yellowy cream. It was the kind of dinner you hardly ever get in Fitzroy Street.

After dinner everybody went to sleep, even the children.

The Queen awoke with a start.

'Good gracious!' she cried, 'what a time we've slept! I must rush off and dress for the banquet. I shan't have much more than time.'

'Hasn't Ritti-Marduk got back with our sister and the Psammead yet?' Anthea asked.

'I QUITE forgot to ask. I'm sorry,' said the Queen. 'And of course they wouldn't announce her unless I told them to, except during justice hours. I expect she's waiting outside. I'll see.'

Ritti-Marduk came in a moment later.

'I regret,' he said, 'that I have been unable to find your sister. The beast she bears with her in a basket has bitten the child of the guard, and your sister and the beast set out to come to you. The police say they have a clue. No doubt we shall have news of her in a few weeks.' He bowed and withdrew.

The horror of this threefold loss—Jane, the Psammead, and the Amulet—gave the children something to talk about while the Queen was dressing. I shall not report their conversation; it was very gloomy. Everyone repeated himself several times, and the discussion ended in each of them blaming the other two for having let Jane go. You know the sort of talk it was, don't you? At last Cyril said—

'After all, she's with the Psammead, so SHE'S all right. The Psammead is jolly careful of itself too. And it isn't as if we were in any danger. Let's try to buck up and enjoy the banquet.'

They did enjoy the banquet. They had a beautiful bath, which was delicious, were heavily oiled all over, including their hair, and that was most unpleasant. Then, they dressed again and were presented to the King, who was most affable. The banquet was long; there were all sorts of nice things to eat, and everybody seemed to eat and drink a good deal. Everyone lay on cushions and couches, ladies on one side and gentlemen on the other; and after the eating was done each lady went and sat by some gentleman, who seemed to be her sweetheart or her husband, for they were very affectionate to each other. The Court dresses had gold threads woven in them, very bright and beautiful.

The middle of the room was left clear, and different people came and did amusing things. There were conjurers and jugglers and snake-charmers, which last Anthea did not like at all.

When it got dark torches were lighted. Cedar splinters dipped in oil blazed in copper dishes set high on poles.

Then there was a dancer, who hardly danced at all, only just struck attitudes. She had hardly any clothes, and was not at all pretty. The children were rather bored by her, but everyone else was delighted, including the King.

'By the beard of Nimrod!' he cried, 'ask what you like girl, and you shall have it!'

'I want nothing,' said the dancer; 'the honour of having pleased the King may-he-live-for-ever is reward enough for me.'

And the King was so pleased with this modest and sensible reply that he gave her the gold collar off his own neck.

'I say!' said Cyril, awed by the magnificence of the gift.

'It's all right,' whispered the Queen, 'it's not his best collar by any means. We always keep a stock of cheap jewellery for these occasions. And now—you promised to sing us something. Would you like my minstrels to accompany you?'

'No, thank you,' said Anthea quickly. The minstrels had been playing off and on all the time, and their music reminded Anthea of the band she and the others had once had on the fifth of November—with penny horns, a tin whistle, a tea-tray, the tongs, a policeman's rattle, and a toy drum. They had enjoyed this band very much at the time. But it was quite different when someone else was making the same kind of music. Anthea understood now that Father had not been really heartless and unreasonable when he had told them to stop that infuriating din.

'What shall we sing?' Cyril was asking.

'Sweet and low?' suggested Anthea.

'Too soft—I vote for "Who will o'er the downs". Now then—one, two, three.

> 'Oh, who will o'er the downs so free,
> Oh, who will with me ride,
> Oh, who will up and follow me,
> To win a blooming bride?
>
> Her father he has locked the door,
> Her mother keeps the key;
> But neither bolt nor bar shall keep

My own true love from me.'

Jane, the alto, was missing, and Robert, unlike the mother of the lady in the song, never could 'keep the key', but the song, even so, was sufficiently unlike anything any of them had ever heard to rouse the Babylonian Court to the wildest enthusiasm.

'More, more,' cried the King; 'by my beard, this savage music is a new thing. Sing again!'

So they sang:

'I saw her bower at twilight gray,
'Twas guarded safe and sure.
I saw her bower at break of day,
'Twas guarded then no more.

The varlets they were all asleep,
And there was none to see
The greeting fair that passed there
Between my love and me.'

Shouts of applause greeted the ending of the verse, and the King would not be satisfied till they had sung all their part-songs (they only knew three) twice over, and ended up with 'Men of Harlech' in unison. Then the King stood up in his royal robes with his high, narrow crown on his head and shouted—

'By the beak of Nisroch, ask what you will, strangers from the land where the sun never sets!'

'We ought to say it's enough honour, like the dancer did,' whispered Anthea

'No, let's ask for IT,' said Robert.

'No, no, I'm sure the other's manners,' said Anthea. But Robert, who was excited by the music, and the flaring torches, and the applause and the opportunity, spoke up before the others could stop him.

'Give us the half of the Amulet that has on it the name UR HEKAU SETCHEH,' he said, adding as an afterthought, 'O King, live-for-ever.'

As he spoke the great name those in the pillared hall fell on their faces, and lay still. All but the Queen who crouched amid her cushions with her head in her hands, and the King, who stood upright, perfectly still, like the statue of a king in stone. It was only for a moment though. Then his great voice thundered out—

'Guard, seize them!'

Instantly, from nowhere as it seemed, sprang eight soldiers in bright armour inlaid with gold, and tunics of red and white. Very splendid they were, and very alarming.

'Impious and sacrilegious wretches!' shouted the King. 'To the dungeons with them! We will find a way, tomorrow, to make them speak. For without doubt they can tell us where to find the lost half of It.'

A wall of scarlet and white and steel and gold closed up round the children and hurried them away among the many pillars of the great hall. As they went they heard the voices of the courtiers loud in horror.

'You've done it this time,' said Cyril with extreme bitterness.

'Oh, it will come right. It MUST. It always does,' said Anthea desperately.

They could not see where they were going, because the guard surrounded them so closely, but the ground under their feet, smooth marble at first, grew rougher like stone, then it was loose earth and sand, and they felt the night air. Then there was more stone, and steps down.

'It's my belief we really ARE going to the deepest dungeon below the castle moat this time,' said Cyril.

And they were. At least it was not below a moat, but below the river Euphrates, which was just as bad if not worse. In a most unpleasant place it was. Dark, very, very damp, and with an odd, musty smell rather like the shells of oysters. There was a torch—that is to say, a copper basket on a high stick with oiled wood burning in it. By its light the children saw that the walls were green, and that trickles of water ran down them and dripped from the roof. There were things on the floor that looked like newts, and in the dark corners creepy, shiny things moved sluggishly, uneasily, horribly.

Robert's heart sank right into those really reliable boots of his. Anthea and Cyril each had a private struggle with that inside disagreeableness which is part of all of us, and which is sometimes called the Old Adam—and both were victors. Neither of them said to Robert (and both tried hard not even to think it), 'This is YOUR doing.' Anthea had the additional temptation to add, 'I told you so.' And she resisted it successfully.

'Sacrilege, and impious cheek,' said the captain of the guard to the gaoler. 'To be kept during the King's pleasure. I expect he means to get some pleasure out of them tomorrow! He'll tickle them up!'

'Poor little kids,' said the gaoler.

'Oh, yes,' said the captain. 'I've got kids of my own too. But it doesn't do to let domestic sentiment interfere with one's public duties. Good night.'

The soldiers tramped heavily off in their white and red and steel and gold. The gaoler, with a bunch of big keys in his hand, stood looking pityingly at the children. He shook his head twice and went out.

'Courage!' said Anthea. 'I know it will be all right. It's only a dream REALLY, you know. It MUST be! I don't believe about time being only a something or other of thought. It IS a dream, and we're bound to wake up all right and safe.'

'Humph,' said Cyril bitterly. And Robert suddenly said—

'It's all my doing. If it really IS all up do please not keep a down on me about it, and tell Father— Oh, I forgot.'

What he had forgotten was that his father was 3,000 miles and 5,000 or more years away from him.

'All right, Bobs, old man,' said Cyril; and Anthea got hold of Robert's hand and squeezed it.

Then the gaoler came back with a platter of hard, flat cakes made of coarse grain, very different from the cream-and-juicy-date feasts of the palace; also a pitcher of water.

'There,' he said.

'Oh, thank you so very much. You ARE kind,' said Anthea feverishly.

'Go to sleep,' said the gaoler, pointing to a heap of straw in a corner; 'tomorrow comes soon enough.'

'Oh, dear Mr Gaoler,' said Anthea, 'whatever will they do to us tomorrow?'

'They'll try to make you tell things,' said the gaoler grimly, 'and my advice is if you've nothing to tell, make up something. Then perhaps they'll sell you to the Northern nations. Regular savages THEY are. Good night.'

'Good night,' said three trembling voices, which their owners strove in vain to render firm. Then he went out, and the three were left alone in the damp, dim vault.

'I know the light won't last long,' said Cyril, looking at the flickering brazier.

'Is it any good, do you think, calling on the name when we haven't got the charm?' suggested Anthea.

'I shouldn't think so. But we might try.'

So they tried. But the blank silence of the damp dungeon remained unchanged.

'What was the name the Queen said?' asked Cyril suddenly. 'Nisbeth—Nesbit—something? You know, the slave of the great names?'

'Wait a sec,' said Robert, 'though I don't know why you want it. Nusroch—Nisrock—Nisroch—that's it.'

Then Anthea pulled herself together. All her muscles tightened, and the muscles of her mind and soul, if you can call them that, tightened too.

'UR HEKAU SETCHEH,' she cried in a fervent voice. 'Oh, Nisroch, servant of the Great Ones, come and help us!'

There was a waiting silence. Then a cold, blue light awoke in the corner where the straw was—and in the light they saw coming towards them a strange and terrible figure. I won't try to describe it, because the drawing shows it, exactly as it was, and exactly as the old Babylonians carved it on their stones, so that you can see it in our own British Museum at this day. I will just say that it had eagle's wings and an eagle's head and the body of a man.

It came towards them, strong and unspeakably horrible.

'Oh, go away,' cried Anthea; but Cyril cried, 'No; stay!'

The creature hesitated, then bowed low before them on the damp floor of the dungeon.

'Speak,' it said, in a harsh, grating voice like large rusty keys being turned in locks. 'The servant of the Great Ones is YOUR servant. What is your need that you call on the name of Nisroch?'

'We want to go home,' said Robert.

'No, no,' cried Anthea; 'we want to be where Jane is.'

Nisroch raised his great arm and pointed at the wall of the dungeon. And, as he pointed, the wall disappeared, and instead of the damp, green, rocky surface, there shone and glowed a room with rich hangings of red silk embroidered with golden water-lilies, with cushioned couches and great mirrors of polished steel; and in it was the Queen, and before her, on a red pillow, sat the Psammead, its fur hunched up in an irritated, discontented way. On a blue-covered couch lay Jane fast asleep.

'Walk forward without fear,' said Nisroch. 'Is there aught else that the Servant of the great Name can do for those who speak that name?'

'No—oh, no,' said Cyril. 'It's all right now. Thanks ever so.'

'You are a dear,' cried Anthea, not in the least knowing what she was saying. 'Oh, thank you thank you. But DO go NOW!'

She caught the hand of the creature, and it was cold and hard in hers, like a hand of stone.

'Go forward,' said Nisroch. And they went.

'Oh, my good gracious,' said the Queen as they stood before her. 'How did you get here? I KNEW you were magic. I meant to let you out the first thing in the morning, if I could slip away—but thanks be to Dagon, you've managed it for yourselves. You must get away. I'll wake my chief lady and she shall call Ritti-Marduk, and he'll let you out the back way, and—'

'Don't rouse anybody for goodness' sake,' said Anthea, 'except Jane, and I'll rouse her.'

She shook Jane with energy, and Jane slowly awoke.

'Ritti-Marduk brought them in hours ago, really,' said the Queen, 'but I wanted to have the Psammead all to myself for a bit. You'll excuse the little natural deception?—it's part of the Babylonish character, don't you know? But I don't want anything to happen to you. Do let me rouse someone.'

'No, no, no,' said Anthea with desperate earnestness. She thought she knew enough of what the Babylonians were like when they were roused. 'We can go by our own magic. And you will tell the King it wasn't the gaoler's fault. It was Nisroch.'

'Nisroch!' echoed the Queen. 'You are indeed magicians.'

Jane sat up, blinking stupidly.

'Hold It up, and say the word,' cried Cyril, catching up the Psammead, which mechanically bit him, but only very slightly.

'Which is the East?' asked Jane.

'Behind me,' said the Queen. 'Why?'

'Ur Hekau Setcheh,' said Jane sleepily, and held up the charm.

And there they all were in the dining-room at 300, Fitzroy Street.

'Jane,' cried Cyril with great presence of mind, 'go and get the plate of sand down for the Psammead.'

Jane went.

'Look here!' he said quickly, as the sound of her boots grew less loud on the stairs, 'don't let's tell her about the dungeon and all that. It'll only frighten her so that she'll never want to go anywhere else.'

'Righto!' said Cyril; but Anthea felt that she could not have said a word to save her life.

'Why did you want to come back in such a hurry?' asked Jane, returning with the plate of sand. 'It was awfully jolly in Babylon, I think! I liked it no end.'

'Oh, yes,' said Cyril carelessly. 'It was jolly enough, of course, but I thought we'd been there long enough. Mother always says you oughtn't to wear out your welcome!'

Chapter 8. The Queen in London

'Now tell us what happened to you,' said Cyril to Jane, when he and the others had told her all about the Queen's talk and the banquet, and the variety entertainment, carefully stopping short before the beginning of the dungeon part of the story.

'It wasn't much good going,' said Jane, 'if you didn't even try to get the Amulet.'

'We found out it was no go,' said Cyril; 'it's not to be got in Babylon. It was lost before that. We'll go to some other jolly friendly place, where everyone is kind and pleasant, and look for it there. Now tell us about your part.'

'Oh,' said Jane, 'the Queen's man with the smooth face—what was his name?'

'Ritti-Marduk,' said Cyril.

'Yes,' said Jane, 'Ritti-Marduk, he came for me just after the Psammead had bitten the guard-of-the-gate's wife's little boy, and he took me to the Palace. And we had supper with the new little Queen from Egypt. She is a dear—not much older than you. She told me heaps about Egypt. And we played ball after supper. And then the Babylon Queen sent for me. I like her too. And she talked to the Psammead and I went to sleep. And then you woke me up. That's all.'

The Psammead, roused from its sound sleep, told the same story.

'But,' it added, 'what possessed you to tell that Queen that I could give wishes? I sometimes think you were born without even the most rudimentary imitation of brains.'

The children did not know the meaning of rudimentary, but it sounded a rude, insulting word.

'I don't see that we did any harm,' said Cyril sulkily.

'Oh, no,' said the Psammead with withering irony, 'not at all! Of course not! Quite the contrary! Exactly so! Only she happened to wish that she might soon find herself in your country. And soon may mean any moment.'

'Then it's your fault,' said Robert, 'because you might just as well have made "soon" mean some moment next year or next century.'

'That's where you, as so often happens, make the mistake,' rejoined the Sand-fairy. '*I* couldn't mean anything but what SHE meant by "soon". It wasn't my wish. And what SHE meant was the next time the King happens to go out lion hunting. So she'll have a whole day, and perhaps two, to do as she wishes with. SHE doesn't know about time only being a mode of thought.'

'Well,' said Cyril, with a sigh of resignation, 'we must do what we can to give her a good time. She was jolly decent to us. I say, suppose we were to go to St James's Park after dinner and feed those ducks that we never did feed. After all that Babylon and all those years ago, I feel as if I should like to see something REAL, and NOW. You'll come, Psammead?'

'Where's my priceless woven basket of sacred rushes?' asked the Psammead morosely. 'I can't go out with nothing on. And I won't, what's more.'

And then everybody remembered with pain that the bass bag had, in the hurry of departure from Babylon, not been remembered.

'But it's not so extra precious,' said Robert hastily. 'You can get them given to you for nothing if you buy fish in Farringdon Market.'

'Oh,' said the Psammead very crossly indeed, 'so you presume on my sublime indifference to the things of this disgusting modern world, to fob me off with a travelling equipage that costs you nothing. Very well, I shall go to sand. Please don't wake me.'

And it went then and there to sand, which, as you know, meant to bed. The boys went to St James's Park to feed the ducks, but they went alone.

Anthea and Jane sat sewing all the afternoon. They cut off half a yard from each of their best green Liberty sashes. A towel cut in two formed a lining; and they sat and sewed and sewed and sewed. What they were making was a bag for the Psammead. Each worked at a half of the bag. jane's half had four-leaved shamrocks embroidered on it. They were the only things she could do (because she had been taught how at school, and, fortunately, some of the silk she had been taught with was left over). And even so, Anthea had to draw the pattern for her. Anthea's side of the bag had letters on it—worked hastily but affectionately in chain stitch. They were something like this:

PSAMS TRAVEL CAR

She would have put 'travelling carriage', but she made the letters too big, so there was no room. The bag was made INTO a bag with old Nurse's sewing machine, and the strings of it were Anthea's and Jane's best red hair ribbons. At tea-time, when the boys had come home with a most unfavourable report of the St James's Park ducks, Anthea ventured to awaken the Psammead, and to show it its new travelling bag.

'Humph,' it said, sniffing a little contemptuously, yet at the same time affectionately, 'it's not so dusty.'

The Psammead seemed to pick up very easily the kind of things that people said nowadays. For a creature that had in its time associated with Megatheriums and Pterodactyls, its quickness was really wonderful.

'It's more worthy of me,' it said, 'than the kind of bag that's given away with a pound of plaice. When do you propose to take me out in it?'

'I should like a rest from taking you or us anywhere,' said Cyril. But Jane said—

'I want to go to Egypt. I did like that Egyptian Princess that came to marry the King in Babylon. She told me about the larks they have in Egypt. And the cats. Do let's go there. And I told her what the bird things on the Amulet were like. And she said it was Egyptian writing.'

The others exchanged looks of silent rejoicing at the thought of their cleverness in having concealed from Jane the terrors they had suffered in the dungeon below the Euphrates.

'Egypt's so nice too,' Jane went on, 'because of Doctor Brewer's Scripture History. I would like to go there when Joseph was dreaming those curious dreams, or when Moses was doing wonderful things with snakes and sticks.'

'I don't care about snakes,' said Anthea shuddering.

'Well, we needn't be in at that part, but Babylon was lovely! We had cream and sweet, sticky stuff. And I expect Egypt's the same.'

There was a good deal of discussion, but it all ended in everybody's agreeing to Jane's idea. And next morning directly after breakfast (which was kippers and very nice) the Psammead was invited to get into his travelling carriage.

The moment after it had done so, with stiff, furry reluctance, like that of a cat when you want to nurse it, and its ideas are not the same as yours, old Nurse came in.

'Well, chickies,' she said, 'are you feeling very dull?'

'Oh, no, Nurse dear,' said Anthea; 'we're having a lovely time. We're just going off to see some old ancient relics.'

'Ah,' said old Nurse, 'the Royal Academy, I suppose? Don't go wasting your money too reckless, that's all.'

She cleared away the kipper bones and the tea-things, and when she had swept up the crumbs and removed the cloth, the Amulet was held up and the order given—just as Duchesses (and other people) give it to their coachmen.

'To Egypt, please!' said Anthea, when Cyril had uttered the wonderful Name of Power.

'When Moses was there,' added Jane.

And there, in the dingy Fitzroy Street dining-room, the Amulet grew big, and it was an arch, and through it they saw a blue, blue sky and a running river.

'No, stop!' said Cyril, and pulled down Jane's hand with the Amulet in it.

'What silly cuckoos we all are,' he said. 'Of course we can't go. We daren't leave home for a single minute now, for fear that minute should be THE minute.'

'What minute be WHAT minute?' asked Jane impatiently, trying to get her hand away from Cyril.

'The minute when the Queen of Babylon comes,' said Cyril. And then everyone saw it.

For some days life flowed in a very slow, dusty, uneventful stream.

The children could never go out all at once, because they never knew when the King of Babylon would go out lion hunting and leave his Queen free to pay them that surprise visit to which she was, without doubt, eagerly looking forward.

So they took it in turns, two and two, to go out and to stay in.

The stay-at-homes would have been much duller than they were but for the new interest taken in them by the learned gentleman.

He called Anthea in one day to show her a beautiful necklace of purple and gold beads.

'I saw one like that,' she said, 'in—'

'In the British Museum, perhaps?'

'I like to call the place where I saw it Babylon,' said Anthea cautiously.

'A pretty fancy,' said the learned gentleman, 'and quite correct too, because, as a matter of fact, these beads did come from Babylon.' The other three were all out that day. The boys had been going to the Zoo, and Jane had said so plaintively, 'I'm sure I am fonder of rhinoceroses than either of you are,' that Anthea had told her to run along then. And she had run, catching the boys before that part of the road where Fitzroy Street suddenly becomes Fitzroy Square.

'I think Babylon is most frightfully interesting,' said Anthea. 'I do have such interesting dreams about it—at least, not dreams exactly, but quite as wonderful.'

'Do sit down and tell me,' said he. So she sat down and told. And he asked her a lot of questions, and she answered them as well as she could.

'Wonderful—wonderful!' he said at last. 'One's heard of thought-transference, but I never thought *I* had any power of that sort. Yet it must be that, and very bad for YOU, I should think. Doesn't your head ache very much?'

He suddenly put a cold, thin hand on her forehead.

'No thank you, not at all,' said she.

'I assure you it is not done intentionally,' he went on. 'Of course I know a good deal about Babylon, and I unconsciously communicate it to you; you've heard of thought-reading, but some of the things you say, I don't understand; they never enter my head, and yet they're so astoundingly probable.'

'It's all right,' said Anthea reassuringly. '*I* understand. And don't worry. It's all quite simple really.'

It was not quite so simple when Anthea, having heard the others come in, went down, and before she had had time to ask how they had liked the Zoo, heard a noise outside, compared to which the wild beasts' noises were gentle as singing birds.

'Good gracious!' cried Anthea, 'what's that?'

The loud hum of many voices came through the open window. Words could be distinguished.

"Ere's a guy!'

'This ain't November. That ain't no guy. It's a ballet lady, that's what it is.'

'Not it—it's a bloomin' looney, I tell you.'

Then came a clear voice that they knew.

'Retire, slaves!' it said.

'What's she a saying of?' cried a dozen voices. 'Some blamed foreign lingo,' one voice replied.

The children rushed to the door. A crowd was on the road and pavement.

In the middle of the crowd, plainly to be seen from the top of the steps, were the beautiful face and bright veil of the Babylonian Queen.

'Jimminy!' cried Robert, and ran down the steps, 'here she is!'

'Here!' he cried, 'look out—let the lady pass. She's a friend of ours, coming to see us.'

'Nice friend for a respectable house,' snorted a fat woman with marrows on a handcart.

All the same the crowd made way a little. The Queen met Robert on the pavement, and Cyril joined them, the Psammead bag still on his arm.

'Here,' he whispered; 'here's the Psammead; you can get wishes.'

'*I* wish you'd come in a different dress, if you HAD to come,' said Robert; 'but it's no use my wishing anything.'

'No,' said the Queen. 'I wish I was dressed—no, I don't—I wish THEY were dressed properly, then they wouldn't be so silly.'

The Psammead blew itself out till the bag was a very tight fit for it; and suddenly every man, woman, and child in that crowd felt that it had not enough clothes on. For, of course, the Queen's idea of proper dress was the dress that had been proper for the working-classes 3,000 years ago in Babylon—and there was not much of it.

'Lawky me!' said the marrow-selling woman, 'whatever could a-took me to come out this figure?' and she wheeled her cart away very quickly indeed.

'Someone's made a pretty guy of you—talk of guys,' said a man who sold bootlaces.

'Well, don't you talk,' said the man next to him. 'Look at your own silly legs; and where's your boots?'

'I never come out like this, I'll take my sacred,' said the bootlace-seller. 'I wasn't quite myself last night, I'll own, but not to dress up like a circus.'

The crowd was all talking at once, and getting rather angry. But no one seemed to think of blaming the Queen.

Anthea bounded down the steps and pulled her up; the others followed, and the door was shut. 'Blowed if I can make it out!' they heard. 'I'm off home, I am.'

And the crowd, coming slowly to the same mind, dispersed, followed by another crowd of persons who were not dressed in what the Queen thought was the proper way.

'We shall have the police here directly,' said Anthea in the tones of despair. 'Oh, why did you come dressed like that?'

The Queen leaned against the arm of the horse-hair sofa.

'How else can a queen dress I should like to know?' she questioned.

'Our Queen wears things like other people,' said Cyril.

'Well, I don't. And I must say,' she remarked in an injured tone, 'that you don't seem very glad to see me now I HAVE come. But perhaps it's the surprise that makes you behave like this. Yet you ought to be used to surprises. The way you vanished! I shall never forget it. The best magic I've ever seen. How did you do it?'

'Oh, never mind about that now,' said Robert. 'You see you've gone and upset all those people, and I expect they'll fetch the police. And we don't want to see you collared and put in prison.'

'You can't put queens in prison,' she said loftily. 'Oh, can't you?' said Cyril. 'We cut off a king's head here once.'

'In this miserable room? How frightfully interesting.'

'No, no, not in this room; in history.'

'Oh, in THAT,' said the Queen disparagingly. 'I thought you'd done it with your own hands.'

The girls shuddered.

'What a hideous city yours is,' the Queen went on pleasantly, 'and what horrid, ignorant people. Do you know they actually can't understand a single word I say.'

'Can you understand them?' asked Jane.

'Of course not; they speak some vulgar, Northern dialect. I can understand YOU quite well.'

I really am not going to explain AGAIN how it was that the children could understand other languages than their own so thoroughly, and talk them, too, so that it felt and sounded (to them) just as though they were talking English.

'Well,' said Cyril bluntly, 'now you've seen just how horrid it is, don't you think you might as well go home again?' 'Why, I've seen simply nothing yet,' said the Queen, arranging her starry veil. 'I wished to be at your door, and I was. Now I must go and see your King and Queen.'

'Nobody's allowed to,' said Anthea in haste; 'but look here, we'll take you and show you anything you'd like to see—anything you CAN see,' she added kindly, because she remembered how nice the Queen had been to them in Babylon, even if she had been a little deceitful in the matter of Jane and Psammead.

'There's the Museum,' said Cyril hopefully; 'there are lots of things from your country there. If only we could disguise you a little.'

'I know,' said Anthea suddenly. 'Mother's old theatre cloak, and there are a lot of her old hats in the big box.'

The blue silk, lace-trimmed cloak did indeed hide some of the Queen's startling splendours, but the hat fitted very badly. It had pink roses in it; and there was something about the coat or the hat or the Queen, that made her look somehow not very respectable.

'Oh, never mind,' said Anthea, when Cyril whispered this. 'The thing is to get her out before Nurse has finished her forty winks. I should think she's about got to the thirty-ninth wink by now.'

'Come on then,' said Robert. 'You know how dangerous it is. Let's make haste into the Museum. If any of those people you made guys of do fetch the police, they won't think of looking for you there.'

The blue silk coat and the pink-rosed hat attracted almost as much attention as the royal costume had done; and the children were uncommonly glad to get out of the noisy streets into the grey quiet of the Museum.

'Parcels and umbrellas to be left here,' said a man at the counter.

The party had no umbrellas, and the only parcel was the bag containing the Psammead, which the Queen had insisted should be brought.

'I'M not going to be left,' said the Psammead softly, 'so don't you think it.'

'I'll wait outside with you,' said Anthea hastily, and went to sit on the seat near the drinking fountain.

'Don't sit so near that nasty fountain,' said the creature crossly; 'I might get splashed.'

Anthea obediently moved to another seat and waited. Indeed she waited, and waited, and waited, and waited, and waited. The Psammead dropped into an uneasy slumber. Anthea had long ceased to watch the swing-door that always let out the wrong person, and she was herself almost asleep, and still the others did not come back.

It was quite a start when Anthea suddenly realized that they HAD come back, and that they were not alone. Behind them was quite a crowd of men in uniform, and several gentlemen were there. Everyone seemed very angry.

'Now go,' said the nicest of the angry gentlemen. 'Take the poor, demented thing home and tell your parents she ought to be properly looked after.'

'If you can't get her to go we must send for the police,' said the nastiest gentleman.

'But we don't wish to use harsh measures,' added the nice one, who was really very nice indeed, and seemed to be over all the others.

'May I speak to my sister a moment first?' asked Robert.

The nicest gentleman nodded, and the officials stood round the Queen, the others forming a sort of guard while Robert crossed over to Anthea.

'Everything you can think of,' he replied to Anthea's glance of inquiry. 'Kicked up the most frightful shine in there. Said those necklaces and earrings and things in the glass cases were all hers—would have them out of the cases. Tried to break the glass—she did break one bit! Everybody in the place has been at her. No good. I only got her out by telling her that was the place where they cut queens' heads off.'

'Oh, Bobs, what a whacker!'

'You'd have told a whackinger one to get her out. Besides, it wasn't. I meant MUMMY queens. How do you know they don't cut off mummies' heads to see how the embalming is done? What I want to say is, can't you get her to go with you quietly?'

'I'll try,' said Anthea, and went up to the Queen.

'Do come home,' she said; 'the learned gentleman in our house has a much nicer necklace than anything they've got here. Come and see it.'

The Queen nodded.

'You see,' said the nastiest gentleman, 'she does understand English.'

'I was talking Babylonian, I think,' said Anthea bashfully.

'My good child,' said the nice gentleman, 'what you're talking is not Babylonian, but nonsense. You just go home at once, and tell your parents exactly what has happened.'

Anthea took the Queen's hand and gently pulled her away. The other children followed, and the black crowd of angry gentlemen stood on the steps watching them. It was when the little party of disgraced children, with the Queen who had disgraced them, had reached the middle of the courtyard that her eyes fell on the bag where the Psammead was. She stopped short.

'I wish,' she said, very loud and clear, 'that all those Babylonian things would come out to me here—slowly, so that those dogs and slaves can see the working of the great Queen's magic.'

'Oh, you ARE a tiresome woman,' said the Psammead in its bag, but it puffed itself out.

Next moment there was a crash. The glass swing doors and all their framework were smashed suddenly and completely. The crowd of angry gentlemen sprang aside when they saw what had done this.

But the nastiest of them was not quick enough, and he was roughly pushed out of the way by an enormous stone bull that was floating steadily through the door. It came and stood beside the Queen in the middle of the courtyard.

It was followed by more stone images, by great slabs of carved stone, bricks, helmets, tools, weapons, fetters, wine-jars, bowls, bottles, vases, jugs, saucers, seals, and the round long things, something like rolling pins with marks on them like the print of little bird-feet, necklaces, collars, rings, armlets, earrings—heaps and heaps and heaps of things, far more than anyone had time to count, or even to see distinctly.

All the angry gentlemen had abruptly sat down on the Museum steps except the nice one. He stood with his hands in his pockets just as though he was quite used to seeing great stone bulls and all sorts of small Babylonish objects float out into the Museum yard.

But he sent a man to close the big iron gates.

A journalist, who was just leaving the museum, spoke to Robert as he passed.

'Theosophy, I suppose?' he said. 'Is she Mrs Besant?'

'YES,' said Robert recklessly.

The journalist passed through the gates just before they were shut.

He rushed off to Fleet Street, and his paper got out a new edition within half an hour.

MRS BESANT AND THEOSOPHY

IMPERTINENT MIRACLE AT THE BRITISH MUSEUM.

People saw it in fat, black letters on the boards carried by the sellers of newspapers. Some few people who had nothing better to do went down to the Museum on the tops of omnibuses. But by the time they got there there was nothing to be seen. For the Babylonian Queen had suddenly seen the closed gates, had felt the threat of them, and had said—

'I wish we were in your house.'

And, of course, instantly they were.

The Psammead was furious.

'Look here,' it said, 'they'll come after you, and they'll find ME. There'll be a National Cage built for me at Westminster, and I shall have to work at politics. Why wouldn't you leave the things in their places?'

'What a temper you have, haven't you?' said the Queen serenely. 'I wish all the things were back in their places. Will THAT do for you?'

The Psammead swelled and shrank and spoke very angrily.

'I can't refuse to give your wishes,' it said, 'but I can Bite. And I will if this goes on. Now then.'

'Ah, don't,' whispered Anthea close to its bristling ear; 'it's dreadful for us too. Don't YOU desert us. Perhaps she'll wish herself at home again soon.'

'Not she,' said the Psammead a little less crossly.

'Take me to see your City,' said the Queen.

The children looked at each other.

'If we had some money we could take her about in a cab. People wouldn't notice her so much then. But we haven't.'

'Sell this,' said the Queen, taking a ring from her finger.

'They'd only think we'd stolen it,' said Cyril bitterly, 'and put us in prison.'

'All roads lead to prison with you, it seems,' said the Queen.

'The learned gentleman!' said Anthea, and ran up to him with the ring in her hand.

'Look here,' she said, 'will you buy this for a pound?'

'Oh!' he said in tones of joy and amazement, and took the ring into his hand. 'It's my very own,' said Anthea; 'it was given to me to sell.'

'I'll lend you a pound,' said the learned gentleman, 'with pleasure; and I'll take care of the ring for you. Who did you say gave it to you?'

'We call her,' said Anthea carefully, 'the Queen of Babylon.'

'Is it a game?' he asked hopefully.

'It'll be a pretty game if I don't get the money to pay for cabs for her,' said Anthea.

'I sometimes think,' he said slowly, 'that I am becoming insane, or that—'

'Or that I am; but I'm not, and you're not, and she's not.'

'Does she SAY that she's the Queen of Babylon?' he uneasily asked.

'Yes,' said Anthea recklessly.

'This thought-transference is more far-reaching than I imagined,' he said. 'I suppose I have unconsciously influenced HER, too. I never thought my Babylonish studies would bear fruit like this. Horrible! There are more things in heaven and earth—'

'Yes,' said Anthea, 'heaps more. And the pound is the thing *I* want more than anything on earth.'

He ran his fingers through his thin hair.

'This thought-transference!' he said. 'It's undoubtedly a Babylonian ring—or it seems so to me. But perhaps I have hypnotized myself. I will see a doctor the moment I have corrected the last proofs of my book.'

'Yes, do!' said Anthea, 'and thank you so very much.'

She took the sovereign and ran down to the others.

And now from the window of a four-wheeled cab the Queen of Babylon beheld the wonders of London. Buckingham Palace she thought uninteresting; Westminster Abbey and the Houses of Parliament little better. But she liked the Tower, and the River, and the ships filled her with wonder and delight.

'But how badly you keep your slaves. How wretched and poor and neglected they seem,' she said, as the cab rattled along the Mile End Road.

'They aren't slaves; they're working-people,' said Jane.

'Of course they're working. That's what slaves are. Don't you tell me. Do you suppose I don't know a slave's face when I see it?

Why don't their masters see that they're better fed and better clothed? Tell me in three words.'

No one answered. The wage-system of modern England is a little difficult to explain in three words even if you understand it—which the children didn't.

'You'll have a revolt of your slaves if you're not careful,' said the Queen.

'Oh, no,' said Cyril; 'you see they have votes—that makes them safe not to revolt. It makes all the difference. Father told me so.'

'What is this vote?' asked the Queen. 'Is it a charm? What do they do with it?'

'I don't know,' said the harassed Cyril; 'it's just a vote, that's all! They don't do anything particular with it.'

'I see,' said the Queen; 'a sort of plaything. Well, I wish that all these slaves may have in their hands this moment their fill of their favourite meat and drink.'

Instantly all the people in the Mile End Road, and in all the other streets where poor people live, found their hands full of things to eat and drink. From the cab window could be seen persons carrying every kind of food, and bottles and cans as well. Roast meat, fowls, red lobsters, great yellowy crabs, fried fish, boiled pork, beef-steak puddings, baked onions, mutton pies; most of the young people had oranges and sweets and cake. It made an enormous change in the look of the Mile End Road—brightened it up, so to speak, and brightened up, more than you can possibly imagine, the faces of the people.

'Makes a difference, doesn't it?' said the Queen.

'That's the best wish you've had yet,' said Jane with cordial approval.

Just by the Bank the cabman stopped.

'I ain't agoin' to drive you no further,' he said. 'Out you gets.'

They got out rather unwillingly.

'I wants my tea,' he said; and they saw that on the box of the cab was a mound of cabbage, with pork chops and apple sauce, a duck, and a spotted currant pudding. Also a large can.

'You pay me my fare,' he said threateningly, and looked down at the mound, muttering again about his tea.

'We'll take another cab,' said Cyril with dignity. 'Give me change for a sovereign, if you please.'

But the cabman, as it turned out, was not at all a nice character. He took the sovereign, whipped up his horse, and disappeared in the stream of cabs and omnibuses and wagons, without giving them any change at all.

Already a little crowd was collecting round the party.

'Come on,' said Robert, leading the wrong way.

The crowd round them thickened. They were in a narrow street where many gentlemen in black coats and without hats were standing about on the pavement talking very loudly.

'How ugly their clothes are,' said the Queen of Babylon. 'They'd be rather fine men, some of them, if they were dressed decently, especially the ones with the beautiful long, curved noses. I wish they were dressed like the Babylonians of my court.'

And of course, it was so.

The moment the almost fainting Psammead had blown itself out every man in Throgmorton Street appeared abruptly in Babylonian full dress.

All were carefully powdered, their hair and beards were scented and curled, their garments richly embroidered. They wore rings and armlets, flat gold collars and swords, and impossible-looking head-dresses.

A stupefied silence fell on them.

'I say,' a youth who had always been fair-haired broke that silence, 'it's only fancy of course—something wrong with my eyes—but you chaps do look so rum.'

'Rum,' said his friend. 'Look at YOU. You in a sash! My hat! And your hair's gone black and you've got a beard. It's my belief we've been poisoned. You do look a jackape.'

'Old Levinstein don't look so bad. But how was it DONE—that's what I want to know. How was it done? Is it conjuring, or what?'

'I think it is chust a ver' bad tream,' said old Levinstein to his clerk; 'all along Bishopsgate I haf seen the gommon people have their hants full of food—GOOT food. Oh yes, without doubt a very bad tream!'

'Then I'm dreaming too, Sir,' said the clerk, looking down at his legs with an expression of loathing. 'I see my feet in beastly sandals as plain as plain.'

'All that goot food wasted,' said old Mr Levinstein. A bad tream—a bad tream.'

The Members of the Stock Exchange are said to be at all times a noisy lot. But the noise they made now to express their disgust at the costumes of ancient Babylon was far louder than their ordinary row. One had to shout before one could hear oneself speak.

'I only wish,' said the clerk who thought it was conjuring—he was quite close to the children and they trembled, because they knew that whatever he wished would come true. 'I only wish we knew who'd done it.'

And, of course, instantly they did know, and they pressed round the Queen.

'Scandalous! Shameful! Ought to be put down by law. Give her in charge. Fetch the police,' two or three voices shouted at once.

The Queen recoiled.

'What is it?' she asked. 'They sound like caged lions—lions by the thousand. What is it that they say?'

'They say "Police!",' said Cyril briefly. 'I knew they would sooner or later. And I don't blame them, mind you.'

'I wish my guards were here!' cried the Queen. The exhausted Psammead was panting and trembling, but the Queen's guards in red and green garments, and brass and iron gear, choked Throgmorton Street, and bared weapons flashed round the Queen.

'I'm mad,' said a Mr Rosenbaum; 'dat's what it is—mad!'

'It's a judgement on you, Rosy,' said his partner. 'I always said you were too hard in that matter of Flowerdew. It's a judgement, and I'm in it too.'

The members of the Stock Exchange had edged carefully away from the gleaming blades, the mailed figures, the hard, cruel Eastern faces.

But Throgmorton Street is narrow, and the crowd was too thick for them to get away as quickly as they wished.

'Kill them,' cried the Queen. 'Kill the dogs!'

The guards obeyed.

'It IS all a dream,' cried Mr Levinstein, cowering in a doorway behind his clerk.

'It isn't,' said the clerk. 'It isn't. Oh, my good gracious! those foreign brutes are killing everybody. Henry Hirsh is down now, and Prentice is cut in two—oh, Lord! and Huth, and there goes Lionel Cohen with his head off, and Guy Nickalls has lost his head now. A dream? I wish to goodness it was all a dream.'

And, of course, instantly it was! The entire Stock Exchange rubbed its eyes and went back to close, to over, and either side of seven-eights, and Trunks, and Kaffirs, and Steel Common, and Contangoes, and Backwardations, Double Options, and all the interesting subjects concerning which they talk in the Street without ceasing.

No one said a word about it to anyone else. I think I have explained before that business men do not like it to be known that they have been dreaming in business hours. Especially mad dreams including such dreadful things as hungry people getting dinners, and the destruction of the Stock Exchange.

The children were in the dining-room at 300, Fitzroy Street, pale and trembling. The Psammead crawled out of the embroidered bag, and lay flat on the table, its leg stretched out, looking more like a dead hare than anything else.

'Thank Goodness that's over,' said Anthea, drawing a deep breath.

'She won't come back, will she?' asked Jane tremulously.

'No,' said Cyril. 'She's thousands of years ago. But we spent a whole precious pound on her. It'll take all our pocket-money for ages to pay that back.'

'Not if it was ALL a dream,' said Robert.

'The wish said ALL a dream, you know, Panther; you cut up and ask if he lent you anything.'

'I beg your pardon,' said Anthea politely, following the sound of her knock into the presence of the learned gentleman, 'I'm so sorry to trouble you, but DID you lend me a pound today?'

'No,' said he, looking kindly at her through his spectacles. 'But it's extraordinary that you should ask me, for I dozed for a few moments this afternoon, a thing I very rarely do, and I dreamed quite distinctly that you brought me a ring that you said belonged to the Queen of Babylon, and that I lent you a sovereign and that you left one of the Queen's rings here. The ring was a magnificent specimen.' He sighed. 'I wish it hadn't been a dream,' he said smiling. He was really learning to smile quite nicely.

Anthea could not be too thankful that the Psammead was not there to grant his wish.

Chapter 9. Atlantis

You will understand that the adventure of the Babylonian queen in London was the only one that had occupied any time at all. But the children's time was very fully taken up by talking over all the wonderful things seen and done in the Past, where, by the power of the Amulet, they seemed to spend hours and hours, only to find when they got back to London that the whole thing had been briefer than a lightning flash.

They talked of the Past at their meals, in their walks, in the dining-room, in the first-floor drawing-room, but most of all on the stairs. It was an old house; it had once been a fashionable one, and was a fine one still. The banister rails of the stairs were excellent for sliding down, and in the corners of the landings were big alcoves that had once held graceful statues, and now quite often held the graceful forms of Cyril, Robert, Anthea, and Jane.

One day Cyril and Robert in tight white underclothing had spent a pleasant hour in reproducing the attitudes of statues seen either in the British Museum, or in Father's big photograph book. But the show ended abruptly because Robert wanted to be the Venus of Milo, and for this purpose pulled at the sheet which served for drapery at the very moment when Cyril, looking really quite like the Discobolos—with a gold and white saucer for the disc—was standing on one foot, and under that one foot was the sheet.

Of course the Discobolos and his disc and the would-be Venus came down together, and everyone was a good deal hurt, especially the saucer, which would never be the same again, however neatly one might join its uneven bits with Seccotine or the white of an egg.

'I hope you're satisfied,' said Cyril, holding his head where a large lump was rising.

'Quite, thanks,' said Robert bitterly. His thumb had caught in the banisters and bent itself back almost to breaking point.

'I AM so sorry, poor, dear Squirrel,' said Anthea; 'and you were looking so lovely. I'll get a wet rag. Bobs, go and hold your hand under the hot-water tap. It's what ballet girls do with their legs when they hurt them. I saw it in a book.'

'What book?' said Robert disagreeably. But he went.

When he came back Cyril's head had been bandaged by his sisters, and he had been brought to the state of mind where he was able reluctantly to admit that he supposed Robert hadn't done it on purpose.

Robert replying with equal suavity, Anthea hastened to lead the talk away from the accident.

'I suppose you don't feel like going anywhere through the Amulet,' she said.

'Egypt!' said Jane promptly. 'I want to see the pussy cats.'

'Not me—too hot,' said Cyril. 'It's about as much as I can stand here—let alone Egypt.' It was indeed, hot, even on the second landing, which was the coolest place in the house. 'Let's go to the North Pole.'

'I don't suppose the Amulet was ever there—and we might get our fingers frost-bitten so that we could never hold it up to get home again. No thanks,' said Robert.

'I say,' said Jane, 'let's get the Psammead and ask its advice. It will like us asking, even if we don't take it.'

The Psammead was brought up in its green silk embroidered bag, but before it could be asked anything the door of the learned gentleman's room opened and the voice of the visitor who had been lunching with him was heard on the stairs. He seemed to be speaking with the door handle in his hand.

'You see a doctor, old boy,' he said; 'all that about thought-transference is just simply twaddle. You've been over-working. Take a holiday. Go to Dieppe.'

'I'd rather go to Babylon,' said the learned gentleman.

'I wish you'd go to Atlantis some time, while we're about it, so as to give me some tips for my Nineteenth Century article when you come home.'

'I wish I could,' said the voice of the learned gentleman. 'Goodbye. Take care of yourself.'

The door was banged, and the visitor came smiling down the stairs—a stout, prosperous, big man. The children had to get up to let him pass.

'Hullo, Kiddies,' he said, glancing at the bandages on the head of Cyril and the hand of Robert, 'been in the wars?'

'It's all right,' said Cyril. 'I say, what was that Atlantic place you wanted him to go to? We couldn't help hearing you talk.'

'You talk so VERY loud, you see,' said Jane soothingly.

'Atlantis,' said the visitor, 'the lost Atlantis, garden of the Hesperides. Great continent—disappeared in the sea. You can read about it in Plato.'

'Thank you,' said Cyril doubtfully.

'Were there any Amulets there?' asked Anthea, made anxious by a sudden thought.

'Hundreds, I should think. So HE'S been talking to you?'

'Yes, often. He's very kind to us. We like him awfully.'

'Well, what he wants is a holiday; you persuade him to take one. What he wants is a change of scene. You see, his head is crusted so thickly inside with knowledge about Egypt and Assyria and things that you can't hammer anything into it unless you keep hard at it all day long for days and days. And I haven't time. But you live in the house. You can hammer almost incessantly. Just try your hands, will you? Right. So long!'

He went down the stairs three at a time, and Jane remarked that he was a nice man, and she thought he had little girls of his own.

'I should like to have them to play with,' she added pensively.

The three elder ones exchanged glances. Cyril nodded.

'All right. LET'S go to Atlantis,' he said.

'Let's go to Atlantis and take the learned gentleman with us,' said Anthea; 'he'll think it's a dream, afterwards, but it'll certainly be a change of scene.'

'Why not take him to nice Egypt?' asked Jane.

'Too hot,' said Cyril shortly.

'Or Babylon, where he wants to go?'

'I've had enough of Babylon,' said Robert, 'at least for the present. And so have the others. I don't know why,' he added, forestalling the question on Jane's lips, 'but somehow we have. Squirrel, let's take off these beastly bandages and get into flannels. We can't go in our unders.'

'He WISHED to go to Atlantis, so he's got to go some time; and he might as well go with us,' said Anthea.

This was how it was that the learned gentleman, permitting himself a few moments of relaxation in his chair, after the fatigue of listening to opinions (about Atlantis and many other things) with which he did not at all agree, opened his eyes to find his four young friends standing in front of him in a row.

'Will you come,' said Anthea, 'to Atlantis with us?'

'To know that you are dreaming shows that the dream is nearly at an end,' he told himself; 'or perhaps it's only a game, like "How many miles to Babylon?".' So he said aloud: 'Thank you very much, but I have only a quarter of an hour to spare.'

'It doesn't take any time,' said Cyril; 'time is only a mode of thought, you know, and you've got to go some time, so why not with us?'

'Very well,' said the learned gentleman, now quite certain that he was dreaming.

Anthea held out her soft, pink hand. He took it. She pulled him gently to his feet. Jane held up the Amulet.

'To just outside Atlantis,' said Cyril, and Jane said the Name of Power.

'You owl!' said Robert, 'it's an island. Outside an island's all water.'

'I won't go. I WON'T,' said the Psammead, kicking and struggling in its bag.

But already the Amulet had grown to a great arch. Cyril pushed the learned gentleman, as undoubtedly the first-born, through the arch—not into water, but on to a wooden floor, out of doors. The others followed. The Amulet grew smaller again, and there they all were, standing on the deck of a ship whose sailors were busy making her fast with chains to rings on a white quay-side. The rings and the chains were of a metal that shone red-yellow like gold.

Everyone on the ship seemed too busy at first to notice the group of newcomers from Fitzroy Street. Those who seemed to be officers were shouting orders to the men.

They stood and looked across the wide quay to the town that rose beyond it. What they saw was the most beautiful sight any of them had ever seen—or ever dreamed of.

The blue sea sparkled in soft sunlight; little white-capped waves broke softly against the marble breakwaters that guarded the shipping of a great city from the wilderness of winter winds and seas. The quay was of marble, white and sparkling with a veining bright as gold. The city was of marble, red and white. The greater buildings that seemed to be temples and palaces were roofed with what looked like gold and silver, but most of the roofs were of copper that glowed golden-red on the houses on the hills among which the city stood, and shaded into marvellous tints of green and blue and purple where they had been touched by the salt sea spray and the fumes of the dyeing and smelting works of the lower town.

Broad and magnificent flights of marble stairs led up from the quay to a sort of terrace that seemed to run along for miles, and beyond rose the town built on a hill.

The learned gentleman drew a long breath. 'Wonderful!' he said, 'wonderful!'

'I say, Mr—what's your name,' said Robert. 'He means,' said Anthea, with gentle politeness, 'that we never can remember your name. I know it's Mr De Something.'

'When I was your age I was called Jimmy,' he said timidly. 'Would you mind? I should feel more at home in a dream like this if I— Anything that made me seem more like one of you.'

'Thank you—Jimmy,' said Anthea with an effort. It seemed such a cheek to be saying Jimmy to a grown-up man. 'Jimmy, DEAR,' she added, with no effort at all. Jimmy smiled and looked pleased.

But now the ship was made fast, and the Captain had time to notice other things. He came towards them, and he was dressed in the best of all possible dresses for the seafaring life.

'What are you doing here?' he asked rather fiercely. 'Do you come to bless or to curse?'

'To bless, of course,' said Cyril. 'I'm sorry if it annoys you, but we're here by magic. We come from the land of the sun-rising,' he went on explanatorily.

'I see,' said the Captain; no one had expected that he would. 'I didn't notice at first, but of course I hope you're a good omen. It's needed. And this,' he pointed to the learned gentleman, 'your slave, I presume?'

'Not at all,' said Anthea; 'he's a very great man. A sage, don't they call it? And we want to see all your beautiful city, and your temples and things, and then we shall go back, and he will tell his friend, and his friend will write a book about it.'

'What,' asked the Captain, fingering a rope, 'is a book?'

'A record—something written, or,' she added hastily, remembering the Babylonian writing, 'or engraved.'

Some sudden impulse of confidence made Jane pluck the Amulet from the neck of her frock.

'Like this,' she said.

The Captain looked at it curiously, but, the other three were relieved to notice, without any of that overwhelming interest which the mere name of it had roused in Egypt and Babylon.

'The stone is of our country,' he said; 'and that which is engraved on it, it is like our writing, but I cannot read it. What is the name of your sage?'

'Ji-jimmy,' said Anthea hesitatingly.

The Captain repeated, 'Ji-jimmy. Will you land?' he added. 'And shall I lead you to the Kings?'

'Look here,' said Robert, 'does your King hate strangers?'

'Our Kings are ten,' said the Captain, 'and the Royal line, unbroken from Poseidon, the father of us all, has the noble tradition to do honour to strangers if they come in peace.'

'Then lead on, please,' said Robert, 'though I SHOULD like to see all over your beautiful ship, and sail about in her.'

'That shall be later,' said the Captain; 'just now we're afraid of a storm—do you notice that odd rumbling?'

'That's nothing, master,' said an old sailor who stood near; 'it's the pilchards coming in, that's all.'

'Too loud,' said the Captain.

There was a rather anxious pause; then the Captain stepped on to the quay, and the others followed him.

'Do talk to him—Jimmy,' said Anthea as they went; 'you can find out all sorts of things for your friend's book.'

'Please excuse me,' he said earnestly. 'If I talk I shall wake up; and besides, I can't understand what he says.'

No one else could think of anything to say, so that it was in complete silence that they followed the Captain up the marble steps and through the streets of the town. There were streets and shops and houses and markets.

'It's just like Babylon,' whispered Jane, 'only everything's perfectly different.'

'It's a great comfort the ten Kings have been properly brought up—to be kind to strangers,' Anthea whispered to Cyril.

'Yes,' he said, 'no deepest dungeons here.'

There were no horses or chariots in the street, but there were handcarts and low trolleys running on thick log-wheels, and porters carrying packets on their heads, and a good many of the people were riding on what looked like elephants, only the great beasts were hairy, and they had not that mild expression we are accustomed to meet on the faces of the elephants at the Zoo.

'Mammoths!' murmured the learned gentleman, and stumbled over a loose stone.

The people in the streets kept crowding round them as they went along, but the Captain always dispersed the crowd before it grew uncomfortably thick by saying—

'Children of the Sun God and their High Priest—come to bless the City.'

And then the people would draw back with a low murmur that sounded like a suppressed cheer.

Many of the buildings were covered with gold, but the gold on the bigger buildings was of a different colour, and they had sorts of steeples of burnished silver rising above them.

'Are all these houses real gold?' asked Jane.

'The temples are covered with gold, of course,' answered the Captain, 'but the houses are only oricalchum. It's not quite so expensive.'

The learned gentleman, now very pale, stumbled along in a dazed way, repeating:

'Oricalchum—oricalchum.'

'Don't be frightened,' said Anthea; 'we can get home in a minute, just by holding up the charm. Would you rather go back now? We could easily come some other day without you.'

'Oh, no, no,' he pleaded fervently; 'let the dream go on. Please, please do.'

'The High Ji-jimmy is perhaps weary with his magic journey,' said the Captain, noticing the blundering walk of the learned gentleman; 'and we are yet very far from the Great Temple, where today the Kings make sacrifice.'

He stopped at the gate of a great enclosure. It seemed to be a sort of park, for trees showed high above its brazen wall.

The party waited, and almost at once the Captain came back with one of the hairy elephants and begged them to mount.

This they did.

It was a glorious ride. The elephant at the Zoo—to ride on him is also glorious, but he goes such a very little way, and then he goes back again, which is always dull. But this great hairy beast went on and on and on along streets and through squares and gardens. It was a glorious city; almost everything was built of marble, red, or white, or black. Every now and then the party crossed a bridge.

It was not till they had climbed to the hill which is the centre of the town that they saw that the whole city was divided into twenty circles, alternately land and water, and over each of the water circles were the bridges by which they had come.

And now they were in a great square. A vast building filled up one side of it; it was overlaid with gold, and had a dome of silver. The rest of the buildings round the square were of oricalchum. And it looked more splendid than you can possibly imagine, standing up bold and shining in the sunlight.

'You would like a bath,' said the Captain, as the hairy elephant went clumsily down on his knees. 'It's customary, you know, before entering the Presence. We have baths for men, women, horses, and cattle. The High Class Baths are here. Our Father Poseidon gave us a spring of hot water and one of cold.'

The children had never before bathed in baths of gold.

'It feels very splendid,' said Cyril, splashing.

'At least, of course, it's not gold; it's or—what's its name,' said Robert. 'Hand over that towel.'

The bathing hall had several great pools sunk below the level of the floor; one went down to them by steps.

'Jimmy,' said Anthea timidly, when, very clean and boiled-looking, they all met in the flowery courtyard of the Public, 'don't you think all this seems much more like NOW than Babylon or Egypt—? Oh, I forgot, you've never been there.'

'I know a little of those nations, however,' said he, 'and I quite agree with you. A most discerning remark—my dear,' he added awkwardly; 'this city certainly seems to indicate a far higher level of civilization than the Egyptian or Babylonish, and—'

'Follow me,' said the Captain. 'Now, boys, get out of the way.' He pushed through a little crowd of boys who were playing with dried chestnuts fastened to a string.

'Ginger!' remarked Robert, 'they're playing conkers, just like the kids in Kentish Town Road!'

They could see now that three walls surrounded the island on which they were. The outermost wall was of brass, the Captain told them; the next, which looked like silver, was covered with tin; and the innermost one was of oricalchum.

And right in the middle was a wall of gold, with golden towers and gates.

'Behold the Temples of Poseidon,' said the Captain. 'It is not lawful for me to enter. I will await your return here.'

He told them what they ought to say, and the five people from Fitzroy Street took hands and went forward. The golden gates slowly opened.

'We are the children of the Sun,' said Cyril, as he had been told, 'and our High Priest, at least that's what the Captain calls him. We have a different name for him at home.' 'What is his name?' asked a white-robed man who stood in the doorway with his arms extended.

'Ji-jimmy,' replied Cyril, and he hesitated as Anthea had done. It really did seem to be taking a great liberty with so learned a gentleman. 'And we have come to speak with your Kings in the Temple of Poseidon—does that word sound right?' he whispered anxiously.

'Quite,' said the learned gentleman. 'It's very odd I can understand what you say to them, but not what they say to you.'

'The Queen of Babylon found that too,' said Cyril; 'it's part of the magic.'

'Oh, what a dream!' said the learned gentleman.

The white-robed priest had been joined by others, and all were bowing low.

'Enter,' he said, 'enter, Children of the Sun, with your High Ji-jimmy.'

In an inner courtyard stood the Temple—all of silver, with gold pinnacles and doors, and twenty enormous statues in bright gold of men and women. Also an immense pillar of the other precious yellow metal.

They went through the doors, and the priest led them up a stair into a gallery from which they could look down on to the glorious place.

'The ten Kings are even now choosing the bull. It is not lawful for me to behold,' said the priest, and fell face downward on the floor outside the gallery. The children looked down.

The roof was of ivory adorned with the three precious metals, and the walls were lined with the favourite oricalchum.

At the far end of the Temple was a statue group, the like of which no one living has ever seen.

It was of gold, and the head of the chief figure reached to the roof. That figure was Poseidon, the Father of the City. He stood in a great chariot drawn by six enormous horses, and round about it were a hundred mermaids riding on dolphins.

Ten men, splendidly dressed and armed only with sticks and ropes, were trying to capture one of some fifteen bulls who ran this way and that about the floor of the Temple. The children held their breath, for the bulls looked dangerous, and the great horned heads were swinging more and more wildly.

Anthea did not like looking at the bulls. She looked about the gallery, and noticed that another staircase led up from it to a still higher storey; also that a door led out into the open air, where there seemed to be a balcony.

So that when a shout went up and Robert whispered, 'Got him,' and she looked down and saw the herd of bulls being driven out of the Temple by whips, and the ten Kings following, one of them spurring with his stick a black bull that writhed and fought in the grip of a lasso, she answered the boy's agitated, 'Now we shan't see anything more,' with—

'Yes we can, there's an outside balcony.'

So they crowded out.

But very soon the girls crept back.

'I don't like sacrifices,' Jane said. So she and Anthea went and talked to the priest, who was no longer lying on his face, but sitting on the top step mopping his forehead with his robe, for it was a hot day.

'It's a special sacrifice,' he said; 'usually it's only done on the justice days every five years and six years alternately. And then they drink the cup of wine with some of the bull's blood in it, and swear to judge truly. And they wear the sacred blue robe, and put out all the Temple fires. But this today is because the City's so upset by the odd noises from the sea, and the god inside the big mountain speaking with his thunder-voice. But all that's happened so often before. If anything could make ME uneasy it wouldn't be THAT.'

'What would it be?' asked Jane kindly.

'It would be the Lemmings.'

'Who are they—enemies?'

'They're a sort of rat; and every year they come swimming over from the country that no man knows, and stay here awhile, and then swim away. This year they haven't come. You know rats won't stay on a ship that's going to be wrecked. If anything horrible were going to happen to us, it's my belief those Lemmings would know; and that may be why they've fought shy of us.'

'What do you call this country?' asked the Psammead, suddenly putting its head out of its bag.

'Atlantis,' said the priest.

'Then I advise you to get on to the highest ground you can find. I remember hearing something about a flood here. Look here, you'—it turned to Anthea; 'let's get home. The prospect's too wet for my whiskers.' The girls obediently went to find their brothers, who were leaning on the balcony railings.

'Where's the learned gentleman?' asked Anthea.

'There he is—below,' said the priest, who had come with them. 'Your High Ji-jimmy is with the Kings.'

The ten Kings were no longer alone. The learned gentleman—no one had noticed how he got there—stood with them on the steps of an altar, on which lay the dead body of the black bull. All the rest of the courtyard was thick with people, seemingly of all classes, and all were shouting, 'The sea—the sea!'

'Be calm,' said the most kingly of the Kings, he who had lassoed the bull. 'Our town is strong against the thunders of the sea and of the sky!'

'I want to go home,' whined the Psammead.

'We can't go without HIM,' said Anthea firmly.

'Jimmy,' she called, 'Jimmy!' and waved to him. He heard her, and began to come towards her through the crowd. They could see from the balcony the sea-captain edging his way out from among the people. And his face was dead white, like paper.

'To the hills!' he cried in a loud and terrible voice. And above his voice came another voice, louder, more terrible—the voice of the sea.

The girls looked seaward.

Across the smooth distance of the sea something huge and black rolled towards the town. It was a wave, but a wave a hundred feet in height, a wave that looked like a mountain—a wave rising higher and higher till suddenly it seemed to break in two—one half of it rushed out to sea again; the other—

'Oh!' cried Anthea, 'the town—the poor people!'

'It's all thousands of years ago, really,' said Robert but his voice trembled. They hid their eyes for a moment. They could not bear to look down, for the wave had broken on the face of the town, sweeping over the quays and docks, overwhelming the great storehouses and factories, tearing gigantic stones from forts and bridges, and using them as battering rams against the temples. Great ships were swept over the roofs of the houses and dashed down halfway up the hill among ruined gardens and broken buildings. The water ground brown fishing-boats to powder on the golden roofs of Palaces.

Then the wave swept back towards the sea.

'I want to go home,' cried the Psammead fiercely.

'Oh, yes, yes!' said Jane, and the boys were ready—but the learned gentleman had not come.

Then suddenly they heard him dash up to the inner gallery, crying—

'I MUST see the end of the dream.' He rushed up the higher flight.

The others followed him. They found themselves in a sort of turret—roofed, but open to the air at the sides.

The learned gentleman was leaning on the parapet, and as they rejoined him the vast wave rushed back on the town. This time it rose higher—destroyed more.

'Come home,' cried the Psammead; 'THAT'S the LAST, I know it is! That's the last—over there.' It pointed with a claw that trembled.

'Oh, come!' cried Jane, holding up the Amulet.

'I WILL SEE the end of the dream,' cried the learned gentleman.

'You'll never see anything else if you do,' said Cyril. 'Oh, JIMMY!' appealed Anthea. 'I'll NEVER bring you out again!'

'You'll never have the chance if you don't go soon,' said the Psammead.

'I WILL see the end of the dream,' said the learned gentleman obstinately.

The hills around were black with people fleeing from the villages to the mountains. And even as they fled thin smoke broke from the great white peak, and then a faint flash of flame. Then the volcano began to throw up its mysterious fiery inside parts. The earth trembled; ashes and sulphur showered down; a rain of fine pumice-stone fell like snow on all the dry land. The elephants from the forest rushed up towards the peaks; great lizards thirty yards long broke from the mountain pools and rushed down towards the sea. The snows melted and rushed down, first in avalanches, then in roaring torrents. Great rocks cast up by the volcano fell splashing in the sea miles away.

'Oh, this is horrible!' cried Anthea. 'Come home, come home!'

'The end of the dream,' gasped the learned gentleman.

'Hold up the Amulet,' cried the Psammead suddenly. The place where they stood was now crowded with men and women, and the children were strained tight against the parapet. The turret rocked and swayed; the wave had reached the golden wall.

Jane held up the Amulet.

'Now,' cried the Psammead, 'say the word!'

And as Jane said it the Psammead leaped from its bag and bit the hand of the learned gentleman.

At the same moment the boys pushed him through the arch and all followed him.

He turned to look back, and through the arch he saw nothing but a waste of waters, with above it the peak of the terrible mountain with fire raging from it.

He staggered back to his chair.

'What a ghastly dream!' he gasped. 'Oh, you're here, my—er—dears. Can I do anything for you?'

'You've hurt your hand,' said Anthea gently; 'let me bind it up.'

The hand was indeed bleeding rather badly.

The Psammead had crept back to its bag. All the children were very white.

'Never again,' said the Psammead later on, 'will I go into the Past with a grown-up person! I will say for you four, you do do as you're told.'

'We didn't even find the Amulet,' said Anthea later still.

'Of course you didn't; it wasn't there. Only the stone it was made of was there. It fell on to a ship miles away that managed to escape and got to Egypt. *I* could have told you that.'

'I wish you had,' said Anthea, and her voice was still rather shaky. 'Why didn't you?'

'You never asked me,' said the Psammead very sulkily. 'I'm not the sort of chap to go shoving my oar in where it's not wanted.'

'Mr Ji-jimmy's friend will have something worth having to put in his article now,' said Cyril very much later indeed.

'Not he,' said Robert sleepily. 'The learned Ji-jimmy will think it's a dream, and it's ten to one he never tells the other chap a word about it at all.'

Robert was quite right on both points. The learned gentleman did. And he never did.

Chapter 10. The Little Black Girl and Julius Caesar

A great city swept away by the sea, a beautiful country devastated by an active volcano—these are not the sort of things you see every day of the week. And when you do see them, no matter how many other wonders you may have seen in your time, such sights are rather apt to take your breath away. Atlantis had certainly this effect on the breaths of Cyril, Robert, Anthea, and Jane.

They remained in a breathless state for some days. The learned gentleman seemed as breathless as anyone; he spent a good deal of what little breath he had in telling Anthea about a wonderful dream he had. 'You would hardly believe,' he said, 'that anyone COULD have such a detailed vision.'

But Anthea could believe it, she said, quite easily.

He had ceased to talk about thought-transference. He had now seen too many wonders to believe that.

In consequence of their breathless condition none of the children suggested any new excursions through the Amulet. Robert voiced the mood of the others when he said that they were 'fed up' with Amulet for a bit. They undoubtedly were.

As for the Psammead, it went to sand and stayed there, worn out by the terror of the flood and the violent exercise it had had to take in obedience to the inconsiderate wishes of the learned gentleman and the Babylonian queen.

The children let it sleep. The danger of taking it about among strange people who might at any moment utter undesirable wishes was becoming more and more plain.

And there are pleasant things to be done in London without any aid from Amulets or Psammeads. You can, for instance visit the Tower of London, the Houses of Parliament, the National Gallery, the Zoological Gardens, the various Parks, the Museums at South Kensington, Madame Tussaud's Exhibition of Waxworks, or the Botanical Gardens at Kew. You can go to Kew by river steamer—and this is the way that the children would have gone if they had gone at all. Only they never did, because it was when they were discussing the arrangements for the journey, and what they should take with them to eat and how much of it, and what the whole thing would cost, that the adventure of the Little Black Girl began to happen.

The children were sitting on a seat in St James's Park. They had been watching the pelican repulsing with careful dignity the advances of the seagulls who are always so anxious to play games with it. The pelican thinks, very properly, that it hasn't the figure for games, so it spends most of its time pretending that that is not the reason why it won't play.

The breathlessness caused by Atlantis was wearing off a little. Cyril, who always wanted to understand all about everything, was turning things over in his mind.

'I'm not; I'm only thinking,' he answered when Robert asked him what he was so grumpy about. 'I'll tell you when I've thought it all out.'

'If it's about the Amulet I don't want to hear it,' said Jane.

'Nobody asked you to,' retorted Cyril mildly, 'and I haven't finished my inside thinking about it yet. Let's go to Kew in the meantime.'

'I'd rather go in a steamer,' said Robert; and the girls laughed.

'That's right,' said Cyril, 'BE funny. I would.'

'Well, he was, rather,' said Anthea.

'I wouldn't think, Squirrel, if it hurts you so,' said Robert kindly.

'Oh, shut up,' said Cyril, 'or else talk about Kew.'

'I want to see the palms there,' said Anthea hastily, 'to see if they're anything like the ones on the island where we united the Cook and the Burglar by the Reverend Half-Curate.'

All disagreeableness was swept away in a pleasant tide of recollections, and 'Do you remember ...?' they said. 'Have you forgotten ...?'

'My hat!' remarked Cyril pensively, as the flood of reminiscence ebbed a little; 'we have had some times.'

'We have that,' said Robert.

'Don't let's have any more,' said Jane anxiously.

'That's what I was thinking about,' Cyril replied; and just then they heard the Little Black Girl sniff. She was quite close to them.

She was not really a little black girl. She was shabby and not very clean, and she had been crying so much that you could hardly see, through the narrow chink between her swollen lids, how very blue her eyes were. It was her dress that was black, and it was too big and too long for her, and she wore a speckled black-ribboned sailor hat that would have fitted a much bigger head than her little flaxen one. And she stood looking at the children and sniffing.

'Oh, dear!' said Anthea, jumping up. 'Whatever is the matter?'

She put her hand on the little girl's arm. It was rudely shaken off.

'You leave me be,' said the little girl. 'I ain't doing nothing to you.'

'But what is it?' Anthea asked. 'Has someone been hurting you?'

'What's that to you?' said the little girl fiercely. 'YOU'RE all right.'

'Come away,' said Robert, pulling at Anthea's sleeve. 'She's a nasty, rude little kid.'

'Oh, no,' said Anthea. 'She's only dreadfully unhappy. What is it?' she asked again.

'Oh, YOU'RE all right,' the child repeated; 'YOU ain't agoin' to the Union.'

'Can't we take you home?' said Anthea; and Jane added, 'Where does your mother live?'

'She don't live nowheres—she's dead—so now!' said the little girl fiercely, in tones of miserable triumph. Then she opened her swollen eyes widely, stamped her foot in fury, and ran away. She ran no further than to the next bench, flung herself down there and began to cry without even trying not to.

Anthea, quite at once, went to the little girl and put her arms as tight as she could round the hunched-up black figure.

'Oh, don't cry so, dear, don't, don't!' she whispered under the brim of the large sailor hat, now very crooked indeed. 'Tell Anthea all about it; Anthea'll help you. There, there, dear, don't cry.'

The others stood at a distance. One or two passers-by stared curiously.

The child was now only crying part of the time; the rest of the time she seemed to be talking to Anthea.

Presently Anthea beckoned Cyril.

'It's horrible!' she said in a furious whisper, 'her father was a carpenter and he was a steady man, and never touched a drop except on a Saturday, and he came up to London for work, and there wasn't any, and then he died; and her name is Imogen, and she's nine come next November. And now her mother's dead, and she's to stay tonight with Mrs Shrobsall—that's a landlady that's been kind—and tomorrow the Relieving Officer is coming for her, and she's going into the Union; that means the Workhouse. It's too terrible. What can we do?'

'Let's ask the learned gentleman,' said Jane brightly.

And as no one else could think of anything better the whole party walked back to Fitzroy Street as fast as it could, the little girl holding tight to Anthea's hand and now not crying any more, only sniffing gently.

The learned gentleman looked up from his writing with the smile that had grown much easier to him than it used to be. They were quite at home in his room now; it really seemed to welcome them. Even the mummy-case appeared to smile as if in its distant superior ancient Egyptian way it were rather pleased to see them than not.

Anthea sat on the stairs with Imogen, who was nine come next November, while the others went in and explained the difficulty.

The learned gentleman listened with grave attention.

'It really does seem rather rough luck,' Cyril concluded, 'because I've often heard about rich people who wanted children most awfully—though I know *I* never should—but they do. There must be somebody who'd be glad to have her.'

'Gipsies are awfully fond of children,' Robert hopefully said. 'They're always stealing them. Perhaps they'd have her.'

'She's quite a nice little girl really,' Jane added; 'she was only rude at first because we looked jolly and happy, and she wasn't. You understand that, don't you?'

'Yes,' said he, absently fingering a little blue image from Egypt. 'I understand that very well. As you say, there must be some home where she would be welcome.' He scowled thoughtfully at the little blue image.

Anthea outside thought the explanation was taking a very long time.

She was so busy trying to cheer and comfort the little black girl that she never noticed the Psammead who, roused from sleep by her voice, had shaken itself free of sand, and was coming crookedly up the stairs. It was close to her before she saw it. She picked it up and settled it in her lap.

'What is it?' asked the black child. 'Is it a cat or a organ-monkey, or what?'

And then Anthea heard the learned gentleman say—

'Yes, I wish we could find a home where they would be glad to have her,' and instantly she felt the Psammead begin to blow itself out as it sat on her lap.

She jumped up lifting the Psammead in her skirt, and holding Imogen by the hand, rushed into the learned gentleman's room.

'At least let's keep together,' she cried. 'All hold hands—quick!'

The circle was like that formed for the Mulberry Bush or Ring-o'-Roses. And Anthea was only able to take part in it by holding in her teeth the hem of her frock which, thus supported, formed a bag to hold the Psammead.

'Is it a game?' asked the learned gentleman feebly. No one answered.

There was a moment of suspense; then came that curious upside-down, inside-out sensation which one almost always feels when transported from one place to another by magic. Also there was that dizzy dimness of sight which comes on these occasions.

The mist cleared, the upside-down, inside-out sensation subsided, and there stood the six in a ring, as before, only their twelve feet, instead of standing on the carpet of the learned gentleman's room, stood on green grass. Above them, instead of the dusky ceiling of the Fitzroy Street floor, was a pale blue sky. And where the walls had been and the painted mummy-case, were tall dark green trees, oaks and ashes, and in between the trees and under them tangled bushes and creeping ivy. There were beech-trees too, but there was nothing under them but their own dead red drifted leaves, and here and there a delicate green fern-frond.

And there they stood in a circle still holding hands, as though they were playing Ring-o'-Roses or the Mulberry Bush. just six people hand in hand in a wood. That sounds simple, but then you must remember that they did not know WHERE the wood was, and what's more, they didn't know WHEN then wood was. There was a curious sort of feeling that made the learned gentleman say—

'Another dream, dear me!' and made the children almost certain that they were in a time a very long while ago. As for little Imogen, she said, 'Oh, my!' and kept her mouth very much open indeed.

'Where are we?' Cyril asked the Psammead.

'In Britain,' said the Psammead.

'But when?' asked Anthea anxiously.

'About the year fifty-five before the year you reckon time from,' said the Psammead crossly. 'Is there anything else you want to know?' it added, sticking its head out of the bag formed by Anthea's blue linen frock, and turning its snail's eyes to right and left. 'I've been here before—it's very little changed.' 'Yes, but why here?' asked Anthea.

'Your inconsiderate friend,' the Psammead replied, 'wished to find some home where they would be glad to have that unattractive and immature female human being whom you have picked up—gracious knows how. In Megatherium days properly brought-up children didn't talk to shabby strangers in parks. Your thoughtless friend wanted a place where someone would be glad to have this undesirable stranger. And now here you are!'

'I see we are,' said Anthea patiently, looking round on the tall gloom of the forest. 'But why HERE? Why NOW?'

'You don't suppose anyone would want a child like that in YOUR times—in YOUR towns?' said the Psammead in irritated tones. 'You've got your country into such a mess that there's no room for half your children—and no one to want them.'

'That's not our doing, you know,' said Anthea gently.

'And bringing me here without any waterproof or anything,' said the Psammead still more crossly, 'when everyone knows how damp and foggy Ancient Britain was.'

'Here, take my coat,' said Robert, taking it off. Anthea spread the coat on the ground and, putting the Psammead on it, folded it round so that only the eyes and furry ears showed.

'There,' she said comfortingly. 'Now if it does begin to look like rain, I can cover you up in a minute. Now what are we to do?'

The others who had stopped holding hands crowded round to hear the answer to this question. Imogen whispered in an awed tone—

'Can't the organ monkey talk neither! I thought it was only parrots!'

'Do?' replied the Psammead. 'I don't care what you do!' And it drew head and ears into the tweed covering of Robert's coat.

The others looked at each other.

'It's only a dream,' said the learned gentleman hopefully; 'something is sure to happen if we can prevent ourselves from waking up.'

And sure enough, something did.

The brooding silence of the dark forest was broken by the laughter of children and the sound of voices.

'Let's go and see,' said Cyril.

'It's only a dream,' said the learned gentleman to Jane, who hung back; 'if you don't go with the tide of a dream—if you resist—you wake up, you know.'

There was a sort of break in the undergrowth that was like a silly person's idea of a path. They went along this in Indian file, the learned gentleman leading.

Quite soon they came to a large clearing in the forest. There were a number of houses—huts perhaps you would have called them—with a sort of mud and wood fence.

'It's like the old Egyptian town,' whispered Anthea.

And it was, rather.

Some children, with no clothes on at all, were playing what looked like Ring-o'-Roses or Mulberry Bush. That is to say, they were dancing round in a ring, holding hands. On a grassy bank several women, dressed in blue and white robes and tunics of beast-skins sat watching the playing children.

The children from Fitzroy Street stood on the fringe of the forest looking at the games. One woman with long, fair braided hair sat a little apart from the others, and there was a look in her eyes as she followed the play of the children that made Anthea feel sad and sorry.

'None of those little girls is her own little girl,' thought Anthea.

The little black-clad London child pulled at Anthea's sleeve.

'Look,' she said, 'that one there—she's precious like mother; mother's 'air was somethink lovely, when she 'ad time to comb it out. Mother wouldn't never a-beat me if she'd lived 'ere—I don't suppose there's e'er a public nearer than Epping, do you, Miss?'

In her eagerness the child had stepped out of the shelter of the forest. The sad-eyed woman saw her. She stood up, her thin face lighted up with a radiance like sunrise, her long, lean arms stretched towards the London child.

'Imogen!' she cried—at least the word was more like that than any other word—'Imogen!'

There was a moment of great silence; the naked children paused in their play, the women on the bank stared anxiously.

'Oh, it IS mother—it IS!' cried Imogen-from-London, and rushed across the cleared space. She and her mother clung together—so closely, so strongly that they stood an instant like a statue carved in stone.

Then the women crowded round. 'It IS my Imogen!' cried the woman.

'Oh it is! And she wasn't eaten by wolves. She's come back to me. Tell me, my darling, how did you escape? Where have you been? Who has fed and clothed you?'

'I don't know nothink,' said Imogen.

'Poor child!' whispered the women who crowded round, 'the terror of the wolves has turned her brain.'

'But you know ME?' said the fair-haired woman.

And Imogen, clinging with black-clothed arms to the bare neck, answered—

'Oh, yes, mother, I know YOU right 'nough.'

'What is it? What do they say?' the learned gentleman asked anxiously.

'You wished to come where someone wanted the child,' said the Psammead. 'The child says this is her mother.'

'And the mother?'

'You can see,' said the Psammead.

'But is she really? Her child, I mean?'

'Who knows?' said the Psammead; 'but each one fills the empty place in the other's heart. It is enough.'

'Oh,' said the learned gentleman, 'this is a good dream. I wish the child might stay in the dream.'

The Psammead blew itself out and granted the wish. So Imogen's future was assured. She had found someone to want her.

'If only all the children that no one wants,' began the learned gentleman—but the woman interrupted. She came towards them.

'Welcome, all!' she cried. 'I am the Queen, and my child tells me that you have befriended her; and this I well believe, looking on your faces. Your garb is strange, but faces I can read. The child is bewitched, I see that well, but in this she speaks truth. Is it not so?'

The children said it wasn't worth mentioning.

I wish you could have seen all the honours and kindnesses lavished on the children and the learned gentleman by those ancient Britons.

You would have thought, to see them, that a child was something to make a fuss about, not a bit of rubbish to be hustled about the streets and hidden away in the Workhouse. It wasn't as grand as the entertainment at Babylon, but somehow it was more satisfying.

'I think you children have some wonderful influence on me,' said the learned gentleman. 'I never dreamed such dreams before I knew you.'

It was when they were alone that night under the stars where the Britons had spread a heap Of dried fern for them to sleep on, that Cyril spoke.

'Well,' he said, 'we've made it all right for Imogen, and had a jolly good time. I vote we get home again before the fighting begins.'

'What fighting?' asked Jane sleepily.

'Why, Julius Caesar, you little goat,' replied her kind brother. 'Don't you see that if this is the year fifty-five, Julius Caesar may happen at any moment.'

'I thought you liked Caesar,' said Robert.

'So I do—in the history. But that's different from being killed by his soldiers.'

'If we saw Caesar we might persuade him not to,' said Anthea.

'YOU persuade CAESAR,' Robert laughed.

The learned gentleman, before anyone could stop him, said, 'I only wish we could see Caesar some time.'

And, of course, in just the little time the Psammead took to blow itself out for wish-giving, the five, or six counting the Psammead, found themselves in Caesar's camp, just outside Caesar's tent. And they saw Caesar. The Psammead must have taken advantage of the loose wording of the learned gentleman's wish, for it was not the same time of day as that on which the wish had been uttered among the dried ferns. It was sunset, and the great man sat on a chair outside his tent gazing over the sea towards Britain—everyone knew without being told that it was towards Britain. Two golden eagles on the top of posts stood on each side of the tent, and on the flaps of the tent which was very gorgeous to look at were the letters S.P.Q.R.

The great man turned unchanged on the newcomers the august glance that he had turned on the violet waters of the Channel. Though they had suddenly appeared out of nothing, Caesar never showed by the faintest movement of an eyelid, by the least tightening of that firm mouth, that they were not some long expected embassy. He waved a calm hand towards the sentinels, who sprang weapons in hand towards the newcomers.

'Back!' he said in a voice that thrilled like music. 'Since when has Caesar feared children and students?'

To the children he seemed to speak in the only language they knew; but the learned gentleman heard—in rather a strange accent, but quite intelligibly—the lips of Caesar speaking in the Latin tongue, and in that tongue, a little stiffly, he answered—

'It is a dream, O Caesar.'

'A dream?' repeated Caesar. 'What is a dream?'

'This,' said the learned gentleman.

'Not it,' said Cyril, 'it's a sort of magic. We come out of another time and another place.'

'And we want to ask you not to trouble about conquering Britain,' said Anthea; 'it's a poor little place, not worth bothering about.'

'Are you from Britain?' the General asked. 'Your clothes are uncouth, but well woven, and your hair is short as the hair of Roman citizens, not long like the hair of barbarians, yet such I deem you to be.' 'We're not,' said Jane with angry eagerness;

'we're not barbarians at all. We come from the country where the sun never sets, and we've read about you in books; and our country's full of fine things—St Paul's, and the Tower of London, and Madame Tussaud's Exhibition, and—' Then the others stopped her.

'Don't talk nonsense,' said Robert in a bitter undertone.

Caesar looked at the children a moment in silence. Then he called a soldier and spoke with him apart. Then he said aloud—

'You three elder children may go where you will within the camp. Few children are privileged to see the camp of Caesar. The student and the smaller girl-child will remain here with me.'

Nobody liked this; but when Caesar said a thing that thing was so, and there was an end to it. So the three went.

Left alone with Jane and the learned gentleman, the great Roman found it easy enough to turn them inside out. But it was not easy, even for him, to make head or tail of the insides of their minds when he had got at them.

The learned gentleman insisted that the whole thing was a dream, and refused to talk much, on the ground that if he did he would wake up.

Jane, closely questioned, was full of information about railways, electric lights, balloons, men-of-war, cannons, and dynamite.

'And do they fight with swords?' asked the General.

'Yes, swords and guns and cannons.'

Caesar wanted to know what guns were.

'You fire them,' said Jane, 'and they go bang, and people fall down dead.'

'But what are guns like?'

Jane found them hard to describe.

'But Robert has a toy one in his pocket,' she said. So the others were recalled.

The boys explained the pistol to Caesar very fully, and he looked at it with the greatest interest. It was a two-shilling pistol, the one that had done such good service in the old Egyptian village.

'I shall cause guns to be made,' said Caesar, 'and you will be detained till I know whether you have spoken the truth. I had just decided that Britain was not worth the bother of invading. But what you tell me decides me that it is very much worth while.'

'But it's all nonsense,' said Anthea. 'Britain is just a savage sort of island—all fogs and trees and big rivers. But the people are kind. We know a little girl there named Imogen. And it's no use your making guns because you can't fire them without gunpowder, and that won't be invented for hundreds of years, and we don't know how to make it, and we can't tell you. Do go straight home, dear Caesar, and let poor little Britain alone.'

'But this other girl-child says—' said Caesar.

'All Jane's been telling you is what it's going to be,' Anthea interrupted, 'hundreds and hundreds of years from now.'

'The little one is a prophetess, eh?' said Caesar, with a whimsical look. 'Rather young for the business, isn't she?'

'You can call her a prophetess if you like,' said Cyril, 'but what Anthea says is true.'

'Anthea?' said Caesar. 'That's a Greek name.'

'Very likely,' said Cyril, worriedly. 'I say, I do wish you'd give up this idea of conquering Britain. It's not worth while, really it isn't!'

'On the contrary,' said Caesar, 'what you've told me has decided me to go, if it's only to find out what Britain is really like. Guards, detain these children.'

'Quick,' said Robert, 'before the guards begin detaining. We had enough of that in Babylon.'

Jane held up the Amulet away from the sunset, and said the word. The learned gentleman was pushed through and the others more quickly than ever before passed through the arch back into their own times and the quiet dusty sitting-room of the learned gentleman.

It is a curious fact that when Caesar was encamped on the coast of Gaul—somewhere near Boulogne it was, I believe—he was sitting before his tent in the glow of the sunset, looking out over the violet waters of the English Channel. Suddenly he started, rubbed his eyes, and called his secretary. The young man came quickly from within the tent.

'Marcus,' said Caesar. 'I have dreamed a very wonderful dream. Some of it I forget, but I remember enough to decide what was not before determined. Tomorrow the ships that have been brought round from the Ligeris shall be provisioned. We shall sail for this three-cornered island. First, we will take but two legions.

This, if what we have heard be true, should suffice. But if my dream be true, then a hundred legions will not suffice. For the dream I dreamed was the most wonderful that ever tormented the brain even of Caesar. And Caesar has dreamed some strange things in his time.'

'And if you hadn't told Caesar all that about how things are now, he'd never have invaded Britain,' said Robert to Jane as they sat down to tea.

'Oh, nonsense,' said Anthea, pouring out; 'it was all settled hundreds of years ago.'

'I don't know,' said Cyril. 'Jam, please. This about time being only a thingummy of thought is very confusIng. If everything happens at the same time—'

'It CAN'T!' said Anthea stoutly, 'the present's the present and the past's the past.'

'Not always,' said Cyril.

'When we were in the Past the present was the future. Now then!' he added triumphantly.

And Anthea could not deny it.

'I should have liked to see more of the camp,' said Robert.

'Yes, we didn't get much for our money—but Imogen is happy, that's one thing,' said Anthea. 'We left her happy in the Past. I've often seen about people being happy in the Past, in poetry books. I see what it means now.'

'It's not a bad idea,' said the Psammead sleepily, putting its head out of its bag and taking it in again suddenly, 'being left in the Past.'

Everyone remembered this afterwards, when—

Chapter 11. Before Pharaoh

It was the day after the adventure of Julius Caesar and the Little Black Girl that Cyril, bursting into the bathroom to wash his hands for dinner (you have no idea how dirty they were, for he had been playing shipwrecked mariners all the morning on the leads at the back of the house, where the water-cistern is), found Anthea leaning her elbows on the edge of the bath, and crying steadily into it.

'Hullo!' he said, with brotherly concern, 'what's up now? Dinner'll be cold before you've got enough salt-water for a bath.'

'Go away,' said Anthea fiercely. 'I hate you! I hate everybody!'

There was a stricken pause.

'*I* didn't know,' said Cyril tamely.

'Nobody ever does know anything,' sobbed Anthea.

'I didn't know you were waxy. I thought you'd just hurt your fingers with the tap again like you did last week,' Cyril carefully explained.

'Oh—fingers!' sneered Anthea through her sniffs.

'Here, drop it, Panther,' he said uncomfortably. 'You haven't been having a row or anything?'

'No,' she said. 'Wash your horrid hands, for goodness' sake, if that's what you came for, or go.'

Anthea was so seldom cross that when she was cross the others were always more surprised than angry.

Cyril edged along the side of the bath and stood beside her. He put his hand on her arm.

'Dry up, do,' he said, rather tenderly for him. And, finding that though she did not at once take his advice she did not seem to resent it, he put his arm awkwardly across her shoulders and rubbed his head against her ear.

'There!' he said, in the tone of one administering a priceless cure for all possible sorrows. 'Now, what's up?'

'Promise you won't laugh?'

'I don't feel laughish myself,' said Cyril, dismally.

'Well, then,' said Anthea, leaning her ear against his head, 'it's Mother.'

'What's the matter with Mother?' asked Cyril, with apparent want of sympathy. 'She was all right in her letter this morning.'

'Yes; but I want her so.'

'You're not the only one,' said Cyril briefly, and the brevity of his tone admitted a good deal.

'Oh, yes,' said Anthea, 'I know. We all want her all the time. But I want her now most dreadfully, awfully much. I never wanted anything so much. That Imogen child—the way the ancient British Queen cuddled her up! And Imogen wasn't me, and the Queen was Mother. And then her letter this morning! And about The Lamb liking the salt bathing! And she bathed him in this very bath the night before she went away—oh, oh, oh!'

Cyril thumped her on the back.

'Cheer up,' he said. 'You know my inside thinking that I was doing? Well, that was partly about Mother. We'll soon get her back. If you'll chuck it, like a sensible kid, and wash your face, I'll tell you about it. That's right. You let me get to the tap. Can't you stop crying? Shall I put the door-key down your back?'

'That's for noses,' said Anthea, 'and I'm not a kid any more than you are,' but she laughed a little, and her mouth began to get back into its proper shape. You know what an odd shape your mouth gets into when you cry in earnest.

'Look here,' said Cyril, working the soap round and round between his hands in a thick slime of grey soapsuds. 'I've been thinking. We've only just PLAYED with the Amulet so far. We've got to work it now—WORK it for all it's worth. And it isn't only Mother either. There's Father out there all among the fighting. I don't howl about it, but I THINK—Oh, bother the soap!' The grey-lined soap had squirted out under the pressure of his fingers, and had hit Anthea's chin with as much force as though it had been shot from a catapult.

'There now,' she said regretfully, 'now I shall have to wash my face.'

'You'd have had to do that anyway,' said Cyril with conviction. 'Now, my idea's this. You know missionaries?'

'Yes,' said Anthea, who did not know a single one.

'Well, they always take the savages beads and brandy, and stays, and hats, and braces, and really useful things—things the savages haven't got, and never heard about. And the savages love them for their kind generousness, and give them pearls, and shells, and ivory, and cassowaries. And that's the way—'

'Wait a sec,' said Anthea, splashing. 'I can't hear what you're saying. Shells and—'

'Shells, and things like that. The great thing is to get people to love you by being generous. And that's what we've got to do. Next time we go into the Past we'll regularly fit out the expedition. You remember how the Babylonian Queen froze on to that pocket-book? Well, we'll take things like that. And offer them in exchange for a sight of the Amulet.'

'A sight of it is not much good.'

'No, silly. But, don't you see, when we've seen it we shall know where it is, and we can go and take it in the night when everybody is asleep.'

'It wouldn't be stealing, would it?' said Anthea thoughtfully, 'because it will be such an awfully long time ago when we do it. Oh, there's that bell again.'

As soon as dinner was eaten (it was tinned salmon and lettuce, and a jam tart), and the cloth cleared away, the idea was explained to the others, and the Psammead was aroused from sand, and asked what it thought would be good merchandise with which to buy the affection of say, the Ancient Egyptians, and whether it thought the Amulet was likely to be found in the Court of Pharaoh.

But it shook its head, and shot out its snail's eyes hopelessly.

'I'm not allowed to play in this game,' it said. 'Of course I COULD find out in a minute where the thing was, only I mayn't. But I may go so far as to own that your idea of taking things with you isn't a bad one. And I shouldn't show them all at once. Take small things and conceal them craftily about your persons.'

This advice seemed good. Soon the table was littered over with things which the children thought likely to interest the Ancient Egyptians. Anthea brought dolls, puzzle blocks, a wooden tea-service, a green leather case with Necessaire written on it in gold letters. Aunt Emma had once given it to Anthea, and it had then contained scissors, penknife, bodkin, stiletto, thimble, corkscrew, and glove-buttoner. The scissors, knife, and thimble, and penknife were, of course, lost, but the other things were there and as good as new. Cyril contributed lead soldiers, a cannon, a catapult, a tin-opener, a tie-clip, and a tennis ball, and a padlock—no key. Robert collected a candle ('I don't suppose they ever saw a self-fitting paraffin one,' he said), a penny Japanese pin-tray, a rubber stamp with his father's name and address on it, and a piece of putty.

Jane added a key-ring, the brass handle of a poker, a pot that had held cold-cream, a smoked pearl button off her winter coat, and a key—no lock.

'We can't take all this rubbish,' said Robert, with some scorn. 'We must just each choose one thing.'

The afternoon passed very agreeably in the attempt to choose from the table the four most suitable objects. But the four children could not agree what was suitable, and at last Cyril said—

'Look here, let's each be blindfolded and reach out, and the first thing you touch you stick to.'

This was done.

Cyril touched the padlock.

Anthea got the Necessaire.

Robert clutched the candle.

Jane picked up the tie-clip.

'It's not much,' she said. 'I don't believe Ancient Egyptians wore ties.'

'Never mind,' said Anthea. 'I believe it's luckier not to really choose. In the stories it's always the thing the wood-cutter's son picks up in the forest, and almost throws away because he thinks it's no good, that turns out to be the magic thing in the end; or else someone's lost it, and he is rewarded with the hand of the King's daughter in marriage.'

'I don't want any hands in marriage, thank you.' said Cyril firmly.

'Nor yet me,' said Robert. 'It's always the end of the adventures when it comes to the marriage hands.'

'ARE we ready?' said Anthea.

'It IS Egypt we're going to, isn't it?—nice Egypt?' said Jane. 'I won't go anywhere I don't know about—like that dreadful big-wavy burning-mountain city,' she insisted.

Then the Psammead was coaxed into its bag. 'I say,' said Cyril suddenly, 'I'm rather sick of kings. And people notice you so in palaces. Besides the Amulet's sure to be in a Temple. Let's just go among the common people, and try to work ourselves up by degrees. We might get taken on as Temple assistants.'

'Like beadles,' said Anthea, 'or vergers. They must have splendid chances of stealing the Temple treasures.'

'Righto!' was the general rejoinder. The charm was held up. It grew big once again, and once again the warm golden Eastern light glowed softly beyond it.

As the children stepped through it loud and furious voices rang in their ears. They went suddenly from the quiet of Fitzroy Street dining-room into a very angry Eastern crowd, a crowd much too angry to notice them. They edged through it to the wall of a house and stood there. The crowd was of men, women, and children. They were of all sorts of complexions, and pictures of them might have been coloured by any child with a shilling paint-box. The colours that child would have used for complexions would have been yellow ochre, red ochre, light red, sepia, and indian ink. But their faces were painted already—black eyebrows and lashes, and some red lips. The women wore a sort of pinafore with shoulder straps, and loose things wound round their heads and shoulders. The men wore very little clothing—for they were the working people—and the Egyptian boys and girls wore nothing at all, unless you count the little ornaments hung on chains round their necks and waists. The children saw all this before they could hear anything distinctly.

Everyone was shouting so.

But a voice sounded above the other voices, and presently it was speaking in a silence.

'Comrades and fellow workers,' it said, and it was the voice of a tall, coppery-coloured man who had climbed into a chariot that had been stopped by the crowd. Its owner had bolted, muttering something about calling the Guards, and now the man spoke from it. 'Comrades and fellow workers, how long are we to endure the tyranny of our masters, who live in idleness and luxury on the fruit of our toil? They only give us a bare subsistence wage, and they live on the fat of the land. We labour all our lives to keep them in wanton luxury. Let us make an end of it!'

A roar of applause answered him.

'How are you going to do it?' cried a voice.

'You look out,' cried another, 'or you'll get yourself into trouble.'

'I've heard almost every single word of that,' whispered Robert, 'in Hyde Park last Sunday!'

'Let us strike for more bread and onions and beer, and a longer mid-day rest,' the speaker went on. 'You are tired, you are hungry, you are thirsty. You are poor, your wives and children are pining for food. The barns of the rich are full to bursting with the corn we want, the corn our labour has grown. To the granaries!'

'To the granaries!' cried half the crowd; but another voice shouted clear above the tumult, 'To Pharaoh! To the King! Let's present a petition to the King! He will listen to the voice of the oppressed!'

For a moment the crowd swayed one way and another—first towards the granaries and then towards the palace. Then, with a rush like that of an imprisoned torrent suddenly set free, it surged along the street towards the palace, and the children were carried with it. Anthea found it difficult to keep the Psammead from being squeezed very uncomfortably.

The crowd swept through the streets of dull-looking houses with few windows, very high up, across the market where people were not buying but exchanging goods. In a momentary pause Robert saw a basket of onions exchanged for a hair comb and five fish for a string of beads. The people in the market seemed better off than those in the crowd; they had finer clothes, and more of them. They were the kind of people who, nowadays, would have lived at Brixton or Brockley.

'What's the trouble now?' a languid, large-eyed lady in a crimped, half-transparent linen dress, with her black hair very much braided and puffed out, asked of a date-seller.

'Oh, the working-men—discontented as usual,' the man answered. 'Listen to them. Anyone would think it mattered whether they had a little more or less to eat. Dregs of society!' said the date-seller.

'Scum!' said the lady.

'And I've heard THAT before, too,' said Robert.

At that moment the voice of the crowd changed, from anger to doubt, from doubt to fear. There were other voices shouting; they shouted defiance and menace, and they came nearer very quickly. There was the rattle of wheels and the pounding of hoofs. A voice shouted, 'Guards!'

'The Guards! The Guards!' shouted another voice, and the crowd of workmen took up the cry. 'The Guards! Pharaoh's Guards!' And swaying a little once more, the crowd hung for a moment as it were balanced. Then as the trampling hoofs came nearer the workmen fled dispersed, up alleys and into the courts of houses, and the Guards in their embossed leather chariots swept down the street at the gallop, their wheels clattering over the stones, and their dark-coloured, blue tunics blown open and back with the wind of their going.

'So THAT riot's over,' said the crimped-linen-dressed lady; 'that's a blessing! And did you notice the Captain of the Guard? What a very handsome man he was, to be sure!'

The four children had taken advantage of the moment's pause before the crowd turned to fly, to edge themselves and drag each other into an arched doorway.

Now they each drew a long breath and looked at the others.

'We're well out of THAT,' said Cyril.

'Yes,' said Anthea, 'but I do wish the poor men hadn't been driven back before they could get to the King. He might have done something for them.'

'Not if he was the one in the Bible he wouldn't,' said Jane. 'He had a hard heart.'

'Ah, that was the Moses one,' Anthea explained. 'The Joseph one was quite different. I should like to see Pharaoh's house. I wonder whether it's like the Egyptian Court in the Crystal Palace.'

'I thought we decided to try to get taken on in a Temple,' said Cyril in injured tones.

'Yes, but we've got to know someone first. Couldn't we make friends with a Temple doorkeeper—we might give him the padlock or something. I wonder which are temples and which are palaces,' Robert added, glancing across the market-place to where an enormous gateway with huge side buildings towered towards the sky. To right and left of it were other buildings only a little less magnificent.

'Did you wish to seek out the Temple of Amen Ra?' asked a soft voice behind them, 'or the Temple of Mut, or the Temple of Khonsu?'

They turned to find beside them a young man. He was shaved clean from head to foot, and on his feet were light papyrus sandals. He was clothed in a linen tunic of white, embroidered heavily in colours. He was gay with anklets, bracelets, and armlets of gold, richly inlaid. He wore a ring on his finger, and he had a short jacket of gold embroidery something like the Zouave soldiers wear, and on his neck was a gold collar with many amulets hanging from it. But among the amulets the children could see none like theirs.

'It doesn't matter which Temple,' said Cyril frankly.

'Tell me your mission,' said the young man. 'I am a divine father of the Temple of Amen Ra and perhaps I can help you.'

'Well,' said Cyril, 'we've come from the great Empire on which the sun never sets.'

'I thought somehow that you'd come from some odd, out-of-the-way spot,' said the priest with courtesy.

'And we've seen a good many palaces. We thought we should like to see a Temple, for a change,' said Robert.

The Psammead stirred uneasily in its embroidered bag.

'Have you brought gifts to the Temple?' asked the priest cautiously.

'We HAVE got some gifts,' said Cyril with equal caution. 'You see there's magic mixed up in it. So we can't tell you everything. But we don't want to give our gifts for nothing.'

'Beware how you insult the god,' said the priest sternly. 'I also can do magic. I can make a waxen image of you, and I can say words which, as the wax image melts before the fire, will make you dwindle away and at last perish miserably.'

'Pooh!' said Cyril stoutly, 'that's nothing. *I* can make FIRE itself!'

'I should jolly well like to see you do it,' said the priest unbelievingly.

'Well, you shall,' said Cyril, 'nothing easier. Just stand close round me.'

'Do you need no preparation—no fasting, no incantations?' The priest's tone was incredulous.

'The incantation's quite short,' said Cyril, taking the hint; 'and as for fasting, it's not needed in MY sort of magic. Union Jack, Printing Press, Gunpowder, Rule Britannia! Come, Fire, at the end of this little stick!'

He had pulled a match from his pocket, and as he ended the incantation which contained no words that it seemed likely the Egyptian had ever heard he stooped in the little crowd of his relations and the priest and struck the match on his boot. He stood up, shielding the flame with one hand.

'See?' he said, with modest pride. 'Here, take it into your hand.'

'No, thank you,' said the priest, swiftly backing. 'Can you do that again?'

'Yes.'

'Then come with me to the great double house of Pharaoh. He loves good magic, and he will raise you to honour and glory. There's no need of secrets between initiates,' he went on confidentially. 'The fact is, I am out of favour at present owing to a little matter of failure of prophecy. I told him a beautiful princess would be sent to him from Syria, and, lo! a woman thirty years old arrived. But she WAS a beautiful woman not so long ago. Time is only a mode of thought, you know.'

The children thrilled to the familiar words.

'So you know that too, do you?' said Cyril.

'It is part of the mystery of all magic, is it not?' said the priest. 'Now if I bring you to Pharaoh the little unpleasantness I spoke of will be forgotten. And I will ask Pharaoh, the Great House, Son of the Sun, and Lord of the South and North, to decree that you shall lodge in the Temple. Then you can have a good look round, and teach me your magic. And I will teach you mine.'

This idea seemed good—at least it was better than any other which at that moment occurred to anybody, so they followed the priest through the city.

The streets were very narrow and dirty. The best houses, the priest explained, were built within walls twenty to twenty-five feet high, and such windows as showed in the walls were very high up. The tops of palm-trees showed above the walls. The poor people's houses were little square huts with a door and two windows, and smoke coming out of a hole in the back.

'The poor Egyptians haven't improved so very much in their building since the first time we came to Egypt,' whispered Cyril to Anthea.

The huts were roofed with palm branches, and everywhere there were chickens, and goats, and little naked children kicking about in the yellow dust. On one roof was a goat, who had climbed up and was eating the dry palm-leaves with snorts and head-tossings of delight. Over every house door was some sort of figure or shape.

'Amulets,' the priest explained, 'to keep off the evil eye.'

'I don't think much of your "nice Egypt",' Robert whispered to Jane; 'it's simply not a patch on Babylon.'

'Ah, you wait till you see the palace,' Jane whispered back.

The palace was indeed much more magnificent than anything they had yet seen that day, though it would have made but a poor show beside that of the Babylonian King. They came to it through a great square pillared doorway of sandstone that stood in a high brick wall. The shut doors were of massive cedar, with bronze hinges, and were studded with bronze nails. At the side was a little door and a wicket gate, and through this the priest led the children. He seemed to know a word that made the sentries make way for him.

Inside was a garden, planted with hundreds of different kinds of trees and flowering shrubs, a lake full of fish, with blue lotus flowers at the margin, and ducks swimming about cheerfully, and looking, as Jane said, quite modern.

'The guard-chamber, the store-houses, the queen's house,' said the priest, pointing them out.

They passed through open courtyards, paved with flat stones, and the priest whispered to a guard at a great inner gate.

'We are fortunate,' he said to the children, 'Pharaoh is even now in the Court of Honour. Now, don't forget to be overcome with respect and admiration. It won't do any harm if you fall flat on your faces. And whatever you do, don't speak until you're spoken to.'

'There used to be that rule in our country,' said Robert, 'when my father was a little boy.'

At the outer end of the great hall a crowd of people were arguing with and even shoving the Guards, who seemed to make it a rule not to let anyone through unless they were bribed to do it. The children heard several promises of the utmost richness, and wondered whether they would ever be kept.

All round the hall were pillars of painted wood. The roof was of cedar, gorgeously inlaid. About half-way up the hall was a wide, shallow step that went right across the hall; then a little farther on another; and then a steep flight of narrower steps, leading right up to the throne on which Pharaoh sat. He sat there very splendid, his red and white double crown on his head, and his sceptre in his hand. The throne had a canopy of wood and wooden pillars painted in bright colours. On a low, broad bench that ran all round the hall sat the friends, relatives, and courtiers of the King, leaning on richly-covered cushions.

The priest led the children up the steps till they all stood before the throne; and then, suddenly, he fell on his face with hands outstretched. The others did the same, Anthea falling very carefully because of the Psammead.

'Raise them,' said the voice of Pharaoh, 'that they may speak to me.'

The officers of the King's household raised them.

'Who are these strangers?' Pharaoh asked, and added very crossly, 'And what do you mean, Rekh-mara, by daring to come into my presence while your innocence is not established?'

'Oh, great King,' said the young priest, 'you are the very image of Ra, and the likeness of his son Horus in every respect. You know the thoughts of the hearts of the gods and of men, and you have divined that these strangers are the children of the children of the vile and conquered Kings of the Empire where the sun never sets. They know a magic not known to the Egyptians. And they come with gifts in their hands as tribute to Pharaoh, in whose heart is the wisdom of the gods, and on his lips their truth.'

'That is all very well,' said Pharaoh, 'but where are the gifts?'

The children, bowing as well as they could in their embarrassment at finding themselves the centre of interest in a circle more grand, more golden and more highly coloured than they could have imagined possible, pulled out the padlock, the Necessaire, and the tie-clip. 'But it's not tribute all the same,' Cyril muttered. 'England doesn't pay tribute!'

Pharaoh examined all the things with great interest when the chief of the household had taken them up to him. 'Deliver them to the Keeper of the Treasury,' he said to one near him. And to the children he said—

'A small tribute, truly, but strange, and not without worth. And the magic, O Rekh-mara?'

'These unworthy sons of a conquered nation ...' began Rekh-mara.

'Nothing of the kind!' Cyril whispered angrily.

'... of a vile and conquered nation, can make fire to spring from dry wood—in the sight of all.'

'I should jolly well like to see them do it,' said Pharaoh, just as the priest had done.

So Cyril, without more ado, did it.

'Do more magic,' said the King, with simple appreciation.

'He cannot do any more magic,' said Anthea suddenly, and all eyes were turned on her, 'because of the voice of the free people who are shouting for bread and onions and beer and a long mid-day rest. If the people had what they wanted, he could do more.'

'A rude-spoken girl,' said Pharaoh. 'But give the dogs what they want,' he said, without turning his head. 'Let them have their rest and their extra rations. There are plenty of slaves to work.'

A richly-dressed official hurried out.

'You will be the idol of the people,' Rekh-mara whispered joyously; 'the Temple of Amen will not contain their offerings.'

Cyril struck another match, and all the court was overwhelmed with delight and wonder. And when Cyril took the candle from his pocket and lighted it with the match, and then held the burning candle up before the King the enthusiasm knew no bounds.

'Oh, greatest of all, before whom sun and moon and stars bow down,' said Rekh-mara insinuatingly, 'am I pardoned? Is my innocence made plain?'

'As plain as it ever will be, I daresay,' said Pharaoh shortly. 'Get along with you. You are pardoned. Go in peace.' The priest went with lightning swiftness.

'And what,' said the King suddenly, 'is it that moves in that sack?

Show me, oh strangers.'

There was nothing for it but to show the Psammead.

'Seize it,' said Pharaoh carelessly. 'A very curious monkey. It will be a nice little novelty for my wild beast collection.'

And instantly, the entreaties of the children availing as little as the bites of the Psammead, though both bites and entreaties were fervent, it was carried away from before their eyes.

'Oh, DO be careful!' cried Anthea. 'At least keep it dry! Keep it in its sacred house!'

She held up the embroidered bag.

'It's a magic creature,' cried Robert; 'it's simply priceless!'

'You've no right to take it away,' cried Jane incautiously. 'It's a shame, a barefaced robbery, that's what it is!'

There was an awful silence. Then Pharaoh spoke.

'Take the sacred house of the beast from them,' he said, 'and imprison all. Tonight after supper it may be our pleasure to see more magic. Guard them well, and do not torture them—yet!'

'Oh, dear!' sobbed Jane, as they were led away. 'I knew exactly what it would be! Oh, I wish you hadn't!'

'Shut up, silly,' said Cyril. 'You know you WOULD come to Egypt. It was your own idea entirely. Shut up. It'll be all right.'

'I thought we should play ball with queens,' sobbed Jane, 'and have no end of larks! And now everything's going to be perfectly horrid!'

The room they were shut up in WAS a room, and not a dungeon, as the elder ones had feared. That, as Anthea said, was one comfort. There were paintings on the wall that at any other time would have been most interesting. And a sort of low couch, and chairs. When they were alone Jane breathed a sigh of relief. 'Now we can get home all right,' she said.

'And leave the Psammead?' said Anthea reproachfully.

'Wait a sec. I've got an idea,' said Cyril. He pondered for a few moments. Then he began hammering on the heavy cedar door. It opened, and a guard put in his head.

'Stop that row,' he said sternly, 'or—'

'Look here,' Cyril interrupted, 'it's very dull for you isn't it?just doing nothing but guard us. Wouldn't you like to see some magic? We're not too proud to do it for you. Wouldn't you like to see it?'

'I don't mind if I do,' said the guard.

'Well then, you get us that monkey of ours that was taken away, and we'll show you.'

'How do I know you're not making game of me?' asked the soldier. 'Shouldn't wonder if you only wanted to get the creature so as to set it on me. I daresay its teeth and claws are poisonous.'

'Well, look here,' said Robert. 'You see we've got nothing with us? You just shut the door, and open it again in five minutes, and we'll have got a magic—oh, I don't know—a magic flower in a pot for you.'

'If you can do that you can do anything,' said the soldier, and he went out and barred the door.

Then, of course, they held up the Amulet. They found the East by holding it up, and turning slowly till the Amulet began to grow big, walked home through it, and came back with a geranium in full scarlet flower from the staircase window of the Fitzroy Street house.

'Well!' said the soldier when he came in. 'I really am—!'

'We can do much more wonderful things than that—oh, ever so much,' said Anthea persuasively, 'if we only have our monkey. And here's twopence for yourself.'

The soldier looked at the twopence.

'What's this?' he said.

Robert explained how much simpler it was to pay money for things than to exchange them as the people were doing in the market. Later on the soldier gave the coins to his captain, who, later still, showed them to Pharaoh, who of course kept them and was much struck with the idea. That was really how coins first came to be used in Egypt. You will not believe this, I daresay, but really, if you believe the rest of the story, I don't see why you shouldn't believe this as well.

'I say,' said Anthea, struck by a sudden thought, 'I suppose it'll be all right about those workmen? The King won't go back on what he said about them just because he's angry with us?'

'Oh, no,' said the soldier, 'you see, he's rather afraid of magic. He'll keep to his word right enough.'

'Then THAT'S all right,' said Robert; and Anthea said softly and coaxingly—

'Ah, DO get us the monkey, and then you'll see some lovely magic. Do—there's a nice, kind soldier.'

'I don't know where they've put your precious monkey, but if I can get another chap to take on my duty here I'll see what I can do,' he said grudgingly, and went out.

'Do you mean,' said Robert, 'that we're going off without even TRYING for the other half of the Amulet?'

'I really think we'd better,' said Anthea tremulously. 'Of course the other half of the Amulet's here somewhere or our half wouldn't have brought us here. I do wish we could find it. It is a pity we don't know any REAL magic. Then we could find out. I do wonder where it is—exactly.'

If they had only known it, something very like the other half of the Amulet was very near them. It hung round the neck of someone, and that someone was watching them through a chink, high up in the wall, specially devised for watching people who were imprisoned. But they did not know.

There was nearly an hour of anxious waiting. They tried to take an interest in the picture on the wall, a picture of harpers playing very odd harps and women dancing at a feast. They examined the painted plaster floor, and the chairs were of white painted wood with coloured stripes at intervals.

But the time went slowly, and everyone had time to think of how Pharaoh had said, 'Don't torture them—YET.'

'If the worst comes to the worst,' said Cyril, 'we must just bunk, and leave the Psammead. I believe it can take care of itself well enough. They won't kill it or hurt it when they find it can speak and give wishes. They'll build it a temple, I shouldn't wonder.'

'I couldn't bear to go without it,' said Anthea, 'and Pharaoh said "After supper", that won't be just yet. And the soldier WAS curious. I'm sure we're all right for the present.'

All the same, the sounds of the door being unbarred seemed one of the prettiest sounds possible.

'Suppose he hasn't got the Psammead?' whispered Jane.

But that doubt was set at rest by the Psammead itself; for almost before the door was open it sprang through the chink of it into Anthea's arms, shivering and hunching up its fur.

'Here's its fancy overcoat,' said the soldier, holding out the bag, into which the Psammead immediately crept.

'Now,' said Cyril, 'what would you like us to do? Anything you'd like us to get for you?'

'Any little trick you like,' said the soldier. 'If you can get a strange flower blooming in an earthenware vase you can get anything, I suppose,' he said. 'I just wish I'd got two men's loads of jewels from the King's treasury. That's what I've always wished for.'

At the word 'WISH' the children knew that the Psammead would attend to THAT bit of magic. It did, and the floor was littered with a spreading heap of gold and precious stones.

'Any other little trick?' asked Cyril loftily. 'Shall we become invisible? Vanish?'

'Yes, if you like,' said the soldier; 'but not through the door, you don't.'

He closed it carefully and set his broad Egyptian back against it.

'No! no!' cried a voice high up among the tops of the tall wooden pillars that stood against the wall. There was a sound of someone moving above.

The soldier was as much surprised as anybody.

'That's magic, if you like,' he said.

And then Jane held up the Amulet, uttering the word of Power. At the sound of it and at the sight of the Amulet growing into the great arch the soldier fell flat on his face among the jewels with a cry of awe and terror.

The children went through the arch with a quickness born of long practice. But Jane stayed in the middle of the arch and looked back.

The others, standing on the dining-room carpet in Fitzroy Street, turned and saw her still in the arch. 'Someone's holding her,' cried Cyril. 'We must go back.'

But they pulled at Jane's hands just to see if she would come, and, of course, she did come.

Then, as usual, the arch was little again and there they all were.

'Oh, I do wish you hadn't!' Jane said crossly. "It WAS so interesting. The priest had come in and he was kicking the soldier, and telling him he'd done it now, and they must take the jewels and flee for their lives.'

'And did they?'

'I don't know. You interfered,' said Jane ungratefully. 'I SHOULD have liked to see the last of it.'

As a matter of fact, none of them had seen the last of it—if by 'it' Jane meant the adventure of the Priest and the Soldier.

Chapter 12. The Sorry-present and the Expelled Little Boy

'Look here, said Cyril, sitting on the dining-table and swinging his legs; 'I really have got it.'

'Got what?' was the not unnatural rejoinder of the others.

Cyril was making a boat with a penknife and a piece of wood, and the girls were making warm frocks for their dolls, for the weather was growing chilly.

'Why, don't you see? It's really not any good our going into the Past looking for that Amulet. The Past's as full of different times as—as the sea is of sand. We're simply bound to hit upon the wrong time. We might spend our lives looking for the Amulet and never see a sight of it. Why, it's the end of September already. It's like looking for a needle in—'

'A bottle of hay—I know,' interrupted Robert; 'but if we don't go on doing that, what ARE we to do?'

'That's just it,' said Cyril in mysterious accents. 'Oh, BOTHER!'

Old Nurse had come in with the tray of knives, forks, and glasses, and was getting the tablecloth and table-napkins out of the chiffonier drawer.

'It's always meal-times just when you come to anything interesting.'

'And a nice interesting handful YOU'D be, Master Cyril,' said old Nurse, 'if I wasn't to bring your meals up to time. Don't you begin grumbling now, fear you get something to grumble AT.'

'I wasn't grumbling,' said Cyril quite untruly; 'but it does always happen like that.'

'You deserve to HAVE something happen,' said old Nurse. 'Slave, slave, slave for you day and night, and never a word of thanks. ...'

'Why, you do everything beautifully,' said Anthea.

'It's the first time any of you's troubled to say so, anyhow,' said Nurse shortly.

'What's the use of SAYING?' inquired Robert. 'We EAT our meals fast enough, and almost always two helps. THAT ought to show you!'

'Ah!' said old Nurse, going round the table and putting the knives and forks in their places; 'you're a man all over, Master Robert. There was my poor Green, all the years he lived with me I never could get more out of him than "It's all right!" when I asked him if he'd fancied his dinner. And yet, when he lay a-dying, his last words to me was, "Maria, you was always a good cook!"' She ended with a trembling voice.

'And so you are,' cried Anthea, and she and Jane instantly hugged her.

When she had gone out of the room Anthea said—

'I know exactly how she feels. Now, look here! Let's do a penance to show we're sorry we didn't think about telling her before what nice cooking she does, and what a dear she is.'

'Penances are silly,' said Robert.

'Not if the penance is something to please someone else. I didn't mean old peas and hair shirts and sleeping on the stones. I mean we'll make her a sorry-present,' explained Anthea. 'Look here! I vote Cyril doesn't tell us his idea until we've done something for old Nurse. It's worse for us than him,' she added hastily, 'because he knows what it is and we don't. Do you all agree?'

The others would have been ashamed not to agree, so they did. It was not till quite near the end of dinner—mutton fritters and blackberry and apple pie—that out of the earnest talk of the four came an idea that pleased everybody and would, they hoped, please Nurse.

Cyril and Robert went out with the taste of apple still in their mouths and the purple of blackberries on their lips—and, in the case of Robert, on the wristband as well—and bought a big sheet of cardboard at the stationers. Then at the plumber's shop, that has tubes and pipes and taps and gas-fittings in the window, they bought a pane of glass the same size as the cardboard. The man cut it with a very interesting tool that had a bit of diamond at the end, and he gave them, out of his own free generousness, a large piece of putty and a small piece of glue.

While they were out the girls had floated four photographs of the four children off their cards in hot water. These were now stuck in a row along the top of the cardboard. Cyril put the glue to melt in a jampot, and put the jampot in a saucepan and saucepan on the fire, while Robert painted a wreath of poppies round the photographs. He painted rather well and very quickly, and poppies are easy to do if you've once been shown how. Then Anthea drew some printed letters and Jane coloured them. The words were:

'With all our loves to shew
We like the thigs to eat.'

And when the painting was dry they all signed their names at the bottom and put the glass on, and glued brown paper round the edge and over the back, and put two loops of tape to hang it up by.

Of course everyone saw when too late that there were not enough letters in 'things', so the missing 'n' was put in. It was impossible, of course, to do the whole thing over again for just one letter.

'There!' said Anthea, placing it carefully, face up, under the sofa. 'It'll be hours before the glue's dry. Now, Squirrel, fire ahead!'

'Well, then,' said Cyril in a great hurry, rubbing at his gluey hands with his pocket handkerchief. 'What I mean to say is this.'

There was a long pause.

'Well,' said Robert at last, 'WHAT is it that you mean to say?'

'It's like this,' said Cyril, and again stopped short.

'Like WHAT?' asked Jane.

'How can I tell you if you will all keep on interrupting?' said Cyril sharply.

So no one said any more, and with wrinkled frowns he arranged his ideas.

'Look here,' he said, 'what I really mean is—we can remember now what we did when we went to look for the Amulet. And if we'd found it we should remember that too.'

'Rather!' said Robert. 'Only, you see we haven't.'

'But in the future we shall have.'

'Shall we, though?' said Jane.

'Yes—unless we've been made fools of by the Psammead. So then, where we want to go to is where we shall remember about where we did find it.'

'I see,' said Robert, but he didn't.

'*I* don't,' said Anthea, who did, very nearly. 'Say it again, Squirrel, and very slowly.'

'If,' said Cyril, very slowly indeed, 'we go into the future—after we've found the Amulet—'

'But we've got to find it first,' said Jane.

'Hush!' said Anthea.

'There will be a future,' said Cyril, driven to greater clearness by the blank faces of the other three, 'there will be a time AFTER we've found it. Let's go into THAT time—and then we shall remember HOW we found it. And then we can go back and do the finding really.'

'I see,' said Robert, and this time he did, and I hope YOU do.

'Yes,' said Anthea. 'Oh, Squirrel, how clever of you!'

'But will the Amulet work both ways?' inquired Robert.

'It ought to,' said Cyril, 'if time's only a thingummy of whatsitsname. Anyway we might try.'

'Let's put on our best things, then,' urged Jane. 'You know what people say about progress and the world growing better and brighter. I expect people will be awfully smart in the future.'

'All right,' said Anthea, 'we should have to wash anyway, I'm all thick with glue.'

When everyone was clean and dressed, the charm was held up.

'We want to go into the future and see the Amulet after we've found it,' said Cyril, and Jane said the word of Power. They walked through the big arch of the charm straight into the British Museum.

They knew it at once, and there, right in front of them, under a glass case, was the Amulet—their own half of it, as well as the other half they had never been able to find—and the two were joined by a pin of red stone that formed a hinge.

'Oh, glorious!' cried Robert. 'Here it is!'

'Yes,' said Cyril, very gloomily, 'here it is. But we can't get it out.'

'No,' said Robert, remembering how impossible the Queen of Babylon had found it to get anything out of the glass cases in the Museum—except by Psammead magic, and then she hadn't been able to take anything away with her; 'no—but we remember where we got it, and we can—'

'Oh, DO we?' interrupted Cyril bitterly, 'do YOU remember where we got it?'

'No,' said Robert, 'I don't exactly, now I come to think of it.'

Nor did any of the others!

'But WHY can't we?' said Jane.

'Oh, *I* don't know,' Cyril's tone was impatient, 'some silly old enchanted rule I suppose. I wish people would teach you magic at school like they do sums—or instead of. It would be some use having an Amulet then.'

'I wonder how far we are in the future,' said Anthea; the Museum looks just the same, only lighter and brighter, somehow.'

'Let's go back and try the Past again,' said Robert.

'Perhaps the Museum people could tell us how we got it,' said Anthea with sudden hope. There was no one in the room, but in the next gallery, where the Assyrian things are and still were, they found a kind, stout man in a loose, blue gown, and stockinged legs.

'Oh, they've got a new uniform, how pretty!' said Jane.

When they asked him their question he showed them a label on the case. It said, 'From the collection of—.' A name followed, and it was the name of the learned gentleman who, among themselves, and to his face when he had been with them at the other side of the Amulet, they had called Jimmy.

'THAT'S not much good,' said Cyril, 'thank you.'

'How is it you're not at school?' asked the kind man in blue. 'Not expelled for long I hope?'

'We're not expelled at all,' said Cyril rather warmly.

'Well, I shouldn't do it again, if I were you,' said the man, and they could see he did not believe them. There is no company so little pleasing as that of people who do not believe you.

'Thank you for showing us the label,' said Cyril. And they came away.

As they came through the doors of the Museum they blinked at the sudden glory of sunlight and blue sky. The houses opposite the Museum were gone. Instead there was a big garden, with trees and flowers and smooth green lawns, and not a single notice to tell you not to walk on the grass and not to destroy the trees and shrubs and not to pick the flowers. There were comfortable seats all about, and arbours covered with roses, and long, trellised walks, also rose-covered. Whispering, splashing fountains fell into full white marble basins, white statues gleamed among the leaves, and the pigeons that swept about among the branches or pecked on the smooth, soft gravel were not black and tumbled like the Museum pigeons are now, but bright and clean and sleek as birds of new silver. A good many people were sitting on the seats, and on the grass babies were rolling and kicking and playing—with very little on indeed. Men, as well as women, seemed to be in charge of the babies and were playing with them.

'It's like a lovely picture,' said Anthea, and it was. For the people's clothes were of bright, soft colours and all beautifully and very simply made. No one seemed to have any hats or bonnets, but there were a great many Japanese-looking sunshades. And among the trees were hung lamps of coloured glass.

'I expect they light those in the evening,' said Jane. 'I do wish we lived in the future!'

They walked down the path, and as they went the people on the benches looked at the four children very curiously, but not rudely or unkindly. The children, in their turn, looked—I hope they did not stare—at the faces of these people in the beautiful soft clothes. Those faces were worth looking at. Not that they were all handsome, though even in the matter of handsomeness they had the advantage of any set of people the children had ever seen. But it was the expression of their faces that made them worth looking at. The children could not tell at first what it was.

'I know,' said Anthea suddenly. 'They're not worried; that's what it is.'

And it was. Everybody looked calm, no one seemed to be in a hurry, no one seemed to be anxious, or fretted, and though some did seem to be sad, not a single one looked worried.

But though the people looked kind everyone looked so interested in the children that they began to feel a little shy and turned out of the big main path into a narrow little one that wound among trees and shrubs and mossy, dripping springs.

It was here, in a deep, shadowed cleft between tall cypresses, that they found the expelled little boy. He was lying face downward on the mossy turf, and the peculiar shaking of his shoulders was a thing they had seen, more than once, in each other. So Anthea kneeled down by him and said—

'What's the matter?'

'I'm expelled from school,' said the boy between his sobs.

This was serious. People are not expelled for light offences.

'Do you mind telling us what you'd done?'

'I—I tore up a sheet of paper and threw it about in the playground,' said the child, in the tone of one confessing an unutterable baseness. 'You won't talk to me any more now you know that,' he added without looking up.

'Was that all?' asked Anthea.

'It's about enough,' said the child; 'and I'm expelled for the whole day!'

'I don't quite understand,' said Anthea, gently. The boy lifted his face, rolled over, and sat up .

'Why, whoever on earth are you?' he said.

'We're strangers from a far country,' said Anthea. 'In our country it's not a crime to leave a bit of paper about.'

'It is here,' said the child. 'If grown-ups do it they're fined. When we do it we're expelled for the whole day.'

'Well, but,' said Robert, 'that just means a day' s holiday.'

'You MUST come from a long way off,' said the little boy. 'A holiday's when you all have play and treats and jolliness, all of you together. On your expelled days no one'll speak to you. Everyone sees you're an Expelleder or you'd be in school.'

'Suppose you were ill?'

'Nobody is—hardly. If they are, of course they wear the badge, and everyone is kind to you. I know a boy that stole his sister's illness badge and wore it when he was expelled for a day. HE got expelled for a week for that. It must be awful not to go to school for a week.'

'Do you LIKE school, then?' asked Robert incredulously.

'Of course I do. It's the loveliest place there is. I chose railways for my special subject this year, there are such splendid models and things, and now I shall be all behind because of that torn-up paper.'

'You choose your own subject?' asked Cyril.

'Yes, of course. Where DID you come from? Don't you know ANYTHING?'

'No,' said Jane definitely; 'so you'd better tell us.'

'Well, on Midsummer Day school breaks up and everything's decorated with flowers, and you choose your special subject for next year. Of course you have to stick to it for a year at least. Then there are all your other subjects, of course, reading, and painting, and the rules of Citizenship.'

'Good gracious!' said Anthea.

'Look here,' said the child, jumping up, 'it's nearly four. The expelledness only lasts till then. Come home with me. Mother will tell you all about everything.'

'Will your mother like you taking home strange children?' asked Anthea.

'I don't understand,' said the child, settling his leather belt over his honey-coloured smock and stepping out with hard little bare feet. 'Come on.'

So they went.

The streets were wide and hard and very clean. There were no horses, but a sort of motor carriage that made no noise. The

Thames flowed between green banks, and there were trees at the edge, and people sat under them, fishing, for the stream was clear as crystal. Everywhere there were green trees and there was no smoke. The houses were set in what seemed like one green garden.

The little boy brought them to a house, and at the window was a good, bright mother-face. The little boy rushed in, and through the window they could see him hugging his mother, then his eager lips moving and his quick hands pointing.

A lady in soft green clothes came out, spoke kindly to them, and took them into the oddest house they had ever seen. It was very bare, there were no ornaments, and yet every single thing was beautiful, from the dresser with its rows of bright china, to the thick squares of Eastern-looking carpet on the floors. I can't describe that house; I haven't the time. And I haven't heart either, when I think how different it was from our houses. The lady took them all over it. The oddest thing of all was the big room in the middle. It had padded walls and a soft, thick carpet, and all the chairs and tables were padded. There wasn't a single thing in it that anyone could hurt itself with.

'What ever's this for?—lunatics?' asked Cyril.

The lady looked very shocked.

'No! It's for the children, of course,' she said. 'Don't tell me that in your country there are no children's rooms.'

'There are nurseries,' said Anthea doubtfully, 'but the furniture's all cornery and hard, like other rooms.'

'How shocking!' said the lady; 'you must be VERY much behind the times in your country! Why, the children are more than half of the people; it's not much to have one room where they can have a good time and not hurt themselves.'

'But there's no fireplace,' said Anthea.

'Hot-air pipes, of course,' said the lady. 'Why, how could you have a fire in a nursery? A child might get burned.'

'In our country,' said Robert suddenly, 'more than 3,000 children are burned to death every year. Father told me,' he added, as if apologizing for this piece of information, 'once when I'd been playing with fire.'

The lady turned quite pale.

'What a frightful place you must live in!' she said. 'What's all the furniture padded for?' Anthea asked, hastily turning the subject.

'Why, you couldn't have little tots of two or three running about in rooms where the things were hard and sharp! They might hurt themselves.'

Robert fingered the scar on his forehead where he had hit it against the nursery fender when he was little.

'But does everyone have rooms like this, poor people and all?' asked Anthea.

'There's a room like this wherever there's a child, of course,' said the lady. 'How refreshingly ignorant you are!—no, I don't mean ignorant, my dear. Of course, you're awfully well up in ancient History. But I see you haven't done your Duties of Citizenship Course yet.'

'But beggars, and people like that?' persisted Anthea 'and tramps and people who haven't any homes?'

'People who haven't any homes?' repeated the lady. 'I really DON'T understand what you're talking about.'

'It's all different in our country,' said Cyril carefully; and I have read it used to be different in London. Usedn't people to have no homes and beg because they were hungry? And wasn't London very black and dirty once upon a time? And the Thames all muddy and filthy? And narrow streets, and—'

'You must have been reading very old-fashioned books,' said the lady. 'Why, all that was in the dark ages! My husband can tell you more about it than I can. He took Ancient History as one of his special subjects.'

'I haven't seen any working people,' said Anthea.

'Why, we're all working people,' said the lady; 'at least my husband's a carpenter.'

'Good gracious!' said Anthea; 'but you're a lady!'

'Ah,' said the lady, 'that quaint old word! Well, my husband WILL enjoy a talk with you. In the dark ages everyone was allowed to have a smoky chimney, and those nasty horses all over the streets, and all sorts of rubbish thrown into the Thames. And, of course, the sufferings of the people will hardly bear thinking of. It's very learned of you to know it all. Did you make Ancient History your special subject?'

'Not exactly,' said Cyril, rather uneasily. 'What is the Duties of Citizenship Course about?'

'Don't you REALLY know? Aren't you pretending—just for fun? Really not? Well, that course teaches you how to be a good citizen, what you must do and what you mayn't do, so as to do your full share of the work of making your town a beautiful and happy place for people to live in. There's a quite simple little thing they teach the tiny children. How does it go ...?

> 'I must not steal and I must learn,
> Nothing is mine that I do not earn.
> I must try in work and play
> To make things beautiful every day.
> I must be kind to everyone,
> And never let cruel things be done.
> I must be brave, and I must try
> When I am hurt never to cry,
> And always laugh as much as I can,
> And be glad that I'm going to be a man
> To work for my living and help the rest
> And never do less than my very best.'

'That's very easy,' said Jane. '*I* could remember that.'

'That's only the very beginning, of course,' said the lady; 'there are heaps more rhymes. There's the one beginning—

> 'I must not litter the beautiful street
> With bits of paper or things to eat;

I must not pick the public flowers,
They are not MINE, but they are OURS.'

'And "things to eat" reminds me—are you hungry? Wells, run and get a tray of nice things.'

'Why do you call him "Wells"?' asked Robert, as the boy ran off.

'It's after the great reformer—surely you've heard of HIM? He lived in the dark ages, and he saw that what you ought to do is to find out what you want and then try to get it. Up to then people had always tried to tinker up what they'd got. We've got a great many of the things he thought of. Then "Wells" means springs of clear water. It's a nice name, don't you think?'

Here Wells returned with strawberries and cakes and lemonade on a tray, and everybody ate and enjoyed.

'Now, Wells,' said the lady, 'run off or you'll be late and not meet your Daddy.'

Wells kissed her, waved to the others, and went.

'Look here,' said Anthea suddenly, 'would you like to come to OUR country, and see what it's like? It wouldn't take you a minute.'

The lady laughed. But Jane held up the charm and said the word.

'What a splendid conjuring trick!' cried the lady, enchanted with the beautiful, growing arch.

'Go through,' said Anthea.

The lady went, laughing. But she did not laugh when she found herself, suddenly, in the dining-room at Fitzroy Street.

'Oh, what a HORRIBLE trick!' she cried. 'What a hateful, dark, ugly place!'

She ran to the window and looked out. The sky was grey, the street was foggy, a dismal organ-grinder was standing opposite the door, a beggar and a man who sold matches were quarrelling at the edge of the pavement on whose greasy black surface people hurried along, hastening to get to the shelter of their houses.

'Oh, look at their faces, their horrible faces!' she cried. 'What's the matter with them all?'

'They're poor people, that's all,' said Robert.

'But it's NOT all! They're ill, they're unhappy, they're wicked! Oh, do stop it, there's dear children. It's very, very clever. Some sort of magic-lantern trick, I suppose, like I've read of. But DO stop it. Oh! their poor, tired, miserable, wicked faces!'

The tears were in her eyes. Anthea signed to Jane. The arch grew, they spoke the words, and pushed the lady through it into her own time and place, where London is clean and beautiful, and the Thames runs clear and bright, and the green trees grow, and no one is afraid, or anxious, or in a hurry. There was a silence. Then—

'I'm glad we went,' said Anthea, with a deep breath.

'I'll never throw paper about again as long as I live,' said Robert.

'Mother always told us not to,' said Jane.

'I would like to take up the Duties of Citizenship for a special subject,' said Cyril. 'I wonder if Father could put me through it. I shall ask him when he comes home.'

'If we'd found the Amulet, Father could be home NOW,' said Anthea, 'and Mother and The Lamb.'

'Let's go into the future AGAIN,' suggested Jane brightly. 'Perhaps we could remember if it wasn't such an awful way off.'

So they did. This time they said, 'The future, where the Amulet is, not so far away.'

And they went through the familiar arch into a large, light room with three windows. Facing them was the familiar mummy-case. And at a table by the window sat the learned gentleman. They knew him at once, though his hair was white. He was one of the faces that do not change with age. In his hand was the Amulet—complete and perfect.

He rubbed his other hand across his forehead in the way they were so used to.

'Dreams, dreams!' he said; 'old age is full of them!'

'You've been in dreams with us before now,' said Robert, 'don't you remember?'

'I do, indeed,' said he. The room had many more books than the Fitzroy Street room, and far more curious and wonderful Assyrian and Egyptian objects. 'The most wonderful dreams I ever had had you in them.'

'Where,' asked Cyril, 'did you get that thing in your hand?'

'If you weren't just a dream,' he answered, smiling, you'd remember that you gave it to me.'

'But where did we get it?' Cyril asked eagerly.

'Ah, you never would tell me that,' he said, 'You always had your little mysteries. You dear children! What a difference you made to that old Bloomsbury house! I wish I could dream you oftener. Now you're grown up you're not like you used to be.'

'Grown up?' said Anthea.

The learned gentleman pointed to a frame with four photographs in it.

'There you are,' he said.

The children saw four grown-up people's portraits—two ladies, two gentlemen—and looked on them with loathing.

'Shall we grow up like THAT?' whispered Jane. 'How perfectly horrid!'

'If we're ever like that, we shan't know it's horrid, I expect,' Anthea with some insight whispered back. 'You see, you get used to yourself while you're changing. It's—it's being so sudden makes it seem so frightful now.'

The learned gentleman was looking at them with wistful kindness. 'Don't let me undream you just yet,' he said. There was a pause.

'Do you remember WHEN we gave you that Amulet?' Cyril asked suddenly.

'You know, or you would if you weren't a dream, that it was on the 3rd December, 1905. I shall never forget THAT day.'

'Thank you,' said Cyril, earnestly; 'oh, thank you very much.'

'You've got a new room,' said Anthea, looking out of the window, 'and what a lovely garden!'

'Yes,' said he, 'I'm too old now to care even about being near the Museum. This is a beautiful place. Do you know—I can hardly believe you're just a dream, you do look so exactly real. Do you know ...' his voice dropped, 'I can say it to YOU, though, of course, if I said it to anyone that wasn't a dream they'd call me mad; there was something about that Amulet you gave me—something very mysterious.'

'There was that,' said Robert.

'Ah, I don't mean your pretty little childish mysteries about where you got it. But about the thing itself. First, the wonderful dreams I used to have, after you'd shown me the first half of it! Why, my book on Atlantis, that I did, was the beginning of my fame and my fortune, too. And I got it all out of a dream! And then, "Britain at the Time of the Roman Invasion"—that was only a pamphlet, but it explained a lot of things people hadn't understood.'

'Yes,' said Anthea, 'it would.'

'That was the beginning. But after you'd given me the whole of the Amulet—ah, it was generous of you!—then, somehow, I didn't need to theorize, I seemed to KNOW about the old Egyptian civilization. And they can't upset my theories'—he rubbed his thin hands and laughed triumphantly—'they can't, though they've tried. Theories, they call them, but they're more like—I don't know—more like memories. I KNOW I'm right about the secret rites of the Temple of Amen.'

'I'm so glad you're rich,' said Anthea. 'You weren't, you know, at Fitzroy Street.'

'Indeed I wasn't,' said he, 'but I am now. This beautiful house and this lovely garden—I dig in it sometimes; you remember, you used to tell me to take more exercise? Well, I feel I owe it all to you—and the Amulet.'

'I'm so glad,' said Anthea, and kissed him. He started.

'THAT didn't feel like a dream,' he said, and his voice trembled.

'It isn't exactly a dream,' said Anthea softly, 'it's all part of the Amulet—it's a sort of extra special, real dream, dear Jimmy.'

'Ah,' said he, 'when you call me that, I know I'm dreaming. My little sister—I dream of her sometimes. But it's not real like this. Do you remember the day I dreamed you brought me the Babylonish ring?'

'We remember it all,' said Robert. 'Did you leave Fitzroy Street because you were too rich for it?'

'Oh, no!' he said reproachfully. 'You know I should never have done such a thing as that. Of course, I left when your old Nurse died and—what's the matter!'

'Old Nurse DEAD?' said Anthea. 'Oh, NO!'

'Yes, yes, it's the common lot. It's a long time ago now.'

Jane held up the Amulet in a hand that twittered.

'Come!' she cried, 'oh, come home! She may be dead before we get there, and then we can't give it to her. Oh, come!'

'Ah, don't let the dream end now!' pleaded the learned gentleman.

'It must,' said Anthea firmly, and kissed him again.

'When it comes to people dying,' said Robert, 'good-bye! I'm so glad you're rich and famous and happy.'

'DO come!' cried Jane, stamping in her agony of impatience. And they went. Old Nurse brought in tea almost as soon as they were back in Fitzroy Street. As she came in with the tray, the girls rushed at her and nearly upset her and it.

'Don't die!' cried Jane, 'oh, don't!' and Anthea cried, 'Dear, ducky, darling old Nurse, don't die!'

'Lord, love you!' said Nurse, 'I'm not agoin' to die yet a while, please Heaven! Whatever on earth's the matter with the chicks?'

'Nothing. Only don't!'

She put the tray down and hugged the girls in turn. The boys thumped her on the back with heartfelt affection.

'I'm as well as ever I was in my life,' she said. 'What nonsense about dying! You've been a sitting too long in the dusk, that's what it is. Regular blind man's holiday. Leave go of me, while I light the gas.'

The yellow light illuminated four pale faces. 'We do love you so,' Anthea went on, 'and we've made you a picture to show you how we love you. Get it out, Squirrel.'

The glazed testimonial was dragged out from under the sofa and displayed.

'The glue's not dry yet,' said Cyril, 'look out!'

'What a beauty!' cried old Nurse. 'Well, I never! And your pictures and the beautiful writing and all. Well, I always did say your hearts was in the right place, if a bit careless at times. Well! I never did! I don't know as I was ever pleased better in my life.'

She hugged them all, one after the other. And the boys did not mind it, somehow, that day.

'How is it we can remember all about the future, NOW?' Anthea woke the Psammead with laborious gentleness to put the question. 'How is it we can remember what we saw in the future, and yet, when we WERE in the future, we could not remember the bit of the future that was past then, the time of finding the Amulet?'

'Why, what a silly question!' said the Psammead, 'of course you cannot remember what hasn't happened yet.'

'But the FUTURE hasn't happened yet,' Anthea persisted, 'and we remember that all right.'

'Oh, that isn't what's happened, my good child,' said the Psammead, rather crossly, 'that's prophetic vision. And you remember dreams, don't you? So why not visions? You never do seem to understand the simplest thing.'

It went to sand again at once.

Anthea crept down in her nightgown to give one last kiss to old Nurse, and one last look at the beautiful testimonial hanging, by its tapes, its glue now firmly set, in glazed glory on the wall of the kitchen.

'Good-night, bless your loving heart,' said old Nurse, 'if only you don't catch your deather-cold!'

Chapter 13. The Shipwreck on the Tin Islands

'Blue and red,' said Jane softly, 'make purple.'

'Not always they don't,' said Cyril, 'it has to be crimson lake and Prussian blue. If you mix Vermilion and Indigo you get the most loathsome slate colour.'

'Sepia's the nastiest colour in the box, I think,' said Jane, sucking her brush.

They were all painting. Nurse in the flush of grateful emotion, excited by Robert's border of poppies, had presented each of the four with a shilling paint-box, and had supplemented the gift with a pile of old copies of the Illustrated London News.

'Sepia,' said Cyril instructively, 'is made out of beastly cuttlefish.'

'Purple's made out of a fish, as well as out of red and blue,' said Robert. 'Tyrian purple was, I know.'

'Out of lobsters?' said Jane dreamily. 'They're red when they're boiled, and blue when they aren't. If you mixed live and dead lobsters you'd get Tyrian purple.'

'*I* shouldn't like to mix anything with a live lobster,' said Anthea, shuddering.

'Well, there aren't any other red and blue fish,' said Jane; 'you'd have to.'

'I'd rather not have the purple,' said Anthea.

'The Tyrian purple wasn't that colour when it came out of the fish, nor yet afterwards, it wasn't,' said Robert; 'it was scarlet really, and Roman Emperors wore it. And it wasn't any nice colour while the fish had it. It was a yellowish-white liquid of a creamy consistency.'

'How do you know?' asked Cyril.

'I read it,' said Robert, with the meek pride of superior knowledge.

'Where?' asked Cyril.

'In print,' said Robert, still more proudly meek.

'You think everything's true if it's printed,' said Cyril, naturally annoyed, 'but it isn't. Father said so. Quite a lot of lies get printed, especially in newspapers.'

'You see, as it happens,' said Robert, in what was really a rather annoying tone, 'it wasn't a newspaper, it was in a book.'

'How sweet Chinese white is!' said Jane, dreamily sucking her brush again.

'I don't believe it,' said Cyril to Robert.

'Have a suck yourself,' suggested Robert.

'I don't mean about the Chinese white. I mean about the cream fish turning purple and—"

'Oh!' cried Anthea, jumping up very quickly, 'I'm tired of painting. Let's go somewhere by Amulet. I say let's let IT choose.'

Cyril and Robert agreed that this was an idea. Jane consented to stop painting because, as she said, Chinese white, though certainly sweet, gives you a queer feeling in the back of the throat if you paint with it too long.

The Amulet was held up. 'Take us somewhere,' said Jane, 'anywhere you like in the Past—but somewhere where you are.' Then she said the word.

Next moment everyone felt a queer rocking and swaying—something like what you feel when you go out in a fishing boat. And that was not wonderful, when you come to think of it, for it was in a boat that they found themselves. A queer boat, with high bulwarks pierced with holes for oars to go through. There was a high seat for the steersman, and the prow was shaped like the head of some great animal with big, staring eyes. The boat rode at anchor in a bay, and the bay was very smooth. The crew were dark, wiry fellows with black beards and hair. They had no clothes except a tunic from waist to knee, and round caps with knobs on the top. They were very busy, and what they were doing was so interesting to the children that at first they did not even wonder where the Amulet had brought them. And the crew seemed too busy to notice the children. They were fastening rush baskets to a long rope with a great piece of cork at the end, and in each basket they put mussels or little frogs. Then they cast out the rope, the baskets sank, but the cork floated. And all about on the blue water were other boats and all the crews of all the boats were busy with ropes and baskets and frogs and mussels.

'Whatever are you doing?' Jane suddenly asked a man who had rather more clothes than the others, and seemed to be a sort of captain or overseer. He started and stared at her, but he had seen too many strange lands to be very much surprised at these queerly-dressed stowaways.

'Setting lines for the dye shell-fish,' he said shortly. 'How did you get here?'

'A sort of magic,' said Robert carelessly. The Captain fingered an Amulet that hung round his neck.

'What is this place?' asked Cyril.

'Tyre, of course,' said the man. Then he drew back and spoke in a low voice to one of the sailors.

'Now we shall know about your precious cream-jug fish,' said Cyril.

'But we never SAID come to Tyre,' said Jane.

'The Amulet heard us talking, I expect. I think it's MOST obliging of it,' said Anthea.

'And the Amulet's here too,' said Robert. 'We ought to be able to find it in a little ship like this. I wonder which of them's got it.'

'Oh—look, look!' cried Anthea suddenly. On the bare breast of one of the sailors gleamed something red. It was the exact counterpart of their precious half-Amulet.

A silence, full of emotion, was broken by Jane.

'Then we've found it!' she said. 'Oh do let's take it and go home!'

'Easy to say "take it",' said Cyril; 'he looks very strong.'

He did—yet not so strong as the other sailors.

'It's odd,' said Anthea musingly, 'I do believe I've seen that man somewhere before.'

'He's rather like our learned gentleman,' said Robert, 'but I'll tell you who he's much more like—' At that moment that sailor looked up. His eyes met Robert's—and Robert and the others had no longer any doubt as to where they had seen him before. It was Rekh-mara, the priest who had led them to the palace of Pharaoh—and whom Jane had looked back at through the arch, when he was counselling Pharaoh's guard to take the jewels and fly for his life.

Nobody was quite pleased, and nobody quite knew why.

Jane voiced the feelings of all when she said, fingering THEIR Amulet through the folds of her frock, 'We can go back in a minute if anything nasty happens.'

For the moment nothing worse happened than an offer of food—figs and cucumbers it was, and very pleasant.

'I see,' said the Captain, 'that you are from a far country. Since you have honoured my boat by appearing on it, you must stay here till morning. Then I will lead you to one of our great ones. He loves strangers from far lands.'

'Let's go home,' Jane whispered, 'all the frogs are drowning NOW. I think the people here are cruel.'

But the boys wanted to stay and see the lines taken up in the morning.

'It's just like eel-pots and lobster-pots,' said Cyril, 'the baskets only open from outside—I vote we stay.'

So they stayed.

'That's Tyre over there,' said the Captain, who was evidently trying to be civil. He pointed to a great island rock, that rose steeply from the sea, crowned with huge walls and towers. There was another city on the mainland.

'That's part of Tyre, too,' said the Captain; 'it's where the great merchants have their pleasure-houses and gardens and farms.'

'Look, look!' Cyril cried suddenly; 'what a lovely little ship!'

A ship in full sail was passing swiftly through the fishing fleet. The Captain's face changed. He frowned, and his eyes blazed with fury.

'Insolent young barbarian!' he cried. 'Do you call the ships of Tyre LITTLE? None greater sail the seas. That ship has been on a three years' voyage. She is known in all the great trading ports from here to the Tin Islands. She comes back rich and glorious. Her very anchor is of silver.'

'I'm sure we beg your pardon,' said Anthea hastily. 'In our country we say "little" for a pet name. Your wife might call you her dear little husband, you know.'

'I should like to catch her at it,' growled the Captain, but he stopped scowling.

'It's a rich trade,' he went on. 'For cloth ONCE dipped, second-best glass, and the rough images our young artists carve for practice, the barbarian King in Tessos lets us work the silver mines. We get so much silver there that we leave them our iron anchors and come back with silver ones.'

'How splendid!' said Robert. 'Do go on. What's cloth once dipped?'

'You MUST be barbarians from the outer darkness,' said the Captain scornfully. 'All wealthy nations know that our finest stuffs are twice dyed—dibaptha. They're only for the robes of kings and priests and princes.'

'What do the rich merchants wear,' asked Jane, with interest, 'in the pleasure-houses?'

'They wear the dibaptha. OUR merchants ARE princes,' scowled the skipper.

'Oh, don't be cross, we do so like hearing about things. We want to know ALL about the dyeing,' said Anthea cordially.

'Oh, you do, do you?' growled the man. 'So that's what you're here for? Well, you won't get the secrets of the dye trade out of ME.'

He went away, and everyone felt snubbed and uncomfortable. And all the time the long, narrow eyes of the Egyptian were watching, watching. They felt as though he was watching them through the darkness, when they lay down to sleep on a pile of cloaks.

Next morning the baskets were drawn up full of what looked like whelk shells.

The children were rather in the way, but they made themselves as small as they could. While the skipper was at the other end of the boat they did ask one question of a sailor, whose face was a little less unkind than the others.

'Yes,' he answered, 'this is the dye-fish. It's a sort of murex—and there's another kind that they catch at Sidon and then, of course, there's the kind that's used for the dibaptha. But that's quite different. It's—'

'Hold your tongue!' shouted the skipper. And the man held it.

The laden boat was rowed slowly round the end of the island, and was made fast in one of the two great harbours that lay inside a long breakwater. The harbour was full of all sorts of ships, so that Cyril and Robert enjoyed themselves much more than their sisters. The breakwater and the quays were heaped with bales and baskets, and crowded with slaves and sailors. Farther along some men were practising diving.

'That's jolly good,' said Robert, as a naked brown body cleft the water.

'I should think so,' said the skipper. 'The pearl-divers of Persia are not more skilful. Why, we've got a fresh-water spring that comes out at the bottom of the sea. Our divers dive down and bring up the fresh water in skin bottles! Can your barbarian divers do as much?'

'I suppose not,' said Robert, and put away a wild desire to explain to the Captain the English system of waterworks, pipes, taps, and the intricacies of the plumbers' trade.

As they neared the quay the skipper made a hasty toilet. He did his hair, combed his beard, put on a garment like a jersey with short sleeves, an embroidered belt, a necklace of beads, and a big signet ring.

'Now,' said he, 'I'm fit to be seen. Come along!'

'Where to?' said Jane cautiously.

'To Pheles, the great sea-captain, said the skipper, 'the man I told you of, who loves barbarians.'

Then Rekh-mara came forward, and, for the first time, spoke.

'I have known these children in another land,' he said. 'You know my powers of magic. It was my magic that brought these barbarians to your boat. And you know how they will profit you. I read your thoughts. Let me come with you and see the end of them, and then I will work the spell I promised you in return for the little experience you have so kindly given me on your boat.'

The skipper looked at the Egyptian with some disfavour.

'So it was YOUR doing,' he said. 'I might have guessed it. Well, come on.'

So he came, and the girls wished he hadn't. But Robert whispered—

'Nonsense—as long as he's with us we've got some chance of the Amulet. We can always fly if anything goes wrong.'

The morning was so fresh and bright; their breakfast had been so good and so unusual; they had actually seen the Amulet round the Egyptian's neck. One or two, or all these things, suddenly raised the children's spirits. They went off quite cheerfully through the city gate—it was not arched, but roofed over with a great flat stone—and so through the street, which smelt horribly of fish and garlic and a thousand other things even less agreeable. But far worse than the street scents was the scent of the factory, where the skipper called in to sell his night's catch. I wish I could tell you all about that factory, but I haven't time, and perhaps after all you aren't interested in dyeing works. I will only mention that Robert was triumphantly proved to be right. The dye WAS a yellowish-white liquid of a creamy consistency, and it smelt more strongly of garlic than garlic itself does.

While the skipper was bargaining with the master of the dye works the Egyptian came close to the children, and said, suddenly and softly—

'Trust me.'

'I wish we could,' said Anthea.

'You feel,' said the Egyptian, 'that I want your Amulet. That makes you distrust me.'

'Yes,' said Cyril bluntly.

'But you also, you want my Amulet, and I am trusting you.'

'There's something in that,' said Robert.

'We have the two halves of the Amulet,' said the Priest, 'but not yet the pin that joined them. Our only chance of getting that is to remain together. Once part these two halves and they may never be found in the same time and place. Be wise. Our interests are the same.'

Before anyone could say more the skipper came back, and with him the dye-master. His hair and beard were curled like the men's in Babylon, and he was dressed like the skipper, but with added grandeur of gold and embroidery. He had necklaces of beads and silver, and a glass amulet with a man's face, very like his own, set between two bull's heads, as well as gold and silver bracelets and armlets. He looked keenly at the children. Then he said—

'My brother Pheles has just come back from Tarshish. He's at his garden house—unless he's hunting wild boar in the marshes. He gets frightfully bored on shore.'

'Ah,' said the skipper, 'he's a true-born Phoenician. "Tyre, Tyre for ever! Oh, Tyre rules the waves!" as the old song says. I'll go at once, and show him my young barbarians.'

'I should,' said the dye-master. 'They are very rum, aren't they? What frightful clothes, and what a lot of them! Observe the covering of their feet. Hideous indeed.'

Robert could not help thinking how easy, and at the same time pleasant, it would be to catch hold of the dye-master's feet and tip him backward into the great sunken vat just near him. But if he had, flight would have had to be the next move, so he restrained his impulse.

There was something about this Tyrian adventure that was different from all the others. It was, somehow, calmer. And there was the undoubted fact that the charm was there on the neck of the Egyptian.

So they enjoyed everything to the full, the row from the Island City to the shore, the ride on the donkeys that the skipper hired at the gate of the mainland city, and the pleasant country—palms and figs and cedars all about. It was like a garden—clematis, honeysuckle, and jasmine clung about the olive and mulberry trees, and there were tulips and gladiolus, and clumps of mandrake, which has bell-flowers that look as though they were cut out of dark blue jewels. In the distance were the mountains of Lebanon. The house they came to at last was rather like a bungalow—long and low, with pillars all along the front. Cedars and sycamores grew near it and sheltered it pleasantly.

Everyone dismounted, and the donkeys were led away.

'Why is this like Rosherville?' whispered Robert, and instantly supplied the answer.

'Because it's the place to spend a happy day.'

'It's jolly decent of the skipper to have brought us to such a ripping place,' said Cyril.

'Do you know,' said Anthea, 'this feels more real than anything else we've seen? It's like a holiday in the country at home.'

The children were left alone in a large hall. The floor was mosaic, done with wonderful pictures of ships and sea-beasts and fishes. Through an open doorway they could see a pleasant courtyard with flowers.

'I should like to spend a week here,' said Jane, 'and donkey ride every day.'

Everyone was feeling very jolly. Even the Egyptian looked pleasanter than usual. And then, quite suddenly, the skipper came back with a joyous smile. With him came the master of the house. He looked steadily at the children and nodded twice.

'Yes,' he said, 'my steward will pay you the price. But I shall not pay at that high rate for the Egyptian dog.'

The two passed on.

'This,' said the Egyptian, 'is a pretty kettle of fish.'

'What is?' asked all the children at once.

'Our present position,' said Rekh-mara. 'Our seafaring friend,' he added, 'has sold us all for slaves!'

A hasty council succeeded the shock of this announcement. The Priest was allowed to take part in it. His advice was 'stay', because they were in no danger, and the Amulet in its completeness must be somewhere near, or, of course, they could not have come to that place at all. And after some discussion they agreed to this.

The children were treated more as guests than as slaves, but the Egyptian was sent to the kitchen and made to work.

Pheles, the master of the house, went off that very evening, by the King's orders, to start on another voyage. And when he was gone his wife found the children amusing company, and kept them talking and singing and dancing till quite late. 'To distract my mind from my sorrows,' she said.

'I do like being a slave,' remarked Jane cheerfully, as they curled up on the big, soft cushions that were to be their beds.

It was black night when they were awakened, each by a hand passed softly over its face, and a low voice that whispered—

'Be quiet, or all is lost.'

So they were quiet.

'It's me, Rekh-mara, the Priest of Amen,' said the whisperer. 'The man who brought us has gone to sea again, and he has taken my Amulet from me by force, and I know no magic to get it back. Is there magic for that in the Amulet you bear?'

Everyone was instantly awake by now.

'We can go after him,' said Cyril, leaping up; 'but he might take OURS as well; or he might be angry with us for following him.'

'I'll see to THAT,' said the Egyptian in the dark. 'Hide your Amulet well.'

There in the deep blackness of that room in the Tyrian country house the Amulet was once more held up and the word spoken.

All passed through on to a ship that tossed and tumbled on a wind-blown sea. They crouched together there till morning, and Jane and Cyril were not at all well. When the dawn showed, dove-coloured, across the steely waves, they stood up as well as they could for the tumbling of the ship. Pheles, that hardy sailor and adventurer, turned quite pale when he turned round suddenly and saw them.

'Well!' he said, 'well, I never did!'

'Master,' said the Egyptian, bowing low, and that was even more difficult than standing up, 'we are here by the magic of the sacred Amulet that hangs round your neck.'

'I never did!' repeated Pheles. 'Well, well!'

'What port is the ship bound for?' asked Robert, with a nautical air.

But Pheles said, 'Are you a navigator?' Robert had to own that he was not.

'Then,' said Pheles, 'I don't mind telling you that we're bound for the Tin Isles. Tyre alone knows where the Tin Isles are. It is a splendid secret we keep from all the world. It is as great a thing to us as your magic to you.'

He spoke in quite a new voice, and seemed to respect both the children and the Amulet a good deal more than he had done before.

'The King sent you, didn't he?' said Jane.

'Yes,' answered Pheles, 'he bade me set sail with half a score brave gentlemen and this crew. You shall go with us, and see many wonders.' He bowed and left them.

'What are we going to do now?' said Robert, when Pheles had caused them to be left along with a breakfast of dried fruits and a sort of hard biscuit.

'Wait till he lands in the Tin Isles,' said Rekh-mara, 'then we can get the barbarians to help us. We will attack him by night and tear the sacred Amulet from his accursed heathen neck,' he added, grinding his teeth.

'When shall we get to the Tin Isles?' asked Jane.

'Oh—six months, perhaps, or a year,' said the Egyptian cheerfully.

'A year of THIS?' cried Jane, and Cyril, who was still feeling far too unwell to care about breakfast, hugged himself miserably and shuddered. It was Robert who said—

'Look here, we can shorten that year. Jane, out with the Amulet! Wish that we were where the Amulet will be when the ship is twenty miles from the Tin Island. That'll give us time to mature our plans.'

It was done—the work of a moment—and there they were on the same ship, between grey northern sky and grey northern sea. The sun was setting in a pale yellow line. It was the same ship, but it was changed, and so were the crew. Weather-worn and dirty were the sailors, and their clothes torn and ragged. And the children saw that, of course, though they had skipped the nine months, the ship had had to live through them. Pheles looked thinner, and his face was rugged and anxious.

'Ha!' he cried, 'the charm has brought you back! I have prayed to it daily these nine months—and now you are here? Have you no magic that can help?'

'What is your need?' asked the Egyptian quietly.

'I need a great wave that shall whelm away the foreign ship that follows us. A month ago it lay in wait for us, by the pillars of the gods, and it follows, follows, to find out the secret of Tyre—the place of the Tin Islands. If I could steer by night I could escape them yet, but tonight there will be no stars.'

'My magic will not serve you here,' said the Egyptian.

But Robert said, 'My magic will not bring up great waves, but I can show you how to steer without stars.'

He took out the shilling compass, still, fortunately, in working order, that he had bought off another boy at school for fivepence, a piece of indiarubber, a strip of whalebone, and half a stick of red sealing-wax.

And he showed Pheles how it worked. And Pheles wondered at the compass's magic truth.

'I will give it to you,' Robert said, 'in return for that charm about your neck.'

Pheles made no answer. He first laughed, snatched the compass from Robert's hand, and turned away still laughing.

'Be comforted,' the Priest whispered, 'our time will come.'

The dusk deepened, and Pheles, crouched beside a dim lantern, steered by the shilling compass from the Crystal Palace.

No one ever knew how the other ship sailed, but suddenly, in the deep night, the look-out man at the stern cried out in a terrible voice—

'She is close upon us!'

'And we,' said Pheles, 'are close to the harbour.' He was silent a moment, then suddenly he altered the ship's course, and then he stood up and spoke.

'Good friends and gentlemen,' he said, 'who are bound with me in this brave venture by our King's command, the false, foreign ship is close on our heels. If we land, they land, and only the gods know whether they might not beat us in fight, and themselves survive to carry back the tale of Tyre's secret island to enrich their own miserable land. Shall this be?'

'Never!' cried the half-dozen men near him. The slaves were rowing hard below and could not hear his words.

The Egyptian leaped upon him; suddenly, fiercely, as a wild beast leaps. 'Give me back my Amulet,' he cried, and caught at the charm. The chain that held it snapped, and it lay in the Priest's hand.

Pheles laughed, standing balanced to the leap of the ship that answered the oarstroke.

'This is no time for charms and mummeries,' he said. 'We've lived like men, and we'll die like gentlemen for the honour and glory of Tyre, our splendid city. "Tyre, Tyre for ever! It's Tyre that rules the waves." I steer her straight for the Dragon rocks, and we go down for our city, as brave men should. The creeping cowards who follow shall go down as slaves—and slaves they shall be to us—when we live again. Tyre, Tyre for ever!'

A great shout went up, and the slaves below joined in it.

'Quick, the Amulet,' cried Anthea, and held it up. Rekh-mara held up the one he had snatched from Pheles. The word was spoken, and the two great arches grew on the plunging ship in the shrieking wind under the dark sky. From each Amulet a great and beautiful green light streamed and shone far out over the waves. It illuminated, too, the black faces and jagged teeth of the great rocks that lay not two ships' lengths from the boat's peaked nose.

'Tyre, Tyre for ever! It's Tyre that rules the waves!' the voices of the doomed rose in a triumphant shout. The children scrambled through the arch, and stood trembling and blinking in the Fitzroy Street parlour, and in their ears still sounded the whistle of the wind, and the rattle of the oars, the crash of the ships bow on the rocks, and the last shout of the brave gentlemen-adventurers who went to their deaths singing, for the sake of the city they loved.

'And so we've lost the other half of the Amulet again,' said Anthea, when they had told the Psammead all about it.

'Nonsense, pooh!' said the Psammead. 'That wasn't the other half. It was the same half that you've got—the one that wasn't crushed and lost.'

'But how could it be the same?' said Anthea gently.

'Well, not exactly, of course. The one you've got is a good many years older, but at any rate it's not the other one. What did you say when you wished?'

'I forget,' said Jane.

'I don't,' said the Psammead. 'You said, "Take us where YOU are"—and it did, so you see it was the same half.'

'I see,' said Anthea.

'But you mark my words,' the Psammead went on, 'you'll have trouble with that Priest yet.'

'Why, he was quite friendly,' said Anthea.

'All the same you'd better beware of the Reverend Rekh-mara.'

'Oh, I'm sick of the Amulet,' said Cyril, 'we shall never get it.'

'Oh yes we shall,' said Robert. 'Don't you remember December 3rd?'

'Jinks!' said Cyril, 'I'd forgotten that.'

'I don't believe it,' said Jane, 'and I don't feel at all well.'

'If I were you,' said the Psammead, 'I should not go out into the Past again till that date. You'll find it safer not to go where you're likely to meet that Egyptian any more just at present.'

'Of course we'll do as you say,' said Anthea soothingly, 'though there's something about his face that I really do like.'

'Still, you don't want to run after him, I suppose,' snapped the Psammead. 'You wait till the 3rd, and then see what happens.'

Cyril and Jane were feeling far from well, Anthea was always obliging, so Robert was overruled. And they promised. And none of them, not even the Psammead, at all foresaw, as you no doubt do quite plainly, exactly what it was that WOULD happen on that memorable date.

Chapter 14. The Heart's Desire

If I only had time I could tell you lots of things. For instance, how, in spite of the advice of the Psammead, the four children did, one very wet day, go through their Amulet Arch into the golden desert, and there find the great Temple of Baalbec and meet with the Phoenix whom they never thought to see again. And how the Phoenix did not remember them at all until it went into a sort of prophetic trance—if that can be called remembering. But, alas! I HAVEN'T time, so I must leave all that out though it was a wonderfully thrilling adventure. I must leave out, too, all about the visit of the children to the Hippodrome with the Psammead in its travelling bag, and about how the wishes of the people round about them were granted so suddenly and surprisingly that at last the Psammead had to be taken hurriedly home by Anthea, who consequently missed half the performance. Then there was the time when, Nurse having gone to tea with a friend out Ivalunk way, they were playing 'devil in the dark'—and in the midst of that most creepy pastime the postman's knock frightened Jane nearly out of her life. She took in the letters, however, and put them in the back of the hat-stand drawer, so that they should be safe. And safe they were, for she never thought of them again for weeks and weeks.

One really good thing happened when they took the Psammead to a magic-lantern show and lecture at the boys' school at Camden Town. The lecture was all about our soldiers in South Africa. And the lecturer ended up by saying, 'And I hope every boy in this room has in his heart the seeds of courage and heroism and self-sacrifice, and I wish that every one of you may grow up to be noble and brave and unselfish, worthy citizens of this great Empire for whom our soldiers have freely given their lives.'

And, of course, this came true—which was a distinct score for Camden Town.

As Anthea said, it was unlucky that the lecturer said boys, because now she and Jane would have to be noble and unselfish, if at all, without any outside help. But Jane said, 'I daresay we are already because of our beautiful natures. It's only boys that have to be made brave by magic'—which nearly led to a first-class row.

And I daresay you would like to know all about the affair of the fishing rod, and the fish-hooks, and the cook next door—which was amusing from some points of view, though not perhaps the cook's—but there really is no time even for that.

The only thing that there's time to tell about is the Adventure of Maskelyne and Cooke's, and the Unexpected Apparition—which is also the beginning of the end.

It was Nurse who broke into the gloomy music of the autumn rain on the window panes by suggesting a visit to the Egyptian Hall, England's Home of Mystery. Though they had good, but private reasons to know that their own particular personal mystery was of a very different brand, the four all brightened at the idea. All children, as well as a good many grown-ups, love conjuring.

'It's in Piccadilly,' said old Nurse, carefully counting out the proper number of shillings into Cyril's hand, 'not so very far down on the left from the Circus. There's big pillars outside, something like Carter's seed place in Holborn, as used to be Day and Martin's blacking when I was a gell. And something like Euston Station, only not so big.'

'Yes, I know,' said everybody.

So they started.

But though they walked along the left-hand side of Piccadilly they saw no pillared building that was at all like Carter's seed warehouse or Euston Station or England's Home of Mystery as they remembered it.

At last they stopped a hurried lady, and asked her the way to Maskelyne and Cooke's.

'I don't know, I'm sure,' she said, pushing past them. 'I always shop at the Stores.' Which just shows, as Jane said, how ignorant grown-up people are.

It was a policeman who at last explained to them that England's Mysteries are now appropriately enough enacted at St George's Hall.

So they tramped to Langham Place, and missed the first two items in the programme. But they were in time for the most wonderful magic appearances and disappearances, which they could hardly believe—even with all their knowledge of a larger magic—was not really magic after all.

'If only the Babylonians could have seen THIS conjuring,' whispered Cyril. 'It takes the shine out of their old conjurer, doesn't it?'

'Hush!' said Anthea and several other members of the audience.

Now there was a vacant seat next to Robert. And it was when all eyes were fixed on the stage where Mr Devant was pouring out glasses of all sorts of different things to drink, out of one kettle with one spout, and the audience were delightedly tasting them, that Robert felt someone in that vacant seat. He did not feel someone sit down in it. It was just that one moment there was no one sitting there, and the next moment, suddenly, there was someone.

Robert turned. The someone who had suddenly filled that empty place was Rekh-mara, the Priest of Amen!

Though the eyes of the audience were fixed on Mr David Devant, Mr David Devant's eyes were fixed on the audience. And it happened that his eyes were more particularly fixed on that empty chair. So that he saw quite plainly the sudden appearance, from nowhere, of the Egyptian Priest.

'A jolly good trick,' he said to himself, 'and worked under my own eyes, in my own hall. I'll find out how that's done.' He had never seen a trick that he could not do himself if he tried.

By this time a good many eyes in the audience had turned on the clean-shaven, curiously-dressed figure of the Egyptian Priest.

'Ladies and gentlemen,' said Mr Devant, rising to the occasion, 'this is a trick I have never before performed. The empty seat, third from the end, second row, gallery—you will now find occupied by an Ancient Egyptian, warranted genuine.'

He little knew how true his words were.

And now all eyes were turned on the Priest and the children, and the whole audience, after a moment's breathless surprise, shouted applause. Only the lady on the other side of Rekh-mara drew back a little. She KNEW no one had passed her, and, as she said later, over tea and cold tongue, 'it was that sudden it made her flesh creep.'

Rekh-mara seemed very much annoyed at the notice he was exciting.

'Come out of this crowd,' he whispered to Robert. 'I must talk with you apart.'

'Oh, no,' Jane whispered. 'I did so want to see the Mascot Moth, and the Ventriloquist.'

'How did you get here?' was Robert's return whisper.

'How did you get to Egypt and to Tyre?' retorted Rekh-mara. 'Come, let us leave this crowd.'

'There's no help for it, I suppose,' Robert shrugged angrily. But they all got up.

'Confederates!' said a man in the row behind. 'Now they go round to the back and take part in the next scene.'

'I wish we did,' said Robert.

'Confederate yourself!' said Cyril. And so they got away, the audience applauding to the last.

In the vestibule of St George's Hall they disguised Rekh-mara as well as they could, but even with Robert's hat and Cyril's Inverness cape he was too striking a figure for foot-exercise in the London streets. It had to be a cab, and it took the last, least money of all of them. They stopped the cab a few doors from home, and then the girls went in and engaged old Nurse's attention by an account of the conjuring and a fervent entreaty for dripping-toast with their tea, leaving the front door open so that while Nurse was talking to them the boys could creep quietly in with Rekh-mara and smuggle him, unseen, up the stairs into their bedroom.

When the girls came up they found the Egyptian Priest sitting on the side of Cyril's bed, his hands on his knees, looking like a statue of a king.

'Come on,' said Cyril impatiently. 'He won't begin till we're all here. And shut the door, can't you?'

When the door was shut the Egyptian said—

'My interests and yours are one.'

'Very interesting,' said Cyril, 'and it'll be a jolly sight more interesting if you keep following us about in a decent country with no more clothes on than THAT!'

'Peace,' said the Priest. 'What is this country? and what is this time?'

'The country's England,' said Anthea, 'and the time's about 6,000 years later than YOUR time.'

'The Amulet, then,' said the Priest, deeply thoughtful, 'gives the power to move to and fro in time as well as in space?'

'That's about it,' said Cyril gruffly. 'Look here, it'll be tea-time directly. What are we to do with you?'

'You have one-half of the Amulet, I the other,' said Rekh-mara. 'All that is now needed is the pin to join them.'

'Don't you think it,' said Robert. 'The half you've got is the same half as the one we've got.'

'But the same thing cannot be in the same place and the same time, and yet be not one, but twain,' said the Priest. 'See, here is my half.' He laid it on the Marcella counterpane. 'Where is yours?'

Jane watching the eyes of the others, unfastened the string of the Amulet and laid it on the bed, but too far off for the Priest to seize it, even if he had been so dishonourable. Cyril and Robert stood beside him, ready to spring on him if one of his hands had moved but ever so little towards the magic treasure that was theirs. But his hands did not move, only his eyes opened very wide, and so did everyone else's for the Amulet the Priest had now quivered and shook; and then, as steel is drawn to the magnet, it was drawn across the white counterpane, nearer and nearer to the Amulet, warm from the neck of Jane. And then, as one drop of water mingles with another on a rain-wrinkled window-pane, as one bead of quick-silver is drawn into another bead, Rekh-mara's Amulet slipped into the other one, and, behold! there was no more but the one Amulet!

'Black magic!' cried Rekh-mara, and sprang forward to snatch the Amulet that had swallowed his. But Anthea caught it up, and at the same moment the Priest was jerked back by a rope thrown over his head. It drew, tightened with the pull of his forward leap, and bound his elbows to his sides. Before he had time to use his strength to free himself, Robert had knotted the cord behind him and tied it to the bedpost. Then the four children, overcoming the priest's wrigglings and kickings, tied his legs with more rope.

'I thought,' said Robert, breathing hard, and drawing the last knot tight, 'he'd have a try for OURS, so I got the ropes out of the box-room, so as to be ready.'

The girls, with rather white faces, applauded his foresight.

'Loosen these bonds!' cried Rekh-mara in fury, 'before I blast you with the seven secret curses of Amen-Ra!'

'We shouldn't be likely to loose them AFTER,' Robert retorted.

'Oh, don't quarrel!' said Anthea desperately. 'Look here, he has just as much right to the thing as we have. This,' she took up the Amulet that had swallowed the other one, 'this has got his in it as well as being ours. Let's go shares.'

'Let me go!' cried the Priest, writhing.

'Now, look here,' said Robert, 'if you make a row we can just open that window and call the police—the guards, you know—and tell them you've been trying to rob us. NOW will you shut up and listen to reason?'

'I suppose so,' said Rekh-mara sulkily.

But reason could not be spoken to him till a whispered counsel had been held in the far corner by the washhand-stand and the towel-horse, a counsel rather long and very earnest.

At last Anthea detached herself from the group, and went back to the Priest.

'Look here,' she said in her kind little voice, 'we want to be friends. We want to help you. Let's make a treaty. Let's join together to get the Amulet—the whole one, I mean. And then it shall belong to you as much as to us, and we shall all get our hearts' desire.'

'Fair words,' said the Priest, 'grow no onions.'

'WE say, "Butter no parsnips",' Jane put in. 'But don't you see we WANT to be fair? Only we want to bind you in the chains of honour and upright dealing.'

'Will you deal fairly by us?' said Robert.

'I will,' said the Priest. 'By the sacred, secret name that is written under the Altar of Amen-Ra, I will deal fairly by you. Will you, too, take the oath of honourable partnership?'

'No,' said Anthea, on the instant, and added rather rashly. 'We don't swear in England, except in police courts, where the guards are, you know, and you don't want to go there. But when we SAY we'll do a thing—it's the same as an oath to us—we do it. You trust us, and we'll trust you.' She began to unbind his legs, and the boys hastened to untie his arms.

When he was free he stood up, stretched his arms, and laughed.

'Now,' he said, 'I am stronger than you and my oath is void. I have sworn by nothing, and my oath is nothing likewise. For there IS no secret, sacred name under the altar of Amen-Ra.'

'Oh, yes there is!' said a voice from under the bed. Everyone started—Rekh-mara most of all.

Cyril stooped and pulled out the bath of sand where the Psammead slept. 'You don't know everything, though you ARE a Divine Father of the Temple of Amen,' said the Psammead shaking itself till the sand fell tinkling on the bath edge. 'There IS a secret, sacred name beneath the altar of Amen-Ra. Shall I call on that name?'

'No, no!' cried the Priest in terror.

'No,' said Jane, too. 'Don't let's have any calling names.'

'Besides,' said Rekh-mara, who had turned very white indeed under his natural brownness, 'I was only going to say that though there isn't any name under—'

'There IS,' said the Psammead threateningly.

'Well, even if there WASN'T, I will be bound by the wordless oath of your strangely upright land, and having said that I will be your friend—I will be it.'

'Then that's all right,' said the Psammead; 'and there's the tea-bell. What are you going to do with your distinguished partner? He can't go down to tea like that, you know.'

'You see we can't do anything till the 3rd of December,' said Anthea, 'that's when we are to find the whole charm. What can we do with Rekh-mara till then?'

'Box-room,' said Cyril briefly, 'and smuggle up his meals. It will be rather fun.'

'Like a fleeing Cavalier concealed from exasperated Roundheads,' said Robert. 'Yes.'

So Rekh-mara was taken up to the box-room and made as comfortable as possible in a snug nook between an old nursery fender and the wreck of a big four-poster. They gave him a big rag-bag to sit on, and an old, moth-eaten fur coat off the nail on the door to keep him warm. And when they had had their own tea they took him some. He did not like the tea at all, but he liked the bread and butter, and cake that went with it. They took it in turns to sit with him during the evening, and left him fairly happy and quite settled for the night.

But when they went up in the morning with a kipper, a quarter of which each of them had gone without at breakfast, Rekh-mara was gone! There was the cosy corner with the rag-bag, and the moth-eaten fur coat—but the cosy corner was empty.

'Good riddance!' was naturally the first delightful thought in each mind. The second was less pleasing, because everyone at once remembered that since his Amulet had been swallowed up by theirs—which hung once more round the neck of Jane—he could have no possible means of returning to his Egyptian past. Therefore he must be still in England, and probably somewhere quite near them, plotting mischief.

The attic was searched, to prevent mistakes, but quite vainly.

'The best thing we can do,' said Cyril, 'is to go through the half Amulet straight away, get the whole Amulet, and come back.'

'I don't know,' Anthea hesitated. 'Would that be quite fair? Perhaps he isn't really a base deceiver. Perhaps something's happened to him.'

'Happened?' said Cyril, 'not it! Besides, what COULD happen?'

'I don't know,' said Anthea. 'Perhaps burglars came in the night, and accidentally killed him, and took away the—all that was mortal of him, you know—to avoid discovery.'

'Or perhaps,' said Cyril, 'they hid the—all that was mortal, in one of those big trunks in the box-room. SHALL WE GO BACK AND LOOK?' he added grimly.

'No, no!' Jane shuddered. 'Let's go and tell the Psammead and see what it says.'

'No,' said Anthea, 'let's ask the learned gentleman. If anything has happened to Rekh-mara a gentleman's advice would be more useful than a Psammead's. And the learned gentleman'll only think it's a dream, like he always does.'

They tapped at the door, and on the 'Come in' entered. The learned gentleman was sitting in front of his untasted breakfast.

Opposite him, in the easy chair, sat Rekh-mara!

'Hush!' said the learned gentleman very earnestly, 'please, hush! or the dream will go. I am learning ... Oh, what have I not learned in the last hour!'

'In the grey dawn,' said the Priest, 'I left my hiding-place, and finding myself among these treasures from my own country, I remained. I feel more at home here somehow.'

'Of course I know it's a dream,' said the learned gentleman feverishly, 'but, oh, ye gods! what a dream! By jove! ...'

'Call not upon the gods,' said the Priest, 'lest ye raise greater ones than ye can control. Already,' he explained to the children, 'he and I are as brothers, and his welfare is dear to me as my own.'

'He has told me,' the learned gentleman began, but Robert interrupted. This was no moment for manners.

'Have you told him,' he asked the Priest, 'all about the Amulet?'

'No,' said Rekh-mara.

'Then tell him now. He is very learned. Perhaps he can tell us what to do.'

Rekh-mara hesitated, then told—and, oddly enough, none of the children ever could remember afterwards what it was that he did tell. Perhaps he used some magic to prevent their remembering.

When he had done the learned gentleman was silent, leaning his elbow on the table and his head on his hand.

'Dear Jimmy,' said Anthea gently, 'don't worry about it. We are sure to find it today, somehow.'

'Yes,' said Rekh-mara, 'and perhaps, with it, Death.'

'It's to bring us our hearts' desire,' said Robert.

'Who knows,' said the Priest, 'what things undreamed-of and infinitely desirable lie beyond the dark gates?'

'Oh, DON'T,' said Jane, almost whimpering.

The learned gentleman raised his head suddenly.

'Why not,' he suggested, 'go back into the Past? At a moment when the Amulet is unwatched. Wish to be with it, and that it shall be under your hand.'

It was the simplest thing in the world! And yet none of them had ever thought of it.

'Come,' cried Rekh-mara, leaping up. 'Come NOW!'

'May—may I come?' the learned gentleman timidly asked. 'It's only a dream, you know.'

'Come, and welcome, oh brother,' Rekh-mara was beginning, but Cyril and Robert with one voice cried, 'NO.'

'You weren't with us in Atlantis,' Robert added, 'or you'd know better than to let him come.'

'Dear Jimmy,' said Anthea, 'please don't ask to come. We'll go and be back again before you have time to know that we're gone.'

'And he, too?'

'We must keep together,' said Rekh-mara, 'since there is but one perfect Amulet to which I and these children have equal claims.'

Jane held up the Amulet—Rekh-mara went first—and they all passed through the great arch into which the Amulet grew at the Name of Power.

The learned gentleman saw through the arch a darkness lighted by smoky gleams. He rubbed his eyes. And he only rubbed them for ten seconds.

The children and the Priest were in a small, dark chamber. A square doorway of massive stone let in gleams of shifting light, and the sound of many voices chanting a slow, strange hymn. They stood listening. Now and then the chant quickened and the light grew brighter, as though fuel had been thrown on a fire.

'Where are we?' whispered Anthea.

'And when?' whispered Robert.

'This is some shrine near the beginnings of belief,' said the Egyptian shivering. 'Take the Amulet and come away. It is cold here in the morning of the world.'

And then Jane felt that her hand was on a slab or table of stone, and, under her hand, something that felt like the charm that had so long hung round her neck, only it was thicker. Twice as thick.

'It's HERE!' she said, 'I've got it!' And she hardly knew the sound of her own voice.

'Come away,' repeated Rekh-mara.

'I wish we could see more of this Temple,' said Robert resistingly.

'Come away,' the Priest urged, 'there is death all about, and strong magic. Listen.'

The chanting voices seemed to have grown louder and fiercer, and light stronger.

'They are coming!' cried Rekh-mara. 'Quick, quick, the Amulet!'

Jane held it up.

'What a long time you've been rubbing your eyes!' said Anthea; 'don't you see we've got back?' The learned gentleman merely stared at her.

'Miss Anthea—Miss Jane!' It was Nurse's voice, very much higher and squeaky and more exalted than usual.

'Oh, bother!' said everyone. Cyril adding, 'You just go on with the dream for a sec, Mr Jimmy, we'll be back directly. Nurse'll come up if we don't. SHE wouldn't think Rekh-mara was a dream.'

Then they went down. Nurse was in the hall, an orange envelope in one hand, and a pink paper in the other.

'Your Pa and Ma's come home. "Reach London 11.15. Prepare rooms as directed in letter", and signed in their two names.'

'Oh, hooray! hooray! hooray!' shouted the boys and Jane. But Anthea could not shout, she was nearer crying.

'Oh,' she said almost in a whisper, 'then it WAS true. And we HAVE got our hearts' desire.'

'But I don't understand about the letter,' Nurse was saying. 'I haven't HAD no letter.'

'OH!' said Jane in a queer voice, 'I wonder whether it was one of those ... they came that night—you know, when we were playing "devil in the dark"—and I put them in the hat-stand drawer, behind the clothes-brushes and'—she pulled out the drawer as she spoke—'and here they are!'

There was a letter for Nurse and one for the children. The letters told how Father had done being a war-correspondent and was coming home; and how Mother and The Lamb were going to meet him in Italy and all come home together; and how The Lamb and Mother were quite well; and how a telegram would be sent to tell the day and the hour of their home-coming.

'Mercy me!' said old Nurse. 'I declare if it's not too bad of You, Miss Jane. I shall have a nice to-do getting things straight for your Pa and Ma.'

'Oh, never mind, Nurse,' said Jane, hugging her; 'isn't it just too lovely for anything!'

'We'll come and help you,' said Cyril. 'There's just something upstairs we've got to settle up, and then we'll all come and help you.'

'Get along with you,' said old Nurse, but she laughed jollily. 'Nice help YOU'D be. I know you. And it's ten o'clock now.'

There was, in fact, something upstairs that they had to settle. Quite a considerable something, too. And it took much longer than they expected.

A hasty rush into the boys' room secured the Psammead, very sandy and very cross.

'It doesn't matter how cross and sandy it is though,' said Anthea, 'it ought to be there at the final council.'

'It'll give the learned gentleman fits, I expect,' said Robert, 'when he sees it.'

But it didn't.

'The dream is growing more and more wonderful,' he exclaimed, when the Psammead had been explained to him by Rekh-mara. 'I have dreamed this beast before.'

'Now,' said Robert, 'Jane has got the half Amulet and I've got the whole. Show up, Jane.'

Jane untied the string and laid her half Amulet on the table, littered with dusty papers, and the clay cylinders marked all over with little marks like the little prints of birds' little feet. Robert laid down the whole Amulet, and Anthea gently restrained the eager hand of the learned gentleman as it reached out yearningly towards the 'perfect specimen'.

And then, just as before on the Marcella quilt, so now on the dusty litter of papers and curiosities, the half Amulet quivered and shook, and then, as steel is drawn to a magnet, it was drawn across the dusty manuscripts, nearer and nearer to the perfect Amulet, warm from the pocket of Robert. And then, as one drop of water mingles with another when the panes of the window are wrinkled with rain, as one bead of mercury is drawn into another bead, the half Amulet, that was the children's and was also Rekh-mara's,—slipped into the whole Amulet, and, behold! there was only one—the perfect and ultimate Charm.

'And THAT'S all right,' said the Psammead, breaking a breathless silence.

'Yes,' said Anthea, 'and we've got our hearts' desire. Father and Mother and The Lamb are coming home today.'

'But what about me?' said Rekh-mara.

'What IS your heart's desire?' Anthea asked.

'Great and deep learning,' said the Priest, without a moment's hesitation. 'A learning greater and deeper than that of any man of my land and my time. But learning too great is useless. If I go back to my own land and my own age, who will believe my tales of what I have seen in the future? Let me stay here, be the great knower of all that has been, in that our time, so living to me, so old to you, about which your learned men speculate unceasingly, and often, HE tells me, vainly.'

'If I were you,' said the Psammead, 'I should ask the Amulet about that. It's a dangerous thing, trying to live in a time that's not your own. You can't breathe an air that's thousands of centuries ahead of your lungs without feeling the effects of it, sooner or later. Prepare the mystic circle and consult the Amulet.'

'Oh, WHAT a dream!' cried the learned gentleman. 'Dear children, if you love me—and I think you do, in dreams and out of them—prepare the mystic circle and consult the Amulet!'

They did. As once before, when the sun had shone in August splendour, they crouched in a circle on the floor. Now the air outside was thick and yellow with the fog that by some strange decree always attends the Cattle Show week. And in the street costers were shouting. 'Ur Hekau Setcheh,' Jane said the Name of Power. And instantly the light went out, and all the sounds went out too, so that there was a silence and a darkness, both deeper than any darkness or silence that you have ever even dreamed of imagining. It was like being deaf or blind, only darker and quieter even than that.

Then out of that vast darkness and silence came a light and a voice. The light was too faint to see anything by, and the voice was too small for you to hear what it said. But the light and the voice grew. And the light was the light that no man may look on and live, and the voice was the sweetest and most terrible voice in the world. The children cast down their eyes. And so did everyone.

'I speak,' said the voice. 'What is it that you would hear?'

There was a pause. Everyone was afraid to speak.

'What are we to do about Rekh-mara?' said Robert suddenly and abruptly. 'Shall he go back through the Amulet to his own time, or—'

'No one can pass through the Amulet now,' said the beautiful, terrible voice, 'to any land or any time. Only when it was imperfect could such things be. But men may pass through the perfect charm to the perfect union, which is not of time or space.'

'Would you be so very kind,' said Anthea tremulously, 'as to speak so that we can understand you? The Psammead said something about Rekh-mara not being able to live here, and if he can't get back—' She stopped, her heart was beating desperately in her throat, as it seemed.

'Nobody can continue to live in a land and in a time not appointed,' said the voice of glorious sweetness. 'But a soul may live, if in that other time and land there be found a soul so akin to it as to offer it refuge, in the body of that land and time, that thus they two may be one soul in one body.'

The children exchanged discouraged glances. But the eyes of Rekh-mara and the learned gentleman met, and were kind to each other, and promised each other many things, secret and sacred and very beautiful.

Anthea saw the look. 'Oh, but,' she said, without at all meaning to say it, 'dear Jimmy's soul isn't at all like Rekh-mara's. I'm certain it isn't. I don't want to be rude, but it ISN'T, you know. Dear Jimmy's soul is as good as gold, and—'

'Nothing that is not good can pass beneath the double arch of my perfect Amulet,' said the voice. 'If both are willing, say the word of Power, and let the two souls become one for ever and ever more.'

'Shall I?' asked Jane.

'Yes.'

'Yes.'

The voices were those of the Egyptian Priest and the learned gentleman, and the voices were eager, alive, thrilled with hope and the desire of great things.

So Jane took the Amulet from Robert and held it up between the two men, and said, for the last time, the word of Power.

'Ur Hekau Setcheh.'

The perfect Amulet grew into a double arch; the two arches leaned to each other making a great A.

'A stands for Amen,' whispered Jane; 'what he was a priest of.'

'Hush!' breathed Anthea.

The great double arch glowed in and through the green light that had been there since the Name of Power had first been spoken—it glowed with a light more bright yet more soft than the other light—a glory and splendour and sweetness unspeakable. 'Come!' cried Rekh-mara, holding out his hands.

'Come!' cried the learned gentleman, and he also held out his hands.

Each moved forward under the glowing, glorious arch of the perfect Amulet.

Then Rekh-mara quavered and shook, and as steel is drawn to a magnet he was drawn, under the arch of magic, nearer and nearer to the learned gentleman. And, as one drop of water mingles with another, when the window-glass is rain-wrinkled, as one quick-silver bead is drawn to another quick-silver bead, Rekh-mara, Divine Father of the Temple of Amen-Ra, was drawn into, slipped into, disappeared into, and was one with Jimmy, the good, the beloved, the learned gentleman.

And suddenly it was good daylight and the December sun shone. The fog has passed away like a dream.

The Amulet was there—little and complete in jane's hand, and there were the other children and the Psammead, and the learned gentleman. But Rekh-mara—or the body of Rekh-mara—was not there any more. As for his soul ...

'Oh, the horrid thing!' cried Robert, and put his foot on a centipede as long as your finger, that crawled and wriggled and squirmed at the learned gentleman's feet.

'THAT,' said the Psammead, 'WAS the evil in the soul of Rekh-mara.'

There was a deep silence.

'Then Rekh-mara's HIM now?' said Jane at last.

'All that was good in Rekh-mara,' said the Psammead.

'HE ought to have his heart's desire, too,' said Anthea, in a sort of stubborn gentleness.

'HIS heart's desire,' said the Psammead, 'is the perfect Amulet you hold in your hand. Yes—and has been ever since he first saw the broken half of it.'

'We've got ours,' said Anthea softly.

'Yes,' said the Psammead—its voice was crosser than they had ever heard it—'your parents are coming home. And what's to become of ME? I shall be found out, and made a show of, and degraded in every possible way. I KNOW they'll make me go into Parliament—hateful place—all mud and no sand. That beautiful Baalbec temple in the desert! Plenty of good sand there, and no politics! I wish I were there, safe in the Past—that I do.'

'I wish you were,' said the learned gentleman absently, yet polite as ever.

The Psammead swelled itself up, turned its long snail's eyes in one last lingering look at Anthea—a loving look, she always said, and thought—and—vanished.

'Well,' said Anthea, after a silence, 'I suppose it's happy. The only thing it ever did really care for was SAND.'

'My dear children,' said the learned gentleman, 'I must have fallen asleep. I've had the most extraordinary dream.'

'I hope it was a nice one,' said Cyril with courtesy.

'Yes.... I feel a new man after it. Absolutely a new man.'

There was a ring at the front-door bell. The opening of a door. Voices.

'It's THEM!' cried Robert, and a thrill ran through four hearts.

'Here!' cried Anthea, snatching the Amulet from Jane and pressing it into the hand of the learned gentleman. 'Here—it's yours—your very own—a present from us, because you're Rekhmara as well as ... I mean, because you're such a dear.'

She hugged him briefly but fervently, and the four swept down the stairs to the hall, where a cabman was bringing in boxes, and where, heavily disguised in travelling cloaks and wraps, was their hearts' desire—three-fold—Mother, Father, and The Lamb.

'Bless me!' said the learned gentleman, left alone, 'bless me! What a treasure! The dear children! It must be their affection that has given me these luminous apercus. I seem to see so many things now—things I never saw before! The dear children! The dear, dear children!'

The Story of the Treasure Seekers

Being the adventures of the Bastable children in search of a fortune

To Oswald Barron Without whom this book could never have been written

The Treasure Seekers is dedicated in memory of childhoods identical but for the accidents of time and space

Chapter 1. The Council of Ways and Means

This is the story of the different ways we looked for treasure, and I think when you have read it you will see that we were not lazy about the looking.

There are some things I must tell before I begin to tell about the treasure-seeking, because I have read books myself, and I know how beastly it is when a story begins, "'Alas!" said Hildegarde with a deep sigh, "we must look our last on this ancestral home"'—and then some one else says something—and you don't know for pages and pages where the home is, or who Hildegarde is, or anything about it. Our ancestral home is in the Lewisham Road. It is semi-detached and has a garden, not a large one. We are the Bastables. There are six of us besides Father. Our Mother is dead, and if you think we don't care because I don't tell you much about her you only show that you do not understand people at all. Dora is the eldest. Then Oswald—and then Dicky. Oswald won the Latin prize at his preparatory school—and Dicky is good at sums. Alice and Noel are twins: they are ten, and Horace Octavius is my youngest brother. It is one of us that tells this story—but I shall not tell you which: only at the very end perhaps I will. While the story is going on you may be trying to guess, only I bet you don't. It was Oswald who first thought of looking for treasure. Oswald often thinks of very interesting things. And directly he thought of it he did not keep it to himself, as some boys would have done, but he told the others, and said—

'I'll tell you what, we must go and seek for treasure: it is always what you do to restore the fallen fortunes of your House.'

Dora said it was all very well. She often says that. She was trying to mend a large hole in one of Noel's stockings. He tore it on a nail when we were playing shipwrecked mariners on top of the chicken-house the day H. O. fell off and cut his chin: he has the scar still. Dora is the only one of us who ever tries to mend anything. Alice tries to make things sometimes. Once she knitted a red scarf for Noel because his chest is delicate, but it was much wider at one end than the other, and he wouldn't wear it. So we used it as a pennon, and it did very well, because most of our things are black or grey since Mother died; and scarlet was a nice change. Father does not like you to ask for new things. That was one way we had of knowing that the fortunes of the ancient House of Bastable were really fallen. Another way was that there was no more pocket-money—except a penny now and then to the little ones, and people did not come to dinner any more, like they used to, with pretty dresses, driving up in cabs—and the carpets got holes in them—and when the legs came off things they were not sent to be mended, and we gave *up* having the gardener except for the front garden, and not that very often. And the silver in the big oak plate-chest that is lined with green baize all went away to the shop to have the dents and scratches taken out of it, and it never came back. We think Father hadn't enough money to pay the silver man for taking out the dents and scratches. The new spoons and forks were yellowy-white, and not so heavy as the old ones, and they never shone after the first day or two.

Father was very ill after Mother died; and while he was ill his business-partner went to Spain—and there was never much money afterwards. I don't know why. Then the servants left and there was only one, a General. A great deal of your comfort and happiness depends on having a good General. The last but one was nice: she used to make jolly good currant puddings for us, and let us have the dish on the floor and pretend it was a wild boar we were killing with our forks. But the General we have now nearly always makes sago puddings, and they are the watery kind, and you cannot pretend anything with them, not even islands, like you do with porridge.

Then we left off going to school, and Father said we should go to a good school as soon as he could manage it. He said a holiday would do us all good. We thought he was right, but we wished he had told us he couldn't afford it. For of course we knew.

Then a great many people used to come to the door with envelopes with no stamps on them, and sometimes they got very angry, and said they were calling for the last time before putting it in other hands. I asked Eliza what that meant, and she kindly explained to me, and I was so sorry for Father.

And once a long, blue paper came; a policeman brought it, and we were so frightened. But Father said it was all right, only when he went up to kiss the girls after they were in bed they said he had been crying, though I'm sure that's not true. Because only cowards and snivellers cry, and my Father is the bravest man in the world.

So you see it was time we looked for treasure and Oswald said so, and Dora said it was all very well. But the others agreed with Oswald. So we held a council. Dora was in the chair—the big dining-room chair, that we let the fireworks off from, the Fifth of November when we had the measles and couldn't do it in the garden. The hole has never been mended, so now we have that chair in the nursery, and I think it was cheap at the blowing-up we boys got when the hole was burnt.

'We must do something,' said Alice, 'because the exchequer is empty.' She rattled the money-box as she spoke, and it really did rattle because we always keep the bad sixpence in it for luck.

'Yes—but what shall we do?' said Dicky. 'It's so jolly easy to say let's do *something*.' Dicky always wants everything settled exactly. Father calls him the Definite Article.

'Let's read all the books again. We shall get lots of ideas out of them.' It was Noel who suggested this, but we made him shut up, because we knew well enough he only wanted to get back to his old books. Noel is a poet. He sold some of his poetry once—and it was printed, but that does not come in this part of the story.

Then Dicky said, 'Look here. We'll be quite quiet for ten minutes by the clock—and each think of some way to find treasure. And when we've thought we'll try all the ways one after the other, beginning with the eldest.'

'I shan't be able to think in ten minutes, make it half an hour,' said H. O. His real name is Horace Octavius, but we call him H. O. because of the advertisement, and it's not so very long ago he was afraid to pass the hoarding where it says 'Eat H. O.' in big letters. He says it was when he was a little boy, but I remember last Christmas but one, he woke in the middle of the night crying and howling, and they said it was the pudding. But he told me afterwards he had been dreaming that they really *had* come to eat H. O., and it couldn't have been the pudding, when you come to think of it, because it was so very plain.

Well, we made it half an hour—and we all sat quiet, and thought and thought. And I made up my mind before two minutes were over, and I saw the others had, all but Dora, who is always an awful time over everything. I got pins and needles in my leg from sitting still so long, and when it was seven minutes H. O. cried out—'Oh, it must be more than half an hour!'

H. O. is eight years old, but he cannot tell the clock yet. Oswald could tell the clock when he was six.

We all stretched ourselves and began to speak at once, but Dora put up her hands to her ears and said—

'One at a time, please. We aren't playing Babel.' (It is a very good game. Did you ever play it?)

So Dora made us all sit in a row on the floor, in ages, and then she pointed at us with the finger that had the brass thimble on. Her silver one got lost when the last General but two went away. We think she must have forgotten it was Dora's and put it in her box by mistake. She was a very forgetful girl. She used to forget what she had spent money on, so that the change was never quite right.

Oswald spoke first. 'I think we might stop people on Blackheath—with crape masks and horse-pistols—and say "Your money or your life! Resistance is useless, we are armed to the teeth"—like Dick Turpin and Claude Duval. It wouldn't matter about not having horses, because coaches have gone out too.'

Dora screwed up her nose the way she always does when she is going to talk like the good elder sister in books, and said, 'That would be very wrong: it's like pickpocketing or taking pennies out of Father's great- coat when it's hanging in the hall.'

I must say I don't think she need have said that, especially before the little ones—for it was when I was only four.

But Oswald was not going to let her see he cared, so he said—

'Oh, very well. I can think of lots of other ways. We could rescue an old gentleman from deadly Highwaymen.'

'There aren't any,' said Dora.

'Oh, well, it's all the same—from deadly peril, then. There's plenty of that. Then he would turn out to be the Prince of Wales, and he would say, "My noble, my cherished preserver! Here is a million pounds a year. Rise up, Sir Oswald Bastable."'

But the others did not seem to think so, and it was Alice's turn to say.

She said, 'I think we might try the divining-rod. I'm sure I could do it. I've often read about it. You hold a stick in your hands, and when you come to where there is gold underneath the stick kicks about. So you know. And you dig.'

'Oh,' said Dora suddenly, 'I have an idea. But I'll say last. I hope the divining-rod isn't wrong. I believe it's wrong in the Bible.'

'So is eating pork and ducks,' said Dicky. 'You can't go by that.'

'Anyhow, we'll try the other ways first,' said Dora. 'Now, H. O.'

'Let's be Bandits,' said H. O. 'I dare say it's wrong but it would be fun pretending.'

'I'm sure it's wrong,' said Dora.

And Dicky said she thought everything wrong. She said she didn't, and Dicky was very disagreeable. So Oswald had to make peace, and he said—

'Dora needn't play if she doesn't want to. Nobody asked her. And, Dicky, don't be an idiot: do dry up and let's hear what Noel's idea is.'

Dora and Dicky did not look pleased, but I kicked Noel under the table to make him hurry up, and then he said he didn't think he wanted to play any more. That's the worst of it. The others are so jolly ready to quarrel. I told Noel to be a man and not a snivelling pig, and at last he said he had not made up his mind whether he would print his poetry in a book and sell it, or find a princess and marry her.

'Whichever it is,' he added, 'none of you shall want for anything, though Oswald did kick me, and say I was a snivelling pig.'

'I didn't,' said Oswald, 'I told you not to be.' And Alice explained to him that that was quite the opposite of what he thought. So he agreed to drop it.

Then Dicky spoke.

'You must all of you have noticed the advertisements in the papers, telling you that ladies and gentlemen can easily earn two pounds a week in their spare time, and to send two shillings for sample and instructions, carefully packed free from observation. Now that we don't go to school all our time is spare time. So I should think we could easily earn twenty pounds a week each. That would do us very well. We'll try some of the other things first, and directly we have any money we'll send for the sample and instructions. And I have another idea, but I must think about it before I say.'

We all said, 'Out with it—what's the other idea?'

But Dicky said, 'No.' That is Dicky all over. He never will show you anything he's making till it's quite finished, and the same with his inmost thoughts. But he is pleased if you seem to want to know, so Oswald said—

'Keep your silly old secret, then. Now, Dora, drive ahead. We've all said except you.'

Then Dora jumped up and dropped the stocking and the thimble (it rolled away, and we did not find it for days), and said—

'Let's try my way *now*. Besides, I'm the eldest, so it's only fair. Let's dig for treasure. Not any tiresome divining-rod—but just plain digging. People who dig for treasure always find it. And then we shall be rich and we needn't try your ways at all. Some of them are rather difficult: and I'm certain some of them are wrong—and we must always remember that wrong things—'

But we told her to shut up and come on, and she did.

I couldn't help wondering as we went down to the garden, why Father had never thought of digging there for treasure instead of going to his beastly office every day.

Chapter 2. Digging for Treasure

I am afraid the last chapter was rather dull. It is always dull in books when people talk and talk, and don't do anything, but I was obliged to put it in, or else you wouldn't have understood all the rest. The best part of books is when things are happening. That is the best part of real things too. This is why I shall not tell you in this story about all the days when nothing happened. You will not catch me saying, 'thus the sad days passed slowly by'—or 'the years rolled on their weary course'—or 'time went on'—because it is silly; of course time goes on—whether you say so or not. So I shall just tell you the nice, interesting parts—and in between you will understand that we had our meals and got up and went to bed, and dull things like that. It would be sickening to write all that down, though of course it happens. I said so to Albert-next-door's uncle, who writes books, and he said, 'Quite right, that's what we call selection, a necessity of true art.' And he is very clever indeed. So you see.

I have often thought that if the people who write books for children knew a little more it would be better. I shall not tell you anything about us except what I should like to know about if I was reading the story and you were writing it. Albert's uncle says I ought to have put this in the preface, but I never read prefaces, and it is not much good writing things just for people to skip. I wonder other authors have never thought of this.

Well, when we had agreed to dig for treasure we all went down into the cellar and lighted the gas. Oswald would have liked to dig there, but it is stone flags. We looked among the old boxes and broken chairs and fenders and empty bottles and things, and at last we found the spades we had to dig in the sand with when we went to the seaside three years ago. They are not silly, babyish, wooden spades, that split if you look at them, but good iron, with a blue mark across the top of the iron part, and yellow wooden handles. We wasted a little time getting them dusted, because the girls wouldn't dig with spades that had cobwebs on them. Girls would never do for African explorers or anything like that, they are too beastly particular.

It was no use doing the thing by halves. We marked out a sort of square in the mouldy part of the garden, about three yards across, and began to dig. But we found nothing except worms and stones—and the ground was very hard.

So we thought we'd try another part of the garden, and we found a place in the big round flower bed, where the ground was much softer. We thought we'd make a smaller hole to begin with, and it was much better. We dug and dug and dug, and it was jolly hard work! We got very hot digging, but we found nothing.

Presently Albert-next-door looked over the wall. We do not like him very much, but we let him play with us sometimes, because his father is dead, and you must not be unkind to orphans, even if their mothers are alive. Albert is always very tidy. He wears frilly collars and velvet knickerbockers. I can't think how he can bear to.

So we said, 'Hallo!'

And he said, 'What are you up to?'

'We're digging for treasure,' said Alice; 'an ancient parchment revealed to us the place of concealment. Come over and help us. When we have dug deep enough we shall find a great pot of red clay, full of gold and precious jewels.'

Albert-next-door only sniggered and said, 'What silly nonsense!' He cannot play properly at all. It is very strange, because he has a very nice uncle. You see, Albert-next-door doesn't care for reading, and he has not read nearly so many books as we have, so he is very foolish and ignorant, but it cannot be helped, and you just have to put up with it when you want him to do anything. Besides, it is wrong to be angry with people for not being so clever as you are yourself. It is not always their faults.

So Oswald said, 'Come and dig! Then you shall share the treasure when we've found it.'

But he said, 'I shan't—I don't like digging—and I'm just going in to my tea.'

'Come along and dig, there's a good boy,' Alice said. 'You can use my spade. It's much the best—'

So he came along and dug, and when once he was over the wall we kept him at it, and we worked as well, of course, and the hole got deep. Pincher worked too—he is our dog and he is very good at digging. He digs for rats in the dustbin sometimes, and gets very dirty. But we love our dog, even when his face wants washing.

'I expect we shall have to make a tunnel,' Oswald said, 'to reach the rich treasure.' So he jumped into the hole and began to dig at one side. After that we took it in turns to dig at the tunnel, and Pincher was most useful in scraping the earth out of the tunnel—he does it with his back feet when you say 'Rats!' and he digs with his front ones, and burrows with his nose as well.

At last the tunnel was nearly a yard long, and big enough to creep along to find the treasure, if only it had been a bit longer. Now it was Albert's turn to go in and dig, but he funked it.

'Take your turn like a man,' said Oswald—nobody can say that Oswald doesn't take his turn like a man. But Albert wouldn't. So we had to make him, because it was only fair.

'It's quite easy,' Alice said. 'You just crawl in and dig with your hands. Then when you come out we can scrape out what you've done, with the spades. Come—be a man. You won't notice it being dark in the tunnel if you shut your eyes tight. We've all been in except Dora—and she doesn't like worms.'

'I don't like worms neither.' Albert-next-door said this; but we remembered how he had picked a fat red and black worm up in his fingers and thrown it at Dora only the day before. So we put him in.

But he would not go in head first, the proper way, and dig with his hands as we had done, and though Oswald was angry at the time, for he hates snivellers, yet afterwards he owned that perhaps it was just as well. You should never be afraid to own that perhaps you were mistaken—but it is cowardly to do it unless you are quite sure you are in the wrong.

'Let me go in feet first,' said Albert-next-door. 'I'll dig with my boots—I will truly, honour bright.'

So we let him get in feet first—and he did it very slowly and at last he was in, and only his head sticking out into the hole; and all the rest of him in the tunnel.

'Now dig with your boots,' said Oswald; 'and, Alice, do catch hold of Pincher, he'll be digging again in another minute, and perhaps it would be uncomfortable for Albert if Pincher threw the mould into his eyes.'

You should always try to think of these little things. Thinking of other people's comfort makes them like you. Alice held Pincher, and we all shouted, 'Kick! dig with your feet, for all you're worth!'

So Albert-next-door began to dig with his feet, and we stood on the ground over him, waiting—and all in a minute the ground gave way, and we tumbled together in a heap: and when we got up there was a little shallow hollow where we had been standing, and Albert-next-door was underneath, stuck quite fast, because the roof of the tunnel had tumbled in on him. He is a horribly unlucky boy to have anything to do with.

It was dreadful the way he cried and screamed, though he had to own it didn't hurt, only it was rather heavy and he couldn't move his legs. We would have dug him out all right enough, in time, but he screamed so we were afraid the police would come, so Dicky climbed over the wall, to tell the cook there to tell Albert-next-door's uncle he had been buried by mistake, and to come and help dig him out.

Dicky was a long time gone. We wondered what had become of him, and all the while the screaming went on and on, for we had taken the loose earth off Albert's face so that he could scream quite easily and comfortably.

Presently Dicky came back and Albert-next-door's uncle came with him. He has very long legs, and his hair is light and his face is brown. He has been to sea, but now he writes books. I like him.

He told his nephew to stow it, so Albert did, and then he asked him if he was hurt—and Albert had to say he wasn't, for though he is a coward, and very unlucky, he is not a liar like some boys are.

'This promises to be a protracted if agreeable task,' said Albert-next- door's uncle, rubbing his hands and looking at the hole with Albert's head in it. 'I will get another spade,' so he fetched the big spade out of the next-door garden tool-shed, and began to dig his nephew out.

'Mind you keep very still,' he said, 'or I might chunk a bit out of you with the spade.' Then after a while he said—

'I confess that I am not absolutely insensible to the dramatic interest of the situation. My curiosity is excited. I own that I should like to know how my nephew happened to be buried. But don't tell me if you'd rather not. I suppose no force was used?'

'Only moral force,' said Alice. They used to talk a lot about moral force at the High School where she went, and in case you don't know what it means I'll tell you that it is making people do what they don't want to, just by slanging them, or laughing at them, or promising them things if they're good.

'Only moral force, eh?' said Albert-next-door's uncle. 'Well?'

'Well,' Dora said, 'I'm very sorry it happened to Albert—I'd rather it had been one of us. It would have been my turn to go into the tunnel, only I don't like worms, so they let me off. You see we were digging for treasure.'

'Yes,' said Alice, 'and I think we were just coming to the underground passage that leads to the secret hoard, when the tunnel fell in on Albert. He *is* so unlucky,' and she sighed.

Then Albert-next-door began to scream again, and his uncle wiped his face—his own face, not Albert's—with his silk handkerchief, and then he put it in his trousers pocket. It seems a strange place to put a handkerchief, but he had his coat and waistcoat off and I suppose he wanted the handkerchief handy. Digging is warm work.

He told Albert-next-door to drop it, or he wouldn't proceed further in the matter, so Albert stopped screaming, and presently his uncle finished digging him out. Albert did look so funny, with his hair all dusty and his velvet suit covered with mould and his face muddy with earth and crying.

We all said how sorry we were, but he wouldn't say a word back to us. He was most awfully sick to think he'd been the one buried, when it might just as well have been one of us. I felt myself that it was hard lines.

'So you were digging for treasure,' said Albert-next-door's uncle, wiping his face again with his handkerchief. 'Well, I fear that your chances of success are small. I have made a careful study of the whole subject. What I don't know about buried treasure is not worth knowing. And I never knew more than one coin buried in any one garden—and that is generally—Hullo—what's that?'

He pointed to something shining in the hole he had just dragged Albert out of. Oswald picked it up. It was a half-crown. We looked at each other, speechless with surprise and delight, like in books.

'Well, that's lucky, at all events,' said Albert-next-door's uncle.

'Let's see, that's fivepence each for you.'

'It's fourpence—something; I can't do fractions,' said Dicky; 'there are seven of us, you see.'

'Oh, you count Albert as one of yourselves on this occasion, eh?'

'Of course,' said Alice; 'and I say, he was buried after all. Why shouldn't we let him have the odd somethings, and we'll have fourpence each.'

We all agreed to do this, and told Albert-next-door we would bring his share as soon as we could get the half-crown changed. He cheered up a little at that, and his uncle wiped his face again—he did look hot—and began to put on his coat and waistcoat.

When he had done it he stooped and picked up something. He held it up, and you will hardly believe it, but it is quite true—it was another half-crown!

'To think that there should be two!' he said; 'in all my experience of buried treasure I never heard of such a thing!'

I wish Albert-next-door's uncle would come treasure-seeking with us regularly; he must have very sharp eyes: for Dora says she was looking just the minute before at the very place where the second half-crown was picked up from, and *she* never saw it.

Chapter 3. Being Detectives

The next thing that happened to us was very interesting. It was as real as the half-crowns—not just pretending. I shall try to write it as like a real book as I can. Of course we have read Mr Sherlock Holmes, as well as the yellow-covered books with pictures outside that are so badly printed; and you get them for fourpence-halfpenny at the bookstall when the corners of them are beginning to curl up and get dirty, with people looking to see how the story ends when they are waiting for trains. I think this is most unfair to the boy at the bookstall. The books are written by a gentleman named Gaboriau, and Albert's uncle says they are the worst translations in the world—and written in vile English. Of course they're not like Kipling, but they're jolly good stories. And we had just been reading a book by Dick Diddlington—that's not his right name, but I know all about libel actions, so I shall not say what his name is really, because his books are rot. Only they put it into our heads to do what I am going to narrate.

It was in September, and we were not to go to the seaside because it is so expensive, even if you go to Sheerness, where it is all tin cans and old boots and no sand at all. But every one else went, even the people next door—not Albert's side, but the other. Their servant told Eliza they were all going to Scarborough, and next day sure enough all the blinds were down and the shutters up, and the milk was not left any more. There is a big horse-chestnut tree between their garden and ours, very useful for getting conkers out of and for making stuff to rub on your chilblains. This prevented our seeing whether the blinds were down at the back as well, but Dicky climbed to the top of the tree and looked, and they were.

It was jolly hot weather, and very stuffy indoors—we used to play a good deal in the garden. We made a tent out of the kitchen clothes- horse and some blankets off our beds, and though it was quite as hot in the tent as in the house it was a very different sort of hotness. Albert's uncle called it the Turkish Bath. It is not nice to be kept from the seaside, but we know that we have much to be thankful for. We might be poor little children living in a crowded alley where even at summer noon hardly a ray of sunlight penetrates; clothed in rags and with bare feet—though I do not mind holes in my clothes myself, and bare feet would not be at all bad in this sort of weather. Indeed we do, sometimes, when we are playing at things which require it. It was shipwrecked mariners that day, I remember, and we were all in the blanket tent. We had just finished eating the things we had saved, at the peril of our lives, from the st-sinking vessel. They were rather nice things. Two-pennyworth of coconut candy—it was got in Greenwich, where it is four ounces a penny—three apples, some macaroni—the straight sort that is so useful to suck things through—some raw rice, and a large piece of cold suet pudding that Alice nicked from the larder when she went to get the rice and macaroni. And when we had finished some one said—

'I should like to be a detective.'

I wish to be quite fair, but I cannot remember exactly who said it. Oswald thinks he said it, and Dora says it was Dicky, but Oswald is too much of a man to quarrel about a little thing like that.

'I should like to be a detective,' said—perhaps it was Dicky, but I think not—'and find out strange and hidden crimes.'

'You have to be much cleverer than you are,' said H. O.

'Not so very,' Alice said, 'because when you've read the books you know what the things mean: the red hair on the handle of the knife, or the grains of white powder on the velvet collar of the villain's overcoat. I believe we could do it.'

'I shouldn't like to have anything to do with murders,' said Dora; 'somehow it doesn't seem safe—'

'And it always ends in the poor murderer being hanged,' said Alice.

We explained to her why murderers have to be hanged, but she only said, 'I don't care. I'm sure no one would ever do murdering *twice*. Think of the blood and things, and what you would see when you woke up in the night! I shouldn't mind being a detective to lie in wait for a gang of coiners, now, and spring upon them unawares, and secure them—single- handed, you know, or with only my faithful bloodhound.'

She stroked Pincher's ears, but he had gone to sleep because he knew well enough that all the suet pudding was finished. He is a very sensible dog. 'You always get hold of the wrong end of the stick,' Oswald said. 'You can't choose what crimes you'll be a detective about. You just have to get a suspicious circumstance, and then you look for a clue and follow it up. Whether it turns out a murder or a missing will is just a fluke.'

'That's one way,' Dicky said. 'Another is to get a paper and find two advertisements or bits of news that fit. Like this: "Young Lady Missing," and then it tells about all the clothes she had on, and the gold locket she wore, and the colour of her hair, and all that; and then in another piece of the paper you see, "Gold locket found," and then it all comes out.'

We sent H. O. for the paper at once, but we could not make any of the things fit in. The two best were about how some burglars broke into a place in Holloway where they made preserved tongues and invalid delicacies, and carried off a lot of them. And on another page there was, 'Mysterious deaths in Holloway.'

Oswald thought there was something in it, and so did Albert's uncle when we asked him, but the others thought not, so Oswald agreed to drop it. Besides, Holloway is a long way off. All the time we were talking about the paper Alice seemed to be thinking about something else, and when we had done she said—

'I believe we might be detectives ourselves, but I should not like to get anybody into trouble.'

'Not murderers or robbers?' Dicky asked.

'It wouldn't be murderers,' she said; 'but I *have* noticed something strange. Only I feel a little frightened. Let's ask Albert's uncle first.'

Alice is a jolly sight too fond of asking grown-up people things. And we all said it was tommyrot, and she was to tell us.

'Well, promise you won't do anything without me,' Alice said, and we promised. Then she said—

'This is a dark secret, and any one who thinks it is better not to be involved in a career of crime-discovery had better go away ere yet it be too late.'

So Dora said she had had enough of tents, and she was going to look at the shops. H. O. went with her because he had twopence to spend. They thought it was only a game of Alice's but Oswald knew by the way she spoke. He can nearly always tell. And when people are not telling the truth Oswald generally knows by the way they look with their eyes. Oswald is not proud of being able to do this. He knows it is through no merit of his own that he is much cleverer than some people.

When they had gone, the rest of us got closer together and said—

'Now then.'

'Well,' Alice said, 'you know the house next door? The people have gone to Scarborough. And the house is shut up. But last night *I saw a light in the windows*.'

We asked her how and when, because her room is in the front, and she couldn't possibly have seen. And then she said—

'I'll tell you if you boys will promise not ever to go fishing again without me.'

So we had to promise.

Then she said—

'It was last night. I had forgotten to feed my rabbits and I woke up and remembered it. And I was afraid I should find them dead in the morning, like Oswald did.'

'It wasn't my fault,' Oswald said; 'there was something the matter with the beasts. I fed them right enough.'

Alice said she didn't mean that, and she went on—

'I came down into the garden, and I saw a light in the house, and dark figures moving about. I thought perhaps it was burglars, but Father hadn't come home, and Eliza had gone to bed, so I couldn't do anything. Only I thought perhaps I would tell the rest of you.'

'Why didn't you tell us this morning?' Noel asked. And Alice explained that she did not want to get any one into trouble, even burglars. 'But we might watch to-night,' she said, 'and see if we see the light again.'

'They might have been burglars,' Noel said. He was sucking the last bit of his macaroni. 'You know the people next door are very grand. They won't know us—and they go out in a real private carriage sometimes. And they have an "At Home" day, and people come in cabs. I daresay they have piles of plate and jewellery and rich brocades, and furs of price and things like that. Let us keep watch to-night.'

'It's no use watching to-night,' Dicky said; 'if it's only burglars they won't come again. But there are other things besides burglars that are discovered in empty houses where lights are seen moving.'

'You mean coiners,' said Oswald at once. 'I wonder what the reward is for setting the police on their track?'

Dicky thought it ought to be something fat, because coiners are always a desperate gang; and the machinery they make the coins with is so heavy and handy for knocking down detectives.

Then it was tea-time, and we went in; and Dora and H. O. had clubbed their money together and bought a melon; quite a big one, and only a little bit squashy at one end. It was very good, and then we washed the seeds and made things with them and with pins and cotton. And nobody said any more about watching the house next door.

Only when we went to bed Dicky took off his coat and waistcoat, but he stopped at his braces, and said—

'What about the coiners?'

Oswald had taken off his collar and tie, and he was just going to say the same, so he said, 'Of course I meant to watch, only my collar's rather tight, so I thought I'd take it off first.'

Dicky said he did not think the girls ought to be in it, because there might be danger, but Oswald reminded him that they had promised Alice, and that a promise is a sacred thing, even when you'd much rather not. So Oswald got Alice alone under pretence of showing her a caterpillar— Dora does not like them, and she screamed and ran away when Oswald offered to show it her. Then Oswald explained, and Alice agreed to come and watch if she could. This made us later than we ought to have been, because Alice had to wait till Dora was quiet and then creep out very slowly, for fear of the boards creaking. The girls sleep with their room-door open for fear of burglars. Alice had kept on her clothes under her nightgown when Dora wasn't looking, and presently we got down, creeping past Father's study, and out at the glass door that leads on to the veranda and the iron steps into the garden. And we went down very quietly, and got into the chestnut-tree; and then I felt that we had only been playing what Albert's uncle calls our favourite instrument—I mean the Fool. For the house next door was as dark as dark. Then suddenly we heard a sound—it came from the gate at the end of the garden. All the gardens have gates; they lead into a kind of lane that runs behind them. It is a sort of back way, very convenient when you don't want to say exactly where you are going. We heard the gate at the end of the next garden click, and Dicky nudged Alice so that she would have fallen out of the tree if it had not been for Oswald's extraordinary presence of mind. Oswald squeezed Alice's arm tight, and we all looked; and the others were rather frightened because really we had not exactly expected anything to happen except perhaps a light. But now a muffled figure, shrouded in a dark cloak, came swiftly up the path of the next-door garden. And we could see that under its cloak the figure carried a mysterious burden. The figure was dressed to look like a woman in a sailor hat.

We held our breath as it passed under the tree where we were, and then it tapped very gently on the back door and was let in, and then a light appeared in the window of the downstairs back breakfast-room. But the shutters were up.

Dicky said, 'My eye!' and wouldn't the others be sick to think they hadn't been in this! But Alice didn't half like it—and as she is a girl I do not blame her. Indeed, I thought myself at first that perhaps it would be better to retire for the present, and return later with a strongly armed force.

'It's not burglars,' Alice whispered; 'the mysterious stranger was bringing things in, not taking them out. They must be coiners—and oh, Oswald!—don't let's! The things they coin with must hurt very much. Do let's go to bed!'

But Dicky said he was going to see; if there was a reward for finding out things like this he would like to have the reward.

'They locked the back door,' he whispered, 'I heard it go. And I could look in quite well through the holes in the shutters and be back over the wall long before they'd got the door open, even if they started to do it at once.'

There were holes at the top of the shutters the shape of hearts, and the yellow light came out through them as well as through the chinks of the shutters.

Oswald said if Dicky went he should, because he was the eldest; and Alice said, 'If any one goes it ought to be me, because I thought of it.'

So Oswald said, 'Well, go then'; and she said, 'Not for anything!' And she begged us not to, and we talked about it in the tree till we were all quite hoarse with whispering.

At last we decided on a plan of action.

Alice was to stay in the tree, and scream 'Murder!' if anything happened. Dicky and I were to get down into the next garden and take it in turns to peep.

So we got down as quietly as we could, but the tree made much more noise than it does in the day, and several times we paused, fearing that all was discovered. But nothing happened.

There was a pile of red flower-pots under the window and one very large one was on the window-ledge. It seemed as if it was the hand of Destiny had placed it there, and the geranium in it was dead, and there was nothing to stop your standing on it—so Oswald did. He went first because he is the eldest, and though Dicky tried to stop him because he thought of it first it could not be, on account of not being able to say anything.

So Oswald stood on the flower-pot and tried to look through one of the holes. He did not really expect to see the coiners at their fell work, though he had pretended to when we were talking in the tree. But if he had seen them pouring the base molten metal into tin moulds the shape of half-crowns he would not have been half so astonished as he was at the spectacle now revealed.

At first he could see little, because the hole had unfortunately been made a little too high, so that the eye of the detective could only see the Prodigal Son in a shiny frame on the opposite wall. But Oswald held on to the window-frame and stood on tiptoe and then he *saw*.

There was no furnace, and no base metal, no bearded men in leathern aprons with tongs and things, but just a table with a table-cloth on it for supper, and a tin of salmon and a lettuce and some bottled beer. And there on a chair was the cloak and the hat of the mysterious stranger, and the two people sitting at the table were the two youngest grown-up daughters of the lady next door, and one of them was saying—

'So I got the salmon three-halfpence cheaper, and the lettuces are only six a penny in the Broadway, just fancy! We must save as much as ever we can on our housekeeping money if we want to go away decent next year.'

And the other said, 'I wish we could *all* go *every* year, or else—Really, I almost wish—'

And all the time Oswald was looking Dicky was pulling at his jacket to make him get down and let Dicky have a squint. And just as she said 'I almost,' Dicky pulled too hard and Oswald felt himself toppling on the giddy verge of the big flower-pots. Putting forth all his strength our hero strove to recover his equi-what's-its-name, but it was now lost beyond recall.

'You've done it this time!' he said, then he fell heavily among the flower-pots piled below. He heard them crash and rattle and crack, and then his head struck against an iron pillar used for holding up the next-door veranda. His eyes closed and he knew no more.

Now you will perhaps expect that at this moment Alice would have cried 'Murder!' If you think so you little know what girls are. Directly she was left alone in that tree she made a bolt to tell Albert's uncle all about it and bring him to our rescue in case the coiner's gang was a very desperate one. And just when I fell, Albert's uncle was getting over the wall. Alice never screamed at all when Oswald fell, but Dicky thinks he heard Albert's uncle say, 'Confound those kids!' which would not have been kind or polite, so I hope he did not say it.

The people next door did not come out to see what the row was. Albert's uncle did not wait for them to come out. He picked up Oswald and carried the insensible body of the gallant young detective to the wall, laid it on the top, and then climbed over and bore his lifeless burden into our house and put it on the sofa in Father's study. Father was out, so we needn't have *crept* so when we were getting into the garden. Then Oswald was restored to consciousness, and his head tied up, and sent to bed, and next day there was a lump on his young brow as big as a turkey's egg, and very uncomfortable.

Albert's uncle came in next day and talked to each of us separately. To Oswald he said many unpleasant things about ungentlemanly to spy on ladies, and about minding your own business; and when I began to tell him what I had heard he told me to shut up, and altogether he made me more uncomfortable than the bump did.

Oswald did not say anything to any one, but next day, as the shadows of eve were falling, he crept away, and wrote on a piece of paper, 'I want to speak to you,' and shoved it through the hole like a heart in the top of the next-door shutters. And the youngest young lady put an eye to the heart-shaped hole, and then opened the shutter and said 'Well?' very crossly. Then Oswald said—

'I am very sorry, and I beg your pardon. We wanted to be detectives, and we thought a gang of coiners infested your house, so we looked through your window last night. I saw the lettuce, and I heard what you said about the salmon being three-halfpence cheaper, and I know it is very dishonourable to pry into other people's secrets, especially ladies', and I never will again if you will forgive me this once.'

Then the lady frowned and then she laughed, and then she said—

'So it was you tumbling into the flower-pots last night? We thought it was burglars. It frightened us horribly. Why, what a bump on your poor head!'

And then she talked to me a bit, and presently she said she and her sister had not wished people to know they were at home, because—And then she stopped short and grew very red, and I said, 'I thought you were all at Scarborough; your servant told Eliza so. Why didn't you want people to know you were at home?'

The lady got redder still, and then she laughed and said—

'Never mind the reason why. I hope your head doesn't hurt much. Thank you for your nice, manly little speech. *You've* nothing to be ashamed of, at any rate.' Then she kissed me, and I did not mind. And then she said, 'Run away now, dear. I'm going to—I'm going to pull up the blinds and open the shutters, and I want to do it at *once*, before it gets dark, so that every one can see we're at home, and not at Scarborough.'

Chapter 4. Good Hunting

When we had got that four shillings by digging for treasure we ought, by rights, to have tried Dicky's idea of answering the advertisement about ladies and gentlemen and spare time and two pounds a week, but there were several things we rather wanted.

Dora wanted a new pair of scissors, and she said she was going to get them with her eight-pence. But Alice said—

'You ought to get her those, Oswald, because you know you broke the points off hers getting the marble out of the brass thimble.'

It was quite true, though I had almost forgotten it, but then it was H. O. who jammed the marble into the thimble first of all. So I said—

'It's H. O.'s fault as much as mine, anyhow. Why shouldn't he pay?'

Oswald didn't so much mind paying for the beastly scissors, but he hates injustice of every kind.

'He's such a little kid,' said Dicky, and of course H. O. said he wasn't a little kid, and it very nearly came to being a row between them. But Oswald knows when to be generous; so he said—

'Look here! I'll pay sixpence of the scissors, and H. O. shall pay the rest, to teach him to be careful.'

H. O. agreed: he is not at all a mean kid, but I found out afterwards that Alice paid his share out of her own money.

Then we wanted some new paints, and Noel wanted a pencil and a halfpenny account-book to write poetry with, and it does seem hard never to have any apples. So, somehow or other nearly all the money got spent, and we agreed that we must let the advertisement run loose a little longer.

'I only hope,' Alice said, 'that they won't have got all the ladies and gentlemen they want before we have got the money to write for the sample and instructions.'

And I was a little afraid myself, because it seemed such a splendid chance; but we looked in the paper every day, and the advertisement was always there, so we thought it was all right.

Then we had the detective try-on—and it proved no go; and then, when all the money was gone, except a halfpenny of mine and twopence of Noel's and three-pence of Dicky's and a few pennies that the girls had left, we held another council.

Dora was sewing the buttons on H. O.'s Sunday things. He got himself a knife with his money, and he cut every single one of his best buttons off. You've no idea how many buttons there are on a suit. Dora counted them. There are twenty-four, counting the little ones on the sleeves that don't undo.

Alice was trying to teach Pincher to beg; but he has too much sense when he knows you've got nothing in your hands, and the rest of us were roasting potatoes under the fire. We had made a fire on purpose, though it was rather warm. They are very good if you cut away the burnt parts—but you ought to wash them first, or you are a dirty boy.

'Well, what can we do?' said Dicky. 'You are so fond of saying "Let's do something!" and never saying what.'

'We can't try the advertisement yet. Shall we try rescuing some one?' said Oswald. It was his own idea, but he didn't insist on doing it, though he is next to the eldest, for he knows it is bad manners to make people do what you want, when they would rather not.

'What was Noel's plan?' Alice asked.

'A Princess or a poetry book,' said Noel sleepily. He was lying on his back on the sofa, kicking his legs. 'Only I shall look for the Princess all by myself. But I'll let you see her when we're married.'

'Have you got enough poetry to make a book?' Dicky asked that, and it was rather sensible of him, because when Noel came to look there were only seven of his poems that any of us could understand. There was the 'Wreck of the Malabar', and the poem he wrote when Eliza took us to hear the Reviving Preacher, and everybody cried, and Father said it must have been the Preacher's Eloquence. So Noel wrote:

O Eloquence and what art thou?
Ay what art thou? because we cried
And everybody cried inside
When they came out their eyes were red—
And it was your doing Father said.

But Noel told Alice he got the first line and a half from a book a boy at school was going to write when he had time. Besides this there were the 'Lines on a Dead Black Beetle that was poisoned'—

O Beetle how I weep to see
Thee lying on thy poor back!
It is so very sad indeed.
You were so shiny and black.
I wish you were alive again
But Eliza says wishing it is nonsense and a shame.

It was very good beetle poison, and there were hundreds of them lying dead—but Noel only wrote a piece of poetry for one of them. He said he hadn't time to do them all, and the worst of it was he didn't know which one he'd written it to—so Alice couldn't bury the beetle and put the lines on its grave, though she wanted to very much.

Well, it was quite plain that there wasn't enough poetry for a book.

'We might wait a year or two,' said Noel. 'I shall be sure to make some more some time. I thought of a piece about a fly this morning that knew condensed milk was sticky.'

'But we want the money *now*,' said Dicky, 'and you can go on writing just the same. It will come in some time or other.'

'There's poetry in newspapers,' said Alice. 'Down, Pincher! you'll never be a clever dog, so it's no good trying.'

'Do they pay for it?' Dicky thought of that; he often thinks of things that are really important, even if they are a little dull.

'I don't know. But I shouldn't think any one would let them print their poetry without. I wouldn't I know.' That was Dora; but Noel said he wouldn't mind if he didn't get paid, so long as he saw his poetry printed and his name at the end.

'We might try, anyway,' said Oswald. He is always willing to give other people's ideas a fair trial.

So we copied out 'The Wreck of the Malabar' and the other six poems on drawing-paper—Dora did it, she writes best—and Oswald drew a picture of the Malabar going down with all hands. It was a full-rigged schooner, and all the ropes and sails were correct; because my cousin is in the Navy, and he showed me.

We thought a long time whether we'd write a letter and send it by post with the poetry—and Dora thought it would be best. But Noel said he couldn't bear not to know at once if the paper would print the poetry, So we decided to take it.

I went with Noel, because I am the eldest, and he is not old enough to go to London by himself. Dicky said poetry was rot—and he was glad he hadn't got to make a fool of himself. That was because there was not enough money for him to go with us. H. O. couldn't come either, but he came to the station to see us off, and waved his cap and called out 'Good hunting!' as the train started.

There was a lady in spectacles in the corner. She was writing with a pencil on the edges of long strips of paper that had print all down them. When the train started she asked—

'What was that he said?'

So Oswald answered—

'It was "Good hunting"—it's out of the Jungle Book!' 'That's very pleasant to hear,' the lady said; 'I am very pleased to meet people who know their Jungle Book. And where are you off to—the Zoological Gardens to look for Bagheera?'

We were pleased, too, to meet some one who knew the Jungle Book.

So Oswald said—

'We are going to restore the fallen fortunes of the House of Bastable— and we have all thought of different ways—and we're going to try them all. Noel's way is poetry. I suppose great poets get paid?'

The lady laughed—she was awfully jolly—and said she was a sort of poet, too, and the long strips of paper were the proofs of her new book of stories. Because before a book is made into a real book with pages and a cover, they sometimes print it all on strips of paper, and the writer make marks on it with a pencil to show the printers what idiots they are not to understand what a writer means to have printed.

We told her all about digging for treasure, and what we meant to do. Then she asked to see Noel's poetry—and he said he didn't like—so she said, 'Look here—if you'll show me yours I'll show you some of mine.' So he agreed.

The jolly lady read Noel's poetry, and she said she liked it very much. And she thought a great deal of the picture of the Malabar. And then she said, 'I write serious poetry like yours myself; too, but I have a piece here that I think you will like because it's about a boy.' She gave it to us—and so I can copy it down, and I will, for it shows that some grown-up ladies are not so silly as others. I like it better than Noel's poetry, though I told him I did not, because he looked as if he was going to cry. This was very wrong, for you should always speak the truth, however unhappy it makes people. And I generally do. But I did not want him crying in the railway carriage. The lady's piece of poetry:

Oh when I wake up in my bed
And see the sun all fat and red,
I'm glad to have another day
For all my different kinds of play.

There are so many things to do—
The things that make a man of you,
If grown-ups did not get so vexed
And wonder what you will do next.

I often wonder whether they
Ever made up our kinds of play—
If they were always good as gold
And only did what they were told.

They like you best to play with tops
And toys in boxes, bought in shops;
They do not even know the names
Of really interesting games.

They will not let you play with fire
Or trip your sister up with wire,
They grudge the tea-tray for a drum,
Or booby-traps when callers come.

They don't like fishing, and it's true
You sometimes soak a suit or two:
They look on fireworks, though they're dry,
With quite a disapproving eye.

They do not understand the way
To get the most out of your day:
They do not know how hunger feels
Nor what you need between your meals.

And when you're sent to bed at night,
They're happy, but they're not polite.
For through the door you hear them say:
'*He's* done *his* mischief for the day!'

She told us a lot of other pieces but I cannot remember them, and she talked to us all the way up, and when we got nearly to Cannon Street she said—

'I've got two new shillings here! Do you think they would help to smooth the path to Fame?'

Noel said, 'Thank you,' and was going to take the shilling. But Oswald, who always remembers what he is told, said—

'Thank you very much, but Father told us we ought never to take anything from strangers.'

'That's a nasty one,' said the lady—she didn't talk a bit like a real lady, but more like a jolly sort of grown-up boy in a dress and hat—'a very nasty one! But don't you think as Noel and I are both poets I might be considered a sort of relation? You've heard of brother poets, haven't you? Don't you think Noel and I are aunt and nephew poets, or some relationship of that kind?'

I didn't know what to say, and she went on—

'It's awfully straight of you to stick to what your Father tells you, but look here, you take the shillings, and here's my card. When you get home tell your Father all about it, and if he says No, you can just bring the shillings back to me.'

So we took the shillings, and she shook hands with us and said, 'Good- bye, and good hunting!'

We did tell Father about it, and he said it was all right, and when he looked at the card he told us we were highly honoured, for the lady wrote better poetry than any other lady alive now. We had never heard of her, and she seemed much too jolly for a poet. Good old Kipling! We owe him those two shillings, as well as the Jungle books!

Chapter 5. The Poet and the Editor

It was not bad sport—being in London entirely on our own hook. We asked the way to Fleet Street, where Father says all the newspaper offices are. They said straight on down Ludgate Hill—but it turned out to be quite another way. At least *we* didn't go straight on.

We got to St Paul's. Noel *would* go in, and we saw where Gordon was buried—at least the monument. It is very flat, considering what a man he was.

When we came out we walked a long way, and when we asked a policeman he said we'd better go back through Smithfield. So we did. They don't burn people any more there now, so it was rather dull, besides being a long way, and Noel got very tired. He's a peaky little chap; it comes of being a poet, I think. We had a bun or two at different shops—out of the shillings—and it was quite late in the afternoon when we got to Fleet Street. The gas was lighted and the electric lights. There is a jolly Bovril sign that comes off and on in different coloured lamps. We went to the Daily Recorder office, and asked to see the Editor. It is a big office, very bright, with brass and mahogany and electric lights.

They told us the Editor wasn't there, but at another office. So we went down a dirty street, to a very dull-looking place. There was a man there inside, in a glass case, as if he was a museum, and he told us to write down our names and our business. So Oswald wrote—

OSWALD BASTABLE
NOEL BASTABLE
BUSINESS VERY PRIVATE INDEED

Then we waited on the stone stairs; it was very draughty. And the man in the glass case looked at us as if we were the museum instead of him. We waited a long time, and then a boy came down and said—

'The Editor can't see you. Will you please write your business?' And he laughed. I wanted to punch his head.

But Noel said, 'Yes, I'll write it if you'll give me a pen and ink, and a sheet of paper and an envelope.'

The boy said he'd better write by post. But Noel is a bit pig-headed; it's his worst fault. So he said—'No, I'll write it *now*.' So I backed him up by saying—

'Look at the price penny stamps are since the coal strike!'

So the boy grinned, and the man in the glass case gave us pen and paper, and Noel wrote. Oswald writes better than he does; but Noel would do it; and it took a very long time, and then it was inky.

DEAR MR EDITOR,
I want you to print my poetry and pay for it,
and I am a friend of Mrs Leslie's; she is a poet too.

Your affectionate friend,
NOEL BASTABLE.

He licked the envelope a good deal, so that that boy shouldn't read it going upstairs; and he wrote 'Very private' outside, and gave the letter to the boy. I thought it wasn't any good; but in a minute the grinning boy came back, and he was quite respectful, and said—'The Editor says, please will you step up?'

We stepped up. There were a lot of stairs and passages, and a queer sort of humming, hammering sound and a very funny smell. The boy was now very polite, and said it was the ink we smelt, and the noise was the printing machines.

After going through a lot of cold passages we came to a door; the boy opened it, and let us go in. There was a large room, with a big, soft, blue-and-red carpet, and a roaring fire, though it was only October; and a large table with drawers, and littered with papers, just like the one in Father's study. A gentleman was sitting at one side of the table; he had a light moustache and light eyes, and he looked very young to be an editor—not nearly so old as Father. He looked very tired and sleepy, as if he had got up very early in the morning; but he was kind, and we liked him. Oswald thought he looked clever. Oswald is considered a judge of faces.

'Well,' said he, 'so you are Mrs Leslie's friends?'

'I think so,' said Noel; 'at least she gave us each a shilling, and she wished us "good hunting!"'

'Good hunting, eh? Well, what about this poetry of yours? Which is the poet?'

I can't think how he could have asked! Oswald is said to be a very manly-looking boy for his age. However, I thought it would look duffing to be offended, so I said—

'This is my brother Noel. He is the poet.' Noel had turned quite pale. He is disgustingly like a girl in some ways. The Editor told us to sit down, and he took the poems from Noel, and began to read them. Noel got paler and paler; I really thought he was going to faint, like he did when I held his hand under the cold-water tap, after I had accidentally cut him with my chisel. When the Editor had read the first poem—it was the one about the beetle—he got up and stood with his back to us. It was not manners; but Noel thinks he did it 'to conceal his emotion,' as they do in books. He read all the poems, and then he said—

'I like your poetry very much, young man. I'll give you—let me see; how much shall I give you for it?'

'As much as ever you can,' said Noel. 'You see I want a good deal of money to restore the fallen fortunes of the house of Bastable.'

The gentleman put on some eye-glasses and looked hard at us. Then he sat down.

'That's a good idea,' said he. 'Tell me how you came to think of it. And, I say, have you had any tea? They've just sent out for mine.'

He rang a tingly bell, and the boy brought in a tray with a teapot and a thick cup and saucer and things, and he had to fetch another tray for us, when he was told to; and we had tea with the Editor of the Daily Recorder. I suppose it was a very proud moment for Noel, though I did not think of that till afterwards. The Editor asked us a lot of questions, and we told him a good deal, though of course I did not tell a stranger all our reasons for thinking that the family fortunes wanted restoring. We stayed about half an hour, and when we were going away he said again—

'I shall print all your poems, my poet; and now what do you think they're worth?'

'I don't know,' Noel said. 'You see I didn't write them to sell.'

'Why did you write them then?' he asked.

Noel said he didn't know; he supposed because he wanted to.

'Art for Art's sake, eh?' said the Editor, and he seemed quite delighted, as though Noel had said something clever.

'Well, would a guinea meet your views?' he asked.

I have read of people being at a loss for words, and dumb with emotion, and I've read of people being turned to stone with astonishment, or joy, or something, but I never knew how silly it looked till I saw Noel standing staring at the Editor with his mouth open. He went red and he went white, and then he got crimson, as if you were rubbing more and more crimson lake on a palette. But he didn't say a word, so Oswald had to say—

'I should jolly well think so.'

So the Editor gave Noel a sovereign and a shilling, and he shook hands with us both, but he thumped Noel on the back and said—

'Buck up, old man! It's your first guinea, but it won't be your last. Now go along home, and in about ten years you can bring me some more poetry. Not before—see? I'm just taking this poetry of yours because I like it very much; but we don't put poetry in this paper at all. I shall have to put it in another paper I know of.'

'What *do* you put in your paper?' I asked, for Father always takes the Daily Chronicle, and I didn't know what the Recorder was like. We chose it because it has such a glorious office, and a clock outside lighted up.

'Oh, news,' said he, 'and dull articles, and things about Celebrities. If you know any Celebrities, now?'

Noel asked him what Celebrities were.

'Oh, the Queen and the Princes, and people with titles, and people who write, or sing, or act—or do something clever or wicked.'

'I don't know anybody wicked,' said Oswald, wishing he had known Dick Turpin, or Claude Duval, so as to be able to tell the Editor things about them. 'But I know some one with a title—Lord Tottenham.'

'The mad old Protectionist, eh? How did you come to know him?'

'We don't know him to speak to. But he goes over the Heath every day at three, and he strides along like a giant—with a black cloak like Lord Tennyson's flying behind him, and he talks to himself like one o'clock.'

'What does he say?' The Editor had sat down again, and he was fiddling with a blue pencil.

'We only heard him once, close enough to understand, and then he said, "The curse of the country, sir—ruin and desolation!" And then he went striding along again, hitting at the furze-bushes as if they were the heads of his enemies.'

'Excellent descriptive touch,' said the Editor. 'Well, go on.'

'That's all I know about him, except that he stops in the middle of the Heath every day, and he looks all round to see if there's any one about, and if there isn't, he takes his collar off.'

The Editor interrupted—which is considered rude—and said—

'You're not romancing?'

'I beg your pardon?' said Oswald. 'Drawing the long bow, I mean,' said the Editor.

Oswald drew himself up, and said he wasn't a liar.

The Editor only laughed, and said romancing and lying were not at all the same; only it was important to know what you were playing at. So Oswald accepted his apology, and went on.

'We were hiding among the furze-bushes one day, and we saw him do it. He took off his collar, and he put on a clean one, and he threw the other among the furze-bushes. We picked it up afterwards, and it was a beastly paper one!'

'Thank you,' said the Editor, and he got up and put his hand in his pocket. 'That's well worth five shillings, and there they are. Would you like to see round the printing offices before you go home?'

I pocketed my five bob, and thanked him, and I said we should like it very much. He called another gentleman and said something we couldn't hear. Then he said good-bye again; and all this time Noel hadn't said a word. But now he said, 'I've made a poem about you. It is called "Lines to a Noble Editor." Shall I write it down?'

The Editor gave him the blue pencil, and he sat down at the Editor's table and wrote. It was this, he told me afterwards as well as he could remember—

> May Life's choicest blessings be your lot
> I think you ought to be very blest
> For you are going to print my poems—
> And you may have this one as well as the rest.

'Thank you,' said the Editor. 'I don't think I ever had a poem addressed to me before. I shall treasure it, I assure you.'

Then the other gentleman said something about Maecenas, and we went off to see the printing office with at least one pound seven in our pockets.

It *was* good hunting, and no mistake!

But he never put Noel's poetry in the Daily Recorder. It was quite a long time afterwards we saw a sort of story thing in a magazine, on the station bookstall, and that kind, sleepy-looking Editor had written it, I suppose. It was not at all amusing. It said a lot about Noel and me, describing us all wrong, and saying how we had tea with the Editor; and all Noel's poems were in the story thing. I think myself the Editor seemed to make game of them, but Noel was quite pleased to see them printed—so that's all right. It wasn't my poetry anyhow, I am glad to say.

Chapter 6. Noel's Princess

She happened quite accidentally. We were not looking for a Princess at all just then; but Noel had said he was going to find a Princess all by himself; and marry her—and he really did. Which was rather odd, because when people say things are going to befall, very often they don't. It was different, of course, with the prophets of old.

We did not get any treasure by it, except twelve chocolate drops; but we might have done, and it was an adventure, anyhow.

Greenwich Park is a jolly good place to play in, especially the parts that aren't near Greenwich. The parts near the Heath are first-rate. I often wish the Park was nearer our house; but I suppose a Park is a difficult thing to move.

Sometimes we get Eliza to put lunch in a basket, and we go up to the Park. She likes that—it saves cooking dinner for us; and sometimes she says of her own accord, 'I've made some pasties for you, and you might as well go into the Park as not. It's a lovely day.'

She always tells us to rinse out the cup at the drinking-fountain, and the girls do; but I always put my head under the tap and drink. Then you are an intrepid hunter at a mountain stream—and besides, you're sure it's clean. Dicky does the same, and so does H. O. But Noel always drinks out of the cup. He says it is a golden goblet wrought by enchanted gnomes.

The day the Princess happened was a fine, hot day, last October, and we were quite tired with the walk up to the Park.

We always go in by the little gate at the top of Croom's Hill. It is the postern gate that things always happen at in stories. It was dusty walking, but when we got in the Park it was ripping, so we rested a bit, and lay on our backs, and looked up at the trees, and wished we could play monkeys. I have done it before now, but the Park-keeper makes a row if he catches you.

When we'd rested a little, Alice said—

'It was a long way to the enchanted wood, but it is very nice now we are there. I wonder what we shall find in it?'

'We shall find deer,' said Dicky, 'if we go to look; but they go on the other side of the Park because of the people with buns.'

Saying buns made us think of lunch, so we had it; and when we had done we scratched a hole under a tree and buried the papers, because we know it spoils pretty places to leave beastly, greasy papers lying about. I remember Mother teaching me and Dora that, when we were quite little. I wish everybody's parents would teach them this useful lesson, and the same about orange peel.

When we'd eaten everything there was, Alice whispered—

'I see the white witch bear yonder among the trees! Let's track it and slay it in its lair.'

'I am the bear,' said Noel; so he crept away, and we followed him among the trees. Often the witch bear was out of sight, and then you didn't know where it would jump out from; but sometimes we saw it, and just followed.

'When we catch it there'll be a great fight,' said Oswald; 'and I shall be Count Folko of Mont Faucon.'

'I'll be Gabrielle,' said Dora. She is the only one of us who likes doing girl's parts.

'I'll be Sintram,' said Alice; 'and H. O. can be the Little Master.'

'What about Dicky?'

'Oh, I can be the Pilgrim with the bones.'

'Hist!' whispered Alice. 'See his white fairy fur gleaming amid yonder covert!'

And I saw a bit of white too. It was Noel's collar, and it had come undone at the back.

We hunted the bear in and out of the trees, and then we lost him altogether; and suddenly we found the wall of the Park—in a place where I'm sure there wasn't a wall before. Noel wasn't anywhere about, and there was a door in the wall. And it was open; so we went through.

'The bear has hidden himself in these mountain fastnesses,' Oswald said. 'I will draw my good sword and after him.'

So I drew the umbrella, which Dora always will bring in case it rains, because Noel gets a cold on the chest at the least thing—and we went on.

The other side of the wall it was a stable yard, all cobble-stones.

There was nobody about—but we could hear a man rubbing down a horse and hissing in the stable; so we crept very quietly past, and Alice whispered—

''Tis the lair of the Monster Serpent; I hear his deadly hiss! Beware! Courage and despatch!'

We went over the stones on tiptoe, and we found another wall with another door in it on the other side. We went through that too, on tiptoe. It really was an adventure. And there we were in a shrubbery, and we saw something white through the trees. Dora said it was the white bear. That is so like Dora. She always begins to take part in a play just when the rest of us are getting tired of it. I don't mean this unkindly, because I am very fond of Dora. I cannot forget how kind she was when I had bronchitis; and ingratitude is a dreadful vice. But it is quite true.

'It is not a bear,' said Oswald; and we all went on, still on tiptoe, round a twisty path and on to a lawn, and there was Noel. His collar had come undone, as I said, and he had an inky mark on his face that he made just before we left the house, and he wouldn't let Dora wash it off, and one of his bootlaces was coming down. He was standing looking at a little girl; she was the funniest little girl you ever saw.

She was like a china doll—the sixpenny kind; she had a white face, and long yellow hair, done up very tight in two pigtails; her forehead was very big and lumpy, and her cheeks came high up, like little shelves under her eyes. Her eyes were small and blue. She had on a funny black frock, with curly braid on it, and button boots that went almost up to her knees. Her legs were very thin. She was sitting in a hammock chair nursing a blue kitten—not a sky-blue one, of course, but the colour of a new slate pencil. As we came up we heard her say to Noel—'Who are you?'

Noel had forgotten about the bear, and he was taking his favourite part, so he said—'I'm Prince Camaralzaman.'

The funny little girl looked pleased—

'I thought at first you were a common boy,' she said. Then she saw the rest of us and said—

'Are you all Princesses and Princes too?'

Of course we said 'Yes,' and she said—

'I am a Princess also.' She said it very well too, exactly as if it were true. We were very glad, because it is so seldom you meet any children who can begin to play right off without having everything explained to them. And even then they will say they are going to 'pretend to be' a lion, or a witch, or a king. Now this little girl just said 'I *am* a Princess.' Then she looked at Oswald and said, 'I fancy I've seen you at Baden.'

Of course Oswald said, 'Very likely.'

The little girl had a funny voice, and all her words were quite plain, each word by itself; she didn't talk at all like we do.

H. O. asked her what the cat's name was, and she said 'Katinka.' Then Dicky said—

'Let's get away from the windows; if you play near windows some one inside generally knocks at them and says "Don't".'

The Princess put down the cat very carefully and said—

'I am forbidden to walk off the grass.'

'That's a pity,' said Dora.

'But I will if you like,' said the Princess.

'You mustn't do things you are forbidden to do,' Dora said; but Dicky showed us that there was some more grass beyond the shrubs with only a gravel path between. So I lifted the Princess over the gravel, so that she should be able to say she hadn't walked off the grass. When we got to the other grass we all sat down, and the Princess asked us if we liked 'dragees' (I know that's how you spell it, for I asked Albert- next-door's uncle).

We said we thought not, but she pulled a real silver box out of her pocket and showed us; they were just flat, round chocolates. We had two each. Then we asked her her name, and she began, and when she began she went on, and on, and on, till I thought she was never going to stop. H. O. said she had fifty names, but Dicky is very good at figures, and he says there were only eighteen. The first were Pauline, Alexandra, Alice, and Mary was one, and Victoria, for we all heard that, and it ended up with Hildegarde Cunigonde something or other, Princess of something else.

When she'd done, H. O. said, 'That's jolly good! Say it again!' and she did, but even then we couldn't remember it. We told her our names, but she thought they were too short, so when it was Noel's turn he said he was Prince Noel Camaralzaman Ivan Constantine Charlemagne James John Edward Biggs Maximilian Bastable Prince of Lewisham, but when she asked him to say it again of course he could only get the first two names right, because he'd made it up as he went on.

So the Princess said, 'You are quite old enough to know your own name.' She was very grave and serious.

She told us that she was the fifth cousin of Queen Victoria. We asked who the other cousins were, but she did not seem to understand. She went on and said she was seven times removed. She couldn't tell us what that meant either, but Oswald thinks it means that the Queen's cousins are so fond of her that they will keep coming bothering, so the Queen's servants have orders to remove them. This little girl must have been very fond of the Queen to try so often to see her, and to have been seven times removed. We could see that it is considered something to be proud of; but we thought it was hard on the Queen that her cousins wouldn't let her alone.

Presently the little girl asked us where our maids and governesses were.

We told her we hadn't any just now. And she said—

'How pleasant! And did you come here alone?'

'Yes,' said Dora; 'we came across the Heath.'

'You are very fortunate,' said the little girl. She sat very upright on the grass, with her fat little hands in her lap. 'I should like to go on the Heath. There are donkeys there, with white saddle covers. I should like to ride them, but my governess will not permit.'

'I'm glad we haven't a governess,' H. O. said. 'We ride the donkeys whenever we have any pennies, and once I gave the man another penny to make it gallop.'

'You are indeed fortunate!' said the Princess again, and when she looked sad the shelves on her cheeks showed more than ever. You could have laid a sixpence on them quite safely if you had had one.

'Never mind,' said Noel; 'I've got a lot of money. Come out and have a ride now.' But the little girl shook her head and said she was afraid it would not be correct.

Dora said she was quite right; then all of a sudden came one of those uncomfortable times when nobody can think of anything to say, so we sat and looked at each other. But at last Alice said we ought to be going.

'Do not go yet,' the little girl said. 'At what time did they order your carriage?'

'Our carriage is a fairy one, drawn by griffins, and it comes when we wish for it,' said Noel.

The little girl looked at him very queerly, and said, 'That is out of a picture-book.'

Then Noel said he thought it was about time he was married if we were to be home in time for tea. The little girl was rather stupid over it, but she did what we told her, and we married them with Dora's pocket- handkerchief for a veil, and the ring off the back of one of the buttons on H. O.'s blouse just went on her little finger.

Then we showed her how to play cross-touch, and puss in the corner, and tag. It was funny, she didn't know any games but battledore and shuttlecock and les graces. But she really began to laugh at last and not to look quite so like a doll.

She was Puss and was running after Dicky when suddenly she stopped short and looked as if she was going to cry. And we looked too, and there were two prim ladies with little mouths and tight hair. One of them said in quite an awful voice, 'Pauline, who are these children?' and her voice was gruff; with very curly R's.

The little girl said we were Princes and Princesses—which was silly, to a grown-up person that is not a great friend of yours.

The gruff lady gave a short, horrid laugh, like a husky bark, and said—

'Princes, indeed! They're only common children!'

Dora turned very red and began to speak, but the little girl cried out 'Common children! Oh, I am so glad! When I am grown up I'll always play with common children.'

And she ran at us, and began to kiss us one by one, beginning with Alice; she had got to H. O. when the horrid lady said—'Your Highness— go indoors at once!'

The little girl answered, 'I won't!'

Then the prim lady said—'Wilson, carry her Highness indoors.'

And the little girl was carried away screaming, and kicking with her little thin legs and her buttoned boots, and between her screams she shrieked:

'Common children! I am glad, glad, glad! Common children! Common children!'

The nasty lady then remarked—'Go at once, or I will send for the police!'

So we went. H. O. made a face at her and so did Alice, but Oswald took off his cap and said he was sorry if she was annoyed about anything; for Oswald has always been taught to be polite to ladies, however nasty. Dicky took his off, too, when he saw me do it; he says he did it first, but that is a mistake. If I were really a common boy I should say it was a lie.

Then we all came away, and when we got outside Dora said, 'So she was really a Princess. Fancy a Princess living *there*!'

'Even Princesses have to live somewhere,' said Dicky.

'And I thought it was play. And it was real. I wish I'd known! I should have liked to ask her lots of things,' said Alice.

H. O. said he would have liked to ask her what she had for dinner and whether she had a crown.

I felt, myself, we had lost a chance of finding out a great deal about kings and queens. I might have known such a stupid-looking little girl would never have been able to pretend, as well as that.

So we all went home across the Heath, and made dripping toast for tea.

When we were eating it Noel said, 'I wish I could give *her* some! It is very good.'

He sighed as he said it, and his mouth was very full, so we knew he was thinking of his Princess. He says now that she was as beautiful as the day, but we remember her quite well, and she was nothing of the kind.

Chapter 7. Being Bandits

Noel was quite tiresome for ever so long after we found the Princess. He would keep on wanting to go to the Park when the rest of us didn't, and though we went several times to please him, we never found that door open again, and all of us except him knew from the first that it would be no go.

So now we thought it was time to do something to rouse him from the stupor of despair, which is always done to heroes when anything baffling has occurred. Besides, we were getting very short of money again—the fortunes of your house cannot be restored (not so that they will last, that is), even by the one pound eight we got when we had the 'good hunting.' We spent a good deal of that on presents for Father's birthday. We got him a paper-weight, like a glass bun, with a picture of Lewisham Church at the bottom; and a blotting-pad, and a box of preserved fruits, and an ivory penholder with a view of Greenwich Park in the little hole where you look through at the top. He was most awfully pleased and surprised, and when he heard how Noel and Oswald had earned the money to buy the things he was more surprised still. Nearly all the rest of our money went to get fireworks for the Fifth of November. We got six Catherine wheels and four rockets; two hand-lights, one red and one green; a sixpenny maroon; two Roman-candles—they cost a shilling; some Italian streamers, a fairy fountain, and a tourbillon that cost eighteen-pence and was very nearly worth it.

But I think crackers and squibs are a mistake. It's true you get a lot of them for the money, and they are not bad fun for the first two or three dozen, but you get jolly sick of them before you've let off your sixpenn'orth. And the only amusing way is not allowed: it is putting them in the fire.

It always seems a long time till the evening when you have got fireworks in the house, and I think as it was a rather foggy day we should have decided to let them off directly after breakfast, only Father had said he would help us to let them off at eight o'clock after he had had his dinner, and you ought never to disappoint your father if you can help it.

You see we had three good reasons for trying H. O.'s idea of restoring the fallen fortunes of our house by becoming bandits on the Fifth of November. We had a fourth reason as well, and that was the best reason of the lot. You remember Dora thought it would be wrong to be bandits. And the Fifth of November came while Dora was away at Stroud staying with her godmother. Stroud is in Gloucestershire. We were determined to do it while she was out of the way, because we did not think it wrong, and besides we meant to do it anyhow.

We held a Council, of course, and laid our plans very carefully. We let H. O. be Captain, because it was his idea. Oswald was Lieutenant. Oswald was quite fair, because he let H. O. call himself Captain; but Oswald is the eldest next to Dora, after all.

Our plan was this. We were all to go up on to the Heath. Our house is in the Lewisham Road, but it's quite close to the Heath if you cut up the short way opposite the confectioner's, past the nursery gardens and the cottage hospital, and turn to the left again and afterwards to the right. You come out then at the top of the hill, where the big guns are with the iron fence round them, and where the bands play on Thursday evenings in the summer.

We were to lurk in ambush there, and waylay an unwary traveller. We were to call upon him to surrender his arms, and then bring him home and put him in the deepest dungeon below the castle moat; then we were to load him with chains and send to his friends for ransom.

You may think we had no chains, but you are wrong, because we used to keep two other dogs once, besides Pincher, before the fall of the fortunes of the ancient House of Bastable. And they were quite big dogs.

It was latish in the afternoon before we started. We thought we could lurk better if it was nearly dark. It was rather foggy, and we waited a good while beside the railings, but all the belated travellers were either grown up or else they were Board School children. We weren't going to get into a row with grown-up people—especially strangers—and no true bandit would ever stoop to ask a ransom from the relations of the poor and needy. So we thought it better to wait.

As I said, it was Guy Fawkes Day, and if it had not been we should never have been able to be bandits at all, for the unwary traveller we did catch had been forbidden to go out because he had a cold in his head. But he would run out to follow a guy, without even putting on a coat or a comforter, and it was a very damp, foggy afternoon and nearly dark, so you see it was his own fault entirely, and served him jolly well right.

We saw him coming over the Heath just as we were deciding to go home to tea. He had followed that guy right across to the village (we call Blackheath the village; I don't know why), and he was coming back dragging his feet and sniffing.

'Hist, an unwary traveller approaches!' whispered Oswald.

'Muffle your horses' heads and see to the priming of your pistols,' muttered Alice. She always will play boys' parts, and she makes Ellis cut her hair short on purpose. Ellis is a very obliging hairdresser.

'Steal softly upon him,' said Noel; 'for lo! 'tis dusk, and no human eyes can mark our deeds.'

So we ran out and surrounded the unwary traveller. It turned out to be Albert-next-door, and he was very frightened indeed until he saw who we were.

'Surrender!' hissed Oswald, in a desperate-sounding voice, as he caught the arm of the Unwary. And Albert-next-door said, 'All right! I'm surrendering as hard as I can. You needn't pull my arm off.'

We explained to him that resistance was useless, and I think he saw that from the first. We held him tight by both arms, and we marched him home down the hill in a hollow square of five.

He wanted to tell us about the guy, but we made him see that it was not proper for prisoners to talk to the guard, especially about guys that the prisoner had been told not to go after because of his cold.

When we got to where we live he said, 'All right, I don't want to tell you. You'll wish I had afterwards. You never saw such a guy.'

'I can see *you*!' said H. O. It was very rude, and Oswald told him so at once, because it is his duty as an elder brother. But H. O. is very young and does not know better yet, and besides it wasn't bad for H. O.

Albert-next-door said, 'You haven't any manners, and I want to go in to my tea. Let go of me!'

But Alice told him, quite kindly, that he was not going in to his tea, but coming with us.

'I'm not,' said Albert-next-door; 'I'm going home. Leave go! I've got a bad cold. You're making it worse.' Then he tried to cough, which was very silly, because we'd seen him in the morning, and he'd told us where the cold was that he wasn't to go out with. When he had tried to cough, he said, 'Leave go of me! You see my cold's getting worse.'

'You should have thought of that before,' said Dicky; 'you're coming in with us.'

'Don't be a silly,' said Noel; 'you know we told you at the very beginning that resistance was useless. There is no disgrace in yielding. We are five to your one.'

By this time Eliza had opened the door, and we thought it best to take him in without any more parlaying. To parley with a prisoner is not done by bandits.

Directly we got him safe into the nursery, H. O. began to jump about and say, 'Now you're a prisoner really and truly!'

And Albert-next-door began to cry. He always does. I wonder he didn't begin long before—but Alice fetched him one of the dried fruits we gave Father for his birthday. It was a green walnut. I have noticed the walnuts and the plums always get left till the last in the box; the apricots go first, and then the figs and pears; and the cherries, if there are any.

So he ate it and shut up. Then we explained his position to him, so that there should be no mistake, and he couldn't say afterwards that he had not understood.

'There will be no violence,' said Oswald—he was now Captain of the Bandits, because we all know H. O. likes to be Chaplain when we play prisoners—'no violence. But you will be confined in a dark, subterranean dungeon where toads and snakes crawl, and but little of the light of day filters through the heavily mullioned windows. You will be loaded with chains. Now don't begin again, Baby, there's nothing to cry about; straw will be your pallet; beside you the gaoler will set a ewer—a ewer is only a jug, stupid; it won't eat you—a ewer with water; and a mouldering crust will be your food.'

But Albert-next-door never enters into the spirit of a thing. He mumbled something about tea-time.

Now Oswald, though stern, is always just, and besides we were all rather hungry, and tea was ready. So we had it at once, Albert-next-door and all—and we gave him what was left of the four-pound jar of apricot jam we got with the money Noel got for his poetry. And we saved our crusts for the prisoner.

Albert-next-door was very tiresome. Nobody could have had a nicer prison than he had. We fenced him into a corner with the old wire nursery fender and all the chairs, instead of putting him in the coal- cellar as we had first intended. And when he said the dog-chains were cold the girls were kind enough to warm his fetters thoroughly at the fire before we put them on him.

We got the straw cases of some bottles of wine someone sent Father one Christmas—it is some years ago, but the cases are quite good. We unpacked them very carefully and pulled them to pieces and scattered the straw about. It made a lovely straw pallet, and took ever so long to make—but Albert-next-door has yet to learn what gratitude really is. We got the bread trencher for the wooden platter where the prisoner's crusts were put—they were not mouldy, but we could not wait till they got so, and for the ewer we got the toilet jug out of the spare-room where nobody ever sleeps. And even then Albert-next-door couldn't be happy like the rest of us. He howled and cried and tried to get out, and he knocked the ewer over and stamped on the mouldering crusts. Luckily there was no water in the ewer because we had forgotten it, only dust and spiders. So we tied him up with the clothes-line from the back kitchen, and we had to hurry up, which was a pity for him. We might have had him rescued by a devoted page if he hadn't been so tiresome. In fact Noel was actually dressing up for the page when Albert-next-door kicked over the prison ewer.

We got a sheet of paper out of an old exercise-book, and we made H. O. prick his own thumb, because he is our little brother and it is our duty to teach him to be brave. We none of us mind pricking ourselves; we've done it heaps of times. H. O. didn't like it, but he agreed to do it, and I helped him a little because he was so slow, and when he saw the red bead of blood getting fatter and bigger as I squeezed his thumb he was very pleased, just as I had told him he would be.

This is what we wrote with H. O.'s blood, only the blood gave out when we got to 'Restored', and we had to write the rest with crimson lake, which is not the same colour, though I always use it, myself, for painting wounds.

While Oswald was writing it he heard Alice whispering to the prisoner that it would soon be over, and it was only play. The prisoner left off howling, so I pretended not to hear what she said. A Bandit Captain has to overlook things sometimes. This was the letter—

> 'Albert Morrison is held a prisoner by Bandits.
> On payment of three thousand pounds he will be
> restored to his sorrowing relatives, and all
> will be forgotten and forgiven.'

I was not sure about the last part, but Dicky was certain he had seen it in the paper, so I suppose it must have been all right.

We let H. O. take the letter; it was only fair, as it was his blood it was written with, and told him to leave it next door for Mrs Morrison.

H. O. came back quite quickly, and Albert-next-door's uncle came with him.

'What is all this, Albert?' he cried. 'Alas, alas, my nephew! Do I find you the prisoner of a desperate band of brigands?'

'Bandits,' said H. O; 'you know it says bandits.'

'I beg your pardon, gentlemen,' said Albert-next-door's uncle, 'bandits it is, of course. This, Albert, is the direct result of the pursuit of the guy on an occasion when your doting mother had expressly warned you to forgo the pleasures of the chase.'

Albert said it wasn't his fault, and he hadn't wanted to play.

'So ho!' said his uncle, 'impenitent too! Where's the dungeon?'

We explained the dungeon, and showed him the straw pallet and the ewer and the mouldering crusts and other things.

'Very pretty and complete,' he said. 'Albert, you are more highly privileged than ever I was. No one ever made me a nice dungeon when I was your age. I think I had better leave you where you are.'

Albert began to cry again and said he was sorry, and he would be a good boy.

'And on this old familiar basis you expect me to ransom you, do you? Honestly, my nephew, I doubt whether you are worth it. Besides, the sum mentioned in this document strikes me as excessive: Albert really is *not* worth three thousand pounds. Also by a strange and unfortunate chance I haven't the money about me. Couldn't you take less?'

We said perhaps we could.

'Say eightpence,' suggested Albert-next-door's uncle, 'which is all the small change I happen to have on my person.'

'Thank you very much,' said Alice as he held it out; 'but are you sure you can spare it? Because really it was only play.'

'Quite sure. Now, Albert, the game is over. You had better run home to your mother and tell her how much you've enjoyed yourself.'

When Albert-next-door had gone his uncle sat in the Guy Fawkes armchair and took Alice on his knee, and we sat round the fire waiting till it would be time to let off our fireworks. We roasted the chestnuts he sent Dicky out for, and he told us stories till it was nearly seven. His stories are first-rate—he does all the parts in different voices. At last he said—

'Look here, young-uns. I like to see you play and enjoy yourselves, and I don't think it hurts Albert to enjoy himself too.'

'I don't think he did much,' said H. O. But I knew what Albert-next- door's uncle meant because I am much older than H. O. He went on—

'But what about Albert's mother? Didn't you think how anxious she would be at his not coming home? As it happens I saw him come in with you, so we knew it was all right. But if I hadn't, eh?'

He only talks like that when he is very serious, or even angry. Other times he talks like people in books—to us, I mean.

We none of us said anything. But I was thinking. Then Alice spoke.

Girls seem not to mind saying things that we don't say. She put her arms round Albert-next-door's uncle's neck and said—

'We're very, very sorry. We didn't think about his mother. You see we try very hard not to think about other people's mothers because—'

Just then we heard Father's key in the door and Albert-next-door's uncle kissed Alice and put her down, and we all went down to meet Father. As we went I thought I heard Albert-next-door's uncle say something that sounded like 'Poor little beggars!'

He couldn't have meant us, when we'd been having such a jolly time, and chestnuts, and fireworks to look forward to after dinner and everything!

Chapter 8. Being Editors

It was Albert's uncle who thought of our trying a newspaper. He said he thought we should not find the bandit business a paying industry, as a permanency, and that journalism might be.

We had sold Noel's poetry and that piece of information about Lord Tottenham to the good editor, so we thought it would not be a bad idea to have a newspaper of our own. We saw plainly that editors must be very rich and powerful, because of the grand office and the man in the glass case, like a museum, and the soft carpets and big writing-table. Besides our having seen a whole handful of money that the editor pulled out quite carelessly from his trousers pocket when he gave me my five bob.

Dora wanted to be editor and so did Oswald, but he gave way to her because she is a girl, and afterwards he knew that it is true what it says in the copy-books about Virtue being its own Reward. Because you've no idea what a bother it is. Everybody wanted to put in everything just as they liked, no matter how much room there was on the page. It was simply awful! Dora put up with it as long as she could and then she said if she wasn't let alone she wouldn't go on being editor; they could be the paper's editors themselves, so there.

Then Oswald said, like a good brother: 'I will help you if you like, Dora,' and she said, 'You're more trouble than all the rest of them! Come and be editor and see how you like it. I give it up to you.' But she didn't, and we did it together. We let Albert-next-door be sub-editor, because he had hurt his foot with a nail in his boot that gathered.

When it was done Albert-next-door's uncle had it copied for us in typewriting, and we sent copies to all our friends, and then of course there was no one left that we could ask to buy it. We did not think of that until too late. We called the paper the Lewisham Recorder; Lewisham because we live there, and Recorder in memory of the good editor. I could write a better paper on my head, but an editor is not allowed to write all the paper. It is very hard, but he is not. You just have to fill up with what you can get from other writers. If I ever have time I will write a paper all by myself. It won't be patchy. We had no time to make it an illustrated paper, but I drew the ship going down with all hands for the first copy. But the typewriter can't draw ships, so it was left out in the other copies. The time the first paper took to write out no one would believe! This was the Newspaper:

THE LEWISHAM RECORDER

EDITORS: DORA AND OSWALD BASTABLE

EDITORIAL NOTE

Every paper is written for some reason. Ours is because we want to sell it and get money. If what we have written brings happiness to any sad heart we shall not have laboured in vain. But we want the money too. Many papers are content with the sad heart and the happiness, but we are not like that, and it is best not to be deceitful. EDITORS.

There will be two serial stories; One by Dicky and one by all of us. In a serial story you only put in one chapter at a time. But we shall put all our serial story at once, if Dora has time to copy it. Dicky's will come later on.

SERIAL STORY
BY US ALL

CHAPTER I—by Dora

The sun was setting behind a romantic-looking tower when two strangers might have been observed descending the crest of the hill. The eldest, a man in the prime of life; the other a handsome youth who reminded everybody of Quentin Durward. They approached the Castle, in which the fair Lady Alicia awaited her deliverers. She leaned from the castellated window and waved her lily hand as they approached. They returned her signal, and retired to seek rest and refreshment at a neighbouring hostelry.

CHAPTER II—by Alice

The Princess was very uncomfortable in the tower, because her fairy godmother had told her all sorts of horrid things would happen if she didn't catch a mouse every day, and she had caught so many mice that now there were hardly any left to catch. So she sent her carrier pigeon to ask the noble Strangers if they could send her a few mice—because she would be of age in a few days and then it wouldn't matter. So the fairy godmother—- (I'm very sorry, but there's no room to make the chapters any longer.-ED.)

CHAPTER III—by the Sub-Editor

(I can't—I'd much rather not—I don't know how.)

CHAPTER IV—by Dicky

I must now retrace my steps and tell you something about our hero. You must know he had been to an awfully jolly school, where they had turkey and goose every day for dinner, and never any mutton, and as many helps of pudding as a fellow cared to send up his plate for—so of course they had all grown up very strong, and before he left school he challenged the Head to have it out man to man, and he gave it him, I tell you. That was the education that made him able to fight Red Indians, and to be the stranger who might have been observed in the first chapter.

CHAPTER V—by Noel

I think it's time something happened in this story. So then the dragon he came out, blowing fire out of his nose, and he said—

'Come on, you valiant man and true, I'd like to have a set-to along of you!'

(That's bad English.—ED. I don't care; it's what the dragon said. Who told you dragons didn't talk bad English?—Noel.)

So the hero, whose name was Noeloninuris, replied—

'My blade is sharp, my axe is keen,
You're not nearly as big as a good many
dragons I've seen.'

(Don't put in so much poetry, Noel. It's not fair, because none of the others can do it.—ED.)

And then they went at it, and he beat the dragon, just as he did the Head in Dicky's part of the Story, and so he married the Princess, and they lived—- (No they didn't—not till the last chapter.—ED.)

CHAPTER VI—by H. O.

I think it's a very nice Story—but what about the mice? I don't want to say any more. Dora can have what's left of my chapter.

CHAPTER VII—by the Editors

And so when the dragon was dead there were lots of mice, because he used to kill them for his tea but now they rapidly multiplied and ravaged the country, so the fair lady Alicia, sometimes called the Princess, had to say she would not marry any one unless they could rid the country of this plague of mice. Then the Prince, whose real name didn't begin with N, but was Osrawalddo, waved his magic sword, and the dragon stood before them, bowing gracefully. They made him promise to be good, and then they forgave him; and when the wedding breakfast came, all the bones were saved for him. And so they were married and lived happy ever after.

(What became of the other stranger?—NOEL. The dragon ate him because he asked too many questions.—EDITORS.)

This is the end of the story.

INSTRUCTIVE

It only takes four hours and a quarter now to get from London to Manchester; but I should not think any one would if they could help it.

A DREADFUL WARNING. A wicked boy told me a very instructive thing about ginger. They had opened one of the large jars, and he happened to take out quite a lot, and he made it all right by dropping marbles in, till there was as much ginger as before. But he told me that on the Sunday, when it was coming near the part where there is only juice generally, I had no idea what his feelings were. I don't see what he could have said when they asked him. I should be sorry to act like it.

SCIENTIFIC

Experiments should always be made out of doors. And don't use benzoline.—DICKY. (That was when he burnt his eyebrows off.—ED.)

The earth is 2,400 miles round, and 800 through—at least I think so, but perhaps it's the other way.—DICKY. (You ought to have been sure before you began.—ED.)

SCIENTIFIC COLUMN

In this so-called Nineteenth Century Science is but too little considered in the nurseries of the rich and proud. But we are not like that.

It is not generally known that if you put bits of camphor in luke-warm water it will move about. If you drop sweet oil in, the camphor will dart away and then stop moving. But don't drop any till you are tired of it, because the camphor won't any more afterwards. Much amusement and instruction is lost by not knowing things like this.

If you put a sixpence under a shilling in a wine-glass, and blow hard down the side of the glass, the sixpence will jump up and sit on the top of the shilling. At least I can't do it myself, but my cousin can. He is in the Navy.

ANSWERS TO CORRESPONDENTS

Noel. You are very poetical, but I am sorry to say it will not do.

Alice. Nothing will ever make your hair curl, so it's no use. Some people say it's more important to tidy up as you go along. I don't mean you in particular, but every one.

H. O. We never said you were tubby, but the Editor does not know any cure.

Noel. If there is any of the paper over when this newspaper is finished, I will exchange it for your shut-up inkstand, or the knife that has the useful thing in it for taking stones out of horses' feet, but you can't have it without.

H. O. There are many ways how your steam engine might stop working. You might ask Dicky. He knows one of them. I think it is the way yours stopped.

Noel. If you think that by filling the garden with sand you can make crabs build their nests there you are not at all sensible.

You have altered your poem about the battle of Waterloo so often, that we cannot read it except where the Duke waves his sword and says some thing we can't read either. Why did you write it on blotting-paper with purple chalk?—ED. (Because YOU KNOW WHO sneaked my pencil.—NOEL.)

POETRY

The Assyrian came down like a wolf on the fold,
And the way he came down was awful, I'm told;
But it's nothing to the way one of the Editors comes down on
m
e,
If I crumble my bread-and-butter or spill my tea.
N
OEL.

CURIOUS FACTS

If you hold a guinea-pig up by his tail his eyes drop out.

You can't do half the things yourself that children in books do, making models or soon. I wonder why?—ALICE.

If you take a date's stone out and put in an almond and eat them together, it is prime. I found this out.—SUB-EDITOR.

If you put your wet hand into boiling lead it will not hurt you if you draw it out quickly enough. I have never tried this.—DORA.

THE PURRING CLASS

(Instructive Article)

If I ever keep a school everything shall be quite different. Nobody shall learn anything they don't want to. And sometimes instead of having masters and mistresses we will have cats, and we will dress up in cat skins and learn purring. 'Now, my dears,' the old cat will say, 'one, two, three all purr together,' and we shall purr like anything.

She won't teach us to mew, but we shall know how without teaching. Children do know some things without being taught.—ALICE.

POETRY (Translated into French by Dora)

Quand j'etais jeune et j'etais fou
J'achetai un violon pour dix-huit sous
Et tous les airs que je jouai
Etait over the hills and far away.

Another piece of it

Mercie jolie vache qui fait
Bon lait pour mon dejeuner
Tous les matins tous les soirs
Mon pain je mange, ton lait je boire.

RECREATIONS

It is a mistake to think that cats are playful. I often try to get a cat to play with me, and she never seems to care about the game, no matter how little it hurts.—H. O.

Making pots and pans with clay is fun, but do not tell the grown-ups. It is better to surprise them; and then you must say at once how easily it washes off—much easier than ink.—DICKY.

SAM REDFERN, OR THE BUSH RANGER'S BURIAL

By Dicky

'Well, Annie, I have bad news for you,' said Mr Ridgway, as he entered the comfortable dining-room of his cabin in the Bush.

'Sam Redfern the Bushranger is about this part of the Bush just now. I hope he will not attack us with his gang.'

'I hope not,' responded Annie, a gentle maiden of some sixteen summers.

Just then came a knock at the door of the hut, and a gruff voice asked them to open the door.

'It is Sam Redfern the Bushranger, father,' said the girl.

'The same,' responded the voice, and the next moment the hall door was smashed in, and Sam Redfern sprang in, followed by his gang.

CHAPTER II

Annie's Father was at once overpowered, and Annie herself lay bound with cords on the drawing-room sofa. Sam Redfern set a guard round the lonely hut, and all human aid was despaired of. But you never know. Far away in the Bush a different scene was being enacted.

'Must be Injuns,' said a tall man to himself as he pushed his way through the brushwood. It was Jim Carlton, the celebrated detective. 'I know them,' he added; 'they are Apaches.' just then ten Indians in full war-paint appeared. Carlton raised his rifle and fired, and slinging their scalps on his arm he hastened towards the humble log hut where resided his affianced bride, Annie Ridgway, sometimes known as the Flower of the Bush.

CHAPTER III

The moon was low on the horizon, and Sam Redfern was seated at a drinking bout with some of his boon companions.

They had rifled the cellars of the hut, and the rich wines flowed like water in the golden goblets of Mr Ridgway.

But Annie had made friends with one of the gang, a noble, good-hearted man who had joined Sam Redfern by mistake, and she had told him to go and get the police as quickly as possible.

'Ha! ha!' cried Redfern, 'now I am enjoying myself!' He little knew that his doom was near upon him.

Just then Annie gave a piercing scream, and Sam Redfern got up, seizing his revolver. 'Who are you?' he cried, as a man entered.

'I am Jim Carlton, the celebrated detective,' said the new arrival.

Sam Redfern's revolver dropped from his nerveless fingers, but the next moment he had sprung upon the detective with the well-known activity of the mountain sheep, and Annie shrieked, for she had grown to love the rough Bushranger.

(To be continued at the end of the paper if there is room.)

SCHOLASTIC

A new slate is horrid till it is washed in milk. I like the green spots on them to draw patterns round. I know a good way to make a slate- pencil squeak, but I won't put it in because I don't want to make it common.—SUB-EDITOR.

Peppermint is a great help with arithmetic. The boy who was second in the Oxford Local always did it. He gave me two. The examiner said to him, 'Are you eating peppermints?' And he said, 'No, Sir.'

He told me afterwards it was quite true, because he was only sucking one. I'm glad I wasn't asked. I should never have thought of that, and I could have had to say 'Yes.'—OSWALD.

THE WRECK OF THE 'MALABAR'

By Noel

(Author of 'A Dream of Ancient Ancestors.') He isn't really—but he put it in to make it seem more real.

Hark! what is that noise of rolling
Waves and thunder in the air?
'Tis the death-knell of the sailors
And officers and passengers of the good ship Malabar.

It was a fair and lovely noon
When the good ship put out of port
And people said 'ah little we think
How soon she will be the elements' sport.'

She was indeed a lovely sight
Upon the billows with sails spread.
But the captain folded his gloomy arms,
Ah—if she had been a life-boat instead!

See the captain stern yet gloomy
Flings his son upon a rock,
Hoping that there his darling boy
May escape the wreck.

Alas in vain the loud winds roared
And nobody was saved.
That was the wreck of the Malabar,
Then let us toll for the brave.
NOEL.

GARDENING NOTES

It is useless to plant cherry-stones in the hope of eating the fruit, because they don't!

Alice won't lend her gardening tools again, because the last time Noel left them out in the rain, and I don't like it. He said he didn't.

SEEDS AND BULBS

These are useful to play at shop with, until you are ready. Not at dinner-parties, for they will not grow unless uncooked. Potatoes are not grown with seed, but with chopped-up potatoes. Apple trees are grown from twigs, which is less wasteful.

Oak trees come from acorns. Every one knows this. When Noel says he could grow one from a peach stone wrapped up in oak leaves, he shows that he knows nothing about gardening but marigolds, and when I passed by his garden I thought they seemed just like weeds now the flowers have been picked.

A boy once dared me to eat a bulb.

Dogs are very industrious and fond of gardening. Pincher is always planting bones, but they never grow up. There couldn't be a bone tree. I think this is what makes him bark so unhappily at night. He has never tried planting dog-biscuit, but he is fonder of bones, and perhaps he wants to be quite sure about them first.

SAM REDFERN, OR THE BUSHRANGER'S BURIAL

By Dicky

CHAPTER IV AND LAST

This would have been a jolly good story if they had let me finish it at the beginning of the paper as I wanted to. But now I have forgotten how I meant it to end, and I have lost my book about Red Indians, and all my Boys of England have been sneaked. The girls say 'Good riddance!' so I expect they did it. They want me just to put in which Annie married, but I shan't, so they will never know.

We have now put everything we can think of into the paper. It takes a lot of thinking about. I don't know how grown-ups manage to write all they do. It must make their heads ache, especially lesson books.

Albert-next-door only wrote one chapter of the serial story, but he could have done some more if he had wanted to. He could not write out any of the things because he cannot spell. He says he can, but it takes him such a long time he might just as well not be able. There are one or two things more. I am sick of it, but Dora says she will write them in.

LEGAL ANSWER WANTED. A quantity of excellent string is offered if you know whether there really is a law passed about not buying gunpowder under thirteen.—DICKY.

The price of this paper is one shilling each, and sixpence extra for the picture of the Malabar going down with all hands. If we sell one hundred copies we will write another paper.

* * *

And so we would have done, but we never did. Albert-next-door's uncle gave us two shillings, that was all. You can't restore fallen fortunes with two shillings!

Chapter 9. The G. B.

Being editors is not the best way to wealth. We all feel this now, and highwaymen are not respected any more like they used to be.

I am sure we had tried our best to restore our fallen fortunes. We felt their fall very much, because we knew the Bastables had been rich once. Dora and Oswald can remember when Father was always bringing nice things home from London, and there used to be turkeys and geese and wine and cigars come by the carrier at Christmas-time, and boxes of candied fruit and French plums in ornamental boxes with silk and velvet and gilding on them. They were called prunes, but the prunes you buy at the grocer's are quite different. But now there is seldom anything nice brought from London, and the turkey and the prune people have forgotten Father's address.

'How *can* we restore those beastly fallen fortunes?' said Oswald. 'We've tried digging and writing and princesses and being editors.'

'And being bandits,' said H. O.

'When did you try that?' asked Dora quickly. 'You know I told you it was wrong.'

'It wasn't wrong the way we did it,' said Alice, quicker still, before Oswald could say, 'Who asked you to tell us anything about it?' which would have been rude, and he is glad he didn't. 'We only caught Albert- next-door.'

'Oh, Albert-next-door!' said Dora contemptuously, and I felt more comfortable; for even after I didn't say, 'Who asked you, and cetera,' I was afraid Dora was going to come the good elder sister over us. She does that a jolly sight too often.

Dicky looked up from the paper he was reading and said, 'This sounds likely,' and he read out—

> 'L100 secures partnership in lucrative business for sale of
> useful patent. £10 weekly.
> No personal attendance necessary.
> Jobbins, 300, Old Street Road.'

'I wish we could secure that partnership,' said Oswald. He is twelve, and a very thoughtful boy for his age.

Alice looked up from her painting. She was trying to paint a fairy queen's frock with green bice, and it wouldn't rub. There is something funny about green bice. It never will rub off; no matter how expensive your paintbox is—and even boiling water is very little use.

She said, 'Bother the bice! And, Oswald, it's no use thinking about that. Where are we to get a hundred pounds?'

'Ten pounds a week is five pounds to us,' Oswald went on—he had done the sum in his head while Alice was talking—'because partnership means halves. It would be A1.'

Noel sat sucking his pencil—he had been writing poetry as usual. I saw the first two lines—

I wonder why Green Bice

Is never very nice.

Suddenly he said, 'I wish a fairy would come down the chimney and drop a jewel on the table—a jewel worth just a hundred pounds.'

'She might as well give you the hundred pounds while she was about it,' said Dora.

'Or while she was about it she might as well give us five pounds a week,' said Alice.

'Or fifty,' said I.

'Or five hundred,' said Dicky.

I saw H. O. open his mouth, and I knew he was going to say, 'Or five thousand,' so I said—

'Well, she won't give us fivepence, but if you'd only do as I am always saying, and rescue a wealthy old gentleman from deadly peril he would give us a pot of money, and we could have the partnership and five pounds a week. Five pounds a week would buy a great many things.'

Then Dicky said, 'Why shouldn't we borrow it?' So we said, 'Who from?' and then he read this out of the paper—

MONEY PRIVATELY WITHOUT FEES
THE BOND STREET BANK
Manager, Z. Rosenbaum.

> Advances cash from £20 to £10,000 on ladies' or gentlemen's note of hand alone, without security. No fees. No inquiries. Absolute privacy guaranteed.

'What does it all mean?' asked H. O.

'It means that there is a kind gentleman who has a lot of money, and he doesn't know enough poor people to help, so he puts it in the paper that he will help them, by lending them his money—that's it, isn't it, Dicky?'

Dora explained this and Dicky said, 'Yes.' And H. O. said he was a Generous Benefactor, like in Miss Edgeworth. Then Noel wanted to know what a note of hand was, and Dicky knew that, because he had read it in a book, and it was just a letter saying you will pay the money when you can, and signed with your name.

'No inquiries!' said Alice. 'Oh—Dicky—do you think he would?'

'Yes, I think so,' said Dicky. 'I wonder Father doesn't go to this kind gentleman. I've seen his name before on a circular in Father's study.'

'Perhaps he has.' said Dora.

But the rest of us were sure he hadn't, because, of course, if he had, there would have been more money to buy nice things. Just then Pincher jumped up and knocked over the painting-water. He is a very careless dog. I wonder why painting-water is always such an ugly colour? Dora ran for a duster to wipe it up, and H. O. dropped drops of the water on his hands and said he had got the plague. So we played at the plague for a bit, and I was an Arab physician with a bath-towel turban, and cured the plague with magic acid-drops. After that it was time for dinner, and after dinner we talked it all over and settled that we would go and see the Generous Benefactor the very next day. But we thought perhaps the G. B.—it is short for Generous Benefactor—would not like it if there were so many of us. I have often noticed that it is the worst of our being six—people think six a great many, when it's children. That sentence looks wrong somehow. I mean they don't mind six pairs of boots, or six pounds of apples, or six oranges, especially in equations, but they seem to think you ought not to have five brothers and sisters. Of course Dicky was to go, because it was his idea. Dora had to go to Blackheath to see an old lady, a friend of Father's, so she couldn't go. Alice said *she* ought to go, because it said, 'Ladies *and* gentlemen,' and perhaps the G. B. wouldn't let us have the money unless there were both kinds of us.

H. O. said Alice wasn't a lady; and she said *he* wasn't going, anyway. Then he called her a disagreeable cat, and she began to cry.

But Oswald always tries to make up quarrels, so he said—

'You're little sillies, both of you!'

And Dora said, 'Don't cry, Alice; he only meant you weren't a grown-up lady.'

Then H. O. said, 'What else did you think I meant, Disagreeable?'

So Dicky said, 'Don't be disagreeable yourself, H. O. Let her alone and say you're sorry, or I'll jolly well make you!'

So H. O. said he was sorry. Then Alice kissed him and said she was sorry too; and after that H. O. gave her a hug, and said, 'Now I'm *really and truly* sorry,' So it was all right.

Noel went the last time any of us went to London, so he was out of it, and Dora said she would take him to Blackheath if we'd take H. O. So as there'd been a little disagreeableness we thought it was better to take him, and we did. At first we thought we'd tear our oldest things a bit more, and put some patches of different colours on them, to show the G. B. how much we wanted money. But Dora said that would be a sort of cheating, pretending we were poorer than we are. And Dora is right sometimes, though she is our elder sister. Then we thought we'd better wear our best things, so that the G. B. might see we weren't so very poor that he couldn't trust us to pay his money back when we had it. But Dora said that would be wrong too. So it came to our being quite honest, as Dora said, and going just as we were, without even washing our faces and hands; but when I looked at H. O. in the train I wished we had not been quite so particularly honest.

Every one who reads this knows what it is like to go in the train, so I shall not tell about it—though it was rather fun, especially the part where the guard came for the tickets at Waterloo, and H. O. was under the seat and pretended to be a dog without a ticket. We went to Charing Cross, and we just went round to Whitehall to see the soldiers and then by St James's for the same reason—and when we'd looked in the shops a bit we got to Brook Street, Bond Street. It was a brass plate on a door next to a shop—a very grand place, where they sold bonnets and hats— all very bright and smart, and no tickets on them to tell you the price. We rang a bell and a boy opened the door and we asked for Mr Rosenbaum. The boy was not polite; he did not ask us in. So then Dicky gave him his visiting card; it was one of Father's really, but the name is the same, Mr Richard Bastable, and we others wrote our names underneath. I happened to have a piece of pink chalk in my pocket and we wrote them with that.

Then the boy shut the door in our faces and we waited on the step. But presently he came down and asked our business. So Dicky said—

'Money advanced, young shaver! and don't be all day about it!'

And then he made us wait again, till I was quite stiff in my legs, but Alice liked it because of looking at the hats and bonnets, and at last the door opened, and the boy said—

'Mr Rosenbaum will see you,' so we wiped our feet on the mat, which said so, and we went up stairs with soft carpets and into a room. It was a beautiful room. I wished then we had put on our best things, or at least washed a little. But it was too late now.

The room had velvet curtains and a soft, soft carpet, and it was full of the most splendid things. Black and gold cabinets, and china, and statues, and pictures. There was a picture of a cabbage and a pheasant and a dead hare that was just like life, and I would have given worlds to have it for my own. The fur was so natural I should never have been tired of looking at it; but Alice liked the one of the girl with the broken jug best. Then besides the pictures there were clocks and candlesticks and vases, and gilt looking-glasses, and boxes of cigars and scent and things littered all over the chairs and tables. It was a wonderful place, and in the middle of all the splendour was a little old gentleman with a very long black coat and a very long white beard and a hookey nose—like a falcon. And he put on a pair of gold spectacles and looked at us as if he knew exactly how much our clothes were worth.

And then, while we elder ones were thinking how to begin, for we had all said 'Good morning' as we came in, of course, H. O. began before we could stop him. He said:

'Are you the G. B.?'

'The *what*?' said the little old gentleman.

'The G. B.,' said H. O., and I winked at him to shut up, but he didn't see me, and the G. B. did. He waved his hand at *me* to shut up, so I had to, and H. O. went on—'It stands for Generous Benefactor.'

The old gentleman frowned. Then he said, 'Your Father sent you here, I suppose?'

'No he didn't,' said Dicky. 'Why did you think so?'

The old gentleman held out the card, and I explained that we took that because Father's name happens to be the same as Dicky's.

'Doesn't he know you've come?'

'No,' said Alice, 'we shan't tell him till we've got the partnership, because his own business worries him a good deal and we don't want to bother him with ours till it's settled, and then we shall give him half our share.'

The old gentleman took off his spectacles and rumpled his hair with his hands, then he said, 'Then what *did* you come for?'

'We saw your advertisement,' Dicky said, 'and we want a hundred pounds on our note of hand, and my sister came so that there should be both kinds of us; and we want it to buy a partnership with in the lucrative business for sale of useful patent. No personal attendance necessary.'

'I don't think I quite follow you,' said the G. B. 'But one thing I should like settled before entering more fully into the matter: why did you call me Generous Benefactor?'

'Well, you see,' said Alice, smiling at him to show she wasn't frightened, though I know really she was, awfully, 'we thought it was so *very* kind of you to try to find out the poor people who want money and to help them and lend them your money.'

'Hum!' said the G. B. 'Sit down.'

He cleared the clocks and vases and candlesticks off some of the chairs, and we sat down. The chairs were velvety, with gilt legs. It was like a king's palace.

'Now,' he said, 'you ought to be at school, instead of thinking about money. Why aren't you?'

We told him that we should go to school again when Father could manage it, but meantime we wanted to do something to restore the fallen fortunes of the House of Bastable. And we said we thought the lucrative patent would be a very good thing. He asked a lot of questions, and we told him everything we didn't think Father would mind our telling, and at last he said—

'You wish to borrow money. When will you repay it?'

'As soon as we've got it, of course,' Dicky said.

Then the G. B. said to Oswald, 'You seem the eldest,' but I explained to him that it was Dicky's idea, so my being eldest didn't matter. Then he said to Dicky—'You are a minor, I presume?'

Dicky said he wasn't yet, but he had thought of being a mining engineer some day, and going to Klondike.

'Minor, not miner,' said the G. B. 'I mean you're not of age?'

'I shall be in ten years, though,' said Dicky. 'Then you might repudiate the loan,' said the G. B., and Dicky said 'What?'

Of course he ought to have said 'I beg your pardon. I didn't quite catch what you said'—that is what Oswald would have said. It is more polite than 'What.'

'Repudiate the loan,' the G. B repeated. 'I mean you might say you would not pay me back the money, and the law could not compel you to do so.'

'Oh, well, if you think we're such sneaks,' said Dicky, and he got up off his chair. But the G. B. said, 'Sit down, sit down; I was only joking.'

Then he talked some more, and at last he said—'I don't advise you to enter into that partnership. It's a swindle. Many advertisements are. And I have not a hundred pounds by me to-day to lend you. But I will lend you a pound, and you can spend it as you like. And when you are twenty-one you shall pay me back.'

'I shall pay you back long before that,' said Dicky. 'Thanks, awfully! And what about the note of hand?'

'Oh,' said the G. B., 'I'll trust to your honour. Between gentlemen, you know—and ladies'—he made a beautiful bow to Alice—'a word is as good as a bond.'

Then he took out a sovereign, and held it in his hand while he talked to us. He gave us a lot of good advice about not going into business too young, and about doing our lessons—just swatting a bit, on our own hook, so as not to be put in a low form when we went back to school. And all the time he was stroking the sovereign and looking at it as if he thought it very beautiful. And so it was, for it was a new one. Then at last he held it out to Dicky, and when Dicky put out his hand for it the G. B. suddenly put the sovereign back in his pocket.

'No,' he said, 'I won't give you the sovereign. I'll give you fifteen shillings, and this nice bottle of scent. It's worth far more than the five shillings I'm charging you for it. And, when you can, you shall pay me back the pound, and sixty per cent interest—sixty per cent, sixty per cent.'

'What's that?' said H. O.

The G. B. said he'd tell us that when we paid back the sovereign, but sixty per cent was nothing to be afraid of. He gave Dicky the money. And the boy was made to call a cab, and the G. B. put us in and shook hands with us all, and asked Alice to give him a kiss, so she did, and H. O. would do it too, though his face was dirtier than ever. The G. B. paid the cabman and told him what station to go to, and so we went home.

That evening Father had a letter by the seven-o'clock post. And when he had read it he came up into the nursery. He did not look quite so unhappy as usual, but he looked grave.

'You've been to Mr Rosenbaum's,' he said.

So we told him all about it. It took a long time, and Father sat in the armchair. It was jolly. He doesn't often come and talk to us now. He has to spend all his time thinking about his business. And when we'd told him all about it he said—

'You haven't done any harm this time, children; rather good than harm, indeed. Mr Rosenbaum has written me a very kind letter.'

'Is he a friend of yours, Father?' Oswald asked. 'He is an acquaintance,' said my father, frowning a little, 'we have done some business together. And this letter—' he stopped and then said: 'No; you didn't do any harm to-day; but I want you for the future not to do anything so serious as to try to buy a partnership without consulting me, that's all. I don't want to interfere with your plays and pleasures; but you will consult me about business matters, won't you?'

Of course we said we should be delighted, but then Alice, who was sitting on his knee, said, 'We didn't like to bother you.'

Father said, 'I haven't much time to be with you, for my business takes most of my time. It is an anxious business—but I can't bear to think of your being left all alone like this.'

He looked so sad we all said we liked being alone. And then he looked sadder than ever.

Then Alice said, 'We don't mean that exactly, Father. It is rather lonely sometimes, since Mother died.'

Then we were all quiet a little while. Father stayed with us till we went to bed, and when he said good night he looked quite cheerful. So we told him so, and he said—

'Well, the fact is, that letter took a weight off my mind.' I can't think what he meant—but I am sure the G. B. would be pleased if he could know he had taken a weight off somebody's mind. He is that sort of man, I think.

We gave the scent to Dora. It is not quite such good scent as we thought it would be, but we had fifteen shillings—and they were all good, so is the G. B.

And until those fifteen shillings were spent we felt almost as jolly as though our fortunes had been properly restored. You do not notice your general fortune so much, as long as you have money in your pocket. This is why so many children with regular pocket-money have never felt it their duty to seek for treasure. So, perhaps, our not having pocket- money was a blessing in disguise. But the disguise was quite impenetrable, like the villains' in the books; and it seemed still more so when the fifteen shillings were all spent. Then at last the others agreed to let Oswald try his way of seeking for treasure, but they were not at all keen about it, and many a boy less firm than Oswald would have chucked the whole thing. But Oswald knew that a hero must rely on himself alone. So he stuck to it, and presently the others saw their duty, and backed him up.

Chapter 10. Lord Tottenham

Oswald is a boy of firm and unswerving character, and he had never wavered from his first idea. He felt quite certain that the books were right, and that the best way to restore fallen fortunes was to rescue an old gentleman in distress. Then he brings you up as his own son: but if you preferred to go on being your own father's son I expect the old gentleman would make it up to you some other way. In the books the least thing does it—you put up the railway carriage window—or you pick up his purse when he drops it—or you say a hymn when he suddenly asks you to, and then your fortune is made.

The others, as I said, were very slack about it, and did not seem to care much about trying the rescue. They said there wasn't any deadly peril, and we should have to make one before we could rescue the old gentleman from it, but Oswald didn't see that that mattered. However, he thought he would try some of the easier ways first, by himself.

So he waited about the station, pulling up railway carriage windows for old gentlemen who looked likely—but nothing happened, and at last the porters said he was a nuisance. So that was no go. No one ever asked him to say a hymn, though he had learned a nice short one, beginning 'New every morning'—and when an old gentleman did drop a two-shilling piece just by Ellis's the hairdresser's, and Oswald picked it up, and was just thinking what he should say when he returned it, the old gentleman caught him by the collar and called him a young thief. It would have been very unpleasant for Oswald if he hadn't happened to be a very brave boy, and knew the policeman on that beat very well indeed. So the policeman backed him up, and the old gentleman said he was sorry, and offered Oswald sixpence. Oswald refused it with polite disdain, and nothing more happened at all.

When Oswald had tried by himself and it had not come off, he said to the others, 'We're wasting our time, not trying to rescue the old gentleman in deadly peril. Come—buck up! Do let's do something!'

It was dinner-time, and Pincher was going round getting the bits off the plates. There were plenty because it was cold-mutton day. And Alice said—

'It's only fair to try Oswald's way—he has tried all the things the others thought of. Why couldn't we rescue Lord Tottenham?'

Lord Tottenham is the old gentleman who walks over the Heath every day in a paper collar at three o'clock—and when he gets halfway, if there is no one about, he changes his collar and throws the dirty one into the furze-bushes.

Dicky said, 'Lord Tottenham's all right—but where's the deadly peril?'

And we couldn't think of any. There are no highwaymen on Blackheath now, I am sorry to say. And though Oswald said half of us could be highwaymen and the other half rescue party, Dora kept on saying it would be wrong to be a highwayman—and so we had to give that up.

Then Alice said, 'What about Pincher?'

And we all saw at once that it could be done.

Pincher is very well bred, and he does know one or two things, though we never could teach him to beg. But if you tell him to hold on—he will do it, even if you only say 'Seize him!' in a whisper.

So we arranged it all. Dora said she wouldn't play; she said she thought it was wrong, and she knew it was silly—so we left her out, and she went and sat in the dining-room with a goody-book, so as to be able to say she didn't have anything to do with it, if we got into a row over it.

Alice and H. O. were to hide in the furze-bushes just by where Lord Tottenham changes his collar, and they were to whisper, 'Seize him!' to Pincher; and then when Pincher had seized Lord Tottenham we were to go and rescue him from his deadly peril. And he would say, 'How can I reward you, my noble young preservers?' and it would be all right.

So we went up to the Heath. We were afraid of being late. Oswald told the others what Procrastination was—so they got to the furze-bushes a little after two o'clock, and it was rather cold. Alice and H. O. and Pincher hid, but Pincher did not like it any more than they did, and as we three walked up and down we heard him whining. And Alice kept saying, 'I *am* so cold! Isn't he coming yet?' And H. O. wanted to come out and jump about to warm himself. But we told him he must learn to be a Spartan boy, and that he ought to be very thankful he hadn't got a beastly fox eating his inside all the time. H. O. is our little brother, and we are not going to let it be our fault if he grows up a milksop. Besides, it was not really cold. It was his knees—he wears socks. So they stayed where they were. And at last, when even the other three who were walking about were beginning to feel rather chilly, we saw Lord Tottenham's big black cloak coming along, flapping in the wind like a great bird. So we said to Alice—

'Hist! he approaches. You'll know when to set Pincher on by hearing Lord Tottenham talking to himself—he always does while he is taking off his collar.'

Then we three walked slowly away whistling to show we were not thinking of anything. Our lips were rather cold, but we managed to do it.

Lord Tottenham came striding along, talking to himself. People call him the mad Protectionist. I don't know what it means—but I don't think people ought to call a Lord such names.

As he passed us he said, 'Ruin of the country, sir! Fatal error, fatal error!' And then we looked back and saw he was getting quite near where Pincher was, and Alice and H. O. We walked on—so that he shouldn't think we were looking—and in a minute we heard Pincher's bark, and then nothing for a bit; and then we looked round, and sure enough good old Pincher had got Lord Tottenham by the trouser leg and was holding on like billy-ho, so we started to run.

Lord Tottenham had got his collar half off—it was sticking out sideways under his ear—and he was shouting, 'Help, help, murder!' exactly as if some one had explained to him beforehand what he was to do. Pincher was growling and snarling and holding on. When we got to him I stopped and said—

'Dicky, we must rescue this good old man.'

Lord Tottenham roared in his fury, 'Good old man be—' something or othered. 'Call the dog off.'

So Oswald said, 'It is a dangerous task—but who would hesitate to do an act of true bravery?'

And all the while Pincher was worrying and snarling, and Lord Tottenham shouting to us to get the dog away. He was dancing about in the road with Pincher hanging on like grim death; and his collar flapping about, where it was undone.

Then Noel said, 'Haste, ere yet it be too late.' So I said to Lord Tottenham—

'Stand still, aged sir, and I will endeavour to alleviate your distress.'

He stood still, and I stooped down and caught hold of Pincher and whispered, 'Drop it, sir; drop it!'

So then Pincher dropped it, and Lord Tottenham fastened his collar again—he never does change it if there's any one looking—and he said—

'I'm much obliged, I'm sure. Nasty vicious brute! Here's something to drink my health.'

But Dicky explained that we are teetotallers, and do not drink people's healths. So Lord Tottenham said, 'Well, I'm much obliged any way. And now I come to look at you—of course, you're not young ruffians, but gentlemen's sons, eh? Still, you won't be above taking a tip from an old boy—I wasn't when I was your age,' and he pulled out half a sovereign.

It was very silly; but now we'd done it I felt it would be beastly mean to take the old boy's chink after putting him in such a funk. He didn't say anything about bringing us up as his own sons—so I didn't know what to do. I let Pincher go, and was just going to say he was very welcome, and we'd rather not have the money, which seemed the best way out of it, when that beastly dog spoiled the whole show. Directly I let him go he began to jump about at us and bark for joy, and try to lick our faces. He was so proud of what he'd done. Lord Tottenham opened his eyes and he just said, 'The dog seems to know you.'

And then Oswald saw it was all up, and he said, 'Good morning,' and tried to get away. But Lord Tottenham said—

'Not so fast!' And he caught Noel by the collar. Noel gave a howl, and Alice ran out from the bushes. Noel is her favourite. I'm sure I don't know why. Lord Tottenham looked at her, and he said—

'So there are more of you!' And then H. O. came out.

'Do you complete the party?' Lord Tottenham asked him. And H. O. said there were only five of us this time.

Lord Tottenham turned sharp off and began to walk away, holding Noel by the collar. We caught up with him, and asked him where he was going, and he said, 'To the Police Station.' So then I said quite politely, 'Well, don't take Noel; he's not strong, and he easily gets upset. Besides, it wasn't his doing. If you want to take any one take me—it was my very own idea.'

Dicky behaved very well. He said, 'If you take Oswald I'll go too, but don't take Noel; he's such a delicate little chap.'

Lord Tottenham stopped, and he said, 'You should have thought of that before.' Noel was howling all the time, and his face was very white, and Alice said—

'Oh, do let Noel go, dear, good, kind Lord Tottenham; he'll faint if you don't, I know he will, he does sometimes. Oh, I wish we'd never done it! Dora said it was wrong.'

'Dora displayed considerable common sense,' said Lord Tottenham, and he let Noel go. And Alice put her arm round Noel and tried to cheer him up, but he was all trembly, and as white as paper.

Then Lord Tottenham said—

'Will you give me your word of honour not to try to escape?'

So we said we would.

'Then follow me,' he said, and led the way to a bench. We all followed, and Pincher too, with his tail between his legs—he knew something was wrong. Then Lord Tottenham sat down, and he made Oswald and Dicky and H. O. stand in front of him, but he let Alice and Noel sit down. And he said—

'You set your dog on me, and you tried to make me believe you were saving me from it. And you would have taken my half-sovereign. Such conduct is most—No—you shall tell me what it is, sir, and speak the truth.'

So I had to say it was most ungentlemanly, but I said I hadn't been going to take the half-sovereign.

'Then what did you do it for?' he asked. 'The truth, mind.'

So I said, 'I see now it was very silly, and Dora said it was wrong, but it didn't seem so till we did it. We wanted to restore the fallen fortunes of our house, and in the books if you rescue an old gentleman from deadly peril, he brings you up as his own son—or if you prefer to be your father's son, he starts you in business, so that you end in wealthy affluence; and there wasn't any deadly peril, so we made Pincher into one—and so—' I was so ashamed I couldn't go on, for it did seem an awfully mean thing. Lord Tottenham said—

'A very nice way to make your fortune—by deceit and trickery. I have a horror of dogs. If I'd been a weak man the shock might have killed me. What do you think of yourselves, eh?'

We were all crying except Oswald, and the others say he was; and Lord Tottenham went on—'Well, well, I see you're sorry. Let this be a lesson to you; and we'll say no more about it. I'm an old man now, but I was young once.'

Then Alice slid along the bench close to him, and put her hand on his arm: her fingers were pink through the holes in her woolly gloves, and said, 'I think you're very good to forgive us, and we are really very, very sorry. But we wanted to be like the children in the books—only we never have the chances they have. Everything they do turns out all right. But we *are* sorry, very, very. And I know Oswald wasn't going to take the half-sovereign. Directly you said that about a tip from an old boy I began to feel bad inside, and I whispered to H. O. that I wished we hadn't.'

Then Lord Tottenham stood up, and he looked like the Death of Nelson, for he is clean shaved and it is a good face, and he said—

'Always remember never to do a dishonourable thing, for money or for anything else in the world.'

And we promised we would remember. Then he took off his hat, and we took off ours, and he went away, and we went home. I never felt so cheap in all my life! Dora said, 'I told you so,' but we didn't mind even that so much, though it was indeed hard to bear. It was what Lord Tottenham had said about ungentlemanly. We didn't go on to the Heath for a week after that; but at last we all went, and we waited for him by the bench. When he came along Alice said, 'Please, Lord Tottenham, we have not been on the Heath for a week, to be a punishment because you let us off. And we have brought you a present each if you will take them to show you are willing to make it up.'

He sat down on the bench, and we gave him our presents. Oswald gave him a sixpenny compass—he bought it with my own money on purpose to give him. Oswald always buys useful presents. The needle would not move after I'd had it a day or two, but Lord Tottenham used to be an admiral, so he will be able to make that go all right. Alice had made him a shaving-case, with a rose worked on it. And H. O. gave him his knife—the same one he once cut all the buttons off his best suit with. Dicky gave him his prize, Naval Heroes, because it was the best thing he had, and Noel gave him a piece of poetry he had made himself—

When sin and shame bow down the brow
Then people feel just like we do now.
We are so sorry with grief and pain
We never will be so ungentlemanly again.

Lord Tottenham seemed very pleased. He thanked us, and talked to us for a bit, and when he said good-bye he said—

'All's fair weather now, mates,' and shook hands.

And whenever we meet him he nods to us, and if the girls are with us he takes off his hat, so he can't really be going on thinking us ungentlemanly now.

Chapter 11. Castilian Amoroso

One day when we suddenly found that we had half a crown we decided that we really ought to try Dicky's way of restoring our fallen fortunes while yet the deed was in our power. Because it might easily have happened to us never to have half a crown again. So we decided to dally no longer with being journalists and bandits and things like them, but to send for sample and instructions how to earn two pounds a week each in our spare time. We had seen the advertisement in the paper, and we had always wanted to do it, but we had never had the money to spare before, somehow. The advertisement says: 'Any lady or gentleman can easily earn two pounds a week in their spare time. Sample and instructions, two shillings. Packed free from observation.' A good deal of the half-crown was Dora's. It came from her godmother; but she said she would not mind letting Dicky have it if he would pay her back before Christmas, and if we were sure it was right to try to make our fortune that way. Of course that was quite easy, because out of two pounds a week in your spare time you can easily pay all your debts, and have almost as much left as you began with; and as to the right we told her to dry up.

Dicky had always thought that this was really the best way to restore our fallen fortunes, and we were glad that now he had a chance of trying because of course we wanted the two pounds a week each, and besides, we were rather tired of Dicky's always saying, when our ways didn't turn out well, 'Why don't you try the sample and instructions about our spare time?'

When we found out about our half-crown we got the paper. Noel was playing admirals in it, but he had made the cocked hat without tearing the paper, and we found the advertisement, and it said just the same as ever. So we got a two-shilling postal order and a stamp, and what was left of the money it was agreed we would spend in ginger-beer to drink success to trade.

We got some nice paper out of Father's study, and Dicky wrote the letter, and we put in the money and put on the stamp, and made H. O. post it. Then we drank the ginger-beer, and then we waited for the sample and instructions. It seemed a long time coming, and the postman got quite tired of us running out and stopping him in the street to ask if it had come.

But on the third morning it came. It was quite a large parcel, and it was packed, as the advertisement said it would be, 'free from observation.' That means it was in a box; and inside the box was some stiff browny cardboard, crinkled like the galvanized iron on the tops of chicken-houses, and inside that was a lot of paper, some of it printed and some scrappy, and in the very middle of it all a bottle, not very large, and black, and sealed on the top of the cork with yellow sealing- wax.

We looked at it as it lay on the nursery table, and while all the others grabbed at the papers to see what the printing said, Oswald went to look for the corkscrew, so as to see what was inside the bottle. He found the corkscrew in the dresser drawer—it always gets there, though it is supposed to be in the sideboard drawer in the dining-room—and when he got back the others had read most of the printed papers.

'I don't think it's much good, and I don't think it's quite nice to sell wine,' Dora said 'and besides, it's not easy to suddenly begin to sell things when you aren't used to it.'

'I don't know,' said Alice; 'I believe I could.' They all looked rather down in the mouth, though, and Oswald asked how you were to make your two pounds a week.

'Why, you've got to get people to taste that stuff in the bottle. It's sherry—Castilian Amoroso its name is—and then you get them to buy it, and then you write to the people and tell them the other people want the wine, and then for every dozen you sell you get two shillings from the wine people, so if you sell twenty dozen a week you get your two pounds. I don't think we shall sell as much as that,' said Dicky.

'We might not the first week,' Alice said, 'but when people found out how nice it was, they would want more and more. And if we only got ten shillings a week it would be something to begin with, wouldn't it?'

Oswald said he should jolly well think it would, and then Dicky took the cork out with the corkscrew. The cork broke a good deal, and some of the bits went into the bottle. Dora got the medicine glass that has the teaspoons and tablespoons marked on it, and we agreed to have a teaspoonful each, to see what it was like.

'No one must have more than that,' Dora said, 'however nice it is.'

Dora behaved rather as if it were her bottle. I suppose it was, because she had lent the money for it.

Then she measured out the teaspoonful, and she had first go, because of being the eldest. We asked at once what it was like, but Dora could not speak just then.

Then she said, 'It's like the tonic Noel had in the spring; but perhaps sherry ought to be like that.'

Then it was Oswald's turn. He thought it was very burny; but he said nothing. He wanted to see first what the others would say.

Dicky said his was simply beastly, and Alice said Noel could taste next if he liked.

Noel said it was the golden wine of the gods, but he had to put his handkerchief up to his mouth all the same, and I saw the face he made.

Then H. O. had his, and he spat it out in the fire, which was very rude and nasty, and we told him so.

Then it was Alice's turn. She said, 'Only half a teaspoonful for me, Dora. We mustn't use it all up.' And she tasted it and said nothing.

Then Dicky said: 'Look here, I chuck this. I'm not going to hawk round such beastly stuff. Any one who likes can have the bottle. Quis?'

And Alice got out 'Ego' before the rest of us. Then she said, 'I know what's the matter with it. It wants sugar.'

And at once we all saw that that was all there was the matter with the stuff. So we got two lumps of sugar and crushed it on the floor with one of the big wooden bricks till it was powdery, and mixed it with some of the wine up to the tablespoon mark, and it was quite different, and not nearly so nasty.

'You see it's all right when you get used to it,' Dicky said. I think he was sorry he had said 'Quis?' in such a hurry.

'Of course,' Alice said, 'it's rather dusty. We must crush the sugar carefully in clean paper before we put it in the bottle.'

Dora said she was afraid it would be cheating to make one bottle nicer than what people would get when they ordered a dozen bottles, but Alice said Dora always made a fuss about everything, and really it would be quite honest.

'You see,' she said, 'I shall just tell them, quite truthfully, what we have done to it, and when their dozens come they can do it for themselves.'

So then we crushed eight more lumps, very cleanly and carefully between newspapers, and shook it up well in the bottle, and corked it up with a screw of paper, brown and not news, for fear of the poisonous printing ink getting wet and dripping down into the wine and killing people. We made Pincher have a taste, and he sneezed for ever so long, and after that he used to go under the sofa whenever we showed him the bottle.

Then we asked Alice who she would try and sell it to. She said: 'I shall ask everybody who comes to the house. And while we are doing that, we can be thinking of outside people to take it to. We must be careful: there's not much more than half of it left, even counting the sugar.'

We did not wish to tell Eliza—I don't know why. And she opened the door very quickly that day, so that the Taxes and a man who came to our house by mistake for next door got away before Alice had a chance to try them with the Castilian Amoroso. But about five Eliza slipped out for half an hour to see a friend who was making her a hat for Sunday, and while she was gone there was a knock. Alice went, and we looked over the banisters. When she opened the door, she said at once, 'Will you walk in, please?' The person at the door said, 'I called to see your Pa, miss. Is he at home?'

Alice said again, 'Will you walk in, please?'

Then the person—it sounded like a man—said, 'He is in, then?'

But Alice only kept on saying, 'Will you walk in, please?' so at last the man did, rubbing his boots very loudly on the mat.

Then Alice shut the front door, and we saw that it was the butcher, with an envelope in his hand. He was not dressed in blue, like when he is cutting up the sheep and things in the shop, and he wore knickerbockers. Alice says he came on a bicycle. She led the way into the dining-room, where the Castilian Amoroso bottle and the medicine glass were standing on the table all ready.

The others stayed on the stairs, but Oswald crept down and looked through the door-crack.

'Please sit down,' said Alice quite calmly, though she told me afterwards I had no idea how silly she felt. And the butcher sat down. Then Alice stood quite still and said nothing, but she fiddled with the medicine glass and put the screw of brown paper straight in the Castilian bottle.

'Will you tell your Pa I'd like a word with him?' the butcher said, when he got tired of saying nothing.

'He'll be in very soon, I think,' Alice said.

And then she stood still again and said nothing. It was beginning to look very idiotic of her, and H. O. laughed. I went back and cuffed him for it quite quietly, and I don't think the butcher heard.

But Alice did, and it roused her from her stupor. She spoke suddenly, very fast indeed—so fast that I knew she had made up what she was going to say before. She had got most of it out of the circular.

She said, 'I want to call your attention to a sample of sherry wine I have here. It is called Castilian something or other, and at the price it is unequalled for flavour and bouquet.'

The butcher said, 'Well—I never!'

And Alice went on, 'Would you like to taste it?'

'Thank you very much, I'm sure, miss,' said the butcher.

Alice poured some out.

The butcher tasted a very little. He licked his lips, and we thought he was going to say how good it was. But he did not. He put down the medicine glass with nearly all the stuff left in it (we put it back in the bottle afterwards to save waste) and said, 'Excuse me, miss, but isn't it a little sweet?—for sherry I mean?'

'The *Real* isn't,' said Alice. 'If you order a dozen it will come quite different to that—we like it best with sugar. I wish you *would* order some.' The butcher asked why.

Alice did not speak for a minute, and then she said—

'I don't mind telling *you*: you are in business yourself, aren't you? We are trying to get people to buy it, because we shall have two shillings for every dozen we can make any one buy. It's called a purr something.'

'A percentage. Yes, I see,' said the butcher, looking at the hole in the carpet.

'You see there are reasons,' Alice went on, 'why we want to make our fortunes as quickly as we can.'

'Quite so,' said the butcher, and he looked at the place where the paper is coming off the wall.

'And this seems a good way,' Alice went on. 'We paid two shillings for the sample and instructions, and it says you can make two pounds a week easily in your leisure time.'

'I'm sure I hope you may, miss,' said the butcher. And Alice said again would he buy some?

'Sherry is my favourite wine,' he said. Alice asked him to have some more to drink.

'No, thank you, miss,' he said; 'it's my favourite wine, but it doesn't agree with me; not the least bit. But I've an uncle drinks it. Suppose I ordered him half a dozen for a Christmas present? Well, miss, here's the shilling commission, anyway,' and he pulled out a handful of money and gave her the shilling.

'But I thought the wine people paid that,' Alice said.

But the butcher said not on half-dozens they didn't. Then he said he didn't think he'd wait any longer for Father—but would Alice ask Father to write him?

Alice offered him the sherry again, but he said something about 'Not for worlds!'—and then she let him out and came back to us with the shilling, and said, 'How's that?'

And we said 'A1.'

And all the evening we talked of our fortune that we had begun to make.

Nobody came next day, but the day after a lady came to ask for money to build an orphanage for the children of dead sailors. And we saw her. I went in with Alice. And when we had explained to her that we had only a shilling and we wanted it for something else, Alice suddenly said, 'Would you like some wine?'

And the lady said, 'Thank you very much,' but she looked surprised.

She was not a young lady, and she had a mantle with beads, and the beads had come off in places—leaving a browny braid showing, and she had printed papers about the dead sailors in a sealskin bag, and the seal had come off in places, leaving the skin bare. We gave her a tablespoonful of the wine in a proper wine-glass out of the sideboard, because she was a lady. And when she had tasted it she got up in a very great hurry, and shook out her dress and snapped her bag shut, and said, 'You naughty, wicked children! What do you mean by playing a trick like this? You ought to be ashamed of yourselves! I shall write to your Mamma about it. You dreadful little girl!—you might have poisoned me. But your Mamma. . .'

Then Alice said, 'I'm very sorry; the butcher liked it, only he said it was sweet. And please don't write to Mother. It makes Father so unhappy when letters come for her!'—and Alice was very near crying.

'What do you mean, you silly child?' said the lady, looking quite bright and interested. 'Why doesn't your Father like your Mother to have letters—eh?'

And Alice said, 'OH, you . . . !' and began to cry, and bolted out of the room.

Then I said, 'Our Mother is dead, and will you please go away now?'

The lady looked at me a minute, and then she looked quite different, and she said, 'I'm very sorry. I didn't know. Never mind about the wine. I daresay your little sister meant it kindly.' And she looked round the room just like the butcher had done. Then she said again, 'I didn't know—I'm very sorry . . .'

So I said, 'Don't mention it,' and shook hands with her, and let her out. Of course we couldn't have asked her to buy the wine after what she'd said. But I think she was not a bad sort of person. I do like a person to say they're sorry when they ought to be—especially a grown-up. They do it so seldom. I suppose that's why we think so much of it.

But Alice and I didn't feel jolly for ever so long afterwards. And when I went back into the dining-room I saw how different it was from when Mother was here, and we are different, and Father is different, and nothing is like it was. I am glad I am not made to think about it every day.

I went and found Alice, and told her what the lady had said, and when she had finished crying we put away the bottle and said we would not try to sell any more to people who came. And we did not tell the others—we only said the lady did not buy any—but we went up on the Heath, and some soldiers went by and there was a Punch-and-judy show, and when we came back we were better.

The bottle got quite dusty where we had put it, and perhaps the dust of ages would have laid thick and heavy on it, only a clergyman called when we were all out. He was not our own clergyman—Mr Bristow is our own clergyman, and we all love him, and we would not try to sell sherry to people we like, and make two pounds a week out of them in our spare time. It was another clergyman, just a stray one; and he asked Eliza if the dear children would not like to come to his little Sunday school. We always spend Sunday afternoons with Father. But as he had left the name of his vicarage with Eliza, and asked her to tell us to come, we thought we would go and call on him, just to explain about Sunday afternoons, and we thought we might as well take the sherry with us.

'I won't go unless you all go too,' Alice said, 'and I won't do the talking.'

Dora said she thought we had much better not go; but we said 'Rot!' and it ended in her coming with us, and I am glad she did.

Oswald said he would do the talking if the others liked, and he learned up what to say from the printed papers.

We went to the Vicarage early on Saturday afternoon, and rang at the bell. It is a new red house with no trees in the garden, only very yellow mould and gravel. It was all very neat and dry. Just before we rang the bell we heard some one inside call 'Jane! Jane!' and we thought we would not be Jane for anything. It was the sound of the voice that called that made us sorry for her.

The door was opened by a very neat servant in black, with a white apron; we saw her tying the strings as she came along the hall, through the different-coloured glass in the door. Her face was red, and I think she was Jane.

We asked if we could see Mr Mallow.

The servant said Mr Mallow was very busy with his sermon just then, but she would see.

But Oswald said, 'It's all right. He asked us to come.'

So she let us all in and shut the front door, and showed us into a very tidy room with a bookcase full of a lot of books covered in black cotton with white labels, and some dull pictures, and a harmonium. And Mr Mallow was writing at a desk with drawers, copying something out of a book. He was stout and short, and wore spectacles.

He covered his writing up when we went in—I didn't know why. He looked rather cross, and we heard Jane or somebody being scolded outside by the voice. I hope it wasn't for letting us in, but I have had doubts.

'Well,' said the clergyman, 'what is all this about?'

'You asked us to call,' Dora said, 'about your little Sunday school. We are the Bastables of Lewisham Road.'

'Oh—ah, yes,' he said; 'and shall I expect you all to-morrow?'

He took up his pen and fiddled with it, and he did not ask us to sit down. But some of us did.

'We always spend Sunday afternoon with Father,' said Dora; 'but we wished to thank you for being so kind as to ask us.'

'And we wished to ask you something else!' said Oswald; and he made a sign to Alice to get the sherry ready in the glass. She did—behind Oswald's back while he was speaking.

'My time is limited,' said Mr Mallow, looking at his watch; 'but still—' Then he muttered something about the fold, and went on: 'Tell me what is troubling you, my little man, and I will try to give you any help in my power. What is it you want?'

Then Oswald quickly took the glass from Alice, and held it out to him, and said, 'I want your opinion on that.'

'On *that*,' he said. 'What is it?'

'It is a shipment,' Oswald said; 'but it's quite enough for you to taste.' Alice had filled the glass half-full; I suppose she was too excited to measure properly.

'A shipment?' said the clergyman, taking the glass in his hand.

'Yes,' Oswald went On; 'an exceptional opportunity. Full-bodied and nutty.'

'It really does taste rather like one kind of Brazil-nut.' Alice put her oar in as usual.

The Vicar looked from Alice to Oswald, and back again, and Oswald went on with what he had learned from the printing. The clergyman held the glass at half-arm's-length, stiffly, as if he had caught cold.

'It is of a quality never before offered at the price. Old Delicate Amoro—what's its name—'

'Amorolio,' said H. O.

'Amoroso,' said Oswald. 'H. O., you just shut up—Castilian Amoroso— it's a true after-dinner wine, stimulating and yet. . .'

'*Wine*?' said Mr Mallow, holding the glass further off. 'Do you *know*,' he went on, making his voice very thick and strong (I expect he does it like that in church), 'have you never been *taught* that it is the drinking of *wine* and *spirits*—yes, and *beer*, which makes half the homes in England full of *wretched* little children, and *degraded*, *miserable* parents?'

'Not if you put sugar in it,' said Alice firmly; 'eight lumps and shake the bottle. We have each had more than a teaspoonful of it, and we were not ill at all. It was something else that upset H. O. Most likely all those acorns he got out of the Park.'

The clergyman seemed to be speechless with conflicting emotions, and just then the door opened and a lady came in. She had a white cap with lace, and an ugly violet flower in it, and she was tall, and looked very strong, though thin. And I do believe she had been listening at the door.

'But why,' the Vicar was saying, 'why did you bring this dreadful fluid, this curse of our country, to *me* to taste?'

'Because we thought you might buy some,' said Dora, who never sees when a game is up. 'In books the parson loves his bottle of old port; and new sherry is just as good—with sugar—for people who like sherry. And if you would order a dozen of the wine, then we should get two shillings.'

The lady said (and it *was* the voice), 'Good gracious! Nasty, sordid little things! Haven't they any one to teach them better?'

And Dora got up and said, 'No, we are not those things you say; but we are sorry we came here to be called names. We want to make our fortune just as much as Mr Mallow does—only no one would listen to us if we preached, so it's no use our copying out sermons like him.'

And I think that was smart of Dora, even if it was rather rude.

Then I said perhaps we had better go, and the lady said, 'I should think so!'

But when we were going to wrap up the bottle and glass the clergyman said, 'No; you can leave that,' and we were so upset we did, though it wasn't his after all.

We walked home very fast and not saying much, and the girls went up to their rooms. When I went to tell them tea was ready, and there was a teacake, Dora was crying like anything and Alice hugging her. I am afraid there is a great deal of crying in this chapter, but I can't help it. Girls will sometimes; I suppose it is their nature, and we ought to be sorry for their affliction.

'It's no good,' Dora was saying, 'you all hate me, and you think I'm a prig and a busybody, but I do try to do right—oh, I do! Oswald, go away; don't come here making fun of me!'

So I said, 'I'm not making fun, Sissy; don't cry, old girl.'

Mother taught me to call her Sissy when we were very little and before the others came, but I don't often somehow, now we are old. I patted her on the back, and she put her head against my sleeve, holding on to Alice all the time, and she went on. She was in that laughy-cryey state when people say things they wouldn't say at other times.

'Oh dear, oh dear—I do try, I do. And when Mother died she said, "Dora, take care of the others, and teach them to be good, and keep them out of trouble and make them happy." She said, "Take care of them for me, Dora dear." And I have tried, and all of you hate me for it; and today I let you do this, though I knew all the time it was silly.'

I hope you will not think I was a muff but I kissed Dora for some time. Because girls like it. And I will never say again that she comes the good elder sister too much. And I have put all this in though I do hate telling about it, because I own I have been hard on Dora, but I never will be again. She is a good old sort; of course we never knew before about what Mother told her, or we wouldn't have ragged her as we did. We did not tell the little ones, but I got Alice to speak to Dicky, and we three can sit on the others if requisite.

This made us forget all about the sherry; but about eight o'clock there was a knock, and Eliza went, and we saw it was poor Jane, if her name was Jane, from the Vicarage. She handed in a brown-paper parcel and a letter. And three minutes later Father called us into his study.

On the table was the brown-paper parcel, open, with our bottle and glass on it, and Father had a letter in his hand. He pointed to the bottle and sighed, and said, 'What have you been doing now?' The letter in his hand was covered with little black writing, all over the four large pages.

So Dicky spoke up, and he told Father the whole thing, as far as he knew it, for Alice and I had not told about the dead sailors' lady.

And when he had done, Alice said, 'Has Mr Mallow written to you to say he will buy a dozen of the sherry after all? It is really not half bad with sugar in it.'

Father said no, he didn't think clergymen could afford such expensive wine; and he said *he* would like to taste it. So we gave him what there was left, for we had decided coming home that we would give up trying for the two pounds a week in our spare time.

Father tasted it, and then he acted just as H. O. had done when he had his teaspoonful, but of course we did not say anything. Then he laughed till I thought he would never stop.

I think it was the sherry, because I am sure I have read somewhere about 'wine that maketh glad the heart of man'. He had only a very little, which shows that it was a good after-dinner wine, stimulating, and yet. . . I forget the rest.

But when he had done laughing he said, 'It's all right, kids. Only don't do it again. The wine trade is overcrowded; and besides, I thought you promised to consult me before going into business?'

'Before buying one I thought you meant,' said Dicky. 'This was only on commission.' And Father laughed again. I am glad we got the Castilian Amoroso, because it did really cheer Father up, and you cannot always do that, however hard you try, even if you make jokes, or give him a comic paper.

Chapter 12. The Nobleness of Oswald

The part about his nobleness only comes at the end, but you would not understand it unless you knew how it began. It began, like nearly everything about that time, with treasure-seeking.

Of course as soon as we had promised to consult my Father about business matters we all gave up wanting to go into business. I don't know how it is, but having to consult about a thing with grown-up people, even the bravest and the best, seems to make the thing not worth doing afterwards.

We don't mind Albert's uncle chipping in sometimes when the thing's going on, but we are glad he never asked us to promise to consult him about anything. Yet Oswald saw that my Father was quite right; and I daresay if we had had that hundred pounds we should have spent it on the share in that lucrative business for the sale of useful patent, and then found out afterwards that we should have done better to spend the money in some other way. My Father says so, and he ought to know. We had several ideas about that time, but having so little chink always stood in the way.

This was the case with H. O.'s idea of setting up a coconut-shy on this side of the Heath, where there are none generally. We had no sticks or wooden balls, and the greengrocer said he could not book so many as twelve dozen coconuts without Mr Bastable's written order. And as we did not wish to consult my Father it was decided to drop it. And when Alice dressed up Pincher in some of the dolls' clothes and we made up our minds to take him round with an organ as soon as we had taught him to dance, we were stopped at once by Dicky's remembering how he had once heard that an organ cost seven hundred pounds. Of course this was the big church kind, but even the ones on three legs can't be got for one-and-sevenpence, which was all we had when we first thought of it. So we gave that up too.

It was a wet day, I remember, and mutton hash for dinner—very tough with pale gravy with lumps in it. I think the others would have left a good deal on the sides of their plates, although they know better, only Oswald said it was a savoury stew made of the red deer that Edward shot. So then we were the Children of the New Forest, and the mutton tasted much better. No one in the New Forest minds venison being tough and the gravy pale.

Then after dinner we let the girls have a dolls' tea-party, on condition they didn't expect us boys to wash up; and it was when we were drinking the last of the liquorice water out of the little cups that Dicky said—

'This reminds me.'

So we said, 'What of?'

Dicky answered us at once, though his mouth was full of bread with liquorice stuck in it to look like cake. You should not speak with your mouth full, even to your own relations, and you shouldn't wipe your mouth on the back of your hand, but on your handkerchief, if you have one. Dicky did not do this. He said—

'Why, you remember when we first began about treasure-seeking, I said I had thought of something, only I could not tell you because I hadn't finished thinking about it.'

We said 'Yes.'

'Well, this liquorice water—'

'Tea,' said Alice softly.

'Well, tea then—made me think.' He was going on to say what it made him think, but Noel interrupted and cried out, 'I say; let's finish off this old tea-party and have a council of war.'

So we got out the flags and the wooden sword and the drum, and Oswald beat it while the girls washed up, till Eliza came up to say she had the jumping toothache, and the noise went through her like a knife. So of course Oswald left off at once. When you are polite to Oswald he never refuses to grant your requests.

When we were all dressed up we sat down round the camp fire, and Dicky began again.

'Every one in the world wants money. Some people get it. The people who get it are the ones who see things. I have seen one thing.'

Dicky stopped and smoked the pipe of peace. It is the pipe we did bubbles with in the summer, and somehow it has not got broken yet. We put tea-leaves in it for the pipe of peace, but the girls are not allowed to have any. It is not right to let girls smoke. They get to think too much of themselves if you let them do everything the same as men. Oswald said, 'Out with it.'

'I see that glass bottles only cost a penny. H. O., if you dare to snigger I'll send you round selling old bottles, and you shan't have any sweets except out of the money you get for them. And the same with you, Noel.'

'Noel wasn't sniggering,' said Alice in a hurry; 'it is only his taking so much interest in what you were saying makes him look like that. Be quiet, H. O., and don't you make faces, either. Do go on, Dicky dear.'

So Dicky went on.

'There must be hundreds of millions of bottles of medicines sold every year. Because all the different medicines say, "Thousands of cures daily," and if you only take that as two thousand, which it must be, at least, it mounts up. And the people who sell them must make a great deal of money by them because they are nearly always two-and-ninepence the bottle, and three-and-six for one nearly double the size. Now the bottles, as I was saying, don't cost anything like that.'

'It's the medicine costs the money,' said Dora; 'look how expensive jujubes are at the chemist's, and peppermints too.'

'That's only because they're nice,' Dicky explained; 'nasty things are not so dear. Look what a lot of brimstone you get for a penny, and the same with alum. We would not put the nice kinds of chemist's things in our medicine.'

Then he went on to tell us that when we had invented our medicine we would write and tell the editor about it, and he would put it in the paper, and then people would send their two-and-ninepence and three-and- six for the bottle nearly double the size, and then when the medicine had cured them they would write to the paper and their letters would be printed, saying how they had been suffering for years, and never thought to get about again, but thanks to the blessing of our ointment—'

Dora interrupted and said, 'Not ointment—it's so messy.' And Alice thought so too. And Dicky said he did not mean it, he was quite decided to let it be in bottles. So now it was all settled, and we did not see at the time that this would be a sort of going into business, but afterwards when Albert's uncle showed us we saw it, and we were sorry. We only had to invent the medicine. You might think that was easy, because of the number of them you see every day in the paper, but it is much harder than you think. First we had to decide what sort of illness we should like to cure, and a 'heated discussion ensued', like in Parliament.

Dora wanted it to be something to make the complexion of dazzling fairness, but we remembered how her face came all red and rough when she used the Rosabella soap that was advertised to make the darkest complexion fair as the lily, and she agreed that perhaps it was better not. Noel wanted to make the medicine first and then find out what it would cure, but Dicky thought not, because there are so many more medicines than there are things the matter with us, so it would be easier to choose the disease first. Oswald would have liked wounds. I still think it was a good idea, but Dicky said, 'Who has wounds, especially now there aren't any wars? We shouldn't sell a bottle a day!' So Oswald gave in because he knows what manners are, and it was Dicky's idea. H. O. wanted a cure for the uncomfortable feeling that they give you powders for, but we explained to him that grown-up people do not have this feeling, however much they eat, and he agreed. Dicky said he did not care a straw what the loathsome disease was, as long as we hurried up and settled on something. Then Alice said—

'It ought to be something very common, and only one thing. Not the pains in the back and all the hundreds of things the people have in somebody's syrup. What's the commonest thing of all?'

And at once we said, 'Colds.'

So that was settled.

Then we wrote a label to go on the bottle. When it was written it would not go on the vinegar bottle that we had got, but we knew it would go small when it was printed. It was like this:

BASTABLE'S
CERTAIN CURE FOR COLDS
Coughs, Asthma, Shortness of Breath, and all infections of the Chest

One dose gives immediate relief
It will cure your cold in one bottle
Especially the larger size at 3s. 6d.
Order at once of the Makers
To prevent disappointment

Makers:

D., O., R., A., N., and H. O. BASTABLE
150, Lewisham Road, S.E.

(A halfpenny for all bottles returned)

Of course the next thing was for one of us to catch a cold and try what cured it; we all wanted to be the one, but it was Dicky's idea, and he said he was not going to be done out of it, so we let him. It was only fair. He left off his undershirt that very day, and next morning he stood in a draught in his nightgown for quite a long time. And we damped his day-shirt with the nail-brush before he put it on. But all was vain. They always tell you that these things will give you cold, but we found it was not so.

So then we all went over to the Park, and Dicky went right into the water with his boots on, and stood there as long as he could bear it, for it was rather cold, and we stood and cheered him on. He walked home in his wet clothes, which they say is a sure thing, but it was no go, though his boots were quite spoiled. And three days after Noel began to cough and sneeze.

So then Dicky said it was not fair.

'I can't help it,' Noel said. 'You should have caught it yourself, then it wouldn't have come to me.'

And Alice said she had known all along Noel oughtn't to have stood about on the bank cheering in the cold.

Noel had to go to bed, and then we began to make the medicines; we were sorry he was out of it, but he had the fun of taking the things.

We made a great many medicines. Alice made herb tea. She got sage and thyme and savory and marjoram and boiled them all up together with salt and water, but she *would* put parsley in too. Oswald is sure parsley is not a herb. It is only put on the cold meat and you are not supposed to eat it. It kills parrots to eat parsley, I believe. I expect it was the parsley that disagreed so with Noel. The medicine did not seem to do the cough any good.

Oswald got a pennyworth of alum, because it is so cheap, and some turpentine which every one knows is good for colds, and a little sugar and an aniseed ball. These were mixed in a bottle with water, but Eliza threw it away and said it was nasty rubbish, and I hadn't any money to get more things with.

Dora made him some gruel, and he said it did his chest good; but of course that was no use, because you cannot put gruel in bottles and say it is medicine. It would not be honest, and besides nobody would believe you.

Dick mixed up lemon-juice and sugar and a little of the juice of the red flannel that Noel's throat was done up in. It comes out beautifully in hot water. Noel took this and he liked it. Noel's own idea was liquorice-water, and we let him have it, but it is too plain and black to sell in bottles at the proper price.

Noel liked H. O.'s medicine the best, which was silly of him, because it was only peppermints melted in hot water, and a little cobalt to make it look blue. It was all right, because H. O.'s paint-box is the French kind, with Couleurs non Veneneuses on it. This means you may suck your brushes if you want to, or even your paints if you are a very little boy.

It was rather jolly while Noel had that cold. He had a fire in his bedroom which opens out of Dicky's and Oswald's, and the girls used to read aloud to Noel all day; they will not read aloud to you when you are well. Father was away at Liverpool on business, and Albert's uncle was at Hastings. We were rather glad of this, because we wished to give all the medicines a fair trial, and grown-ups are but too fond of interfering. As if we should have given him anything poisonous!

His cold went on—it was bad in his head, but it was not one of the kind when he has to have poultices and can't sit up in bed. But when it had been in his head nearly a week, Oswald happened to tumble over Alice on the stairs. When we got up she was crying.

'Don't cry silly!' said Oswald; 'you know I didn't hurt you.' I was very sorry if I had hurt her, but you ought not to sit on the stairs in the dark and let other people tumble over you. You ought to remember how beastly it is for them if they do hurt you.

'Oh, it's not that, Oswald,' Alice said. 'Don't be a pig! I am so miserable. Do be kind to me.'

So Oswald thumped her on the back and told her to shut up.

'It's about Noel,' she said. 'I'm sure he's very ill; and playing about with medicines is all very well, but I know he's ill, and Eliza won't send for the doctor: she says it's only a cold. And I know the doctor's bills are awful. I heard Father telling Aunt Emily so in the summer. But he *is* ill, and perhaps he'll die or something.'

Then she began to cry again. Oswald thumped her again, because he knows how a good brother ought to behave, and said, 'Cheer up.' If we had been in a book Oswald would have embraced his little sister tenderly, and mingled his tears with hers.

Then Oswald said, 'Why not write to Father?'

And she cried more and said, 'I've lost the paper with the address. H. O. had it to draw on the back of, and I can't find it now; I've looked everywhere. I'll tell you what I'm going to do. No I won't. But I'm going out. Don't tell the others. And I say, Oswald, do pretend I'm in if Eliza asks. Promise.'

'Tell me what you're going to do,' I said. But she said 'No'; and there was a good reason why not. So I said I wouldn't promise if it came to that. Of course I meant to all right. But it did seem mean of her not to tell me.

So Alice went out by the side door while Eliza was setting tea, and she was a long time gone; she was not in to tea. When Eliza asked Oswald where she was he said he did not know, but perhaps she was tidying her corner drawer. Girls often do this, and it takes a long time. Noel coughed a good bit after tea, and asked for Alice.

Oswald told him she was doing something and it was a secret. Oswald did not tell any lies even to save his sister. When Alice came back she was very quiet, but she whispered to Oswald that it was all right. When it was rather late Eliza said she was going out to post a letter. This always takes her an hour, because she *will* go to the post-office across the Heath instead of the pillar-box, because once a boy dropped fusees in our pillar-box and burnt the letters. It was not any of us; Eliza told us about it. And when there was a knock at the door a long time after we thought it was Eliza come back, and that she had forgotten the back-door key. We made H. O. go down to open the door, because it is his place to run about: his legs are younger than ours. And we heard boots on the stairs besides H. O.'s, and we listened spellbound till the door opened, and it was Albert's uncle. He looked very tired.

'I am glad you've come,' Oswald said. 'Alice began to think Noel—'

Alice stopped me, and her face was very red, her nose was shiny too, with having cried so much before tea.

She said, 'I only said I thought Noel ought to have the doctor. Don't you think he ought?' She got hold of Albert's uncle and held on to him.

'Let's have a look at you, young man,' said Albert's uncle, and he sat down on the edge of the bed. It is a rather shaky bed, the bar that keeps it steady underneath got broken when we were playing burglars last winter. It was our crowbar. He began to feel Noel's pulse, and went on talking.

'It was revealed to the Arab physician as he made merry in his tents on the wild plains of Hastings that the Presence had a cold in its head. So he immediately seated himself on the magic carpet, and bade it bear him hither, only pausing in the flight to purchase a few sweetmeats in the bazaar.'

He pulled out a jolly lot of chocolate and some butterscotch, and grapes for Noel. When we had all said thank you, he went on.

'The physician's are the words of wisdom: it's high time this kid was asleep. I have spoken. Ye have my leave to depart.'

So we bunked, and Dora and Albert's uncle made Noel comfortable for the night.

Then they came to the nursery which we had gone down to, and he sat down in the Guy Fawkes chair and said, 'Now then.'

Alice said, 'You may tell them what I did. I daresay they'll all be in a wax, but I don't care.'

'I think you were very wise,' said Albert's uncle, pulling her close to him to sit on his knee. 'I am very glad you telegraphed.'

So then Oswald understood what Alice's secret was. She had gone out and sent a telegram to Albert's uncle at Hastings. But Oswald thought she might have told him. Afterwards she told me what she had put in the telegram. It was, 'Come home. We have given Noel a cold, and I think we are killing him.' With the address it came to tenpence-halfpenny.

Then Albert's uncle began to ask questions, and it all came out, how Dicky had tried to catch the cold, but the cold had gone to Noel instead, and about the medicines and all. Albert's uncle looked very serious.

'Look here,' he said, 'You're old enough not to play the fool like this. Health is the best thing you've got; you ought to know better than to risk it. You might have killed your little brother with your precious medicines. You've had a lucky escape, certainly. But poor Noel!'

'Oh, do you think he's going to die?' Alice asked that, and she was crying again.

'No, no,' said Albert's uncle; 'but look here. Do you see how silly you've been? And I thought you promised your Father—' And then he gave us a long talking-to. He can make you feel most awfully small. At last he stopped, and we said we were very sorry, and he said, 'You know I promised to take you all to the pantomime?'

So we said, 'Yes,' and knew but too well that now he wasn't going to. Then he went on—

'Well, I will take you if you like, or I will take Noel to the sea for a week to cure his cold. Which is it to be?'

Of course he knew we should say, 'Take Noel' and we did; but Dicky told me afterwards he thought it was hard on H. O.

Albert's uncle stayed till Eliza came in, and then he said good night in a way that showed us that all was forgiven and forgotten.

And we went to bed. It must have been the middle of the night when Oswald woke up suddenly, and there was Alice with her teeth chattering, shaking him to wake him.

'Oh, Oswald!' she said, 'I am so unhappy. Suppose I should die in the night!'

Oswald told her to go to bed and not gas. But she said, 'I must tell you; I wish I'd told Albert's uncle. I'm a thief, and if I die to-night I know where thieves go to.' So Oswald saw it was no good and he sat up in bed and said—'Go ahead.' So Alice stood shivering and said—'I hadn't enough money for the telegram, so I took the bad sixpence out of the exchequer. And I paid for it with that and the fivepence I had. And I wouldn't tell you, because if you'd stopped me doing it I couldn't have borne it; and if you'd helped me you'd have been a thief too. Oh, what shall I do?'

Oswald thought a minute, and then he said—

'You'd better have told me. But I think it will be all right if we pay it back. Go to bed. Cross with you? No, stupid! Only another time you'd better not keep secrets.'

So she kissed Oswald, and he let her, and she went back to bed.

The next day Albert's uncle took Noel away, before Oswald had time to persuade Alice that we ought to tell him about the sixpence. Alice was very unhappy, but not so much as in the night: you can be very miserable in the night if you have done anything wrong and you happen to be awake. I know this for a fact.

None of us had any money except Eliza, and she wouldn't give us any unless we said what for; and of course we could not do that because of the honour of the family. And Oswald was anxious to get the sixpence to give to the telegraph people because he feared that the badness of that sixpence might have been found out, and that the police might come for Alice at any moment. I don't think I ever had such an unhappy day. Of course we could have written to Albert's uncle, but it would have taken a long time, and every moment of delay added to Alice's danger. We thought and thought, but we couldn't think of any way to get that sixpence. It seems a small sum, but you see Alice's liberty depended on it. It was quite late in the afternoon when I met Mrs Leslie on the Parade. She had a brown fur coat and a lot of yellow flowers in her hands. She stopped to speak to me, and asked me how the Poet was. I told her he had a cold, and I wondered whether she would lend me sixpence if I asked her, but I could not make up my mind how to begin to say it. It is a hard thing to say—much harder than you would think. She talked to me for a bit, and then she suddenly got into a cab, and said—

'I'd no idea it was so late,' and told the man where to go. And just as she started she shoved the yellow flowers through the window and said, 'For the sick poet, with my love,' and was driven off.

Gentle reader, I will not conceal from you what Oswald did. He knew all about not disgracing the family, and he did not like doing what I am going to say: and they were really Noel's flowers, only he could not have sent them to Hastings, and Oswald knew he would say 'Yes' if Oswald asked him. Oswald sacrificed his family pride because of his little sister's danger. I do not say he was a noble boy—I just tell you what he did, and you can decide for yourself about the nobleness.

He put on his oldest clothes—they're much older than any you would think he had if you saw him when he was tidy—and he took those yellow chrysanthemums and he walked with them to Greenwich Station and waited for the trains bringing people from London. He sold those flowers in penny bunches and got tenpence. Then he went to the telegraph office at Lewisham, and said to the lady there:

'A little girl gave you a bad sixpence yesterday. Here are six good pennies.'

The lady said she had not noticed it, and never mind, but Oswald knew that 'Honesty is the best Policy', and he refused to take back the pennies. So at last she said she should put them in the plate on Sunday. She is a very nice lady. I like the way she does her hair.

Then Oswald went home to Alice and told her, and she hugged him, and said he was a dear, good, kind boy, and he said 'Oh, it's all right.'

We bought peppermint bullseyes with the fourpence I had over, and the others wanted to know where we got the money, but we would not tell.

Only afterwards when Noel came home we told him, because they were his flowers, and he said it was quite right. He made some poetry about it. I only remember one bit of it.

> The noble youth of high degree
> Consents to play a menial part,
> All for his sister Alice's sake,
> Who was so dear to his faithful heart.

But Oswald himself has never bragged about it. We got no treasure out of this, unless you count the peppermint bullseyes.

Chapter 13. The Robber and the Burglar

A day or two after Noel came back from Hastings there was snow; it was jolly. And we cleared it off the path. A man to do it is sixpence at least, and you should always save when you can. A penny saved is a penny earned. And then we thought it would be nice to clear it off the top of the portico, where it lies so thick, and the edges as if they had been cut with a knife. And just as we had got out of the landing-window on to the portico, the Water Rates came up the path with his book that he tears the thing out of that says how much you have got to pay, and the little ink-bottle hung on to his buttonhole in case you should pay him. Father says the Water Rates is a sensible man, and knows it is always well to be prepared for whatever happens, however unlikely. Alice said afterwards that she rather liked the Water Rates, really, and Noel said he had a face like a good vizier, or the man who rewards the honest boy for restoring the purse, but we did not think about these things at the time, and as the Water Rates came up the steps, we shovelled down a great square slab of snow like an avalanche—and it fell right on his head. Two of us thought of it at the same moment, so it was quite a large avalanche. And when the Water Rates had shaken himself he rang the bell. It was Saturday, and Father was at home. We know now that it is very wrong and ungentlemanly to shovel snow off porticoes on to the Water Rates, or any other person, and we hope he did not catch a cold, and we are very sorry. We apologized to the Water Rates when Father told us to. We were all sent to bed for it.

We all deserved the punishment, because the others would have shovelled down snow just as we did if they'd thought of it—only they are not so quick at thinking of things as we are. And even quite wrong things sometimes lead to adventures; as every one knows who has ever read about pirates or highwaymen.

Eliza hates us to be sent to bed early, because it means her having to bring meals up, and it means lighting the fire in Noel's room ever so much earlier than usual. He had to have a fire because he still had a bit of a cold. But this particular day we got Eliza into a good temper by giving her a horrid brooch with pretending amethysts in it, that an aunt once gave to Alice, so Eliza brought up an extra scuttle of coals, and when the greengrocer came with the potatoes (he is always late on Saturdays) she got some chestnuts from him. So that when we heard Father go out after his dinner, there was a jolly fire in Noel's room, and we were able to go in and be Red Indians in blankets most comfortably. Eliza had gone out; she says she gets things cheaper on Saturday nights. She has a great friend, who sells fish at a shop, and he is very generous, and lets her have herrings for less than half the natural price.

So we were all alone in the house; Pincher was out with Eliza, and we talked about robbers. And Dora thought it would be a dreadful trade, but Dicky said—

'I think it would be very interesting. And you would only rob rich people, and be very generous to the poor and needy, like Claude Duval.' Dora said, 'It is wrong to be a robber.'

'Yes,' said Alice, 'you would never know a happy hour. Think of trying to sleep with the stolen jewels under your bed, and remembering all the quantities of policemen and detectives that there are in the world!'

'There are ways of being robbers that are not wrong,' said Noel; 'if you can rob a robber it is a right act.'

'But you can't,' said Dora; 'he is too clever, and besides, it's wrong anyway.'

'Yes you can, and it isn't; and murdering him with boiling oil is a right act, too, so there!' said Noel. 'What about Ali Baba? Now then!' And we felt it was a score for Noel.

'What would you do if there *was* a robber?' said Alice.

H. O. said he would kill him with boiling oil; but Alice explained that she meant a real robber—now—this minute—in the house.

Oswald and Dicky did not say; but Noel said he thought it would only be fair to ask the robber quite politely and quietly to go away, and then if he didn't you could deal with him.

Now what I am going to tell you is a very strange and wonderful thing, and I hope you will be able to believe it. I should not, if a boy told me, unless I knew him to be a man of honour, and perhaps not then unless he gave his sacred word. But it is true, all the same, and it only shows that the days of romance and daring deeds are not yet at an end.

Alice was just asking Noel *how* he would deal with the robber who wouldn't go if he was asked politely and quietly, when we heard a noise downstairs—quite a plain noise, not the kind of noise you fancy you hear. It was like somebody moving a chair. We held our breath and listened and then came another noise, like some one poking a fire. Now, you remember there was no one *to* poke a fire or move a chair downstairs, because Eliza and Father were both out. They could not have come in without our hearing them, because the front door is as hard to shut as the back one, and whichever you go in by you have to give a slam that you can hear all down the street.

H. O. and Alice and Dora caught hold of each other's blankets and looked at Dicky and Oswald, and every one was quite pale. And Noel whispered—

'It's ghosts, I know it is'—and then we listened again, but there was no more noise. Presently Dora said in a whisper—

'Whatever shall we do? Oh, whatever shall we do—what *shall* we do?' And she kept on saying it till we had to tell her to shut up.

O reader, have you ever been playing Red Indians in blankets round a bedroom fire in a house where you thought there was no one but you—and then suddenly heard a noise like a chair, and a fire being poked, downstairs? Unless you have you will not be able to imagine at all what it feels like. It was not like in books; our hair did not stand on end at all, and we never said 'Hist!' once, but our feet got very cold, though we were in blankets by the fire, and the insides of Oswald's hands got warm and wet, and his nose was cold like a dog's, and his ears were burning hot.

The girls said afterwards that they shivered with terror, and their teeth chattered, but we did not see or hear this at the time.

'Shall we open the window and call police?' said Dora; and then Oswald suddenly thought of something, and he breathed more freely and he said—

'I *know* it's not ghosts, and I don't believe it's robbers. I expect it's a stray cat got in when the coals came this morning, and she's been hiding in the cellar, and now she's moving about. Let's go down and see.'

The girls wouldn't, of course; but I could see that they breathed more freely too. But Dicky said, 'All right; I will if you will.'

H. O. said, 'Do you think it's *really* a cat?' So we said he had better stay with the girls. And of course after that we had to let him and Alice both come. Dora said if we took Noel down with his cold, she would scream 'Fire!' and 'Murder!' and she didn't mind if the whole street heard.

So Noel agreed to be getting his clothes on, and the rest of us said we would go down and look for the cat.

Now Oswald *said* that about the cat, and it made it easier to go down, but in his inside he did not feel at all sure that it might not be robbers after all. Of course, we had often talked about robbers before, but it is very different when you sit in a room and listen and listen and listen; and Oswald felt somehow that it would be easier to go down and see what it was, than to wait, and listen, and wait, and wait, and listen, and wait, and then perhaps to hear *it*, whatever it was, come creeping slowly up the stairs as softly as *it* could with *its* boots off, and the stairs creaking, towards the room where we were with the door open in case of Eliza coming back suddenly, and all dark on the landings. And then it would have been just as bad, and it would have lasted longer, and you would have known you were a coward besides. Dicky says he felt all these same things. Many people would say we were young heroes to go down as we did; so I have tried to explain, because no young hero wishes to have more credit than he deserves.

The landing gas was turned down low—just a blue bead—and we four went out very softly, wrapped in our blankets, and we stood on the top of the stairs a good long time before we began to go down. And we listened and listened till our ears buzzed.

And Oswald whispered to Dicky, and Dicky went into our room and fetched the large toy pistol that is a foot long, and that has the trigger broken, and I took it because I am the eldest; and I don't think either of us thought it was the cat now. But Alice and H. O. did. Dicky got the poker out of Noel's room, and told Dora it was to settle the cat with when we caught her.

Then Oswald whispered, 'Let's play at burglars; Dicky and I are armed to the teeth, we will go first. You keep a flight behind us, and be a reinforcement if we are attacked. Or you can retreat and defend the women and children in the fortress, if you'd rather.'

But they said they would be a reinforcement.

Oswald's teeth chattered a little when he spoke. It was not with anything else except cold.

So Dicky and Oswald crept down, and when we got to the bottom of the stairs, we saw Father's study door just ajar, and the crack of light. And Oswald was so pleased to see the light, knowing that burglars prefer the dark, or at any rate the dark lantern, that he felt really sure it *was* the cat after all, and then he thought it would be fun to make the others upstairs think it was really a robber. So he cocked the pistol— you can cock it, but it doesn't go off—and he said, 'Come on, Dick!' and he rushed at the study door and burst into the room, crying, 'Surrender! you are discovered! Surrender, or I fire! Throw up your hands!'

And, as he finished saying it, he saw before him, standing on the study hearthrug, a Real Robber. There was no mistake about it. Oswald was sure it was a robber, because it had a screwdriver in its hands, and was standing near the cupboard door that H. O. broke the lock off; and there were gimlets and screws and things on the floor. There is nothing in that cupboard but old ledgers and magazines and the tool chest, but of course, a robber could not know that beforehand.

When Oswald saw that there really was a robber, and that he was so heavily armed with the screwdriver, he did not feel comfortable. But he kept the pistol pointed at the robber, and—you will hardly believe it, but it is true—the robber threw down the screwdriver clattering on the other tools, and he *did* throw up his hands, and said—

'I surrender; don't shoot me! How many of you are there?'

So Dicky said, 'You are outnumbered. Are you armed?'

And the robber said, 'No, not in the least.'

And Oswald said, still pointing the pistol, and feeling very strong and brave and as if he was in a book, 'Turn out your pockets.'

The robber did: and while he turned them out, we looked at him. He was of the middle height, and clad in a black frock-coat and grey trousers. His boots were a little gone at the sides, and his shirt-cuffs were a bit frayed, but otherwise he was of gentlemanly demeanour. He had a thin, wrinkled face, with big, light eyes that sparkled, and then looked soft very queerly, and a short beard. In his youth it must have been of a fair golden colour, but now it was tinged with grey. Oswald was sorry for him, especially when he saw that one of his pockets had a large hole in it, and that he had nothing in his pockets but letters and string and three boxes of matches, and a pipe and a handkerchief and a thin tobacco pouch and two pennies. We made him put all the things on the table, and then he said—

'Well, you've caught me; what are you going to do with me? Police?'

Alice and H. O. had come down to be reinforcements, when they heard a shout, and when Alice saw that it was a Real Robber, and that he had surrendered, she clapped her hands and said, 'Bravo, boys!' and so did H. O. And now she said, 'If he gives his word of honour not to escape, I shouldn't call the police: it seems a pity. Wait till Father comes home.'

The robber agreed to this, and gave his word of honour, and asked if he might put on a pipe, and we said 'Yes,' and he sat in Father's armchair and warmed his boots, which steamed, and I sent H. O. and Alice to put on some clothes and tell the others, and bring down Dicky's and my knickerbockers, and the rest of the chestnuts.

And they all came, and we sat round the fire, and it was jolly. The robber was very friendly, and talked to us a great deal.

'I wasn't always in this low way of business,' he said, when Noel said something about the things he had turned out of his pockets. 'It's a great come-down to a man like me. But, if I must be caught, it's something to be caught by brave young heroes like you. My stars! How you did bolt into the room,—"Surrender, and up with your hands!" You might have been born and bred to the thief-catching.'

Oswald is sorry if it was mean, but he could not own up just then that he did not think there was any one in the study when he did that brave if rash act. He has told since.

'And what made you think there was any one in the house?' the robber asked, when he had thrown his head back, and laughed for quite half a minute. So we told him. And he applauded our valour, and Alice and H. O. explained that they would have said 'Surrender,' too, only they were reinforcements. The robber ate some of the chestnuts—and we sat and wondered when Father would come home, and what he would say to us for our intrepid conduct. And the robber told us of all the things he had done before he began to break into houses. Dicky picked up the tools from the floor, and suddenly he said—

'Why, this is Father's screwdriver and his gimlets, and all! Well, I do call it jolly cheek to pick a man's locks with his own tools!'

'True, true,' said the robber. 'It is cheek, of the jolliest! But you see I've come down in the world. I was a highway robber once, but horses are so expensive to hire—five shillings an hour, you know—and I couldn't afford to keep them. The highwayman business isn't what it was.'

'What about a bike?' said H. O.

But the robber thought cycles were low—and besides you couldn't go across country with them when occasion arose, as you could with a trusty steed. And he talked of highwaymen as if he knew just how we liked hearing it.

Then he told us how he had been a pirate captain—and how he had sailed over waves mountains high, and gained rich prizes—and how he *did* begin to think that here he had found a profession to his mind.

'I don't say there are no ups and downs in it,' he said, 'especially in stormy weather. But what a trade! And a sword at your side, and the Jolly Roger flying at the peak, and a prize in sight. And all the black mouths of your guns pointed at the laden trader—and the wind in your favour, and your trusty crew ready to live and die for you! Oh—but it's a grand life!'

I did feel so sorry for him. He used such nice words, and he had a gentleman's voice.

'I'm sure you weren't brought up to be a pirate,' said Dora. She had dressed even to her collar—and made Noel do it too—but the rest of us were in blankets with just a few odd things put on anyhow underneath.

The robber frowned and sighed.

'No,' he said, 'I was brought up to the law. I was at Balliol, bless your hearts, and that's true anyway.' He sighed again, and looked hard at the fire.

'That was my Father's college,' H. O. was beginning, but Dicky said—'Why did you leave off being a pirate?'

'A pirate?' he said, as if he had not been thinking of such things.

'Oh, yes; why I gave it up because—because I could not get over the dreadful sea-sickness.'

'Nelson was sea-sick,' said Oswald.

'Ah,' said the robber; 'but I hadn't his luck or his pluck, or something. He stuck to it and won Trafalgar, didn't he? "Kiss me, Hardy"—and all that, eh? *I* couldn't stick to it—I had to resign. And nobody kissed *me*.'

I saw by his understanding about Nelson that he was really a man who had been to a good school as well as to Balliol.

Then we asked him, 'And what did you do then?'

And Alice asked if he was ever a coiner, and we told him how we had thought we'd caught the desperate gang next door, and he was very much interested and said he was glad he had never taken to coining.

'Besides, the coins are so ugly nowadays,' he said, 'no one could really find any pleasure in making them. And it's a hole-and-corner business at the best, isn't it?—and it must be a very thirsty one—with the hot metal and furnaces and things.'

And again he looked at the fire.

Oswald forgot for a minute that the interesting stranger was a robber, and asked him if he wouldn't have a drink. Oswald has heard Father do this to his friends, so he knows it is the right thing. The robber said he didn't mind if he did. And that is right, too.

And Dora went and got a bottle of Father's ale—the Light Sparkling Family—and a glass, and we gave it to the robber. Dora said she would be responsible.

Then when he had had a drink he told us about bandits, but he said it was so bad in wet weather. Bandits' caves were hardly ever properly weathertight. And bush-ranging was the same.

'As a matter of fact,' he said, 'I was bush-ranging this afternoon, among the furze-bushes on the Heath, but I had no luck. I stopped the Lord Mayor in his gilt coach, with all his footmen in plush and gold lace, smart as cockatoos. But it was no go. The Lord Mayor hadn't a stiver in his pockets. One of the footmen had six new pennies: the Lord Mayor always pays his servants' wages in new pennies. I spent fourpence of that in bread and cheese, that on the table's the tuppence. Ah, it's a poor trade!' And then he filled his pipe again.

We had turned out the gas, so that Father should have a jolly good surprise when he did come home, and we sat and talked as pleasant as could be. I never liked a new man better than I liked that robber. And I felt so sorry for him. He told us he had been a war-correspondent and an editor, in happier days, as well as a horse-stealer and a colonel of dragoons.

And quite suddenly, just as we were telling him about Lord Tottenham and our being highwaymen ourselves, he put up his hand and said 'Shish!' and we were quiet and listened.

There was a scrape, scrape, scraping noise; it came from downstairs.

'They're filing something,' whispered the robber, 'here—shut up, give me that pistol, and the poker. There is a burglar now, and no mistake.'

'It's only a toy one and it won't go off,' I said, 'but you can cock it.'

Then we heard a snap. 'There goes the window bar,' said the robber softly. 'Jove! what an adventure! You kids stay here, I'll tackle it.'

But Dicky and I said we should come. So he let us go as far as the bottom of the kitchen stairs, and we took the tongs and shovel with us. There was a light in the kitchen; a very little light. It is curious we never thought, any of us, that this might be a plant of our robber's to get away. We never thought of doubting his word of honour. And we were right.

That noble robber dashed the kitchen door open, and rushed in with the big toy pistol in one hand and the poker in the other, shouting out just like Oswald had done—

'Surrender! You are discovered! Surrender, or I'll fire! Throw up your hands!' And Dicky and I rattled the tongs and shovel so that he might know there were more of us, all bristling with weapons.

And we heard a husky voice in the kitchen saying—

'All right, governor! Stow that scent sprinkler. I'll give in. Blowed if I ain't pretty well sick of the job, anyway.'

Then we went in. Our robber was standing in the grandest manner with his legs very wide apart, and the pistol pointing at the cowering burglar. The burglar was a large man who did not mean to have a beard, I think, but he had got some of one, and a red comforter, and a fur cap, and his face was red and his voice was thick. How different from our own robber! The burglar had a dark lantern, and he was standing by the plate-basket. When we had lit the gas we all thought he was very like what a burglar ought to be.

He did not look as if he could ever have been a pirate or a highwayman, or anything really dashing or noble, and he scowled and shuffled his feet and said: 'Well, go on: why don't yer fetch the pleece?'

'Upon my word, I don't know,' said our robber, rubbing his chin. 'Oswald, why don't we fetch the police?'

It is not every robber that I would stand Christian names from, I can tell you but just then I didn't think of that. I just said—'Do you mean I'm to fetch one?'

Our robber looked at the burglar and said nothing.

Then the burglar began to speak very fast, and to look different ways with his hard, shiny little eyes.

'Lookee 'ere, governor,' he said, 'I was stony broke, so help me, I was. And blessed if I've nicked a haporth of your little lot. You know yourself there ain't much to tempt a bloke,' he shook the plate-basket as if he was angry with it, and the yellowy spoons and forks rattled. 'I was just a-looking through this 'ere Bank-ollerday show, when you come. Let me off, sir. Come now, I've got kids of my own at home, strike me if I ain't—same as yours—I've got a nipper just about 'is size, and what'll come of them if I'm lagged? I ain't been in it long, sir, and I ain't 'andy at it.'

'No,' said our robber; 'you certainly are not.' Alice and the others had come down by now to see what was happening. Alice told me afterwards they thought it really was the cat this time.

'No, I ain't 'andy, as you say, sir, and if you let me off this once I'll chuck the whole blooming bizz; rake my civvy, I will. Don't be hard on a cove, mister; think of the missis and the kids. I've got one just the cut of little missy there bless 'er pretty 'eart.'

'Your family certainly fits your circumstances very nicely,' said our robber. Then Alice said—

'Oh, do let him go! If he's got a little girl like me, whatever will she do? Suppose it was Father!'

'I don't think he's got a little girl like you, my dear,' said our robber, 'and I think he'll be safer under lock and key.'

'You ask yer Father to let me go, miss,' said the burglar; ''e won't 'ave the 'art to refuse you.'

'If I do,' said Alice, 'will you promise never to come back?'

'Not me, miss,' the burglar said very earnestly, and he looked at the plate-basket again, as if that alone would be enough to keep him away, our robber said afterwards.

'And will you be good and not rob any more?' said Alice.

'I'll turn over a noo leaf, miss, so help me.'

Then Alice said—'Oh, do let him go! I'm sure he'll be good.'

But our robber said no, it wouldn't be right; we must wait till Father came home. Then H. O. said, very suddenly and plainly:

'I don't think it's at all fair, when you're a robber yourself.'

The minute he'd said it the burglar said, 'Kidded, by gum!'—and then our robber made a step towards him to catch hold of him, and before you had time to think 'Hullo!' the burglar knocked the pistol up with one hand and knocked our robber down with the other, and was off out of the window like a shot, though Oswald and Dicky did try to stop him by holding on to his legs.

And that burglar had the cheek to put his head in at the window and say, 'I'll give yer love to the kids and the missis'—and he was off like winking, and there were Alice and Dora trying to pick up our robber, and asking him whether he was hurt, and where. He wasn't hurt at all, except a lump at the back of his head. And he got up, and we dusted the kitchen floor off him. Eliza is a dirty girl.

Then he said, 'Let's put up the shutters. It never rains but it pours. Now you've had two burglars I daresay you'll have twenty.' So we put up the shutters, which Eliza has strict orders to do before she goes out, only she never does, and we went back to Father's study, and the robber said, 'What a night we are having!' and put his boots back in the fender to go on steaming, and then we all talked at once. It was the most wonderful adventure we ever had, though it wasn't treasure-seeking—at least not ours. I suppose it was the burglar's treasure-seeking, but he didn't get much—and our robber said he didn't believe a word about those kids that were so like Alice and me.

And then there was the click of the gate, and we said, 'Here's Father,' and the robber said, 'And now for the police.'

Then we all jumped up. We did like him so much, and it seemed so unfair that he should be sent to prison, and the horrid, lumping big burglar not.

And Alice said, 'Oh, *no*—run! Dicky will let you out at the back door. Oh, do go, go *now*.'

And we all said, 'Yes, *go*,' and pulled him towards the door, and gave him his hat and stick and the things out of his pockets.

But Father's latchkey was in the door, and it was too late.

Father came in quickly, purring with the cold, and began to say, 'It's all right, Foulkes, I've got—' And then he stopped short and stared at us. Then he said, in the voice we all hate, 'Children, what is the meaning of all this?' And for a minute nobody spoke.

Then my Father said, 'Foulkes, I must really apologize for these very naughty—' And then our robber rubbed his hands and laughed, and cried out:

'You're mistaken, my dear sir, I'm not Foulkes; I'm a robber, captured by these young people in the most gallant manner. "Hands up, surrender, or I fire," and all the rest of it. My word, Bastable, but you've got some kids worth having! I wish my Denny had their pluck.'

Then we began to understand, and it was like being knocked down, it was so sudden. And our robber told us he wasn't a robber after all. He was only an old college friend of my Father's, and he had come after dinner, when Father was just trying to mend the lock H. O. had broken, to ask Father to get him a letter to a doctor about his little boy Denny, who was ill. And Father had gone over the Heath to Vanbrugh Park to see some rich people he knows and get the letter. And he had left Mr Foulkes to wait till he came back, because it was important to know at once whether Father could get the letter, and if he couldn't Mr Foulkes would have had to try some one else directly.

We were dumb with amazement.

Our robber told my Father about the other burglar, and said he was sorry he'd let him escape, but my Father said, 'Oh, it's all right: poor beggar; if he really had kids at home: you never can tell—forgive us our debts, don't you know; but tell me about the first business. It must have been moderately entertaining.'

Then our robber told my Father how I had rushed into the room with a pistol, crying out . . . but you know all about that. And he laid it on so thick and fat about plucky young-uns, and chips off old blocks, and things like that, that I felt I was purple with shame, even under the blanket. So I swallowed that thing that tries to prevent you speaking when you ought to, and I said, 'Look here, Father, I didn't really think there was any one in the study. We thought it was a cat at first, and then I thought there was no one there, and I was just larking. And when I said surrender and all that, it was just the game, don't you know?'

Then our robber said, 'Yes, old chap; but when you found there really *was* someone there, you dropped the pistol and bunked, didn't you, eh?'

And I said, 'No; I thought, "Hullo! here's a robber! Well, it's all up, I suppose, but I may as well hold on and see what happens."'

And I was glad I'd owned up, for Father slapped me on the back, and said I was a young brick, and our robber said I was no funk anyway, and though I got very hot under the blanket I liked it, and I explained that the others would have done the same if they had thought of it.

Then Father got up some more beer, and laughed about Dora's responsibility, and he got out a box of figs he had bought for us, only he hadn't given it to us because of the Water Rates, and Eliza came in and brought up the bread and cheese, and what there was left of the neck of mutton—cold wreck of mutton, Father called it—and we had a feast— like a picnic—all sitting anywhere, and eating with our fingers. It was prime. We sat up till past twelve o'clock, and I never felt so pleased to think I was not born a girl. It was hard on the others; they would have done just the same if they'd thought of it. But it does make you feel jolly when your pater says you're a young brick!

When Mr Foulkes was going, he said to Alice, 'Good-bye, Hardy.'

And Alice understood, of course, and kissed him as hard as she could.

And she said, 'I wanted to, when you said no one kissed you when you left off being a pirate.' And he said, 'I know you did, my dear.' And Dora kissed him too, and said, 'I suppose none of these tales were true?'

And our robber just said, 'I tried to play the part properly, my dear.'

And he jolly well did play it, and no mistake. We have often seen him since, and his boy Denny, and his girl Daisy, but that comes in another story.

And if any of you kids who read this ever had two such adventures in one night you can just write and tell me. That's all.

Chapter 14. The Divining-rod

You have no idea how uncomfortable the house was on the day when we sought for gold with the divining-rod. It was like a spring-cleaning in the winter-time. All the carpets were up, because Father had told Eliza to make the place decent as there was a gentleman coming to dinner the next day. So she got in a charwoman, and they slopped water about, and left brooms and brushes on the stairs for people to tumble over. H. O. got a big bump on his head in that way, and when he said it was too bad, Eliza said he should keep in the nursery then, and not be where he'd no business. We bandaged his head with a towel, and then he stopped crying and played at being England's wounded hero dying in the cockpit, while every man was doing his duty, as the hero had told them to, and Alice was Hardy, and I was the doctor, and the others were the crew. Playing at Hardy made us think of our own dear robber, and we wished he was there, and wondered if we should ever see him any more.

We were rather astonished at Father's having anyone to dinner, because now he never seems to think of anything but business. Before Mother died people often came to dinner, and Father's business did not take up so much of his time and was not the bother it is now. And we used to see who could go furthest down in our nightgowns and get nice things to eat, without being seen, out of the dishes as they came out of the dining-room. Eliza can't cook very nice things. She told Father she was a good plain cook, but he says it was a fancy portrait. We stayed in the nursery till the charwoman came in and told us to be off—she was going to make one job of it, and have our carpet up as well as all the others, now the man was here to beat them. It came up, and it was very dusty— and under it we found my threepenny-bit that I lost ages ago, which shows what Eliza is. H. O. had got tired of being the wounded hero, and Dicky was so tired of doing nothing that Dora said she knew he'd begin to tease Noel in a minute; then of course Dicky said he wasn't going to tease anybody—he was going out to the Heath. He said he'd heard that nagging women drove a man from his home, and now he found it was quite true. Oswald always tries to be a peacemaker, so he told Dicky to shut up and not make an ass of himself. And Alice said, 'Well, Dora began'— And Dora tossed her chin up and said it wasn't any business of Oswald's any way, and no one asked Alice's opinion. So we all felt very uncomfortable till Noel said, 'Don't let's quarrel about nothing. You know let dogs delight—and I made up another piece while you were talking—

> Quarrelling is an evil thing,
> It fills with gall life's cup;
> For when once you begin
> It takes such a long time to make it up.'

We all laughed then and stopped jawing at each other. Noel is very funny with his poetry. But that piece happened to come out quite true. You begin to quarrel and then you can't stop; often, long before the others are ready to cry and make it up, I see how silly it is, and I want to laugh; but it doesn't do to say so—for it only makes the others crosser than they were before. I wonder why that is?

Alice said Noel ought to be poet laureate, and she actually went out in the cold and got some laurel leaves—the spotted kind—out of the garden, and Dora made a crown and we put it on him. He was quite pleased; but the leaves made a mess, and Eliza said, 'Don't.' I believe that's a word grown-ups use more than any other. Then suddenly Alice thought of that old idea of hers for finding treasure, and she said—'Do let's try the divining-rod.'

So Oswald said, 'Fair priestess, we do greatly desire to find gold beneath our land, therefore we pray thee practise with the divining-rod, and tell us where we can find it.'

'Do ye desire to fashion of it helms and hauberks?' said Alice.

'Yes,' said Noel; 'and chains and ouches.'

'I bet you don't know what an "ouch" is,' said Dicky.

'Yes I do, so there!' said Noel. 'It's a carcanet. I looked it out in the dicker, now then!' We asked him what a carcanet was, but he wouldn't say.

'And we want to make fair goblets of the gold,' said Oswald.

'Yes, to drink coconut milk out of,' said H. O.

'And we desire to build fair palaces of it,' said Dicky.

'And to buy things,' said Dora; 'a great many things. New Sunday frocks and hats and kid gloves and—'

She would have gone on for ever so long only we reminded her that we hadn't found the gold yet.

By this Alice had put on the nursery tablecloth, which is green, and tied the old blue and yellow antimacassar over her head, and she said—

'If your intentions are correct, fear nothing and follow me.'

And she went down into the hall. We all followed chanting 'Heroes.' It is a gloomy thing the girls learnt at the High School, and we always use it when we want a priestly chant.

Alice stopped short by the hat-stand, and held up her hands as well as she could for the tablecloth, and said—

'Now, great altar of the golden idol, yield me the divining-rod that I may use it for the good of the suffering people.'

The umbrella-stand was the altar of the golden idol, and it yielded her the old school umbrella. She carried it between her palms.

'Now,' she said, 'I shall sing the magic chant. You mustn't say anything, but just follow wherever I go—like follow my leader, you know—and when there is gold underneath the magic rod will twist in the hand of the priestess like a live thing that seeks to be free. Then you will dig, and the golden treasure will be revealed. H. O., if you make that clatter with your boots they'll come and tell us not to. Now come on all of you.'

So she went upstairs and down and into every room. We followed her on tiptoe, and Alice sang as she went. What she sang is not out of a book—Noel made it up while she was dressing up for the priestess.

> Ashen rod cold
> That here I hold,
> Teach me where to find the gold.

When we came to where Eliza was, she said, 'Get along with you'; but Dora said it was only a game, and we wouldn't touch anything, and our boots were quite clean, and Eliza might as well let us. So she did.

It was all right for the priestess, but it was a little dull for the rest of us, because she wouldn't let us sing, too; so we said we'd had enough of it, and if she couldn't find the gold we'd leave off and play something else. The priestess said, 'All right, wait a minute,' and went on singing. Then we all followed her back into the nursery, where the carpet was up and the boards smelt of soft soap. Then she said, 'It moves, it moves! Once more the choral hymn!' So we sang 'Heroes' again, and in the middle the umbrella dropped from her hands.

'The magic rod has spoken,' said Alice; 'dig here, and that with courage and despatch.' We didn't quite see how to dig, but we all began to scratch on the floor with our hands, but the priestess said, 'Don't be so silly! It's the place where they come to do the gas. The board's loose. Dig an you value your lives, for ere sundown the dragon who guards this spoil will return in his fiery fury and make you his unresisting prey.'

So we dug—that is, we got the loose board up. And Alice threw up her arms and cried—

'See the rich treasure—the gold in thick layers, with silver and diamonds stuck in it!'

'Like currants in cake,' said H. O.

'It's a lovely treasure,' said Dicky yawning. 'Let's come back and carry it away another day.'

But Alice was kneeling by the hole.

'Let me feast my eyes on the golden splendour,' she said, 'hidden these long centuries from the human eye. Behold how the magic rod has led us to treasures more—Oswald, don't push so!—more bright than ever monarch—I say, there *is* something down there, really. I saw it shine!'

We thought she was kidding, but when she began to try to get into the hole, which was much too small, we saw she meant it, so I said, 'Let's have a squint,' and I looked, but I couldn't see anything, even when I lay down on my stomach. The others lay down on their stomachs too and tried to see, all but Noel, who stood and looked at us and said we were the great serpents come down to drink at the magic pool. He wanted to be the knight and slay the great serpents with his good sword—he even drew the umbrella ready—but Alice said, 'All right, we will in a minute. But now—I'm sure I saw it; do get a match, Noel, there's a dear.'

'What did you see?' asked Noel, beginning to go for the matches very slowly.

'Something bright, away in the corner under the board against the beam.'

'Perhaps it was a rat's eye,' Noel said, 'or a snake's,' and we did not put our heads quite so close to the hole till he came back with the matches.

Then I struck a match, and Alice cried, 'There it is!' And there it was, and it was a half-sovereign, partly dusty and partly bright. We think perhaps a mouse, disturbed by the carpets being taken up, may have brushed the dust of years from part of the half-sovereign with his tail. We can't imagine how it came there, only Dora thinks she remembers once when H. O. was very little Mother gave him some money to hold, and he dropped it, and it rolled all over the floor. So we think perhaps this was part of it. We were very glad. H. O. wanted to go out at once and buy a mask he had seen for fourpence. It had been a shilling mask, but now it was going very cheap because Guy Fawkes' Day was over, and it was a little cracked at the top. But Dora said, 'I don't know that it's our money. Let's wait and ask Father.'

But H. O. did not care about waiting, and I felt for him. Dora is rather like grown-ups in that way; she does not seem to understand that when you want a thing you do want it, and that you don't wish to wait, even a minute.

So we went and asked Albert-next-door's uncle. He was pegging away at one of the rotten novels he has to write to make his living, but he said we weren't interrupting him at all.

'My hero's folly has involved him in a difficulty,' he said. 'It is his own fault. I will leave him to meditate on the incredible fatuity—the hare-brained recklessness—which have brought him to this pass. It will be a lesson to him. I, meantime, will give myself unreservedly to the pleasures of your conversation.'

That's one thing I like Albert's uncle for. He always talks like a book, and yet you can always understand what he means. I think he is more like us, inside of his mind, than most grown-up people are. He can pretend beautifully. I never met anyone else so good at it, except our robber, and we began it, with him. But it was Albert's uncle who first taught us how to make people talk like books when you're playing things, and he made us learn to tell a story straight from the beginning, not starting in the middle like most people do. So now Oswald remembered what he had been told, as he generally does, and began at the beginning, but when he came to where Alice said she was the priestess, Albert's uncle said—

'Let the priestess herself set forth the tale in fitting speech.'

So Alice said, 'O high priest of the great idol, the humblest of thy slaves took the school umbrella for a divining-rod, and sang the song of inver—what's-it's-name?'

'Invocation perhaps?' said Albert's uncle. 'Yes; and then I went about and about and the others got tired, so the divining-rod fell on a certain spot, and I said, "Dig", and we dug—it was where the loose board is for the gas men—and then there really and truly was a half- sovereign lying under the boards, and here it is.'

Albert's uncle took it and looked at it.

'The great high priest will bite it to see if it's good,' he said, and he did. 'I congratulate you,' he went on; 'you are indeed among those favoured by the Immortals. First you find half-crowns in the garden, and now this. The high priest advises you to tell your Father, and ask if you may keep it. My hero has become penitent, but impatient. I must pull him out of this scrape. Ye have my leave to depart.'

Of course we know from Kipling that that means, 'You'd better bunk, and be sharp about it,' so we came away. I do like Albert's uncle.

I shall be like that when I'm a man. He gave us our Jungle books, and he is awfully clever, though he does have to write grown-up tales.

We told Father about it that night. He was very kind. He said we might certainly have the half-sovereign, and he hoped we should enjoy ourselves with our treasure-trove.

Then he said, 'Your dear Mother's Indian Uncle is coming to dinner here to-morrow night. So will you not drag the furniture about overhead, please, more than you're absolutely obliged; and H. O. might wear slippers or something. I can always distinguish the note of H. O.'s boots.'

We said we would be very quiet, and Father went on—

'This Indian Uncle is not used to children, and he is coming to talk business with me. It is really important that he should be quiet. Do you think, Dora, that perhaps bed at six for H. O. and Noel—'

But H. O. said, 'Father, I really and truly won't make a noise. I'll stand on my head all the evening sooner than disturb the Indian Uncle with my boots.'

And Alice said Noel never made a row anyhow. So Father laughed and said, 'All right.' And he said we might do as we liked with the half- sovereign. 'Only for goodness' sake don't try to go in for business with it,' he said. 'It's always a mistake to go into business with an insufficient capital.'

We talked it over all that evening, and we decided that as we were not to go into business with our half-sovereign it was no use not spending it at once, and so we might as well have a right royal feast. The next day we went out and bought the things. We got figs, and almonds and raisins, and a real raw rabbit, and Eliza promised to cook it for us if we would wait till tomorrow, because of the Indian Uncle coming to dinner. She was very busy cooking nice things for him to eat. We got the rabbit because we are so tired of beef and mutton, and Father hasn't a bill at the poultry shop. And we got some flowers to go on the dinner-table for Father's party. And we got hardbake and raspberry noyau and peppermint rock and oranges and a coconut, with other nice things. We put it all in the top long drawer. It is H. O.'s play drawer, and we made him turn his things out and put them in Father's old portmanteau. H. O. is getting old enough now to learn to be unselfish, and besides, his drawer wanted tidying very badly. Then we all vowed by the honour of the ancient House of Bastable that we would not touch any of the feast till Dora gave the word next day. And we gave H. O. some of the hardbake, to make it easier for him to keep his vow. The next day was the most rememorable day in all our lives, but we didn't know that then. But that is another story. I think that is such a useful way to know when you can't think how to end up a chapter. I learnt it from another writer named Kipling. I've mentioned him before, I believe, but he deserves it!

Chapter 15. 'Lo, the Poor Indian!'

It was all very well for Father to ask us not to make a row because the Indian Uncle was coming to talk business, but my young brother's boots are not the only things that make a noise. We took his boots away and made him wear Dora's bath slippers, which are soft and woolly, and hardly any soles to them; and of course we wanted to see the Uncle, so we looked over the banisters when he came, and we were as quiet as mice—but when Eliza had let him in she went straight down to the kitchen and made the most awful row you ever heard, it sounded like the Day of judgement, or all the saucepans and crockery in the house being kicked about the floor, but she told me afterwards it was only the tea-tray and one or two cups and saucers, that she had knocked over in her flurry. We heard the Uncle say, 'God bless my soul!' and then he went into Father's study and the door was shut—we didn't see him properly at all that time.

I don't believe the dinner was very nice. Something got burned I'm sure—for we smelt it. It was an extra smell, besides the mutton.

I know that got burned. Eliza wouldn't have any of us in the kitchen except Dora—till dinner was over. Then we got what was left of the dessert, and had it on the stairs—just round the corner where they can't see you from the hall, unless the first landing gas is lighted. Suddenly the study door opened and the Uncle came out and went and felt in his greatcoat pocket. It was his cigar-case he wanted. We saw that afterwards. We got a much better view of him then. He didn't look like an Indian but just like a kind of brown, big Englishman, and of course he didn't see us, but we heard him mutter to himself—

'Shocking bad dinner! Eh!—what?'

When he went back to the study he didn't shut the door properly. That door has always been a little tiresome since the day we took the lock off to get out the pencil sharpener H. O. had shoved into the keyhole. We didn't listen—really and truly—but the Indian Uncle has a very big voice, and Father was not going to be beaten by a poor Indian in talking or anything else—so he spoke up too, like a man, and I heard him say it was a very good business, and only wanted a little capital—and he said it as if it was an imposition he had learned, and he hated having to say it. The Uncle said, 'Pooh, pooh!' to that, and then he said he was afraid that what that same business wanted was not capital but management. Then I heard my Father say, 'It is not a pleasant subject: I am sorry I introduced it. Suppose we change it, sir. Let me fill your glass.' Then the poor Indian said something about vintage—and that a poor, broken-down man like he was couldn't be too careful. And then Father said, 'Well, whisky then,' and afterwards they talked about Native Races and Imperial something or other and it got very dull.

So then Oswald remembered that you must not hear what people do not intend you to hear—even if you are not listening and he said, 'We ought not to stay here any longer. Perhaps they would not like us to hear—'

Alice said, 'Oh, do you think it could possibly matter?' and went and shut the study door softly but quite tight. So it was no use staying there any longer, and we went to the nursery.

Then Noel said, 'Now I understand. Of course my Father is making a banquet for the Indian, because he is a poor, broken-down man. We might have known that from "Lo, the poor Indian!" you know.'

We all agreed with him, and we were glad to have the thing explained, because we had not understood before what Father wanted to have people to dinner for—and not let us come in.

'Poor people are very proud,' said Alice, 'and I expect Father thought the Indian would be ashamed, if all of us children knew how poor he was.'

Then Dora said, 'Poverty is no disgrace. We should honour honest Poverty.'

And we all agreed that that was so.

'I wish his dinner had not been so nasty,' Dora said, while Oswald put lumps of coal on the fire with his fingers, so as not to make a noise. He is a very thoughtful boy, and he did not wipe his fingers on his trouser leg as perhaps Noel or H. O. would have done, but he just rubbed them on Dora's handkerchief while she was talking.

'I am afraid the dinner was horrid.' Dora went on. 'The table looked very nice with the flowers we got. I set it myself, and Eliza made me borrow the silver spoons and forks from Albert-next-door's Mother.'

'I hope the poor Indian is honest,' said Dicky gloomily, 'when you are a poor, broken-down man silver spoons must be a great temptation.'

Oswald told him not to talk such tommy-rot because the Indian was a relation, so of course he couldn't do anything dishonourable. And Dora said it was all right any way, because she had washed up the spoons and forks herself and counted them, and they were all there, and she had put them into their wash-leather bag, and taken them back to Albert-next-door's Mother.

'And the brussels sprouts were all wet and swimmy,' she went on, 'and the potatoes looked grey—and there were bits of black in the gravy—and the mutton was bluey-red and soft in the middle. I saw it when it came out. The apple-pie looked very nice—but it wasn't quite done in the apply part. The other thing that was burnt—you must have smelt it, was the soup.'

'It is a pity,' said Oswald; 'I don't suppose he gets a good dinner every day.'

'No more do we,' said H. O., 'but we shall to-morrow.'

I thought of all the things we had bought with our half-sovereign—the rabbit and the sweets and the almonds and raisins and figs and the coconut: and I thought of the nasty mutton and things, and while I was thinking about it all Alice said—

'Let's ask the poor Indian to come to dinner with *us* to-morrow.' I should have said it myself if she had given me time.

We got the little ones to go to bed by promising to put a note on their dressing-table saying what had happened, so that they might know the first thing in the morning, or in the middle of the night if they happened to wake up, and then we elders arranged everything.

I waited by the back door, and when the Uncle was beginning to go Dicky was to drop a marble down between the banisters for a signal, so that I could run round and meet the Uncle as he came out.

This seems like deceit, but if you are a thoughtful and considerate boy you will understand that we could not go down and say to the Uncle in the hall under Father's eye, 'Father has given you a beastly, nasty dinner, but if you will come to dinner with us tomorrow, we will show you our idea of good things to eat.' You will see, if you think it over, that this would not have been at all polite to Father.

So when the Uncle left, Father saw him to the door and let him out, and then went back to the study, looking very sad, Dora says.

As the poor Indian came down our steps he saw me there at the gate.

I did not mind his being poor, and I said, 'Good evening, Uncle,' just as politely as though he had been about to ascend into one of the gilded chariots of the rich and affluent, instead of having to walk to the station a quarter of a mile in the mud, unless he had the money for a tram fare.

'Good evening, Uncle.' I said it again, for he stood staring at me. I don't suppose he was used to politeness from boys—some boys are anything but—especially to the Aged Poor.

So I said, 'Good evening, Uncle,' yet once again. Then he said—

'Time you were in bed, young man. Eh!—what?'

Then I saw I must speak plainly with him, man to man. So I did. I said—

'You've been dining with my Father, and we couldn't help hearing you say the dinner was shocking. So we thought as you're an Indian, perhaps you're very poor'—I didn't like to tell him we had heard the dreadful truth from his own lips, so I went on, 'because of "Lo, the poor Indian"—you know—and you can't get a good dinner every day. And we are very sorry if you're poor; and won't you come and have dinner with us to-morrow—with us children, I mean? It's a very, very good dinner— rabbit, and hardbake, and coconut—and you needn't mind us knowing you're poor, because we know honourable poverty is no disgrace, and—' I could have gone on much longer, but he interrupted me to say—'Upon my word! And what's your name, eh?'

'Oswald Bastable,' I said; and I do hope you people who are reading this story have not guessed before that I was Oswald all the time.

'Oswald Bastable, eh? Bless my soul!' said the poor Indian. 'Yes, I'll dine with you, Mr Oswald Bastable, with all the pleasure in life. Very kind and cordial invitation, I'm sure. Good night, sir. At one o'clock, I presume?'

'Yes, at one,' I said. 'Good night, sir.'

Then I went in and told the others, and we wrote a paper and put it on the boy's dressing-table, and it said—

'The poor Indian is coming at one. He seemed very grateful to me for my kindness.'

We did not tell Father that the Uncle was coming to dinner with us, for the polite reason that I have explained before. But we had to tell Eliza; so we said a friend was coming to dinner and we wanted everything very nice. I think she thought it was Albert-next-door, but she was in a good temper that day, and she agreed to cook the rabbit and to make a pudding with currants in it. And when one o'clock came the Indian Uncle came too. I let him in and helped him off with his greatcoat, which was all furry inside, and took him straight to the nursery. We were to have dinner there as usual, for we had decided from the first that he would enjoy himself more if he was not made a stranger of. We agreed to treat him as one of ourselves, because if we were too polite, he might think it was our pride because he was poor.

He shook hands with us all and asked our ages, and what schools we went to, and shook his head when we said we were having a holiday just now. I felt rather uncomfortable—I always do when they talk about schools— and I couldn't think of anything to say to show him we meant to treat him as one of ourselves. I did ask if he played cricket. He said he had not played lately. And then no one said anything till dinner came in. We had all washed our faces and hands and brushed our hair before he came in, and we all looked very nice, especially Oswald, who had had his hair cut that very morning. When Eliza had brought in the rabbit and gone out again, we looked at each other in silent despair, like in books. It seemed as if it were going to be just a dull dinner like the one the poor Indian had had the night before; only, of course, the things to eat would be nicer. Dicky kicked Oswald under the table to make him say something—and he had his new boots on, too!—but Oswald did not kick back; then the Uncle asked—

'Do you carve, sir, or shall I?'

Suddenly Alice said—

'Would you like grown-up dinner, Uncle, or play-dinner?'

He did not hesitate a moment, but said, 'Play-dinner, by all means. Eh!—what?' and then we knew it was all right.

So we at once showed the Uncle how to be a dauntless hunter. The rabbit was the deer we had slain in the green forest with our trusty yew bows, and we toasted the joints of it, when the Uncle had carved it, on bits of firewood sharpened to a point. The Uncle's piece got a little burnt, but he said it was delicious, and he said game was always nicer when you had killed it yourself. When Eliza had taken away the rabbit bones and brought in the pudding, we waited till she had gone out and shut the door, and then we put the dish down on the floor and slew the pudding in the dish in the good old-fashioned way. It was a wild boar at bay, and very hard indeed to kill, even with forks. The Uncle was very fierce indeed with the pudding, and jumped and howled when he speared it, but when it came to his turn to be helped, he said, 'No, thank you; think of my liver. Eh!—what?'

But he had some almonds and raisins—when we had climbed to the top of the chest of drawers to pluck them from the boughs of the great trees; and he had a fig from the cargo that the rich merchants brought in their ship—the long drawer was the ship—and the rest of us had the sweets and the coconut. It was a very glorious and beautiful feast, and when it was over we said we hoped it was better than the dinner last night. And he said:

'I never enjoyed a dinner more.' He was too polite to say what he really thought about Father's dinner. And we saw that though he might be poor, he was a true gentleman.

He smoked a cigar while we finished up what there was left to eat, and told us about tiger shooting and about elephants. We asked him about wigwams, and wampum, and mocassins, and beavers, but he did not seem to know, or else he was shy about talking of the wonders of his native land.

We liked him very much indeed, and when he was going at last, Alice nudged me, and I said—'There's one and threepence farthing left out of our half-sovereign. Will you take it, please, because we do like you very much indeed, and we don't want it, really; and we would rather you had it.' And I put the money into his hand.

'I'll take the threepenny-bit,' he said, turning the money over and looking at it, 'but I couldn't rob you of the rest. By the way, where did you get the money for this most royal spread—half a sovereign you said—eh, what?'

We told him all about the different ways we had looked for treasure, and when we had been telling some time he sat down, to listen better and at last we told him how Alice had played at divining-rod, and how it really had found a half-sovereign.

Then he said he would like to see her do it again. But we explained that the rod would only show gold and silver, and that we were quite sure there was no more gold in the house, because we happened to have looked very carefully.

'Well, silver, then,' said he; 'let's hide the plate-basket, and little Alice shall make the divining-rod find it. Eh!—what?'

'There isn't any silver in the plate-basket now,' Dora said. 'Eliza asked me to borrow the silver spoons and forks for your dinner last night from Albert-next-door's Mother. Father never notices, but she thought it would be nicer for you. Our own silver went to have the dents taken out; and I don't think Father could afford to pay the man for doing it, for the silver hasn't come back.'

'Bless my soul!' said the Uncle again, looking at the hole in the big chair that we burnt when we had Guy Fawkes' Day indoors. 'And how much pocket-money do you get? Eh!—what?'

'We don't have any now,' said Alice; 'but indeed we don't want the other shilling. We'd much rather you had it, wouldn't we?'

And the rest of us said, 'Yes.' The Uncle wouldn't take it, but he asked a lot of questions, and at last he went away. And when he went he said—

'Well, youngsters, I've enjoyed myself very much. I shan't forget your kind hospitality. Perhaps the poor Indian may be in a position to ask you all to dinner some day.'

Oswald said if he ever could we should like to come very much, but he was not to trouble to get such a nice dinner as ours, because we could do very well with cold mutton and rice pudding. We do not like these things, but Oswald knows how to behave. Then the poor Indian went away.

We had not got any treasure by this party, but we had had a very good time, and I am sure the Uncle enjoyed himself.

We were so sorry he was gone that we could none of us eat much tea; but we did not mind, because we had pleased the poor Indian and enjoyed ourselves too. Besides, as Dora said, 'A contented mind is a continual feast,' so it did not matter about not wanting tea.

Only H. O. did not seem to think a continual feast was a contented mind, and Eliza gave him a powder in what was left of the red-currant jelly Father had for the nasty dinner.

But the rest of us were quite well, and I think it must have been the coconut with H. O. We hoped nothing had disagreed with the Uncle, but we never knew.

Chapter 16. The End of the Treasure-seeking

Now it is coming near the end of our treasure-seeking, and the end was so wonderful that now nothing is like it used to be. It is like as if our fortunes had been in an earthquake, and after those, you know, everything comes out wrong-way up.

The day after the Uncle speared the pudding with us opened in gloom and sadness. But you never know. It was destined to be a day when things happened. Yet no sign of this appeared in the early morning. Then all was misery and upsetness. None of us felt quite well; I don't know why: and Father had one of his awful colds, so Dora persuaded him not to go to London, but to stay cosy and warm in the study, and she made him some gruel. She makes it better than Eliza does; Eliza's gruel is all little lumps, and when you suck them it is dry oatmeal inside.

We kept as quiet as we could, and I made H. O. do some lessons, like the G. B. had advised us to. But it was very dull. There are some days when you seem to have got to the end of all the things that could ever possibly happen to you, and you feel you will spend all the rest of your life doing dull things just the same way. Days like this are generally wet days. But, as I said, you never know.

Then Dicky said if things went on like this he should run away to sea, and Alice said she thought it would be rather nice to go into a convent. H. O. was a little disagreeable because of the powder Eliza had given him, so he tried to read two books at once, one with each eye, just because Noel wanted one of the books, which was very selfish of him, so it only made his headache worse. H. O. is getting old enough to learn by experience that it is wrong to be selfish, and when he complained about his head Oswald told him whose fault it was, because I am older than he is, and it is my duty to show him where he is wrong. But he began to cry, and then Oswald had to cheer him up because of Father wanting to be quiet. So Oswald said—

'They'll eat H. O. if you don't look out!' And Dora said Oswald was too bad.

Of course Oswald was not going to interfere again, so he went to look out of the window and see the trams go by, and by and by H. O. came and looked out too, and Oswald, who knows when to be generous and forgiving, gave him a piece of blue pencil and two nibs, as good as new, to keep.

As they were looking out at the rain splashing on the stones in the street they saw a four-wheeled cab come lumbering up from the way the station is. Oswald called out—

'Here comes the coach of the Fairy Godmother. It'll stop here, you see if it doesn't!'

So they all came to the window to look. Oswald had only said that about stopping and he was stricken with wonder and amaze when the cab really did stop. It had boxes on the top and knobby parcels sticking out of the window, and it was something like going away to the seaside and something like the gentleman who takes things about in a carriage with the wooden shutters up, to sell to the drapers' shops. The cabman got down, and some one inside handed out ever so many parcels of different shapes and sizes, and the cabman stood holding them in his arms and grinning over them.

Dora said, 'It is a pity some one doesn't tell him this isn't the house.' And then from inside the cab some one put out a foot feeling for the step, like a tortoise's foot coming out from under his shell when you are holding him off the ground, and then a leg came and more parcels, and then Noel cried—

'It's the poor Indian!'

And it was.

Eliza opened the door, and we were all leaning over the banisters. Father heard the noise of parcels and boxes in the hall, and he came out without remembering how bad his cold was. If you do that yourself when you have a cold they call you careless and naughty. Then we heard the poor Indian say to Father—

'I say, Dick, I dined with your kids yesterday—as I daresay they've told you. Jolliest little cubs I ever saw! Why didn't you let me see them the other night? The eldest is the image of poor Janey—and as to young Oswald, he's a man! If he's not a man, I'm a nigger! Eh!—what? And Dick, I say, I shouldn't wonder if I could find a friend to put a bit into that business of yours—eh?'

Then he and Father went into the study and the door was shut—and we went down and looked at the parcels. Some were done up in old, dirty newspapers, and tied with bits of rag, and some were in brown paper and string from the shops, and there were boxes. We wondered if the Uncle had come to stay and this was his luggage, or whether it was to sell. Some of it smelt of spices, like merchandise—and one bundle Alice felt certain was a bale. We heard a hand on the knob of the study door after a bit, and Alice said—

'Fly!' and we all got away but H. O., and the Uncle caught him by the leg as he was trying to get upstairs after us.

'Peeping at the baggage, eh?' said the Uncle, and the rest of us came down because it would have been dishonourable to leave H. O. alone in a scrape, and we wanted to see what was in the parcels.

'I didn't touch,' said H. O. 'Are you coming to stay? I hope you are.'

'No harm done if you did touch,' said the good, kind, Indian man to all of us. 'For all these parcels are *for you*.'

I have several times told you about our being dumb with amazement and terror and joy, and things like that, but I never remember us being dumber than we were when he said this.

The Indian Uncle went on: 'I told an old friend of mine what a pleasant dinner I had with you, and about the threepenny-bit, and the divining- rod, and all that, and he sent all these odds and ends as presents for you. Some of the things came from India.'

'Have you come from India, Uncle?' Noel asked; and when he said 'Yes' we were all very much surprised, for we never thought of his being that sort of Indian. We thought he was the Red kind, and of course his not being accounted for his ignorance of beavers and things.

He got Eliza to help, and we took all the parcels into the nursery and he undid them and undid them and undid them, till the papers lay thick on the floor. Father came too and sat in the Guy Fawkes chair. I cannot begin to tell you all the things that kind friend of Uncle's had sent us. He must be a very agreeable person.

There were toys for the kids and model engines for Dick and me, and a lot of books, and Japanese china tea-sets for the girls, red and white and gold—there were sweets by the pound and by the box—and long yards and yards of soft silk from India, to make frocks for the girls—and a real Indian sword for Oswald and a book of Japanese pictures for Noel, and some ivory chess men for Dicky: the castles of the chessmen are elephant-and-castles. There is a railway station called that; I never knew what it meant before. The brown paper and string parcels had boxes of games in them—and big cases of preserved fruits and things. And the shabby old newspaper parcels and the boxes had the Indian things in. I never saw so many beautiful things before. There were carved fans and silver bangles and strings of amber beads, and necklaces of uncut gems— turquoises and garnets, the Uncle said they were—and shawls and scarves of silk, and cabinets of brown and gold, and ivory boxes and silver trays, and brass things. The Uncle kept saying, 'This is for you, young man,' or 'Little Alice will like this fan,'or 'Miss Dora would look well in this green silk, I think. Eh!—what?'

And Father looked on as if it was a dream, till the Uncle suddenly gave him an ivory paper-knife and a box of cigars, and said, 'My old friend sent you these, Dick; he's an old friend of yours too, he says.' And he winked at my Father, for H. O. and I saw him. And my Father winked back, though he has always told us not to.

That was a wonderful day. It was a treasure, and no mistake! I never saw such heaps and heaps of presents, like things out of a fairy-tale— and even Eliza had a shawl. Perhaps she deserved it, for she did cook the rabbit and the pudding; and Oswald says it is not her fault if her nose turns up and she does not brush her hair. I do not think Eliza likes brushing things. It is the same with the carpets. But Oswald tries to make allowances even for people who do not wash their ears.

The Indian Uncle came to see us often after that, and his friend always sent us something. Once he tipped us a sovereign each—the Uncle brought it; and once he sent us money to go to the Crystal Palace, and the Uncle took us; and another time to a circus; and when Christmas was near the Uncle said—

'You remember when I dined with you, some time ago, you promised to dine with me some day, if I could ever afford to give a dinner-party. Well, I'm going to have one—a Christmas party. Not on Christmas Day, because every one goes home then—but on the day after. Cold mutton and rice pudding. You'll come? Eh!—what?'

We said we should be delighted, if Father had no objection, because that is the proper thing to say, and the poor Indian, I mean the Uncle, said, 'No, your Father won't object—he's coming too, bless your soul!'

We all got Christmas presents for the Uncle. The girls made him a handkerchief case and a comb bag, out of some of the pieces of silk he had given them. I got him a knife with three blades; H. O. got a siren whistle, a very strong one, and Dicky joined with me in the knife, and Noel would give the Indian ivory box that Uncle's friend had sent on the wonderful Fairy Cab day. He said it was the very nicest thing he had, and he was sure Uncle wouldn't mind his not having bought it with his own money.

I think Father's business must have got better—perhaps Uncle's friend put money in it and that did it good, like feeding the starving. Anyway we all had new suits, and the girls had the green silk from India made into frocks, and on Boxing Day we went in two cabs—Father and the girls in one, and us boys in the other.

We wondered very much where the Indian Uncle lived, because we had not been told. And we thought when the cab began to go up the hill towards the Heath that perhaps the Uncle lived in one of the poky little houses up at the top of Greenwich. But the cab went right over the Heath and in at some big gates, and through a shrubbery all white with frost like a fairy forest, because it was Christmas time. And at last we stopped before one of those jolly, big, ugly red houses with a lot of windows, that are so comfortable inside, and on the steps was the Indian Uncle, looking very big and grand, in a blue cloth coat and yellow sealskin waistcoat, with a bunch of seals hanging from it.

'I wonder whether he has taken a place as butler here?' said Dicky.

'A poor, broken-down man—'

Noel thought it was very likely, because he knew that in these big houses there were always thousands of stately butlers.

The Uncle came down the steps and opened the cab door himself, which I don't think butlers would expect to have to do. And he took us in. It was a lovely hall, with bear and tiger skins on the floor, and a big clock with the faces of the sun and moon dodging out when it was day or night, and Father Time with a scythe coming out at the hours, and the name on it was 'Flint. Ashford. 1776'; and there was a fox eating a stuffed duck in a glass case, and horns of stags and other animals over the doors.

'We'll just come into my study first,' said the Uncle, 'and wish each other a Merry Christmas.' So then we knew he wasn't the butler, but it must be his own house, for only the master of the house has a study.

His study was not much like Father's. It had hardly any books, but swords and guns and newspapers and a great many boots, and boxes half unpacked, with more Indian things bulging out of them.

We gave him our presents and he was awfully pleased. Then he gave us his Christmas presents. You must be tired of hearing about presents, but I must remark that all the Uncle's presents were watches; there was a watch for each of us, with our names engraved inside, all silver except H. O.'s, and that was a Waterbury, 'To match his boots,' the Uncle said. I don't know what he meant.

Then the Uncle looked at Father, and Father said, 'You tell them, sir.'

So the Uncle coughed and stood up and made a speech. He said—

'Ladies and gentlemen, we are met together to discuss an important subject which has for some weeks engrossed the attention of the honourable member opposite and myself.'

I said, 'Hear, hear,' and Alice whispered, 'What happened to the guinea- pig?' Of course you know the answer to that.

The Uncle went on—

'I am going to live in this house, and as it's rather big for me, your Father has agreed that he and you shall come and live with me. And so, if you're agreeable, we're all going to live here together, and, please God, it'll be a happy home for us all. Eh!—what?'

He blew his nose and kissed us all round. As it was Christmas I did not mind, though I am much too old for it on other dates. Then he said, 'Thank you all very much for your presents; but I've got a present here I value more than anything else I have.'

I thought it was not quite polite of him to say so, till I saw that what he valued so much was a threepenny-bit on his watch-chain, and, of course, I saw it must be the one we had given him.

He said, 'You children gave me that when you thought I was the poor Indian, and I'll keep it as long as I live. And I've asked some friends to help us to be jolly, for this is our house-warming. Eh!—what?'

Then he shook Father by the hand, and they blew their noses; and then Father said, 'Your Uncle has been most kind—most—'

But Uncle interrupted by saying, 'Now, Dick, no nonsense!' Then H. O. said, 'Then you're not poor at all?' as if he were very disappointed. The Uncle replied, 'I have enough for my simple wants, thank you, H. O.; and your Father's business will provide him with enough for yours. Eh!—what?'

Then we all went down and looked at the fox thoroughly, and made the Uncle take the glass off so that we could see it all round and then the Uncle took us all over the house, which is the most comfortable one I have ever been in. There is a beautiful portrait of Mother in Father's sitting-room. The Uncle must be very rich indeed. This ending is like what happens in Dickens's books; but I think it was much jollier to happen like a book, and it shows what a nice man the Uncle is, the way he did it all.

Think how flat it would have been if the Uncle had said, when we first offered him the one and threepence farthing, 'Oh, I don't want your dirty one and three-pence! I'm very rich indeed.' Instead of which he saved up the news of his wealth till Christmas, and then told us all in one glorious burst. Besides, I can't help it if it is like Dickens, because it happens this way. Real life is often something like books.

Presently, when we had seen the house, we were taken into the drawing- room, and there was Mrs Leslie, who gave us the shillings and wished us good hunting, and Lord Tottenham, and Albert-next-door's Uncle—and Albert-next-door, and his Mother (I'm not very fond of her), and best of all our own Robber and his two kids, and our Robber had a new suit on. The Uncle told us he had asked the people who had been kind to us, and Noel said, 'Where is my noble editor that I wrote the poetry to?'

The Uncle said he had not had the courage to ask a strange editor to dinner; but Lord Tottenham was an old friend of Uncle's, and he had introduced Uncle to Mrs Leslie, and that was how he had the pride and pleasure of welcoming her to our house-warming. And he made her a bow like you see on a Christmas card.

Then Alice asked, 'What about Mr Rosenbaum? He was kind; it would have been a pleasant surprise for him.'

But everybody laughed, and Uncle said—

'Your father has paid him the sovereign he lent you. I don't think he could have borne another pleasant surprise.'

And I said there was the butcher, and he was really kind; but they only laughed, and Father said you could not ask all your business friends to a private dinner.

Then it was dinner-time, and we thought of Uncle's talk about cold mutton and rice. But it was a beautiful dinner, and I never saw such a dessert! We had ours on plates to take away into another sitting-room, which was much jollier than sitting round the table with the grown-ups. But the Robber's kids stayed with their Father. They were very shy and frightened, and said hardly anything, but looked all about with very bright eyes. H. O. thought they were like white mice; but afterwards we got to know them very well, and in the end they were not so mousy. And there is a good deal of interesting stuff to tell about them; but I shall put all that in another book, for there is no room for it in this one. We played desert islands all the afternoon and drank Uncle's health in ginger wine. It was H. O. that upset his over Alice's green silk dress, and she never even rowed him. Brothers ought not to have favourites, and Oswald would never be so mean as to have a favourite sister, or, if he had, wild horses should not make him tell who it was.

And now we are to go on living in the big house on the Heath, and it is very jolly.

Mrs Leslie often comes to see us, and our own Robber and Albert-next- door's uncle. The Indian Uncle likes him because he has been in India too and is brown; but our Uncle does not like Albert-next-door. He says he is a muff. And I am to go to Rugby, and so are Noel and H. O., and perhaps to Balliol afterwards. Balliol is my Father's college. It has two separate coats of arms, which many other colleges are not allowed. Noel is going to be a poet and Dicky wants to go into Father's business.

The Uncle is a real good old sort; and just think, we should never have found him if we hadn't made up our minds to be Treasure Seekers! Noel made a poem about it—

> Lo! the poor Indian from lands afar,
> Comes where the treasure seekers are;
> We looked for treasure, but we find
> The best treasure of all is the Uncle good and kind.

I thought it was rather rot, but Alice would show it to the Uncle, and he liked it very much. He kissed Alice and he smacked Noel on the back, and he said, 'I don't think I've done so badly either, if you come to that, though I was never a regular professional treasure seeker. Eh!— what?'

The Would-Be-Goods

Being the Further Adventures of the Treasure Seekers

To my Dear Son Fabian Bland

Chapter 1. The Jungle

'Children are like jam: all very well in the proper place, but you can't stand them all over the shop—eh, what?'

These were the dreadful words of our Indian uncle. They made us feel very young and angry; and yet we could not be comforted by calling him names to ourselves, as you do when nasty grown-ups say nasty things, because he is not nasty, but quite the exact opposite when not irritated. And we could not think it ungentlemanly of him to say we were like jam, because, as Alice says, jam is very nice indeed—only not on furniture and improper places like that. My father said, 'Perhaps they had better go to boarding-school.' And that was awful, because we know Father disapproves of boarding-schools. And he looked at us and said, 'I am ashamed of them, sir!'

Your lot is indeed a dark and terrible one when your father is ashamed of you. And we all knew this, so that we felt in our chests just as if we had swallowed a hard-boiled egg whole. At least, this is what Oswald felt, and Father said once that Oswald, as the eldest, was the representative of the family, so, of course, the others felt the same.

And then everybody said nothing for a short time. At last Father said—

'You may go—but remember—'

The words that followed I am not going to tell you. It is no use telling you what you know before—as they do in schools. And you must all have had such words said to you many times. We went away when it was over. The girls cried, and we boys got out books and began to read, so that nobody should think we cared. But we felt it deeply in our interior hearts, especially Oswald, who is the eldest and the representative of the family.

We felt it all the more because we had not really meant to do anything wrong. We only thought perhaps the grown-ups would not be quite pleased if they knew, and that is quite different. Besides, we meant to put all the things back in their proper places when we had done with them before anyone found out about it. But I must not anticipate (that means telling the end of the story before the beginning. I tell you this because it is so sickening to have words you don't know in a story, and to be told to look it up in the dicker).

We are the Bastables—Oswald, Dora, Dicky, Alice, Noel, and H. O. If you want to know why we call our youngest brother H. O. you can jolly well read The Treasure Seekers and find out. We were the Treasure Seekers, and we sought it high and low, and quite regularly, because we particularly wanted to find it. And at last we did not find it, but we were found by a good, kind Indian uncle, who helped Father with his business, so that Father was able to take us all to live in a jolly big red house on Blackheath, instead of in the Lewisham Road, where we lived when we were only poor but honest Treasure Seekers. When we were poor but honest we always used to think that if only Father had plenty of business, and we did not have to go short of pocket money and wear shabby clothes (I don't mind this myself, but the girls do), we should be happy and very, very good.

And when we were taken to the beautiful big Blackheath house we thought now all would be well, because it was a house with vineries and pineries, and gas and water, and shrubberies and stabling, and replete with every modern convenience, like it says in Dyer & Hilton's list of Eligible House Property. I read all about it, and I have copied the words quite right.

It is a beautiful house, all the furniture solid and strong, no casters off the chairs, and the tables not scratched, and the silver not dented; and lots of servants, and the most decent meals every day—and lots of pocket-money.

But it is wonderful how soon you get used to things, even the things you want most. Our watches, for instance. We wanted them frightfully; but when I had mine a week or two, after the mainspring got broken and was repaired at Bennett's in the village, I hardly cared to look at the works at all, and it did not make me feel happy in my heart any more, though, of course, I should have been very unhappy if it had been taken away from me. And the same with new clothes and nice dinners and having enough of everything. You soon get used to it all, and it does not make you extra happy, although, if you had it all taken away, you would be very dejected. (That is a good word, and one I have never used before.) You get used to everything, as I said, and then you want something more. Father says this is what people mean by the deceitfulness of riches; but Albert's uncle says it is the spirit of progress, and Mrs Leslie said some people called it 'divine discontent'. Oswald asked them all what they thought one Sunday at dinner. Uncle said it was rot, and what we wanted was bread and water and a licking; but he meant it for a joke. This was in the Easter holidays.

We went to live at the Red House at Christmas. After the holidays the girls went to the Blackheath High School, and we boys went to the Prop. (that means the Proprietary School). And we had to swot rather during term; but about Easter we knew the deceitfulness of riches in the vac., when there was nothing much on, like pantomimes and things. Then there was the summer term, and we swotted more than ever; and it was boiling hot, and masters' tempers got short and sharp, and the girls used to wish the exams came in cold weather. I can't think why they don't. But I suppose schools don't think of sensible thinks like that. They teach botany at girls' schools.

Then the Midsummer holidays came, and we breathed again—but only for a few days. We began to feel as if we had forgotten something, and did not know what it was. We wanted something to happen—only we didn't exactly know what. So we were very pleased when Father said—

'I've asked Mr Foulkes to send his children here for a week or two. You know—the kids who came at Christmas. You must be jolly to them, and see that they have a good time, don't you know.'

We remembered them right enough—they were little pinky, frightened things, like white mice, with very bright eyes. They had not been to our house since Christmas, because Denis, the boy, had been ill, and they had been with an aunt at Ramsgate.

Alice and Dora would have liked to get the bedrooms ready for the honoured guests, but a really good housemaid is sometimes more ready to say 'Don't' than even a general. So the girls had to chuck it. Jane only let them put flowers in the pots on the visitors' mantelpieces, and then they had to ask the gardener which kind they might pick, because nothing worth gathering happened to be growing in our own gardens just then.

Their train got in at 12.27. We all went to meet them. Afterwards I thought that was a mistake, because their aunt was with them, and she wore black with beady things and a tight bonnet, and she said, when we took our hats off— 'Who are you?' quite crossly.

We said, 'We are the Bastables; we've come to meet Daisy and Denny.'

The aunt is a very rude lady, and it made us sorry for Daisy and Denny when she said to them—

'Are these the children? Do you remember them?' We weren't very tidy, perhaps, because we'd been playing brigands in the shrubbery; and we knew we should have to wash for dinner as soon as we got back, anyhow. But still—

Denny said he thought he remembered us. But Daisy said, 'Of course they are,' and then looked as if she was going to cry.

So then the aunt called a cab, and told the man where to drive, and put Daisy and Denny in, and then she said—

'You two little girls may go too, if you like, but you little boys must walk.'

So the cab went off, and we were left. The aunt turned to us to say a few last words. We knew it would have been about brushing your hair and wearing gloves, so Oswald said, 'Good-bye', and turned haughtily away, before she could begin, and so did the others. No one but that kind of black beady tight lady would say 'little boys'. She is like Miss Murdstone in David Copperfield. I should like to tell her so; but she would not understand. I don't suppose she has ever read anything but Markham's History and Mangnall's Questions—improving books like that.

When we got home we found all four of those who had ridden in the cab sitting in our sitting-room—we don't call it nursery now—looking very thoroughly washed, and our girls were asking polite questions and the others were saying 'Yes' and 'No', and 'I don't know'. We boys did not say anything. We stood at the window and looked out till the gong went for our dinner. We felt it was going to be awful—and it was. The newcomers would never have done for knight-errants, or to carry the Cardinal's sealed message through the heart of France on a horse; they would never have thought of anything to say to throw the enemy off the scent when they got into a tight place.

They said 'Yes, please', and 'No, thank you'; and they ate very neatly, and always wiped their mouths before they drank, as well as after, and never spoke with them full.

And after dinner it got worse and worse.

We got out all our books and they said 'Thank you', and didn't look at them properly. And we got out all our toys, and they said 'Thank you, it's very nice' to everything. And it got less and less pleasant, and towards teatime it came to nobody saying anything except Noel and H. O.—and they talked to each other about cricket.

After tea Father came in, and he played 'Letters' with them and the girls, and it was a little better; but while late dinner was going on—I shall never forget it. Oswald felt like the hero of a book—'almost at the end of his resources'. I don't think I was ever glad of bedtime before, but that time I was.

When they had gone to bed (Daisy had to have all her strings and buttons undone for her, Dora told me, though she is nearly ten, and Denny said he couldn't sleep without the gas being left a little bit on) we held a council in the girls' room. We all sat on the bed—it is a mahogany fourposter with green curtains very good for tents, only the housekeeper doesn't allow it, and Oswald said—

'This is jolly nice, isn't it?'

'They'll be better to-morrow,' Alice said, 'they're only shy.'

Dicky said shy was all very well, but you needn't behave like a perfect idiot.

'They're frightened. You see we're all strange to them,' Dora said.

'We're not wild beasts or Indians; we shan't eat them. What have they got to be frightened of?' Dicky said this.

Noel told us he thought they were an enchanted prince and princess who'd been turned into white rabbits, and their bodies had got changed back but not their insides.

But Oswald told him to dry up.

'It's no use making things up about them,' he said. 'The thing is: what are we going to DO? We can't have our holidays spoiled by these snivelling kids.'

'No,' Alice said, 'but they can't possibly go on snivelling for ever. Perhaps they've got into the habit of it with that Murdstone aunt. She's enough to make anyone snivel.'

'All the same,' said Oswald, 'we jolly well aren't going to have another day like today. We must do something to rouse them from their snivelling leth—what's its name?—something sudden and—what is it?—decisive.'

'A booby trap,' said H. O., 'the first thing when they get up, and an apple-pie bed at night.'

But Dora would not hear of it, and I own she was right.

'Suppose,' she said, 'we could get up a good play— like we did when we were Treasure Seekers.'

We said, well what? But she did not say.

'It ought to be a good long thing—to last all day,' Dicky said, 'and if they like they can play, and if they don't—'

'If they don't, I'll read to them,' Alice said.

But we all said 'No, you don't—if you begin that way you'll have to go on.'

And Dicky added, 'I wasn't going to say that at all. I was going to say if they didn't like it they could jolly well do the other thing.'

We all agreed that we must think of something, but we none of us could, and at last the council broke up in confusion because Mrs Blake—she is the housekeeper—came up and turned off the gas.

But next morning when we were having breakfast, and the two strangers were sitting there so pink and clean, Oswald suddenly said—

'I know; we'll have a jungle in the garden.'

And the others agreed, and we talked about it till brek was over. The little strangers only said 'I don't know' whenever we said anything to them.

After brekker Oswald beckoned his brothers and sisters mysteriously apart and said—

'Do you agree to let me be captain today, because I thought of it?'

And they said they would.

Then he said, 'We'll play Jungle Book, and I shall be Mowgli. The rest of you can be what you like—Mowgli's father and mother, or any of the beasts.'

'I don't suppose they know the book,' said Noel. 'They don't look as if they read anything, except at lesson times.'

'Then they can go on being beasts all the time,' Oswald said. 'Anyone can be a beast.'

So it was settled.

And now Oswald—Albert's uncle has sometimes said he is clever at arranging things—began to lay his plans for the jungle. The day was indeed well chosen. Our Indian uncle was away; Father was away; Mrs Blake was going away, and the housemaid had an afternoon off. Oswald's first conscious act was to get rid of the white mice—I mean the little good visitors. He explained to them that there would be a play in the afternoon, and they could be what they liked, and gave them the Jungle Book to read the stories he told them to—all the ones about Mowgli. He led the strangers to a secluded spot among the sea-kale pots in the kitchen garden and left them. Then he went back to the others, and we had a jolly morning under the cedar talking about what we would do when Blakie was gone. She went just after our dinner.

When we asked Denny what he would like to be in the play, it turned out he had not read the stories Oswald told him at all, but only the 'White Seal' and 'Rikki Tikki'.

We then agreed to make the jungle first and dress up for our parts afterwards. Oswald was a little uncomfortable about leaving the strangers alone all the morning, so he said Denny should be his aide-de-camp, and he was really quite useful. He is rather handy with his fingers, and things that he does up do not come untied. Daisy might have come too, but she wanted to go on reading, so we let her, which is the truest manners to a visitor. Of course the shrubbery was to be the jungle, and the lawn under the cedar a forest glade, and then we began to collect the things. The cedar lawn is just nicely out of the way of the windows. It was a jolly hot day—the kind of day when the sunshine is white and the shadows are dark grey, not black like they are in the evening.

We all thought of different things. Of course first we dressed up pillows in the skins of beasts and set them about on the grass to look as natural as we could. And then we got Pincher, and rubbed him all over with powdered slate-pencil, to make him the right colour for Grey Brother. But he shook it all off, and it had taken an awful time to do. Then Alice said—

'Oh, I know!' and she ran off to Father's dressing-room, and came back with the tube of creme d'amande pour la barbe et les mains, and we squeezed it on Pincher and rubbed it in, and then the slate-pencil stuff stuck all right, and he rolled in the dust-bin of his own accord, which made him just the right colour. He is a very clever dog, but soon after he went off and we did not find him till quite late in the afternoon. Denny helped with Pincher, and with the wild-beast skins, and when Pincher was finished he said—

'Please, may I make some paper birds to put in the trees? I know how.'

And of course we said 'Yes', and he only had red ink and newspapers, and quickly he made quite a lot of large paper birds with red tails. They didn't look half bad on the edge of the shrubbery.

While he was doing this he suddenly said, or rather screamed, 'Oh?'

And we looked, and it was a creature with great horns and a fur rug—something like a bull and something like a minotaur—and I don't wonder Denny was frightened. It was Alice, and it was first-class.

Up to now all was not yet lost beyond recall. It was the stuffed fox that did the mischief—and I am sorry to own it was Oswald who thought of it. He is not ashamed of having THOUGHT of it. That was rather clever of him. But he knows now that it is better not to take other people's foxes and things without asking, even if you live in the same house with them.

It was Oswald who undid the back of the glass case in the hall and got out the fox with the green and grey duck in its mouth, and when the others saw how awfully like life they looked on the lawn, they all rushed off to fetch the other stuffed things. Uncle has a tremendous lot of stuffed things. He shot most of them himself—but not the fox, of course. There was another fox's mask, too, and we hung that in a bush to look as if the fox was peeping out. And the stuffed birds we fastened on to the trees with string. The duck-bill—what's its name?—looked very well sitting on his tail with the otter snarling at him. Then Dicky had an idea; and though not nearly so much was said about it afterwards as there was about the stuffed things, I think myself it was just as bad, though it was a good idea, too. He just got the hose and put the end over a branch of the cedar-tree. Then we got the steps they clean windows with, and let the hose rest on the top of the steps and run. It was to be a waterfall, but it ran between the steps and was only wet and messy; so we got Father's mackintosh and uncle's and covered the steps with them, so that the water ran down all right and was glorious, and it ran away in a stream across the grass where we had dug a little channel for it—and the otter and the duck-bill-thing were as if in their native haunts. I hope all this is not very dull to read about. I know it was jolly good fun to do. Taking one thing with another, I don't know that we ever had a better time while it lasted.

We got all the rabbits out of the hutches and put pink paper tails on to them, and hunted them with horns made out of The Times. They got away somehow, and before they were caught next day they had eaten a good many lettuces and other things. Oswald is very sorry for this. He rather likes the gardener.

Denny wanted to put paper tails on the guinea-pigs, and it was no use our telling him there was nothing to tie the paper on to. He thought we were kidding until we showed him, and then he said, 'Well, never mind', and got the girls to give him bits of the blue stuff left over from their dressing-gowns.

'I'll make them sashes to tie round their little middles,' he said. And he did, and the bows stuck up on the tops of their backs. One of the guinea-pigs was never seen again, and the same with the tortoise when we had done his shell with vermilion paint. He crawled away and returned no more. Perhaps someone collected him and thought he was an expensive kind unknown in these cold latitudes.

The lawn under the cedar was transformed into a dream of beauty, what with the stuffed creatures and the paper-tailed things and the waterfall. And Alice said—

'I wish the tigers did not look so flat.' For of course with pillows you can only pretend it is a sleeping tiger getting ready to make a spring out at you. It is difficult to prop up tiger-skins in a life-like manner when there are no bones inside them, only pillows and sofa cushions.

'What about the beer-stands?' I said. And we got two out of the cellar. With bolsters and string we fastened insides to the tigers—and they were really fine. The legs of the beer-stands did for tigers' legs. It was indeed the finishing touch.

Then we boys put on just our bathing drawers and vests—so as to be able to play with the waterfall without hurting our clothes. I think this was thoughtful. The girls only tucked up their frocks and took their shoes and stockings off. H. O. painted his legs and his hands with Condy's fluid—to make him brown, so that he might be Mowgli, although Oswald was captain and had plainly said he was going to be Mowgli himself. Of course the others weren't going to stand that. So Oswald said—

'Very well. Nobody asked you to brown yourself like that. But now you've done it, you've simply got to go and be a beaver, and live in the dam under the waterfall till it washes off.'

He said he didn't want to be beavers. And Noel said—

'Don't make him. Let him be the bronze statue in the palace gardens that the fountain plays out of.'

So we let him have the hose and hold it up over his head. It made a lovely fountain, only he remained brown. So then Dicky and Oswald and I did ourselves brown too, and dried H. O. as well as we could with our handkerchiefs, because he was just beginning to snivel. The brown did not come off any of us for days.

Oswald was to be Mowgli, and we were just beginning to arrange the different parts. The rest of the hose that was on the ground was Kaa, the Rock Python, and Pincher was Grey Brother, only we couldn't find him. And while most of us were talking, Dicky and Noel got messing about with the beer-stand tigers.

And then a really sad event instantly occurred, which was not really our fault, and we did not mean to.

That Daisy girl had been mooning indoors all the afternoon with the Jungle Books, and now she came suddenly out, just as Dicky and Noel had got under the tigers and were shoving them along to fright each other. Of course, this is not in the Mowgli book at all: but they did look jolly like real tigers, and I am very far from wishing to blame the girl, though she little knew what would be the awful consequence of her rash act. But for her we might have got out of it all much better than we did. What happened was truly horrid.

As soon as Daisy saw the tigers she stopped short, and uttering a shriek like a railway whistle she fell flat on the ground.

'Fear not, gentle Indian maid,' Oswald cried, thinking with surprise that perhaps after all she did know how to play, 'I myself will protect thee.' And he sprang forward with the native bow and arrows out of uncle's study.

The gentle Indian maiden did not move.

'Come hither,' Dora said, 'let us take refuge in yonder covert while this good knight does battle for us.' Dora might have remembered that we were savages, but she did not. And that is Dora all over. And still the Daisy girl did not move.

Then we were truly frightened. Dora and Alice lifted her up, and her mouth was a horrid violet-colour and her eyes half shut. She looked horrid. Not at all like fair fainting damsels, who are always of an interesting pallor. She was green, like a cheap oyster on a stall.

We did what we could, a prey to alarm as we were. We rubbed her hands and let the hose play gently but perseveringly on her unconscious brow. The girls loosened her dress, though it was only the kind that comes down straight without a waist. And we were all doing what we could as hard as we could, when we heard the click of the front gate. There was no mistake about it.

'I hope whoever it is will go straight to the front door,' said Alice. But whoever it was did not. There were feet on the gravel, and there was the uncle's voice, saying in his hearty manner—

'This way. This way. On such a day as this we shall find our young barbarians all at play somewhere about the grounds.'

And then, without further warning, the uncle, three other gentlemen and two ladies burst upon the scene.

We had no clothes on to speak of—I mean us boys. We were all wet through. Daisy was in a faint or a fit, or dead, none of us then knew which. And all the stuffed animals were there staring the uncle in the face. Most of them had got a sprinkling, and the otter and the duck-bill brute were simply soaked. And three of us were dark brown. Concealment, as so often happens, was impossible.

The quick brain of Oswald saw, in a flash, exactly how it would strike the uncle, and his brave young blood ran cold in his veins. His heart stood still.

'What's all this—eh, what?' said the tones of the wronged uncle.

Oswald spoke up and said it was jungles we were playing, and he didn't know what was up with Daisy. He explained as well as anyone could, but words were now in vain.

The uncle had a Malacca cane in his hand, and we were but ill prepared to meet the sudden attack. Oswald and H. O. caught it worst. The other boys were under the tigers—and of course my uncle would not strike a girl. Denny was a visitor and so got off.

But it was bread and water for us for the next three days, and our own rooms. I will not tell you how we sought to vary the monotonousness of imprisonment. Oswald thought of taming a mouse, but he could not find one. The reason of the wretched captives might have given way but for the gutter that you can crawl along from our room to the girls'. But I will not dwell on this because you might try it yourselves, and it really is dangerous. When my father came home we got the talking to, and we said we were sorry—and we really were—especially about Daisy, though she had behaved with muffishness, and then it was settled that we were to go into the country and stay till we had grown into better children.

Albert's uncle was writing a book in the country; we were to go to his house. We were glad of this—Daisy and Denny too. This we bore nobly. We knew we had deserved it. We were all very sorry for everything, and we resolved that for the future we WOULD be good.

I am not sure whether we kept this resolution or not. Oswald thinks now that perhaps we made a mistake in trying so very hard to be good all at once. You should do everything by degrees.

P.S.—It turned out Daisy was not really dead at all. It was only fainting—so like a girl.

N.B.—Pincher was found on the drawing-room sofa.

Appendix.—I have not told you half the things we did for the jungle—for instance, about the elephants' tusks and the horse-hair sofa-cushions, and uncle's fishing-boots.

Chapter 2. The Would-Be-Goods

When we were sent down into the country to learn to be good we felt it was rather good business, because we knew our being sent there was really only to get us out of the way for a little while, and we knew right enough that it wasn't a punishment, though Mrs Blake said it was, because we had been punished thoroughly for taking the stuffed animals out and making a jungle on the lawn with them, and the garden hose. And you cannot be punished twice for the same offence. This is the English law; at least I think so. And at any rate no one would punish you three times, and we had had the Malacca cane and the solitary confinement; and the uncle had kindly explained to us that all ill-feeling between him and us was wiped out entirely by the bread and water we had endured. And what with the bread and water and being prisoners, and not being able to tame any mice in our prisons, I quite feel that we had suffered it up thoroughly, and now we could start fair.

I think myself that descriptions of places are generally dull, but I have sometimes thought that was because the authors do not tell you what you truly want to know. However, dull or not, here goes—because you won't understand anything unless I tell you what the place was like.

The Moat House was the one we went to stay at. There has been a house there since Saxon times. It is a manor, and a manor goes on having a house on it whatever happens. The Moat House was burnt down once or twice in ancient centuries—I don't remember which—but they always built a new one, and Cromwell's soldiers smashed it about, but it was patched up again. It is a very odd house: the front door opens straight into the dining-room, and there are red curtains and a black-and-white marble floor like a chess-board, and there is a secret staircase, only it is not secret now—only rather rickety. It is not very big, but there is a watery moat all round it with a brick bridge that leads to the front door. Then, on the other side of the moat there is the farm, with barns and oast houses and stables, or things like that. And the other way the garden lawn goes on till it comes to the churchyard. The churchyard is not divided from the garden at all except by a little grass bank. In the front of the house there is more garden, and the big fruit garden is at the back.

The man the house belongs to likes new houses, so he built a big one with conservatories and a stable with a clock in a turret on the top, and he left the Moat House. And Albert's uncle took it, and my father was to come down sometimes from Saturday to Monday, and Albert's uncle was to live with us all the time, and he would be writing a book, and we were not to bother him, but he would give an eye to us. I hope all this is plain. I have said it as short as I can.

We got down rather late, but there was still light enough to see the big bell hanging at the top of the house. The rope belonging to it went right down the house, through our bedroom to the dining-room. H. O. saw the rope and pulled it while he was washing his hands for supper, and Dicky and I let him, and the bell tolled solemnly. Father shouted to him not to, and we went down to supper.

But presently there were many feet trampling on the gravel, and Father went out to see. When he came back he said— 'The whole village, or half of it, has come up to see why the bell rang. It's only rung for fire or burglars. Why can't you kids let things alone?'

Albert's uncle said—

'Bed follows supper as the fruit follows the flower. They'll do no more mischief to-night, sir. To-morrow I will point out a few of the things to be avoided in this bucolic retreat.'

So it was bed directly after supper, and that was why we did not see much that night.

But in the morning we were all up rather early, and we seemed to have awakened in a new world rich in surprises beyond the dreams of anybody, as it says in the quotation.

We went everywhere we could in the time, but when it was breakfast-time we felt we had not seen half or a quarter. The room we had breakfast in was exactly like in a story—black oak panels and china in corner cupboards with glass doors. These doors were locked. There were green curtains, and honeycomb for breakfast. After brekker my father went back to town, and Albert's uncle went too, to see publishers. We saw them to the station, and Father gave us a long list of what we weren't to do. It began with 'Don't pull ropes unless you're quite sure what will happen at the other end,' and it finished with 'For goodness sake, try to keep out of mischief till I come down on Saturday'. There were lots of other things in between.

We all promised we would. And we saw them off and waved till the train was quite out of sight. Then we started to walk home. Daisy was tired so Oswald carried her home on his back. When we got home she said—

'I do like you, Oswald.'

She is not a bad little kid; and Oswald felt it was his duty to be nice to her because she was a visitor. Then we looked all over everything. It was a glorious place. You did not know where to begin. We were all a little tired before we found the hayloft, but we pulled ourselves together to make a fort with the trusses of hay—great square things—and we were having a jolly good time, all of us, when suddenly a trap-door opened and a head bobbed up with a straw in its mouth. We knew nothing about the country then, and the head really did scare us rather, though, of course, we found out directly that the feet belonging to it were standing on the bar of the loose-box underneath. The head said—

'Don't you let the governor catch you a-spoiling of that there hay, that's all.' And it spoke thickly because of the straw.

It is strange to think how ignorant you were in the past. We can hardly believe now that once we really did not know that it spoiled hay to mess about with it. Horses don't like to eat it afterwards.

Always remember this.

When the head had explained a little more it went away, and we turned the handle of the chaff-cutting machine, and nobody got hurt, though the head HAD said we should cut our fingers off if we touched it.

And then we sat down on the floor, which is dirty with the nice clean dirt that is more than half chopped hay, and those there was room for hung their legs down out of the top door, and we looked down at the farmyard, which is very slushy when you get down into it, but most interesting.

Then Alice said—

'Now we're all here, and the boys are tired enough to sit still for a minute, I want to have a council.'

We said what about? And she said, 'I'll tell you.' H. O., don't wriggle so; sit on my frock if the straws tickle your legs.'

You see he wears socks, and so he can never be quite as comfortable as anyone else.

'Promise not to laugh' Alice said, getting very red, and looking at Dora, who got red too.

We did, and then she said:

'Dora and I have talked this over, and Daisy too, and we have written it down because it is easier than saying it. Shall I read it? or will you, Dora?'

Dora said it didn't matter; Alice might. So Alice read it, and though she gabbled a bit we all heard it. I copied it afterwards. This is what she read:

NEW SOCIETY FOR BEING GOOD IN

'I, Dora Bastable, and Alice Bastable, my sister, being of sound mind and body, when we were shut up with bread and water on that jungle day, we thought a great deal about our naughty sins, and we made our minds up to be good for ever after. And we talked to Daisy about it, and she had an idea. So we want to start a society for being good in. It is Daisy's idea, but we think so too.'

'You know,' Dora interrupted, 'when people want to do good things they always make a society. There are thousands—there's the Missionary Society.'

'Yes,' Alice said, 'and the Society for the Prevention of something or other, and the Young Men's Mutual Improvement Society, and the S.P.G.'

'What's S.P.G.?' Oswald asked.

'Society for the Propagation of the Jews, of course,' said Noel, who cannot always spell.

'No, it isn't; but do let me go on.'

Alice did go on.

'We propose to get up a society, with a chairman and a treasurer and secretary, and keep a journal-book saying what we've done. If that doesn't make us good it won't be my fault.'

'The aim of the society is nobleness and goodness, and great and unselfish deeds. We wish not to be such a nuisance to grown-up people and to perform prodigies of real goodness. We wish to spread our wings'—here Alice read very fast. She told me afterwards Daisy had helped her with that part, and she thought when she came to the wings they sounded rather silly—'to spread our wings and rise above the kind of interesting things that you ought not to do, but to do kindnesses to all, however low and mean.'

Denny was listening carefully. Now he nodded three or four times.

'Little words of kindness' (he said),
'Little deeds of love,
Make this earth an eagle
Like the one above.'

This did not sound right, but we let it pass, because an eagle does have wings, and we wanted to hear the rest of what the girls had written. But there was no rest.

'That's all,' said Alice, and Daisy said— 'Don't you think it's a good idea?'

'That depends,' Oswald answered, 'who is president and what you mean by being good.'

Oswald did not care very much for the idea himself, because being good is not the sort of thing he thinks it is proper to talk about, especially before strangers. But the girls and Denny seemed to like it, so Oswald did not say exactly what he thought, especially as it was Daisy's idea. This was true politeness.

'I think it would be nice,' Noel said, 'if we made it a sort of play. Let's do the Pilgrim's Progress.'

We talked about that for some time, but it did not come to anything, because we all wanted to be Mr Greatheart, except H. O., who wanted to be the lions, and you could not have lions in a Society for Goodness.

Dicky said he did not wish to play if it meant reading books about children who die; he really felt just as Oswald did about it, he told me afterwards. But the girls were looking as if they were in Sunday school, and we did not wish to be unkind.

At last Oswald said, 'Well, let's draw up the rules of the society, and choose the president and settle the name.'

Dora said Oswald should be president, and he modestly consented. She was secretary, and Denny treasurer if we ever had any money.

Making the rules took us all the afternoon. They were these:

RULES

1. Every member is to be as good as possible.

2. There is to be no more jaw than necessary about being good. (Oswald and Dicky put that rule in.)

3. No day must pass without our doing some kind action to a suffering fellow-creature.

4. We are to meet every day, or as often as we like.

5. We are to do good to people we don't like as often as we can.

6. No one is to leave the Society without the consent of all the rest of us.

7. The Society is to be kept a profound secret from all the world except us.

8. The name of our Society is—

And when we got as far as that we all began to talk at once. Dora wanted it called the Society for Humane Improvement; Denny said the Society for Reformed Outcast Children; but Dicky said, No, we really were not so bad as all that.

Then H. O. said, 'Call it the Good Society.'

'Or the Society for Being Good In,' said Daisy.

'Or the Society of Goods,' said Noel.

'That's priggish,' said Oswald; 'besides, we don't know whether we shall be so very.'

'You see,' Alice explained, 'we only said if we COULD we would be good.'

'Well, then,' Dicky said, getting up and beginning to dust the chopped hay off himself, 'call it the Society of the Wouldbegoods and have done with it.'

Oswald thinks Dicky was getting sick of it and wanted to make himself a little disagreeable. If so, he was doomed to disappointment. For everyone else clapped hands and called out, 'That's the very thing!' Then the girls went off to write out the rules, and took H. O. with them, and Noel went to write some poetry to put in the minute book. That's what you call the book that a society's secretary writes what it does in. Denny went with him to help. He knows a lot of poetry. I think he went to a lady's school where they taught nothing but that. He was rather shy of us, but he took to Noel. I can't think why. Dicky and Oswald walked round the garden and told each other what they thought of the new society.

'I'm not sure we oughtn't to have put our foot down at the beginning,' Dicky said. 'I don't see much in it, anyhow.'

'It pleases the girls,' Oswald said, for he is a kind brother.

'But we're not going to stand jaw, and "words in season", and "loving sisterly warnings". I tell you what it is, Oswald, we'll have to run this thing our way, or it'll be jolly beastly for everybody.'

Oswald saw this plainly.

'We must do something,' Dicky said; it's very very hard, though. Still, there must be SOME interesting things that are not wrong.'

'I suppose so,' Oswald said, 'but being good is so much like being a muff, generally. Anyhow I'm not going to smooth the pillows of the sick, or read to the aged poor, or any rot out of Ministering Children.'

'No more am I,' Dicky said. He was chewing a straw like the head had in its mouth, 'but I suppose we must play the game fair. Let's begin by looking out for something useful to do—

something like mending things or cleaning them, not just showing off.'

'The boys in books chop kindling wood and save their pennies to buy tea and tracts.'

'Little beasts!' said Dick. 'I say, let's talk about something else.' And Oswald was glad to, for he was beginning to feel jolly uncomfortable.

We were all rather quiet at tea, and afterwards Oswald played draughts with Daisy and the others yawned. I don't know when we've had such a gloomy evening. And everyone was horribly polite, and said 'Please' and 'Thank you' far more than requisite.

Albert's uncle came home after tea. He was jolly, and told us stories, but he noticed us being a little dull, and asked what blight had fallen on our young lives. Oswald could have answered and said, 'It is the Society of the Wouldbegoods that is the blight,' but of course he didn't and Albert's uncle said no more, but he went up and kissed the girls when they were in bed, and asked them if there was anything wrong. And they told him no, on their honour.

The next morning Oswald awoke early. The refreshing beams of the morning sun shone on his narrow white bed and on the sleeping forms of his dear little brothers and Denny, who had got the pillow on top of his head and was snoring like a kettle when it sings. Oswald could not remember at first what was the matter with him, and then he remembered the Wouldbegoods, and wished he hadn't. He felt at first as if there was nothing you could do, and even hesitated to buzz a pillow at Denny's head. But he soon saw that this could not be. So he chucked his boot and caught Denny right in the waistcoat part, and thus the day began more brightly than he had expected.

Oswald had not done anything out of the way good the night before, except that when no one was looking he polished the brass candlestick in the girls' bedroom with one of his socks. And he might just as well have let it alone, for the servants cleaned it again with the other things in the morning, and he could never find the sock afterwards. There were two servants. One of them had to be called Mrs Pettigrew instead of Jane and Eliza like others. She was cook and managed things.

After breakfast Albert's uncle said—

'I now seek the retirement of my study. At your peril violate my privacy before 1.30 sharp. Nothing short of bloodshed will warrant the intrusion, and nothing short of man—or rather boy—slaughter shall avenge it.'

So we knew he wanted to be quiet, and the girls decided that we ought to play out of doors so as not to disturb him; we should have played out of doors anyhow on a jolly fine day like that.

But as we were going out Dicky said to Oswald—

'I say, come along here a minute, will you?'

So Oswald came along, and Dicky took him into the other parlour and shut the door, and Oswald said—

'Well, spit it out: what is it?'

He knows that is vulgar, and he would not have said it to anyone but his own brother. Dicky said—

'It's a pretty fair nuisance. I told you how it would be.' And Oswald was patient with him, and said—

'What is? Don't be all day about it.'

Dicky fidgeted about a bit, and then he said—

'Well, I did as I said. I looked about for something useful to do. And you know that dairy window that wouldn't open—only a little bit like that? Well, I mended the catch with wire and whip cord and it opened wide.'

'And I suppose they didn't want it mended,' said Oswald. He knew but too well that grown-up people sometimes like to keep things far different from what we would, and you catch it if you try to do otherwise.

'I shouldn't have minded THAT,' Dicky said, 'because I could easily have taken it all off again if they'd only said so. But the sillies went and propped up a milk-pan against the window. They never took the trouble to notice I had mended it. So the wretched thing pushed the window open all by itself directly they propped it up, and it tumbled through into the moat, and they are most awfully waxy. All the men are out in the fields and they haven't any spare milk-pans. If I were a farmer, I must say I wouldn't stick at an extra milk-pan or two. Accidents must happen sometimes. I call it mean.'

Dicky spoke in savage tones. But Oswald was not so unhappy, first because it wasn't his fault, and next because he is a far-seeing boy.

'Never mind,' he said kindly. 'Keep your tail up. We'll get the beastly milk-pan out all right. Come on.' He rushed hastily to the garden and gave a low, signifying whistle, which the others know well enough to mean something extra being up.

And when they were all gathered round him he spoke.

'Fellow countrymen,' he said, 'we're going to have a rousing good time.'

'It's nothing naughty, is it,' Daisy asked, 'like the last time you had that was rousingly good?'

Alice said 'Shish', and Oswald pretended not to hear.

'A precious treasure,' he said, 'has inadvertently been laid low in the moat by one of us.'

'The rotten thing tumbled in by itself,' Dicky said.

Oswald waved his hand and said, 'Anyhow, it's there. It's our duty to restore it to its sorrowing owners. I say, look here—we're going to drag the moat.'

Everyone brightened up at this. It was our duty and it was interesting too. This is very uncommon.

So we went out to where the orchard is, at the other side of the moat. There were gooseberries and things on the bushes, but we did not take any till we had asked if we might. Alice went and asked. Mrs Pettigrew said, 'Law! I suppose so; you'd eat 'em anyhow, leave or no leave.'

She little knows the honourable nature of the house of Bastable. But she has much to learn.

The orchard slopes gently down to the dark waters of the moat. We sat there in the sun and talked about dragging the moat, till Denny said, 'How DO you drag moats?'

And we were speechless, because, though we had read many times about a moat being dragged for missing heirs and lost wills, we really had never thought about exactly how it was done.

'Grappling-irons are right, I believe,' Denny said, 'but I don't suppose they'd have any at the farm.'

And we asked, and found they had never even heard of them. I think myself he meant some other word, but he was quite positive.

So then we got a sheet off Oswald's bed, and we all took our shoes and stockings off, and we tried to see if the sheet would drag the bottom of the moat, which is shallow at that end. But it would keep floating on the top of the water, and when we tried sewing stones into one end of it, it stuck on something in the bottom, and when we got it up it was torn. We were very sorry, and the sheet was in an awful mess; but the girls said they were sure they could wash it in the basin in their room, and we thought as we had torn it anyway, we might as well go on. That washing never came off.

'No human being,' Noel said, 'knows half the treasures hidden in this dark tarn.'

And we decided we would drag a bit more at that end, and work gradually round to under the dairy window where the milk-pan was. We could not see that part very well, because of the bushes that grow between the cracks of the stones where the house goes down into the moat. And opposite the dairy window the barn goes straight down into the moat too. It is like pictures of Venice; but you cannot get opposite the dairy window anyhow.

We got the sheet down again when we had tied the torn parts together in a bunch with string, and Oswald was just saying—

'Now then, my hearties, pull together, pull with a will! One, two, three,' when suddenly Dora dropped her bit of the sheet with a piercing shriek and cried out—

'Oh! it's all wormy at the bottom. I felt them wriggle.' And she was out of the water almost before the words were out of her mouth.

The other girls all scuttled out too, and they let the sheet go in such a hurry that we had no time to steady ourselves, and one of us went right in, and the rest got wet up to our waistbands. The one who went right in was only H. O.; but Dora made an awful fuss and said it was our fault. We told her what we thought, and it ended in the girls going in with H. O. to change his things. We had some more gooseberries while they were gone. Dora was in an awful wax when she went away, but she is not of a sullen disposition though sometimes hasty, and when they all came back we saw it was all right, so we said—

'What shall we do now?'

Alice said, 'I don't think we need drag any more. It is wormy. I felt it when Dora did. And besides, the milk-pan is sticking a bit of itself out of the water. I saw it through the dairy window.'

'Couldn't we get it up with fish-hooks?' Noel said. But Alice explained that the dairy was now locked up and the key taken out. So then Oswald said—

'Look here, we'll make a raft. We should have to do it some time, and we might as well do it now. I saw an old door in that corner stable that they don't use. You know. The one where they chop the wood.'

We got the door.

We had never made a raft, any of us, but the way to make rafts is better described in books, so we knew what to do.

We found some nice little tubs stuck up on the fence of the farm garden, and nobody seemed to want them for anything just then, so we took them. Denny had a box of tools someone had given him for his last birthday; they were rather rotten little things, but the gimlet worked all right, so we managed to make holes in the edges of the tubs and fasten them with string under the four corners of the old door. This took us a long time. Albert's uncle asked us at dinner what we had been playing at, and we said it was a secret, and it was nothing wrong. You see we wished to atone for Dicky's mistake before anything more was said. The house has no windows in the side that faces the orchard.

The rays of the afternoon sun were beaming along the orchard grass when at last we launched the raft. She floated out beyond reach with the last shove of the launching. But Oswald waded out and towed her back; he is not afraid of worms. Yet if he had known of the other things that were in the bottom of that moat he would have kept his boots on. So would the others, especially Dora, as you will see.

At last the gallant craft rode upon the waves. We manned her, though not up to our full strength, because if more than four got on the water came up too near our knees, and we feared she might founder if over-manned.

Daisy and Denny did not want to go on the raft, white mice that they were, so that was all right. And as H. O. had been wet through once he was not very keen. Alice promised Noel her best paint-brush if he'd give up and not go, because we knew well that the voyage was fraught with deep dangers, though the exact danger that lay in wait for us under the dairy window we never even thought of.

So we four elder ones got on the raft very carefully; and even then, every time we moved the water swished up over the raft and hid our feet. But I must say it was a jolly decent raft.

Dicky was captain, because it was his adventure. We had hop-poles from the hop-garden beyond the orchard to punt with. We made the girls stand together in the middle and hold on to each other to keep steady. Then we christened our gallant vessel. We called it the Richard, after Dicky, and also after the splendid admiral who used to eat wine-glasses and died after the Battle of the Revenge in Tennyson's poetry.

Then those on shore waved a fond adieu as well as they could with the dampness of their handkerchiefs, which we had had to use to dry our legs and feet when we put on our stockings for dinner, and slowly and stately the good ship moved away from shore, riding on the waves as though they were her native element.

We kept her going with the hop-poles, and we kept her steady in the same way, but we could not always keep her steady enough, and we could not always keep her in the wind's eye. That is to say, she went where we did not want, and once she bumped her corner against the barn wall, and all the crew had to sit down suddenly to avoid falling overboard into a watery grave. Of course then the waves swept her decks, and when we got up again we said that we should have to change completely before tea.

But we pressed on undaunted, and at last our saucy craft came into port, under the dairy window and there was the milk-pan, for whose sake we had endured such hardships and privations, standing up on its edge quite quietly.

The girls did not wait for orders from the captain, as they ought to have done; but they cried out, 'Oh, here it is!' and then both reached out to get it. Anyone who has pursued a naval career will see that of course the raft capsized. For a moment it felt like standing on the roof of the house, and the next moment the ship stood up on end and shot the whole crew into the dark waters.

We boys can swim all right. Oswald has swum three times across the Ladywell Swimming Baths at the shallow end, and Dicky is nearly as good; but just then we did not think of this; though, of course, if the water had been deep we should have.

As soon as Oswald could get the muddy water out of his eyes he opened them on a horrid scene.

Dicky was standing up to his shoulders in the inky waters; the raft had righted itself, and was drifting gently away towards the front of the house, where the bridge is, and Dora and Alice were rising from the deep, with their hair all plastered over their faces—like Venus in the Latin verses.

There was a great noise of splashing. And besides that a feminine voice, looking out of the dairy window and screaming—

'Lord love the children!'

It was Mrs Pettigrew. She disappeared at once, and we were sorry we were in such a situation that she would be able to get at Albert's uncle before we could. Afterwards we were not so sorry.

Before a word could be spoken about our desperate position Dora staggered a little in the water, and suddenly shrieked, 'Oh, my foot! oh, it's a shark! I know it is—or a crocodile!'

The others on the bank could hear her shrieking, but they could not see us properly; they did not know what was happening. Noel told me afterwards he never could care for that paint-brush.

Of course we knew it could not be a shark, but I thought of pike, which are large and very angry always, and I caught hold of Dora. She screamed without stopping. I shoved her along to where there was a ledge of brickwork, and shoved her up, till she could sit on it, then she got her foot out of the water, still screaming.

It was indeed terrible. The thing she thought was a shark came up with her foot, and it was a horrid, jagged, old meat-tin, and she had put her foot right into it. Oswald got it off, and directly he did so blood began to pour from the wounds. The tin edges had cut it in several spots. It was very pale blood, because her foot was wet, of course.

She stopped screaming, and turned green, and I thought she was going to faint, like Daisy did on the jungle day.

Oswald held her up as well as he could, but it really was one of the least agreeable moments in his life. For the raft was gone, and she couldn't have waded back anyway, and we didn't know how deep the moat might be in other places.

But Mrs Pettigrew had not been idle. She is not a bad sort really.

Just as Oswald was wondering whether he could swim after the raft and get it back, a boat's nose shot out from under a dark archway a little further up under the house. It was the boathouse, and Albert's uncle had got the punt and took us back in it. When we had regained the dark arch where the boat lives we had to go up the cellar stairs. Dora had to be carried.

There was but little said to us that day. We were sent to bed—those who had not been on the raft the same as the others, for they owned up all right, and Albert's uncle is the soul of justice.

Next day but one was Saturday. Father gave us a talking to—with other things.

The worst was when Dora couldn't get her shoe on, so they sent for the doctor, and Dora had to lie down for ever so long. It was indeed poor luck.

When the doctor had gone Alice said to me—

'It IS hard lines, but Dora's very jolly about it. Daisy's been telling her about how we should all go to her with our little joys and sorrows and things, and about the sweet influence from a sick bed that can be felt all over the house, like in What Katy Did, and Dora said she hoped she might prove a blessing to us all while she's laid up.'

Oswald said he hoped so, but he was not pleased. Because this sort of jaw was exactly the sort of thing he and Dicky didn't want to have happen.

The thing we got it hottest for was those little tubs off the garden railings. They turned out to be butter-tubs that had been put out there 'to sweeten'.

But as Denny said, 'After the mud in that moat not all the perfumes of somewhere or other could make them fit to use for butter again.'

I own this was rather a bad business. Yet we did not do it to please ourselves, but because it was our duty. But that made no difference to our punishment when Father came down. I have known this mistake occur before.

Chapter 3. Bill's Tombstone

There were soldiers riding down the road, on horses two and two. That is the horses were two and two, and the men not. Because each man was riding one horse and leading another. To exercise them. They came from Chatham Barracks. We all drew up in a line outside the churchyard wall, and saluted as they went by, though we had not read Toady Lion then. We have since. It is the only decent book I have ever read written by Toady Lion's author. The others are mere piffle. But many people like them. In Sir Toady Lion the officer salutes the child.

There was only a lieutenant with those soldiers, and he did not salute me. He kissed his hand to the girls; and a lot of the soldiers behind kissed theirs too. We waved ours back.

Next day we made a Union Jack out of pocket-handkerchiefs and part of a red flannel petticoat of the White Mouse's, which she did not want just then, and some blue ribbon we got at the village shop.

Then we watched for the soldiers, and after three days they went by again, by twos and twos as before. It was A1.

We waved our flag, and we shouted. We gave them three cheers. Oswald can shout loudest. So as soon as the first man was level with us (not the advance guard, but the first of the battery)—he shouted—

'Three cheers for the Queen and the British Army!' And then we waved the flag, and bellowed. Oswald stood on the wall to bellow better, and Denny waved the flag because he was a visitor, and so politeness made us let him enjoy the fat of whatever there was going.

The soldiers did not cheer that day; they only grinned and kissed their hands.

The next day we all got up as much like soldiers as we could. H. O. and Noel had tin swords, and we asked Albert's uncle to let us wear some of the real arms that are on the wall in the dining-room.

And he said, 'Yes', if we would clean them up afterwards. But we jolly well cleaned them up first with Brooke's soap and brick dust and vinegar, and the knife polish (invented by the great and immortal Duke of Wellington in his spare time when he was not conquering Napoleon. Three cheers for our Iron Duke!), and with emery paper and wash leather and whitening. Oswald wore a cavalry sabre in its sheath. Alice and the Mouse had pistols in their belts, large old flint-locks, with bits of red flannel behind the flints. Denny had a naval cutlass, a very beautiful blade, and old enough to have been at Trafalgar. I hope it was. The others had French sword-bayonets that were used in the Franco-German war. They are very bright when you get them bright, but the sheaths are hard to polish. Each sword-bayonet has the name on the blade of the warrior who once wielded it. I wonder where they are now. Perhaps some of them died in the war. Poor chaps! But it is a very long time ago.

I should like to be a soldier. It is better than going to the best schools, and to Oxford afterwards, even if it is Balliol you go to. Oswald wanted to go to South Africa for a bugler, but father would not let him. And it is true that Oswald does not yet know how to bugle, though he can play the infantry 'advance', and the 'charge' and the 'halt' on a penny whistle. Alice taught them to him with the piano, out of the red book Father's cousin had when he was in the Fighting Fifth. Oswald cannot play the 'retire', and he would scorn to do so. But I suppose a bugler has to play what he is told, no matter how galling to the young boy's proud spirit.

The next day, being thoroughly armed, we put on everything red, white and blue that we could think of— night-shirts are good for white, and you don't know what you can do with red socks and blue jerseys till you try—and we waited by the churchyard wall for the soldiers. When the advance guard (or whatever you call it of artillery—it's that for infantry, I know) came by, we got ready, and when the first man of the first battery was level with us Oswald played on his penny whistle the 'advance' and the 'charge'—and then shouted—

'Three cheers for the Queen and the British Army!' This time they had the guns with them. And every man of the battery cheered too. It was glorious. It made you tremble all over. The girls said it made them want to cry—but no boy would own to this, even if it were true. It is babyish to cry. But it was glorious, and Oswald felt differently to what he ever did before.

Then suddenly the officer in front said, 'Battery! Halt!' and all the soldiers pulled their horses up, and the great guns stopped too. Then the officer said, 'Sit at ease,' and something else, and the sergeant repeated it, and some of the men got off their horses and lit their pipes, and some sat down on the grass edge of the road, holding their horses' bridles.

We could see all the arms and accoutrements as plain as plain.

Then the officer came up to us. We were all standing on the wall that day, except Dora, who had to sit, because her foot was bad, but we let her have the three-edged rapier to wear, and the blunderbuss to hold as well—it has a brass mouth and is like in Mr Caldecott's pictures.

He was a beautiful man the officer. Like a Viking. Very tall and fair, with moustaches very long, and bright blue eyes. He said—

'Good morning.'

So did we.

Then he said—

'You seem to be a military lot.'

We said we wished we were.

'And patriotic,' said he.

Alice said she should jolly well think so.

Then he said he had noticed us there for several days, and he had halted the battery because he thought we might like to look at the guns.

Alas! there are but too few grown-up people so far-seeing and thoughtful as this brave and distinguished officer.

We said, 'Oh, yes', and then we got off the wall, and that good and noble man showed us the string that moves the detonator and the breech-block (when you take it out and carry it away the gun is in vain to the enemy, even if he takes it); and he let us look down the gun to see the rifling, all clean and shiny—and he showed us the ammunition boxes, but there was nothing in them. He also told us how the gun was unlimbered (this means separating the gun from the ammunition carriage), and how quick it could be done—but he did not make the men do this then, because they were resting. There were six guns. Each had painted on the carriage, in white letters, 15 Pr., which the captain told us meant fifteen-pounder.

'I should have thought the gun weighed more than fifteen pounds,' Dora said. 'It would if it was beef, but I suppose wood and gun are lighter.'

And the officer explained to her very kindly and patiently that 15 Pr. meant the gun could throw a SHELL weighing fifteen pounds.

When we had told him how jolly it was to see the soldiers go by so often, he said—

'You won't see us many more times. We're ordered to the front; and we sail on Tuesday week; and the guns will be painted mud-colour, and the men will wear mud-colour too, and so shall I.'

The men looked very nice, though they were not wearing their busbies, but only Tommy caps, put on all sorts of ways.

We were very sorry they were going, but Oswald, as well as others, looked with envy on those who would soon be allowed—being grown up, and no nonsense about your education—to go and fight for their Queen and country.

Then suddenly Alice whispered to Oswald, and he said—

'All right; but tell him yourself.'

So Alice said to the captain—

'Will you stop next time you pass?'

He said, 'I'm afraid I can't promise that.'

Alice said, 'You might; there's a particular reason.'

He said, 'What?' which was a natural remark; not rude, as it is with children. Alice said—

'We want to give the soldiers a keepsake and will write to ask my father. He is very well off just now. Look here--if we're not on the wall when you come by, don't stop; but if we are, please, PLEASE do!'

The officer pulled his moustache and looked as if he did not know; but at last he said 'Yes', and we were very glad, though but Alice and Oswald knew the dark but pleasant scheme at present fermenting in their youthful nuts.

The captain talked a lot to us. At last Noel said—

'I think you are like Diarmid of the Golden Collar. But I should like to see your sword out, and shining in the sun like burnished silver.'

The captain laughed and grasped the hilt of his good blade. But Oswald said hurriedly—

'Don't. Not yet. We shan't ever have a chance like this. If you'd only show us the pursuing practice! Albert's uncle knows it; but he only does it on an armchair, because he hasn't a horse.'

And that brave and swagger captain did really do it. He rode his horse right into our gate when we opened it, and showed us all the cuts, thrusts, and guards. There are four of each kind. It was splendid. The morning sun shone on his flashing blade, and his good steed stood with all its legs far apart and stiff on the lawn.

Then we opened the paddock gate, and he did it again, while the horse galloped as if upon the bloody battlefield among the fierce foes of his native land, and this was far more ripping still.

Then we thanked him very much, and he went away, taking his men with him. And the guns of course.

Then we wrote to my father, and he said 'Yes', as we knew he would, and next time the soldiers came by —but they had no guns this time, only the captive Arabs of the desert—we had the keepsakes ready in a wheelbarrow, and we were on the churchyard wall.

And the bold captain called an immediate halt.

Then the girls had the splendid honour and pleasure of giving a pipe and four whole ounces of tobacco to each soldier.

Then we shook hands with the captain, and the sergeant and the corporals, and the girls kissed the captain—I can't think why girls will kiss everybody— and we all cheered for the Queen. It was grand. And I wish my father had been there to see how much you can do with £12 if you order the things from the Stores.

We have never seen those brave soldiers again.

I have told you all this to show you how we got so keen about soldiers, and why we sought to aid and abet the poor widow at the white cottage in her desolate and oppressedness.

Her name was Simpkins, and her cottage was just beyond the churchyard, on the other side from our house. On the different military occasions which I have remarked upon this widow woman stood at her garden gate and looked on. And after the cheering she rubbed her eyes with her apron. Alice noticed this slight but signifying action.

We feel quite sure Mrs Simpkins liked soldiers, and so we felt friendly to her. But when we tried to talk to her she would not. She told us to go along with us, do, and not bother her. And Oswald, with his usual delicacy and good breeding, made the others do as she said.

But we were not to be thus repulsed with impunity. We made complete but cautious inquiries, and found out that the reason she cried when she saw soldiers was that she had only one son, a boy. He was twenty-two, and he had gone to the War last April. So that she thought of him when she saw the soldiers, and that was why she cried. Because when your son is at the wars you always think he is being killed. I don't know why. A great many of them are not. If I had a son at the wars I should never think he was dead till I heard he was, and perhaps not then, considering everything. After we had found this out we held a council.

Dora said, 'We must do something for the soldier's widowed mother.'

We all agreed, but added 'What?'

Alice said, 'The gift of money might be deemed an insult by that proud, patriotic spirit. Besides, we haven't more than eighteenpence among us.'

We had put what we had to father's £12 to buy the baccy and pipes.

The Mouse then said, 'Couldn't we make her a flannel petticoat and leave it without a word upon her doorstep?'

But everyone said, 'Flannel petticoats in this weather?' so that was no go.

Noel said he would write her a poem, but Oswald had a deep, inward feeling that Mrs Simpkins would not understand poetry. Many people do not.

H. O. said, 'Why not sing "Rule Britannia" under her window after she had gone to bed, like waits,' but no one else thought so.

Denny thought we might get up a subscription for her among the wealthy and affluent, but we said again that we knew money would be no balm to the haughty mother of a brave British soldier.

'What we want,' Alice said, 'is something that will be a good deal of trouble to us and some good to her.'

'A little help is worth a deal of poetry,' said Denny.

I should not have said that myself. Noel did look sick.

' What DOES she do that we can help in?' Dora asked. 'Besides, she won't let us help.'

H. O. said, 'She does nothing but work in the garden. At least if she does anything inside you can't see it, because she keeps the door shut.'

Then at once we saw. And we agreed to get up the very next day, ere yet the rosy dawn had flushed the east, and have a go at Mrs Simpkins's garden.

We got up. We really did. But too often when you mean to, overnight, it seems so silly to do it when you come to waking in the dewy morn. We crept downstairs with our boots in our hands. Denny is rather unlucky, though a most careful boy. It was he who dropped his boot, and it went blundering down the stairs, echoing like thunderbolts, and waking up Albert's uncle. But when we explained to him that we were going to do some gardening he let us, and went back to bed.

Everything is very pretty and different in the early morning, before people are up. I have been told this is because the shadows go a different way from what they do in the awake part of the day. But I don't know. Noel says the fairies have just finished tidying up then. Anyhow it all feels quite otherwise.

We put on our boots in the porch, and we got our gardening tools and we went down to the white cottage. It is a nice cottage, with a thatched roof, like in the drawing copies you get at girls' schools, and you do the thatch—if you can—with a B.B. pencil. If you cannot, you just leave it. It looks just as well, somehow, when it is mounted and framed.

We looked at the garden. It was very neat. Only one patch was coming up thick with weeds. I could see groundsel and chickweed, and others that I did not know. We set to work with a will. We used all our tools—spades, forks, hoes, and rakes—and Dora worked with the trowel, sitting down, because her foot was hurt. We cleared the weedy patch beautifully, scraping off all the nasty weeds and leaving the nice clean brown dirt. We worked as hard as ever we could. And we were happy, because it was unselfish toil, and no one thought then of putting it in the Book of Golden Deeds, where we had agreed to write down our virtuous actions and the good doings of each other, when we happen to notice them.

We had just done, and we were looking at the beautiful production of our honest labour, when the cottage door burst open, and the soldier's widowed mother came out like a wild tornado, and her eyes looked like upas trees—death to the beholder.

'You wicked, meddlesome, nasty children!' she said, ain't you got enough of your own good ground to runch up and spoil, but you must come into MY little lot?'

Some of us were deeply alarmed, but we stood firm.

'We have only been weeding your garden,' Dora said; 'we wanted to do something to help you.'

'Dratted little busybodies,' she said. It was indeed hard, but everyone in Kent says 'dratted' when they are cross. 'It's my turnips,' she went on, 'you've hoed up, and my cabbages. My turnips that my boy sowed afore he went. There, get along with you do, afore I come at you with my broom-handle.'

She did come at us with her broom-handle as she spoke, and even the boldest turned and fled. Oswald was even the boldest. 'They looked like weeds right enough,' he said.

And Dicky said, 'It all comes of trying to do golden deeds.' This was when we were out in the road.

As we went along, in a silence full of gloomy remorse, we met the postman. He said—

'Here's the letters for the Moat,' and passed on hastily. He was a bit late.

When we came to look through the letters, which were nearly all for Albert's uncle, we found there was a postcard that had got stuck in a magazine wrapper. Alice pulled it out. It was addressed to Mrs Simpkins. We honourably only looked at the address, although it is allowed by the rules of honourableness to read postcards that come to your house if you like, even if they are not for you.

After a heated discussion, Alice and Oswald said they were not afraid, whoever was, and they retraced their steps, Alice holding the postcard right way up, so that we should not look at the lettery part of it, but only the address.

With quickly-beating heart, but outwardly unmoved, they walked up to the white cottage door.

It opened with a bang when we knocked.

'Well?' Mrs Simpkins said, and I think she said it what people in books call 'sourly'.

Oswald said, 'We are very, very sorry we spoiled your turnips, and we will ask my father to try and make it up to you some other way.'

She muttered something about not wanting to be beholden to anybody.

'We came back,' Oswald went on, with his always unruffled politeness, 'because the postman gave us a postcard in mistake with our letters, and it is addressed to you.'

'We haven't read it,' Alice said quickly. I think she needn't have said that. Of course we hadn't. But perhaps girls know better than we do what women are likely to think you capable of.

The soldier's mother took the postcard (she snatched it really, but 'took' is a kinder word, considering everything) and she looked at the address a long time. Then she turned it over and read what was on the back. Then she drew her breath in as far as it would go, and caught hold of the door-post. Her face got awful. It was like the wax face of a dead king I saw once at Madame Tussaud's.

Alice understood. She caught hold of the soldier's mother's hand and said—

'Oh, NO—it's NOT your boy Bill!'

And the woman said nothing, but shoved the postcard into Alice's hand, and we both read it—and it WAS her boy Bill.

Alice gave her back the card. She had held on to the woman's hand all the time, and now she squeezed the hand, and held it against her face. But she could not say a word because she was crying so. The soldier's mother took the card again and she pushed Alice away, but it was not an unkind push, and she went in and shut the door; and as Alice and Oswald went down the road Oswald looked back, and one of the windows of the cottage had a white blind. Afterwards the other windows had too. There were no blinds really to the cottage. It was aprons and things she had pinned up.

Alice cried most of the morning, and so did the other girls. We wanted to do something for the soldier's mother, but you can do nothing when people's sons are shot. It is the most dreadful thing to want to do something for people who are unhappy, and not to know what to do.

It was Noel who thought of what we COIULD do at last.

He said, 'I suppose they don't put up tombstones to soldiers when they die in war. But there—I mean Oswald said, 'Of course not.'

Noel said, 'I daresay you'll think it's silly, but I don't care. Don't you think she'd like it, if we put one up to HIM? Not in the churchyard, of course, because we shouldn't be let, but in our garden, just where it joins on to the churchyard?'

And we all thought it was a first-rate idea.

This is what we meant to put on the tombstone:

'Here lies

BILL SIMPKINS

Who died fighting for Queen

and Country.'

'A faithful son,
A son so dear,
A soldier brave
Lies buried here.'

Then we remembered that poor brave Bill was really buried far away in the Southern hemisphere, if at all. So we altered it to—

'A soldier brave
We weep for here.'

Then we looked out a nice flagstone in the stable-yard, and we got a cold chisel out of the Dentist's toolbox, and began.

But stone-cutting is difficult and dangerous work.

Oswald went at it a bit, but he chipped his thumb, and it bled so he had to chuck it. Then Dicky tried, and then Denny, but Dicky hammered his finger, and Denny took all day over every stroke, so that by tea-time we had only done the H, and about half the E—and the E was awfully crooked. Oswald chipped his thumb over the H.

We looked at it the next morning, and even the most sanguinary of us saw that it was a hopeless task.

Then Denny said, 'Why not wood and paint?' and he showed us how. We got a board and two stumps from the carpenter's in the village, and we painted it all white, and when that was dry Denny did the words on it.

It was something like this:

'IN MEMORY OF

BILL SIMPKINS

DEAD FOR QUEEN AND COUNTRY.

HONOUR TO HIS NAME AND ALL

OTHER BRAVE SOLDIERS.'

We could not get in what we meant to at first, so we had to give up the poetry.

We fixed it up when it was dry. We had to dig jolly deep to get the posts to stand up, but the gardener helped us.

Then the girls made wreaths of white flowers, roses and Canterbury bells, and lilies and pinks, and sweet-peas and daisies, and put them over the posts. And I think if Bill Simpkins had known how sorry we were, he would have been glad. Oswald only hopes if he falls on the wild battlefield, which is his highest ambition, that somebody will be as sorry about him as he was about Bill, that's all!

When all was done, and what flowers there were over from the wreaths scattered under the tombstone between the posts, we wrote a letter to Mrs Simpkins, and said—

DEAR MRS SIMPKINS—

We are very, very sorry about the turnips and things, and we beg your pardon humbly. We have put up a tombstone to your brave son.

And we signed our names. Alice took the letter.

The soldier's mother read it, and said something about our oughting to know better than to make fun of people's troubles with our tombstones and tomfoolery.

Alice told me she could not help crying.

She said—

'It's not! it's NOT! Dear, DEAR Mrs Simpkins, do come with me and see! You don't know how sorry we are about Bill. Do come and see.

We can go through the churchyard, and the others have all gone in, so as to leave it quiet for you. Do come.'

And Mrs Simpkins did. And when she read what we had put up, and Alice told her the verse we had not had room for, she leant against the wall by the grave— I mean the tombstone— and Alice hugged her, and they both cried bitterly. The poor soldier's mother was very, very pleased, and she forgave us about the turnips, and we were friends after that, but she always liked Alice the best. A great many people do, somehow.

After that we used to put fresh flowers every day on Bill's tombstone, and I do believe his mother was pleased, though she got us to move it away from the churchyard edge and put it in a corner of our garden under a laburnum, where people could not see it from the church. But you could from the road, though I think she thought you couldn't. She came every day to look at the new wreaths. When the white flowers gave out we put coloured, and she liked it just as well.

About a fortnight after the erecting of the tombstone the girls were putting fresh wreaths on it when a soldier in a red coat came down the road, and he stopped and looked at us. He walked with a stick, and he had a bundle in a blue cotton handkerchief, and one arm in a sling.

And he looked again, and he came nearer, and he leaned on the wall, so that he could read the black printing on the white paint.

And he grinned all over his face, and he said—

'Well, I AM blessed!'

And he read it all out in a sort of half whisper, and when he came to the end, where it says, 'and all such brave soldiers', he said—

'Well, I really AM!' I suppose he meant he really was blessed. Oswald thought it was like the soldier's cheek, so he said—

'I daresay you aren't so very blessed as you think. What's it to do with you, anyway, eh, Tommy?'

Of course Oswald knew from Kipling that an infantry soldier is called that. The soldier said—

'Tommy yourself, young man. That's ME!' and he pointed to the tombstone.

We stood rooted to the spot. Alice spoke first.

'Then you're Bill, and you're not dead,' she said. 'Oh, Bill, I am so glad! Do let ME tell your mother.'

She started running, and so did we all. Bill had to go slowly because of his leg, but I tell you he went as fast as ever he could.

We all hammered at the soldier's mother's door, and shouted—

'Come out! come out!' and when she opened the door we were going to speak, but she pushed us away, and went tearing down the garden path like winking. I never saw a grown-up woman run like it, because she saw Bill coming.

She met him at the gate, running right into him, and caught hold of him, and she cried much more than when she thought he was dead.

And we all shook his hand and said how glad we were.

The soldier's mother kept hold of him with both hands, and I couldn't help looking at her face. It was like wax that had been painted on both pink cheeks, and the eyes shining like candles. And when we had all said how glad we were, she said—

'Thank the dear Lord for His mercies,' and she took her boy Bill into the cottage and shut the door.

We went home and chopped up the tombstone with the wood-axe and had a blazing big bonfire, and cheered till we could hardly speak.

The postcard was a mistake; he was only missing. There was a pipe and a whole pound of tobacco left over from our keepsake to the other soldiers. We gave it to Bill. Father is going to have him for under-gardener when his wounds get well. He'll always be a bit lame, so he cannot fight any more.

Chapter 4. The Tower of Mystery

It was very rough on Dora having her foot bad, but we took it in turns to stay in with her, and she was very decent about it. Daisy was most with her. I do not dislike Daisy, but I wish she had been taught how to play. Because Dora is rather like that naturally, and sometimes I have thought that Daisy makes her worse.

I talked to Albert's uncle about it one day, when the others had gone to church, and I did not go because of ear-ache, and he said it came from reading the wrong sort of books partly—she has read Ministering Children, and Anna Ross, or The Orphan of Waterloo, and Ready Work for Willing Hands, and Elsie, or Like a Little Candle, and even a horrid little blue book about the something or other of Little Sins. After this conversation Oswald took care she had plenty of the right sort of books to read, and he was surprised and pleased when she got up early one morning to finish Monte Cristo. Oswald felt that he was really being useful to a suffering fellow-creature when he gave Daisy books that were not all about being good.

A few days after Dora was laid up, Alice called a council of the Wouldbegoods, and Oswald and Dicky attended with darkly-clouded brows. Alice had the minute-book, which was an exercise-book that had not much written in it. She had begun at the other end. I hate doing that myself, because there is so little room at the top compared with right way up.

Dora and a sofa had been carried out on to the lawn, and we were on the grass. It was very hot and dry. We had sherbet. Alice read:

'"Society of the Wouldbegoods.

'"We have not done much. Dicky mended a window, and we got the milk-pan out of the moat that dropped through where he mended it. Dora, Oswald, Dicky and me got upset in the moat. This was not goodness. Dora's foot was hurt. We hope to do better next time."'

Then came Noel's poem:

> 'We are the Wouldbegoods Society,
> We are not good yet, but we mean to try,
> And if we try, and if we don't succeed,
> It must mean we are very bad indeed.'

This sounded so much righter than Noel's poetry generally does, that Oswald said so, and Noel explained that Denny had helped him.

'He seems to know the right length for lines of poetry. I suppose it comes of learning so much at school,' Noel said.

Then Oswald proposed that anybody should be allowed to write in the book if they found out anything good that anyone else had done, but not things that were public acts; and nobody was to write about themselves, or anything other people told them, only what they found out.

After a brief jaw the others agreed, and Oswald felt, not for the first time in his young life, that he would have made a good diplomatic hero to carry despatches and outwit the other side. For now he had put it out of the minute-book's power to be the kind of thing readers of Ministering Children would have wished.

'And if anyone tells other people any good thing he's done he is to go to Coventry for the rest of the day.'

And Denny remarked, 'We shall do good by stealth, and blush to find it shame.'

After that nothing was written in the book for some time. I looked about, and so did the others, but I never caught anyone in the act of doing anything extra; though several of the others have told me since of things they did at this time, and really wondered nobody had noticed.

I think I said before that when you tell a story you cannot tell everything. It would be silly to do it. Because ordinary kinds of play are dull to read about; and the only other thing is meals, and to dwell on what you eat is greedy and not like a hero at all. A hero is always contented with a venison pasty and a horn of sack. All the same, the meals were very interesting; with things you do not get at home—Lent pies with custard and currants in them, sausage rolls and fiede cakes, and raisin cakes and apple turnovers, and honeycomb and syllabubs, besides as much new milk as you cared about, and cream now and then, and cheese always on the table for tea. Father told Mrs Pettigrew to get what meals she liked, and she got these strange but attractive foods.

In a story about Wouldbegoods it is not proper to tell of times when only some of us were naughty, so I will pass lightly over the time when Noel got up the kitchen chimney and brought three bricks and an old starling's nest and about a ton of soot down with him when he fell. They never use the big chimney in the summer, but cook in the wash-house. Nor do I wish to dwell on what H. O. did when he went into the dairy. I do not know what his motive was. But Mrs Pettigrew said SHE knew; and she locked him in, and said if it was cream he wanted he should have enough, and she wouldn't let him out till tea-time. The cat had also got into the dairy for some reason of her own, and when H. O. was tired of whatever he went in for he poured all the milk into the churn and tried to teach the cat to swim in it. He must have been desperate. The cat did not even try to learn, and H. O. had the scars on his hands for weeks. I do not wish to tell tales of H. O., for he is very young, and whatever he does he always catches it for; but I will just allude to our being told not to eat the greengages in the garden. And we did not. And whatever H. O. did was Noel's fault—for Noel told H. O. that greengages would grow again all right if you did not bite as far as the stone, just as wounds are not mortal except when you are pierced through the heart. So the two of them bit bites out of every greengage they could reach. And of course the pieces did not grow again.

Oswald did not do things like these, but then he is older than his brothers. The only thing he did just about then was making a booby-trap for Mrs Pettigrew when she had locked H. O. up in the dairy, and unfortunately it was the day she was going out in her best things, and part of the trap was a can of water. Oswald was not willingly vicious; it was but a light and thoughtless act which he had every reason to be sorry for afterwards. And he is sorry even without those reasons, because he knows it is ungentlemanly to play tricks on women.

I remember Mother telling Dora and me when we were little that you ought to be very kind and polite to servants, because they have to work very hard, and do not have so many good times as we do. I used to think about Mother more at the Moat House than I did at Blackheath, especially in the garden. She was very fond of flowers, and she used to tell us about the big garden where she used to live; and I remember Dora and I helped her to plant seeds. But it is no use wishing. She would have liked that garden, though.

The girls and the white mice did not do anything boldly wicked—though of course they used to borrow Mrs Pettigrew's needles, which made her very nasty. Needles that are borrowed might just as well be stolen. But I say no more.

I have only told you these things to show the kind of events which occurred on the days I don't tell you about. On the whole, we had an excellent time.

It was on the day we had the pillow-fight that we went for the long walk. Not the Pilgrimage—that is another story. We did not mean to have a pillow-fight. It is not usual to have them after breakfast, but Oswald had come up to get his knife out of the pocket of his Etons, to cut some wire we were making rabbit snares of. It is a very good knife, with a file in it, as well as a corkscrew and other things—and he did not come down at once, because he was detained by having to make an apple-pie bed for Dicky. Dicky came up after him to see what he was up to, and when he did see he buzzed a pillow at Oswald, and the fight began. The others, hearing the noise of battle from afar, hastened to the field of action, all except Dora, who couldn't because of being laid up with her foot, and Daisy, because she is a little afraid of us still, when we are all together. She thinks we are rough. This comes of having only one brother.

Well, the fight was a very fine one. Alice backed me up, and Noel and H. O. backed Dicky, and Denny heaved a pillow or two; but he cannot shy straight, so I don't know which side he was on.

And just as the battle raged most fiercely, Mrs Pettigrew came in and snatched the pillows away, and shook those of the warriors who were small enough for it. SHE was rough if you like. She also used language I should have thought she would be above. She said, Drat you!' and 'Drabbit you!' The last is a thing I have never heard said before. She said—

'There's no peace of your life with you children. Drat your antics! And that poor, dear, patient gentleman right underneath, with his headache and his handwriting: and you rampaging about over his head like young bull-calves. I wonder you haven't more sense, a great girl like you.'

She said this to Alice, and Alice answered gently, as we are told to do—

'I really am awfully sorry; we forgot about the headache. Don't be cross, Mrs Pettigrew; we didn't mean to; we didn't think.'

'You never do,' she said, and her voice, though grumpy, was no longer violent. 'Why on earth you can't take yourselves off for the day I don't know.'

We all said, 'But may we?'

She said, 'Of course you may. Now put on your boots and go for a good long walk. And I'll tell you what—I'll put you up a snack, and you can have an egg to your tea to make up for missing your dinner. Now don't go clattering about the stairs and passages, there's good children. See if you can't be quiet this once, and give the good gentleman a chance with his copying.'

She went off. Her bark is worse than her bite. She does not understand anything about writing books, though. She thinks Albert's uncle copies things out of printed books, when he is really writing new ones. I wonder how she thinks printed books get made first of all. Many servants are like this.

She gave us the 'snack' in a basket, and sixpence to buy milk with. She said any of the farms would let us have it, only most likely it would be skim. We thanked her politely, and she hurried us out of the front door as if we'd been chickens on a pansy bed.

(I did not know till after I had left the farm gate open, and the hens had got into the garden, that these feathered bipeds display a great partiality for the young buds of plants of the genus viola, to which they are extremely destructive. I was told that by the gardener. I looked it up in the gardening book afterwards to be sure he was right. You do learn a lot of things in the country.)

We went through the garden as far as the church, and then we rested a bit in the porch, and just looked into the basket to see what the 'snack' was. It proved to be sausage rolls and queen cakes, and a Lent pie in a round tin dish, and some hard-boiled eggs, and some apples. We all ate the apples at once, so as not to have to carry them about with us. The churchyard smells awfully good. It is the wild thyme that grows on the graves. This is another thing we did not know before we came into the country.

Then the door of the church tower was ajar, and we all went up; it had always been locked before when we had tried it.

We saw the ringers' loft where the ends of the bellropes hang down with long, furry handles to them like great caterpillars, some red, and some blue and white, but we did not pull them. And then we went up to where the bells are, very big and dusty among large dirty beams; and four windows with no glass, only shutters like Venetian blinds, but they won't pull up. There were heaps of straws and sticks on the window ledges. We think they were owls' nests, but we did not see any owls.

Then the tower stairs got very narrow and dark, and we went on up, and we came to a door and opened it suddenly, and it was like being hit in the face, the light was so sudden. And there we were on the top of the tower, which is flat, and people have cut their names on it, and a turret at one corner, and a low wall all round, up and down, like castle battlements. And we looked down and saw the roof of the church, and the leads, and the churchyard, and our garden, and the Moat House, and the farm, and Mrs Simpkins's cottage, looking very small, and other farms looking like toy things out of boxes, and we saw corn-fields and meadows and pastures. A pasture is not the same thing as a meadow, whatever you may think. And we saw the tops of trees and hedges, looking like the map of the United States, and villages, and a tower that did not look very far away standing by itself on the top of a hill. Alice pointed to it, and said—

'What's that?'

'It's not a church,' said Noel, 'because there's no churchyard. Perhaps it's a tower of mystery that covers the entrance to a subterranean vault with treasure in it.'

Dicky said, 'Subterranean fiddlestick!' and 'A waterworks, more likely.'

Alice thought perhaps it was a ruined castle, and the rest of its crumbling walls were concealed by ivy, the growth of years.

Oswald could not make his mind up what it was, so he said, 'Let's go and see! We may as well go there as anywhere.'

So we got down out of the church tower and dusted ourselves, and set out.

The Tower of Mystery showed quite plainly from the road, now that we knew where to look for it, because it was on the top of a hill. We began to walk. But the tower did not seem to get any nearer. And it was very hot.

So we sat down in a meadow where there was a stream in the ditch and ate the 'snack'. We drank the pure water from the brook out of our hands, because there was no farm to get milk at just there, and it was too much fag to look for one—and, besides, we thought we might as well save the sixpence.

Then we started again, and still the tower looked as far off as ever. Denny began to drag his feet, though he had brought a walking-stick which none of the rest of us had, and said—

'I wish a cart would come along. We might get a lift.'

He knew all about getting lifts, of course, from having been in the country before. He is not quite the white mouse we took him for at first. Of course when you live in Lewisham or Blackheath you learn other things. If you asked for a lift in Lewisham, High Street, your only reply would be jeers. We sat down on a heap of stones, and decided that we would ask for a lift from the next cart, whichever way it was going. It was while we were waiting that Oswald found out about plantain seeds being good to eat.

When the sound of wheels came we remarked with joy that the cart was going towards the Tower of Mystery. It was a cart a man was going to fetch a pig home in. Denny said—

'I say, you might give us a lift. Will you?'

The man who was going for the pig said—

'What, all that little lot?' but he winked at Alice, and we saw that he meant to aid us on our way. So we climbed up, and he whipped up the horse and asked us where we were going. He was a kindly old man, with a face like a walnut shell, and white hair and beard like a jack-in-the-box.

'We want to get to the tower,' Alice said. 'Is it a ruin, or not?'

'It ain't no ruin,' the man said; 'no fear of that! The man wot built it he left so much a year to be spent on repairing of it! Money that might have put bread in honest folks' mouths.'

We asked was it a church then, or not.

'Church?' he said. 'Not it. It's more of a tombstone, from all I can make out. They do say there was a curse on him that built it, and he wasn't to rest in earth or sea. So he's buried half-way up the tower—if you can call it buried.'

'Can you go up it?' Oswald asked.

'Lord love you! yes; a fine view from the top they say. I've never been up myself, though I've lived in sight of it, boy and man, these sixty-three years come harvest.'

Alice asked whether you had to go past the dead and buried person to get to the top of the tower, and could you see the coffin.

'No, no,' the man said; 'that's all hid away behind a slab of stone, that is, with reading on it. You've no call to be afraid, missy. It's daylight all the way up. But I wouldn't go there after dark, so I wouldn't. It's always open, day and night, and they say tramps sleep there now and again. Anyone who likes can sleep there, but it wouldn't be me.'

We thought that it would not be us either, but we wanted to go more than ever, especially when the man said—

'My own great-uncle of the mother's side, he was one of the masons that set up the stone slab. Before then it was thick glass, and you could see the dead man lying inside, as he'd left it in his will. He was lying there in a glass coffin with his best clothes—blue satin and silver, my uncle said, such as was all the go in his day, with his wig on, and his sword beside him, what he used to wear. My uncle said his hair had grown out from under his wig, and his beard was down to the toes of him. My uncle he always upheld that that dead man was no deader than you and me, but was in a sort of fit, a transit, I think they call it, and looked for him to waken into life again some day. But the doctor said not. It was only something done to him like Pharaoh in the Bible afore he was buried.'

Alice whispered to Oswald that we should be late for tea, and wouldn't it be better to go back now directly. But he said—

'If you're afraid, say so; and you needn't come in anyway—but I'm going on.'

The man who was going for the pig put us down at a gate quite near the tower—at least it looked so until we began to walk again. We thanked him, and he said—

'Quite welcome,' and drove off.

We were rather quiet going through the wood. What we had heard made us very anxious to see the tower— all except Alice, who would keep talking about tea, though not a greedy girl by nature. None of the others encouraged her, but Oswald thought himself that we had better be home before dark.

As we went up the path through the wood we saw a poor wayfarer with dusty bare feet sitting on the bank.

He stopped us and said he was a sailor, and asked for a trifle to help him to get back to his ship.

I did not like the look of him much myself, but Alice said, 'Oh, the poor man, do let's help him, Oswald.' So we held a hurried council, and decided to give him the milk sixpence. Oswald had it in his purse, and he had to empty the purse into his hand to find the sixpence, for that was not all the money he had, by any means. Noel said afterwards that he saw the wayfarer's eyes fastened greedily upon the shining pieces as Oswald returned them to his purse. Oswald has to own that he purposely let the man see that he had more money, so that the man might not feel shy about accepting so large a sum as sixpence.

The man blessed our kind hearts and we went on.

The sun was shining very brightly, and the Tower of Mystery did not look at all like a tomb when we got to it. The bottom Storey was on arches, all open, and ferns and things grew underneath. There was a round stone stair going up in the middle. Alice began to gather ferns while we went up, but when we had called out to her that it was as the pig-man had said, and daylight all the way up, she said—

'All right. I'm not afraid. I'm only afraid of being late home,' and came up after us. And perhaps, though not downright manly truthfulness, this was as much as you could expect from a girl.

There were holes in the little tower of the staircase to let light in. At the top of it was a thick door with iron bolts. We shot these back, and it was not fear but caution that made Oswald push open the door so very slowly and carefully.

Because, of course, a stray dog or cat might have got shut up there by accident, and it would have startled Alice very much if it had jumped out on us.

When the door was opened we saw that there was no such thing. It was a room with eight sides. Denny says it is the shape called octogenarian; because a man named Octagius invented it. There were eight large arched windows with no glass, only stone-work, like in churches. The room was full of sunshine, and you could see the blue sky through the windows, but nothing else, because they were so high up. It was so bright we began to think the pig-man had been kidding us. Under one of the windows was a door. We went through, and there was a little passage and then a turret-twisting stair, like in the church, but quite light with windows. When we had gone some way up this, we came to a sort of landing, and there was a block of stone let into the wall—polished—Denny said it was Aberdeen graphite, with gold letters cut in it. It said—

> 'Here lies the body of Mr Richard Ravenal
> Born 1720. Died 1779.'

and a verse of poetry:

> 'Here lie I, between earth and sky,
> Think upon me, dear passers-by,
> And you who do my tombstone see
> Be kind to say a prayer for me.'

'How horrid!' Alice said. 'Do let's get home.'

'We may as well go to the top,' Dicky said, 'just to say we've been.'

And Alice is no funk—so she agreed; though I could see she did not like it.

Up at the top it was like the top of the church tower, only octogenarian in shape, instead of square.

Alice got all right there; because you cannot think much about ghosts and nonsense when the sun is shining bang down on you at four o'clock in the afternoon, and you can see red farm-roofs between the trees, and the safe white roads, with people in carts like black ants crawling.

It was very jolly, but we felt we ought to be getting back, because tea is at five, and we could not hope to find lifts both ways.

So we started to go down. Dicky went first, then Oswald, then Alice—and H. O. had just stumbled over the top step and saved himself by Alice's back, which nearly upset Oswald and Dicky, when the hearts of all stood still, and then went on by leaps and bounds, like the good work in missionary magazines.

For, down below us, in the tower where the man whose beard grew down to his toes after he was dead was buried, there was a noise—a loud noise. And it was like a door being banged and bolts fastened. We tumbled over each other to get back into the open sunshine on the top of the tower, and Alice's hand got jammed between the edge of the doorway and H. O.'s boot; it was bruised black and blue, and another part bled, but she did not notice it till long after.

We looked at each other, and Oswald said in a firm voice (at least, I hope it was)—

'What was that?'

'He HAS waked up,' Alice said. 'Oh, I know he has. Of course there is a door for him to get out by when he wakes. He'll come up here. I know he will.'

Dicky said, and his voice was not at all firm (I noticed that at the time), 'It doesn't matter, if he's ALIVE.'

'Unless he's come to life a raving lunatic,' Noel said, and we all stood with our eyes on the doorway of the turret—and held our breath to hear.

But there was no more noise.

Then Oswald said—and nobody ever put it in the Golden Deed book, though they own that it was brave and noble of him—he said—

'Perhaps it was only the wind blowing one of the doors to. I'll go down and see, if you will, Dick.'

Dicky only said—

'The wind doesn't shoot bolts.'

'A bolt from the blue,' said Denny to himself, looking up at the sky. His father is a sub-editor. He had gone very red, and he was holding on to Alice's hand. Suddenly he stood up quite straight and said—

'I'm not afraid. I'll go and see.'

THIS was afterwards put in the Golden Deed book. It ended in Oswald and Dicky and Denny going. Denny went first because he said he would rather— and Oswald understood this and let him. If Oswald had pushed first it would have been like Sir Lancelot refusing to let a young knight win his spurs. Oswald took good care to go second himself, though. The others never understood this. You don't expect it from girls; but I did think father would have understood without Oswald telling him, which of course he never could.

We all went slowly.

At the bottom of the turret stairs we stopped short. Because the door there was bolted fast and would not yield to shoves, however desperate and united.

Only now somehow we felt that Mr Richard Ravenal was all right and quiet, but that some one had done it for a lark, or perhaps not known about anyone being up there. So we rushed up, and Oswald told the others in a few hasty but well-chosen words, and we all leaned over between the battlements, and shouted, 'Hi! you there!'

Then from under the arches of the quite-downstairs part of the tower a figure came forth—and it was the sailor who had had our milk sixpence. He looked up and he spoke to us. He did not speak loud, but he spoke loud enough for us to hear every word quite plainly. He said—

'Drop that.'

Oswald said, 'Drop what?'

He said, 'That row.'

Oswald said, 'Why?'

He said, 'Because if you don't I'll come up and make you, and pretty quick too, so I tell you.'

Dicky said, 'Did you bolt the door?'

The man said, 'I did so, my young cock.'

Alice said—and Oswald wished to goodness she had held her tongue, because he saw right enough the man was not friendly—'Oh, do come and let us out—do, please.'

While she was saying it Oswald suddenly saw that he did not want the man to come up. So he scurried down the stairs because he thought he had seen something on the door on the top side, and sure enough there were two bolts, and he shot them into their sockets. This bold act was not put in the Golden Deed book, because when Alice wanted to, the others said it was not GOOD of Oswald to think of this, but only CLEVER. I think sometimes, in moments of danger and disaster, it is as good to be clever as it is to be good. But Oswald would never demean himself to argue about this.

When he got back the man was still standing staring up. Alice said—

'Oh, Oswald, he says he won't let us out unless we give him all our money. And we might be here for days and days and all night as well. No one knows where we are to come and look for us. Oh, do let's give it him ALL.'

She thought the lion of the English nation, which does not know when it is beaten, would be ramping in her brother's breast. But Oswald kept calm. He said—

'All right,' and he made the others turn out their pockets. Denny had a bad shilling, with a head on both sides, and three halfpence. H. O. had a halfpenny. Noel had a French penny, which is only good for chocolate machines at railway stations. Dicky had tenpence-halfpenny, and Oswald had a two-shilling piece of his own that he was saving up to buy a gun with. Oswald tied the whole lot up in his handkerchief, and looking over the battlements, he said—

'You are an ungrateful beast. We gave you sixpence freely of our own will.'

The man did look a little bit ashamed, but he mumbled something about having his living to get. Then Oswald said—

'Here you are. Catch!' and he flung down the handkerchief with the money in it.

The man muffed the catch—butter-fingered idiot!— but he picked up the handkerchief and undid it, and when he saw what was in it he swore dreadfully. The cad!

'Look here,' he called out, 'this won't do, young shaver. I want those there shiners I see in your pus! Chuck 'em along!'

Then Oswald laughed. He said—

'I shall know you again anywhere, and you'll be put in prison for this. Here are the SHINERS.' And he was so angry he chucked down purse and all. The shiners were not real ones, but only card-counters that looked like sovereigns on one side. Oswald used to carry them in his purse so as to look affluent. He does not do this now.

When the man had seen what was in the purse he disappeared under the tower, and Oswald was glad of what he had done about the bolts—and he hoped they were as strong as the ones on the other side of the door.

They were.

We heard the man kicking and pounding at the door, and I am not ashamed to say that we were all holding on to each other very tight. I am proud, however, to relate that nobody screamed or cried.

After what appeared to be long years, the banging stopped, and presently we saw the brute going away among the trees. Then Alice did cry, and I do not blame her. Then Oswald said—

'It's no use. Even if he's undone the door, he may be in ambush. We must hold on here till somebody comes.'

Then Alice said, speaking chokily because she had not quite done crying—

'Let's wave a flag.'

By the most fortunate accident she had on one of her Sunday petticoats, though it was Monday. This petticoat is white. She tore it out at the gathers, and we tied it to Denny's stick, and took turns to wave it. We had laughed at his carrying a stick before, but we were very sorry now that we had done so.

And the tin dish the Lent pie was baked in we polished with our handkerchiefs, and moved it about in the sun so that the sun might strike on it and signal our distress to some of the outlying farms.

This was perhaps the most dreadful adventure that had then ever happened to us. Even Alice had now stopped thinking of Mr Richard Ravenal, and thought only of the lurker in ambush.

We all felt our desperate situation keenly. I must say Denny behaved like anything but a white mouse. When it was the others' turn to wave, he sat on the leads of the tower and held Alice's and Noel's hands, and said poetry to them—yards and yards of it. By some strange fatality it seemed to comfort them. It wouldn't have me.

He said 'The Battle of the Baltic', and 'Gray's Elegy', right through, though I think he got wrong in places, and the 'Revenge', and Macaulay's thing about Lars Porsena and the Nine Gods. And when it was his turn he waved like a man.

I will try not to call him a white mouse any more. He was a brick that day, and no mouse.

The sun was low in the heavens, and we were sick of waving and very hungry, when we saw a cart in the road below. We waved like mad, and shouted, and Denny screamed exactly like a railway whistle, a thing none of us had known before that he could do.

And the cart stopped. And presently we saw a figure with a white beard among the trees. It was our Pig-man.

We bellowed the awful truth to him, and when he had taken it in—he thought at first we were kidding— he came up and let us out.

He had got the pig; luckily it was a very small one— and we were not particular. Denny and Alice sat on the front of the cart with the Pig-man, and the rest of us got in with the pig, and the man drove us right home. You may think we talked it over on the way. Not us. We went to sleep, among the pig, and before long the Pig-man stopped and got us to make room for Alice and Denny. There was a net over the cart. I never was so sleepy in my life, though it was not more than bedtime.

Generally, after anything exciting, you are punished—but this could not be, because we had only gone for a walk, exactly as we were told.

There was a new rule made, though. No walks except on the high-roads, and we were always to take Pincher and either Lady, the deer-hound, or Martha, the bulldog. We generally hate rules, but we did not mind this one.

Father gave Denny a gold pencil-case because he was first to go down into the tower. Oswald does not grudge Denny this, though some might think he deserved at least a silver one. But Oswald is above such paltry jealousies.

Chapter 5. The Waterworks

This is the story of one of the most far-reaching and influentially naughty things we ever did in our lives. We did not mean to do such a deed. And yet we did do it. These things will happen with the best-regulated consciences.

The story of this rash and fatal act is intimately involved—which means all mixed up anyhow—with a private affair of Oswald's, and the one cannot be revealed without the other. Oswald does not particularly want his story to be remembered, but he wishes to tell the truth, and perhaps it is what father calls a wholesome discipline to lay bare the awful facts.

It was like this.

On Alice's and Noel's birthday we went on the river for a picnic. Before that we had not known that there was a river so near us. Afterwards father said he wished we had been allowed to remain on our pristine ignorance, whatever that is. And perhaps the dark hour did dawn when we wished so too. But a truce to vain regrets.

It was rather a fine thing in birthdays. The uncle sent a box of toys and sweets, things that were like a vision from another and a brighter world. Besides that Alice had a knife, a pair of shut-up scissors, a silk handkerchief, a book—it was The Golden Age and is A1 except where it gets mixed with grown-up nonsense. Also a work-case lined with pink plush, a boot-bag, which no one in their senses would use because it had flowers in wool all over it. And she had a box of chocolates and a musical box that played 'The Man who broke' and two other tunes, and two pairs of kid gloves for church, and a box of writing-paper—pink—with 'Alice' on it in gold writing, and an egg coloured red that said 'A. Bastable' in ink on one side. These gifts were the offerings of Oswald, Dora, Dicky, Albert's uncle, Daisy, Mr Foulkes (our own robber), Noel, H. O., father and Denny. Mrs Pettigrew gave the egg. It was a kindly housekeeper's friendly token.

I shall not tell you about the picnic on the river because the happiest times form but dull reading when they are written down. I will merely state that it was prime. Though happy, the day was uneventful. The only thing exciting enough to write about was in one of the locks, where there was a snake—a viper. It was asleep in a warm sunny corner of the lock gate, and when the gate was shut it fell off into the water.

Alice and Dora screamed hideously. So did Daisy, but her screams were thinner.

The snake swam round and round all the time our boat was in the lock. It swam with four inches of itself—the head end—reared up out of the water, exactly like Kaa in the Jungle Book—so we know Kipling is a true author and no rotter. We were careful to keep our hands well inside the boat. A snake's eyes strike terror into the boldest breast.

When the lock was full father killed the viper with a boat-hook. I was sorry for it myself. It was indeed a venomous serpent. But it was the first we had ever seen, except at the Zoo. And it did swim most awfully well.

Directly the snake had been killed H. O. reached out for its corpse, and the next moment the body of our little brother was seen wriggling conclusively on the boat's edge. This exciting spectacle was not of a lasting nature. He went right in. Father clawed him out. He is very unlucky with water.

Being a birthday, but little was said. H. O. was wrapped in everybody's coats, and did not take any cold at all.

This glorious birthday ended with an iced cake and ginger wine, and drinking healths. Then we played whatever we liked. There had been rounders during the afternoon. It was a day to be for ever marked by memory's brightest what's-its-name.

I should not have said anything about the picnic but for one thing. It was the thin edge of the wedge. It was the all-powerful lever that moved but too many events. You see, WE WERE NO LONGER STRANGERS TO THE RIVER.

And we went there whenever we could. Only we had to take the dogs, and to promise no bathing without grown-ups. But paddling in back waters was allowed. I say no more.

I have not numerated Noel's birthday presents because I wish to leave something to the imagination of my young readers. (The best authors always do this.) If you will take the large, red catalogue of the Army and Navy Stores, and just make a list of about fifteen of the things you would like best—prices from 2s. to 25s.—you will get a very good idea of Noel's presents, and it will help you to make up your mind in case you are asked just before your next birthday what you really NEED.

One of Noel's birthday presents was a cricket ball. He cannot bowl for nuts, and it was a first-rate ball. So some days after the birthday Oswald offered him to exchange it for a coconut he had won at the fair, and two pencils (new), and a brand-new note-book. Oswald thought, and he still thinks, that this was a fair exchange, and so did Noel at the time, and he agreed to it, and was quite pleased till the girls said it wasn't fair, and Oswald had the best of it. And then that young beggar Noel wanted the ball back, but Oswald, though not angry, was firm.

'You said it was a bargain, and you shook hands on it,' he said, and he said it quite kindly and calmly.

Noel said he didn't care. He wanted his cricket ball back. And the girls said it was a horrid shame.

If they had not said that, Oswald might yet have consented to let Noel have the beastly ball, but now, of course, he was not going to. He said—

'Oh, yes, I daresay. And then you would be wanting the coconut and things again the next minute.'

'No, I shouldn't,' Noel said. It turned out afterwards he and H. O. had eaten the coconut, which only made it worse. And it made them worse too—which is what the book calls poetic justice.

Dora said, 'I don't think it was fair,' and even Alice said—

'Do let him have it back, Oswald.'

I wish to be just to Alice. She did not know then about the coconut having been secretly wolfed up.

We were in the garden. Oswald felt all the feelings of the hero when the opposing forces gathered about him are opposing as hard as ever they can. He knew he was not unfair, and he did not like to be jawed at just because Noel had eaten the coconut and wanted the ball back. Though Oswald did not know then about the eating of the coconut, but he felt the injustice in his soul all the same.

Noel said afterwards he meant to offer Oswald something else to make up for the coconut, but he said nothing about this at the time.

'Give it me, I say,' Noel said.

And Oswald said, 'Shan't!'

Then Noel called Oswald names, and Oswald did not answer back but just kept smiling pleasantly, and carelessly throwing up the ball and catching it again with an air of studied indifference.

It was Martha's fault that what happened happened. She is the bull-dog, and very stout and heavy. She had just been let loose and she came bounding along in her clumsy way, and jumped up on Oswald, who is beloved by all dumb animals. (You know how sagacious they are.) Well, Martha knocked the ball out of Oswald's hands, and it fell on the grass, and Noel pounced on it like a hooded falcon on its prey. Oswald would scorn to deny that he was not going to stand this, and the next moment the two were rolling over on the grass, and very soon Noel was made to bite the dust. And serve him right. He is old enough to know his own mind.

Then Oswald walked slowly away with the ball, and the others picked Noel up, and consoled the beaten, but Dicky would not take either side.

And Oswald went up into his own room and lay on his bed, and reflected gloomy reflections about unfairness.

Presently he thought he would like to see what the others were doing without their knowing he cared. So he went into the linen-room and looked out of its window, and he saw they were playing Kings and Queens—and Noel had the biggest paper crown and the longest stick sceptre.

Oswald turned away without a word, for it really was sickening.

Then suddenly his weary eyes fell upon something they had not before beheld. It was a square trap-door in the ceiling of the linen-room.

Oswald never hesitated. He crammed the cricket ball into his pocket and climbed up the shelves and unbolted the trap-door, and shoved it up, and pulled himself up through it. Though above all was dark and smelt of spiders, Oswald fearlessly shut the trap-door down again before he struck a match. He always carries matches. He is a boy fertile in every subtle expedient. Then he saw he was in the wonderful, mysterious place between the ceiling and the roof of the house. The roof is beams and tiles. Slits of light show through the tiles here and there. The ceiling, on its other and top side, is made of rough plaster and beams. If you walk on the beams it is all right—if you walk on the plaster you go through with your feet. Oswald found this out later, but some fine instinct now taught the young explorer where he ought to tread and where not. It was splendid. He was still very angry with the others and he was glad he had found out a secret they jolly well didn't know.

He walked along a dark, narrow passage. Every now and then cross-beams barred his way, and he had to creep under them. At last a small door loomed before him with cracks of light under and over. He drew back the rusty bolts and opened it. It opened straight on to the leads, a flat place between two steep red roofs, with a parapet two feet high back and front, so that no one could see you. It was a place no one could have invented better than, if they had tried, for hiding in.

Oswald spent the whole afternoon there. He happened to have a volume of Percy's Anecdotes in his pocket, the one about lawyers, as well as a few apples. While he read he fingered the cricket ball, and presently it rolled away, and he thought he would get it by-and-by.

When the tea-bell rang he forgot the ball and went hurriedly down, for apples do not keep the inside from the pangs of hunger.

Noel met him on the landing, got red in the face, and said—

'It wasn't QUITE fair about the ball, because H. O. and I had eaten the coconut. YOU can have it.'

'I don't want your beastly ball,' Oswald said, 'only I hate unfairness. However, I don't know where it is just now. When I find it you shall have it to bowl with as often as you want.'

'Then you're not waxy?'

And Oswald said 'No' and they went in to tea together. So that was all right. There were raisin cakes for tea.

Next day we happened to want to go down to the river quite early. I don't know why; this is called Fate, or Destiny. We dropped in at the 'Rose and Crown' for some ginger-beer on our way. The landlady is a friend of ours and lets us drink it in her back parlour, instead of in the bar, which would be improper for girls.

We found her awfully busy, making pies and jellies, and her two sisters were hurrying about with great hams, and pairs of chickens, and rounds of cold beef and lettuces, and pickled salmon and trays of crockery and glasses.

'It's for the angling competition,' she said.

We said, 'What's that?'

'Why,' she said, slicing cucumber like beautiful machinery while she said it, 'a lot of anglers come down some particular day and fish one particular bit of the river. And the one that catches most fish gets the prize. They're fishing the pen above Stoneham Lock. And they all come here to dinner. So I've got my hands full and a trifle over.'

We said, 'Couldn't we help?'

But she said, 'Oh, no, thank you. Indeed not, please. I really am so I don't know which way to turn. Do run along, like dears.'

So we ran along like these timid but graceful animals.

Need I tell the intellectual reader that we went straight off to the pen above Stoneham Lock to see the anglers competing? Angling is the same thing as fishing.

I am not going to try and explain locks to you. If you've never seen a lock you could never understand even if I wrote it in words of one syllable and pages and pages long. And if you have, you'll understand without my telling you. It is harder than Euclid if you don't know beforehand. But you might get a grown-up person to explain it to you with books or wooden bricks.

I will tell you what a pen is because that is easy. It is the bit of river between one lock and the next. In some rivers 'pens' are called 'reaches', but pen is the proper word.

We went along the towing-path; it is shady with willows, aspens, alders, elders, oaks and other trees. On the banks are flowers—yarrow, meadow-sweet, willow herb, loosestrife, and lady's bed-straw. Oswald learned the names of all these trees and plants on the day of the picnic. The others didn't remember them, but Oswald did. He is a boy of what they call relenting memory.

The anglers were sitting here and there on the shady bank among the grass and the different flowers I have named. Some had dogs with them, and some umbrellas, and some had only their wives and families.

We should have liked to talk to them and ask how they liked their lot, and what kinds of fish there were, and whether they were nice to eat, but we did not like to.

Denny had seen anglers before and he knew they liked to be talked to, but though he spoke to them quite like to equals he did not ask the things we wanted to know. He just asked whether they'd had any luck, and what bait they used.

And they answered him back politely. I am glad I am not an angler.

It is an immovable amusement, and, as often as not, no fish to speak of after all.

Daisy and Dora had stayed at home: Dora's foot was nearly well but they seem really to like sitting still. I think Dora likes to have a little girl to order about. Alice never would stand it. When we got to Stoneham Lock Denny said he should go home and fetch his fishing-rod. H. O. went with him. This left four of us—Oswald, Alice, Dicky, and Noel. We went on down the towing-path. The lock shuts up (that sounds as if it was like the lock on a door, but it is very otherwise) between one pen of the river and the next; the pen where the anglers were was full right up over the roots of the grass and flowers. But the pen below was nearly empty.

'You can see the poor river's bones,' Noel said.

And so you could.

Stones and mud and dried branches, and here and there an old kettle or a tin pail with no bottom to it, that some bargee had chucked in.

From walking so much along the river we knew many of the bargees. Bargees are the captains and crews of the big barges that are pulled up and down the river by slow horses. The horses do not swim. They walk on the towing-path, with a rope tied to them, and the other end to the barge. So it gets pulled along. The bargees we knew were a good friendly sort, and used to let us go all over the barges when they were in a good temper. They were not at all the sort of bullying, cowardly fiends in human form that the young hero at Oxford fights a crowd of, single-handed, in books.

The river does not smell nice when its bones are showing. But we went along down, because Oswald wanted to get some cobbler's wax in Falding village for a bird-net he was making.

But just above Falding Lock, where the river is narrow and straight, we saw a sad and gloomy sight—a big barge sitting flat on the mud because there was not water enough to float her.

There was no one on board, but we knew by a red flannel waistcoat that was spread out to dry on top that the barge belonged to friends of ours.

Then Alice said, 'They have gone to find the man who turns on the water to fill the pen. I daresay they won't find him. He's gone to his dinner, I shouldn't wonder. What a lovely surprise it would be if they came back to find their barge floating high and dry on a lot of water! DO let's do it. It's a long time since any of us did a kind action deserving of being put in the Book of Golden Deeds.'

We had given that name to the minute-book of that beastly 'Society of the Wouldbegoods'. Then you could think of the book if you wanted to without remembering the Society. I always tried to forget both of them.

Oswald said, 'But how? YOU don't know how. And if you did we haven't got a crowbar.'

I cannot help telling you that locks are opened with crowbars. You push and push till a thing goes up and the water runs through. It is rather like the little sliding door in the big door of a hen-house.

'I know where the crowbar is,' Alice said. 'Dicky and I were down here yesterday when you were su—' She was going to say sulking, I know, but she remembered manners ere too late so Oswald bears her no malice. She went on: 'Yesterday, when you were upstairs. And we saw the water-tender open the lock and the weir sluices. It's quite easy, isn't it, Dicky?'

'As easy as kiss your hand,' said Dicky; 'and what's more, I know where he keeps the other thing he opens the sluices with. I votes we do.'

'Do let's, if we can,' Noel said, 'and the bargees will bless the names of their unknown benefactors. They might make a song about us, and sing it on winter nights as they pass round the wassail bowl in front of the cabin fire.'

Noel wanted to very much; but I don't think it was altogether for generousness, but because he wanted to see how the sluices opened. Yet perhaps I do but wrong the boy.

We sat and looked at the barge a bit longer, and then Oswald said, well, he didn't mind going back to the lock and having a look at the crowbars. You see Oswald did not propose this; he did not even care very much about it when Alice suggested it.

But when we got to Stoneham Lock, and Dicky dragged the two heavy crowbars from among the elder bushes behind a fallen tree, and began to pound away at the sluice of the lock, Oswald felt it would not be manly to stand idly apart. So he took his turn.

It was very hard work but we opened the lock sluices, and we did not drop the crowbar into the lock either, as I have heard of being done by older and sillier people.

The water poured through the sluices all green and solid, as if it had been cut with a knife, and where it fell on the water underneath the white foam spread like a moving counterpane. When we had finished the lock we did the weir—which is wheels and chains— and the water pours through over the stones in a magnificent waterfall and sweeps out all round the weir-pool.

The sight of the foaming waterfalls was quite enough reward for our heavy labours, even without the thought of the unspeakable gratitude that the bargees would feel to us when they got back to their barge and found her no longer a stick-in-the-mud, but bounding on the free bosom of the river.

When we had opened all the sluices we gazed awhile on the beauties of Nature, and then went home, because we thought it would be more truly noble and good not to wait to be thanked for our kind and devoted action—and besides, it was nearly dinner-time and Oswald thought it was going to rain.

On the way home we agreed not to tell the others, because it would be like boasting of our good acts.

'They will know all about it,' Noel said, 'when they hear us being blessed by the grateful bargees, and the tale of the Unknown Helpers is being told by every village fireside. And then they can write it in the Golden Deed book.'

So we went home. Denny and H. O. had thought better of it, and they were fishing in the moat. They did not catch anything.

Oswald is very weather-wise—at least, so I have heard it said, and he had thought there would be rain. There was. It came on while we were at dinner—a great, strong, thundering rain, coming down in sheets—the first rain we had had since we came to the Moat House.

We went to bed as usual. No presentiment of the coming awfulness clouded our young mirth. I remember Dicky and Oswald had a wrestling match, and Oswald won.

In the middle of the night Oswald was awakened by a hand on his face. It was a wet hand and very cold. Oswald hit out, of course, but a voice said, in a hoarse, hollow whisper—

'Don't be a young ass! Have you got any matches? My bed's full of water; it's pouring down from the ceiling.'

Oswald's first thoughts was that perhaps by opening those sluices we had flooded some secret passage which communicated with the top of Moat House, but when he was properly awake he saw that this could not be, on account of the river being so low.

He had matches. He is, as I said before, a boy full of resources. He struck one and lit a candle, and Dicky, for it was indeed he, gazed with Oswald at the amazing spectacle.

Our bedroom floor was all wet in patches. Dicky's bed stood in a pond, and from the ceiling water was dripping in rich profusion at a dozen different places. There was a great wet patch in the ceiling, and that was blue, instead of white like the dry part, and the water dripped from different parts of it.

In a moment Oswald was quite unmanned.

'Krikey!' he said, in a heart-broken tone, and remained an instant plunged in thought.

'What on earth are we to do?' Dicky said.

And really for a short time even Oswald did not know. It was a blood-curdling event, a regular facer. Albert's uncle had gone to London that day to stay till the next. Yet something must be done.

The first thing was to rouse the unconscious others from their deep sleep, because the water was beginning to drip on to their beds, and though as yet they knew it not, there was quite a pool on Noel's bed, just in the hollow behind where his knees were doubled up, and one of H. O.'s boots was full of water, that surged wildly out when Oswald happened to kick it over.

We woke them—a difficult task, but we did not shrink from it.

Then we said, 'Get up, there is a flood! Wake up, or you will be drowned in your beds! And it's half past two by Oswald's watch.'

They awoke slowly and very stupidly. H. O. was the slowest and stupidest.

The water poured faster and faster from the ceiling.

We looked at each other and turned pale, and Noel said—

'Hadn't we better call Mrs Pettigrew?'

But Oswald simply couldn't consent to this. He could not get rid of the feeling that this was our fault somehow for meddling with the river, though of course the clear star of reason told him it could not possibly be the case.

We all devoted ourselves, heart and soul, to the work before us. We put the bath under the worst and wettest place, and the jugs and basins under lesser streams, and we moved the beds away to the dry end of the room. Ours is a long attic that runs right across the house.

But the water kept coming in worse and worse. Our nightshirts were wet through, so we got into our other shirts and knickerbockers, but preserved bareness in our feet. And the floor kept on being half an inch deep in water, however much we mopped it up.

We emptied the basins out of the window as fast as they filled, and we baled the bath with a jug without pausing to complain how hard the work was. All the same, it was more exciting than you can think. But in Oswald's dauntless breast he began to see that they would HAVE to call Mrs Pettigrew.

A new waterfall broke out between the fire-grate and the mantelpiece, and spread in devastating floods. Oswald is full of ingenious devices. I think I have said this before, but it is quite true; and perhaps even truer this time than it was last time I said it.

He got a board out of the box-room next door, and rested one end in the chink between the fireplace and the mantelpiece, and laid the other end on the back of a chair, then we stuffed the rest of the chink with our nightgowns, and laid a towel along the plank, and behold, a noble stream poured over the end of the board right into the bath we put there ready. It was like Niagara, only not so round in shape. The first lot of water that came down the chimney was very dirty. The wind whistled outside. Noel said, 'If it's pipes burst, and not the rain, it will be nice for the water-rates.' Perhaps it was only natural after this for Denny to begin with his everlasting poetry. He stopped mopping up the water to say:

'By this the storm grew loud apace,
The water-rats were shrieking,
And in the howl of Heaven each face
Grew black as they were speaking.'

Our faces were black, and our hands too, but we did not take any notice; we only told him not to gas but to go on mopping. And he did. And we all did.

But more and more water came pouring down. You would not believe so much could come off one roof.

When at last it was agreed that Mrs Pettigrew must be awakened at all hazards, we went and woke Alice to do the fatal errand.

When she came back, with Mrs Pettigrew in a nightcap and red flannel petticoat, we held our breath.

But Mrs Pettigrew did not even say, 'What on earth have you children been up to NOW?' as Oswald had feared.

She simply sat down on my bed and said—

'Oh, dear! oh, dear! oh, dear!' ever so many times.

Then Denny said, 'I once saw holes in a cottage roof. The man told me it was done when the water came through the thatch. He said if the water lies all about on the top of the ceiling, it breaks it down, but if you make holes the water will only come through the holes and you can put pails under the holes to catch it.'

So we made nine holes in the ceiling with the poker, and put pails, baths and tubs under, and now there was not so much water on the floor. But we had to keep on working like niggers, and Mrs Pettigrew and Alice worked the same.

About five in the morning the rain stopped; about seven the water did not come in so fast, and presently it only dripped slowly. Our task was done.

This is the only time I was ever up all night. I wish it happened oftener. We did not go back to bed then, but dressed and went down. We all went to sleep in the afternoon, though. Quite without meaning to.

Oswald went up on the roof, before breakfast, to see if he could find the hole where the rain had come in. He did not find any hole, but he found the cricket ball jammed in the top of a gutter pipe which he afterwards knew ran down inside the wall of the house and ran into the moat below. It seems a silly dodge, but so it was.

When the men went up after breakfast to see what had caused the flood they said there must have been a good half-foot of water on the leads the night before for it to have risen high enough to go above the edge of the lead, and of course when it got above the lead there was nothing to stop it running down under it, and soaking through the ceiling. The parapet and the roofs kept it from tumbling off down the sides of the house in the natural way. They said there must have been some obstruction in the pipe which ran down into the house, but whatever it was the water had washed it away, for they put wires down, and the pipe was quite clear.

While we were being told this Oswald's trembling fingers felt at the wet cricket ball in his pocket. And he KNEW, but he COULD not tell. He heard them wondering what the obstruction could have been, and all the time he had the obstruction in his pocket, and never said a single word.

I do not seek to defend him. But it really was an awful thing to have been the cause of; and Mrs Pettigrew is but harsh and hasty. But this, as Oswald knows too well, is no excuse for his silent conduct.

That night at tea Albert's uncle was rather silent too. At last he looked upon us with a glance full of intelligence, and said—

'There was a queer thing happened yesterday. You know there was an angling competition. The pen was kept full on purpose. Some mischievous busybody went and opened the sluices and let all the water out. The anglers' holiday was spoiled. No, the rain wouldn't have spoiled it anyhow, Alice; anglers LIKE rain. The 'Rose and Crown' dinner was half of it wasted because the anglers were so furious that a lot of them took the next train to town. And this is the worst of all—a barge, that was on the mud in the pen below, was lifted and jammed across the river and the water tilted her over, and her cargo is on the river bottom. It was coals.'

During this speech there were four of us who knew not where to turn our agitated glances. Some of us tried bread-and-butter, but it seemed dry and difficult, and those who tried tea choked and spluttered and were sorry they had not let it alone. When the speech stopped Alice said, 'It was us.'

And with deepest feelings she and the rest of us told all about it.

Oswald did not say much. He was turning the obstruction round and round in his pocket, and wishing with all his sentiments that he had owned up like a man when Albert's uncle asked him before tea to tell him all about what had happened during the night.

When they had told all, Albert's uncle told us four still more plainly, and exactly, what we had done, and how much pleasure we had spoiled, and how much of my father's money we had wasted—because he would have to pay for the coals being got up from the bottom of the river, if they could be, and if not, for the price of the coals. And we saw it ALL.

And when he had done Alice burst out crying over her plate and said—

'It's no use! We HAVE tried to be good since we've been down here. You don't know how we've tried! And it's all no use. I believe we are the wickedest children in the whole world, and I wish we were all dead!'

This was a dreadful thing to say, and of course the rest of us were all very shocked. But Oswald could not help looking at Albert's uncle to see how he would take it.

He said very gravely, 'My dear kiddie, you ought to be sorry, and I wish you to be sorry for what you've done. And you will be punished for it.' (We were; our pocket-money was stopped and we were forbidden to go near the river, besides impositions miles long.) 'But,' he went on, 'you mustn't give up trying to be good. You are extremely naughty and tiresome, as you know very well.'

Alice, Dicky, and Noel began to cry at about this time.

'But you are not the wickedest children in the world by any means.'

Then he stood up and straightened his collar, and put his hands in his pockets.

'You're very unhappy now,' he said, 'and you deserve to be. But I will say one thing to you.'

Then he said a thing which Oswald at least will never forget (though but little he deserved it, with the obstruction in his pocket, unowned up to all the time).

He said, 'I have known you all for four years—and you know as well as I do how many scrapes I've seen you in and out of—but I've never known one of you tell a lie, and I've never known one of you do a mean or dishonourable action. And when you have done wrong you are always sorry. Now this is something to stand firm on. You'll learn to be good in the other ways some day.'

He took his hands out of his pockets, and his face looked different, so that three of the four guilty creatures knew he was no longer adamant, and they threw themselves into his arms. Dora, Denny, Daisy, and H. O., of course, were not in it, and I think they thanked their stars.

Oswald did not embrace Albert's uncle. He stood there and made up his mind he would go for a soldier. He gave the wet ball one last squeeze, and took his hand out of his pocket, and said a few words before going to enlist. He said—

'The others may deserve what you say. I hope they do, I'm sure. But I don't, because it was my rotten cricket ball that stopped up the pipe and caused the midnight flood in our bedroom. And I knew it quite early this morning. And I didn't own up.'

Oswald stood there covered with shame, and he could feel the hateful cricket ball heavy and cold against the top of his leg, through the pocket.

Albert's uncle said—and his voice made Oswald hot all over, but not with shame—he said—

I shall not tell you what he said. It is no one's business but Oswald's; only I will own it made Oswald not quite so anxious to run away for a soldier as he had been before.

That owning up was the hardest thing I ever did. They did put that in the Book of Golden Deeds, though it was not a kind or generous act, and did no good to anyone or anything except Oswald's own inside feelings. I must say I think they might have let it alone. Oswald would rather forget it. Especially as Dicky wrote it in and put this:

'Oswald acted a lie, which, he knows, is as bad as telling one. But he owned up when he needn't have, and this condones his sin. We think he was a thorough brick to do it.'

Alice scratched this out afterwards and wrote the record of the incident in more flattering terms. But Dicky had used Father's ink, and she used Mrs Pettigrew's, so anyone can read his underneath the scratching outs.

The others were awfully friendly to Oswald, to show they agreed with Albert's uncle in thinking I deserved as much share as anyone in any praise there might be going.

It was Dora who said it all came from my quarrelling with Noel about that rotten cricket ball; but Alice, gently yet firmly, made her shut up.

I let Noel have the ball. It had been thoroughly soaked, but it dried all right. But it could never be the same to me after what it had done and what I had done.

I hope you will try to agree with Albert's uncle and not think foul scorn of Oswald because of this story. Perhaps you have done things nearly as bad yourself sometimes. If you have, you will know how 'owning up' soothes the savage breast and alleviates the gnawings of remorse.

If you have never done naughty acts I expect it is only because you never had the sense to think of anything.

Chapter 6. The Circus

The ones of us who had started the Society of the Wouldbegoods began, at about this time, to bother.

They said we had not done anything really noble— not worth speaking of, that is—for over a week, and that it was high time to begin again—'with earnest endeavour', Daisy said. So then Oswald said—

'All right; but there ought to be an end to everything. Let's each of us think of one really noble and unselfish act, and the others shall help to work it out, like we did when we were Treasure Seekers. Then when everybody's had their go-in we'll write every single thing down in the Golden Deed book, and we'll draw two lines in red ink at the bottom, like Father does at the end of an account. And after that, if anyone wants to be good they can jolly well be good on our own, if at all.'

The ones who had made the Society did not welcome this wise idea, but Dicky and Oswald were firm.

So they had to agree. When Oswald is really firm, opposingness and obstinacy have to give way.

Dora said, 'It would be a noble action to have all the school-children from the village and give them tea and games in the paddock. They would think it so nice and good of us.'

But Dicky showed her that this would not be OUR good act, but Father's, because he would have to pay for the tea, and he had already stood us the keepsakes for the soldiers, as well as having to stump up heavily over the coal barge. And it is in vain being noble and generous when someone else is paying for it all the time, even if it happens to be your father. Then three others had ideas at the same time and began to explain what they were.

We were all in the dining-room, and perhaps we were making a bit of a row. Anyhow, Oswald for one, does not blame Albert's uncle for opening his door and saying—

'I suppose I must not ask for complete silence. That were too much. But if you could whistle, or stamp with your feet, or shriek or howl—anything to vary the monotony of your well-sustained conversation.'

Oswald said kindly, 'We're awfully sorry. Are you busy?'

'Busy?' said Albert's uncle. 'My heroine is now hesitating on the verge of an act which, for good or ill, must influence her whole subsequent career. You wouldn't like her to decide in the middle of such a row that she can't hear herself think?'

We said, 'No, we wouldn't.'

Then he said, 'If any outdoor amusement should commend itself to you this bright mid-summer day.' So we all went out.

Then Daisy whispered to Dora—they always hang together. Daisy is not nearly so white-micey as she was at first, but she still seems to fear the deadly ordeal of public speaking. Dora said—

'Daisy's idea is a game that'll take us all day. She thinks keeping out of the way when he's making his heroine decide right would be a noble act, and fit to write in the Golden Book; and we might as well be playing something at the same time.'

We all said 'Yes, but what?'

There was a silent interval.

'Speak up, Daisy, my child.' Oswald said; 'fear not to lay bare the utmost thoughts of that faithful heart.'

Daisy giggled. Our own girls never giggle—they laugh right out or hold their tongues. Their kind brothers have taught them this. Then Daisy said—

'If we could have a sort of play to keep us out of the way. I once read a story about an animal race. Everybody had an animal, and they had to go how they liked, and the one that got in first got the prize. There was a tortoise in it, and a rabbit, and a peacock, and sheep, and dogs, and a kitten.'

This proposal left us cold, as Albert's uncle says, because we knew there could not be any prize worth bothering about. And though you may be ever ready and willing to do anything for nothing, yet if there's going to be a prize there must BE a prize and there's an end of it.

Thus the idea was not followed up. Dicky yawned and said, 'Let's go into the barn and make a fort.'

So we did, with straw. It does not hurt straw to be messed about with like it does hay.

The downstairs—I mean down-ladder—part of the barn was fun too, especially for Pincher. There was as good ratting there as you could wish to see. Martha tried it, but she could not help running kindly beside the rat, as if she was in double harness with it. This is the noble bull-dog's gentle and affectionate nature coming out. We all enjoyed the ratting that day, but it ended, as usual, in the girls crying because of the poor rats. Girls cannot help this; we must not be waxy with them on account of it, they have their nature, the same as bull-dogs have, and it is this that makes them so useful in smoothing the pillows of the sick-bed and tending wounded heroes.

However, the forts, and Pincher, and the girls crying, and having to be thumped on the back, passed the time very agreeably till dinner. There was roast mutton with onion sauce, and a roly-poly pudding.

Albert's uncle said we had certainly effaced ourselves effectually, which means we hadn't bothered.

So we determined to do the same during the afternoon, for he told us his heroine was by no means out of the wood yet.

And at first it was easy. Jam roly gives you a peaceful feeling and you do not at first care if you never play any runabout game ever any more. But after a while the torpor begins to pass away. Oswald was the first to recover from his.

He had been lying on his front part in the orchard, but now he turned over on his back and kicked his legs up, and said—

'I say, look here; let's do something.'

Daisy looked thoughtful. She was chewing the soft yellow parts of grass, but I could see she was still thinking about that animal race. So I explained to her that it would be very poor fun without a tortoise and a peacock, and she saw this, though not willingly.

It was H. O. who said—

'Doing anything with animals is prime, if they only will. Let's have a circus!'

At the word the last thought of the pudding faded from Oswald's memory, and he stretched himself, sat up, and said—

'Bully for H. O. Let's!'

The others also threw off the heavy weight of memory, and sat up and said 'Let's!' too.

Never, never in all our lives had we had such a gay galaxy of animals at our command. The rabbits and the guinea-pigs, and even all the bright, glass-eyed, stuffed denizens of our late-lamented jungle paled into insignificance before the number of live things on the farm.

(I hope you do not think that the words I use are getting too long. I know they are the right words. And Albert's uncle says your style is always altered a bit by what you read. And I have been reading the Vicomte de Bragelonne. Nearly all my new words come out of those.)

'The worst of a circus is,' Dora said, 'that you've got to teach the animals things. A circus where the performing creatures hadn't learned performing would be a bit silly. Let's give up a week to teaching them and then have the circus.'

Some people have no idea of the value of time. And Dora is one of those who do not understand that when you want to do a thing you do want to, and not to do something else, and perhaps your own thing, a week later.

Oswald said the first thing was to collect the performing animals.

'Then perhaps,' he said, 'we may find that they have hidden talents hitherto unsuspected by their harsh masters.'

So Denny took a pencil and wrote a list of the animals required. This is it:

LIST OF ANIMALS REQUISITE FOR THE
CIRCUS WE ARE GOING TO HAVE

1 Bull for bull-fight. 1 Horse for ditto (if possible). 1 Goat to do Alpine feats of daring. 1 Donkey to play see-saw. 2 White pigs—one to be Learned, and the other to play with the clown. Turkeys, as many as possible, because they can make a noise that sounds like an audience applauding. The dogs, for any odd parts. 1 Large black pig—to be the Elephant in the procession. Calves (several) to be camels, and to stand on tubs.

Daisy ought to have been captain because it was partly her idea, but she let Oswald be, because she is of a retiring character. Oswald said—

'The first thing is to get all the creatures together; the paddock at the side of the orchard is the very place, because the hedge is good all round. When we've got the performers all there we'll make a programme, and then dress for our parts. It's a pity there won't be any audience but the turkeys.'

We took the animals in their right order, according to Denny's list. The bull was the first. He is black. He does not live in the cowhouse with the other horned people; he has a house all to himself two fields away. Oswald and Alice went to fetch him. They took a halter to lead the bull by, and a whip, not to hurt the bull with, but just to make him mind.

The others were to try to get one of the horses while we were gone.

Oswald as usual was full of bright ideas.

'I daresay,' he said, 'the bull will be shy at first, and he'll have to be goaded into the arena.'

'But goads hurt,' Alice said.

'They don't hurt the bull,' Oswald said; 'his powerful hide is too thick.'

'Then why does he attend to it,' Alice asked, 'if it doesn't hurt?'

'Properly-brought-up bulls attend because they know they ought,' Oswald said. 'I think I shall ride the bull,' the brave boy went on. 'A bull-fight, where an intrepid rider appears on the bull, sharing its joys and sorrows. It would be something quite new.'

'You can't ride bulls,' Alice said; 'at least, not if their backs are sharp like cows.'

But Oswald thought he could. The bull lives in a house made of wood and prickly furze bushes, and he has a yard to his house. You cannot climb on the roof of his house at all comfortably.

When we got there he was half in his house and half out in his yard, and he was swinging his tail because of the flies which bothered. It was a very hot day.

'You'll see,' Alice said, 'he won't want a goad. He'll be so glad to get out for a walk he'll drop his head in my hand like a tame fawn, and follow me lovingly all the way.'

Oswald called to him. He said, 'Bull! Bull! Bull! Bull!' because we did not know the animal's real name. The bull took no notice; then Oswald picked up a stone and threw it at the bull, not angrily, but just to make it pay attention. But the bull did not pay a farthing's worth of it. So then Oswald leaned over the iron gate of the bull's yard and just flicked the bull with the whiplash. And then the bull DID pay attention. He started when the lash struck him, then suddenly he faced round, uttering a roar like that of the wounded King of Beasts, and putting his head down close to his feet he ran straight at the iron gate where we were standing.

Alice and Oswald mechanically turned away; they did not wish to annoy the bull any more, and they ran as fast as they could across the field so as not to keep the others waiting.

As they ran across the field Oswald had a dream-like fancy that perhaps the bull had rooted up the gate with one paralysing blow, and was now tearing across the field after him and Alice, with the broken gate balanced on its horns. We climbed the stile quickly and looked back; the bull was still on the right side of the gate.

Oswald said, 'I think we'll do without the bull. He did not seem to want to come. We must be kind to dumb animals.'

Alice said, between laughing and crying—

'Oh, Oswald, how can you!' But we did do without the bull, and we did not tell the others how we had hurried to get back. We just said, 'The bull didn't seem to care about coming.'

The others had not been idle. They had got old Clover, the cart-horse, but she would do nothing but graze, so we decided not to use her in the bull-fight, but to let her be the Elephant. The Elephant's is a nice quiet part, and she was quite big enough for a young one. Then the black pig could be Learned, and the other two could be something else. They had also got the goat; he was tethered to a young tree.

The donkey was there. Denny was leading him in the halter. The dogs were there, of course—they always are.

So now we only had to get the turkeys for the applause and the calves and pigs.

The calves were easy to get, because they were in their own house. There were five. And the pigs were in their houses too. We got them out after long and patient toil, and persuaded them that they wanted to go into the paddock, where the circus was to be. This is done by pretending to drive them the other way. A pig only knows two ways—the way you want him to go, and the other. But the turkeys knew thousands of different ways, and tried them all. They made such an awful row, we had to drop all ideas of ever hearing applause from their lips, so we came away and left them.

'Never mind,' H. O. said, 'they'll be sorry enough afterwards, nasty, unobliging things, because now they won't see the circus. I hope the other animals will tell them about it.'

While the turkeys were engaged in baffling the rest of us, Dicky had found three sheep who seemed to wish to join the glad throng, so we let them.

Then we shut the gate of the paddock, and left the dumb circus performers to make friends with each other while we dressed.

Oswald and H. O. were to be clowns. It is quite easy with Albert's uncle's pyjamas, and flour on your hair and face, and the red they do the brick-floors with.

Alice had very short pink and white skirts, and roses in her hair and round her dress. Her dress was the pink calico and white muslin stuff off the dressing-table in the girls' room fastened with pins and tied round the waist with a small bath towel. She was to be the Dauntless Equestrienne, and to give her enhancing act a barebacked daring, riding either a pig or a sheep, whichever we found was freshest and most skittish. Dora was dressed for the Haute ecole, which means a riding-habit and a high hat. She took Dick's topper that he wears with his Etons, and a skirt of Mrs Pettigrew's. Daisy, dressed the same as Alice, taking the muslin from Mrs Pettigrew's dressing-table without saying anything beforehand. None of us would have advised this, and indeed we were thinking of trying to put it back, when Denny and Noel, who were wishing to look like highwaymen, with brown-paper top-boots and slouch hats and Turkish towel cloaks, suddenly stopped dressing and gazed out of the window.

'Krikey!' said Dick, 'come on, Oswald!' and he bounded like an antelope from the room.

Oswald and the rest followed, casting a hasty glance through the window. Noel had got brown-paper boots too, and a Turkish towel cloak. H. O. had been waiting for Dora to dress him up for the other clown. He had only his shirt and knickerbockers and his braces on. He came down as he was—as indeed we all did. And no wonder, for in the paddock, where the circus was to be, a blood-thrilling thing had transpired. The dogs were chasing the sheep. And we had now lived long enough in the country to know the fell nature of our dogs' improper conduct.

We all rushed into the paddock, calling to Pincher, and Martha, and Lady. Pincher came almost at once. He is a well-brought-up dog—Oswald trained him. Martha did not seem to hear. She is awfully deaf, but she did not matter so much, because the sheep could walk away from her easily. She has no pace and no wind. But Lady is a deer-hound. She is used to pursuing that fleet and antlered pride of the forest—the stag—and she can go like billyo. She was now far away in a distant region of the paddock, with a fat sheep just before her in full flight. I am sure if ever anybody's eyes did start out of their heads with horror, like in narratives of adventure, ours did then.

There was a moment's pause of speechless horror. We expected to see Lady pull down her quarry, and we know what a lot of money a sheep costs, to say nothing of its own personal feelings.

Then we started to run for all we were worth. It is hard to run swiftly as the arrow from the bow when you happen to be wearing pyjamas belonging to a grown-up person—as I was—but even so I beat Dicky. He said afterwards it was because his brown-paper boots came undone and tripped him up. Alice came in third. She held on the dressing-table muslin and ran jolly well. But ere we reached the fatal spot all was very nearly up with the sheep. We heard a plop; Lady stopped and looked round. She must have heard us bellowing to her as we ran. Then she came towards us, prancing with happiness, but we said 'Down!' and 'Bad dog!' and ran sternly on.

When we came to the brook which forms the northern boundary of the paddock we saw the sheep struggling in the water. It is not very deep, and I believe the sheep could have stood up, and been well in its depth, if it had liked, but it would not try.

It was a steepish bank. Alice and I got down and stuck our legs into the water, and then Dicky came down, and the three of us hauled that sheep up by its shoulders till it could rest on Alice and me as we sat on the bank. It kicked all the time we were hauling. It gave one extra kick at last, that raised it up, and I tell you that sopping wet, heavy, panting, silly donkey of a sheep sat there on our laps like a pet dog; and Dicky got his shoulder under it at the back and heaved constantly to keep it from flumping off into the water again, while the others fetched the shepherd.

When the shepherd came he called us every name you can think of, and then he said—

'Good thing master didn't come along. He would ha' called you some tidy names.'

He got the sheep out, and took it and the others away. And the calves too. He did not seem to care about the other performing animals.

Alice, Oswald and Dick had had almost enough circus for just then, so we sat in the sun and dried ourselves and wrote the programme of the circus. This was it:

PROGRAMME

1. Startling leap from the lofty precipice by the performing sheep. Real water, and real precipice. The gallant rescue. O. A. and D. Bastable. (We thought we might as well put that in though it was over and had happened accidentally.)

2. Graceful bare-backed equestrienne act on the trained pig, Eliza. A. Bastable. 3. Amusing clown interlude, introducing trained dog, Pincher, and the other white pig. H. O. and O. Bastable.

4. The See-Saw. Trained donkeys. (H. O. said we had only one donkey, so Dicky said H. O. could be the other. When peace was restored we went on to 5.)

5. Elegant equestrian act by D. Bastable. Haute ecole, on Clover, the incomparative trained elephant from the plains of Venezuela.

6. Alpine feat of daring. The climbing of the Andes, by Billy, the well-known acrobatic goat. (We thought we could make the Andes out of hurdles and things, and so we could have but for what always happens. (This is the unexpected. (This is a saying Father told me—but I see I am three deep in brackets so I will close them before I get into any more).).).

7. The Black but Learned Pig. ('I daresay he knows something,' Alice said, 'if we can only find out what.' We DID find out all too soon.)

We could not think of anything else, and our things were nearly dry—all except Dick's brown-paper top-boots, which were mingled with the gurgling waters of the brook.

We went back to the seat of action—which was the iron trough where the sheep have their salt put—and began to dress up the creatures.

We had just tied the Union Jack we made out of Daisy's flannel petticoat and cetera, when we gave the soldiers the baccy, round the waist of the Black and Learned Pig, when we heard screams from the back part of the house, and suddenly we saw that Billy, the acrobatic goat, had got loose from the tree we had tied him to. (He had eaten all the parts of its bark that he could get at, but we did not notice it until next day, when led to the spot by a grown-up.)

The gate of the paddock was open. The gate leading to the bridge that goes over the moat to the back door was open too. We hastily proceeded in the direction of the screams, and, guided by the sound, threaded our way into the kitchen. As we went, Noel, ever fertile in melancholy ideas, said he wondered whether Mrs Pettigrew was being robbed, or only murdered.

In the kitchen we saw that Noel was wrong as usual. It was neither. Mrs Pettigrew, screaming like a steam-siren and waving a broom, occupied the foreground. In the distance the maid was shrieking in a hoarse and monotonous way, and trying to shut herself up inside a clothes-horse on which washing was being aired.

On the dresser—which he had ascended by a chair—was Billy, the acrobatic goat, doing his Alpine daring act. He had found out his Andes for himself, and even as we gazed he turned and tossed his head in a way that showed us some mysterious purpose was hidden beneath his calm exterior. The next moment he put his off-horn neatly behind the end plate of the next to the bottom row, and ran it along against the wall. The plates fell crashing on to the soup tureen and vegetable dishes which adorned the lower range of the Andes.

Mrs Pettigrew's screams were almost drowned in the discarding crash and crackle of the falling avalanche of crockery.

Oswald, though stricken with horror and polite regret, preserved the most dauntless coolness.

Disregarding the mop which Mrs Pettigrew kept on poking at the goat in a timid yet cross way, he sprang forward, crying out to his trusty followers, 'Stand by to catch him!'

But Dick had thought of the same thing, and ere Oswald could carry out his long-cherished and general-like design, Dicky had caught the goat's legs and tripped it up. The goat fell against another row of plates, righted itself hastily in the gloomy ruins of the soup tureen and the sauce-boats, and then fell again, this time towards Dicky. The two fell heavily on the ground together. The trusty followers had been so struck by the daring of Dicky and his lion-hearted brother, that they had not stood by to catch anything.

The goat was not hurt, but Dicky had a sprained thumb and a lump on his head like a black marble door-knob. He had to go to bed.

I will draw a veil and asterisks over what Mrs Pettigrew said. Also Albert's uncle, who was brought to the scene of ruin by her screams. Few words escaped our lips. There are times when it is not wise to argue; however, little what has occurred is really our fault.

When they had said what they deemed enough and we were let go, we all went out. Then Alice said distractedly, in a voice which she vainly strove to render firm—

'Let's give up the circus. Let's put the toys back in the boxes—no, I don't mean that—the creatures in their places—and drop the whole thing. I want to go and read to Dicky.'

Oswald has a spirit that no reverses can depreciate. He hates to be beaten. But he gave in to Alice, as the others said so too, and we went out to collect the performing troop and sort it out into its proper places.

Alas! we came too late. In the interest we had felt about whether Mrs Pettigrew was the abject victim of burglars or not, we had left both gates open again. The old horse—I mean the trained elephant from Venezuela—was there all right enough. The dogs we had beaten and tied up after the first act, when the intrepid sheep bounded, as it says in the programme. The two white pigs were there, but the donkey was gone. We heard his hoofs down the road, growing fainter and fainter, in the direction of the 'Rose and Crown'. And just round the gatepost we saw a flash of red and white and blue and black that told us, with dumb signification, that the pig was off in exactly the opposite direction. Why couldn't they have gone the same way? But no, one was a pig and the other was a donkey, as Denny said afterwards.

Daisy and H. O. started after the donkey; the rest of us, with one accord, pursued the pig—I don't know why. It trotted quietly down the road; it looked very black against the white road, and the ends on the top, where the Union Jack was tied, bobbed brightly as it trotted. At first we thought it would be easy to catch up to it. This was an error.

When we ran faster it ran faster; when we stopped it stopped and looked round at us, and nodded. (I daresay you won't swallow this, but you may safely. It's as true as true, and so's all that about the goat. I give you my sacred word of honour.) I tell you the pig nodded as much as to say—

'Oh, yes. You think you will, but you won't!' and then as soon as we moved again off it went. That pig led us on and on, o'er miles and miles of strange country. One thing, it did keep to the roads. When we met people, which wasn't often, we called out to them to help us, but they only waved their arms and roared with laughter. One chap on a bicycle almost tumbled off his machine, and then he got off it and propped it against a gate and sat down in the hedge to laugh properly. You remember Alice was still dressed up as the gay equestrienne in the dressing-table pink and white, with rosy garlands, now very droopy, and she had no stockings on, only white sand-shoes, because she thought they would be easier than boots for balancing on the pig in the graceful bare-backed act.

Oswald was attired in red paint and flour and pyjamas, for a clown. It is really IMPOSSIBLE to run speedfully in another man's pyjamas, so Oswald had taken them off, and wore his own brown knickerbockers belonging to his Norfolks. He had tied the pyjamas round his neck, to carry them easily. He was afraid to leave them in a ditch, as Alice suggested, because he did not know the roads, and for aught he recked they might have been infested with footpads. If it had been his own pyjamas it would have been different. (I'm going to ask for pyjamas next winter, they are so useful in many ways.)

Noel was a highwayman in brown-paper gaiters and bath towels and a cocked hat of newspaper. I don't know how he kept it on. And the pig was encircled by the dauntless banner of our country. All the same, I think if I had seen a band of youthful travellers in bitter distress about a pig I should have tried to lend a helping hand and not sat roaring in the hedge, no matter how the travellers and the pig might have been dressed.

It was hotter than anyone would believe who has never had occasion to hunt the pig when dressed for quite another part. The flour got out of Oswald's hair into his eyes and his mouth. His brow was wet with what the village blacksmith's was wet with, and not his fair brow alone. It ran down his face and washed the red off in streaks, and when he rubbed his eyes he only made it worse. Alice had to run holding the equestrienne skirts on with both hands, and I think the brown-paper boots bothered Noel from the first. Dora had her skirt over her arm and carried the topper in her hand. It was no use to tell ourselves it was a wild boar hunt—we were long past that.

At last we met a man who took pity on us. He was a kind-hearted man. I think, perhaps, he had a pig of his own—or, perhaps, children. Honour to his name!

He stood in the middle of the road and waved his arms. The pig right-wheeled through a gate into a private garden and cantered up the drive. We followed. What else were we to do, I should like to know?

The Learned Black Pig seemed to know its way. It turned first to the right and then to the left, and emerged on a lawn.

'Now, all together!' cried Oswald, mustering his failing voice to give the word of command. 'Surround him!—cut off his retreat!'

We almost surrounded him. He edged off towards the house.

'Now we've got him!' cried the crafty Oswald, as the pig got on to a bed of yellow pansies close against the red house wall.

All would even then have been well, but Denny, at the last, shrank from meeting the pig face to face in a manly way. He let the pig pass him, and the next moment, with a squeak that said 'There now!' as plain as words, the pig bolted into a French window. The pursuers halted not. This was no time for trivial ceremony. In another moment the pig was a captive. Alice and Oswald had their arms round him under the ruins of a table that had had teacups on it, and around the hunters and their prey stood the startled members of a parish society for making clothes for the poor heathen, that that pig had led us into the very midst of. They were reading a missionary report or something when we ran our quarry to earth under their table. Even as he crossed the threshold I heard something about 'black brothers being already white to the harvest'. All the ladies had been sewing flannel things for the poor blacks while the curate read aloud to them. You think they screamed when they saw the Pig and Us? You are right.

On the whole, I cannot say that the missionary people behaved badly. Oswald explained that it was entirely the pig's doing, and asked pardon quite properly for any alarm the ladies had felt; and Alice said how sorry we were but really it was NOT our fault this time. The curate looked a bit nasty, but the presence of ladies made him keep his hot blood to himself.

When we had explained, we said, 'Might we go?' The curate said, 'The sooner the better.' But the Lady of the House asked for our names and addresses, and said she should write to our Father. (She did, and we heard of it too.) They did not do anything to us, as Oswald at one time believed to be the curate's idea. They let us go.

And we went, after we had asked for a piece of rope to lead the pig by.

'In case it should come back into your nice room,' Alice said. 'And that would be such a pity, wouldn't it?'

A little girl in a starched pinafore was sent for the rope. And as soon as the pig had agreed to let us tie it round his neck we came away. The scene in the drawing-room had not been long. The pig went slowly,

'Like the meandering brook,' Denny said. Just by the gate the shrubs rustled and opened, and the little girl came out. Her pinafore was full of cake.

'Here,' she said. 'You must be hungry if you've come all that way. I think they might have given you some tea after all the trouble you've had.' We took the cake with correct thanks.

'I wish I could play at circuses,' she said. 'Tell me about it.'

We told her while we ate the cake; and when we had done she said perhaps it was better to hear about than do, especially the goat's part and Dicky's.

'But I do wish auntie had given you tea,' she said.

We told her not to be too hard on her aunt, because you have to make allowances for grown-up people. When we parted she said she would never forget us, and Oswald gave her his pocket button-hook and corkscrew combined for a keepsake.

Dicky's act with the goat (which is true, and no kid) was the only thing out of that day that was put in the Golden Deed book, and he put that in himself while we were hunting the pig.

Alice and me capturing the pig was never put in. We would scorn to write our own good actions, but I suppose Dicky was dull with us all away; and you must pity the dull, and not blame them.

I will not seek to unfold to you how we got the pig home, or how the donkey was caught (that was poor sport compared to the pig). Nor will I tell you a word of all that was said and done to the intrepid hunters of the Black and Learned. I have told you all the interesting part. Seek not to know the rest. It is better buried in obliquity.

Chapter 7. Being Beavers; or, The Young Explorers (Arctic or Otherwise)

You read in books about the pleasures of London, and about how people who live in the country long for the gay whirl of fashion in town because the country is so dull. I do not agree with this at all. In London, or at any rate Lewisham, nothing happens unless you make it happen; or if it happens it doesn't happen to you, and you don't know the people it does happen to. But in the country the most interesting events occur quite freely, and they seem to happen to you as much as to anyone else. Very often quite without your doing anything to help.

The natural and right ways of earning your living in the country are much jollier than town ones, too; sowing and reaping, and doing things with animals, are much better sport than fishmongering or bakering or oil-shopping, and those sort of things, except, of course, a plumber's and gasfitter's, and he is the same in town or country—most interesting and like an engineer.

I remember what a nice man it was that came to cut the gas off once at our old house in Lewisham, when my father's business was feeling so poorly. He was a true gentleman, and gave Oswald and Dicky over two yards and a quarter of good lead piping, and a brass tap that only wanted a washer, and a whole handful of screws to do what we liked with. We screwed the back door up with the screws, I remember, one night when Eliza was out without leave. There was an awful row. We did not mean to get her into trouble. We only thought it would be amusing for her to find the door screwed up when she came down to take in the milk in the morning. But I must not say any more about the Lewisham house. It is only the pleasures of memory, and nothing to do with being beavers, or any sort of exploring.

I think Dora and Daisy are the kind of girls who will grow up very good, and perhaps marry missionaries. I am glad Oswald's destiny looks at present as if it might be different.

We made two expeditions to discover the source of the Nile (or the North Pole), and owing to their habit of sticking together and doing dull and praiseable things, like sewing, and helping with the cooking, and taking invalid delicacies to the poor and indignant, Daisy and Dora were wholly out of it both times, though Dora's foot was now quite well enough to have gone to the North Pole or the Equator either. They said they did not mind the first time, because they like to keep themselves clean; it is another of their queer ways. And they said they had had a better time than us. (It was only a clergyman and his wife who called, and hot cakes for tea.) The second time they said they were lucky not to have been in it. And perhaps they were right. But let me to my narrating. I hope you will like it. I am going to try to write it a different way, like the books they give you for a prize at a girls' school—I mean a 'young ladies' school', of course—not a high school. High schools are not nearly so silly as some other kinds. Here goes:

'"Ah, me!" sighed a slender maiden of twelve summers, removing her elegant hat and passing her tapery fingers lightly through her fair tresses, "how sad it is—is it not?—to see able-bodied youths and young ladies wasting the precious summer hours in idleness and luxury."

'The maiden frowned reproachingly, but yet with earnest gentleness, at the group of youths and maidens who sat beneath an umbragipeaous beech tree and ate black currants.

'"Dear brothers and sisters," the blushing girl went on, "could we not, even now, at the eleventh hour, turn to account these wasted lives of ours, and seek some occupation at once improving and agreeable?"

'"I do not quite follow your meaning, dear sister," replied the cleverest of her brothers, on whose brow—'

It's no use. I can't write like these books. I wonder how the books' authors can keep it up.

What really happened was that we were all eating black currants in the orchard, out of a cabbage leaf, and Alice said—

'I say, look here, let's do something. It's simply silly to waste a day like this. It's just on eleven. Come on!'

And Oswald said, 'Where to?'

This was the beginning of it.

The moat that is all round our house is fed by streams. One of them is a sort of open overflow pipe from a good-sized stream that flows at the other side of the orchard.

It was this stream that Alice meant when she said—

'Why not go and discover the source of the Nile?'

Of course Oswald knows quite well that the source of the real live Egyptian Nile is no longer buried in that mysteriousness where it lurked undisturbed for such a long time. But he was not going to say so. It is a great thing to know when not to say things.

'Why not have it an Arctic expedition?' said Dicky; 'then we could take an ice-axe, and live on blubber and things. Besides, it sounds cooler.'

'Vote! vote!' cried Oswald. So we did. Oswald, Alice, Noel, and Denny voted for the river of the ibis and the crocodile. Dicky, H. O., and the other girls for the region of perennial winter and rich blubber.

So Alice said, 'We can decide as we go. Let's start anyway.'

The question of supplies had now to be gone into. Everybody wanted to take something different, and nobody thought the other people's things would be the slightest use. It is sometimes thus even with grown-up expeditions. So then Oswald, who is equal to the hardest emergency that ever emerged yet, said—

'Let's each get what we like. The secret storehouse can be the shed in the corner of the stableyard where we got the door for the raft. Then the captain can decide who's to take what.'

This was done. You may think it but the work of a moment to fit out an expedition, but this is not so, especially when you know not whether your exploring party is speeding to Central Africa or merely to the world of icebergs and the Polar bear.

Dicky wished to take the wood-axe, the coal hammer, a blanket, and a mackintosh.

H. O. brought a large faggot in case we had to light fires, and a pair of old skates he had happened to notice in the box-room, in case the expedition turned out icy.

Noel had nicked a dozen boxes of matches, a spade, and a trowel, and had also obtained—I know not by what means—a jar of pickled onions.

Denny had a walking-stick—we can't break him of walking with it—a book to read in case he got tired of being a discoverer, a butterfly net and a box with a cork in it, a tennis ball, if we happened to want to play rounders in the pauses of exploring, two towels and an umbrella in the event of camping or if the river got big enough to bathe in or to be fallen into.

Alice had a comforter for Noel in case we got late, a pair of scissors and needle and cotton, two whole candles in case of caves.

And she had thoughtfully brought the tablecloth off the small table in the dining-room, so that we could make all the things up into one bundle and take it in turns to carry it.

Oswald had fastened his master mind entirely on grub. Nor had the others neglected this.

All the stores for the expedition were put down on the tablecloth and the corners tied up. Then it was more than even Oswald's muscley arms could raise from the ground, so we decided not to take it, but only the best-selected grub. The rest we hid in the straw loft, for there are many ups and downs in life, and grub is grub at any time, and so are stores of all kinds. The pickled onions we had to leave, but not for ever.

Then Dora and Daisy came along with their arms round each other's necks as usual, like a picture on a grocer's almanac, and said they weren't coming.

It was, as I have said, a blazing hot day, and there were differences of opinion among the explorers about what eatables we ought to have taken, and H. O. had lost one of his garters and wouldn't let Alice tie it up with her handkerchief, which the gentle sister was quite willing to do. So it was a rather gloomy expedition that set off that bright sunny day to seek the source of the river where Cleopatra sailed in Shakespeare (or the frozen plains Mr Nansen wrote that big book about).

But the balmy calm of peaceful Nature soon made the others less cross—Oswald had not been cross exactly but only disinclined to do anything the others wanted—and by the time we had followed the stream a little way, and had seen a water-rat and shied a stone or two at him, harmony was restored. We did not hit the rat.

You will understand that we were not the sort of people to have lived so long near a stream without plumbing its depths. Indeed it was the same stream the sheep took its daring jump into the day we had the circus. And of course we had often paddled in it—in the shallower parts. But now our hearts were set on exploring. At least they ought to have been, but when we got to the place where the stream goes under a wooden sheep-bridge, Dicky cried, 'A camp! a camp!' and we were all glad to sit down at once. Not at all like real explorers, who know no rest, day or night, till they have got there (whether it's the North Pole, or the central point of the part marked 'Desert of Sahara' on old-fashioned maps).

The food supplies obtained by various members were good and plenty of it. Cake, hard eggs, sausage-rolls, currants, lemon cheese-cakes, raisins, and cold apple dumplings. It was all very decent, but Oswald could not help feeling that the source of the Nile (or North Pole) was a long way off, and perhaps nothing much when you got there.

So he was not wholly displeased when Denny said, as he lay kicking into the bank when the things to eat were all gone—

'I believe this is clay: did you ever make huge platters and bowls out of clay and dry them in the sun? Some people did in a book called Foul Play, and I believe they baked turtles, or oysters, or something, at the same time.'

He took up a bit of clay and began to mess it about, like you do putty when you get hold of a bit. And at once the heavy gloom that had hung over the explorers became expelled, and we all got under the shadow of the bridge and messed about with clay.

'It will be jolly!' Alice said, 'and we can give the huge platters to poor cottagers who are short of the usual sorts of crockery. That would really be a very golden deed.'

It is harder than you would think when you read about it, to make huge platters with clay. It flops about as soon as you get it any size, unless you keep it much too thick, and then when you turn up the edges they crack. Yet we did not mind the trouble. And we had all got our shoes and stockings off. It is impossible to go on being cross when your feet are in cold water; and there is something in the smooth messiness of clay, and not minding how dirty you get, that would soothe the savagest breast that ever beat.

After a bit, though, we gave up the idea of the huge platter and tried little things. We made some platters—they were like flower-pot saucers; and Alice made a bowl by doubling up her fists and getting Noel to slab the clay on outside. Then they smoothed the thing inside and out with wet fingers, and it was a bowl—at least they said it was. When we'd made a lot of things we set them in the sun to dry, and then it seemed a pity not to do the thing thoroughly. So we made a bonfire, and when it had burnt down we put our pots on the soft, white, hot ashes among the little red sparks, and kicked the ashes over them and heaped more fuel over the top. It was a fine fire.

Then tea-time seemed as if it ought to be near, and we decided to come back next day and get our pots.

As we went home across the fields Dicky looked back and said—

'The bonfire's going pretty strong.'

We looked. It was. Great flames were rising to heaven against the evening sky. And we had left it,a smouldering flat heap.

'The clay must have caught alight,' H. O. said. 'Perhaps it's the kind that burns. I know I've heard of fireclay. And there's another sort you can eat.'

'Oh, shut up!' Dicky said with anxious scorn.

With one accord we turned back. We all felt THE feeling—the one that means something fatal being up and it being your fault.

'Perhaps, Alice said, 'a beautiful young lady in a muslin dress was passing by, and a spark flew on to her, and now she is rolling in agony enveloped in flames.'

We could not see the fire now, because of the corner of the wood, but we hoped Alice was mistaken.

But when we got in sight of the scene of our pottering industry we saw it was as bad nearly as Alice's wild dream. For the wooden fence leading up to the bridge had caught fire, and it was burning like billy oh.

Oswald started to run; so did the others. As he ran he said to himself, 'This is no time to think about your clothes. Oswald, be bold!'

And he was.

Arrived at the site of the conflagration, he saw that caps or straw hats full of water, however quickly and perseveringly given, would never put the bridge out, and his eventful past life made him know exactly the sort of wigging you get for an accident like this.

So he said, 'Dicky, soak your jacket and mine in the stream and chuck them along. Alice, stand clear, or your silly girl's clothes'll catch as sure as fate.'

Dicky and Oswald tore off their jackets, so did Denny, but we would not let him and H. O. wet theirs. Then the brave Oswald advanced warily to the end of the burning rails and put his wet jacket over the end bit, like a linseed poultice on the throat of a suffering invalid who has got bronchitis. The burning wood hissed and smouldered, and Oswald fell back, almost choked with the smoke. But at once he caught up the other wet jacket and put it on another place, and of course it did the trick as he had known it would do. But it was a long job, and the smoke in his eyes made the young hero obliged to let Dicky and Denny take a turn as they had bothered to do from the first. At last all was safe; the devouring element was conquered. We covered up the beastly bonfire with clay to keep it from getting into mischief again, and then Alice said—

'Now we must go and tell.'

'Of course,' Oswald said shortly. He had meant to tell all the time.

So we went to the farmer who has the Moat House Farm, and we went at once, because if you have any news like that to tell it only makes it worse if you wait about. When we had told him he said—

'You little —-.' I shall not say what he said besides that, because I am sure he must have been sorry for it next Sunday when he went to church, if not before.

We did not take any notice of what he said, but just kept on saying how sorry we were; and he did not take our apology like a man, but only said he daresayed, just like a woman does. Then he went to look at his bridge, and we went in to our tea. The jackets were never quite the same again.

Really great explorers would never be discouraged by the daresaying of a farmer, still less by his calling them names he ought not to. Albert's uncle was away so we got no double slating; and next day we started again to discover the source of the river of cataracts (or the region of mountain-like icebergs).

We set out, heavily provisioned with a large cake Daisy and Dora had made themselves, and six bottles of ginger-beer. I think real explorers most likely have their ginger-beer in something lighter to carry than stone bottles. Perhaps they have it by the cask, which would come cheaper; and you could make the girls carry it on their back, like in pictures of the daughters of regiments.

We passed the scene of the devouring conflagration, and the thought of the fire made us so thirsty we decided to drink the ginger-beer and leave the bottles in a place of concealment. Then we went on, determined to reach our destination, Tropic or Polar, that day.

Denny and H. O. wanted to stop and try to make a fashionable watering-place at that part where the stream spreads out like a small-sized sea, but Noel said, 'No.' We did not like fashionableness.

'YOU ought to, at any rate,' Denny said. 'A Mr Collins wrote an Ode to the Fashions, and he was a great poet.'

'The poet Milton wrote a long book about Satan,' Noel said, 'but I'm not bound to like HIM.' I think it was smart of Noel.

'People aren't obliged to like everything they write about even, let alone read,' Alice said. 'Look at "Ruin seize thee, ruthless king!" and all the pieces of poetry about war, and tyrants, and slaughtered saints—and the one you made yourself about the black beetle, Noel.'

By this time we had got by the pondy place and the danger of delay was past; but the others went on talking about poetry for quite a field and a half, as we walked along by the banks of the stream. The stream was broad and shallow at this part, and you could see the stones and gravel at the bottom, and millions of baby fishes, and a sort of skating-spiders walking about on the top of the water. Denny said the water must be ice for them to be able to walk on it, and this showed we were getting near the North Pole. But Oswald had seen a kingfisher by the wood, and he said it was an ibis, so this was even.

When Oswald had had as much poetry as he could bear he said, 'Let's be beavers and make a dam.' And everybody was so hot they agreed joyously, and soon our clothes were tucked up as far as they could go and our legs looked green through the water, though they were pink out of it.

Making a dam is jolly good fun, though laborious, as books about beavers take care to let you know.

Dicky said it must be Canada if we were beavers, and so it was on the way to the Polar system, but Oswald pointed to his heated brow, and Dicky owned it was warm for Polar regions. He had brought the ice-axe (it is called the wood chopper sometimes), and Oswald, ever ready and able to command, set him and Denny to cut turfs from the bank while we heaped stones across the stream. It was clayey here, or of course dam making would have been vain, even for the best-trained beaver. When we had made a ridge of stones we laid turfs against them—nearly across the stream, leaving about two feet for the water to go through—then more stones, and then lumps of clay stamped down as hard as we could. The industrious beavers spent hours over it, with only one easy to eat cake in. And at last the dam rose to the level of the bank. Then the beavers collected a great heap of clay, and four of them lifted it and dumped it down in the opening where the water was running. It did splash a little, but a true-hearted beaver knows better than to mind a bit of a wetting, as Oswald told Alice at the time. Then with more clay the work was completed. We must have used tons of clay; there was quite a big long hole in the bank above the dam where we had taken it out.

When our beaver task was performed we went on, and Dicky was so hot he had to take his jacket off and shut up about icebergs.

I cannot tell you about all the windings of the stream; it went through fields and woods and meadows, and at last the banks got steeper and higher, and the trees overhead darkly arched their mysterious branches, and we felt like the princes in a fairy tale who go out to seek their fortunes.

And then we saw a thing that was well worth coming all that way for; the stream suddenly disappeared under a dark stone archway, and however much you stood in the water and stuck your head down between your knees you could not see any light at the other end.

The stream was much smaller than where we had been beavers.

Gentle reader, you will guess in a moment who it was that said—

'Alice, you've got a candle. Let's explore.' This gallant proposal met but a cold response. The others said they didn't care much about it, and what about tea?

I often think the way people try to hide their cowardliness behind their teas is simply beastly.

Oswald took no notice. He just said, with that dignified manner, not at all like sulking, which he knows so well how to put on—

'All right. I'M going. If you funk it you'd better cut along home and ask your nurses to put you to bed.' So then, of course, they agreed to go. Oswald went first with the candle. It was not comfortable; the architect of that dark subterranean passage had not imagined anyone would ever be brave enough to lead a band of beavers into its inky recesses, or he would have built it high enough to stand upright in. As it was, we were bent almost at a right angle, and this is very awkward if for long.

But the leader pressed dauntlessly on, and paid no attention to the groans of his faithful followers, nor to what they said about their backs.

It really was a very long tunnel, though, and even Oswald was not sorry to say, 'I see daylight.' The followers cheered as well as they could as they splashed after him. The floor was stone as well as the roof, so it was easy to walk on. I think the followers would have turned back if it had been sharp stones or gravel.

And now the spot of daylight at the end of the tunnel grew larger and larger, and presently the intrepid leader found himself blinking in the full sun, and the candle he carried looked simply silly. He emerged, and the others too, and they stretched their backs and the word 'krikey' fell from more than one lip. It had indeed been a cramping adventure. Bushes grew close to the mouth of the tunnel, so we could not see much landscape, and when we had stretched our backs we went on upstream and nobody said they'd had jolly well enough of it, though in more than one young heart this was thought.

It was jolly to be in the sunshine again. I never knew before how cold it was underground. The stream was getting smaller and smaller.

Dicky said, 'This can't be the way. I expect there was a turning to the North Pole inside the tunnel, only we missed it. It was cold enough there.'

But here a twist in the stream brought us out from the bushes, and Oswald said—

'Here is strange, wild, tropical vegetation in the richest profusion. Such blossoms as these never opened in a frigid what's-its-name.'

It was indeed true. We had come out into a sort of marshy, swampy place like I think, a jungle is, that the stream ran through, and it was simply crammed with queer plants, and flowers we never saw before or since. And the stream was quite thin. It was torridly hot, and softish to walk on. There were rushes and reeds and small willows, and it was all tangled over with different sorts of grasses—and pools here and there. We saw no wild beasts, but there were more different kinds of wild flies and beetles than you could believe anybody could bear, and dragon-flies and gnats. The girls picked a lot of flowers. I know the names of some of them, but I will not tell you them because this is not meant to be instructing. So I will only name meadow-sweet, yarrow, loose-strife, lady's bed-straw and willow herb—both the larger and the lesser.

Everyone now wished to go home. It was much hotter there than in natural fields. It made you want to tear all your clothes off and play at savages, instead of keeping respectable in your boots.

But we had to bear the boots because it was so brambly.

It was Oswald who showed the others how flat it would be to go home the same way we came; and he pointed out the telegraph wires in the distance and said—

'There must be a road there, let's make for it,' which was quite a simple and ordinary thing to say, and he does not ask for any credit for it. So we sloshed along, scratching our legs with the brambles, and the water squelched in our boots, and Alice's blue muslin frock was torn all over in those crisscross tears which are considered so hard to darn.

We did not follow the stream any more. It was only a trickle now, so we knew we had tracked it to its source. And we got hotter and hotter and hotter, and the dews of agony stood in beads on our brows and rolled down our noses and off our chins. And the flies buzzed, and the gnats stung, and Oswald bravely sought to keep up Dicky's courage, when he tripped on a snag and came down on a bramble bush, by saying—

'You see it IS the source of the Nile we've discovered. What price North Poles now?'

Alice said, 'Ah, but think of ices! I expect Oswald wishes it HAD been the Pole, anyway.'

Oswald is naturally the leader, especially when following up what is his own idea, but he knows that leaders have other duties besides just leading. One is to assist weak or wounded members of the expedition, whether Polar or Equatorish.

So the others had got a bit ahead through Oswald lending the tottering Denny a hand over the rough places. Denny's feet hurt him, because when he was a beaver his stockings had dropped out of his pocket, and boots without stockings are not a bed of luxuriousness. And he is often unlucky with his feet.

Presently we came to a pond, and Denny said—

'Let's paddle.'

Oswald likes Denny to have ideas; he knows it is healthy for the boy, and generally he backs him up, but just now it was getting late and the others were ahead, so he said—

'Oh, rot! come on.'

Generally the Dentist would have; but even worms will turn if they are hot enough, and if their feet are hurting them. 'I don't care, I shall!' he said.

Oswald overlooked the mutiny and did not say who was leader. He just said—

'Well don't be all day about it,' for he is a kind-hearted boy and can make allowances. So Denny took off his boots and went into the pool. 'Oh, it's ripping!' he said. 'You ought to come in.'

'It looks beastly muddy,' said his tolerating leader.

'It is a bit,' Denny said, 'but the mud's just as cool as the water, and so soft, it squeezes between your toes quite different to boots.'

And so he splashed about, and kept asking Oswald to come along in.

But some unseen influence prevented Oswald doing this; or it may have been because both his bootlaces were in hard knots.

Oswald had cause to bless the unseen influence, or the bootlaces, or whatever it was.

Denny had got to the middle of the pool, and he was splashing about, and getting his clothes very wet indeed, and altogether you would have thought his was a most envious and happy state. But alas! the brightest cloud had a waterproof lining. He was just saying—

'You are a silly, Oswald. You'd much better—' when he gave a blood-piercing scream, and began to kick about.

'What's up?' cried the ready Oswald; he feared the worst from the way Denny screamed, but he knew it could not be an old meat tin in this quiet and jungular spot, like it was in the moat when the shark bit Dora.

'I don't know, it's biting me. Oh, it's biting me all over my legs! Oh, what shall I do? Oh, it does hurt! Oh! oh! oh!' remarked Denny, among his screams, and he splashed towards the bank. Oswald went into the water and caught hold of him and helped him out. It is true that Oswald had his boots on, but I trust he would not have funked the unknown terrors of the deep, even without his boots, I am almost sure he would not have.

When Denny had scrambled and been hauled ashore, we saw with horror and amaze that his legs were stuck all over with large black, slug-looking things. Denny turned green in the face—and even Oswald felt a bit queer, for he knew in a moment what the black dreadfulnesses were. He had read about them in a book called Magnet Stories, where there was a girl called Theodosia, and she could play brilliant trebles on the piano in duets, but the other girl knew all about leeches which is much more useful and golden deedy. Oswald tried to pull the leeches off, but they wouldn't, and Denny howled so he had to stop trying. He remembered from the Magnet Stories how to make the leeches begin biting—the girl did it with cream—but he could not remember how to stop them, and they had not wanted any showing how to begin.

'Oh, what shall I do? What shall I do? Oh, it does hurt! Oh, oh!' Denny observed, and Oswald said—

'Be a man! Buck up! If you won't let me take them off you'll just have to walk home in them.'

At this thought the unfortunate youth's tears fell fast. But Oswald gave him an arm, and carried his boots for him, and he consented to buck up, and the two struggled on towards the others, who were coming back, attracted by Denny's yells. He did not stop howling for a moment, except to breathe. No one ought to blame him till they have had eleven leeches on their right leg and six on their left, making seventeen in all, as Dicky said, at once.

It was lucky he did yell, as it turned out, because a man on the road—where the telegraph wires were—was interested by his howls, and came across the marsh to us as hard as he could. When he saw Denny's legs he said—

'Blest if I didn't think so,' and he picked Denny up and carried him under one arm, where Denny went on saying 'Oh!' and 'It does hurt' as hard as ever.

Our rescuer, who proved to be a fine big young man in the bloom of youth, and a farm-labourer by trade, in corduroys, carried the wretched sufferer to the cottage where he lived with his aged mother; and then Oswald found that what he had forgotten about the leeches was SALT. The young man in the bloom of youth's mother put salt on the leeches, and they squirmed off, and fell with sickening, slug-like flops on the brick floor.

Then the young man in corduroys and the bloom, etc., carried Denny home on his back, after his legs had been bandaged up, so that he looked like 'wounded warriors returning'.

It was not far by the road, though such a long distance by the way the young explorers had come.

He was a good young man, and though, of course, acts of goodness are their own reward, still I was glad he had the two half-crowns Albert's uncle gave him, as well as his own good act. But I am not sure Alice ought to have put him in the Golden Deed book which was supposed to be reserved for Us.

Perhaps you will think this was the end of the source of the Nile (or North Pole). If you do, it only shows how mistaken the gentlest reader may be.

The wounded explorer was lying with his wounds and bandages on the sofa, and we were all having our tea, with raspberries and white currants, which we richly needed after our torrid adventures, when Mrs Pettigrew, the housekeeper, put her head in at the door and said—

'Please could I speak to you half a moment, sir?' to Albert's uncle. And her voice was the kind that makes you look at each other when the grown-up has gone out, and you are silent, with your bread-and-butter halfway to the next bite, or your teacup in mid flight to your lips.

It was as we suppose. Albert's uncle did not come back for a long while. We did not keep the bread-and-butter on the wing all that time, of course, and we thought we might as well finish the raspberries and white currants. We kept some for Albert's uncle, of course, and they were the best ones too but when he came back he did not notice our thoughtful unselfishness.

He came in, and his face wore the look that means bed, and very likely no supper.

He spoke, and it was the calmness of white-hot iron, which is something like the calmness of despair. He said—

'You have done it again. What on earth possessed you to make a dam?'

'We were being beavers,' said H. O., in proud tones. He did not see as we did where Albert's uncle's tone pointed to.

'No doubt,' said Albert's uncle, rubbing his hands through his hair. 'No doubt! no doubt! Well, my beavers, you may go and build dams with your bolsters. Your dam stopped the stream; the clay you took for it left a channel through which it has run down and ruined about seven pounds' worth of freshly-reaped barley. Luckily the farmer found it out in time or you might have spoiled seventy pounds' worth. And you burned a bridge yesterday.'

We said we were sorry. There was nothing else to say, only Alice added, 'We didn't MEAN to be naughty.'

'Of course not,' said Albert's uncle, 'you never do. Oh, yes, I'll kiss you—but it's bed and it's two hundred lines to-morrow, and the line is—"Beware of Being Beavers and Burning Bridges. Dread Dams." It will be a capital exercise in capital B's and D's.'

We knew by that that, though annoyed, he was not furious; we went to bed.

I got jolly sick of capital B's and D's before sunset on the morrow. That night, just as the others were falling asleep, Oswald said—

'I say.'

'Well,' retorted his brother.

'There is one thing about it,' Oswald went on, 'it does show it was a rattling good dam anyhow.'

And filled with this agreeable thought, the weary beavers (or explorers, Polar or otherwise) fell asleep.

Chapter 8. The High-Born Babe

It really was not such a bad baby—for a baby. Its face was round and quite clean, which babies' faces are not always, as I daresay you know by your own youthful relatives; and Dora said its cape was trimmed with real lace, whatever that may be—I don't see myself how one kind of lace can be realler than another. It was in a very swagger sort of perambulator when we saw it; and the perambulator was standing quite by itself in the lane that leads to the mill.

'I wonder whose baby it is,' Dora said. 'Isn't it a darling, Alice?'

Alice agreed to its being one, and said she thought it was most likely the child of noble parents stolen by gipsies.

'These two, as likely as not,' Noel said. 'Can't you see something crime-like in the very way they're lying?'

They were two tramps, and they were lying on the grass at the edge of the lane on the shady side fast asleep, only a very little further on than where the Baby was. They were very ragged, and their snores did have a sinister sound.

'I expect they stole the titled heir at dead of night, and they've been travelling hot-foot ever since, so now they're sleeping the sleep of exhaustedness,' Alice said. 'What a heart-rending scene when the patrician mother wakes in the morning and finds the infant aristocrat isn't in bed with his mamma.'

The Baby was fast asleep or else the girls would have kissed it. They are strangely fond of kissing. The author never could see anything in it himself.

'If the gipsies DID steal it,' Dora said 'perhaps they'd sell it to us. I wonder what they'd take for it.'

'What could you do with it if you'd got it?' H. O. asked.

'Why, adopt it, of course,' Dora said. 'I've often thought I should enjoy adopting a baby. It would be a golden deed, too. We've hardly got any in the book yet.'

'I should have thought there were enough of us,' Dicky said.

'Ah, but you're none of you babies,' said Dora.

'Unless you count H. O. as a baby: he behaves jolly like one sometimes.'

This was because of what had happened that morning when Dicky found H. O. going fishing with a box of worms, and the box was the one Dicky keeps his silver studs in, and the medal he got at school, and what is left of his watch and chain. The box is lined with red velvet and it was not nice afterwards. And then H. O. said Dicky had hurt him, and he was a beastly bully, and he cried. We thought all this had been made up, and were sorry to see it threaten to break out again. So Oswald said—

'Oh, bother the Baby! Come along, do!'

And the others came.

We were going to the miller's with a message about some flour that hadn't come, and about a sack of sharps for the pigs.

After you go down the lane you come to a clover-field, and then a cornfield, and then another lane, and then it is the mill. It is a jolly fine mill: in fact it is two—water and wind ones—one of each kind—with a house and farm buildings as well. I never saw a mill like it, and I don't believe you have either.

If we had been in a story-book the miller's wife would have taken us into the neat sanded kitchen where the old oak settle was black with time and rubbing, and dusted chairs for us—old brown Windsor chairs—and given us each a glass of sweet-scented cowslip wine and a thick slice of rich home-made cake. And there would have been fresh roses in an old china bowl on the table. As it was, she asked us all into the parlour and gave us Eiffel Tower lemonade and Marie biscuits. The chairs in her parlour were 'bent wood', and no flowers, except some wax ones under a glass shade, but she was very kind, and we were very much obliged to her. We got out to the miller, though, as soon as we could; only Dora and Daisy stayed with her, and she talked to them about her lodgers and about her relations in London.

The miller is a MAN. He showed us all over the mills—both kinds—and let us go right up into the very top of the wind-mill, and showed us how the top moved round so that the sails could catch the wind, and the great heaps of corn, some red and some yellow (the red is English wheat), and the heaps slice down a little bit at a time into a square hole and go down to the mill-stones. The corn makes a rustling soft noise that is very jolly—something like the noise of the sea—and you can hear it through all the other mill noises.

Then the miller let us go all over the water-mill. It is fairy palaces inside a mill. Everything is powdered over white, like sugar on pancakes when you are allowed to help yourself. And he opened a door and showed us the great water-wheel working on slow and sure, like some great, round, dripping giant, Noel said, and then he asked us if we fished.

'Yes,' was our immediate reply.

'Then why not try the mill-pool?' he said, and we replied politely; and when he was gone to tell his man something we owned to each other that he was a trump.

He did the thing thoroughly. He took us out and cut us ash saplings for rods; he found us in lines and hooks, and several different sorts of bait, including a handsome handful of meal-worms, which Oswald put loose in his pocket.

When it came to bait, Alice said she was going home with Dora and Daisy. Girls are strange, mysterious, silly things. Alice always enjoys a rat hunt until the rat is caught, but she hates fishing from beginning to end. We boys have got to like it. We don't feel now as we did when we turned off the water and stopped the competition of the competing anglers. We had a grand day's fishing that day. I can't think what made the miller so kind to us. Perhaps he felt a thrill of fellow-feeling in his manly breast for his fellow-sportsmen, for he was a noble fisherman himself.

We had glorious sport—eight roach, six dace, three eels, seven perch, and a young pike, but he was so very young the miller asked us to put him back, and of course we did. 'He'll live to bite another day,' said the miller.

The miller's wife gave us bread and cheese and more Eiffel Tower lemonade, and we went home at last, a little damp, but full of successful ambition, with our fish on a string.

It had been a strikingly good time—one of those times that happen in the country quite by themselves. Country people are much more friendly than town people. I suppose they don't have to spread their friendly feelings out over so many persons, so it's thicker, like a pound of butter on one loaf is thicker than on a dozen. Friendliness in the country is not scrape, like it is in London. Even Dicky and H. O. forgot the affair of honour that had taken place in the morning. H. O. changed rods with Dicky because H. O.'s was the best rod, and Dicky baited H. O.'s hook for him, just like loving, unselfish brothers in Sunday School magazines.

We were talking fishlikely as we went along down the lane and through the cornfield and the cloverfield, and then we came to the other lane where we had seen the Baby. The tramps were gone, and the perambulator was gone, and, of course, the Baby was gone too.

'I wonder if those gipsies HAD stolen the Baby?' Noel said dreamily. He had not fished much, but he had made a piece of poetry. It was this:

'How I wish
I was a fish.
I would not look
At your hook,
But lie still and be cool
At the bottom of the pool
And when you went to look
At your cruel hook,
You would not find me there,
So there!'

'If they did steal the Baby,' Noel went on, 'they will be tracked by the lordly perambulator. You can disguise a baby in rags and walnut juice, but there isn't any disguise dark enough to conceal a perambulator's person.'

'You might disguise it as a wheel-barrow,' said Dicky.

'Or cover it with leaves,' said H. O., 'like the robins.'

We told him to shut up and not gibber, but afterwards we had to own that even a young brother may sometimes talk sense by accident.

For we took the short cut home from the lane—it begins with a large gap in the hedge and the grass and weeds trodden down by the hasty feet of persons who were late for church and in too great a hurry to go round by the road. Our house is next to the church, as I think I have said before, some time.

The short cut leads to a stile at the edge of a bit of wood (the Parson's Shave, they call it, because it belongs to him). The wood has not been shaved for some time, and it has grown out beyond the stile and here, among the hazels and chestnuts and young dogwood bushes, we saw something white. We felt it was our duty to investigate, even if the white was only the under side of the tail of a dead rabbit caught in a trap.

It was not—it was part of the perambulator. I forget whether I said that the perambulator was enamelled white—not the kind of enamelling you do at home with Aspinall's and the hairs of the brush come out and it is gritty-looking, but smooth, like the handles of ladies very best lace parasols. And whoever had abandoned the helpless perambulator in that lonely spot had done exactly as H. O. said, and covered it with leaves, only they were green and some of them had dropped off.

The others were wild with excitement. Now or never, they thought, was a chance to be real detectives. Oswald alone retained a calm exterior. It was he who would not go straight to the police station.

He said: 'Let's try and ferret out something for ourselves before we tell the police. They always have a clue directly they hear about the finding of the body. And besides, we might as well let Alice be in anything there is going. And besides, we haven't had our dinners yet.'

This argument of Oswald's was so strong and powerful—his arguments are often that, as I daresay you have noticed—that the others agreed. It was Oswald, too, who showed his artless brothers why they had much better not take the deserted perambulator home with them.

'The dead body, or whatever the clue is, is always left exactly as it is found,' he said, 'till the police have seen it, and the coroner, and the inquest, and the doctor, and the sorrowing relations. Besides, suppose someone saw us with the beastly thing, and thought we had stolen it; then they would say, "What have you done with the Baby?" and then where should we be?' Oswald's brothers could not answer this question, but once more Oswald's native eloquence and far-seeing discerningness conquered.

'Anyway,' Dicky said, 'let's shove the derelict a little further under cover.'

So we did.

Then we went on home. Dinner was ready and so were Alice and Daisy, but Dora was not there.

'She's got a— well, she's not coming to dinner anyway,' Alice said when we asked. 'She can tell you herself afterwards what it is she's got.'

Oswald thought it was headache, or pain in the temper, or in the pinafore, so he said no more, but as soon as Mrs Pettigrew had helped us and left the room he began the thrilling tale of the forsaken perambulator. He told it with the greatest thrillingness anyone could have, but Daisy and Alice seemed almost unmoved. Alice said—

'Yes, very strange,' and things like that, but both the girls seemed to be thinking of something else. They kept looking at each other and trying not to laugh, so Oswald saw they had got some silly secret and he said—

'Oh, all right! I don't care about telling you. I only thought you'd like to be in it. It's going to be a really big thing, with policemen in it, and perhaps a judge.'

'In what?' H. O. said; 'the perambulator?'

Daisy choked and then tried to drink, and spluttered and got purple, and had to be thumped on the back. But Oswald was not appeased. When Alice said, 'Do go on, Oswald. I'm sure we all like it very much,' he said—

'Oh, no, thank you,' very politely. 'As it happens,' he went on, 'I'd just as soon go through with this thing without having any girls in it.'

'In the perambulator?' said H. O. again.

'It's a man's job,' Oswald went on, without taking any notice of H. O.

'Do you really think so,' said Alice, 'when there's a baby in it?'

'But there isn't,' said H. O., 'if you mean in the perambulator.'

'Blow you and your perambulator,' said Oswald, with gloomy forbearance.

Alice kicked Oswald under the table and said—

'Don't be waxy, Oswald. Really and truly Daisy and I HAVE got a secret, only it's Dora's secret, and she wants to tell you herself. If it was mine or Daisy's we'd tell you this minute, wouldn't we, Mouse?'

'This very second,' said the White Mouse.

And Oswald consented to take their apologies.

Then the pudding came in, and no more was said except asking for things to be passed—sugar and water, and bread and things.

Then when the pudding was all gone, Alice said—

'Come on.'

And we came on. We did not want to be disagreeable, though really we were keen on being detectives and sifting that perambulator to the very dregs. But boys have to try to take an interest in their sisters' secrets, however silly. This is part of being a good brother.

Alice led us across the field where the sheep once fell into the brook, and across the brook by the plank. At the other end of the next field there was a sort of wooden house on wheels, that the shepherd sleeps in at the time of year when lambs are being born, so that he can see that they are not stolen by gipsies before the owners have counted them.

To this hut Alice now led her kind brothers and Daisy's kind brother. 'Dora is inside,' she said, 'with the Secret. We were afraid to have it in the house in case it made a noise.'

The next moment the Secret was a secret no longer, for we all beheld Dora, sitting on a sack on the floor of the hut, with the Secret in her lap.

It was the High-born Babe!

Oswald was so overcome that he sat down suddenly, just like Betsy Trotwood did in David Copperfield, which just shows what a true author Dickens is.

'You've done it this time,' he said. 'I suppose you know you're a baby-stealer?'

'I'm not,' Dora said. 'I've adopted him.'

'Then it was you,' Dicky said, 'who scuttled the perambulator in the wood?'

'Yes,' Alice said; 'we couldn't get it over the stile unless Dora put down the Baby, and we were afraid of the nettles for his legs. His name is to be Lord Edward.'

'But, Dora—really, don't you think—'

'If you'd been there you'd have done the same,' said Dora firmly. 'The gipsies had gone. Of course something had frightened them and they fled from justice. And the little darling was awake and held out his arms to me. No, he hasn't cried a bit, and I know all about babies; I've often nursed Mrs Simpkins's daughter's baby when she brings it up on Sundays. They have bread and milk to eat. You take him, Alice, and I'll go and get some bread and milk for him.'

Alice took the noble brat. It was horribly lively, and squirmed about in her arms, and wanted to crawl on the floor. She could only keep it quiet by saying things to it a boy would be ashamed even to think of saying, such as 'Goo goo', and 'Did ums was', and 'Ickle ducksums, then'.

When Alice used these expressions the Baby laughed and chuckled and replied—

'Daddadda', 'Bababa', or 'Glueglue'.

But if Alice stopped her remarks for an instant the thing screwed its face up as if it was going to cry, but she never gave it time to begin.

It was a rummy little animal.

Then Dora came back with the bread and milk, and they fed the noble infant. It was greedy and slobbery, but all three girls seemed unable to keep their eyes and hands off it. They looked at it exactly as if it was pretty.

We boys stayed watching them. There was no amusement left for us now, for Oswald saw that Dora's Secret knocked the bottom out of the perambulator.

When the infant aristocrat had eaten a hearty meal it sat on Alice's lap and played with the amber heart she wears that Albert's uncle brought her from Hastings after the business of the bad sixpence and the nobleness of Oswald.

'Now,' said Dora, 'this is a council, so I want to be business-like. The Duckums Darling has been stolen away; its wicked stealers have deserted the Precious. We've got it. Perhaps its ancestral halls are miles and miles away. I vote we keep the little Lovey Duck till it's advertised for.'

'If Albert's uncle lets you,' said Dicky darkly.

'Oh, don't say "you" like that,' Dora said; 'I want it to be all of our baby. It will have five fathers and three mothers, and a grandfather and a great Albert's uncle, and a great grand-uncle. I'm sure Albert's uncle will let us keep it—at any rate till it's advertised for.'

'And suppose it never is,' Noel said.

'Then so much the better,' said Dora, 'the little Duckyux.'

She began kissing the baby again. Oswald, ever thoughtful, said— 'Well, what about your dinner?'

'Bother dinner!' Dora said—so like a girl. 'Will you all agree to be his fathers and mothers?'

'Anything for a quiet life,' said Dicky, and Oswald said—

'Oh, yes, if you like. But you'll see we shan't be allowed to keep it.'

'You talk as if he was rabbits or white rats,' said Dora, 'and he's not—he's a little man, he is.'

'All right, he's no rabbit, but a man. Come on and get some grub, Dora,' rejoined the kind-hearted Oswald, and Dora did, with Oswald and the other boys. Only Noel stayed with Alice. He really seemed to like the baby. When I looked back he was standing on his head to amuse it, but the baby did not seem to like him any better whichever end of him was up.

Dora went back to the shepherd's house on wheels directly she had had her dinner. Mrs Pettigrew was very cross about her not being in to it, but she had kept her some mutton hot all the same. She is a decent sort. And there were stewed prunes. We had some to keep Dora company. Then we boys went fishing again in the moat, but we caught nothing.

Just before tea-time we all went back to the hut, and before we got half across the last field we could hear the howling of the Secret.

'Poor little beggar,' said Oswald, with manly tenderness. 'They must be sticking pins in it.'

We found the girls and Noel looking quite pale and breathless. Daisy was walking up and down with the Secret in her arms. It looked like Alice in Wonderland nursing the baby that turned into a pig. Oswald said so, and added that its screams were like it too.

'What on earth is the matter with it?' he said.

'*I* don't know,' said Alice. 'Daisy's tired, and Dora and I are quite worn out. He's been crying for hours and hours. YOU take him a bit.'

'Not me,' replied Oswald, firmly, withdrawing a pace from the Secret.

Dora was fumbling with her waistband in the furthest corner of the hut.

'I think he's cold,' she said. 'I thought I'd take off my flannelette petticoat, only the horrid strings got into a hard knot. Here, Oswald, let's have your knife.'

With the word she plunged her hand into Oswald's jacket pocket, and next moment she was rubbing her hand like mad on her dress, and screaming almost as loud as the Baby. Then she began to laugh and to cry at the same time. This is called hysterics.

Oswald was sorry, but he was annoyed too. He had forgotten that his pocket was half full of the meal-worms the miller had kindly given him. And, anyway, Dora ought to have known that a man always carries his knife in his trousers pocket and not in his jacket one.

Alice and Daisy rushed to Dora. She had thrown herself down on the pile of sacks in the corner. The titled infant delayed its screams for a moment to listen to Dora's, but almost at once it went on again.

'Oh, get some water!' said Alice. 'Daisy, run!'

The White Mouse, ever docile and obedient, shoved the baby into the arms of the nearest person, who had to take it or it would have fallen a wreck to the ground. This nearest person was Oswald. He tried to pass it on to the others, but they wouldn't. Noel would have, but he was busy kissing Dora and begging her not to. So our hero, for such I may perhaps term him, found himself the degraded nursemaid of a small but furious kid.

He was afraid to lay it down, for fear in its rage it should beat its brains out against the hard earth, and he did not wish, however innocently, to be the cause of its hurting itself at all. So he walked earnestly up and down with it, thumping it unceasingly on the back, while the others attended to Dora, who presently ceased to yell.

Suddenly it struck Oswald that the High-born also had ceased to yell. He looked at it, and could hardly believe the glad tidings of his faithful eyes. With bated breath he hastened back to the sheep-house.

The others turned on him, full of reproaches about the meal-worms and Dora, but he answered without anger.

'Shut up,' he said in a whisper of imperial command. 'Can't you see it's GONE TO SLEEP?'

As exhausted as if they had all taken part in all the events of a very long Athletic Sports, the youthful Bastables and their friends dragged their weary limbs back across the fields. Oswald was compelled to go on holding the titled infant, for fear it should wake up if it changed hands, and begin to yell again. Dora's flannelette petticoat had been got off somehow—how I do not seek to inquire—and the Secret was covered with it. The others surrounded Oswald as much as possible, with a view to concealment if we met Mrs Pettigrew. But the coast was clear. Oswald took the Secret up into his bedroom. Mrs Pettigrew doesn't come there much, it's too many stairs.

With breathless precaution Oswald laid it down on his bed. It sighed, but did not wake. Then we took it in turns to sit by it and see that it did not get up and fling itself out of bed, which, in one of its furious fits, it would just as soon have done as not.

We expected Albert's uncle every minute.

At last we heard the gate, but he did not come in, so we looked out and saw that there he was talking to a distracted-looking man on a piebald horse—one of the miller's horses.

A shiver of doubt coursed through our veins. We could not remember having done anything wrong at the miller's. But you never know. And it seemed strange his sending a man up on his own horse. But when we had looked a bit longer our fears went down and our curiosity got up. For we saw that the distracted one was a gentleman.

Presently he rode off, and Albert's uncle came in. A deputation met him at the door—all the boys and Dora, because the baby was her idea.

'We've found something,' Dora said, 'and we want to know whether we may keep it.'

The rest of us said nothing. We were not so very extra anxious to keep it after we had heard how much and how long it could howl. Even Noel had said he had no idea a baby could yell like it. Dora said it only cried because it was sleepy, but we reflected that it would certainly be sleepy once a day, if not oftener.

'What is it?' said Albert's uncle. 'Let's see this treasure-trove. Is it a wild beast?'

'Come and see,' said Dora, and we led him to our room.

Alice turned down the pink flannelette petticoat with silly pride, and showed the youthful heir fatly and pinkly sleeping.

'A baby!' said Albert's uncle. 'THE Baby! Oh, my cat's alive!'

That is an expression which he uses to express despair unmixed with anger.

'Where did you?— but that doesn't matter. We'll talk of this later.'

He rushed from the room, and in a moment or two we saw him mount his bicycle and ride off.

Quite shortly he returned with the distracted horse- man.

It was HIS baby, and not titled at all. The horseman and his wife were the lodgers at the mill. The nursemaid was a girl from the village.

She SAID she only left the Baby five minutes while she went to speak to her sweetheart who was gardener at the Red House. But we knew she left it over an hour, and nearly two.

I never saw anyone so pleased as the distracted horseman.

When we were asked we explained about having thought the Baby was the prey of gipsies, and the distracted horseman stood hugging the Baby, and actually thanked us.

But when he had gone we had a brief lecture on minding our own business. But Dora still thinks she was right. As for Oswald and most of the others, they agreed that they would rather mind their own business all their lives than mind a baby for a single hour.

If you have never had to do with a baby in the frenzied throes of sleepiness you can have no idea what its screams are like.

If you have been through such a scene you will understand how we managed to bear up under having no baby to adopt. Oswald insisted on having the whole thing written in the Golden Deed book. Of course his share could not be put in without telling about Dora's generous adopting of the forlorn infant outcast, and Oswald could not and cannot forget that he was the one who did get that baby to sleep.

What a time Mr and Mrs Distracted Horseman must have of it, though—especially now they've sacked the nursemaid.

If Oswald is ever married—I suppose he must be some day—he will have ten nurses to each baby. Eight is not enough. We know that because we tried, and the whole eight of us were not enough for the needs of that deserted infant who was not so extra high-born after all.

Chapter 9. Hunting the Fox

It is idle to expect everyone to know everything in the world without being told. If we had been brought up in the country we should have known that it is not done—to hunt the fox in August. But in the Lewisham Road the most observing boy does not notice the dates when it is proper to hunt foxes.

And there are some things you cannot bear to think that anybody would think you would do; that is why I wish to say plainly at the very beginning that none of us would have shot a fox on purpose even to save our skins. Of course, if a man were at bay in a cave, and had to defend girls from the simultaneous attack of a herd of savage foxes it would be different. A man is bound to protect girls and take care of them—they can jolly well take care of themselves really it seems to me—still, this is what Albert's uncle calls one of the 'rules of the game', so we are bound to defend them and fight for them to the death, if needful. Denny knows a quotation which says—

> 'What dire offence from harmless causes springs,
> What mighty contests rise from trefoil things.'

He says this means that all great events come from three things—threefold, like the clover or trefoil, and the causes are always harmless. Trefoil is short for threefold.

There were certainly three things that led up to the adventure which is now going to be told you. The first was our Indian uncle coming down to the country to see us. The second was Denny's tooth. The third was only our wanting to go hunting; but if you count it in it makes the thing about the trefoil come right. And all these causes were harmless.

It is a flattering thing to say, and it was not Oswald who said it, but Dora. She said she was certain our uncle missed us, and that he felt he could no longer live without seeing his dear ones (that was us).

Anyway, he came down, without warning, which is one of the few bad habits that excellent Indian man has, and this habit has ended in unpleasantness more than once, as when we played jungles.

However, this time it was all right. He came on rather a dull kind of day, when no one had thought of anything particularly amusing to do. So that, as it happened to be dinner-time and we had just washed our hands and faces, we were all spotlessly clean (compared with what we are sometimes, I mean, of course).

We were just sitting down to dinner, and Albert's uncle was just plunging the knife into the hot heart of the steak pudding, when there was the rumble of wheels, and the station fly stopped at the garden gate. And in the fly, sitting very upright, with his hands on his knees, was our Indian relative so much beloved. He looked very smart, with a rose in his buttonhole. How different from what he looked in other days when he helped us to pretend that our currant pudding was a wild boar we were killing with our forks. Yet, though tidier, his heart still beat kind and true. You should not judge people harshly because their clothes are tidy. He had dinner with us, and then we showed him round the place, and told him everything we thought he would like to hear, and about the Tower of Mystery, and he said—

'It makes my blood boil to think of it.'

Noel said he was sorry for that, because everyone else we had told it to had owned, when we asked them, that it froze their blood.

'Ah,' said the Uncle, 'but in India we learn how to freeze our blood and boil it at the same time.'

In those hot longitudes, perhaps, the blood is always near boiling-point, which accounts for Indian tempers, though not for the curry and pepper they eat. But I must not wander; there is no curry at all in this story. About temper I will not say.

Then Uncle let us all go with him to the station when the fly came back for him; and when we said good-bye he tipped us all half a quid, without any insidious distinctions about age or considering whether you were a boy or a girl. Our Indian uncle is a true-born Briton, with no nonsense about him.

We cheered him like one man as the train went off, and then we offered the fly-driver a shilling to take us back to the four cross-roads, and the grateful creature did it for nothing because, he said, the gent had tipped him something like. How scarce is true gratitude! So we cheered the driver too for this rare virtue, and then went home to talk about what we should do with our money. I cannot tell you all that we did with it, because money melts away 'like snow-wreaths in thaw-jean', as Denny says, and somehow the more you have the more quickly it melts. We all went into Maidstone, and came back with the most beautiful lot of brown-paper parcels, with things inside that supplied long-felt wants. But none of them belongs to this narration, except what Oswald and Denny clubbed to buy.

This was a pistol, and it took all the money they both had, but when Oswald felt the uncomfortable inside sensation that reminds you who it is and his money that are soon parted he said to himself—

'I don't care. We ought to have a pistol in the house, and one that will go off, too — not those rotten flintlocks. Suppose there should be burglars and us totally unarmed?'

We took it in turns to have the pistol, and we decided always to practise with it far from the house, so as not to frighten the grown-ups, who are always much nervouser about firearms than we are.

It was Denny's idea getting it; and Oswald owns it surprised him, but the boy was much changed in his character. We got it while the others were grubbing at the pastry-cook's in the High Street, and we said nothing till after tea, though it was hard not to fire at the birds on the telegraph wires as we came home in the train.

After tea we called a council in the straw-loft, and Oswald said—

'Denny and I have got a secret.'

'I know what it is,' Dicky said contemptibly. 'You've found out that shop in Maidstone where peppermint rock is four ounces a penny. H. O. and I found it out before you did.'

Oswald said, 'You shut-up. If you don't want to hear the secret you'd better bunk. I'm going to administer the secret oath.'

This is a very solemn oath, and only used about real things, and never for pretending ones, so Dicky said—

'Oh, all right; go ahead! I thought you were only rotting.'

So they all took the secret oath. Noel made it up long before, when he had found the first thrush's nest we ever saw in the Blackheath garden:

> 'I will not tell, I will not reveal,
> I will not touch, or try to steal;
> And may I be called a beastly sneak,
> If this great secret I ever repeat.'

It is a little wrong about the poetry, but it is a very binding promise. They all repeated it, down to H. O.

'Now then,' Dicky said, 'what's up?'

Oswald, in proud silence, drew the pistol from his breast and held it out, and there was a murmur of awful amazement and respect from every one of the council. The pistol was not loaded, so we let even the girls have it to look at. And then Dicky said, 'Let's go hunting.'

And we decided that we would. H. O. wanted to go down to the village and get penny horns at the shop for the huntsmen to wind, like in the song, but we thought it would be more modest not to wind horns or anything noisy, at any rate not until we had run down our prey. But his talking of the song made us decide that it was the fox we wanted to hunt. We had not been particular which animal we hunted before that.

Oswald let Denny have first go with the pistol, and when we went to bed he slept with it under his pillow, but not loaded, for fear he should have a nightmare and draw his fell weapon before he was properly awake.

Oswald let Denny have it, because Denny had toothache, and a pistol is consoling though it does not actually stop the pain of the tooth. The toothache got worse, and Albert's uncle looked at it, and said it was very loose, and Denny owned he had tried to crack a peach-stone with it. Which accounts. He had creosote and camphor, and went to bed early, with his tooth tied up in red flannel.

Oswald knows it is right to be very kind when people are ill, and he forbore to wake the sufferer next morning by buzzing a pillow at him, as he generally does. He got up and went over to shake the invalid, but the bird had flown and the nest was cold. The pistol was not in the nest either, but Oswald found it afterwards under the looking-glass on the dressing-table. He had just awakened the others (with a hair-brush because they had not got anything the matter with their teeth), when he heard wheels, and, looking out, beheld Denny and Albert's uncle being driven from the door in the farmer's high cart with the red wheels.

We dressed extra quick, so as to get downstairs to the bottom of the mystery. And we found a note from Albert's uncle. It was addressed to Dora, and said—

'Denny's toothache got him up in the small hours. He's off to the dentist to have it out with him, man to man. Home to dinner.'

Dora said, 'Denny's gone to the dentist.'

'I expect it's a relation,' H. O. said. 'Denny must be short for Dentist.'

I suppose he was trying to be funny—he really does try very hard. He wants to be a clown when he grows up. The others laughed.

'I wonder,' said Dicky, 'whether he'll get a shilling or half-a-crown for it.'

Oswald had been meditating in gloomy silence, now he cheered up and said—

'Of course! I'd forgotten that. He'll get his tooth money, and the drive too. So it's quite fair for us to have the fox-hunt while he's gone. I was thinking we should have to put it off.'

The others agreed that it would not be unfair.

'We can have another one another time if he wants to,' Oswald said.

We know foxes are hunted in red coats and on horseback—but we could not do this—but H. O. had the old red football jersey that was Albert's uncle's when he was at Loretto. He was pleased.

'But I do wish we'd had horns,' he said grievingly. 'I should have liked to wind the horn.'

'We can pretend horns,' Dora said; but he answered, 'I didn't want to pretend. I wanted to wind something.'

'Wind your watch,' Dicky said. And that was unkind, because we all know H. O.'s watch is broken, and when you wind it, it only rattles inside without going in the least.

We did not bother to dress up much for the hunting expedition—just cocked hats and lath swords; and we tied a card on to H. O.'s chest with 'Moat House Fox-Hunters' on it; and we tied red flannel round all the dogs' necks to show they were fox-hounds. Yet it did not seem to show it plainly; somehow it made them look as if they were not fox-hounds, but their own natural breeds—only with sore throats.

Oswald slipped the pistol and a few cartridges into his pocket. He knew, of course, that foxes are not shot; but as he said—

'Who knows whether we may not meet a bear or a crocodile.'

We set off gaily. Across the orchard and through two cornfields, and along the hedge of another field, and so we got into the wood, through a gap we had happened to make a day or two before, playing 'follow my leader'.

The wood was very quiet and green; the dogs were happy and most busy. Once Pincher started a rabbit. We said, 'View Halloo!' and immediately started in pursuit; but the rabbit went and hid, so that even Pincher could not find him, and we went on. But we saw no foxes. So at last we made Dicky be a fox, and chased him down the green rides. A wide walk in a wood is called a ride, even if people never do anything but walk in it.

We had only three hounds—Lady, Pincher and Martha—so we joined the glad throng and were being hounds as hard as we could, when we suddenly came barking round a corner in full chase and stopped short, for we saw that our fox had stayed his hasty flight. The fox was stooping over something reddish that lay beside the path, and he cried—

'I say, look here!' in tones that thrilled us throughout.

Our fox—whom we must now call Dicky, so as not to muddle the narration—pointed to the reddy thing that the dogs were sniffing at.

'It's a real live fox,' he said. And so it was. At least it was real—only it was quite dead—and when Oswald lifted it up its head was bleeding. It had evidently been shot through the brain and expired instantly. Oswald explained this to the girls when they began to cry at the sight of the poor beast; I do not say he did not feel a bit sorry himself.

The fox was cold, but its fur was so pretty, and its tail and its little feet. Dicky strung the dogs on the leash; they were so much interested we thought it was better.

'It does seem horrid to think it'll never see again out of its poor little eyes,' Dora said, blowing her nose.

'And never run about through the wood again, lend me your hanky, Dora' said Alice.

'And never be hunted or get into a hen-roost or a trap or anything exciting, poor little thing,' said Dicky.

The girls began to pick green chestnut leaves to cover up the poor fox's fatal wound, and Noel began to walk up and down making faces, the way he always does when he's making poetry. He cannot make one without the other. It works both ways, which is a comfort.

'What are we going to do now?' H. O. said; 'the huntsman ought to cut off its tail, I'm quite certain. Only, I've broken the big blade of my knife, and the other never was any good.'

The girls gave H. O. a shove, and even Oswald said, 'Shut up', for somehow we all felt we did not want to play fox-hunting any more that day. When his deadly wound was covered the fox hardly looked dead at all.

'Oh, I wish it wasn't true!' Alice said.

Daisy had been crying all the time, and now she said, 'I should like to pray God to make it not true.'

But Dora kissed her, and told her that was no good —only she might pray God to take care of the fox's poor little babies, if it had had any, which I believe she has done ever since.

'If only we could wake up and find it was a horrid dream,' Alice said.

It seems silly that we should have cared so much when we had really set out to hunt foxes with dogs, but it is true. The fox's feet looked so helpless. And there was a dusty mark on its side that I know would not have been there if it had been alive and able to wash itself.

Noel now said, 'This is the piece of poetry':

'Here lies poor Reynard who is slain,
He will not come to life again.
I never will the huntsman's horn
Wind since the day that I was born
Until the day I die—
For I don't like hunting, and this is why.'

'Let's have a funeral,' said H. O. This pleased everybody, and we got Dora to take off her petticoat to wrap the fox in, so that we could carry it to our garden and bury it without bloodying our jackets. Girls' clothes are silly in one way, but I think they are useful too. A boy cannot take off more than his jacket and waistcoat in any emergency, or he is at once entirely undressed. But I have known Dora take off two petticoats for useful purposes and look just the same outside afterwards.

We boys took it in turns to carry the fox. It was very heavy. When we got near the edge of the wood Noel said—

'It would be better to bury it here, where the leaves can talk funeral songs over its grave for ever, and the other foxes can come and cry if they want to.' He dumped the fox down on the moss under a young oak tree as he spoke.

'If Dicky fetched the spade and fork we could bury it here, and then he could tie up the dogs at the same time.'

'You're sick of carrying it,' Dicky remarked, 'that's what it is.' But he went on condition the rest of us boys went too.

While we were gone the girls dragged the fox to the edge of the wood; it was a different edge to the one we went in by—close to a lane—and while they waited for the digging or fatigue party to come back, they collected a lot of moss and green things to make the fox's long home soft for it to lie in. There are no flowers in the woods in August, which is a pity.

When we got back with the spade and fork we dug a hole to bury the fox in. We did not bring the dogs back, because they were too interested in the funeral to behave with real, respectable calmness.

The ground was loose and soft and easy to dig when we had scraped away the broken bits of sticks and the dead leaves and the wild honeysuckle; Oswald used the fork and Dicky had the spade. Noel made faces and poetry—he was struck so that morning—and the girls sat stroking the clean parts of the fox's fur till the grave was deep enough. At last it was; then Daisy threw in the leaves and grass, and Alice and Dora took the poor dead fox by his two ends and we helped to put him in the grave. We could not lower him slowly—he was dropped in, really. Then we covered the furry body with leaves, and Noel said the Burial Ode he had made up. He says this was it, but it sounds better now than it did then, so I think he must have done something to it since:

THE FOX'S BURIAL ODE

'Dear Fox, sleep here, and do not wake,
We picked these leaves for your sake
You must not try to rise or move,
We give you this with our love.

Close by the wood where once you grew
Your mourning friends have buried you.
If you had lived you'd not have been
(Been proper friends with us, I mean),

But now you're laid upon the shelf,
Poor fox, you cannot help yourself,
So, as I say, we are your loving friends—
And here your Burial Ode, dear Foxy, ends.

P. S.—When in the moonlight bright
The foxes wander of a night,
They'll pass your grave and fondly think of you,
Exactly like we mean to always do.

So now, dear fox, adieu!
Your friends are few
But true
To you.

Adieu!'

When this had been said we filled in the grave and covered the top of it with dry leaves and sticks to make it look like the rest of the wood. People might think it was a treasure, and dig it up, if they thought there was anything buried there, and we wished the poor fox to sleep sound and not to be disturbed.

The interring was over. We folded up Dora's bloodstained pink cotton petticoat, and turned to leave the sad spot.

We had not gone a dozen yards down the lane when we heard footsteps and a whistle behind us, and a scrabbling and whining, and a gentleman with two fox-terriers had called a halt just by the place where we had laid low the 'little red rover'.

The gentleman stood in the lane, but the dogs were digging—we could see their tails wagging and see the dust fly. And we SAW WHERE. We ran back.

'Oh, please, do stop your dogs digging there!' Alice said.

The gentleman said 'Why?'

'Because we've just had a funeral, and that's the grave.'

The gentleman whistled, but the fox-terriers were not trained like Pincher, who was brought up by Oswald. The gentleman took a stride through the hedge gap.

'What have you been burying—pet dicky bird, eh?' said the gentleman, kindly. He had riding breeches and white whiskers.

We did not answer, because now, for the first time, it came over all of us, in a rush of blushes and uncomfortableness, that burying a fox is a suspicious act. I don't know why we felt this, but we did.

Noel said dreamily—

'We found his murdered body in the wood,
And dug a grave by which the mourners stood.'

But no one heard him except Oswald, because Alice and Dora and Daisy were all jumping about with the jumps of unrestrained anguish, and saying, 'Oh, call them off! Do! do!—oh, don't, don't! Don't let them dig.'

Alas! Oswald was, as usual, right. The ground of the grave had not been trampled down hard enough, and he had said so plainly at the time, but his prudent counsels had been overruled. Now these busy-bodying, meddling, mischief-making fox-terriers (how different from Pincher, who minds his own business unless told otherwise) had scratched away the earth and laid bare the reddish tip of the poor corpse's tail.

We all turned to go without a word, it seemed to be no use staying any longer.

But in a moment the gentleman with the whiskers had got Noel and Dicky each by an ear—they were nearest him. H. O. hid in the hedge. Oswald, to whose noble breast sneakishness is, I am thankful to say, a stranger, would have scorned to escape, but he ordered his sisters to bunk in a tone of command which made refusal impossible.

'And bunk sharp, too' he added sternly. 'Cut along home.'

So they cut. The white-whiskered gentleman now encouraged his angry fox-terriers, by every means at his command, to continue their vile and degrading occupation; holding on all the time to the ears of Dicky and Noel, who scorned to ask for mercy. Dicky got purple and Noel got white. It was Oswald who said—

'Don't hang on to them, sir. We won't cut. I give you my word of honour.'

'YOUR word of honour,' said the gentleman, in tones for which, in happier days, when people drew their bright blades and fought duels, I would have had his heart's dearest blood. But now Oswald remained calm and polite as ever.

'Yes, on my honour,' he said, and the gentleman dropped the ears of Oswald's brothers at the sound of his firm, unswerving tones. He dropped the ears and pulled out the body of the fox and held it up.

The dogs jumped up and yelled.

'Now,' he said, 'you talk very big about words of honour. Can you speak the truth?'

Dickie said, 'If you think we shot it, you're wrong. We know better than that.'

The white-whiskered one turned suddenly to H. O. and pulled him out of the hedge.

'And what does that mean?' he said, and he was pink with fury to the ends of his large ears, as he pointed to the card on H. O.'s breast, which said, 'Moat House Fox-Hunters'.

Then Oswald said, 'We WERE playing at fox-hunting, but we couldn't find anything but a rabbit that hid, so my brother was being the fox; and then we found the fox shot dead, and I don't know who did it; and we were sorry for it and we buried it—and that's all.'

'Not quite,' said the riding-breeches gentleman, with what I think you call a bitter smile, 'not quite. This is my land and I'll have you up for trespass and damage. Come along now, no nonsense! I'm a magistrate and I'm Master of the Hounds. A vixen, too! What did you shoot her with? You're too young to have a gun. Sneaked your Father's revolver, I suppose?'

Oswald thought it was better to be goldenly silent. But it was vain. The Master of the Hounds made him empty his pockets, and there was the pistol and the cartridges.

The magistrate laughed a harsh laugh of successful disagreeableness.

'All right,' said he, 'where's your licence? You come with me. A week or two in prison.'

I don't believe now he could have done it, but we all thought then he could and would, what's more.

So H. O. began to cry, but Noel spoke up. His teeth were chattering yet he spoke up like a man.

He said, 'You don't know us. You've no right not to believe us till you've found us out in a lie. We don't tell lies. You ask Albert's uncle if we do.'

'Hold your tongue,' said the White-Whiskered. But Noel's blood was up.

'If you do put us in prison without being sure,' he said, trembling more and more, 'you are a horrible tyrant like Caligula, and Herod, or Nero, and the Spanish Inquisition, and I will write a poem about it in prison, and people will curse you for ever.'

'Upon my word,' said White Whiskers. 'We'll see about that,' and he turned up the lane with the fox hanging from one hand and Noel's ear once more reposing in the other.

I thought Noel would cry or faint. But he bore up nobly—exactly like an early Christian martyr.

The rest of us came along too. I carried the spade and Dicky had the fork. H. O. had the card, and Noel had the magistrate. At the end of the lane there was Alice. She had bunked home, obeying the orders of her thoughtful brother, but she had bottled back again like a shot, so as not to be out of the scrape. She is almost worthy to be a boy for some things.

She spoke to Mr Magistrate and said—

'Where are you taking him?'

The outraged majesty of the magistrate said, 'To prison, you naughty little girl.'

Alice said, 'Noel will faint. Somebody once tried to take him to prison before—about a dog. Do please come to our house and see our uncle—at least he's not—but it's the same thing. We didn't kill the fox, if that's what you think—indeed we didn't. Oh, dear, I do wish you'd think of your own little boys and girls if you've got any, or else about when you were little. You wouldn't be so horrid if you did.'

I don't know which, if either, of these objects the fox-hound master thought of, but he said—

'Well, lead on,' and he let go Noel's ear and Alice snuggled up to Noel and put her arm round him.

It was a frightened procession, whose cheeks were pale with alarm—except those between white whiskers, and they were red—that wound in at our gate and into the hall among the old oak furniture, and black and white marble floor and things.

Dora and Daisy were at the door. The pink petticoat lay on the table, all stained with the gore of the departed. Dora looked at us all, and she saw that it was serious. She pulled out the big oak chair and said, 'Won't you sit down?' very kindly to the white- whiskered magistrate.

He grunted, but did as she said.

Then he looked about him in a silence that was not comforting, and so did we. At last he said—

'Come, you didn't try to bolt. Speak the truth, and I'll say no more.'

We said we had.

Then he laid the fox on the table, spreading out the petticoat under it, and he took out a knife and the girls hid their faces. Even Oswald did not care to look. Wounds in battle are all very well, but it's different to see a dead fox cut into with a knife.

Next moment the magistrate wiped something on his handkerchief and then laid it on the table, and put one of my cartridges beside it. It was the bullet that had killed the fox.

'Look here!' he said. And it was too true. The bullets were the same.

A thrill of despair ran through Oswald. He knows now how a hero feels when he is innocently accused of a crime and the judge is putting on the black cap, and the evidence is convulsive and all human aid is despaired of.

'I can't help it,' he said, 'we didn't kill it, and that's all there is to it.'

The white-whiskered magistrate may have been master of the fox-hounds, but he was not master of his temper, which is more important, I should think, than a lot of beastly dogs.

He said several words which Oswald would never repeat, much less in his own conversing, and besides that he called us 'obstinate little beggars'.

Then suddenly Albert's uncle entered in the midst of a silence freighted with despairing reflections. The M.F.H. got up and told his tale: it was mainly lies, or, to be more polite, it was hardly any of it true, though I supposed he believed it.

'I am very sorry, sir' said Albert's uncle, looking at the bullets. 'You'll excuse my asking for the children's version?'

'Oh, certainly, sir, certainly,' fuming, the fox-hound magistrate replied.

Then Albert's uncle said, 'Now Oswald, I know I can trust you to speak the exact truth.'

So Oswald did.

Then the white-whiskered fox-master laid the bullets before Albert's uncle, and I felt this would be a trial to his faith far worse than the rack or the thumb-screw in the days of the Armada.

And then Denny came in. He looked at the fox on the table.

'You found it, then?' he said.

The M.F.H. would have spoken but Albert's uncle said, 'One moment, Denny; you've seen this fox before?'

'Rather,' said Denny; 'I—'

But Albert's uncle said, 'Take time. Think before you speak and say the exact truth. No, don't whisper to Oswald. This boy,' he said to the injured fox-master, 'has been with me since seven this morning. His tale, whatever it is, will be independent evidence.'

But Denny would not speak, though again and again Albert's uncle told him to.

'I can't till I've asked Oswald something,' he said at last. White Whiskers said, 'That looks bad—eh?'

But Oswald said, 'Don't whisper, old chap. Ask me whatever you like, but speak up.'

So Denny said, 'I can't without breaking the secret oath.'

So then Oswald began to see, and he said, 'Break away for all you're worth, it's all right.'

And Denny said, drawing relief's deepest breath, 'Well then, Oswald and I have got a pistol—shares—and I had it last night. And when I couldn't sleep last night because of the toothache I got up and went out early this morning. And I took the pistol. And I loaded it just for fun. And down in the wood I heard a whining like a dog, and I went, and there was the poor fox caught in an iron trap with teeth. And I went to let it out and it bit me—look, here's the place—and the pistol went off and the fox died, and I am so sorry.'

'But why didn't you tell the others?'

'They weren't awake when I went to the dentist's.'

'But why didn't you tell your uncle if you've been with him all the morning?'

'It was the oath,' H. O. said—

> 'May I be called a beastly sneak
> If this great secret I ever repeat.'

White Whiskers actually grinned.

'Well,' he said, 'I see it was an accident, my boy.' Then he turned to us and said—

'I owe you an apology for doubting your word—all of you. I hope it's accepted.'

We said it was all right and he was to never mind.

But all the same we hated him for it. He tried to make up for his unbelievingness afterwards by asking Albert's uncle to shoot rabbits; but we did not really forgive him till the day when he sent the fox's brush to Alice, mounted in silver with a note about her plucky conduct in standing by her brothers.

We got a lecture about not playing with firearms, but no punishment, because our conduct had not been exactly sinful, Albert's uncle said, but merely silly.

The pistol and the cartridges were confiscated.

I hope the house will never be attacked by burglars. When it is, Albert's uncle will only have himself to thank if we are rapidly overpowered, because it will be his fault that we shall have to meet them totally unarmed, and be their almost unresisting prey.

Chapter 10. The Sale of Antiquities

It began one morning at breakfast. It was the fifteenth of August—the birthday of Napoleon the Great, Oswald Bastable, and another very nice writer. Oswald was to keep his birthday on the Saturday, so that his Father could be there. A birthday when there are only many happy returns is a little like Sunday or Christmas Eve. Oswald had a birthday-card or two—that was all; but he did not repine, because he knew they always make it up to you for putting off keeping your birthday, and he looked forward to Saturday.

Albert's uncle had a whole stack of letters as usual, and presently he tossed one over to Dora, and said, 'What do you say, little lady? Shall we let them come?'

But Dora, butter-fingered as ever, missed the catch, and Dick and Noel both had a try for it, so that the letter went into the place where the bacon had been, and where now only a frozen-looking lake of bacon fat was slowly hardening, and then somehow it got into the marmalade, and then H. O. got it, and Dora said—

'I don't want the nasty thing now—all grease and stickiness.' So H. O. read it aloud—

MAIDSTONE SOCIETY OF ANTIQUITIES AND FIELD CLUB
Aug. 14, 1900

'DEAR SIR,—At a meeting of the—'

H. O. stuck fast here, and the writing was really very bad, like a spider that has been in the ink-pot crawling in a hurry over the paper without stopping to rub its feet properly on the mat. So Oswald took the letter. He is above minding a little marmalade or bacon. He began to read. It ran thus:

'It's not Antiquities, you little silly,' he said; 'it's Antiquaries.'

'The other's a very good word,' said Albert's uncle, 'and I never call names at breakfast myself—it upsets the digestion, my egregious Oswald.'

'That's a name though,' said Alice, 'and you got it out of "Stalky", too. Go on, Oswald.'

So Oswald went on where he had been interrupted:

'MAIDSTONE SOCIETY OF "ANTIQUARIES" AND FIELD CLUB
Aug. 14, 1900.

'DEAR SIR,—At a meeting of the Committee of this Society it was agreed that a field day should be held on Aug. 20, when the Society proposes to visit the interesting church of Ivybridge and also the Roman remains in the vicinity. Our president, Mr Longchamps, F.R.S., has obtained permission to open a barrow in the Three Trees pasture. We venture to ask whether you would allow the members of the Society to walk through your grounds and to inspect—from without, of course—your beautiful house, which is, as you are doubtless aware, of great historic interest, having been for some years the residence of the celebrated Sir Thomas Wyatt.

—I am, dear Sir, yours faithfully,
EDWARD K. TURNBULL (Hon. Sec.).'

'Just so,' said Albert's uncle; 'well, shall we permit the eye of the Maidstone Antiquities to profane these sacred solitudes, and the foot of the Field Club to kick up a dust on our gravel?'

'Our gravel is all grass,' H. O. said.

And the girls said, 'Oh, do let them come!' It was Alice who said—

'Why not ask them to tea? They'll be very tired coming all the way from Maidstone.'

'Would you really like it?' Albert's uncle asked. 'I'm afraid they'll be but dull dogs, the Antiquities, stuffy old gentlemen with amphorae in their buttonholes instead of orchids, and pedigrees poking out of all their pockets.'

We laughed—because we knew what an amphorae is. If you don't you might look it up in the dicker. It's not a flower, though it sounds like one out of the gardening book, the kind you never hear of anyone growing.

Dora said she thought it would be splendid.

'And we could have out the best china,' she said, 'and decorate the table with flowers. We could have tea in the garden. We've never had a party since we've been here.'

'I warn you that your guests may be boresome; however, have it your own way,' Albert's uncle said; and he went off to write the invitation to tea to the Maidstone Antiquities. I know that is the wrong word but somehow we all used it whenever we spoke of them, which was often.

In a day or two Albert's uncle came in to tea with a lightly-clouded brow.

'You've let me in for a nice thing,' he said. 'I asked the Antiquities to tea, and I asked casually how many we might expect. I thought we might need at least the full dozen of the best teacups. Now the secretary writes accepting my kind invitation—'

'Oh, good!' we cried. 'And how many are coming?' 'Oh, only about sixty,' was the groaning rejoinder. 'Perhaps more, should the weather be exceptionally favourable.'

Though stunned at first, we presently decided that we were pleased.

We had never, never given such a big party.

The girls were allowed to help in the kitchen, where Mrs Pettigrew made cakes all day long without stopping. They did not let us boys be there, though I cannot see any harm in putting your finger in a cake before it is baked, and then licking your finger, if you are careful to put a different finger in the cake next time. Cake before it is baked is delicious—like a sort of cream.

Albert's uncle said he was the prey of despair. He drove in to Maidstone one day. When we asked him where he was going, he said—

'To get my hair cut: if I keep it this length I shall certainly tear it out by double handfuls in the extremity of my anguish every time I think of those innumerable Antiquities.'

But we found out afterwards that he really went to borrow china and things to give the Antiquities their tea out of; though he did have his hair cut too, because he is the soul of truth and honour.

Oswald had a very good sort of birthday, with bows and arrows as well as other presents. I think these were meant to make up for the pistol that was taken away after the adventure of the fox-hunting. These gave us boys something to do between the birthday-keeping, which was on the Saturday, and the Wednesday when the Antiquities were to come.

We did not allow the girls to play with the bows and arrows, because they had the cakes that we were cut off from: there was little or no unpleasantness over this.

On the Tuesday we went down to look at the Roman place where the Antiquities were going to dig. We sat on the Roman wall and ate nuts. And as we sat there, we saw coming through the beet-field two labourers with picks and shovels, and a very young man with thin legs and a bicycle. It turned out afterwards to be a free-wheel, the first we had ever seen.

They stopped at a mound inside the Roman wall, and the men took their coats off and spat on their hands.

We went down at once, of course. The thin-legged bicyclist explained his machine to us very fully and carefully when we asked him, and then we saw the men were cutting turfs and turning them over and rolling them up and putting them in a heap. So we asked the gentleman with the thin legs what they were doing. He said—

'They are beginning the preliminary excavation in readiness for to-morrow.'

'What's up to-morrow?' H. O. asked.

'To-morrow we propose to open this barrow and examine it.'

'Then YOU'RE the Antiquities?' said H. O.

'I'm the secretary,' said the gentleman, smiling, but narrowly.

'Oh, you're all coming to tea with us,' Dora said, and added anxiously, 'how many of you do you think there'll be?'

'Oh, not more than eighty or ninety, I should think,' replied the gentleman.

This took our breath away and we went home. As we went, Oswald, who notices many things that would pass unobserved by the light and careless, saw Denny frowning hard. So he said, 'What's up?'

'I've got an idea,' the Dentist said. 'Let's call a council.' The Dentist had grown quite used to our ways now. We had called him Dentist ever since the fox-hunt day. He called a council as if he had been used to calling such things all his life, and having them come, too; whereas we all know that his former existing was that of a white mouse in a trap, with that cat of a Murdstone aunt watching him through the bars.

(That is what is called a figure of speech. Albert's uncle told me.)

Councils are held in the straw-loft. As soon as we were all there, and the straw had stopped rustling after our sitting down, Dicky said—

'I hope it's nothing to do with the Wouldbegoods?'

'No,' said Denny in a hurry: 'quite the opposite.'

'I hope it's nothing wrong,' said Dora and Daisy together.

'It's—it's "Hail to thee, blithe spirit—bird thou never wert",' said Denny. 'I mean, I think it's what is called a lark.'

'You never know your luck. Go on, Dentist,' said Dicky.

'Well, then, do you know a book called The Daisy Chain?'

We didn't.

'It's by Miss Charlotte M. Yonge,' Daisy interrupted, 'and it's about a family of poor motherless children who tried so hard to be good, and they were confirmed, and had a bazaar, and went to church at the Minster, and one of them got married and wore black watered silk and silver ornaments. So her baby died, and then she was sorry she had not been a good mother to it. And— ' Here Dicky got up and said he'd got some snares to attend to, and he'd receive a report of the Council after it was over. But he only got as far as the trap-door, and then Oswald, the fleet of foot, closed with him, and they rolled together on the floor, while all the others called out 'Come back! Come back!' like guinea-hens on a fence.

Through the rustle and bustle and hustle of the struggle with Dicky, Oswald heard the voice of Denny murmuring one of his everlasting quotations—

'"Come back, come back!" he cried in Greek, "Across the stormy water, And I'll forgive your Highland cheek, My daughter, O my daughter!"'

When quiet was restored and Dicky had agreed to go through with the Council, Denny said—

'The Daisy Chain is not a bit like that really. It's a ripping book. One of the boys dresses up like a lady and comes to call, and another tries to hit his little sister with a hoe. It's jolly fine, I tell you.'

Denny is learning to say what he thinks, just like other boys. He would never have learnt such words as 'ripping' and 'jolly fine' while under the auntal tyranny.

Since then I have read The Daisy Chain. It is a first-rate book for girls and little boys.

But we did not want to talk about The Daisy Chain just then, so Oswald said—

'But what's your lark?' Denny got pale pink and said—

'Don't hurry me. I'll tell you directly. Let me think a minute.'

Then he shut his pale pink eyelids a moment in thought, and then opened them and stood up on the straw and said very fast—

'Friends, Romans, countrymen, lend me your ears, or if not ears, pots. You know Albert's uncle said they were going to open the barrow, to look for Roman remains to-morrow. Don't you think it seems a pity they shouldn't find any?'

'Perhaps they will,' Dora said.

But Oswald saw, and he said 'Primus! Go ahead, old man.'

The Dentist went ahead.

'In The Daisy Chain,' he said, 'they dug in a Roman encampment and the children went first and put some pottery there they'd made themselves, and Harry's old medal of the Duke of Wellington. The doctor helped them to some stuff to partly efface the inscription, and all the grown-ups were sold. I thought we might—

> 'You may break, you may shatter
> The vase if you will;
> But the scent of the Romans
> Will cling round it still.'

Denny sat down amid applause. It really was a great idea, at least for HIM. It seemed to add just what was wanted to the visit of the Maidstone Antiquities. To sell the Antiquities thoroughly would be indeed splendiferous. Of course Dora made haste to point out that we had not got an old medal of the Duke of Wellington, and that we hadn't any doctor who would 'help us to stuff to efface', and etcetera; but we sternly bade her stow it. We weren't going to do EXACTLY like those Daisy Chain kids.

The pottery was easy. We had made a lot of it by the stream—which was the Nile when we discovered its source—and dried it in the sun, and then baked it under a bonfire, like in Foul Play. And most of the things were such queer shapes that they should have done for almost anything—Roman or Greek, or even Egyptian or antediluvian, or household milk-jugs of the cavemen, Albert's uncle said. The pots were, fortunately, quite ready and dirty, because we had already buried them in mixed sand and river mud to improve the colour, and not remembered to wash it off.

So the Council at once collected it all—and some rusty hinges and some brass buttons and a file without a handle; and the girl Councillors carried it all concealed in their pinafores, while the men members carried digging tools. H. O. and Daisy were sent on ahead as scouts to see if the coast was clear. We have learned the true usefulness of scouts from reading about the Transvaal War. But all was still in the hush of evening sunset on the Roman ruin.

We posted sentries, who were to lie on their stomachs on the walls and give a long, low, signifying whistle if aught approached.

Then we dug a tunnel, like the one we once did after treasure, when we happened to bury a boy. It took some time; but never shall it be said that a Bastable grudged time or trouble when a lark was at stake. We put the things in as naturally as we could, and shoved the dirt back, till everything looked just as before. Then we went home, late for tea. But it was in a good cause; and there was no hot toast, only bread-and-butter, which does not get cold with waiting.

That night Alice whispered to Oswald on the stairs, as we went up to bed—

'Meet me outside your door when the others are asleep. Hist! Not a word.'

Oswald said, 'No kid?' And she replied in the affirmation.

So he kept awake by biting his tongue and pulling his hair—for he shrinks from no pain if it is needful and right.

And when the others all slept the sleep of innocent youth, he got up and went out, and there was Alice dressed.

She said, 'I've found some broken things that look ever so much more Roman—they were on top of the cupboard in the library. If you'll come with me, we'll bury them just to see how surprised the others will be.'

It was a wild and daring act, but Oswald did not mind.

He said—

'Wait half a shake.' And he put on his knickerbockers and jacket, and slipped a few peppermints into his pocket in case of catching cold. It is these thoughtful expedients which mark the born explorer and adventurer.

It was a little cold; but the white moonlight was very fair to see, and we decided we'd do some other daring moonlight act some other day. We got out of the front door, which is never locked till Albert's uncle goes to bed at twelve or one, and we ran swiftly and silently across the bridge and through the fields to the Roman ruin.

Alice told me afterwards she should have been afraid if it had been dark. But the moonlight made it as bright as day is in your dreams.

Oswald had taken the spade and a sheet of newspaper.

We did not take all the pots Alice had found—but just the two that weren't broken—two crooked jugs, made of stuff like flower-pots are made of. We made two long cuts with the spade and lifted the turf up and scratched the earth under, and took it out very carefully in handfuls on to the newspaper, till the hole was deepish. Then we put in the jugs, and filled it up with earth and flattened the turf over. Turf stretches like elastic. This we did a couple of yards from the place where the mound was dug into by the men, and we had been so careful with the newspaper that there was no loose earth about.

Then we went home in the wet moonlight—at least the grass was very wet—chuckling through the peppermint, and got up to bed without anyone knowing a single thing about it.

The next day the Antiquities came. It was a jolly hot day, and the tables were spread under the trees on the lawn, like a large and very grand Sunday-school treat. There were dozens of different kinds of cake, and bread-and-butter, both white and brown, and gooseberries and plums and jam sandwiches. And the girls decorated the tables with flowers—blue larkspur and white Canterbury bells. And at about three there was a noise of people walking in the road, and presently the Antiquities began to come in at the front gate, and stood about on the lawn by twos and threes and sixes and sevens, looking shy and uncomfy, exactly like a Sunday-school treat. Presently some gentlemen came, who looked like the teachers; they were not shy, and they came right up to the door. So Albert's uncle, who had not been too proud to be up in our room with us watching the people on the lawn through the netting of our short blinds, said—

'I suppose that's the Committee. Come on!'

So we all went down—we were in our Sunday things—and Albert's uncle received the Committee like a feudal system baron, and we were his retainers.

He talked about dates, and king posts and gables, and mullions, and foundations, and records, and Sir Thomas Wyatt, and poetry, and Julius Caesar, and Roman remains, and lych gates and churches, and dog's-tooth moulding till the brain of Oswald reeled. I suppose that Albert's uncle remarked that all our mouths were open, which is a sign of reels in the brain, for he whispered—

'Go hence, and mingle unsuspected with the crowd!'

So we went out on to the lawn, which was now crowded with men and women and one child. This was a girl; she was fat, and we tried to talk to her, though we did not like her. (She was covered in red velvet like an arm-chair.) But she wouldn't. We thought at first she was from a deaf-and-dumb asylum, where her kind teachers had only managed to teach the afflicted to say 'Yes' and 'No'. But afterwards we knew better, for Noel heard her say to her mother, 'I wish you hadn't brought me, mamma. I didn't have a pretty teacup, and I haven't enjoyed my tea one bit.' And she had had five pieces of cake, besides little cakes and nearly a whole plate of plums, and there were only twelve pretty teacups altogether.

Several grown-ups talked to us in a most uninterested way, and then the President read a paper about the Moat House, which we couldn't understand, and other people made speeches we couldn't understand either, except the part about kind hospitality, which made us not know where to look.

Then Dora and Alice and Daisy and Mrs Pettigrew poured out the tea, and we handed cups and plates.

Albert's uncle took me behind a bush to see him tear what was left of his hair when he found there were one hundred and twenty-three Antiquities present, and I heard the President say to the Secretary that 'tea always fetched them'.

Then it was time for the Roman ruin, and our hearts beat high as we took our hats—it was exactly like Sunday—and joined the crowded procession of eager Antiquities. Many of them had umbrellas and overcoats, though the weather was fiery and without a cloud. That is the sort of people they were. The ladies all wore stiff bonnets, and no one took their gloves off, though, of course, it was quite in the country, and it is not wrong to take your gloves off there.

We had planned to be quite close when the digging went on; but Albert's uncle made us a mystic sign and drew us apart.

Then he said: 'The stalls and dress circle are for the guests. The hosts and hostesses retire to the gallery, whence, I am credibly informed, an excellent view may be obtained.'

So we all went up on the Roman walls, and thus missed the cream of the lark; for we could not exactly see what was happening. But we saw that things were being taken from the ground as the men dug, and passed round for the Antiquities to look at. And we knew they must be our Roman remains; but the Antiquities did not seem to care for them much, though we heard sounds of pleased laughter. And at last Alice and I exchanged meaning glances when the spot was reached where we had put in the extras. Then the crowd closed up thick, and we heard excited talk and we knew we really HAD sold the Antiquities this time.

Presently the bonnets and coats began to spread out and trickle towards the house and we were aware that all would soon be over. So we cut home the back way, just in time to hear the President saying to Albert's uncle—

'A genuine find—most interesting. Oh, really, you ought to have ONE. Well, if you insist—'

And so, by slow and dull degrees, the thick sprinkling of Antiquities melted off the lawn; the party was over, and only the dirty teacups and plates, and the trampled grass and the pleasures of memory were left.

We had a very beautiful supper—out of doors, too— with jam sandwiches and cakes and things that were over; and as we watched the setting monarch of the skies—I mean the sun— Alice said—

'Let's tell.'

We let the Dentist tell, because it was he who hatched the lark, but we helped him a little in the narrating of the fell plot, because he has yet to learn how to tell a story straight from the beginning.

When he had done, and we had done, Albert's uncle said, 'Well, it amused you; and you'll be glad to learn that it amused your friends the Antiquities.'

'Didn't they think they were Roman?' Daisy said; 'they did in The Daisy Chain.'

'Not in the least,' said Albert's uncle; 'but the Treasurer and Secretary were charmed by your ingenious preparations for their reception.'

'We didn't want them to be disappointed,' said Dora.

'They weren't,' said Albert's uncle. 'Steady on with those plums, H.O. A little way beyond the treasure you had prepared for them they found two specimens of REAL Roman pottery which sent every man-jack of them home thanking his stars he had been born a happy little Antiquary child.'

'Those were our jugs,' said Alice, 'and we really HAVE sold the Antiquities. She unfolded the tale about our getting the jugs and burying them in the moonlight, and the mound; and the others listened with deeply respectful interest. 'We really have done it this time, haven't we?' she added in tones of well-deserved triumph.

But Oswald had noticed a queer look about Albert's uncle from almost the beginning of Alice's recital; and he now had the sensation of something being up, which has on other occasions frozen his noble blood. The silence of Albert's uncle now froze it yet more Arcticly.

'Haven't we?' repeated Alice, unconscious of what her sensitive brother's delicate feelings had already got hold of. 'We have done it this time, haven't we?'

'Since you ask me thus pointedly,' answered Albert's uncle at last, 'I cannot but confess that I think you have indeed done it. Those pots on the top of the library cupboard ARE Roman pottery. The amphorae which you hid in the mound are probably—I can't say for certain, mind—priceless. They are the property of the owner of this house. You have taken them out and buried them. The President of the Maidstone Antiquarian Society has taken them away in his bag. Now what are you going to do?'

Alice and I did not know what to say, or where to look. The others added to our pained position by some ungenerous murmurs about our not being so jolly clever as we thought ourselves.

There was a very far from pleasing silence. Then Oswald got up. He said—

'Alice, come here a sec; I want to speak to you.'

As Albert's uncle had offered no advice, Oswald disdained to ask him for any.

Alice got up too, and she and Oswald went into the garden, and sat down on the bench under the quince tree, and wished they had never tried to have a private lark of their very own with the Antiquities —'A Private Sale', Albert's uncle called it afterwards. But regrets, as nearly always happens, were vain. Something had to be done.

But what?

Oswald and Alice sat in silent desperateness, and the voices of the gay and careless others came to them from the lawn, where, heartless in their youngness, they were playing tag. I don't know how they could. Oswald would not like to play tag when his brother and sister were in a hole, but Oswald is an exception to some boys.

But Dicky told me afterwards he thought it was only a joke of Albert's uncle's.

The dusk grew dusker, till you could hardly tell the quinces from the leaves, and Alice and Oswald still sat exhausted with hard thinking, but they could not think of anything. And it grew so dark that the moonlight began to show.

Then Alice jumped up—just as Oswald was opening his mouth to say the same thing—and said, 'Of course—how silly! I know. Come on in, Oswald.' And they went on in.

Oswald was still far too proud to consult anyone else. But he just asked carelessly if Alice and he might go into Maidstone the next day to buy some wire-netting for a rabbit-hutch, and to see after one or two things.

Albert's uncle said certainly. And they went by train with the bailiff from the farm, who was going in about some sheep-dip and too buy pigs. At any other time Oswald would not have been able to bear to leave the bailiff without seeing the pigs bought. But now it was different. For he and Alice had the weight on their bosoms of being thieves without having meant it—and nothing, not even pigs, had power to charm the young but honourable Oswald till that stain had been wiped away.

So he took Alice to the Secretary of the Maidstone Antiquities' house, and Mr Turnbull was out, but the maid-servant kindly told us where the President lived, and ere long the trembling feet of the unfortunate brother and sister vibrated on the spotless gravel of Camperdown Villa.

When they asked, they were told that Mr Longchamps was at home. Then they waited, paralysed with undescribed emotions, in a large room with books and swords and glass bookcases with rotten-looking odds and ends in them. Mr Longchamps was a collector. That means he stuck to anything, no matter how ugly and silly, if only it was old.

He came in rubbing his hands, and very kind. He remembered us very well, he said, and asked what he could do for us.

Oswald for once was dumb. He could not find words in which to own himself the ass he had been. But Alice was less delicately moulded. She said—

'Oh, if you please, we are most awfully sorry, and we hope you'll forgive us, but we thought it would be such a pity for you and all the other poor dear Antiquities to come all that way and then find nothing Roman—so we put some pots and things in the barrow for you to find.'

'So I perceived,' said the President, stroking his white beard and smiling most agreeably at us; 'a harmless joke, my dear! Youth's the season for jesting. There's no harm done—pray think no more about it. It's very honourable of you to come and apologize, I'm sure.'

His brow began to wear the furrowed, anxious look of one who would fain be rid of his guests and get back to what he was doing before they interrupted him.

Alice said, 'We didn't come for that. It's MUCH worse. Those were two REAL true Roman jugs you took away; we put them there; they aren't ours. We didn't know they were real Roman. We wanted to sell the Antiquities—I mean Antiquaries—and we were sold ourselves.'

'This is serious,' said the gentleman. 'I suppose you'd know the—the "jugs" if you saw them again?'

'Anywhere,' said Oswald, with the confidential rashness of one who does not know what he is talking about.

Mr Longchamps opened the door of a little room leading out of the one we were in, and beckoned us to follow. We found ourselves amid shelves and shelves of pottery of all sorts; and two whole shelves —small ones—were filled with the sort of jug we wanted.

'Well,' said the President, with a veiled menacing sort of smile, like a wicked cardinal, 'which is it?'

Oswald said, 'I don't know.'

Alice said, 'I should know if I had it in my hand.'

The President patiently took the jugs down one after another, and Alice tried to look inside them. And one after another she shook her head and gave them back. At last she said, 'You didn't WASH them?'

Mr Longchamps shuddered and said 'No'.

'Then,' said Alice, 'there is something written with lead-pencil inside both the jugs. I wish I hadn't. I would rather you didn't read it. I didn't know it would be a nice old gentleman like you would find it. I thought it would be the younger gentleman with the thin legs and the narrow smile.'

'Mr Turnbull.' The President seemed to recognize the description unerringly. 'Well, well—boys will be boys—girls, I mean. I won't be angry. Look at all the "jugs" and see if you can find yours.'

Alice did—and the next one she looked at she said, 'This is one'—and two jugs further on she said, 'This is the other.'

'Well,' the President said, 'these are certainly the specimens which I obtained yesterday. If your uncle will call on me I will return them to him. But it's a disappointment. Yes, I think you must let me look inside.'

He did. And at the first one he said nothing. At the second he laughed.

'Well, well,' he said, 'we can't expect old heads on young shoulders. You're not the first who went forth to shear and returned shorn. Nor, it appears, am I. Next time you have a Sale of Antiquities, take care that you yourself are not "sold". Good-day to you, my dear. Don't let the incident prey on your mind,' he said to Alice. 'Bless your heart, I was a boy once myself, unlikely as you may think it. Good-bye.'

We were in time to see the pigs bought after all.

I asked Alice what on earth it was she'd scribbled inside the beastly jugs, and she owned that just to make the lark complete she had written 'Sucks' in one of the jugs, and 'Sold again, silly', in the other.

But we know well enough who it was that was sold. And if ever we have any Antiquities to tea again, they shan't find so much as a Greek waistcoat button if we can help it.

Unless it's the President, for he did not behave at all badly. For a man of his age I think he behaved exceedingly well. Oswald can picture a very different scene having been enacted over those rotten pots if the President had been an otherwise sort of man.

But that picture is not pleasing, so Oswald will not distress you by drawing it for you. You can most likely do it easily for yourself.

Chapter 11. The Benevolent Bar

The tramp was very dusty about the feet and legs, and his clothes were very ragged and dirty, but he had cheerful twinkly grey eyes, and he touched his cap to the girls when he spoke to us, though a little as though he would rather not.

We were on the top of the big wall of the Roman ruin in the Three Tree pasture. We had just concluded a severe siege with bows and arrows—the ones that were given us to make up for the pistol that was confiscated after the sad but not sinful occasion when it shot a fox.

To avoid accidents that you would be sorry for afterwards, Oswald, in his thoughtfulness, had decreed that everyone was to wear wire masks.

Luckily there were plenty of these, because a man who lived in the Moat House once went to Rome, where they throw hundreds and thousands at each other in play, and call it a Comfit Battle or Battaglia di Confetti (that's real Italian). And he wanted to get up that sort of thing among the village people—but they were too beastly slack, so he chucked it.

And in the attic were the wire masks he brought home with him from Rome, which people wear to prevent the nasty comfits getting in their mouths and eyes.

So we were all armed to the teeth with masks and arrows, but in attacking or defending a fort your real strength is not in your equipment, but in your power of Shove. Oswald, Alice, Noel and Denny defended the fort. We were much the strongest side, but that was how Dicky and Oswald picked up.

The others got in, it is true, but that was only because an arrow hit Dicky on the nose, and it bled quarts as usual, though hit only through the wire mask. Then he put into dock for repairs, and while the defending party weren't looking he sneaked up the wall at the back and shoved Oswald off, and fell on top of him, so that the fort, now that it had lost its gallant young leader, the life and soul of the besieged party, was of course soon overpowered, and had to surrender.

Then we sat on the top and ate some peppermints Albert's uncle brought us a bag of from Maidstone when he went to fetch away the Roman pottery we tried to sell the Antiquities with.

The battle was over, and peace raged among us as we sat in the sun on the big wall and looked at the fields, all blue and swimming in the heat.

We saw the tramp coming through the beetfield. He made a dusty blot on the fair scene.

When he saw us he came close to the wall, and touched his cap, as I have said, and remarked—

'Excuse me interrupting of your sports, young gentlemen and ladies, but if you could so far oblige as to tell a labouring man the way to the nearest pub. It's a dry day and no error.'

'The "Rose and Crown" is the best pub,' said Dicky, 'and the landlady is a friend of ours. It's about a mile if you go by the field path.'

'Lor' love a duck!' said the tramp, 'a mile's a long way, and walking's a dry job this 'ere weather.' We said we agreed with him.

'Upon my sacred,' said the tramp, 'if there was a pump handy I believe I'd take a turn at it—I would indeed, so help me if I wouldn't! Though water always upsets me and makes my 'and shaky.'

We had not cared much about tramps since the adventure of the villainous sailor-man and the Tower of Mystery, but we had the dogs on the wall with us (Lady was awfully difficult to get up, on account of her long deer-hound legs), and the position was a strong one, and easy to defend. Besides the tramp did not look like that bad sailor, nor talk like it. And we considerably outnumbered the tramp, anyway.

Alice nudged Oswald and said something about Sir Philip Sidney and the tramp's need being greater than his, so Oswald was obliged to go to the hole in the top of the wall where we store provisions during sieges and get out the bottle of ginger-beer which he had gone without when the others had theirs so as to drink it when he got really thirsty. Meanwhile Alice said—

'We've got some ginger-beer; my brother's getting it. I hope you won't mind drinking out of our glass. We can't wash it, you know—unless we rinse it out with a little ginger-beer.'

'Don't ye do it, miss,' he said eagerly; 'never waste good liquor on washing.'

The glass was beside us on the wall. Oswald filled it with ginger-beer and handed down the foaming tankard to the tramp. He had to lie on his young stomach to do this.

The tramp was really quite polite—one of Nature's gentlemen, and a man as well, we found out afterwards. He said—

'Here's to you!' before he drank. Then he drained the glass till the rim rested on his nose.

'Swelp me, but I WAS dry,' he said. 'Don't seem to matter much what it is, this weather, do it?—so long as it's suthink wet. Well, here's thanking you.'

'You're very welcome,' said Dora; 'I'm glad you liked it.'

'Like it?'—said he. 'I don't suppose you know what it's like to have a thirst on you. Talk of free schools and free libraries, and free baths and wash-houses and such! Why don't someone start free DRINKS? He'd be a ero, he would. I'd vote for him any day of the week and one over. Ef yer don't objec I'll set down a bit and put on a pipe.'

He sat down on the grass and began to smoke. We asked him questions about himself, and he told us many of his secret sorrows—especially about there being no work nowadays for an honest man. At last he dropped asleep in the middle of a story about a vestry he worked for that hadn't acted fair and square by him like he had by them, or it (I don't know if vestry is singular or plural), and we went home. But before we went we held a hurried council and collected what money we could from the little we had with us (it was ninepence-halfpenny), and wrapped it in an old envelope Dicky had in his pocket and put it gently on the billowing middle of the poor tramp's sleeping waistcoat, so that he would find it when he woke. None of the dogs said a single syllable while we were doing this, so we knew they believed him to be poor but honest, and we always find it safe to take their word for things like that.

As we went home a brooding silence fell upon us; we found out afterwards that those words of the poor tramp's about free drinks had sunk deep in all our hearts, and rankled there.

After dinner we went out and sat with our feet in the stream. People tell you it makes your grub disagree with you to do this just after meals, but it never hurts us. There is a fallen willow across the stream that just seats the eight of us, only the ones at the end can't get their feet into the water properly because of the bushes, so we keep changing places. We had got some liquorice root to chew. This helps thought. Dora broke a peaceful silence with this speech—

'Free drinks.'

The words awoke a response in every breast.

'I wonder someone doesn't,' H. O. said, leaning back till he nearly toppled in, and was only saved by Oswald and Alice at their own deadly peril.

'Do for goodness sake sit still, H. O.,' observed Alice. 'It would be a glorious act! I wish WE could.'

'What, sit still?' asked H. O.

'No, my child,' replied Oswald, 'most of us can do that when we try. Your angel sister was only wishing to set up free drinks for the poor and thirsty.'

'Not for all of them,' Alice said, 'just a few. Change places now, Dicky. My feet aren't properly wet at all.'

It is very difficult to change places safely on the willow. The changers have to crawl over the laps of the others, while the rest sit tight and hold on for all they're worth. But the hard task was accomplished and then Alice went on—

'And we couldn't do it for always, only a day or two—just while our money held out. Eiffel Tower lemonade's the best, and you get a jolly lot of it for your money too. There must be a great many sincerely thirsty persons go along the Dover Road every day.'

'It wouldn't be bad. We've got a little chink between us,' said Oswald.

'And then think how the poor grateful creatures would linger and tell us about their inmost sorrows. It would be most frightfully interesting. We could write all their agonied life histories down afterwards like All the Year Round Christmas numbers. Oh, do let's!'

Alice was wriggling so with earnestness that Dicky thumped her to make her calm.

'We might do it, just for one day,' Oswald said, 'but it wouldn't be much—only a drop in the ocean compared with the enormous dryness of all the people in the whole world. Still, every little helps, as the mermaid said when she cried into the sea.'

'I know a piece of poetry about that,' Denny said.

> 'Small things are best.
> Care and unrest
> To wealth and rank are given,
> But little things
> On little wings—

do something or other, I forget what, but it means the same as Oswald was saying about the mermaid.'

'What are you going to call it?' asked Noel, coming out of a dream.

'Call what?'

'The Free Drinks game.'

> 'It's a horrid shame
> If the Free Drinks game
> Doesn't have a name.
> You would be to blame
> If anyone came
> And—'

'Oh, shut up!' remarked Dicky. 'You've been making that rot up all the time we've been talking instead of listening properly.' Dicky hates poetry. I don't mind it so very much myself, especially Macaulay's and Kipling's and Noel's.

'There was a lot more—"lame" and "dame" and name" and "game" and things—and now I've forgotten it,' Noel said in gloom.

'Never mind,' Alice answered, 'it'll come back to you in the silent watches of the night; you see if it doesn't. But really, Noel's right, it OUGHT to have a name.'

'Free Drinks Company.' 'Thirsty Travellers' Rest.' 'The Travellers' Joy.'

These names were suggested, but not cared for extra.

Then someone said—I think it was Oswald— 'Why not "The House Beautiful"?'

'It can't be a house, it must be in the road. It'll only be a stall.'

'The "Stall Beautiful" is simply silly,' Oswald said.

'The "Bar Beautiful" then,' said Dicky, who knows what the 'Rose and Crown' bar is like inside, which of course is hidden from girls.

'Oh, wait a minute,' cried the Dentist, snapping his fingers like he always does when he is trying to remember things. 'I thought of something, only Daisy tickled me and it's gone—I know—let's call it the Benevolent Bar!'

It was exactly right, and told the whole truth in two words. 'Benevolent' showed it was free and 'Bar' showed what was free; e.g. things to drink. The 'Benevolent Bar' it was.

We went home at once to prepare for the morrow, for of course we meant to do it the very next day. Procrastination is you know what—and delays are dangerous. If we had waited long we might have happened to spend our money on something else.

The utmost secrecy had to be observed, because Mrs Pettigrew hates tramps. Most people do who keep fowls. Albert's uncle was in London till the next evening, so we could not consult him, but we know he is always chock full of intelligent sympathy with the poor and needy.

Acting with the deepest disguise, we made an awning to cover the Benevolent Bar keepers from the searching rays of the monarch of the skies. We found some old striped sun-blinds in the attic, and the girls sewed them together. They were not very big when they were done, so we added the girls' striped petticoats. I am sorry their petticoats turn up so constantly in my narrative, but they really are very useful, especially when the band is cut off. The girls borrowed Mrs Pettigrew's sewing-machine; they could not ask her leave without explanations, which we did not wish to give just then, and she had lent it to them before. They took it into the cellar to work it, so that she should not hear the noise and ask bothering questions.

They had to balance it on one end of the beer-stand. It was not easy. While they were doing the sewing we boys went out and got willow poles and chopped the twigs off, and got ready as well as we could to put up the awning.

When we returned a detachment of us went down to the shop in the village for Eiffel Tower lemonade. We bought seven-and-sixpence worth; then we made a great label to say what the bar was for. Then there was nothing else to do except to make rosettes out of a blue sash of Daisy's to show we belonged to the Benevolent Bar.

The next day was as hot as ever. We rose early from our innocent slumbers, and went out to the Dover Road to the spot we had marked down the day before. It was at a cross-roads, so as to be able to give drinks to as many people as possible.

We hid the awning and poles behind the hedge and went home to brekker.

After break we got the big zinc bath they wash clothes in, and after filling it with clean water we just had to empty it again because it was too heavy to lift. So we carried it vacant to the trysting-spot and left H. O. and Noel to guard it while we went and fetched separate pails of water; very heavy work, and no one who wasn't really benevolent would have bothered about it for an instant. Oswald alone carried three pails. So did Dicky and the Dentist. Then we rolled down some empty barrels and stood up three of them by the roadside, and put planks on them. This made a very first-class table, and we covered it with the best tablecloth we could find in the linen cupboard. We brought out several glasses and some teacups—not the best ones, Oswald was firm about that—and the kettle and spirit-lamp and the tea-pot, in case any weary tramp-woman fancied a cup of tea instead of Eiffel Tower. H. O. and Noel had to go down to the shop for tea; they need not have grumbled; they had not carried any of the water. And their having to go the second time was only because we forgot to tell them to get some real lemons to put on the bar to show what the drink would be like when you got it. The man at the shop kindly gave us tick for the lemons, and we cashed up out of our next week's pocket-money.

Two or three people passed while we were getting things ready, but no one said anything except the man who said, 'Bloomin' Sunday-school treat', and as it was too early in the day for anyone to be thirsty we did not stop the wayfarers to tell them their thirst could be slaked without cost at our Benevolent Bar.

But when everything was quite ready, and our blue rosettes fastened on our breasts over our benevolent hearts, we stuck up the great placard we had made with 'Benevolent Bar. Free Drinks to all Weary Travellers', in white wadding on red calico, like Christmas decorations in church. We had meant to fasten this to the edge of the awning, but we had to pin it to the front of the tablecloth, because I am sorry to say the awning went wrong from the first. We could not drive the willow poles into the road; it was much too hard. And in the ditch it was too soft, besides being no use. So we had just to cover our benevolent heads with our hats, and take it in turns to go into the shadow of the tree on the other side of the road. For we had pitched our table on the sunny side of the way, of course, relying on our broken-reed-like awning, and wishing to give it a fair chance.

Everything looked very nice, and we longed to see somebody really miserable come along so as to be able to allieve their distress.

A man and woman were the first: they stopped and stared, but when Alice said, 'Free drinks! Free drinks! Aren't you thirsty?' they said, 'No thank you,' and went on. Then came a person from the village—he didn't even say 'Thank you' when we asked him, and Oswald began to fear it might be like the awful time when we wandered about on Christmas Day trying to find poor persons and persuade them to eat our Conscience pudding.

But a man in a blue jersey and a red bundle eased Oswald's fears by being willing to drink a glass of lemonade, and even to say, 'Thank you, I'm sure' quite nicely.

After that it was better. As we had foreseen, there were plenty of thirsty people walking along the Dover Road, and even some from the cross-road.

We had had the pleasure of seeing nineteen tumblers drained to the dregs ere we tasted any ourselves. Nobody asked for tea.

More people went by than we gave lemonade to. Some wouldn't have it because they were too grand. One man told us he could pay for his own liquor when he was dry, which, praise be, he wasn't over and above, at present; and others asked if we hadn't any beer, and when we said 'No', they said it showed what sort we were—as if the sort was not a good one, which it is.

And another man said, 'Slops again! You never get nothing for nothing, not this side of heaven you don't. Look at the bloomin' blue ribbon on 'em! Oh, Lor'!' and went on quite sadly without having a drink.

Our Pig-man who helped us on the Tower of Mystery day went by and we hailed him, and explained it all to him and gave him a drink, and asked him to call as he came back. He liked it all, and said we were a real good sort. How different from the man who wanted the beer. Then he went on.

One thing I didn't like, and that was the way boys began to gather. Of course we could not refuse to give drinks to any traveller who was old enough to ask for it, but when one boy had had three glasses of lemonade and asked for another, Oswald said—

'I think you've had jolly well enough. You can't be really thirsty after all that lot.'

The boy said, 'Oh, can't I? You'll just see if I can't,' and went away. Presently he came back with four other boys, all bigger than Oswald; and they all asked for lemonade. Oswald gave it to the four new ones, but he was determined in his behaviour to the other one, and wouldn't give him a drop. Then the five of them went and sat on a gate a little way off and kept laughing in a nasty way, and whenever a boy went by they called out—

'I say, 'ere's a go,' and as often as not the new boy would hang about with them. It was disquieting, for though they had nearly all had lemonade we could see it had not made them friendly.

A great glorious glow of goodness gladdened (those go all together and are called alliteration) our hearts when we saw our own tramp coming down the road. The dogs did not growl at him as they had at the boys or the beer-man. (I did not say before that we had the dogs with us, but of course we had, because we had promised never to go out without them.) Oswald said, 'Hullo,' and the tramp said, 'Hullo.' Then Alice said, 'You see we've taken your advice; we're giving free drinks. Doesn't it all look nice?'

'It does that,' said the tramp. 'I don't mind if I do.'

So we gave him two glasses of lemonade succeedingly, and thanked him for giving us the idea. He said we were very welcome, and if we'd no objection he'd sit down a bit and put on a pipe. He did, and after talking a little more he fell asleep. Drinking anything seemed to end in sleep with him. I always thought it was only beer and things made people sleepy, but he was not so. When he was asleep he rolled into the ditch, but it did not wake him up.

The boys were getting very noisy, and they began to shout things, and to make silly noises with their mouths, and when Oswald and Dicky went over to them and told them to just chuck it, they were worse than ever. I think perhaps Oswald and Dicky might have fought and settled them—though there were eleven, yet back to back you can always do it against overwhelming numbers in a book—only Alice called out—

'Oswald, here's some more, come back!'

We went. Three big men were coming down the road, very red and hot, and not amiable-looking. They stopped in front of the Benevolent Bar and slowly read the wadding and red-stuff label.

Then one of them said he was blessed, or something like that, and another said he was too. The third one said, 'Blessed or not, a drink's a drink. Blue ribbon, though, by —' (a word you ought not to say, though it is in the Bible and the catechism as well). 'Let's have a liquor, little missy.'

The dogs were growling, but Oswald thought it best not to take any notice of what the dogs said, but to give these men each a drink. So he did. They drank, but not as if they cared about it very much, and then they set their glasses down on the table, a liberty no one else had entered into, and began to try and chaff Oswald. Oswald said in an undervoice to H. O.—

'Just take charge. I want to speak to the girls a sec. Call if you want anything.' And then he drew the others away, to say he thought there'd been enough of it, and considering the boys and new three men, perhaps we'd better chuck it and go home. We'd been benevolent nearly four hours anyway.

While this conversation and the objections of the others were going on, H. O. perpetuated an act which nearly wrecked the Benevolent Bar.

Of course Oswald was not an eye or ear witness of what happened, but from what H. O. said in the calmer moments of later life, I think this was about what happened. One of the big disagreeable men said to H. O.—

'Ain't got such a thing as a drop o' spirit, 'ave yer?'

H. O. said no, we hadn't, only lemonade and tea.

'Lemonade and tea! blank' (bad word I told you about) 'and blazes,' replied the bad character, for such he afterwards proved to be. 'What's THAT then?'

He pointed to a bottle labelled Dewar's whisky, which stood on the table near the spirit-kettle.

'Oh, is THAT what you want?' said H. O. kindly.

The man is understood to have said he should bloomin' well think so, but H. O. is not sure about the 'bloomin'.

He held out his glass with about half the lemonade in it, and H. O. generously filled up the tumbler out of the bottle, labelled Dewar's whisky. The man took a great drink, and then suddenly he spat out what happened to be left in his mouth just then, and began to swear. It was then that Oswald and Dicky rushed upon the scene.

The man was shaking his fist in H. O.'s face, and H. O. was still holding on to the bottle we had brought out the methylated spirit in for the lamp, in case of anyone wanting tea, which they hadn't. 'If I was Jim,' said the second ruffian, for such indeed they were, when he had snatched the bottle from H. O. and smelt it, 'I'd chuck the whole show over the hedge, so I would, and you young gutter-snipes after it, so I wouldn't.'

Oswald saw in a moment that in point of strength, if not numbers, he and his party were out-matched, and the unfriendly boys were drawing gladly near. It is no shame to signal for help when in distress—the best ships do it every day. Oswald shouted 'Help, help!' Before the words were out of his brave yet trembling lips our own tramp leapt like an antelope from the ditch and said—

'Now then, what's up?'

The biggest of the three men immediately knocked him down. He lay still.

The biggest then said, 'Come on—any more of you? Come on!'

Oswald was so enraged at this cowardly attack that he actually hit out at the big man—and he really got one in just above the belt. Then he shut his eyes, because he felt that now all was indeed up. There was a shout and a scuffle, and Oswald opened his eyes in astonishment at finding himself still whole and unimpaired. Our own tramp had artfully simulated insensibleness, to get the men off their guard, and then had suddenly got his arms round a leg each of two of the men, and pulled them to the ground, helped by Dicky, who saw his game and rushed in at the same time, exactly like Oswald would have done if he had not had his eyes shut ready to meet his doom.

The unpleasant boys shouted, and the third man tried to help his unrespectable friends, now on their backs involved in a desperate struggle with our own tramp, who was on top of them, accompanied by Dicky. It all happened in a minute, and it was all mixed up. The dogs were growling and barking—Martha had one of the men by the trouser leg and Pincher had another; the girls were screaming like mad and the strange boys shouted and laughed (little beasts!), and then suddenly our Pig-man came round the corner, and two friends of his with him. He had gone and fetched them to take care of us if anything unpleasant occurred. It was a very thoughtful, and just like him.

'Fetch the police!' cried the Pig-man in noble tones, and H. O. started running to do it. But the scoundrels struggled from under Dicky and our tramp, shook off the dogs and some bits of trouser, and fled heavily down the road.

Our Pig-man said, 'Get along home!' to the disagreeable boys, and 'Shoo'd' them as if they were hens, and they went. H. O. ran back when they began to go up the road, and there we were, all standing breathless in tears on the scene of the late desperate engagement. Oswald gives you his word of honour that his and Dicky's tears were tears of pure rage. There are such things as tears of pure rage. Anyone who knows will tell you so.

We picked up our own tramp and bathed the lump on his forehead with lemonade. The water in the zinc bath had been upset in the struggle. Then he and the Pig-man and his kind friends helped us carry our things home.

The Pig-man advised us on the way not to try these sort of kind actions without getting a grown-up to help us. We've been advised this before, but now I really think we shall never try to be benevolent to the poor and needy again. At any rate not unless we know them very well first.

We have seen our own tramp often since. The Pig-man gave him a job. He has got work to do at last. The Pig-man says he is not such a very bad chap, only he will fall asleep after the least drop of drink. We know that is his failing. We saw it at once. But it was lucky for us he fell asleep that day near our benevolent bar.

I will not go into what my father said about it all. There was a good deal in it about minding your own business—there generally is in most of the talkings-to we get. But he gave our tramp a sovereign, and the Pig-man says he went to sleep on it for a solid week.

Chapter 12. The Canterbury Pilgrims

The author of these few lines really does hope to goodness that no one will be such an owl as to think from the number of things we did when we were in the country, that we were wretched, neglected little children, whose grown-up relations sparkled in the bright haunts of pleasure, and whirled in the giddy what's-its-name of fashion, while we were left to weep forsaken at home. It was nothing of the kind, and I wish you to know that my father was with us a good deal—and Albert's uncle (who is really no uncle of ours, but only of Albert next door when we lived in Lewisham) gave up a good many of his valuable hours to us. And the father of Denny and Daisy came now and then, and other people, quite as many as we wished to see. And we had some very decent times with them; and enjoyed ourselves very much indeed, thank you. In some ways the good times you have with grown-ups are better than the ones you have by yourselves. At any rate they are safer. It is almost impossible, then, to do anything fatal without being pulled up short by a grown-up ere yet the deed is done. And, if you are careful, anything that goes wrong can be looked on as the grown-up's fault. But these secure pleasures are not so interesting to tell about as the things you do when there is no one to stop you on the edge of the rash act.

It is curious, too, that many of our most interesting games happened when grown-ups were far away. For instance when we were pilgrims.

It was just after the business of the Benevolent Bar, and it was a wet day. It is not easy to amuse yourself indoors on a wet day as older people seem to think, especially when you are far removed from your own home, and haven't got all your own books and things. The girls were playing Halma—which is a beastly game—Noel was writing poetry, H. O. was singing 'I don't know what to do' to the tune of 'Canaan's happy shore'. It goes like this, and is very tiresome to listen to—

> 'I don't know what to do—oo—oo—oo!
> I don't know what to do—oo—oo!
> It IS a beastly rainy day
> And I don't know what to do.'

The rest of us were trying to make him shut up. We put a carpet bag over his head, but he went on inside it; and then we sat on him, but he sang under us; we held him upside down and made him crawl head first under the sofa, but when, even there, he kept it up, we saw that nothing short of violence would induce him to silence, so we let him go. And then he said we had hurt him, and we said we were only in fun, and he said if we were he wasn't, and ill feeling might have grown up even out of a playful brotherly act like ours had been, only Alice chucked the Halma and said—

'Let dogs delight. Come on—let's play something.'

Then Dora said, 'Yes, but look here. Now we're together I do want to say something. What about the Wouldbegoods Society?'

Many of us groaned, and one said, 'Hear! hear!' I will not say which one, but it was not Oswald.

'No, but really,' Dora said, 'I don't want to be preachy—but you know we DID say we'd try to be good. And it says in a book I was reading only yesterday that NOT being naughty is not enough. You must BE good. And we've hardly done anything. The Golden Deed book's almost empty.'

'Couldn't we have a book of leaden deeds?' said Noel, coming out of his poetry, 'then there'd be plenty for Alice to write about if she wants to, or brass or zinc or aluminium deeds? We shan't ever fill the book with golden ones.'

H. O. had rolled himself in the red tablecloth and said Noel was only advising us to be naughty, and again peace waved in the balance. But Alice said, 'Oh, H. O., DON'T—he didn't mean that; but really and truly, I wish wrong things weren't so interesting. You begin to do a noble act, and then it gets so exciting, and before you know where you are you are doing something wrong as hard as you can lick.'

'And enjoying it too' Dick said.

'It's very curious,' Denny said, 'but you don't seem to be able to be certain inside yourself whether what you're doing is right if you happen to like doing it, but if you don't like doing it you know quite well. I only thought of that just now. I wish Noel would make a poem about it.'

'I am,' Noel said; 'it began about a crocodile but it is finishing itself up quite different from what I meant it to at first. Just wait a minute.'

He wrote very hard while his kind brothers and sisters and his little friends waited the minute he had said, and then he read:

> 'The crocodile is very wise,
> He lives in the Nile with little eyes,
> He eats the hippopotamus too,
> And if he could he would eat up you.
>
> 'The lovely woods and starry skies
> He looks upon with glad surprise!
> He sees the riches of the east,
> And the tiger and lion, kings of beast.
>
> 'So let all be good and beware
> Of saying shan't and won't and don't care;
> For doing wrong is easier far
> Than any of the right things I know about are.

And I couldn't make it king of beasts because of it not rhyming with east, so I put the s off beasts on to king. It comes even in the end.'

We all said it was a very nice piece of poetry. Noel gets really ill if you don't like what he writes, and then he said, 'If it's trying that's wanted, I don't care how hard we TRY to be good, but we may as well do it some nice way. Let's be Pilgrim's Progress, like I wanted to at first.'

And we were all beginning to say we didn't want to, when suddenly Dora said, 'Oh, look here! I know. We'll be the Canterbury Pilgrims. People used to go pilgrimages to make themselves good.'

'With peas in their shoes,' the Dentist said. 'It's in a piece of poetry—only the man boiled his peas—which is quite unfair.'

'Oh, yes,' said H. O., 'and cocked hats.'

'Not cocked—cockled'—it was Alice who said this. 'And they had staffs and scrips, and they told each other tales. We might as well.'

Oswald and Dora had been reading about the Canterbury Pilgrims in a book called A Short History of the English People. It is not at all short really—three fat volumes—but it has jolly good pictures. It was written by a gentleman named Green. So Oswald said—

'All right. I'll be the Knight.'

'I'll be the wife of Bath,' Dora said. 'What will you be, Dicky?'

'Oh, I don't care, I'll be Mr Bath if you like.'

'We don't know much about the people,' Alice said. 'How many were there?'

'Thirty,' Oswald replied, 'but we needn't be all of them. There's a Nun-Priest.'

'Is that a man or a woman?'

Oswald said he could not be sure by the picture, but Alice and Noel could be it between them. So that was settled. Then we got the book and looked at the dresses to see if we could make up dresses for the parts. At first we thought we would, because it would be something to do, and it was a very wet day; but they looked difficult, especially the Miller's. Denny wanted to be the Miller, but in the end he was the Doctor, because it was next door to Dentist, which is what we call him for short. Daisy was to be the Prioress—because she is good, and has 'a soft little red mouth', and H. O. WOULD be the Manciple (I don't know what that is), because the picture of him is bigger than most of the others, and he said Manciple was a nice portmanteau word—half mandarin and half disciple.

'Let's get the easiest parts of the dresses ready first.' Alice said—'the pilgrims' staffs and hats and the cockles.'

So Oswald and Dicky braved the fury of the elements and went into the wood beyond the orchard to cut ash-sticks. We got eight jolly good long ones. Then we took them home, and the girls bothered till we changed our clothes, which were indeed sopping with the elements we had faced.

Then we peeled the sticks. They were nice and white at first, but they soon got dirty when we carried them. It is a curious thing: however often you wash your hands they always seem to come off on anything white. And we nailed paper rosettes to the tops of them. That was the nearest we could get to cockle-shells.

'And we may as well have them there as on our hats,' Alice said. 'And let's call each other by our right names to-day, just to get into it. Don't you think so, Knight?'

'Yea, Nun-Priest,' Oswald was replying, but Noel said she was only half the Nun-Priest, and again a threat of unpleasantness darkened the air. But Alice said—

'Don't be a piggy-wiggy, Noel, dear; you can have it all, I don't want it. I'll just be a plain pilgrim, or Henry who killed Becket.'

So she was called the Plain Pilgrim, and she did not mind.

We thought of cocked hats, but they are warm to wear, and the big garden hats that make you look like pictures on the covers of plantation songs did beautifully. We put cockle-shells on them. Sandals we did try, with pieces of oil-cloth cut the shape of soles and fastened with tape, but the dust gets into your toes so, and we decided boots were better for such a long walk. Some of the pilgrims who were very earnest decided to tie their boots with white tape crossed outside to pretend sandals. Denny was one of these earnest palmers. As for dresses, there was no time to make them properly, and at first we thought of nightgowns; but we decided not to, in case people in Canterbury were not used to that sort of pilgrim nowadays. We made up our minds to go as we were—or as we might happen to be next day.

You will be ready to believe we hoped next day would be fine. It was.

Fair was the morn when the pilgrims arose and went down to breakfast. Albert's uncle had had brekker early and was hard at work in his study. We heard his quill pen squeaking when we listened at the door. It is not wrong to listen at doors when there is only one person inside, because nobody would tell itself secrets aloud when it was alone.

We got lunch from the housekeeper, Mrs Pettigrew. She seems almost to LIKE us all to go out and take our lunch with us. Though I should think it must be very dull for her all alone. I remember, though, that Eliza, our late general at Lewisham, was just the same. We took the dear dogs of course. Since the Tower of Mystery happened we are not allowed to go anywhere without the escort of these faithful friends of man. We did not take Martha, because bull-dogs do not like walks. Remember this if you ever have one of those valuable animals.

When we were all ready, with our big hats and cockle-shells, and our staves and our tape sandals, the pilgrims looked very nice.

'Only we haven't any scrips,' Dora said. 'What is a scrip?'

'I think it's something to read. A roll of parchment or something.'

So we had old newspapers rolled up, and carried them in our hands. We took the Globe and the Westminster Gazette because they are pink and green. The Dentist wore his white sandshoes, sandalled with black tape, and bare legs. They really looked almost as good as bare feet.

'We OUGHT to have peas in our shoes,' he said. But we did not think so. We knew what a very little stone in your boot will do, let alone peas.

Of course we knew the way to go to Canterbury, because the old Pilgrims' Road runs just above our house. It is a very pretty road, narrow, and often shady. It is nice for walking, but carts do not like it because it is rough and rutty; so there is grass growing in patches on it.

I have said that it was a fine day, which means that it was not raining, but the sun did not shine all the time.

''Tis well, O Knight,' said Alice, 'that the orb of day shines not in undi—what's-its-name?—splendour.'

'Thou sayest sooth, Plain Pilgrim,' replied Oswald. ''Tis jolly warm even as it is.'

'I wish I wasn't two people,' Noel said, 'it seems to make me hotter. I think I'll be a Reeve or something.'

But we would not let him, and we explained that if he hadn't been so beastly particular Alice would have been half of him, and he had only himself to thank if being all of a Nun-Priest made him hot.

But it WAS warm certainly, and it was some time since we'd gone so far in boots. Yet when H. O. complained we did our duty as pilgrims and made him shut up. He did as soon as Alice said that about whining and grizzling being below the dignity of a Manciple.

It was so warm that the Prioress and the wife of Bath gave up walking with their arms round each other in their usual silly way (Albert's uncle calls it Laura Matildaing), and the Doctor and Mr Bath had to take their jackets off and carry them.

I am sure if an artist or a photographer, or any person who liked pilgrims, had seen us he would have been very pleased. The paper cockle-shells were first-rate, but it was awkward having them on the top of the staffs, because they got in your way when you wanted the staff to use as a walking-stick.

We stepped out like a man all of us, and kept it up as well as we could in book-talk, and at first all was merry as a dinner-bell; but presently Oswald, who was the 'very perfect gentle knight', could not help noticing that one of us was growing very silent and rather pale, like people are when they have eaten something that disagrees with them before they are quite sure of the fell truth.

So he said, 'What's up, Dentist, old man?' quite kindly and like a perfect knight, though, of course, he was annoyed with Denny. It is sickening when people turn pale in the middle of a game and everything is spoiled, and you have to go home, and tell the spoiler how sorry you are that he is knocked up, and pretend not to mind about the game being spoiled.

Denny said, 'Nothing', but Oswald knew better.

Then Alice said, 'Let's rest a bit, Oswald, it IS hot.'

'Sir Oswald, if you please, Plain Pilgrim,' returned her brother dignifiedly. 'Remember I'm a knight.'

So then we sat down and had lunch, and Denny looked better. We played adverbs, and twenty questions, and apprenticing your son, for a bit in the shade, and then Dicky said it was time to set sail if we meant to make the port of Canterbury that night. Of course, pilgrims reck not of ports, but Dicky never does play the game thoughtfully.

We went on. I believe we should have got to Canterbury all right and quite early, only Denny got paler and paler, and presently Oswald saw, beyond any doubt, that he was beginning to walk lame.

'Shoes hurt you, Dentist?' he said, still with kind striving cheerfulness.

'Not much—it's all right,' returned the other.

So on we went—but we were all a bit tired now—and the sun was hotter and hotter; the clouds had gone away. We had to begin to sing to keep up our spirits. We sang 'The British Grenadiers' and 'John Brown's Body', which is grand to march to, and a lot of others. We were just starting on 'Tramp, tramp, tramp, the boys are marching', when Denny stopped short. He stood first on one foot and then on the other, and suddenly screwed up his face and put his knuckles in his eyes and sat down on a heap of stones by the roadside. When we pulled his hands down he was actually crying. The author does not wish to say it is babyish to cry.

'Whatever is up?' we all asked, and Daisy and Dora petted him to get him to say, but he only went on howling, and said it was nothing, only would we go on and leave him, and call for him as we came back.

Oswald thought very likely something had given Denny the stomach-ache, and he did not like to say so before all of us, so he sent the others away and told them to walk on a bit.

Then he said, 'Now, Denny, don't be a young ass. What is it? Is it stomach-ache?'

And Denny stopped crying to say 'No!' as loud as he could.

'Well, then,' Oswald said, 'look here, you're spoiling the whole thing. Don't be a jackape, Denny. What is it?'

'You won't tell the others if I tell you?'

'Not if you say not,' Oswald answered in kindly tones.

'Well, it's my shoes.'

'Take them off, man.'

'You won't laugh?'

'NO!' cried Oswald, so impatiently that the others looked back to see why he was shouting. He waved them away, and with humble gentleness began to undo the black-tape sandals.

Denny let him, crying hard all the time.

When Oswald had got off the first shoe the mystery was made plain to him.

'Well! Of all the—' he said in proper indignation.

Denny quailed—though he said he did not—but then he doesn't know what quailing is, and if Denny did not quail then Oswald does not know what quailing is either.

For when Oswald took the shoe off he naturally chucked it down and gave it a kick, and a lot of little pinky yellow things rolled out. And Oswald look closer at the interesting sight. And the little things were SPLIT peas.

'Perhaps you'll tell me,' said the gentle knight, with the politeness of despair, 'why on earth you've played the goat like this?'

'Oh, don't be angry,' Denny said; and now his shoes were off, he curled and uncurled his toes and stopped crying. 'I KNEW pilgrims put peas in their shoes—and—oh, I wish you wouldn't laugh!'

'I'm not,' said Oswald, still with bitter politeness.

'I didn't want to tell you I was going to, because I wanted to be better than all of you, and I thought if you knew I was going to you'd want to too, and you wouldn't when I said it first. So I just put some peas in my pocket and dropped one or two at a time into my shoes when you weren't looking.'

In his secret heart Oswald said, 'Greedy young ass.' For it IS greedy to want to have more of anything than other people, even goodness.

Outwardly Oswald said nothing.

'You see'—Denny went on—'I do want to be good. And if pilgriming is to do you good, you ought to do it properly. I shouldn't mind being hurt in my feet if it would make me good for ever and ever. And besides, I wanted to play the game thoroughly. You always say I don't.'

The breast of the kind Oswald was touched by these last words.

'I think you're quite good enough,' he said. 'I'll fetch back the others—no, they won't laugh.'

And we all went back to Denny, and the girls made a fuss with him. But Oswald and Dicky were grave and stood aloof. They were old enough to see that being good was all very well, but after all you had to get the boy home somehow.

When they said this, as agreeably as they could, Denny said—

'It's all right—someone will give me a lift.'

'You think everything in the world can be put right with a lift,' Dicky said, and he did not speak lovingly.

'So it can,' said Denny, 'when it's your feet. I shall easily get a lift home.'

'Not here you won't,' said Alice. 'No one goes down this road; but the high road's just round the corner, where you see the telegraph wires.'

Dickie and Oswald made a sedan chair and carried Denny to the high road, and we sat down in a ditch to wait. For a long time nothing went by but a brewer's dray. We hailed it, of course, but the man was so sound asleep that our hails were vain, and none of us thought soon enough about springing like a flash to the horses' heads, though we all thought of it directly the dray was out of sight.

So we had to keep on sitting there by the dusty road, and more than one pilgrim was heard to say it wished we had never come. Oswald was not one of those who uttered this useless wish.

At last, just when despair was beginning to eat into the vital parts of even Oswald, there was a quick tap-tapping of horses' feet on the road, and a dogcart came in sight with a lady in it all alone.

We hailed her like the desperate shipwrecked mariners in the long-boat hail the passing sail.

She pulled up. She was not a very old lady—twenty-five we found out afterwards her age was—and she looked jolly.

'Well,' she said, 'what's the matter?'

'It's this poor little boy,' Dora said, pointing to the Dentist, who had gone to sleep in the dry ditch, with his mouth open as usual. 'His feet hurt him so, and will you give him a lift?'

'But why are you all rigged out like this?' asked the lady, looking at our cockle-shells and sandals and things. We told her.

'And how has he hurt his feet?' she asked. And we told her that.

She looked very kind. 'Poor little chap,' she said. 'Where do you want to go?'

We told her that too. We had no concealments from this lady.

'Well,' she said, 'I have to go on to—what is its name?'

'Canterbury,' said H. O.

'Well, yes, Canterbury,' she said; 'it's only about half a mile. I'll take the poor little pilgrim—and, yes, the three girls. You boys must walk. Then we'll have tea and see the sights, and I'll drive you home—at least some of you. How will that do?'

We thanked her very much indeed, and said it would do very nicely.

Then we helped Denny into the cart, and the girls got up, and the red wheels of the cart spun away through the dust.

'I wish it had been an omnibus the lady was driving,' said H. O., 'then we could all have had a ride.'

'Don't you be so discontented,' Dicky said. And Noel said—

'You ought to be jolly thankful you haven't got to carry Denny all the way home on your back. You'd have had to if you'd been out alone with him.'

When we got to Canterbury it was much smaller than we expected, and the cathedral not much bigger than the Church that is next to the Moat House. There seemed to be only one big street, but we supposed the rest of the city was hidden away somewhere. There was a large inn, with a green before it, and the red-wheeled dogcart was standing in the stableyard and the lady, with Denny and the others, sitting on the benches in the porch, looking out for us. The inn was called the 'George and Dragon', and it made me think of the days when there were coaches and highwaymen and foot-pads and jolly landlords, and adventures at country inns, like you read about.

'We've ordered tea,' said the lady. 'Would you like to wash your hands?'

We saw that she wished us to, so we said yes, we would. The girls and Denny were already much cleaner than when we parted from them.

There was a courtyard to the inn and a wooden staircase outside the house. We were taken up this, and washed our hands in a big room with a fourpost wooden bed and dark red hangings—just the sort of hangings that would not show the stains of gore in the dear old adventurous times.

Then we had tea in a great big room with wooden chairs and tables, very polished and old.

It was a very nice tea, with lettuces, and cold meat, and three kinds of jam, as well as cake, and new bread, which we are not allowed at home.

While tea was being had, the lady talked to us. She was very kind.

There are two sorts of people in the world, besides others; one sort understand what you're driving at, and the other don't. This lady was the one sort.

After everyone had had as much to eat as they could possibly want, the lady said, 'What was it you particularly wanted to see at Canterbury?'

'The cathedral,' Alice said, 'and the place where Thomas A Becket was murdered.'

'And the Danejohn,' said Dicky.

Oswald wanted to see the walls, because he likes the Story of St Alphege and the Danes.

'Well, well,' said the lady, and she put on her hat; it was a really sensible one—not a blob of fluffy stuff and feathers put on sideways and stuck on with long pins, and no shade to your face, but almost as big as ours, with a big brim and red flowers, and black strings to tie under your chin to keep it from blowing off.

Then we went out all together to see Canterbury. Dicky and Oswald took it in turns to carry Denny on their backs. The lady called him 'The Wounded Comrade'.

We went first to the church. Oswald, whose quick brain was easily aroused to suspicions, was afraid the lady might begin talking in the church, but she did not. The church door was open. I remember mother telling us once it was right and good for churches to be left open all day, so that tired people could go in and be quiet, and say their prayers, if they wanted to. But it does not seem respectful to talk out loud in church. (See Note A.)

When we got outside the lady said, 'You can imagine how on the chancel steps began the mad struggle in which Becket, after hurling one of his assailants, armour and all, to the ground—'

'It would have been much cleverer,' H. O. interrupted, 'to hurl him without his armour, and leave that standing up.'

'Go on,' said Alice and Oswald, when they had given H. O. a withering glance. And the lady did go on. She told us all about Becket, and then about St Alphege, who had bones thrown at him till he died, because he wouldn't tax his poor people to please the beastly rotten Danes.

And Denny recited a piece of poetry he knows called 'The Ballad of Canterbury'.

It begins about Danish warships snake-shaped, and ends about doing as you'd be done by. It is long, but it has all the beef-bones in it, and all about St Alphege.

Then the lady showed us the Danejohn, and it was like an oast-house. And Canterbury walls that Alphege defied the Danes from looked down on a quite common farmyard. The hospital was like a barn, and other things were like other things, but we went all about and enjoyed it very much. The lady was quite amusing, besides sometimes talking like a real cathedral guide I met afterwards. (See Note B.) When at last we said we thought Canterbury was very small considering, the lady said—

'Well, it seemed a pity to come so far and not at least hear something about Canterbury.'

And then at once we knew the worst, and Alice said—

'What a horrid sell!' But Oswald, with immediate courteousness, said—

'I don't care. You did it awfully well.' And he did not say, though he owns he thought of it—

'I knew it all the time,' though it was a great temptation. Because really it was more than half true. He had felt from the first that this was too small for Canterbury. (See Note C.)

The real name of the place was Hazelbridge, and not Canterbury at all. We went to Canterbury another time. (See Note D.) We were not angry with the lady for selling us about it being Canterbury, because she had really kept it up first-rate. And she asked us if we minded, very handsomely, and we said we liked it. But now we did not care how soon we got home. The lady saw this, and said—

'Come, our chariots are ready, and our horses caparisoned.'

That is a first-rate word out of a book. It cheered Oswald up, and he liked her for using it, though he wondered why she said chariots. When we got back to the inn I saw her dogcart was there, and a grocer's cart too, with B. Munn, grocer, Hazelbridge, on it. She took the girls in her cart, and the boys went with the grocer. His horse was a very good one to go, only you had to hit it with the wrong end of the whip. But the cart was very bumpety.

The evening dews were falling—at least, I suppose so, but you do not feel dew in a grocer's cart—when we reached home. We all thanked the lady very much, and said we hoped we should see her again some day. She said she hoped so.

The grocer drove off, and when we had all shaken hands with the lady and kissed her, according as we were boys or girls, or little boys, she touched up her horse and drove away.

She turned at the corner to wave to us, and just as we had done waving, and were turning into the house, Albert's uncle came into our midst like a whirling wind. He was in flannels, and his shirt had no stud in at the neck, and his hair was all rumpled up and his hands were inky, and we knew he had left off in the middle of a chapter by the wildness of his eye.

'Who was that lady?' he said. 'Where did you meet her?'

Mindful, as ever, of what he was told, Oswald began to tell the story from the beginning.

'The other day, protector of the poor,' he began; 'Dora and I were reading about the Canterbury pilgrims ...'

Oswald thought Albert's uncle would be pleased to find his instructions about beginning at the beginning had borne fruit, but instead he interrupted.

'Stow it, you young duffer! Where did you meet her?'

Oswald answered briefly, in wounded accents, 'Hazelbridge.'

Then Albert's uncle rushed upstairs three at a time, and as he went he called out to Oswald—

'Get out my bike, old man, and blow up the back tyre.'

I am sure Oswald was as quick as anyone could have been, but long ere the tyre was thoroughly blowed Albert's uncle appeared, with a collar-stud and tie and blazer, and his hair tidy, and wrenching the unoffending machine from Oswald's surprised fingers.

Albert's uncle finished pumping up the tyre, and then flinging himself into the saddle he set off, scorching down the road at a pace not surpassed by any highwayman, however black and high-mettled his steed. We were left looking at each other. 'He must have recognized her,' Dicky said.

'Perhaps,' Noel said, 'she is the old nurse who alone knows the dark secret of his highborn birth.'

'Not old enough, by chalks,' Oswald said.

'I shouldn't wonder,' said Alice, 'if she holds the secret of the will that will make him rolling in long-lost wealth.'

'I wonder if he'll catch her,' Noel said. 'I'm quite certain all his future depends on it. Perhaps she's his long-lost sister, and the estate was left to them equally, only she couldn't be found, so it couldn't be shared up.'

'Perhaps he's only in love with her,' Dora said, 'parted by cruel Fate at an early age, he has ranged the wide world ever since trying to find her.'

'I hope to goodness he hasn't—anyway, he's not ranged since we knew him—never further than Hastings,' Oswald said. 'We don't want any of that rot.'

'What rot?' Daisy asked. And Oswald said—

'Getting married, and all that sort of rubbish.'

And Daisy and Dora were the only ones that didn't agree with him. Even Alice owned that being bridesmaids must be fairly good fun. It's no good. You may treat girls as well as you like, and give them every comfort and luxury, and play fair just as if they were boys, but there is something unmanly about the best of girls. They go silly, like milk goes sour, without any warning.

When Albert's uncle returned he was very hot, with a beaded brow, but pale as the Dentist when the peas were at their worst.

'Did you catch her?' H. O. asked.

Albert's uncle's brow looked black as the cloud that thunder will presently break from. 'No,' he said.

'Is she your long-lost nurse?' H. O. went on, before we could stop him.

'Long-lost grandmother! I knew the lady long ago in India,' said Albert's uncle, as he left the room, slamming the door in a way we should be forbidden to.

And that was the end of the Canterbury Pilgrimage.

As for the lady, we did not then know whether she was his long-lost grandmother that he had known in India or not, though we thought she seemed youngish for the part. We found out afterwards whether she was or not, but that comes in another part. His manner was not the one that makes you go on asking questions. The Canterbury Pilgriming did not exactly make us good, but then, as Dora said, we had not done anything wrong that day. So we were twenty-four hours to the good.

Note A.

— Afterwards we went and saw real Canterbury. It is very large. A disagreeable man showed us round the cathedral, and jawed all the time quite loud as if it wasn't a church. I remember one thing he said. It was this:

'This is the Dean's Chapel; it was the Lady Chapel in the wicked days when people used to worship the Virgin Mary.'

And H. O. said, 'I suppose they worship the Dean now?'

Some strange people who were there laughed out loud. I think this is worse in church than not taking your cap off when you come in, as H.O. forgot to do, because the cathedral was so big he didn't think it was a church.

Note B. (See Note C.)

Note C. (See Note D.)

Note D. (See Note E.)

Note E. (See Note A.)

This ends the Canterbury Pilgrims.

Chapter 13. The Dragon's Teeth; or, Army-seed

Albert's uncle was out on his bicycle as usual. After the day when we became Canterbury Pilgrims and were brought home in the dog-cart with red wheels by the lady he told us was his long-lost grandmother he had known years ago in India, he spent not nearly so much of his time in writing, and he used to shave every morning instead of only when requisite, as in earlier days. And he was always going out on his bicycle in his new Norfolk suit. We are not so unobserving as grown-up people make out. We knew well enough he was looking for the long-lost. And we jolly well wished he might find her. Oswald, always full of sympathy with misfortune, however undeserved, had himself tried several times to find the lady. So had the others. But all this is what they call a digression; it has nothing to do with the dragon's teeth I am now narrating.

It began with the pig dying—it was the one we had for the circus, but it having behaved so badly that day had nothing to do with its illness and death, though the girls said they felt remorse, and perhaps if we hadn't made it run so that day it might have been spared to us. But Oswald cannot pretend that people were right just because they happen to be dead, and as long as that pig was alive we all knew well enough that it was it that made us run—and not us it.

The pig was buried in the kitchen garden. Bill, that we made the tombstone for, dug the grave, and while he was away at his dinner we took a turn at digging, because we like to be useful, and besides, when you dig you never know what you may turn up. I knew a man once that found a gold ring on the point of his fork when he was digging potatoes, and you know how we found two half-crowns ourselves once when we were digging for treasure.

Oswald was taking his turn with the spade, and the others were sitting on the gravel and telling him how to do it.

'Work with a will,' Dicky said, yawning.

Alice said, 'I wish we were in a book. People in books never dig without finding something. I think I'd rather it was a secret passage than anything.'

Oswald stopped to wipe his honest brow ere replying.

'A secret's nothing when you've found it out. Look at the secret staircase. It's no good, not even for hide-and-seek, because of its squeaking. I'd rather have the pot of gold we used to dig for when we were little.' It was really only last year, but you seem to grow old very quickly after you have once passed the prime of your youth, which is at ten, I believe.

'How would you like to find the mouldering bones of Royalist soldiers foully done to death by nasty Ironsides?' Noel asked, with his mouth full of plum.

'If they were really dead it wouldn't matter,' Dora said. 'What I'm afraid of is a skeleton that can walk about and catch at your legs when you're going upstairs to bed.' 'Skeletons can't walk,' Alice said in a hurry; 'you know they can't, Dora.'

And she glared at Dora till she made her sorry she had said what she had. The things you are frightened of, or even those you would rather not meet in the dark, should never be mentioned before the little ones, or else they cry when it comes to bed-time, and say it was because of what you said.

'We shan't find anything. No jolly fear,' said Dicky.

And just then my spade I was digging with struck on something hard, and it felt hollow. I did really think for one joyful space that we had found that pot of gold. But the thing, whatever it was, seemed to be longish; longer, that is, than a pot of gold would naturally be. And as I uncovered it I saw that it was not at all pot-of-gold-colour, but like a bone Pincher has buried. So Oswald said—

'It IS the skeleton.'

The girls all drew back, and Alice said, 'Oswald, I wish you wouldn't.'

A moment later the discovery was unearthed, and Oswald lifted it up, with both hands.

'It's a dragon's head,' Noel said, and it certainly looked like it.

It was long and narrowish and bony, and with great yellow teeth sticking in the jaw.

Bill came back just then and said it was a horse's head, but H. O. and Noel would not believe it, and Oswald owns that no horse he has ever seen had a head at all that shape.

But Oswald did not stop to argue, because he saw a keeper who showed me how to set snares going by, and he wanted to talk to him about ferrets, so he went off and Dicky and Denny and Alice with him. Also Daisy and Dora went off to finish reading Ministering Children. So H. O. and Noel were left with the bony head. They took it away.

The incident had quite faded from the mind of Oswald next day. But just before breakfast Noel and H. O. came in, looking hot and anxious. They had got up early and had not washed at all—not even their hands and faces. Noel made Oswald a secret signal. All the others saw it, and with proper delicate feeling pretended not to have.

When Oswald had gone out with Noel and H. O. in obedience to the secret signal, Noel said—

'You know that dragon's head yesterday?'

'Well?' Oswald said quickly, but not crossly—the two things are quite different.

'Well, you know what happened in Greek history when some chap sowed dragon's teeth?'

'They came up armed men,' said H. O., but Noel sternly bade him shut up, and Oswald said 'Well,' again. If he spoke impatiently it was because he smelt the bacon being taken in to breakfast.

'Well,' Noel went on, 'what do you suppose would have come up if we'd sowed those dragon's teeth we found yesterday?'

'Why, nothing, you young duffer,' said Oswald, who could now smell the coffee. 'All that isn't History it's Humbug. Come on in to brekker.'

'It's NOT humbug,' H. O. cried, 'it is history. We DID sow—'

'Shut up,' said Noel again. 'Look here, Oswald. We did sow those dragon's teeth in Randall's ten-acre meadow, and what do you think has come up?'

'Toadstools I should think,' was Oswald's contemptible rejoinder.

'They have come up a camp of soldiers,' said Noel—ARMED MEN. So you see it WAS history. We have sowed army-seed, just like Cadmus, and it has come up. It was a very wet night. I daresay that helped it along.'

Oswald could not decide which to disbelieve—his brother or his ears. So, disguising his doubtful emotions without a word, he led the way to the bacon and the banqueting hall.

He said nothing about the army-seed then, neither did Noel and H. O. But after the bacon we went into the garden, and then the good elder brother said—

'Why don't you tell the others your cock-and-bull story?'

So they did, and their story was received with warm expressions of doubt. It was Dicky who observed—

'Let's go and have a squint at Randall's ten-acre, anyhow. I saw a hare there the other day.'

We went. It is some little way, and as we went, disbelief reigned superb in every breast except Noel's and H. O.'s, so you will see that even the ready pen of the present author cannot be expected to describe to you his variable sensations when he got to the top of the hill and suddenly saw that his little brothers had spoken the truth. I do not mean that they generally tell lies, but people make mistakes sometimes, and the effect is the same as lies if you believe them.

There WAS a camp there with real tents and soldiers in grey and red tunics. I daresay the girls would have said coats. We stood in ambush, too astonished even to think of lying in it, though of course we know that this is customary. The ambush was the wood on top of the little hill, between Randall's ten-acre meadow and Sugden's Waste Wake pasture.

'There would be cover here for a couple of regiments,' whispered Oswald, who was, I think, gifted by Fate with the far-seeingness of a born general.

Alice merely said 'Hist', and we went down to mingle with the troops as though by accident, and seek for information.

The first man we came to at the edge of the camp was cleaning a sort of cauldron thing like witches brew bats in.

We went up to him and said, 'Who are you? Are you English, or are you the enemy?'

'We're the enemy,' he said, and he did not seem ashamed of being what he was. And he spoke English with quite a good accent for a foreigner.

'The enemy!' Oswald echoed in shocked tones. It is a terrible thing to a loyal and patriotic youth to see an enemy cleaning a pot in an English field, with English sand, and looking as much at home as if he was in his foreign fastnesses.

The enemy seemed to read Oswald's thoughts with deadly unerringness. He said—

'The English are somewhere over on the other side of the hill. They are trying to keep us out of Maidstone.'

After this our plan of mingling with the troops did not seem worth going on with. This soldier, in spite of his unerringness in reading Oswald's innermost heart, seemed not so very sharp in other things, or he would never have given away his secret plans like this, for he must have known from our accents that we were Britons to the backbone. Or perhaps (Oswald thought this, and it made his blood at once boil and freeze, which our uncle had told us was possible, but only in India), perhaps he thought that Maidstone was already as good as taken and it didn't matter what he said. While Oswald was debating within his intellect what to say next, and how to say it so as to discover as many as possible of the enemy's dark secrets, Noel said—

'How did you get here? You weren't here yesterday at tea-time.'

The soldier gave the pot another sandy rub, and said—

'I daresay it does seem quick work—the camp seems as if it had sprung up in the night, doesn't it?—like a mushroom.'

Alice and Oswald looked at each other, and then at the rest of us. The words 'sprung up in the night' seemed to touch a string in every heart.

'You see,' whispered Noel, 'he won't tell us how he came here. NOW, is it humbug or history?'

Oswald, after whisperedly requesting his young brother to dry up and not bother, remarked, 'Then you're an invading army?'

'Well,' said the soldier, 'we're a skeleton battalion, as a matter of fact, but we're invading all right enough.'

And now indeed the blood of the stupidest of us froze, just as the quick-witted Oswald's had done earlier in the interview. Even H. O. opened his mouth and went the colour of mottled soap; he is so fat that this is the nearest he can go to turning pale. Denny said, 'But you don't look like skeletons.'

The soldier stared, then he laughed and said, 'Ah, that's the padding in our tunics. You should see us in the grey dawn taking our morning bath in a bucket.' It was a dreadful picture for the imagination. A skeleton, with its bones all loose most likely, bathing anyhow in a pail. There was a silence while we thought it over.

Now, ever since the cleaning-cauldron soldier had said that about taking Maidstone, Alice had kept on pulling at Oswald's jacket behind, and he had kept on not taking any notice. But now he could not stand it any longer, so he said—

'Well, what is it?'

Alice drew him aside, or rather, she pulled at his jacket so that he nearly fell over backwards, and then she whispered, 'Come along, don't stay parlaying with the foe. He's only talking to you to gain time.'

'What for?' said Oswald.

'Why, so that we shouldn't warn the other army, you silly,' Alice said, and Oswald was so upset by what she said, that he forgot to be properly angry with her for the wrong word she used.

'But we ought to warn them at home,' she said—' suppose the Moat House was burned down, and all the supplies commandeered for the foe?'

Alice turned boldly to the soldier. 'DO you burn down farms?' she asked.

'Well, not as a rule,' he said, and he had the cheek to wink at Oswald, but Oswald would not look at him. 'We've not burned a farm since—oh, not for years.'

'A farm in Greek history it was, I expect,' Denny murmured. 'Civilized warriors do not burn farms nowadays,' Alice said sternly, 'whatever they did in Greek times. You ought to know that.'

The soldier said things had changed a good deal since Greek times.

So we said good morning as quickly as we could: it is proper to be polite even to your enemy, except just at the moments when it has really come to rifles and bayonets or other weapons.

The soldier said 'So long!' in quite a modern voice, and we retraced our footsteps in silence to the ambush—I mean the wood. Oswald did think of lying in the ambush then, but it was rather wet, because of the rain the night before, that H. O. said had brought the army-seed up. And Alice walked very fast, saying nothing but 'Hurry up, can't you!' and dragging H. O. by one hand and Noel by the other. So we got into the road.

Then Alice faced round and said, 'This is all our fault. If we hadn't sowed those dragon's teeth there wouldn't have been any invading army.'

I am sorry to say Daisy said, 'Never mind, Alice, dear. WE didn't sow the nasty things, did we, Dora?'

But Denny told her it was just the same. It was WE had done it, so long as it was any of us, especially if it got any of us into trouble. Oswald was very pleased to see that the Dentist was beginning to understand the meaning of true manliness, and about the honour of the house of Bastable, though of course he is only a Foulkes. Yet it is something to know he does his best to learn.

If you are very grown-up, or very clever, I daresay you will now have thought of a great many things. If you have you need not say anything, especially if you're reading this aloud to anybody. It's no good putting in what you think in this part, because none of us thought anything of the kind at the time.

We simply stood in the road without any of your clever thoughts, filled with shame and distress to think of what might happen owing to the dragon's teeth being sown. It was a lesson to us never to sow seed without being quite sure what sort it is. This is particularly true of the penny packets, which sometimes do not come up at all, quite unlike dragon's teeth.

Of course H. O. and Noel were more unhappy than the rest of us. This was only fair.

'How can we possibly prevent their getting to Maidstone?' Dickie said. 'Did you notice the red cuffs on their uniforms? Taken from the bodies of dead English soldiers, I shouldn't wonder.'

'If they're the old Greek kind of dragon's-teeth soldiers, they ought to fight each other to death,' Noel said; 'at least, if we had a helmet to throw among them.'

But none of us had, and it was decided that it would be of no use for H. O. to go back and throw his straw hat at them, though he wanted to. Denny said suddenly—

'Couldn't we alter the sign-posts, so that they wouldn't know the way to Maidstone?'

Oswald saw that this was the time for true generalship to be shown.

He said—

'Fetch all the tools out of your chest—Dicky go too, there's a good chap, and don't let him cut his legs with the saw.' He did once, tumbling over it. 'Meet us at the cross-roads, you know, where we had the Benevolent Bar. Courage and dispatch, and look sharp about it.'

When they had gone we hastened to the crossroads, and there a great idea occurred to Oswald. He used the forces at his command so ably that in a very short time the board in the field which says 'No thoroughfare. Trespassers will be prosecuted' was set up in the middle of the road to Maidstone. We put stones, from a heap by the road, behind it to make it stand up.

Then Dicky and Denny came back, and Dicky shinned up the sign-post and sawed off the two arms, and we nailed them up wrong, so that it said 'To Maidstone' on the Dover Road, and 'To Dover' on the road to Maidstone. We decided to leave the Trespassers board on the real Maidstone road, as an extra guard.

Then we settled to start at once to warn Maidstone.

Some of us did not want the girls to go, but it would have been unkind to say so. However, there was at least one breast that felt a pang of joy when Dora and Daisy gave out that they would rather stay where they were and tell anybody who came by which was the real road.

'Because it would be so dreadful if someone was going to buy pigs or fetch a doctor or anything in a hurry and then found they had got to Dover instead of where they wanted to go to,' Dora said. But when it came to dinner-time they went home, so that they were entirely out of it. This often happens to them by some strange fatalism.

We left Martha to take care of the two girls, and Lady and Pincher went with us. It was getting late in the day, but I am bound to remember no one said anything about their dinners, whatever they may have thought. We cannot always help our thoughts. We happened to know it was roast rabbits and currant jelly that day.

We walked two and two, and sang the 'British Grenadiers' and 'Soldiers of the queen' so as to be as much part of the British Army as possible. The Cauldron-Man had said the English were the other side of the hill. But we could not see any scarlet anywhere, though we looked for it as carefully as if we had been fierce bulls.

But suddenly we went round a turn in the road and came plump into a lot of soldiers. Only they were not red-coats. They were dressed in grey and silver. And it was a sort of furzy-common place, and three roads branching out. The men were lying about, with some of their belts undone, smoking pipes and cigarettes.

'It's not British soldiers,' Alice said. 'Oh dear, oh dear, I'm afraid it's more enemy. You didn't sow the army-seed anywhere else, did you, H. O. dear?'

H. O. was positive he hadn't. 'But perhaps lots more came up where we did sow them,' he said; 'they're all over England by now very likely. *I* don't know how many men can grow out of one dragon's tooth.'

Then Noel said, 'It was my doing anyhow, and I'm not afraid,' and he walked straight up to the nearest soldier, who was cleaning his pipe with a piece of grass, and said—

'Please, are you the enemy?' The man said—

'No, young Commander-in-Chief, we're the English.'

Then Oswald took command. 'Where is the General?' he said.

'We're out of generals just now, Field-Marshal,' the man said, and his voice was a gentleman's voice. 'Not a single one in stock. We might suit you in majors now —and captains are quite cheap. Competent corporals going for a song. And we have a very nice colonel, too quiet to ride or drive.'

Oswald does not mind chaff at proper times. But this was not one.

'You seem to be taking it very easy,' he said with disdainful expression.

'This IS an easy,' said the grey soldier, sucking at his pipe to see if it would draw.

'I suppose YOU don't care if the enemy gets into Maidstone or not!' exclaimed Oswald bitterly. 'If I were a soldier I'd rather die than be beaten.'

The soldier saluted. 'Good old patriotic sentiment' he said, smiling at the heart-felt boy.

But Oswald could bear no more. 'Which is the Colonel?' he asked.

'Over there—near the grey horse.'

'The one lighting a cigarette?' H. O. asked.

'Yes—but I say, kiddie, he won't stand any jaw. There's not an ounce of vice about him, but he's peppery. He might kick out. You'd better bunk.'

'Better what?' asked H. O.

'Bunk, bottle, scoot, skip, vanish, exit,' said the soldier.

'That's what you'd do when the fighting begins,' said H. O. He is often rude like that—but it was what we all thought, all the same.

The soldier only laughed.

A spirited but hasty altercation among ourselves in whispers ended in our allowing Alice to be the one to speak to the Colonel. It was she who wanted to. 'However peppery he is he won't kick a girl,' she said, and perhaps this was true.

But of course we all went with her. So there were six of us to stand in front of the Colonel. And as we went along we agreed that we would salute him on the word three. So when we got near, Dick said, 'One, two, three', and we all saluted very well—except H. O., who chose that minute to trip over a rifle a soldier had left lying about, and was only saved from falling by a man in a cocked hat who caught him deftly by the back of his jacket and stood him on his legs.

'Let go, can't you,' said H. O. 'Are you the General?'

Before the Cocked Hat had time to frame a reply, Alice spoke to the Colonel. I knew what she meant to say, because she had told me as we threaded our way among the resting soldiery. What she really said was—

'Oh, how CAN you!'

'How can I WHAT?' said the Colonel, rather crossly.

'Why, SMOKE?' said Alice.

'My good children, if you're an infant Band of Hope, let me recommend you to play in some other backyard,' said the Cock-Hatted Man.

H. O. said, 'Band of Hope yourself'—but no one noticed it.

'We're NOT a Band of Hope,' said Noel. 'We're British, and the man over there told us you are. And Maidstone's in danger, and the enemy not a mile off, and you stand SMOKING.' Noel was standing crying, himself, or something very like it.

'It's quite true,' Alice said.

The Colonel said, 'Fiddle-de-dee.'

But the Cocked-Hatted Man said, 'What was the enemy like?' We told him exactly. And even the Colonel then owned there might be something in it.

'Can you show me the place where they are on the map?' he asked.

'Not on the map, we can't,' said Dicky—'at least, I don't think so, but on the ground we could. We could take you there in a quarter of an hour.'

The Cocked-Hatted One looked at the Colonel, who returned his scrutiny, then he shrugged his shoulders.

'Well, we've got to do something,' he said, as if to himself. 'Lead on, Macduff.'

The Colonel roused his soldiery from their stupor of pipes by words of command which the present author is sorry he can't remember.

Then he bade us boys lead the way. I tell you it felt fine, marching at the head of a regiment. Alice got a lift on the Cocked-Hatted One's horse. It was a red-roan steed of might, exactly as if it had been in a ballad. They call a grey-roan a 'blue' in South Africa, the Cocked-Hatted One said.

We led the British Army by unfrequented lanes till we got to the gate of Sugden's Waste Wake pasture. Then the Colonel called a whispered halt, and choosing two of us to guide him, the dauntless and discerning commander went on, on foot, with an orderly. He chose Dicky and Oswald as guides. So we led him to the ambush, and we went through it as quietly as we could. But twigs do crackle and snap so when you are reconnoitring, or anxious to escape detection for whatever reason.

Our Colonel's orderly crackled most. If you're not near enough to tell a colonel by the crown and stars on his shoulder-strap, you can tell him by the orderly behind him, like 'follow my leader'.

'Look out!' said Oswald in a low but commanding whisper, 'the camp's down in that field. You can see if you take a squint through this gap.'

The speaker took a squint himself as he spoke, and drew back, baffled beyond the power of speech. While he was struggling with his baffledness the British Colonel had his squint. He also drew back, and said a word that he must have known was not right—at least when he was a boy.

'I don't care,' said Oswald, 'they were there this morning. White tents like mushrooms, and an enemy cleaning a cauldron.'

'With sand,' said Dicky.

'That's most convincing,' said the Colonel, and I did not like the way he said it.

'I say,' Oswald said, 'let's get to the top corner of the ambush—the wood, I mean. You can see the crossroads from there.'

We did, and quickly, for the crackling of branches no longer dismayed our almost despairing spirits.

We came to the edge of the wood, and Oswald's patriotic heart really did give a jump, and he cried, 'There they are, on the Dover Road.'

Our miscellaneous signboard had done its work.

'By Jove, young un, you're right! And in quarter column, too! We've got em on toast—on toast—egad!' I never heard anyone not in a book say 'egad' before, so I saw something really out of the way was indeed up.

The Colonel was a man of prompt and decisive action. He sent the orderly to tell the Major to advance two companies on the left flank and take cover. Then we led him back through the wood the nearest way, because he said he must rejoin the main body at once. We found the main body very friendly with Noel and H. O. and the others, and Alice was talking to the Cocked-Hatted One as if she had known him all her life.

'I think he's a general in disguise,' Noel said. 'He's been giving us chocolate out of a pocket in his saddle.'

Oswald thought about the roast rabbit then—and he is not ashamed to own it—yet he did not say a word. But Alice is really not a bad sort. She had saved two bars of chocolate for him and Dicky. Even in war girls can sometimes be useful in their humble way.

The Colonel fussed about and said, 'Take cover there!' and everybody hid in the ditch, and the horses and the Cocked Hat, with Alice, retreated down the road out of sight. We were in the ditch too. It was muddy—but nobody thought of their boots in that perilous moment. It seemed a long time we were crouching there. Oswald began to feel the water squelching in his boots, so we held our breath and listened. Oswald laid his ear to the road like a Red Indian. You would not do this in time of peace, but when your country is in danger you care but little about keeping your ears clean. His backwoods' strategy was successful. He rose and dusted himself and said— 'They're coming!'

It was true. The footsteps of the approaching foe were now to be heard quite audibly, even by ears in their natural position. The wicked enemy approached. They were marching with a careless swaggeringness that showed how little they suspected the horrible doom which was about to teach them England's might and supremeness.

Just as the enemy turned the corner so that we could see them, the Colonel shouted— 'Right section, fire!' and there was a deafening banging.

The enemy's officer said something, and then the enemy got confused and tried to get into the fields through the hedges. But all was vain. There was firing now from our men, on the left as well as the right. And then our Colonel strode nobly up to the enemy's Colonel and demanded surrender. He told me so afterwards. His exact words are only known to himself and the other Colonel. But the enemy's Colonel said, 'I would rather die than surrender,' or words to that effect.

Our Colonel returned to his men and gave the order to fix bayonets, and even Oswald felt his manly cheek turn pale at the thought of the amount of blood to be shed. What would have happened can never now be revealed. For at this moment a man on a piebald horse came clattering over a hedge—as carelessly as if the air was not full of lead and steel at all. Another man rode behind him with a lance and a red pennon on it. I think he must have been the enemy's General coming to tell his men not to throw away their lives on a forlorn hope, for directly he said they were captured the enemy gave in and owned that they were. The enemy's Colonel saluted and ordered his men to form quarter column again. I should have thought he would have had about enough of that myself.

He had now given up all thought of sullen resistance to the bitter end. He rolled a cigarette for himself, and had the foreign cheek to say to our Colonel—

'By Jove, old man, you got me clean that time! Your scouts seem to have marked us down uncommonly neatly.'

It was a proud moment when our Colonel laid his military hand on Oswald's shoulder and said—

'This is my chief scout' which were high words, but not undeserved, and Oswald owns he felt red with gratifying pride when he heard them.

'So you are the traitor, young man,' said the wicked Colonel, going on with his cheek.

Oswald bore it because our Colonel had, and you should be generous to a fallen foe, but it is hard to be called a traitor when you haven't.

He did not treat the wicked Colonel with silent scorn as he might have done, but he said—

'We aren't traitors. We are the Bastables and one of us is a Foulkes. We only mingled unsuspected with the enemy's soldiery and learned the secrets of their acts, which is what Baden-Powell always does when the natives rebel in South Africa; and Denis Foulkes thought of altering the sign-posts to lead the foe astray. And if we did cause all this fighting, and get Maidstone threatened with capture and all that, it was only because we didn't believe Greek things could happen in Great Britain and Ireland, even if you sow dragon's teeth, and besides, some of us were not asked about sowing them.'

Then the Cocked-Hatted One led his horse and walked with us and made us tell him all about it, and so did the Colonel. The wicked Colonel listened too, which was only another proof of his cheek.

And Oswald told the tale in the modest yet manly way that some people think he has, and gave the others all the credit they deserved. His narration was interrupted no less than four times by shouts of 'Bravo!' in which the enemy's Colonel once more showed his cheek by joining. By the time the story was told we were in sight of another camp. It was the British one this time. The Colonel asked us to have tea in his tent, and it only shows the magnanimosity of English chivalry in the field of battle that he asked the enemy's Colonel too. With his usual cheek he accepted. We were jolly hungry.

When everyone had had as much tea as they possibly could, the Colonel shook hands with us all, and to Oswald he said—

'Well, good-bye, my brave scout. I must mention your name in my dispatches to the War Office.'

H. O. interrupted him to say, 'His name's Oswald Cecil Bastable, and mine is Horace Octavius.' I wish H. O. would learn to hold his tongue. No one ever knows Oswald was christened Cecil as well, if he can possibly help it. YOU didn't know it till now.

'Mr Oswald Bastable,' the Colonel went on—he had the decency not to take any notice of the 'Cecil' -'you would be a credit to any regiment. No doubt the War Office will reward you properly for what you have done for your country. But meantime, perhaps, you'll accept five shillings from a grateful comrade-in-arms.' Oswald felt heart-felt sorry to wound the good Colonel's feelings, but he had to remark that he had only done his duty, and he was sure no British scout would take five bob for doing that. 'And besides,' he said, with that feeling of justice which is part of his young character, 'it was the others just as much as me.'

'Your sentiments, Sir,' said the Colonel who was one of the politest and most discerning colonels I ever saw, 'your sentiments do you honour. But, Bastables all, and—and non-Bastables' (he couldn't remember Foulkes; it's not such an interesting name as Bastable, of course) -'at least you'll accept a soldier's pay?'

'Lucky to touch it, a shilling a day!' Alice and Denny said together. And the Cocked-Hatted Man said something about knowing your own mind and knowing your own Kipling.

'A soldier,' said the Colonel, 'would certainly be lucky to touch it. You see there are deductions for rations. Five shillings is exactly right, deducting twopence each for six teas.'

This seemed cheap for the three cups of tea and the three eggs and all the strawberry jam and bread-and-butter Oswald had had, as well as what the others ate, and Lady's and Pincher's teas, but I suppose soldiers get things cheaper than civilians, which is only right.

Oswald took the five shillings then, there being no longer any scruples why he should not.

Just as we had parted from the brave Colonel and the rest we saw a bicycle coming. It was Albert's uncle. He got off and said—

'What on earth have you been up to? What were you doing with those volunteers?'

We told him the wild adventures of the day, and he listened, and then he said he would withdraw the word volunteers if we liked.

But the seeds of doubt were sown in the breast of Oswald. He was now almost sure that we had made jolly fools of ourselves without a moment's pause throughout the whole of this eventful day. He said nothing at the time, but after supper he had it out with Albert's uncle about the word which had been withdrawn.

Albert's uncle said, of course, no one could be sure that the dragon's teeth hadn't come up in the good old-fashioned way, but that, on the other hand, it was barely possible that both the British and the enemy were only volunteers having a field-day or sham fight, and he rather thought the Cocked-Hatted Man was not a general, but a doctor. And the man with a red pennon carried behind him MIGHT have been the umpire.

Oswald never told the others a word of this. Their young breasts were all panting with joy because they had saved their country; and it would have been but heartless unkindness to show them how silly they had been. Besides, Oswald felt he was much too old to have been so taken in—if he HAD been. Besides, Albert's uncle did say that no one could be sure about the dragon's teeth.

The thing that makes Oswald feel most that, perhaps, the whole thing was a beastly sell, was that we didn't see any wounded. But he tries not to think of this. And if he goes into the army when he grows up, he will not go quite green. He has had experience of the arts of war and the tented field. And a real colonel has called him 'Comrade-in-Arms', which is exactly what Lord Roberts called his own soldiers when he wrote home about them.

Chapter 14. Albert's Uncle's Grandmother; or, the long-lost

The shadow of the termination now descended in sable thunder-clouds upon our devoted nobs. As Albert's uncle said, 'School now gaped for its prey'. In a very short space of time we should be wending our way back to Blackheath, and all the variegated delightfulness of the country would soon be only preserved in memory's faded flowers. (I don't care for that way of writing very much. It would be an awful swot to keep it up— looking out the words and all that.)

To speak in the language of everyday life, our holiday was jolly nearly up. We had had a ripping time, but it was all but over. We really did feel sorry— though, of course, it was rather decent to think of getting back to Father and being able to tell the other chaps about our raft, and the dam, and the Tower of Mystery, and things like that.

When but a brief time was left to us, Oswald and Dicky met by chance in an apple-tree. (That sounds like 'consequences', but it is mere truthfulness.) Dicky said—

'Only four more days.'

Oswald said, 'Yes.'

'There's one thing,' Dickie said, 'that beastly society. We don't want that swarming all over everything when we get home. We ought to dissolve it before we leave here.'

The following dialogue now took place:

Oswald—'Right you are. I always said it was piffling rot.'

Dicky—'So did I.'

Oswald—'Let's call a council. But don't forget we've jolly well got to put our foot down.'

Dicky assented, and the dialogue concluded with apples.

The council, when called, was in but low spirits. This made Oswald's and Dicky's task easier. When people are sunk in gloomy despair about one thing, they will agree to almost anything about something else. (Remarks like this are called philosophic generalizations, Albert's uncle says.) Oswald began by saying—

'We've tried the society for being good in, and perhaps it's done us good. But now the time has come for each of us to be good or bad on his own, without hanging on to the others.'

> 'The race is run by one and one,
> But never by two and two,'

the Dentist said.

The others said nothing.

Oswald went on: 'I move that we chuck—I mean dissolve— the Wouldbegoods Society; its appointed task is done. If it's not well done, that's ITS fault and not ours.'

Dicky said, 'Hear! hear! I second this prop.'

The unexpected Dentist said, 'I third it. At first I thought it would help, but afterwards I saw it only made you want to be naughty, just because you were a Wouldbegood.'

Oswald owns he was surprised. We put it to the vote at once, so as not to let Denny cool. H. O. and Noel and Alice voted with us, so Daisy and Dora were what is called a hopeless minority. We tried to cheer their hopelessness by letting them read the things out of the Golden Deed book aloud. Noel hid his face in the straw so that we should not see the faces he made while he made poetry instead of listening, and when the Wouldbegoods was by vote dissolved for ever he sat up, straws in his hair, and said—

THE EPITAPH

'The Wouldbegoods are dead and gone
But not the golden deeds they have done
These will remain upon Glory's page
To be an example to every age,
And by this we have got to know
How to be good upon our ow—N.

N is for Noel, that makes the rhyme and the sense both right. O, W, N, own; do you see?'

We saw it, and said so, and the gentle poet was satisfied. And the council broke up. Oswald felt that a weight had been lifted from his expanding chest, and it is curious that he never felt so inclined to be good and a model youth as he did then. As he went down the ladder out of the loft he said—

'There's one thing we ought to do, though, before we go home. We ought to find Albert's uncle's long-lost grandmother for him.'

Alice's heart beat true and steadfast. She said, 'That's just exactly what Noel and I were saying this morning. Look out, Oswald, you wretch, you're kicking chaff into my eyes.' She was going down the ladder just under me.

Oswald's younger sister's thoughtful remark ended in another council. But not in the straw loft. We decided to have a quite new place, and disregarded H. O.'s idea of the dairy and Noel's of the cellars. We had the new council on the secret staircase, and there we settled exactly what we ought to do. This is the same thing, if you really wish to be good, as what you are going to do. It was a very interesting council, and when it was over Oswald was so pleased to think that the Wouldbegoods was unrecoverishly dead that he gave Denny and Noel, who were sitting on the step below him, a good-humoured, playful, gentle, loving, brotherly shove, and said, 'Get along down, it's tea-time!'

No reader who understands justice and the real rightness of things, and who is to blame for what, will ever think it could have been Oswald's fault that the two other boys got along down by rolling over and over each other, and bursting the door at the bottom of the stairs open by their revolving bodies. And I should like to know whose fault it was that Mrs Pettigrew was just on the other side of that door at that very minute? The door burst open, and the Impetuous bodies of Noel and Denny rolled out of it into Mrs Pettigrew, and upset her and the tea-tray. Both revolving boys were soaked with tea and milk, and there were one or two cups and things smashed. Mrs Pettigrew was knocked over, but none of her bones were broken. Noel and Denny were going to be sent to bed, but Oswald said it was all his fault. He really did this to give the others a chance of doing a refined golden deed by speaking the truth and saying it was not his fault. But you cannot really count on anyone. They did not say anything, but only rubbed the lumps on their late-revolving heads. So it was bed for Oswald, and he felt the injustice hard.

But he sat up in bed and read The Last of the Mohicans, and then he began to think. When Oswald really thinks he almost always thinks of something. He thought of something now, and it was miles better than the idea we had decided on in the secret staircase, of advertising in the Kentish Mercury and saying if Albert's uncle's long-lost grandmother would call at the Moat House she might hear of something much to her advantage.

What Oswald thought of was that if we went to Hazelbridge and asked Mr B. Munn, Grocer, that drove us home in the cart with the horse that liked the wrong end of the whip best, he would know who the lady was in the red hat and red wheels that paid him to drive us home that Canterbury night. He must have been paid, of course, for even grocers are not generous enough to drive perfect strangers, and five of them too, about the country for nothing. Thus we may learn that even unjustness and sending the wrong people to bed may bear useful fruit, which ought to be a great comfort to everyone when they are unfairly treated. Only it most likely won't be. For if Oswald's brothers and sisters had nobly stood by him as he expected, he would not have had the solitary reflections that led to the great scheme for finding the grandmother.

Of course when the others came up to roost they all came and squatted on Oswald's bed and said how sorry they were. He waived their apologies with noble dignity, because there wasn't much time, and said he had an idea that would knock the council's plan into a cocked hat. But he would not tell them what it was. He made them wait till next morning. This was not sulks, but kind feeling. He wanted them to have something else to think of besides the way they hadn't stood by him in the bursting of the secret staircase door and the tea-tray and the milk.

Next morning Oswald kindly explained, and asked who would volunteer for a forced march to Hazelbridge. The word volunteer cost the young Oswald a pang as soon as he had said it, but I hope he can bear pangs with any man living. 'And mind,' he added, hiding the pang under a general-like severeness, 'I won't have anyone in the expedition who has anything in his shoes except his feet.'

This could not have been put more delicately and decently. But Oswald is often misunderstood. Even Alice said it was unkind to throw the peas up at Denny. When this little unpleasantness had passed away (it took some time because Daisy cried, and Dora said, 'There now, Oswald!') there were seven volunteers, which, with Oswald, made eight, and was, indeed, all of us. There were no cockle-shells, or tape-sandals, or staves, or scrips, or anything romantic and pious about the eight persons who set out for Hazelbridge that morning, more earnestly wishful to be good and deedful—at least Oswald, I know, was—than ever they had been in the days of the beastly Wouldbegood Society. It was a fine day. Either it was fine nearly all last summer, which is how Oswald remembers it, or else nearly all the interesting things we did came on fine days.

With hearts light and gay, and no peas in anyone's shoes, the walk to Hazelbridge was perseveringly conducted. We took our lunch with us, and the dear dogs. Afterwards we wished for a time that we had left one of them at home. But they did so want to come, all of them, and Hazelbridge is not nearly as far as Canterbury, really, so even Martha was allowed to put on her things—I mean her collar—and come with us. She walks slowly, but we had the day before us so there was no extra hurry.

At Hazelbridge we went into B. Munn's grocer's shop and asked for ginger-beer to drink. They gave it us, but they seemed surprised at us wanting to drink it there, and the glass was warm—it had just been washed. We only did it, really, so as to get into conversation with B. Munn, grocer, and extract information without rousing suspicion. You cannot be too careful. However, when we had said it was first-class ginger-beer, and paid for it, we found it not so easy to extract anything more from B. Munn, grocer; and there was an anxious silence while he fiddled about behind the counter among the tinned meats and sauce bottles, with a fringe of hobnailed boots hanging over his head.

H. O. spoke suddenly. He is like the sort of person who rushes in where angels fear to tread, as Denny says (say what sort of person that is). He said—

'I say, you remember driving us home that day. Who paid for the cart?'

Of course B. Munn, grocer, was not such a nincompoop (I like that word, it means so many people I know) as to say right off. He said—

'I was paid all right, young gentleman. Don't you terrify yourself.'

People in Kent say terrify when they mean worry. So Dora shoved in a gentle oar. She said—

'We want to know the kind lady's name and address, so that we can write and thank her for being so jolly that day.'

B. Munn, grocer, muttered something about the lady's address being goods he was often asked for. Alice said, 'But do tell us. We forgot to ask her. She's a relation of a second-hand uncle of ours, and I do so want to thank her properly. And if you've got any extra-strong peppermints at a penny an ounce, we should like a quarter of a pound.'

This was a master-stroke. While he was weighing out the peppermints his heart got soft, and just as he was twisting up the corner of the paper bag, Dora said, 'What lovely fat peppermints! Do tell us.'

And B. Munn's heart was now quite melted, he said—

'It's Miss Ashleigh, and she lives at The Cedars—about a mile down the Maidstone Road.'

We thanked him, and Alice paid for the peppermints. Oswald was a little anxious when she ordered such a lot, but she and Noel had got the money all right, and when we were outside on Hazelbridge Green (a good deal of it is gravel, really), we stood and looked at each other. Then Dora said—

'Let's go home and write a beautiful letter and all sign it.'

Oswald looked at the others. Writing is all very well, but it's such a beastly long time to wait for anything to happen afterwards.

The intelligent Alice divined his thoughts, and the Dentist divined hers—he is not clever enough yet to divine Oswald's—and the two said together—

'Why not go and see her?'

'She did say she would like to see us again some day,' Dora replied. So after we had argued a little about it we went.

And before we had gone a hundred yards down the dusty road Martha began to make us wish with all our hearts we had not let her come. She began to limp, just as a pilgrim, who I will not name, did when he had the split peas in his silly palmering shoes.

So we called a halt and looked at her feet. One of them was quite swollen and red. Bulldogs almost always have something the matter with their feet, and it always comes on when least required. They are not the right breed for emergencies.

There was nothing for it but to take it in turns to carry her. She is very stout, and you have no idea how heavy she is. A half-hearted unadventurous person name no names, but Oswald, Alice, Noel, H. O., Dicky, Daisy, and Denny will understand me) said, why not go straight home and come another day without Martha? But the rest agreed with Oswald when he said it was only a mile, and perhaps we might get a lift home with the poor invalid. Martha was very grateful to us for our kindness. She put her fat white arms round the person's neck who happened to be carrying her. She is very affectionate, but by holding her very close to you you can keep her from kissing your face all the time. As Alice said, 'Bulldogs do give you such large, wet, pink kisses.'

A mile is a good way when you have to take your turn at carrying Martha.

At last we came to a hedge with a ditch in front of it, and chains swinging from posts to keep people off the grass and out of the ditch, and a gate with 'The Cedars' on it in gold letters. All very neat and tidy, and showing plainly that more than one gardener was kept. There we stopped. Alice put Martha down, grunting with exhaustedness, and said—

'Look here, Dora and Daisy, I don't believe a bit that it's his grandmother. I'm sure Dora was right, and it's only his horrid sweetheart. I feel it in my bones. Now, don't you really think we'd better chuck it; we're sure to catch it for interfering. We always do.'

'The cross of true love never did come smooth,' said the Dentist. 'We ought to help him to bear his cross.'

'But if we find her for him, and she's not his grandmother, he'll MARRY her,' Dicky said in tones of gloominess and despair.

Oswald felt the same, but he said, 'Never mind. We should all hate it, but perhaps Albert's uncle MIGHT like it. You can never tell. If you want to do a really unselfish action and no kid, now's your time, my late Wouldbegoods.'

No one had the face to say right out that they didn't want to be unselfish.

But it was with sad hearts that the unselfish seekers opened the long gate and went up the gravel drive between the rhododendrons and other shrubberies towards the house.

I think I have explained to you before that the eldest son of anybody is called the representative of the family if his father isn't there. This was why Oswald now took the lead. When we got to the last turn of the drive it was settled that the others were to noiselessly ambush in the rhododendrons, and Oswald was to go on alone and ask at the house for the grandmother from India—I mean Miss Ashleigh.

So he did, but when he got to the front of the house and saw how neat the flower-beds were with red geraniums, and the windows all bright and speckless with muslin blinds and brass rods, and a green parrot in a cage in the porch, and the doorstep newly whited, lying clean and untrodden in the sunshine, he stood still and thought of his boots and how dusty the roads were, and wished he had not gone into the farmyard after eggs before starting that morning. As he stood there in anxious uncertainness he heard a low voice among the bushes. It said, 'Hist! Oswald here!' and it was the voice of Alice.

So he went back to the others among the shrubs and they all crowded round their leader full of importable news.

'She's not in the house; she's HERE,' Alice said in a low whisper that seemed nearly all S's. 'Close by—she went by just this minute with a gentleman.'

'And they're sitting on a seat under a tree on a little lawn, and she's got her head on his shoulder, and he's holding her hand. I never saw anyone look so silly in all my born,' Dicky said.

'It's sickening,' Denny said, trying to look very manly with his legs wide apart.

'I don't know,' Oswald whispered. 'I suppose it wasn't Albert's uncle?'

'Not much,' Dicky briefly replied.

'Then don't you see it's all right. If she's going on like that with this fellow she'll want to marry him, and Albert's uncle is safe. And we've really done an unselfish action without having to suffer for it afterwards.'

With a stealthy movement Oswald rubbed his hands as he spoke in real joyfulness. We decided that we had better bunk unnoticed. But we had reckoned without Martha. She had strolled off limping to look about her a bit in the shrubbery. 'Where's Martha?' Dora suddenly said.

'She went that way,' pointingly remarked H. O.

'Then fetch her back, you young duffer! What did you let her go for?' Oswald said. 'And look sharp. Don't make a row.'

He went. A minute later we heard a hoarse squeak from Martha—the one she always gives when suddenly collared from behind—and a little squeal in a lady-like voice, and a man say 'Hallo!' and then we knew that H. O. had once more rushed in where angels might have thought twice about it. We hurried to the fatal spot, but it was too late. We were just in time to hear H. O. say—

'I'm sorry if she frightened you. But we've been looking for you. Are you Albert's uncle's long-lost grandmother?'

'NO,' said our lady unhesitatingly.

It seemed vain to add seven more agitated actors to the scene now going on. We stood still. The man was standing up. He was a clergyman, and I found out afterwards he was the nicest we ever knew except our own Mr Briston at Lewisham, who is now a canon or a dean, or something grand that no one ever sees. At present I did not like him. He said, 'No, this lady is nobody's grandmother. May I ask in return how long it is since you escaped from the lunatic asylum, my poor child, and whence your keeper is?'

H. O. took no notice of this at all, except to say, 'I think you are very rude, and not at all funny, if you think you are.'

The lady said, 'My dear, I remember you now perfectly. How are all the others, and are you pilgrims again to-day?'

H. O. does not always answer questions. He turned to the man and said—

'Are you going to marry the lady?'

'Margaret,' said the clergyman, 'I never thought it would come to this: he asks me my intentions.'

'If you ARE,' said H. O., 'it's all right, because if you do Albert's uncle can't—at least, not till you're dead. And we don't want him to.'

'Flattering, upon my word,' said the clergyman, putting on a deep frown. 'Shall I call him out, Margaret, for his poor opinion of you, or shall I send for the police?'

Alice now saw that H. O., though firm, was getting muddled and rather scared. She broke cover and sprang into the middle of the scene.

'Don't let him rag H. O. any more,' she said, 'it's all our faults. You see, Albert's uncle was so anxious to find you, we thought perhaps you were his long-lost heiress sister or his old nurse who alone knew the secret of his birth, or something, and we asked him, and he said you were his long-lost grandmother he had known in India. And we thought that must be a mistake and that really you were his long-lost sweetheart. And we tried to do a really unselfish act and find you for him. Because we don't want him to be married at all.'

'It isn't because we don't like YOU,' Oswald cut in, now emerging from the bushes, 'and if he must marry, we'd sooner it was you than anyone. Really we would.'

'A generous concession, Margaret,' the strange clergyman uttered, 'most generous, but the plot thickens. It's almost pea-soup-like now. One or two points clamour for explanation. Who are these visitors of yours? Why this Red Indian method of paying morning calls? Why the lurking attitude of the rest of the tribe which I now discern among the undergrowth? Won't you ask the rest of the tribe to come out and join the glad throng?'

Then I liked him better. I always like people who know the same songs we do, and books and tunes and things.

The others came out. The lady looked very uncomfy, and partly as if she was going to cry. But she couldn't help laughing too, as more and more of us came out.

'And who,' the clergyman went on, 'who in fortune's name is Albert? And who is his uncle? And what have they or you to do in this galere—I mean garden?'

We all felt rather silly, and I don't think I ever felt more than then what an awful lot there were of us.

'Three years' absence in Calcutta or elsewhere may explain my ignorance of these details, but still—'

'I think we'd better go,' said Dora. 'I'm sorry if we've done anything rude or wrong. We didn't mean to. Good-bye. I hope you'll be happy with the gentleman, I'm sure.'

'I HOPE so too,' said Noel, and I know he was thinking how much nicer Albert's uncle was. We turned to go. The lady had been very silent compared with what she was when she pretended to show us Canterbury. But now she seemed to shake off some dreamy silliness, and caught hold of Dora by the shoulder.

'No, dear, no,' she said, 'it's all right, and you must have some tea—we'll have it on the lawn. John, don't tease them any more. Albert's uncle is the gentleman I told you about. And, my dear children, this is my brother that I haven't seen for three years.'

'Then he's a long-lost too,' said H. O.

The lady said 'Not now' and smiled at him.

And the rest of us were dumb with confounding emotions. Oswald was particularly dumb. He might have known it was her brother, because in rotten grown-up books if a girl kisses a man in a shrubbery that is not the man you think she's in love with; it always turns out to be a brother, though generally the disgrace of the family and not a respectable chaplain from Calcutta.

The lady now turned to her reverend and surprising brother and said, 'John, go and tell them we'll have tea on the lawn.'

When he was gone she stood quite still a minute. Then she said, 'I'm going to tell you something, but I want to put you on your honour not to talk about it to other people. You see it isn't everyone I would tell about it. He, Albert's uncle, I mean, has told me a lot about you, and I know I can trust you.'

We said 'Yes', Oswald with a brooding sentiment of knowing all too well what was coming next.

The lady then said, 'Though I am not Albert's uncle's grandmother I did know him in India once, and we were going to be married, but we had a—a—misunderstanding.'

'Quarrel?' Row?' said Noel and H. O. at once.

'Well, yes, a quarrel, and he went away. He was in the Navy then. And then ... well, we were both sorry, but well, anyway, when his ship came back we'd gone to Constantinople, then to England, and he couldn't find us. And he says he's been looking for me ever since.'

'Not you for him?' said Noel.

'Well, perhaps,' said the lady.

And the girls said 'Ah!' with deep interest. The lady went on more quickly, 'And then I found you, and then he found me, and now I must break it to you. Try to bear up.'

She stopped. The branches cracked, and Albert's uncle was in our midst. He took off his hat. 'Excuse my tearing my hair,' he said to the lady, 'but has the pack really hunted you down?'

'It's all right,' she said, and when she looked at him she got miles prettier quite suddenly. 'I was just breaking to them ...'

'Don't take that proud privilege from me,' he said. 'Kiddies, allow me to present you to the future Mrs Albert's uncle, or shall we say Albert's new aunt?'

* * *

There was a good deal of explaining done before tea—about how we got there, I mean, and why. But after the first bitterness of disappointment we felt not nearly so sorry as we had expected to. For Albert's uncle's lady was very jolly to us, and her brother was awfully decent, and showed us a lot of first-class native curiosities and things, unpacking them on purpose; skins of beasts, and beads, and brass things, and shells from different savage lands besides India. And the lady told the girls that she hoped they would like her as much as she liked them, and if they wanted a new aunt she would do her best to give satisfaction in the new situation. And Alice thought of the Murdstone aunt belonging to Daisy and Denny, and how awful it would have been if Albert's uncle had married HER. And she decided, she told me afterwards, that we might think ourselves jolly lucky it was no worse.

Then the lady led Oswald aside, pretending to show him the parrot which he had explored thoroughly before, and told him she was not like some people in books. When she was married she would never try to separate her husband from his bachelor friends, she only wanted them to be her friends as well.

Then there was tea, and thus all ended in amicableness, and the reverend and friendly drove us home in a wagonette. But for Martha we shouldn't have had tea, or explanations, or lift or anything. So we honoured her, and did not mind her being so heavy and walking up and down constantly on our laps as we drove home.

And that is all the story of the long-lost grandmother and Albert's uncle. I am afraid it is rather dull, but it was very important (to him), so I felt it ought to be narrated. Stories about lovers and getting married are generally slow. I like a love-story where the hero parts with the girl at the garden-gate in the gloaming and goes off and has adventures, and you don't see her any more till he comes home to marry her at the end of the book. And I suppose people have to marry. Albert's uncle is awfully old—more than thirty, and the lady is advanced in years—twenty-six next Christmas. They are to be married then. The girls are to be bridesmaids in white frocks with fur. This quite consoles them. If Oswald repines sometimes, he hides it. What's the use? We all have to meet our fell destiny, and Albert's uncle is not extirpated from this awful law.

Now the finding of the long-lost was the very last thing we did for the sake of its being a noble act, so that is the end of the Wouldbegoods, and there are no more chapters after this. But Oswald hates books that finish up without telling you the things you might want to know about the people in the book. So here goes.

We went home to the beautiful Blackheath house. It seemed very stately and mansion-like after the Moat House, and everyone was most frightfully pleased to see us.

Mrs Pettigrew CRIED when we went away. I never was so astonished in my life. She made each of the girls a fat red pincushion like a heart, and each of us boys had a knife bought out of the housekeeping (I mean housekeeper's own) money.

Bill Simpkins is happy as sub-under-gardener to Albert's uncle's lady's mother. They do keep three gardeners—I knew they did. And our tramp still earns enough to sleep well on from our dear old Pig-man.

Our last three days were entirely filled up with visits of farewell sympathy to all our many friends who were so sorry to lose us. We promised to come and see them next year. I hope we shall.

Denny and Daisy went back to live with their father at Forest Hill. I don't think they'll ever be again the victims of the Murdstone aunt—who is really a great-aunt and about twice as much in the autumn of her days as our new Albert's-uncle aunt. I think they plucked up spirit enough to tell their father they didn't like her—which they'd never thought of doing before. Our own robber says their holidays in the country did them both a great deal of good. And he says us Bastables have certainly taught Daisy and Denny the rudiments of the art of making home happy. I believe they have thought of several quite new naughty things entirely on their own—and done them too—since they came back from the Moat House.

I wish you didn't grow up so quickly. Oswald can see that ere long he will be too old for the kind of games we can all play, and he feels grown-upness creeping inordiously upon him. But enough of this.

And now, gentle reader, farewell. If anything in these chronicles of the Wouldbegoods should make you try to be good yourself, the author will be very glad, of course. But take my advice and don't make a society for trying in. It is much easier without.

And do try to forget that Oswald has another name besides Bastable. The one beginning with C., I mean. Perhaps you have not noticed what it was. If so, don't look back for it. It is a name no manly boy would like to be called by—if he spoke the truth. Oswald is said to be a very manly boy, and he despises that name, and will never give it to his own son when he has one. Not if a rich relative offered to leave him an immense fortune if he did. Oswald would still be firm. He would, on the honour of the House of Bastable.

The Enchanted Castle

To Margaret Ostler with love from E. Nesbit

Peggy, you came from the heath and moor,
And you brought their airs through my open door;
You brought the blossom of youth to blow
In the Latin Quarter of Soho.
For the sake of that magic I send you here
A tale of enchantments, Peggy dear,
A bit of my work, and a bit of my heart...
The bit that you left when we had to part.

Royalty Chambers, Soho, W. 25 September 1907

There were three of them Jerry, Jimmy, and Kathleen. Of course, Jerry's name was Gerald, and not Jeremiah, whatever you may think; and Jimmy's name was James; and Kathleen was never called by her name at all, but Cathy, or Catty, or Puss Cat, when her brothers were pleased with her, and Scratch Cat when they were not pleased. And they were at school in a little town in the West of England the boys at one school, of course, and the girl at another, because the sensible habit of having boys and girls at the same school is not yet as common as I hope it will be some day. They used to see each other on Saturdays and Sundays at the house of a kind maiden lady; but it was one of those houses where it is impossible to play. You know the kind of house, don't you? There is a sort of a something about that kind of house that makes you hardly able even to talk to each other when you are left alone, and playing seems unnatural and affected. So they looked forward to the holidays, when they should all go home and be together all day long, in a house where playing was natural and conversation possible, and where the Hampshire forests and fields were full of interesting things to do and see. Their Cousin Betty was to be there too, and there were plans. Betty's school broke up before theirs, and so she got to the Hampshire home first, and the moment she got there she began to have measles, so that my three couldn't go home at all. You may imagine their feelings. The thought of seven weeks at Miss Hervey's was not to be borne, and all three wrote home and said so. This astonished their parents very much, because they had always thought it was so nice for the children to have dear Miss Hervey's to go to. However, they were "jolly decent about it", as Jerry said, and after a lot of letters and telegrams, it was arranged that the boys should go and stay at Kathleen's school, where there were now no girls left and no mistresses except the French one.

"It'll be better than being at Miss Hervey's," said Kathleen, when the boys came round to ask Mademoiselle when it would be convenient for them to come; "and, besides, our school's not half so ugly as yours. We do have tablecloths on the tables and curtains at the windows, and yours is all deal boards, and desks, and inkiness."

When they had gone to pack their boxes Kathleen made all the rooms as pretty as she could with flowers in jam jars marigolds chiefly, because there was nothing much else in the back garden. There were geraniums in the front garden, and calceolarias and lobelias; of course, the children were not allowed to pick these.

"We ought to have some sort of play to keep us going through the holidays," said Kathleen, when tea was over, and she had unpacked and arranged the boys clothes in the painted chests of drawers, feeling very grown-up and careful as she neatly laid the different sorts of clothes in tidy little heaps in the drawers. "Suppose we write a book."

"You couldn't," said Jimmy.

"I didn't mean me, of course," said Kathleen, a little injured; "I meant us."

"Too much fag," said Gerald briefly.

"If we wrote a book," Kathleen persisted, "about what the insides of schools really are like, people would read it and say how clever we were."

"More likely expel us," said Gerald. "No; we'll have an out-of-doors game bandits, or something like that. It wouldn't be bad if we could get a cave and keep stores in it, and have our meals there."

"There aren't any caves," said Jimmy, who was fond of contradicting everyone. "And, besides, your precious Mamselle won't let us go out alone, as likely as not."

"Oh, we'll see about that," said Gerald. "I'll go and talk to her like a father."

"Like that?" Kathleen pointed the thumb of scorn at him, and he looked in the glass.

"To brush his hair and his clothes and to wash his face and hands was to our hero but the work of a moment," said Gerald, and went to suit the action to the word.

It was a very sleek boy, brown and thin and interesting-looking, that knocked at the door of the parlour where Mademoiselle sat reading a yellow-covered book and wishing vain wishes. Gerald could always make himself look interesting at a moment's notice, a very useful accomplishment in dealing with strange grown-ups. It was done by opening his grey eyes rather wide, allowing the corners of his mouth to droop, and assuming a gentle, pleading expression, resembling that of the late little Lord Fauntleroy who must, by the way, be quite old now, and an awful prig.

"Entrez!" said Mademoiselle, in shrill French accents. So he entered.

"Eh bien?" she said rather impatiently.

"I hope I am not disturbing you," said Gerald, in whose mouth, it seemed, butter would not have melted.

"But no," she said, somewhat softened. "What is it that you desire?"

"I thought I ought to come and say how do you do," said Gerald, "because of you being the lady of the house."

He held out the newly-washed hand, still damp and red. She took it.

"You are a very polite little boy," she said.

"Not at all," said Gerald, more polite than ever. "I am so sorry for you. It must be dreadful to have us to look after in the holidays."

"But not at all," said Mademoiselle in her turn. "I am sure you will be very good childrens."

Gerald's look assured her that he and the others would be as near angels as children could be without ceasing to be human."We'll try," he said earnestly.

"Can one do anything for you?" asked the French governess kindly.

"Oh, no, thank you," said Gerald. "We don't want to give you any trouble at all. And I was thinking it would be less trouble for you if we were to go out into the woods all day tomorrow and take our dinner with us something cold, you know so as not to be a trouble to the cook."

"You are very considerate," said Mademoiselle coldly. Then Gerald's eyes smiled; they had a trick of doing this when his lips were quite serious. Mademoiselle caught the twinkle, and she laughed and Gerald laughed too.

"Little deceiver!" she said. "Why not say at once you want to be free of surveillance, how you say overwatching without pretending it is me you wish to please?"

"You have to be careful with grown-ups, " said Gerald, "but it isn't all pretence either. We don't want to trouble you and we don't want you to"

"To trouble you. Eh bien! Your parents, they permit these days at woods?"

"Oh, yes," said Gerald truthfully.

"Then I will not be more a dragon than the parents. I will forewarn the cook. Are you content?"

"Rather!" said Gerald. "Mademoiselle, you are a dear."

"A deer?" she repeated "a stag?"

"No, a cherie," said Gerald "a regular A1 cherie. And you shan't repent it. Is there anything we can do for you wind your wool, or find your spectacles, or ?"

"He thinks me a grandmother!" said Mademoiselle, laughing more than ever. "Go then, and be not more naughty than you must."

"Well, what luck?" the others asked.

"It's all right," said Gerald indifferently. "I told you it would be. The ingenuous youth won the regard of the foreign governess, who in her youth had been the beauty of her humble village."

"I don't believe she ever was. She's too stern," said Kathleen.

"Ah!" said Gerald, "that's only because you don't know how to manage her. She wasn't stern with me."

"I say, what a humbug you are though, aren't you?" said Jimmy.

"No, I'm a dip what's-its-name? Something like an ambassador. Dipsoplomatist that's what I am. Anyhow, we've got our day, and if we don't find a cave in it my name's not Jack Robinson."

Mademoiselle, less stern than Kathleen had ever seen her, presided at supper, which was bread and treacle spread several hours before, and now harder and drier than any other food you can think of. Gerald was very polite in handing her butter and cheese, and pressing her to taste the bread and treacle.

"Bah! it is like sand in the mouth of a dryness! Is it possible this pleases you?"

"No," said Gerald, "it is not possible, but it is not polite for boys to make remarks about their food!"

She laughed, but there was no more dried bread and treacle for supper after that.

"How do you do it?" Kathleen whispered admiringly as they said good night.

"Oh, it's quite easy when you've once got a grownup to see what you're after. You'll see, I shall drive her with a rein of darning cotton after this."

Next morning Gerald got up early and gathered a little bunch of pink carnations from a plant which he found hidden among the marigolds. He tied it up with black cotton and laid it on Mademoiselle's plate. She smiled and looked quite handsome as she stuck the flowers in her belt.

"Do you think it's quite decent," Jimmy asked later "sort of bribing people to let you do as you like with flowers and things and passing them the salt?"

"It's not that," said Kathleen suddenly. "I know what Gerald means, only I never think of the things in time myself. You see, if you want grown-ups to be nice to you the least you can do is to be nice to them and think of little things to please them. I never think of any myself. Jerry does; that's why all the old ladies like him. It's not bribery. It's a sort of honesty like paying for things."

"Well, anyway," said Jimmy, putting away the moral question, "we've got a ripping day for the woods."

They had.

The wide High Street, even at the busy morning hour almost as quiet as a dream-street, lay bathed in sunshine; the leaves shone fresh from last night's rain, but the road was dry, and in the sunshine the very dust of it sparkled like diamonds. The beautiful old houses, standing stout and strong, looked as though they were basking in the sunshine and enjoying it.

"But are there any woods?" asked Kathleen as they passed the market-place.

"It doesn't much matter about woods," said Gerald dreamily, "we're sure to find something. One of the chaps told me his father said when he was a boy there used to be a little cave under the bank in a lane near the Salisbury Road; but he said there was an enchanted castle there too, so perhaps the cave isn't true either." "If we were to get horns," said Kathleen, "and to blow them very hard all the way, we might find a magic castle."

"If you've got the money to throw away on horns..." said Jimmy contemptuously.

"Well, I have, as it happens, so there!" said Kathleen. And the horns were bought in a tiny shop with a bulging window full of a tangle of toys and sweets and cucumbers and sour apples.

And the quiet square at the end of the town where the church is, and the houses of the most respectable people, echoed to the sound of horns blown long and loud. But none of the houses turned into enchanted castles. Away they went along the Salisbury Road, which was very hot and dusty, so they agreed to drink one of the bottles of ginger-beer.

"We might as well carry the ginger-beer inside us as inside the bottle," said Jimmy, "and we can hide the bottle and call for it as we come back.

Presently they came to a place where the road, as Gerald said, went two ways at once.

"That looks like adventures," said Kathleen; and they took the right-hand road, and the next time they took a turning it was a left-hand one, "so as to be quite fair," Jimmy said, and then a right-hand one and then a left, and so on, till they were completely lost.

"Completely," said Kathleen; "how jolly!"

And now trees arched overhead, and the banks of the road were high and bushy. The adventurers had long since ceased to blow their horns. It was too tiring to go on doing that, when there was no one to be annoyed by it.

"Oh, kriky!" observed Jimmy suddenly, "let's sit down a bit and have some of our dinner. We might call it lunch, you know," he added persuasively.

So they sat down in the hedge and ate the ripe red gooseberries that were to have been their dessert.

And as they sat and rested and wished that their boots did not feel so full of feet, Gerald leaned back against the bushes, and the bushes gave way so that he almost fell over backward. Something had yielded to the pressure of his back, and there was the sound of something heavy that fell.

"Oh, Jimminy!" he remarked, recovering himself suddenly; "there's something hollow in there the stone I was leaning against simply went!"

"I wish it was a cave," said Jimmy; "but of course it isn't."

"If we blow the horns perhaps it will be," said Kathleen, and hastily blew her own.

Gerald reached his hand through the bushes. "I can't feel anything but air," he said; "it's just a hole full of emptiness. The other two pulled back the bushes. There certainly was a hole in the bank. "I'm going to go in," observed Gerald.

"Oh, don't!" said his sister. "I wish you wouldn't. Suppose there were snakes!"

"Not likely," said Gerald, but he leaned forward and struck a match. "It is a cave!" he cried, and put his knee on the mossy stone he had been sitting on, scrambled over it, and disappeared.

A breathless pause followed.

"You all right?" asked Jimmy.

"Yes; come on. You'd better come feet first there's a bit of a drop."

"I'll go next," said Kathleen, and went feet first, as advised. The feet waved wildly in the air.

"Look out!" said Gerald in the dark; "you'll have my eye out. Put your feet down, girl, not up. It's no use trying to fly here there's no room."

He helped her by pulling her feet forcibly down and then lifting her under the arms. She felt rustling dry leaves under her boots, and stood ready to receive Jimmy, who came in head first, like one diving into an unknown sea.

"It is a cave," said Kathleen.

"The young explorers," explained Gerald, blocking up the hole of entrance with his shoulders, "dazzled at first by the darkness of the cave, could see nothing."

"Darkness doesn't dazzle," said Jimmy.

"I wish we'd got a candle," said Kathleen.

"Yes, it does," Gerald contradicted "could see nothing. But their dauntless leader, whose eyes had grown used to the dark while the clumsy forms of the others were bunging up the entrance, had made a discovery.

"Oh, what!" Both the others were used to Gerald's way of telling a story while he acted it, but they did sometimes wish that he didn't talk quite so long and so like a book in moments of excitement.

"He did not reveal the dread secret to his faithful followers till one and all had given him their word of honour to be calm."

"We'll be calm all right," said Jimmy impatiently."Well, then," said Gerald, ceasing suddenly to be a book and becoming a boy, "there's a light over there look behind you!"

They looked. And there was. A faint greyness on the brown walls of the cave, and a brighter greyness cut off sharply by a dark line, showed that round a turning or angle of the cave there was daylight.

"Attention!" said Gerald; at least, that was what he meant, though what he said was "Shun!" as becomes the son of a soldier. The others mechanically obeyed.

"You will remain at attention till I give the word "Slow march!' on which you will advance cautiously in open order, following your hero leader, taking care not to tread on the dead and wounded."

"I wish you wouldn't!" said Kathleen.

"There aren't any," said Jimmy, feeling for her hand in the dark; "he only means, take care not to tumble over stones and things"

Here he found her hand, and she screamed.

"It's only me," said Jimmy. "I thought you'd like me to hold it. But you're just like a girl."

Their eyes had now begun to get accustomed to the darkness, and all could see that they were in a rough stone cave, that went straight on for about three or four yards and then turned sharply to the right.

"Death or victory!" remarked Gerald. "Now, then — Slow march!"

He advanced carefully, picking his way among the loose earth and stones that were the floor of the cave.

"A sail, a sail!" he cried, as he turned the corner.

"How splendid!" Kathleen drew a long breath as she came out into the sunshine.

"I don't see any sail," said Jimmy, following.

The narrow passage ended in a round arch all fringed with ferns and creepers. They passed through the arch into a deep, narrow gully whose banks were of stones, moss-covered; and in the crannies grew more ferns and long grasses. Trees growing on the top of the bank arched across, and the sunlight came through in changing patches of brightness, turning the gully to a roofed corridor of goldy-green. The path, which was of greeny-grey flagstones where heaps of leaves had drifted, sloped steeply down, and at the end of it was another round arch, quite dark inside, above which rose rocks and grass and bushes.

"It's like the outside of a railway tunnel," said James.

"It's the entrance to the enchanted castle," said Kathleen. "Let's blow the horns."

"Dry up!" said Gerald. "The bold Captain, reproving the silly chatter of his subordinates,"

"I like that!" said Jimmy, indignant.

"I thought you would," resumed Gerald "of his subordinates, bade them advance with caution and in silence, because after all there might be somebody about, and the other arch might be an ice-house or something dangerous.

"What?" asked Kathleen anxiously.

"Bears, perhaps," said Gerald briefly.

"There aren't any bears without bars in England, anyway," said Jimmy. "They call bears bars in America," he added absently.

"Quick march!" was Gerald's only reply.

And they marched. Under the drifted damp leaves the path was firm and stony to their shuffling feet. At the dark arch they stopped.

"There are steps down," said Jimmy.

"It is an ice-house," said Gerald.

"Don't let's," said Kathleen.

"Our hero," said Gerald, "who nothing could dismay, raised the faltering hopes of his abject minions by saying that he was jolly well going on, and they could do as they liked about it."

"If you call names," said Jimmy, "you can go on by yourself. He added, "So there!"

"It's part of the game, silly," explained Gerald kindly. "You can be Captain tomorrow, so you'd better hold your jaw now, and begin to think about what names you'll call us when it's your turn."

Very slowly and carefully they went down the steps. A vaulted stone arched over their heads. Gerald struck a match when the last step was found to have no edge, and to be, in fact, the beginning of a passage, turning to the left.

"This," said Jimmy, "will take us back into the road."

"Or under it," said Gerald. "We've come down eleven steps."

They went on, following their leader, who went very slowly for fear, as he explained, of steps. The passage was very dark.

"I don't half like it!" whispered Jimmy.

Then came a glimmer of daylight that grew and grew, and presently ended in another arch that looked out over a scene so like a picture out of a book about Italy that everyone's breath was taken away, and they simply walked forward silent and staring. A short avenue of cypresses led, widening as it went, to a marble terrace that lay broad and white in the sunlight. The children, blinking, leaned their arms on the broad, flat balustrade and gazed. Immediately below them was a lake just like a lake in "The Beauties of Italy" a lake with swans and an island and weeping willows; beyond it were green slopes dotted with groves of trees, and amid the trees gleamed the white limbs of statues. Against a little hill to the left was a round white building with pillars, and to the right a waterfall came tumbling down among mossy stones to splash into the lake. Steps fed from the terrace to the water, and other steps to the green lawns beside it. Away across the grassy slopes deer were feeding, and in the distance where the groves of trees thickened into what looked almost a forest were enormous shapes of grey stone, like nothing that the children had ever seen before.

"That chap at school," said Gerald.

"It is an enchanted castle," said Kathleen.

"I don't see any castle," said Jimmy.

"What do you call that, then?" Gerald pointed to where, beyond a belt of lime-trees, white towers and turrets broke the blue of the sky.

"There doesn't seem to be anyone about," said Kathleen, "and yet it's all so tidy. I believe it is magic"

"Magic mowing machines," Jimmy suggested.

"If we were in a book it would be an enchanted castle — certain to be," said Kathleen.

"It is an enchanted castle," said Gerald in hollow tones.

"But there aren't any" Jimmy was quite positive.

"How do you know? Do you think there's nothing in the world but what you've seen?" His scorn was crushing.

"I think magic went out when people began to have steam-engines," Jimmy insisted, "and newspapers, and telephones and wireless telegraphing."

"Wireless is rather like magic when you come to think of it," said Gerald.

"Oh, that sort!" Jimmy's contempt was deep.

"Perhaps there's given up being magic because people didn't believe in it any more," said Kathleen.

"Well, don't let's spoil the show with any silly old not believing," said Gerald with decision. "I'm going to believe in magic as hard as I can. This is an enchanted garden, and that's an enchanted castle, and I'm jolly well going to explore."

The dauntless knight then led the way, leaving his ignorant squires to follow or not, just as they jolly well chose. He rolled off the balustrade and strode firmly down towards the lawn, his boots making, as they went, a clatter full of determination. The others followed. There never was such a garden out of a picture or a fairy-tale. They passed quite close by the deer, who only raised their pretty heads to look, and did not seem startled at all. And after a long stretch of turf they passed under the heaped-up heavy masses of lime-trees and came into a rose-garden, bordered with thick, close-cut yew hedges, and lying red and pink and green and white in the sun, like a giant's many-coloured, highly-scented pocket-handkerchief.

"I know we shall meet a gardener in a minute, and he'll ask what we re doing here. And then what will you say?" Kathleen asked with her nose in a rose.

"I shall say we have lost our way, and it will be quite true," said Gerald.

But they did not meet a gardener or anybody else, and the feeling of magic got thicker and thicker, till they were almost afraid of the sound of their feet in the great silent place. Beyond the rose garden was a yew hedge with an arch cut in it, and it was the beginning of a maze like the one in Hampton Court.

"Now," said Gerald, "you mark my words. In the middle of this maze we shall find the secret enchantment. Draw your swords, my merry men all, and hark forward tallyho in the utmost silence. Which they did. It was very hot in the maze, between the close yew hedges, and the way to the maze's heart was hidden well. Again and again they found themselves at the black yew arch that opened on the rose garden, and they were all glad that they had brought large, clean pocket-handkerchiefs with them. It was when they found themselves there for the fourth time that Jimmy suddenly cried, "Oh, I wish ' and then stopped short very suddenly. "Oh!" he added in quite a different voice, "where's the dinner?" And then in a stricken silence they all remembered that the basket with the dinner had been left at the entrance of the cave. Their thoughts dwelt fondly on the slices of cold mutton, the six tomatoes, the bread and butter, the screwed-up paper of salt, the apple turnovers, and the little thick glass that one drank the ginger-beer out of.

"Let's go back," said Jimmy, "now this minute, and get our things and have our dinner."

"Let's have one more try at the maze. I hate giving things up," said Gerald.

"I am so hungry!" said Jimmy.

"Why didn't you say so before?" asked Gerald bitterly.

"I wasn't before."

"Then you can't be now. You don't get hungry all in a minute. What's that?"

That was a gleam of red that lay at the foot of the yew-hedge a thin little line, that you would hardly have noticed unless you had been staring in a fixed and angry way at the roots of the hedge.

It was a thread of cotton. Gerald picked it up. One end of it was tied to a thimble with holes in it, and the other—

"There is no other end," said Gerald, with firm triumph. "It's a clue that's what it is. What price cold mutton now? I've always felt something magic would happen some day, and now it has."

"I expect the gardener put it there," said Jimmy.

"With a Princess's silver thimble on it? Look! there's a crown on the thimble."

There was.

"Come," said Gerald in low, urgent tones, "if you are adventurers be adventurers; and anyhow, I expect someone has gone along the road and bagged the mutton hours ago."

He walked forward, winding the red thread round his fingers as he went. And it was a clue, and it led them right into the middle of the maze. And in the very middle of the maze they came upon the wonder.

The red clue led them up two stone steps to a round grass plot. There was a sun-dial in the middle, and all round against the yew hedge a low, wide marble seat. The red clew ran straight across the grass and by the sun-dial, and ended in a small brown hand with jewelled rings on every finger. The hand was, naturally, attached to an arm, and that had many bracelets on it, sparkling with red and blue and green stones. The arm wore a sleeve of pink and gold brocaded silk, faded a little here and there but still extremely imposing, and the sleeve was part of a dress, which was worn by a lady who lay on the stone seat asleep in the sun. The rosy gold dress fell open over an embroidered petticoat of a soft green colour. There was old yellow lace the colour of scalded cream, and a thin white veil spangled with silver stars covered the face.

"It's the enchanted Princess," said Gerald, now really impressed. "I told you so."

"It's the Sleeping Beauty," said Kathleen. "It is look how old-fashioned her clothes are, like the pictures of Marie Antoinette's ladies in the history book. She has slept for a hundred years. Oh, Gerald, you're the eldest; you must be the Prince, and we never knew it."

"She isn't really a Princess," said Jimmy. But the others laughed at him, partly because his saying things like that was enough to spoil any game, and partly because they really were not at all sure that it was not a Princess who lay there as still as the sunshine. Every stage of the adventure the cave, the wonderful gardens, the maze, the clue, had deepened the feeling of magic, till now Kathleen and Gerald were almost completely bewitched.

"Lift the veil up," Jerry, said Kathleen in a whisper, "if she isn't beautiful we shall know she can't be the Princess.

"Lift it yourself," said Gerald.

"I expect you're forbidden to touch the figures," said Jimmy.

"It's not wax, silly," said his brother.

"No," said his sister, "wax wouldn't be much good in this sun. And, besides, you can see her breathing. It's the Princess right enough." She very gently lifted the edge of the veil and turned it back. The Princess's face was small and white between long plaits of black hair. Her nose was straight and her brows finely traced. There were a few freckles on cheekbones and nose.

"No wonder," whispered Kathleen, "sleeping all these years in all this sun! Her mouth was not a rosebud. But all the same "Isn't she lovely!" Kathleen murmured. "Not so dusty," Gerald was understood to reply. "Now, Jerry," said Kathleen firmly, "you're the eldest."

"Of course I am," said Gerald uneasily.

"Well, you've got to wake the Princess."

"She's not a Princess," said Jimmy, with his hands in the pockets of his knickerbockers; "she's only a little girl dressed up."

"But she's in long dresses," urged Kathleen.

"Yes, but look what a little way down her frock her feet come. She wouldn't be any taller than Jerry if she was to stand up."

"Now then," urged Kathleen. "Jerry, don't be silly. You've got to do it."

"Do what?" asked Gerald, kicking his left boot with his right.

"Why, kiss her awake, of course."

"Not me!" was Gerald's unhesitating rejoinder.

"Well, someone's got to."

"She'd go for me as likely as not the minute she woke up," said Gerald anxiously.

"I'd do it like a shot," said Kathleen, "but I don't suppose it ud make any difference me kissing her."

She did it; and it didn't. The Princess still lay in deep slumber.

"Then you must, Jimmy. I dare say you'll do. Jump back quickly before she can hit you."

"She won't hit him, he's such a little chap," said Gerald.

"Little yourself!" said Jimmy. "I don't mind kissing her. I'm not a coward, like Some People. Only if I do, I'm going to be the dauntless leader for the rest of the day."

"No, look here hold on!" cried Gerald, "perhaps I'd better " But, in the meantime, Jimmy had planted a loud, cheerful-sounding kiss on the Princess's pale cheek, and now the three stood breathless, awaiting the result.

And the result was that the Princess opened large, dark eyes, stretched out her arms, yawned a little, covering her mouth with a small brown hand, and said, quite plainly and distinctly, and without any room at all for mistake:

"Then the hundred years are over? How the yew hedges have grown! Which of you is my Prince that aroused me from my deep sleep of so many long years?"

"I did," said Jimmy fearlessly, for she did not look as though she were going to slap anyone.

"My noble preserver!" said the Princess, and held out her hand. Jimmy shook it vigorously.

"But I say," said he, "you aren't really a Princess, are you?"

"Of course I am," she answered; "who else could I be? Look at my crown!" She pulled aside the spangled veil, and showed beneath it a coronet of what even Jimmy could not help seeing to be diamonds.

"But " said Jimmy.

"Why," she said, opening her eyes very wide, "you must have known about my being here, or you'd never have come. How did you get past the dragons?"

Gerald ignored the question. "I say," he said, "do you really believe in magic, and all that?"

"I ought to," she said, "if anybody does. Look, here's the place where I pricked my finger with the spindle." She showed a little scar on her wrist.

"Then this really is an enchanted castle?"

"Of course it is," said the Princess. "How stupid you are!" She stood up, and her pink brocaded dress lay in bright waves about her feet.

"I said her dress would be too long," said Jimmy.

"It was the right length when I went to sleep," said the Princess; "it must have grown in the hundred years."

"I don't believe you're a Princess at all," said Jimmy; "at least "

"Don't bother about believing it, if you don't like," said the Princess. "It doesn't so much matter what you believe as what I am. She turned to the others.

"Let's go back to the castle," she said, "and I'll show you all my lovely jewels and things. Wouldn't you like that?"

"Yes, said Gerald with very plain hesitation. "But "

"But what?" The Princess's tone was impatient.

"But we're most awfully hungry."

"Oh, so am I!" cried the Princess.

"We've had nothing to eat since breakfast."

"And it's three now," said the Princess, looking at the sun-dial. "Why, you've had nothing to eat for hours and hours and hours. But think of me! I haven't had anything to eat for a hundred years. Come along to the castle."

"The mice will have eaten everything," said Jimmy sadly. He saw now that she really was a Princess.

"Not they," cried the Princess joyously. "You forget everything's enchanted here. Time simply stood still for a hundred years. Come along, and one of you must carry my train, or I shan't be able to move now it's grown such a frightful length."

When you are young so many things are difficult to believe, and yet the dullest people will tell you that they are true such things, for instance, as that the earth goes round the sun, and that it is not flat but round. But the things that seem really likely, like fairy-tales and magic, are, so say the grown-ups, not true at all. Yet they are so easy to believe, especially when you see them happening. And, as I am always telling you, the most wonderful things happen to all sorts of people, only you never hear about them because the people think that no one will believe their stories, and so they don't tell them to any one except me. And they tell me, because they know that I can believe anything.

When Jimmy had awakened the Sleeping Princess, and she had invited the three children to go with her to her palace and get something to eat, they all knew quite surely that they had come into a place of magic happenings. And they walked in a slow procession along the grass towards the castle. The Princess went first, and Kathleen carried her shining train; then came Jimmy, and Gerald came last. They were all quite sure that they had walked right into the middle of a fairy-tale, and they were the more ready to believe it because they were so tired and hungry. They were, in fact, so hungry and tired that they hardly noticed where they were going, or observed the beauties of the formal gardens through which the pink-silk Princess was leading them. They were in a sort of dream, from which they only partially awakened to find themselves in a big hail, with suits of armour and old flags round the walls, the skins of beasts on the floor, and heavy oak tables and benches ranged along it.

The Princess entered, slow and stately, but once inside she twitched her sheeny train out of Jimmy's hand and turned to the three.

"You just wait here a minute," she said, "and mind you don't talk while I'm away. This castle is crammed with magic, and I don't know what will happen if you talk." And with that, picking up the thick goldy-pink folds under her arms, she ran out, as Jimmy said afterwards, "most unprincesslike," showing as she ran black stockings and black strap shoes.

Jimmy wanted very much to say that he didn't believe anything would happen, only he was afraid something would happen if he did, so he merely made a face and put out his tongue. The others pretended not to see this, which was much more crushing than anything they could have said. So they sat in silence, and Gerald ground the heel of his boot upon the marble floor. Then the Princess came back, very slowly and kicking her long skirts in front of her at every step. She could not hold them up now because of the tray she carried.

It was not a silver tray, as you might have expected, but an oblong tin one. She set it down noisily on the end of the long table and breathed a sigh of relief..

"Oh! it was heavy," she said. I don't know what fairy feast the children's fancy had been busy with. Anyhow, this was nothing like it. The heavy tray held a loaf of bread, a lump of cheese, and a brown jug of water. The rest of its heaviness was just plates and mugs and knives.

"Come along," said the Princess hospitably. "I couldn't find anything but bread and cheese but it doesn't matter, because everything's magic here, and unless you have some dreadful secret fault the bread and cheese will turn into anything you like. What would you like?" she asked Kathleen.

"Roast chicken," said Kathleen, without hesitation.

The pinky Princess cut a slice of bread and laid it on a dish.

"There you are," she said, "roast chicken. Shall I carve it, or will you?"

"You, please," said Kathleen, and received a piece of dry bread on a plate.

"Green peas?" asked the Princess, cut a piece of cheese and laid it beside the bread.

Kathleen began to eat the bread, cutting it up with knife and fork as you would eat chicken. It was no use owning that she didn't see any chicken and peas, or anything but cheese and dry bread, because that would be owning that she had some dreadful secret fault.

"If I have, it is a secret, even from me," she told herself.

The others asked for roast beef and cabbage and got it, she supposed, though to her it only looked like dry bread and Dutch cheese.

"I do wonder what my dreadful secret fault is," she thought, as the Princess remarked that, as for her, she could fancy a slice of roast peacock. "This one, she added, lifting a second mouthful of dry bread on her fork, "is quite delicious."

"It's a game, isn't it?" asked Jimmy suddenly.

"What's a game?" asked the Princess, frowning.

"Pretending it's beef the bread and cheese, I mean."

"A game? But it is beef. Look at it," said the Princess, opening her eyes very wide.

"Yes, of course," said Jimmy feebly. "I was only joking."

Bread and cheese is not perhaps so good as roast beef or chicken or peacock (I'm not sure about the peacock. I never tasted peacock, did you?); but bread and cheese is, at any rate, very much better than nothing when you have gone on having nothing since breakfast (gooseberries and ginger-beer hardly count) and it is long past your proper dinner-time. Everyone ate and drank and felt much better.

"Now," said the Princess, brushing the bread crumbs off her green silk lap, "if you're sure you won't have any more meat you can come and see my treasures. Sure you won't take the least bit more chicken? No? Then follow me."

She got up and they followed her down the long hall to the end where the great stone stairs ran up at each side and joined in a broad flight leading to the gallery above. Under the stairs was a hanging of tapestry.

"Beneath this arras," said the Princess, "is the door leading to my private apartments." She held the tapestry up with both hands, for it was heavy, and showed a little door that had been hidden by it.

"The key," she said, "hangs above."

And so it did, on a large rusty nail.

"Put it in," said the Princess, "and turn it." Gerald did so, and the great key creaked and grated in the lock.

"Now push," she said; "push hard, all of you. They pushed hard, all of them. The door gave way, and they fell over each other into the dark space beyond.

The Princess dropped the curtain and came after them, closing the door behind her.

"Look out!" she said; "look out!" there are two steps down.

"Thank you," said Gerald, rubbing his knee at the bottom of the steps. "We found that out for ourselves."

"I'm sorry," said the Princess, "but you can't have hurt yourselves much. Go straight on. There aren't any more steps."

They went straight on in the dark.

"When you come to the door just turn the handle and go in. Then stand still till I find the matches. I know where they are."

"Did they have matches a hundred years ago?" asked Jimmy.

"I meant the tinder-box," said the Princess quickly. "We always called it the matches. Don't you? Here, let me go first."

She did, and when they had reached the door she was waiting for them with a candle in her hand. She thrust it on Gerald.

"Hold it steady," she said, and undid the shutters of a long window, so that first a yellow streak and then a blazing great oblong of light flashed at them and the room was full of sunshine.

"It makes the candle look quite silly," said Jimmy. "So it does, said the Princess, and blew out the candle. Then she took the key from the outside of the door, put it in the inside keyhole, and turned it.

The room they were in was small and high. Its domed ceiling was of deep blue with gold stars painted on it. The walls were of wood, panelled and carved, and there was no furniture in it whatever.

"This," said the Princess, "is my treasure chamber." "But where, asked Kathleen politely, "are the treasures?"

"Don't you see them?" asked the Princess.

"No, we don't," said Jimmy bluntly. "You don't come that bread-and-cheese game with me not twice over, you don't!"

"If you really don't see them," said the Princess, "I suppose I shall have to say the charm. Shut your eyes, please. And give me your word of honour you won't look till I tell you, and that you'll never tell anyone what you've seen."

Their words of honour were something that the children would rather not have given just then, but they gave them all the same, and shut their eyes tight.

"Wiggadil yougadoo begadee leegadeeve nowgadow?" said the Princess rapidly; and they heard the swish of her silk train moving across the room. Then there was a creaking, rustling noise.

"She's locking us in!" cried Jimmy.

"Your word of honour," gasped Gerald.

"Oh, do be quick!" moaned Kathleen.

"You may look," said the voice of the Princess. And they looked. The room was not the same room, yet yes, the starry-vaulted blue ceiling was there, and below it half a dozen feet of the dark panelling, but below that the walls of the room blazed and sparkled with white and blue and red and green and gold and silver. Shelves ran round the room, and on them were gold cups and silver dishes, and platters and goblets set with gems, ornaments of gold and silver, tiaras of diamonds, necklaces of rubies, strings of emeralds and pearls, all set out in unimaginable splendour against a background of faded blue velvet. It was like the Crown jewels that you see when your kind uncle takes you to the Tower, only there seemed to be far more jewels than you or anyone else has ever seen together at the Tower or anywhere else.

The three children remained breathless, open-mouthed, staring at the sparkling splendours all about them, while the Princess stood, her arm stretched out in a gesture of command, and a proud smile on her lips.

"My word!" said Gerald, in a low whisper. But no one spoke out loud. They waited as if spellbound for the Princess to speak.

She spoke.

"What price bread-and-cheese games now?" she asked triumphantly. "Can I do magic, or can't I?"

"You can; oh, you can!" said Kathleen.

"May we may we touch?" asked Gerald.

"All that's mine is yours," said the Princess, with a generous wave of her brown hand, and added quickly, "Only, of course, you mustn't take anything away with you."

"We're not thieves!" said Jimmy. The others were already turning over the wonderful things on the blue velvet shelves.

"Perhaps not," said the Princess, "but you're a very unbelieving little boy. You think I can't see inside you, but I can. I know what you've been thinking."

"What?" asked Jimmy.

"Oh, you know well enough," said the Princess. "You're thinking about the bread and cheese that I changed into beef, and about your secret fault. I say, let's all dress up and you be princes and princesses too."

"To crown our hero," said Gerald, lifting a gold crown with a cross on the top, "was the work of a moment." He put the crown on his head, and added a collar of Ss and a zone of sparkling emeralds, which would not quite meet round his middle. He turned from fixing it by an ingenious adaptation of his belt to find the others already decked with diadems, necklaces, and rings.

"How splendid you look!" said the Princess, "and how I wish your clothes were prettier. What ugly clothes people wear nowadays! A hundred years ago "

Kathleen stood quite still with a diamond bracelet raised in her hand.

"I say," she said. "The King and Queen?"

"What King and Queen?" asked the Princess.

"Your father and mother, your sorrowing parents," said Kathleen. "They'll have waked up by now. Won't they be wanting to see you, after a hundred years, you know?"

"Oh ah yes," said the Princess slowly. "I embraced my rejoicing parents when I got the bread and cheese. They're having their dinner. They won't expect me yet. Here," she added, hastily putting a ruby bracelet on Kathleen's arm, "see how splendid that is!"

Kathleen would have been quite content to go on all day trying on different jewels and looking at herself in the little silver-framed mirror that the Princess took from one of the shelves, but the boys were soon weary of this amusement.

"Look here," said Gerald, "if you're sure your father and mother won't want you, let's go out and have a jolly good game of something. You could play besieged castles awfully well in that maze unless you can do any more magic tricks."

"You forget," said the Princess, "I'm grown up. I don't play games. And I don't like to do too much magic at a time, it's so tiring. Besides, it'll take us ever so long to put all these things back in their proper places."

It did. The children would have laid the jewels just anywhere; but the Princess showed them that every necklace, or ring, or bracelet had its own home on the velvet a slight hollowing in the shelf beneath, so that each stone fitted into its own little nest.

As Kathleen was fitting the last shining ornament into its proper place, she saw that part of the shelf near it held, not bright jewels, but rings and brooches and chains, as well as queer things that she did not know the names of, and all were of dull metal and odd shapes.

"What's all this rubbish?" she asked.

"Rubbish, indeed!" said the Princess. "Why those are all magic things! This bracelet anyone who wears it has got to speak the truth. This chain makes you as strong as ten men; if you wear this spur your horse will go a mile a minute; or if you're walking it's the same as seven-league boots."

"What does this brooch do?" asked Kathleen, reaching out her hand. The princess caught her by the wrist.

"You mustn't touch," she said; "if anyone but me touches them all the magic goes out at once and never comes back. That brooch will give you any wish you like."

"And this ring?" Jimmy pointed.

"Oh, that makes you invisible."

"What's this?" asked Gerald, showing a curious buckle.

"Oh, that undoes the effect of all the other charms."

"Do you mean really?" Jimmy asked. "You're not just kidding?"

"Kidding indeed!" repeated the Princess scornfully. "I should have thought I'd shown you enough magic to prevent you speaking to a Princess like that!"

"I say," said Gerald, visibly excited. "You might show us how some of the things act. Couldn't you give us each a wish?"

The Princess did not at once answer. And the minds of the three played with granted wishes brilliant yet thoroughly reasonable, the kind of wish that never seems to occur to people in fairy-tales when they suddenly get a chance to have their three wishes granted.

"No," said the Princess suddenly, "no; I can't give wishes to you, it only gives me wishes. But I'll let you see the ring make me invisible. Only you must shut your eyes while I do it."

They shut them.

"Count fifty," said the Princess, "and then you may look. And then you must shut them again, and count fifty, and I'll reappear."

Gerald counted, aloud. Through the counting one could hear a creaking, rustling sound.

"Forty-seven, forty-eight, forty-nine, fifty!" said Gerald, and they opened their eyes.

They were alone in the room. The jewels had vanished and so had the Princess.

"She's gone out by the door, of course," said Jimmy, but the door was locked.

"That is magic," said Kathleen breathlessly. "Maskelyne and Devant can do that trick, said Jimmy. "And I want my tea."

"Your tea!" Gerald's tone was full of contempt. "The lovely Princess, he went on, "reappeared as soon as our hero had finished counting fifty. One, two, three, four ,"

Gerald and Kathleen had both closed their eyes. But somehow Jimmy hadn't. He didn't mean to cheat, he just forgot. And as Gerald's count reached twenty he saw a panel under the window open slowly.

"Her," he said to himself. "I knew it was a trick!" and at once shut his eyes, like an honourable little boy.

On the word "fifty" six eyes opened. And the panel was closed and there was no Princess.

"She hasn't pulled it off this time," said Gerald. "Perhaps you'd better count again," said Kathleen. "I believe there's a cupboard under the window," said Jimmy, "and she's hidden in it. Secret panel, you know."

"You looked! That's cheating," said the voice of the Princess so close to his ear that he quite jumped.

"I didn't cheat."

"Where on earth," "Whatever," said all three together. For still there was no Princess to be seen.

"Come back visible, Princess dear," said Kathleen. "Shall we shut our eyes and count again?"

"Don't be silly!" said the voice of the Princess, and it sounded very cross.

"We're not silly," said Jimmy, and his voice was cross too. "Why can't you come back and have done with it? You know you're only hiding."

"Don't!" said Kathleen gently. "She is invisible, you know."

"So should I be if I got into the cupboard," said Jimmy.

"Oh yes," said the sneering tone of the Princess, "you think yourselves very clever, I dare say. But I don't mind. We'll play that you can't see me, if you like."

"Well, but we can't," said Gerald. "It's no use getting in a wax. If you're hiding, as Jimmy says, you'd better come out. If you've really turned invisible, you'd better make yourself visible again."

"Do you really mean," asked a voice quite changed, but still the Princess's, "that you can't see me?"

"Can't you see we can't?" asked Jimmy rather unreasonably.

The sun was blazing in at the window; the eight-sided room was very hot, and everyone was getting cross.

"You can't see me?" There was the sound of a sob in the voice of the invisible Princess.

"No, I tell you," said Jimmy, "and I want my tea and "

What he was saying was broken off short, as one might break a stick of sealing wax. And then in the golden afternoon a really quite horrid thing happened: Jimmy suddenly leaned backwards, then forwards, his eyes opened wide and his mouth too. Backward and forward he went, very quickly and abruptly, then stood still.

"Oh, he's in a fit! Oh, Jimmy, dear Jimmy!" cried Kathleen, hurrying to him. "What is it, dear, what is it?"

"It's not a fit," gasped Jimmy angrily. "She shook me."

"Yes, said the voice of the Princess, "and I'll shake him again if he keeps on saying he can't see me."

"You'd better shake me," said Gerald angrily. "I'm nearer your own size."

And instantly she did. But not for long. The moment Gerald felt hands on his shoulders he put up his own and caught those other hands by the wrists. And there he was, holding wrists that he couldn't see. It was a dreadful sensation. An invisible kick made him wince, but he held tight to the wrists.

"Cathy," he cried, "come and hold her legs; she's kicking me."

"Where?" cried Kathleen, anxious to help. "I don't see any legs."

"This is her hands I've got," cried Gerald. "She is invisible right enough. Get hold of this hand, and then you can feel your way down to her legs."

Kathleen did so. I wish I could make you understand how very, very uncomfortable and frightening it is to feel, in broad daylight, hands and arms that you can't see.

"I won't have you hold my legs," said the invisible Princess, struggling violently.

"What are you so cross about?" Gerald was quite calm. "You said you'd be invisible and you are."

"I'm not."

"You are really. Look in the glass."

"I'm not; I can't be."

"Look in the glass," Gerald repeated, quite unmoved.

"Let go, then," she said.

Gerald did, and the moment he had done so he found it impossible to believe that he really had been holding invisible hands.

"You're just pretending not to see me," said the Princess anxiously, "aren't you? Do say you are. You've had your joke with me. Don't keep it up. I don't like it."

"On our sacred word of honour," said Gerald, "you're still invisible.

There was a silence. Then, "Come," said the Princess. "I'll let you out, and you can go. I'm tired of playing with you."

They followed her voice to the door, and through it, and along the little passage into the hall. No one said anything. Everyone felt very uncomfortable.

"Let's get out of this," whispered Jimmy as they got to the end of the hall.

But the voice of the Princess said: "Come out this way; it's quicker. I think you're perfectly hateful. I'm sorry I ever played with you. Mother always told me not to play with strange children."

A door abruptly opened, though no hand was seen to touch it. "Come through, can't you!" said the voice of the Princess.

It was a little ante-room, with long, narrow mirrors between its long, narrow windows.

"Good-bye, said Gerald. "Thanks for giving us such a jolly time. Let's part friends, he added, holding out his hand.

An unseen hand was slowly put in his, which closed on it, vice-like.

"Now," he said, "you've jolly well got to look in the glass and own that we're not liars."

He led the invisible Princess to. one of the mirrors, and held her in front of it by the shoulders.

"Now," he said, "you just look for yourself." There was a silence, and then a cry of despair rang through the room.

"Oh oh oh! I am invisible. Whatever shall I do?"

"Take the ring off," said Kathleen, suddenly practical.

Another silence.

"I can't!" cried the Princess. "It won't come off. But it can't be the ring; rings don't make you invisible."

"You said this one did," said Kathleen, "and it has."

"But it can't," said the Princess. "I was only playing at magic. I just hid in the secret cupboard, it was only a game. Oh, whatever shall I do?"

"A game?" said Gerald slowly; "but you can do magic — the invisible jewels, you made them come visible."

"Oh, it's only a secret spring and the panelling slides up. Oh, what am I to do?"

Kathleen moved towards the voice and gropingly got her arms round a pink-silk waist that she couldn't see. Invisible arms clasped her, a hot invisible cheek was laid against hers, and warm invisible tears lay wet between the two faces.

"Don't cry, dear," said Kathleen; "let me go and tell the King and Queen."

"The ?"

"Your royal father and mother."

"Oh, don't mock me!" said the poor Princess. "You know that was only a game, too, like ,"

"Like the bread and cheese," said Jimmy triumphantly. "I knew that was!"

"But your dress and being asleep in the maze, and ,"

"Oh, I dressed up for fun, because everyone's away at the fair, and I put the clue just to make it all more real. I was playing at Fair Rosamond first, and then I heard you talking in the maze, and I thought what fun; and now I'm invisible, and I shall never come right again, never I know I shan't! It serves me right for lying, but I didn't really think you'd believe it, not more than half, that is," she added hastily, trying to be truthful.

"But if you're not the Princess, who are you?" asked Kathleen, still embracing the unseen.

"I'm — my aunt lives here," said the invisible Princess. "She may be home any time. Oh, what shall I do?"

"Perhaps she knows some charm "

"Oh, nonsense!" said the voice sharply; "she doesn't believe in charms. She would be so vexed. Oh, I daren't let her see me like this!" she added wildly.

"And all of you here, too. She'd be so dreadfully cross."

The beautiful magic castle that the children had believed in now felt as though it were tumbling about their ears. All that was left was the invisibleness of the Princess. But that, you will own, was a good deal.

"I just said it," moaned the voice, "and it came true. I wish I'd never played at magic. I wish I'd never played at anything at all."

"Oh, don't say that," Gerald said kindly. "Let's go out into the garden, near the lake, where it's cool, and we'll hold a solemn council. You'll like that, won't you?"

"Oh!" cried Kathleen suddenly, "the buckle; that makes magic come undone!"

"It doesn't really," murmured the voice that seemed to speak without lips. "I only just said that."

"You only 'just said' about the ring," said Gerald. "Anyhow, let's try."

"Not you me," said the voice. "You go down to the Temple of Flora, by the lake. I'll go back to the jewel-room by myself. Aunt might see you."

"She won't see you," said Jimmy.

"Don't rub it in," said Gerald. "Where is the Temple of Flora?"

"That's the way," the voice said; "down those steps and along the winding path through the shrubbery. You can't miss it. It's white marble, with a statue goddess inside."

The three children went down to the white marble Temple of Flora that stood close against the side of the little hill, and sat down in its shadowy inside. It had arches all round except against the hill behind the statue, and it was cool and restful.

They had not been there five minutes before the feet of a runner sounded loud on the gravel. A shadow, very black and distinct, fell on the white marble floor.

"Your shadow's not invisible, anyhow," said Jimmy.

"Oh, bother my shadow!" the voice of the Princess replied. "We left the key inside the door, and it's shut itself with the wind, and it's a spring lock!"

There was a heartfelt pause.

Then Gerald said, in his most business-like manner: "Sit down, Princess, and we'll have a thorough good palaver about it."

"I shouldn't wonder," said Jimmy, "if we was to wake up and find it was dreams."

"No such luck," said the voice.

"Well," said Gerald, "first of all, what's your name, and if you're not a Princess, who are you?"

"I'm I'm," said a voice broken with sobs, "I'm the housekeeper's niece at the castle and my name's Mabel Prowse."

"That's exactly what I thought," said Jimmy, without a shadow of truth, because how could he? The others were silent. It was a moment full of agitation and confused ideas.

"Well, anyhow," said Gerald, "you belong here."

"Yes," said the voice, and it came from the floor, as though its owner had flung herself down in the madness of despair. "Oh yes, I belong here right enough, but what's the use of belonging anywhere if you're invisible?"

Those of my readers who have gone about much with an invisible companion will not need to be told how awkward the whole business is. For one thing, however much you may have been convinced that your companion is invisible, you will, I feel sure, have found yourself every now and then saying, "This must be a dream!" or "I know I shall wake up in half a sec!" And this was the case with Gerald, Kathleen, and Jimmy as they sat in the white marble Temple of Flora, looking out through its arches at the sunshiny park and listening to the voice of the enchanted Princess, who really was not a Princess at all, but just the housekeeper's niece, Mabel Prowse; though, as Jimmy said, "she was enchanted, right enough."

"It's no use talking," she said again and again, and the voice came from an empty-looking space between two pillars; "I never believed anything would happen, and now it has."

"Well," said Gerald kindly, "can we do anything for you? Because, if not, I think we ought to be going."

"Yes," said Jimmy; "I do want my tea!"

"Tea!" said the unseen Mabel scornfully. "Do you mean to say you'd go off to your teas and leave me after getting me into this mess?"

"Well, of all the unfair Princesses I ever met!" Gerald began. But Kathleen interrupted

"Oh, don't rag her," she said. "Think how horrid it must be to be invisible!"

"I don't think," said the hidden Mabel, "that my aunt likes me very much as it is. She wouldn't let me go to the fair because I'd forgotten to put back some old trumpery shoe that Queen Elizabeth wore. I got it out from the glass case to try it on."

"Did it fit?" asked Kathleen, with interest

"No — it was much too small," said Mabel. "I don't believe it ever fitted anyone."

"I do want my tea!" said Jimmy

"I do really think perhaps we ought to go," said Gerald. "You see, it isn't as if we could do anything for you."

"You'll have to tell your aunt," said Kathleen kindly

"No, no, no!" moaned Mabel invisibly; "take me with you. I'll leave her a note to say I've run away to sea."

"Girls don't run away to sea."

They might," said the stone floor between the pillars, "as stowaways, if nobody wanted a cabin boy — cabin girl, I mean."

"I'm sure you oughtn't," said Kathleen firmly.

"Well, what am I to do?"

"Really," said Gerald, "I don't know what the girl can do. Let her come home with us and have "

"Tea oh, yes," said Jimmy, jumping up.

"And have a good council."

"After tea," said Jimmy

"But her aunt'll find she's gone."

"So she would if I stayed."

"Oh, come on," said Jimmy.

"But the aunt'll think something's happened to her."

"So it has."

"And she'll tell the police, and they'll look everywhere for me."

"They'll never find you," said Gerald. "Talk of impenetrable disguises!"

"I'm sure," said Mabel, "Aunt would much rather never see me again than see me like this. She'd never get over it; it might kill her — she has spasms as it is. I'll write to her, and we'll put it in the big letter-box at the gate as we go out. Has anyone got a bit of pencil and a scrap of paper?"

Gerald had a note-book, with leaves of the shiny kind which you have to write on, not with a blacklead pencil, but with an ivory thing with a point of real lead. And it won't write on any other paper except the kind that is in the book, and this is often very annoying when you are in a hurry. Then was seen the strange spectacle of a little ivory stick, with a leaden point, standing up at an odd, impossible-looking slant, and moving along all by itself as ordinary pencils do when you are writing with them

"May we look over?" asked Kathleen.

There was no answer. The pencil went on writing.

"Mayn't we look over?" Kathleen said again."

Of course you may!" said the voice near the paper. "I nodded, didn't I? Oh, I forgot, my nodding's invisible too."The pencil was forming round, clear letters on the page torn out of the note-book. This is what it wrote:

"DEAR AUNT, I am afraid you will not see me again for some time. A lady in a motor-car has adopted me, and we are going straight to the coast and then in a ship. It is useless to try to follow me. Farewell, and may you be happy. I hope you enjoyed the fair

MABEL."

"But that's all lies," said Jimmy bluntly.

"No, it isn't; it's fancy," said Mabel. "If I said I've become invisible, she'd think that was a lie, anyhow.""

"Oh, come along," said Jimmy; "you can quarrel just as well walking."

Gerald folded up the note as a lady in India had taught him to do years before, and Mabel led them by another and very much nearer way out of the park. And the walk home was a great deal shorter, too, than the walk out had been.

The sky had clouded over while they were in the Temple of Flora, and the first spots of rain fell as they got back to the house, very late indeed for tea.

Mademoiselle was looking out of the window, and came herself to open the door

"But it is that you are in lateness, in lateness!" she cried. "You have had a misfortune no? All goes well?"

"We are very sorry indeed," said Gerald. "It took us longer to get home than we expected. I do hope you haven't been anxious. I have been thinking about you most of the way home."

"Go, then," said the French lady, smiling; "you shall have them in the same time the tea and the supper."

Which they did.

"How could you say you were thinking about her all the time?" said a voice just by Gerald's ear, when Mademoiselle had left them alone with the bread and butter and milk and baked apples. "It was just as much a lie as me being adopted by a motor lady."

"No, it wasn't," said Gerald, through bread and butter. "I was thinking about whether she'd be in a wax or not. So there!"

There were only three plates, but Jimmy let Mabel have his, and shared with Kathleen. It was rather horrid to see the bread and butter waving about in the air, and bite after bite disappearing from it apparently by no human agency; and the spoon rising with apple in it and returning to the plate empty. Even the tip of the spoon disappeared as long as it was in Mabel's unseen mouth; so that at times it looked as though its bowl had been broken off

Everyone was very hungry, and more bread and butter had to be fetched. Cook grumbled when the plate was filled for the third time.

"I tell you what," said Jimmy; "I did want my tea."

"I tell you what," said Gerald; "it'll be jolly difficult to give Mabel any breakfast. Mademoiselle will be here then. She'd have a fit if she saw bits of forks with bacon on them vanishing, and then the forks coming back out of vanishment, and the bacon lost for ever."

"We shall have to buy things to eat and feed our poor captive in secret," said Kathleen.

"Our money won't last long," said Jimmy, in gloom. "Have you got any money?"

He turned to where a mug of milk was suspended in the air without visible means of support.

"I've not got much money," was the reply from near the milk, "but I've got heaps of ideas."

"We must talk about everything in the morning," said Kathleen. "We must just say good night to Mademoiselle, and then you shall sleep in my bed, Mabel. I'll lend you one of my nightgowns."

"I'll get my own tomorrow," said Mabel cheerfully.

"You'll go back to get things?"

"Why not? Nobody can see me. I think I begin to see all sorts of amusing things coming along. It's not half bad being invisible."

It was extremely odd, Kathleen thought, to see the Princess's clothes coming out of nothing. First the gauzy veil appeared hanging in the air. Then the sparkling coronet suddenly showed on the top of the chest of drawers. Then a sleeve of the pinky gown showed, then another, and then the whole gown lay on the floor in a glistening ring as the unseen legs of Mabel stepped out of it. For each article of clothing became visible as Mabel took it off. The nightgown, lifted from the bed, disappeared a bit at a time.

"Get into bed," said Kathleen, rather nervously.

The bed creaked and a hollow appeared in the pillow. Kathleen put out the gas and got into bed; all this magic had been rather upsetting, and she was just the least bit frightened, but in the dark she found it was not so bad. Mabel's arms went round her neck the moment she got into bed, and the two little girls kissed in the kind darkness, where the visible and the invisible could meet on equal terms.

"Good night," said Mabel. "You're a darling, Cathy; you've been most awfully good to me, and I shan't forget it. I didn't like to say so before the boys, because I know boys think you're a muff if you're grateful. But I am. Good night."

Kathleen lay awake for some time. She was just getting sleepy when she remembered that the maid who would call them in the morning would see those wonderful Princess clothes.

"I'll have to get up and hide them," she said. "What a bother!"

And as she lay thinking what a bother it was she happened to fall asleep, and when she woke again it was bright morning, and Eliza was standing in front of the chair where Mabel's clothes lay, gazing at the pink Princess-frock that lay on the top of her heap and saying, "Law!"

"Oh, don't touch, please!" Kathleen leaped out of bed as Eliza was reaching out her hand.

"Where on earth did you get hold of that?"

"We're going to use it for acting," said Kathleen, on the desperate inspiration of the moment. "It's lent me for that."

"You might show me, miss," suggested Eliza.

"Oh, please not!" said Kathleen, standing in front of the chair in her nightgown. "You shall see us act when we are dressed up. There! And you won't tell anyone, will you?"

"Not if you're a good little girl," said Eliza. "But you be sure to let me see when you do dress up. But where ..."

Here a bell rang and Eliza had to go, for it was the postman, and she particularly wanted to see him.

"And now," said Kathleen, pulling on her first stocking, "we shall have to do the acting. Everything seems very difficult."

"Acting isn't," said Mabel; and an unsupported stocking waved in the air and quickly vanished. "I shall love it.,"

"You forget," said Kathleen gently, "invisible actresses can't take part in plays unless they're magic ones."

"Oh," cried a voice from under a petticoat that hung in the air, "I've got such an idea!"

"Tell it us after breakfast," said Kathleen, as the water in the basin began to splash about and to drip from nowhere back into itself. "And oh! I do wish you hadn't written such whoppers to your aunt. I'm sure we oughtn't to tell lies for anything."

"What's the use of telling the truth if nobody believes you?" came from among the splashes

"I don't know," said Kathleen, "but I'm sure we ought to tell the truth."

"You can, if you like," said a voice from the folds of a towel that waved lonely in front of the wash-hand stand

"All right. We will, then, first thing after brek your brek, I mean. You'll have to wait up here till we can collar something and bring it up to you. Mind you dodge Eliza when she comes to make the bed."

The invisible Mabel found this a fairly amusing game; she further enlivened it by twitching out the corners of tucked-up sheets and blankets when Eliza wasn't looking.

"Drat the clothes!" said Eliza; "anyone ud think the things was bewitched."

She looked about for the wonderful Princess clothes she had glimpsed earlier in the morning. But Kathleen had hidden them in a perfectly safe place under the mattress, which she knew Eliza never turned.

Eliza hastily brushed up from the floor those bits of fluff which come from goodness knows where in the best regulated houses. Mabel, very hungry and exasperated at the long absence of the others at their breakfast, could not forbear to whisper suddenly in Eliza's ear:

"Always sweep under the mats."

The maid started and turned pale. "I must be going silly," she murmured; "though it's just what mother always used to say. Hope I ain't going dotty, like Aunt Emily. Wonderful what you can fancy, ain't it?"

She took up the hearth-rug all the same, swept under it, and under the fender. So thorough was she, and so pale, that Kathleen, entering with a chunk of bread raided by Gerald from the pantry window, exclaimed:

"Not done yet. I say, Eliza, you do look ill! What's the matter?"

"I thought I'd give the room a good turn-out," said Eliza, still very pale.

"Nothing's happened to upset you?" Kathleen asked. She had her own private fears.

"Nothing only my fancy, miss," said Eliza. "I always was fanciful from a child dreaming of the pearly gates and them little angels with nothing on only their heads and wings so cheap to dress, I always think, compared with children."

When she was got rid of, Mabel ate the bread and drank water from the tooth-mug.

"I'm afraid it tastes of cherry tooth-paste rather," said Kathleen apologetically.

"It doesn't matter," a voice replied from the tilted mug; "it's more interesting than water. I should think red wine in ballads was rather like this."

"We've got leave for the day again," said Kathleen, when the last bit of bread had vanished, "and Gerald feels like I do about lies, So we're going to tell your aunt where you really are."

"She won't believe you."

"That doesn't matter, if we speak the truth," said Kathleen primly.

"I expect you'll be sorry for it," said Mabel; "but come on and, I say, do be careful not to shut me in the door as you go out. You nearly did just now."

In the blazing sunlight that flooded the High Street four shadows to three children seemed dangerously noticeable. A butcher's boy looked far too earnestly at the extra shadow, and his big, liver-coloured lurcher snuffed at the legs of that shadow's mistress and whined uncomfortably.

"Get behind me," said Kathleen; "then our two shadows will look like one."

But Mabel's shadow, very visible, fell on Kathleen's back, and the ostler of the Davenant Arms looked up to see what big bird had cast that big shadow.

A woman driving a cart with chickens and ducks in it called out: "Halloa, missy, ain't you blacked yer back, neither! What you been leaning up against?"

Everyone was glad when they got out of the town.

Speaking the truth to Mabel's aunt did not turn out at all as anyone even Mabel expected. The aunt was discovered reading a pink novelette at the window of the housekeeper's room, which, framed in clematis and green creepers, looked out on a nice little courtyard to which Mabel led the party.

"Excuse me," said Gerald, "but I believe you've lost your niece?"

"Not lost, my boy," said the aunt, who was spare and tall, with a drab fringe and a very genteel voice.

"We could tell you something about her," said Gerald.

"Now," replied the aunt, in a warning voice, "no complaints, please. My niece has gone, and I am sure no one thinks less than I do of her little pranks. If she's played any tricks on you it's only her lighthearted way. Go away, children, I'm busy."

"Did you get her note?" asked Kathleen.

The aunt showed rather more interest than before, but she still kept her finger in the novelette.

"Oh," she said, "so you witnessed her departure? Did she seem glad to go?"

"Quite," said Gerald truthfully.

"Then I can only be glad that she is provided for," said the aunt. "I dare say you were surprised. These romantic adventures do occur in our family. Lord Yalding selected me out of eleven applicants for the post of housekeeper here. I've not the slightest doubt the child was changed at birth and her rich relatives have claimed her."

"But aren't you going to do anything tell the police, or"

"Shish!" said Mabel.

"I won't shish," said Jimmy. "Your Mabel's invisible that's all it is. She's just beside me now."

"I detest untruthfulness," said the aunt severely, "in all its forms. Will you kindly take that little boy away? I am quite satisfied about Mabel."

"Well," said Gerald, "you are an aunt and no mistake! But what will Mabel's father and mother say?"

"Mabel's father and mother are dead," said the aunt calmly, and a little sob sounded close to Gerald's ear.

"All right," he said, "we'll be off. But don't you go saying we didn't tell you the truth, that's all."

"You have told me nothing," said the aunt, "none of you, except that little boy, who has told me a silly falsehood."

"We meant well," said Gerald gently. "You don't mind our having come through the grounds, do you? we're very careful not to touch anything."

"No visitors are allowed," said the aunt, glancing down at her novel rather impatiently.

"Ah! but you wouldn't count us visitors," said Gerald in his best manner. "We're friends of Mabel's. Our father's Colonel of the 7th."

"Indeed!" said the aunt.

"And our aunt's Lady Sandling, so you can be sure we wouldn't hurt anything on the estate."

"I'm sure you wouldn't hurt a fly," said the aunt absently. "Good-bye. Be good children."

And on this they got away quickly.

"Why," said Gerald, when they were outside the little court, "your aunt's as mad as a hatter. Fancy not caring what becomes of you, and fancy believing that rot about the motor lady!"

"I knew she'd believe it when I wrote it," said Mabel modestly. "She's not mad, only she's always reading novelettes, I read the books in the big library. Oh, it's such a jolly room such a queer smell, like boots, and old leather books sort of powdery at the edges. I'll take you there some day. Now your consciences are all right about my aunt, I'll tell you my great idea. Let's get down to the Temple of Flora. I'm glad you got aunt's permission for the grounds. It would be so awkward for you to have to be always dodging behind bushes when one of the gardeners came along."

"Yes," said Gerald modestly, "I thought of that."

The day was as bright as yesterday had been, and from the white marble temple the Italian-looking landscape looked more than ever like a steel engraving coloured by hand, or an oleographic imitation of one of Turner's pictures.

When the three children were comfortably settled on the steps that led up to the white statue, the voice of the fourth child said sadly: "I'm not ungrateful, but I'm rather hungry. And you can't be always taking things for me through your larder window. If you like, I'll go back and live in the castle. It's supposed to be haunted. I suppose I could haunt it as well as anyone else. I am a sort of ghost now, you know. I will if you like."

"Oh no," said Kathleen kindly; "you must stay with us.

"But about food. I'm not ungrateful, really I'm not, but breakfast is breakfast, and bread's only bread."

"If you could get the ring off, you could go back."

"Yes," said Mabel's voice, "but you see, I can't. I tried again last night in bed, and again this morning. And it's like stealing, taking things out of your larder even if it's only bread."

"Yes, it is," said Gerald, who had carried out this bold enterprise.

"Well, now, what we must do is to earn some money."

Jimmy remarked that this was all very well. But Gerald and Kathleen listened attentively.

"What I mean to say," the voice went on, "I'm really sure is all for the best, me being invisible. We shall have adventures you see if we don t."

"Adventures," said the bold buccaneer, "are not always profitable." It was Gerald who murmured this.

"This one will be, anyhow, you see. Only you mustn't all go. Look here, if Jerry could make himself look common "

"That ought to be easy," said Jimmy. And Kathleen told him not to be so jolly disagreeable.

"I'm not," said Jimmy, "only "

"Only he has an inside feeling that this Mabel of yours is going to get us into trouble," put in Gerald. "Like La Belle Dame Sans Merci, and he does not want to be found in future ages alone and palely loitering in the middle of sedge and things."

"I won't get you into trouble, indeed I won't," said the voice. "Why, we're a band of brothers for life, after the way you stood by me yesterday. What I mean is Gerald can go to the fair and do conjuring."

"He doesn't know any," said Kathleen.

"I should do it really," said Mabel, "but Jerry could look like doing it move things without touching them and all that. But it wouldn't do for all three of you to go. The more there are of children the younger they look, I think, and the more people wonder what they re doing all alone by themselves."

"The accomplished conjurer deemed these the words of wisdom," said Gerald; and answered the dismal "Well, but what about us? of his brother and sister by suggesting that they should mingle unsuspected with the crowd. "But don't let on that you know me," he said; "and try to look as if you belonged to some of the grown-ups at the fair. If you don't, as likely as not you'll have the kind policemen taking the little lost children by the hand and leading them home to their stricken relations — French governess, I mean."

"Let's go now," said the voice that they never could get quite used to hearing, coming out of different parts of the air as Mabel moved from one place to another. So they went.

The fair was held on a waste bit of land, about half a mile from the castle gates. When they got near enough to hear the steam-organ of the merry-go-round, Gerald suggested that as he had ninepence he should go ahead and get something to eat, the amount spent to be paid back out of any money they might make by conjuring. The others waited in the shadows of a deep-banked lane, and he came back, quite soon, though long after they had begun to say what a long time he had been gone. He brought some Barcelona nuts, red-streaked apples, small sweet yellow pears, pale pasty gingerbread, a whole quarter of a pound of peppermint bulls-eyes, and two bottles of ginger-beer.

"It's what they call an investment," he said, when Kathleen said something about extravagance. "We shall all need special nourishing to keep our strength up, especially the bold conjurer."

They ate and drank. It was a very beautiful meal, and the far-off music of the steam-organ added the last touch of festivity to the scene. The boys were never tired of seeing Mabel eat, or rather of seeing the strange, magic-looking vanishment of food which was all that showed of Mabel's eating. They were entranced by the spectacle, and pressed on her more than her just share of the feast, just for the pleasure of seeing it disappear.

"My aunt!" said Gerald, again and again; "that ought to knock 'em!"

It did.

Jimmy and Kathleen had the start of the others, and when they got to the fair they mingled with the crowd, and were as unsuspected as possible.

They stood near a large lady who was watching the Coconut shies, and presently saw a strange figure with its hands in its pockets strolling across the trampled yellowy grass among the bits of drifting paper and the sticks and straws that always litter the ground of an English fair. It was Gerald, but at first they hardly knew him. He had taken off his tie, and round his head, arranged like a turban, was the crimson school-scarf that had supported his white flannels. The tie, one supposed, had taken on the duties of the handkerchief. And his face and hands were a bright black, like very nicely polished stoves!

Everyone turned to look at him.

"He's just like a conjurer!" whispered Jimmy. "I don't suppose it'll ever come off, do you?"

They followed him at a distance, and when he went close to the door of a small tent, against whose door-post a long-faced melancholy woman was lounging, they stopped and tried to look as though they belonged to a farmer who strove to send up a number by banging with a big mallet on a wooden block.

Gerald went up to the woman.

"Taken much?" he asked, and was told, but not harshly, to go away with his impudence.

"I'm in business myself," said Gerald, "I'm a conjurer, from India."

"Not you!" said the woman; "you ain't no conjurer. Why, the backs of yer ears is all white."

"Are they?" said Gerald. "How clever of you to see that!" He rubbed them with his hands. "That better?"

"That's all right. What's your little game?"

"Conjuring, really and truly," said Gerald. "There's smaller boys than me put on to it in India. Look here, I owe you one for telling me about my ears. If you like to run the show for me I'll go shares. Let me have your tent to perform in, and you do the patter at the door.

"Lor love you! I can't do no patter. And you're getting at me. Let's see you do a bit of conjuring, since you're so clever an all."

"Right you are," said Gerald firmly. "You see this apple? Well, I'll make it move slowly through the air, and then when I say "Go!" it'll vanish."

"Yes into your mouth! Get away with your nonsense."

"You're too clever to be so unbelieving," said Gerald. "Look here!"

He held out one of the little apples, and the woman saw it move slowly and unsupported along the air.

"Now go!" cried Gerald, to the apple, and it went. "How's that?" he asked, in tones of triumph.

The woman was glowing with excitement, and her eyes shone. "The best I ever see!" she whispered. "I'm on, mate, if you know any more tricks like that."

"Heaps," said Gerald confidently; "hold out your hand." The woman held it out; and from nowhere, as it seemed, the apple appeared and was laid on her hand. The apple was rather damp.

She looked at it a moment, and then whispered:

"Come on! there's to be no one in it but just us two. But not in the tent. You take a pitch here, 'longside the tent. It's worth twice the money in the open air."

"But people won't pay if they can see it all for nothing."

"Not for the first turn, but they will after, you see. And you'll have to do the patter."

"Will you lend me your shawl?" Gerald asked. She unpinned it it was a red and black plaid and he spread it on the ground as he had seen Indian conjurers do, and seated himself cross-legged behind it.

"I mustn't have anyone behind me, that's all," he said; and the woman hastily screened off a little enclosure for him by hanging old sacks to two of the guy-ropes of the tent. "Now I'm ready, he said. The woman got a drum from the inside of the tent and beat it. Quite soon a little crowd had collected.

"Ladies and gentlemen," said Gerald, "I come from India, and I can do a conjuring entertainment the like of which you've never seen. When I see two shillings on the shawl I'll begin."

"I dare say you will!" said a bystander; and there were several short, disagreeable laughs.

"Of course," said Gerald, "if you can't afford two shillings between you" there were about thirty people in the crowd by now "I say no more."

Two or three pennies fell on the shawl, then a few more then the fall of copper ceased.

"Ninepence," said Gerald. "Well, I've got a generous nature. You'll get such a ninepennyworth as you've never had before. I don't wish to deceive you I have an accomplice, but my accomplice is invisible."

The crowd snorted.

"By the aid of that accomplice," Gerald went on, "I will read any letter that any of you may have in your pocket. If one of you will just step over the rope and stand beside me, my invisible accomplice will read that letter over his shoulder."

A man stepped forward, a ruddy-faced, horsy-looking person. He pulled a letter from his pocket and stood plain in the sight of all, in a place where everyone saw that no one could see over his shoulder.

"Now!" said Gerald. There was a moment's pause. Then from quite the other side of the enclosure came a faint, faraway, sing-song voice. It said:

"SIR Yours of the fifteenth duly to hand. With regard to the mortgage on your land, we regret our inability "

"Stow it!" cried the man, turning threateningly on Gerald.

He stepped out of the enclosure explaining that there was nothing of that sort in his letter; but nobody believed him, and a buzz of interested chatter began in the crowd, ceasing abruptly when Gerald began to speak.

"Now," said he, laying the nine pennies down on the shawl, "you keep your eyes on those pennies, and one by one you'll see them disappear."

And of course they did. Then one by one they were laid down again by the invisible hand of Mabel. The crowd clapped loudly. "Bravo!" "That's something like!" "Show us another!" cried the people in the front rank. And those behind pushed forward.

"Now," said Gerald, "you've seen what I can do, but I don't do any more till I see five shillings on this carpet."

And in two minutes seven-and-threepence lay there and Gerald did a little more conjuring.

When the people in front didn't want to give any more money, Gerald asked them to stand back and let the others have a look in. I wish I had time to tell you of all the tricks he did the grass round his enclosure was absolutely trampled off by the feet of the people who thronged to look at him. There is really hardly any limit to the wonders you can do if you have an invisible accomplice. All sorts of things were made to move about, apparently by themselves, and even to vanish into the folds of Mabel's clothing. The woman stood by, looking more and more pleasant as she saw the money come tumbling in, and beating her shabby drum every time Gerald stopped conjuring.

The news of the conjurer had spread all over the fair. The crowd was frantic with admiration. The man who ran the coconut shies begged Gerald to throw in his lot with him; the owner of the rifle gallery offered him free board and lodging and go shares; and a brisk, broad lady, in stiff black silk and a violet bonnet, tried to engage him for the forthcoming Bazaar for Reformed Bandsmen.

And all this time the others mingled with the crowd quite unobserved, for who could have eyes for anyone but Gerald? It was getting quite late, long past tea-time, and Gerald, who was getting very tired indeed, and was quite satisfied with his share of the money, was racking his brains for a way to get out of it.

"How are we to hook it?" he murmured, as Mabel made his cap disappear from his head by the simple process of taking it off and putting it in her pocket.

"They'll never let us get away. I didn't think of that before."

"Let me think!" whispered Mabel; and next moment she said, close to his ear: "Divide the money, and give her something for the shawl. Put the money on it and say. . ." She told him what to say.

Gerald's pitch was in the shade of the tent; otherwise, of course, everyone would have seen the shadow of the invisible Mabel as she moved about making things vanish.

Gerald told the woman to divide the money, which she did honestly enough.

"Now," he said, while the impatient crowd pressed closer and closer, "I'll give you five bob for your shawl.

"Seven-and-six," said the woman mechanically.

"Righto!" said Gerald, putting his heavy share of the money in his trouser pocket.

"This shawl will now disappear," he said, picking it up. He handed it to Mabel, who put it on; and, of course, it disappeared. A roar of applause went up from the audience.

"Now," he said, "I come to the last trick of all. I shall take three steps backwards and vanish. He took three steps backwards, Mabel wrapped the invisible shawl round him, and he did not vanish. The shawl, being invisible, did not conceal him in the least.

"Yah!" cried a boy's voice in the crowd. "Look at "im! "E knows "e can't do it."

"I wish I could put you in my pocket," said Mabel. The crowd was crowding closer. At any moment they might touch Mabel, and then anything might happen simply anything. Gerald took hold of his hair with both hands, as his way was when he was anxious or discouraged. Mabel, in invisibility, wrung her hands, as people are said to do in books that is, she clasped them and squeezed very tight.

"Oh!" she whispered suddenly, "it's loose. I can get it off."

"Not "

"Yes the ring."

"Come on, young master. Give us summat for our money," a farm labourer shouted.

"I will," said Gerald. "This time I really will vanish. Slip round into the tent," he whispered to Mabel.

"Push the ring under the canvas. Then slip out at the back and join the others. When I see you with them I'll disappear. Go slow, and I'll catch you up."

"It's me," said a pale and obvious Mabel in the ear of Kathleen. "He's got the ring; come on, before the crowd begins to scatter."

As they went out of the gate they heard a roar of surprise and annoyance rise from the crowd, and knew that this time Gerald really had disappeared.

They had gone a mile before they heard footsteps on the road, and looked back. No one was to be seen.

Next moment Gerald's voice spoke out of clear, empty-looking space.

"Halloa!" it said gloomily.

"How horrid!" cried Mabel; "you did make me jump! Take the ring off; it makes me feel quite creepy, you being nothing but a voice."

"So did you us," said Jimmy.

"Don't take it off yet," said Kathleen, who was really rather thoughtful for her age, "because you're still blackleaded, I suppose, and you might be recognized, and eloped with by gypsies, so that you should go on doing conjuring for ever and ever."

"I should take it off," said Jimmy; "it's no use going about invisible, and people seeing us with Mabel and saying we've eloped with her."

"Yes," said Mabel impatiently, "that would be simply silly. And, besides, I want my ring."

"It's not yours any more than ours, anyhow," said Jimmy.

"Yes, it is," said Mabel.

"Oh, stow it!" said the weary voice of Gerald beside her. "What's the use of jawing?"

"I want the ring," said Mabel, rather mulishly.

"Want" the words came out of the still evening air "want must be your master. You can't have the ring. I can't get it off!"

The difficulty was not only that Gerald had got the ring on and couldn't get it off, and was therefore invisible, but that Mabel, who had been invisible and therefore possible to be smuggled into the house, was now plain to be seen and impossible for smuggling purposes.

The children would have not only to account for the apparent absence of one of themselves, but for the obvious presence of a perfect stranger.

"I can't go back to aunt. I can't and I won't," said Mabel firmly, "not if I was visible twenty times over."

"She'd smell a rat if you did," Gerald owned "about the motor-car, I mean, and the adopting lady. And what we're to say to Mademoiselle about you !" He tugged at the ring.

"Suppose you told the truth," said Mabel meaningly.

"She wouldn't believe it," said Cathy; "or, if she did, she'd go stark, staring, raving mad."

"No," said Gerald's voice, "we daren't tell her. But she's really rather decent. Let's ask her to let you stay the night because it's too late for you to get home."

"That's all right," said Jimmy, "but what about you?"

"I shall go to bed," said Gerald, "with a bad headache. Oh, that's not a lie! I've got one right enough. It's the sun, I think. I know blacklead attracts the concentration of the sun."

"More likely the pears and the gingerbread," said Jimmy unkindly. "Well, let's get along. I wish it was me was invisible. I'd do something different from going to bed with a silly headache, I know that."

"What would you do?" asked the voice of Gerald just behind him.

"Do keep in one place, you silly cuckoo!" said Jimmy. "You make me feel all jumpy. He had indeed jumped rather violently. "Here, walk between Cathy and me.

"What would you do?" repeated Gerald, from that apparently unoccupied position.

"I'd be a burglar," said Jimmy.

Cathy and Mabel in one breath reminded him how wrong burgling was, and Jimmy replied:

"Well, then a detective."

"There's got to be something to detect before you can begin detectiving," said Mabel.

"Detectives don't always detect things," said Jimmy, very truly. "If I couldn't be any other kind I'd be a baffled detective. You could be one all right, and have no end of larks just the same. Why don't you do it?"

"It's exactly what I am going to do," said Gerald. "We'll go round by the police-station and see what they've got in the way of crimes."

They did, and read the notices on the board outside. Two dogs had been lost, a purse, and a portfolio of papers "of no value to any but the owner." Also Houghton Grange had been broken into and a quantity of silver plate stolen. "Twenty pounds reward offered for any information that may lead to the recovery of the missing property."

"That burglary's my lay," said Gerald; "I'll detect that. Here comes Johnson," he added; "he's going off duty. Ask him about it. The fell detective, being invisible, was unable to pump the constable, but the young brother of our hero made the inquiries in quite a creditable manner. Be creditable, Jimmy."

Jimmy hailed the constable.

"Halloa, Johnson!" he said.

And Johnson replied: "Halloa, young shaver!"

"Shaver yourself!" said Jimmy, but without malice.

"What are you doing this time of night?" the constable asked jocosely. "All the dicky birds is gone to their little nesteses."

"We've been to the fair," said Kathleen. "There was a conjurer there. I wish you could have seen him."

"Heard about him," said Johnson; "all fake, you know. The quickness of the 'and deceives the hi."

Such is fame. Gerald, standing in the shadow, jingled the loose money in his pocket to console himself.

"What's that?" the policeman asked quickly.

"Our money jingling," said Jimmy, with perfect truth.

"It's well to be some people," Johnson remarked; "wish I'd got my pockets full to jingle with."

"Well, why haven't you?" asked Mabel. "Why don't you get that twenty pounds reward?"

"I'll tell you why I don't. Because in this "ere realm of liberty, and Britannia ruling the waves, you ain't allowed to arrest a chap on suspicion, even if you know puffickly well who done the job."

"What a shame!" said Jimmy warmly. "And who do you think did it?"

"I don't think I know." Johnson's voice was ponderous as his boots. "It's a man what's known to the police on account of a heap o crimes he's done, but we never can't bring it 'ome to 'im, nor yet get sufficient evidence to convict."

"Well, said Jimmy, "when I've left school I'll come to you and be apprenticed, and be a detective. Just now I think we'd better get home and detect our supper. Good night!"

They watched the policeman's broad form disappear through the swing door of the police-station; and as it settled itself into quiet again the voice of Gerald was heard complaining bitterly.

"You've no more brains than a halfpenny bun," he said; "no details about how and when the silver was taken."

"But he told us he knew," Jimmy urged.

"Yes, that's all you've got out of him. A silly policeman's silly idea. Go home and detect your precious supper! It's all you're fit for."

"What'll you do about supper?" Mabel asked.

"Buns!" said Gerald, "halfpenny buns. They'll make me think of my dear little brother and sister. Perhaps you've got enough sense to buy buns? I can't go into a shop in this state."

"Don't you be so disagreeable," said Mabel with spirit.

"We did our best. If I were Cathy you should whistle for your nasty buns."

"If you were Cathy the gallant young detective would have left home long ago. Better the cabin of a tramp steamer than the best family mansion that's got a brawling sister in it," said Gerald. "You are a bit of an outsider at present, my gentle maiden. Jimmy and Cathy know well enough when their bold leader is chaffing and when he isn't."

"Not when we can't see your face we don't," said Cathy, in tones of relief. "I really thought you were in a flaring wax, and so did Jimmy, didn't you?"

"Oh, rot!" said Gerald. "Come on! This way to the bun shop."

They went, And it was while Cathy and Jimmy were in the shop and the others were gazing through the glass at the jam tarts and Swiss rolls and Victoria sandwiches and Bath buns under the spread yellow muslin in the window, that Gerald discoursed in Mabel's ear of the plans and hopes of one entering on a detective career.

"I shall keep my eyes open tonight, I can tell you," he began. "I shall keep my eyes skinned, and no jolly error. The invisible detective may not only find out about the purse and the silver, but detect some crime that isn't even done yet. And I shall hang about until I see some suspicious-looking characters leave the town, and follow them furtively and catch them red-handed, with their hands full of priceless jewels, and hand them over."

"Oh!" cried Mabel, so sharply and suddenly that Gerald was roused from his dream to express sympathy.

"Pain?" he said quite kindly. "It's the apples — they were rather hard."

"Oh, it's not that," said Mabel very earnestly. "Oh, how awful! I never thought of that before."

"Never thought of what?" Gerald asked impatiently.

"The window."

"What window?"

"The panelled-room window. At home, you know at the castle. That settles it I must go home. We left it open and the shutters as well, and all the jewels and things there. Auntie'll never go in; she never does. That settles it; I must go home now this minute."

Here the others issued from the shop, bun-bearing, and the situation was hastily explained to them.

"So you see I must go," Mabel ended.

And Kathleen agreed that she must.

But Jimmy said he didn't see what good it would do. "Because the key's inside the door, anyhow."

"She will be cross," said Mabel sadly. "She'll have to get the gardeners to get a ladder and "

"Hooray!" said Gerald. "Here's me! Nobler and more secret than gardeners or ladders was the invisible Jerry. I'll climb in at the window it's all ivy, I know I could and shut the window and the shutters all sereno, put the key back on the nail, and slip out unperceived the back way, threading my way through the maze of unconscious retainers. There'll be plenty of time. I don't suppose burglars begin their fell work until the night is far advanced."

"Won't you be afraid?" Mabel asked. "Will it be safe? Suppose you were caught?"

"As houses. I can't be," Gerald answered, and wondered that the question came from Mabel and not from Kathleen, who was usually inclined to fuss a little annoyingly about the danger and folly of adventures.

But all Kathleen said was, "Well, good-bye; we'll come and see you tomorrow, Mabel. The floral temple at half-past ten. I hope you won't get into an awful row about the motor-car lady."

"Let's detect our supper now," said Jimmy.

"All right," said Gerald a little bitterly. It is hard to enter on an adventure like this and to find the sympathetic interest of years suddenly cut off at the meter, as it were. Gerald felt that he ought, at a time like this, to have been the centre of interest. And he wasn't. They could actually talk about supper. Well, let them. He didn't care! He spoke with sharp sternness: "Leave the pantry window undone for me to get in by when I've done my detecting. Come on, Mabel." He caught her hand. "Bags I the buns, though," he added, by a happy afterthought, and snatching the bag, pressed it on Mabel, and the sound of four boots echoed on the pavement of the High Street as the outlines of the running Mabel grew small with distance.

Mademoiselle was in the drawing-room. She was sitting by the window in the waning light reading letters.

"Ah, vous voici!" she said unintelligibly. "You are again late; and my little Gerald, where is he?"

This was an awful moment. Jimmy's detective scheme had not included any answer to this inevitable question. The silence was unbroken till Jimmy spoke.

"He said he was going to bed because he had a headache." And this, of course, was true.

"This poor Gerald!" said Mademoiselle. "Is it that I should mount him some supper?"

"He never eats anything when he's got one of his headaches," Kathleen said. And this also was the truth.

Jimmy and Kathleen went to bed, wholly untroubled by anxiety about their brother, and Mademoiselle pulled out the bundle of letters and read them amid the ruins of the simple supper.

"It is ripping being out late like this," said Gerald through the soft summer dusk.

"Yes," said Mabel, a solitary-looking figure plodding along the high-road. "I do hope auntie won't be very furious."

"Have another bun," suggested Gerald kindly, and a sociable munching followed.

It was the aunt herself who opened to a very pale and trembling Mabel the door which is appointed for the entrances and exits of the domestic staff at Yalding Towers. She looked over Mabel's head first, as if she expected to see someone taller. Then a very small voice said:

"Aunt!"

The aunt started back, then made a step towards Mabel.

"You naughty, naughty girl!" she cried angrily; "how could you give me such a fright? I've a good mind to keep you in bed for a week for this, miss. Oh, Mabel, thank Heaven you're safe!" And with that the aunt's arms went round Mabel and Mabel's round the aunt in such a hug as they had never met in before.

"But you didn't seem to care a bit this morning," said Mabel, when she had realized that her aunt really had been anxious, really was glad to have her safe home again.

"How do you know?"

"I was there listening. Don't be angry, auntie."

"I feel as if I could never be angry with you again, now I've got you safe," said the aunt surprisingly.

"But how was it?" Mabel asked.

"My dear," said the aunt impressively, "I've been in a sort of trance. I think I must be going to be ill. I've always been fond of you, but I didn't want to spoil you. But yesterday, about half-past three, I was talking about you to Mr. Lewson, at the fair, and quite suddenly I felt as if you didn't matter at all. And I felt the same when I got your letter and when those children came. And today in the middle of tea I suddenly woke up and realized that you were gone. It was awful. I think I must be going to be ill. Oh, Mabel, why did you do it?"

"It was a joke," said Mabel feebly. And then the two went in and the door was shut.

"That's most uncommon odd," said Gerald, outside; "looks like more magic to me. I don't feel as if we d got to the bottom of this yet, by any manner of means. There's more about this castle than meets the eye."

There certainly was. For this castle happened to be ... but it would not be fair to Gerald to tell you more about it than he knew on that night when he went alone and invisible through the shadowy great grounds of it to look for the open window of the panelled room. He knew that night no more than I have told you; but as he went along the dewy lawns and through the groups of shrubs and trees, where pools lay like giant looking-glasses reflecting the quiet stars, and the white limbs of statues gleamed against a background of shadow, he began to feel well, not excited, not surprised, not anxious, but different.

The incident of the invisible Princess had surprised, the incident of the conjuring had excited, and the sudden decision to be a detective had brought its own anxieties; but all these happenings, though wonderful and unusual, had seemed to be, after all, inside the circle of possible things wonderful as the chemical experiments are where two liquids poured together make fire, surprising as legerdemain, thrilling as a juggler's display, but nothing more. Only now a new feeling came to him as he walked through those gardens; by day those gardens were like dreams, at night they were like visions. He could not see his feet as he walked, but he saw the movement of the dewy grass-blades that his feet displaced. And he had that extraordinary feeling so difficult to describe, and yet so real and so unforgettable, the feeling that he was in another world, that had covered up and hidden the old world as a carpet covers a floor. The floor was there all right, underneath, but what he walked on was the carpet that covered it, and that carpet was drenched in magic, as the turf was drenched in dew.

The feeling was very wonderful; perhaps you will feel it some day. There are still some places in the world where it can be felt, but they grow fewer every year.

The enchantment of the garden held him.

"I'll not go in yet," he told himself; "it's too early. And perhaps I shall never be here at night again. I suppose it is the night that makes everything look so different."

Something white moved under a weeping willow; white hands parted the long, rustling leaves. A white figure came out, a creature with horns and goat's legs and the head and arms of a boy. And Gerald was not afraid. That was the most wonderful thing of all, though he would never have owned it. The white thing stretched its limbs, rolled on the grass, righted itself and frisked away across the lawn. Still something white gleamed under the willow; three steps nearer and Gerald saw that it was the pedestal of a statue empty.

"They come alive," he said; and another white shape came out of the Temple of Flora and disappeared in the laurels. "The statues come alive."

There was a crunching of the little stones in the gravel of the drive. Something enormously long and darkly grey came crawling towards him, slowly, heavily. The moon came out just in time to show its shape. It was one of those great lizards that you see at the Crystal Palace, made in stone, of the same awful size which they were millions of years ago when they were masters of the world, before Man was.

"It can't see me," said Gerald. "I am not afraid. It's come to life, too."

As it writhed past him he reached out a hand and touched the side of its gigantic tail. It was of stone. It had not "come alive" as he had fancied, but was alive in its stone. It turned, however, at the touch; but Gerald also had turned, and was running with all his speed towards the house. Because at that stony touch Fear had come into the garden and almost caught him. It was Fear that he ran from, and not the moving stone beast.

He stood panting under the fifth window; when he had climbed to the window-ledge by the twisted ivy that clung to the wall, he looked back over the grey slope there was a splashing at the fish-pool that had mirrored the stars the shape of the great stone beast was wallowing in the shallows among the lily-pads.

Once inside the room, Gerald turned for another look. The fish-pond lay still and dark, reflecting the moon. Through a gap in the drooping willow the moonlight fell on a statue that stood calm and motionless on its pedestal. Everything was in its place now in the garden. Nothing moved or stirred.

"How extraordinarily rum!" said Gerald. "I shouldn't have thought you could go to sleep walking through a garden and dream like that."

He shut the window, lit a match, and closed the shutters. Another match showed him the door. He turned the key, went out, locked the door again, hung the key on its usual nail, and crept to the end of the passage. Here he waited, safe in his invisibility, till the dazzle of the matches should have gone from his eyes, and he be once more able to find his way by the moonlight that fell in bright patches on the floor through the barred, unshuttered windows of the hall.

"Wonder where the kitchen is," said Gerald. He had quite forgotten that he was a detective. He was only anxious to get home and tell the others about that extraordinarily odd dream that he had had in the gardens. "I suppose it doesn't matter what doors I open. I'm invisible all right still, I suppose? Yes; can't see my hand before my face." He held up a hand for the purpose. "Here goes!"

He opened many doors, wandered into long rooms with furniture dressed in brown holland covers that looked white in that strange light, rooms with chandeliers hanging in big bags from the high ceilings, rooms whose walls were alive with pictures, rooms whose walls were deadened with rows on rows of old books, state bedrooms in whose great plumed four-posters Queen Elizabeth had no doubt slept. (That Queen, by the way, must have been very little at home, for she seems to have slept in every old house in England.) But he could not find the kitchen. At last a door opened on stone steps that went up there was a narrow stone passage steps that went down a door with a light under it. It was, somehow, difficult to put out one's hand to that door and open it.

"Nonsense!" Gerald told himself, "don't be an ass! Are you invisible, or aren't you?"

Then he opened the door, and someone inside said something in a sudden rough growl.

Gerald stood back, flattened against the wall, as a man sprang to the doorway and flashed a lantern into the passage.

"All right," said the man, with almost a sob of relief. "It was only the door swung open, it's that heavy that's all."

"Blow the door!" said another growling voice; "blessed if I didn't think it was a fair cop that time."

They closed the door again. Gerald did not mind. In fact, he rather preferred that it should be so. He didn't like the look of those men. There was an air of threat about them. In their presence even invisibility seemed too thin a disguise. And Gerald had seen as much as he wanted to see. He had seen that he had been right about the gang. By wonderful luck beginner's luck, a card-player would have told him he had discovered a burglary on the very first night of his detective career. The men were taking silver out of two great chests, wrapping it in rags, and packing it in baize sacks. The door of the room was of iron six inches thick. It was, in fact, the strong-room, and these men had picked the lock. The tools they had done it with lay on the floor, on a neat cloth roll, such as wood-carvers keep their chisels in.

"Hurry up!" Gerald heard. "You needn't take all night over it."

The silver rattled slightly. "You're a rattling of them trays like bloomin' castanets," said the gruffest voice. Gerald turned and went away, very carefully and very quickly. And it is a most curious thing that, though he couldn't find the way to the servants wing when he had nothing else to think of, yet now, with his mind full, so to speak, of silver forks and silver cups, and the question of who might be coming after him down those twisting passages, he went straight as an arrow to the door that led from the hall to the place he wanted to get to.

As he went the happenings took words in his mind.

"The fortunate detective," he told himself, "having succeeded beyond his wildest dreams, himself left the spot in search of assistance."

But what assistance? There were, no doubt, men in the house, also the aunt; but he could not warn them.

He was too hopelessly invisible to carry any weight with strangers. The assistance of Mabel would not be of much value. The police? Before they could be got and the getting of them presented difficulties the burglars would have cleared away with their sacks of silver.

Gerald stopped and thought hard; he held his head with both hands to do it. You know the way the same as you sometimes do for simple equations or the dates of the battles of the Civil War.

Then with pencil, note-book, a window-ledge, and all the cleverness he could find at the moment, he wrote: "You know the room where the silver is. Burglars are burgling it, the thick door is picked. Send a man for police. I will follow the burglars if they get away ere police arrive on the spot."

He hesitated a moment, and ended "From a Friend this is not a sell."

This letter, tied tightly round a stone by means of a shoelace, thundered through the window of the room where Mabel and her aunt, in the ardour of reunion, were enjoying a supper of unusual charm — stewed plums, cream, sponge-cakes, custard in cups, and cold bread-and-butter pudding.

Gerald, in hungry invisibility, looked wistfully at the supper before he threw the stone. He waited till the shrieks had died away, saw the stone picked up, the warning letter read.

"Nonsense!" said the aunt, growing calmer. "How wicked! Of course it's a hoax."

"Oh! do send for the police, like he says," wailed Mabel.

"Like who says?" snapped the aunt.

"Whoever it is," Mabel moaned.

"Send for the police at once," said Gerald, outside, in the manliest voice he could find. "You'll only blame yourself if you don't. I can't do any more for you."

"I — I'll set the dogs on you!" cried the aunt.

"Oh, auntie, don't!" Mabel was dancing with agitation. "It's true, I know it's true. Do do wake Bates!"

"I don't believe a word of it," said the aunt. No more did Bates when, owing to Mabel's persistent worryings, he was awakened. But when he had seen the paper, and had to choose whether he'd go to the strong-room and see that there really wasn't anything to believe or go for the police on his bicycle, he chose the latter course.

When the police arrived the strong-room door stood ajar, and the silver, or as much of it as the three men could carry, was gone.

Gerald's note-book and pencil came into play again later on that night. It was five in the morning before he crept into bed, tired out and cold as a stone.

"Master Gerald!" it was Eliza's voice in his ears "it's seven o clock and another fine day, and there's been another burglary. My cats alive!" she screamed, as she drew up the blind and turned towards the bed; "look at his bed, all crocked with black, and him not there!" "Oh, Jiminy!" It was a scream this time. Kathleen came running from her room; Jimmy sat up in his bed and rubbed his eyes.

"Whatever is it?" Kathleen cried.

"I dunno when I 'ad such a turn." Eliza sat down heavily on a box as she spoke. "First thing his bed all empty and black as the chimley back, and him not in it, and then when I looks again he is in it all the time. I must be going silly. I thought as much when I heard them haunting angel voices yesterday morning. But I'll tell Mamselle of you, my lad, with your tricks, you may rely on that. Blacking yourself all over and crocking up your clean sheets and pillow-cases. It's going back of beyond, this is."

"Look here," said Gerald slowly; "I'm going to tell you something."

Eliza simply snorted, and that was rude of her; but then, she had had a shock and had not got over it.

"Can you keep a secret?" asked Gerald, very earnest through the grey of his partly rubbed-off blacklead.

"Yes," said Eliza.

"Then keep it and I'll give you two bob."

"But what was you going to tell me?"

"That. About the two bob and the secret. And you keep your mouth shut."

"I didn't ought to take it," said Eliza, holding out her hand eagerly. "Now you get up, and mind you wash all the corners, Master Gerald."

"Oh, I'm so glad you're safe," said Kathleen, when Eliza had gone.

"You didn't seem to care much last night," said Gerald coldly.

"I can't think how I let you go. I didn't care last night. But when I woke this morning and remembered!"

"There, that'll do it'll come off on you," said Gerald through the reckless hugging of his sister.

"How did you get visible?" Jimmy asked.

"It just happened when she called me the ring came off."

"Tell us all about everything," said Kathleen.

"Not yet," said Gerald mysteriously.

"Where's the ring?" Jimmy asked after breakfast. "I want to have a try now."

"I — I forgot it," said Gerald; "I expect it's in the bed somewhere.

But it wasn't. Eliza had made the bed.

"I'll swear there ain't no ring there," she said. "I should 'a seen it if there had'a been."

"Search and research proving vain," said Gerald, when every corner of the bedroom had been turned out and the ring had not been found, "the noble detective hero of our tale remarked that he would have other fish to fry in half a jiff, and if the rest of you want to hear about last night..."

"Let's keep it till we get to Mabel," said Kathleen heroically.

"The assignation was ten-thirty, wasn't it? Why shouldn't Gerald gas as we go along? I don't suppose anything very much happened, anyhow." This, of course, was Jimmy.

"That shows," remarked Gerald sweetly, "how much you know. The melancholy Mabel will await the tryst without success, as far as this one is concerned. 'Fish, fish, other fish other fish I fry!'" he warbled to the tune of 'Cherry Ripe', till Kathleen could have pinched him.

Jimmy turned coldly away, remarking, "When you've quite done."

But Gerald went on singing

> "Where the lips of Johnson smile,
> There's the land of Cherry Isle.
> Other fish, other fish,
> Fish I fry.
> Stately Johnson, come and buy!"

"How can you," asked Kathleen, "be so aggravating?"

"I don't know," said Gerald, returning to prose.

"Want of sleep or intoxication of success, I mean. Come where no one can hear us.

> 'Oh, come to some island where no one can hear,
> And beware of the keyhole that's glued to an ear,'"

he whispered, opened the door suddenly, and there, sure enough, was Eliza, stooping without. She flicked feebly at the wainscot with a duster, but concealment was vain.

"You know what listeners never hear," said Jimmy severely.

"I didn't, then so there!" said Eliza, whose listening ears were crimson. So they passed out, and up the High Street, to sit on the churchyard wall and dangle their legs. And all the way Gerald's lips were shut into a thin, obstinate line.

"Now," said Kathleen. "Oh, Jerry, don't be a goat! I'm simply dying to hear what happened."

"That's better," said Gerald, and he told his story. As he told it some of the white mystery and magic of the moonlit gardens got into his voice and his words, so that when he told of the statues that came alive, and the great beast that was alive through all its stone, Kathleen thrilled responsive, clutching his arm, and even Jimmy ceased to kick the wall with his boot heels, and listened open-mouthed.

Then came the thrilling tale of the burglars, and the warning letter flung into the peaceful company of Mabel, her aunt, and the bread-and-butter pudding. Gerald told the story with the greatest enjoyment and such fullness of detail that the church clock chimed half-past eleven as he said, "Having done all that human agency could do, and further help being despaired of, our gallant young detective Hullo, there's Mabel!"

There was. The tail-board of a cart shed her almost at their feet.

"I couldn't wait any longer," she explained, "when you didn't come. And I got a lift. Has anything more happened?" The burglars had gone when Bates got to the strong-room.

"You don't mean to say all that wheeze is real?" Jimmy asked.

"Of course it's real," said Kathleen. "Go on, Jerry. He's just got to where he threw the stone into your bread-and-butter pudding, Mabel. Go on.

Mabel climbed on to the wall. "You've got visible again quicker than I did," she said.

Gerald nodded and resumed:

"Our story must be told in as few words as possible, owing to the fish-frying taking place at twelve, and it's past the half-hour now. Having left his missive to do its warning work, Gerald de Sherlock Holmes sped back, wrapped in invisibility, to the spot where by the light of their dark-lanterns the burglars were still still burgling with the utmost punctuality and despatch. I didn't see any sense in running into danger, so I just waited outside the passage where the steps are you know?"

Mabel nodded.

"Presently they came out, very cautiously, of course, and looked about them. They didn't see me so deeming themselves unobserved they passed in silent Indian file along the passage one of the sacks of silver grazed my front part and out into the night."

"But which way?"

"Through the little looking-glass room where you looked at yourself when you were invisible. The hero followed swiftly on his invisible tennis-shoes. The three miscreants instantly sought the shelter of the groves and passed stealthily among the rhododendrons and across the park," and his voice dropped and he looked straight before him at the pinky convolvulus netting a heap of stones beyond the white dust of the road "the stone things that come alive, they kept looking out from between bushes and under trees and I saw them all right, but they didn't see me. They saw the burglars though, right enough; but the burglars couldn't see them. Rum, wasn't it?"

"The stone things?" Mabel had to have them explained to her.

"I never saw them come alive," she said, "and I've been in the gardens in the evening as often as often.

"I saw them," said Gerald stiffly.

"I know, I know," Mabel hastened to put herself right with him; "what I mean to say is I shouldn't wonder if they're only visible when you're invisible — the liveness of them, I mean, not the stoniness."

Gerald understood, and I'm sure I hope you do.

"I shouldn't wonder if you're right," he said. "The castle garden's enchanted right enough; but what I should like to know is how and why. I say, come on, I've got to catch Johnson before twelve. We'll walk as far as the market and then we'll have to run for it."

"But go on with the adventure," said Mabel. "You can talk as we go." "Oh, do it is so awfully thrilling!"

This pleased Gerald, of course.

"Well, I just followed, you know, like in a dream, and they got out the cavy way you know, where we got in and I jolly well thought I'd lost them; I had to wait till they'd moved off down the road so that they shouldn't hear me rattling the stones, and I had to tear to catch them up. I took my shoes off, I expect my stockings are done for. And I followed and followed and followed and they went through the place where the poor people live, and right down to the river. And

I say, we must run for it."

So the story stopped and the running began.

They caught Johnson in his own back-yard washing at a bench against his own back-door.

"Look here, Johnson," Gerald said, "what'll you give me if I put you up to winning that fifty pounds reward?"

"Halves," said Johnson promptly, "and a clout 'long-side your head if you was coming any of your nonsense over me."

"It's not nonsense," said Gerald very impressively. "If you'll let us in I'll tell you all about it. And when you've caught the burglars and got the swag back you just give me a quid for luck. I won't ask for more."

"Come along in, then," said Johnson, "if the young ladies'll excuse the towel. But I bet you do want something more off of me. Else why not claim the reward yourself?"

"Great is the wisdom of Johnson he speaks winged words." The children were all in the cottage now, and the door was shut. "I want you never to let on who told you. Let them think it was your own unaided pluck and far-sightedness."

"Sit you down," said Johnson, "and if you're kidding you'd best send the little gells home afore I begin on you."

"I am not kidding," replied Gerald loftily, "never less. And anyone but a policeman would see why I don't want anyone to know it was me. I found it out at dead of night, in a place where I wasn't supposed to be; and there'd be a beastly row if they found out at home about me being out nearly all night. Now do you see, my bright-eyed daisy?"

Johnson was now too interested, as Jimmy said afterwards, to mind what silly names he was called. He said he did see and asked to see more.

"Well, don't you ask any questions, then. I'll tell you all it's good for you to know. Last night about eleven I was at Yalding Towers. No it doesn't matter how I got there or what I got there for and there was a window open and I got in, and there was a light. And it was in the strong-room, and there were three men, putting silver in a bag."

"Was it you give the warning, and they sent for the police?" Johnson was leaning eagerly forward, a hand on each knee.

"Yes, that was me. You can let them think it was you, if you like. You were off duty, weren't you?"

"I was," said Johnson, "in the arms of Murphy "

"Well, the police didn't come quick enough. But I was there a lonely detective. And I followed them."

"You did?"

"And I saw them hide the booty and I know the other stuff from Houghton's Court's in the same place, and I heard them arrange about when to take it away."

"Come and show me where," said Johnson, jumping up so quickly that his Windsor arm-chair fell over backwards, with a crack, on the red-brick floor.

"Not so," said Gerald calmly; "if you go near the spot before the appointed time you'll find the silver, but you'll never catch the thieves."

"You're right there." The policeman picked up his chair and sat down in it again. "Well?"

"Well, there's to be a motor to meet them in the lane beyond the boat-house by Sadler's Rents at one o clock tonight. They'll get the things out at half-past twelve and take them along in a boat. So now's your chance to fill your pockets with chink and cover yourself with honour and glory."

"So help me!" Johnson was pensive and doubtful still "So help me! You couldn't have made all this up out of your head."

"Oh yes, I could. But I didn't. Now look here. It's the chance of your lifetime, Johnson! A quid for me, and a still tongue for you, and the job's done. Do you agree?"

"Oh, I agree right enough," said Johnson. "I agree. But if you're coming any of your larks ..."

"Can't you see he isn't?" Kathleen put in impatiently. "He's not a liar, we none of us are."

"If you're not on, say so," said Gerald, "and I'll find another policeman with more sense."

"I could split about you being out all night," said Johnson.

"But you wouldn't be so ungentlemanly," said Mabel brightly. "Don't you be so unbelieving, when we're trying to do you a good turn."

"If I were you," Gerald advised, "I'd go to the place where the silver is, with two other men. You could make a nice little ambush in the wood-yard, it's close there. And I'd have two or three more men up trees in the lane to wait for the motor-car."

"You ought to have been in the force, you ought," said Johnson admiringly; "but s'pose it was a hoax!"

"Well, then you'd have made an ass of yoursel.f I don't suppose it'd be the first time," said Jimmy.

"Are you on?" said Gerald in haste. "Hold your jaw, Jimmy, you idiot!"

"Yes," said Johnson.

"Then when you're on duty you go down to the wood-yard, and the place where you see me blow my nose is the place. The sacks are tied with string to the posts under the water. You just stalk by in your dignified beauty and make a note of the spot. That's where glory waits you, and when Fame elates you and you're a sergeant, please remember me."

Johnson said he was blessed. He said it more than once, and then remarked that he was on, and added that he must be off that instant minute.

Johnson's cottage lies just out of the town beyond the blacksmith's forge and the children had come to it through the wood. They went back the same way, and then down through the town, and through its narrow, unsavoury streets to the towing-path by the timber yard. Here they ran along the trunks of the big trees, peeped into the saw-pit, and — the men were away at dinner and this was a favourite play place of every boy within miles — made themselves a see-saw with a fresh cut, sweet-smelling pine plank and an elm-root.

"What a ripping place!" said Mabel, breathless on the seesaw's end. "I believe I like this better than pretending games or even magic."

"So do I," said Jimmy. "Jerry, don't keep sniffing so you'll have no nose left."

"I can't help it," Gerald answered; "I daren't use my hankey for fear Johnson's on the lookout somewhere unseen. I wish I'd thought of some other signal." Sniff! "No, nor I shouldn't want to now if I hadn't got not to. That's what's so rum. The moment I got down here and remembered what I'd said about the signal I began to have a cold and... Thank goodness! Here he is."

The children, with a fine air of unconcern, abandoned the see-saw. "Follow my leader!" Gerald cried, and ran along a barked oak trunk, the others following. In and out and round about ran the file of children, over heaps of logs, under the jutting ends of piled planks, and just as the policeman's heavy boots trod the towing-path Gerald halted at the end of a little landing-stage of rotten boards, with a rickety handrail, cried "Pax!" and blew his nose with loud fervour.

"Morning," he said immediately.

"Morning," said Johnson. "Got a cold, ain't you?"

"Ah! I shouldn't have a cold if I'd got boots like yours," returned Gerald admiringly. "Look at them. Anyone ud know your fairy footstep a mile off. How do you ever get near enough to anyone to arrest them?" He skipped off the landing-stage, whispered as he passed Johnson, "Courage, promptitude, and dispatch. That's the place," and was off again, the active leader of an active procession.

"We've brought a friend home to dinner," said Kathleen, when Eliza opened the door. "Where's Mademoiselle?"

"Gone to see Yalding Towers. Today's show day, you know. An just you hurry over your dinners. It's my afternoon out, and my gentleman friend don't like it if he's kept waiting."

"All right, we'll eat like lightning," Gerald promised. "Set another place, there's an angel."

They kept their word. The dinner — it was minced veal and potatoes and rice-pudding, perhaps the dullest food in the world — was over in a quarter of an hour.

"And now," said Mabel, when Eliza and a jug of hot water had disappeared up the stairs together, "where's the ring? I ought to put it back."

"I haven't had a turn yet," said Jimmy. "When we find it Cathy and I ought to have turns same as you and Gerald did."

"When you find it ?" Mabel's pale face turned paler between her dark locks.

"I'm very sorry — we're all very sorry," began Kathleen, and then the story of the losing had to be told.

"You couldn't have looked properly," Mabel protested. "It can't have vanished."

"You don't know what it can do no more do we. It's no use getting your quills up, fair lady. Perhaps vanishing itself is just what it does do. You see, it came off my hand in the bed. We looked everywhere."

"Would you mind if I looked?" Mabel's eyes implored her little hostess. "You see, if it's lost it's my fault. It's almost the same as stealing. That Johnson would say it was just the same. I know he would."

"Let's all look again," said Cathy, jumping up. "We were rather in a hurry this morning."

So they looked, and they looked. In the bed, under the bed, under the carpet, under the furniture. They shook the curtains, they explored the corners, and found dust and flue, but no ring. They looked, and they looked. Everywhere they looked. Jimmy even looked fixedly at the ceiling, as though he thought the ring might have bounced up there and stuck. But it hadn't.

"Then," said Mabel at last, "your housemaid must have stolen it. That's all. I shall tell her I think so."

And she would have done it too, but at that moment the front door banged and they knew that Eliza had gone forth in all the glory of her best things to meet her "gentleman friend" .

"It's no use," Mabel was almost in tears; "look here will you leave me alone? Perhaps you others looking distracts me. And I'll go over every inch of the room by myself."

"Respecting the emotion of their guest, the kindly charcoal-burners withdrew," said Gerald. And they closed the door softly from the outside on Mabel and her search.

They waited for her, of course, politeness demanded it, and besides, they had to stay at home to let Mademoiselle in; though it was a dazzling day, and Jimmy had just remembered that Gerald's pockets were full of the money earned at the fair, and that nothing had yet been bought with that money, except a few buns in which he had had no share. And of course they waited impatiently.

It seemed about an hour, and was really quite ten minutes, before they heard the bedroom door open and Mabel's feet on the stairs.

"She hasn't found it," Gerald said.

"How do you know?" Jimmy asked.

"The way she walks," said Gerald. You can, in fact, almost always tell whether the thing has been found that people have gone to look for by the sound of their feet as they return. Mabel's feet said "No go" as plain as they could speak. And her face confirmed the cheerless news.

A sudden and violent knocking at the back door prevented anyone from having to be polite about how sorry they were, or fanciful about being sure the ring would turn up soon.

All the servants except Eliza were away on their holidays, so the children went together to open the door, because, as Gerald said, if it was the baker they could buy a cake from him and eat it for dessert. "That kind of dinner sort of needs dessert," he said.

But it was not the baker. When they opened the door they saw in the paved court where the pump is, and the dust-bin, and the water-butt, a young man, with his hat very much on one side, his mouth open under his fair bristly mustache, and his eyes as nearly round as human eyes can be. He wore a suit of a bright mustard colour, a blue necktie, and a goldish watch-chain across his waistcoat. His body was thrown back and his right arm stretched out towards the door, and his expression was that of a person who is being dragged somewhere against his will. He looked so strange that Kathleen tried to shut the door in his face, murmuring, "Escaped insane." But the door would not close. There was something in the way.

"Leave go of me!" said the young man.

"Ho yus! I'll leave go of you!" It was the voice of Eliza but no Eliza could be seen.

"Who's got hold of you?" asked Kathleen.

"She has, miss," replied the unhappy stranger.

"Who's she?" asked Kathleen, to gain time, as she afterwards explained, for she now knew well enough that what was keeping the door open was Eliza's unseen foot.

"My fyongsay, miss. At least it sounds like her voice, and it feels like her bones, but something's come over me, miss, an I can't see her."

"That's what he keeps on saying," said Eliza's voice. "E's my gentleman friend; is 'e gone dotty, or is it me?"

"Both, I shouldn't wonder," said Jimmy.

"Now," said Eliza, "you call yourself a man; you look me in the face and say you can't see me."

"Well I can't," said the wretched gentleman friend.

"If I'd stolen a ring," said Gerald, looking at the sky, "I should go indoors and be quiet, not stand at the back door and make an exhibition of myself."

"Not much exhibition about her," whispered Jimmy; "good old ring!"

"I haven't stolen anything," said the gentleman friend. "Here, you leave me be. It's my eyes has gone wrong. Leave go of me, d'ye hear?"

Suddenly his hand dropped and he staggered back against the water-butt. Eliza had "left go" of him. She pushed past the children, shoving them aside with her invisible elbows. Gerald caught her by the arm with one hand, felt for her ear with the other, and whispered, "You stand still and don't say a word. If you do well, what's to stop me from sending for the police?"

Eliza did not know what there was to stop him. So she did as she was told, and stood invisible and silent, save for a sort of blowing, snorting noise peculiar to her when she was out of breath.

The mustard-coloured young man had recovered his balance, and stood looking at the children with eyes, if possible, rounder than before.

"What is it?" he gasped feebly. "What's up? What's it all about?"

"If you don't know, I'm afraid we can't tell you," said Gerald politely.

"Have I been talking very strange-like?" he asked, taking off his hat and passing his hand over his forehead.

"Very," said Mabel.

"I hope I haven't said anything that wasn't good manners," he said anxiously.

"Not at all," said Kathleen. "You only said your fiancee had hold of your hand, and that you couldn't see her."

"No more I can."

"No more can we," said Mabel.

"But I couldn't have dreamed it, and then come along here making a penny show of myself like this, could I?"

"You know best," said Gerald courteously.

"But," the mustard-coloured victim almost screamed, "do you mean to tell me..."

"I don't mean to tell you anything," said Gerald quite truly, "but I'll give you a bit of advice. You go home and lie down a bit and put a wet rag on your head. You'll be all right tomorrow."

"But I haven't "

"I should," said Mabel; "the sun's very hot, you know."

"I feel all right now," he said, "but well, I can only say I'm sorry, that's all I can say. I've never been taken like this before, miss. I'm not subject to it, don't you think that. But I could have sworn Eliza — Ain't she gone out to meet me?"

"Eliza's in-doors," said Mabel. "She can't come out to meet anybody today."

"You won't tell her about me carrying on this way, will you, miss? It might set her against me if she thought I was liable to fits, which I never was from a child."

"We won't tell Eliza anything about you."

"And you'll overlook the liberty?"

"Of course. We know you couldn't help it," said Kathleen. "You go home and lie down. I'm sure you must need it. Good afternoon."

"Good afternoon, I'm sure, miss," he said dreamily. "All the same I can feel the print of her finger-bones on my hand while I'm saying it. And you won't let it get round to my boss my employer I mean? Fits of all sorts are against a man in any trade."

"No, no, no, it's all right good-bye," said everyone. And a silence fell as he went slowly round the water-butt and the green yard-gate shut behind him. The silence was broken by Eliza.

"Give me up!" she said. "Give me up to break my heart in a prison cell!"

There was a sudden splash, and a round wet drop lay on the doorstep.

"Thunder shower," said Jimmy; but it was a tear from Eliza.

"Give me up," she went on, "give me up" splash "but don't let me be took here in the town where I'm known and respected" splash. "I'll walk ten miles to be took by a strange police not Johnson as keeps company with my own cousin" splash. "But I do thank you for one thing. You didn't tell Elf as I'd stolen the ring. And I didn't splash I only sort of borrowed it, it being my day out, and my gentleman friend such a toff, like you can see for yourselves."

The children had watched, spellbound, the interesting tears that became visible as they rolled off the invisible nose of the miserable Eliza. Now Gerald roused himself, and spoke.

"It's no use your talking," he said. "We can't see you!"

"That's what he said," said Eliza's voice, "but "

"You can't see yourself," Gerald went on. "Where's your hand?"

Eliza, no doubt, tried to see it, and of course failed; for instantly, with a shriek that might have brought the police if there had been any about, she went into a violent fit of hysterics. The children did what they could, everything that they had read of in books as suitable to such occasions, but it is extremely difficult to do the right thing with an invisible housemaid in strong hysterics and her best clothes. That was why the best hat was found, later on, to be completely ruined, and why the best blue dress was never quite itself again. And as they were burning bits of the feather dusting-brush as nearly under Eliza's nose as they could guess, a sudden spurt of flame and a horrible smell, as the flame died between the quick hands of Gerald, showed but too plainly that Eliza's feather boa had tried to help.

It did help. Eliza "came to" with a deep sob and said, "Don't burn me real ostrich stole; I'm better now."

They helped her up and she sat down on the bottom step, and the children explained to her very carefully and quite kindly that she really was invisible, and that if you steal or even borrow rings you can never be sure what will happen to you.

"But 'ave I got to go on stopping like this," she moaned, when they had fetched the little mahogany looking-glass from its nail over the kitchen sink, and convinced her that she was really invisible, "for ever and ever? An we was to a bin married come Easter. No one won't marry a gell as 'e can't see. It ain't likely."

"No, not for ever and ever," said Mabel kindly, "but you've got to go through with it like measles. I expect you'll be all right tomorrow."

"Tonight, I think," said Gerald.

"We'll help you all we can, and not tell anyone," said Kathleen.

"Not even the police," said Jimmy.

"Now let's get Mademoiselle's tea ready," said Gerald.

"And ours," said Jimmy.

"No," said Gerald, "we'll have our tea out. We'll have a picnic and we'll take Eliza. I'll go out and get the cakes."

"I shan't eat no cake, Master Jerry," said Eliza's voice, "so don't you think it. You'd see it going down inside my chest. It wouldn't he what I should call nice of me to have cake showing through me in the open air. Oh, it's a dreadful judgment just for a borrow!"

They reassured her, set the tea, deputed Kathleen to let in Mademoiselle who came home tired and a little sad, it seemed, waited for her and Gerald and the cakes, and started off for Yalding Towers.

"Picnic parties aren't allowed," said Mabel.

"Ours will be," said Gerald briefly. "Now, Eliza, you catch on to Kathleen's arm and I'll walk behind to conceal your shadow. My aunt! take your hat off; it makes your shadow look like I don't know what. People will think we're the county lunatic asylum turned loose."

It was then that the hat, becoming visible in Kathleen's hand, showed how little of the sprinkled water had gone where it was meant to go on Eliza's face.

"Me best 'at," said Eliza, and there was a silence with sniffs in it.

"Look here," said Mabel, "you cheer up. Just you think this is all a dream. It's just the kind of thing you might dream if your conscience bad got pains in it about the ring."

"But will I wake up again?"

"Oh yes, you'll wake up again. Now we're going to bandage your eyes and take you through a very small door, and don't you resist, or we'll bring a policeman into the dream like a shot."

I have not time to describe Eliza's entrance into the cave. She went head first: the girls propelled and the boys received her. If Gerald had not thought of tying her hands someone would certainly have been scratched. As it was Mabel's hand was scraped between the cold rock and a passionate boot-heel. Nor will I tell you all that she said as they led her along the fern-bordered gully and through the arch into the wonderland of Italian scenery. She had but little language left when they removed her bandage under a weeping willow where a statue of Diana, bow in hand, stood poised on one toe a most unsuitable attitude for archery, I have always thought.

"Now," said Gerald, "it's all over nothing but niceness now and cake and things."

"It's time we did have our tea," said Jimmy. And it was.

Eliza, once convinced that her chest, though invisible, was not transparent, and that her companions could not by looking through it count how many buns she had eaten, made an excellent meal. So did the others. If you want really to enjoy your tea, have minced veal and potatoes and rice-pudding for dinner, with several hours of excitement to follow, and take your tea late.

The soft, cool green and grey of the garden were changing. The green grew golden, the shadows black, and the lake where the swans were mirrored upside down, under the Temple of Phoebus, was bathed in rosy light from the little fluffy clouds that lay opposite the sunset.

"It is pretty," said Eliza, "just like a picture-postcard, ain't it? The tuppenny kind."

"I ought to be getting home," said Mabel.

"I can't go home like this. I'd stay and be a savage and live in that white hut if it had any walls and doors," said Eliza.

"She means the Temple of Dionysus," said Mabel, pointing to it.

The sun set suddenly behind the line of black fir-trees on the top of the slope, and the white temple, that had been pink, turned grey.

"It would be a very nice place to live in even as it is," said Kathleen.

"Draughty," said Eliza, "and law, what a lot of steps to clean! What they make houses for without no walls to 'em? Who'd live in," She broke off, stared, and added: "What's that?"

"What?"

"That white thing coming down the steps. Why, it's a young man in statooary."

"The statues do come alive here, after sunset," said Gerald in very matter-of-fact tones.

"I see they do." Eliza did not seem at all surprised or alarmed. "There's another of 'em. Look at them little wings to his feet like pigeons."

"I expect that's Mercury," said Gerald.

"It's 'Hermes' under the statue that's got wings on its feet, said Mabel, "but "

"I don't see any statues," said Jimmy. "What are you punching me for?"

"Don't you see?" Gerald whispered; but he need not have been so troubled, for all Eliza's attention was with her wandering eyes that followed hither and thither the quick movements of unseen statues. "Don't you see? The statues come alive when the sun goes down and you can't see them unless you're invisible and if you do see them you're not frightened unless you touch them."

"Let's get her to touch one and see," said Jimmy.

"E's lep into the water," said Eliza in a rapt voice. "My, can't he swim neither! And the one with the pigeons wings is flying all over the lake having larks with 'im. I do call that pretty. It's like cupids as you see on wedding-cakes. And here's another of 'em, a little chap with long ears and a baby deer galloping alongside! An look at the lady with the biby, throwing it up and catching it like as if it was a ball. I wonder she ain't afraid. But it's pretty to see 'em."

The broad park lay stretched before the children in growing greyness and a stillness that deepened. Amid the thickening shadows they could see the statues gleam white and motionless. But Eliza saw other things. She watched in silence presently, and they watched silently, and the evening fell like a veil that grew heavier and blacker. And it was night. And the moon came up above the trees.

"Oh," cried Eliza suddenly, "here's the dear little boy with the deer — he's coming right for me, bless his heart!"

Next moment she was screaming, and her screams grew fainter and there was the sound of swift boots on gravel.

"Come on!" cried Gerald; "she touched it, and then she was frightened, Just like I was. Run! She'll send everyone in the town mad if she gets there like that. Just a voice and boots! Run! Run!

They ran. But Eliza had the start of them. Also when she ran on the grass they could not hear her footsteps and had to wait for the sound of leather on far-away gravel. Also she was driven by fear, and fear drives fast.

She went, it seemed, the nearest way, invisibly through the waxing moonlight, seeing she only knew what amid the glades and groves.

"I'll stop here; see you tomorrow," gasped Mabel, as the loud pursuers followed Eliza's clatter across the terrace. "She's gone through the stable yard."

"The back way," Gerald panted as they turned the corner of their own street, and he and Jimmy swung in past the water-butt.

An unseen but agitated presence seemed to be fumbling with the locked back-door. The church clock struck the half-hour.

"Half-past nine," Gerald had just breath to say. "Pull at the ring. Perhaps it'll come off now."

He spoke to the bare doorstep. But it was Eliza, dishevelled, breathless, her hair coming down, her collar crooked, her dress twisted and disordered, who suddenly held out a hand a hand that they could see; and in the hand, plainly visible in the moonlight, the dark circle of the magic ring.

"Alf a mo!" said Eliza's gentleman friend next morning. He was waiting for her when she opened the door with pail and hearthstone in her hand. "Sorry you couldn't come out yesterday."

"So'm I." Eliza swept the wet flannel along the top step. "What did you do?"

"I 'ad a bit of a headache," said the gentleman friend. "I laid down most of the afternoon. What were you up to?"

"Oh, nothing pertickler," said Eliza.

"Then it was all a dream, she said, when he was gone; "but it'll be a lesson to me nòt to meddle with anybody's old ring again in a hurry."

"So they didn't tell 'er about me behaving like I did," said he as he went "sun, I suppose like our Army in India. I hope I ain't going to be liable to it, that's all!"

Johnson was the hero of the hour. It was he who had tracked the burglars, laid his plans, and recovered the lost silver. He had not thrown the stone — public opinion decided that Mabel and her aunt must have been mistaken in supposing that there was a stone at all. But he did not deny the warning letter. It was Gerald who went out after breakfast to buy the newspaper, and who read aloud to the others the two columns of fiction which were the Liddlesby Observer's report of the facts. As he read every mouth opened wider and wider, and when he ceased with "this gifted fellow-townsman with detective instincts which out-rival those of Messrs. Lecoq and Holmes, and whose promotion is now assured," there was quite a blank silence.

"Well," said Jimmy, breaking it, "he doesn't stick it on neither, does he?"

"I feel," said Kathleen, "as if it was our fault — as if it was us had told all these whoppers; because if it hadn't been for you they couldn't have, Jerry. How could he say all that?"

"Well," said Gerald, trying to be fair, "you know, after all, the chap had to say something. I'm glad I..." He stopped abruptly.

"You're glad you what?"

"No matter," said he, with an air of putting away affairs of state. "Now, what are we going to do today? The faithful Mabel approaches; she will want her ring. And you and Jimmy want it too. Oh, I know. Mademoiselle hasn't had any attention paid to her for more days than our hero likes to confess."

"I wish you wouldn't always call yourself 'our hero', said Jimmy; "you aren't mine, anyhow."

"You're both of you mine," said Kathleen hastily.

"Good little girl." Gerald smiled annoyingly. "Keep baby brother in a good temper till Nursie comes back."

"You're not going out without us?" Kathleen asked in haste.

"I haste away,
'Tis market day,"

sang Gerald,

"And in the market there
Buy roses for my fair.

If you want to come too, get your boots on, and look slippy about it."

"I don't want to come," said Jimmy, and sniffed.

Kathleen turned a despairing look on Gerald.

"Oh, James, James," said Gerald sadly, "how difficult you make it for me to forget that you're my little brother! If ever I treat you like one of the other chaps, and rot you like I should Turner or Moberley or any of my pals well, this is what comes of it."

"You don't call them your baby brothers," said Jimmy, and truly.

"No; and I'll take precious good care I don't call you it again. Come on, my hero and heroine. The devoted Mesrour is your salaaming slave."

The three met Mabel opportunely at the corner of the square where every Friday the stalls and the awnings and the green umbrellas were pitched, and poultry, pork, pottery, vegetables, drapery, sweets, toys, tools, mirrors, and all sorts of other interesting merchandise were spread out on trestle tables, piled on carts whose horses were stabled and whose shafts were held in place by piled wooden cases, or laid out, as in the case of crockery and hardware, on the bare flag-stones of the market-place.

The sun was shining with great goodwill, and, as Mabel remarked, "all Nature looked smiling and gay." There were a few bunches of flowers among the vegetables, and the children hesitated, balanced in choice.

"Mignonette is sweet," said Mabel.

"Roses are roses," said Kathleen.

"Carnations are tuppence," said Jimmy; and Gerald, sniffing among the bunches of tightly-tied tea-roses, agreed that this settled it.

So the carnations were bought, a bunch of yellow ones, like sulphur, a bunch of white ones like clotted cream, and a bunch of red ones like the cheeks of the doll that Kathleen never played with. They took the carnations home, and Kathleen's green hair-ribbon came in beautifully for tying them up, which was hastily done on the doorstep.

Then discreetly Gerald knocked at the door of the drawing-room, where Mademoiselle seemed to sit all day.

"Entrez!" came her voice; and Gerald entered. She was not reading, as usual, but bent over a sketch-book; on the table was an open colour-box of un-English appearance, and a box of that slate-coloured liquid so familiar alike to the greatest artist in watercolours and to the humblest child with a sixpenny paintbox.

"With all of our loves," said Gerald, laying the flowers down suddenly before her.

"But it is that you are a dear child. For this it must that I embrace you no?" And before Gerald could explain that he was too old, she kissed him with little quick French pecks on the two cheeks.

"Are you painting?" he asked hurriedly, to hide his annoyance at being treated like a baby.

"I achieve a sketch of yesterday," she answered; and before he had time to wonder what yesterday would look like in a picture she showed him a beautiful and exact sketch of Yalding Towers.

"Oh, I say ripping!" was the critic's comment. "I say, mayn't the others come and see?" The others came, including Mabel, who stood awkwardly behind the rest, and looked over Jimmy's shoulder.

"I say, you are clever," said Gerald respectfully.

"To what good to have the talent, when one must pass one's life at teaching the infants?" said Mademoiselle.

"It must be fairly beastly," Gerald owned.

"You, too, see the design?" Mademoiselle asked Mabel, adding: "A friend from the town, yes?"

"How do you do?" said Mabel politely. "No, I'm not from the town. I live at Yalding Towers."

The name seemed to impress Mademoiselle very much. Gerald anxiously hoped in his own mind that she was not a snob.

"Yalding Towers," she repeated, "but this is very extraordinary. Is it possible that you are then of the family of Lord Yalding?"

"He hasn't any family," said Mabel; "he's not married."

"I would say are you how you say? Cousin? Sister? Niece?"

"No," said Mabel, flushing hotly, "I'm nothing grand at all. I'm Lord Yalding's housekeeper's niece."

"But you know Lord Yalding, is it not?"

"No," said Mabel, "I've never seen him."

"He comes then never to his chateau?"

"Not since I've lived there. But he's coming next week."

"Why lives he not there?" Mademoiselle asked.

"Auntie says he's too poor," said Mabel, and proceeded to tell the tale as she had heard it in the housekeeper's room: how Lord Yalding's uncle had left all the money he could leave away from Lord Yalding to Lord Yalding's second cousin, and poor Lord Yalding had only just enough to keep the old place in repair, and to live very quietly indeed somewhere else, but not enough to keep the house open or to live there; and how he couldn't sell the house because it was "in tale".

"What is it then in tail?" asked Mademoiselle.

"In a tale that the lawyers write out," said Mabel, proud of her knowledge and flattered by the deep interest of the French governess; "and when once they've put your house in one of their tales you can't sell it or give it away, but you have to leave it to your son, even if you don't want to."

"But how his uncle could he be so cruel to leave him the chateau and no money?" Mademoiselle asked; and Kathleen and Jimmy stood amazed at the sudden keenness of her interest in what seemed to them the dullest story.

"Oh, I can tell you that too," said Mabel. "Lord Yalding wanted to marry a lady his uncle didn't want him to, a barmaid or a ballet lady or something, and he wouldn't give her up, and his uncle said, 'Well then,' and left everything to the cousin."

"And you say he is not married."

"No, the lady went into a convent; I expect she's bricked-up alive by now."

"Bricked?"

"In a wall, you know, " said Mabel, pointing explainingly at the pink and gilt roses of the wall-paper, "shut up to kill them. That's what they do to you in convents."

"Not at all," said Mademoiselle; "in convents are very kind good women; there is but one thing in convents that is detestable, the locks on the doors. Sometimes people cannot get out, especially when they are very young and their relations have placed them there for their welfare and happiness. But brick — how you say it? — enwalling ladies to kill them. No it does itself never. And this lord, he did not then seek his lady?"

"Oh, yes he sought her right enough," Mabel assured her; "but there are millions of convents, you know, and he had no idea where to look, and they sent back his letters from the post-office, and "

"Ciel!" cried Mademoiselle, "but it seems that one knows all in the housekeeper's saloon."

"Pretty well all," said Mabel simply.

"And you think he will find her? No?"

"Oh, he'll find her all right," said Mabel, "when he's old and broken down, you know and dying; and then a gentle Sister of Charity will soothe his pillow, and just when he's dying she'll reveal herself and say: 'My own lost love!' and his face will light up with a wonderful joy and he'll expire with her beloved name on his parched lips."

Mademoiselle's was the silence of sheer astonishment. "You do the prophecy, it appears?" she said at last. "Oh no," said Mabel; "I got that out of a book. I can tell you lots more fatal love-stories any time you like."

The French governess gave a little jump, as though she had suddenly remembered something.

"It is nearly dinner-time," she said. "Your friend Mabelle, yes will be your convivial, and in her honour we will make a little feast. My beautiful flowers, put them to the water, Kathleen. I run to buy the cakes. Wash the hands, all, and be ready when I return."

Smiling and nodding to the children, she left them, and ran up the stairs.

"Just as if she was young," said Kathleen.

"She is young," said Mabel. "Heaps of ladies have offers of marriage when they're no younger than her. I've seen lots of weddings too, with much older brides. And why didn't you tell me she was so beautiful?"

"Is she?" asked Kathleen.

"Of course she is; and what a darling to think of cakes for me, and calling me a convivial!"

"Look here," said Gerald, "I call this jolly decent of her. You know, governesses never have more than the meanest pittance, just enough to sustain life, and here she is spending her little all on us. Supposing we just don't go out today, but play with her instead. I expect she's most awfully bored really."

"Would she really like it?" Kathleen wondered. "Aunt Emily says grown-ups never really like playing. They do it to please us."

"They little know," Gerald answered, "how often we do it to please them."

"We've got to do that dressing-up with the Princess clothes anyhow we said we would," said Kathleen. "Let's treat her to that."

"Rather near tea-time," urged Jimmy, "so that there'll be a fortunate interruption and the play won't go on for ever."

"I suppose all the things are safe?" Mabel asked.

"Quite. I told you where I put them. Come on, Jimmy; let's help lay the table. We'll get Eliza to put out the best china."

They went.

"It was lucky," said Gerald, struck by a sudden thought, "that the burglars didn't go for the diamonds in the treasure-chamber."

"They couldn't," said Mabel almost in a whisper; "they didn't know about them. I don't believe anybody knows about them, except me and you, and you're sworn to secrecy. " This, you will remember, had been done almost at the beginning. "I know aunt doesn't know. I just found out the spring by accident. Lord Yalding's kept the secret well."

"I wish I'd got a secret like that to keep," said Gerald.

"If the burglars do know," said Mabel, "it'll all come out at the trial. Lawyers make you tell everything you know at trials, and a lot of lies besides."

"There won't be any trial," said Gerald, kicking the leg of the piano thoughtfully.

"No trial?"

"It said in the paper," Gerald went on slowly, "'The miscreants must have received warning from a confederate, for the admirable preparations to arrest them as they returned for their ill-gotten plunder were unavailing. But the police have a clue.'"

"What a pity!" said Mabel.

"You needn't worry, they haven't got any old clue," said Gerald, still attentive to the piano leg.

"I didn't mean the clue; I meant the confederate."

"It's a pity you think he's a pity, because he was me," said Gerald, standing up and leaving the piano leg alone. He looked straight before him, as the boy on the burning deck may have looked.

"I couldn't help it," he said. "I know you'll think I'm a criminal, but I couldn't do it. I don't know how detectives can. I went over a prison once, with father; and after I'd given the tip to Johnson I remembered that, and I just couldn't. I know I'm a beast, and not worthy to be a British citizen."

"I think it was rather nice of you," said Mabel kindly. "How did you warn them?"

"I just shoved a paper under the man's door — the one that I knew where he lived — to tell him to lie low."

"Oh! do tell me what did you put on it exactly?" Mabel warmed to this new interest.

"It said: 'The police know all except your names. Be virtuous and you are safe. But if there's any more burgling I shall split and you may rely on that from a friend.' I know it was wrong, but I couldn't help it. Don't tell the others. They wouldn't understand why I did it. I don't understand it myself."

"I do," said Mabel: "it's because you've got a kind and noble heart."

"Kind fiddlestick, my good child!" said Gerald, suddenly losing the burning boy expression and becoming in a flash entirely himself. "Cut along and wash your hands; you're as black as ink."

"So are you," said Mabel, "and I'm not. It's dye with me. Auntie was dyeing a blouse this morning. It told you how in Home Drivel and she's as black as ink too, and the blouse is all streaky. Pity the ring won't make just parts of you invisible — the dirt, for instance."

"Perhaps," Gerald said unexpectedly, "it won't make even all of you invisible again."

"Why not? You haven't been doing anything to it have you?" Mabel sharply asked.

"No; but didn't you notice you were invisible twenty-one hours; I was fourteen hours invisible, and Eliza only seven that's seven less each time. And now we've come to —"

"How frightfully good you are at sums!" said Mabel, awe-struck.

"You see, it's got seven hours less each time, and seven from seven is nought; it's got to be something different this time. And then afterwards it can't be minus seven, because I don't see how, unless it made you more visible — thicker, you know."

"Don't!" said Mabel; "you make my head go round."

"And there's another odd thing," Gerald went on; "when you're invisible your relations don't love you. Look at your aunt, and Cathy never turning a hair at me going burgling. We haven't got to the bottom of that ring yet. Crikey! Here's Mademoiselle with the cakes. Run, bold bandits, wash for your lives!"

They ran.

It was not cakes only; it was plums and grapes and jam tarts and soda-water and raspberry vinegar, and chocolates in pretty boxes and pure, thick, rich cream in brown jugs, also a big bunch of roses. Mademoiselle was strangely merry for a governess. She served out the cakes and tarts with a liberal hand, made wreaths of the flowers for all their heads — she was not eating much herself — drank the health of Mabel, as the guest of the day, in the beautiful pink drink that comes from mixing raspberry vinegar and soda-water, and actually persuaded Jimmy to wear his wreath, on the ground that the Greek gods as well as the goddesses always wore wreaths at a feast.

There never was such a feast provided by any French governess since French governesses began. There were jokes and stories and laughter. Jimmy showed all those tricks with forks and corks and matches and apples which are so deservedly popular. Mademoiselle told them stories of her own schooldays when she was "a quite little girl with two tight tresses so", and when they could not understand the tresses, called for paper and pencil and drew the loveliest little picture of herself when she was a child with two short fat pig-tails sticking out from her head like knitting-needles from a ball of dark worsted. Then she drew pictures of everything they asked for, till Mabel pulled Gerald's jacket and whispered: "The acting!"

"Draw us the front of a theatre," said Gerald tactfully "a French theatre."

"They are the same thing as the English theatres," Mademoiselle told him.

"Do you like acting — the theatre, I mean?"

"But yes I love it."

"All right," said Gerald briefly. "We'll act a play for you now this afternoon if you like."

"Eliza will be washing up," Cathy whispered, "and she was promised to see it."

"Or this evening," said Gerald "and please, Mademoiselle, may Eliza come in and look on?"

"But certainly," said Mademoiselle; "amuse yourselves well, my children."

"But it's you," said Mabel suddenly, "that we want to amuse. Because we love you very much don't we, all of you?"

"Yes," the chorus came unhesitatingly. Though the others would never have thought of saying such a thing on their own account. Yet, as Mabel said it, they found to their surprise that it was true.

"Tiens!" said Mademoiselle, "you love the old French governess? Impossible," and she spoke rather indistinctly.

"You're not old," said Mabel; "at least not so very, " she added brightly, "and you're as lovely as a Princess."

"Go then, flatteress!" said Mademoiselle, laughing; and Mabel went. The others were already half-way up the stairs.

Mademoiselle sat in the drawing-room as usual, and it was a good thing that she was not engaged in serious study, for it seemed that the door opened and shut almost ceaselessly all throughout the afternoon. Might they have the embroidered antimacassars and the sofa cushions? Might they have the clothes-line out of the washhouse? Eliza said they mightn't, but might they? Might they have the sheepskin hearth-rugs? Might they have tea in the garden, because they had almost got the stage ready in the dining-room, and Eliza wanted to set tea? Could Mademoiselle lend them any coloured clothes scarves or dressing-gowns, or anything bright? Yes, Mademoiselle could, and did — silk things, surprisingly lovely for a governess to have.

Had Mademoiselle any rouge? They had always heard that French ladies... No. Mademoiselle hadn't and to judge by the colour of her face, Mademoiselle didn't need it. Did Mademoiselle think the chemist sold rouge or had she any false hair to spare? At this challenge Mademoiselle's pale fingers pulled out a dozen hairpins, and down came the loveliest blue-black hair, hanging to her knees in straight, heavy lines.

"No, you terrible infants," she cried. "I have not the false hair, nor the rouge. And my teeth you want them also, without doubt?"

She showed them in a laugh.

"I said you were a Princess," said Mabel, "and now I know. You're Rapunzel. Do always wear your hair like that! May we have the peacock fans, please, off the mantelpiece, and the things that loop back the curtains, and all the handkerchiefs you've got?"

Mademoiselle denied them nothing. They had the fans and the handkerchiefs and some large sheets of expensive drawing-paper out of the school cupboard, and Mademoiselle's best sable paint-brush and her paint-box.

"Who would have thought," murmured Gerald, pensively sucking the brush and gazing at the paper mask he had just painted, "that she was such a brick in disguise? I wonder why crimson lake always tastes just like Liebig's Extract."

Everything was pleasant that day somehow. There are some days like that, you know, when everything goes well from the very beginning; all the things you want are in their places, nobody misunderstands you, and all that you do turns out admirably. How different from those other days which we all know too well, when your shoe-lace breaks, your comb is mislaid, your brush spins on its back on the floor and lands under the bed where you can't get at it, you drop the soap, your buttons come off, an eyelash gets into your eye, you have used your last clean handkerchief, your collar is frayed at the edge and cuts your neck, and at the very last moment your suspender breaks, and there is no string. On such a day as this you are naturally late for breakfast, and everyone thinks you did it on purpose. And the day goes on and on, getting worse and worse, you mislay your exercise-book, you drop your arithmetic in the mud, your pencil breaks, and when you open your knife to sharpen the pencil you split your nail. On such a day you jam your thumb in doors, and muddle the messages you are sent on by grown-ups. You upset your tea, and your bread-and-butter won't hold together for a moment. And when at last you get to bed — usually in disgrace — it is no comfort at all to you to know that not a single bit of it is your own fault.

This day was not one of those days, as you will have noticed. Even the tea in the garden — there was a bricked bit by a rockery that made a steady floor for the tea-table — was most delightful, though the thoughts of four out of the five were busy with the coming play, and the fifth had thoughts of her own that had had nothing to do with tea or acting.

Then there was an interval of slamming doors, interesting silences, feet that flew up and down stairs.

It was still good daylight when the dinner-bell rang. The signal had been agreed upon at tea-time, and carefully explained to Eliza. Mademoiselle laid down her book and passed out of the sunset-yellowed hail into the faint yellow gaslight of the dining-room. The giggling Eliza held the door open before her, and followed her in. The shutters had been closed — streaks of daylight showed above and below them. The green-and-black tablecloths of the school dining-tables were supported on the clothes-line from the backyard. The line sagged in a graceful curve, but it answered its purpose of supporting the curtains which concealed that part of the room which was the stage.

Rows of chairs had been placed across the other end of the room all the chairs in the house, as it seemed and Mademoiselle started violently when she saw that fully half a dozen of these chairs were occupied. And by the queerest people, too an old woman with a poke bonnet tied under her chin with a red handkerchief, a lady in a large straw hat wreathed in flowers and the oddest hands that stuck out over the chair in front of her, several men with strange, clumsy figures, and all with hats on.

"But," whispered Mademoiselle, through the chinks of the tablecloths, "you have then invited other friends? You should have asked me, my children."

Laughter and something like a "hurrah" answered her from behind the folds of the curtaining tablecloths.

"All right, Mademoiselle Rapunzel," cried Mabel; "turn the gas up. It's only part of the entertainment."

Eliza, still giggling, pushed through the lines of chairs, knocking off the hat of one of the visitors as she did so, and turned up the three incandescent burners.

Mademoiselle looked at the figure seated nearest to her, stooped to look more closely, half laughed, quite screamed, and sat down suddenly.

"Oh!" she cried, "they are not alive!"

Eliza, with a much louder scream, had found out the same thing and announced it differently. "They ain't got no insides," said she. The seven members of the audience seated among the wilderness of chairs had, indeed, no insides to speak of. Their bodies were bolsters and rolled-up blankets, their spines were broom-handles, and their arm and leg bones were hockey sticks and umbrellas. Their shoulders were the wooden crosspieces that Mademoiselle used for keeping her jackets in shape; their hands were gloves stuffed out with handkerchiefs; and their faces were the paper masks painted in the afternoon by the untutored brush of Gerald, tied on to the round heads made of the ends of stuffed bolster-cases. The faces were really rather dreadful. Gerald had done his best, but even after his best had been done you would hardly have known they were faces, some of them, if they hadn't been in the positions which faces usually occupy, between the collar and the hat. Their eyebrows were furious with lamp-black frowns their eyes the size, and almost the shape, of five-shilling pieces, and on their lips and cheeks had been spent much crimson lake and nearly the whole of a half-pan of vermilion.

"You have made yourself an auditors, yes? Bravo!" cried Mademoiselle, recovering herself and beginning to clap. And to the sound of that clapping the curtain went up or, rather, apart. A voice said, in a breathless, choked way, "Beauty and the Beast," and the stage was revealed.

It was a real stage too the dining-tables pushed close together and covered with pink-and-white counterpanes. It was a little unsteady and creaky to walk on, but very imposing to look at. The scene was simple, but convincing. A big sheet of cardboard, bent square, with slits cut in it and a candle behind, represented, quite transparently, the domestic hearth; a round hat-tin of Eliza's, supported on a stool with a night-light under it, could not have been mistaken, save by wilful malice, for anything but a copper. A waste-paper basket with two or three school dusters and an overcoat in it, and a pair of blue pyjamas over the back of a chair, put the finishing touch to the scene. It did not need the announcement from the wings, "The laundry at Beauty's home." It was so plainly a laundry and nothing else.

In the wings: "They look just like a real audience, don't they?" whispered Mabel. "Go on, Jimmy don't forget the Merchant has to be pompous and use long words."

Jimmy, enlarged by pillows under Gerald's best overcoat which had been intentionally bought with a view to his probable growth during the two years which it was intended to last him, a Turkish towel turban on his head and an open umbrella over it, opened the first act in a simple and swift soliloquy:

"I am the most unlucky merchant that ever was. I was once the richest merchant in Bagdad, but I lost all my ships, and now I live in a poor house that is all to bits; you can see how the rain comes through the roof, and my daughters take in washing. And,"

The pause might have seemed long, but Gerald rustled in, elegant in Mademoiselle's pink dressing-gown and the character of the eldest daughter.

"A nice drying day," he minced. "Pa dear, put the umbrella the other way up. It'll save us going out in the rain to fetch water. Come on, sisters, dear father's got us a new wash-tub. Here's luxury!"

Round the umbrella, now held the wrong way up, the three sisters knelt and washed imaginary linen. Kathleen wore a violet skirt of Eliza's, a blue blouse of her own, and a cap of knotted handkerchiefs. A white nightdress girt with a white apron and two red carnations in Mabel's black hair left no doubt as to which of the three was Beauty.

The scene went very well. The final dance with waving towels was all that there is of charming, Mademoiselle said; and Eliza was so much amused that, as she said, she got quite a nasty stitch along of laughing so hearty.

You know pretty well what Beauty and the Beast would be like acted by four children who had spent the afternoon in arranging their costumes and so had left no time for rehearsing what they had to say. Yet it delighted them, and it charmed their audience. And what more can any play do, even Shakespeare's? Mabel, in her Princess clothes, was a resplendent Beauty; and Gerald a Beast who wore the drawing-room hearthrugs with an air of indescribable distinction. If Jimmy was not a talkative merchant, he made it up with a stoutness practically unlimited, and Kathleen surprised and delighted even herself by the quickness with which she changed from one to the other of the minor characters fairies, servants, and messengers. It was at the end of the second act that Mabel, whose costume, having reached the height of elegance, could not be bettered and therefore did not need to be changed, said to Gerald, sweltering under the weighty magnificence of his beast-skin:

"I say, you might let us have the ring back."

"I'm going to," said Gerald, who had quite forgotten it. "I'll give it you in the next scene. Only don't lose it, or go putting it on. You might go out all together and never be seen again, or you might get seven times as visible as anyone else, so that all the rest of us would look like shadows beside you, you'd be so thick, or ,"

"Ready!" said Kathleen, bustling in, once more a wicked sister.

Gerald managed to get his hand into his pocket under his hearthrug, and when he rolled his eyes in agonies of sentiment, and said, "Farewell, dear Beauty! Return quickly, for if you remain long absent from your faithful beast he will assuredly perish," he pressed a ring into her hand and added: "This is a magic ring that will give you anything you wish. When you desire to return to your own disinterested beast, put on the ring and utter your wish. Instantly you will be by my side."

Beauty-Mabel took the ring, and it was the ring.

The curtains closed to warm applause from two pairs of hands.

The next scene went splendidly. The sisters were almost too natural in their disagreeableness, and Beauty's annoyance when they splashed her Princess's dress with real soap and water was considered a miracle of good acting. Even the merchant rose to something more than mere pillows, and the curtain fell on his pathetic assurance that in the absence of his dear Beauty he was wasting away to a shadow. And again two pairs of hands applauded.

"Here, Mabel, catch hold," Gerald appealed from under the weight of a towel-horse, the tea-urn, the tea-tray, and the green baize apron of the boot boy, which together with four red geraniums from the landing, the pampas-grass from the drawing-room fireplace, and the india-rubber plants from the drawing-room window were to represent the fountains and garden of the last act. The applause had died away.

"I wish," said Mabel, taking on herself the weight of the tea-urn, "I wish those creatures we made were alive. We should get something like applause then."

"I'm jolly glad they aren't, said Gerald, arranging the baize and the towel-horse. "Brutes! It makes me feel quite silly when I catch their paper eyes."

The curtains were drawn back. There lay the hearthrug-coated beast, in flat abandonment among the tropic beauties of the garden, the pampas-grass shrubbery, the india-rubber plant bushes, the geranium-trees and the urn fountain. Beauty was ready to make her great entry in all the thrilling splendour of despair. And then suddenly it all happened.

Mademoiselle began it: she applauded the garden scene with hurried little clappings of her quick French hands. Eliza's fat red palms followed heavily, and then someone else was clapping, six or seven people, and their clapping made a dull padded sound. Nine faces instead of two were turned towards the stage, and seven out of the nine were painted, pointed paper faces. And every hand and every face was alive. The applause grew louder as Mabel glided forward, and as she paused and looked at the audience her unstudied pose of horror and amazement drew forth applause louder still; but it was not loud enough to drown the shrieks of Mademoiselle and Eliza as they rushed from the room, knocking chairs over and crushing each other in the doorway. Two distant doors banged, Mademoiselle's door and Eliza's door.

"Curtain! curtain! quick!" cried Beauty-Mabel, in a voice that wasn't Mabel's or the Beauty's. "Jerry those things have come alive. Oh, whatever shall we do?"

Gerald in his hearthrugs leaped to his feet. Again that flat padded applause marked the swish of cloths on clothes-line as Jimmy and Kathleen drew the curtains.

"What's up?" they asked as they drew.

"You've done it this time!" said Gerald to the pink, perspiring Mabel. "Oh, bother these strings!"

"Can't you burst them? I've done it?" retorted Mabel. "I like that!"

"More than I do," said Gerald.

"Oh, it's all right," said Mabel. "Come on. We must go and pull the things to pieces then they can't go on being alive."

"It's your fault, anyhow," said Gerald with every possible absence of gallantry. "Don't you see? It's turned into a wishing ring. I knew something different was going to happen. Get my knife out of my pocket this string's in a knot. Jimmy, Cathy, those Ugly-Wuglies have come alive because Mabel wished it. Cut out and pull them to pieces."

Jimmy and Cathy peeped through the curtain and recoiled with white faces and staring eyes. "Not me!" was the brief rejoinder of Jimmy. Cathy said, "Not much!" And she meant it, anyone could see that.

And now, as Gerald, almost free of the hearthrugs, broke his thumb-nail on the stiffest blade of his knife, a thick rustling and a sharp, heavy stumping sounded beyond the curtain.

"They're going out!" screamed Kathleen "walking out on their umbrella and broomstick legs. You can't stop them, Jerry, they re too awful!"

"Everybody in the town'll be insane by tomorrow night if we don't stop them," cried Gerald. "Here, give me the ring I'll unwish them."

He caught the ring from the unresisting Mabel, cried, "I wish the Uglies weren't alive," and tore through the door. He saw, in fancy, Mabel's wish undone, and the empty hall strewed with limp bolsters, hats, umbrellas, coats and gloves, prone abject properties from which the brief life had gone out for ever. But the hall was crowded with live things, strange things all horribly short as broom sticks and umbrellas are short. A limp hand gesticulated. A pointed white face with red cheeks looked up at him, and wide red lips said something, he could not tell what. The voice reminded him of the old beggar down by the bridge who had no roof to his mouth. These creatures had no roofs to their mouths, of course they had no "Aa oo re o me me oo a oo ho el?" said the voice again. And it had said it four times before Gerald could collect himself sufficiently to understand that this horror alive, and most likely quite uncontrollable was saying, with a dreadful calm, polite persistence: "Can you recommend me to a good hotel?"

"Can you recommend me to a good hotel?" The speaker had no inside to his head. Gerald had the best of reasons for knowing it. The speaker's coat had no shoulders inside it only the cross-bar that a jacket is slung on by careful ladies. The hand raised in interrogation was not a hand at all; it was a glove lumpily stuffed with pocket-handkerchiefs; and the arm attached to it was only Kathleen's school umbrella. Yet the whole thing was alive, and was asking a definite, and for anybody else, anybody who really was a body, a reasonable question.

With a sensation of inward sinking, Gerald realized that now or never was the time for him to rise to the occasion. And at the thought he inwardly sank more deeply than before. It seemed impossible to rise in the very smallest degree.

"I beg your pardon" was absolutely the best he could do; and the painted, pointed paper face turned to him once more, and once more said: "Aa oo re o me me oo a oo ho el?"

"You want a hotel?" Gerald repeated stupidly, "a good hotel?"

"A oo ho el," reiterated the painted lips.

"I'm awfully sorry," Gerald went on one can always be polite, of course, whatever happens, and politeness came natural to him "but all our hotels shut so early about eight, I think."

"Och em er," said the Ugly-Wugly. Gerald even now does not understand how that practical joke hastily wrought of hat, overcoat, paper face and limp hands could have managed, by just being alive, to become perfectly respectable, apparently about fifty years old, and obviously well known and respected in his own suburb the kind of man who travels first class and smokes expensive cigars. Gerald knew this time, without need of repetition, that the Ugly-Wugly had said: "Knock 'em up."

"You can't," Gerald explained; "they re all stone deaf every single person who keeps a hotel in this town. It's," he wildly plunged "it's a County Council law. Only deaf people are allowed to keep hotels. It's because of the hops in the beer," he found himself adding; "you know, hops are so good for ear-ache."

"I o wy ollo oo," said the respectable Ugly-Wugly; and Gerald was not surprised to find that the thing did "not quite follow him."

"It is a little difficult at first," he said. The other Ugly-Wuglies were crowding round. The lady in the poke bonnet said (Gerald found he was getting quite clever at understanding the conversation of those who had no roofs to their mouths):

"If not a hotel, a lodging."

"My lodging is on the cold ground," sang itself unbidden and unavailing in Gerald's ear. Yet stay, was it unavailing?

"I do know a lodging," he said slowly, "but," The tallest of the Ugly-Wuglies pushed forward. He was dressed in the old brown overcoat and top-hat which always hung on the school hat-stand to discourage possible burglars by deluding them into the idea that there was a gentleman-of-the-house, and that he was at home. He had an air at once more sporting and less reserved than that of the first speaker, and anyone could see that he was not quite a gentleman.

"Wa I wo oo oh," he began, but the lady Ugly-Wugly in the flower-wreathed hat interrupted him. She spoke more distinctly than the others, owing, as Gerald found afterwards, to the fact that her mouth had been drawn open, and the flap cut from the aperture had been folded back so that she really had something like a roof to her mouth, though it was only a paper one.

"What I want to know," Gerald understood her to say, "is where are the carriages we ordered?"

"I don't know," said Gerald, "but I'll find out. But we ought to be moving," he added; "you see, the performance is over, and they want to shut up the house and put the lights out. Let's be moving."

"Eh ech e oo-ig," repeated the respectable Ugly-Wugly, and stepped towards the front door.

"Oo urn oo," said the flower-wreathed one; and Gerald assures me that her vermilion lips stretched in a smile.

"I shall be delighted," said Gerald with earnest courtesy, "to do anything, of course. Things do happen so awkwardly when you least expect it. I could go with you, and get you a lodging, if you'd only wait a few moments in the in the yard. It's quite a superior sort of yard, he went on, as a wave of surprised disdain passed over their white paper faces not a common yard, you know; the pump," he added madly, "has just been painted green all over, and the dustbin is enamelled iron."

The Ugly-Wuglies turned to each other in consultation, and Gerald gathered that the greenness of the pump and the enamelled character of the dustbin made, in their opinion, all the difference.

"I'm awfully sorry," he urged eagerly, "to have to ask you to wait, but you see I've got an uncle who's quite mad, and I have to give him his gruel at half-past nine. He won't feed out of any hand but mine." Gerald did not mind what he said. The only people one is allowed to tell lies to are the Ugly-Wuglies; they are all clothes and have no insides, because they are not human beings, but only a sort of very real visions, and therefore cannot be really deceived, though they may seem to be.

Through the back door that has the blue, yellow, red, and green glass in it, down the iron steps into the yard, Gerald led the way, and the Ugly-Wuglies trooped after him. Some of them had boots, but the ones whose feet were only broomsticks or umbrellas found the open-work iron stairs very awkward.

"If you wouldn't mind," said Gerald, "just waiting under the balcony? My uncle is so very mad. If he were to see see any strangers I mean, even aristocratic ones I couldn't answer for the consequences."

"Perhaps, said the flower-hatted lady nervously, "it would be better for us to try and find a lodging ourselves?"

"I wouldn't advise you to," said Gerald as grimly as he knew how; "the police here arrest all strangers. It's the new law the Liberals have just made," he added convincingly, "and you'd get the sort of lodging you wouldn't care for. I couldn't bear to think of you in a prison dungeon," he added tenderly.

"I ah wi oo er papers," said the respectable Ugly-Wugly, and added something that sounded like "disgraceful state of things."

However, they ranged themselves under the iron balcony. Gerald gave one last look at them and wondered, in his secret heart, why he was not frightened, though in his outside mind he was congratulating himself on his bravery. For the things did look rather horrid. In that light it was hard to believe that they were really only clothes and pillows and sticks with no insides. As he went up the steps he heard them talking among themselves in that strange language of theirs, all oo's and ah's; and he thought he distinguished the voice of the respectable Ugly-Wugly saying, "Most gentlemanly lad," and the wreathed-hatted lady answering warmly: "Yes, indeed."

The coloured-glass door closed behind him. Behind him was the yard, peopled by seven impossible creatures. Before him lay the silent house, peopled, as he knew very well, by five human beings as frightened as human beings could be. You think, perhaps, that Ugly-Wuglies are nothing to be frightened of. That's only because you have never seen one come alive. You must make one — any old suit of your father's, and a hat that he isn't wearing, a bolster or two, a painted paper face, a few sticks and a pair of boots will do the trick; get your father to lend you a wishing ring, give it back to him when it has done its work, and see how you feel then.

Of course the reason why Gerald was not afraid was that he had the ring; and, as you have seen, the wearer of that is not frightened by anything unless he touches that thing. But Gerald knew well enough how the others must be feeling. That was why he stopped for a moment in the hall to try and imagine what would have been most soothing to him if he had been as terrified as he knew they were.

"Cathy! I say! What ho, Jimmy! Mabel ahoy!" he cried in a loud, cheerful voice that sounded very unreal to himself.

The dining-room door opened a cautious inch.

"I say such larks!" Gerald went on, shoving gently at the door with his shoulder. "Look out! what are you keeping the door shut for?"

"Are you alone?" asked Kathleen in hushed, breathless tones.

"Yes, of course. Don't be a duffer!"

The door opened, revealing three scared faces and the disarranged chairs where that odd audience had sat.

"Where are they? Have you unwished them? We heard them talking. Horrible!"

"They're in the yard," said Gerald with the best imitation of joyous excitement that he could manage. "It is such fun! They're just like real people, quite kind and jolly. It's the most ripping lark. Don't let on to Mademoiselle and Eliza. I'll square them. Then Kathleen and Jimmy must go to bed, and I'll see Mabel home, and as soon as we get outside I must find some sort of lodging for the Ugly-Wuglies — they are such fun though. I do wish you could all go with me."

"Fun?" echoed Kathleen dismally and doubting.

"Perfectly killing," Gerald asserted resolutely. "Now, you just listen to what I say to Mademoiselle and Eliza, and back me up for all you're worth.

"But," said Mabel, "you can't mean that you're going to leave me alone directly we get out, and go off with those horrible creatures. They look like fiends."

"You wait till you've seen them close," Gerald advised. "Why, they're just ordinary — the first thing one of them did was to ask me to recommend it to a good hotel! I couldn't understand it at first, because it has no roof to its mouth, of course."

It was a mistake to say that, Gerald knew it at once.

Mabel and Kathleen were holding hands in a way that plainly showed how a few moments ago they had been clinging to each other in an agony of terror. Now they clung again. And Jimmy, who was sitting on the edge of what had been the stage, kicking his boots against the pink counterpane, shuddered visibly.

"It doesn't matter," Gerald explained "about the roofs, I mean; you soon get to understand. I heard them say I was a gentlemanly lad as I was coming away. They wouldn't have cared to notice a little thing like that if they'd been fiends, you know."

"It doesn't matter how gentlemanly they think you; if you don't see me home you aren't, that's all. Are you going to?" Mabel demanded.

"Of course I am. We shall have no end of a lark. Now for Mademoiselle."

He had put on his coat as he spoke and now ran up the stairs. The others, herding in the hall, could hear his light-hearted there's-nothing-unusual-the-matter-whatever-did-you-bolt-like-that-for knock at Mademoiselle's door, the reassuring "It's only me Gerald, you know," the pause, the opening of the door, and the low-voiced parley that followed; then Mademoiselle and Gerald at Eliza's door, voices of reassurance; Eliza's terror, bluntly voluble, tactfully soothed.

"Wonder what lies he's telling them," Jimmy grumbled.

"Oh! not lies," said Mabel; "he's only telling them as much of the truth as it's good for them to know."

"If you'd been a man," said Jimmy witheringly, "you'd have been a beastly Jesuit, and hid up chimneys."

"If I were only just a boy," Mabel retorted, "I shouldn't be scared out of my life by a pack of old coats."

"I'm so sorry you were frightened," Gerald's honeyed tones floated down the staircase; "we didn't think about you being frightened. And it was a good trick, wasn't it?"

"There!" whispered Jimmy, "he's been telling her it was a trick of ours."

"Well, so it was," said Mabel stoutly.

"It was indeed a wonderful trick," said Mademoiselle; "and how did you move the mannikins?"

"Oh, we've often done it with strings, you know," Gerald explained.

"That's true, too," Kathleen whispered.

"Let us see you do once again this trick so remarkable," said Mademoiselle, arriving at the bottom-stair mat.

"Oh, I've cleared them all out," said Gerald. ("So he has, from Kathleen aside to Jimmy.) "We were so sorry you were startled; we thought you wouldn't like to see them again."

"Then," said Mademoiselle brightly, as she peeped into the untidy dining-room and saw that the figures had indeed vanished, "if we supped and discoursed of your beautiful piece of theatre?"

Gerald explained fully how much his brother and sister would enjoy this. As for him Mademoiselle would see that it was his duty to escort Mabel home, and kind as it was of Mademoiselle to ask her to stay the night, it could not be, on account of the frenzied and anxious affection of Mabel's aunt. And it was useless to suggest that Eliza should see Mabel home, because Eliza was nervous at night unless accompanied by her gentleman friend.

So Mabel was hatted with her own hat and cloaked with a cloak that was not hers; and she and Gerald went out by the front door, amid kind last words and appointments for the morrow.

The moment that front door was shut Gerald caught Mabel by the arm and led her briskly to the corner of the side street which led to the yard. Just round the corner he stopped.

"Now," he said, "what I want to know is are you an idiot or aren't you?"

"Idiot yourself!" said Mabel, but mechanically, for she saw that he was in earnest.

"Because I'm not frightened of the Ugly-Wuglies. They're as harmless as tame rabbits. But an idiot might be frightened, and give the whole show away. If you're an idiot, say so, and I'll go back and tell them you're afraid to walk home, and that I'll go and let your aunt know you're stopping."

"I'm not an idiot," said Mabel; "and," she added, glaring round her with the wild gaze of the truly terror-stricken, "I'm not afraid of anything."

"I'm going to let you share my difficulties and dangers," said Gerald; "at least, I'm inclined to let you. I wouldn't do as much for my own brother, I can tell you. And if you queer my pitch I'll never speak to you again or let the others either."

"You're a beast, that's what you are! I don't need to be threatened to make me brave. I am."

"Mabel," said Gerald, in low, thrilling tones, for he saw that the time had come to sound another note, "I know you're brave. I believe in you, That's why I've arranged it like this. I'm certain you've got the heart of a lion under that black-and-white exterior. Can I trust you? To the death?"

Mabel felt that to say anything but "Yes" was to throw away a priceless reputation for courage. So "Yes" was what she said.

"Then wait here. You're close to the lamp. And when you see me coming with them, remember they're as harmless as serpents, I mean doves. Talk to them just like you would to anyone else. See?"

He turned to leave her, but stopped at her natural question:

"What hotel did you say you were going to take them to?"

"Oh, Jimminy!" the harassed Gerald caught at his hair with both hands. "There! you see, Mabel, you're a help already." he had, even at that moment, some tact left. "I clean forgot! I meant to ask you — isn't there any lodge or anything in the

Castle grounds where I could put them for the night? The charm will break, you know, some time, like being invisible did, and they'll just be a pack of coats and things that we can easily carry home any day. Is there a lodge or anything?"

"There's a secret passage," Mabel began but at the moment the yard-door opened and an Ugly-Wugly put out its head and looked anxiously down the street.

"Righto!" Gerald ran to meet it. It was all Mabel could do not to run in an opposite direction with an opposite motive. It was all she could do, but she did it, and was proud of herself as long as ever she remembered that night.

And now, with all the silent precaution necessitated by the near presence of an extremely insane uncle, the Ugly-Wuglies, a grisly band, trooped out of the yard door.

"Walk on your toes, dear," the bonneted Ugly-Wugly whispered to the one with a wreath; and even at that thrilling crisis Gerald wondered how she could, since the toes of one foot were but the end of a golf club and of the other the end of a hockey-stick.

Mabel felt that there was no shame in retreating to the lamp-post at the street corner, but, once there, she made herself halt and no one but Mabel will ever know how much making that took. Think of it — to stand there, firm and quiet, and wait for those hollow, unbelievable things to come up to her, clattering on the pavement with their stumpy feet or borne along noiselessly, as in the case of the flower-hatted lady, by a skirt that touched the ground, and had, Mabel knew very well, nothing at all inside it.

She stood very still; the insides of her hands grew cold and damp, but still she stood, saying over and over again: "They're not true — they can't be true. It's only a dream they aren't really true. They can't be." And then Gerald was there, and all the Ugly-Wuglies crowding round, and Gerald saying: "This is one of our friends — Mabel, the Princess in the play, you know. Be a man!" he added in a whisper for her ear alone.

Mabel, all her nerves stretched tight as banjo strings, had an awful instant of not knowing whether she would be able to be a man or whether she would be merely a shrieking and running little mad girl. For the respectable Ugly-Wugly shook her limply by the hand.

("He can't be true," she told herself), and the rose-wreathed one took her arm with a soft-padded glove at the end of an umbrella arm, and said: "You dear, clever little thing! Do walk with me!" in a gushing, girlish way, and in speech almost wholly lacking in consonants.

Then they all walked up the High Street as if, as Gerald said, they were anybody else.

It was a strange procession, but Liddlesby goes early to bed, and the Liddlesby police, in common with those of most other places, wear boots that one can hear a mile off. If such boots had been heard, Gerald would have had time to turn back and head them off. He felt now that he could not resist a flush of pride in Mabel's courage as he heard her polite rejoinders to the still more polite remarks of the amiable Ugly-Wuglies. He did not know how near she was to the scream that would throw away the whole thing and bring the police and the residents out to the ruin of everybody.

They met no one, except one man, who murmured, "Guy Fawkes, swelp me!" and crossed the road hurriedly; and when, next day, he told what he had seen, his wife disbelieved him, and also said it was a judgement on him, which was unreasonable.

Mabel felt as though she were taking part in a very completely arranged nightmare, but Gerald was in it too — Gerald, who had asked if she was an idiot. Well, she wasn't. But she soon would be, she felt. Yet she went on answering the courteous vowel-talk of these impossible people. She had often heard her aunt speak of impossible people. Well, now she knew what they were like.

Summer twilight had melted into summer moonlight. The shadows of the Ugly-Wuglies on the white road were much more horrible than their more solid selves. Mabel wished it had been a dark night, and then corrected the wish with a hasty shudder.

Gerald, submitting to a searching interrogatory from the tall-hatted Ugly-Wugly as to his schools, his sports, pastimes, and ambitions, wondered how long the spell would last. The ring seemed to work in sevens. Would these things have seven hours'life or fourteen or twenty-one?"His mind lost itself in the intricacies of the seven-times table (a teaser at the best of times) and only found itself with a shock when the procession found itself at the gates of the Castle grounds.

Locked of course.

"You see," he explained, as the Ugly-Wuglies vainly shook the iron gates with incredible hands; "it's so very late. There is another way. But you have to climb through a hole."

"The ladies," the respectable Ugly-Wugly began objecting; but the ladies with one voice affirmed that they loved adventures. "So frightfully thrilling," added the one who wore roses.

So they went round by the road, and coming to the hole it was a little difficult to find in the moonlight, which always disguises the most familiar things Gerald went first with the bicycle lantern which he had snatched as his pilgrims came out of the yard; the shrinking Mabel followed, and then the Ugly-Wuglies, with hollow rattlings of their wooden limbs against the stone, crept through, and with strange vowel-sounds of general amazement, manly courage, and feminine nervousness, followed the light along the passage through the fern-hung cutting and under the arch.

When they emerged on the moonlit enchantment of the Italian garden a quite intelligible "Oh!" of surprised admiration broke from more than one painted paper lip; and the respectable Ugly-Wugly was understood to say that it must be quite a show-place by George, sir! yes.

Those marble terraces and artfully serpentining gravel walks surely never had echoed to steps so strange. No shadows so wildly unbelievable had, for all its enchantments, ever fallen on those smooth, grey, dewy lawns. Gerald was thinking this, or something like it (what he really thought was, "I bet there never was such ado as this, even here!), when he saw the statue of Hermes leap from its pedestal and run towards him and his company with all the lively curiosity of a street boy eager to be in at a street fight. He saw, too, that he was the only one who perceived that white advancing presence. And he knew that it was the ring that let him see what by others could not be seen. He slipped it from his finger. Yes; Hermes was on his pedestal, still as the snow man you make in the Christmas holidays. He put the ring on again, and there was Hermes, circling round the group and gazing deep in each unconscious Ugly-Wugly face.

"This seems a very superior hotel," the tall-hatted Ugly-Wugly was saying; "the grounds are laid out with what you might call taste."

"We should have to go in by the back door," said Mabel suddenly. "The front door's locked at half-past nine."

A short, stout Ugly-Wugly in a yellow and blue cricket cap, who had hardly spoken, muttered something about an escapade, and about feeling quite young again.

And now they had skirted the marble-edged pool where the goldfish swam and glimmered, and where the great prehistoric beast had come down to bathe and drink. The water flashed white diamonds in the moonlight, and Gerald alone of them all saw that the scaly-plated vast lizard was even now rolling and wallowing there among the lily pads.

They hastened up the steps of the Temple of Flora. The back of it, where no elegant arch opened to the air, was against one of those sheer hills, almost cliffs, that diversified the landscape of that garden. Mabel passed behind the statue of the goddess, fumbled a little, and then Gerald's lantern, flashing like a searchlight, showed a very high and very narrow doorway: the stone that was the door, and that had closed it, revolved slowly under the touch of Mabel's fingers.

"This way," she said, and panted a little. The back of her neck felt cold and goose-fleshy.

"You lead the way, my lad, with the lantern," said the suburban Ugly-Wugly in his bluff, agreeable way.

"I I must stay behind to close the door," said Gerald.

"The Princess can do that. We'll help her," said the wreathed one with effusion; and Gerald thought her horribly officious.

He insisted gently that he would be the one responsible for the safe shutting of that door.

"You wouldn't like me to get into trouble, I'm sure," he urged; and the Ugly-Wuglies, for the last time kind and reasonable, agreed that this, of all things, they would most deplore.

"You take it," Gerald urged, pressing the bicycle lamp on the elderly Ugly-Wugly; "you're the natural leader. Go straight ahead. Are there any steps?" he asked Mabel in a whisper.

"Not for ever so long," she whispered back. "It goes on for ages, and then twists round."

"Whispering," said the smallest Ugly-Wugly suddenly, "ain't manners."

"He hasn't any, anyhow," whispered the lady Ugly-Wugly; "don't mind him — quite a self-made man," and squeezed Mabel's arm with horrible confidential flabbiness.

The respectable Ugly-Wugly leading with the lamp, the others following trustfully, one and all disappeared into that narrow doorway; and Gerald and Mabel standing without, hardly daring to breathe lest a breath should retard the procession, almost sobbed with relief. Prematurely, as it turned out. For suddenly there was a rush and a scuffle inside the passage, and as they strove to close the door the Ugly-Wuglies fiercely pressed to open it again. Whether they saw something in the dark passage that alarmed them, whether they took it into their empty heads that this could not be the back way to any really respectable hotel, or whether a convincing sudden instinct warned them that they were being tricked, Mabel and Gerald never knew. But they knew that the Ugly- Wuglies were no longer friendly and commonplace, that a fierce change had come over them. Cries of "No, No!" "We won't go on!" "Make him lead!" broke the dreamy stillness of the perfect night. There were screams from ladies voices, the hoarse, determined shouts of strong Ugly-Wuglies roused to resistance, and, worse than all, the steady pushing open of that narrow stone door that had almost closed upon the ghastly crew. Through the chink of it they could be seen, a writhing black crowd against the light of the bicycle lamp; a padded hand reached round the door; stick-boned arms stretched out angrily towards the world that that door, if it closed, would shut them off from for ever. And the tone of their consonantless speech was no longer conciliatory and ordinary; it was threatening, full of the menace of unbearable horrors.

The padded hand fell on Gerald's arm, and instantly all the terrors that he had, so far, only known in imagination became real to him, and he saw, in the sort of flash that shows drowning people their past lives, what it was that he had asked of Mabel, and that she had given.

"Push, push for your life!" he cried, and setting his heel against the pedestal of Flora, pushed manfully.

"I can't any more oh, I can't!" moaned Mabel, and tried to use her heel likewise but her legs were too short.

"They mustn't get out, they mustn't!" Gerald panted.

"You'll know it when we do," came from inside the door in tones which fury and mouth-rooflessness would have made unintelligible to any ears but those sharpened by the wild fear of that unspeakable moment.

"What's up, there?" cried suddenly a new voice a voice with all its consonants comforting, clean-cut, and ringing, and abruptly a new shadow fell on the marble floor of Flora's temple.

"Come and help push!" Gerald's voice only just reached the newcomer. "If they get out they'll kill us all."

A strong, velveteen-covered shoulder pushed suddenly between the shoulders of Gerald and Mabel; a stout man's heel sought the aid of the goddess's pedestal; the heavy, narrow door yielded slowly, it closed, its spring clicked, and the furious, surging, threatening mass of Ugly-Wuglies was shut in, and Gerald and Mabel oh, incredible relief! were shut out. Mabel threw herself on the marble floor, sobbing slow, heavy sobs of achievement and exhaustion. If I had been there I should have looked the other way, so as not to see whether Gerald yielded himself to the same abandonment.

The newcomer (he appeared to be a gamekeeper Gerald decided later) looked down on, well, certainly on Mabel, and said:

"Come on, don't be a little duffer." (He may have said, "a couple of little duffers .) "Who is it, and what's it all about?"

"I can't possibly tell you," Gerald panted.

"We shall have to see about that, shan't we," said the newcomer amiably. "Come out into the moonlight and let's review the situation."

Gerald, even in that topsy-turvy state of his world, found time to think that a gamekeeper who used such words as that had most likely a romantic past. But at the same time he saw that such a man would be far less easy to "square" with an unconvincing tale than Eliza, or Johnson, or even Mademoiselle. In fact, he seemed, with the only tale that they had to tell, practically unsquarable.

Gerald got up if he was not up already, or still up and pulled at the limp and now hot hand of the sobbing Mabel; and as he did so the unsquarable one took his hand, and thus led both children out from under the shadow of Flora's dome into the bright white moonlight that carpeted Flora's steps. Here he sat down, a child on each side of him, drew a hand of each through his velveteen arm, pressed them to his velveteen sides in a friendly, reassuring way, and said: "Now then! Go ahead!"

Mabel merely sobbed. We must excuse her. She had been very brave, and I have no doubt that all heroines, from Joan of Arc to Grace Darling, have had their sobbing moments.

But Gerald said: "It's no use. If I made up a story you'd see through it."

"That's a compliment to thy discernment, anyhow," said the stranger. "What price telling me the truth?"

"If we told you the truth," said Gerald, "you wouldn't believe it."

"Try me," said the velveteen one. He was clean-shaven, and had large eyes that sparkled when the moonlight touched them.

"I can't," said Gerald, and it was plain that he spoke the truth. "You'd either think we were mad, and get us shut up, or else... Oh, it's no good. Thank you for helping us, and do let us go home."

"I wonder," said the stranger musingly, "whether you have any imagination."

"Considering that we invented them " Gerald hotly began, and stopped with late prudence.

"If by 'them' you mean the people whom I helped you to imprison in yonder tomb," said the Stranger, loosing Mabel's hand to put his arm round her, "remember that I saw and heard them. And with all respect to your imagination, I doubt whether any invention of yours would be quite so convincing."

Gerald put his elbows on his knees and his chin in his hands.

"Collect yourself," said the one in velveteen; "and while you are collecting, let me just put the thing from my point of view. I think you hardly realize my position. I come down from London to take care of a big estate."

"I thought you were a gamekeeper," put in Gerald.

Mabel put her head on the stranger's shoulder. "Hero in disguise, then, I know," she sniffed.

"Not at all," said he; "bailiff would be nearer the mark. On the very first evening I go out to take the moonlit air, and approaching a white building, hear sounds of an agitated scuffle, accompanied by frenzied appeals for assistance. Carried away by the enthusiasm of the moment, I do assist and shut up goodness knows who behind a stone door. Now, is it unreasonable that I should ask who it is that I've shut up, helped to shut up, I mean, and who it is that I've assisted?"

"It's reasonable enough," Gerald admitted.

"Well then," said the stranger.

"Well then," said Gerald, "the fact is — No," he added after a pause, "the fact is, I simply can't tell you."

"Then I must ask the other side," said Velveteens. "Let me go I'll undo that door and find out for myself."

"Tell him," said Mabel, speaking for the first time. "Never mind if he believes or not. We can't have them let out."

"Very well," said Gerald, "I'll tell him. Now look here, Mr. Bailiff, will you promise us on an English gentleman's word of honour because, of course, I can see you're that, bailiff or not — will you promise that you won't tell any one what we tell you and that you won't have us put in a lunatic asylum, however mad we sound?"

"Yes," said the stranger, "I think I can promise that. But if you've been having a sham fight or anything and shoved the other side into that hole, don't you think you'd better let them out? They'll be most awfully frightened, you know. After all, I suppose they are only children."

"Wait till you hear," Gerald answered. "They're not children — not much! Shall I just tell about them or begin at the beginning?"

"The beginning, of course," said the stranger.

Mabel lifted her head from his velveteen shoulder and said, "Let me begin, then. I found a ring, and I said it would make me invisible. I said it in play. And it did. I was invisible twenty-one hours. Never mind where I got the ring. Now, Gerald, you go on."

Gerald went on; for quite a long time he went on, for the story was a splendid one to tell.

"And so," he ended, "we got them in there; and when seven hours are over, or fourteen, or twenty-one, or something with a seven in it, they'll just be old coats again. They came alive at half-past nine. I think they'll stop being it in seven hours that's half-past four. Now will you let us go home?"

"I'll see you home," said the stranger in a quite new tone of exasperating gentleness. "Come let's be going."

"You don't believe us," said Gerald. "Of course you don t. Nobody could. But I could make you believe if I chose."

All three stood up, and the stranger stared in Gerald's eyes till Gerald answered his thought.

"No, I don't look mad, do I?"

"No, you aren't. But, come, you're an extraordinarily sensible boy; don't you think you may be sickening for a fever or something?"

"And Cathy and Jimmy and Mademoiselle and Eliza, and the man who said 'Guy Fawkes, swelp me!' and you, you saw them move — you heard them call out. Are you sickening for anything?"

"No, or at least not for anything but information. Come, and I'll see you home."

"Mabel lives at the Towers," said Gerald, as the stranger turned into the broad drive that leads to the big gate.

"No relation to Lord Yalding," said Mabel hastily "housekeeper's niece." She was holding on to his hand all the way. At the servants entrance she put up her face to be kissed, and went in.

"Poor little thing!" said the bailiff, as they went down the drive towards the gate.

He went with Gerald to the door of the school.

"Look here," said Gerald at parting. "I know what you're going to do. You're going to try to undo that door."

"Discerning!" said the stranger.

"Well don't. Or, anyway, wait till daylight and let us be there. We can get there by ten."

"All right I'll meet you there by ten," answered the stranger. "By George! you're the rummest kids I ever met."

"We are rum," Gerald owned, "but so would you be if — Goodnight."

As the four children went over the smooth lawn towards Flora's Temple they talked, as they had talked all the morning, about the adventures of last night and of Mabel's bravery. It was not ten, but half-past twelve; for Eliza, backed by Mademoiselle, had insisted on their "clearing up," and clearing up very thoroughly, the "litter" of last night.

"You're a Victoria Cross heroine, dear," said Cathy warmly. "You ought to have a statue put up to you."

"It would come alive if you put it here," said Gerald grimly.

"I shouldn't have been afraid," said Jimmy.

"By daylight," Gerald assured him, "everything looks so jolly different."

"I do hope he'll be there," Mabel said; "he was such a dear, Cathy a perfect bailiff, with the soul of a gentleman."

"He isn't there, though," said Jimmy. "I believe you just dreamed him, like you did the statues coming alive."

They went up the marble steps in the sunshine, and it was difficult to believe that this was the place where only in last night's moonlight fear had laid such cold hands on the hearts of Mabel and Gerald.

"Shall we open the door," suggested Kathleen, "and begin to carry home the coats?"

"Let's listen first," said Gerald; "perhaps they aren't only coats yet."

They laid ears to the hinges of the stone door, behind which last night the Ugly-Wuglies had shrieked and threatened. All was still as the sweet morning itself. It was as they turned away that they saw the man they had come to meet. He was on the other side of Flora's pedestal. But he was not standing up. He lay there, quite still, on his back, his arms flung wide.

"Oh, look!" cried Cathy, and pointed. His face was a queer greenish colour, and on his forehead there was a cut; its edges were blue, and a little blood had trickled from it on to the white of the marble.

At the same time Mabel pointed too but she did not cry out as Cathy had done. And what she pointed at was a big glossy-leaved rhododendron bush, from which a painted pointed paper face peered out very white, very red, in the sunlight and, as the children gazed, shrank back into the cover of the shining leaves.

It was but too plain. The unfortunate bailiff must have opened the door before the spell had faded, while yet the Ugly Wuglies were something more than mere coats and hats and sticks. They had rushed out upon him, and had done this. He lay there insensible was it a golf-club or a hockey-stick that had made that horrible cut on his forehead? Gerald wondered. The girls had rushed to the sufferer; already his head was in Mabel's lap. Kathleen had tried to get it on to hers, but Mabel was too quick for her.

Jimmy and Gerald both knew what was the first thing needed by the unconscious, even before Mabel impatiently said: "Water! water!"

"What in?" Jimmy asked, looking doubtfully at his hands, and then down the green slope to the marble-bordered pool where the water-lilies were.

"Your hat — anything," said Mabel.

The two boys turned away.

"Suppose they come after us," said Jimmy.

"What come after us?" Gerald snapped rather than asked.

"The Ugly-Wuglies," Jimmy whispered..

"Who's afraid?" Gerald inquired.

But he looked to right and left very carefully, and chose the way that did not lead near the bushes. He scooped water up in his straw hat and returned to Flora's Temple, carrying it carefully in both hands. When he saw how quickly it ran through the straw he pulled his handkerchief from his breast pocket with his teeth and dropped it into the hat. It was with this that the girls wiped the blood from the bailiff's brow.

"We ought to have smelling salts," said Kathleen, half in tears. "I know we ought."

"They would be good," Mabel owned.

"Hasn't your aunt any?"

"Yes, but..."

"Don't be a coward," said Gerald; "think of last night. They wouldn't hurt you. He must have insulted them or something. Look here, you run. We'll see that nothing runs after you."

There was no choice but to relinquish the head of the interesting invalid to Kathleen; so Mabel did it, cast one glaring glance round the rhododendron bordered slope, and fled towards the castle.

The other three bent over the still unconscious bailiff.

"He's not dead, is he?" asked Jimmy anxiously.

"No," Kathleen reassured him, "his heart's heating. Mabel and I felt it in his wrist, where doctors do. How frightfully good-looking he is!"

"Not so dusty," Gerald admitted.

"I never know what you mean by good-looking," said Jimmy, and suddenly a shadow fell on the marble beside them and a fourth voice spoke not Mabel s; her hurrying figure, though still in sight, was far away.

The children looked up into the face of the eldest of the Ugly-Wuglies, the respectable one. Jimmy and Kathleen screamed. I am sorry, but they did.

"Hush!" said Gerald savagely: he was still wearing the ring. "Hold your tongues! I'll get him away," he added in a whisper.

"Very sad affair this," said the respectable Ugly-Wugly. He spoke with a curious accent; there was something odd about his r's, and his m's and n's were those of a person labouring under an almost intolerable cold in the head. But it was not the dreadful "oo" and "ah" voice of the night before. Kathleen and Jimmy stooped over the bailiff. Even that prostrate form, being human, seemed some little protection. But Gerald, strong in the fearlessness that the ring gave to its wearer, looked full into the face of the Ugly-Wugly and started. For though the face was almost the same as the face he had himself painted on the school drawing-paper, it was not the same. For it was no longer paper. It was a real face, and the hands, lean and almost transparent as they were, were real hands. As it moved a little to get a better view of the bailiff it was plain that it had legs, arms live legs and arms, and a self-supporting backbone. It was alive indeed with a vengeance.

"How did it happen?" Gerald asked, with an effort of calmness a successful effort.

"Most regrettable," said the Ugly-Wugly. "The others must have missed the way last night in the passage. They never found the hotel."

"Did you?" asked Gerald blankly.

"Of course," said the Ugly-Wugly. "Most respectable, exactly as you said. Then when I came away I didn't come the front way because I wanted to revisit this sylvan scene by daylight, and the hotel people didn't seem to know how to direct me to it. I found the others all at this door, very angry. They'd been here all night, trying to get out. Then the door opened — this gentleman must have opened it — and before I could protect him, that underbred man in the high hat — you remember,"

Gerald remembered.

"Hit him on the head, and he fell where you see him. The others dispersed, and I myself was just going for assistance when I saw you."

Here Jimmy was discovered to be in tears and Kathleen white as any drawing-paper.

"What's the matter, my little man?" said the respectable Ugly-Wugly kindly. Jimmy passed instantly from tears to yells.

"Here, take the ring!" said Gerald in a furious whisper, and thrust it on to Jimmy's hot, damp, resisting finger. Jimmy's voice stopped short in the middle of a howl. And Gerald in a cold flash realized what it was that Mabel had gone through the night before. But it was daylight, and Gerald was not a coward.

"We must find the others," he said.

"I imagine," said the elderly Ugly-Wugly, "that they have gone to bathe. Their clothes are in the wood."

He pointed stiffly.

"You two go and see," said Gerald. "I'll go on dabbing this chap's head."

In the wood Jimmy, now fearless as any lion, discovered four heaps of clothing, with broomsticks, hockeysticks, and masks complete all that had gone to make up the gentlemen Ugly-Wuglies of the night before. On a stone seat well in the sun sat the two lady Ugly-Wuglies, and Kathleen approached them gingerly. Valour is easier in the sunshine than at night, as we all know. When she and Jimmy came close to the bench, they saw that the Ugly-Wuglies were only Ugly-Wuglies such as they had often made. There was no life in them. Jimmy shook them to pieces, and a sigh of relief burst from Kathleen.

"The spell's broken, you see," she said; "and that old gentleman, he's real. He only happens to be like the Ugly-Wugly we made."

"He's got the coat that hung in the hall on, anyway," said Jimmy.

"No, it's only like it. Let's get back to the unconscious stranger."

They did, and Gerald begged the elderly Ugly-Wugly to retire among the bushes with Jimmy; "because, said he, "I think the poor bailiff's coming round, and it might upset him to see strangers and Jimmy'll keep you company. He's the best one of us to go with you," he added hastily.

And this, since Jimmy had the ring, was certainly true.

So the two disappeared behind the rhododendrons. Mabel came back with the salts just as the bailiff opened his eyes.

"It's just like life," she said; "I might just as well not have gone. However," She knelt down at once and held the bottle under the sufferer's nose till he sneezed and feebly pushed her hand away with the faint question: "What's up now?"

"You've hurt your head," said Gerald. "Lie still."

"No more smelling-bottle," he said weakly, and lay.

Quite soon he sat up and looked round him. There was an anxious silence. Here was a grown-up who knew last night's secret, and none of the children were at all sure what the utmost rigour of the law might be in a case where people, no matter how young, made Ugly-Wuglies, and brought them to life — dangerous, fighting, angry life. What would he say what would he do?" He said: "What an odd thing! Have I been insensible long?"

"Hours," said Mabel earnestly.

"Not long," said Kathleen.

"We don't know. We found you like it," said Gerald.

"I'm all right now," said the bailiff, and his eye fell on the blood-stained handkerchief. "I say, I did give my head a bang. And you've been giving me first aid. Thank you most awfully. But it is rum."

"What's rum?" politeness obliged Gerald to ask.

"Well, I suppose it isn't really rum. I expect I saw you just before I fainted, or whatever it was, but I've dreamed the most extraordinary dream while I've been insensible and you were in it."

"Nothing but us?" asked Mabel breathlessly.

"Oh, lots of things impossible things but you were real enough."

Everyone breathed deeply in relief. It was indeed, as they agreed later, a lucky let-off.

"Are you sure you're all right?" they all asked, as he got on his feet.

"Perfectly, thank you." He glanced behind Flora's statue as he spoke. "Do you know, I dreamed there was a door there, but of course there isn't. I don't know how to thank you," he added, looking at them with what the girls called his beautiful, kind eyes; "it's lucky for me you came along. You come here whenever you like, you know," he added. "I give you the freedom of the place."

"You're the new bailiff, aren't you?" said Mabel.

"Yes. How did you know?" he asked quickly; but they did not tell him how they knew. Instead, they found out which way he was going, and went the other way after warm handshakes and hopes on both sides that they would meet again soon.

"I'll tell you what," said Gerald, as they watched the tall, broad figure of the bailiff grow smaller across the hot green of the grass slope, "have you got any idea of how we're going to spend the day? Because I have."

The others hadn't.

"We'll get rid of that Ugly-Wugly oh, we'll find a way right enough and directly we've done it we'll go home and seal up the ring in an envelope so that its teeth'll be drawn and it'll be powerless to have unforeseen larks with us. Then we'll get out on the roof, and have a quiet day books and apples. I'm about fed up with adventures, so I tell you."

The others told him the same thing.

"Now, think," said he "think as you never thought before how to get rid of that Ugly-Wugly."

Everyone thought, but their brains were tired with anxiety and distress, and the thoughts they thought were, as Mabel said, not worth thinking, let alone saying.

"I suppose Jimmy's all right," said Kathleen anxiously.

"Oh, he's all right: he's got the ring," said Gerald.

"I hope he won't go wishing anything rotten," said Mabel, but Gerald urged her to shut up and let him think.

"I think I think best sitting down," he said, and sat; "and sometimes you can think best aloud. The Ugly-Wugly's real don't make any mistake about that. And he got made real inside that passage. If we could get him back there he might get changed again, and then we could take the coats and things back."

"Isn't there any other way?" Kathleen asked; and Mabel, more candid, said bluntly: "I'm not going into that passage, so there!"

"Afraid! In broad daylight," Gerald sneered.

"It wouldn't be broad daylight in there," said Mabel, and Kathleen shivered.

"If we went to him and suddenly tore his coat off," said she "he is only coats he couldn't go on being real then.

"Couldn't he!" said Gerald. "You don't know what he's like under the coat."

Kathleen shivered again. And all this time the sun was shining gaily and the white statues and the green trees and the fountains and terraces looked as cheerfully romantic as a scene in a play.

"Anyway," said Gerald, "we'll try to get him back, and shut the door. That's the most we can hope for. And then apples, and Robinson Crusoe or the Swiss Family, or any book you like that's got no magic in it. Now, we've just got to do it. And he's not horrid now; really he isn't. He's real, you see."

"I suppose that makes all the difference," said Mabel, and tried to feel that perhaps it did.

"And it's broad daylight, just look at the sun," Gerald insisted. "Come on!"

He took a hand of each, and they walked resolutely towards the bank of rhododendrons behind which Jimmy and the Ugly-Wugly had been told to wait, and as they went Gerald said: "He's real" "The sun's shining" "It'll all be over in a minute." And he said these things again and again, so that there should be no mistake about them.

As they neared the bushes the shining leaves rustled, shivered, and parted, and before the girls had time to begin to hang back Jimmy came blinking out into the sunlight. The boughs closed behind him, and they did not stir or rustle for the appearance of anyone else. Jimmy was alone.

"Where is it?" asked the girls in one breath.

"Walking up and down in a fir-walk," said Jimmy, "doing sums in a book. He says he's most frightfully rich, and he's got to get up to town to the Stocks or something where they change papers into gold if you're clever, he says. I should like to go to the Stocks-change, wouldn't you?"

"I don't seem to care very much about changes, said Gerald. "I've had enough. Show us where he is — we must get rid of him."

"He's got a motor-car," Jimmy went on, parting the warm varnished-looking rhododendron leaves, "and a garden with a tennis-court and a lake and a carriage and pair, and he goes to Athens for his holiday sometimes, just like other people go to Margate."

"The best thing," said Gerald, following through the bushes, "will be to tell him the shortest way out is through that hotel that he thinks he found last night. Then we get him into the passage, give him a push, fly back, and shut the door."

"He'll starve to death in there," said Kathleen, "if he's really real."

"I expect it doesn't last long, the ring magics don't — anyway, it's the only thing I can think of."

"He's frightfully rich," Jimmy went on unheeding amid the cracking of the bushes; "he's building a public library for the people where he lives, and having his portrait painted to put in it. He thinks they'll like that."

The belt of rhododendrons was passed, and the children had reached a smooth grass walk bordered by tall pines and firs of strange different kinds. "He's just round that corner," said Jimmy. "He's simply rolling in money. He doesn't know what to do with it. He's been building a horse-trough and drinking fountain with a bust of himself on top. Why doesn't he build a private swimming-bath close to his bed, so that he can just roll off into it of a morning? I wish I was rich; I'd soon show him."

"That's a sensible wish," said Gerald. "I wonder we didn't think of doing that. Oh, criky!" he added, and with reason. For there, in the green shadows of the pine-walk, in the woodland silence, broken only by rustling leaves and the agitated breathing of the three unhappy others, Jimmy got his wish. By quick but perfectly plain-to-be-seen degrees Jimmy became rich. And the horrible thing was that though they could see it happening they did not know what was happening, and could not have stopped it if they had. All they could see was Jimmy, their own Jimmy, whom they had larked with and quarrelled with and made it up with ever since they could remember, Jimmy continuously and horribly growing old. The whole thing was over in a few seconds. Yet in those few seconds they saw him grow to a youth, a young man, a middle-aged man; and then, with a sort of shivering shock, unspeakably horrible and definite, he seemed to settle down into an elderly gentleman, handsomely but rather dowdily dressed, who was looking down at them through spectacles and asking them the nearest way to the railway-station. If they had not seen the change take place, in all its awful details, they would never have guessed that this stout, prosperous, elderly gentleman with the high hat, the frock-coat, and the large red seal dangling from the curve of a portly waistcoat, was their own Jimmy. But, as they had seen it, they knew the dreadful truth.

"Oh, Jimmy, don't!" cried Mabel desperately.

Gerald said: "This is perfectly beastly," and Kathleen broke into wild weeping.

"Don't cry, little girl!" said That-which-had-been Jimmy; "and you, boy, can't you give a civil answer to a civil question?"

"He doesn't know us!" wailed Kathleen.

"Who doesn't know you?" said That-which-had-been impatiently.

"You y-you don't!" Kathleen sobbed.

"I certainly don't," returned That-which "but surely that need not distress you so deeply."

"Oh, Jimmy, Jimmy, Jimmy!" Kathleen sobbed louder than before.

"He doesn't know us," Gerald owned, "or look here, Jimmy, you aren't kidding, are you? Because if you are it's simply abject rot."

"My name is Mr. —," said That-which-had-been-Jimmy, and gave the name correctly. By the way, it will perhaps be shorter to call this elderly stout person who was Jimmy grown rich by some simpler name than I have just used. Let us call him 'That', short for 'That-which-had-been Jimmy'.

"What are we to do?" whispered Mabel, awestruck; and aloud she said: "Oh, Mr. James, or whatever you call yourself, do give me the ring." For on That's finger the fatal ring showed plain.

"Certainly not," said That firmly. "You appear to be a very grasping child."

"But what are you going to do?" Gerald asked in the flat tones of complete hopelessness.

"Your interest is very flattering," said That. "Will you tell me, or won't you, the way to the nearest railway station?"

"No," said Gerald, "we won't."

"Then," said That, still politely, though quite plainly furious, "perhaps you'll tell me the way to the nearest lunatic asylum?"

"Oh, no, no, no!" cried Kathleen. "You're not so bad as that."

"Perhaps not. But you are," That retorted; "if you're not lunatics you're idiots. However, I see a gentleman ahead who is perhaps sane. In fact, I seem to recognize him." A gentleman, indeed, was now to be seen approaching. It was the elderly Ugly-Wugly.

"Oh! don't you remember Jerry?" Kathleen cried, "and Cathy, your own Cathy Puss Cat? Dear, dear Jimmy, don't be so silly!"

"Little girl," said That, looking at her crossly through his spectacles, "I am sorry you have not been better brought up." And he walked stiffly towards the Ugly-Wugly. Two hats were raised, a few words were exchanged, and two elderly figures walked side by side down the green pine-walk, followed by three miserable children, horrified, bewildered, alarmed, and, what is really worse than anything, quite at their wits end.

"He wished to be rich, so of course he is," said Gerald; "he'll have money for tickets and everything. And when the spell breaks — it's sure to break, isn't it? he'll find himself somewhere awful — perhaps in a really good hotel and not know how he got there."

"I wonder how long the Ugly-Wuglies lasted," said Mabel.

"Yes," Gerald answered, "that reminds me. You two must collect the coats and things. Hide them, anywhere you like, and we'll carry them home tomorrow — if there is any tomorrow," he added darkly.

"Oh, don't!" said Kathleen, once more breathing heavily on the verge of tears: "you wouldn't think everything could be so awful, and the sun shining like it does."

"Look here," said Gerald, "of course I must stick to Jimmy. You two must go home to Mademoiselle and tell her Jimmy and I have gone off in the train with a gentleman — say he looked like an uncle. He does look like some kind of uncle. There'll be a beastly row afterwards, but it's got to be done."

"It all seems thick with lies," said Kathleen; "you don't seem to be able to get a word of truth in edgewise hardly."

"Don't you worry," said her brother; "they aren't lies, they're as true as anything else in this magic rot we've got mixed up in. It's like telling lies in a dream; you can't help it."

"Well, all I know is I wish it would stop."

"Lot of use your wishing that is," said Gerald, exasperated. "So long. I've got to go, and you've got to stay. If it's any comfort to you, I don't believe any of it's real: it can't be; it's too thick. Tell Mademoiselle Jimmy and I will be back to tea. If we don't happen to be I can't help it. I can't help anything, except perhaps Jimmy." He started to run, for the girls had lagged, and the Ugly-Wugly and That (late Jimmy) had quickened their pace.

The girls were left looking after them.

"We've got to find these clothes," said Mabel, "simply got to. I used to want to be a heroine. It's different when it really comes to being, isn't it?"

"Yes, very," said Kathleen. "Where shall we hide the clothes when we've got them? Not that passage?"

"Never!" said Mabel firmly; "we'll hide them inside the great stone dinosaurus. He's hollow."

"He comes alive in his stone," said Kathleen.

"Not in the sunshine he doesn't," Mabel told her confidently, "and not without the ring."

"There won't be any apples and books today," said Kathleen.

"No, but we'll do the babiest thing we can do the minute we get home. We'll have a dolls tea-party. That'll make us feel as if there wasn't really any magic."

"It'll have to be a very strong tea party, then," said Kathleen doubtfully.

And now we see Gerald, a small but quite determined figure, paddling along in the soft white dust of the sunny road, in the wake of two elderly gentlemen. His hand, in his trousers pocket, buries itself with a feeling of satisfaction in the heavy mixed coinage that is his share of the profits of his conjuring at the fair. His noiseless tennis-shoes bear him to the station, where, unobserved, he listens at the ticket office to the voice of That-which-was-James. "One first London," it says and Gerald, waiting till That and the Ugly-Wugly have strolled on to the platform, politely conversing of politics and the Kaffir market, takes a third return to London. The train strides in, squeaking and puffing. The watched take their seats in a carriage blue-lined. The watcher springs into a yellow wooden compartment. A whistle sounds, a flag is waved. The train pulls itself together, strains, jerks, and starts.

"I don't understand," says Gerald, alone in his third-class carriage, "how railway trains and magic can go on at the same time."

And yet they do.

Mabel and Kathleen, nervously peering among the rhododendron bushes and the bracken and the fancy fir-trees, find six several heaps of coats, hats, skirts, gloves, golf-clubs, hockey-sticks, broom-handles. They carry them, panting and damp, for the mid-day sun is pitiless, up the hill to where the stone dinosaurus looms immense among a forest of larches. The dinosaurus has a hole in his stomach. Kathleen shows Mabel how to "make a back" and climbs up on it into the cold, stony inside of the monster. Mabel hands up the clothes and the sticks.

"There's lots of room," says Kathleen; "its tail goes down into the ground. It's like a secret passage."

"Suppose something comes out of it and jumps out at you," says Mabel, and Kathleen hurriedly descends.

The explanations to Mademoiselle promise to be difficult, but, as Kathleen said afterwards, any little thing is enough to take a grown-up's attention off. A figure passes the window just as they are explaining that it really did look exactly like an uncle that the boys have gone to London with.

"Who's that?" says Mademoiselle suddenly, pointing, too, which everyone knows is not manners.

It is the bailiff coming back from the doctor's with antiseptic plaster on that nasty cut that took so long a-bathing this morning. They tell her it is the bailiff at Yalding Towers, and she says, "Ciel!" (Sky!) and asks no more awkward questions about the boys. Lunch, very late, is a silent meal. After lunch Mademoiselle goes out, in a hat with many pink roses, carrying a rose-lined parasol. The girls, in dead silence, organize a dolls tea-party, with real tea. At the second cup Kathleen bursts into tears. Mabel, also weeping, embraces her.

"I wish," sobs Kathleen, "oh, I do wish I knew where the boys were! It would be such a comfort."

Gerald knew where the boys were, and it was no comfort to him at all. If you come to think of it, he was the only person who could know where they were, because Jimmy didn't know that he was a boy and indeed he wasn't really and the Ugly-Wugly couldn't be expected to know anything real, such as where boys were. At the moment when the second cup of dolls tea — very strong, but not strong enough to drown care in — was being poured out by the trembling hand of Kathleen, Gerald was lurking (there really is no other word for it) on the staircase of Aldermanbury Buildings, Old Broad Street. On the floor below him was a door bearing the legend "MR. U. W. UGLI, Stock and Share Broker (and at the Stock Exchange)" and on the floor above was another door, on which was the name of Gerald's little brother, now grown suddenly rich in so magic and tragic a way. There were no explaining words under Jimmy's name. Gerald could not guess what walk in life it was to which That (which had been Jimmy) owed its affluence. He had seen, when the door opened to admit his brother, a tangle of clerks and mahogany desks. Evidently That had a large business.

What was Gerald to do? What could he do?

It is almost impossible, especially for one so young as Gerald, to enter a large London office and explain that the elderly and respected head of it is not what he seems, but is really your little brother, who has been suddenly advanced to age and wealth by a tricky wishing ring. If you think it's a possible thing, try it, that's all. Nor could he knock at the door of Mr. U. W. Ugli, Stock and Share Broker (and at the Stock Exchange), and inform his clerks that their chief was really nothing but old clothes that had accidentally come alive, and by some magic, which he couldn't attempt to explain, become real during a night spent at a really good hotel which had no existence.

The situation bristled, as you see, with difficulties. And it was so long past Gerald's proper dinner-time that his increasing hunger was rapidly growing to seem the most important difficulty of all. It is quite possible to starve to death on the staircase of a London building if the people you are watching for only stay long enough in their offices. The truth of this came home to Gerald more and more painfully.

A boy with hair like a new front door mat came whistling up the stairs. He had a dark blue bag in his hands.

"I'll give you a tanner for yourself if you'll get me a tanner's worth of buns," said Gerald, with that prompt decision common to all great commanders.

"Show us yer tanners," the boy rejoined with at least equal promptness. Gerald showed them. "All right; hand over."

"Payment on delivery," said Gerald, using words from the drapers which he had never thought to use.

The boy grinned admiringly.

"Knows 'is wy abaht," he said; "ain't no flies on 'im."

"Not many," Gerald owned with modest pride. "Cut along, there's a good chap. I've got to wait here. I'll take care of your bag if you like."

"Nor yet there ain't no flies on me neither," remarked the boy, shouldering it. "I been up to the confidence trick for years ever since I was your age."

With this parting shot he went, and returned in due course bun-laden. Gerald gave the sixpence and took the buns. When the boy, a minute later, emerged from the door of Mr. U. W. Ugli, Stock and Share Broker (and at the Stock Exchange), Gerald stopped him.

"What sort of chap's that?" he asked, pointing the question with a jerk of an explaining thumb.

"Awful big pot," said the boy; "up to his eyes in oof. Motor and all that."

"Know anything about the one on the next landing?"

"He's bigger than what this one is. Very old firm. Special cellar in the Bank of England to put his chink in, all in bins like against the wall at the corn-chandler's. Jimminy, I wouldn't mind 'alf an hour in there, and the doors open and the police away at a beano. Not much! Neither. You'll bust if you eat all them buns."

"Have one?" Gerald responded, and held out the bag.

"They say in our office," said the boy, paying for the bun honourably with unasked information, "as these two is all for cutting each other's throats, oh, only in the way of business, been at it for years."

Gerald wildly wondered what magic and how much had been needed to give history and a past to these two things of yesterday, the rich Jimmy and the Ugly-Wugly. If he could get them away would all memory of them fade in this boy's mind, for instance, in the minds of all the people who did business with them in the City? Would the mahogany-and-clerk-furnished offices fade away? Were the clerks real? Was the mahogany? Was he himself real? Was the boy?

"Can you keep a secret?" he asked the other boy. "Are you on for a lark?"

"I ought to be getting back to the office," said the boy.

"Get then!" said Gerald.

"Don't you get stuffy," said the boy. "I was just a-going to say it didn't matter. I know how to make my nose bleed if I'm a bit late."

Gerald congratulated him on this accomplishment, at once so useful and so graceful, and then said: "Look here. I'll give you five bob honest."

"What for?" was the boy's natural question.

"If you'll help me. "

"Fire ahead."

"I'm a private inquiry," said Gerald.

"Tec? You don't look it."

"What's the good of being one if you look it?" Gerald asked impatiently, beginning on another bun. "That old chap on the floor above — he's wanted."

"Police?" asked the boy with fine carelessness.

"No, sorrowing relations."

"'Return to,'" said the boy; "'all forgotten and forgiven.' I see."

"And I've got to get him to them, somehow. Now, if you could go in and give him a message from someone who wanted to meet him on business,"

"Hold on!" said the boy. "I know a trick worth two of that. You go in and see old Ugli. He'd give his ears to have the old boy out of the way for a day or two. They were saying so in our office only this morning."

"Let me think," said Gerald, laying down the last bun on his knee expressly to hold his head in his hands.

"Don't you forget to think about my five bob," said the boy.

Then there was a silence on the stairs, broken only by the cough of a clerk in That's office, and the clickety-clack of a typewriter in the office of Mr. U. W. Ugli.

Then Gerald rose up and finished the bun.

"You're right," he said. "I'll chance it. Here's your five bob."

He brushed the bun crumbs from his front, cleared his throat, and knocked at the door of Mr. U. W. Ugli. It opened and he entered.

The door-mat boy lingered, secure in his power to account for his long absence by means of his well-trained nose, and his waiting was rewarded. He went down a few steps, round the bend of the stairs, and heard the voice of Mr. U. W. Ugli, so well known on that staircase (and on the Stock Exchange) say in soft, cautious accents:

"Then I'll ask him to let me look at the ring and I'll drop it. You pick it up. But remember, it's a pure accident, and you don't know me. I can't have my name mixed up in a thing like this. You're sure he's really unhinged?"

"Quite," said Gerald; "he's quite mad about that ring. He'll follow it anywhere. I know he will. And think of his sorrowing relations."

"I do, I do," said Mr. Ugli kindly; "that's all I do think of, of course."

He went up the stairs to the other office, and Gerald heard the voice of That telling his clerks that he was going out to lunch. Then the horrible Ugly-Wugly and Jimmy, hardly less horrible in the eyes of Gerald, passed down the stairs where, in the dusk of the lower landing, two boys were making themselves as undistinguishable as possible, and so out into the street, talking of stocks and shares, bears and bulls. The two boys followed.

"I say," the door-mat-headed boy whispered admiringly, "whatever are you up to?"

"You'll see," said Gerald recklessly. "Come on!"

"You tell me. I must be getting back."

"Well, I'll tell you, but you won't believe me. That old gentleman's not really old at all, he's my young brother suddenly turned into what you see. The other's not real at all. He's only just old clothes and nothing inside."

"He looks it, I must say," the boy admitted; "but I say, you do stick it on, don't you?"

"Well, my brother was turned like that by a magic ring."

"There ain't no such thing as magic," said the boy. "I learnt that at school."

"All right," said Gerald. "Good-bye."

"Oh, go ahead!" said the boy; "you do stick it on, though."

"Well, that magic ring. If I can get hold of it I shall just wish we were all in a certain place. And we shall be. And then I can deal with both of them."

"Deal?"

"Yes, the ring won't unwish anything you've wished. That undoes itself with time, like a spring uncoiling. But it'll give you a brand-new wish I'm almost certain of it. Anyhow, I'm going to chance it."

"You are a rotter, aren't you?" said the boy respectfully.

"You wait and see," Gerald repeated.

"I say, you aren't going into this swell place! You can't?"

The boy paused, appalled at the majesty of Pym's.

"Yes, I am they can't turn us out as long as we behave. You come along, too. I'll stand lunch."

I don't know why Gerald clung so to this boy. He wasn't a very nice boy. Perhaps it was because he was the only person Gerald knew in London to speak to — except That-which-had-been-

Jimmy and the Ugly-Wugly; and he did not want to talk to either of them.

What happened next happened so quickly that, as Gerald said later, it was "just like magic". The restaurant was crowded. Busy men were hastily bolting the food hurriedly brought by busy waitresses. There was a clink of forks and plates, the gurgle of beer from bottles, the hum of talk, and the smell of many good things to eat.

"Two chops, please," Gerald had just said, playing with a plainly shown handful of money, so as to leave no doubt of his honourable intentions. Then at the next table he heard the words, "Ah, yes, curious old family heirloom," the ring was drawn off the finger of That, and Mr. U. W. Ugli, murmuring something about a unique curio, reached his impossible hand out for it. The door-mat-headed boy was watching breathlessly.

"There's a ring right enough," he owned. And then the ring slipped from the hand of Mr. U. W. Ugli and skidded along the floor. Gerald pounced on it like a greyhound on a hare. He thrust the dull circlet on his finger and cried out aloud in that crowded place:

"I wish Jimmy and I were inside that door behind the statue of Flora."

It was the only safe place he could think of.

The lights and sounds and scents of the restaurant died away as a wax-drop dies in fire a rain-drop in water. I don't know, and Gerald never knew, what happened in that restaurant. There was nothing about it in the papers, though Gerald looked anxiously for 'Extraordinary Disappearance of well-known City Man.' What the door-mat-headed boy did or thought I don't know either. No more does Gerald. But he would like to know, whereas I don't care tuppence. The world went on all right, anyhow, whatever he thought or did. The lights and the sounds and the scents of Pym's died out. In place of the light there was darkness; in place of the sounds there was silence; and in place of the scent of beef, pork, mutton, fish, veal, cabbage, onions, carrots, beer, and tobacco there was the musty, damp scent of a place underground that has been long shut up.

Gerald felt sick and giddy, and there was something at the back of his mind that he knew would make him feel sicker and giddier as soon as he should have the sense to remember what it was. Meantime it was important to think of proper words to soothe the City man that had once been Jimmy to keep him quiet till Time, like a spring uncoiling, should bring the reversal of the spell make all things as they were and as they ought to be. But he fought in vain for words. There were none. Nor were they needed. For through the deep darkness came a voice and it was not the voice of that City man who had been Jimmy, but the voice of that very Jimmy who was Gerald's little brother, and who had wished that unlucky wish for riches that could only be answered by changing all that was Jimmy, young and poor, to all that Jimmy, rich and old, would have been. Another voice said: "Jerry, Jerry! Are you awake? I've had such a rum dream."

And then there was a moment when nothing was said or done.

Gerald felt through the thick darkness, and the thick silence, and the thick scent of old earth shut up, and he got hold of Jimmy's hand.

"It's all right, Jimmy, old chap," he said; "it's not a dream now. It's that beastly ring again. I had to wish us here, to get you back at all out of your dream."

"Wish us where?" Jimmy held on to the hand in a way that in the daylight of life he would have been the first to call babyish.

"Inside the passage behind the Flora statue," said Gerald, adding, "it's all right, really."

"Oh, I dare say it's all right," Jimmy answered through the dark, with an irritation not strong enough to make him loosen his hold of his brother's hand. "But how are we going to get out?"

Then Gerald knew what it was that was waiting to make him feel more giddy than the lightning flight from Cheapside to Yalding Towers had been able to make him. But he said stoutly:

"I'll wish us out, of course." Though all the time he knew that the ring would not undo its given wishes.

It didn't.

Gerald wished. He handed the ring carefully to Jimmy, through the thick darkness. And Jimmy wished.

And there they still were, in that black passage behind Flora, that had led in the case of one Ugly-Wugly at least to 'a good hotel'. And the stone door was shut. And they did not know even which way to turn to it.

"If I only had some matches!" said Gerald.

"Why didn't you leave me in the dream?" Jimmy almost whimpered. "It was light there, and I was just going to have salmon and cucumber."

"I," rejoined Gerald in gloom, "was just going to have steak and fried potatoes."

The silence, and the darkness, and the earthy scent were all they had now.

"I always wondered what it would be like," said Jimmy in low, even tones, "to be buried alive. And now I know! Oh!" his voice suddenly rose to a shriek, "it isn't true, it isn't! It's a dream that's what it is!"

There was a pause while you could have counted ten. Then "Yes," said Gerald bravely, through the scent and the silence and the darkness, "it's just a dream, Jimmy, old chap. We'll just hold on, and call out now and then just for the lark of the thing. But it's really only a dream, of course."

"Of course", said Jimmy in the silence and the darkness and the scent of old earth.

There is a curtain, thin as gossamer, clear as glass, strong as iron, that hangs for ever between the world of magic and the world that seems to us to be real. And when once people have found one of the little weak spots in that curtain which are marked by magic rings, and amulets, and the like, almost anything may happen. Thus it is not surprising that Mabel and Kathleen, conscientiously conducting one of the dullest dolls tea-parties at which either had ever assisted, should suddenly, and both at once, have felt a strange, unreasonable, but quite irresistible desire to return instantly to the Temple of Flora even at the cost of leaving the dolls tea-service in an unwashed state, and only half the raisins eaten. They went, as one has to go when the magic impulse drives one, against their better judgement, against their wills almost.

And the nearer they came to the Temple of Flora, in the golden hush of the afternoon, the more certain each was that they could not possibly have done otherwise.

And this explains exactly how it was that when Gerald and Jimmy, holding hands in the darkness of the passage, uttered their first concerted yell, "just for the lark of the thing", that yell was instantly answered from outside.

A crack of light showed in that part of the passage where they had least expected the door to be. The stone door itself swung slowly open, and they were out of it, in the Temple of Flora, blinking in the good daylight, an unresisting prey to Kathleen's embraces and the questionings of Mabel.

"And you left that Ugly-Wugly loose in London," Mabel pointed out; "you might have wished it to be with you, too."

"It's all right where it is," said Gerald. "I couldn't think of everything. And besides, no, thank you! Now we'll go home and seal up the ring in an envelope."

"I haven't done anything with the ring yet," said Kathleen.

"I shouldn't think you'd want to when you see the sort of things it does with you," said Gerald.

"It wouldn't do things like that if I was wishing with it," Kathleen protested,

"Look here," said Mabel, "let's just put it back in the treasure-room and have done with it. I oughtn't ever to have taken it away, really. It's a sort of stealing. It's quite as bad, really, as Eliza borrowing it to astonish her gentleman friend with."

"I don't mind putting it back if you like," said Gerald, "only if any of us do think of a sensible wish you'll let us have it out again, of course?"

"Of course, of course," Mabel agreed.

So they trooped up to the castle, and Mabel once more worked the spring that let down the panelling and showed the jewels, and the ring was put back among the odd dull ornaments that Mabel had once said were magic.

"How innocent it looks!" said Gerald. "You wouldn't think there was any magic about it. It's just like an old silly ring. I wonder if what Mabel said about the other things is true! Suppose we try."

"Don't!" said Kathleen. "I think magic things are spiteful. They just enjoy getting you into tight places."

"I'd like to try," said Mabel, "only well, everything's been rather upsetting, and I've forgotten what I said anything was."

So had the others. Perhaps that was why, when Gerald said that a bronze buckle laid on the foot would have the effect of seven-league boots, it didn't; when Jimmy, a little of the City man he had been clinging to him still, said that the steel collar would ensure your always having money in your pockets, his own remained empty; and when Mabel and Kathleen invented qualities of the most delightful nature for various rings and chains and brooches, nothing at all happened.

"It's only the ring that's magic," said Mabel at last; "and, I say!" she added, in quite a different voice.

"What?"

"Suppose even the ring isn't!"

"But we know it is."

"I don't," said Mabel. "I believe it's not today at all. I believe it's the other day we've just dreamed all these things. It's the day I made up that nonsense about the ring."

"No, it isn't," said Gerald; "you were in your Princess-clothes then."

"What Princess-clothes?" said Mabel, opening her dark eyes very wide.

"Oh, don't be silly," said Gerald wearily.

"I'm not silly," said Mabel; "and I think it's time you went. I'm sure Jimmy wants his tea."

"Of course I do," said Jimmy. "But you had got the Princess-clothes that day. Come along; let's shut up the shutters and leave the ring in its long home."

"What ring?" said Mabel.

"Don't take any notice of her," said Gerald. "She's only trying to be funny."

"No, I'm not," said Mabel; "but I'm inspired like a Python or a Sibylline lady. What ring?"

"The wishing-ring," said Kathleen; "the invisibility ring."

"Don't you see now," said Mabel, her eyes wider than ever, "the ring's what you say it is? That's how it came to make us invisible I just said it. Oh, we can't leave it here, if that's what it is. It isn't stealing, really, when it's as valuable as that, you see. Say what it is.

"It's a wishing-ring," said Jimmy.

"We've had that before and you had your silly wish," said Mabel, more and more excited. "I say it isn't a wishing-ring. I say it's a ring that makes the wearer four yards high."

She had caught up the ring as she spoke, and even as she spoke the ring showed high above the children's heads on the finger of an impossible Mabel, who was, indeed, twelve feet high.

"Now you've done it!" said Gerald and he was right. It was in vain that Mabel asserted that the ring was a wishing-ring. It quite clearly wasn't; it was what she had said it was.

"And you can't tell at all how long the effect will last," said Gerald. "Look at the invisibleness." This is difficult to do, but the others understood him.

"It may last for days," said Kathleen. "Oh, Mabel, it was silly of you!"

"That's right, rub it in," said Mabel bitterly; "you should have believed me when I said it was what I said it was. Then I shouldn't have had to show you, and I shouldn't be this silly size. What am I to do now, I should like to know?"

"We must conceal you till you get your right size again that's all," said Gerald practically.

"Yes but where?" said Mabel, stamping a foot twenty-four inches long.

"In one of the empty rooms. You wouldn't be afraid?"

"Of course not," said Mabel. "Oh, I do wish we'd just put the ring back and left it."

"Well, it wasn't us that didn't," said Jimmy, with more truth than grammar.

"I shall put it back now," said Mabel, tugging at it.

"I wouldn't if I were you," said Gerald thoughtfully. "You don't want to stay that length, do you? And unless the ring's on your finger when the time's up, I dare say it wouldn't act."

The exalted Mabel sullenly touched the spring. The panels slowly slid into place, and all the bright jewels were hidden. Once more the room was merely eight-sided, panelled, sunlit, and unfurnished.

"Now," said Mabel, "where am I to hide? It's a good thing auntie gave me leave to stay the night with you. As it is, one of you will have to stay the night with me. I'm not going to be left alone, the silly height I am."

Height was the right word; Mabel had said "four yards high" and she was four yards high. But she was hardly any thicker than when her height was four feet seven, and the effect was, as Gerald remarked, "wonderfully worm-like". Her clothes had, of course, grown with her, and she looked like a little girl reflected in one of those long bent mirrors at Rosherville Gardens, that make stout people look so happily slender, and slender people so sadly scraggy. She sat down suddenly on the floor, and it was like a four-fold foot-rule folding itself up.

"It's no use sitting there, girl," said Gerald.

"I'm not sitting here," retorted Mabel; "I only got down so as to be able to get through the door. It'll have to be hands and knees through most places for me now, I suppose."

"Aren't you hungry?" Jimmy asked suddenly.

"I don't know," said Mabel desolately; "it's it's such a long way off!"

"Well, I'll scout," said Gerald; "if the coast's clear."

"Look here," said Mabel, "I think I'd rather be out of doors till it gets dark."

"You can't. Someone's certain to see you."

"Not if I go through the yew-hedge," said Mabel. "There's a yew-hedge with a passage along its inside like the box-hedge in The Luck of the Vails."

"In what?"

"The Luck of the Vails. It's a ripping book. It was that book first set me on to hunt for hidden doors in panels and things. If I crept along that on my front, like a serpent it comes out amongst the rhododendrons, close by the dinosaurus, we could camp there.

"There's tea," said Gerald, who had had no dinner.

"That's just what there isn't," said Jimmy, who had had none either.

"Oh, you won't desert me!" said Mabel. "Look here I'll write to auntie. She'll give you the things for a picnic, if she's there and awake. If she isn't, one of the maids will."

So she wrote on a leaf of Gerald's invaluable pocketbook: "DEAREST AUNTIE Please may we have some things for a picnic? Gerald will bring them. I would come myself, but I am a little tired. I think I have been growing rather fast. Your loving niece, MABEL." "P.S. Lots, please, because some of us are very hungry."

It was found difficult, but possible, for Mabel to creep along the tunnel in the yew-hedge. Possible, but slow, so that the three had hardly had time to settle themselves among the rhododendrons and to wonder bitterly what on earth Gerald was up to, to be such a time gone, when he returned, panting under the weight of a covered basket. He dumped it down on the fine grass carpet, groaned, and added, "But it's worth it. Where's our Mabel?"

The long, pale face of Mabel peered out from rhododendron leaves, very near the ground.

"I look just like anybody else like this, don't I?" she asked anxiously; "all the rest of me's miles away, under different bushes."

"We've covered up the bits between the bushes with bracken and leaves," said Kathleen, avoiding the question; "don't wriggle, Mabel, or you'll waggle them off."

Jimmy was eagerly unpacking the basket. It was a generous tea. A long loaf, butter in a cabbage-leaf, a bottle of milk, a bottle of water, cake, and large, smooth, yellow gooseberries in a box that had once held an extra-sized bottle of somebody's matchless something for the hair and moustache. Mabel cautiously advanced her incredible arms from the rhododendron and leaned on one of her spindly elbows, Gerald cut bread and butter, while Kathleen obligingly ran round, at Mabel's request, to see that the green coverings had not dropped from any of the remoter parts of Mabel's person. Then there was a happy, hungry silence, broken only by those brief, impassioned suggestions natural to such an occasion:

"More cake, please."

"Milk ahoy, there."

"Chuck us the goosegogs."

Everyone grew calmer, more contented with their lot. A pleasant feeling, half tiredness and half restfulness, crept to the extremities of the party. Even the unfortunate Mabel was conscious of it in her remote feet, that lay crossed under the third rhododendron to the north-north-west of the tea-party. Gerald did but voice the feelings of the others when he said, not without regret:

"Well, I'm a new man, but I couldn't eat so much as another goosegog if you paid me."

"I could," said Mabel; "yes, I know they re all gone, and I've had my share. But I could. It's me being so long, I suppose."

A delicious after-food peace filled the summer air. At a little distance the green-lichened grey of the vast stone dinosaurus showed through the shrubs. He, too, seemed peaceful and happy. Gerald caught his stone eye through a gap in the foliage. His glance seemed somehow sympathetic.

"I dare say he liked a good meal in his day," said Gerald, stretching luxuriously.

"Who did?"

"The dino what's-his-name," said Gerald.

"He had a meal today," said Kathleen, and giggled.

"Yes didn't he?" said Mabel, giggling also.

"You mustn't laugh lower than your chest," said Kathleen anxiously, "or your green stuff will joggle off."

"What do you mean a meal?" Jimmy asked suspiciously. "What are you sniggering about?"

"He had a meal. Things to put in his inside," said Kathleen, still giggling.

"Oh, be funny if you want to," said Jimmy, suddenly cross. "We don't want to know do we, Jerry?"

"I do," said Gerald witheringly; "I'm dying to know. Wake me, you girls, when you've finished pretending you're not going to tell."

He tilted his hat over his eyes, and lay back in the attitude of slumber.

"Oh, don't be stupid!" said Kathleen hastily. "It's only that we fed the dinosaurus through the hole in his stomach with the clothes the Ugly-Wuglies were made of!"

"We can take them home with us, then," said Gerald, chewing the white end of a grass stalk, "so that's all right."

"Look here," said Kathleen suddenly; "I've got an idea. Let me have the ring a bit. I won't say what the idea is, in case it doesn't come off, and then you'd say I was silly. I'll give it back before we go."

"Oh, but you aren't going yet!" said Mabel, pleading. She pulled off the ring. "Of course, she added earnestly, "I'm only too glad for you to try any idea, however silly it is."

Now, Kathleen's idea was quite simple. It was only that perhaps the ring would change its powers if someone else renamed it someone who was not under the power of its enchantment. So the moment it had passed from the long, pale hand of Mabel to one of her own fat, warm, red paws, she jumped up, crying "Let's go and empty the dinosaurus now, and started to run swiftly towards that prehistoric monster. She had a good start. She wanted to say aloud, yet so that the others could not hear her, "This is a wishing-ring. It gives you any wish you choose. And she did say it. And no one heard her, except the birds and a squirrel or two, and perhaps a stone faun, whose pretty face seemed to turn a laughing look on her as she raced past its pedestal.

The way was uphill; it was sunny, and Kathleen had run her hardest, though her brothers caught her up before she reached the great black shadow of the dinosaurus. So that when she did reach that shadow she was very hot indeed and not in any state to decide calmly on the best wish to ask for.

"I'll get up and move the things down, because I know exactly where I put them," she said.

Gerald made a back, Jimmy assisted her to climb up, and she disappeared through the hole into the dark inside of the monster. In a moment a shower began to descend from the opening a shower of empty waistcoats, trousers with wildly waving legs, and coats with sleeves uncontrolled.

"Heads below!" called Kathleen, and down came walking-sticks and golf-sticks and hockey-sticks and broom-sticks, rattling and chattering to each other as they came.

"Come on," said Jimmy.

"Hold on a bit," said Gerald. "I'm coming up. He caught the edge of the hole above in his hands and jumped. Just as he got his shoulders through the opening and his knees on the edge he heard Kathleen's boots on the floor of the dinosaurus's inside, and Kathleen's voice saying: "Isn't it jolly cool in here? I suppose statues are always cool. I do wish I was a statue. Oh!"

The "oh" was a cry of horror and anguish. And it seemed to be cut off very short by a dreadful stony silence.

"What's up?" Gerald asked. But in his heart he knew. He climbed up into the great hollow. In the little light that came up through the hole he could see something white against the grey of the creature's sides. He felt in his pockets, still kneeling, struck a match, and when the blue of its flame changed to clear yellow he looked up to see what he had known he would see the face of Kathleen, white, stony, and lifeless. Her hair was white, too, and her hands, clothes, shoes everything was white, with the hard, cold whiteness of marble. Kathleen had her wish: she was a statue. There was a long moment of perfect stillness in the inside of the dinosaurus. Gerald could not speak. It was too sudden, too terrible. It was worse than anything that had happened yet. Then he turned and spoke down out of that cold, stony silence to Jimmy, in the green, sunny, rustling, live world outside.

"Jimmy, he said, in tones perfectly ordinary and matter of fact, "Kathleen's gone and said that ring was a wishing-ring. And so it was, of course. I see now what she was up to, running like that. And then the young duffer went and wished she was a statue."

"And she is?" asked Jimmy, below.

"Come up and have a look," said Gerald. And Jimmy came, partly with a pull from Gerald and partly with a jump of his own.

"She's a statue, right enough," he said, in awestruck tones. "Isn't it awful!"

"Not at all," said Gerald firmly. "Come on let's go and tell Mabel."

To Mabel, therefore, who had discreetly remained with her long length screened by rhododendrons, the two boys returned and broke the news. They broke it as one breaks a bottle with a pistol-shot.

"Oh, my goodness!" said Mabel, and writhed through her long length so that the leaves and fern tumbled off in little showers, and she felt the sun suddenly hot on the backs of her legs. "What next? Oh, my goodness!"

"She'll come all right," said Gerald, with outward calm.

"Yes; but what about me?" Mabel urged. "I haven't got the ring. And my time will be up before hers is. Couldn't you get it back? Can't you get it off her hand? I'd put it back on her hand the very minute I was my right size again faithfully I would."

"Well, it's nothing to blub about," said Jimmy, answering the sniffs that had served her in this speech for commas and full-stops; "not for you, anyway."

"Ah! you don't know," said Mabel; "you don't know what it is to be as long as I am. Do — do try and get the ring. After all, it is my ring more than any of the rest of yours, anyhow, because I did find it, and I did say it was magic."

The sense of justice always present in the breast of Gerald awoke to this appeal.

"I expect the ring's turned to stone — her boots have, and all her clothes. But I'll go and see. Only if I can't, I can't, and it's no use your making a silly fuss."

The first match lighted inside the dinosaurus showed the ring dark on the white hand of the statuesque Kathleen.

The fingers were stretched straight out. Gerald took hold of the ring, and, to his surprise, it slipped easily off the cold, smooth marble finger.

"I say, Cathy, old girl, I am sorry," he said, and gave the marble hand a squeeze. Then it came to him that perhaps she could hear him. So he told the statue exactly what he and the others meant to do. This helped to clear up his ideas as to what he and the others did mean to do. So that when, after thumping the statue hearteningly on its marble back, he returned to the rhododendrons, he was able to give his orders with the clear precision of a born leader, as he later said. And since the others had, neither of them, thought of any plans, his plan was accepted, as the plans of born leaders are apt to be.

"Here's your precious ring," he said to Mabel. "Now you're not frightened of anything, are you?"

"No," said Mabel, in surprise. "I'd forgotten that. Look here, I'll stay here or farther up in the wood if you'll leave me all the coats, so that I shan't be cold in the night. Then I shall be here when Kathleen comes out of the stone again."

"Yes," said Gerald, "that was exactly the born leader's idea."

"You two go home and tell Mademoiselle that Kathleen's staying at the Towers. She is."

"Yes," said Jimmy, "she certainly is."

"The magic goes in seven-hour lots," said Gerald; "your invisibility was twenty-one hours, mine fourteen, Eliza's seven. When it was a wishing-ring it began with seven. But there's no knowing what number it will be really. So there's no knowing which of you will come right first. Anyhow, we'll sneak out by the cistern window and come down the trellis, after we've said good night to Mademoiselle, and come and have a look at you before we go to bed. I think you'd better come close up to the dinosaurus and we'll leaf you over before we go."

Mabel crawled into cover of the taller trees, and there stood up looking as slender as a poplar and as unreal as the wrong answer to a sum in long division. It was to her an easy matter to crouch beneath the dinosaurus, to put her head up through the opening, and thus to behold the white form of Kathleen.

"It's all right, dear," she told the stone image; "I shall be quite close to you. You call me as soon as you feel you're coming right again."

The statue remained motionless, as statues usually do, and Mabel withdrew her head, lay down, was covered up, and left. The boys went home. It was the only reasonable thing to do. It would never have done for Mademoiselle to become anxious and set the police on their track. Everyone felt that. The shock of discovering the missing Kathleen, not only in a dinosaurus's stomach, but, further, in a stone statue of herself, might well have unhinged the mind of any constable, to say nothing of the mind of Mademoiselle, which, being foreign, would necessarily be a mind more light and easy to upset. While as for Mabel...

"Well, to look at her as she is now," said Gerald, "why, it would send any one off their chump except us."

"We're different, said Jimmy; "our chumps have had to jolly well get used to things. It would take a lot to upset us now."

"Poor old Cathy! all the same," said Gerald.

"Yes, of course," said Jimmy.

The sun had died away behind the black trees and the moon was rising. Mabel, her preposterous length covered with coats, waistcoats, and trousers laid along it, slept peacefully in the chill of the evening. Inside the dinosaurus Kathleen, alive in her marble, slept too. She had heard Gerald's words had seen the lighted matches. She was Kathleen just the same as ever, only she was Kathleen in a case of marble that would not let her move. It would not have let her cry, even if she wanted to. But she had not wanted to cry. Inside, the marble was not cold or hard. It seemed, somehow, to be softly lined with warmth and pleasantness and safety. Her back did not ache with stooping. Her limbs were not stiff with the hours that they had stayed moveless. Everything was well — better than well. One had only to wait quietly and quite comfortably and one would come out of this stone case, and once more be the Kathleen one had always been used to being. So she waited happily and calmly, and presently waiting changed to not waiting to not anything; and, close held in the soft inwardness of the marble, she slept as peacefully and calmly as though she had been lying in her own bed.

She was awakened by the fact that she was not lying in her own bed was not, indeed, lying at all by the fact that she was standing and that her feet had pins and needles in them. Her arms, too, held out in that odd way, were stiff and tired. She rubbed her eyes, yawned, and remembered. She had been a statue a statue inside the stone dinosaurus.

"Now I'm alive again," was her instant conclusion, "and I'll get out of it."

She sat down, put her feet through the hole that showed faintly grey in the stone beast's underside, and as she did so a long, slow lurch threw her sideways on the stone where she sat. The dinosaurus was moving!

"Oh!" said Kathleen inside it, "how dreadful! It must be moonlight, and it's come alive, like Gerald said.

It was indeed moving. She could see through the hole the changing surface of grass and bracken and moss as it waddled heavily along. She dared not drop through the hole while it moved, for fear it should crush her to death with its gigantic feet. And with that thought came another: where was Mabel? Somewhere somewhere near? Suppose one of the great feet planted itself on some part of Mabel's inconvenient length? Mabel being the size she was now it would be quite difficult not to step on some part or other of her, if she should happen to be in one's way — quite difficult, however much one tried. And the dinosaurus would not try: Why should it? Kathleen hung in an agony over the round opening. The huge beast swung from side to side. It was going faster; it was no good, she dared not jump out. Anyhow, they must be quite away from Mabel by now. Faster and faster went the dinosaurus. The floor of its stomach sloped. They were going downhill. Twigs cracked and broke as it pushed through a belt of evergreen oaks; gravel crunched, ground beneath its stony feet. Then stone met stone. There was a pause. A splash! They were close to water the lake where by moonlight Hermes fluttered and Janus and the dinosaurus swam together. Kathleen dropped swiftly through the hole on to the flat marble that edged the basin, rushed sideways, and stood panting in the shadow of a statue's pedestal. Not a moment too soon, for even as she crouched the monster lizard slipped heavily into the water, drowning a thousand smooth, shining lily pads, and swam away towards the central island.

"Be still, little lady. I leap!" The voice came from the pedestal, and next moment Phoebus had jumped from the pedestal in his little temple, clearing the steps, and landing a couple of yards away.

"You are new," said Phoebus over his graceful shoulder. "I should not have forgotten you if once I had seen you."

"I am," said Kathleen, "quite, quite new. And I didn't know you could talk."

"Why not?" Phoebus laughed. "You can talk."

"But I'm alive."

"Am not I?" he asked.

"Oh, yes, I suppose so," said Kathleen, distracted, but not afraid; "only I thought you had to have the ring on before one could even see you move."

Phoebus seemed to understand her, which was rather to his credit, for she had certainly not expressed herself with clearness.

"Ah! that's for mortals," he said. "We can hear and see each other in the few moments when life is ours. That is a part of the beautiful enchantment."

"But I am a mortal," said Kathleen.

"You are as modest as you are charming," said Phoebus Apollo absently; "the white water calls me! I go," and the next moment rings of liquid silver spread across the lake, widening and widening, from the spot where the white joined hands of the Sun-god had struck the water as he dived.

Kathleen turned and went up the hill towards the rhododendron bushes. She must find Mabel, and they must go home at once. If only Mabel was of a size that one could conveniently take home with one! Most likely, at this hour of enchantments, she was. Kathleen, heartened by the thought, hurried on. She passed through the rhododendron bushes, remembered the pointed painted paper face that had looked out from the glossy leaves, expected to be frightened and wasn't. She found Mabel easily enough, and much more easily than she would have done had Mabel been as she wished to find her. For quite a long way off in the moonlight, she could see that long and worm-like form, extended to its full twelve feet and covered with coats and trousers and waistcoats. Mabel looked like a drain-pipe that has been covered in sacks in frosty weather. Kathleen touched her long cheek gently, and she woke.

"What's up?" she said sleepily.

"It's only me," Kathleen explained.

"How cold your hands are!" said Mabel.

"Wake up," said Kathleen, "and let's talk."

"Can't we go home now? I'm awfully tired, and it's so long since tea-time."

"You're too long to go home yet," said Kathleen sadly, and then Mabel remembered.

She lay with closed eyes then suddenly she stirred and cried out:

"Oh! Cathy, I feel so funny — like one of those horn snakes when you make it go short to get it into its box. I am, yes I know I am "

She was; and Kathleen, watching her, agreed that it was exactly like the shortening of a horn spiral snake between the closing hands of a child. Mabel's distant feet drew near Mabel's long, lean arms grew shorter Mabel's face was no longer half a yard long.

"You're coming right you are! Oh, I am so glad!" cried Kathleen.

"I know I am," said Mabel; and as she said it she became once more Mabel, not only in herself which, of course, she had been all the time, but in her outward appearance.

"You are all right. Oh, hooray! hooray! I am so glad!" said Kathleen kindly; "and now we'll go home at once, dear."

"Go home?" said Mabel, slowly sitting up and staring at Kathleen with her big dark eyes. "Go home like that?"

"Like what?" Kathleen asked impatiently.

"Why, you," was Mabel's odd reply.

"I'm all right," said Kathleen. "Come on."

"Do you mean to say you don't know?" said Mabel. "Look at yourself your hands your dress everything."

Kathleen looked at her hands. They were of marble whiteness. Her dress, too her shoes, her stockings, even the ends of her hair. She was white as new-fallen snow.

"What is it?" she asked, beginning to tremble. "What am I all this horrid colour for?"

"Don't you see? Oh, Cathy, don't you see? You've not come right. You're a statue still."

"I'm not! I'm alive! I'm talking to you."

"I know you are, darling," said Mabel, soothing her as one soothes a fractious child. "That's because it's moonlight."

"But you can see I'm alive."

"Of course I can. I've got the ring."

"But I'm all right; I know I am."

"Don't you see," said Mabel gently, taking her white marble hand, "you're not all right? It's moonlight, and you're a statue, and you've just come alive with all the other statues. And when the moon goes down you'll just be a statue again. That's the difficulty, dear, about our going home again. You're just a statue still, only you've come alive with the other marble things. Where's the dinosaurus?"

"In his bath," said Kathleen, "and so are all the other stone beasts."

"Well," said Mabel, trying to look on the bright side of things, "then we've got one thing, at any rate, to be thankful for!"

"If," said Kathleen, sitting disconsolate in her marble, "if I am really a statue come alive, I wonder you're not afraid of me."

"I've got the ring," said Mabel with decision. "Cheer up, dear! you will soon be better. Try not to think about it."

She spoke as you speak to a child that has cut its finger, or fallen down on the garden path, and rises up with grazed knees to which gravel sticks intimately.

"I know," Kathleen absently answered.

"And I've been thinking," said Mabel brightly, "we might find out a lot about this magic place, if the other statues aren't too proud to talk to us."

"They aren't," Kathleen assured her; "at least, Phoebus wasn't. He was most awfully polite and nice."

"Where is he?" Mabel asked.

"In the lake — he was," said Kathleen.

"Then let's go down there," said Mabel. "Oh, Cathy! it is jolly being your own proper thickness again." She jumped up, and the withered ferns and branches that had covered her long length and had been gathered closely upon her as she shrank to her proper size fell as forest leaves do when sudden storms tear them. But the white Kathleen did not move.

The two sat on the grey moonlit grass with the quiet of the night all about them. The great park was still as a painted picture; only the splash of the fountains and the far-off whistle of the Western express broke the silence, which, at the same time, then deepened.

"What cheer, little sister!" said a voice behind them a golden voice. They turned quick, startled heads, as birds, surprised, might turn. There in the moonlight stood Phoebus, dripping still from the lake, and smiling at them, very gentle, very friendly.

"Oh, it's you!" said Kathleen.

"None other," said Phoebus cheerfully. "Who is your friend, the earth-child?"

"This is Mabel," said Kathleen.

Mabel got up and bowed, hesitated, and held out a hand.

"I am your slave, little lady," said Phoebus, enclosing it in marble fingers. "But I fail to understand how you can see us, and why you do not fear."

Mabel held up the hand that wore the ring.

"Quite sufficient explanation," said Phoebus; "but since you have that, why retain your mottled earthy appearance? Become a statue, and swim with us in the lake."

"I can't swim," said Mabel evasively.

"Nor yet me," said Kathleen.

"You can," said Phoebus. "All statues that come to life are proficient in all athletic exercises. And you, child of the dark eyes and hair like night, wish yourself a statue and join our revels."

"I'd rather not, if you will excuse me," said Mabel cautiously. "You see ... this ring ... you wish for things, and you never know how long they're going to last. It would be jolly and all that to be a statue now, but in the morning I should wish I hadn't."

"Earth-folk often do, they say," mused Phoebus. "But, child, you seem ignorant of the powers of your ring. Wish exactly, and the ring will exactly perform. If you give no limit of time, strange enchantments woven by Arithmos the outcast god of numbers will creep in and spoil the spell. Say thus: "I wish that till the dawn I may be a statue of living marble, even as my child friend, and that after that time I may be as before Mabel of the dark eyes and night-coloured hair."

"Oh, yes, do, it would be so jolly!" cried Kathleen. "Do, Mabel! And if we're both statues, shall we be afraid of the dinosaurus?"

"In the world of living marble fear is not," said Phoebus. "Are we not brothers, we and the dinosaurus brethren alike wrought of stone and life?"

"And could I swim if I did?"

"Swim, and float, and dive and with the ladies of Olympus spread the nightly feast, eat of the food of the gods, drink their cup, listen to the song that is undying, and catch the laughter of immortal lips."

"A feast!" said Kathleen. "Oh, Mabel, do! You would if you were as hungry as I am."

"But it won't be real food," urged Mabel.

"It will be real to you, as to us," said Phoebus; "there is no other realness even in your many-coloured world."

Still Mabel hesitated. Then she looked at Kathleen's legs and suddenly said: "Very well, I will. But first I'll take off my shoes and stockings. Marble boots look simply awful, especially the laces. And a marble stocking that's coming down — and mine do!"

She had pulled off shoes and stockings and pinafore. "Mabel has the sense of beauty," said Phoebus approvingly. "Speak the spell, child, and I will lead you to the ladies of Olympus."

Mabel, trembling a little, spoke it, and there were two little live statues in the moonlit glade. Tall Phoebus took a hand of each.

"Come run!" he cried. And they ran.

"Oh it is jolly!" Mabel panted. "Look at my white feet in the grass! I thought it would feel stiff to be a statue, but it doesn't."

"There is no stiffness about the immortals," laughed the Sun-god. "For tonight you are one of us."

And with that they ran down the slope to the lake.

"Jump!" he cried, and they jumped, and the water splashed up round three white, gleaming shapes.

"Oh! I can swim!" breathed Kathleen.

"So can I," said Mabel.

"Of course you can," said Phoebus. "Now three times round the lake, and then make for the island."

Side by side the three swam, Phoebus swimming gently to keep pace with the children. Their marble clothes did not seem to interfere at all with their swimming, as your clothes would if you suddenly jumped into the basin of the Trafalgar Square fountains and tried to swim there. And they swam most beautifully, with that perfect ease and absence of effort or tiredness which you must have noticed about your own swimming in dreams. And it was the most lovely place to swim in; the water-lilies, whose long, snaky stalks are so inconvenient to ordinary swimmers, did not in the least interfere with the movements of marble arms and legs. The moon was high in the clear sky-dome. The weeping willows, cypresses, temples, terraces, banks of trees and shrubs, and the wonderful old house, all added to the romantic charm of the scene.

"This is the nicest thing the ring has brought us yet," said Mabel, through a languid but perfect side-stroke.

"I thought you'd enjoy it," said Phoebus kindly; "now once more round, and then the island."

They landed on the island amid a fringe of rushes, yarrow, willow-herb, loose-strife, and a few late, scented, powdery, creamy heads of meadow-sweet. The island was bigger than it looked from the bank, and it seemed covered with trees and shrubs. But when, Phoebus leading the way, they went into the shadow of these, they perceived that beyond the trees lay a light, much nearer to them than the other side of the island could possibly be. And almost at once they were through the belt of trees, and could see where the light came from. The trees they had just passed among made a dark circle round a big cleared space, standing up thick and dark, like a crowd round a football field, as Kathleen remarked.

First came a wide, smooth ring of lawn, then marble steps going down to a round pool, where there were no water-lilies, only gold and silver fish that darted here and there like flashes of quicksilver and dark flames. And the enclosed space of water and marble and grass was lighted with a clear, white, radiant light, seven times stronger than the whitest moonlight, and in the still waters of the pool seven moons lay reflected. One could see that they were only reflections by the way their shape broke and changed as the gold and silver fish rippled the water with moving fin and tail that steered.

The girls looked up at the sky, almost expecting to see seven moons there. But no, the old moon shone alone, as she had always shone on them.

"There are seven moons," said Mabel blankly, and pointed, which is not manners.

"Of course," said Phoebus kindly; "everything in our world is seven times as much so as in yours."

"But there aren't seven of you," said Mabel.

No, but I am seven times as much," said the Sun-god. "You ee, there's numbers, and there's quantity, to say nothing of uality. You see that, I'm sure."

Not quite," said Kathleen.

Explanations always weary me," Phoebus interrupted. "Shall ve join the ladies?"

)n the further side of the pool was a large group, so white that t seemed to make a great white hole in the trees. Some twenty r thirty figures there were in the group all statues and all alive. Some were dipping their white feet among the gold and silver ish, and sending ripples across the faces of the seven moons. Some were pelting each other with roses roses so sweet that the irls could smell them even across the pool. Others were olding hands and dancing in a ring, and two were sitting on he steps playing cat's-cradle which is a very ancient game ndeed with a thread of white marble.

As the new-comers advanced a shout of greeting and gay aughter went up. "Late again, Phoebus!" someone called out. And another: "Did one of your horses cast a shoe?" And yet nother called out something about laurels.

I bring two guests," said Phoebus, and instantly the statues rowded round, stroking the girls hair, patting their cheeks, nd calling them the prettiest love-names.

'Are the wreaths ready, Hebe?" the tallest and most splendid of he ladies called out. "Make two more!"

And almost directly Hebe came down the steps, her round arms ung thick with rose-wreaths. There was one for each marble ead.

Everyone now looked seven times more beautiful than before, which, in the case of the gods and goddesses, is saying a good leal. The children remembered how at the raspberry vinegar 'east Mademoiselle had said that gods and goddesses always wore wreaths for meals.

Hebe herself arranged the roses on the girls' heads, and Aphrodite Urania, the dearest lady in the world, with a voice ike mother's at those moments when you love her most, took hem by the hands and said: "Come, we must get the feast eady. Eros, Psyche, Hebe, Ganymede, all you young people can rrange the fruit."

'I don't see any fruit," said Kathleen, as four slender forms lisengaged themselves from the white crowd and came towards hem.

'You will though," said Eros, a really nice boy, as the girls nstantly agreed; "you've only got to pick it."

'Like this," said Psyche, lifting her marble arms to a willow branch. She reached out her hand to the children it held a ripe pomegranate.

"I see," said Mabel. "You just..." She laid her fingers to the willow branch and the firm softness of a big peach was within them.

"Yes, just that," laughed Psyche, who was a darling, as any one could see.

After this Hebe gathered a few silver baskets from a convenient alder, and the four picked fruit industriously. Meanwhile the elder statues were busy plucking golden goblets and jugs and dishes from the branches of ash-trees and young oaks and filling them with everything nice to eat and drink that anyone could possibly want, and these were spread on the steps. It was a celestial picnic. Then everyone sat or lay down and the feast began. And oh! the taste of the food served on those dishes, the sweet wonder of the drink that melted from those gold cups on the white lips of the company! And the fruit there is no fruit like it grown on earth, just as there is no laughter like the laughter of those lips, no songs like the songs that stirred the silence of that night of wonder.

"Oh!" cried Kathleen, and through her fingers the juice of her third peach fell like tears on the marble steps. "I do wish the boys were here!"

"I do wonder what they're doing," said Mabel.

"At this moment," said Hermes, who had just made a wide ring of flight, as a pigeon does, and come back into the circle "at this moment they are wandering desolately near the home of the dinosaurus, having escaped from their home by a window, in search of you. They fear that you have perished, and they would weep if they did not know that tears do not become a man, however youthful."

Kathleen stood up and brushed the crumbs of ambrosia from her marble lap.

"Thank you all very much, she said. "It was very kind of you to have us, and we've enjoyed ourselves very much, but I think we ought to go now, please.

"If it is anxiety about your brothers," said Phoebus obligingly, "it is the easiest thing in the world for them to join you. Lend me your ring a moment."

He took it from Kathleen's half-reluctant hand, dipped it in the reflection of one of the seven moons, and gave it back. She clutched it. "Now," said the Sun-god, "wish for them that which Mabel wished for herself. Say..."

"I know," Kathleen interrupted. "I wish that the boys may be statues of living marble like Mabel and me till dawn, and afterwards be like they are now."

"If you hadn't interrupted," said Phoebus "but there, we can't expect old heads on shoulders of young marble. You should have wished them here and... but no matter. Hermes, old chap, cut across and fetch them, and explain things as you come."

He dipped the ring again in one of the reflected moons before he gave it back to Kathleen.

"There," he said, "now it's washed clean ready for the next magic."

"It is not our custom to question guests," said Hera the queen, turning her great eyes on the children; "but that ring excites, I am sure, the interest of us all."

"It is the ring," said Phoebus.

"That, of course," said Hera; "but if it were not inhospitable to ask questions I should ask: How came it into the hands of these earth-children?"

"That," said Phoebus, "is a long tale. After the feast the story, and after the story the song."

Hermes seemed to have "explained everything" quite fully; for when Gerald and Jimmy in marble whiteness arrived, each clinging to one of the god's winged feet, and so borne through the air, they were certainly quite at ease. They made their best bows to the goddesses and took their places as unembarrassed as though they had had Olympian suppers every night of their lives. Hebe had woven wreaths of roses ready for them, and as Kathleen watched them eating and drinking, perfectly at home in their marble, she was very glad that amid the welling springs of immortal peach-juice she had not forgotten her brothers.

"And now," said Hera, when the boys had been supplied with everything they could possibly desire, and more than they could eat "now for the story."

"Yes," said Mabel intensely; and Kathleen said, "Oh yes; now for the story. How splendid!"

"The story," said Phoebus unexpectedly, "will be told by our guests."

"Oh no!" said Kathleen, shrinking.

"The lads, maybe, are bolder," said Zeus the king, taking off his rose-wreath, which was a little tight, and rubbing his compressed ears.

"I really can't," said Gerald; "besides, I don't know any stories."

"Nor yet me," said Jimmy.

"It's the story of how we got the ring that they want," said Mabel in a hurry. "I'll tell it if you like, Once upon a time there was a little girl called Mabel," she added yet more hastily, and went on with the tale all the tale of the enchanted castle, or almost all, that you have read in these pages. The marble Olympians listened enchanted — almost as enchanted as the castle itself — and the soft moonlit moments fell past like pearls dropping into a deep pool.

"And so," Mabel ended abruptly, "Kathleen wished for the boys and the Lord Hermes fetched them and here we all are."

A burst of interested comment and question blossomed out round the end of the story, suddenly broken off short by Mabel.

"But," said she, brushing it aside, as it grew thinner, "now we want you to tell us."

"To tell you ?"

"How you come to be alive, and how you know about the ring and everything you do know."

"Everything I know?" Phoebus laughed it was to him that she had spoken and not his lips only but all the white lips curled in laughter. "The span of your life, my earth-child, would not contain the words I should speak, to tell you all I know."

"Well, about the ring anyhow, and how you come alive," said Gerald; "you see, it's very puzzling to us."

"Tell them, Phoebus," said the dearest lady in the world; "don't tease the children."

So Phoebus, leaning back against a heap of leopard-skins that Dionysus had lavishly plucked from a spruce fir, told.

"All statues," he said, "can come alive when the moon shines, if they so choose. But statues that are placed in ugly cities do not choose. Why should they weary themselves with the contemplation of the hideous?"

"Quite so," said Gerald politely, to fill the pause.

"In your beautiful temples," the Sun-god went on, "the images of your priests and of your warriors who lie cross-legged on their tombs come alive and walk in their marble about their temples, and through the woods and fields. But only on one night in all the year can any see them. You have beheld us because you held the ring, and are of one brotherhood with us in your marble, but on that one night all may behold us."

"And when is that?" Gerald asked, again polite, in a pause.

"At the festival of the harvest," said Phoebes. "On that night as the moon rises it strikes one beam of perfect light on to the altar in certain temples. One of these temples is in Hellas buried under the fall of a mountain which Zeus, being angry hurled down upon it. One is in this land; it is in this great garden."

"Then," said Gerald, much interested, "if we were to come up to that temple on that night, we could see you, even without being statues or having the ring?"

"Even so," said Phoebus. "More, any question asked by a mortal we are on that night bound to answer."

"And the night is when?"

"Ah!" said Phoebus, and laughed. "Wouldn't you like to know!"

Then the great marble King of the Gods yawned, stroked his long beard, and said: "Enough of stories, Phoebus. Tune your lyre."

"But the ring," said Mabel in a whisper, as the Sun-god tuned the white strings of a sort of marble harp that lay at his feet "about how you know all about the ring?"

"Presently," the Sun-god whispered back. "Zeus must be obeyed; but ask me again before dawn, and I will tell you all I know of it." Mabel drew back, and leaned against the comfortable knees of one Demeter. Kathleen and Psyche sat holding hands. Gerald and Jimmy lay at full length, chins on elbows, gazing at the Sun-god; and even as he held the lyre, before ever his fingers began to sweep the strings, the spirit of music hung in the air, enchanting, enslaving, silencing all thought but the thought of itself, all desire but the desire to listen to it.

Then Phoebus struck the strings and softly plucked melody from them, and all the beautiful dreams of all the world came fluttering close with wings like doves wings; and all the lovely thoughts that sometimes hover near, but not so near that you can catch them, now came home as to their nests in the hearts of those who listened. And those who listened forgot time and space, and how to be sad, and how to be naughty, and it seemed that the whole world lay like a magic apple in the hand of each listener, and that the whole world was good and beautiful.

And then, suddenly, the spell was shattered. Phoebus struck a broken chord, followed by an instant of silence; then he sprang up, crying, "The dawn! the dawn! To your pedestals, O gods!"

In an instant the whole crowd of beautiful marble people had leaped to its feet, had rushed through the belt of wood that cracked and rustled as they went, and the children heard them splash, in the water beyond. They heard, too, the gurgling breathing of a great beast, and knew that the dinosaurus, too, was returning to his own place.

Only Hermes had time, since one flies more swiftly than one swims, to hover above them for one moment, and to whisper with a mischievous laugh:

"In fourteen days from now, at the Temple of Strange Stones."

"What's the secret of the ring?" gasped Mabel.

"The ring is the heart of the magic," said Hermes. "Ask at the moonrise on the fourteenth day, and you shall know all."

With that he waved the snowy caduceus and rose in the air supported by his winged feet. And as he went the seven reflected moons died out and a chill wind began to blow, a grey light grew and grew, the birds stirred and twittered, and the marble slipped away from the children like a skin that shrivels in fire, and they were statues no more, but flesh and blood children as they used to be, standing knee-deep in brambles and long coarse grass. There was no smooth lawn, no marble steps, no seven-mooned fish-pond. The dew lay thick on the grass and the brambles, and it was very cold.

"We ought to have gone with them," said Mabel with chattering teeth. "We can't swim now we re not marble. And I suppose this is the island?"

It was and they couldn't swim.

They knew it. One always knows those sort of things somehow without trying. For instance, you know perfectly that you can't fly. There are some things that there is no mistake about.

The dawn grew brighter and the outlook more black every moment.

"There isn't a boat, I suppose?" Jimmy asked.

"No," said Mabel, "not on this side of the lake; there's one in the boat-house, of course if you could swim there."

"You know I can't," said Jimmy.

"Can't anyone think of anything?" Gerald asked, shivering.

"When they find we've disappeared they'll drag all the water for miles round, said Jimmy hopefully, "in case we've fallen in and sunk to the bottom. When they come to drag this we can yell and be rescued."

"Yes, dear, that will be nice," was Gerald's bitter comment.

"Don't be so disagreeable," said Mabel with a tone so strangely cheerful that the rest stared at her in amazement.

"The ring," she said. "Of course we've only got to wish ourselves home with it. Phoebus washed it in the moon ready for the next wish.

"You didn't tell us about that," said Gerald in accents of perfect good temper. "Never mind. Where is the ring?"

"You had it," Mabel reminded Kathleen.

"I know I had," said that child in stricken tones, "but I gave it to Psyche to look at and and she's got it on her finger!"

Everyone tried not to be angry with Kathleen. All partly succeeded.

"If we ever get off this beastly island," said Gerald,

"I suppose you can find Psyche's statue and get it off again?"

"No I can't," Mabel moaned. "I don't know where the statue is. I've never seen it. It may be in Hellas, wherever that is or anywhere, for anything I know."

No one had anything kind to say, and it is pleasant to record that nobody said anything. And now it was grey daylight, and the sky to the north was flushing in pale pink and lavender.

The boys stood moodily, hands in pockets. Mabel and Kathleen seemed to find it impossible not to cling together, and all about their legs the long grass was icy with dew.

A faint sniff and a caught breath broke the silence. "Now, look here," said Gerald briskly, "I won't have it. Do you hear? Snivelling's no good at all. No, I'm not a pig. It's for your own good. Let's make a tour of the island. Perhaps there's a boat hidden somewhere among the overhanging boughs.

"How could there be?" Mabel asked.

"Someone might have left it there, I suppose," said Gerald.

"But how would they have got off the island?"

"In another boat, of course," said Gerald; "come on." Downheartedly, and quite sure that there wasn't and couldn't be any boat, the four children started to explore the island. How often each one of them had dreamed of islands, how often wished to be stranded on one! Well, now they were. Reality is sometimes quite different from dreams, and not half so nice. It was worst of all for Mabel, whose shoes and stockings were far away on the mainland. The coarse grass and brambles were very cruel to bare legs and feet.

They stumbled through the wood to the edge of the water, but it was impossible to keep close to the edge of the island, the branches grew too thickly. There was a narrow, grassy path that wound in and out among the trees, and this they followed, dejected and mournful. Every moment made it less possible for them to hope to get back to the school-house unnoticed. And if they were missed and beds found in their present unslept-in state well, there would be a row of some sort, and, as Gerald said, "Farewell to liberty!"

"Of course we can get off all right," said Gerald. "Just all shout when we see a gardener or a keeper on the mainland. But if we do, concealment is at an end and all is absolutely up!"

"Yes," said everyone gloomily.

"Come, buck up!" said Gerald, the spirit of the born general beginning to reawaken in him. "We shall get out of this scrape all right, as we've got out of others; you know we shall. See, the sun's coming out. You feel all right and jolly now, don't you?"

"Yes, oh yes!" said everyone, in tones of unmixed misery.

The sun was now risen, and through a deep cleft in the hills it sent a strong shaft of light straight at the island. The yellow light, almost level, struck through the stems of the trees and dazzled the children's eyes. This, with the fact that he was not looking where he was going, as Jimmy did not fail to point out later, was enough to account for what now happened to Gerald, who was leading the melancholy little procession. He stumbled, clutched at a tree-trunk, missed his clutch, and disappeared, with a yell and a clatter; and Mabel, who came next, only pulled herself up just in time not to fall down a steep flight of moss-grown steps that seemed to open suddenly in the ground at her feet.

"Oh, Gerald!" she called down the steps; "are you hurt?"

"No," said Gerald, out of sight and crossly, for he was hurt, rather severely; "it's steps, and there's a passage."

"There always is," said Jimmy.

"I knew there was a passage," said Mabel; "it goes under the water and comes out at the Temple of Flora. Even the gardeners know that, but they won't go down, for fear of snakes."

"Then we can get out that way — I do think you might have said so," Gerald's voice came up to say.

"I didn't think of it," said Mabel. "At least... And I suppose it goes past the place where the Ugly-Wugly found its good hotel."

"I'm not going," said Kathleen positively, "not in the dark, I'm not. So I tell you!"

"Very well, baby," said Gerald sternly, and his head appeared from below very suddenly through interlacing brambles. "No one asked you to go in the dark. We'll leave you here if you like, and return and rescue you with a boat. Jimmy, the bicycle lamp!" He reached up a hand for it.

Jimmy produced from his bosom, the place where lamps are always kept in fairy stories (see Aladdin and others) a bicycle lamp.

"We brought it," he explained, "so as not to break our shins over bits of long Mabel among the rhododendrons."

"Now," said Gerald very firmly, striking a match and opening the thick, rounded glass front of the bicycle lamp, "I don't know what the rest of you are going to do, but I'm going down these steps and along this passage. If we find the good hotel well, a good hotel never hurt anyone yet."

"It's no good, you know," said Jimmy weakly; "you know jolly well you can't get out of that Temple of Flora door, even if you get to it."

"I don't know," said Gerald, still brisk and commander-like; "there's a secret spring inside that door most likely. We hadn't a lamp last time to look for it, remember."

"If there's one thing I do hate its undergroundness," said Mabel.

"You're not a coward," said Gerald, with what is known as diplomacy. "You're brave, Mabel. Don't I know it!" You hold Jimmy's hand and I'll hold Cathy's. Now then."

"I won't have my hand held," said Jimmy, of course. "I'm not a kid."

"Well, Cathy will. Poor little Cathy! Nice brother Jerry'll hold poor Cathy's hand."

Gerald's bitter sarcasm missed fire here, for Cathy gratefully caught the hand he held out in mockery. She was too miserable to read his mood, as she mostly did. "Oh, thank you, Jerry dear," she said gratefully; "you are a dear, and I will try not to be frightened." And for quite a minute Gerald shamedly felt that he had not been quite, quite kind.

So now, leaving the growing goldness of the sunrise, the four went down the stone steps that led to the underground and underwater passage, and everything seemed to grow dark and then to grow into a poor pretence of light again, as the splendour of dawn gave place to the small dogged lighting of the bicycle lamp. The steps did indeed lead to a passage, the beginnings of it choked with the drifted dead leaves of many old autumns. But presently the passage took a turn, there were more steps, down, down, and then the passage was empty and straight lined above and below and on each side with slabs of marble, very clear and clean. Gerald held Cathy's hand with more of kindness and less of exasperation than he had supposed possible.

And Cathy, on her part, was surprised to find it possible to be so much less frightened than she expected.

The flame of the bull's-eye threw ahead a soft circle of misty light — the children followed it silently. Till, silently and suddenly, the light of the bull's-eye behaved as the flame of a candle does when you take it out into the sunlight to light a bonfire, or explode a train of gunpowder, or what not. Because now, with feelings mixed indeed, of wonder, and interest, and awe, but no fear, the children found themselves in a great hall, whose arched roof was held up by two rows of round pillars, and whose every corner was filled with a soft, searching, lovely light, filling every cranny, as water fills the rocky secrecies of hidden sea-caves.

"How beautiful!" Kathleen whispered, breathing hard into the tickled ear of her brother, and Mabel caught the hand of Jimmy and whispered, "I must hold your hand, I must hold on to something, silly, or I shan't believe it's real."

For this hall in which the children found themselves was the most beautiful place in the world. I won't describe it, because it does not look the same to any two people, and you wouldn't understand me if I tried to tell you how it looked to any one of these four. But to each it seemed the most perfect thing possible. I will only say that all round it were great arches. Kathleen saw them as Moorish, Mabel as Tudor, Gerald as Norman, and Jimmy as Churchwarden Gothic. (If you don't know what these are, ask your uncle who collects brasses, and he will explain, or perhaps Mr. Millar will draw the different kinds of arches for you.) And through these arches one could see many things oh! but many things. Through one appeared an olive garden, and in it two lovers who held each other's hands, under an Italian moon; through another a wild sea, and a ship to whom the wild, racing sea was slave. A third showed a king on his throne, his courtiers obsequious about him; and yet a fourth showed a really good hotel, with the respectable Ugly-Wugly sunning himself on the front doorsteps. There was a mother, bending over a wooden cradle. There was an artist gazing entranced on the picture his wet brush seemed to have that moment completed, a general dying on a field where Victory had planted the standard he loved, and these things were not pictures, but the truest truths, alive, and, as anyone could see, immortal.

Many other pictures there were that these arches framed. And all showed some moment when life had sprung to fire and flower the best that the soul of man could ask or man's destiny grant. And the really good hotel had its place here too, because there are some souls that ask no higher thing of life than "a really good hotel" .

"Oh, I am glad we came; I am, I am!" Kathleen murmured, and held fast to her brother's hand.

They went slowly up the hall, the ineffectual bull's-eye, held by Jimmy, very crooked indeed, showing almost as a shadow in this big, glorious light.

And then, when the hall's end was almost reached, the children saw where the light came from. It glowed and spread itself from one place, and in that place stood the one statue that Mabel "did not know where to find" the statue of Psyche. They went on, slowly, quite happy, quite bewildered. And when they came close to Psyche they saw that on her raised hand the ring showed dark.

Gerald let go Kathleen's hand, put his foot on the pediment, his knee on the pedestal. He stood up, dark and human, beside the white girl with the butterfly wings.

"I do hope you don't mind," he said, and drew the ring off very gently. Then, as he dropped to the ground, "Not here," he said. "I don't know why, but not here."

And they all passed behind the white Psyche, and once more the bicycle lamp seemed suddenly to come to life again as Gerald held it in front of him, to be the pioneer in the dark passage that led from the Hall of... but they did not know, then, what it was the Hall of.

Then, as the twisting passage shut in on them with a darkness that pressed close against the little light of the bicycle lamp, Kathleen said, "Give me the ring. I know exactly what to say."

Gerald gave it with not extreme readiness.

"I wish," said Kathleen slowly, "that no one at home may know that we've been out tonight, and I wish we were safe in our own beds, undressed, and in our nightgowns, and asleep."

And the next thing any of them knew, it was good, strong, ordinary daylight not just sunrise, but the kind of daylight you are used to being called in, and all were in their own beds. Kathleen had framed the wish most sensibly. The only mistake had been in saying "in our own beds" because, of course, Mabel's own bed was at Yalding Towers, and to this day Mabel's drab-haired aunt cannot understand how Mabel, who was staying the night with that child in the town she was so taken up with, hadn't come home at eleven, when the aunt locked up, and yet she was in her bed in the morning. For though not a clever woman, she was not stupid enough to be able to believe any one of the eleven fancy explanations which the distracted Mabel offered in the course of the morning. The first (which makes twelve) of these explanations was The Truth, and of course the aunt was far too clever to believe That!

It was show-day at Yalding Castle, and it seemed good to the children to go and visit Mabel, and, as Gerald put it, to mingle unsuspected with the crowd; to gloat over all the things which they knew and which the crowd didn't know about the castle and the sliding panels, the magic ring and the statues that came alive. Perhaps one of the pleasantest things about magic happenings is the feeling which they give you of knowing what other people not only don't know but wouldn't, so to speak, believe if they did.

On the white road outside the gates of the castle was a dark spattering of breaks and wagonettes and dogcarts. Three or four waiting motor-cars puffed fatly where they stood, and bicycles sprawled in heaps along the grassy hollow by the red brick wall. And the people who had been brought to the castle by the breaks and wagonettes, and dog-carts and bicycles and motors, as well as those who had walked there on their own unaided feet, were scattered about the grounds, or being shown over those parts of the castle which were, on this one day of the week, thrown open to visitors.

There were more visitors than usual today because it had somehow been whispered about that Lord Yalding was down, and that the holland covers were to be taken off the state furniture so that a rich American who wished to rent the castle, to live in, might see the place in all its glory.

It certainly did look very splendid. The embroidered satin, gilded leather and tapestry of the chairs, which had been hidden by brown holland, gave to the rooms a pleasant air of being lived in. There were flowering plants and pots of roses here and there on tables or window-ledges. Mabel's aunt prided herself on her tasteful touch in the home, and had studied the arrangement of flowers in a series of articles in Home Drivel called "How to Make Home High-class on Nine-pence a Week".

The great crystal chandeliers, released from the bags that at ordinary times shrouded them, gleamed with grey and purple splendour. The brown linen sheets had been taken off the state beds, and the red ropes that usually kept the low crowd in its proper place had been rolled up and hidden away.

"It's exactly as if we were calling on the family," said the grocer's daughter from Salisbury to her friend who was in the millinery.

"If the Yankee doesn't take it, what do you say to you and me setting up here when we get spliced?" the draper's assistant asked his sweetheart. And she said: "Oh, Reggie, how can you! you are too funny."

All the afternoon the crowd in its smart holiday clothes, pink blouses, and light-coloured suits, flowery hats, and scarves beyond description passed through and through the dark hall, the magnificent drawing-rooms and boudoirs and picture-galleries. The chattering crowd was awed into something like quiet by the calm, stately bedchambers, where men had been born, and died; where royal guests had lain in long-ago summer nights, with big bow-pots of elder-flowers set on the hearth to ward off fever and evil spells. The terrace, where in old days dames in ruffs had sniffed the sweet-brier and southern-wood of the borders below, and ladies, bright with rouge and powder and brocade, had walked in the swing of their hooped skirts, the terrace now echoed to the sound of brown boots, and the tap-tap of high-heeled shoes at two and eleven three, and high laughter and chattering voices that said nothing that the children wanted to hear. These spoiled for them the quiet of the enchanted castle, and outraged the peace of the garden of enchantments.

"It isn't such a lark after all," Gerald admitted, as from the window of the stone summer-house at the end of the terrace they watched the loud colours and heard the loud laughter. "I do hate to see all these people in our garden."

"I said that to that nice bailiff-man this morning," said Mabel, setting herself on the stone floor, "and he said it wasn't much to let them come once a week. He said Lord Yalding ought to let them come when they liked — said he would if he lived there."

"That's all he knows!" said Jimmy. "Did he say anything else?"

"Lots," said Mabel. "I do like him! I told him,"

"You didn't!"

"Yes. I told him lots about our adventures. The humble bailiff is a beautiful listener."

"We shall be locked up for beautiful lunatics if you let your jaw get the better of you, my Mabel child."

"Not us!" said Mabel. "I told it you know the way every word true, and yet so that nobody believes any of it. When I'd quite done he said I'd got a real littery talent, and I promised to put his name on the beginning of the first book I write when I grow up."

"You don't know his name," said Kathleen. "Let's do something with the ring."

"Imposs!" said Gerald. "I forgot to tell you, but I met Mademoiselle when I went back for my garters and she's coming to meet us and walk back with us."

"What did you say?"

"I said," said Gerald deliberately, "that it was very kind of her. And so it was. Us not wanting her doesn't make it not kind her coming."

"It may be kind, but it's sickening too," said Mabel, "because now I suppose we shall have to stick here and wait for her; and I promised we'd meet the bailiff-man. He's going to bring things in a basket and have a picnic-tea with us."

"Where?"

"Beyond the dinosaurus. He said he'd tell me all about the anteddy-something animals it means before Noah's Ark; there are lots besides the dinosaurus in return for me telling him my agreeable fictions. Yes, he called them that."

"When?"

"As soon as the gates shut. That's five."

"We might take Mademoiselle along," suggested Gerald.

"She d be too proud to have tea with a bailiff, I expect; you never know how grown-ups will take the simplest things." It was Kathleen who said this.

"Well, I'll tell you what," said Gerald, lazily turning on the stone bench. "You all go along, and meet your bailiff. A picnic's a picnic. And I'll wait for Mademoiselle."

Mabel remarked joyously that this was jolly decent of Gerald, to which he modestly replied: "Oh, rot!"

Jimmy added that Gerald rather liked sucking-up to people.

"Little boys don't understand diplomacy," said Gerald calmly; "sucking-up is simply silly. But it's better to be good than pretty and —"

"How do you know?" Jimmy asked.

"And," his brother went on, "you never know when a grown-up may come in useful. Besides, they like it. You must give them some little pleasures. Think how awful it must be to be old. My hat!"

"I hope I shan't be an old maid," said Kathleen.

"I don't mean to be," said Mabel briskly. "I'd rather marry a travelling tinker."

"It would be rather nice," Kathleen mused, "to marry the Gypsy King and go about in a caravan telling fortunes and hung round with baskets and brooms."

"Oh, if I could choose," said Mabel, "of course I'd marry a brigand, and live in his mountain fastnesses, and be kind to his captives and help them to escape and —"

"You'll be a real treasure to your husband," said Gerald.

"Yes," said Kathleen, "or a sailor would be nice. You'd watch for his ship coming home and set the lamp in the dormer window to light him home through the storm; and when he was drowned at sea you'd be most frightfully sorry, and go every day to lay flowers on his daisied grave."

"Yes," Mabel hastened to say, "or a soldier, and then you'd go to the wars with short petticoats and a cocked hat and a barrel round your neck like a St. Bernard dog. There's a picture of a soldier's wife on a song auntie's got. It's called 'The Veevandyear'."

"When I marry," Kathleen quickly said.

"When I marry," said Gerald, "I'll marry a dumb girl, or else get the ring to make her so that she can't speak unless she's spoken to. Let's have a squint. "

He applied his eye to the stone lattice.

"They're moving off," he said. "Those pink and purple hats are nodding off in the distant prospect; and the funny little man with the beard like a goat is going a different way from everyone else — the gardeners will have to head him off. I don't see Mademoiselle, though. The rest of you had better bunk. It doesn't do to run any risks with picnics. The deserted hero of our tale, alone and unsupported, urged on his brave followers to pursue the commissariat waggons, he himself remaining at the post of danger and difficulty, because he was born to stand on burning decks whence all but he had fled, and to lead forlorn hopes when despaired of by the human race!"

"I think I'll marry a dumb husband," said Mabel, "and there shan't be any heroes in my books when I write them, only a heroine. Come on, Cathy."

Coming out of that cool, shadowy summer-house into the sunshine was like stepping into an oven, and the stone of the terrace was burning to the children's feet.

"I know now what a cat on hot bricks feels like," said Jimmy.

The antediluvian animals are set in a beech-wood on a slope at least half a mile across the park from the castle. The grandfather of the present Lord Yalding had them set there in the middle of last century, in the great days of the late Prince Consort, the Exhibition of 1851, Sir Joseph Paxton, and the Crystal Palace. Their stone flanks, their wide, ungainly wings, their lozenged crocodile-like backs show grey through the trees a long way off.

Most people think that noon is the hottest time of the day. They are wrong. A cloudless sky gets hotter and hotter all the afternoon, and reaches its very hottest at five. I am sure you must all have noticed this when you are going out to tea anywhere in your best clothes, especially if your clothes are starched and you happen to have a rather long and shadeless walk.

Kathleen, Mabel, and Jimmy got hotter and hotter, and went more and more slowly. They had almost reached that stage of resentment and discomfort when one "wishes one hadn't come" before they saw, below the edge of the beech-wood, the white waved handkerchief of the bailiff.

That banner, eloquent of tea, shade, and being able to sit down, put new heart into them. They mended their pace, and a final desperate run landed them among the drifted coppery leaves and bare grey and green roots of the beech-wood.

"Oh, glory!" said Jimmy, throwing himself down. "How do you do?"

The bailiff looked very nice, the girls thought. He was not wearing his velveteens, but a grey flannel suit that an Earl need not have scorned; and his straw hat would have done no discredit to a Duke; and a Prince could not have worn a prettier green tie. He welcomed the children warmly. And there were two baskets dumped heavy and promising among the beech-leaves.

He was a man of tact. The hot, instructive tour of the stone antediluvians, which had loomed with ever-lessening charm before the children, was not even mentioned.

"You must be desert-dry," he said, "and you'll be hungry, too, when you've done being thirsty. I put on the kettle as soon as I discerned the form of my fair romancer in the extreme offing."

The kettle introduced itself with puffings and bubblings from the hollow between two grey roots where it sat on a spirit-lamp.

"Take off your shoes and stockings, won't you?" said the bailiff in matter-of-course tones, just as old ladies ask each other to take off their bonnets; "there's a little baby canal just over the ridge."

The joys of dipping one's feet in cool running water after a hot walk have yet to be described. I could write pages about them. There was a mill-stream when I was young with little fishes in it, and dropped leaves that spun round, and willows and alders that leaned over it and kept it cool, and but this is not the story of my life.

When they came back, on rested, damp, pink feet, tea was made and poured out — delicious tea with as much milk as ever you wanted, out of a beer bottle with a screw top, and cakes, and gingerbread, and plums, and a big melon with a lump of ice in its heart — a tea for the gods!

This thought must have come to Jimmy, for he said suddenly, removing his face from inside a wide-bitten crescent of melon-rind:

"Your feast's as good as the feast of the Immortals, almost."

"Explain your recondite allusion," said the grey-flannelled host; and Jimmy, understanding him to say, "What do you mean?" replied with the whole tale of that wonderful night when the statues came alive, and a banquet of unearthly splendour and deliciousness was plucked by marble hands from the trees of the lake island.

When he had done the bailiff said: "Did you get all this out of a book?"

"No," said Jimmy, "it happened."

"You are an imaginative set of young dreamers,. aren't you?" the bailiff asked, handing the plums to Kathleen, who smiled, friendly but embarrassed. Why couldn't Jimmy have held his tongue?

"No, we're not," said that indiscreet one obstinately; "everything I've told you did happen, and so did the things Mabel told you."

The bailiff looked a little uncomfortable. "All right, old chap," he said. And there was a short, uneasy silence. "Look here," said Jimmy, who seemed for once to have got the bit between his teeth, "do you believe me or not?"

"Don't be silly, Jimmy!" Kathleen whispered.

"Because, if you don't I'll make you believe."

"Don't!" said Mabel and Kathleen together.

"Do you or don't you?" Jimmy insisted, lying on his front with his chin on his hands, his elbows on a moss-cushion, and his bare legs kicking among the beech leaves.

"I think you tell adventures awfully well," said the bailiff cautiously.

"Very well," said Jimmy, abruptly sitting up, "you don't believe me. Nonsense, Cathy! he's a gentleman, even if he is a bailiff."

"Thank you!" said the bailiff with eyes that twinkled.

"You won't tell, will you?" Jimmy urged.

"Tell what?"

"Anything."

"Certainly not. I am, as you say, the soul of honour."

"Then Cathy, give me the ring."

"Oh, no!" said the girls together.

Kathleen did not mean to give up the ring; Mabel did not mean that she should; Jimmy certainly used no force. Yet presently he held it in his hand. It was his hour. There are times like that for all of us, when what we say shall be done is done.

"Now," said Jimmy, "this is the ring Mabel told you about. I say it is a wishing-ring. And if you will put it on your hand and wish, whatever you wish will happen."

"Must I wish out loud?"

"Yes I think so."

"Don't wish for anything silly," said Kathleen, making the best of the situation, "like its being fine on Tuesday or its being your favourite pudding for dinner tomorrow. Wish for something you really want."

"I will," said the bailiff. "I'll wish for the only thing I really want. I wish my I wish — my friend were here."

The three who knew the power of the ring looked round to see the bailiff's friend appear; a surprised man that friend would be, they thought, and perhaps a frightened one. They had all risen, and stood ready to soothe and reassure the newcomer. But no startled gentleman appeared in the wood, only, coming quietly through the dappled sun and shadow under the beech-trees, Mademoiselle and Gerald, Mademoiselle in a white gown, looking quite nice and like a picture, Gerald hot and polite.

"Good afternoon," said that dauntless leader of forlorn hopes. "I persuaded Mademoiselle —"

That sentence was never finished, for the bailiff and the French governess were looking at each other with the eyes of tired travellers who find, quite without expecting it, the desired end of a very long journey.

And the children saw that even if they spoke it would not make any difference.

"You!" said the bailiff.

"Mais . . . c'est donc vous," said Mademoiselle, in a funny choky voice.

And they stood still and looked at each other, "like stuck pigs" as Jimmy said later, for quite a long time.

"Is she your friend?" Jimmy asked.

"Yes — oh yes," said the bailiff. "You are my friend, are you not?"

"But yes," Mademoiselle said softly. "I am your friend."

"There! you see," said Jimmy, "the ring does do what I said."

"We won't quarrel about that," said the bailiff. "You can say it's the ring. For me it's a coincidence — the happiest, the dearest ,"

"Then you?" said the French governess.

"Of course," said the bailiff. "Jimmy, give your brother some tea. Mademoiselle, come and walk in the woods: there are a thousand things to say."

"Eat then, my Gerald," said Mademoiselle, now grown young, and astonishingly like a fairy princess. "I return all at the hour, and we re-enter together. It is that we must speak each other. It is long time that we have not seen us, me and Lord Yalding!"

"So he was Lord Yalding all the time," said Jimmy, breaking a stupefied silence as the white gown and the grey flannels disappeared among the beech trunks. "Landscape painter sort of dodge — silly, I call it. And fancy her being a friend of his, and his wishing she was here! Different from us, eh? Good old ring!"

"His friend!" said Mabel with strong scorn; "Don't you see she's his lover? Don't you see she's the lady that was bricked up in the convent, because he was so poor, and he couldn't find her. And now the ring's made them live happy ever after. I am glad! Aren't you, Cathy?"

"Rather!" said Kathleen; "it's as good as marrying a sailor or a bandit."

"It's the ring did it," said Jimmy. "If the American takes the house he'll pay lots of rent, and they can live on that."

"I wonder if they'll be married tomorrow!" said Mabel.

"Wouldn't if be fun if we were bridesmaids," said Cathy.

"May I trouble you for the melon," said Gerald. "Thanks! Why didn't we know he was Lord Yalding? Apes and moles that we were!"

"I've known since last night," said Mabel calmly; "only I promised not to tell. I can keep a secret, can't I?"

"Too jolly well," said Kathleen, a little aggrieved.

"He was disguised as a bailiff," said Jimmy; "that's why we didn't know."

"Disguised as a fiddle-stick-end," said Gerald. "Ha, ha! I see something old Sherlock Holmes never saw, nor that idiot Watson, either. If you want a really impenetrable disguise, you ought to disguise yourself as what you really are. I'll remember that."

"It's like Mabel, telling things so that you can't believe them," said Cathy.

"I think Mademoiselle's jolly lucky," said Mabel.

"She's not so bad. He might have done worse," said Gerald. "Plums, please!"

There was quite plainly magic at work. Mademoiselle next morning was a changed governess. Her cheeks were pink, her lips were red, her eyes were larger and brighter, and she had done her hair in an entirely new way, rather frivolous and very becoming.

"Mamselle's coming out!" Eliza remarked.

Immediately after breakfast Lord Yalding called with a wagonette that wore a smart blue cloth coat, and was drawn by two horses whose coats were brown and shining and fitted them even better than the blue cloth coat fitted the wagonette, and the whole party drove in state and splendour to Yalding Towers.

Arrived there, the children clamoured for permission to explore the castle thoroughly, a thing that had never yet been possible. Lord Yalding, a little absent in manner, but yet quite cordial, consented. Mabel showed the others all the secret doors and unlikely passages and stairs that she had discovered. It was a glorious morning. Lord Yalding and Mademoiselle went through the house, it is true, but in a rather half-hearted way. Quite soon they were tired, and went out through the French windows of the drawing-room and through the rose garden, to sit on the curved stone seat in the middle of the maze, where once, at the beginning of things, Gerald, Kathleen, and Jimmy had found the sleeping Princess who wore pink silk and diamonds.

The children felt that their going left to the castle a more spacious freedom, and explored with more than Arctic enthusiasm. It was as they emerged from the little rickety secret staircase that led from the powdering-room of the state suite to the gallery of the hall that they came suddenly face to face with the odd little man who had a beard like a goat and had taken the wrong turning yesterday.

"This part of the castle is private," said Mabel, with great presence of mind, and shut the door behind her.

"I am aware of it," said the goat-faced stranger, "but I have the permission of the Earl of Yalding to examine the house at my leisure."

"Oh!" said Mabel. "I beg your pardon. We all do. We didn't know."

"You are relatives of his lordship, I should surmise?" asked the goat-faced.

"Not exactly," said Gerald. "Friends".

The gentleman was thin and very neatly dressed; he had small, merry eyes and a face that was brown and dry-looking.

"You are playing some game, I should suppose?"

"No, sir," said Gerald, "only exploring."

"May a stranger propose himself as a member of your Exploring Expedition?" asked the gentleman, smiling a tight but kind smile.

The children looked at each other.

"You see," said Gerald, "it's rather difficult to explain but you see what I mean, don't you?"

"He means," said Jimmy, "that we can't take you into an exploring party without we know what you want to go for."

"Are you a photographer?" asked Mabel, "or is it some newspaper's sent you to write about the Towers?"

"I understand your position," said the gentleman. "I am not a photographer, nor am I engaged by any journal. I am a man of independent means, travelling in this country with the intention of renting a residence. My name is Jefferson D. Conway."

"Oh!" said Mabel; "then you're the American millionaire."

"I do not like the description, young lady," said Mr. Jefferson D. Conway. "I am an American citizen, and I am not without means. This is a fine property, a very fine property. If it were for sale ,"

"It isn't, it can't be," Mabel hastened to explain. "The lawyers have put it in a tale, so Lord Yalding can't sell it. But you could take it to live in, and pay Lord Yalding a good millionairish rent, and then he could marry the French governess."

"Shish!" said Kathleen and Mr. Jefferson D. Conway together, and he added: "Lead the way, please; and I should suggest that the exploration be complete and exhaustive."

Thus encouraged, Mabel led the millionaire through all the castle. He seemed pleased, yet disappointed too.

"It is a fine mansion," he said at last when they had come back to the point from which they had started; "but I should suppose, in a house this size, there would mostly be a secret stairway, or a priests hiding place, or a ghost?"

"There are," said Mabel briefly, "but I thought Americans didn't believe in anything but machinery and newspapers." She touched the spring of the panel behind her, and displayed the little tottery staircase to the American. The sight of it worked a wonderful transformation in him. He became eager, alert, very keen.

"Say!" he cried, over and over again, standing in the door that led from the powdering-room to the state bed-chamber. "But this is great — great!"

The hopes of everyone ran high. It seemed almost certain that the castle would be let for a millionairish rent and Lord Yalding be made affluent to the point of marriage.

"If there were a ghost located in this ancestral pile, I'd close with the Earl of Yalding today, now, on the nail," Mr. Jefferson D. Conway went on.

"If you were to stay till tomorrow, and sleep in this room, I expect you'd see the ghost," said Mabel.

"There is a ghost located here then?" he said joyously.

"They say," Mabel answered, "that old Sir Rupert, who lost his head in Henry the Eighth's time, walks of a night here, with his head under his arm. But we've not seen that. What we have seen is the lady in a pink dress with diamonds in her hair. She carries a lighted taper," Mabel hastily added. The others, now suddenly aware of Mabel's plan, hastened to assure the American in accents of earnest truth that they had all seen the lady with the pink gown.

He looked at them with half-closed eyes that twinkled.

"Well," he said, "I calculate to ask the Earl of Yalding to permit me to pass a night in his ancestral best bed-chamber. And if I hear so much as a phantom footstep, or hear so much as a ghostly sigh, I'll take the place."

"I am glad!" said Cathy.

"You appear to be very certain of your ghost," said the American, still fixing them with little eyes that shone. "Let me tell you, young gentlemen, that I carry a gun, and when I see a ghost, I shoot."

He pulled a pistol out of his hip-pocket, and looked at it lovingly.

"And I am a fair average shot," he went on, walking across the shiny floor of the state bed-chamber to the open window. "See that big red rose, like a tea-saucer?"

They saw.

The next moment a loud report broke the stillness, and the red petals of the shattered rose strewed balustrade and terrace.

The American looked from one child to another. Every face was perfectly white.

"Jefferson D. Conway made his little pile by strict attention to business, and keeping his eyes skinned," he added. "Thank you for all your kindness."

"Suppose you'd done it, and he'd shot you!" said Jimmy cheerfully. "That would have been an adventure, wouldn't it?"

"I'm going to do it still," said Mabel, pale and defiant. "Let's find Lord Yalding and get the ring back."

Lord Yalding had had an interview with Mabel's aunt, and lunch for six was laid in the great dark hall, among the armour and the oak furniture a beautiful lunch served on silver dishes. Mademoiselle, becoming every moment younger and more like a Princess, was moved to tears when Gerald rose, lemonade-glass in hand, and proposed the health of "Lord and Lady Yalding".

When Lord Yalding had returned thanks in a speech full of agreeable jokes the moment seemed to Gerald propitious, and he said:

"The ring, you know you don't believe in it, but we do. May we have it back?"

And got it.

Then, after a hasty council, held in the panelled jewel-room, Mabel said: "This is a wishing-ring, and I wish all the American's weapons of all sorts were here."

Instantly the room was full six feet up the wall of a tangle and mass of weapons, swords, spears, arrows, tomahawks, fowling pieces, blunderbusses, pistols, revolvers, scimitars, kreeses every kind of weapon you can think of and the four children wedged in among all these weapons of death hardly dared to breathe.

"He collects arms, I expect," said Gerald, "and the arrows are poisoned, I shouldn't wonder. Wish them back where they came from, Mabel, for goodness sake, and try again."

Mabel wished the weapons away, and at once the four children stood safe in a bare panelled room. But, "no," Mabel said, "I can't stand it. We'll work the ghost another way. I wish the American may think he sees a ghost when he goes to bed. Sir Rupert with his head under his arm will do."

"Is it tonight he sleeps there?"

"I don't know. I wish he may see Sir Rupert every night that'll make it all serene."

"It's rather dull," said Gerald; "we shan't know whether he's seen Sir Rupert or not."

"We shall know in the morning, when he takes the house."

This being settled, Mabel's aunt was found to be desirous of Mabel's company, so the others went home.

It was when they were at supper that Lord Yalding suddenly appeared, and said: "Mr. Jefferson Conway wants you boys to spend the night with him in the state chamber. I've had beds put up. You don't mind, do you? He seems to think you've got some idea of playing ghost-tricks on him."

It was difficult to refuse, so difficult that it proved impossible.

Ten o clock found the boys each in a narrow white bed that looked quite absurdly small in that high, dark chamber, and in face of that tall gaunt four-poster hung with tapestry and ornamented with funereal-looking plumes.

"I hope to goodness there isn't a real ghost," Jimmy whispered.

"Not likely," Gerald whispered back.

"But I don't want to see Sir Rupert's ghost with its head under its arm," Jimmy insisted.

"You won't. The most you'll see'll be the millionaire seeing it. Mabel said he was to see it, not us. Very likely you'll sleep all night and not see anything. Shut your eyes and count up to a million and don't be a goat!"

As soon as Mabel had learned from her drab-haired aunt that this was indeed the night when Mr. Jefferson D. Conway would sleep at the castle she had hastened to add a wish, "that Sir Rupert and his head may appear tonight in the state bedroom."

Jimmy shut his eyes and began to count a million. Before he had counted it he fell asleep. So did his brother.

They were awakened by the loud echoing bang of a pistol shot. Each thought of the shot that had been fired that morning, and opened eyes that expected to see a sunshiny terrace and red-rose petals strewn upon warm white stone.

Instead, there was the dark, lofty state chamber, lighted but little by six tall candles; there was the American in shirt and trousers, a smoking pistol in his hand; and there, advancing from the door of the powdering-room, a figure in doublet and hose, a ruff round its neck and no head! The head, sure enough, was there; but it was under the right arm, held close in the slashed-velvet sleeve of the doublet. The face looking from under the arm wore a pleasant smile. Both boys, I am sorry to say, screamed. The American fired again. The bullet passed through Sir Rupert, who advanced without appearing to notice it.

Then, suddenly, the lights went out. The next thing the boys knew it was morning. A grey daylight shone blankly through the tall windows and wild rain was beating upon the glass, and the American was gone.

"Where are we?" said Jimmy, sitting up with tangled hair and looking round him. "Oh, I remember. Ugh! it was horrid. I'm about fed up with that ring, so I don't mind telling you."

"Nonsense!" said Gerald. "I enjoyed it. I wasn't a bit frightened, were you?"

"No," said Jimmy, "of course I wasn't.

"We've done the trick," said Gerald later when they learned that the American had breakfasted early with Lord Yalding and taken the first train to London; "he's gone to get rid of his other house, and take this one. The old ring's beginning to do really useful things."

"Perhaps you'll believe in the ring now," said Jimmy to Lord Yalding, whom he met later on in the picture-gallery; "it's all our doing that Mr. Jefferson saw the ghost. He told us he'd take the house if he saw a ghost, so of course we took care he did see one."

"Oh, you did, did you?" said Lord Yalding in rather an odd voice. "I'm very much obliged, I'm sure."

"Don't mention it," said Jimmy kindly. "I thought you'd be pleased and him too."

"Perhaps you'll be interested to learn," said Lord Yalding, putting his hands in his pockets and staring down at Jimmy, "that Mr. Jefferson D. Conway was so pleased with your ghost that he got me out of bed at six o clock this morning to talk about it."

"Oh, ripping!" said Jimmy. "What did he say?"

"He said, as far as I can remember," said Lord Yalding, still in the same strange voice "he said: "My lord, your ancestral pile is Al. It is, in fact, The Limit. Its luxury is palatial, its grounds are nothing short of Edenesque. No expense has been spared, I should surmise. Your ancestors were whole-hoggers. They have done the thing as it should be done every detail attended to. I like your tapestry, and I like your oak, and I like your secret stairs. But I think your ancestors should have left well enough alone, and stopped at that." So I said they had, as far as I knew, and he shook his head and said:

"No, Sir. Your ancestors take the air of a night with their heads under their arms. A ghost that sighed or glided or rustled I could have stood, and thanked you for it, and considered it in the rent. But a ghost that bullets go through while it stands grinning with a bare neck and its head loose under its own arm and little boys screaming and fainting in their beds no! What I say is, If this is a British hereditary high-toned family ghost, excuse me!" And he went off by the early train.

"I say," the stricken Jimmy remarked, "I am sorry, and I don't think we did faint, really I don't but we thought it would be just what you wanted. And perhaps someone else will take the house."

"I don't know anyone else rich enough," said Lord Yalding. "Mr. Conway came the day before he said he would, or you'd never have got hold of him. And I don't know how you did it, and I don't want to know. It was a rather silly trick."

There was a gloomy pause. The rain beat against the long windows.

"I say" Jimmy looked up at Lord Yalding with the light of a new idea in his round face "I say, if you're hard up, why don't you sell your jewels?"

"I haven't any jewels, you meddlesome young duffer," said Lord Yalding quite crossly; and taking his hands out of his pockets, he began to walk away.

"I mean the ones in the panelled room with the stars in the ceiling," Jimmy insisted, following him.

"There aren't any," said Lord Yalding shortly; "and if this is some more ring-nonsense I advise you to be careful, young man. I've had about as much as I care for."

"It's not ring-nonsense, said Jimmy: "there are shelves and shelves of beautiful family jewels. You can sell them and ,"

"Oh, no!" cried Mademoiselle, appearing like an oleograph of a duchess in the door of the picture-gallery; "don't sell the family jewels "

"There aren't any, my lady," said Lord Yalding, going towards her. "I thought you were never coming."

"Oh, aren't there!" said Mabel, who had followed Mademoiselle. "You just come and see,"

"Let us see what they will to show us," cried Mademoiselle, for Lord Yalding did not move; "it should at least be amusing."

"It is," said Jimmy.

So they went, Mabel and Jimmy leading, while Mademoiselle and Lord Yalding followed, hand in hand.

"It's much safer to walk hand in hand," said Lord Yalding; "with these children at large one never knows what may happen next."

It would be interesting, no doubt, to describe the feelings of Lord Yalding as he followed Mabel and Jimmy through his ancestral halls, but I have no means of knowing at all what he felt. Yet one must suppose that he felt something: bewilderment, perhaps, mixed with a faint wonder, and a desire to pinch himself to see if he were dreaming. Or he may have pondered the rival questions, "Am I mad? Are they mad?" without being at all able to decide which he ought to try to answer, let alone deciding what, in either case, the answer ought to be. You see, the children did seem to believe in the odd stories they told and the wish had come true, and the ghost had appeared. He must have thought... but all this is vain; I don't really know what he thought any more than you do.

Nor can I give you any clue to the thoughts and feelings of Mademoiselle. I only know that she was very happy, but anyone would have known that if they had seen her face. Perhaps this is as good a moment as any to explain that when her guardian had put her in a convent so that she should not sacrifice her fortune by marrying a poor lord, her guardian had secured that fortune (to himself) by going off with it to South America. Then, having no money left, Mademoiselle had to work for it. So she went out as governess, and took the situation she did take because it was near Lord Yalding's home. She wanted to see him, even though she thought he had forsaken her and did not love her any more. And now she had seen him. I dare say she thought about some of these things as she went along through his house, her hand held in his. But of course I can't be sure.

Jimmy's thoughts, of course, I can read like any old book. He thought, "Now he'll have to believe me." That Lord Yalding should believe him had become, quite unreasonably, the most important thing in the world to Jimmy. He wished that Gerald and Kathleen were there to share his triumph, but they were helping Mabel's aunt to cover the grand furniture up, and so were out of what followed. Not that they missed much, for when Mabel proudly said, "Now you'll see, and the others came close round her in the little panelled room, there was a pause, and then nothing happened at all!

"There's a secret spring here somewhere," said Mabel, fumbling with fingers that had suddenly grown hot and damp.

"Where?" said Lord Yalding.

"Here," said Mabel impatiently, "only I can't find it."

And she couldn't. She found the spring of the secret panel under the window all right, but that seemed to everyone dull compared with the jewels that everyone had pictured and two at least had seen. But the spring that made the oak panelling slide away and displayed jewels plainly to any eye worth a king's ransom this could not be found. More, it was simply not there. There could be no doubt of that. Every inch of the panelling was felt by careful fingers. The earnest protests of Mabel and Jimmy died away presently in a silence made painful by the hotness of one's ears, the discomfort of not liking to meet anyone's eyes, and the resentful feeling that the spring was not behaving in at all a sportsmanlike way, and that, in a word, this was not cricket.

"You see!" said Lord Yalding severely. "Now you've had your joke, if you call it a joke, and I've had enough of the whole silly business. Give me the ring — it's mine, I suppose, since you say you found it somewhere here — and don't let's hear another word about all this rubbish of magic and enchantment."

"Gerald's got the ring," said Mabel miserably.

"Then go and fetch him," said Lord Yalding "both of you."

The melancholy pair retired, and Lord Yalding spent the time of their absence in explaining to Mademoiselle how very unimportant jewels were compared with other things.

The four children came back together.

"We've had enough of this ring business," said Lord Yalding. "Give it to me and we'll say no more about it."

"I — I can't get it off," said Gerald. "It it always did have a will of its own."

"I'll soon get it off," said Lord Yalding. But he didn't. "We'll try soap," he said firmly. Four out of his five hearers knew just exactly how much use soap would be.

"They won't believe about the jewels," wailed Mabel, suddenly dissolved in tears, "and I can't find the spring. I've felt all over — we all have — it was just here, and..."

Her fingers felt it as she spoke; and as she ceased to speak the carved panels slid away, and the blue velvet shelves laden with jewels were disclosed to the unbelieving eyes of Lord Yalding and the lady who was to be his wife.

"Jove!" said Lord Yalding.

"Misericorde!" said the lady.

"But why now?" gasped Mabel. "Why not before?"

"I expect it's magic," said Gerald. "There's no real spring here, and it couldn't act because the ring wasn't here. You know Phoebus told us the ring was the heart of all the magic."

"Shut it up and take the ring away and see."

They did, and Gerald was (as usual, he himself pointed out) proved to be right. When the ring was away there was no spring; when the ring was in the room there (as Mabel urged) was the spring all right enough.

"So you see," said Mabel to Lord Yalding.

"I see that the spring's very artfully concealed," said that dense peer. "I think it was very clever indeed of you to find it. And if those jewels are real,"

"Of course they're real," said Mabel indignantly.

"Well, anyway," said Lord Yalding, "thank you all very much. I think it's clearing up. I'll send the wagonette home with you after lunch. And if you don't mind, I'll have the ring."

Half an hour of soap and water produced no effect whatever, except to make the finger of Gerald very red and very sore. Then Lord Yalding said something very impatient indeed, and then Gerald suddenly became angry and said: "Well, I'm sure I wish it would come off," and of course instantly, "slick as butter" , as he later pointed out, off it came.

"Thank you," said Lord Yalding.

"And I believe now he thinks I kept it on on purpose," said Gerald afterwards when, at ease on the leads at home, they talked the whole thing out over a tin of preserved pineapple and a bottle of ginger-beer apiece. "There's no pleasing some people. He wasn't in such a fiery hurry to order that wagonette after he found that Mademoiselle meant to go when we did. But I liked him better when he was a humble bailiff. Take him for all in all, he does not look as if we should like him again.

"He doesn't know what's the matter with him," said Kathleen, leaning back against the tiled roof, "it's really the magic — it's like sickening with measles."

Don't you remember how cross Mabel was at first about the invisibleness?"

"Rather!" said Jimmy.

"It's partly that," said Gerald, trying to be fair, "and partly it's the being in love. It always makes people like idiots, a chap at school told me. His sister was like that — quite rotten, you know. And she used to be quite a decent sort before she was engaged."

At tea and at supper Mademoiselle was radiant as attractive as a lady on a Christmas card, as merry as a marmoset, and as kind as you would always be yourself if you could take the trouble. At breakfast, an equal radiance, kindness, attraction, merriment. Then Lord Yalding came to see her. The meeting took place in the drawing-room; the children with deep discreetness remained shut in the school-room till Gerald, going up to his room for a pencil, surprised Eliza with her ear glued to the drawing-room key-hole.

After that Gerald sat on the top stair with a book.

He could not hear any of the conversation in the drawing-room, but he could command a view of the door, and in this way be certain that no one else heard any of it. Thus it was that when the drawing-room door opened Gerald was in a position to see Lord Yalding come out. "Our young hero, as he said later, "coughed with infinite tact to show that he was there," but Lord Yalding did not seem to notice. He walked in a blind sort of way to the hat-stand, fumbled clumsily with the umbrellas and macintoshes, found his straw hat and looked at it gloomily, crammed it on his head and went out, banging the door behind him in the most reckless way.

He left the drawing-room door open, and Gerald, though he had purposely put himself in a position where one could hear nothing from the drawing-room when the door was shut, could hear something quite plainly now that the door was open. That something, he noticed with deep distress and disgust, was the sound of sobs and sniffs. Mademoiselle was quite certainly crying.

"Jimminy!" he remarked to himself, "they haven't lost much time. Fancy their beginning to quarrel already! I hope I'll never have to be anybody's lover."

But this was no time to brood on the terrors of his own future. Eliza might at any time occur. She would not for a moment hesitate to go through that open door, and push herself into the very secret sacred heart of Mademoiselle's grief. It seemed to Gerald better that he should be the one to do this. So he went softly down the worn green Dutch carpet of the stairs and into the drawing-room, shutting the door softly and securely behind him.

"It is all over," Mademoiselle was saying, her face buried in the beady arum-lilies on a red ground worked for a cushion cover by a former pupil: "he will not marry me!"

Do not ask me how Gerald had gained the lady's confidence. He had, as I think I said almost at the beginning, very pretty ways with grown-ups, when he chose. Anyway, he was holding her hand, almost as affectionately as if she had been his mother with a headache, and saying "Don't!" and "Don't cry!" and "It'll be all right, you see if it isn't" in the most comforting way you can imagine, varying the treatment with gentle thumps on the back and entreaties to her to tell him all about it.

This wasn't mere curiosity, as you might think. The entreaties were prompted by Gerald's growing certainty that whatever was the matter was somehow the fault of that ring. And in this Gerald was ("once more", as he told himself) right.

The tale, as told by Mademoiselle, was certainly an unusual one. Lord Yalding, last night after dinner, had walked in the park "to think of —"

"Yes, I know," said Gerald; "and he had the ring on. And he saw —"

"He saw the monuments become alive," sobbed Mademoiselle; "his brain was troubled by the ridiculous accounts of fairies that you tell him. He sees Apollon and Aphrodite alive on their marble. He remembers him of your story. He wish himself a statue. Then he becomes mad — imagines to himself that your story of the island is true, plunges in the lake, swims among the beasts of the Ark of Noe, feeds with gods on an island. At dawn the madness become less. He think the Pantheon vanish. But him, no he thinks himself statue, hiding from gardeners in his garden till nine less a quarter. Then he thinks to wish himself no more a statue and perceives that he is flesh and blood. A bad dream, but he has lost the head with the tales you tell. He say it is no dream but he is fool mad how you say? And a mad man must not marry. There is no hope. I am at despair! And the life is vain!"

"There is," said Gerald earnestly. "I assure you there is hope, I mean. And life's as right as rain really. And there's nothing to despair about. He's not mad, and it's not a dream. It's magic. It really and truly is."

"The magic exists not," Mademoiselle moaned; "it is that he is mad. It is the joy to re-see me after so many days. Oh, la-la-la-la-la!"

"Did he talk to the gods?" Gerald asked gently.

"It is there the most mad of all his ideas. He say that Mercure give him rendezvous at some temple tomorrow when the moon raise herself."

"Right," cried Gerald, "righto! Dear nice, kind, pretty Mademoiselle Rapunzel, don't be a silly little duffer" he lost himself for a moment among the consoling endearments he was accustomed to offer to Kathleen in moments of grief and emotion, but hastily added: "I mean, do not be a lady who weeps causelessly. Tomorrow he will go to that temple. I will go. Thou shalt go, he will go. We will go, you will go, let 'em all go! And, you see, it's going to be absolutely all right. He'll see he isn't mad, and you'll understand all about everything. Take my handkerchief, it's quite a clean one as it happens; I haven't even unfolded it. Oh! do stop crying, there's a dear, darling, long-lost lover."

This flood of eloquence was not without effect. She took his handkerchief, sobbed, half smiled, dabbed at her eyes, and said: "Oh, naughty! Is it some trick you play him, like the ghost?"

"I can't explain," said Gerald, "but I give you my word of honour — you know what an Englishman's word of honour is, don't you? even if you are French — that everything is going to be exactly what you wish. I've never told you a lie. Believe me!"

"It is curious," said she, drying her eyes, "but I do." And once again, so suddenly that he could not have resisted, she kissed him. I think, however, that in this her hour of sorrow he would have thought it mean to resist.

"It pleases her and it doesn't hurt me much," would have been his thought.

And now it is near moonrise. The French governess, half-doubting, half-hoping, but wholly longing to be near Lord Yalding even if he be as mad as a March hare, and the four children (they have collected Mabel by an urgent letter-card posted the day before) are going over the dewy grass. The moon has not yet risen, but her light is in the sky mixed with the pink and purple of the sunset. The west is heavy with ink-clouds and rich colour, but the east, where the moon rises, is clear as a rock-pool.

They go across the lawn and through the beech wood and come at last, through a tangle of underwood and bramble, to a little level tableland that rises out of the flat hill-top, one tableland out of another. Here is the ring of vast rugged stones, one pierced with a curious round hole, worn smooth at its edges. In the middle of the circle is a great flat stone, alone, desolate, full of meaning, a stone that is covered thick with the memory of old faiths and creeds long since forgotten. Something dark moves in the circle. The French girl breaks from the children, goes to it, clings to its arm. It is Lord Yalding, and he is telling her to go.

"Never of the life!" she cries. "If you are mad I am mad too, for I believe the tale these children tell. And I am here to be with thee and see with thee whatever the rising moon shall show us."

The children, holding hands by the flat stone, more moved by the magic in the girl's voice than by any magic of enchanted rings, listen, trying not to listen.

"Are you not afraid?" Lord Yalding is saying.

"Afraid? With you?" she laughs. He put his arm round her. The children hear her sigh.

"Are you afraid," he says, "my darling?"

Gerald goes across the wide turf ring expressly to say: "You can't be afraid if you are wearing the ring. And I'm sorry, but we can hear every word you say."

She laughs again. "It makes nothing," she says "you know already if we love each other."

Then he puts the ring on her finger, and they stand together. The white of his flannel coat sleeve marks no line on the white of her dress; they stand as though cut out of one block of marble.

Then a faint greyness touches the top of that round hole, creeps up the side. Then the hole is a disc of light a moonbeam strikes straight through it across the grey green of the circle that the stones mark, and as the moon rises the moonbeam slants downward. The children have drawn back till they stand close to the lovers. The moonbeam slants more and more; now it touches the far end of the stone, now it draws nearer and nearer to the middle of it, now at last it touches the very heart and centre of that central stone. And then it is as though a spring were touched, a fountain of light released. Everything changes or, rather, everything is revealed. There are no more secrets. The plan of the world seems plain, like an easy sum that one writes in big figures on a child's slate. One wonders how one can ever have wondered about anything. Space is not; every place that one has seen or dreamed of is here. Time is not; into this instant is crowded all that one has ever done or dreamed of doing. It is a moment and it is eternity. It is the centre of the universe and it is the universe itself. The eternal light rests on and illuminates the eternal heart of things.

None of the six human beings who saw that moon-rising were ever able to think about it as having anything to do with time. Only for one instant could that moon-ray have rested full on the centre of that stone.

And yet there was time for many happenings.

From that height one could see far out over the quiet park and sleeping gardens, and through the grey green of them shapes moved, approaching.

The great beasts came first: strange forms that were when the world was new — gigantic lizards with wings, dragons they lived as in men's memories, mammoths, strange vast birds, they crawled up the hill and ranged themselves outside the circle. Then, not from the garden but from very far away, came the stone gods of Egypt and Assyria — bull-bodied, bird-winged, hawk-headed, cat-headed, all in stone, and all alive and alert; strange, grotesque figures from the towers of cathedrals, figures of angels with folded wings, figures of beasts with wings wide spread; sphinxes; uncouth idols from Southern palm-fringed islands; and, last of all, the beautiful marble shapes of the gods and goddesses who had held their festival on the lake-island, and bidden Lord Yalding and the children to this meeting.

Not a word was spoken. Each stone shape came gladly and quietly into the circle of light and understanding, as children, tired with a long ramble, creep quietly through the open door into the firelit welcome of home.

The children had thought to ask many questions. And it had been promised that the questions should be answered. Yet now no one spoke a word, because all had come into the circle of the real magic where all things are understood without speech.

Afterwards none of them could ever remember at all what had happened. But they never forgot that they had been somewhere where everything was easy and beautiful. And people who can remember even that much are never quite the same again. And when they came to talk of it next day they found that to each some little part of that night's great enlightenment was left.

All the stone creatures drew closer round the stone — the light where the moonbeam struck — it seemed to break away in spray such as water makes when it falls from a height. All the crowd was bathed in whiteness. A deep hush lay over the vast assembly.

Then a wave of intention swept over the mighty crowd. All the faces, bird, beast, Greek statue, Babylonian monster, human child and human lover, turned upward, the radiant light illumined them and one word broke from all.

"The light!" they cried, and the sound of their voice was like the sound of a great wave; "the light! the light!"

And then the light was not any more, and, soft as floating thistle-down, sleep was laid on the eyes of all but the immortals.

The grass was chill and dewy and the clouds had veiled the moon. The lovers and the children were standing together, all clinging close, not for fear, but for love.

"I want," said the French girl softly, "to go to the cave on the island."

Very quietly through the gentle brooding night they went down to the boat-house, loosed the clanking chain, and dipped oars among the drowned stars and lilies. They came to the island, and found the steps.

"I brought candles," said Gerald, "in case."

So, lighted by Gerald's candles, they went down into the Hall of Psyche and there glowed the light spread from her statue, and all was as the children had seen it before.

It is the Hall of Granted Wishes.

"The ring," said Lord Yalding.

"The ring," said his lover, "is the magic ring given long ago to a mortal, and it is what you say it is. It was given to your ancestor by a lady of my house that he might build her a garden and a house like her own palace and garden in her own land. So that this place is built partly by his love and partly by that magic. She never lived to see it; that was the price of the magic."

It must have been English that she spoke, for otherwise how could the children have understood her? Yet the words were not like Mademoiselle's way of speaking.

"Except from children," her voice went on, "the ring exacts a payment. You paid for me, when I came by your wish, by this terror of madness that you have since known. Only one wish is free."

"And that wish is ,"

"The last," she said. "Shall I wish?"

"Yes — wish," they said, all of them.

"I wish, then," said Lord Yalding's lover, "that all the magic this ring has wrought may be undone, and that the ring itself may be no more and no less than a charm to bind thee and me together for evermore."

She ceased. And as she ceased the enchanted light died away, the windows of granted wishes went out, like magic-lantern pictures. Gerald's candle faintly lighted a rudely arched cave, and where Psyche's statue had been was a stone with something carved on it.

Gerald held the light low.

"It is her grave," the girl said.

Next day no one could remember anything at all exactly. But a good many things were changed. There was no ring but the plain gold ring that Mademoiselle found clasped in her hand when she woke in her own bed in the morning. More than half the jewels in the panelled room were gone, and those that remained had no panelling to cover them; they just lay bare on the velvet-covered shelves. There was no passage at the back of the Temple of Flora. Quite a lot of the secret passages and hidden rooms had disappeared. And there were not nearly so many statues in the garden as everyone had supposed. And large pieces of the castle were missing and had to be replaced at great expense.

From which we may conclude that Lord Yalding's ancestor had used the ring a good deal to help him in his building.

However, the jewels that were left were quite enough to pay for everything.

The suddenness with which all the ring-magic was undone was such a shock to everyone concerned that they now almost doubt that any magic ever happened.

But it is certain that Lord Yalding married the French governess and that a plain gold ring was used in the ceremony, and this, if you come to think of it, could be no other than the magic ring, turned, by that last wish, into a charm to keep him and his wife together for ever.

Also, if all this story is nonsense and a make-up, if Gerald and Jimmy and Kathleen and Mabel have merely imposed on my trusting nature by a pack of unlikely inventions, how do you account for the paragraph which appeared in the evening papers the day after the magic of the moon-rising?

"MYSTERIOUS DISAPPEARANCE OF A WELL-KNOWN CITY MAN,"

it said, and then went on to say how a gentleman, well known and much respected in financial circles, had vanished, leaving no trace.

"Mr. U. W. Ugli," the papers continued, "had remained late, working at his office as was his occasional habit. The office door was found locked, and on its being broken open the clothes of the unfortunate gentleman were found in a heap on the floor, together with an umbrella, a walking stick, a golf club, and, curiously enough, a feather brush, such as housemaids use for dusting. Of his body, however, there was no trace. The police are stated to have a clue."

If they have, they have kept it to themselves. But I do not think they can have a clue, because, of course, that respected gentleman was the Ugly-Wugly who became real when, in search of a really good hotel, he got into the Hall of Granted Wishes. And if none of this story ever happened, how is it that those four children are such friends with Lord and Lady Yalding, and stay at The Towers almost every holidays?

It is all very well for all of them to pretend that the whole of this story is my own invention: facts are facts, and you can't explain them away.

Lightning Source UK Ltd.
Milton Keynes UK
22 December 2009

147810UK00001B/81/A